1Q84: BOOKS ONE, TWO AND THREE

Haruki Murakami was born in Kyoto in 1949 and
now lives near Tokyo. He is the author of many
novels as well as short stories and non-fiction. His
works include *Norwegian Wood, The Wind-Up
Bird Chronicle, Kafka on the Shore, After Dark*
and *What I Talk About When I Talk About
Running*. His work has been translated into more
than forty languages, and the most recent of his
many international honours is the Jerusalem Prize,
whose previous recipients include J.M. Coetzee,
Milan Kundera, and V.S. Naipaul.

OTHER WORKS BY HARUKI MURAKAMI

Fiction

After Dark

After the Quake

Blind Willow, Sleeping Woman

Dance Dance Dance

The Elephant Vanishes

*Hard-Boiled Wonderland and the End of the
World*

Kafka on the Shore

Norwegian Wood

South of the Border, West of the Sun

Sputnik Sweetheart

A Wild Sheep Chase

The Wind-Up Bird Chronicle

Non-fiction

*Underground: The Tokyo Gas Attack and the
Japanese Psyche*

What I Talk About When I Talk About Running

HARUKI MURAKAMI

1Q84

TRANSLATED FROM THE JAPANESE BY
Jay Rubin and Philip Gabriel

VINTAGE BOOKS
London

Published by Vintage 2012

4 6 8 10 9 7 5 3

right © Haruki Murakami: Books One and Two 2009, Book Three 2010
English translation copyright © Haruki Murakami 2011
Books One and Two translated by Jay Rubin
Book Three translated by Philip Gabriel

First published in three volumes with the title *1Q84* in 2009 and 2010
by Shinchosa Publishing Co Ltd, Tokyo

Adapted from the multi-volume Japanese edition with the participation
of the author

First published in Great Britain in 2011 by Harvill Secker

Vintage
Random House, 20 Vauxhall Bridge Road,
London SW1V 2SA

www.vintage-books.co.uk

Addresses for companies within The Random House Group Limited can be
found at: www.randomhouse.co.uk/offices.htm

The Random House Group Limited Reg. No. 954009

A CIP catalogue record for this book
is available from the British Library

ISBN 9780099578079

Printed and bound in Germany by GGP Media GmbH, Pössneck

It's a Barnum and Bailey world,

just as phony as it can be,

But it wouldn't be make-believe

if you believed in me

"It's Only a Paper Moon,"

– Billy Rose and E. Y. "Yip" Harburg

1Q
84

BOOK 1 APRIL–JUNE

CHAPTER 1

Aomame

DON'T LET APPEARANCES FOOL YOU

The taxi's radio was tuned to a classical FM broadcast. Janáček's *Sinfonietta* – probably not the ideal music to hear in a taxi caught in traffic. The middle-aged driver didn't seem to be listening very closely, either. With his mouth clamped shut, he stared straight ahead at the endless line of cars stretching out on the elevated expressway, like a veteran fisherman standing in the bow of his boat, reading the ominous confluence of two currents. Aomame settled into the broad back seat, closed her eyes, and listened to the music.

How many people could recognize Janáček's *Sinfonietta* after hearing just the first few bars? Probably somewhere between "very few" and "almost none." But for some reason, Aomame was one of the few who could.

Janáček composed his little symphony in 1926. He originally wrote the opening as a fanfare for a gymnastics festival. Aomame imagined 1926 Czechoslovakia: The First World War had ended, and the country was freed from the long rule of the Hapsburg Dynasty. As they enjoyed the peaceful respite visiting central Europe, people drank Pilsner beer in cafés and manufactured handsome light machine guns. Two years earlier, in utter obscurity, Franz Kafka had left the world behind. Soon Hitler would come out of nowhere and gobble up this beautiful little country in the blink of an eye, but at the time no one knew what hardships lay in store for them. This may be the most important proposition revealed by history: "At the time, no one knew what was coming." Listening to Janáček's music, Aomame imagined the carefree winds sweeping across the plains of Bohemia and thought about the vicissitudes of history.

In 1926 Japan's Taisho Emperor died, and the era name was changed to Showa. It was the beginning of a terrible, dark time in this country, too. The short interlude of modernism and democracy was ending, giving way to fascism.

Aomame loved history as much as she loved sports. She rarely read fiction, but history books could keep her occupied for hours. What she liked about history was the way all its facts were linked with particular dates and places. She did not find it especially difficult to remember historical dates. Even if she did not learn them by rote memorization, once she grasped the relationship of an event to its time and to the events preceding and following it, the date would come to her automatically. In both middle school and high school, she had always gotten the top grade on history exams. It puzzled her to hear someone say he had trouble learning dates. How could something so simple be a problem for anyone?

"Aomame" was her real name. Her grandfather on her father's side came from some little mountain town or village in Fukushima Prefecture, where there were supposedly a number of people who bore the name, written with exactly the same characters as the word for "green peas" and pronounced with the same four syllables, "Ah-oh-mah-meh." She had never been to the place, however. Her father had cut his ties with his family before her birth, just as her mother had done with her own family, so she had never met any of her grandparents. She didn't travel much, but on those rare occasions when she stayed in an unfamiliar city or town, she would always open the hotel's phone book to see if there were any Aomames in ~~~~~ had never found a single one, and whenever she trie~ area. She she felt like a lonely castaway on the open sea. ~ failed,

Telling people her name was always a bother. ~ the name left her lips, the other person looked p~s confused.

"Miss Aomame?"

"Yes. Just like 'green peas.' "

Employers required her to have business cards p~ which only made things worse. People would stare at th~ as if she had thrust a letter at them bearing bad news. Wh~ she announced her name on the telephone, she would often hear suppressed laughter. In waiting rooms at the doctor's or at public offices, people would look up at the sound of her name, curious to see what someone called "Green Peas" could look like.

Some people would get the name of the plant wrong and call her "Edamame" or "Soramame," whereupon she would gently correct them: "No, I'm not soybeans or fava beans, just green peas. Pretty close, though. Aomame." How many times in her thirty years had she heard the same remarks, the same feeble jokes about her name? *My life might have been totally different if I hadn't been born with this name. If I had had an ordinary name like Sato or Tanaka or Suzuki, I could have lived a slightly more relaxed life or looked at people with somewhat more forgiving eyes. Perhaps.*

Eyes closed, Aomame listened to the music, allowing the lovely unison of the brasses to sink into her brain. Just then it occurred to her that the sound quality was too good for a radio in a taxicab. Despite the rather low volume at which it was playing, the sound had true depth, and the overtones were clearly audible. She opened her eyes and leaned forward to study the dashboard stereo. The jet-black device shone with a proud gloss. She couldn't make out its brand name, but it

...sly high end, with lots of knobs and switches, the ...nerals of the station readout clear against the black ...his was not the kind of stereo you expected to see in ...inary fleet cab.

...e looked around at the cab's interior. She had been too ...orbed in her own thoughts to notice until now, but this ...as no ordinary taxi. The high quality of the trim was evident, and the seat was especially comfortable. Above all, it was quiet. The car probably had extra sound insulation to keep noise out, like a soundproofed music studio. The driver probably owned his own cab. Many such owner-drivers would spare no expense on the upkeep of their automobiles. Moving only her eyes, Aomame searched for the driver's registration card, without success. This did not seem to be an illegal unlicensed cab, though. It had a standard taxi meter, which was ticking off the proper fare: 2,150 yen so far. Still, the registration card showing the driver's name was nowhere to be found.

"What a nice car," Aomame said, speaking to the driver's back. "So quiet. What kind is it?"

"Toyota Crown Royal Saloon," the driver replied succinctly.

"The music sounds great in here."

"It's a very quiet car. That's one reason I chose it. Toyota has some of the best sound-insulating technology in the world."

Aomame nodded and leaned back in her seat. There was something about the driver's way of speaking that bothered her, as though he were leaving something important unsaid. For example (and this is just one example), his remark on Toyota's impeccable sound insulation might be taken to mean that some other Toyota feature was less than impeccable. And each time he finished a sentence, there was a tiny but meaningful lump of silence left behind. This lump floated there, enclosed in the car's restricted space like an imaginary miniature cloud, giving Aomame a strangely unsettled feeling.

"It certainly is a quiet car," Aomame declared, to sweep the little cloud away. "And the stereo looks especi ne."

"Decisiveness was key when I bought it," the said, like a retired staff officer explaining a past milit "I have to spend so much time in here, I want the ess. available. And – " d

Aomame waited for what was to follow, but n lowed. She closed her eyes again and concentra music. She knew nothing about Janáček as a perso was quite sure that he never imagined that in 1984 would be listening to his composition in a hushe Crown Royal Saloon on the gridlocked elevated Met Expressway in Tokyo.

Why, though, Aomame wondered, had she instantl ognized the piece to be Janáček's *Sinfonietta*? And how she know it had been composed in 1926? She was not classical music fan, and she had no personal recollections involving Janáček, yet the moment she heard the opening bars, all her knowledge of the piece came to her by reflex, like a flock of birds swooping through an open window. The music gave her an odd, wrenching kind of feeling. There was no pain or unpleasantness involved, just a sensation that all the elements of her body were being physically wrung out. Aomame had no idea what was going on. *Could* Sinfonietta *actually be giving me this weird feeling?*

"Janáček," Aomame said half-consciously, though after the word emerged from her lips, she wanted to take it back.

"What's that, ma'am?"

"Janáček. The man who wrote this music."

"Never heard of him."

"Czech composer."

"Well-well," the driver said, seemingly impressed.

"Do you own this cab?" Aomame asked, hoping to change the subject.

he driver answered. After a brief pause, he added, "I \e. My second one."

"It's comfortable seats."

nk you, ma'am." Turning his head slightly in her direc- asked, "By the way, are you in a hurry?"

ave to meet someone in Shibuya. That's why I asked you ke the expressway."

What time is your meeting?"

Four thirty," Aomame said.

"Well, it's already three forty-five. You'll never make it."

"Is the backup that bad?"

"Looks like a major accident up ahead. This is no ordinary traffic jam. We've hardly moved for quite a while."

She wondered why the driver was not listening to traffic reports. The expressway had been brought to a standstill. He should be listening to updates on the taxi drivers' special radio station.

"You can tell it's an accident without hearing a traffic report?" Aomame asked.

"You can't trust them," he said with a hollow ring to his voice. "They're half lies. The Expressway Corporation only releases reports that suit its agenda. If you really want to know what's happening here and now, you've got to use your own eyes and your own judgment."

"And your judgment tells you that we'll be stuck here?"

"For quite a while," the driver said with a nod. "I can guarantee you that. When it backs up solid like this, the expressway is sheer hell. Is your meeting an important one?"

Aomame gave it some thought. "Yes, very. I have to see a client."

"That's a shame. You're probably not going to make it."

The driver shook his head a few times as if trying to ease a stiff neck. The wrinkles on the back of his neck moved like some kind of ancient creature. Half-consciously watching the movement, Aomame found herself thinking of the sharp object in the bottom of her shoulder bag. A touch of sweat came to her palms.

"What do you think I should do?" she asked.

"There's nothing you *can* do up here on the expressway – not until we get to the next exit. If we were down on the city streets, you could just step out of the cab and take the subway."

"What is the next exit?"

"Ikejiri. We might not get there before the sun goes down, though."

Before the sun goes down? Aomame imagined herself locked in this cab until sunset. The Janáček was still playing. Muted strings came to the foreground as if to soothe her heightened anxiety. That earlier wrenching sensation had largely subsided. What could that have been?

Aomame had caught the cab near Kinuta and told the driver to take the elevated expressway from Yohga. The flow of traffic had been smooth at first, but suddenly backed up just before Sangenjaya, after which they had hardly moved. The outbound lanes were moving fine. Only the side headed toward downtown Tokyo was tragically jammed. Inbound Expressway Number 3 would not normally back up at three in the afternoon, which was why Aomame had directed the driver to take it.

"Time charges don't add up on the expressway," the driver said, speaking toward his rearview mirror. "So don't let the fare worry you. I suppose you need to get to your meeting, though?"

"Yes, of course. But there's nothing I can do about it, is there?"

He glanced at her in the mirror. He was wearing pale sunglasses. The way the light was shining in, Aomame could not make out his expression.

"Well, in fact, there might be a way. You *could* take the

subway to Shibuya from here, but you'd have to do something a little . . . extreme."

"Something extreme?"

"It's not something I can openly advise you to do."

Aomame said nothing. She waited for more with narrowed eyes.

"Look over there. See that turnout just ahead?" he asked, pointing. "See? Near that Esso sign."

Aomame strained to see through the windshield until she focused on a space to the left of the two-lane roadway where broken-down cars could pull off. The elevated roadway had no shoulder but instead had emergency turnouts at regular intervals. Aomame saw that the turnout was outfitted with a yellow emergency phone box for contacting the Metropolitan Expressway Public Corporation office. The turnout itself was empty at the moment. On top of a building beyond the oncoming lanes there was a big billboard advertising Esso gasoline with a smiling tiger holding a gas hose.

"To tell you the truth, there's a stairway leading from the turnout down to street level. It's for drivers who have to abandon their cars in a fire or earthquake and climb down to the street. Usually only maintenance workers use it. If you were to climb down that stairway, you'd be near a Tokyu Line station. From there, it's nothing to Shibuya."

"I had no idea these Metropolitan Expressways had emergency stairs," Aomame said.

"Not many people do."

"But wouldn't I get in trouble using it without permission when there's no real emergency?"

The driver paused a moment. Then he said, "I wonder. I don't know all the rules of the Corporation, but you wouldn't be hurting anybody. They'd probably look the other way, don't you think? Anyway, they don't have people watching every exit. The Metropolitan Expressway Public Corporation is

famous for having a huge staff but nobo[...]
work."

"What kind of stairway is it?"

"Hmm, kind of like a fire escape. You k[...]
you see on the backs of old buildings. It's [...]
gerous or anything. It's maybe three stories[...]
climb down. There's a barrier at the openir[...]
high. Anybody who wanted to could get ov[...]

"Have you ever used one of these stairw[...]

Instead of replying, the driver directed [...]
his rearview mirror, a smile that could be [...]
ways.

"It's strictly up to you," he said, tapping [...]
ing wheel in time to the music. "If you j[...]
and relax and enjoy the music, I'm fine wit[...]
well resign ourselves to the fact that we're no[...]
soon. All I'm saying is that there *are* emergenc[...]
can take if you have urgent business."

Aomame frowned and glanced at her watch. Sh[...]
and studied the surrounding cars. On the right w[...]
Mitsubishi Pajero wagon with a thin layer of white [...]
bored-looking young man in the front passenger sea[...]
smoking a cigarette with his window open. He had long [...]
a tanned face, and wore a dark red windbreaker. The car's l[...]
gage compartment was filled with a number of worn surf[...]
boards. In front of him was a gray Saab 900, its dark-tinted
windows closed tight, preventing any glimpse of who might
be inside. The body was so immaculately polished, you could
probably see your face in it.

The car ahead was a red Suzuki Alto with a Nerima Ward
license plate and a dented bumper. A young mother sat gripping the wheel. Her small child was standing on the seat next
to her, moving back and forth to dispel its boredom. The
mother's annoyance showed on her face as she cautioned the

omame could see her mouth moving. The
ed from ten minutes earlier. In those ten
d probably advanced less than ten yards.

ht hard, arranging everything in order of
d hardly any time to reach a conclusion. As
this, the final movement of the Janáček was

all Ray-Ban sunglasses partway out of her
ook three thousand-yen bills from her walls to the driver, she said, "I'll get out here.
for this appointment."

ed and took the money. "Would you like a

eep the change."

ch," he said. "Be careful, it looks windy out

il," Aomame said.

the driver said, facing the mirror, "please
hings are not what they seem."

are not what they seem, Aomame repeated mentally.
o you mean by that?" she asked with knitted brows.

e driver chose his words carefully: "It's just that you're
ut to do something *out of the ordinary.* Am I right? Peo-
e do not ordinarily climb down the emergency stairs of the
Metropolitan Expressway in the middle of the day – especially
women."

"I suppose you're right."

"Right. And after you *do* something like that, the everyday
look of things might seem to change a little. Things may look
different to you than they did before. I've had that experience
myself. But don't let appearances fool you. There's always only
one reality."

Aomame thought about what he was saying, and in the
course of her thinking, the Janáček ended and the audience

broke into immediate applause. This was obviously a live recording. The applause was long and enthusiastic. There were even occasional calls of "Bravo!" She imagined the smiling conductor bowing repeatedly to the standing audience. He would then raise his head, raise his arms, shake hands with the concertmaster, turn away from the audience, raise his arms again in praise of the orchestra, face front, and take another deep bow. As she listened to the long recorded applause, it sounded less like applause and more like an endless Martian sandstorm.

"There is always, as I said, only one reality," the driver repeated slowly, as if underlining an important passage in a book.

"Of course," Aomame said. He was right. A physical object could only be in one place at one time. Einstein proved that. Reality was utterly coolheaded and utterly lonely.

Aomame pointed toward the car stereo. "Great sound."

The driver nodded. "What was the name of that composer again?"

"Janáček."

"Janáček," the driver repeated, as if committing an important password to memory. Then he pulled the lever that opened the passenger door. "Be careful," he said. "I hope you get to your appointment on time."

Aomame stepped out of the cab, gripping the strap of her large leather shoulder bag. The applause was still going. She started walking carefully along the left edge of the elevated road toward the emergency turnout some ten meters ahead. Each time a large truck roared by on the opposite side, she felt the surface of the road shake – or, rather, undulate – through her high heels, as if she were walking on the deck of an aircraft carrier on a stormy sea.

The little girl in the front seat of the red Suzuki Alto stuck her head out of her window and stared, open-mouthed, at

Aomame passing by. Then she turned to her mother and asked, "Mommy, what is that lady doing? Where's she going? I want to get out and walk too. Please, Mommy! Pleeease!" The mother responded to her cries in silence, shaking her head and shooting an accusatory glance at Aomame. The girl's loud pleading and the mother's glance were the only responses to her that Aomame noticed. The other drivers just sat at the wheel smoking and watching her make her way with determined steps between the cars and the side wall. They knit their brows and squinted as if looking at a too-bright object but seemed to have temporarily suspended all judgment. For someone to be walking on the Metropolitan Expressway was by no means an everyday event, with or without the usual flow of traffic, so it took them some time to process the sight as an actual occurrence – all the more so because the walker was a young woman in high heels and a miniskirt.

Aomame pulled in her chin, kept her gaze fixed straight ahead, her back straight, and her pace steady. Her chestnut-colored Charles Jourdan heels clicked against the road's surface, and the skirts of her coat waved in the breeze. April had begun, but there was still a chill in the air and a hint of roughness to come. Aomame wore a beige spring coat over her green light wool Junko Shimada suit. A black leather bag hung over her shoulder, and her shoulder-length hair was impeccably trimmed and shaped. She wore no accessories of any kind. Five foot six inches tall, she carried not an ounce of excess fat. Every muscle in her body was well toned, but her coat kept that fact hidden.

A detailed examination of her face from the front would reveal that the size and shape of her ears were significantly different, the left one much bigger and malformed. No one ever noticed this, however, because her hair nearly always covered her ears. Her lips formed a tight straight line, suggesting that she was not easily approachable. Also contributing to this impression were her small, narrow nose, somewhat protruding cheekbones, broad forehead, and long, straight eyebrows. All of these were arranged to sit in a pleasing oval shape, however, and while tastes differ, few would object to calling her a beautiful woman. The one problem with her face was its extreme paucity of expression. Her firmly closed lips only formed a smile when absolutely necessary. Her eyes had the cool, vigilant stare of a superior deck officer. Thanks to these features, no one ever had a vivid impression of her face. She attracted attention not so much because of the qualities of her features but rather because of the naturalness and grace with which her expression moved. In that sense, Aomame resembled an insect skilled at biological mimicry. What she most wanted was to blend in with her background by changing color and shape, to remain inconspicuous and not easily remembered. This was how she had protected herself since childhood.

Whenever something caused her to frown or grimace, however, her features underwent dramatic changes. The muscles of her face tightened, pulling in several directions at once and emphasizing the lack of symmetry in the overall structure. Deep wrinkles formed in her skin, her eyes suddenly drew inward, her nose and mouth became violently distorted, her jaw twisted to the side, and her lips curled back, exposing Aomame's large white teeth. Instantly, she became a wholly different person, as if a cord had broken, dropping the mask that normally covered her face. The shocking transformation terrified anyone who saw it, so she was careful never to frown in the presence of a stranger. She would contort her face only when she was alone or when she was threatening a man who displeased her.

Reaching the turnout, Aomame stopped and looked around. It took only a moment for her to find the emergency stairway. As the driver had said, there was a metal barrier across the entrance. It was a little more than waist high, and it was locked. Stepping over it in a tight miniskirt could be a slight problem, but only if she cared about being seen. Without hesitating, she slipped her high heels off and shoved them into her shoulder bag. She would probably ruin her stockings by walking in bare feet, but she could easily buy another pair.

People stared at her in silence as she removed her shoes and coat. From the open window of the black Toyota Celica parked next to the turnout, Michael Jackson's high-pitched voice provided her with background music. "Billie Jean" was playing. She felt as if she were performing a striptease. *So what? Let them look all they want. They must be bored waiting for the traffic jam to end. Sorry, though, folks, this is all I'll be taking off today.*

Aomame slung the bag across her chest to keep it from falling. Some distance away she could see the brand-new black Toyota Crown Royal Saloon in which she had been riding, its windshield reflecting the blinding glare of the afternoon sun. She could not make out the face of the driver, but she knew he must be watching.

Don't let appearances fool you. There's always only one reality.

Aomame took in a long, deep breath, and slowly let it out. Then, to the tune of "Billie Jean," she swung her leg over the metal barrier. Her miniskirt rode up to her hips. *Who gives a damn? Let them look all they want. Seeing what's under my skirt doesn't let them really see me as a person.* Besides, her legs were the part of her body of which Aomame was the most proud.

Stepping down once she was on the other side of the barrier, Aomame straightened her skirt, brushed the dust from her hands, put her coat back on, slung her bag across her chest again, and pushed her sunglasses more snugly against her face. The emergency stairway lay before her – a metal stairway painted gray. Plain, practical, functional. Not made for use by miniskirted women wearing only stockings on their otherwise bare feet. Nor had Junko Shimada designed Aomame's suit for use on the emergency escape stairs of Tokyo Metropolitan Expressway Number 3. Another huge truck roared down the outbound side of the expressway, shaking the stairs. The breeze whistled through gaps in the stairway's metal framework. But in any case, there it was, before her: the stairway. All that was left for her to do was climb down to the street.

Aomame turned for one last look at the double line of cars packed on the expressway, scanning them from left to right, then right to left, like a speaker on a podium looking for questions from the audience now that she had finished her talk. There had been no movement at all. Trapped on the expressway with nothing else to occupy them, people were watching her every move, wondering what this woman on the far side of the barrier would do next. Aomame lightly pulled in her chin, bit her lower lip, and took stock of her audience through the dark green lenses of her sunglasses.

You couldn't begin to imagine who I am, where I'm going, or what I'm about to do, Aomame said to her audience without moving her lips. *All of you are trapped here. You can't go anywhere, forward or back. But I'm not like you. I have work to do. I have a mission to accomplish. And so, with your permission, I shall move ahead.*

Aomame had the urge at the end to treat her assembled throng to one of her special scowls, but she managed to stop herself. There was no time for such things now. Once she let herself frown, it took both time and effort to regain her original expression.

Aomame turned her back on her silent audience and, with careful steps, began to descend the emergency stairway, feeling the chill of the crude metal rungs against the soles of her feet. Also chilling was the early April breeze, which swept her hair back now and then, revealing her misshapen left ear.

CHAPTER 2

Tengo

SOMETHING ELSE IN MIND

Tengo's first memory dated from the time he was one and a half. His mother had taken off her blouse and dropped the shoulder straps of her white slip to let a man who was not his father suck on her breasts. The infant in the crib nearby was probably Tengo himself. He was observing the scene as a third person. Or could the infant have been his twin? No, not likely. It was one-and-a-half-year-old Tengo. He knew this intuitively. The infant was asleep, its eyes closed, its little breaths deep and regular. The vivid ten-second scene was seared into the wall of his consciousness, his earliest memory in life. Nothing came before or after it. It stood out alone, like the steeple of a town visited by a flood, thrusting up above the muddy water.

Tengo made a point of asking people how old they were at the time of their first memory. For most people it was four or five. Three at the very earliest. A child had to be at least three to begin observing a surrounding scene with a degree of rationality. In the stage before that, everything registered as incomprehensible chaos. The world was a mushy bowl of loose gruel, lacking framework or handholds. It flowed past our open windows without forming memories in the brain.

Surely a one-and-a-half-year-old infant was unable to grasp what it meant for a man who was not his father to be sucking his mother's breasts. That much was clear. So if this memory of Tengo's was genuine, the scene must have been seared into his retinas as a pure image free of judgment – the way a camera records objects on film, mechanically, as a blend of light and shadow. And as his consciousness matured, the fixed image held in reserve would have been analyzed bit by bit, and meaning applied to it. But is such a thing even possible? Was the infant brain capable of preserving images like that?

Or was this simply a false memory of Tengo's? Was it just something that his mind had later decided – for whatever purpose or plan – to make up on its own? Tengo had given plenty of thought to the possibility that this memory might be a fabrication, but he had arrived at the conclusion that it probably was not. It was too vivid and too deeply compelling to be fake. The light, the smells, the beating of his heart: these felt overwhelmingly real, not like imitations. And besides, it explained many things – both logically and emotionally – to assume that the scene was real.

This vivid ten-second image would come to him without warning and without consideration of either time or place. He could be riding on the subway or writing formulas on the blackboard or having a meal or (as now) sitting and talking to someone across a table, and it would envelop him like a soundless tsunami. By the time he noticed, it would be directly in front of him, and his arms and legs would be paralyzed. The flow of time stopped. The air grew thin, and he had trouble breathing. He lost all connection with the people and things around him. The tsunami's liquid wall swallowed him whole. And though it felt to him as if the world were being closed off in darkness, he experienced no loss of awareness. It was just a sense of having been switched to a new track. Parts of his mind were, if anything, sharpened by the change. He felt no terror, but he could not keep his eyes open. His eyelids were clamped shut. Sounds grew distant, and the familiar image was projected onto the screen of his consciousness again and again. Sweat gushed from every part of his body and the armpits of his undershirt grew damp. He trembled all over, and his heartbeat grew faster and louder.

If he was with someone when it happened, Tengo would feign momentary dizziness. It was, in fact, like a dizzy spell. Everything would return to normal in time. He would pull his handkerchief from his pocket and press it to his mouth. Waiting for the "dizziness" to pass, he would raise a hand to signal to the other person that it was nothing to worry about. Sometimes it would all be over in thirty seconds, at other times it went on for over a minute. As long as it lasted, the same image would be repeated as if on a tape machine set on automatic. His mother would drop her shoulder straps and some man would start sucking on her hardened nipples. She would close her eyes and heave a deep sigh. The warm, familiar scent of mother's milk hovered faintly in the air. Smell is an infant's most acute sense. The sense of smell reveals a great deal – sometimes it reveals everything. The scene was soundless, the air a dense liquid. All he could hear was the soft beating of his own heart.

Look at this, they say. *Look at this and nothing else,* they say. *You are here. You can't go anywhere else,* they say. The message is played over and over.

This "attack" was a long one. Tengo closed his eyes, covered his mouth with his handkerchief as always, and gritted his teeth. He had no idea how long it went on. All he could do was guess, based on how worn out he felt afterward. He felt physically drained, more fatigued than he had ever felt before. Some time had to go by before he could open his eyes. His mind wanted to wake up, but his muscles and internal organs resisted. He might as well have been a hibernating animal trying to wake up in the wrong season.

"Tengo, Tengo!" someone was calling. The muffled voice

seemed to reach him from the depths of a cave. It finally dawned on Tengo that he was hearing his own name. "What's wrong, Tengo? Is it happening to you again? Are you all right?" The voice sounded closer now.

Tengo finally opened his eyes, managed to focus them, and stared at his own right hand gripping the edge of the table. Now he could be sure that the world still existed in one piece and that he was still a part of it. Some numbness remained, but the hand was certainly his. So, too, was the smell of sweat emanating from him, an oddly harsh odor like a zoo animal's.

His throat was dry. Tengo reached for the glass on the table and drank half its contents, carefully trying not to spill any. After a momentary rest to catch his breath, he drank the remainder. His mind was gradually coming back to where it belonged and his senses were returning to normal. He set the empty glass down and wiped his mouth with his handkerchief.

"Sorry," he said. "I'm okay now."

He knew that the man across from him was Komatsu and that they had been talking at a café near Tokyo's Shinjuku Station. The sounds of other nearby conversations now sounded like normal voices. The couple at the neighboring table were staring at him, obviously concerned. The waitress stood by with a worried expression on her face as though she expected her customer to vomit. Tengo looked up and nodded to her, smiling as if to signal, "Don't worry, no problem."

"That wasn't some kind of *fit*, was it?" Komatsu asked.

"No, it's nothing, a kind of dizzy spell. A bad one," Tengo replied. His voice still didn't sound like his own, though it was getting closer.

"It'd be terrible if that happened while you were driving or something," Komatsu said, looking directly at him.

"I don't drive."

"That's good. I know a guy with a cedar pollen allergy who started sneezing at the wheel and smashed into a telephone pole. Of course, your thing is not just sneezing. I was shocked the first time. I'm more or less used to it now, though."

"Sorry."

Tengo picked up his coffee cup and gulped down what was left. He tasted nothing, just felt some lukewarm liquid passing down his throat.

"Want to order another glass of water?" Komatsu asked.

Tengo shook his head. "No, I'm okay now."

Komatsu took a pack of Marlboros from his jacket pocket, put one in his mouth, and lit up with the café's matches. Then he glanced at his watch.

"What were we talking about again?" Tengo asked, trying to get back to normal.

"Good question," Komatsu said, staring off into space, thinking – or pretending to. Tengo could not be sure which. There was a good deal of acting involved in the way Komatsu spoke and gestured. "That's it – the girl Fuka-Eri. We were just getting started on her and *Air Chrysalis.*"

Tengo nodded. That was it. He was just beginning to give his opinion on Fuka-Eri and her novella, *Air Chrysalis,* when the "attack" hit him.

Komatsu said, "I was going to tell you about that odd one-word pen name of hers."

"It is odd, isn't it? The 'Fuka' sounds like part of a family name, and the 'Eri' could be an ordinary girl's name: 'Eri' or 'Eriko.' "

"That's exactly what it is. Her family name is 'Fukada,' and her real first name is 'Eriko,' so she put them together: 'Fuka' plus 'Eri' equals 'Fuka-Eri.' "

Tengo pulled the manuscript from his briefcase and laid it on the table, resting his hand atop the sheaf of paper to re-affirm its presence.

"As I mentioned briefly on the phone, the best thing about this *Air Chrysalis* is that it's not an imitation of anyone. It has absolutely none of the usual new writer's sense of 'I want to be another so-and-so.' The style, for sure, is rough, and the writing is clumsy. She even gets the title wrong: she's confusing 'chrysalis' and 'cocoon.' You could pick it apart completely if you wanted to. But the story itself has real power: it draws you in. The overall plot is a fantasy, but the descriptive detail is incredibly real. The balance between the two is excellent. I don't know if words like 'originality' or 'inevitability' fit here, and I suppose I might agree if someone insisted it's not at that level, but finally, after you work your way through the thing, with all its faults, it leaves a real impression – it *gets* to you in some strange, inexplicable way that may be a little disturbing."

Komatsu kept his eyes on Tengo, saying nothing. He was waiting to hear more.

Tengo went on. "I'd hate to see this thing dropped from the competition just because the style is clumsy. I've read tons of submissions over the years – or maybe I should say 'skimmed' rather than 'read.' A few of them were fairly well written, of course, but most of them were just awful. And out of all those manuscripts, this *Air Chrysalis* is the only one that moved me the least bit. It's the only one that ever made me want to read it again."

"Well, well," Komatsu said, and then, as if he found this all rather boring, he released a stream of smoke through his pursed lips. Tengo had known Komatsu too long to be deceived by such a display, however. Komatsu was a man who often adopted an expression that was either unrelated to – or exactly the opposite of – what he was actually feeling. And so Tengo was prepared to wait him out.

"I read it, too," Komatsu said after a short pause. "Right after you called me. The writing is incredibly bad. It's ungrammatical, and in some places you have no idea what she's trying to say. She should go back to school and learn how to write a decent sentence before she starts writing fiction."

"But you *did* read it to the end, didn't you?"

Komatsu smiled. It was the kind of smile he might have found way in the back of a normally unopened drawer. "You're right, I did read it all the way through – much to my own surprise. I *never* read these new writer prize submissions from beginning to end. I even *re*read some parts of this one. Let's just say the planets were in perfect alignment. I'll grant it that much."

"Which means it *has* something, don't you think?"

Komatsu set his cigarette in an ashtray and rubbed the side of his nose with the middle finger of his right hand. He did not, however, answer Tengo's question.

Tengo said, "She's just seventeen, a high school kid. She still doesn't have the discipline to read and write fiction, that's all. It's practically impossible for this work to take the new writers' prize, I know, but it's good enough to put on the short list. *You* can make that happen, I'm sure. So then she can win next time."

"Hmm," Komatsu said with another noncommittal answer and a yawn. He took a drink from his water glass. "Think about it, Tengo. Imagine if I put it on the short list. The members of the selection committee would faint – or more likely have a shit fit. But they would definitely not read it all the way through. All four of them are active writers, busy with their own work. They'd skim the first couple of pages and toss it out as if it were some grade school composition. I could plead with them to give it another try, and guarantee them it would be brilliant with a little polishing here and there, but who's going to listen to me? Even supposing I could 'make it happen,' I'd only want to do that for something with more promise."

"So you're saying we should drop it just like that?"

"No, that is not what I'm saying," Komatsu said, rubbing the side of his nose. "I've got something else in mind for this story."

"Something else in mind," Tengo said. He sensed something ominous in Komatsu's tone.

"You're saying we should count on her *next* work as a winner," Komatsu said. "I'd like to be able to do that, too, of course. One of an editor's greatest joys is nurturing a young writer over time. It's a thrill to look at the clear night sky and discover a new star before anybody else sees it. But to tell you the truth, Tengo, I don't believe this girl *has* a next work in her. Not to boast, but I've been making my living in this business for twenty years now. I've seen writers come and go. And if I've learned anything, it's how to tell the difference between writers who *have* a next work in them, and those who don't. And if you ask me, this girl doesn't have one. Her next work is not going to make it, and neither will the one after that or the one after that. First of all, look at this style. No amount of work is going to make it any better. It's never going to happen. And the reason it's never going to happen is that the writer herself doesn't give a damn about style: she shows absolutely no *intention* of wanting to write well, of wanting to improve her writing. Good style happens in one of two ways: the writer either has an inborn talent or is willing to work herself to death to get it. And this girl, Fuka-Eri, belongs to neither type. Don't ask me why, but style as such simply doesn't interest her. What she does have, though, is the desire to tell a story – a fairly strong desire. I grant her that. Even in this raw form, it was able to draw you in, Tengo, and it made me read the manuscript all the way through. That alone is impressive, you could say. But she has no future as a novelist. None. I hate to disappoint you, but that's my honest opinion."

Tengo had to admit that Komatsu could be right. The man possessed good editorial instincts, if nothing else.

"Still, it wouldn't hurt to give her a chance, would it?" Tengo asked.

"You mean, throw her in, see if she sinks or swims?"

"In a word."

"I've done too much of that already. I don't want to watch anybody else drown."

"Well, what about me?"

"You at least are willing to work hard," Komatsu said cautiously. "As far as I can tell, you don't cut corners. You're very modest when it comes to the act of writing. And why? Because you *like* to write. I value that in you. It's the single most important quality for somebody who wants to be a writer."

"But not, in itself, enough."

"No, of course, not in itself enough. There also has to be that 'special something,' an indefinable quality, something I can't quite put my finger on. That's the part of fiction I value more highly than anything else. Stuff I understand perfectly doesn't interest me. Obviously. It's very simple."

Tengo fell silent for a while. Then he said, "Does Fuka-Eri's writing have something you don't understand perfectly?"

"Yes, it does, of course. She has something important. I don't know what it is exactly, but she has it, that much is clear. It's obvious to you, and it's obvious to me. Anybody can see it, like the smoke from a bonfire on a windless afternoon. But whatever she has, Tengo, she probably can't carry it on her own."

"Meaning, if we throw her in the water, she'll drown?"

"Exactly."

"And that's why you don't want to put her on the short list."

"That is exactly why." Komatsu contorted his lips and folded his hands on the table. "Which brings us to a point in the conversation where I have to be very careful how I express myself."

Tengo picked up his coffee cup and stared at the puddle inside. Then he put the cup down again. Komatsu still had not spoken. Tengo asked, "Is this where I find out what you mean by 'something else'?"

Komatsu narrowed his eyes like a teacher gazing upon his prize pupil. He nodded slowly and said, "It is."

* * *

There was something inscrutable about this man Komatsu. You couldn't easily tell from his expression or tone of voice what he was thinking or feeling. He appeared to derive a good deal of pleasure from keeping others guessing. Mentally, he was very quick, that was for certain. He was the type of man who had his own sense of logic and reached his own conclusions without regard to the opinions of others. He did not engage in pointless intellectual display, but it was clear that he had read an enormous amount and that his knowledge was both wide-ranging and deep. Nor was it simply a matter of factual knowledge: he had an intuitive eye both for people and for books. His biases played a large role here, but for Komatsu bias was an important element of truth.

He never said a great deal, and he hated long-winded explanations, but when necessary he could present his views logically and precisely. He could also be quite caustic if he felt like it, aiming a quick and merciless jab at his opponent's weakest point. He had very strong opinions about both people and literature; the works and individuals he could not tolerate far outnumbered those he could. Not surprisingly, the number of people who disliked him was far greater than those who thought well of him – which was exactly what he hoped for. Tengo thought that Komatsu enjoyed the isolation – and even relished being openly hated. Komatsu believed that mental acuity was never born from comfortable circumstances.

At forty-five, Komatsu was sixteen years older than Tengo. A dedicated editor of literary magazines, he had established a certain reputation as one of the top people in the industry, but no one knew a thing about his private life. He met with people constantly in his work, but he never spoke of anything personal. Tengo had no idea where he was born or raised, or even where he lived. They often had long conversations, but such topics never came up. People were puzzled that a difficult man like Komatsu was able to solicit manuscripts from writers – he had no friends to speak of and displayed only contempt for the literary world – but over the years he managed, almost effortlessly, to obtain work by famous authors for the magazine, and more than a few issues owed their contents to his efforts. So even if they didn't like him, people respected him.

Rumor had it that when Komatsu was a student in the prestigious University of Tokyo's Department of Literature in 1960, he had been one of the leaders of the huge leftist demonstrations against the U.S.-Japan Security Treaty. He was said to have been near fellow student Michiko Kanba when she was killed by riot police, and to have suffered serious injuries himself. No one knew if this was true, but there was something about Komatsu that made the stories seem convincing. He was tall and gangly, with an oversized mouth and an undersized nose. He had long limbs and nicotine-stained fingers, reminiscent of those failed revolutionary intellectuals in nineteenth-century Russian novels. He rarely smiled, but when he did it was with his whole face. Not that it made him look especially happy – he was more like an old sorcerer chuckling to himself over an ominous prophecy he was about to reveal. Clean and decently groomed, he always wore a tweed jacket, white oxford cloth or pale gray polo shirt, no tie, gray pants, suede shoes – a "uniform" meant to show the world he didn't care about these things. Tengo imagined a half-dozen three-button tweed jackets of a subtly different color, cloth, and pattern that hung, carefully brushed, in Komatsu's closet. Perhaps Komatsu had to attach number tags to distinguish one jacket from another.

Komatsu's fine, wiry hair was beginning to show a touch of gray in front. Tangled on the sides, it was long enough to cover his ears, and it always stayed that length, about a week overdue for a haircut. Tengo wondered how such a thing was possible. At times Komatsu's eyes would take on a sharp glow, like stars glittering in the winter night sky. And if something caused him to clam up, he would maintain his silence like a rock on the far side of the moon. All expression would disappear from his face, and his body seemed to go cold.

Tengo first met Komatsu five years earlier when he was short-listed for the new writers' prize competition of Komatsu's magazine. Komatsu called and said he wanted to get together for a chat. They agreed to meet in a café in Shinjuku (the same one in which they were now sitting). Komatsu told Tengo there was no way his work would take the prize (and in fact it did not). Komatsu himself, however, had enjoyed the story. "I'm not looking for thanks, but I almost never say this to anyone," he said. (This was in fact true, as Tengo came to learn.) "So I'd like you to let me read your next story before you show it to anyone else." Tengo promised to do that.

Komatsu also wanted to learn about Tengo as a person – his experience growing up, what he was doing now. Tengo explained himself as honestly as he could. He was born in the city of Ichikawa in nearby Chiba Prefecture. His mother died of an illness shortly after he was born, or at least that was what his father told him. He had no siblings. His father never remarried but raised Tengo by himself, collecting NHK television subscription fees door to door to make a living. Now, however, his father had Alzheimer's disease and was living in a nursing home on the southern tip of Chiba's Boso Peninsula. Tengo himself had graduated from Tsukuba University's oddly named "School 1 College of Natural Studies Mathematics Major" and was writing fiction while teaching mathematics at a private cram school in Yoyogi. At the time of his graduation he could have taken a position at a prefectural high school near home, but instead chose the relatively free schedule of the Tokyo cram school. He lived alone in a small apartment in the Koenji District west of downtown Tokyo, which gave him an easy half-hour commute to school.

Tengo did not know for certain whether he wanted to be a professional novelist, nor was he sure he had the talent to write fiction. What he did know was that he could not help spending a large part of every day writing fiction. To him, writing was like breathing.

Komatsu said practically nothing as he listened to Tengo's story. He seemed to like Tengo, though it was not clear why. Tengo was a big man (he had been a key member of his judo team in middle school, high school, and college), and he had the eyes of an early-waking farmer. He wore his hair short, seemed always to have a tan, and had cauliflower ears. He looked neither like a youthful devotee of literature nor like a teacher of mathematics, which was also something that Komatsu seemed to like about him.

Whenever Tengo finished a story, he would take it to Komatsu. Komatsu would read it and offer his comments. Tengo would rewrite it following his advice and bring it to Komatsu again, who would provide new instructions, like a coach raising the bar a little at a time. "Your case might take some time," he said. "But we're in no hurry. Just make up your mind to write every single day. And don't throw anything out. It might come in handy later." Tengo agreed to follow Komatsu's advice.

For his part, Komatsu would occasionally send small writing jobs Tengo's way. Anonymously, Tengo wrote copy for the women's magazine produced by Komatsu's publisher. He handled everything: revising letters to the editor, writing background pieces on movies and books, composing horoscopes. His horoscopes were especially popular because they were often right. Once when he wrote, "Beware an early-morning earthquake," there actually was a big earthquake early one morning. Tengo was grateful for the extra income and for the writing practice this work provided. It made him happy to see his writing in print – in any form – displayed in the bookstores.

Eventually Tengo was hired as a screener for the literary magazine's new writers' prize. It was odd for him to be screening other writers' works when he himself was competing for the prize, but he read everything impartially, not terribly concerned about the delicacy of his situation. If nothing else, the experience of reading mounds of badly written fiction gave him an indelible lesson in exactly what constituted badly written fiction. He read around one hundred works each time, choosing ten that might have some point to them to bring to Komatsu with written comments. Five works would make it to the short list, and from those the four-person committee would select the winner.

Tengo was not the only part-time screener, and Komatsu was only one of several editors engaged in assembling the short list. This was all in the name of fairness, but such efforts were not really necessary. No matter how many works were entered in the competition, there were never more than two or three of any value, and no one could possibly miss those. Three of Tengo's stories had made the short list in the past. Each had been chosen not by Tengo himself, of course, but by two other screeners and then by Komatsu, who manned the editorial desk. None had won the prize, but this had not been a crushing blow to Tengo. For one thing, Komatsu had ingrained in him the idea that he just had to give it time. And Tengo himself was not all that eager to become a novelist right away.

If he arranged his teaching schedule well, Tengo was able to spend four days a week at home. He had taught at the same cram school for seven years now, and he was popular with the students because he knew how to convey the subject succinctly and clearly, and he could answer any question on the spot. Tengo surprised himself with his own eloquence. His explanations were clever, his voice carried well, and he could excite the class with a good joke. He had always thought of himself as a poor speaker, and even now he could be at a loss for words when confronted face-to-face. In a small group, he was strictly a listener. In front of a large class, however, his head would clear, and he could speak at length with ease. His own teaching experience gave him renewed awareness of the inscrutability of human beings.

Tengo was not dissatisfied with his salary. It was by no means high, but the school paid in accordance with ability. The students were asked to do course evaluations periodically, and compensation hinged on the results. The school was afraid of having its best teachers lured away (and, in fact, Tengo had been headhunted several times). This never happened at ordinary schools. There, salary was set by seniority, teachers' private lives were subject to the supervision of administrators, and ability and popularity counted for nothing. Tengo actually enjoyed teaching at the cram school. Most of the students went there with the explicit purpose of preparing for the college entrance exams, and they attended his lectures enthusiastically. Teachers had only one duty: to teach their classes. This was exactly what Tengo wanted. He never had to deal with student misbehavior or infractions of school rules. All he had to do was show up in the classroom and teach students how to solve mathematical problems. And the manipulation of pure abstractions using numerical tools came naturally to Tengo.

When he was home, Tengo usually wrote from first thing in the morning until the approach of evening. All he needed to satisfy him was his Mont Blanc pen, his blue ink, and standard manuscript sheets, each page lined with four hundred empty squares ready to accept four hundred characters. Once a week his married girlfriend would come to spend the afternoon with him. Sex with a married woman ten years his senior was stress free and fulfilling, because it couldn't lead to anything. As the sun was setting, he would head out for a long walk, and once the sun was down he would read a book while listening to music. He never watched television. Whenever the NHK fee collector came, he would point out that he had no television set, and politely refuse to pay. "I really don't have one. You can come in and look if you want," he would say, but the collector would never come in. They were not allowed to.

"I have something bigger in mind," Komatsu said.

"Something bigger?"

"Much bigger. Why be satisfied with small-scale stuff like the new writers' prize? As long as we're aiming, why not go for something big?"

Tengo fell silent. He had no idea what Komatsu was getting at, but he sensed something disturbing.

"The Akutagawa Prize!" Komatsu declared after a moment's pause.

"The Akutagawa Prize?" Tengo repeated the words slowly, as if he were writing them in huge characters with a stick on wet sand.

"Come on, Tengo, you can't be *that* out of touch! The Akutagawa Prize! Every writer's dream! Huge headlines in the paper! TV news!"

"Now you're losing me. Are we still talking about Fuka-Eri?"

"Of course we are – Fuka-Eri and *Air Chrysalis*. Have we been discussing anything else?"

Tengo bit his lip as he tried to fathom the meaning behind Komatsu's words. "But you yourself said there's no way *Air Chrysalis* can take the new writers' prize. Haven't we been talking about that all along, how the work will never amount to anything the way it is?"

"Precisely. It'll never amount to anything the way it is. That is for certain."

Tengo needed time to think. "Are you saying it needs to be revised?"

"It's the only way. It's not that unusual for an author to revise a promising work with the advice of an editor. It happens all the time. Only, in this case, rather than the author, someone else will do the revising."

"Someone else?" Tengo asked, but he already knew what Komatsu's answer would be.

"You."

Tengo searched for an appropriate response but couldn't find one. He heaved a sigh and said, "You know as well as I do that this work is going to need more than a little patching here and there. It'll never come together without a fundamental top-to-bottom rewrite."

"Which is why you'll rewrite it from top to bottom. Just use the framework of the story as is. And keep as much of the tone as possible. But change the language – a total remake. You'll be in charge of the actual writing, and I'll be the producer."

"Just like that?" Tengo muttered, as if to himself.

"Look," Komatsu said, picking up a spoon and pointing it at Tengo the way a conductor uses his baton to single out a soloist from the rest of the orchestra. "This Fuka-Eri girl has something special. Anyone can see it reading *Air Chrysalis*. Her imagination is far from ordinary. Unfortunately, though, her writing is hopeless. A total mess. You, on the other hand, know how to write. Your story lines are good. You have taste. You may be built like a lumberjack, but you write with intelligence and sensitivity. And real power. Unlike Fuka-Eri, though, you still haven't grasped exactly what it is you want to write about. Which is why a lot of your stories are missing something at the core. I know you've got something inside you that you need to write about, but you can't get it to come out. It's like a frightened little animal hiding way back in a cave – you know it's in there, but there's no way to catch it until it comes out. Which is why I keep telling you, just give it time."

Tengo shifted awkwardly on the booth's vinyl seat. He said nothing.

"The answer is simple," Komatsu said, still lightly waving his spoon. "We put the two writers together and invent a brand-new one. We add your perfect style to Fuka-Eri's raw story. It's an ideal combination. I know you've got it in you. Why do you think I've been backing you all this time? Just leave the rest to me. With the two of you together, the new writers' prize will be easy, and then we can shoot for the Akutagawa. I haven't been wasting my time in this business all these years. I know how to pull the right strings."

Tengo let his lips part as he stared at Komatsu. Komatsu put his spoon back in his saucer. It made an abnormally loud sound.

"Supposing the story wins the Akutagawa Prize, then what?" Tengo asked, recovering from the shock.

"If it takes the Akutagawa, it'll cause a sensation. Most people don't know the value of a good novel, but they don't want to be left out, so they'll buy it and read it – especially when they hear it was written by a high school girl. If the book sells, it'll make a lot of money. We'll split it three ways. I'll take care of that."

"Never mind the money," Tengo said, his voice flat. "How about your professional ethics as an editor? If the scheme became public, it'd cause an uproar. You'd lose your job."

"It wouldn't come out so easily. I can handle the whole thing very carefully. And even if it did come out, I'd be glad to leave the company. Management doesn't like me, and they've never treated me decently. Finding another job would be no problem for me. Besides, I wouldn't be doing it for the money. I'd be doing it to screw the literary world. Those bastards all huddle together in their gloomy cave and kiss each other's asses, and lick each other's wounds, and trip each other up, all the while spewing this pompous crap about the mission of literature. I want to have a good laugh at their expense. I want to outwit the system and make idiots out of the whole bunch of them. Doesn't that sound like fun to you?"

It did not sound like all that much fun to Tengo. For one thing, he had never actually seen this "literary world." And when he realized that a competent individual like Komatsu had such childish motives for crossing such a dangerous bridge, he was momentarily at a loss for words.

"It sounds like a scam to me," he said at length.

"Coauthorship is not that unusual," Komatsu said with a frown. "Half the magazines' serialized *manga* are coauthored. The staff toss around ideas and make up the story, the artist does simple line drawings, his assistants fill in the details and add color. It's not much different from the way a factory makes alarm clocks. The same sort of thing goes on in the fiction world. Romance novels, for example. With most of those, the publisher hires writers to make up stories following the guidelines they've established. Division of labor: that's the system. Mass production would be impossible any other way. In the self-conscious world of literary fiction, of course, such methods are not openly sanctioned, so as a practical strategy we have to set Fuka-Eri up as our single author. If the deception comes out, it might cause a bit of a scandal, but we wouldn't be breaking the law. We'd just be riding the current of the times. And besides, we're not talking about a Balzac or a Murasaki Shikibu here. All we'd be doing is patching the holes in the story some high school girl wrote and making it a better piece of fiction. What's wrong with that? If the finished work is good and brings pleasure to a lot of readers, then no harm done, don't you agree?"

Tengo gave some thought to what Komatsu was saying, and he answered with care. "I see two problems here. I'm sure there are more than that, but for now let me concentrate on these two. One is that we don't know whether the author, Fuka-Eri, would go along with having someone else rewrite her work. If she says no, of course, that's the end of that. The other problem, assuming she says okay, is whether I could really do a good job of rewriting it. Coauthorship is a very delicate matter; I can't believe things would go as easily as you are suggesting."

"I know you can do it, Tengo," Komatsu said without hesitation, as if he had been anticipating Tengo's reaction. "I have no doubt whatever. I knew it the first time I read *Air Chrysalis*. The first thing that popped into my head was 'Tengo has to rewrite this!' It's perfect for you. It's aching for you to rewrite it. Don't you see?"

Tengo merely shook his head, saying nothing.

"There's no rush," Komatsu said quietly. "This is important. Take two or three days to think about it. Read *Air Chrysalis* again, and give some good, careful thought to what I'm proposing. And – oh yes, let me give you this."

Komatsu withdrew a brown envelope from his breast pocket and handed it to Tengo. Inside the envelope were two standard-size color photos, pictures of a girl. One showed her from the chest up, the other was a full-length snapshot. They seemed to have been taken at the same time. She was standing in front of a stairway somewhere, a broad stone stairway. Classically beautiful features. Long, straight hair. White blouse. Small and slim. Her lips were trying to smile, but her eyes were resisting. Serious eyes. Eyes in search of something. Tengo stared at the two photos. The more he looked, the more he thought about himself at that age, and the more he sensed a small, dull ache in his chest. It was a special ache, something he had not experienced for a very long time.

"That's Fuka-Eri," Komatsu said. "Beautiful girl, don't you think? Sweet and fresh. Seventeen. Perfect. We won't tell anyone that her real name is Eriko Fukada. We'll keep her as 'Fuka-Eri.' The name alone should cause a stir if she wins the Akutagawa Prize, don't you think? She'll have reporters swarming around her like bats at sunset. The books'll sell out overnight."

Tengo wondered how Komatsu had gotten hold of the photos. Entrants were not required to send in photos with their manuscripts. But he decided not to ask, partly because he didn't want to know the answer, whatever it might be.

"You can keep those," Komatsu said. "They might come in handy."

Tengo put them back into the envelope and laid them on the manuscript. Then he said to Komatsu, "I don't know much about how the 'industry' works, but sheer common sense tells me this is a tremendously risky plan. Once you start lying to the public, you have to keep lying. It never ends. It's not easy, either psychologically or practically, to keep tweaking the truth to make it all fit together. If one person who's in on the plan makes one little slip, everybody could be done for. Don't you agree?"

Komatsu pulled out another cigarette and lit it. "You're absolutely right. It *is* risky. There are a few too many uncertainties at this point in time. One slip, and things could get *very* unpleasant for us. I'm perfectly aware of that. But you know, Tengo, taking everything into consideration, my instincts still tell me, 'Go for it!' For the simple reason that you don't get chances like this very often. I've never had one before, and I'm sure I'll never have another one. Comparing this to gambling might not be the best way to look at it, but we've got all the right cards and a mountain of chips. The conditions are perfect. If we let a chance like this slip away, we'll regret it for the rest of our lives."

Tengo stared in silence at Komatsu's utterly sinister smile.

Komatsu continued: "And the most important thing is that we are remaking *Air Chrysalis* into a much better work. It's a story that *should* have been much better written. There's something important in it, something that needs someone to bring it out. I'm sure you think so too, Tengo. Am I wrong? We each contribute our own special talents to the project: we pool our resources for one thing only, and that is *to bring out that important something in the work.* Our motives are pure: we can present them anywhere without shame."

"Well, you can try to rationalize it all you want, you can

invent all kinds of noble-sounding pretexts, but in the end, a scam is a scam."

"Look, Tengo, you're losing sight of one crucial fact," Komatsu said, his mouth opening in a big, wide grin the likes of which Tengo had never seen. "Or should I say you are deliberately choosing not to look at it? And that's the simple fact that *you want to do this.* You already feel that way – 'risk' and 'morality' be damned. I can see it. You're itching to rewrite *Air Chrysalis* with your own hands. *You* want to be the one, not Fuka-Eri, who brings out that special something in the work. I want you to go home now and figure out what you really think. Stand in front of a mirror and give yourself a long, hard look. It's written all over your face."

Tengo felt the air around him growing thin. He glanced at his surroundings. Was the image coming to him again? But no, there was no sign of it. The thinness of the air had come from something else. He pulled his handkerchief from his pocket and wiped the sweat from his brow. Komatsu was always right. Why should that be?

CHAPTER 3

Aomame

SOME CHANGED FACTS

Aomame climbed down the emergency stairway in her stocking feet. The wind whistled past the stairway, which was open to the elements. Snug though her miniskirt was, it filled like a sail with the occasional strong gust from below, providing enough lift to make her steps unsteady. She kept a tight grip on the cold metal pipe that served as a handrail, lowering herself a step at a time, backward, and stopping now and then to brush aside the stray hair hanging down her forehead and to adjust the position of the shoulder bag slung diagonally across her chest.

She had a sweeping view of National Highway 246 running below. The din of the city enveloped her: car engines, blaring horns, the scream of an automobile burglar alarm, an old war song echoing from a right-wing sound truck, a sledgehammer cracking concrete. Riding on the wind, the noise pressed in on her from all directions – above, below, and 360 degrees around. Listening to the racket (not that she wanted to listen, but she was in no position to be covering her ears), she began to feel almost seasick.

Partway down, the stairs became a horizontal catwalk leading back toward the center of the elevated expressway, then angled straight down again.

Just across the road from the open stairway stood a small,

five-story apartment house, a relatively new building covered in brown brick tile. Each apartment had a small balcony facing the emergency stairway, but all the patio doors were shut tight, the blinds or curtains closed. What kind of architect puts balconies on a building that stands nose-to-nose with an elevated expressway? No one would be hanging out their sheets to dry or lingering on the balcony with a gin and tonic to watch the evening rush-hour traffic. Still, on several balconies were stretched the seemingly obligatory nylon clotheslines, and one even had a garden chair and potted rubber plant. The rubber plant was ragged and faded, its leaves disintegrating and marked with brown dry spots. Aomame could not help feeling sorry for the plant. If she were ever reincarnated, let her *not* be reborn as such a miserable rubber plant!

Judging from the spiderwebs clinging to it, the emergency stairway was hardly ever used. To each web clung a small black spider, patiently waiting for its small prey to come along. Not that the spiders had any awareness of being "patient." A spider had no special skill other than building its web, and no lifestyle choice other than sitting still. It would stay in one place waiting for its prey until, in the natural course of things, it shriveled up and died. This was all genetically predetermined. The spider had no confusion, no despair, no regrets. No metaphysical doubt, no moral complications. Probably. *Unlike me. I have to move with a purpose, which is why I'm alone now, climbing down these stupid emergency stairs from Metropolitan Expressway Number 3 where it passes through the useless Sangenjaya neighborhood, even if it means ruining a perfectly good pair of stockings, all the while sweeping away these damned spiderwebs and looking at an ugly rubber plant on somebody's stupid balcony.*

I move, therefore I am.

Climbing down the stairway, Aomame thought about Tamaki Otsuka. She had not been intending to think about Tamaki, but once the thoughts began, she couldn't stop them. Tamaki was her closest friend in high school and a fellow member of the softball team. As teammates, they went to many different places, and did all kinds of things together. They once shared a kind of lesbian experience. The two of them took a summer trip and ended up sleeping together when a small double was the only size bed the hotel could offer. They found themselves touching each other all over. Neither of them was a lesbian, but, spurred on by the special curiosity of two young girls, they experimented boldly. Neither had a boyfriend at the time, and neither had the slightest sexual experience. It was simply one of those things that remain as an "exceptional but interesting" episode in life. But as she brought back the images of herself and Tamaki touching each other that night, Aomame felt some small, deep part of herself growing hot even as she made her way down the windswept stairway. Tamaki's oval-shaped nipples, her sparse pubic hair, the lovely curve of her buttocks, the shape of her clitoris: Aomame recalled them all with strange clarity.

As her mind traced these graphic memories, the brass unison of Janáček's *Sinfonietta* rang like festive background music. The palm of her hand was caressing the curve of Tamaki's waist. At first Tamaki just laughed as if she were being tickled, but soon the laughter stopped, and her breathing changed. The music had initially been composed as a fanfare for an athletic meet. The breeze blew gently over the green meadows of Bohemia in time with the music. Aomame knew when Tamaki's nipples suddenly became erect. And then her own did the same. And then the timpani conjured up a complex musical pattern.

Aomame halted her steps and shook her head several times. *I should not be thinking such thoughts at a time like this. I have to concentrate on climbing down the stairs.* But the thoughts would not go away. The images came to her one after another and with great vividness. The summer night, the narrow bed, the faint smell of perspiration. The words they spoke. The feelings that would not take the form of words. Forgotten promises. Unrealized hopes. Frustrated longings. A gust of wind lifted a lock of her hair and whipped it against her cheek. The pain brought a film of tears to her eyes. Successive gusts soon dried the tears away.

When did that happen, I wonder? But time became confused in her memory, like a tangled string. The straight-line axis was lost, and forward and back, right and left, jumbled together. One drawer took the place of another. She could not recall things that should have come back to her easily. *It is now April 1984. I was born in . . . that's it . . . 1954. I can remember that much.* These dates were engraved in her mind, but as soon as she recalled them, they lost all meaning. She saw white cards imprinted with dates scattering in the wind, flying in all directions. She ran, trying to pick up as many as she could, but the wind was too strong, the sheer number of cards overwhelming. Away they flew: 1954, 1984, 1645, 1881, 2006, 771, 2041 . . . all order lost, all knowledge vanishing, the stairway of intellection crumbling beneath her feet.

Aomame and Tamaki were in bed together. They were seventeen and enjoying their newly granted freedom. This was their first trip together as friends, just the two of them. That fact alone was exciting. They soaked in the hotel's hot spring, split a can of beer from the refrigerator, turned out the lights, and crawled into bed. They were just kidding around at first, poking each other for the fun of it, but at some point Tamaki reached out and grabbed Aomame's nipple through the T-shirt she wore as pajamas. An electric shock ran through Aomame's body. Eventually they stripped off their shirts and panties and were naked in the summer night. *Where did we go on that trip?* She could not recall. It didn't matter. Soon, without either of them being the first to suggest it, they were examining each other's bodies down to the smallest detail. Looking, touching, caressing, kissing, licking, half in jest, half seriously. Tamaki was small and a bit plump with large breasts. Aomame was taller, lean and muscular, with smaller breasts. Tamaki always talked about going on a diet, but Aomame found her attractive just the way she was.

Tamaki's skin was soft and fine. Her nipples swelled in a beautiful oval shape reminiscent of olives. Her pubic hair was fine and sparse, like a delicate willow tree. Aomame's was hard and bristly. They laughed at the difference. They experimented with touching each other in different places and discussed which areas were the most sensitive. Some areas were the same, others were not. Each held out a finger and touched the other's clitoris. Both girls had experienced masturbation – a lot. But now they saw how different it was to be touched by someone else. The breeze swept across the meadows of Bohemia.

Aomame came to a stop and shook her head again. She released a deep sigh and tightened her grip on the metal pipe handrail. *I have to stop thinking about these things. I have to concentrate on climbing down the stairs. By now, I must be more than halfway down. Still, why is there so much noise here? Why is the wind so strong? They both seem to be reprimanding me, punishing me.*

Setting such immediate sensory impressions aside, Aomame began to worry about what might await her at the bottom of the stairway. What if someone were there, demanding that she identify herself and explain her presence? Could she get by with a simple explanation – "The traffic was backed up on the expressway and I have such urgent business that I climbed down the stairs"? Or would there be complications? She didn't want any complications. Not today.

Fortunately, she found no one at ground level to challenge her. The first thing she did was pull her shoes from her bag and step into them. The stairway came down to a vacant patch beneath the elevated expressway, a storage area for construction materials hemmed in between the inbound and outbound lanes of

Route 246 and surrounded by high metal sheeting. A number of steel poles lay on the bare ground, rusting, probably discarded surplus from some construction job. A makeshift plastic roof covered one part of the area where three cloth sacks lay piled. Aomame had no idea what they held, but they had been further protected from the rain by a vinyl cover. The sacks, too, seemed to be construction surplus, thrown there at the end of the job because they were too much trouble to haul away. Beneath the roof, several crushed corrugated cartons, some plastic drink bottles, and a number of *manga* magazines lay on the ground. Aside from a few plastic shopping bags that were being whipped around by the wind, there was nothing else down here.

The area had a metal gate, but a large padlock and several wrappings of chain held it in place. The gate towered over her and was topped with barbed wire. There was no way she could climb over it. Even if she managed to do so, her suit would be torn to shreds. She gave it a few tentative shakes, but it wouldn't budge. There was not even enough space for a cat to squeeze through. Damn. What was the point of locking the place so securely? There was nothing here worth stealing. She frowned and cursed and even spit on the ground. After all her trouble to climb down from the elevated expressway, now she was locked in a storage yard! She glanced at her watch. The time was still okay, but she couldn't go on hanging around in this place forever. And doubling back to the expressway now was out of the question.

The heels of both her stockings were ripped. Checking to make sure that there was no one watching her, she slipped out of her high heels, rolled up her skirt, pulled her stockings down, yanked them off her feet, and stepped into her shoes again. The torn stockings she shoved into her bag. This calmed her somewhat. Now she walked the perimeter of the storage area, paying close attention to every detail. It was about the size of an elementary school classroom, so a full circuit of the place took no time at all. Yes, she had already found the only exit, the locked gate. The metal sheeting that enclosed the space was thin, but the pieces were securely bolted together, and the bolts could not be loosened without tools. Time to give up.

She went over to the roofed area for a closer look at the crushed cartons. They had been arranged as bedding, she realized, with a number of worn blankets rolled up inside. They were not all that old, either. Some street people were probably sleeping here, which explained the bottles and magazines. No doubt about it. Aomame put her mind to work. If they were using this place to spend their nights, it must have some kind of secret entrance. They're good at finding hidden places to ward off the wind and rain, she thought. And they know how to secure secret passageways, like animal trails, for their exclusive use.

Aomame made another round, closely inspecting each metal sheet of the fence and giving it a shake. As she expected, she found one loose spot where a bolt might have slipped out. She tried bending it in different directions. If you changed the angle a little and pulled it inward, a space opened up that was just big enough for a person to squeeze through. The street people probably came in after dark to enjoy sleeping under the roof, but they would have problems if someone caught them in here, so they went out during the daylight hours to find food and collect empty bottles for spare change. Aomame inwardly thanked the nameless nighttime residents. As someone who had to move stealthily, anonymously, behind the scenes in the big city, she felt at one with them.

She crouched down and slipped through the narrow gap, taking great care to avoid catching and tearing her expensive suit on any sharp objects. It was not her favorite suit: it was the only one she owned. She almost never dressed this way, and she never wore heels. Sometimes, however, this particular line of work required her to dress respectably, so she had to avoid ruining the suit.

Fortunately, there was no one outside the fence, either. She checked her clothing once more, resumed a calm expression on her face, and walked to a corner with a traffic signal. Crossing Route 246, she entered a drugstore and bought a new pair of stockings, which she put on in a back room with the permission of the girl at the register. This improved her mood considerably and obliterated the slight discomfort, like seasickness, that had remained in her stomach. Thanking the clerk, she left the store.

The traffic on Route 246 was heavier than usual, probably because word had spread that an accident had stopped traffic on the parallel urban expressway. Aomame abandoned the idea of taking a cab and decided instead to take the Tokyu Shin-Tamagawa Line from a nearby station. That would be a sure thing. She had had enough of taxis stuck in traffic.

As she headed for Sangenjaya Station, she passed a policeman on the street. He was a tall young officer, walking rapidly, heading somewhere in particular. She tensed up for a moment, but he looked straight ahead, apparently in too much of a hurry even to glance at her. Just before they passed each other, Aomame noticed that there was something unusual about his uniform. The jacket was the normal deep navy blue, but its cut was different: the design was more casual, less tight fitting, and in a softer material, the lapels smaller, even the navy color a touch paler. His pistol, too, was a different model. He wore a large automatic at his waist instead of the revolver normally issued to policemen in Japan. Crimes involving firearms were so rare in this country that there was little likelihood that an officer would be caught in a shootout, which meant an old-fashioned six-shooter was adequate. Revolvers were simply made, cheap, reliable, and easy to maintain. But for some reason this officer was carrying the latest model semiautomatic pistol, the kind that could be loaded with sixteen 9mm bullets. Probably a Glock or a Beretta. But how could that be? How could police uniforms and pistols have changed without her being aware of it? It was practically unthinkable. She read the newspaper closely each day. Changes like that would have been featured prominently. And besides, she paid careful attention to police uniforms. Until this morning, just a few hours ago, policemen were still wearing the same old stiff uniforms they always had, and still carrying the same old unsophisticated revolvers. She remembered them clearly. It was very strange.

But Aomame was in no frame of mind to think deeply about such matters. She had a job to do.

When the subway reached Shibuya Station, she deposited her coat in a coin locker, then hurried up Dogenzaka toward the hotel wearing only her suit. It was a decent enough hotel, nothing fancy, but well equipped, clean, with reputable guests. It had a restaurant on the street level, as well as a convenience store. Close to the station. A good location.

She walked in and headed straight for the ladies' room. Fortunately, it was empty. The first thing she did was sit down for a good, long pee, eyes closed, listening to the sound like distant surf, and thinking of nothing in particular. Next she stood at one of the sinks and washed her hands well with soap and water. She brushed her hair and blew her nose. She took out her toothbrush and did a cursory brushing without toothpaste. She had no time to floss. It wasn't that important. She wasn't preparing for a date. She faced the mirror and added a touch of lipstick and eyebrow pencil. Removing her suit jacket, she adjusted the position of her underwire bra, smoothed the wrinkles in her white blouse, and sniffed her armpits. No smell. Then she closed her eyes and recited the usual prayer, the words of which meant nothing. The meaning didn't matter. Reciting was the important thing.

After the prayer she opened her eyes and looked at herself in the mirror. Fine. The picture of the capable businesswoman. Erect posture. Firm mouth. Only the big, bulky shoulder bag seemed out of place. A slim attaché case might have been better, but this bag was more practical. She checked again to make sure she had all the items she needed in the bag. No problem. Everything was where it belonged, easy to find by touch.

Now it was just a matter of carrying out the task as arranged. Head-on. With unwavering conviction and ruthlessness. Aomame undid the top button of her blouse. This would give a glimpse of cleavage when she bent over. If only she had more cleavage to expose!

No one challenged her as she took the elevator to the fourth floor, walked down the corridor, and quickly found Room 426. Taking a clipboard from the bag, she clutched it to her chest and knocked on the door. A light, crisp knock. A brief wait. Another knock, this one a little harder. Grumbling from inside. Door opened a crack. Man's face. Maybe forty. Marine-blue shirt. Gray flannel slacks. Classic look of a businessman working with his tie and jacket off. Red eyes, annoyed. Probably sleep deprived. He seemed surprised to see Aomame in her business suit, probably expecting her to be a maid, here to replenish the minibar.

"I'm terribly sorry to disturb you, sir. My name is Ito, and I'm a member of the hotel management staff. There has been a problem with the air conditioner and I need to do an inspection. May I come in? It won't take more than five minutes," Aomame announced briskly, with a sweet smile.

The man squinted at her in obvious displeasure. "I'm working on something important, a rush job. I'll be leaving the room in another hour. Can I get you to come back then? There's nothing wrong with the air conditioner in this room."

"I'm terribly sorry, sir. It's an emergency involving a short circuit. We need to take care of it as soon as possible, for safety's sake. We're going from room to room. It won't even take five minutes . . ."

"Ah, what the hell," the man said, with a click of his tongue. "I made a point of taking a room so I could work undisturbed."

He pointed to the papers on the desk – a pile of detailed charts and graphs he had printed out, probably materials he was preparing for a late meeting. He had a computer and a calculator, and scratch paper with long lines of figures.

Aomame knew that he worked for a corporation connected with oil. He was a specialist on capital investment in a number of Middle Eastern countries. According to the information she had been given, he was one of the more capable men in the field. She could see it in the way he carried himself. He came from a good family, earned a sizable income, and drove a new Jaguar. After a pampered childhood, he had gone to study abroad, spoke good English and French, and exuded self-confidence. He was the type who could not bear to be told what to do, or to be criticized, especially if the criticism came from a woman. He had no difficulty bossing others around, though, and cracking a few of his wife's ribs with a golf club was no problem at all. As far as he was concerned, the world revolved around him, and without him the earth didn't move at all. He could become furious – violently angry – if anyone interfered with what he was doing or contradicted him in any way.

"Sorry to trouble you, sir," Aomame said, flashing him her best business smile. As if it were a fait accompli, she squeezed halfway into the room, pressing her back against the door, readied her clipboard, and started writing something on it with a ballpoint pen. "That was, uh, Mr. Miyama, I believe . . . ?" she asked. Having seen his photo any number of times, she knew his face well, but it wouldn't hurt to make sure she had the right person. There was no way to correct a mistake.

"Yes, of course. Miyama," he said curtly. He followed this

with a resigned sigh that seemed to say, "All right. Do as you damn please." He took his seat at the desk and, with a ballpoint pen in one hand, picked up whatever document he had been reading. His suit coat and a striped tie lay on the fully made double bed where he had thrown them. They were both obviously very expensive. Aomame walked straight for the closet, her bag hanging from her shoulder. She had been told that the air conditioner switch panel was in there. Inside she found a trench coat of soft material and a dark gray cashmere scarf. The only luggage was a leather briefcase. No change of clothes, no bag for toiletries. He was probably not planning to stay the night. On the desk stood a coffeepot that had obviously been delivered by room service. She pretended to inspect the switch panel for thirty seconds and then called out to Miyama.

"Thank you, Mr. Miyama, for your cooperation. I can't find any problem with the equipment in this room."

"Which is what I was trying to tell you from the start," he grumbled.

"Uh . . . Mr. Miyama . . . ?" she ventured. "Excuse me, but I think you have something stuck to the back of your neck."

"The back of my neck?" he said. He rubbed the area and then stared at the palm of his hand. "I don't think so."

"Please just let me have a look," she said, drawing closer. "Do you mind?"

"Sure, go ahead," he said, looking puzzled. "What is it?"

"A spot of paint, I think. Bright green."

"Paint?"

"I'm not really sure. Judging from the color, it has to be paint. Is it all right if I touch you back there? It may come right off."

"Well, okay," Miyama said, ducking his head forward, exposing the back of his neck to Aomame. It was bare, thanks to what looked like a recent haircut. Aomame took a deep breath and held it, concentrating her attention on her fingers' nimble search for the right spot. She pressed a fingertip there as if to mark the place, then closed her eyes, confirming that her touch was not mistaken. *Yes, this is it. I'd like to take more time if possible to make doubly certain, but it's too late for that now. I'll just have to do my best with the situation I've been given.*

"Sorry, sir, but do you mind holding that position a bit longer? I'll take a penlight from my bag. The lighting in here is not very good."

"Why would I have *paint* back there, of all things?"

"I have no idea, sir. I'll check it right away."

Keeping her finger pressed against the spot on the man's neck, Aomame drew a hard plastic case from her bag, opened it, and took out an object wrapped in thin cloth. With a few deft moves she unfolded the cloth, revealing something like a small ice pick about four inches in length with a compact wooden handle. It *looked* like an ice pick, but it was not meant for cracking ice. Aomame had designed and made it herself. The tip was as sharp and pointed as a needle, and it was protected from breakage by a small piece of cork – cork that had been specially processed to make it as soft as cotton. She carefully plucked the cork from the point and slipped it into her pocket. She then held the exposed point against that special spot on Miyama's neck. *Calm down now, this is it,* Aomame told herself. *I can't be off by even one-hundredth of an inch. One slip and all my efforts will be wasted. Concentration is the key.*

"How much longer is this going to take?" Miyama protested.

"I'm sorry, sir, I'll be through in a moment."

Don't worry, she said to him silently, *it'll all be over before you know it. Wait just a second or two. Then you won't have to think about a thing. You won't have to think about the oil refining system or crude oil market trends or quarterly reports to the investors or Bahrain flight reservations or bribes for officials or presents for your mistress. What a strain it must have been for you to keep these things straight in your head all this time! So please, just wait a minute. I'm hard at work here, giving it all the concentration I can muster. Don't distract me. That's all I ask.*

Once she had settled on the location and set her mind to the task, Aomame raised her right palm in the air, held her breath, and, after a brief pause, brought it straight down – not too forcefully – against the wooden handle. If she applied too much force, the needle might break under the skin, and leaving the needle tip behind was out of the question. The important thing was to bring the palm down lightly, almost tenderly, at exactly the right angle with exactly the right amount of force, without resisting gravity, straight down, as if the fine point of the needle were being sucked into the spot with the utmost naturalness – deeply, smoothly, and with fatal results. The angle and force – or, rather, the restraint of force – were crucial. As long as she was careful about those details, it was as simple as driving a needle into a block of tofu. The needle pierced the skin, thrust into the special spot at the base of the brain, and stopped the heart as naturally as blowing out a candle. Everything ended in a split second, almost too easily. Only Aomame could do this. No one else could find that subtle point by touch. Her fingertips possessed the special intuition that made it possible.

She heard him draw a sharp breath, and then every muscle in his body went stiff. Instantly, she withdrew the needle and just as quickly took out the small gauze pad she had ready in her pocket, pressing it against the wound to prevent the flow of blood. Because the needle was so fine and had remained in his skin for no more than a few seconds, only a minuscule amount of blood could possibly escape through the opening, but she had to take every precaution. She must not leave even the slightest trace of blood. One drop could ruin everything. Caution was Aomame's specialty.

The strength began to drain from Miyama's body, which had momentarily stiffened, like air going out of a basketball.

Keeping her finger on the spot on his neck, Aomame let him slump forward onto the desk. His face lay sideways, pillowed on his documents. His eyes were wide open in apparent surprise, as if his last act had been to witness something utterly amazing. They showed neither fear nor pain, only pure surprise. Something out of the ordinary was happening to him, but he could not comprehend what it was – a pain, an itch, a pleasure, or a divine revelation? There were many different ways of dying in the world, perhaps none of them as easy as this.

This was an easier death than you deserved, Aomame thought with a scowl. *It was just too simple. I probably should have broken a few ribs for you with a five iron and given you plenty of pain before putting you out of your misery. That would have been the right kind of death for a rat like you. It's what you did to your wife. Unfortunately, however, the choice was not mine. My mission was to send this man to the other world as swiftly and surely – and discreetly – as possible. Now, I have accomplished that mission. He was alive until a moment ago, and now he's dead. He crossed the threshold separating life from death without being aware of it himself.*

Aomame held the gauze in place for a full five minutes, patiently, but without pressing hard enough for her finger to leave an indentation. She kept her eyes glued on the second hand of her watch. It was a very long five minutes. If someone had walked in then and seen her pressing her finger against the man's neck while holding the slender murder weapon in the other hand, it would have been all over. She could never have talked her way out of it. A bellhop could bring a pot of coffee. There could be a knock on the door at any moment. But this was an indispensable five minutes. To calm herself, Aomame took several slow deep breaths. *I can't get flustered now. I can't lose my composure. I have to stay the same calm, cool Aomame as always.*

She could hear her heart beating. And in her head, in time

with the beat, resounded the opening fanfare of Janáček's *Sinfonietta*. Soft, silent breezes played across the green meadows of Bohemia. She was aware that she had become split in two. Half of her continued to press the dead man's neck with utter coolness. The other half was filled with fear. She wanted to drop everything and get out of this room *now. I'm here, but I'm not here. I'm in two places at once. It goes against Einstein's theorem, but what the hell. Call it the Zen of the killer.*

The five minutes were finally up. But just to make sure, Aomame gave it one more minute. *I can wait another minute. The greater the rush, the more care one should take with the job.* She endured the extra minute, which seemed as if it would never end. Then she slowly pulled her finger away and examined the wound with her penlight. A mosquito's stinger left a larger hole than this.

Stabbing the special point at the base of the brain with an exceptionally fine needle causes a death that is almost indistinguishable from a natural sudden death. It would look like a heart attack to most ordinary doctors. It hit him without warning while he was working at his desk, and he breathed his last. Overwork and stress. No sign of unnatural causes. No need for an autopsy.

This man was a high-powered operator, but also prone to overwork. He earned a high salary, but he couldn't use it now that he was dead. He wore Armani suits and drove a Jaguar, but finally he was just another ant, working and working until he died without meaning. The very fact that he existed in this world would eventually be forgotten. "Such a shame, he was so young," people might say. Or they might not.

Aomame took the cork from her pocket and placed it on the needle. Wrapping the delicate instrument in the thin cloth again, she returned it to the hard case, which she placed in the bottom of the shoulder bag. She then took a hand towel from the bathroom and wiped any fingerprints she might have left in the room. These would all be on the air conditioner panel and the doorknob. She had been careful not to touch anything else. She returned the towel to the bathroom. Placing the man's cup and coffeepot on the room service tray, she set them in the corridor. This way the bellhop would not have to knock when he came to retrieve them, and the discovery of the body would be delayed that much more. If all went well, the maid would find the body after checkout time tomorrow.

When he failed to show up at tonight's meeting, people might ring the room, but there would be no answer. They might think it odd enough to have the manager open the room, but then again they might not. Things would simply take their course.

Aomame stood before the bathroom mirror to make sure nothing about her clothing was in disarray. She closed the top button of her blouse. She had not had to flash cleavage. The bastard had hardly looked at her. What the hell did other people mean to him? She tried out a medium frown. Then she straightened her hair, massaged her facial muscles with her fingertips to soften them, and flashed the mirror a sweet smile, revealing her recently cleaned white teeth. *All right, then, here I go, out of the dead man's room and back to the real world. Time to adjust the atmospheric pressure. I'm not a cool killer anymore, just a smiling, capable businesswoman in a sharp suit.*

She opened the door a crack, checked to see that there was no one in the corridor, and slipped out. She took the stairs rather than the elevator. No one paid her any mind as she passed through the lobby. Posture erect, she stared straight ahead and walked quickly – though not quickly enough to attract attention. She was a pro, virtually perfect. If only her breasts were a little bigger, she thought with a twinge, she might have been truly perfect. A partial frown. *But hell, you've gotta work with what you've got.*

CHAPTER 4

Tengo

IF THAT IS WHAT YOU WANT TO DO

The phone woke Tengo. The luminous hands of his clock pointed to a little after one a.m. The room was dark, of course. Tengo knew the call was from Komatsu. No one but Komatsu would call him at one in the morning – and keep the phone ringing until he picked it up, however long it took. Komatsu had no sense of time. He would place a call the moment a thought struck him, never considering the hour. It could be the middle of the night or the crack of dawn. The other person could be enjoying his wedding night or lying on his deathbed. The prosaic thought never seemed to enter Komatsu's egg-shaped head that a call from him might be disturbing.

Which is not to say that he did this with everyone. Even Komatsu worked for an organization and collected a salary. He couldn't possibly go around behaving toward everyone with a total disregard for common sense. Only with Tengo could he get away with it. Tengo was, for Komatsu, little more than an extension of Komatsu himself, another arm or leg. If Komatsu was up, Tengo must be up. Tengo normally went to bed at ten o'clock and woke at six, maintaining a generally regular lifestyle. He was a deep sleeper. Once something woke him, though, it was hard for him to get to sleep again. He was high-strung to that extent. He had tried to explain this to Komatsu any number of times, and pleaded with him not to call in the middle of the night, like a farmer begging God not to send swarms of locusts into his fields before harvest time.

"Got it," Komatsu declared. "No more nighttime calls." But his promise had not sunk deep roots in his brain. One rainfall was all it took to wash them out.

Tengo crawled out of bed and, bumping into things, managed to find his way to the phone in the kitchen. All the while, the phone kept up its merciless ringing.

"I talked to Fuka-Eri," Komatsu said. He never bothered with the standard greetings, no "Were you sleeping?" or "Sorry to call so late." Pretty impressive. Tengo couldn't help admiring him.

Tengo frowned in the dark, saying nothing. When roused at night, it took his brain a while to start working.

"Did you hear what I said?"

"Yes, I did."

"It was just a phone call. But I did talk to her. Or *at* her. She just listened. You couldn't exactly call it a conversation. She hardly talks. And she's got an odd way of speaking. You'll see what I mean. Anyhow, I gave her a general outline of my plan, like, what did she think of the idea of going after the new writers' prize by having somebody rewrite *Air Chrysalis* to get it into better shape? I couldn't give her much more than a rough idea on the phone and ask her if she had any interest, assuming we'd meet and talk over the details. I kept it sort of vague. If I got *too* direct about stuff like this, I could put myself in an awkward position."

"And so?"

"No answer."

"No answer?"

Komatsu paused for effect. He put a cigarette between his lips and lit it with a match. Hearing the sounds over the phone, Tengo could imagine the scene vividly. Komatsu never used a lighter.

"Fuka-Eri says she wants to meet you first," Komatsu said,

exhaling. "She didn't say whether or not she was interested in the plan, or whether or not she liked the idea. I guess the main thing is to start by meeting you and talking about it face-to-face. She'll give me her answer after that, she says. The responsibility is all yours, don't you think?"

"And so?"

"Are you free tomorrow evening?"

His classes started in the morning and ended at four. Fortunately (or unfortunately) he had nothing after that. "I'm free," he said.

"Good. I want you to go to the Nakamuraya Café in Shinjuku at six o'clock. I'll reserve a table for you in the back where it's quiet. It'll be in my name and on the company's tab, so eat and drink as much as you like. The two of you can have a nice, long talk."

"Without you?"

"That's the way Fuka-Eri wants it. She says there's no point in meeting me yet."

Tengo kept silent.

"So that's how it is," Komatsu said cheerily. "Give it your best shot, Tengo. You're a big lug, but you make a good impression on people. And besides, you teach at a cram school. You're used to talking to these precocious high school girls. You're the right guy for the job, not me. Flash her a smile, win her over, get her to trust you. I'll be looking forward to the good news."

"Now, wait just a minute. This was all *your* idea. I still haven't even told you if I'll do it. Like I said the other day, this is a tremendously risky plan, and I don't see it working all that well. It could turn into a real scandal. How am I supposed to convince this girl I've never met to go along with it when I myself haven't decided to take it on?"

Komatsu remained silent at his end. Then, after a moment's pause, he said, "Now listen, Tengo. We've already pulled out of the station. You can't stop the train and get off now. I'm totally committed. And you're more than half committed, I'm sure. We share the same fate."

Tengo shook his head. *Share the same fate? When did this melodrama get started?* "Just the other day you told me to take my time and think it over, didn't you?"

"It's been five days since then. You've had plenty of time to think it over. What's your decision?" Komatsu demanded.

Tengo was at a loss for words. "I don't have a decision," he said honestly.

"So then, why don't you try meeting this Fuka-Eri girl and talking it over? You can make up your mind after that."

Tengo pressed his fingertips hard against his temples. His brain was still not working properly. "All right. I'll talk to her. Six o'clock tomorrow at the Shinjuku Nakamuraya. I'll give her *my* explanation of the situation. But I'm not promising any more than that. I can *explain* the plan, but I can't *convince* her of anything."

"That's all I ask, of course."

"So anyway, how much does Fuka-Eri know about me?"

"I filled her in on the general stuff. You're twenty-nine or thirty, a bachelor, you teach math at a Yoyogi cram school. You're a big guy, but not a bad guy. You don't eat young girls. You live a simple lifestyle, you've got gentle eyes. And I like your writing a lot. That's about it."

Tengo sighed. When he tried to think, reality hovered nearby, then retreated into the distance.

"Do you mind if I go back to bed? It's almost one thirty, and I want at least a little sleep before the sun comes up. I've got three classes tomorrow starting in the morning."

"Fine. Good night," Komatsu said. "Sweet dreams." And he hung up.

Tengo stared at the receiver in his hand for a while, then set it down. He wanted to get to sleep right away if possible, and to have good dreams if possible, but he knew it wouldn't be easy after having been dragged out of bed and forced to participate in an unpleasant conversation. He could try drinking himself to sleep, but he wasn't in the mood for alcohol. He ended up drinking a glass of water, getting back in bed, turning on the light, and beginning to read a book. He hoped it would make him sleepy, but he didn't actually fall asleep until almost dawn.

Tengo took the elevated train to Shinjuku after his third class ended. He bought a few books at the Kinokuniya bookstore, and then headed for the Nakamuraya Café. He gave Komatsu's name at the door and was shown to a quiet table in the back. Fuka-Eri was not there yet. Tengo told the waiter he would wait for the other person to come. Would he want something to drink while he waited? He said that he would not. The waiter left a menu and a glass of water on the table. Tengo opened one of his new books and started reading. It was a book on occultism and it detailed the function of curses in Japanese society over the centuries. Curses played a major role in ancient communities. They had made up for the gaps and inconsistencies in the social system. It seemed like an enjoyable time to be alive.

Fuka-Eri had still not come at six fifteen. Unconcerned, Tengo went on reading. It didn't surprise him that she was late. This whole business was so crazy, he couldn't complain to anybody if it took another crazy turn. It would not be strange if she changed her mind and decided not to show up at all. In fact, he would prefer it that way – it would be simpler. He could just report to Komatsu that he waited an hour and she never showed. What would happen after that was no concern of his. He would just eat dinner by himself and go home, and that would satisfy his obligation to Komatsu.

Fuka-Eri arrived at 6:22. The waiter showed her to the table and she sat down across from Tengo. Resting her small hands on the table, not even removing her coat, she stared straight at him. No "Sorry I'm late," or "I hope I didn't keep you waiting too long." Not even a "Hi" or a "Nice to meet you." All she did was look directly at Tengo, her lips forming a tight, straight line. She could have been observing a new landscape from afar. Tengo was impressed.

Fuka-Eri was a small girl, small all over, and her face was more beautiful than in the pictures. Her most attractive facial feature was her deep, striking eyes. Under the gaze of two glistening, pitch-black pupils, Tengo felt uncomfortable. She hardly blinked and seemed almost not to be breathing. Her hair was absolutely straight, as if someone had drawn each individual strand with a ruler, and the shape of her eyebrows matched the hair perfectly. As with many beautiful teenage girls, her expression lacked any trace of everyday life. It also was strangely unbalanced – perhaps because there was a slight difference in the depth of the left and right eyes – causing discomfort in the recipient of her gaze. You couldn't tell what she was thinking. In that sense, she was not the kind of beautiful girl who becomes a model or a pop star. Rather, she had something about her that aroused people and drew them toward her.

Tengo closed his book and laid it to one side. He sat up straight and took a drink of water. Komatsu had been right. If a girl like this took a literary prize, the media would be all over her. It would be a sensation. And then what?

The waiter came and placed a menu and a glass of water in front of her. Still she did not move. Instead of picking up the menu, she went on staring at Tengo. He felt he had no choice but to say something. "Hello." In her presence, he felt bigger than ever.

Fuka-Eri did not return his greeting but continued to stare at him. "I know you," she murmured at last.

"You know me?" Tengo said.

"You teach math."

He nodded. "I do."

"I heard you twice."

"My lectures?"

"Yes."

Her style of speaking had some distinguishing characteristics: sentences shorn of embellishment, a chronic shortage of inflection, a limited vocabulary (or at least what seemed like a limited vocabulary). Komatsu was right: it was odd.

"You mean you're a student at my school?" Tengo asked.

Fuka-Eri shook her head. "Just went for lectures."

"You're not supposed to be able to get in without a student ID."

Fuka-Eri gave a little shrug, as if to say, "Grown-ups shouldn't say such dumb things."

"How were the lectures?" Tengo asked, his second meaningless question.

Fuka-Eri took a drink of water without averting her gaze. She did not answer the question. Tengo guessed he couldn't have made too bad an impression if she came twice. She would have quit after the first one if it hadn't aroused her interest.

"You're in your third year of high school, aren't you?" Tengo asked.

"More or less."

"Studying for college entrance exams?"

She shook her head.

Tengo could not decide whether this meant "I don't want to talk about my college entrance exams" or "I wouldn't be caught dead taking college entrance exams." He recalled Komatsu's remark on how little Fuka-Eri had to say.

The waiter came for their orders. Fuka-Eri still had her coat on. She ordered a salad and bread. "That's all," she said, returning the menu to the waiter. Then, as if it suddenly occurred to her, she added, "And a glass of white wine."

The young waiter seemed about to ask her age, but she gave him a stare that made him turn red, and he swallowed his words. *Impressive*, Tengo thought again. He ordered seafood linguine and decided to join Fuka-Eri in a glass of white wine.

"You're a teacher and a writer," Fuka-Eri said. She seemed to be asking Tengo a question. Apparently, asking questions without question marks was another characteristic of her speech.

"For now," Tengo said.

"You don't look like either."

"Maybe not," he said. He thought of smiling but couldn't quite manage it. "I'm certified as an instructor and I do teach courses at a cram school, but I'm not exactly a teacher. I write fiction, but I've never been published, so I'm not a writer yet, either."

"You're nothing."

Tengo nodded. "Exactly. For the moment, I'm nothing."

"You like math."

Tengo mentally added a question mark to her comment and answered this new question: "I do like math. I've always liked it, and I still like it."

"What about it."

"What do I like about math? Hmm. When I've got figures in front of me, it relaxes me. Kind of like, everything fits where it belongs."

"The calculus part was good."

"You mean in my lecture?"

Fuka-Eri nodded.

"Do you like math?"

She gave her head a quick shake. She did not like math.

"But the part about calculus was good?" he asked.

Fuka-Eri gave another little shrug. "You talked about it like you cared."

"Oh, really?" Tengo said. No one had ever told him this before.

"Like you were talking about somebody important to you," she said.

"I can maybe get even more passionate when I lecture on sequences," Tengo said. "Sequences were a personal favorite of mine in high school math."

"You like sequences," Fuka-Eri asked, without a question mark.

"To me, they're like Bach's *Well-Tempered Clavier*. I never get tired of them. There's always something new to discover."

"I know the *Well-Tempered Clavier*."

"You like Bach?"

Fuka-Eri nodded. "The Professor is always listening to it."

"The Professor? One of your teachers?"

Fuka-Eri did not answer. She looked at Tengo with an expression that seemed to say, "It's too soon to talk about that."

She took her coat off as if it had only now occurred to her to do so. She emerged from it like an insect sloughing off its skin. Without bothering to fold it, she set it on the chair next to hers. She wore a thin crew-neck sweater of pale green and white jeans, with no jewelry or makeup, but still she stood out. She had a slender build, in proportion to which her full breasts could not help but attract attention. They were beautifully shaped as well. Tengo had to caution himself not to look down there, but he couldn't help it. His eyes moved to her chest as if toward the center of a great whirlpool.

The two glasses of white wine arrived. Fuka-Eri took a sip of hers, and then, after thoughtfully studying the glass, she set it on the table. Tengo took a perfunctory sip. Now it was time to talk about important matters.

Fuka-Eri brought her hand to her straight black hair and combed her fingers through it for a while. It was a lovely gesture, and her fingers were lovely, each seemingly moving according to its own will and purpose as if in tune with something occult.

"What do I like about math?" Tengo asked himself aloud again in order to divert his attention from her fingers and her chest. "Math is like water. It has a lot of difficult theories, of course, but its basic logic is very simple. Just as water flows from high to low over the shortest possible distance, figures can only flow in one direction. You just have to keep your eye on them for the route to reveal itself. That's all it takes. You don't have to do a thing. Just concentrate your attention and keep your eyes open, and the figures make everything clear to you. In this whole, wide world, the only thing that treats me so kindly is math."

Fuka-Eri thought about this for a while. "Why do you write fiction," she asked in her expressionless way.

Tengo converted her question into longer sentences: "In other words, if I like math so much, why do I go to all the trouble of writing fiction? Why not just keep doing math? Is that it?"

She nodded.

"Hmm. Real life is different from math. Things in life don't necessarily flow over the shortest possible route. For me, math is – how should I put it? – math is all too natural. It's like beautiful scenery. It's *just there*. There's no need to exchange it with anything else. That's why, when I'm doing math, I sometimes feel I'm turning transparent. And that can be scary."

Fuka-Eri kept looking straight into Tengo's eyes as if she were looking into an empty house with her face pressed up against the glass.

Tengo said, "When I'm writing a story, I use words to transform the surrounding scene into something more natural for me. In other words, I reconstruct it. That way, I can confirm without a doubt that this person known as 'me' exists in the world. This is a totally different process from steeping myself in the world of math."

"You confirm that you exist," Fuka-Eri said.

"I can't say I've been one hundred percent successful at it," Tengo said.

Fuka-Eri did not look convinced by Tengo's explanation, but she said nothing more. She merely brought the glass of wine to her mouth and took soundless little sips as though drinking through a straw.

"If you ask me," Tengo said, "you're in effect doing the same thing. You transform the scenes you see into your own words and reconstruct them. And you confirm your own existence."

Fuka-Eri's hand that held her wineglass stopped moving. She thought about Tengo's remark for a while, but again she offered no opinion.

"You gave shape to that process. In the form of the work you wrote," Tengo added. "If the work succeeds in gaining many people's approval and if they identify with it, then it becomes a literary work with objective value."

Fuka-Eri gave her head a decisive shake. "I'm not interested in form."

"You're not interested in form," Tengo said.

"Form has no *meaning*."

"So then, why did you write the story and submit it for the new writers' prize?"

She put down her wineglass. "I didn't," she said.

To calm himself, Tengo picked up his glass and took a drink of water. "You're saying you didn't submit it?"

Fuka-Eri nodded. "I didn't send it in."

"Well, who did?"

She gave a little shrug, then kept silent for a good fifteen seconds. Finally, she said, "It doesn't matter."

"It doesn't matter," Tengo repeated, emitting a long, slow breath from his pursed lips. *Oh, great. Things really are* not *going to go smoothly. I knew it.*

Several times, Tengo had formed personal relationships with his female cram school students, though always after they had left the school and entered universities, and it was always the girls who took the initiative. They would call and say they wanted to see him. The two of them would meet and go somewhere together. He had no idea what attracted them to him, but ultimately he was a bachelor, and they were no longer his students. He had no good reason to refuse when asked for a date.

Twice the dates had led to sex, but the relationships had eventually faded on their own. Tengo could not quite relax when he was with energetic young college girls. It was like playing with a kitten, fresh and fun at first, but tiring in the end. The girls, too, seemed disappointed to discover that in person, Tengo was not the same as the passionate young math lecturer they encountered in class. He could understand how they felt.

Tengo was able to relax when he was with older women. Not having to take the lead in everything seemed to lift a weight from his shoulders. And many older women liked him. Which is why, after having formed a relationship with a married woman ten years his senior a year ago, he had stopped dating any young girls. By meeting his older girlfriend in his apartment once a week, any desire (or need) he might have for a flesh-and-blood woman was pretty well satisfied. The rest of the week he spent shut up in his room alone, writing, reading, and listening to music; occasionally he would go for a swim in the neighborhood pool. Aside from a little chatting with his colleagues at the cram school, he hardly spoke with anyone. He was not especially dissatisfied with this life. Far from it: for him, it was close to ideal.

But this seventeen-year-old girl, Fuka-Eri, was different. The mere sight of her sent a violent shudder through him. It was the same feeling her photograph had given him when he first saw it, but in the living girl's presence it was far stronger. This was not the pangs of love or sexual desire. A certain *something*, he felt, had managed to work its way in through a tiny opening and was trying to fill a blank space inside him. The void was not one that Fuka-Eri had made. It had always been there inside Tengo. She had merely managed to shine a special light on it.

"You're not interested in writing fiction, and you didn't enter the new writers' competition," Tengo said as if confirming what she had told him.

With her eyes locked on his, Fuka-Eri nodded in agreement. Then she gave a little shrug, as if shielding herself from a cold autumn blast.

"You don't want to be a writer." Tengo was shocked to hear himself asking a question without a question mark. The style was obviously contagious.

"No, I don't," Fuka-Eri said.

At that point their meal arrived – a large bowl of salad and a roll for Fuka-Eri, and seafood linguine for Tengo. Fuka-Eri used her fork to turn over several lettuce leaves, inspecting them as if they were imprinted with newspaper headlines.

"Well, *somebody* sent your *Air Chrysalis* to the publisher for the new writers' competition. I found it when I was screening manuscripts."

"*Air Chrysalis,*" Fuka-Eri said, narrowing her eyes.

"That's the title of the novella you wrote," Tengo said.

Fuka-Eri kept her eyes narrowed, saying nothing.

"That's not the title you gave it?" Tengo asked with an uneasy twinge.

Fuka-Eri gave her head a tiny shake.

He began to feel confused again, but he decided not to pursue the question of the title. The important thing was to make some progress with the discussion at hand.

"Never mind, then. Anyway, it's not a bad title. It has real atmosphere, and it'll attract attention, make people wonder what it could possibly be about. Whoever thought of it, I have no problem with it as a title. I'm not sure about the distinction between 'chrysalis' and 'cocoon,' but that's no big deal. What I'm trying to tell you is that the work really *got* to me, which is why I brought it to Mr. Komatsu. He liked it a lot, too, but he felt that the writing needed work if it was going to be a serious contender for the new writers' prize. The style doesn't quite measure up to the strength of the story, so what he wants to do is have it rewritten, not by you but by me. I haven't decided whether I want to do it or not, and I haven't given him my answer. I'm not sure it's the right thing to do."

Tengo broke off at that point to see Fuka-Eri's reaction. There was no reaction.

"What I'd like to hear from you now is what you think of the idea of me rewriting *Air Chrysalis* instead of you. Even if I decided to do it, it couldn't happen without your agreement and cooperation."

Using her fingers, Fuka-Eri picked a cherry tomato out of her salad and ate it. Tengo stabbed a mussel with his fork and ate that.

"You can do it," Fuka-Eri said simply. She picked up another tomato. "Fix it any way you like."

"Don't you think you should take a little more time to think it over? This is a pretty big decision."

Fuka-Eri shook her head. No need.

"Now, supposing I rewrote your novella," Tengo continued, "I would be careful not to change the story but just strengthen the style. This would probably involve some major changes. But finally, you are the author. It would remain a work by the seventeen-year-old girl named Fuka-Eri. That would not change. If it won the prize, you would get it. Just you. If it were published as a book, you would be the only author listed on the title page. We would be a team – the three of us, you, me, and Mr. Komatsu, the editor. But the only name on the book would be yours. He and I would stay in the background and not say a word, kind of like prop men in a play. Do you understand what I am telling you?"

Fuka-Eri brought a piece of celery to her mouth with her fork. "I understand," she said with a nod.

"*Air Chrysalis* belongs entirely to you. It came out of you. I could never make it mine. I would be nothing but your technical helper, and you would have to keep that fact a complete secret. We'd be engaged in a conspiracy, in other words, to lie to the whole world. Any way you look at it, this is not an easy thing to do, to keep a secret locked up in your heart."

"Whatever you say," Fuka-Eri said.

Tengo pushed his mussel shells to the side of his plate and started to take a forkful of linguine but then reconsidered and stopped. Fuka-Eri picked up a piece of cucumber and bit it carefully, as if tasting something she had never seen before.

Fork in hand, Tengo said, "Let me ask you one more time. Are you sure you have no objection to my rewriting your story?"

"Do what you want," Fuka-Eri said, when she had finished the cucumber.

"Any way I rewrite it is okay with you?"

"Okay."

"Why is that?" he asked. "You don't know a thing about me."

Fuka-Eri gave a little shrug, saying nothing.

The two continued their meal wordlessly. Fuka-Eri gave her full concentration to her salad. Now and then she would butter a piece of bread, eat it, and reach for her wine. Tengo mechanically transported his linguine to his mouth and filled his mind with many possibilities.

Setting his fork down, he said, "You know, when Mr. Komatsu suggested this idea to me, I thought it was crazy, that there was no way it could work. I was planning to turn him down. But after I got home and thought about it for a while, I started to feel more and more that I wanted to give it a try. Ethical questions aside, I began to feel that I wanted to put my own stamp on the novella that you had written. It was – how to put this? – a totally natural, spontaneous desire."

Or rather than a desire, hunger *might be a better way to put it,* Tengo added mentally. Just as Komatsu had predicted, the hunger was becoming increasingly difficult to suppress.

Fuka-Eri said nothing, but from somewhere deep inside her neutral, beautiful eyes, she looked hard at Tengo. She seemed to be struggling to understand the words that Tengo had spoken.

"You want to rewrite the story," she asked.

Tengo looked straight into her eyes. "I think I do."

A faint flash crossed Fuka-Eri's black pupils, as if they were projecting something. Or at least they looked that way to Tengo.

Tengo held his hands out, as if he were supporting an imaginary box in the air. The gesture had no particular meaning, but he needed some kind of imaginary medium like that to convey his feelings. "I don't know how to put it exactly," he said, "but in reading *Air Chrysalis* over and over, I began to feel that I could see what you were seeing. Especially when the Little People appear. Your imagination has some special kind of power. It's entirely original, and quite contagious."

Fuka-Eri quietly set her spoon on her plate and dabbed at her mouth with her napkin.

"The Little People really exist," she said softly.

"They really exist?"

Fuka-Eri paused before she said, "Just like you and me."

"Just like you and me," Tengo repeated.

"You can see them if you try."

Her concise speaking style was strangely persuasive. From every word that came to her lips, he felt a precise, wedge-like thrust. He still could not tell, though, how seriously he should take her. There was something out of the ordinary about her, a screw slightly loose. It was an inborn quality, perhaps. He might be in the presence of an authentic talent in its most natural form, or it could all be an act. Intelligent teenage girls were often instinctively theatrical, purposely eccentric, mouthing highly suggestive words to confuse people. He had seen a number of such cases when it was impossible to distinguish the real thing from acting. Tengo decided to bring the conversation back to reality – or, at least, something closer to reality.

"As long as it's okay with you, I'd like to start rewriting *Air Chrysalis* tomorrow."

"If that is what you want to do."

"It *is* what I want to do," Tengo replied.

"There's someone to meet," Fuka-Eri said.

"Someone you want *me* to meet?"

She nodded.

"Now, who could that be?"

She ignored his question. "To talk to," she added.

"I don't mind," Tengo said, "if it's something I should do."

"Are you free Sunday morning," she asked, without a question mark.

"I am," Tengo said. *It's as if we're talking in semaphore,* he thought.

They finished eating and parted. At the door of the restaurant, Tengo slipped a few ten-yen coins into the pay phone and called Komatsu's work number. He was still in his office, but it took him a while to come to the phone. Tengo waited with the receiver on his ear.

"How did it go?" Komatsu asked right away.

"Fuka-Eri is basically okay with me rewriting *Air Chrysalis,* I think."

"That's great!" Komatsu exclaimed. "Marvelous! To tell you the truth, I was a little worried about you. I mean, you're not exactly the negotiator type."

"I didn't do any negotiating," Tengo said. "I didn't have to convince her. I just explained the main points, and she pretty much decided on her own."

"I don't care how you did it. The results are what count. Now we can go ahead with the plan."

"Except that I have to meet somebody first."

"Meet somebody? Who?"

"I don't know. She wants me to meet this person and talk."

Komatsu kept silent for a few seconds. "So when are you supposed to do that?"

"This Sunday. She's going to take me there."

"There's one important rule when it comes to keeping secrets," Komatsu said gravely. "The fewer people who know the secret, the better. So far, only three of us know about the plan – you, me, and Fuka-Eri. If possible, I'd like to avoid increasing that number. You understand, don't you?"

"In theory," Tengo said.

Komatsu's voice softened as he said, "Anyhow, Fuka-Eri is ready to have you rewrite her manuscript. That's the most important thing. We can work out the rest."

Tengo switched the receiver to his left hand and slowly pressed his right index finger against his temple. "To be honest," he said to Komatsu, "this is making me nervous. I don't have any real grounds for saying so, but I have this strong feeling that I'm being swept up in something out of the ordinary. I didn't feel it when I was with Fuka-Eri, but it's been getting stronger since she left. Call it a premonition, or just a funny feeling, but there is something strange going on here. Something out of the ordinary. I feel it less with my mind than my whole body."

"Was it meeting Fuka-Eri that made you feel this way?"

"Maybe so. She's probably the real thing. This is just my gut feeling, of course."

"You mean that she has real talent?"

"I don't know about her talent," Tengo said. "I've just met her, after all. But she may actually be seeing things that you and I can't see. She might have something special. That's what's bothering me."

"You mean she might have mental issues?"

"She's definitely eccentric, but I don't think she's crazy. There's a logical thread to what she says, more or less. It's just that . . . I don't know . . . something's bothering me."

"In any case, did she take an interest in you?" Komatsu asked.

Tengo searched for the appropriate words with which to answer him, but was unable to find them. "I really can't say about that," he replied.

"Well, she met you, and she must have thought you were qualified to rewrite *Air Chrysalis*. That means she liked you. Good work, Tengo! What happens from here on out, I don't know, either. There is some risk, of course. But risk is the spice of life. Start rewriting the manuscript right away. We don't have any time to lose. I've got to return the rewritten manuscript to the pile of entries as soon as possible, switch it for the original. Can you do the job in ten days?"

Tengo sighed. "What a taskmaster!"

"Don't worry, you don't have to make it absolutely polished. We can still touch it up in the next stage. Just get it into reasonably good shape."

Tengo did a general estimate of the job in his head. "If that's the case, I might be able to pull it off in ten days. It's still going to be a huge job, though."

"Just give it everything you've got," Komatsu urged him cheerfully. "Look at the world through her eyes. You'll be the go-between – connecting Fuka-Eri's world and the real world we live in. I know you can do it, Tengo, I just – "

At this point the last ten-yen coin ran out.

Aomame

A PROFESSION REQUIRING SPECIALIZED TECHNIQUES AND TRAINING

After finishing her job and exiting the hotel, Aomame walked a short distance before catching a cab to yet another hotel, in the Akasaka District. She needed to calm her nerves with alcohol before going home to bed. After all, she had just sent a man to the other side. True, he was a loathsome rat who had no right to complain about being killed, but he was, ultimately, a human being. Her hands still retained the sensation of the life draining out of him. He had expelled his last breath, and the spirit had left his body. Aomame had been to the bar in this Akasaka hotel any number of times. It was the top floor of a high-rise building, had a great view, and a comfortable counter.

She entered the bar a little after seven. A young piano and guitar duo were playing "Sweet Lorraine." Their version was a copy of an old Nat King Cole record, but they weren't bad. As always, she sat at the bar and ordered a gin and tonic and a plate of pistachios. The place was still not crowded – a young couple drinking cocktails as they took in the view, four men in suits who seemed to be discussing a business deal, a middle-aged foreign couple holding martini glasses. She took her time drinking the gin and tonic. She didn't want the alcohol to take effect too quickly. The night ahead was long.

She pulled a book from her shoulder bag and started reading. It was a history of the South Manchurian Railway Company of the 1930s. The line and right-of-way had been ceded to Japan by Russia after the Russo-Japanese War of 1904–1905, after which the company had rapidly expanded its operations, becoming fundamental in Japan's invasion of China. It was broken up by the Soviet army in 1945. Until the outbreak of the Russo-German War in 1941, one could travel between Shimonoseki and Paris in thirteen days via this line and the Trans-Siberian Railway.

Aomame figured that a young woman drinking alone in a hotel bar could not be mistaken for a high-class hooker on the prowl if she was wearing a business suit, had a big shoulder bag parked next to her, and sat there absorbed in a book about the South Manchurian Railway (a hardcover, no less). In fact, Aomame had no idea what kind of outfit a real high-class hooker would wear. If she herself were a prostitute looking for wealthy businessmen, she would probably try her best not to look like a prostitute so as to avoid either making potential clients nervous or having herself ejected from the bar. One way to accomplish that might be to wear a Junko Shimada business suit and white blouse, keep her makeup to a minimum, carry a big, practical shoulder bag, and have a book on the South Manchurian Railway open in front of her. Come to think of it, what she was doing now was not substantially different from a prostitute on the prowl.

As the time passed, the place gradually filled up. Before she knew it, Aomame was surrounded by the buzz of conversation. But none of the customers had what she was looking for. She drank another gin and tonic, ordered some crudités (she hadn't eaten dinner yet), and continued reading. Eventually a man came and sat a few seats away from her at the bar. He was alone. Nicely tanned, he wore an expensively tailored blue-gray suit. His taste in neckties was not bad, either

– neither flashy nor plain. He must have been around fifty, and his hair was more than a little thin. He wore no glasses. She guessed he was in Tokyo on business and, having finished the day's work, wanted a drink before going to bed. Like Aomame herself. The idea was to calm the nerves by introducing a moderate amount of alcohol into the body.

Few men in Tokyo on business stayed in this kind of expensive hotel. Most chose a cheap business hotel, one near a train station, where the bed nearly filled the room, the only view from the window was the wall of the next building, and you couldn't take a shower without bumping your elbows twenty times. The corridor of each floor had vending machines for drinks and toiletries. Either the company wouldn't pay for anything better, or the men were pocketing the travel money left over from staying in such a cheap place. They would drink a beer from the local liquor store before going to bed, and wolf down a bowl of rice and beef for breakfast at the eatery next door.

A different class of people stayed at this hotel. When these men came to Tokyo on business, they never took anything but the bullet train's luxury "green cars," and they stayed only in certain elite hotels. Finishing a job, they would relax in the hotel bar and drink expensive whiskey. Most held management positions in first-rank corporations, or else they were independent businessmen or professionals such as doctors or lawyers. They had reached middle age, and money was no problem for them. They also knew more or less how to have a good time. This was the type that Aomame had in mind.

Aomame herself did not know why, but ever since the time she was twenty, she had been attracted to men with thinning hair. They should not be completely bald but have something left on top. And thin hair was not all it took to please her. They had to have well-shaped heads. Her ideal type was Sean Connery. His beautifully shaped head was sexy. Looking at him was all it took to set her heart racing. The man now sitting at the bar two seats away from her had a very well-shaped head – not as perfect as Sean Connery's, of course, but attractive in its own way. His hairline had receded from the forehead and his sparse remaining hair recalled a frosty meadow in late autumn. Aomame raised her eyes a little from the pages of her book and admired his head shape for a while. His facial features were nothing special. Though not fat, his jowls were just beginning to sag, and he had a hint of bags under his eyes. He was the kind of middle-aged man you see everywhere. But that head shape of his she found very much to her liking.

When the bartender brought him a menu and a warm towel, the man ordered a Scotch highball without looking at the menu. "Do you prefer a certain brand?" the bartender asked. "Not really," the man said. "Anything will be fine." He had a calm, quiet voice and spoke with a soft Kansai accent. Then, as if it had just occurred to him, he asked if they had Cutty Sark. The bartender said they did. *Not bad,* thought Aomame. She liked the fact that he had not chosen Chivas Regal or some sophisticated single malt. It was her personal view that people who are overly choosy about the drinks they order in a bar tend to be sexually bland. She had no idea why this should be so.

Aomame also had a taste for Kansai accents. She especially enjoyed the mismatch between vocabulary and intonation when people born and raised in Kansai came up to Tokyo and tried to use Tokyo words with Kansai pronunciation. She found that special sound to be strangely calming. So now she made up her mind: she would go for this man. She was dying to run her fingers through the few strands of hair he had left. So when the bartender brought him his Cutty Sark highball, she said to the bartender loudly enough so the man was sure to hear her, "Cutty Sark on the rocks, please." "Yes, ma'am, right away," the bartender replied, his face a blank.

The man undid the top button of his shirt and loosened his tie, which was a dark blue with a fine-grained pattern. His suit was also dark blue. He wore a pale blue shirt with a standard collar. She went on reading her book as she waited for her Cutty Sark to come. Discreetly, she undid the top button of her blouse. The jazz duo played "It's Only a Paper Moon." The pianist sang a single chorus. Her drink arrived, and she took a sip. She sensed the man glancing in her direction. She raised her head and looked at him. Casually, as if by chance. When their eyes met, she gave him a faint, almost nonexistent smile, and then immediately faced forward again, pretending to look at the nighttime view.

It was the perfect moment for a man to approach a woman, and she had created it. But this man said nothing. *What the hell is he waiting for?* she wondered. *He's no kid. He should pick up on these subtle hints. Maybe he hasn't got the guts. Maybe he's worried about the age difference. Maybe he thinks I'll ignore him or put him down: bald old coot of fifty has some nerve approaching a woman in her twenties! Damn, he just doesn't get it.*

She closed her book and returned it to her bag. Now she took the initiative.

"You like Cutty Sark?"

He looked shocked, as if he could not grasp the meaning of her question. Then he relaxed his expression. "Oh, yes, Cutty Sark," he said, as if it suddenly came back to him. "I've always liked the label, the sailboat."

"So you like boats."

"Sailboats especially."

Aomame raised her glass. The man raised his highball glass slightly. It was almost a toast.

Aomame slung her bag on her shoulder and, whiskey glass in hand, slipped over two seats to the stool next to his. He seemed a little surprised but struggled not to show it.

"I was supposed to meet an old high school girlfriend of mine here, but it looks like I've been stood up," Aomame said, glancing at her watch. "She's not even calling."

"Maybe she got the date wrong."

"May*be*. She's always been kind of scatterbrained," Aomame said. "I guess I'll wait a little longer. Mind keeping me company? Or would you rather be alone?"

"No, not at all," the man said, though he sounded somewhat uncertain. He knit his brows and looked at her carefully, as if assessing an object to be used as collateral. He seemed to suspect her of being a prostitute. But Aomame was clearly not a prostitute. He relaxed and let his guard down a little.

"Are you staying in this hotel?" he asked.

"No, I live in Tokyo," she said, shaking her head. "I'm just here to meet my friend. And you?"

"In town on business," he said. "From Osaka. For a meeting. A stupid meeting, but the company headquarters are in Osaka, so somebody had to come."

Aomame gave him a perfunctory smile. *I don't give a shit about your business, mister,* she thought, *I just happen to like the shape of your head.*

"I needed a drink after work. I've got one more job to finish up tomorrow morning, and then I head back to Osaka."

"I just finished a big job myself," Aomame said.

"Oh, really? What kind of work do you do?"

"I don't like to talk about my work. It's a kind of specialized profession."

"Specialized profession," the man responded, repeating her words. "A profession requiring specialized techniques and training."

What are you, some kind of walking dictionary? Silently, she challenged him, but she just kept on smiling and said, "Hmm, I wonder . . ."

He took another sip of his highball and a handful of nuts from the bowl. "I'm curious what kind of work you do, but you don't want to talk about it."

She nodded. "Not yet, at least."

"Does it involve words, by any chance? Say, you might be an editor or a university researcher?"

"What makes you think that?"

He straightened the knot of his necktie and redid the top button of his shirt. "I don't know, you seemed pretty absorbed in that big book of yours."

Aomame tapped her fingernail against the edge of her glass. "No, I just like to read. Without any connection to work."

"I give up, then. I can't imagine."

"No, I'm sure you can't," she said, silently adding, "*Ever.*"

He gave her a casual once-over. Pretending to have dropped something, she bent over and gave him a good, long look at her cleavage and perhaps a peek at her white bra with lace trim. Then she straightened up and took another sip of her Cutty Sark on the rocks. The large, rounded chunks of ice clinked against the sides of her glass.

"How about another drink?" he asked. "I'll order one too."

"Please," Aomame replied.

"You can hold your liquor."

Aomame gave him a vague smile but quickly turned serious. "Oh, yes, I wanted to ask you something."

"What would that be?"

"Have policemen's uniforms changed lately? And the type of guns they carry?"

"What do you mean by 'lately'?"

"In the past week," she said.

He gave her an odd look. "Police uniforms and guns both underwent a change, but that was some years back. The jackets went from a stiff, formal style to something more casual, almost like a windbreaker. And they started carrying those new-model automatic pistols. I don't think there have been any changes since then."

"Japanese policemen always carried old-fashioned revolvers, I'm sure. Right up to last week."

The man shook his head. "Now there, you're wrong. They all started carrying automatics quite some time ago."

"Can you say that with absolute certainty?"

Her tone gave him pause. He wrinkled his brow and searched his memory. "Well, if you put it that way, I can't be one hundred percent sure, but I know I saw something in the papers about the switch to new pistols. It caused quite a stir. The usual citizens' groups were complaining to the government that the pistols were too high-powered."

"And this was a while ago?" Aomame asked.

The man called over the middle-aged bartender and asked him when the police changed their uniforms and pistols.

"In the spring two years ago," the bartender replied, without hesitation.

"See?" the man said with a laugh. "Bartenders in first-class hotels know everything!"

The bartender laughed as well. "No, not really," he said. "It just so happens my younger brother is a cop, so I clearly remember that stuff. My brother couldn't stand the new uniforms and was always complaining about them. And he thought the new pistols were too heavy. He's still complaining about those. They're 9mm Beretta automatics. One click and you can switch them to semiautomatic. I'm pretty sure Mitsubishi's making them domestically under license now. We almost never have any out-and-out gun battles in Japan; there's just no need for such a high-powered gun. If anything, the cops have to worry now about having their guns stolen from them. But it was government policy back then to upgrade the force."

"What happened to the old revolvers?" Aomame asked, keeping her voice as calm as she could.

"I'm pretty sure they were all recalled and dismantled," the bartender said. "I remember seeing it on television. It was a huge job dismantling that many pistols and scrapping all that ammunition."

"They should have just sold everything abroad," said the thinning-haired company man.

"The constitution forbids the export of weapons," the bartender pointed out modestly.

"See? Bartenders in first-class hotels – "

Aomame cut the man off and asked, "You're telling me that Japanese police haven't used revolvers *at all* for two years now?"

"As far as I know."

Aomame frowned slightly. *Am I going crazy? I just saw a policeman wearing the old-style uniform and carrying an old revolver this morning. I'm sure I never heard a thing about them getting rid of every single revolver, but I also can't believe that these two middle-aged men are wrong or lying to me. Which means I must be mistaken.*

"Thanks very much. I've heard all I need to about that," she said to the bartender, who gave her a professional smile like a well-timed punctuation mark and went back to work.

"Do you have some special interest in policemen?" the middle-aged man asked her.

"No, not really," Aomame answered, adding vaguely, "It's just that my memory has gotten a little foggy."

They drank their new Cutty Sarks – the man his highball and Aomame hers on the rocks. The man talked about sailboats. He moored his small sailboat in the Nishinomiya yacht harbor, he said. He took it out to the ocean on holidays and weekends. He spoke passionately of how wonderful it was to feel the wind as you sailed alone on the sea. Aomame didn't want to hear about any damned sailboats. Better for him to talk about the history of ball bearings or the distribution of mineral resources in Ukraine. She glanced at her watch and said, "Look, it's getting late. Can I just ask you something straight out?"

"Sure," he replied.

"It's, uh, rather personal."

"I'll answer if I can."

"Do you have a decent-sized cock? Is it on the big side?"

The man's lips parted and his eyes narrowed as he looked at her for a while. He could not quite believe he had heard her correctly. But her face was utterly serious. She was not joking. Her eyes made that clear.

"Let me see," he said, speaking earnestly. "I'm not really sure. I guess it's pretty much normal size. I don't know what to say when you spring it on me like that."

"How old are you?" Aomame asked.

"I just turned fifty-one last month, but . . . ," he said.

"You've been living more than fifty years with a normal brain, you have a decent job, you even own your own sailboat, and still you can't tell whether your cock is bigger or smaller than normal?"

"Well, I suppose it could be a little bigger," he said with a degree of difficulty after giving it some thought.

"You're sure, now?"

"Why are you so concerned?"

"Concerned? Who says I'm concerned?"

"Well, no one, but . . . ," he said, recoiling slightly atop his bar stool. "That seems to be the problem we're discussing at the moment."

"Problem? It's no problem. No problem at all," Aomame declared. "I just happen to like big cocks. Visually speaking. I'm not saying I need a big one to feel anything, no no. Or that I'm okay with anything as long as it's big. All I'm saying is I tend to like 'em on the big side. Is there something wrong with that? People have their likes and dislikes. But ridiculously big ones are no good. They just hurt. Do you see what I mean?"

"Well, then, I might be able to please you with mine. It's somewhat bigger than standard, I think, but it's not ridiculously big, either. It's – shall I say? – just right . . ."

"You're not lying to me, now?"

"What would be the point of lying about something like that?"

"Well, all right, then, maybe you should give me a peek."

"Here?"

Aomame frowned while struggling to control herself. "Here?! Are you crazy? What are you thinking, at your age? You're wearing a good suit and even a tie, but where's your social common sense? You can't just whip out your cock in a place like this. Imagine what the people around you would think! No, we go to your room now, and I let you take your pants off and show me. Just the two of us. That much should be obvious to you."

"So I show you, and then what happens?" he asked worriedly.

"What happens after you show it to me?" Aomame asked, catching her breath and producing a major uncontrolled frown. "We have sex, obviously. What else? I mean, we go to your room, you show me your cock, and I say, 'Thank you very much for showing me such a nice one. Good night,' and I go home? You must have a screw loose somewhere."

The man gasped to see Aomame's face undergoing such dramatic changes before his eyes. A frown from Aomame could make any man shrivel up. Little children might pee in their pants, the impact of her frown was so powerful. *Maybe I overdid it,* she thought. *I really shouldn't frighten him so badly. At least not until I've taken care of business.* She quickly returned her face to its normal state and forced a smile. Then, as if spelling it out for him, she said, "Here's what happens. We go to your room. We get in bed. We have sex. You're not gay or impotent, are you?"

"No, I don't believe so. I have two children . . ."

"Look, nobody's asking you how many kids you've got. Do I look like a census taker? Keep the details to yourself. All I'm asking is whether you can get it up when you're in bed with a woman. Nothing else."

"As far back as I can remember, I've never failed to perform when necessary," he said. "But tell me – are you a professional? Is this your job?"

"No, it is *not* my job, so you can stop that right now. I am not a professional, or a pervert, just an ordinary citizen. An ordinary citizen who wants nothing more than to have inter-course with a member of the opposite sex. There's nothing special about me. I'm totally normal. What could be wrong with that? I've just finished a tough job, the sun is down, I've had a little to drink, and I'd like to let off steam by having sex with a stranger. To calm my nerves. That's what I need. You're a man, you know how I feel."

"Of course I do, but . . ."

"I'm not looking for any money. I'd almost pay *you* if you can satisfy me. And I've got condoms with me, so you don't have to worry. Am I making myself clear?"

"You certainly are, but . . ."

"But what? You don't seem all that eager. Am I not good enough for you?"

"That's not it at all. I just don't get it. You're young and pretty, and I'm old enough to be your father . . ."

"Oh, stop it, will you please? Sure you're a lot older than me, but I'm not your damn daughter, and you're not my damn father. That much is obvious. It sets my nerves on edge to be subjected to such meaningless generalizations. I just like your bald head. I like the way it's shaped. Do you see?"

"Well, I wouldn't exactly call myself *bald*. I know my hair-line is a little . . ."

"Shut *up*, will you?" Aomame said, trying her best not to frown. *I shouldn't scare him too much*, she thought, softening her tone somewhat. "That's really not important."

Look, mister, I don't care what you *think, you are* bald. *If the census had a "bald" category, you'd be in it, no problem. If you go to heaven, you're going to bald heaven. If you go to hell, you're going to bald hell. Have you got that straight? Then stop looking away from the truth. Let's go now. I'm taking you straight to bald heaven, nonstop.*

The man paid the bill and they went to his room.

His penis was in fact somewhat larger than normal, though not too large, as advertised. Aomame's expert handling soon made it big and hard. She took off her blouse and skirt.

"I know you're thinking my breasts are small," she said coldly as she looked down at him in her underwear. "You came through with a good-sized cock and all you get in return is these puny things. I bet you feel cheated."

"Not at all," he reassured her. "They're not that small. And they're really quite beautiful."

"I wonder," she said. "Let me just say this, though. I *never* wear these frilly lace bras. I had to put this one on today for work, to show off a little cleavage."

"What *is* this work of yours?"

"Look, I told you before. I don't want to discuss my job here. I can say this much, though: it's not that easy being a woman."

"Well, it's not that easy being a man, either."

"Maybe not, but you never have to put on a lacy bra when you don't want to."

"True . . ."

"So don't pretend to know what you're talking about. Women have it much tougher than men. Have you ever had to climb down a steep stairway in high heels, or climb over a barricade in a miniskirt?"

"I owe you an apology," the man said simply.

She reached back, unhooked her bra, and threw it on the floor. Then she rolled down her stockings and threw those on the floor as well. Lying down beside him, she started working on his penis again. "Pretty impressive," she said. "Nice shape, just about ideal size, and firm as a tree trunk."

"I'm glad it meets with your approval," he said with apparent relief.

"Now just let big sister do her thing. She'll make this little man of yours twitch with happiness."

"Maybe we should shower first. I'm pretty sweaty."

"Oh, shut up," Aomame said, giving his right testicle a light snap, as if issuing a warning. "I came here to have sex, not take a shower. Got it? We do it first. Fuck like crazy. To hell with a little sweat. I'm not a blushing schoolgirl."

"All right," the man said.

When they were finished and she was caressing the back of the man's exposed neck as he lay facedown, exhausted, Aomame felt a strong urge to plunge her sharp needle into that special place. *Maybe I should really do it,* the thought flashed through her mind. The ice pick was in her bag, wrapped in cloth. The needle that she had spent so much time sharpening was covered by a specially softened cork. It would have been so easy, just a quick shove of her right palm against the wooden handle. He'd be dead before he knew what hit him. No pain. It would be ruled a natural death. But of course she stopped herself. There was no reason to expunge this man from society, aside from the fact that he no longer served any purpose for Aomame. She shook her head and swept the dangerous thought from her mind.

This man is not an especially bad person, she told herself. He was pretty good in bed, too. He had enough control not to ejaculate until he had made her come. The shape of his head and the degree of his baldness were just the way she liked them. The size of his penis was exactly right. He was courteous, had good taste in clothes, and was in no way overbearing. True, he was tremendously boring, which really got on her nerves, but that was not a crime deserving death. Probably.

"Mind if I turn on the television?" she asked.

"Fine," he said, still on his stomach.

Naked in bed, she watched the eleven o'clock news to the end. In the Middle East, Iran and Iraq were still embroiled in their bloody war. It was a quagmire, with no sign of a settlement. In Iraq, young draft dodgers had been strung up on telephone poles as an example to others. The Iranian government was accusing Saddam Hussein of having used nerve gas and biological weapons. In America, Walter Mondale and Gary Hart were battling to become the Democratic candidate for president. Neither looked like the brightest person in the world. Smart presidents usually became the target of assassins, so people with higher-than-average intelligence probably did their best to avoid being elected.

On the moon, the construction of a permanent observation post was making progress. The United States and the Soviet Union were cooperating on this project, for a change, as they had done with the Antarctic observation post. *An observation post on the moon?* Aomame cocked her head. *I haven't heard anything about that. What is wrong with me?* But she decided not to think too deeply about it. There were more pressing problems to consider. A large number of people had died in a mine fire in Kyushu, and the government was looking into the cause. What most surprised Aomame was the fact that people continued to dig coal out of the earth in an age when bases were being built on the moon. America was pushing Japan to open its financial markets. Morgan Stanley and Merrill Lynch were lighting fires under the government in search of new sources of profit. Next there was a feature that introduced a clever cat from Shimane Prefecture that could open a window and let itself out. Once out, it would close the window. The owner had trained the cat to do this. Aomame watched with admiration as the slim black cat turned around, stretched a paw out, and, with a knowing look in its eye, slid the window closed.

There was a great variety of news stories, but no report on the discovery of a body in a Shibuya hotel. After the news, Aomame turned the TV off with the remote control. The room was hushed, the only sound the soft, rhythmic breathing of the man sleeping beside her.

That other man, the one in the hotel room, is probably still slumped over his desk, looking sound asleep, like this one. Without the breathing. That rat can never wake and rise again. Aomame stared at the ceiling, imagining the look of the corpse. She gave her head a slight shake and indulged in a lonely frown. Then she slipped out of bed and gathered her clothing from the floor, piece by piece.

CHAPTER 6

Tengo

DOES THIS MEAN WE'RE GOING PRETTY FAR FROM THE CITY?

The next call from Komatsu came early Friday morning, shortly after five o'clock. Tengo was just then dreaming about crossing a long stone bridge on a river. He was going to retrieve a document that he had forgotten on the opposite shore. He was alone. The river was big and beautiful, with sandbars here and there. The river flowed gently, and willows grew on the sandbars. He could see the elegant shape of trout in the water. The willows' brilliant green leaves hung down, gently touching the water's surface. The scene could have come from a Chinese plate. Tengo woke and looked at the clock by his pillow in the dark. Of course he knew before lifting the receiver who would be calling at such a time.

"Do you have a word processor, Tengo?" Komatsu asked. No "Good morning," no "Were you up?" If he was awake now, Komatsu must have pulled an all-nighter. He had certainly not awakened early to see the sun rise. He must have recalled something he wanted to tell Tengo before going to bed.

"No, of course not," Tengo answered. He was still in pitch darkness, halfway across the long bridge. He rarely had such vivid dreams. "It's nothing to boast about, but I can't afford anything like that."

"Do you know how to use one?"

"I do. I can pretty much handle either a dedicated word processor or a computer. We have them at school. I use them all the time for work."

"Good. I want you to buy one today. I don't know a thing about machines, so I'll leave it to you to pick out the make and model. Send me a bill afterward. I want you to start revising *Air Chrysalis* as soon as possible."

"You know, we're talking about at least 250,000 yen – for a cheap one."

"That's no problem."

Tengo cocked his head in wonderment. "So, you're saying you're going to buy me a word processor?"

"That I am – from my own little private stash. This job deserves at least that much of an investment. We'll never get anything done playing it cheap. As you know, *Air Chrysalis* arrived as a word-processed manuscript, which means we'll have to use a word processor to rewrite it. I want you to make the new one look like the old one. Can you start the rewrite today?"

Tengo thought about it a moment. "I can start it anytime I decide to, but Fuka-Eri wants me to meet someone this Sunday before she gives me permission, and of course I haven't met the person yet. If those negotiations break down, anything we do now could be a complete waste of time and money."

"Never mind, it'll work out. Don't worry about the details. Start working right away. We're in a race against time."

"Are you that sure my interview will go well?"

"That's what my gut tells me," Komatsu said. "I go by the gut. I might not appear to have any talent, but I've got plenty of gut instinct – if I do say so myself. That's how I've survived all these years. By the way, Tengo, do you know what the biggest difference is between talent and gut instinct?"

"I have no idea."

"You can have tons of talent, but it won't necessarily keep you fed. If you have sharp instincts, though, you'll never go hungry."

"I'll keep that in mind," Tengo said.

"All I'm saying is, don't worry. You can start the job today."

"If you say so, it's fine with me. I was just trying to avoid kicking myself for starting too early."

"Let me worry about that. I'll take complete responsibility."

"Okay, then. I'm seeing somebody this afternoon, but I'll be free to start working after that. I can shop for a word processor this morning."

"That's great, Tengo. I'm counting on you. We'll join forces and turn the world upside down."

Tengo's married girlfriend called just after nine, when she was finished dropping her husband and kids off at the train station for their daily commute. She was supposed to be visiting Tengo's apartment that afternoon. They always got together on Fridays.

"I'm just not feeling right," she said. "Sorry, but I don't think I can make it today. See you next week."

"Not feeling right" was her euphemism for her period. She had been raised to prefer delicate, euphemistic expressions. There was nothing delicate or euphemistic about her in bed, but that was another matter. Tengo said he was also sorry to miss her that day, but he supposed it couldn't be helped.

In fact, he was not all that sorry to miss her on this particular Friday. He always enjoyed sex with her, but his feelings were already moving in the direction of rewriting *Air Chrysalis*. Ideas were welling up inside him like life-forms stirring in a primordial sea. *This way, I'm no different from Komatsu,* he thought. *Nothing has been formally settled, and already my feelings are headed in that direction on their own.*

At ten o'clock he went to Shinjuku and bought a Fujitsu word processor with his credit card. It was the latest model, far lighter than earlier versions. He also bought ink ribbon cartridges and paper. He carried everything back to his apartment, set the machine on his desk, and plugged it in. At work he used a full-sized Fujitsu word processor, and the basic functions of this portable model were not much different. To reassure himself of its operation, he launched into the rewriting of *Air Chrysalis*.

He had no well-defined plan for rewriting the novella, no consistent method or guidelines that he had prepared, just a few detailed ideas for certain sections. Tengo was not even sure it was possible to do a logical rewrite of a work of fantasy and feeling. True, as Komatsu had said, the style needed a great deal of improvement, but would it be possible for him to do that without destroying the work's fundamental nature and atmosphere? Wouldn't this be tantamount to giving a butterfly a skeleton? Such thoughts only caused him confusion and anxiety. But events had already started moving, and he had a limited amount of time. He couldn't just sit there, thinking, arms folded. All he could do was deal with one small, concrete problem after another. Perhaps, as he worked on each detail by hand, an overall image would take shape spontaneously.

"I know you can do it, Tengo," Komatsu had declared with confidence, and for some unfathomable reason, Tengo himself was able to swallow Komatsu's words whole – for now. In both word and action, Komatsu could be a questionable character, and he basically thought of no one but himself. If the occasion arose, he would drop Tengo without batting an eyelash. But as Komatsu himself liked to say, he had special instincts as an editor. He made all judgments instantaneously and carried them out decisively, unconcerned what other people might say. This was a quality indispensable to a brilliant commanding officer on the front lines, but it was a quality that Tengo himself did not possess.

It was half past twelve by the time Tengo started rewriting *Air Chrysalis*. He typed the first few pages of the manuscript into the word processor as is, stopping at a convenient break in the story. He would rewrite this block of text first, changing none of the content but thoroughly reworking the style. It was like remodeling a condo. You leave the basic structure intact, keep the kitchen and bathroom in place, but tear out and replace the flooring, ceiling, walls, and partitions. *I'm a skilled carpenter who's been put in charge of everything,* Tengo told himself. *I don't have a blueprint, so all I can do is use my intuition and experience to work on each separate problem that comes up.*

After typing it in, he reread Fuka-Eri's text, adding explanatory material to sections that felt too obscure, improving the flow of the language, and deleting superfluous or redundant passages. Here and there he would change the order of sentences or paragraphs. Fuka-Eri was extremely sparing in her use of adjectives and adverbs, and he wanted to remain consistent with that aspect of her style, but in certain places where he felt more descriptions were necessary, he would supply something appropriate. Her style overall was juvenile and artless, but the good and the bad passages stood out from each other so clearly that choosing among them took far less time and trouble than he had expected. The artlessness made some passages dense and difficult but it gave others a startling freshness. He needed only to throw out and replace the first type, and leave the second in place.

Rewriting her work gave Tengo a renewed sense that Fuka-Eri had written the piece without any intention of leaving behind a work of literature. All she had done was record a story – or, as she had put it, things she had actually witnessed – that she possessed inside her, and it just so happened that she had used words to do it. She might just as well have used something other than words, but she had not come across a more appropriate medium. It was as simple as that. She had never had any literary ambition, no thought of making the finished piece into a commodity, and so she felt no need to pay attention to the details of style, as if she had been making a room for herself and all she needed was walls and a roof to keep the weather out. This was why it made no difference to her how much Tengo reworked her writing. She had already accomplished her objective. When she said, "Fix it any way you like," she was almost certainly expressing her true feelings.

And yet, the sentences and paragraphs that comprised *Air Chrysalis* were by no means the work of an author writing just for herself. If Fuka-Eri's sole objective was to record things she had witnessed or imagined, setting them down as sheer information, she could have accomplished that much with a list. She didn't have to go to the trouble of fashioning a story, which was unmistakably writing that was meant for other people to pick up and read, which was precisely why *Air Chrysalis,* though written without the objective of creating a literary work, and in crude and artless language, still had succeeded in acquiring the power to appeal directly to the heart. The more he read, however, the more convinced Tengo became that those "other people" were almost certainly not the same "general public" that modern literature invariably had in mind.

All right, then, what kind of reader was this meant for?

Tengo had no idea.

All he knew for sure was that *Air Chrysalis* was an utterly unique work of fiction combining enormous strengths with enormous flaws, and that it seemed to possess an objective that was something quite special.

Tengo found that his rewrite was more than doubling the length of the text. The original was far more often underwritten than overwritten, so rewriting it for coherence and consistency could not help but increase its volume. Fuka-Eri's text was so threadbare! True, with its more logical style and consistent point of view, the new version was far easier to read, but the overall flow was becoming strangely sluggish. Its logicality showed through too clearly, dulling the sharpness of the original.

Once he had filled out this first block of text, Tengo's next task was to eliminate from his bloated manuscript everything that was not strictly necessary, to remove every extra bit of fat. Subtraction was a far simpler process than addition, and it reduced the volume of his text by some thirty percent. It was a kind of mind game. He would set a certain time period for expanding the text as much as possible, then set a certain time period for reducing the text as much as possible. As he alternated tenaciously between the two processes, the swings between them gradually shrank in size, until the volume of text naturally settled down where it belonged, arriving at a point where it could be neither expanded nor reduced. He excised any hint of ego, shook off all extraneous embellishments, and sent all transparent signs of imposed logic into the back room. Tengo had a gift for such work. He was a born technician, possessing both the intense concentration of a bird sailing through the air in search of prey and the patience of a donkey hauling water, playing always by the rules of the game.

Tengo had been all but lost in the work for some time when he looked up to find it was nearly three o'clock. Come to think of it, he hadn't eaten lunch yet. He went to the kitchen, put a kettle on to boil, and ground some coffee beans. He ate a few crackers with cheese, followed those with an apple, and when the water boiled, made coffee. Drinking this from a large mug, he distracted himself with thoughts of sex with his older girlfriend. Ordinarily, he would have been doing it with her right about now. He pictured the things that he would be doing, and the things that she would be doing. He closed his eyes, turned his face toward the ceiling, and released a deep sigh heavy with suggestion and possibility.

Tengo then went back to his desk, switched circuits in his brain again, and read through his rewritten opening to *Air Chrysalis* on the word processor's screen the way the general in the opening scene of Stanley Kubrick's *Paths of Glory* makes his rounds inspecting the trenches. He approved of what he found. Not bad. The writing was much improved. He was making headway. But not enough. He still had lots to do. The trench walls were crumbling here and there. The machine guns' ammunition was running out. The barbed wire barriers had noticeable thin spots.

He printed a draft, saved the document, turned off the word processor, and shifted the machine to the side of his desk. Now, with pencil in hand, he did another careful read-through of the text, this time on paper. Again he deleted parts that seemed superfluous, fleshed out passages that felt underwritten, and revised sections until they fit more smoothly into the rest of the story. He selected his words with all the care of a craftsman choosing the perfect piece of tile to fill a narrow gap in a bathroom floor, inspecting the fit from every angle. Where the fit was less than perfect, he adjusted the shape. The slightest difference in nuance could bring the passage to life or kill it.

The exact same text was subtly different to read when viewed on the printed pages rather than on the word processor's screen. The feel of the words he chose would change depending on whether he was writing them on paper in pencil or typing them on the keyboard. It was imperative to do both. He turned the machine on again and typed each penciled correction back into the word-processed document. Then he reread the revised text on the screen. *Not bad,* he told himself. Each sentence possessed the proper weight, which gave the whole thing a natural rhythm.

Tengo sat up straight in his chair, stretched his back, and, turning his face to the ceiling, let out a long breath. His job was by no means done. When he reread the text in a few days, he would find more things that needed fixing. But this was fine for now. His powers of concentration had just about reached their limit. He needed a cooling-off period. The hands of the clock were nearing five, and the light of day was growing dim. He would rewrite the next block tomorrow. It had taken him almost the whole day to rewrite just the first few pages. This was a lot more time-consuming than he had expected it to be. But the process should speed up once the rules were laid down and a rhythm took hold. Besides, the most difficult and time-consuming part would be the opening. Once he got through that, the rest –

Tengo pictured Fuka-Eri and wondered how she would feel when she read the rewritten manuscript. But then he realized that he had no idea how Fuka-Eri would feel about anything. He knew virtually nothing about her other than that she was seventeen, a junior in high school with no interest in taking college entrance exams, spoke in a very odd way, liked white wine, and had a disturbingly beautiful face.

Still, Tengo had begun to have a fairly strong sense that his grasp of the world that Fuka-Eri was trying to depict (or record) in *Air Chrysalis* was generally accurate. The scenes that Fuka-Eri had created with her peculiar, limited vocabulary took on a new clarity and vividness when reworked by Tengo, who paid such careful attention to detail. They flowed now. He could see that. All he had provided the work was a level of technical reinforcement, but the results were utterly natural, as if he himself had written the thing from scratch. Now the story of *Air Chrysalis* was beginning to emerge with tremendous power.

This was a great source of happiness for Tengo. The long hours of mental concentration had left him physically spent but emotionally uplifted. For some time after he had turned off the word processor and left his desk, Tengo could not suppress the desire to keep rewriting the story. He was enjoying the work immensely. At this rate, he might manage not to disappoint Fuka-Eri – though in fact he could not picture Fuka-Eri being either disappointed or pleased. Far from it. He could not even picture her cracking a smile or displaying the slightest hint of displeasure. Her face was devoid of expression. Tengo could not tell whether she lacked expression because she had no feelings or the feelings she had were unconnected to her expression. In any case, she was a mysterious girl.

The heroine of *Air Chrysalis* was probably Fuka-Eri herself in the past. A ten-year-old girl, she lived in a special mountain commune (or commune-like place), where she was assigned to look after a blind goat. All the children in the commune had work assignments. Though the goat was old, it had special meaning for the community, so the girl's duty was to make sure that no harm came to it. She was not allowed to take her eyes off it for a second. One day, however, in a moment of carelessness, she did exactly that, and the goat died. As her punishment, the girl was put in total isolation for ten days, locked in an old storehouse with the goat's corpse.

The goat served as a passageway to this world for the Little People. The girl did not know whether the Little People were good or bad (and neither did Tengo). When night came, the Little People would enter this world through the corpse, and they would go back to the other side when dawn broke. The girl could speak to them. They taught her how to make an air chrysalis.

What most impressed Tengo was the concrete detail with which the blind goat's traits and actions were depicted. These details were what made the work as a whole so vivid. Could Fuka-Eri have actually been the keeper of a blind goat? And could she have actually lived in a mountain commune like the one in the story? Tengo guessed that the answer in both cases was yes. Because if she had never had these experiences, Fuka-Eri was a storyteller of rare, inborn talent.

Tengo decided that he would ask Fuka-Eri about the goat and the commune the next time they met (which was to be on Sunday). Of course she might not answer his questions.

Judging from their previous conversation, it seemed that Fuka-Eri would only answer questions when she felt like it. When she didn't want to answer, or when she clearly had no intention of responding, she simply ignored the questions, as if she had never heard them. Like Komatsu. The two were much alike in that regard. Which made them very different from Tengo. If someone asked Tengo a question, any question, he would do his best to answer it. He had probably been born that way.

His older girlfriend called him at five thirty.

"What did you do today?" she asked.

"I was writing a story all day," he answered, half truthfully. He had not been writing his own fiction. But this was not something he could explain to her in any detail.

"Did it go well?"

"More or less."

"I'm sorry for canceling today on such short notice. I think we can meet next week."

"I'll be looking forward to it."

"Me too," she said.

After that, she talked about her children. She often did that with Tengo. She had two little girls. Tengo had no siblings and obviously no children, so he didn't know much about young children. But that never stopped her from telling Tengo about hers. Tengo rarely initiated a conversation, but he enjoyed listening to other people. And so he listened to her with interest. Her older girl, a second grader, was probably being bullied at school, she said. The girl herself had told her nothing, but the mother of one of the girl's classmates had let her know that this was apparently happening. Tengo had never met the girl, but he had once seen a photograph. She didn't look much like her mother.

"Why are they bullying her?" Tengo asked.

"She often has asthma attacks, so she can't participate in a lot of activities with the other kids. Maybe that's it. She's a sweet little thing, and her grades aren't bad."

"I don't get it," Tengo said. "You'd think they'd take special care of a kid with asthma, not bully her."

"It's never that simple in the kids' world," she said with a sigh. "Kids get shut out just for being different from everyone else. The same kind of thing goes on in the grown-up world, but it's much more direct in the children's world."

"Can you give me a concrete example?"

She gave him several examples, none of which was especially bad in itself, but which, continued on a daily basis, could have a severe impact on a child: hiding things, not speaking to the child, or doing nasty imitations of her. "Did you ever experience bullying when you were a child?"

Tengo thought back to his childhood. "I don't think so," he answered. "Or maybe I just never noticed."

"If you never noticed, it never happened. I mean, the whole *point* of bullying is to make the person notice it's being done to him or her. You can't *have* bullying without the victim noticing."

Even as a child, Tengo had been big and strong, and people treated him with respect, which was probably why he was never bullied. But he had far more serious problems than mere bullying to deal with back then.

"Were you ever bullied?" Tengo asked.

"Never," she declared, but then she seemed to hesitate. "I did *do* some bullying, though."

"You were part of a group that did it?"

"Yes, in the fifth grade. We got together and decided not to talk to one boy. I can't remember why. There must have been a reason, but it probably wasn't a very good one if I can't even remember what it was. I still feel bad about it, though. I'm ashamed to think about it. I wonder why I went and did something like that. I have no idea what made me do it."

This reminded Tengo of a certain event, something from the distant past that he would recall now and then. Something he could never forget. But he decided not to mention it. It would have been a long story. And it was the kind of thing that loses the most important nuances when reduced to words. He had never told anyone about it, and he probably never would.

"Finally," his girlfriend said, "everybody feels safe belonging *not* to the excluded minority but to the excluding majority. You think, *Oh, I'm glad that's not me.* It's basically the same in all periods in all societies. If you belong to the majority, you can avoid thinking about lots of troubling things."

"And those troubling things are all you *can* think about when you're one of the few."

"That's about the size of it," she said mournfully. "But maybe, if you're in a situation like that, you learn to think for yourself."

"Yes, but maybe what you end up thinking for yourself *about* is all those troubling things."

"That's another problem, I suppose."

"Better not think about it too seriously," Tengo said. "I doubt it'll turn out to be that terrible. I'm sure there must be a few kids in her class who know how to use their brains."

"I guess so," she said, and then she spent some time alone with her thoughts. Holding the receiver against his ear, Tengo waited patiently for her to gather her thoughts together.

"Thanks," she said finally. "I feel a little better after talking to you." She seemed to have found some answers.

"I feel a little better too," Tengo said.

"Why's that?"

"Talking to you."

"See you next Friday," she said.

After hanging up, Tengo went out to the neighborhood supermarket. Returning home with a big bag of groceries, he wrapped the vegetables and fish in plastic and put them in the refrigerator. He was preparing dinner to the refrains of an FM music broadcast when the phone rang. Four phone calls in one day was a lot for Tengo. He could probably count the number of days that such a thing happened in any one year. This time it was Fuka-Eri.

"About Sunday," she said, without saying hello.

He could hear car horns honking at the other end. A lot of drivers seemed to be angry about something. She was probably calling from a public phone on a busy street.

"Yes," he said, adding meat to the bones of her bare pronouncement. "Sunday morning – the day after tomorrow – I'll be seeing you and meeting somebody else."

"Nine o'clock. Shinjuku Station. Front end of the train to Tachikawa," she said, setting forth three facts in a row.

"In other words, you want to meet on the outward-bound platform of the Chuo Line where the first car stops, right?"

"Right."

"Where should I buy a ticket to?"

"Anywhere."

"So I should just buy any ticket and adjust the fare where we get off," he said, supplementing material to her words the way he was doing with *Air Chrysalis*. "Does this mean we're going pretty far from the city?"

"What were you just doing," she asked, ignoring his question.

"Making dinner."

"Making what."

"Nothing special, just cooking for myself. Grilling a dried mackerel and grating a daikon radish. Making a miso soup with littlenecks and green onions to eat with tofu. Dousing cucumber slices and wakame seaweed with vinegar. Ending up with rice and nappa pickles. That's all."

"Sounds good."

"I wonder. Nothing special. Pretty much what I eat all the time," Tengo said.

Fuka-Eri kept silent. Long silences did not seem to bother her, but this was not the case for Tengo.

"Oh yes," he said, "I should tell you I started rewriting your *Air Chrysalis* today. I know you haven't given us your final permission, but there's so little time, I'd better get started if we're going to meet the deadline."

"Mr. Komatsu said so," she asked, without a question mark.

"Yes, he is the one who told me to get started."

"Are you and Mr. Komatsu close," she asked.

"Well, sort of," Tengo answered. No one in this world could actually be "close" to Komatsu, Tengo guessed, but trying to explain this to Fuka-Eri would take too long.

"Is the rewrite going well."

"So far, so good."

"That's nice," Fuka-Eri said. She seemed to mean it. It sounded to Tengo as if Fuka-Eri was happy in her own way to hear that the rewriting of her work was going well, but given her limited expression of emotion, she could not go so far as to openly suggest this.

"I hope you'll like what I'm doing," he said.

"Not worried."

"Why not?" Tengo asked.

Fuka-Eri did not answer, lapsing into silence on her end. It seemed like a deliberate kind of silence, designed to make Tengo think, but try as he might, Tengo could come up with no explanation for why she should have such confidence in him.

He spoke to break the silence. "You know, there's something I'd like to ask you. Did you actually live in a commune-type place and take care of a goat? The descriptions are so realistic, I wanted to ask you if these things actually happened."

Fuka-Eri cleared her throat. "I don't talk about the goat."

"That's fine," Tengo said. "You don't have to talk about it if you don't want to. I just thought I'd try asking. Don't worry. For

the author, the work is everything. No explanations needed.
Let's meet on Sunday. Is there anything I should be concerned
about in meeting that person?"

"What do you mean."

"Well . . . like I should dress properly, or bring a gift or
something. You haven't given me any hint what the person is
like."

Fuka-Eri fell silent again, but this time it did not seem
deliberate. She simply could not fathom the purpose of his
question or what prompted him to ask it. His question hadn't
landed in any region of her consciousness. It seemed to have
gone beyond the bounds of meaning, sucked into permanent
nothingness like a lone planetary exploration rocket that has
sailed beyond Pluto.

"Never mind," he said, giving up. "It's not important." It had
been a mistake even to ask Fuka-Eri such a question. He supposed he could pick up a basket of fruit or something along
the way.

"Okay, then, see you at nine o'clock Sunday morning,"
Tengo said.

Fuka-Eri hesitated a few moments, and then hung up without saying anything, no "Good-bye," no "See you Sunday,"
no anything. There was just the click of the connection being
cut. Perhaps she had nodded to Tengo before hanging up the
receiver. Unfortunately, though, body language generally fails
to have its intended effect on the phone. Tengo set down the
receiver, took two deep breaths, switched the circuits of his
brain to something more realistic, and continued with the
preparations for his modest dinner.

CHAPTER 7

Aomame

QUIETLY, SO AS NOT TO WAKE
THE BUTTERFLY

Just after one o'clock Saturday afternoon, Aomame visited
the Willow House. The grounds of the place were dominated
by several large, old willow trees that towered over the surrounding stone wall and swayed soundlessly in the wind
like lost souls. Quite naturally, the people of the neighborhood had long called the old, Western-style home "Willow
House." It stood atop a steep slope in the fashionable Azabu
neighborhood. When Aomame reached the top of the slope,
she noticed a flock of little birds in the willows' uppermost
branches, barely weighing them down. A big cat was napping
on the sun-splashed roof, its eyes half closed. The streets up
here were narrow and crooked, and few cars came this way.
The tall trees gave the quarter a gloomy feel, and time seemed
to slow when you stepped inside. Some embassies were located
here, but few people visited them. Only in the summer would
the atmosphere change dramatically, when the cries of cicadas
pained the ears.

Aomame pressed the button at the gate and stated her name
to the intercom. Then she aimed a tiny smile toward the overhead camera. The iron gate drew slowly open, and once she was
inside it closed behind her. As always, she stepped through the

garden and headed for the front door. Knowing that the security cameras were on her, she walked straight down the path, her back as erect as a fashion model's, chin pulled back. She was dressed casually today in a navy-blue windbreaker over a gray parka and blue jeans, and white basketball shoes. She carried her regular shoulder bag, but without the ice pick, which rested quietly in her dresser drawer when she had no need for it.

Outside the front door stood a number of teak garden chairs, into one of which was squeezed a powerfully built man. He was not especially tall, but his upper body was startlingly well developed. Perhaps forty years of age, he kept his head shaved and wore a well-trimmed moustache. On his broad-shouldered frame was draped a gray suit. His stark white shirt contrasted with his deep gray silk tie and spotless black cordovans. Here was a man who would never be mistaken for a ward office cashier or a car insurance salesman. One glance told Aomame that he was a professional bodyguard, which was in fact his area of expertise, though at times he also served as a driver. A high-ranking karate expert, he could also use weapons effectively when the need arose. He could bare his fangs and be more vicious than anyone, but he was ordinarily calm, cool, and even intellectual. Looking deep into his eyes – if, that is, he allowed you to do so – you could find a warm glow.

In his private life, the man enjoyed toying with machines and gadgets. He collected progressive rock records from the sixties and seventies, and lived in another part of Azabu with his handsome young beautician boyfriend. His name was Tamaru. Aomame could not be sure if this was his family name or his given name or what characters he wrote it with. People just called him "Tamaru."

Still seated in his teak garden chair, Tamaru nodded to Aomame, who took the chair opposite him and greeted him with a simple "Hello."

"I heard a man died in a hotel in Shibuya," Tamaru said, inspecting the shine of his cordovans.

"I didn't know about that," Aomame said.

"Well, it wasn't worth putting in the papers. Just an ordinary heart attack, I guess. Sad case: he was in his early forties."

"Gotta take care of your heart."

Tamaru nodded. "Lifestyle is the important thing," he said. "Irregular hours, stress, sleep deprivation: those things'll kill you."

"Of course, something's gonna kill everybody sooner or later."

"Stands to reason."

"Think there'll be an autopsy?"

Tamaru bent over and flicked a barely visible speck from the instep of his shoe. "Like anybody else, the cops have a million things to do, and they've got a limited budget to work with. They can't start dissecting every corpse that comes to them without a mark on it. And the guy's family probably doesn't want him cut open for no reason after he's quietly passed away."

"His widow, especially."

After a short silence, Tamaru extended his thick, glove-like right hand toward Aomame. She grasped it, and the two shared a firm handshake.

"You must be tired," he said. "You ought to get some rest."

Aomame widened the edges of her mouth somewhat, the way ordinary people do when they smile, but in fact she produced only the slightest suggestion of a smile.

"How's Bun?" she asked.

"She's fine," Tamaru answered. Bun was the female German shepherd that lived in this house, a good-natured dog, and smart, despite a few odd habits.

"Is she still eating her spinach?" Aomame asked.

"As much as ever. And with the price of spinach as high as it's been, that's no small expense!"

"I've never seen a German shepherd that liked spinach before."

"She doesn't know she's a dog."

"What does she think she is?"

"Well, she seems to think she's a special being that transcends classification."

"Superdog?"

"Maybe so."

"Which is why she likes spinach?"

"No, that's another matter. She just likes spinach. Has since she was a pup."

"But maybe that's where she gets these dangerous thoughts of hers."

"Maybe so," Tamaru said. He glanced at his watch. "Say, your appointment today was for one thirty, right?"

Aomame nodded. "Right. There's still some time."

Tamaru eased out of his chair. "Wait here a minute, will you? Maybe we can get you in a little earlier." He disappeared through the front door.

While she waited, Aomame let her eyes wander over the garden's magnificent willow trees. Without a wind to stir them, their branches hung down toward the ground, as if they were people deep in thought.

Tamaru came back a short time later. "I'm going to have you go around to the back. She wants to see you in the hothouse today."

The two of them circled the garden past the willows in the direction of the hothouse, which was behind the main house in a sunny area without trees. Tamaru carefully opened the glass door just far enough for Aomame to squeeze through without letting the butterflies escape. He slipped in after her, quickly shutting the door. This was not a motion that a big man would normally be good at, though he did it very efficiently. He simply didn't *think* of it as a special accomplishment.

Spring had come inside the big, glass hothouse, completely and unreservedly. Flowers of all descriptions were blooming in profusion, but most of them were ordinary varieties that could be seen just about anywhere. Potted gladiolus, anemone, and daisies lined the shelves. Among them were plants that, to Aomame, could only be weeds. She saw not one that might be a prize specimen – no costly orchids, no rare roses, no primary-colored Polynesian blooms. Aomame had no special interest in plants, but the lack of affectation in this hothouse was something she rather liked.

Instead, the place was full of butterflies. The owner of this large glass enclosure seemed to be far more interested in raising unusual butterflies than rare plant specimens. Most of the flowers grown here were rich in the nectar preferred by the butterflies. To keep butterflies in a hothouse calls for a great deal of attention, knowledge, and effort, Aomame had heard, but she had absolutely no idea where such attention had been lavished here.

The dowager, the mistress of the house, would occasionally invite Aomame into the hothouse for private chats, though never at the height of summer. The glass enclosure was ideal to keep from being overheard. Their conversations were not the sort that could be held just anywhere at full volume, and the owner said it calmed her to be surrounded by flowers and butterflies. Aomame could see it on her face. The hothouse was a bit too warm for Aomame, but not unbearable.

The dowager was in her mid-seventies and slightly built. She kept her lovely white hair short. Today she wore a long-sleeved denim work shirt, cream-colored cotton pants, and dirty tennis shoes. With white cotton work gloves on her hands, she was using a large metal watering can to moisten the soil in one pot after another. Everything she wore seemed to be a size too large, but each piece hung on her body with comfortable familiarity. Whenever Aomame looked at her, she could not help but feel a kind of esteem for her natural, unaffected dignity.

Born into one of the fabulously wealthy families that dominated finance and industry prior to World War II, the dowager had married into the aristocracy, but there was nothing showy or pampered about her. When she lost her husband shortly after the war, she helped run a relative's small investment company and displayed an outstanding talent for the stock market. Everyone recognized it as something for which she had a natural gift. Thanks to her efforts, the company developed rapidly, and the personal fortune left to her expanded enormously. With this money, she bought several first-class properties in the city that had been owned by former members of the aristocracy or the imperial family. She had retired ten years earlier, having increased her fortune yet again by well-timed sales of her holdings. Because she had always avoided appearing in public, her name was not widely known, though everyone in financial circles knew of her. It was also rumored that she had strong political connections. On a personal level, she was simply a bright, friendly woman who knew no fear, trusted her instincts, and stuck to her decisions.

When she saw Aomame come in, the dowager put down her watering can and motioned for her to sit in a small iron garden chair near the hothouse entrance. Aomame sat down, and the woman sat in the chair facing her. None of her movements made any sound. She was like a female fox cutting through the forest.

"Shall I bring drinks?" Tamaru asked.

"Some herbal tea for me," the dowager said. "And for you . . . ?" She looked at Aomame.

"I'll have the same."

Tamaru nodded and left the hothouse. After looking around to make sure there were no butterflies nearby, he opened the door a crack, slipped through, and closed the door again with the precision of a ballroom dancer.

The dowager took off her work gloves and set them on a table, carefully placing one on top of the other as she might with silk gloves she had worn to a soirée. Then she looked straight at Aomame with her lustrous black eyes. These were eyes that had witnessed much. Aomame returned her gaze as long as courtesy allowed.

"We seem to have lost a valuable member of society," the dowager said. "Especially well known in oil circles, apparently. Still young, but quite the powerhouse, I hear."

She always spoke softly. Her voice was easily drowned out by a slight gust of wind. People had to pay attention to what she was saying. Aomame often felt the urge to reach over and turn up the volume – if only there were a knob! She had no choice but to listen intently.

Aomame said, "But still, his sudden absence doesn't seem to have inconvenienced anybody. The world just keeps moving along."

The dowager smiled. "There is no one in this world who can't be replaced. A person might have enormous knowledge or ability, but a successor can almost always be found. It would be terrible for us if the world were full of people who couldn't be replaced. Though of course" – and here she raised her right index finger to make a point – "I can't imagine finding anybody to take *your* place."

"You might not find a *person* that easily, but you could probably find a *way* without too much trouble," Aomame noted.

The dowager looked at Aomame calmly, her lips forming a satisfied smile. "That may be true," she said, "but I almost surely could never find anything to take the place of what we are sharing here and now. You are you and only you. I'm very grateful for that. More grateful than I can say."

She bent forward, stretched out her hand, and laid it on

Aomame's. She kept it there for a full ten seconds. Then, with a look of great satisfaction on her face, she withdrew her hand and twisted around to face the other way. A butterfly came fluttering along and landed on the shoulder of her blue work shirt. It was a small, white butterfly with a few crimson spots on its wings. The butterfly seemed to know no fear as it went to sleep on her shoulder.

"I'm sure you've never seen this kind of butterfly," the dowager said, glancing toward her own shoulder. Her voice betrayed a touch of pride. "Even down in Okinawa, you'd have trouble finding one of these. It gets its nourishment from only one type of flower – a special flower that only grows in the mountains of Okinawa. You have to bring the flower here and grow it first if you want to keep this butterfly in Tokyo. It's a *lot* of trouble. Not to mention the expense."

"It seems to be very comfortable with you."

"This little *person* thinks of me as a friend."

"Is it possible to become friends with a butterfly?"

"It is if you first become a part of nature. You suppress your presence as a human being, stay very still, and convince yourself that you are a tree or grass or a flower. It takes time, but once the butterfly lets its guard down, you can become friends quite naturally."

"Do you give them names?" Aomame asked, curious. "Like dogs or cats?"

The dowager gave her head a little shake. "No, I don't give them names, but I can tell one from another by their shapes and patterns. And besides, there wouldn't be much point in giving them names: they die so quickly. These people are your nameless friends for just a little while. I come here every day, say hello to the butterflies, and talk about things with them. When the time comes, though, they just quietly go off and disappear. I'm sure it means they've died, but I can never find their bodies. They don't leave any trace behind. It's as if they've been absorbed by the air. They're dainty little creatures that hardly exist at all: they come out of nowhere, search quietly for a few, limited things, and disappear into nothingness again, perhaps to some other world."

The hothouse air was warm and humid and thick with the smell of plants. Hundreds of butterflies flitted in and out of sight like short-lived punctuation marks in a stream of consciousness without beginning or end. Whenever she came in here, Aomame felt as if she had lost all sense of time.

Tamaru came back with a silver tray bearing a beautiful celadon teapot and two matching cups, cloth napkins, and a small dish of cookies. The aroma of herbal tea mingled with the fragrance of the surrounding flowers.

"Thank you, Tamaru. I'll take over from here," the dowager said.

Tamaru set the tray on the nearby table, gave the dowager a bow, and moved silently away, opening and closing the hothouse door, exiting with the same light steps as before. The woman lifted the teapot lid, inhaling the fragrance inside and checking the degree of openness of the leaves. Then she slowly filled their two cups, taking great care to ensure the equality of their strength.

"It's none of my business, but why don't you put a screen door on the entrance?" Aomame asked.

The dowager raised her head and looked at Aomame. "Screen door?"

"Yes, if you were to add a screen door inside the glass one, you wouldn't have to be so careful every time to make sure no butterflies escaped."

The dowager lifted her saucer with her left hand and, with her right hand, brought her cup to her mouth for a quiet sip of herbal tea. She savored its fragrance and gave a little nod. She returned the cup to the saucer and the saucer to the tray. After dabbing at her mouth with her napkin, she returned the cloth to her lap. At the very least, she took three times as long to accomplish these motions as the ordinary person. Aomame felt she was observing a fairy deep in the forest sipping a life-giving morning dew.

The woman lightly cleared her throat. "I don't like screens," she said.

Aomame waited for the dowager to continue, but she did not. Was her dislike of screens based on a general opposition to things that restricted freedom, or on aesthetic considerations, or on a mere visceral preference that had no special reason behind it? Not that it was an especially important problem. Aomame's question about screens had simply popped into her head.

Like the dowager, Aomame picked up her cup and saucer together and silently sipped her tea. She was not that fond of herbal tea. She preferred coffee as hot and strong as a devil at midnight, but perhaps that was not a drink suited to a hot-house in the afternoon. And so she always ordered the same drink as the mistress of the house when they were in the hot-house. When offered a cookie, she ate one. A gingersnap. Just baked, it had the taste of fresh ginger. Aomame recalled that the dowager had spent some time after the war in England. The dowager also took a cookie and nibbled it in tiny bits, slowly and quietly so as not to wake the rare butterfly sleeping on her shoulder.

"Tamaru will give you the key when you leave," the woman said. "Please mail it back when you're through with it. As always."

"Of course."

A tranquil moment of silence followed. No sounds reached the sealed hothouse from the outside world. The butterfly went on sleeping.

"We haven't done anything wrong," the woman said, look-ing straight at Aomame.

Aomame lightly set her teeth against her lower lip and nodded. "I know."

"Look at what's in that envelope," the woman said.

From an envelope lying on the table Aomame took seven Polaroid photographs and set them in a row, like unlucky tarot cards, beside the fine celadon teapot. They were close-up shots of a young woman's body: her back, breasts, buttocks, thighs, even the soles of her feet. Only her face was missing. Each body part bore marks of violence in the form of lurid welts, raised, almost certainly, by a belt. Her pubic hair had been shaved, the skin marked with what looked like cigarette burns. Aomame found herself scowling. She had seen photos like this in the past, but none as bad.

"You haven't seen these before, have you?"

Aomame shook her head in silence. "I had heard, but this is the first I've seen of them."

"Our man did this," the dowager said. "We've taken care of her three fractures, but one ear is exhibiting symptoms of hearing loss and may never be the same again." She spoke as quietly as ever, but her voice took on a cold, hard edge that seemed to startle the butterfly on her shoulder. It spread its wings and fluttered away.

She continued, "We can't let anyone get away with doing something like this. We simply can't."

Aomame gathered the photos and returned them to the envelope.

"Don't you agree?" the dowager asked.

"I certainly do," said Aomame.

"We did the right thing," the dowager declared.

She left her chair and, perhaps to calm herself, picked up the watering can by her side as if taking in hand a sophisticated weapon. She was somewhat pale now, her eyes sharply focused on a corner of the hothouse. Aomame followed her gaze but saw nothing more unusual than a potted thistle.

"Thank you for coming to see me," the dowager said, still holding the empty watering can. "I appreciate your efforts." This seemed to signal the end of their interview.

Aomame stood and picked up her bag. "Thank you for the tea."

"And let me thank you again," the dowager said.

Aomame gave her a faint smile.

"You don't have anything to worry about," the dowager said. Her voice had regained its gentle tone. A warm glow shone in her eyes. She touched Aomame's arm. "We did the right thing, I'm telling you."

Aomame nodded. The woman always ended their conversations this way. Perhaps she was saying the same thing to herself repeatedly, like a prayer or mantra. "You don't have anything to worry about. We did the right thing, I'm telling you."

After checking to be sure there were no butterflies nearby, Aomame opened the hothouse door just enough to squeeze through, and closed it again. The dowager stayed inside, the watering can in her hand. The air outside was chilling and fresh with the smell of trees and grass. This was the real world. Here time flowed in the normal manner. Aomame inhaled the real world's air deep into her lungs.

She found Tamaru seated in the same teak chair by the front entrance, waiting for her. His task was to hand her a key to a post office box.

"Business finished?" he asked.

"I think so," Aomame replied. She sat down next to him, took the key, and tucked it into a compartment of her shoulder bag.

For a time, instead of speaking, they watched the birds that were visiting the garden. There was still no wind, and the branches of the willows hung motionlessly. Several branches were nearly touching the ground.

"Is the woman doing okay?" Aomame asked.

"Which woman?"

"The wife of the man who suffered the heart attack in the Shibuya hotel."

"Doing okay? Not really. Not yet," Tamaru said with a scowl. "She's still in shock. She can hardly speak. It'll take time."

"What's she like?"

"Early thirties. No kids. Pretty. Seems like a nice person. Stylish. Unfortunately, she won't be wearing bathing suits this summer. Maybe not next year, either. Did you see the Polaroids?"

"Yes, just now."

"Horrible, no?"

"Really," Aomame said.

Tamaru said, "It's such a common pattern. Talented guy, well thought of, good family, impressive career, high social standing."

"But he becomes a different person at home," Aomame said, continuing his thought. "Especially when he drinks, he becomes violent. But only toward women. His wife is the only one he can knock around. To everyone else, he shows only his good side. Everybody thinks of him as a gentle, loving husband. The wife tries to tell people what terrible things he's doing to her, but no one will believe her. The husband knows that, so when he's violent he chooses parts of her body she can't easily show to people, or he's careful not to make bruises. Is this the 'pattern'?"

Tamaru nodded. "Pretty much. Only this guy didn't drink. He was stone-cold sober and out in the open about it. A really ugly case. She wanted a divorce, but he absolutely refused. Who knows? Maybe he loved her. Or maybe he didn't want to let go of such a handy victim. Or maybe he just enjoyed raping his wife."

Tamaru raised one foot, then the other, to check the shine

on his shoes again. Then he continued, "Of course, you can usually get a divorce if you have proof of domestic violence, but it takes time and it takes money. If the husband hires a good lawyer, he can make it very unpleasant for you. The family courts are full, and there's a shortage of judges. If, in spite of all that, you *do* get a divorce, and the judge awards a divorce settlement or alimony, the number of men who actually pay up is small. They can get out of it all kinds of ways. In Japan, ex-husbands almost never get put in jail for not paying. If they demonstrate a *willingness* to pay and cough up a little bit, the courts usually look the other way. Men still have the upper hand in Japanese society."

Aomame said, "Maybe so, but as luck would have it, one of those violent husbands suffered a heart attack in a Shibuya hotel room a few days ago."

" 'As luck would have it' is a bit too direct for me," Tamaru said with a click of the tongue. "I prefer 'Due to heavenly dispensation.' In any case, no doubts have been raised regarding the cause of death, and the amount of life insurance was not so high as to attract attention, so the insurance company won't have any suspicions. They'll probably pay without a hitch. Finally, it's a decent amount of money, enough for her to begin a new life. Plus she'll be saving all the time and money that would have been eaten up by suing for divorce. When it's over, she will have avoided all the complicated, meaningless legal procedures and all the subsequent mental anguish."

"Not to mention that that scummy bastard won't be set loose on some new victim."

"Heavenly dispensation," Tamaru said. "Everything's settled nicely thanks to one heart attack. All's well that ends well."

"Assuming there's an end somewhere," Aomame said.

Tamaru formed some short creases near his mouth that were faintly reminiscent of a smile. "There has to be an end somewhere. It's just that nothing's labeled 'This is the end.' Is the top rung of a ladder labeled 'This is the last rung. Please don't step higher than this'?"

Aomame shook her head.

"It's the same thing," Tamaru said.

Aomame said, "If you use your common sense and keep your eyes open, it becomes clear enough where the end is."

Tamaru nodded. "And even if it doesn't" – he made a falling gesture with his finger " – the end is right there."

They were both quiet for a while as they listened to the birds singing. It was a calm April afternoon without a hint of ill will or violence.

"How many women are living here now?" Aomame asked.

"Four," Tamaru answered, without hesitation.

"All in the same kind of situation?"

"More or less." Tamaru pursed his lips. "But the other three cases are not as serious as hers. Their men are all nasty bastards, as usual, but none are as bad as the character we've been talking about. These guys are lightweights who like to come on strong, not worth bothering you about. We can take care of them ourselves."

"Legally."

"Pretty much – even if we have to lean on them a little. Of course, a heart attack is an entirely 'legal' cause of death."

"Of course," Aomame chimed in.

Tamaru went silent for a while, resting his hands on his knees and looking at the silent branches of the willow trees.

After some hesitation, Aomame decided to broach something with Tamaru. "You know," she said, "there's something I'd like you to tell me."

"What's that?"

"How many years ago did the police get new uniforms and guns?"

Tamaru wrinkled his brow almost imperceptibly. "Where did *that* come from all of a sudden?"

"Nowhere special. It just popped into my head."

Tamaru looked her in the eye. His own eyes were entirely neutral, free of expression. He was leaving himself room to go in any direction with this.

"That big shootout near Lake Motosu between the Yamanashi Prefectural Police and the radical group took place in mid-October of 1981, and the police had their major re-organization the following year. Two years ago."

Aomame nodded without changing her expression. She had absolutely no recollection of such an event, but all she could do now was play along with him.

"It was really bloody. Old-fashioned six-shooters against five Kalashnikov AK-47s. The cops were totally outgunned. Poor guys: three of them were torn up pretty badly. They looked as if they'd been stitched on a sewing machine. The Self-Defense Force got involved right away, sending in their special paratroopers. The cops totally lost face. Prime Minister Nakasone immediately got serious about strengthening police power. There was an overall restructuring, a special weapons force was instituted, and ordinary patrolmen were given high-powered automatic pistols to carry – Beretta Model 92s. Ever fired one?"

Aomame shook her head. Far from it. She had never even fired an air rifle.

"I have," Tamaru said. "A fifteen-shot automatic. It uses 9mm Parabellum rounds. It's one of *the* great pistols. The U.S. Army uses it. It's not cheap, but its selling point is that it's not as expensive as a SIG or a Glock. It's not an easy gun to use, though, is definitely not for amateurs. The old revolvers only weighed 490 grams, but these weigh 850. They're useless in the hands of an untrained Japanese policeman. Fire a high-powered gun like that in a crowded country like Japan, and you end up hurting innocent bystanders."

"Where did you ever fire such a thing?"

"You know, the usual story. Once upon a time I was playing my harp by a spring when a fairy appeared out of nowhere, handed me a Beretta Model 92, and told me to shoot the white rabbit over there for target practice."

"Get serious."

The creases by Tamaru's mouth deepened slightly. "I'm always serious," he said. "In any case, the cops' official guns and uniforms changed two years ago. In the spring. Just about this time of year. Does that answer your question?"

"Two years ago," Aomame said.

Tamaru gave her another sharp look. "You know, if something's bothering you, you'd better tell me. Are the cops involved in something?"

"No, that's not it," Aomame said, waving off his suspicions with both hands. "I was just wondering about their uniforms, like, when they changed."

A period of silence followed, bringing the conversation to a natural end. Tamaru thrust out his right hand again. "Anyhow, I'm glad it all came off without a hitch." Aomame took his hand in hers. *He understands,* she told herself. *After a tough job where your life is on the line, what you need is the warm, quiet encouragement that accompanies the touch of human flesh.*

"Take a break," Tamaru said. "Sometimes you need to stop, take a deep breath, and empty your head. Go to Guam or someplace with a boyfriend."

Aomame stood up, slung her bag over her shoulder, and adjusted the hood of her parka. Tamaru also got to his feet. He was by no means tall, but when he stood up it looked as if a stone wall had suddenly materialized. His solidity always took her by surprise.

Tamaru kept his eyes fixed on her back as she walked away. She could feel him looking at her the whole time. And so she kept her chin pulled in, her back straight, and walked with firm steps as if following a perfectly straight line. But inside, where she could not be seen, she was confused. In places of which she was totally unaware, things about which she was totally unaware were happening one after another. Until a short time before, she had had the world in her hand, without disruptions or inconsistencies. But now it was falling apart.

A shootout at Lake Motosu? Beretta Model 92?

What was happening to her? Aomame could never have missed such important news. This world's system was getting out of whack. Her mind went on churning as she walked. Whatever might have happened, she would have to do something to make the world whole again, to make it logical again. And do it now. Otherwise, outlandish things could happen.

Tamaru could probably see the confusion inside her. He was a cautious man with superb intuition. He was also very dangerous. Tamaru had a profound respect for his employer, and was fiercely loyal to her. He would do anything to protect her. Aomame and Tamaru acknowledged each other's abilities and liked each other – or so it seemed. But if he concluded that Aomame's existence was not to his employer's benefit, for whatever reason, then he would not hesitate to get rid of her. Aomame couldn't blame him for that. It was his job, after all.

The gate opened as she reached the other side of the garden. She gave the friendliest smile she could manage to the security camera, and a little wave as if there were nothing bothering her. Once she was outside the wall, the gate slowly shut behind her. As she descended the steep Azabu slope, Aomame tried to organize her thoughts and make a detailed, comprehensive list of what she should do from this point forward.

CHAPTER 8

Tengo

MEETING NEW PEOPLE
IN NEW PLACES

Most people think of Sunday morning as a time for rest. Throughout his youth, however, Tengo never once thought of Sunday morning as something to enjoy. Instead, it depressed him. When the weekend came, his whole body felt sluggish and achy, and his appetite would disappear. For Tengo, Sunday was like a misshapen moon that showed only its dark side. *If only Sunday would never come!* he would often think as a boy. *How much more fun it would be to have school every day without a break!* He even prayed for Sunday not to come, though his prayers were never answered. Even now, as an adult, dark feelings would inexplicably overtake him when he awoke on a Sunday morning. He felt his joints creaking and wanted to throw up. Such a reaction to Sunday had long since permeated his heart, perhaps in some deep, unconscious region.

Tengo's father was a collector of subscription fees for NHK – Japan's quasi-governmental broadcasting network – and he would take little Tengo with him as he went from door to door. These rounds started before Tengo entered kindergarten and continued through the fifth grade without a single weekend off, excepting only those Sundays when there was a special function at school. Waking at seven, his father would make him scrub his face with soap and water, inspect his ears and nails, and dress him in the cleanest (but least showy) clothes he owned, promising that, in return, he would buy Tengo a yummy treat.

Tengo had no idea whether the other NHK subscription fee collectors kept working on weekends and holidays, but as far as he could remember, his father always did. If anything, he worked with even more enthusiasm than usual, because on Sundays he could often catch people who were usually out during the week.

Tengo's father had several reasons for taking him on his rounds. One was that he could not leave the boy home alone. On weekdays and Saturdays, he could leave Tengo in day-care or kindergarten or elementary school, but these were all closed on Sundays. Another reason, he said, was that it was important for a father to show his son the type of work he did. A child should learn from early on what kind of activity supported his daily life, and he should appreciate the importance of labor. Tengo's father had been sent out to work in the fields, Sunday or no, from the time he was old enough to understand anything, and he had even been kept out of school during the busiest seasons on the farm. To him, such a life was a given.

His third and final reason was a more calculating one, which is why it left the deepest scars on Tengo's heart. His father knew that having a small child with him made his job easier. When a fee collector had a child in hand, people found it more difficult to say to him, "I don't want to pay, so get out of here." With a little person staring up at them, even people determined not to pay would usually end up forking over the money, which was why he saved the most difficult routes for Sunday. Tengo sensed from the beginning that this was the role he was expected to play, and he absolutely hated it. But he also felt that he had to act out his role as cleverly as he could in order to please his father. He might as well have been a trained monkey. If he pleased his father, he would be treated kindly that day.

Tengo's one salvation was that his father's route was fairly far from home. They lived in a suburban residential district outside the city of Ichikawa, but his father's rounds were in the center of the city. The school district was different there as well. At least he was able to avoid doing collections at the homes of his kindergarten and elementary school classmates. Occasionally, though, when walking in the downtown shopping area, he would spot a classmate on the street. When this happened, he would dodge behind his father to keep from being noticed.

Most of Tengo's school friends had fathers who commuted to office jobs in the center of Tokyo. These men thought of Ichikawa as a part of Tokyo that just happened to have been incorporated into Chiba Prefecture. On Monday mornings his school friends would talk excitedly about where they had gone and what they had done on Sunday. They went to amusement parks and zoos and baseball games. In the summer they would go swimming, in the winter skiing. Their fathers would take them for drives or to go hiking. They would share their experiences with enthusiasm, and exchange information about new places. But Tengo had nothing to talk about. He never went to tourist attractions or amusement parks. From morning to evening on Sundays, he and his father would ring the doorbells of strangers' houses, bow their heads, and take money from the people who came to the door. If someone didn't want to pay, his father would threaten or cajole them. With anyone who tried to talk his way out of paying, he would have an argument. Sometimes he would curse at them like stray dogs. Such experiences were not the kind of thing Tengo could share with school friends.

When Tengo was in the third grade, word spread that his

father was an NHK subscription fee collector. Someone had probably seen them making their rounds together. He was, after all, walking all day long behind his father to every corner of the city every Sunday, so it was almost inevitable that he would be spotted at some point (especially now that he was too big to hide behind his father). Indeed, it was surprising that it hadn't happened before.

From that point on, Tengo's nickname became "NHK." He could not help becoming a kind of alien in a society of middle-class children of white-collar workers. Much of what they took for granted, Tengo could not. He lived a different kind of life in a different world. His grades were outstanding, as was his athletic ability. He was big and strong, and the teachers focused on him. So even though he was an "alien," he was never a class outcast. If anything, in most circumstances he was treated with respect. But whenever the other boys invited him to go somewhere or to visit their homes on a Sunday, he had to turn them down. He knew that if he told his father, "Some of the boys are getting together this Sunday at so-and-so's house," it wouldn't make any difference. Soon, people stopped inviting him. Before long he realized that he didn't belong to any groups. He was always alone.

Sunday collection rounds were an absolute rule: no exceptions, no changes. If he caught a cold, if he had a persistent cough, if he was running a little fever, if he had an upset stomach, his father accepted no excuses. Staggering after his father on such days, he would often wish he could fall down and die on the spot. Then, perhaps, his father might think twice about his own behavior; it might occur to him that he had been too strict with his son. For better or worse, though, Tengo was born with a robust constitution. Even if he had a fever or a stomachache or felt nauseous, he always walked the entire long route with his father, never falling down or fainting, and never complaining.

* * *

Tengo's father was repatriated from Manchuria, destitute, when the war ended in 1945. Born the third son of a farming family in the hardscrabble Tohoku region, he joined a homesteaders' group and crossed over to Manchuria in the 1930s with friends from the same prefecture. None of them had swallowed whole the government's claims that Manchuria was a paradise where the land was vast and rich, offering an affluent life to all comers. They knew enough to realize that "paradise" was not to be found anywhere. They were simply poor and hungry. The best they could hope for if they stayed at home was a life on the brink of starvation. The times were terrible, and huge numbers of people were unemployed. The cities offered no hope of finding decent work. This left crossing the sea to Manchuria as virtually the only way to survive. As farmers developing new land, they received basic training in the use of firearms in case of emergency, were given some minimal information about farming conditions in Manchuria, were sent off with three cheers from their villages, and then were transported by train from the port of Dalian to a place near the Manchurian-Mongolian border. There they were given some land and farming implements and small arms, and together started cultivating the earth. The soil was poor and rocky, and in winter everything froze. Sometimes stray dogs were all they had to eat. Even so, with government support the first few years, they managed to get by.

Their lives were finally becoming more stable when, in August 1945, the Soviet Union broke its neutrality treaty with Japan and launched a full-scale invasion of Manchuria. Having ended its operations on the European front, the Soviet army had used the Trans-Siberian Railway to shift a huge military force to the Far East in preparation for the border crossing. Tengo's father had been expecting this to happen, having been secretly informed of the impending situation by a certain official, a man he had become friendly with thanks to a distant connection. The man had told him privately that Japan's weakened Kwantung Army could never stand up to such an invasion, so he should prepare to flee with the clothes on his back as soon as it happened – the sooner the better. The minute he heard the news that the Soviet army had apparently violated the border, he mounted his horse, galloped to the local train station, and boarded the second-to-last train for Dalian. He was the only one among his farming companions to make it back to Japan before the end of the year.

He went to Tokyo after the war and tried making a living as a black marketeer and as a carpenter's apprentice, but nothing seemed to work. He could barely keep himself alive. He was working as a liquor store delivery man in the Asakusa entertainment district when he bumped into an acquaintance from his Manchurian days on the street. It was the official who had warned him of the impending Soviet invasion. The man had originally gone over to work for the postal service in Japan's Manchukuo puppet state, and now that he was back in Japan he had his old job back with the Ministry of Communications. He seemed to like Tengo's father, both because they came from the same village and because he knew what a hard worker he was. He invited him to share a bite.

When the man learned that Tengo's father was having a hard time finding a decent job, he asked if he might be interested in working as a subscription fee collector for NHK. He offered to recommend him to a friend in that department, and Tengo's father gladly accepted. He knew almost nothing about NHK, but he was willing to try anything that promised a steady income. The man wrote him a letter of recommendation and even served as a guarantor for him, smoothing his way to become an NHK subscription fee collector. They gave him training, a uniform, and a quota to fill. People then were just beginning to recover from the shock of defeat and to look for entertainment in their destitute lives. Radio was the most accessible and cheapest form of entertainment; and postwar radio, which offered music, comedy, and sports, was incomparably more popular than its wartime predecessor, with its virtuous exhortations for patriotic self-sacrifice. NHK needed huge numbers of people to go from door to door collecting listeners' fees.

Tengo's father performed his duties with great enthusiasm. His foremost strengths were his sturdy constitution and his perseverance in the face of adversity. Here was a man who had barely eaten a filling meal since birth. To a person like that, the collection of NHK fees was not excruciating work. The most violent curses hurled at him were nothing. Moreover, he felt much satisfaction at belonging to a gigantic organization, even as one of its lowest-ranking members. He worked for one year as a commissioned collector without job security, his only income a percentage of his collections, but his performance and attitude were so outstanding that he was taken directly into the ranks of the full-fledged employees, an almost unheard-of achievement in NHK. Part of this had to do with his superior results in an especially difficult collection area, but also effective here was the influence of his guarantor, the Communications Ministry official. Soon he received a set basic salary plus expenses. He was able to move into a corporation-owned apartment and join the health care plan. The difference in treatment was like night and day. It was the greatest stroke of good fortune he had ever encountered in life. In other words, he had finally worked his way up to the lowest spot on the totem pole.

Young Tengo heard this story from his father so many times that he grew sick of it. His father never sang him lullabies, never read storybooks to him at bedtime. Instead, he would tell the boy stories of his actual experiences – over and over, from his childhood in a poor farm family in Tohoku, through the ultimate (and inevitable) happy ending of his good fortune as a fully fledged NHK fee collector.

His father was a good storyteller. There was no way for Tengo to ascertain how much was based on fact, but the stories were at least coherent and consistent. They were not exactly pregnant with deep meaning, but the details were lively and his father's narrative was strongly colored. There were funny stories, touching stories, and violent stories. There were astounding, preposterous stories and stories that Tengo had trouble following no matter how many times he heard them. If a life was to be measured by the color and variety of its episodes, his father's life could be said to have been rich in its own way, perhaps.

But when they touched on the period after he became a full-fledged NHK employee, his father's stories suddenly lost all color and reality. They lacked detail and wholeness, as if he thought of them as mere sequels not worth telling. He met a woman, married her, and had a child – that is, Tengo. A few months after Tengo was born, his mother fell ill and died. His father raised him alone after that, never remarrying, just working hard for NHK. The End.

How he happened to meet Tengo's mother and marry her, what kind of woman she was, what had caused her death (could it have had something to do with Tengo's birth?), whether her death had been a relatively easy one or she had suffered greatly – his father told him almost nothing about such matters. If Tengo tried asking, his father would just evade the question and, finally, never answer. Most of the time, such questions put him in a foul mood, and he would clam up. Not a single photo of Tengo's mother had survived, and not a single wedding photo. "We couldn't afford a ceremony," he explained, "and I didn't have a camera."

But Tengo fundamentally disbelieved his father's story. His father was hiding the facts, remaking the story. His mother had not died some months after he was born. In his only memory of her, she was still alive when he was one and a half. And near where he was sleeping, she was in the arms of a man other than his father.

His mother took off her blouse, dropped the straps of her slip, and let a man not his father suck on her breasts. Tengo slept next to them, his breathing audible. But at the same time, Tengo was not asleep. He was watching his mother.

This was Tengo's souvenir photograph of his mother. The ten-second scene was burned into his brain with perfect clarity. It was the only concrete information he had about his mother, the one tenuous connection his mind could make with her. They were linked by a hypothetical umbilical cord. His mind floated in the amniotic fluid of memory, listening for echoes of the past. His father, meanwhile, had no idea that such a vivid scene was burned into Tengo's brain or that, like a cow in the meadow, Tengo was endlessly regurgitating fragments of the scene to chew on, a cud from which he obtained essential nutrients. Father and son: each was locked in a deep, dark embrace with his secrets.

It was a clear, pleasant Sunday morning. There was a chill in the mid-April breeze, though, a reminder of how easily the seasons can turn backward. Over a thin, black crew-neck sweater, Tengo wore a herringbone jacket that he had owned since his college days. He also had on beige chino pants and brown Hush Puppies. The shoes were rather new. This was as close as he could come to dapper attire.

When Tengo reached the front end of the outward-bound Chuo Line platform in Shinjuku Station, Fuka-Eri was already there, sitting alone on a bench, utterly still, staring into space with narrowed eyes. She wore a cotton print dress that had to be meant for midsummer. Over the dress she wore a heavy, grass-green winter cardigan, and on her bare feet she wore faded gray sneakers – a somewhat odd combination for the season. The dress was too thin, the cardigan too thick. On her, though, the outfit did not seem especially out of place. Perhaps she was expressing her own special worldview by this mismatch. It was not entirely out of the question. But probably she had just chosen her clothing at random without much thought.

She was not reading a newspaper, she was not reading a book, she was not listening to a Walkman, she was just sitting still, her big, black eyes staring straight ahead. She could have been staring at something or looking at nothing at all. She could have been thinking about something or not thinking at all. From a distance, she looked like a realistic sculpture made of some special material.

"Did I keep you waiting?" Tengo asked.

Fuka-Eri glanced at him and shook her head a centimeter or two from side to side. Her black eyes had a fresh, silken luster but, as before, no perceptible expression. She looked as though she did not want to speak with anyone for the moment, so Tengo gave up on any attempt to keep up a conversation and sat beside her on the bench, saying nothing.

When the train came, Fuka-Eri stood up, and the two of them boarded together. There were few passengers on the weekend rapid-service train, which went all the way out to the mountains of Takao. Tengo and Fuka-Eri sat next to each other, silently watching the cityscape pass the windows on the other side. Fuka-Eri said nothing, as usual, so Tengo kept silent as well. She tugged the collar of her cardigan closed as if preparing for a wave of bitter cold to come, looking straight ahead with her lips drawn into a perfectly straight line.

Tengo took out a small paperback he had brought along and started to read, but after some hesitation he stopped reading. Returning the book to his pocket, he folded his hands on his knees and stared straight ahead, adopting Fuka-Eri's pose as if to keep her company. He considered using the time to think, but he couldn't think of anything to think about. Because he had been concentrating on the rewrite of *Air Chrysalis,* it seemed, his mind refused to form any coherent thoughts. At the core of his brain was a mass of tangled threads.

Tengo watched the scenery streaming past the window and listened to the monotonous sound of the rails. The Chuo Line stretched on and on straight westward, as if following a line drawn on the map with a ruler. In fact, "as if" was probably unnecessary: they must have done just that when they laid it out a hundred years earlier. In this part of the Kanto Plain there was not a single topographical obstruction worth mentioning, which led to the building of a line without a perceivable curve, rise, or fall, and no bridges or tunnels. All they needed back then was a ruler, and all the trains did now was run in a perfectly straight line to the mountains out west.

At some point, Tengo fell asleep. When the swaying of the train woke him, they were slowing down for the stop in Ogikubo Station, no more than ten minutes out of Shinjuku – a short nap. Fuka-Eri was sitting in the same position, staring straight ahead. Tengo had no idea what she was, in fact, looking at. Judging from her air of concentration, she had no intention of getting off the train for some time yet.

"What kind of books do you read?" Tengo asked Fuka-Eri when they had gone another ten minutes and were past Mitaka. He raised the question not only out of sheer boredom but because he had been meaning to ask her about her reading habits.

Fuka-Eri glanced at him and faced forward again. "I don't read books," she answered simply.

"At all?"

She gave him a quick nod.

"Are you just not interested in reading books?" he asked.

"It takes time," she said.

"You don't read books because it takes time?" he asked, not quite sure he was understanding her properly.

Fuka-Eri kept facing forward and offered no reply. Her posture seemed to convey the message that she had no intention of negating his suggestion.

Generally speaking, of course, it does take some time to read a book. It's different from watching television, say, or reading *manga*. The reading of a book is an activity that involves some continuity; it is carried out over a relatively long time frame. But in Fuka-Eri's statement that "it takes time," there seemed to be included a nuance somewhat different from such generalities.

"When you say, 'It takes time,' do you mean . . . it takes a *lot* of time?" Tengo asked.

"A *lot*," Fuka-Eri declared.

"A lot longer than most people?"

Fuka-Eri gave him a sharp nod.

"That must be a problem in school, too. I'm sure you have to read a lot of books for your classes."

"I just fake it," she said coolly.

Somewhere in his head, Tengo heard an ominous knock. He wished he could ignore it, but that was out of the question. He had to know the truth.

"Could what you're talking about be what they call 'dyslexia'?" he asked.

"Dyslexia."

"A learning disability. It means you have trouble making out characters on a page."

"They have mentioned that. Dys – "

"Who mentioned that?"

She gave a little shrug.

"In other words," Tengo went on, searching for the right way to say it, "is this something you've had since you were little?"

Fuka-Eri nodded.

"So that explains why you've hardly read any novels."

"By myself," she said.

This also explained why her writing was free of the influence of any established authors. It made perfect sense.

"You didn't read them 'by yourself,' " Tengo said.

"Somebody read them to me."

"Your father, say, or your mother read books aloud to you?"

Fuka-Eri did not reply to this.

"Maybe you can't read, but you can write just fine, I would think," Tengo asked with growing apprehension.

Fuka-Eri shook her head. "Writing takes time too."

"A *lot* of time?"

Fuka-Eri gave another small shrug. This meant yes.

Tengo shifted his position on the train seat. "Which means, perhaps, that you didn't write the text of *Air Chrysalis* by yourself."

"I didn't."

Tengo let a few seconds go by. A few heavy seconds. "So who did write it?"

"Azami," she said.

"Who's Azami?"

"Two years younger."

There was another short gap. "This other girl wrote *Air Chrysalis* for you."

Fuka-Eri nodded as though this were an absolutely normal thing.

Tengo set the gears of his mind spinning. "In other words, you dictated the story, and Azami wrote it down. Right?"

"Typed it and printed it," Fuka-Eri said.

Tengo bit his lip and tried to put in order the few facts that he had been offered so far. Once he had done the rearranging, he said, "In other words, Azami printed the manuscript and sent it in to the magazine as an entry in the new writer's contest, probably without telling you what she was doing. And she's the one who gave it the title *Air Chrysalis*."

Fuka-Eri cocked her head to one side in a way that signaled neither a clear yes nor a clear no. But she did not contradict him. This probably meant that he generally had the right idea.

"This Azami – is she a friend of yours?"

"Lives with me."

"She's your younger sister?"

Fuka-Eri shook her head. "Professor's daughter."

"The Professor," Tengo said. "Are you saying this Professor also lives with you?"

Fuka-Eri nodded. *Why bother to ask something so obvious?* she seemed to be saying.

"So the person I'm going to meet now must be this 'Professor,' right?"

Fuka-Eri turned toward Tengo and looked at him for a moment as if observing the flow of a distant cloud or considering how best to deal with a slow-learning dog. Then she nodded.

"We are going to meet the Professor," she said in a voice lacking expression.

This brought their conversation to a tentative end. Again Tengo and Fuka-Eri stopped talking and, side by side, watched the cityscape stream past the train window opposite them. Featureless houses without end stretched across the flat, featureless earth, thrusting numberless TV antennas skyward like so many insects. Had the people living in those houses paid their NHK subscription fees? Tengo often found himself wondering about TV and radio reception fees on Sundays. He didn't *want* to think about them, but he had no choice.

Today, on this wonderfully clear mid-April morning, a number of less-than-pleasant facts had come to light. First of all,

Fuka-Eri had not written *Air Chrysalis* herself. If he was to take what she said at face value (and for now he had no reason to think that he should not), Fuka-Eri had merely dictated the story and another girl had written it down. In terms of its production process, it was no different from some of the greatest landmarks in Japanese literary history – the *Kojiki,* with its legendary history of the ruling dynasty, for example, or the colorful narratives of the warring samurai clans of the twelfth century, *The Tale of the Heike.* This fact served to lighten somewhat the guilt he felt about modifying the text of *Air Chrysalis,* but at the same time it made the situation as a whole significantly more complicated.

In addition, Fuka-Eri had a bad case of dyslexia and couldn't even read a book in the normal way. Tengo mentally reviewed his knowledge of dyslexia. He had attended lectures on the disorder when he was taking teacher training courses in college. A person with dyslexia could, in principle, both read and write. The problem had nothing to do with intelligence. Reading simply took time. The person might have no trouble with a short selection, but the longer the passage, the more difficulty the person's information processing faculty encountered, until it could no longer keep up. The link between a character and what it stood for was lost. These were the general symptoms of dyslexia. The causes were still not fully understood, but it was not surprising for there to be one or two dyslexic children in any classroom. Einstein had suffered from dyslexia, as had Thomas Edison and Charles Mingus.

Tengo did not know whether people with dyslexia generally experienced the same difficulties in writing as in reading, but it seemed to be the case with Fuka-Eri. One was just as difficult for her as the other.

What would Komatsu say when he found out about this? Tengo caught himself sighing. This seventeen-year-old girl was congenitally dyslexic and could neither read books nor write extended passages. Even when she engaged in conversation, she could only speak one sentence at a time (assuming she was not doing so intentionally). To make someone like this into a professional novelist (even if only for show) was going to be impossible. Even supposing that Tengo succeeded in rewriting *Air Chrysalis,* that it took the new writers' prize, and that it was published as a book and praised by the critics, they could not go on deceiving the public forever. It might go well at first, but before long people would begin to think that "something" was "funny." If the truth came out at that point, everyone involved would be ruined. Tengo's career as a novelist would be cut short before it had hardly begun.

There was no way they could pull off such a flawed conspiracy. He had felt they were treading on thin ice from the outset, but now he realized that such an expression was far too tepid. The ice was already creaking before they ever stepped on it. The only thing for him to do was go home, call Komatsu, and announce, "I'm withdrawing from the plan. It's just too dangerous for me." This was what anyone with any common sense would do.

But when he started thinking about *Air Chrysalis,* Tengo was split with confusion. As dangerous as Komatsu's plan might be, he could not possibly stop rewriting the novella at this point. He might have been able to give up on the idea before he started working on it, but that was out of the question now. He was up to his neck in it. He was breathing the air of its world, adapting to its gravity. The story's essence had permeated every part of him, to the walls of his viscera. Now the story was begging him to rework it: he could feel it pleading with him for help. This was something that only Tengo could do. It was a job well worth doing, a job he simply *had to do.*

Sitting on the train seat, Tengo closed his eyes and tried to reach some kind of conclusion as to how he should deal with the situation. But no conclusion was forthcoming. No one split with confusion could possibly produce a reasonable conclusion.

"Does Azami take down exactly what you say?" Tengo asked.

"Exactly what I tell her."

"You speak, and she writes it down."

"But I have to speak softly."

"Why do you have to speak softly?"

Fuka-Eri looked around the car. It was almost empty. The only other passengers were a mother and her two small children on the opposite seat a short distance away from Tengo and Fuka-Eri. The three of them appeared to be headed for someplace fun. There existed such happy people in the world.

"So they won't hear me," Fuka-Eri said quietly.

" 'They'?" Tengo asked. Looking at Fuka-Eri's unfocused eyes, it was clear that she was not talking about the mother and children. She was referring to particular people that she knew well and that Tengo did not know at all. "Who are 'they'?" Tengo, too, had lowered his voice.

Fuka-Eri said nothing, but a small wrinkle appeared between her brows. Her lips were clamped shut.

"Are 'they' the Little People?" Tengo asked.

Still no answer.

"Are 'they' somebody who might get mad at you if your story got into print and was released to the public and people started talking about them?"

Fuka-Eri did not answer this question, either. Her eyes were still not focused on any one point. He waited until he was quite sure there would be no answer, and then he asked another question.

"Can you tell me about your 'Professor'? What's he like?"

Fuka-Eri gave him a puzzled look, as if to say, *What is this person talking about?* Then she said, "You will meet the Professor."

"Yes, of course," Tengo said. "You're absolutely right. I'm going to meet him in any case. I should just meet him and decide for myself."

At Kokubunji Station, a group of elderly people dressed in hiking gear got on. There were ten of them altogether, five men and five women in their late sixties and early seventies. They carried backpacks and wore hats and were chattering away like schoolchildren. All carried water bottles, some strapped to their waists, others tucked in the pockets of their backpacks. Tengo wondered if he could possibly reach that age with such a sense of enjoyment. Then he shook his head. No way. He imagined these old folks standing proudly on some mountain-top, drinking from their water bottles.

In spite of their small size, the Little People drank prodigious amounts of water. They preferred to drink rainwater or water from the nearby stream, rather than tap water. And so the girl would scoop water from the stream during daylight hours and give it to the Little People to drink. Whenever it rained, she would collect water in a bucket because the Little People preferred rainwater to water gathered from the stream. They were therefore grateful for the girl's kindness.

Tengo noticed he was having trouble staying focused on any one thought. This was not a good sign. He felt an internal confusion starting. An ominous sandstorm was developing somewhere on the plane of his emotions. This often happened on Sundays.

"Is something wrong," Fuka-Eri asked without a question mark. She seemed able to sense the tension that Tengo was feeling.

"I wonder if I can do it."

"Do what."

"If I can say what I need to say."

"Say what you need to say," Fuka-Eri asked. She seemed to be having trouble understanding what he meant.

"To the Professor."

"Say what you need to say to the Professor," she repeated.

After some hesitation, Tengo confessed. "I keep thinking that things are not going to go smoothly, that everything is going to fall apart," he said.

Fuka-Eri turned in her seat until she was looking directly at Tengo. "Afraid," she asked.

"What am I afraid of?" Tengo rephrased her question.

She nodded silently.

"Maybe I'm just afraid of meeting new people. Especially on a Sunday morning."

"Why Sunday," Fuka-Eri asked.

Tengo's armpits started sweating. He felt a suffocating tightness in the chest. Meeting new people and having new things thrust upon him. And having his present existence threatened by them.

"Why Sunday," Fuka-Eri asked again.

Tengo recalled his boyhood Sundays. After they had walked all day, his father would take him to the restaurant across from the station and tell him to order anything he liked. It was a kind of reward for him, and virtually the only time the frugal pair would eat out. His father would even order a beer (though he almost never drank). Despite the offer, Tengo never felt the slightest bit hungry on these occasions. Ordinarily, he was hungry all the time, but he never enjoyed anything he ate on Sunday. To eat every mouthful of what he had ordered – which he was absolutely required to do – was nothing but torture for him. Sometimes he even came close to vomiting. This was what Sunday meant for Tengo as a boy.

Fuka-Eri looked into Tengo's eyes in search of something. Then she reached out and took his hand. This startled him, but he tried not to let it show on his face.

Fuka-Eri kept her gentle grip on Tengo's hand until the train arrived in Kunitachi Station, near the end of the line. Her hand was unexpectedly hard and smooth, neither hot nor cold. It was maybe half the size of Tengo's hand.

"Don't be afraid. It's not just another Sunday," she said, as if stating a well-known fact.

Tengo thought this might have been the first time he heard her speak two sentences at once.

CHAPTER 9

Aomame

NEW SCENERY, NEW RULES

Aomame went to the ward library closest to home. At the reference desk, she requested the compact edition of the newspaper for the three-month period from September to November, 1981. The clerk pointed out that they had such editions for four newspapers – the *Asahi,* the *Yomiuri,* the *Mainichi,* and the *Nikkei* – and asked which she preferred. The bespectacled middle-aged woman seemed less a regular librarian than a housewife doing part-time work. She was not especially fat, but her wrists were puffy, almost ham-like.

Aomame said she didn't care which newspaper they gave her to read: they were all pretty much the same.

"That may be true, but I really need *you* to decide which you would like," the woman said in a flat voice meant to repel any further argument. Aomame had no intention of arguing, so she chose the *Mainichi,* for no special reason. Sitting in a cubicle, she opened her notebook and, ballpoint pen in hand, started scanning one article after another.

No especially major events had occurred in the early autumn of 1981. Charles and Diana had married that July, and the aftereffects were still in evidence – reports on where they went, what they did, what she wore, what her accessories were like. Aomame of course knew about the wedding, but she had no particular interest in it, and she could not figure out why people were so deeply concerned about the fate of an English prince and princess. Charles looked less like a prince than a high school physics teacher with stomach trouble.

In Poland, Lech Walesa's "Solidarity" movement was deepening its confrontation with the government, and the Soviet government was expressing its "concern." More directly, the Soviets were threatening to send in tanks, just as they had prior to the 1968 "Prague Spring," if the Polish government failed to bring things under control. Aomame generally remembered these events as well. She knew that the Soviet government eventually gave up any thought of interfering in the situation, so there was no need for her to read these articles closely. One thing did catch her attention, though. When President Reagan issued a declaration meant to discourage the Soviets from intervening in Polish internal affairs, he was quoted as saying, "We hope that the tense situation in Poland will not interfere with joint U.S.-Soviet plans to construct a moon base." Construct a moon base? She had never heard of such a plan. Come to think of it, though, there had been some mention of that on the TV news the other day – that night when she had sex with the balding, middle-aged man from Kansai in the Akasaka hotel.

On September 20, the world's largest kite-flying competition took place in Jakarta, with more than ten thousand participants. Aomame was unfamiliar with that particular bit of news, but there was nothing strange about it. Who would remember news about a giant kite-flying competition held in Jakarta three years ago?

On October 6, Egyptian President Anwar Sadat was assassinated by radical Islamic terrorists. Aomame recalled the event with renewed pity for Sadat. She had always been fond of Sadat's bald head, and she felt only revulsion for any kind of religious fundamentalists. The very thought of such people's

intolerant worldview, their inflated sense of their own superiority, and their callous imposition of their own beliefs on
others was enough to fill her with rage. Her anger was almost
uncontrollable. But this had nothing to do with the problem
she was now confronting. She took several deep breaths to
calm her nerves, and then she turned the page.

On October 12, in a residential section of the Itabashi Ward
of Tokyo, an NHK subscription fee collector (aged fifty-six)
became involved in a shouting match with a college student
who refused to pay. Pulling out the butcher knife he always
carried in his briefcase, he stabbed the student in the abdomen, wounding him seriously. The police rushed to the scene
and arrested him on the spot. The collector was standing there
in a daze with the bloody knife in his hand. He offered no
resistance. According to one of his fellow collectors, the man
had been a full-time staff member for six years and was an
extremely serious worker with an outstanding record.

Aomame had no recollection of such an event. She always
took the *Yomiuri* newspaper and read it from cover to cover,
paying close attention to the human interest stories – especially
those involving crimes (which comprised fully half the human
interest stories in the evening edition). There was almost no
way she could have failed to read an article as long as this
one. Of course, *something* could have come up that caused
her to miss it, but this was very unlikely – unlikely, but not
unthinkable.

She knit her brow and mulled over the possibility that she
could have missed such a report. Then she recorded the date
in her notebook, with a summary of the event.

The collector's name was Shinnosuke Akutagawa. Impressive. Sounded like the literary giant Ryunosuke Akutagawa.
There was no photograph of the collector, only of the man
he stabbed, Akira Tagawa, age twenty-one. Tagawa was a
third-year student in the undergraduate law program of Nihon

University and a second-rank practitioner of Japanese swords-manship. Had he been holding a bamboo practice sword at the time, the collector would not have been able to stab him so easily, but ordinary people do not hold bamboo swords in hand when they talk to NHK fee collectors. Of course, ordinary NHK fee collectors don't walk around with butcher knives in their briefcases, either. Aomame followed the next several days' worth of reports on the case but found nothing to indicate that the student had died. He had probably survived.

On October 16 there had been a major accident at a coal mine in Yubari, Hokkaido. A fire broke out at the extraction point one thousand meters underground, and more than fifty miners suffocated. The fire spread upward toward the surface, and another ten men died. To prevent the fire from spreading further, the company pumped the mine full of water without first ascertaining the whereabouts of the remaining miners. The final death toll rose to ninety-three. This was a heartrend-ing event. Coal was a "dirty" energy source, and its extraction was dangerous work. Mining companies were slow to invest in safety equipment, and working conditions were terrible. Accidents were common and miners' lungs were destroyed, but there were many people and businesses that required coal because it was cheap. Aomame had a clear memory of this accident.

The aftermath of the Yubari coal mine accident was still being reported in the paper when Aomame found the event that she was looking for. It had occurred on October 19, 1981. Not until Tamaru told her about it several hours earlier was Aomame aware that such an incident had ever happened. This was simply unimaginable. The headline appeared on the front page of the morning edition in large type:

YAMANASHI GUNFIGHT WITH RADICALS:
3 OFFICERS DIE

A large photo accompanied the article, an aerial shot of the location where the battle had occurred near Lake Motosu, in the hills of Yamanashi Prefecture. There was also a simple map of the site, which was in the mountains away from the developed area of lakeside vacation homes. There were three portrait photos of the dead officers from the Yamanashi Prefectural Police. A Self-Defense Force special paratroop unit dispatched by helicopter. Camouflage fatigues, sniper rifles with scopes, short-barreled automatics.

Aomame scowled hugely. In order to express her feelings properly, she stretched every muscle in her face as far as it would go. Thanks to the partitions on either side of her, no one else sitting at the library tables was able to witness her startling transformation. She then took a deep breath, sucking in all the surrounding air that she possibly could, and letting every bit of it out, like a whale rising to the surface to exchange all the air in its giant lungs. The sound startled the high school student studying at the table behind her, his back to hers, and he spun around to look at her. But he said nothing. He was just frightened.

After distorting her face for a while, Aomame made an effort to relax each of her facial muscles until she had resumed a normal expression. For a long time after that, she tapped at her front teeth with the top end of her ballpoint pen and tried to organize her thoughts. There ought to be a reason. *There has to be a reason. How could I have overlooked such a major event, one that shook the whole of Japan?*

And this incident is not the only one. I didn't know anything about the NHK fee collector's stabbing of the college student. It's absolutely mystifying. I couldn't possibly have missed one major thing after another. I'm too observant, too meticulous for that. I know when something's off by a millimeter. And I know my memory is strong. This is why, in sending a number of men to the "other side," I've never made a single mistake. This is why I've been able to survive. I read the newspaper carefully every day, and when I say "read the newspaper carefully," that means never missing anything that is in any way significant.

The newspaper continued for days to devote major space to the "Lake Motosu Incident." The Self-Defense Force and the Yamanashi Prefectural Police chased down ten escaped radicals, staging a large-scale manhunt in the surrounding hills, killing three of them, severely wounding two, and arresting four (one of whom turned out to be a woman). The last person remained unaccounted for. The paper was filled with reports on the incident, completely obliterating any follow-up reports on the NHK fee collector who stabbed the college student in Itabashi Ward.

Though no one at NHK ever said so, of course, the broadcasters must have been extremely relieved. For if something like the Lake Motosu Incident had not occurred, the media would almost certainly have been screaming about the NHK collections system or raising doubts about the very nature of NHK's quasi-governmental status. At the beginning of that year, information on the ruling Liberal Democratic Party's objections to an NHK special on the Lockheed scandal was leaked, exposing how the NHK had, in response, changed some of the content. After these revelations, much of the nation was – quite reasonably – beginning to doubt the autonomy of NHK programming and to question its political fairness. This in turn gave added impetus to a campaign against paying NHK subscription fees.

Aside from the Lake Motosu Incident and the incident involving the NHK fee collector, Aomame clearly remembered the other events and incidents and accidents that had occurred at the time, and she clearly remembered having read all the newspaper reports about them. Only in those two cases did her powers of recall seem to fail her. Why should that be? Why should there be absolutely nothing left in her memory from those two events alone? *Even supposing this is all due to some malfunction in my brain, could I possibly have erased those two matters so cleanly, leaving everything else intact?*

Aomame closed her eyes and pressed her fingertips against her temples – hard. *Maybe such a thing is, in fact, possible. Maybe my brain is giving rise to some kind of function that is trying to remake reality, that singles out certain news stories and throws a black cloth over them to keep me from seeing or remembering them – the police department's switch to new guns and uniforms, the construction of a joint U.S.-Soviet moon base, an NHK fee collector's stabbing of a college student, a fierce gun battle at Lake Motosu between a radical group and a special detachment of the Self-Defense Force.*

But what do any of these things have in common?

Nothing at all, as far as I can see.

Aomame continued tapping on her teeth with the top end of her ballpoint pen as her mind spun furiously.

She kept this up for a long time until finally, the thought struck her: *Maybe I can look at it this way – the problem is not with me but with the world around me. It's not that my consciousness or mind has given rise to some abnormality, but rather that some kind of incomprehensible power has caused the world around me to change.*

The more she thought about it, the more natural her second hypothesis began to feel to her because, no matter how much she searched for it, she could not find in herself a gap or distortion in her mind.

And so she carried this hypothesis forward:

It's not me but the world that's deranged.

Yes, that settles it.

At some point in time, the world I knew either vanished or withdrew, and another world came to take its place. Like the switching of a track. In other words, my mind, here and now, belongs to the world that was, but the world itself has already changed into something else. So far, the actual changes carried out in that process are limited in number. Most of the new world has been retained from the world I knew, which is why the changes have presented (virtually) no impediments to my daily life – so far. But the changes that have already taken place will almost certainly create other, greater, differences around me as time goes by. Those differences will expand little by little and will, in some cases, destroy the logicality of the actions I take. They could well cause me to commit errors that are – for me – literally fatal.

Parallel worlds.

Aomame scowled as if she had bitten into something horribly sour, though the scowl was not as extreme as the earlier one. She started tapping her ballpoint pen against her teeth again, and released a deep groan. The high school student behind her heard it rattle in her throat, but this time pretended not to hear.

This is starting to sound like science fiction.

Am I just making up a self-serving hypothesis as a form of self-defense? Maybe it's just that I've gone crazy. I see my own mind as perfectly normal, as free of distortion. But don't all mental patients insist that they are perfectly fine and it's the world around them that is crazy? Aren't I just proposing the wild hypothesis of parallel worlds as a way to justify my own madness?

This calls for the detached opinion of a third party.

But going to a psychiatrist for analysis is out of the question. The situation is far too complicated for that, and there's too much that I can't talk about. Take my recent "work," for example, which, without a doubt, is against the law. I mean, I've been secretly killing men with a homemade ice pick. I couldn't possibly tell a doctor about that, even if the men themselves have been utterly despicable, twisted individuals.

Even supposing I could successfully conceal my illegal activities, the legal parts of the life I've led since birth could hardly be called normal, either. My life is like a trunk stuffed with dirty laundry. It contains more than enough material to drive any one human being to mental aberration – maybe two or three people's worth. My sex life alone would do. It's nothing I could talk about to anyone.

No, I can't go to a doctor. I have to solve this on my own.

Let me pursue this hypothesis a little further if I can.

If something like this has actually happened – if, that is, this world I'm standing in now has in fact taken the place of the old one – then when, where, and how did the switching of the tracks occur, in the most concrete sense?

Aomame made another concentrated effort to work her way back through her memory.

She had first become aware of the changes in the world a few days earlier, when she took care of the oil field development specialist in a hotel room in Shibuya. She had left her taxi on the elevated Metropolitan Expressway No. 3, climbed down an emergency escape stairway to Route 246, changed her stockings, and headed for Sangenjaya Station on the Tokyu Line. On the way to the station, she passed a young policeman and noticed for the first time that something about his appearance was different. *That's when it all started. Which means the world switched tracks just before that. The policeman I saw near home that morning was wearing the same old uniform and carrying an old-fashioned revolver.*

Aomame recalled the odd sensation she had felt when she heard the opening of Janáček's *Sinfonietta* in the taxi caught in traffic. She had experienced it as a kind of physical *wrenching*, as if the components of her body were being wrung out like a rag. *Then the driver told me about the Metropolitan Expressway's emergency stairway. I took off my high heels and climbed down. The entire time I climbed down that precarious stairway in my stocking feet with the wind tearing at me, the opening fanfare of Janáček's* Sinfonietta *echoed on and off in my ears. That may have been when it started,* she thought.

There had been something strange about that taxi driver, too. Aomame still remembered his parting words. She reproduced them as precisely as she could in her mind:

After you *do* something like that, the everyday *look* of things might seem to change a little. Things may look *different* to you than they did before. But don't let appearances fool you. There's always only one reality.

At the time, Aomame had found this odd, but she had had no idea what he was trying to tell her, so she hadn't given it much thought. She had been in too much of a hurry to puzzle over riddles. Thinking back on it now, though, his remarks had come out of nowhere, and they were truly strange. They could be taken as cautionary advice or an evocative message. *What was he trying to convey to me?*

And then there was the Janáček music.

How was I able to tell instantly that it was Janáček's Sinfonietta? And how did I know it was composed in 1926? Janáček's Sinfonietta is not such popular music that anyone can recognize it on hearing the first few bars. Nor have I ever been such a passionate fan of classical music. I can't tell Haydn from Beethoven. Yet the moment it came flowing through the car radio, I knew what it was. Why was that, and why should it have given me such an intensely physical – and intensely personal – jolt?

Yes, that jolt was utterly personal. It felt as if something had awakened a memory that had been asleep inside me for years. Something seemed to grab my shoulder and shake me. Which means I might have had a deep connection with that music at some point in my life. The music started playing, threw an automatic switch to "on," and perhaps some kind of memory came fully awake. Janáček's Sinfonietta.

But though she tried to probe her memory, Aomame could come up with nothing else. She looked around, stared at her palms, inspected the shape of her fingernails, and grabbed her breasts through her shirt to check the shape. *No change. Same size and shape. I'm still the same me. The world is still the same world. But something has started to change.* She could feel it. It was like looking for differences between two identical pictures. Two pictures hang on the wall side by side. They look exactly alike, even with careful comparison. But when you examine the tiniest details, minuscule differences become apparent.

Aomame switched mental gears, turned the page of the compact-edition newspaper, and started taking detailed notes on the gun battle at Lake Motosu. There was speculation that the five Chinese-made Kalashnikov AK-47s had been smuggled in through the Korean Peninsula. They were most likely used military surplus in fairly good condition and came with lots of ammunition. The Japan Sea's coast was a long one. Bringing in weapons and ammunition under cover of night and using a spy ship disguised as a fishing vessel was not that difficult. That was how drugs and weapons were brought into Japan in exchange for massive quantities of Japanese yen.

The Yamanashi Prefectural Police had been unaware that the radicals were so heavily armed. They obtained a search warrant on the (purely pro-forma) charge of inflicting bodily injury, and were carrying only their usual weapons when they piled into two patrol cars and a minibus and headed for the "farm." This was the headquarters of a group that called itself Akebono, or "First Light." On the face of it, the group members were simply operating an organic farm. They refused to allow the police to search their property. A confrontation ensued, and at some point it turned into a gun battle.

The Akebono group owned high-powered Chinese-made hand grenades, which fortunately they did not use, purely because they had obtained the grenades so recently that they had not had time to learn how to operate them. If the radicals had used hand grenades, casualties among the police and the

Self-Defense Force would almost certainly have been much greater. Initially, the police did not even bring bulletproof vests with them. Critics singled out the police authorities' poor intelligence analysis and the department's aging weaponry. What most shocked people, however, was the very fact that there still survived in Japan such an armed radical group operating so actively beneath the surface. The late sixties' bombastic calls for "revolution" were already a thing of the past, and everyone assumed that the remnants of the radicals had been wiped out in the police siege of the Asama Mountain Lodge in 1972.

When she had finished taking all her notes, Aomame returned the compact newspaper to the reference counter. Choosing a thick book called *Composers of the World* from the music section, she returned to her table and opened the book to "Janáček."

Leoš Janáček was born in a village in Moravia in 1854 and died in 1928. The article included a picture of him in his later years. Far from bald, his head was covered by a healthy thatch of white hair. It was so thick that Aomame couldn't tell much about the shape of his head. *Sinfonietta* was composed in 1926. Janáček had endured a loveless marriage, but in 1917, at the age of sixty-three, he met and fell in love with a married woman named Kamila. He had been suffering through a slump, but his encounter with Kamila brought back a vigorous creative urge, and he published one late-career masterpiece after another.

He and Kamila were walking in a park one day when they came across an outdoor concert and stopped to listen. Janáček felt a surge of joy go through his entire body, and the motif for his *Sinfonietta* came to him. Something seemed to snap in his head, he recounted years later, and he felt enveloped in ecstasy. By chance, he had been asked around that time to compose a fanfare for a major athletic event. The motif that came to him in the park and the motif of the fanfare became one, and *Sinfonietta* was born. The "small symphony" label is ordinary enough, but the structure is utterly nontraditional, combining the radiant brass of the festive fanfare with the gentle central European string ensemble to produce a unique mood.

Aomame took careful notes on the commentary and the biographical factual material, but the book gave no hint as to what kind of connection there was – or could have been – between herself and this *Sinfonietta*. She left the library and wandered aimlessly through the streets as evening approached, often talking to herself or shaking her head.

Of course, it's all just a hypothesis, Aomame told herself as she walked. *But it's the most compelling hypothesis I can produce at the moment. I'll have to act according to this one, I suppose, until a more compelling hypothesis comes along. Otherwise, I could end up being thrown to the ground somewhere. If only for that reason, I'd better give an appropriate name to this new situation in which I find myself. There's a need, too, for a special name in order to distinguish between this present world and the former world in which the police carried old-fashioned revolvers. Even cats and dogs need names. A newly changed world must need one, too.*

1Q84 – that's what I'll call this new world, Aomame decided. *Q is for "question mark." A world that bears a question.*

Aomame nodded to herself as she walked along.

Like it or not, I'm here now, in the year 1Q84. The 1984 that I knew no longer exists. It's 1Q84 now. The air has changed, the scene has changed. I have to adapt to this world-with-a-question-mark as soon as I can. Like an animal released into a new forest. In order to protect myself and survive, I have to learn the rules of this place and adapt myself to them.

Aomame went to a record store near Jiyugaoka Station to look for Janáček's *Sinfonietta*. Janáček was not a very popular composer. The Janáček section was quite small, and only one record contained *Sinfonietta*, a version with George Szell conducting the Cleveland Orchestra. The A side was Bartók's *Concerto for Orchestra*. She knew nothing about these performances, but since there was no other choice, she bought the LP. She went back to her apartment, took a bottle of Chablis from the refrigerator and opened it, placed the record on the turntable, and lowered the needle into the groove. Drinking the well-chilled wine, she listened to the music. It started with the same bright fanfare. This was the music she had heard in the cab, without a doubt. She closed her eyes and gave the music her complete concentration. The performance was not bad. But nothing happened. It was just music playing. She felt no wrenching of her body. Her perceptions underwent no metamorphosis.

After listening to the piece all the way through, she returned the record to its jacket, sat down on the floor, and leaned against the wall, drinking wine. Alone and absorbed in her thoughts, she could hardly taste the wine. She went to the bathroom sink, washed her face with soap and water, trimmed her eyebrows with a small pair of scissors, and cleaned her ears with a cotton swab.

Either I'm funny or the world's funny, I don't know which. The bottle and lid don't fit. It could be the bottle's fault or the lid's fault. In either case, there's no denying that the fit is bad.

Aomame opened her refrigerator and examined its contents. She hadn't been shopping for some days, so there wasn't much to see. She took out a ripe papaya, cut it in two, and ate it with a spoon. Next she took out three cucumbers, washed them, and ate them with mayonnaise, taking the time to chew slowly. Then she drank a glass of soy milk. That was her entire dinner. It was a simple meal, but ideal for preventing constipation. Constipation was one of the things she hated most in the world, on par with despicable men who commit domestic violence and narrow-minded religious fundamentalists.

When she was through eating, Aomame got undressed and took a hot shower. Stepping out, she dried herself off and looked at her naked body in the full-length mirror on the back of the door. Flat stomach, firm muscles. Lopsided breasts, pubic hair like a poorly tended soccer field. Observing her nakedness, she suddenly recalled that she would be turning thirty in another week. *Another damn birthday. To think I'm going to have my thirtieth birthday in this incomprehensible world, of all places!* She knit her brows.

1Q84.

That was where she was now.

CHAPTER 10

Tengo

A REAL REVOLUTION WITH REAL BLOODSHED

"Transfer," Fuka-Eri said. Then she took Tengo's hand again. This was just before the train pulled into Tachikawa Station.

They stepped off the train and walked down one set of stairs and up another to a different platform. Fuka-Eri never once let go of Tengo's hand. They probably looked like a pair of fond lovers to the people around them. There was quite an age difference, but Tengo looked younger than his actual age. Their size difference also probably amused some onlookers. A happy Sunday-morning date in the spring.

Through the hand holding his, however, Tengo felt no hint of affection for the opposite sex. The strength of her grip never changed. Her fingers had something like the meticulous professionalism of a doctor taking a patient's pulse. It suddenly occurred to Tengo: *Perhaps this girl thinks we can communicate wordlessly through the touch of fingers and palms.* But even supposing such communication had actually taken place, it was all traveling in one direction rather than back and forth. Fuka-Eri's palm might well be absorbing what was in Tengo's mind, but that didn't mean that Tengo could read Fuka-Eri's mind. This did not especially worry Tengo, however. There was nothing in his mind – no thoughts or feelings – that he would be concerned to have her know.

Even if she has no feeling for me as a member of the opposite sex, she must like me to some extent, Tengo surmised. *Or at least she must not have a* bad *impression of me. Otherwise, whatever her purpose, she wouldn't go on holding my hand like this for such a long time.*

Having changed now to the platform for the Oume Line, they boarded the waiting train. This station, Tachikawa, was the beginning of the Oume Line, which headed yet farther toward the hills northwest of Tokyo. The car was surprisingly crowded, full of old folks and family groups in Sunday hiking gear. Tengo and Fuka-Eri stood near the door.

"We seem to have joined an outing," Tengo said, scanning the crowd.

"Is it okay to keep holding your hand," Fuka-Eri asked Tengo. She had not let go even after they boarded the train.

"That's fine," Tengo said. "Of course."

Fuka-Eri seemed relieved and went on holding his hand. Her fingers and palm were as smooth as ever, and free of sweat. They still seemed to be trying to find and verify something inside him.

"You're not afraid anymore," she asked without a question mark.

"No, I'm not," Tengo answered. He was not lying. His Sunday-morning panic attack had certainly lost its force, thanks perhaps to Fuka-Eri's holding his hand. He was no longer sweating, nor could he hear his heart pounding. The hallucination paid him no visit, and his breathing was as calm as usual.

"Good," she said without inflection.

Yes, good, Tengo also thought.

There was a simple, rapidly spoken announcement that the train would soon depart, and the train doors rumbled closed, sending an outsized shudder through the train as if some huge, ancient animal were waking itself from a long sleep. As though it had finally made up its mind, the train pulled slowly away from the platform.

Still holding hands with Fuka-Eri, Tengo watched the scenery go past the train window. At first, it was just the usual residential area scenery, but the farther they went, the more the flat Musashino Plain gave way to views of distant mountains. After nearly a dozen stops, the two-track line narrowed down to a single line of rails, and they had to transfer to a four-car train. The surrounding mountains were becoming increasingly prominent. Now they had gone beyond commuting distance from downtown Tokyo. The hills out here retained the withered look of winter, which brought out the brilliance of the evergreens. The smell of the air was different, too, Tengo realized, as the train doors opened at each new station, and sounds were subtly different. Fields lay by the tracks, and farmhouses increased in number. Pickup trucks seemed to outnumber sedans. *We've really come a long way,* Tengo thought. *How far do we have to go?*

"Don't worry," Fuka-Eri said, as if she had read his mind.

Tengo nodded silently. *I don't know, it feels like I'm going to meet her parents to ask for her hand in marriage,* he thought.

Finally, after five stops on the single-track section of the line, they got off at a station called Futamatao. Tengo had never heard of the place before. *What a strange name. Forked Tail?* The small station was an old wooden building. Five other passengers got off with them. No one got on. People came to Futamatao to breathe the clean air on the mountain trails, not to see a performance of *Man of La Mancha* or go to a disco with a wild reputation or visit an Aston Martin showroom or eat *gratin de homard* at a famous French restaurant. That much was obvious from the clothing of the passengers who left the train here.

There were virtually no shops by the station, and no people. There was, however, one taxi parked there. It probably showed up whenever a train was scheduled to arrive. Fuka-Eri tapped on the window, and the rear door opened. She ducked inside and motioned for Tengo to follow her. The door closed, Fuka-Eri told the driver briefly where she wanted to go, and he nodded in response.

They were not in the taxi very long, but the route was tremendously complicated. They went up one steep hill and down another along a narrow farm road where there was barely enough room to squeeze past other vehicles. The number of curves and corners was beyond counting, but the driver hardly slowed down for any of them. Tengo clutched the door's grip in terror. The taxi finally came to a stop after climbing a hill as frighteningly steep as a ski slope on what seemed to be the peak of a small mountain. It felt less like a taxi trip than a spin on an amusement park ride. Tengo produced two thousand-yen bills from his wallet and received his change and receipt in return.

A black Mitsubishi Pajero and a large, green Jaguar were parked in front of the old Japanese house. The Pajero was shiny and new, but the Jaguar was an old model so coated with white dust that its color was almost obscured. It seemed not to have been driven in some time. The air was startlingly fresh, and a stillness filled the surrounding space. It was a stillness so profound one had to adjust one's hearing to it. The perfectly clear sky seemed to soar upward, and the warmth of the sunlight gently touched any skin directly exposed to it. Tengo heard the high, unfamiliar cry of a bird now and then, but he could not see the bird itself.

The house was large and elegant. It had obviously been built long ago, but it was well cared for. The trees and bushes in the front yard were beautifully trimmed. Several of the trees were so perfectly shaped and matched that they looked like plastic imitations. One large pine cast a broad shadow on the ground. The view from here was unobstructed, but it revealed not a single house as far as the eye could see. Tengo guessed that a person would have to loathe human contact to build a home in such an inconvenient place.

Turning the knob with a clatter, Fuka-Eri walked in through the unlocked front door and signaled for Tengo to follow her. No one came out to greet them. They removed their shoes in the quiet, almost too-large front entry hall. The glossy wooden floor of the corridor felt cool against stocking feet as they walked down it to the large reception room. The windows there revealed a panoramic view of the mountains and of a river meandering far below, the sunlight reflecting on its surface. It was a marvelous view, but Tengo was in no mood to enjoy it. Fuka-Eri sat him down on a large sofa and left the room without a word. The sofa bore the smell of a distant age, but just how distant Tengo could not tell.

The reception room was almost frighteningly free of decoration. There was a low table made from a single thick plank. Nothing lay on it – no ashtray, no tablecloth. No pictures adorned the walls. No clocks, no calendars, no vases. No sideboard, no magazines, no books. The floor had an antique rug so faded that its pattern could not be discerned, and the sofa and easy chairs seemed just as old. There was nothing else, just the large, raft-like sofa on which Tengo was sitting and three matching chairs. There was a large, open-style fireplace, but it showed no signs of having contained a fire recently. For a mid-April morning, the room was downright chilly, as if the cold that had seeped in through the winter had decided to stay for a while. Many long months and years seemed to have passed since the room had made up its mind never to welcome any visitors. Fuka-Eri returned and sat down next to Tengo, still without speaking.

Neither of them said anything for a long time. Fuka-Eri shut herself up in her own enigmatic world, while Tengo tried to calm himself with several quiet deep breaths. Except for the occasional distant bird cry, the room was hushed. Tengo listened to the silence, which seemed to offer several different meanings. It was not simply an absence of sound. The silence seemed to be trying to tell him something about itself. For no reason, he looked at his watch. Raising his face, he glanced at the view outside the window, and then looked at his watch again. Hardly any time had passed. Time always passed slowly on Sunday mornings.

Ten minutes went by like this. Then suddenly, without warning, the door opened and a thinly built man entered the reception room with nervous footsteps. He was probably in his mid-sixties. He was no taller than five foot three, but his excellent posture prevented him from looking unimpressive. His back was as straight as if it had a steel rod in it, and he kept his chin pulled in smartly. His eyebrows were bushy, and he wore black, thick-framed glasses that seemed to have been made to frighten people. His movements suggested an exquisite machine with parts designed for compactness and efficiency. Tengo started to stand and introduce himself, but the man quickly signaled for him to remain seated. Tengo sat back down while the man rushed to lower himself into the facing easy chair, as if in a race with Tengo. For a while, the man simply stared at Tengo, saying nothing. His gaze was not exactly penetrating, but his eyes seemed to take in everything, narrowing and widening like a camera's diaphragm when the photographer adjusts the aperture.

The man wore a deep green sweater over a white shirt and dark gray woolen trousers. Each piece looked as if it had been worn daily for a good ten years or more. They conformed to his body well enough, but they were also a bit threadbare. This was not a person who paid a great deal of attention to his clothes. Nor, perhaps, did he have people close by who did it for him. The thinness of his hair emphasized the rather elongated shape of his head from front to back. He had sunken cheeks and a square jaw. A plump child's tiny lips were the one feature of his that did not quite match the others. His razor had missed a few patches on his face – or possibly it was just the way the light struck him. The mountain sunlight pouring through the windows seemed different from the sunlight Tengo was used to seeing.

"I'm sorry I made you come all this way," the man said. He spoke with an unusually clear intonation, like someone long accustomed to public speaking – and probably about logical topics. "It's not easy for me to leave this place, so all I could do was ask you to go to the trouble of coming here."

Tengo said it was no trouble at all. He told the man his name and apologized for not having a business card.

"My name is Ebisuno," the man said. "I don't have a business card either."

"Mr. 'Ebisuno'?" Tengo asked.

"Everybody calls me 'Professor.' I don't know why, but even my own daughter calls me 'Professor.' "

"What characters do you write your name with?"

"It's an unusual name. I hardly ever see anybody else with it. Eri, write the characters for him, will you?"

Fuka-Eri nodded, took out a kind of notebook, and slowly, painstakingly, wrote the characters for Tengo on a blank sheet with a ballpoint pen. The "Ebisu" part was the character normally used for ancient Japan's wild northern tribes. The "no" was just the usual character for "field." The way Fuka-Eri wrote them, the two characters could have been scratched into a brick with a nail, though they did have a certain style of their own.

"In English, my name could be translated as 'field of savages' – perfect for a cultural anthropologist, which is what I used to be." The Professor's lips formed something akin to a smile, but his eyes lost none of their attentiveness. "I cut my ties with the research life a very long time ago, though. Now, I'm doing something completely different. I'm living in a whole new 'field of savages.' "

To be sure, the Professor's name was an unusual one, but Tengo found it familiar. He was fairly certain there had been a famous scholar named Ebisuno in the late sixties who had published a number of well-received books. He had no idea what the books were about, but the name, at least, remained in some remote corner of his memory. Somewhere along the way, though, he had stopped encountering it.

"I think I've heard your name before," Tengo said tentatively.

"Perhaps," the Professor said, looking off into the distance, as if speaking about someone not present. "In any case, it would have been a long time ago."

Tengo could sense the quiet breathing of Fuka-Eri seated next to him – slow, deep breathing.

"Tengo Kawana," the Professor said as if reading a name tag.

"That's right," Tengo said.

"You majored in mathematics in college, and now you teach math at a cram school in Yoyogi," the Professor said. "But you also write fiction. That's what Eri tells me. Is that about right?"

"Yes, it is," Tengo said.

"You don't look like a math teacher. You don't look like a writer, either."

Tengo gave him a strained smile and said, "Somebody said exactly the same thing to me the other day. It's probably my build."

"I didn't mean it in a bad sense," the Professor said, pressing back the bridge of his black-framed glasses. "There's nothing wrong with not looking like something. It just means you don't fit the stereotype yet."

"I'm honored to have you say that. I'm not a writer yet. I'm still just trying to write fiction."

"Trying."

"It's still trial and error for me."

"I see," the Professor said. Then, as if he had just noticed the chilliness of the room, he rubbed his hands together. "I've also heard that you're going to be revising the novella that Eri wrote in the hopes that she can win a literary magazine's new writers' prize. You're planning to sell her to the public as a writer. Is my interpretation correct?"

"That is basically correct," Tengo said. "An editor named Komatsu came up with the idea. I don't know if the plan is going to work or not. Or whether it's even ethical. My only role is to revise the style of the work, *Air Chrysalis*. I'm just a technician. Komatsu is responsible for everything else."

The Professor concentrated on his thoughts for a while. In the hushed room, Tengo could almost hear his brain working. The Professor then said, "This editor, Mr. Komatsu, came up with the idea, and you're cooperating with him on the technical side."

"Correct."

"I've always been a scholar, and, to tell you the truth, I've never read fiction with much enthusiasm. I don't know anything about customary practice in the world of writing and publishing fiction, but what you people are planning to do sounds to me like a kind of fraud. Am I wrong about that?"

"No, you are not wrong. It sounds like fraud to me, too," Tengo said.

The Professor frowned slightly. "You yourself obviously have ethical doubts about this scheme, and still you are planning to go along with it, out of your own free will."

"Well, it's not exactly my own free will, but I am planning to go along with it. That is correct."

"And why is that?"

"That's what I've been asking myself again and again all week," Tengo said honestly.

The Professor and Fuka-Eri waited in silence for Tengo to continue.

"Reasoning, common sense, instinct – they are all pleading with me to pull out of this as quickly as possible. I'm basically a cautious, commonsensical kind of person. I don't like gambling or taking chances. If anything, I'm a kind of coward. But this is different. I just can't bring myself to say no to Komatsu's plan, as risky as it is. And my only reason is that I'm so strongly drawn to *Air Chrysalis*. If it had been any other work, I would have refused out of hand."

The Professor gave Tengo a quizzical look. "In other words, you have no interest in the fraudulent part of the scheme, but you have a deep interest in the rewriting of the work. Is that it?"

"Exactly. It's more than a 'deep interest.' If *Air Chrysalis* has to be rewritten, I don't want to let anyone else do it."

"I see," the Professor said. Then he made a face, as if he had accidentally put something sour in his mouth. "I see. I think I understand your feelings in the matter. But how about this Komatsu person? What is he in it for? Money? Fame?"

"To tell you the truth, I'm not sure what Komatsu wants," Tengo said. "But I do think it's something bigger than money or fame."

"And what might that be?"

"Well, Komatsu himself might not see it that way, but he is another person who is obsessed with literature. People like him are looking for just one thing, and that is to find, if only once in their lifetimes, a work that is unmistakably the *real thing*. They want to put it on a tray and serve it up to the world."

The Professor kept his gaze fixed on Tengo for a time. Then he said, "In other words, you and he have very different motives – motives that have nothing to do with money or fame."

"I think you're right."

"Whatever your motives might be, though, the plan is, as

you said, a very risky one. If the truth were to come out at some point, it would be sure to cause a scandal, and the public's censure would not be limited to you and Mr. Komatsu. It could deliver a fatal blow to Eri's life at the tender age of seventeen. That's the thing that worries me most about this."

"And you should be worried," Tengo said with a nod. "You're absolutely right."

The space between the Professor's thick, black eyebrows contracted half an inch. "But what you are telling me is that you want to be the one to rewrite *Air Chrysalis* even if it could put Eri in some danger."

"As I said before, that is because my desire comes from a place that reason and common sense can't reach. Of course I would like to protect Eri as much as possible, but I can't promise that she would never be harmed by this. That would be a lie."

"I see," the Professor said. Then he cleared his throat as if to mark a turning point in the discussion. "Well, you seem to be an honest person, at least."

"I'm trying to be as straightforward with you as I can."

The Professor stared at the hands resting on his knees as if he had never seen them before. First he stared at the backs of his hands, and then he flipped them over and stared at his palms. Then he raised his face and said, "So, does this editor, this Mr. Komatsu, think that his plan is really going to work?"

"Komatsu's view is that there are always two sides to everything," Tengo said. "A good side and a not-so-bad side."

The Professor smiled. "A most unusual view. Is this Mr. Komatsu an optimist, or is he self-confident?"

"Neither," Tengo said. "He's just cynical."

The Professor shook his head lightly. "When he gets cynical, he becomes an optimist. Or he becomes self-confident. Is that it?"

"He might have such tendencies."

"A hard man to deal with, it seems."

"He is a pretty hard man to deal with," Tengo said. "But he's no fool."

The Professor let out a long, slow breath. Then he turned to Fuka-Eri. "How about it, Eri? What do you think of this plan?"

Fuka-Eri stared at an anonymous point in space for a while. Then she said, "It's okay."

"In other words, you don't mind letting Mr. Kawana here rewrite *Air Chrysalis*?"

"I don't mind," she said.

"It might cause you a lot of trouble."

Fuka-Eri said nothing in response to this. All she did was tightly grip the collar of her cardigan together at the neck, but the gesture was a direct expression of her firm resolve.

"She's probably right," the Professor said with a touch of resignation.

Tengo stared at her little hands, which were balled into fists.

"There is one other problem, though," the Professor said to Tengo. "You and this Mr. Komatsu plan to publish *Air Chrysalis* and present Eri to the public as a novelist, but she's dyslexic. Did you know that?"

"I got the general idea on the train this morning."

"She was probably born that way. In school, they think she suffers from a kind of retardation, but she's actually quite smart – even wise, in a very profound way. Still, her dyslexia can't help your plan, to put it mildly."

"How many people know about this?"

"Aside from Eri herself, three," the Professor said. "There's me, of course, my daughter Azami, and you. No one else knows."

"You mean to say her teachers don't know?"

"No, they don't. It's a little school in the countryside. They've probably never even heard of dyslexia. And besides, she only went to school for a short time."

"Then we might be able to hide it."

The Professor looked at Tengo for a while, as if judging the value of his face.

"Eri seems to trust you," he said a moment later. "I don't know why, but she does. And I – "

Tengo waited for him to continue.

"And I trust Eri. So if she says it's all right to let you rewrite her novella, all I can do is give my approval. On the other hand, if you really do plan to go ahead with this scheme, there are a few things you should know about Eri." The Professor swept his hand lightly across his right knee several times as if he had found a tiny piece of thread there. "What her childhood was like, for example, and where she spent it, and how I became responsible for raising her. This could take a while to tell."

"I'm listening," Tengo said.

Next to him on the sofa, Fuka-Eri sat up straight, still holding the collar of her cardigan closed at the throat.

"All right, then," the Professor said. "The story goes back to the sixties. Eri's father and I were close friends for a long time. I was ten years older, but we both taught in the same department at the same university. Our personalities and worldviews were very different, but for some reason we got along. Both of us married late, and we both had daughters shortly after we got married. We lived in the same faculty apartment building, and our families were always together. Professionally, too, we were doing very well. People were starting to notice us as 'rising stars of academe.' We often appeared in the media. It was a tremendously exciting time for us.

"Toward the end of the sixties, though, things started to change for the worse. The second renewal of the U.S.-Japan Security Treaty was coming in 1970, and the student movement was opposed to it. They blockaded the university campuses, fought with the riot police, had bloody factional disputes, and as a result, people died. All of this was more than I wanted to deal with, and I decided to leave the university. I had never been that temperamentally suited to the academic life, but once these protests and riots began, I became fed up with it. Establishment, antiestablishment: I didn't care. Ultimately, it was just a clash of organizations, and I simply didn't trust any kind of organization, big or small. You, I would guess, were not yet old enough to be in the university in those days."

"No, the commotion had all died down by the time I started."

"The party was over, you mean."

"Pretty much."

The Professor raised his hands for a moment and then lowered them to his knees again. "So I quit the university, and two years later Eri's father left. At the time, he was a great believer in Mao Zedong's revolutionary ideology and supported China's Cultural Revolution. We heard almost nothing in those days about how terrible and inhumane the Cultural Revolution could be. It even became trendy with some intellectuals to hold up Mao's *Little Red Book*. Eri's father went so far as to organize a group of students into a kind of Red Guard on campus, and he participated in the strike against the university. Some student-believers on other campuses came to join his organization, and for a while, under his leadership, the faction became quite large. Then the university got the riot police to storm the campus. He was holed up there with his students, so he was arrested with them, convicted, and sentenced. This led to his de facto dismissal from the university. Eri was still a little girl then and probably doesn't remember any of this."

Fuka-Eri remained silent.

"Her father's name is Tamotsu Fukada. After leaving the university, he took with him ten core students from his Red Guard unit and they entered the Takashima Academy. Most of the students had been expelled from the university. They all needed someplace to go, and Takashima Academy was not a bad choice for them. The media paid some attention to their movements at the time. Do you know anything about this?"

Tengo shook his head. "No, nothing."

"Fukada's family went with him – meaning his wife and Eri here. They all entered Takashima together. You know about the Takashima Academy, don't you?"

"In general," Tengo said. "It's organized like a commune. They live a completely communal lifestyle and support themselves by farming. Dairy farming, too, on a national scale. They don't believe in personal property and own everything collectively."

"That's it. Fukada was supposedly looking for a utopia in the Takashima system," the Professor said with a frown. "But utopias don't exist, of course, anywhere in any world. Like alchemy or perpetual motion. What Takashima is doing, if you ask me, is making mindless robots. They take the circuits out of people's brains that make it possible for them to think for themselves. Their world is like the one that George Orwell depicted in his novel. I'm sure you realize that there are plenty of people who are looking for exactly that kind of brain death. It makes life a lot easier. You don't have to think about difficult things, just shut up and do what your superiors tell you to do. You never have to starve. To people who are searching for that kind of environment, the Takashima Academy may well be utopia.

"But Fukada is not that kind of person. He likes to think things out for himself, to examine every aspect of an issue. That's how he made his living all those years: it was his profession. He could never be satisfied with a place like Takashima. He knew that much from the start. Kicked out of the university with a bunch of book-smart students in tow, he didn't have anywhere else to go, so he chose Takashima as a temporary refuge. What he was looking for there was not utopia but an understanding of the Takashima system. The first thing they had to do was learn farming techniques. Fukada and his students were all city people. They didn't know any more about farming than I know about rocket science. And there was a lot for them to learn: distribution systems, the possibilities and limits of a self-sufficient economy, practical rules for communal living, and so on. They lived in Takashima for two years, learning everything they could. After that, Fukada took his group with him, left Takashima, and went out on his own."

"Takashima was fun," Fuka-Eri said.

The Professor smiled. "I'm sure Takashima is fun for little children. But when you grow up and reach a certain age and develop an ego, life in Takashima for most young people comes close to a living hell. The leaders use their power to crush people's natural desire to think for themselves. It's foot-binding for the brain."

"Foot-binding," Fuka-Eri asked.

"In the old days in China, they used to cram little girls' feet into tiny shoes to keep them from growing," Tengo explained to her.

She pictured it to herself, saying nothing.

The Professor continued, "The core of Fukada's splinter group, of course, was made up of ex-students who were with him from his Red Guard days, but others came forward too, so the size of the group snowballed beyond anyone's expectations. A good number of people had entered Takashima for idealistic reasons but were dissatisfied and disappointed with what they found: people who had been hoping for a hippie-style communal life, leftists scarred by the university uprisings, people dissatisfied with ordinary life and searching for a new world of spirituality, single people, people who had their families with them like Fukada – a motley crew if ever there was one, and Fukada was their leader. He had a natural gift for leadership, like Moses leading the Israelites. He was smart, eloquent, and had outstanding powers of judgment. He was a charismatic figure – a big man. Just about your size, come to think of it. People placed him at the center of the group as a matter of course, and they followed his judgment."

The Professor held out his arms to indicate the man's physical bulk. Fuka-Eri stared first at the Professor's arms and then at Tengo, but she said nothing.

"Fukada and I are totally different, both in looks and personality. But even given our differences, we were very close friends. We recognized each other's abilities and trusted each other. I can say without exaggeration that ours was a once-in-a-lifetime friendship."

Under Tamotsu Fukada's leadership, the group had found a depopulated village that suited their purposes in the mountains of Yamanashi Prefecture. The village was on the brink of death. The few old people who remained there could not manage the crops themselves and had no one to carry on the farm work after they were gone. The group was able to purchase the fields and houses for next to nothing, including the vinyl greenhouses. The village office provided a subsidy on condition that the group continue to cultivate the established farmland, and they were granted preferential tax treatment for at least the first few years. In addition, Fukada had his own personal source of funds, but Professor Ebisuno had no idea where the money came from.

"Fukada refused to talk about it, and he never revealed the secret to anybody, but *somewhere* he got hold of a considerable amount of cash that was needed to establish the commune. They used the money to buy farm machinery and building materials, and to set up a reserve fund. They repaired the old houses by themselves and built facilities that would enable their thirty members to live. This was in 1974. They called their new commune "Sakigake," or "Forerunner."

Sakigake? The name sounded familiar to Tengo, but he

couldn't remember where he might have heard it before. When his attempt to trace the memory back ended in failure, he felt unusually frustrated.

The Professor continued, "Fukada was resigned to the likelihood that the operation of the commune would be tough for the first several years until they became accustomed to the area, but things went more smoothly than he had expected. They were blessed with good weather and helpful neighbors. People readily took to Fukada as leader, given his sincere personality, and they admired the hardworking young members they saw sweating in the fields. The locals offered useful advice. In this way, the members were able to absorb practical knowledge about farming techniques and learn how to live off the land.

"While they continued to practice what they had learned in Takashima, Sakigake also came up with several of their own innovations. For example, they switched to organic farming, eschewing chemical pesticides and growing their vegetables entirely with organic fertilizers. They also started a mail-order food service pitched directly to affluent urbanites. That way they could charge more per unit. They were the first of the so-called ecological farmers, and they knew how to make the most of it. Having been raised in the city, the commune's members knew that city people would be glad to pay high prices for fresh, tasty vegetables free of pollutants. They created their own distribution system by contracting with delivery companies and simplifying their routes. They were also the first to make a virtue of the fact that they were selling 'un-uniform vegetables with the soil still clinging to them.'"

The professor went on. "I visited Fukada on his farm any number of times. He seemed invigorated by his new surroundings and the chance to try new possibilities there. It was probably the most peaceful, hope-filled time of his life, and his family also appeared to have adapted well to this new way of living.

"More and more people would hear about Sakigake farm and show up there wanting to become members. The name had gradually become more widely known through the mail order business, and the mass media had reported on it as an example of a successful commune. More than a few people were eager to escape from the real world's mad pursuit of money and its flood of information, instead earning their living by the sweat of their brow. Sakigake appealed to them. When these people showed up, Sakigake would interview and investigate them, and give the promising ones membership. They couldn't admit everyone who came. They had to preserve the members' high quality and ethics. They were looking for people with strong farming skills and healthy physiques who could tolerate hard physical labor. They also welcomed women in hopes of keeping something close to a fifty-fifty male-female ratio. Increasing the numbers would mean enlarging the scale of the farm, but there were plenty of extra fields and houses nearby, so that was no problem. Young bachelors made up the core of the farm's membership at first, but the number of people joining with families gradually increased. Among the newcomers were well-educated professionals – doctors, engineers, teachers, accountants, and the like. Such people were heartily welcomed by the community since their professional skills could be put to good use."

Tengo asked, "Did the commune adopt Takashima's type of primitive communist system?"

The Professor shook his head. "No, Fukada avoided the communal ownership of property. Politically, he was a radical, but he was also a coolheaded realist. What he was aiming for was a more flexible community, not a society like an ant colony. His approach was to divide the whole into a number of units, each leading its own flexible communal life. They recognized private property and apportioned out compensation to some extent. If you weren't satisfied with your unit, you could switch

to another one, and you were free to leave Sakigake itself anytime you liked. There was full access to the outside world, too,
and there was virtually no ideological inculcation or brain-
washing. He had learned when they were in Takashima that a
natural, open system would increase productivity."

Under Fukada's leadership, the operation of Sakigake farm
remained on track, but eventually the commune split into two
distinct factions. Such a split was inevitable as long as they
kept Fukada's flexible unit system. On one side was a militant
faction, a revolutionary group based on the Red Guard unit
that Fukada had originally organized. For them, the farming
commune was strictly preparatory for the revolution. Farming
was just a cover for them until the time came for them to take
up arms. That was their unshakable stance.

On the other side was the moderate faction. As the majority,
they shared the militant faction's opposition to capitalism, but
they kept some distance from politics, instead preferring the
creation of a self-sufficient communal life in nature. Insofar as
farming was concerned, each faction shared the same goals,
but whenever it became necessary to make decisions regarding operational policy of the commune as a whole, their opinions split. Often they could find no room for rapprochement,
and this would give rise to violent arguments. The breakup of
the commune was just a matter of time.

Maintaining a neutral stance became increasingly difficult with each passing day. Eventually, Fukada found himself
trapped between the two factions. He was generally aware that
1970s Japan was not the place or time for mounting a revolution. What he had always had in mind was the potential of
a revolution – revolution as a metaphor or hypothesis. He
believed that exercising that kind of antiestablishment, sub-
versive will was indispensable for a healthy society. But his students wanted a real revolution with real bloodshed. Of course

Fukada bore some responsibility for this. He was the one who had planted such baseless myths in their heads. But he never told them that his "revolution" had quotation marks around it.

And so the two factions of the Sakigake commune parted ways. The moderate faction continued to call itself "Sakigake" and remained in the original village, while the militant faction moved to a different, abandoned village a few miles away and made it the base of their revolutionary movement. The Fukada family remained in Sakigake with all the other families. The split was a friendly one. It appears that Fukada obtained the funds for the new commune from his usual unspecified source. Even after their separation, the two farms maintained a cooperative relationship. They traded necessary materials and, for economic reasons, used the same distribution routes for their products. The two small communities had to help each other if they were to survive.

One thing did change, however, shortly after the split: the effective cessation of visits between the old Sakigake members and the new commune. Only Fukada himself continued to correspond with his former radical students. Fukada felt a strong sense of responsibility for them, as the one who had originally organized and led them into the mountains of Yamanashi. In addition, the new commune needed the secret funds that Fukada controlled.

"Fukada was probably in a kind of schizoid state by then," the Professor said. "He no longer believed with his whole heart in the possibility or the romance of the revolution. Neither, however, could he completely disavow it. To do so would mean disavowing his life and confessing his mistakes for all to see. This was something he could not do. He had too much pride, and he worried about the confusion that would surely arise among his students as a result. At that stage, he still wielded a certain degree of control over them.

"This is how he found himself living a life that had him running back and forth between Sakigake and the new commune. He took upon himself the simultaneous duties of leader of one and adviser to the other. So a person who no longer truly believed in the revolution continued to preach revolutionary theory. The members of the new commune carried on with their farm work while they submitted to the harsh discipline of military training and ideological indoctrination. And politically, in contrast to Fukada, they became increasingly radicalized. They adopted a policy of obsessive secrecy, and they no longer allowed outsiders to enter. Aware of their calls for armed revolution, the security police identified them as a group that needed to be watched and placed them under surveillance, though not at a high level of alert."

The Professor stared at his knees again, and then looked up.

"Sakigake split in two in 1976," he went on. "Eri escaped from Sakigake and came to live with us the following year. Around that time the new commune began calling itself 'Akebono.'"

Tengo looked up and narrowed his eyes. "Wait a minute," he said. *Akebono. I'm absolutely certain I've heard that name, too.* But the memory was vague and incoherent. All he could grab hold of were a few fragmentary, fact-like details. "This Akebono . . . didn't they cause some kind of big incident a while ago?"

"Exactly," Professor Ebisuno said, looking at Tengo more intently than he had until now. "We're talking about the famous Akebono, of course, the ones who staged the gun battle with the police in the mountains near Lake Motosu."

Gun battle, Tengo thought. *I remember hearing about that. It was big news. I can't remember the details, though, for some reason, and I'm confused about the sequence of events.* When he strained to recall more, he experienced a wrenching sensation through his whole body, as though his top and bottom halves were being twisted in opposite directions. He felt a dull throbbing deep in his head, and the air around him suddenly went thin. Sounds became muffled as though he were underwater. He was probably about to have an "attack."

"Is something wrong?" the Professor asked with obvious concern. His voice seemed to be coming from a very great distance.

Tengo shook his head and in a strained voice said, "I'm fine. It'll go away soon."

CHAPTER 11

Aomame

THE HUMAN BODY IS A TEMPLE

The number of people who could deliver a kick to the balls with Aomame's mastery must have been few indeed. She had studied kick patterns with great diligence and never missed her daily practice. In kicking the balls, the most important thing was never to hesitate. One had to deliver a lightning attack to the adversary's weakest point and do so mercilessly and with the utmost ferocity – just as when Hitler easily brought down France by striking at the weak point of the Maginot Line. One must not hesitate. A moment of indecision could be fatal.

Generally speaking, there was no other way for a woman to take down a bigger, stronger man one-on-one. This was Aomame's unshakable belief. That part of the body was the weakest point attached to – or, rather, hanging from – the creature known as man, and most of the time, it was not effectively defended. Not to take advantage of that fact was out of the question.

As a woman, Aomame had no concrete idea how much it hurt to suffer a hard kick in the balls, though judging from the reactions and facial expressions of men she had kicked, she could at least imagine it. Not even the strongest or toughest man, it seemed, could bear the pain and the major loss of self-respect that accompanied it.

"It hurts so much you think the end of the world is coming

right now. I don't know how else to put it. It's different from ordinary pain," said a man, after careful consideration, when Aomame asked him to explain it to her.

Aomame gave some thought to his analogy. The end of the world?

"Conversely, then," she said, "would you say that when the end of the world is coming *right now,* it feels like a hard kick in the balls?"

"Never having experienced the end of the world, I can't be sure, but that might be right," the man said, glaring at a point in space with unfocused eyes. "There's just this deep sense of powerlessness. Dark, suffocating, helpless."

Sometime after that, Aomame happened to see the movie *On the Beach* on late-night television. It was an American movie made around 1960. Total war broke out between the U.S. and the USSR and a huge number of missiles were launched between the continents like schools of flying fish. The earth was annihilated, and humanity was wiped out in almost every part of the world. Thanks to the prevailing winds or something, however, the ashes of death still hadn't reached Australia in the Southern Hemisphere, though it was just a matter of time. The extinction of the human race was simply unavoidable. The surviving human beings there could do nothing but wait for the end to come. They chose different ways to live out their final days. That was the plot. It was a dark movie offering no hope of salvation. (Though, watching it, Aomame reconfirmed her belief that everyone, deep in their hearts, is waiting for the end of the world to come.)

In any case, watching the movie in the middle of the night, alone, Aomame felt satisfied that she now had at least some idea of what it felt like to be kicked in the balls.

After graduating from a college of physical education, Aomame spent four years working for a company that manufactured sports drinks and health food. She was a key member of the company's women's softball team (ace pitcher, cleanup batter). The team did fairly well and several times reached the quarterfinals of the national championship playoffs. A month after Tamaki Otsuka died, though, Aomame resigned from the company and marked the end of her softball career. Any desire she might have had to continue with the game had vanished, and she felt a need to start her life anew. With the help of an older friend from college, she found a job as an instructor at a sports club in Tokyo's swank Hiroo District.

Aomame was primarily in charge of classes in muscle training and martial arts. It was a well-known, exclusive club with high membership fees and dues, and many of its members were celebrities. Aomame established several classes in her best area, women's self-defense techniques. She made a large canvas dummy in the shape of a man, sewed a black work glove in the groin area to serve as testicles, and gave female club members thorough training in how to kick in that spot. In the interest of realism, she stuffed two squash balls into the glove. The women were to kick this target swiftly, mercilessly, and repeatedly. Many of them took special pleasure in this training, and their skill improved markedly, but other members (mostly men, of course) viewed the spectacle with a frown and complained to the club's management that she was going overboard. As a result, Aomame was called in and instructed to rein in the ball-kicking practice.

"Realistically speaking, though," she protested, "it's impossible for women to protect themselves against men without resorting to a kick in the testicles. Most men are bigger and stronger than women. A swift testicle attack is a woman's only chance. Mao Zedong said it best. You find your opponent's weak point and make the first move with a concentrated attack. It's the only chance a guerrilla force has of defeating a regular army."

The manager did not take well to her passionate defense. "You know perfectly well that we're one of the few truly exclusive clubs in the metropolitan area," he said with a frown. "Most of our members are celebrities. We have to preserve our dignity in all aspects of our operations. Image is crucial. I don't care what the reason is for these drills of yours, it's less than dignified to have a gang of nubile women kicking a doll in the crotch and screeching their heads off. We've already had at least one case of a potential member touring the club and withdrawing his application after he happened to see your class in action. I don't care what Mao Zedong said – or Genghis Khan, for that matter: a spectacle like that is going to make most men feel anxious and annoyed and upset."

Aomame felt not the slightest regret at having caused male club members to feel anxious and annoyed and upset. Such unpleasant feelings were nothing compared with the pain experienced by a victim of forcible rape. She could not defy her superior's orders, however, and so her self-defense classes had to lower the level of their aggressiveness. She was also forbidden to use the doll. As a result, her drills became much more lukewarm and formal. Aomame herself was hardly pleased by this, and several members raised objections, but as an employee, there was nothing she could do.

It was Aomame's opinion that, if she were unable to deliver an effective kick to the balls when forcefully attacked by a man, there would be very little else left for her to try. In the actual heat of combat, it was virtually impossible to perform such high-level techniques as grabbing your opponent's arm and twisting it behind his back. That only happened in the movies. Rather than attempting such a feat, a woman would be far better off running away without trying to fight.

In any case, Aomame had mastered at least ten separate techniques for kicking men in the balls. She had even gone so far as to have several younger men she knew from college put on protective cups and let her practice on them. "Your kicks really *hurt,* even with the cup on," one of them had screamed in pain. "No more, please!" If the need arose, she knew, she would never hesitate to apply her sophisticated techniques in actual combat. *If there's any guy crazy enough to attack me, I'm going to show him the end of the world – close up. I'm going to let him see the king-dom come with his own eyes. I'm going to send him straight to the Southern Hemisphere and let the ashes of death rain all over him and the kangaroos and the wallabies.*

As she pondered the coming of the kingdom, Aomame sat at the bar taking little sips of her Tom Collins. She would glance at her wristwatch every now and then, pretending that she was here to meet someone, but in fact she had made no such arrangement. She was simply keeping an eye out for a suitable man among the bar's arriving patrons. Her watch said eight thirty. She wore a pale blue blouse beneath a dark brown Cal-vin Klein jacket and a navy-blue miniskirt. Her handmade ice pick was not with her today. It was resting peacefully, wrapped in a towel in her dresser drawer at home.

This was a well-known singles bar in the Roppongi enter-tainment district. Single men came here on the prowl for sin-gle women – or vice versa. A lot of them were foreigners. The bar was meant to look like a place where Hemingway might have hung out in the Bahamas. A stuffed swordfish hung on the wall, and fishing nets dangled from the ceiling. There were lots of photographs of people posing with giant fish they had caught, and there was a portrait of Hemingway. Happy Papa Hemingway. The people who came here were apparently not concerned that the author later suffered from alcoholism and killed himself with a hunting rifle.

Several men approached Aomame that evening, but none she liked. A pair of typically footloose college students invited her to join them, but she couldn't be bothered to respond.

To a thirtyish company employee with creepy eyes she said she was here to meet someone and turned him down flat. She just didn't like young men. They were so aggressive and self-confident, but they had nothing to talk about, and whatever they had to say was boring. In bed, they went at it like animals and had no clue about the true enjoyment of sex. She liked those slightly tired middle-aged men, preferably in the early stages of baldness. They should be clean and free of any hint of vulgarity. And they had to have well-shaped heads. Such men were not easy to find, which meant that she had to be willing to compromise.

Scanning the room, Aomame released a silent sigh. Why were there so damn few "suitable men" around? She thought about Sean Connery. Just imagining the shape of his head, she felt a dull throbbing deep inside. *If Sean Connery were to suddenly pop up here, I would do anything to make him mine. Of course, there's no way in hell that Sean Connery is going to show his face in a Roppongi fake Bahamas singles bar.*

On the bar's big wall television, Queen was performing. Aomame didn't much like Queen's music. She tried her best not to look in that direction. She also tried hard not to listen to the music coming from the speakers. After the Queen video ended, ABBA came on. *Oh, no. Something tells me this is going to be an awful night.*

Aomame had met the dowager of Willow House at the sports club where she worked. The woman was enrolled in Aomame's self-defense class, the short-lived radical one that emphasized attacking the doll. She was a small woman, the oldest member of the class, but her movements were light and her kicks sharp. *In a tight situation, I'm sure she could kick her opponent in the balls without the slightest hesitation. She never speaks more than necessary, and when she does speak she never beats around the bush.* Aomame liked that about her. "At my age, there's no special need for self-defense," the woman said to Aomame with a dignified smile after class.

"Age has nothing to do with it," Aomame snapped back. "It's a question of how you live your life. The important thing is to adopt a stance of always being deadly serious about protecting yourself. You can't go anywhere if you just resign yourself to being attacked. A state of chronic powerlessness eats away at a person."

The dowager said nothing for a while, looking Aomame in the eye. Either Aomame's words or her tone of voice seemed to have made a strong impression on her. She nodded gravely. "You're right. You are absolutely right," she said. "You have obviously done some solid thinking about this."

A few days later, Aomame received an envelope. It had been left at the club's front desk for her. Inside Aomame found a short, beautifully penned note containing the dowager's address and telephone number. "I know you must be very busy," it said, "but I would appreciate hearing from you some-time when you are free."

A man answered the phone – a secretary, it seemed. When Aomame gave her name, he switched her to an extension without a word. The dowager came on the line and thanked her for calling. "If it's not too much bother, I'd like to invite you out for a meal," she said. "I'd like to have a nice, long talk with you, just the two of us."

"With pleasure," Aomame said.

"How would tomorrow night be for you?"

Aomame had no problem with that, but she had to wonder what this elegant older woman could possibly want to speak about with someone like her.

The two had dinner at a French restaurant in a quiet section of Azabu. The dowager had been coming here for a long time, it seemed. They showed her to one of the better tables in the back, and she apparently knew the aging waiter who provided them

with attentive service. She wore a beautifully cut dress of unfig-
ured pale green cloth (perhaps a 1960s Givenchy) and a jade
necklace. Midway through the meal, the manager appeared
and offered her his respectful greetings. Vegetarian cuisine
occupied much of the menu, and the flavors were elegant and
simple. By coincidence, the soup of the day was green pea soup,
as if in honor of Aomame. The dowager had a glass of Chablis,
and Aomame kept her company. The wine was just as elegant
and simple as the food. Aomame ordered a grilled cut of white
fish. The dowager took only vegetables. Her manner of eating
the vegetables was beautiful, like a work of art. "When you get
to be my age, you can stay alive eating very little," she said. "Of
the finest food possible," she added, half in jest.

She wanted Aomame to become her personal trainer,
instructing her in martial arts at her home two or three days a
week. Also, if possible, she wanted Aomame to help her with
muscle stretching.

"Of course I can do that," Aomame said, "but I'll have to ask
you to arrange for the personal training away from the gym
through the club's front desk."

"That's fine," the dowager said, "but let's make scheduling
arrangements directly. There is bound to be confusion if other
people get involved. I'd like to avoid that. Would that be all
right with you?"

"Perfectly all right."

"Then let's start next week," the dowager said.

This was all it took to conclude their business.

The dowager said, "I was tremendously struck by what you
said at the gym the other day. About powerlessness. About
how powerlessness inflicts such damage on people. Do you
remember?"

Aomame nodded. "I do."

"Do you mind if I ask you a question? It will be a very direct
question. To save time."

"Ask whatever you like," Aomame said.

"Are you a feminist, or a lesbian?"

Aomame blushed slightly and shook her head. "I don't think so. My thoughts on such matters are strictly my own. I'm not a doctrinaire feminist, and I'm not a lesbian."

"That's good," the dowager said. As if relieved, she elegantly lifted a forkful of broccoli to her mouth, elegantly chewed it, and took one small sip of wine. Then she said, "Even if you were a feminist or a lesbian, it wouldn't bother me in the least. It wouldn't influence anything. But, if I may say so, your *not* being either will make it easier for us to communicate. Do you see what I'm trying to say?"

"I do," Aomame said.

Aomame went to the dowager's compound twice a week to guide her in martial arts. The dowager had a large, mirrored practice space built years earlier for her little daughter's ballet lessons, and it was there that she and Aomame did their carefully ordered exercises. For someone her age, the dowager was very flexible, and she progressed rapidly. Hers was a small body, but one that had been well cared for over the years. Aomame also taught her the basics of systematic stretching, and gave her massages to loosen her muscles.

Aomame was especially skilled at deep tissue massage. She had earned better grades in that field than anyone else at the college of physical education. The names of all the bones and all the muscles of the human body were engraved in her brain. She knew the function and characteristics of each muscle, both how to tone it and how to keep it toned. It was Aomame's firm belief that the human body was a temple, to be kept as strong and beautiful and clean as possible, whatever one might enshrine there.

Not content with ordinary sports medicine, Aomame learned acupuncture techniques as a matter of personal interest, taking formal training for several years from a Chinese doctor. Impressed with her rapid progress, the doctor told her that she had more than enough skill to be a professional. She was a quick learner, with an unquenchable thirst for detailed knowledge regarding the body's functions. But more than anything, she had fingertips that were endowed with an almost frightening sixth sense. Just as certain people possess perfect pitch or the ability to find underground water veins, Aomame's fingertips could instantly discern the subtle points on the body that influenced its functionality. This was nothing that anyone had taught her. It came to her naturally.

Before long, Aomame and the dowager would follow up their training and massage sessions with a leisurely chat over a cup of tea. Tamaru would always bring the tea utensils on the silver tray. He never spoke a word in Aomame's presence during the first month, until Aomame felt compelled to ask the dowager if by any chance Tamaru was incapable of speaking.

One time, the dowager asked Aomame if she had ever used her testicle-kicking technique in actual self-defense.

"Just once," Aomame answered.

"Did it work?" the dowager asked.

"It had the intended effect," Aomame answered, cautiously and concisely.

"Do you think it would work on Tamaru?"

Aomame shook her head. "Probably not. He knows about things like that. If the other person has the ability to read your movements, there's nothing you can do. The testicle kick only works with amateurs who have no actual fighting experience."

"In other words, you recognize that Tamaru is no amateur."

"How should I put it?" Aomame paused. "He has a special presence. He's not an ordinary person."

The dowager added cream to her tea and stirred it slowly.

"So the man you kicked that time was an amateur, I assume. A big man?"

Aomame nodded but did not say anything. The man had been well built and strong-looking. But he was arrogant, and he had let his guard down with a mere woman. He had never had the experience of being kicked in the balls by a woman, and never imagined such a thing would ever happen to him.

"Did he end up with any wounds?" the dowager asked.

"No, no wounds," Aomame said. "He was just in intense pain for a while."

The dowager remained silent for a moment. Then she asked, "Have you ever attacked a man before? Not just causing him pain but intentionally wounding him?"

"I have," Aomame replied. Lying was not a specialty of hers.

"Can you talk about it?"

Aomame shook her head almost imperceptibly. "I'm sorry, but it's not something I can talk about easily."

"Of course not," the dowager said. "That's fine. There's no need to force yourself."

The two drank their tea in silence, each with her own thoughts.

Finally, the dowager spoke. "But sometime, when you feel like talking about it, do you think I might be able to have you tell me what happened back then?"

Aomame said, "I might be able to tell you sometime. Or I might not, ever. I honestly don't know, myself."

The dowager looked at Aomame for a while. Then she said, "I'm not asking out of mere curiosity."

Aomame kept silent.

"As I see it, you are living with something that you keep hidden deep inside. Something heavy. I felt it from the first time I met you. You have a strong gaze, as if you have made up your mind about something. To tell you the truth, I myself carry such things around inside. Heavy things. That is how I can see it in you. There is no need to hurry, but you will be better off, at some point in time, if you bring it outside yourself. I am nothing if not discreet, and I have several realistic measures at my disposal. If all goes well, I could be of help to you."

Later, when Aomame finally opened up to the dowager, she would also open a new door in her life.

"Hey, what are you drinking?" someone asked near Aomame's ear. The voice belonged to a woman.

Aomame raised her head and looked at the speaker. A young woman with a fifties-style ponytail was sitting on the neighboring barstool. Her dress had a tiny flower pattern, and a small Gucci bag hung from her shoulder. Her nails were carefully manicured in pale pink. By no means fat, the woman was round everywhere, including her face, which radiated a truly friendly warmth, and she had big breasts.

Aomame was somewhat taken aback. She had not been expecting to be approached by a woman. This was a bar for men to approach women.

"Tom Collins," Aomame said.

"Is it good?"

"Not especially. But it's not that strong, and I can sip it."

"I wonder why they call it 'Tom Collins.' "

"I have no idea," Aomame said. "Maybe it's the name of the guy who invented it. Not that it's such an amazing invention."

The woman waved to the bartender and said, "I'll have a Tom Collins too." A few moments later, she had her drink.

"Mind if I sit here?" she asked.

"Not at all. It's an empty seat." *And you're already sitting in it,* Aomame thought without speaking the words.

"You don't have a date to meet anybody here, do you?" the woman asked.

Instead of answering, Aomame studied the woman's face. She guessed the woman was three or four years younger than herself.

"Don't worry, I'm not interested in *that,*" the woman

whispered, as if sharing a secret. "If that's what you're worried about. I prefer men, too. Like you."

"Like me?"

"Well, isn't that why you came here, to find a guy?"

"Do I look like that?"

The woman narrowed her eyes somewhat. "That much is obvious. It's what this place is for. And I'm guessing that neither of us is a pro."

"Of course not," Aomame said.

"Hey, here's an idea. Why don't we team up? It's probably easier for a man to approach two women than one. And we can relax more and sort of feel safer if we're together instead of alone. We look so different, too – I'm more the womanly type, and you have that trim, boyish style – I'm sure we're a good match."

Boyish, Aomame thought. *That's the first time anyone's ever called me that.* "Our taste in men might be different, though," she said. "How's that supposed to work if we're a 'team'?"

The woman pursed her lips in thought. "True, now that you mention it. Taste in men, huh? Hmm. What kind do you like?"

"Middle-aged if possible," Aomame said. "I'm not that into young guys. I like 'em when they're just starting to lose their hair."

"Wow. I get it. Middle-aged, huh? I like 'em young and lively and good-looking. I'm not much interested in middle-aged guys, but I'm willing to go along with you and give it a try. It's all experience. Are middle-aged guys good? At sex, I mean."

"It depends on the guy," Aomame said.

"Of course," the woman replied. Then she narrowed her eyes, as if verifying some kind of theory. "You can't generalize about sex, of course, but if you were to say overall . . ."

"They're not bad. They eventually run out of steam, but while they're at it they take their time. They don't rush it. When they're good, they can make you come a *lot.*"

The woman gave this some thought. "Hmm, I may be getting interested. Maybe I'll try that out."

"You should!"

"Say, have you ever tried four-way sex? You switch partners at some point."

"Never."

"I haven't, either. Interested?"

"Probably not," Aomame said. "Uh, I don't mind teaming up, but if we're going to do stuff together, even temporarily, can you tell me a little more about yourself? Because we could be on completely different wavelengths."

"Good idea," she said. "So, what do you want to know about me?"

"Well, for one thing, what kind of work do you do?"

The woman took a drink of her Tom Collins and set it down on the coaster. Then she dabbed at her lips with a paper napkin. Then she examined the lipstick stains on the napkin.

"This is a pretty good drink," she said. "It has a gin base, right?"

"Gin and lemon juice and soda water."

"True, it's no great invention, but it tastes pretty good."

"I'm glad."

"So, then, what kind of work do I do? That's kind of tough. Even if I tell you the truth, you might not believe me."

"So I'll go first," Aomame said. "I'm an instructor at a sports club. I mostly teach martial arts. Also muscle stretching."

"Martial arts!" the woman exclaimed. "Like Bruce Lee kind of stuff?"

"Kind of."

"Are you good at it?"

"Okay."

The woman smiled and raised her glass as if in a toast. "So, in a pinch, we might be an unbeatable team. I might not look it, but I've been doing aikido for years. To tell you the truth, I'm a policewoman."

"A policewoman?!" Aomame's mouth dropped open, but no further words emerged from it.

"Tokyo Metropolitan Police Department. I don't look the part, do I?"

"Certainly not," Aomame said.

"It's true, though. Absolutely. My name is Ayumi."

"I'm Aomame."

"Aomame. Is that your real name?"

Aomame gave her a solemn nod. "A policewoman? You mean you wear a uniform and carry a gun and ride in a police car and patrol the streets?"

"That's what I'd *like* to be doing. It's what I joined the police force to do. But they won't let me," Ayumi said. She took a handful of pretzels from a nearby bowl and started munching them noisily. "I wear a ridiculous uniform, ride around in one of those mini patrol cars – basically, a motor scooter – and give parking tickets all day. They won't let me carry a pistol, of course. There's no need to fire warning shots at a local citizen who's parked his Toyota Corolla in front of a fire hydrant. I got great marks at shooting practice, but nobody gives a damn about that. Just because I'm a woman, they've got me going around with a piece of chalk on a stick, writing the time and license plate numbers on the asphalt day after day."

"Speaking of pistols, do you fire a Beretta semiautomatic?"

"Sure. They're all Berettas now. They're a little too heavy for me. Fully loaded, they probably weigh close to a kilogram."

"The body of a Beretta alone weighs 850 grams," Aomame said.

Ayumi looked at Aomame like a pawnbroker assessing a wristwatch. "How do you know something like that?" she asked.

"I've always had an interest in guns," Aomame said. "Of course, I've never actually fired one."

"Oh, really?" Ayumi seemed convinced. "I'm really into shooting pistols. True, a Beretta is heavy, but it has less of a recoil than the older guns, so even a small woman can handle one with enough practice. The top guys don't believe it, though. They're convinced that a woman can't handle a pistol. All the higher-ups in the department are male chauvinist fascists. I had super grades in nightstick techniques, too, at least as good as most of the men, but I got no recognition at all. The only thing I ever heard from them was filthy double entendres. 'Say, you really know how to grab that nightstick. Let me know any time you want some extra practice.' Stuff like that. Their brains are like a century and a half behind the times."

Ayumi took a pack of Virginia Slims from her shoulder bag, and with practiced movements eased a cigarette from the pack, put it between her lips, lit it with a slim gold lighter, and slowly exhaled the smoke toward the ceiling.

"Whatever gave you the idea of becoming a police officer?" Aomame asked.

"I never intended to," Ayumi replied. "But I didn't want to do ordinary office work, and I didn't have any professional skills. That really limited my options. So in my senior year of college I took the Metropolitan Police employment exam. A lot of my relatives were cops – my father, my brother, one of my uncles. The police are a kind of nepotistic society, so it's easier to get hired if you're related to a policeman."

"The police family."

"Exactly. Until I actually got into it, though, I had no idea how rife the place was with gender discrimination. Female officers are more or less second-class citizens in the police world. The only jobs they give you to do are handling traffic violations, shuffling papers at a desk, teaching safety education at elementary schools, or patting down female suspects:

boooring! Meanwhile, guys who clearly have less ability than me are sent out to one interesting crime scene after another. The higher-ups talk about 'equal opportunity for the sexes,' but it's all a front, it just doesn't work that way. It kills your desire to do a good job. You know what I mean?"

Aomame said she understood.

"It makes me so mad!"

"Don't you have a boyfriend or something?" Aomame asked.

Ayumi frowned. For a while, she glared at the slim cigarette between her fingers. "It's nearly impossible for a policewoman to have a boyfriend. You work irregular hours, so it's hard to coordinate times with anyone who works a normal business week. And even if things do start to work out, the minute an ordinary guy hears you're a cop, he just scoots away like a crab running from the surf. It's awful, don't you think?"

Aomame said that she did think it was awful.

"Which leaves a workplace romance as the only possibility – except there aren't any decent men there. They're all brain-dead jerks who can only tell dirty jokes. They're either born stupid or they think of nothing else but their advance-ment. And these are the guys responsible for the safety of soci-ety! Japan does not have a bright future."

"Somebody as cute as you should be popular with the men, I would think," Aomame said.

"Well, I'm not exactly *un*popular – as long as I don't reveal my profession. So in places like this I just tell them I work for an insurance company."

"Do you come here often?"

"Not 'often.' Once in a while," Ayumi said. After a moment's reflection, she said, as if revealing a secret, "Every now and then, I start craving sex. To put it bluntly, I want a man. You know, more or less periodically. So then I get all dolled up, put on fancy underwear, and come here. I find a suitable guy and we do it all night. That calms me down for a while. I've just got a healthy sex drive – I'm not a nympho or sex addict or anything, I'm okay once I work off the desire. It doesn't last. The next day I'm hard at work again, handing out parking tickets. How about you?"

Aomame picked up her Tom Collins glass and took a sip. "About the same, I guess."

"No boyfriend?"

"I made up my mind not to have a boyfriend. I don't want the bother."

"Having one man is a bother?"

"Pretty much."

"But sometimes I want to do it so bad I can't stand it," Ayumi said.

"That expression you used a minute ago, 'Work off the desire,' is more my speed."

"How about 'Have an opulent evening'?"

"That's not bad, either," Aomame said.

"In any case, it should be a one-night stand, without any follow-up."

Aomame nodded.

Elbow on the bar, Ayumi propped her chin on her hand and thought about this for a while. "We might have a lot in common," she said.

"Maybe so," Aomame agreed. *Except you're a female cop and I kill people. We're inside and outside the law. I bet that counts as one big difference.*

"Let's play it this way," Ayumi said. "We both work for the same casualty insurance company, but the name of the company is a secret. You're a couple years ahead of me. There was some unpleasantness in the office today, so we came here to drown our sorrows, and now we're feeling pretty good. How's that for our 'situation'?"

"Fine, except I don't know a thing about casualty insurance."

"Leave that to me. I'm good at making up stories."

"It's all yours, then," Aomame said.

"Now, it just so happens that two sort-of-middle-aged guys are sitting at the table right behind us, and they've been looking around with hungry eyes. Can you check 'em out without being obvious about it?"

Aomame glanced back casually as instructed. A table's width away from the bar stood a table with two middle-aged men. Both wore a suit and tie, and both looked like typical company employees out for a drink after a hard day's work. Their suits were not rumpled, and their ties were not in bad taste. Neither man appeared unclean, at least. One was probably just around forty, and the other not yet forty. The older one was thin with an oval face and a receding hairline. The younger one had the look of a former college rugby player who had recently started to put on weight from lack of exercise. His face still retained a certain youthfulness, but he was beginning to grow thick around the chin. They were chatting pleasantly over whiskey-and-waters, but their eyes were very definitely searching the room.

Ayumi began to analyze them. "I'd say they're not used to places like this. They're here looking for a good time, but they don't know how to approach girls. They're probably both married. They have a kind of guilty look about them."

Aomame was impressed with Ayumi's precise powers of observation. She must have taken all this in quite unnoticed while chatting away with Aomame. Maybe it was worth being a member of the police family.

"The one with the thinning hair is more to your taste, isn't he?" Ayumi asked. "I'll take the stocky one, okay?"

Aomame glanced backward again. The head shape of the thin-haired one was more or less acceptable – light-years away from Sean Connery, but worth a passing grade. She couldn't ask too much on a night like this, with nothing but Queen and ABBA to listen to all evening.

"That's fine with me," Aomame said, "but how are you going to get them to invite us to join them?"

"Not by waiting for the sun to come up, that's for sure! We crash their party, all smiles."

"Are you serious?"

"Of course I am! Just leave it to me – I'll go over and start up a conversation. You wait here." Ayumi took a healthy swig of her Tom Collins and rubbed her palms together. Then she slung her Gucci bag over her shoulder and put on a brilliant smile.

"Okay, time for a little nightstick practice."

CHAPTER 12

Tengo

THY KINGDOM COME

The Professor turned to Fuka-Eri and said, "Sorry to bother you, Eri, but could you make us some tea?"

The girl stood up and left the reception room. The door closed quietly behind her. The Professor waited, saying nothing, while Tengo, seated on the sofa, brought his breathing under control and regained a normal state of consciousness. The Professor removed his black-framed glasses and, after wiping them with a not-very-clean-looking handkerchief, put them back on. Beyond the window, some kind of small, black thing shot across the sky. A bird, possibly. Or it might have been someone's soul being blown to the far side of the world.

"I'm sorry," Tengo said. "I'm all right now. Just fine. Please go on with what you were saying."

The Professor nodded and began to speak. "There was nothing left of Akebono after that violent gun battle. That happened in 1981, three years ago – four years after Eri came here to live. But the Akebono problem has nothing to do with what I'm telling you now.

"Eri was ten years old when she started living with us. She just showed up on our doorstep one day without warning, utterly changed from the Eri I had known until then. True, she had never been very talkative, and she would not open up to strangers, but she had always been fond of me and talked freely with me even as a toddler. When she first showed up here, though, she was in no condition to talk to anybody. She seemed to have lost the power to speak at all. The most she could do was nod or shake her head when we asked her questions."

The Professor was speaking more clearly and rapidly now. Tengo sensed that he was trying to move his story ahead while Fuka-Eri was out of the room.

"We could see that Eri had had a terrible time finding her way to us up here in the mountains. She was carrying some cash and a sheet of paper with our address written on it, but she had grown up in those isolated surroundings and she couldn't really speak. Even so, she had managed, with the memo in hand, to make all the necessary transfers and find her way to our doorstep.

"We could see immediately that something awful had happened to her. Azami and the woman who helps me out here took care of her. After Eri had been with us a few days and calmed down somewhat, I called the Sakigake commune and asked to speak with Fukada, but I was told that he was 'unable to come to the phone.' I asked what the reason for that might be, but couldn't get them to tell me. So then I asked to speak to Mrs. Fukada and was told that she couldn't come to the phone either. I couldn't speak with either of them."

"Did you tell the person on the phone that you had Eri with you?"

The Professor shook his head. "No, I had a feeling I'd better keep quiet about that as long as I couldn't tell Fukada directly. Of course after that I tried to get in touch with him any number of times, using every means at my disposal, but nothing worked."

Tengo knit his brow. "You mean to say you haven't been able to contact her parents even once in seven years?"

The Professor nodded. "Not once. Seven years without a word."

"And her parents never once tried to find their daughter's whereabouts in seven years?"

"I know, it's absolutely baffling. The Fukadas loved and treasured Eri more than anything. And if Eri was going to go to someone for help, this was the only possible place. Both Fukada and his wife had cut their ties with their families, and Eri grew up without knowing either set of grandparents. We're the only people she could come to. Her parents had even told her this is where she should come if anything ever happened to them. In spite of that, I haven't heard a word. It's unthinkable."

Tengo asked, "Didn't you say before that Sakigake was an open commune?"

"I did indeed. Sakigake had functioned consistently as an open commune since its founding, but shortly before Eri escaped it had begun moving gradually toward a policy of confinement from the outside. I first became aware of this when I started hearing less frequently from Fukada. He had always been a faithful correspondent, sending me long letters about goings-on in the commune or his current thoughts and feelings. At some point they just stopped coming, and my letters were never answered. I tried calling, but they would never put him on the phone. And the few times they did, we had only the briefest, most limited conversations. Fukada's remarks were brusque, as if he was aware that someone was listening to us."

The Professor clasped his hands on his knees.

"I went out to Sakigake a few times myself. I needed to talk to Fukada about Eri, and since neither letters nor phone calls worked, the only thing left for me to do was to go directly to the place. But they wouldn't let me into the compound. Far from it – they chased me away from the gate. Nothing I said had any effect on them. By then they had built a high fence around the entire compound, and all outsiders were sent packing.

"There was no way to tell from the outside what was happening in the commune. If it were Akebono, I could see the need for secrecy. They were aiming for armed revolution, and they had a lot to hide. But Sakigake was peacefully running an organic farm, and they had always adopted a consistently friendly posture toward the outside world, which was why the locals liked them. But the place had since become an absolute fortress. The attitude and even the facial expressions of the people inside had totally changed. The local people were just as stymied as I was by the change in Sakigake. I was worried sick that something terrible had happened to Fukada and his wife, but all I could do was take Eri under my wing. Since then, seven years have gone by, with the situation as murky as ever."

"You mean, you don't even know if Fukada is alive?" Tengo asked.

"Not even that much," the Professor said with a nod. "I have no way of knowing. I'd rather not think the worst, but I haven't heard a word from Fukada in seven years. Under ordinary circumstances, that would be unthinkable. I can only imagine that something has happened to them." He lowered his voice. "Maybe they're being held in there against their will. Or possibly it's even worse than that."

" 'Even worse'?"

"I'm saying that not even the worst possibility can be excluded. Sakigake is no longer a peaceful farming community."

"Do you think the Sakigake group has started to move in a dangerous direction?"

"I do. The locals tell me that the number of people going in and out of there is much larger than it used to be. Cars are constantly coming and going, most of them with Tokyo license plates, and a lot of them are big luxury sedans you don't often see in the country. The number of people in the commune has also suddenly increased, it seems. So has the number of buildings and facilities, too, all fully equipped. They're increasingly aggressive about buying up the surrounding land at low prices, and bringing in tractors and excavation equipment and concrete mixers and such. They still do farming, which is probably their most important source of income. The Sakigake brand of vegetables is better known than ever, and the commune is shipping them directly to restaurants that capitalize on their use of natural ingredients. They also have contractual agreements with high-quality supermarkets. Their profits must have been rising all the while, but in parallel with that, they have apparently also been making steady progress in *something* other than farming. It's inconceivable that sales of produce are the only thing financing the large-scale expansion they have been undergoing. Whatever this other thing they're developing may be, their absolute secrecy has given the local people the impression that it must be something they can't reveal to the general public."

"Does this mean they've started some kind of political activity again?" Tengo asked.

"I doubt it," the Professor answered without hesitation. "Sakigake always moved on a separate axis from the political realm. It was for that very reason that at one point they had to let the Akebono group go."

"Yes, but after that, something happened inside Sakigake that made it necessary for Eri to escape."

"Something did happen," the Professor said. "Something of great significance. Something that made her leave her parents behind and run away by herself. But she has never said a word about it."

"Maybe she can't put it into words because it was too great a shock, or it somehow scarred her for life."

"No, she's never had that air about her, that she had experienced a great shock or that she was afraid of something or that she was uneasy being alone and separated from her parents.

She's just impassive. Still, she adapted to living here without a problem – almost too easily."

The Professor glanced toward the door and then returned his gaze to Tengo.

"Whatever happened to Eri, I didn't want to pry it out of her. I felt that what she needed was time. So I didn't question her. I pretended I wasn't concerned about her silence. She was always with Azami. After Azami came home from school, they would rush through dinner and shut themselves up in their room. What they would do in there, I have no idea. Maybe they found a way to converse when they were alone together. I just let them do as they pleased, without intruding. Aside from Eri's not speaking, her living with us presented no problem. She was a bright child, and she did what she was told. She and Azami were inseparable. Back then, though, Eri couldn't go to school. She couldn't speak a word. I couldn't very well send her to school that way."

"Was it just you and Azami before that?"

"My wife died about ten years ago," the Professor said, pausing for a moment. "She was killed in a car crash. Instantly. A rear-ender. The two of us were left alone. We have a distant relative, a woman, who lives nearby and helps us run the house. She also looks after both girls. Losing my wife like that was terrible, for Azami and for me. It happened so quickly, we had no way to prepare ourselves. So whatever brought Eri to us, we were glad to have her. Even if we couldn't hold a conversation with her, just having her in the house was strangely calming to both of us. Over these seven years, Eri has, though very slowly, regained the use of words. To other people, she may sound odd or abnormal, but we can see she has made remarkable progress."

"Does she go to school now?" Tengo asked.

"No, not really. She's officially registered, but that's all. Realistically speaking, it was impossible for her to keep up with school. I gave her individual instruction in my spare time, and so did students of mine who came to the house. What she got was very fragmentary, of course, nothing you could call a systematic education. She couldn't read books on her own, so we would read out loud to her whenever we could, and I would give her books on tape. That is about the sum total of the education she has received. But she's a startlingly bright girl. Once she has made up her mind to learn something, she can absorb it very quickly, deeply, and effectively. Her abilities on that score are amazing. But if something doesn't interest her, she won't look at it twice. The difference is huge."

The reception room door was still not opening. It was taking quite a bit of time for Eri to boil water and make tea.

Tengo said, "I gather Eri dictated the story *Air Chrysalis* to Azami. Is that correct?"

"As I said before, Eri and Azami would always shut themselves in their room at night, and I didn't know what they were doing. They had their secrets. It does seem, however, that at some point, Eri's storytelling became a major part of their communication. Azami would take notes or record Eri's story and then type it into the computer in my study. Eri has gradually been recovering her ability to experience emotion since then, I think. Her apathy was like a membrane that covered everything, but that has been fading. Some degree of expression has returned to her face, and she is more like the happy little girl we used to know."

"So she is on the road to recovery?"

"Well, not entirely. It's still very uneven. But in general, you're right. Her recovery may well have begun with her telling of her story."

Tengo thought about this for a time. Then he changed the subject.

"Did you talk to the police about the loss of contact with Mr. and Mrs. Fukada?"

"Yes, I went to the local police. I didn't tell them about Eri, but I did say that I had been unable to get in touch with my friends inside for a long time and I feared they were possibly being held against their will. At the time, they said there was nothing they could do. The Sakigake compound was private property, and without clear evidence that criminal activity had taken place there, they were unable to set foot inside. I kept after them, but they wouldn't listen to me. And then, after 1979, it became truly impossible to mount a criminal investigation inside Sakigake."

"Something happened in 1979?" Tengo asked.

"That was the year that Sakigake was granted official recognition as a religion."

Tengo was astounded. "A religion?!"

"I know. It's incredible. Sakigake was designated a 'Religious Juridical Person' under the Religious Corporation Law. The governor of Yamanashi Prefecture officially granted the title. Once it had the 'Religious Juridical Person' label, Sakigake became virtually immune to any criminal investigation by the police. Such a thing would be a violation of the freedom of religious belief guaranteed by the Constitution. The Prefectural Police couldn't touch them.

"I myself was astounded when I heard about this from the police. I couldn't believe it at first. Even after they showed it to me in writing and I saw it with my own eyes, I had trouble believing it could be true. Fukada was one of my oldest friends. I *knew* him – his character, his personality. As a cultural anthropologist, my ties with religion were by no means shallow. Unlike me, though, Fukada was a totally political being who approached everything with logic and reason. He had, if anything, a visceral disgust for religion. There was no way he would ever accept a 'Religious Juridical Person' designation even if he had strategic reasons for doing so."

"Obtaining such a designation couldn't be very easy, either, I would think."

"That's not necessarily the case," the Professor said. "True, you have to go through a lot of screenings and red tape, but if you pull the right political strings, you can clear such hurdles fairly easily. Drawing distinctions between religions and cults has always been a delicate business. There's no hard and fast definition. Interpretation is everything. And where there is room for interpretation, there is always room for political persuasion. Once you are certified to be a 'Religious Juridical Person,' you can get preferential tax treatment and special legal protections."

"In any case, Sakigake stopped being an ordinary agricultural commune and became a religious organization – a frighteningly closed-off religious organization," Tengo ventured.

"Yes, a 'new religion,' " the Professor said. "Or, to put it more bluntly, a cult."

"I don't get it," Tengo said. "Something major must have occurred for them to have undergone such a radical conversion."

The Professor stared at the backs of his hands, which had a heavy growth of kinky gray hair. "You're right about that, of course," he said. "I've been wondering about it myself for a very long time. I've come up with all sorts of possibilities, but no final answers. What *could* have caused it to happen? But they've adopted a policy of such total secrecy, it's impossible to find out what is going on inside. And not only that, Fukada, who used to be the leader of Sakigake, has never once publicly surfaced since they underwent their conversion."

"And meanwhile, the Akebono faction ceased to exist after their gun battle three years ago," Tengo said.

The Professor nodded. "Sakigake survived once they had cut themselves off from Akebono, and now they're steadily developing as a religion."

"Which means the gunfight was no great blow to Sakigake, I suppose."

"Far from it," the Professor said. "It was good advertising for them. They're smart. They know how to turn things to their best advantage. In any case, this all happened *after* Eri left Sakigake. As I said earlier, it has no direct connection with Eri."

Tengo sensed that the Professor was hoping to change the subject. He asked him, "Have you yourself read *Air Chrysalis*?"

"Of course," the Professor answered.

"What did you think of it?"

"It's a very interesting story," the Professor said. "Very evocative. Evocative of what, though, I'm not sure, to tell you the truth. I don't know what the blind goat is supposed to mean, or the Little People, or the air chrysalis itself."

"Do you think the story is hinting at something that Eri actually experienced or witnessed in Sakigake?"

"Maybe so, but I can't tell how much is real and how much is fantasy. It seems like a kind of myth, or it could be read as an ingenious allegory."

"Eri told me the Little People actually exist," Tengo said.

A thoughtful frown crossed the Professor's face when he heard this. He asked, "Do you think *Air Chrysalis* describes things that actually happened?"

Tengo shook his head. "All I'm trying to say is that every detail in the story is described very realistically, and that this is a great strength of the work as a piece of fiction."

"And by rewriting the story in your own words, with your own style, you are trying to put that *something* the story is hinting at into a clearer form? Is that it?"

"Yes, if all goes well."

"My specialty is cultural anthropology," the Professor said. "I gave up being a scholar some time ago, but I'm still permeated with the spirit of the discipline. One aim of my field is to relativize the images possessed by individuals, discover in these images the factors universal to all human beings, and feed these universal truths back to those same individuals. As a result of this process, people might be able to belong to something even as they maintain their autonomy. Do you see what I'm saying?"

"I think I do."

"Perhaps that same process is what is being demanded of you."

Tengo opened his hands on his knees. "Sounds difficult."

"But it's probably worth a try."

"I'm not even sure I'm qualified to do it."

The Professor looked at Tengo. There was a special gleam in his eye now.

"What I would like to know is what happened to Eri inside Sakigake. I'd also like to know the fate of Fukada and his wife. I've done my best over the past seven years to shed light on these questions, but I haven't managed to grasp a single clue. I always come up against a thick, solid wall standing in my way. The key to unlock the mystery may be hidden in *Air Chrysalis*. As long as there is such a possibility, however slim, I want to pursue it. I have no idea whether you are qualified to do the job, but I do know that you think highly of the story and are deeply involved in it. Perhaps that is qualification enough."

"There is something I have to ask you, though, and I need to receive a clear yes or no from you," Tengo said. "It's what I came to see you about today. Do I have your permission to rewrite *Air Chrysalis*?"

The Professor nodded. Then he said, "I myself am looking forward to reading your rewrite, and I know that Eri seems to have a great deal of faith in you. She doesn't have anyone else she can look to like that – aside from Azami and me, of course. So you ought to give it a try. We'll put the work in your hands. In a word, the answer is yes."

When the Professor stopped speaking, a heavy silence

settled over the room like a finalized destiny. At precisely that moment, Fuka-Eri came in with the tea.

On the way back to the city, Tengo was alone. Fuka-Eri went out to walk the dog. The Professor called a cab that took Tengo to Futamatao Station in time for the next train. Tengo transferred to the Chuo Line at Tachikawa.

When the train reached Mitaka, a mother and her little girl got on and sat across from Tengo. Both were neatly dressed. Their clothing was by no means expensive or new, but all items were clean and well cared for, the whites exceptionally white, and everything nicely ironed. The girl was probably a second or third grader, with large eyes and good features. The mother was quite thin. She wore her hair tied in a bun in back, had black-framed glasses, and carried a faded bag of thick cloth. The bag seemed to be crammed full of something. The mother's features were also nicely symmetrical, but a hint of nervous exhaustion showed at her eyes' outer edges, making her look older than she probably was. It was only mid-April, but she carried a parasol, on which the cloth was wrapped so tightly around the pole that it looked like a dried-out club.

The two sat beside each other in unbroken silence. The mother looked as though she might be devising a plan. The girl seemed at a loss for something to do. She looked at her shoes, at the floor, at ads hanging from the train ceiling, and now and then she stole a glance at Tengo sitting opposite her. His large build and his cauliflower ears seemed to have aroused her interest. Little children often looked at Tengo that way, as if he were some kind of rare but harmless animal. The girl kept her body and head very still, allowing just her eyes to dart around from object to object.

The mother and child left the train at Ogikubo. As the train was slowing to a stop, the mother rose quickly to her feet, parasol in her left hand and cloth bag in her right. She said nothing to the girl, who also quickly left her seat and followed her out of the car. As she was standing, though, the girl took one last look at Tengo. In her eyes, he saw a strange light, a kind of appeal or plea directed at him. It was only a faint, momentary gleam, but Tengo was able to catch it. She was sending out some kind of signal, he felt. Even if this were true, of course, and it was a signal meant for him, there was nothing he could do. He had no knowledge of her situation, nor could he become involved with her. The girl left the train with her mother at Ogikubo Station, and Tengo, still in his seat, continued on toward the next station. Three middle school students now sat where the girl had been sitting. They started jabbering about the practice test they had just taken, but still there lingered in their place the after-image of the silent girl.

The girl's eyes reminded Tengo of another girl, one who had been in Tengo's third- and fourth-grade classes. She, too, had looked at him – stared hard at him – with eyes like this one . . .

The girl's parents had belonged to a religious organization called the Society of Witnesses. A Christian sect, the Witnesses preached the coming of the end of the world. They were fervent proselytizers and lived their lives by the Bible. They would not condone the transfusion of blood, for example. This greatly limited their chances of surviving serious injury in a traffic accident. Undergoing major surgery was virtually impossible for them. On the other hand, when the end of the world came, they could survive as God's chosen people and live a thousand years in a world of ultimate happiness.

Like the little girl on the train, the one whose parents were Witnesses also had big, beautiful eyes. Impressive eyes. Nice features. But her face always seemed to be covered by a kind of opaque membrane. It was meant to expunge her presence. She never spoke to people unless it was absolutely necessary. Her face never showed emotion. She kept her thin lips compressed in a perfectly straight line.

Tengo first took an interest in the girl when he saw her out on weekends with her mother, doing missionary work. Children in Witness families were expected to begin accompanying their parents in missionary activity as soon as they were old enough to walk. From the time she was three, the girl walked from door to door, mostly with her mother, handing out pamphlets titled *Before the Flood* and expounding on the Witnesses' doctrines. The mother would explain in basic language the many signs of coming destruction that were apparent in the present world. She referred to God as "the Lord." At most homes, of course, they would have the door slammed in their faces. This was because their doctrines were simply too narrow-minded, too one-sided, too divorced from reality – or at least from what most people thought of as reality. Once in a great while, however, they would find someone who was willing to listen to them. There were people in the world who wanted someone to talk to – about anything, no matter what. Among these few individuals, there would occasionally be the exceedingly rare person who would actually attend one of their meetings. They would go from house to house, ringing doorbells, in search of that one person in a thousand. They had been entrusted with the sacred duty to guide the world toward an awakening, however minimal, through their continued efforts. The more taxing their duty, the higher the thresholds, and the more radiant was the bliss that would be granted them.

Whenever Tengo saw her, the girl was making the rounds, proselytizing with her mother. In one hand, the mother held a cloth bag stuffed with copies of *Before the Flood,* and the other hand usually held a parasol. The girl followed a few steps behind, lips compressed in a straight line as always, face expressionless. Tengo passed the girl on the street several times this way while he was making the rounds with his father, collecting NHK subscription fees. He would recognize her, and she would recognize him. Whenever this happened, he thought he could see some kind of secret gleam in her eye. Of course, they never spoke. No greeting passed between them. Tengo's father was too busy trying to increase his collections, and the girl's mother was too busy preaching the coming end of the world. The boy and girl simply rushed past each other on the Sunday street in their parents' wake, exchanging momentary glances.

All the children in their class knew that the girl was a Witness believer. "For religious reasons," she never participated in the school's Christmas events or in school outings or study tours when these involved visits to Shinto shrines or Buddhist temples. Nor did she participate in athletic meets or the singing of the school song or the national anthem. Such behavior, which could only be viewed as extreme, served increasingly to isolate the girl from her classmates. The girl was also required to recite – in a loud, clear voice, so that the other children could hear every word – a special prayer before she ate her school lunches. Not surprisingly, her classmates found this utterly creepy. She could not have been all that eager to perform in front of them. But it had been instilled in her that prayers must be recited before meals, and you were not allowed to omit them simply because no other believers were there to observe you. The Lord saw everything – every little thing – from on high.

O Lord in Heaven, may Thy name be praised in utmost purity for ever and ever, and may Thy kingdom come to us. Please forgive our many sins, and bestow Thy blessings upon our humble pathways. Amen.

How strange a thing is memory! Tengo could recall every word of her prayer even though he hadn't heard it for twenty years. **May Thy kingdom come to us.** "What kind of kingdom could that be?" Tengo, as an elementary school boy, had wondered each time he heard the girl's prayer. Did that kingdom have NHK? No, probably not. If there was no NHK, there would be no fee collections, of course. If that was true, maybe the sooner the kingdom came, the better.

Tengo had never said a word to the girl. They were in the same class, but there had been no opportunity for them to talk directly to each other. She always kept to herself, and would not talk to anyone unless she had to. The atmosphere of the classroom provided no opportunity for him to go over and talk to her. In his heart, though, Tengo sympathized with her. On Sundays, children should be allowed to play with other children to their heart's content, not made to go around threatening people until they paid their fees or frightening people with warnings about the impending end of the world. Such work – to the extent that it is necessary at all – should be done by adults.

Tengo did once extend a helping hand to the girl in the wake of a minor incident. It happened in the autumn when they were in the fourth grade. One of the other pupils reprimanded the girl when they were seated at the same table performing an experiment in science. Tengo could not recall exactly what her mistake had been, but as a result a boy made fun of her for "handing out stupid pamphlets door to door." He also called her "Lord." This was a rather unusual development – which is to say that, instead of bullying or teasing her, the other children usually just ignored her, treating her as if she didn't exist. When it came to a joint activity such as a science experiment, however, there was no way for them to exclude her. On this occasion, the boy's words contained a good deal of venom. Tengo was in the group at the next table, but he found it impossible to pretend that he had not heard anything. Exactly why, he could not be sure, but he could not leave it alone.

Tengo went to the other table and told the girl she should join his group. He did this almost reflexively, without deep thought or hesitation. He then gave the girl a detailed explanation of the experiment. She paid close attention to his words, understood them, and corrected her mistake. This was the second year that she and Tengo were in the same class, but it was the first time he ever spoke to her (and the last). Tengo had excellent grades, and he was a big, strong boy, whom the others treated with respect, so no one teased him for having come to the girl's defense – at least not then and there. But later his standing in the class seemed to fall a notch, as though he had caught some of her impurity.

Tengo never let that bother him. He knew that she was just an ordinary girl.

But they never spoke again after that. There was no need – or opportunity – to do so. Whenever their eyes happened to meet, however, a hint of tension would show on her face. He could sense it. Perhaps, he thought, she was bothered by what he had done for her during the science experiment. Maybe she was angry at him and wished that he had just left her alone. He had difficulty judging what she felt about the matter. He was still a child, after all, and could not yet read subtle psychological shifts from a person's expression.

Then, one day, the girl took Tengo's hand. It happened on a sunny afternoon in early December. Beyond the classroom window, he could see the clear sky and a straight, white cloud. Class had been dismissed, and the two of them happened to be the last to leave after the children had finished cleaning the room. No one else was there. She strode quickly across the room, heading straight for Tengo, as if she had just made up her mind about something. She stood next to him and, without the slightest hesitation, grabbed his hand and looked up at him. (He was ten centimeters taller, so she had to look up.) Taken by surprise, Tengo looked back at her. Their eyes met. In hers, he could see a transparent depth that he had never seen before. She went on holding his hand for a very long time, saying nothing, but never once relaxing her powerful grip. Then, without warning, she dropped his hand and dashed out of the classroom, skirts flying.

Tengo had no idea what had just happened to him. He went on standing there, at a loss for words. His first thought was how glad he felt that they had not been seen by anyone. Who knew what kind of commotion it could have caused? He looked around, relieved at first, but then he felt deeply shaken.

The mother and daughter who sat across from him between Mitaka and Ogikubo could well have been Witness believers themselves. They might even have been headed for their usual Sunday missionary activity. But no, they were more likely just a normal mother and daughter on their way to a lesson the girl was taking. The cloth sack might have been holding books of piano music or a calligraphy set. *I'm just being hypersensitive to lots of things,* Tengo thought. He closed his eyes and released a long, slow breath. Time flows in strange ways on Sundays, and sights become mysteriously distorted.

At home, Tengo fixed himself a simple dinner. Come to think of it, he hadn't had lunch. When he was through eating, he thought about calling Komatsu, who would be wanting to hear the results of his meeting. But this was Sunday; Komatsu wouldn't be at the office. Tengo didn't know his home phone number. *Oh well, if he wants to know how it went, he can call me.*

The phone rang as the hands of the clock passed ten and Tengo was thinking of going to bed. He assumed it was Komatsu, but the voice on the phone turned out to be that of his married older girlfriend. "I won't be able to get away very long, but do you mind if I come over for a quick visit the day after tomorrow in the afternoon?" she asked.

He heard some notes on a piano in the background. Her husband must not be home yet, he guessed. "Fine," he said. If she came over, his rewriting of *Air Chrysalis* would be interrupted for a time, but when he heard her voice, Tengo realized how much he desired her. After hanging up he went to the kitchen, poured himself a glass of Wild Turkey, and drank it straight, standing by the sink. Then he went to bed, read a few pages of a book, and fell asleep.

This brought Tengo's long, strange Sunday to an end.

CHAPTER 13

Aomame

A BORN VICTIM

When she woke, she realized what a serious hangover she was going to have. Aomame *never* had hangovers. No matter how much she drank, the next morning her head would be clear and she could go straight into her next activity. This was a point of pride for her. But today was different. She felt a dull throbbing in her temples and she saw everything through a thin haze. It felt as if she had an iron ring tightening around her skull. The hands of the clock had passed ten, and the late-morning light jabbed deep into her eyeballs. A motorcycle tearing down the street out front filled the room with the groaning of a torture machine.

She was naked in her own bed, but she had absolutely no idea how she had managed to make it back. Most of the clothes she had been wearing the night before were scattered all over the floor. She must have torn them off her body. Her shoulder bag was on the desk. Stepping over the scattered clothes, she went to the kitchen and drank one glass of water after another from the tap. Going from there to the bathroom, she washed her face with cold water and looked at her naked body in the big mirror. Close inspection revealed no bruises. She breathed a sigh of relief. Still, her lower body retained a trace of that special feeling that was always there the morning after an intense night of sex – the sweet lassitude that comes from having your insides powerfully churned. She seemed to notice, too, an unfamiliar sensation between her buttocks. *My god,* Aomame thought, pressing her fingers against her temples. *They did it there, too? Damn, I don't remember a thing.*

With her brain still clouded and her hand against the wall, she took a hot shower, scrubbing herself all over with soap and water in hopes of expunging the memory – or the nameless something close to a memory – of last night. She washed her genitals and anus with special care. She also washed her hair. Next she brushed her teeth to rid her mouth of its sticky taste, cringing all the while from the mint flavor of the toothpaste. Finally she picked up last night's underthings and stockings from the bedroom floor and, averting her gaze, threw them in the laundry basket.

She examined the contents of the shoulder bag on the table. The wallet was right where it belonged, as were her credit and ATM cards. Most of her money was in there, too. The only cash she had spent last night, apparently, was for the return taxi fare, and the only things missing from the bag were some of her condoms – four, to be exact. Why four? The wallet contained a folded sheet of memo paper with a Tokyo telephone number. She had absolutely no memory of whose phone number it could be.

She stretched out in bed again and tried to remember what she could about last night. Ayumi went over to the men's table, arranged everything in her charming way, the four had drinks and the mood was good. The rest unfolded in the usual manner. They took two rooms in a nearby business hotel. As planned, Aomame had sex with the thin-haired one, and Ayumi took the big, young one. The sex wasn't bad. Aomame and her man took a bath together and then engaged in a long, deliberate session of oral sex. She made sure he wore a condom before penetration took place.

An hour later the phone rang, and Ayumi asked if it was all right for the two of them to come to the room so they could have another little drink together. Aomame agreed, and a few minutes later Ayumi and her man came in. They ordered a bottle of whiskey and some ice and drank that as a foursome.

What happened after that, Aomame could not clearly recall. She was drunk almost as soon as all four were together again, it seemed. The choice of drink might have done it; Aomame almost never drank whiskey. Or she might have let herself get careless, having a female companion nearby instead of being alone with a man. She vaguely remembered that they changed partners. *I was in bed with the young one, and Ayumi did it with the thin-haired one on the sofa. I'm pretty sure that was it. And after that . . . everything after that is in a deep fog. I can't remember a thing. Oh well, maybe it's better that way. Let me just forget the whole thing. I had some wild sex, that's all. I'll probably never see those guys again.*

But did the second guy wear a condom? That was the one thing that worried Aomame. *I wouldn't want to get pregnant or catch something from such a stupid mistake. It's probably okay, though. I wouldn't slip up on that, even if I was drunk out of my mind.*

Hmm, did I have some work scheduled today? No work. It's Saturday. No work on Saturday. Oh, wait. I do have one thing. At three o'clock I'm supposed to go to the Willow House and do muscle stretching with the dowager. She had to see the doctor for some kind of test yesterday. Tamaru called a few days ago to see if I could switch our appointment to today. I totally forgot. But I've got four and a half hours left until three o'clock. My headache should be gone by then, and my brain will be a lot clearer.

She made herself some hot coffee and forced a few cups into her stomach. Then she spent the rest of the morning in bed, with nothing but a bathrobe on, staring at the ceiling. That was the most she could get herself to do – stare at the ceiling.

Not that the ceiling had anything of interest about it. But she couldn't complain. Ceilings weren't put on rooms to amuse people. The clock advanced to noon, but she still had no appetite. Motorcycle and car engines still echoed in her head. This was her first authentic hangover.

All of that sex did seem to have done her body a lot of good, though. Having a man hold her and gaze at her naked body and caress her and lick her and bite her and penetrate her and give her orgasms had helped release the tension of the spring wound up inside her. True, the hangover felt terrible, but that feeling of release more than made up for it.

But how long am I going to keep this up? Aomame wondered. *How long* can *I keep it up? I'll be thirty soon, and before long forty will come into view.*

She decided not to think about this anymore. *I'll get to it later, when I have more time. Not that I'm faced with any deadlines at the moment. It's just that, to think seriously about such matters, I'm –*

At that point the phone rang. It seemed to roar in Aomame's ears, like a super-express train in a tunnel. She staggered from the bed and lifted the receiver. The hands on the large wall clock were pointing to twelve thirty.

A husky female voice spoke her name. It was Ayumi.

"Yes, it's me," she answered.

"Are you okay? You sound like you've just been run over by a bus."

"That's maybe not far off."

"Hangover?"

"Yeah, a bad one," Aomame said. "How did you know my home phone?"

"You don't remember? You wrote it down for me. Mine should be in your wallet. We were talking about getting together soon."

"Oh, yeah? I don't remember a thing."

"I thought you might not. I was worried about you. That's why I'm calling," Ayumi said. "I wanted to make sure you got home okay. I *did* manage to get you into a cab at Roppongi Crossing and tell the driver your address, though."

Aomame sighed. "I don't remember, but I guess I made it here. I woke up in my own bed."

"Well, that's good."

"What are you doing now?"

"I'm working, what I'm supposed to be doing," Ayumi said. "I've been riding around in a mini patrol and writing parking tickets since ten o'clock. I'm taking a break right now."

"Very impressive," Aomame said. She meant it.

"I'm a little sleep deprived, of course. Last night was fun, though! Best time I ever had, thanks to you."

Aomame pressed her fingertips against her temples. "To tell you the truth, I don't remember much of the second half. After you guys came to our room, I mean."

"What a waste!" Ayumi said in all seriousness. "It was amazing! The four of us did *everything*. You wouldn't believe it. It was like a porno movie. You and I played lesbians. And then – "

Aomame rushed to cut her off. "Never mind all that. I just want to know if I was using condoms. That's what worries me. I can't remember."

"Of course you were. I'm very strict about that. I made absolutely sure, so don't worry. I mean, when I'm not writing tickets I go around to high schools in the ward, holding assemblies for the girls and teaching them, like, the right way to put on condoms. I give very detailed instructions."

"The right way to put on condoms?" Aomame was shocked. "What is a policewoman doing teaching stuff like that to high school kids?"

"Well, the original idea was for me to give information to prevent sex crimes, like the danger of date rape or what to do about gropers on the subway, but I figure as long as I'm at it, I can add my own personal message about condoms. A certain amount of student sex is unavoidable, so I tell them to make sure they avoid pregnancy and venereal disease. I can't say it quite that directly, of course, with their teachers in the room. Anyhow, it's like professional instinct with me. No matter how much I've been drinking, I never forget. So you don't have to worry. You're clean. 'No condom, no penetration.' That's my motto."

"Thank you," Aomame said. "That's a huge relief."

"Hey, want to hear about all the stuff we did?"

"Maybe later," Aomame said, expelling the congealed air that had been sitting in her lungs. "I'll let you tell me the juicy details some other time. If you did it now, my head would split in two."

"Okay, I get it. Next time I see you, then," Ayumi said brightly. "You know, ever since I woke up I've been thinking what a great team we can make. Mind if I call you again? When I get in the mood for another night like last night, I mean."

"Sure," Aomame said.

"Oh, great."

"Thanks for the call."

"Take care of yourself," Ayumi said, and hung up.

Her brain was much clearer by two o'clock, thanks to the black coffee and a nap. Her headache was gone, too, thankfully. All that was left of her hangover was a slight heavy feeling in her muscles. She left the apartment carrying her gym bag – without the special ice pick, of course, just a change of clothes and a towel. Tamaru met her at the front door as usual.

He showed her to a long, narrow sunroom. A large open window faced the garden, but it was covered by a lace curtain for privacy. A row of potted plants stood on the windowsill. Tranquil baroque music played from a small ceiling speaker

– a sonata for recorder and harpsichord. In the middle of the room stood a massage table. The dowager was already lying facedown on top of it, wearing a white robe.

When Tamaru left the room, Aomame changed into looser clothing. The dowager turned her head to watch Aomame change from her perch on the massage table. Aomame was not concerned about being seen naked by a member of the same sex. It was an everyday occurrence for team athletes, and the dowager herself was nearly naked during a massage, which made checking the condition of her muscles that much easier. Aomame took off her cotton pants and blouse, putting on a matching jersey top and bottom. She folded her street clothing and set them down in a corner.

"You're so firm and well toned," the dowager said. Sitting up, she took off her robe, leaving only thin silk on top and bottom.

"Thank you," Aomame said.

"I used to be built like you."

"I can tell that," Aomame said. Even now, in her seventies, the dowager retained physical traces of youth. Her body shape had not disintegrated, and even her breasts had a degree of firmness. Moderate eating and daily exercise had preserved her natural beauty. Aomame guessed that this had been supplemented with a touch of plastic surgery – some periodic wrinkle removal, and some lifting around the eyes and mouth.

"Your body is still quite lovely," Aomame said.

The dowager's lips curled slightly. "Thank you, but it's nothing like it used to be."

Aomame did not reply to this.

"I gained great pleasure from my body back then. I *gave* great pleasure with it, too, if you know what I mean."

"I do," Aomame said.

"And are you enjoying yours?"

"Now and then," Aomame said.

"Now and then may not be enough," the dowager said, lying facedown again. "You have to enjoy it while you're still young. Enjoy it to the fullest. You can use the memories of what you did to warm your body after you get old and can't do it anymore."

Aomame recalled the night before. Her anus still retained a slight feeling of having been penetrated. Would memories of this actually warm her body in old age?

Aomame placed her hands on the dowager's body and concentrated on stretching one set of muscles after another. Now the earlier remaining dullness in her own body was gone. Once she had changed her clothes and touched the dowager's flesh, her nerves had sharpened into clarity.

Aomame's fingers traced the dowager's muscles as though following roads on a map. She remembered in detail the degree of each muscle's tension and stiffness and resistance the way a pianist memorizes a long score. In matters concerning the body, Aomame possessed minute powers of memory. And if she should forget, her fingers remembered. If a muscle felt the slightest bit different than usual, she would stimulate it from various angles using varying degrees of strength, checking to see what kind of response she got from it, whether pain or pleasure or numbness. She would not simply loosen the knots in a pulled muscle but direct the dowager to move it using her own strength. Of course there were parts of the body that could not be relieved merely by her own strength, and for those parts, Aomame concentrated on stretching. What muscles most appreciated and welcomed, however, was daily self-help efforts.

"Does this hurt?" Aomame asked. The dowager's groin muscles were far stiffer than usual – nastily so. Placing her hand in the hollow of the dowager's pelvis, Aomame very slightly bent her thigh at a special angle.

"A *lot*," the dowager said, grimacing.

"Good," Aomame said. "It's good that you feel pain. If it

stopped hurting, you'd have something seriously wrong with you. This is going to hurt a little more. Can you stand it?"

"Yes, of course," the dowager said. There was no need to ask her each time. She could tolerate a great deal of pain. Most of the time, she bore it in silence. She might grimace but she would never cry out. Aomame had often made big, strong men cry out in pain from her massages. She had to admire the dowager's strength of will.

Setting her right elbow against the dowager like a fulcrum, Aomame bent her thigh still farther. The joint moved with a dull snap. The dowager gasped, but she made no sound with her voice.

"That should do it for you," Aomame said. "You'll feel a lot better."

The dowager released a great sigh. Sweat glistened on her forehead. "Thank you," she murmured.

Aomame spent a full hour unknotting muscles all over the dowager's body, stimulating them, stretching them, and loosening joints. The process involved a good deal of pain, but without such pain nothing would be resolved. Both Aomame and the dowager knew this perfectly well, and so they spent the hour almost wordlessly. The recorder sonata ended at some point, and the CD player fell silent. All that could be heard was the calls of birds in the garden.

"My whole body feels so light now!" the dowager said after some time had passed. She was slumped facedown on the massage table, the large towel spread beneath her dark with sweat.

"I'm glad," Aomame said.

"It's such a help to have you with me! I'd hate for you to leave."

"Don't worry, I have no plans to go anywhere just yet."

The dowager seemed to hesitate for a moment, and only after a brief silence she asked, "I don't mean to get too personal, but do you have someone you're in love with?"

"I do," Aomame said.

"I'm glad to hear that."

"Unfortunately, though, he's not in love with me."

"This may be an odd thing to ask, but why do you think he doesn't love you? Objectively speaking, I think you are a fascinating young woman."

"He doesn't even know I exist."

The dowager took a few minutes to think about what Aomame had said.

"Don't you have any desire to convey to him the fact that you *do* exist?"

"Not at this point," Aomame said.

"Is there something standing in the way – something preventing you from taking the initiative?"

"There are a few things, most of which have to do with my own feelings."

The dowager looked at Aomame with apparent admiration. "I've met lots of odd people in my lifetime, but you may be one of the oddest."

Aomame relaxed the muscles around her mouth somewhat. "There's nothing odd about me. I'm just honest about my own feelings."

"You mean that once you've decided on a rule, you follow it?"

"That's it."

"So you're a little stubborn, and you tend to be short-tempered."

"That may be true."

"But last night you went kind of wild."

Aomame blushed. "How do you know that?"

"Looking at your skin. And I can smell it. Your body still has traces of it. Getting old teaches you a lot."

Aomame frowned momentarily. "I need that kind of thing. Now and then. I know it's nothing to brag about."

The dowager reached out and gently placed her hand on Aomame's.

"Of course you need that kind of thing once in a while. Don't worry, I'm not blaming you. It's just that I feel you ought to have a more *ordinary* kind of happiness – marry someone you love, happy ending."

"I wouldn't mind that myself. But it won't be so easy."

"Why not?"

Aomame did not answer this. She had no simple explanation.

"If you ever feel like talking to someone about these personal matters, please talk to me," the dowager said, withdrawing her hand from Aomame's and toweling the sweat from her face. "About anything at all. I might have something I can do for you."

"Thanks very much," Aomame said.

"Some things can't be solved just by going wild every now and then."

"You're absolutely right."

"You are not doing anything that will destroy you?" the dowager said. "Nothing at all? You're sure of that, are you?"

"Yes, I'm sure," Aomame said. *She's right. I'm not doing anything that is going to destroy me. Still, there is something quiet left behind. Like sediment in a bottle of wine.*

Even now, Aomame still recalled the events surrounding the death of Tamaki Otsuka. It tore her apart to think that she could no longer see and talk to Tamaki. Tamaki was the first real friend she ever had. They could tell each other everything. Aomame had had no one like that before Tamaki, and no one since. Nor could anyone take her place. Had she never met Tamaki, Aomame would have led a far more miserable and gloomy life.

She and Tamaki were the same age. They had been teammates in the softball club of their public high school. From middle school into high school, Aomame had been passionately devoted to the game of softball. She had joined reluctantly at first when begged to help fill out a shorthanded team, and her early efforts were halfhearted at best, but eventually softball became her reason for living. She clung to the game the way a person clings to a post when a storm threatens to blow him away. And though she had never realized it before, Aomame was a born athlete. She became a central member of both her middle and high school teams and helped them breeze through one tournament after another. This gave her something very close to self-confidence (but only close: it was not, strictly speaking, self-confidence). Her greatest joy in life was knowing that her importance to the team was by no means small and that, as narrow as that world might be, she had been granted a definite *place* in it. Someone *needed* her.

Aomame was pitcher and cleanup batter – literally *the* central player of the team, both on offense and defense. Tamaki Otsuka played second base, the linchpin of the team, and she also served as captain. Tamaki was small but had great reflexes and knew how to use her brain. She could read all the complications of a situation instantaneously. With each pitch, she knew toward which side to incline her center of gravity, and as soon as the batter connected with the ball, she could gauge the direction of the hit and move to cover the proper position. Not a lot of infielders could do that. Her powers of judgment had saved the team from many a tight spot. She was not a distance hitter like Aomame, but her batting was sharp and precise, and she was quick on her feet. She was also an outstanding leader. She brought the team together as a unit, planned strategy, gave everyone valuable advice, and fired them up on the field. Her coaching was tough, but she won the other players' confidence, as a result of which the team grew stronger day by day. They went as far as the championship game in the Tokyo regional playoffs and even made it to the national interscholastic tournament. Both Aomame and Tamaki were chosen to be on the Kanto area all-star team.

Aomame and Tamaki recognized each other's talents and – without either taking the initiative – naturally drew close until each had become the other's best friend. They spent long hours together on team trips to away games. They told each other about their backgrounds, concealing nothing. When she was a fifth grader, Aomame had made up her mind to break with her parents and had gone to live with an uncle on her mother's side. The uncle's family understood her situation and welcomed her warmly as a member of the household, but it was, ultimately, not her family. She felt lonely and hungry for love. Unsure where she was to find a purpose or meaning to her life, she passed one formless day after another. Tamaki came from a wealthy household of some social standing, but her parents' terrible relationship had turned the home into a wasteland. Her father almost never came home, and her mother often fell into states of mental confusion. She would suffer from terrible headaches, and was unable to leave her bed sometimes for days at a time. Tamaki and her younger brother were all but ignored. They often ate at neighborhood restaurants or fast-food places or made do with ready-made boxed lunches. Each girl, then, had her reasons for becoming obsessed with softball.

Given all their problems, the two lonely girls had a mountain of things to tell each other. When they took a trip together one summer, they touched each other's naked bodies in the hotel bed. It happened just that one time, spontaneously, and neither of them ever talked about it. But because it had happened, their relationship grew all the deeper and all the more conspiratorial.

Aomame kept playing softball after her graduation from high school when she went on to a private college of physical education. Having won a national reputation as an outstanding softball player, she was recruited and given a special scholarship. In college, too, she was a key member of the team. While devoting much energy to softball, she was also interested in sports medicine and started studying it in earnest, along with martial arts.

Tamaki entered the law program in a first-rank private university. She stopped playing softball upon graduating from high school. For an outstanding student like Tamaki, softball was merely a phase. She intended to take the bar exam and become a lawyer. Though their paths in life diverged, Aomame and Tamaki remained best friends. Aomame lived in a college dormitory with free room and board while Tamaki continued commuting from her family home. The place was as much of an emotional wasteland as ever, but at least it gave her economic freedom. The two would meet once a week to share a meal and catch up. They never ran out of things to talk about.

Tamaki lost her virginity in the autumn of her first year in college. The man was one year older than Tamaki, a fellow member of the college tennis club. He invited her to his room after a club party, and there he forced her to have sex with him. Tamaki had liked this man, which was why she had accepted the invitation to his room, but the violence with which he forced her into having sex and his narcissistic, self-centered manner came as a terrible shock. She quit the tennis club and went into a period of depression. The experience left her with a profound feeling of powerlessness. Her appetite disappeared, and she lost fifteen pounds. All she had wanted from the man was a degree of understanding and sympathy. If he had shown a trace of it and had taken the time to prepare her, the mere physical giving of herself to him would have been no great problem. She found it impossible to understand his actions. Why did he have to become so violent? It had been absolutely unnecessary!

Aomame comforted Tamaki and advised her to find a way

to punish him, but Tamaki could not agree. Her own carelessness had been a part of it, she said, and it was too late now to
lodge any complaints. "I bear some responsibility for going to
his room alone," she said. "All I can do now is forget about it."
But it was painfully clear to Aomame how deeply her friend
had been wounded by the incident. This was not about the
mere loss of her virginity but rather the sanctity of an individual human being's soul. No one had the right to invade
such sacred precincts with muddy feet. And once it happened,
that sense of powerlessness could only keep gnawing away at
a person.

Aomame decided to take it upon herself to punish the man.
She got his address from Tamaki and went to his apartment
carrying a softball bat in a plastic blueprint tube. Tamaki was
away for the day in Kanazawa, attending a relative's memorial service or some such thing, which was a perfect alibi.
Aomame checked to be sure the man was not at home. She
used a screwdriver and hammer to break the lock on his
door. Then she wrapped a towel around the bat several times
to dampen the noise and proceeded to smash everything in
the apartment that was smashable – the television, the lamps,
the clocks, the records, the toaster, the vases: she left nothing whole. She cut the telephone cord with scissors, cracked
the spines of all the books and scattered their pages, spread
the entire contents of a toothpaste tube and shaving cream
canister on the rug, poured Worcestershire sauce on the bed,
took notebooks from a drawer and ripped them to pieces,
broke every pen and pencil in two, shattered every lightbulb,
slashed all the curtains and cushions with a kitchen knife,
took scissors to every shirt in the dresser, poured a bottle of
ketchup into the underwear and sock drawers, pulled out the
refrigerator fuse and threw it out a window, ripped the flapper
out of the toilet tank and tore it apart, and crushed the bathtub's showerhead. The destruction was utterly deliberate and

complete. The room looked very much like the recent news photos she had seen of the streets of Beirut after the shelling.

Tamaki was an intelligent girl (with grades in school that Aomame could never hope to match), and in softball she had always been on her toes. Whenever Aomame got herself into a difficult situation on the mound, Tamaki would run over to her, offer her a few quick words of advice, flash her a smile, pat her on the butt with her glove, and go back to her position in the infield. Her view of things was broad, her heart was warm, and she had a good sense of humor. She put a great deal of effort into her schoolwork and could speak with real eloquence. Had she continued with her studies, she would undoubtedly have made a fine lawyer.

In the presence of men, however, Tamaki's powers of judgment fell totally to pieces. Tamaki liked handsome men. She was a sucker for good looks. As Aomame saw it, this tendency of her friend's ranked as a sickness. Tamaki could meet men of marvelous character or with superior talents who were eager to woo her, but if their looks did not meet her standards, she was utterly unmoved. For some reason, the ones who aroused her interest were always sweet-faced men with nothing inside. And when it came to men, she would stubbornly resist anything Aomame might have to say. Tamaki was always ready to accept – and even respect – Aomame's opinions on other matters, but if Aomame criticized her choice of boyfriend, Tamaki simply refused to listen. Aomame eventually gave up trying to advise her. She didn't want to quarrel with Tamaki and destroy their friendship. Ultimately, it was Tamaki's life. All Aomame could do was let her live it. Tamaki became involved with many men during her college years, and each one led to trouble. They would always betray her, wound her, and abandon her, leaving Tamaki each time in a state close to madness. Twice she resorted to abortions. Where relations with the opposite sex were concerned, Tamaki was truly a born victim.

Aomame never had a steady boyfriend. She was asked out on dates now and then, and she thought that a few of the men were not at all bad, but she never let herself become deeply involved.

Tamaki asked her, "Are you going to stay a virgin the rest of your life?"

"I'm too busy for that," Aomame would say. "I can barely keep my life going day to day. I don't have time to be fooling around with a boyfriend."

After graduation, Tamaki stayed on in graduate school to prepare for the bar exam. Aomame went to work for a company that made sports drinks and health food, and she played for the company's softball team. Tamaki continued to commute from home, while Aomame went to live in the company dorm in Yoyogi Hachiman. As in their student days, they would meet for a meal on weekends and talk.

When she was twenty-four, Tamaki married a man two years her senior. As soon as they became engaged, she left graduate school and gave up on continuing her legal studies. He insisted that she do so. Aomame met Tamaki's fiancé only once. He came from a wealthy family, and, just as she had suspected, his features were handsome but utterly lacking in depth. His hobby was sailing. He was a smooth talker and clever in his own way, but there was no substance to his personality, and his words carried no weight. He was, in other words, a typical Tamaki-type boyfriend. But there was more about him, something ominous, that Aomame sensed. She disliked him from the start. And he probably didn't like her much, either.

"This marriage will never work," Aomame said to Tamaki. She hated to offer unwanted advice again, but this was marriage, not playing house. As Tamaki's best and oldest friend, Aomame could not keep silent. This led to their first violent argument. Aomame's opposition to her marriage made Tamaki hysterical, and she screamed harsh words at Aomame, among them words that Aomame least wanted to hear. Aomame did not attend the wedding.

The two of them made up before long. As soon as she came back from her honeymoon, Tamaki showed up at Aomame's without warning and apologized for her behavior. "I want you to forget everything I said that time," she pleaded. "I wasn't myself. I was thinking about you all during my honeymoon." Aomame told her not to worry, that she had already forgotten everything. They held each other close. Soon they were joking and laughing.

But still, after the wedding, there was a sudden decline in the number of occasions when Aomame and Tamaki could meet face-to-face. They exchanged frequent letters and talked on the telephone, but Tamaki seemed to find it difficult to arrange times when the two of them could get together. Her excuse was that she had so much to do at home. "Being a full-time housewife is *hard work*," she would say, but there was something in her tone of voice suggesting that her husband did not want her meeting people outside the house. Also, Tamaki and her husband were living in the same compound as his parents, which seemed to make it difficult for her to go out. Aomame was never invited to Tamaki's new home.

Her married life was going well, Tamaki would tell Aomame whenever she had the chance. "My husband is gentle with me, and his parents are very kind. We're quite comfortable. We often take the yacht out of Enoshima on weekends. I'm not sorry I stopped studying law. I was feeling a lot of pressure over the bar exam. Maybe this ordinary kind of life was the right thing for me all along. I'll probably have a child soon, and then I'll really be just a typical boring mother. I might not have *any* time for you!" Tamaki's voice was always cheery, and Aomame could find no reason to doubt her words. "That's great," she would say, and she really did think it was great. She would certainly prefer to have her premonitions miss the mark than to be on target. Something inside Tamaki had finally settled down where it belonged, she guessed. Or so she tried to believe.

Aomame had no other real friends; as her contact with Tamaki diminished, she became increasingly unsure what to do with each passing day. She could no longer concentrate on softball as she used to. Her very feeling for the game seemed to wane as Tamaki grew more distant from her life. Aomame was twenty-five but still a virgin. Now and then, when she felt unsettled, she would masturbate, but she didn't find this life especially lonely. Deep personal relationships with people were a source of pain for Aomame. Better to keep to herself.

Tamaki committed suicide on a windy late-autumn day three days before her twenty-sixth birthday. She hanged herself at home. Her husband found her the next evening when he returned from a business trip.

"We had no domestic problems, and I never heard of any dissatisfaction on her part. I can't imagine what would have caused her to take her own life," the husband told the police. His parents said much the same thing.

But they were lying. The husband's constant sadistic violence had left Tamaki covered with scars both physical and mental. His actions toward her had verged on the monomaniacal, and his parents generally knew the truth. The police could also tell what had happened from the autopsy, but their suspicions never became public. They called the husband in and questioned him, but the case was clearly a suicide, and at the time of death the husband was hundreds of miles away in Hokkaido. He was never charged with a crime. Tamaki's younger brother subsequently revealed all this to Aomame in confidence.

The violence had been there from the beginning, he said, and it only grew more insistent and more gruesome with the passage of time. But Tamaki had been unable to escape from her nightmare. She had not said a word about it to Aomame because she knew what the answer would be if she asked for advice: Get out of that house *now*. But that was the one thing she could not do.

At the very end, just before she killed herself, Tamaki wrote a long letter to Aomame. It started by saying that she had been wrong and Aomame had been right from the start. She closed the letter this way:

I am living in hell from one day to the next. But there is nothing I can do to escape. I don't know where I would go if I did. I feel utterly powerless, and that feeling is my prison. I entered of my own free will, I locked the door, and I threw away the key. This marriage was of course a mistake, just as you said. But the deepest problem is not in my husband or in my married life. It is inside me. I deserve all the pain I am feeling. I can't blame anyone else. You are my only friend, the only person in the world I can trust. But I am beyond saving now. Please remember me always if you can. If only we could have gone on playing softball together forever!

Aomame felt horribly sick as she read Tamaki's letter. Her body would not stop trembling. She called Tamaki's house several times, but no one took the call. All she got was the machine. She took the train to Setagaya and walked to Tamaki's house in Okusawa. It was on a large plot of land behind a high wall. Aomame rang the intercom bell, but no one answered this, either. There was only the sound of a dog barking inside. All she could do was give up and go home. She had no way of knowing it, but Tamaki had already drawn her last breath. She was hanging alone from a rope she had tied to the stairway handrail. Inside the hushed house, the telephone's bell and the front-door chime had been ringing in emptiness.

Aomame received the news of Tamaki's death with little sense of surprise. Somewhere in the back of her mind, she must have been expecting it. She felt no sadness welling up. She gave the caller a perfunctory answer, hung up, and settled into a chair. After she had been sitting there for a considerable length of time, she felt all the liquids in her body pouring out of her. She could not get out of the chair for a very long time. She telephoned her company to say she felt sick and would not be in for several days. She stayed in her apartment, not eating, not sleeping, hardly drinking even water. She did not attend the funeral. She felt as if, with a distinct click, something had switched places inside her. *This marks a borderline,* she felt strongly. *From now on, I will no longer be the person I was.*

Aomame resolved in her heart to punish the man for what he had done. *Whatever happens, I must be sure to present him with the end of the world. Otherwise, he will do the same thing to someone else.*

Aomame spent a great deal of time formulating a meticulous plan. She had already learned that a needle thrust into a certain point on the back of the neck at a certain angle could kill a person instantly. It was not something that just anyone could do, of course. But she could do it. First, she would have to train herself to find the extremely subtle point by touch in the shortest possible time. Next she would have to have an instrument suited to such a task. She obtained the necessary tools and, over time, fashioned for herself a special implement that looked like a small, slender ice pick. Its needle was as sharp and cold and pointed as a merciless idea. She found many ways to undertake the necessary training, and she did so with great dedication. When she was satisfied with her preparation, she put her plan into action. Unhesitatingly, coolly, and precisely, she brought the kingdom down upon the man. And when she was finished she even intoned a prayer, its phrases falling from her lips almost as a matter of reflex:

O Lord in Heaven, may Thy name be praised in utmost purity for ever and ever, and may Thy kingdom come to us. Please forgive our many sins, and bestow Thy blessings upon our humble pathways. Amen.

It was after this that Aomame came to feel an intense periodic craving for men's bodies.

CHAPTER 14

Tengo

THINGS THAT MOST READERS HAVE NEVER SEEN BEFORE

Komatsu and Tengo had arranged to meet in the usual place, the café near Shinjuku Station. Komatsu arrived twenty minutes late as always. Komatsu never came on time, and Tengo was never late. This was standard practice for them. Komatsu was carrying his leather briefcase and wearing his usual tweed jacket over a navy-blue polo shirt.

"Sorry to keep you waiting," Komatsu said, but he didn't seem at all sorry. He appeared to be in an especially good mood, his smile like a crescent moon at dawn.

Tengo merely nodded without answering.

Komatsu took the chair across from him and said, "Sorry to hurry you. I'm sure it was tough."

"I don't mean to exaggerate, but I didn't know whether I was alive or dead these past ten days," Tengo said.

"You did great, though. You got permission from Fuka-Eri's guardian, and you finished rewriting the story. It's an amazing accomplishment for somebody who lives in his own little world. Now I see you in a whole new light."

Tengo ignored Komatsu's praise. "Did you read the report-thing I wrote on Fuka-Eri's background? The long one."

"I sure did. Of course. Every word. Thanks for writing it. She's got a – what should I say? – a complicated history. It could be part of a roman-fleuve. But what really surprised me was to learn that Professor Ebisuno is her guardian. What a small world! Did he say anything about me?"

"About you?"

"Yes, did the Professor say anything about me?"

"No, nothing special."

"That's strange," Komatsu said, evidently quite puzzled by this. "Professor Ebisuno and I once worked together. I used to go to his university office to pick up his manuscripts. It was a *really* long time ago, of course, when I was just getting started as an editor."

"Maybe he forgot, if it was such a long time ago. He asked me to tell him about you – what sort of person you are."

"No way," Komatsu said with a frown and a shake of the head. "That's impossible. He never forgets a thing. His memory is so good it's almost frightening. He and I talked about all kinds of stuff, I'm sure he remembers. . . . Anyway, he's not an easy guy to deal with. And according to your report, the situation surrounding Fuka-Eri is not going to be easy to deal with, either."

"That's putting it mildly. It's like we're holding a time bomb. Fuka-Eri is in no way ordinary. She's not just another pretty seventeen-year-old. If the novella makes a big splash, the media are going to pounce on this and reveal all kinds of tasty facts. It'll be terrible."

"True, it could be a real Pandora's box," Komatsu said, but he was still smiling.

"So should we cancel the plan?"

"Cancel the plan?!"

"Yes, it'll be too big a deal, and too dangerous. Let's put the original manuscript back in the pile."

"It's not that easy, I'm afraid. Your *Air Chrysalis* rewrite has already gone out to the printers. They're making the galleys. As soon as it's printed it'll go to the editor in chief and the head of publications and the four members of the selection committee. It's too late to say, 'Excuse me, that was a mistake. Please give it back and pretend you never saw it.' "

Tengo sighed.

"What's done is done. We can't turn the clock back," Komatsu said. He put a Marlboro between his lips, narrowed his eyes, and lit the cigarette with the café's matches. "I'll think about what to do next. You don't have to think about anything, Tengo. Even if *Air Chrysalis* takes the prize, we'll keep Fuka-Eri under wraps. She'll be the enigmatic girl writer who doesn't want to appear in public. I can pull it off. As the editor in charge of the story, I'll be her spokesman. Don't worry, I've got it all figured out."

"I don't doubt your abilities, but Fuka-Eri is no ordinary girl. She's not the type to shut up and do as she's told. If she makes up her mind to do something, she'll do it. She doesn't hear what she doesn't want to hear. That's how she's made. It's not going to be as easy as you seem to think."

Komatsu kept silent and went on turning over the matchbox in his hand. Then he said, "In any case, Tengo, we've come this far. All we can do now is make up our minds to keep going. First of all, your rewrite of *Air Chrysalis* is marvelous, really wonderful, far exceeding my expectations. It's almost perfect. I have no doubt that it's going to take the new writers' prize and cause a big sensation. It's too late now for us to bury it. If you ask me, burying a work like that would be a crime. And as I said before, things are moving full speed ahead."

"A crime?!" Tengo exclaimed, looking straight at Komatsu.

"Well, take these words, for example," Komatsu said. " 'Every art and every inquiry, and similarly every action and pursuit, is thought to aim at some good; and for this reason the good has rightly been declared to be that at which all things aim.' "

"What is *that*?"

"Aristotle. *Nicomachean Ethics*. Have you ever read Aristotle?"

"Almost nothing."

"You ought to. I'm sure you'd like it. Whenever I run out of things to read, I read Greek philosophy. I never get tired of the stuff. There's always something new to learn."

"So what's the point of the quotation?"

"The conclusion of things is the good. The good is, in other words, the conclusion at which all things arrive. Let's leave doubt for tomorrow," Komatsu said. "That is the point."

"What does Aristotle have to say about the Holocaust?"

Komatsu's crescent-moon smile further deepened. "Here, Aristotle is mainly talking about things like art and scholarship and crafts."

Tengo had far more than a passing acquaintance with Komatsu. He knew the man's public face, and he had seen his private face as well. Komatsu appeared to be a lone wolf in the literary industry who had always survived by doing as he pleased. Most people were taken in by that image. But if you observed him closely, taking into account the full context of his actions, you could tell that his moves were highly calculated. He was like a player of chess or *shogi* who could see several moves ahead. It was true that he liked to plot outlandish schemes, but he was also careful to draw a line beyond which he would not stray. He was, if anything, a high-strung man whose more outrageous gestures were mostly for show.

Komatsu was careful to protect himself with various kinds of insurance. For example, he wrote a literary column once a week in the evening edition of a major newspaper. In it, he would shower writers with praise or blame. The blame was always expressed in highly acerbic prose, which was a specialty of his. The column appeared under a made-up name, but everyone in the industry knew who was writing it. No one liked being criticized in the newspaper, of course, so writers tried their best not to ruffle his feathers. When asked by him to write something, they avoided turning him down whenever possible. Otherwise, there was no telling what might be said about them in the column.

Tengo was not fond of Komatsu's more calculating side, the way he displayed contempt for the literary world while exploiting its system to his best advantage. Komatsu possessed outstanding editorial instincts, and he had been enormously helpful to Tengo. His advice on the writing of fiction was almost always valuable. But Tengo was careful to keep a certain distance between them. He was determined not to draw too close to Komatsu and then have the ladder pulled out from under him for overstepping certain boundaries. In that sense, Tengo, too, was a cautious individual.

"As I said a minute ago, your rewrite of *Air Chrysalis* is close to perfect. A great job," Komatsu continued. "There's just one part – really, just one – that I'd like to have you redo if possible. Not now, of course. It's fine at the 'new writer' level. But after the committee picks it to win the prize and just before the magazine prints it, at that stage I'd like you to fix it."

"What part?" Tengo asked.

"When the Little People finish making the air chrysalis, there are two moons. The girl looks up to find two moons in the sky. Remember that part?"

"Of course I remember it."

"In my opinion, you haven't written enough about the two moons. I'd like you to give it more concrete detail. That's my only request."

"It *is* a little terse, maybe. I just didn't want to overdo it with detail and destroy the flow of Fuka-Eri's original."

Komatsu raised the hand that had a cigarette tucked between the fingers. "Think of it this way, Tengo. Your readers have seen the sky with one moon in it any number of times, right? But I doubt they've seen a sky with two moons in it side by side. When you introduce things that most readers have *never* seen before into a piece of fiction, you have to describe them with as much precision and in as much detail as possible. What you can eliminate from fiction is the description of things that most readers *have* seen."

"I get it," Tengo said. Komatsu's request made a lot of sense. "I'll fill out the part where the two moons appear."

"Good. Then it *will* be perfect," Komatsu said. He crushed out his cigarette.

"I'm always glad to have you praise my work," Tengo said, "but it's not so simple for me this time."

"You have suddenly matured," Komatsu said slowly, as if pausing for emphasis. "You have matured both as a manipulator of language and as an author. It should be simple enough for you to be glad about that. I'm sure rewriting *Air Chrysalis* taught you a lot about the writing of fiction. It should be a big help the next time you write your own work."

"If there is a next time," Tengo said.

A big grin crossed Komatsu's face. "Don't worry. You did your job. Now it's my turn. You can go back to the bench and take it easy, just watch the game unfold."

The waitress arrived and poured cold water into their glasses. Tengo drank half of his before realizing that he had absolutely no desire for water. He asked Komatsu, "Was it Aristotle who said the human soul is composed of reason, will, and desire?"

"No, that was Plato. Aristotle and Plato were as different as Mel Tormé and Bing Crosby. In any case, things were a lot simpler in the old days," Komatsu said. "Wouldn't it be fun to imagine reason, will, and desire engaged in a fierce debate around a table?"

"I've got a pretty good idea who would lose that one."

"What I like about you," Komatsu said, raising an index finger, "is your sense of humor."

This is not humor, Tengo thought, but he kept it to himself.

* * *

After leaving Komatsu, Tengo walked to Kinokuniya, bought several books, and started reading them over a beer in a nearby bar. This was the sort of moment in which he should have been able to relax most completely.

On this particular night, though, he could not seem to concentrate on his books. The recurring image of his mother floated vaguely before his eyes and would not go away. She had lowered the straps of her white slip from her shoulders, revealing her well-shaped breasts, and was letting a man suck on them. The man was not his father. He was larger and more youthful, and had better features. The infant Tengo was asleep in his crib, eyes closed, his breathing regular. A look of ecstasy suffused his mother's face while the man sucked on her breasts, a look very much like his older girlfriend's when she was having an orgasm.

Once, out of curiosity, Tengo had asked his girlfriend to try wearing a white slip for him. "Glad to," she replied with a smile. "I'll wear one next time if you'd like that. Do you have any other requests? I'll do anything you want. Just ask. Don't be embarrassed."

"Can you wear a white blouse, too? A very simple one."

She showed up the following week wearing a white blouse over a white slip. He took her blouse off, lowered the shoulder straps of the slip, and sucked on her breasts. He adopted the same position and angle as the man in his vision, and when he did this he felt a slight dizziness. His mind misted over, and he lost track of the order of things. In his lower body there was a heavy sensation that rapidly swelled, and no sooner was he aware of it than he shuddered with a violent ejaculation.

"Tengo, what's wrong? Did you come already?" she asked, astounded.

He himself was not sure what had just happened, but then he realized that he had gotten semen on the lower part of her slip.

"I'm sorry," he said. "I wasn't planning to do that."

"Don't apologize," she said cheerily. "I can rinse it right off. It's just the usual stuff. I'm glad it's not soy sauce or red wine!"

She took the slip off, scrubbed the semen-smeared part at the bathroom sink, and hung it over the shower rod to dry.

"Was that too strong?" she asked with a gentle smile, rubbing Tengo's belly with the palm of her hand. "You like white slips, huh, Tengo?"

"Not exactly," Tengo said, but he could not explain to her his real reason for having made the request.

"Just let big sister know any time you've got a fantasy you want to play out, honey. I'll go along with *anything*. I just *love* fantasies! Everybody needs *some* kind of fantasy to go on living, don't you think? You want me to wear a white slip next time, too?"

Tengo shook his head. "No, thanks, once was enough."

Tengo often wondered if the young man sucking on his mother's breasts in his vision might be his biological father. This was because Tengo in no way resembled the man who was supposed to be his father – the stellar NHK collections agent. Tengo was a tall, strapping man with a broad forehead, narrow nose, and tightly balled ears. His father was short and squat and utterly unimpressive. He had a narrow forehead, flat nose, and pointed ears like a horse's. Virtually every facial feature of his contrasted with Tengo's. Where Tengo had a generally relaxed and generous look, his father appeared nervous and tightfisted. Comparing the two of them, people often openly remarked that they did not look like father and son.

Still, it was not their different facial features that made it difficult for Tengo to identify with his father; rather, it was their psychological makeup and tendencies. His father showed no sign at all of what might be called intellectual curiosity. True, his father had not had a decent education. Having been born in poverty, he had not had the opportunity to establish in himself an orderly intellectual system. Tengo felt a degree of pity regarding his father's circumstances. But still, a basic desire to obtain knowledge at a universal level – which Tengo assumed to be a more or less natural urge in people – was lacking in the man. There was a certain practical wisdom at work in him that enabled him to survive, but Tengo could discover no hint of a willingness in his father to raise himself up, to deepen himself, to view a wider, larger world.

But Tengo's father never seemed to suffer discomfort from the narrowness and the stagnant air of his cramped little world. Tengo never once saw him pick up a book at home. They never had newspapers (watching the regular NHK news broadcasts was enough, he would say). He had absolutely no interest in music or movies, and he never took a trip. The only thing that seemed to interest him was his assigned collection route. He would make a map of the area, mark it with colored pens, and examine it whenever he had a spare moment, the way a biologist classifies chromosomes.

By contrast, Tengo was regarded as a math prodigy from early childhood. His grades in arithmetic were always outstanding. He could solve high school math problems by the time he was in the third grade. He won high marks in the other sciences as well without any apparent effort. And whenever *he* had a spare moment, he would devour books. Hugely curious about everything, he would absorb knowledge from a broad range of fields with all the efficiency of a power shovel scooping earth. Whenever he looked at his father, he found it inconceivable that half of the genes that made his existence possible could come from this narrow, uneducated man.

My real father must be somewhere else. This was the conclusion that Tengo reached in boyhood. Like the unfortunate children in a Dickens novel, Tengo must have been led by strange circumstances to be raised by this man. Such a possibility was both a nightmare and a great hope. He became obsessed with Dickens after reading *Oliver Twist,* plowing through every Dickens volume in the library. As he traveled through the world of the stories, he steeped himself in reimagined versions of his own life. The reimaginings (or obsessive fantasies) in his head grew ever longer and more complex. They followed a single pattern, but with infinite variations. In all of them, Tengo would tell himself that this was not the place where he belonged. He had been mistakenly locked in a cage. Someday his real parents, guided by sheer good fortune, would find him. They would rescue him from this cramped and ugly cage and bring him back where he belonged. Then he would have the most beautiful, peaceful, and free Sundays imaginable.

Tengo's father exulted over the boy's outstanding schoolwork. He prided himself on Tengo's excellent grades, and boasted of them to people in the neighborhood. At the same time, however, he showed a certain displeasure regarding Tengo's brightness and talent. Often when Tengo was at his desk, studying, his father would interrupt him, seemingly on purpose. He would order the boy to do chores or nag Tengo about his supposedly offensive behavior. The content of his father's nagging was always the same: he was running himself ragged every day, covering huge distances and sometimes enduring people's curses as a collections agent, while Tengo did nothing but take it easy all the time, living in comfort. "They had me working my tail off around the house when I was your age, and my father and older brother would beat me black and blue for anything at all. They never gave me enough food, and treated me like an animal. I don't want you thinking you're so special just because you got a few good grades." His father would go on like this endlessly.

This man may be envious of me, Tengo began to think after a certain point. *He's jealous – either of me as a person or of the life I'm leading. But does a father really feel jealousy toward his own son?* As a child, Tengo did not judge his father, but he could not help feeling a pathetic kind of meanness that emanated from his father's words and deeds – and this he found almost physically unbearable. Often he felt that this man was not only envious of him, but that he actually hated something in his son. It was not that his father hated Tengo as a person but rather that he hated *something inside* Tengo, something that he could not forgive.

Mathematics gave Tengo an effective means of retreat. By fleeing into a world of numerical expression, he was able to escape from the troublesome cage of reality. As a little boy, he noticed that he could easily move into a mathematical world with the flick of a switch in his head. He remained free as long as he actively explored that realm of infinite consistency. He walked down the gigantic building's twisted corridor, opening one numbered door after another. Each time a new spectacle opened up before him, the ugly traces of the real world would dissipate and then simply disappear. The world governed by numerical expression was, for him, a legitimate and always safe hiding place. As long as he stayed in that world, he could forget or ignore the rules and burdens forced upon him by the real world.

Where mathematics was a magnificent imaginary building, the world of story as represented by Dickens was like a deep, magical forest for Tengo. When mathematics stretched infinitely upward toward the heavens, the forest spread out beneath his gaze in silence, its dark, sturdy roots stretching deep into the earth. In the forest there were no maps, no numbered doorways.

In elementary and middle school, Tengo was utterly absorbed by the world of mathematics. Its clarity and absolute freedom enthralled him, and he also needed them to survive. Once he entered adolescence, however, he began to feel increasingly that this might not be enough. There was no problem as long as he was visiting the world of math, but whenever he returned to the real world (as return he must), he found himself in the same miserable cage. Nothing had improved. Rather, his shackles felt even heavier. So then, what good was mathematics? Wasn't it just a temporary means of escape that made his real-life situation even worse?

As his doubts increased, Tengo began deliberately to put some distance between himself and the world of mathematics, and instead the forest of story began to exert a stronger pull on his heart. Of course, reading novels was just another form of escape. As soon as he closed their pages he had to come back to the real world. But at some point Tengo noticed that returning to reality from the world of a novel was not as devastating a blow as returning from the world of mathematics. Why should that have been? After much deep thought, he reached a conclusion. No matter how clear the relationships of things might become in the forest of story, there was never a clear-cut solution. That was how it differed from math. The role of a story was, in the broadest terms, to transpose a single problem into another form. Depending on the nature and direction of the problem, a solution could be suggested in the narrative. Tengo would return to the real world with that suggestion in hand. It was like a piece of paper bearing the indecipherable text of a magic spell. At times it lacked coherence and served no immediate practical purpose. But it would contain a possibility. Someday he might be able to decipher the spell. That possibility would gently warm his heart from within.

The older he became, the more Tengo was drawn to this kind of narrative suggestion. Mathematics was a great joy for him even now, as an adult. When he was teaching students at the cram school, the same joy he had felt as a child would come welling up naturally. To share the joy of that conceptual freedom with someone was a wonderful thing. But Tengo was no longer able to lose himself so unreservedly in a world of numerical expression. For he knew that no amount of searching in that world would give him the solution he was really looking for.

When he was in the fifth grade, after much careful thinking, Tengo declared that he wanted to stop making the rounds with his father on Sundays to collect the NHK subscription fees. He told his father that he wanted to use the time for studying and reading books and playing with other kids. Just as his father had his own work, he had things that he had to do. He wanted to live a normal life like everybody else.

Tengo said what he needed to say, concisely and coherently.

His father, of course, blew up. He didn't give a damn what other families did, he said; it had nothing to do with them. We have our own way of doing things. And don't you *dare* talk to me about a "normal life," Mr. Know-it-all. What do *you* know about a "normal life"? Tengo did not try to argue with him. He merely stared back in silence, knowing that nothing he said would get through to his father. If that was what Tengo wanted, his father continued, that was what he would get. But if *he* couldn't listen to his father, his father couldn't go on feeding him anymore. Tengo should get the hell out.

Tengo did as he was told. He packed a bag and left home. He had made up his mind. No matter how angry his father got, no matter how much he screamed and shouted, Tengo was not going to be afraid – even if his father raised a hand to him (which he did not do). Now that Tengo had been given permission to leave his cage, he was more relieved than anything else.

But still, there was no way a ten-year-old boy could live on his own. When class was dismissed at the end of the day, he confessed his predicament to his teacher and said he had no place to spend the night. He also explained to her what an emotional burden it had been for him to make the rounds with his father on Sundays collecting NHK subscription fees.

The teacher was a single woman in her mid-thirties. She was far from beautiful and she wore thick, ugly glasses, but she was a fair-minded, warmhearted person. A small woman, she was normally quiet and mild-mannered, but she could be surprisingly quick-tempered; once she let her anger out, she became a different person, and no one could stop her. The difference shocked people. Tengo, however, was fond of her, and her temper tantrums never frightened him.

She heard Tengo out with understanding and sympathy, and she brought him home to spend the night in her house. She spread a blanket on the sofa and had him sleep there. She made him breakfast in the morning. That evening she took him to his father's place for a long talk.

Tengo was told to leave the room, so he was not sure what they said to each other, but finally his father had to sheathe his sword. However extreme his anger might be, he could not leave a ten-year-old boy to wander the streets alone. The duty of a parent to support his child was a matter of law.

As a result of the teacher's talk with his father, Tengo was free to spend Sundays as he pleased. He was required to devote the morning to housework, but he could do anything he wanted after that. This was the first tangible right that Tengo had ever won from his father. His father was too angry to talk to Tengo for a while, but this was of no great concern to the boy. He had won something far more important than that. He had taken his first step toward freedom and independence.

Tengo did not see his fifth-grade teacher for a long time after he left elementary school. He probably could have seen her if he had attended the occasional class reunion, to which he was invited, but he had no intention of showing his face at such gatherings. He had virtually no happy memories from that school. He did, however, think of his teacher now and then and recall what she had done for him.

The next time he saw her, Tengo was in his second year of high school. He belonged to the judo club, but he had injured his calf at the time and was forced to take a two-month break from judo matches. Instead, he was recruited to be a temporary percussionist in the school's brass band. The band was only days away from a competition, but one of their two percussionists suddenly transferred to another school, and the other one came down with a bad case of influenza. All they needed was a human being who could hold two sticks, the music teacher said, pleading with Tengo to help them out of their predicament since his injury had left him with time to kill. There would be several meals in it for Tengo, and the teacher promised to go easy on his grade if he would join the rehearsals.

Tengo had never performed on a percussion instrument nor had any interest in doing so, but once he actually tried playing, he was amazed to find that it was perfectly suited to the way his mind worked. He felt a natural joy in dividing time into small fragments, reassembling them, and transforming them into an effective row of tones. All of the sounds mentally appeared to him in the form of a diagram. He proceeded to grasp the system of one percussion instrument after another the way a sponge soaks up water. His music teacher introduced him to a symphony orchestra's percussionist, from whom he learned the techniques of the timpani. He mastered its general structure and performance technique with only a few hours' lessons. And because the score resembled numerical expression, learning how to read it was no great challenge for him.

The music teacher was delighted to discover Tengo's outstanding musical talent. "You seem to have a natural sense for complex rhythms and a marvelous ear for music," he said. "If you continue to study with professionals, you could become one yourself."

The timpani was a difficult instrument, but it was deep and

compelling in its own special way, its combination of sounds hinting at infinite possibilities. Tengo and his classmates were rehearsing several passages excerpted from Janáček's *Sinfonietta,* as arranged for wind instruments. They were to perform it as their "free-choice piece" in a competition for high school brass bands. Janáček's *Sinfonietta* was a difficult piece for high school musicians, and the timpani figured prominently in the opening fanfare. The music teacher, who doubled as the band leader, had chosen *Sinfonietta* on the assumption that he had two outstanding percussionists to work with, and when he suddenly lost them, he was at his wit's end. Obviously, then, Tengo had a major role to fill, but he felt no pressure and wholeheartedly enjoyed the performance.

The band's performance was flawless (good enough for a top prize, if not the championship), and when it was over, Tengo's old fifth-grade teacher came over to congratulate him on his fine playing.

"I knew it was you right away, Tengo," she said. He recognized this small woman but couldn't recall her name. "The timpani sounded so good, I looked to see who could be playing – and it was *you,* of all people! You're a lot bigger than you used to be, but I recognized your face immediately. When did you start playing?"

Tengo gave her a quick summary of the events that had led up to this performance, which made her all the more impressed. "You're such a talented boy, and in so many ways!"

"Judo is a lot easier for me," Tengo said, smiling.

"So, how's your father?" she asked.

"He's fine," Tengo responded automatically, though he didn't know – and didn't want to know – how his father was doing. By then Tengo was living in a dormitory and hadn't spoken to his father in a very long time.

"Why are you here?" he asked the teacher.

"My niece plays clarinet in another high school's band. She

wanted me to hear her play a solo. Are you going to keep up with your music?"

"I'll go back to judo when my leg gets better. Judo keeps me fed. My school supports judo in a big way. They cover my room and board. The band can't do that."

"I guess you're trying not to depend on your father?"

"Well, you know what he's like," Tengo said.

She smiled at him. "It's too bad, though. With all your talents!"

Tengo looked down at the small woman and remembered the night she put him up at her place. He pictured the plain and practical – but neat and tidy – little apartment in which she lived. The lace curtains and potted plants. The ironing board and open book. The small pink dress hanging on the wall. The smell of the sofa where he slept. And now here she stood before him, he realized, fidgeting like a young girl. He realized, too, that he was no longer a powerless ten-year-old boy but a strapping seventeen-year-old – broad-chested, with stubble to shave and a sex drive in full bloom. He felt strangely calm in the presence of this older woman.

"I'm glad I ran into you," she said.

"I am too," Tengo replied. He really was glad. But he still couldn't remember her name.

CHAPTER 15

Aomame

FIRMLY, LIKE ATTACHING AN ANCHOR TO A BALLOON

Aomame devoted a great deal of attention to her daily diet. Vegetarian dishes were central to the meals she prepared for herself, to which she added seafood, mostly white fish. An occasional piece of chicken was about all the meat she would eat. She chose only fresh ingredients and kept seasonings to a minimum, rejecting high-fat ingredients entirely and keeping her intake of carbohydrates low. Salads she would eat with a touch of olive oil, salt, and lemon juice, never dressings. She did not just eat a lot of vegetables, she also studied their nutritional elements in detail and made sure she was eating a well-balanced selection. She fashioned her own original menus and shared them with sports club members when asked. "Forget about counting calories," she would always advise them. "Once you develop a knack for choosing the proper ingredients and eating in moderation, you don't have to pay attention to numbers."

This is not to say that she clung obsessively to her ascetic menus. If she felt a strong desire for meat, she would pop into a restaurant and order a thick steak or lamb chops. She believed that an unbearable desire for a particular food meant that the body was sending signals for something it truly needed, and she would follow the call of nature.

She enjoyed wine and sake, but she established three days a week when she would not drink at all in order to avoid excessive alcohol intake, as a way to both protect her liver and control the sugar in her bloodstream. For Aomame, her body was sacred, to be kept clean always, without a fleck of dust or the slightest stain. Whatever one enshrined there was another question, to be thought about later.

Aomame had no excess flesh, only muscle. She would confirm this for herself in detail each day, standing stark naked in front of the mirror. Not that she was thrilled at the sight of her own body. Quite the opposite. Her breasts were not big enough, and they were asymmetrical. Her pubic hair grew like a patch of grass that had been trampled by a passing army. She couldn't stop herself from scowling at the sight of her own body, but there was nothing there for her to pinch.

She lived frugally, but her meals were the only things on which she deliberately spent her money. She never compromised on the quality of her groceries, and drank only good-quality wines. On those rare occasions when she ate out, she would choose restaurants that prepared their food with the greatest care. Almost nothing else mattered to her – not clothing, not cosmetics, not accessories. Jeans and a sweater were all she needed for commuting to work at the sports club, and once she was there she would spend the day in a jersey top and bottom – without accessories, of course. She rarely had occasion to go out in fancy clothing. Once Tamaki Otsuka was married, she no longer had any women friends to dine out with. She would wear makeup and dress well when she was out in search of a one-night stand, but that was once a month and didn't require an extensive wardrobe.

When necessary, Aomame would make the rounds of the boutiques in Aoyama to have one "killer dress" made and to buy an accessory or two and a pair of heels to match. That was all she needed. Ordinarily she wore flats and a ponytail. As long as she washed her face well with soap and water and applied moisturizer, she always had a glow. The most important thing was to have a clean, healthy body.

Aomame had been used to living a simple, unadorned life since childhood. Self-denial and moderation were the values pounded into her as long as she could remember. Her family's home was free of all extras, and "waste" was their most commonly used word. They had no television and did not subscribe to a newspaper. Even news was looked upon in her home as a *nonessential*. Meat and fish rarely found their way to the dining table. Her school lunches provided Aomame with the nutrients she needed for development. The other children would complain how tasteless the lunches were, and would leave much of theirs uneaten, but she almost wished she could have what they wasted.

She wore only hand-me-downs. The believers would hold periodic gatherings to exchange their unneeded articles of clothing, as a result of which her parents never once bought her anything new, the only exceptions being things like the gym clothes required by the school. She could not recall ever having worn clothing or shoes that fit her perfectly, and the items she did have were an assemblage of clashing colors and patterns. If the family could not afford any other lifestyle, she would have just resigned herself to the fact, but Aomame's family was by no means poor. Her father was an engineer with a normal income and savings. They chose their exceedingly frugal lifestyle entirely as a matter of belief.

Because the life she led was so very different from those of the children around her, for a long time Aomame could not make friends with anyone. She had neither the clothing nor the money that would have enabled her to go out with a friend. She was never given an allowance, so that even if she had been invited to someone's birthday party (which, for better or worse, never happened), she would not have been able to bring along a little gift.

Because of all this, Aomame hated her parents and deeply despised both the world to which they belonged and the ideology of that world. What she longed for was an *ordinary life* like everybody else's. Not luxury: just a totally normal little life, nothing more. She wanted to hurry up and become an adult so she could leave her parents and live alone – eating what and as much as she wanted, using the money in her purse any way she liked, wearing new clothes of her own choosing, wearing shoes that fit her feet, going where she wanted to go, making lots of friends and exchanging beautifully wrapped presents with them.

Once she became an adult, however, Aomame discovered that she was most comfortable living a life of self-denial and moderation. What she wanted most of all was not to go out with someone all dressed up, but to spend time alone in her room dressed in a jersey top and bottom.

After Tamaki died, Aomame quit the sports drink company, left the dormitory she had been living in, and moved into a one-bedroom rental condo in the lively, freewheeling Jiyuga-oka neighborhood, away from the center of the city. Though hardly spacious, the place looked huge to her. She kept her furnishings to a minimum – except for her extensive collection of kitchen utensils. She had few possessions. She enjoyed reading books, but as soon as she was through with them, she would sell them to a used bookstore. She enjoyed listening to music, but was not a collector of records. She hated to see her belongings pile up. She felt guilty whenever she bought something. *I don't really need this,* she would tell herself. Seeing the nicer clothing and shoes in her closet would give her a pain in the chest and constrict her breathing. Such sights suggestive of freedom and opulence would, paradoxically, remind Aomame of her restrictive childhood.

What did it mean for a person to be free? she would often ask herself. Even if you managed to escape from one cage, weren't you just in another, larger one?

Whenever Aomame sent a designated man into the other world, the dowager of Azabu would provide her with remuneration. A wad of bills, tightly wrapped in blank paper, would be deposited in a post-office box. Aomame would receive the key from Tamaru, retrieve the contents of the box, and later return the key. Without breaking the seal on the pack of bills to count the money, she would throw the package into her bank's safe-deposit box, which now contained two hard bricks of cash.

Aomame was unable to use up her monthly salary from the sports club, and she even had a bit of savings in the bank. She had no use whatever for the dowager's money, which she tried to explain to her the first time she received the remuneration.

"This is a mere external form," the dowager said softly but firmly. "Think of it as a kind of set procedure – a requirement. You are at least required to receive it. If you don't need the money, then you don't have to use it. If you hate the idea of taking it, I don't mind if you donate it anonymously to some charity. You are free to do anything you like with it. But if you ask me, the best thing for you to do would be to keep it untouched for a while, stored away somewhere."

"I just don't like the idea of money changing hands for something like this," Aomame said.

"I understand how you feel, but remember this: thanks to the fact that these terrible men have been so good as to remove themselves from our presence, there has been no need for divorce proceedings or custody battles, and no need for the women to live in fear that their husbands might show up and beat them beyond recognition. Life insurance and survivors' annuities have been paid. Think of the money you get as the *outward form* of the women's gratitude. Without a doubt, you have done the right thing. But your act must not go uncompensated. Do you understand why?"

"No, not really," Aomame replied honestly.

"Because you are neither an angel nor a god. I am quite aware that your actions have been prompted by your pure feelings, and I understand perfectly well that, for that very reason, you do not wish to receive money for what you have done. But pure, unadulterated feelings are dangerous in their own way. It is no easy feat for a flesh-and-blood human being to go on living with such feelings. That is why it is necessary for you to fasten your feelings to the earth – firmly, like attaching an anchor to a balloon. The money is for that. To prevent you from feeling that you can do anything you want as long as it's the right thing and your feelings are pure. Do you see now?"

After thinking about it a while, Aomame nodded. "I don't really understand it very well, but I'll do as you say for now."

The dowager smiled and took a sip of her herbal tea. "Now, don't do anything silly like putting it in your bank account. If the tax people found it, they'd have a great time wondering what it could be. Just put the cash in a safe-deposit box. It will come in handy sometime."

Aomame said that she would follow the dowager's instructions.

Home from the club, she was preparing dinner when the phone rang.

"Hi there, Aomame," a woman's voice said. A slightly husky voice. It was Ayumi.

Pressing the receiver to her ear, Aomame reached out and lowered the gas flame as she spoke: "How's police work these days?"

"I'm handing out parking tickets like crazy. Everybody hates me. No men around, just good, hard work."

"Glad to hear it."

"What are *you* doing now?" Ayumi asked.

"Making supper."

"Are you free the day after tomorrow? At night, I mean."

"I'm free, but I'm not ready for another night like the last one. I need a break."

"Me, too," Ayumi said. "I was just thinking I haven't seen you for a while. I'd like to get together and talk, that's all."

Aomame gave some thought to what Ayumi was suggesting, but she couldn't make up her mind right away.

"You know, you caught me in the middle of stir-frying," she said. "I can't stop now. Can you call me again in half an hour?"

"Sure thing," Ayumi said. "Half an hour it is."

Aomame hung up and finished stir-frying her vegetables. Then she made some miso soup with bean sprouts and had that with brown rice. She drank half a can of beer and poured the rest down the drain. She had washed the dishes and was resting on the sofa when Ayumi called again.

"I thought it might be nice to have dinner together sometime," she said. "I get tired of eating alone."

"Do you always eat alone?"

"I live in a dormitory, with meals included, so I usually eat in a big, noisy crowd. Sometimes, though, I want to have a nice, quiet meal, maybe go someplace a little fancy. But not alone. You know what I mean?"

"Of course I do," Aomame said.

"I just don't have anybody – man or woman – to eat with at times like that. They all like to hang out in cheap bars. With *you*, though, I thought just maybe, if you wouldn't mind . . ."

"No, I wouldn't mind at all," Aomame said. "Let's do it. Let's go have a fancy meal together. I haven't done something like that for a long time."

"Really? I'm thrilled!"

"You said the day after tomorrow is good for you?"

"Right. I'm off duty the day after that. Do you know a nice place?"

Aomame mentioned a certain French restaurant in the Nogizaka neighborhood.

Ayumi gasped. "Are you kidding? It's only the most famous French restaurant in the city. I read in a magazine it's insanely expensive, and you have to wait two months for a reservation. That's no place for anybody on *my* salary!"

"Don't worry, the owner-chef is a member of my gym. I'm his personal trainer, and I kind of advise him on his menus' nutritional values. If I ask him, I'm sure he'll save us a table – and knock the bill way down, too. I can't guarantee we'd get great seats, of course."

"I'd be happy to sit in a closet in that place," Ayumi said.

"You'd better wear your best dress," Aomame advised her.

When she had hung up, Aomame was somewhat shocked to realize that she had grown fond of the young policewoman. She hadn't felt like this about anyone since Tamaki Otsuka died. And though the feelings were utterly different from what she had felt for Tamaki, this was the first time in a very long time that she would share a meal with a friend – or even *want* to do such a thing. To add to which, this other person was a police officer! Aomame sighed. Life was so strange.

Aomame wore a small white cardigan over a blue-gray short-sleeve dress, and she had on her Ferragamo heels. She added earrings and a narrow gold bracelet. Leaving her usual shoulder bag at home (along with the ice pick), she carried a small Bagagerie purse. Ayumi wore a simple black jacket by Comme des Garçons over a scoop-necked brown T-shirt, a flower-patterned flared skirt, the Gucci bag she carried before, small pearl pierced earrings, and brown low-heeled shoes. She looked far lovelier and more elegant than last time – and certainly not like a police officer.

They met at the bar, sipped mimosas, and then were shown to their table, which turned out to be a rather good one. The chef stepped out of the kitchen for a chat with Aomame and noted that the wine would be on the house.

"Sorry, it's already been uncorked, and one tasting's worth is gone. A customer complained about the taste yesterday and we gave him a new bottle, but in fact there is absolutely nothing wrong with this wine. The man is a famous politician who likes to think he's a wine connoisseur, but he doesn't know a damn thing about wine. He did it to show off. 'I'm afraid this might have a slight edge,' he says. We had to humor him. 'Oh, yes, you may be right about that, sir. I'm sure the importer's warehouse is at fault. I'll bring another bottle right away. But bravo, sir! I don't think another person in the country could have caught this!' That was the best way to make everybody happy, as you can imagine. Now, I can't say this too loudly, but we had to inflate the bill a little to cover our loss. He was on an expense account, after all. In any case, there's no way a restaurant with our reputation could serve a returned bottle."

"Except to us, you mean."

The chef winked. "You don't mind, do you?"

"Of course not," Aomame said.

"Not at all," Ayumi chimed in.

"Is this lovely lady your younger sister, by any chance?" the chef asked Aomame.

"Does she look it?" Aomame asked back.

"I don't see a physical resemblance, but there's a certain atmosphere . . ."

"She's my friend," Aomame said. "My police officer friend."

"Really?" He looked again at Ayumi with an expression of disbelief. "You mean, with a pistol and everything?"

"I've never shot anyone," Ayumi said.

"I don't think I said anything incriminating, did I?"

Ayumi shook her head. "Not a thing."

The chef smiled and clasped his hands across his chest. "In any case, this is a highly respected Burgundy that we can serve to anyone with confidence. From a noble domain, a good year. I won't say how many ten-thousand-yen bills we'd ordinarily have to charge for this one."

The chef withdrew and the waiter approached to pour their wine. Aomame and Ayumi toasted each other, the clink of their glasses a distant echo of heavenly bells.

"Oh! I've never tasted such delicious wine before!" Ayumi said, her eyes narrowed after her first sip. "Who could possibly object to a wine like this?"

"You can always find somebody to complain about anything," Aomame said.

The two women studied the menu. Ayumi went through every item twice with the sharp gaze of a smart lawyer reading a major contract: was she missing something important, a clever loophole? She mentally scrutinized all the provisos and stipulations and pondered their likely repercussions, carefully weighing profit and loss.

Aomame enjoyed watching this spectacle from across the table. "Have you decided?" she asked.

"Pretty much," Ayumi said.

"So, what are you going to order?"

"I'll have the mussels, the three-onion salad, and the Bordeaux-braised Iwate veal stew. How about you?"

"I'd like the lentil soup, the warm spring green salad, and the parchment- baked monkfish with polenta. Not much of a match for a red wine, but it's free, so I can't complain."

"Mind sharing a little?"

"Not at all," Aomame said. "And if *you* don't mind, let's share the deep-fried shrimp to start."

"Marvelous!"

"If we're through choosing, we'd better close the menus," Aomame said. "Otherwise the waiter will never come."

"True," Ayumi said, closing her menu with apparent regret and setting it on the table. The waiter came over immediately and took their order.

"Whenever I finish ordering in a restaurant, I feel like I got the wrong thing," Ayumi said when the waiter was gone. "How about you?"

"Even if you *do* order the wrong thing, it's just food. It's no big deal compared with mistakes in life."

"No, of course not," Ayumi said. "But still, it's important to me. It's been that way ever since I was little. Always after I've ordered I start having regrets – 'Oh, if only I had ordered the fried shrimp instead of a hamburger!' Have you always been so cool?"

"Well, for various reasons, my family never ate out. Ever. As far back as I can remember, I never set foot in a restaurant, and I never had the experience until much later of choosing food from a menu and ordering what I wanted to eat. I just had to shut up and eat what I was served day after day. I wasn't allowed to complain if the food was tasteless or if it didn't fill me up or if I hated it. To tell you the truth, even now, I really don't care what I eat, as long as it's healthy."

"Really? Can that be true? I don't know much about your situation, but you sure don't look it. To me, you look like somebody who's been used to coming to places like this since you were little."

This Aomame owed entirely to the guidance of Tamaki Otsuka. How to behave in an elegant restaurant, how to choose your food without making a fool of yourself, how to order wine, how to request dessert, how to deal with your waiter, how to use your cutlery properly: Tamaki knew about all these things, and she taught them all in great detail to Aomame. She also taught Aomame how to choose her clothing, how to wear accessories, and how to use makeup. These were all new discoveries for Aomame. Tamaki grew up in an affluent

Yamanote household. A socialite, her mother was exceedingly particular about manners and clothing, as a result of which Tamaki had internalized all that knowledge as early as her high school days. She could socialize comfortably with grown-ups. Aomame absorbed this knowledge voraciously; she would have been a far different person if she had never met an excellent teacher like Tamaki. She often felt that Tamaki was still alive and lurking inside of her.

Ayumi seemed a little anxious at first, but each sip of wine relaxed her.

"Uh, I want to ask you something," Ayumi said. "You don't have to answer if you don't want to, but I just feel like asking. You won't get mad, will you?"

"No, I won't get mad."

"It's kind of a strange question, but I don't have any ulterior motive in asking it. I want you to understand that. I'm just a curious person. But some people get really angry about these things."

"Don't worry, I won't get angry."

"Are you sure? That's what everybody says, and then they blow up."

"I'm special, so don't worry."

"Did you ever have the experience of having a man do funny things to you when you were little?"

Aomame shook her head. "No, I don't think so. Why?"

"I just wanted to ask. If it never happened to you, fine," Ayumi said. Then she changed the subject. "Tell me, have you ever had a lover? I mean, someone you were seriously involved with?"

"Never."

"Not even once?"

"Not even once," Aomame said. Then, after some hesitation, she added, "To tell you the truth, I was a virgin until I turned twenty-six."

Ayumi was at a loss for words. She put down her knife and

fork, dabbed at her mouth with her napkin, and stared at Aomame with narrowed eyes.

"A beautiful woman like you? I can't believe it."

"I just wasn't interested."

"Not interested in men?"

"I did have one person I fell in love with," Aomame said. "It happened when I was ten. I held his hand."

"You fell in love with a boy when you were ten? That's all?"

"That's all."

Ayumi picked up her knife and fork and seemed deep in thought as she sliced one of her shrimp. "So, where is the boy now? What's he doing?"

Aomame shook her head. "I don't know. We were in the same third- and fourth-grade classes in Ichikawa in Chiba, but I moved to a school in Tokyo in the fifth grade, and I never saw him again, never heard anything about him. All I know is that, if he's still alive, he should be twenty-nine years old now. He'll probably turn thirty this fall."

"Are you telling me you never thought about trying to find out where he is or what he's doing? It wouldn't be that hard, you know."

Aomame gave another firm shake of her head. "I never felt like taking the initiative to find out."

"That's so strange. If it were me, I'd do everything I could to locate him. If you love him that much, you should track him down and tell him so to his face."

"I don't want to do that," Aomame said. "What I want is for the two of us to meet somewhere by chance one day, like, passing on the street, or getting on the same bus."

"Destiny. A chance encounter."

"More or less," Aomame said, taking a sip of wine. "That's when I'll open up to him. 'The only one I've ever loved in this life is you.'"

"How romantic!" Ayumi said, astonished. "But the odds

of a meeting like that are pretty low, I'd say. And besides, you haven't seen him for twenty years. He might look completely different. You could pass him on the street and never know."

Aomame shook her head. "I'd know. His face might have changed, but I'd know him at a glance. I couldn't miss him."

"How can you be so sure?"

"I'm sure."

"So you go on waiting, believing that this chance encounter is bound to happen."

"Which is why I always pay attention when I walk down the street."

"Incredible," Ayumi said. "But as much as you love him, you don't mind having sex with other men – at least after you turned twenty-six."

Aomame thought about this for a moment. Then she said, "That's all just in passing. It doesn't last."

A short silence ensued, during which both women concentrated on their food. Then Ayumi said, "Sorry if this is getting too personal, but did something happen to you when you were twenty-six?"

Aomame nodded. "Something did happen. And it changed me completely. But I can't talk about it here and now. Sorry."

"That's perfectly okay," Ayumi said. "Did I put you in a bad mood asking all these questions?"

"Not in the least," Aomame said.

The waiter brought the starters, and they ate for a while in silence. Their conversation picked up again after they had put their spoons down and the waiter cleared their bowls from the table.

"Aren't you afraid, though?" Ayumi asked Aomame.

"Afraid of what?"

"Don't you see? You and he might never cross paths again. Of course, a chance meeting *could* occur, and I hope it happens. I really do, for your sake. But realistically speaking, you have to see there's a huge possibility you'll never be able to meet him again. And even if you *do* meet, he might already be married to somebody else. He might have two kids. Isn't that so? And in that case, you may have to live the rest of your life alone, never being joined with the one person you love in all the world. Don't you find that scary?"

Aomame stared at the red wine in her glass. "Maybe I do," she said. "But at least I *have* someone I love."

"Even if he never loved you?"

"If you can love someone with your whole heart, even one person, then there's salvation in life. Even if you can't get together with that person."

Ayumi thought this over for a while. The waiter approached and refilled their wineglasses. Taking a sip, Aomame thought, *Ayumi is right. Who could possibly object to a wine like this?*

"You're amazing," Ayumi said, "the way you can put this in such a philosophical perspective."

"I'm not being philosophical. I'm just telling you what I honestly think."

"I was in love with somebody once," Ayumi said with a confidential air. "Right after I graduated from high school. The boy I first had sex with. He was three years older than me. But he dumped me for somebody else right away. I went kind of wild after that. It was really hard on me. I got over him, but I still haven't recovered from the wild part. He was a real two-timing bastard, a smooth talker. But I really loved him."

Aomame nodded, and Ayumi picked up her wineglass and took a drink.

"He still calls me once in a while, says he wants to get together. All he wants is my body, of course. I know that. So I don't see him. I know it would just be another mess if I did. Or should I say my *brain* knows it, but my body always reacts. It wants him *so* badly! When these things build up, I let myself go crazy again. I wonder if you know what I mean."

"I certainly do," Aomame said.

"He's really an awful guy, pretty nasty, and he's not that good in bed, either. But at least he's not scared of me, and while I'm with him he treats me well."

"Feelings like that don't give you any choice, do they?" Aomame said. "They come at you whenever they want to. It's not like choosing food from a menu."

"It is in one way: you have regrets after you make a mistake."

They shared a laugh.

Aomame said, "It's the same with menus and men and just about anything else: we *think* we're choosing things for ourselves, but in fact we may not be choosing anything. It could be that everything's decided in advance and we *pretend* we're making choices. Free will may be an illusion. I often think that."

"If that's true, life is pretty dark."

"Maybe so."

"But *if* you can love someone with your whole heart – even if he's a terrible person and even if he doesn't love you back – life is not a hell, at least, though it might be kind of dark. Is that what you're saying?" Ayumi asked.

"Exactly."

"But still," Ayumi said, "it seems to me that this world has a serious shortage of both logic and kindness."

"You may be right," Aomame said. "But it's too late to trade it in for another one."

"The exchange window expired a long time ago," Ayumi said.

"And the receipt's been thrown away."

"You said it."

"Oh, well, no problem," Aomame said. "The world's going to end before we know it."

"Sounds like fun."

"And the kingdom is going to come."

"I can hardly wait," Ayumi said.

*　　*　　*

They ate dessert, drank espresso, and split the bill (which was amazingly cheap). Then they dropped into a neighborhood bar for cocktails.

"Oh, look at *him* over there," Ayumi said. "He's your type, isn't he?"

Aomame swung her gaze in that direction. A tall, middle-aged man was drinking a martini alone at the end of the bar. He looked like a high school scholar-athlete who had entered middle age virtually unchanged. His hair was beginning to thin, but he still had a youthful face.

"He may be, but we're not having anything to do with men today," Aomame declared. "And besides, this is a classy bar."

"I know. I just wanted to see what you'd say."

"We'll do that next time."

Ayumi looked at Aomame. "Does that mean you'll go with me next time? Searching for men, I mean."

"For sure," Aomame said. "Let's do it."

"Great! Something tells me that together, we can do anything!"

Aomame was drinking a daiquiri, Ayumi a Tom Collins.

"Oh, by the way," Aomame said, "on the phone the other day you said we were doing lesbian stuff. What kind of stuff?"

"Oh, *that*," Ayumi said. "It was nothing special. We just faked it a bit to liven things up. You really don't remember anything? You were pretty hot."

"Not a thing. My memory is wiped clean."

"We were naked and touching each other's breasts and kissing down there and – "

"Kissing down there?!" Aomame exclaimed. After the words escaped her lips, she nervously glanced around. She had spoken too loudly in the quiet bar, but fortunately no one seemed to have heard what she said.

"Don't worry, like I said, we were faking it. No tongues."

"Oh, man," Aomame sighed, pressing her temples. "What the hell was *that* all about?"

"I'm sorry," Ayumi said.

"It's not your fault. I should never have let myself get so drunk."

"But really, Aomame, you were so sweet and clean down there. Like new."

"Well, of course, I really *am* almost new down there."

"You mean you don't use it all that often?"

Aomame nodded. "That's exactly what I mean. So, tell me: are you interested in women?"

Ayumi shook her head. "No, I never did anything like that before. Really. But I was pretty drunk, too, and I figured I wouldn't mind doing a little of that stuff as long as it was with you. Faking it. Just for fun. How about you?"

"No, I don't have those kinds of feelings, either. Once, though, when I was in high school, I kind of did stuff like that with a good friend of mine. Neither of us had been planning it. It just sort of happened."

"It's probably not that unusual. Did you *feel* anything that time?"

"I did, I think," Aomame answered honestly. "But only that once. I also felt it was wrong and never did anything like it again."

"You mean you think lesbian sex is wrong?"

"No, not at all. I'm not saying lesbian sex is wrong or dirty or anything. I mean I just felt I shouldn't get into that kind of a relationship with that particular friend. I didn't want to change an important friendship into anything so physical."

"I see," Ayumi said. "You know, if it's okay with you, would you mind putting me up tonight? I don't feel like going back to the dorm. The minute I walk in there it will just ruin the elegant mood we've managed to create this evening."

Aomame took her last sip of daiquiri and set her glass on the bar. "I don't mind putting you up, but no fooling around."

"No, no, that's fine, I'm not looking for that. I just want to stay with you a little longer. I don't care where you put me to bed. I can sleep anywhere – even on the floor. And I'm off duty tomorrow, so we can hang out in the morning, too."

They took the subway back to Aomame's apartment in Jiyuga-oka, arriving just before eleven. Both were pleasantly drunk and sleepy. Aomame put bedding on the sofa and lent Ayumi a pair of pajamas.

"Can I get in bed with you for a minute or two?" Ayumi asked. "I want to stay close to you just a little bit longer. No funny business, I promise."

"I don't mind," Aomame said, struck by the fact that a woman who had killed three men would be lying in bed with an active-duty policewoman. Life was so strange!

Ayumi crawled under the covers and wrapped her arms around Aomame, her firm breasts pressing against Aomame's arm, her breath smelling of alcohol and toothpaste. "Don't you think my breasts are too big?" she asked Aomame.

"Not at all. They're beautiful."

"Sure, but, I don't know, big boobs make you look stupid, don't you think? Mine bounce when I run, and I'm too embarrassed to hang my bras out to dry – they're like two big salad bowls."

"Men seem to like them like that."

"And even my nipples are too big." Ayumi unbuttoned her pajama top and pulled out a breast. "Look. This is a big nipple! Don't you think it's odd?"

Aomame looked at Ayumi's nipple. It was certainly not small, but not so big as to cause concern, maybe a little bit bigger than Tamaki's. "It's nice. Did somebody tell you your nipples are too big?"

"Yeah, one guy. He said they're the biggest he's ever seen in his life."

"I'm sure he hadn't seen very many. *Yours* are ordinary. *Mine* are too small."

"No, I like your breasts. They're very elegantly shaped, and they give this *intellectual* impression."

"That's ridiculous. They're too small, and they're different sizes. I have trouble buying bras because one side is bigger than the other."

"Really? I guess we all have our issues."

"Exactly. Now go to sleep," Aomame said.

Ayumi stretched her arm down and started to put a finger into Aomame's pajamas. Aomame grabbed her hand.

"No, you promised."

"Sorry," Ayumi said, pulling her hand back. "You're right, I did promise, didn't I? I must be drunk. But I'm crazy about you. Like some mousy little high school girl."

Aomame said nothing.

Almost whispering, Ayumi said, "What I think is that you're saving the one thing that's most important to you for that boy. It's true, isn't it? I envy you. That you've got somebody to save yourself for."

She could be right, Aomame thought. *But what* is *the one thing that's most important to me?*

"Now go to sleep," Aomame said. "I'll hold you until you fall asleep."

"Thank you," Ayumi said. "Sorry for putting you to so much trouble."

"Don't apologize. This is no trouble."

Aomame continued to feel Ayumi's warm breath against her side. A dog howled in the distance, and someone slammed a window shut. All the while, Aomame kept stroking Ayumi's hair.

Aomame slipped out of bed after Ayumi was sound asleep. She would be the one sleeping on the sofa tonight, it seemed. She took a bottle of mineral water from the refrigerator and drank two glasses from it. Then she stepped out onto her small balcony and sat in an aluminum chair, looking at the neighborhood stretched out below. It was a soft spring night. The breeze carried the roar of distant streets like a man-made ocean. The glitter of neon had diminished somewhat now that midnight had passed.

I'm fond of this girl Ayumi, no doubt about it. I want to be as good to her as I can. After Tamaki died, I made up my mind to live without deep ties to anyone. I never once felt that I wanted a new friend. But for some reason I feel my heart opening to Ayumi. I can even confess my true feelings to her with a certain degree of honesty. She is totally different from you, of course, Aomame said to the Tamaki inside. *You are special. I grew up with you. No one else can compare.*

Aomame leaned her head back and looked up at the sky for a time. Even as her eyes took in the sky, her mind wandered through distant memories. The time she spent with Tamaki, the talking they did, and the touching. . . . Soon, she began to sense that the night sky she saw above her was somehow different from the sky she was used to seeing. The strangeness of it was subtle but undeniable.

Some time had to pass before she was able to grasp what the difference was. And even after she had grasped it, she had to work hard to accept it. What her vision had seized upon, her mind could not easily confirm.

There were two moons in the sky – a small moon and a large one. They were floating there side by side. The large one was the usual moon that she had always seen. It was nearly full, and yellow. But there was another moon right next to it. It had an unfamiliar shape. It was somewhat lopsided, and greenish, as though thinly covered with moss. This was what her vision had seized upon.

Aomame stared at the two moons with narrowed eyes. Then she closed her eyes, let a moment pass, took a deep breath, and opened her eyes again, expecting to find that everything had returned to normal and there was only one moon. But nothing had changed. The light was not playing tricks on her, nor had her eyesight gone strange. There could be no doubt that two moons were clearly floating in the sky side by side – a yellow one and a green one.

She thought of waking Ayumi to ask if there really were two moons up there, but she decided against it. Ayumi might say, "Of *course* there are two moons in the sky. They increased in number last year." Or then again, she might say, "What are you talking about? There's only one moon up there. Something must be wrong with your eyes." Neither response would solve the problem now facing her. Both would only deepen it.

Aomame raised her hands to cover the lower half of her face, and she continued staring at the two moons. *Something is happening, for sure*, she thought. Her heartbeat sped up. *Something's wrong with the world, or something's wrong with me: one or the other. The bottle and the cap don't fit: is the problem with the bottle or the cap?*

She went back inside, locked the balcony door, and drew the curtain. She took a bottle of brandy from the cabinet and poured herself a glassful. Ayumi was sleeping nicely in bed, her breathing deep and even. Aomame kept watch over her and took a sip of brandy now and then. Planting her elbows on the kitchen table, she struggled not to think about what lay beyond the curtain.

Maybe the world really is ending, she thought.

"And the kingdom is coming," Aomame muttered to herself.

"I can hardly wait," somebody said somewhere.

CHAPTER 16

Tengo

I'M GLAD YOU LIKED IT

Tengo had spent ten days reworking *Air Chrysalis* before handing it over to Komatsu as a newly finished work, following which he was visited by a string of calm, tranquil days. He taught three days a week at the cram school, and got together once a week with his married girlfriend. The rest of his time he spent doing housework, taking walks, and writing his own novel. April passed like this. The cherry blossoms scattered, new buds appeared on the trees, the magnolias reached full bloom, and the seasons moved along in stages. The days flowed by smoothly, regularly, uneventfully. This was the life that Tengo most wanted, each week linking automatically and seamlessly with the next.

Amid all the sameness, however, one change became evident. A good change. Tengo was aware that, as he went on writing his novel, a new wellspring was forming inside him. Not that its water was gushing forth: it was more like a tiny spring among the rocks. The flow may have been limited, but it was continuous, welling up drop by drop. He was in no hurry. He felt no pressure. All he had to do was wait patiently for the water to collect in the rocky basin until he could scoop it up. Then he would sit at his desk, turning what he had scooped into words, and the story would advance quite naturally.

The concentrated work of rewriting *Air Chrysalis* might have dislodged a rock that had been blocking his wellspring until now. Tengo had no idea why that should be so, but he had a definite sense that a heavy lid had finally come off. He felt as though his body had become lighter, that he had emerged from a cramped space and could now stretch his arms and legs freely. *Air Chrysalis* had probably stimulated something that had been deep inside him all along.

Tengo sensed, too, that something very like desire was growing inside him. This was the first time in his life he had ever experienced such a feeling. All through high school and college, his judo coach and older teammates would often say to him, "You have the talent and the strength, and you practice enough, but you just don't have the desire." They were probably right. He lacked that drive to win at all costs, which is why he would often make it to the semifinals and the finals but lose the all-important championship match. He exhibited these tendencies in everything, not just judo. He was more placid than determined. It was the same with his fiction. He could write with some style and make up reasonably interesting stories, but his work lacked the strength to grab the reader by the throat. Something was missing. And so he would always make it to the short list but never take the new writers' prize, as Komatsu had said.

After he finished rewriting *Air Chrysalis*, however, Tengo was truly chagrined for the first time in his life. While engaged in the rewrite, he had been totally absorbed in the process, moving his hands without thinking. Once he had completed the work and handed it to Komatsu, however, Tengo was assaulted by a profound sense of powerlessness. Once the powerlessness began to abate, a kind of rage surged up from deep inside him. The rage was directed at Tengo himself. *I used another person's story to create a rewrite that amounts to a literary fraud, and I did it with far more passion than I bring to my own work. Isn't a writer someone who finds the story hidden inside and uses the proper words to express it? Aren't you ashamed of yourself? You should be able to write something as good as* Air Chrysalis *if you make up your mind to do it. Isn't that true?*

But he had to prove it to himself.

Tengo decided to discard the manuscript he had written thus far and start a brand-new story from scratch. He closed his eyes and, for a long time, listened closely to the dripping of the little spring inside him. Eventually the words began to come naturally to him. Little by little, taking all the time he needed, he began to form them into sentences.

In early May Komatsu called him for the first time in quite a while. The phone rang just before nine o'clock at night.

"It's all set," Komatsu said, with a note of excitement in his voice. This was rare for him.

Tengo could not tell at first what Komatsu was talking about. "What's all set?"

"What else? *Air Chrysalis* took the new writers' award a few minutes ago. The committee reached a unanimous decision, with none of the usual debate. I guess you could say it was inevitable, it's such a powerful work. In any case, things have started to move. We're in this together from now on, Tengo. Let's give it our best shot."

Tengo glanced at the calendar on the wall. Come to think of it, today *was* the day the screening committee was going to pick the winner. Tengo had been so absorbed in writing his own novel, he had lost all sense of time.

"So what happens now?" Tengo asked. "In terms of the prize schedule, I mean."

"Tomorrow the newspapers announce it – every paper in the country. They'll probably have photos, too. A pretty seventeen-year-old girl wins: that alone will cause a sensation. Don't take this the wrong way, but that has a lot more news value than if the new writers' prize had gone to some thirty-year-old cram school teacher who looks like a bear coming out of hibernation."

"Way more," Tengo said.

"Then comes the award ceremony on May 16 in a Shinbashi hotel. The press conference is all arranged."

"Will Fuka-Eri be there?"

"I'm sure she will, this time at least. There's no way the winner of a new writers' prize wouldn't be present at the award ceremony. If we can get through that without any major mishaps, we can then adopt a policy of total secrecy. 'Sorry, but the author does not wish to make public appearances.' We can hold them at bay like that, and the truth will never come out."

Tengo tried to imagine Fuka-Eri holding a press conference in a hotel ballroom. A row of microphones, cameras flashing. He couldn't picture it.

"Do you really need to have a press conference?" he asked Komatsu.

"We'll have to, at least once, to keep up appearances."

"It's bound to be a disaster!"

"Which is why it's your job, Tengo, to make sure it doesn't turn into a disaster."

Tengo went silent. Ominous dark clouds appeared on the horizon.

"Hey, are you still there?" Komatsu asked.

"I'm here," Tengo said. "What does that mean – it's *my job*?"

"You have to drill Fuka-Eri on how a press conference works and how to deal with it. Pretty much the same sorts of questions come up every time, so you should prepare answers for questions they're likely to ask, and have her memorize them word for word. You teach at a cram school. You must know how to do stuff like that."

"You want *me* to do it?"

"Of course. She trusts you, for some reason. She'll listen to you. There's no way I can do it. She hasn't even agreed to meet me."

Tengo sighed. He wished he could cut all ties with *Air Chrysalis*. He had done everything asked of him, and now he just wanted to concentrate on his own work. Something told him, however, that it was not going to be that simple, and he knew that bad premonitions have a far higher accuracy rate than good ones.

"Are you free in the evening the day after tomorrow?" Komatsu asked.

"I am."

"Six o'clock at the usual café in Shinjuku. Fuka-Eri will be there."

"I can't do what you're asking me to do," Tengo said to Komatsu. "I don't know anything about press conferences. I've never even seen one."

"You want to be a novelist, right? So imagine it. Isn't that the job of the novelist – to imagine things he's never seen?"

"Yes, but aren't you the one who told me all I had to do was rewrite *Air Chrysalis,* that you'd take care of everything else after that, that I could just sit on the sidelines and watch the rest of the game?"

"Look, I'd gladly do it if I could. I'm not crazy about asking people to do things for me, but that's exactly what I'm doing now, pleading with you to do this job because I can't do it. Don't you see? It's as if we're in a boat shooting the rapids. I've got my hands full steering the rudder, so I'm letting you take the oar. If you tell me you can't do it, the boat's going to capsize and we all might go under, including Fuka-Eri. You don't want that to happen, do you?"

Tengo sighed again. Why did he always get himself backed into a corner where he couldn't refuse? "Okay, I'll do my best. But I can't promise it's going to work."

"That's all I'm asking," Komatsu said. "I'll owe you big for this. I mean, Fuka-Eri seems to have made up her mind not to talk to anyone but you. And there's one more thing. You and I have to set up a new company."

"A company?"

"Company, office, firm – call it anything you like. To handle Fuka-Eri's literary activities. A paper company, of course. Officially, Fuka-Eri will be paid by the company. We'll have Professor Ebisuno be her representative and you'll be a company employee. We can make up some kind of title for you, it doesn't matter, but the main thing is the company will pay you. I'll be in on it, too, but without revealing my name. If people found out that I was involved, *that* would cause some serious trouble. Anyway, that's how we divide up the profits. All I need is for you to put your seal on a few documents, and I'll take care of the rest. I know a good lawyer."

Tengo thought about what Komatsu was telling him. "Can you please just drop me from your plan? I don't need to be paid. I enjoyed rewriting *Air Chrysalis,* and I learned a lot from it. I'm glad that Fuka-Eri got the prize and I'll do my best to prepare her for the press conference. But that's all. I don't want to have anything to do with this convoluted 'company' arrangement. That would be straight-up fraud."

"You can't turn back now, Tengo," Komatsu said. "Straight-up fraud? Maybe so. But you must have known that from the start when we decided to pull the wool over people's eyes with this half-invented author, Fuka-Eri. Am I right? Of course something like this is going to involve money, and that's going to require a sophisticated system to handle it. This is not child's play. It's too late to start saying you don't want to have anything to do with it, that it's too dangerous, that you don't need money. If you were going to get out of the boat, you should have done it before, while the stream was still gentle. You can't do it now. We need an official head count to set up a company, and I can't start bringing in new people now who don't know what's going on. You have to do it. You're right in the thick of what's happening now."

Tengo racked his brain without producing a single useful thought. "I do have one question, though," he said to Komatsu. "Judging from what you're saying, Professor Ebisuno intends to give his full approval to the plan. It sounds as if he's already agreed to set up the fake company and act as a representative."

"As Fuka-Eri's guardian, the Professor understands and approves of the entire situation and has given us the green light. I called him as soon as you told me about your talk with him. He remembered me, of course. I think he didn't say anything about me because he wanted to get your uncensored opinion of me. He said you impressed him as a sharp observer of people. What in the world did you tell him about me?"

"What does Professor Ebisuno have to gain from participating in this plan? He can't possibly be doing it for the money."

"You're right about that. He's not the kind of guy to be influenced by a little spare change."

"So why would he let himself get involved in such a risky plan? Does he have something to gain from it?"

"I don't know any better than you do. He's a hard one to read."

"And so are you. That gives us a lot of deep motives to guess about."

"Well, anyway," Komatsu said, "the Professor may look like just another innocent old guy, but in fact he's quite inscrutable."

"How much does Fuka-Eri know about the plan?"

"She doesn't know – and she doesn't need to know – anything about the behind-the-scenes stuff. She trusts Professor Ebisuno and she likes you. That's why I'm asking you for more help."

Tengo shifted the phone from one hand to the other. He felt a need to trace the progress of the current situation. "By the way, Professor Ebisuno is not a scholar anymore, is he?

He left the university, and he's not writing books or anything."

"True, he's cut all ties with academia. He was an outstanding scholar, but he doesn't seem to miss the academic world. But then, he never did want much to do with authority or the organization. He was always something of a maverick."

"What sort of work is he doing now?"

"I think he's a stockbroker," Komatsu said. "Or, if that sounds too old-fashioned, he's an investment consultant. He manages money for people, and while he moves it around for them, he makes his own profit on the side. He stays holed up on the mountaintop, issuing suggestions to buy or sell. His instinct for it is frighteningly good. He also excels at analyzing data and has put together his own system. It was just a hobby for him at first, but it became his main profession. So that's the story. He's pretty famous in those circles. One thing's for sure: he's not hurting for money."

"I don't see any connection between cultural anthropology and stock trading," Tengo said.

"In general, there is no connection, but there is for him."

"And he's a hard one to read."

"Exactly."

Tengo pressed his fingertips against his temples. Then, resigning himself to his fate, he said, "I'll meet Fuka-Eri at the usual café in Shinjuku at six o'clock the day after tomorrow, and we'll prepare for the press conference. That's what you want me to do, right?"

"That's the plan," Komatsu said. "You know, Tengo, don't think too hard about this stuff for the time being. Just go with the flow. Things like this don't happen all that often in one lifetime. This is the magnificent world of a picaresque novel. Just brace yourself and enjoy the smell of evil. We're shooting the rapids. And when we go over the falls, let's do it together in grand style!"

*   *   *

Tengo met Fuka-Eri at the Shinjuku café in the evening two days later. She wore a slim pair of jeans and a thin summer sweater that clearly revealed the outline of her breasts. Her hair hung down long and straight, and her skin had a fresh glow. The male customers kept glancing in her direction. Tengo could feel their gazes. Fuka-Eri herself, though, seemed totally unaware of them. When this girl was announced as the winner of a literary magazine's new writers' prize, it would almost certainly cause a commotion.

Fuka-Eri had already received word that she had won the prize, but she seemed neither pleased nor excited by it. She didn't care one way or the other. It was a summerlike day, but she ordered hot cocoa and clutched the cup in both hands, savoring every drop. No one had told her about the upcoming press conference, but when Tengo explained, she had no reaction.

"You *do* know what a press conference is, don't you?"

"Press conference . . ." Fuka-Eri repeated the words.

"You sit up on the podium and answer questions from a bunch of newspaper and magazine reporters. They'll take your picture. There might even be TV cameras. The whole country will see reports on the questions and answers. It's very unusual for a seventeen-year-old girl to win a literary magazine's new writers' award. It'll be big news. They'll make a big deal of the fact that the committee's decision was unanimous. That almost never happens."

"Questions and answers," Fuka-Eri asked.

"They ask the questions, you give the answers."

"What kind of questions."

"All kinds of questions. About the work, about you, about your private life, your hobbies, your plans for the future. It might be a good idea to prepare answers now for those kinds of questions."

"Why."

"It's safer that way. So you aren't at a loss for answers and don't say anything that might invite misunderstanding. It wouldn't hurt to get ready for it now. Kind of like a rehearsal."

Fuka-Eri drank her cocoa in silence. Then she looked at Tengo with eyes that said, "I'm really not interested in doing such a thing, but if you think it's necessary . . ." Her eyes could be more eloquent – or at least speak more full sentences – than her words. But she could hardly conduct a press conference with her eyes.

Tengo took a piece of paper from his briefcase and unfolded it on the table. It contained a list of questions that were likely to come up at the press conference. Tengo had put a lot of time and thought into compiling it the night before.

"I'll ask a question, and you answer me as if I'm a newspaper reporter, okay?"

Fuka-Eri nodded.

"Have you written lots of stories before?"

"Lots," Fuka-Eri replied.

"When did you start writing?"

"A long time ago."

"That's fine," Tengo said. "Short answers are good. No need to add anything extra. Like, the fact that Azami did the writing for you. Okay?"

Fuka-Eri nodded.

"You shouldn't say anything about that. It's just our little secret, yours and mine."

"I won't say anything about that," Fuka-Eri said.

"Did you think you'd win when you submitted your work for the new writers' prize?"

She smiled but said nothing.

"So you don't want to answer that?"

"No."

"That's fine. Just keep quiet and smile when you don't want to answer. They're stupid questions, anyway."

Fuka-Eri nodded again.

"Where did you get the story line for *Air Chrysalis*?"

"From the blind goat."

"Good answer. What are your friends at school saying about your winning the prize?"

"I don't go to school."

"Why don't you go to school?"

No answer.

"Do you plan to keep writing fiction?"

Silence again.

Tengo drank the last of his coffee and returned the cup to the saucer. From the speakers recessed in the café's ceiling, a string performance of soundtrack music from *The Sound of Music* played at low volume.

Raindrops on roses and whiskers on kittens . . .

"Are my answers bad," Fuka-Eri asked.

"Not at all," Tengo said. "Not at all. They're fine."

"Good," Fuka-Eri said.

Tengo meant it. Even though she could not speak more than a sentence at a time and some punctuation marks were missing, her answers were, in a sense, perfect. The best thing was her instant response to every question. Also good was the way she looked directly into the eyes of the questioner without blinking. This proved that her answers were honest and their shortness was not meant as a put-down. Another bonus was that no one was likely to be able to grasp her precise meaning. That was the main thing that Tengo was hoping for – that she should give an impression of sincerity even as she mystified her listeners.

"Your favorite novel is . . . ?"

"*The Tale of the Heike*."

Tengo was astounded. To think that a thirteenth-century samurai war chronicle should be her favorite "novel"! What a great answer!

"What do you like about *The Tale of the Heike*?"

"Everything."

"How about another favorite?"

"*Tales of Times Now Past.*"

"But that's even older! Don't you read any new literature?"

Fuka-Eri gave it a moment of thought before saying, " 'Sansho the Bailiff.' "

Wonderful! Ogai Mori must have written that one around 1915. This was what she thought of as "new literature."

"Do you have any hobbies?"

"Listening to music."

"What kind of music?"

"I like Bach."

"Anything in particular?"

"BWV 846 to 893."

Tengo mulled that one over. "*The Well-Tempered Clavier,* Books I and II."

"Yes."

"Why did you answer with the BWV numbers?"

"They're easier to remember."

The Well-Tempered Clavier was truly heavenly music for mathematicians. It was composed of prelude and fugue pairs in major and minor keys using all twelve tones of the scale, twenty-four pieces per book, forty-eight pieces in all, comprising a perfect cycle.

"How about other works?" Tengo asked.

"BWV 244."

Tengo could not immediately recall which work of Bach's had a BWV number of 244.

Fuka-Eri began to sing.

> Buß' und Reu'
> Buß' und Reu'
> Knirscht das Sündenherz entzwei

Buß' und Reu'
Buß' und Reu'
Knirscht das Sündenherz entzwei
Knirscht das Sündenherz entzwei
Buß' und Reu'
Buß' und Reu'
Knirscht das Sündenherz entzwei
Buß' und Reu'
Knirscht das Sündenherz entzwei
Daß die Tropfen meiner Zähren
Angenehme Spezerei
Treuer Jesu, dir gebären.

Tengo was momentarily dumbstruck. Her singing was not exactly on key, but her German pronunciation was amazingly clear and precise.

" 'St. Matthew Passion,' " Tengo said. "You know it by heart."

"No I don't," the girl said.

Tengo wanted to say something, but the words would not come to him. All he could do was look down at his notes and move on to the next question.

"Do you have a boyfriend?"

Fuka-Eri shook her head.

"Why not?"

"I don't want to get pregnant."

"It's possible to have a boyfriend without getting pregnant."

Fuka-Eri said nothing but instead blinked several times.

"Why don't you want to get pregnant?"

Fuka-Eri kept her mouth clamped shut. Tengo felt sorry for having asked such a stupid question.

"Okay, let's stop," Tengo said, returning the list to his briefcase. "We don't really know what they're going to ask, and you'll be fine answering them any way you like. You can do it."

"That's good," Fuka-Eri said with apparent relief.

"I'm sure you think it's a waste of time to prepare these answers."

Fuka-Eri gave a little shrug.

"I agree with you. I'm not doing this because I want to. Mr. Komatsu asked me to do it."

Fuka-Eri nodded.

"But," Tengo said, "*please* don't tell anyone that I rewrote *Air Chrysalis*. You understand that, don't you?"

Fuka-Eri nodded twice. "I wrote it by myself."

"In any case, *Air Chrysalis* is your work alone and no one else's. That has been clear from the outset."

"I wrote it by myself," Fuka-Eri said again.

"Did you read my rewritten *Air Chrysalis*?"

"Azami read it to me."

"How did you like it?"

"You're a good writer."

"Which means you liked it, I suppose?"

"It's like I wrote it," Fuka-Eri said.

Tengo looked at her. She picked up her cocoa cup and took a sip. He had to struggle not to look at the lovely swell of her chest.

"I'm glad to hear that," he said. "I really enjoyed rewriting *Air Chrysalis*. Of course, it was very hard work trying not to destroy what you'd done with it. So it's very important to me to know whether you liked the finished product or not."

Fuka-Eri nodded silently. Then, as if trying to ascertain something, she brought her hand up to her small, well-formed earlobe.

The waitress approached and refilled their water glasses. Tengo took a swallow to moisten his throat. Then, screwing up his courage, he gave voice to a thought that he had been toying with for a while.

"I have my own request to make of you now, if you don't mind."

"What's that."

"I'd like you to go to the press conference in the same clothes you're wearing today."

Fuka-Eri gave him a puzzled look. Then she looked down to check each article of clothing she had on, as if she had been unaware until this moment of what she was wearing.

"You want me to go wearing this," she asked.

"Right. I'd like you to go to the press conference wearing exactly what you're wearing now."

"Why."

"It looks good on you. It shows off the shape of your chest beautifully. This is strictly my own hunch, but I suspect the reporters won't be able to stop themselves from looking down there and they'll forget to ask you tough questions. Of course, if you don't like the idea, that's fine. I'm not insisting."

Fuka-Eri said, "Azami picks all my clothes."

"Not you?"

"I don't care what I wear."

"So Azami picked your outfit today?"

"Azami picked it."

"Even so, it looks great on you."

"So this outfit makes my chest look good," she asked without a question mark.

"Most definitely. It's a real attention-getter."

"This sweater and bra are a good match."

Fuka-Eri looked straight into his eyes. Tengo felt himself blushing.

"I can't tell what kind of matching is involved, but the, uh, *effect* is excellent."

Fuka-Eri was still staring into Tengo's eyes. Gravely, she asked, "You can't stop yourself from looking down there."

"It's true, I must confess," Tengo said.

Fuka-Eri pulled on the collar of her sweater and all but stuck her nose inside as she looked down, apparently to check out what kind of bra she had on today. Then she focused her eyes on Tengo's bright red face for a moment as if looking at some kind of curiosity. "I will do as you say," she said a moment later.

"Thank you," Tengo said, bringing their session to an end.

Tengo walked Fuka-Eri to Shinjuku Station. Many people on the street had their jackets off. A few women wore sleeveless tops. The bustle of people combined with the traffic created the liberated sound unique to the city. A fresh early-summer breeze swept down the street. Tengo was mystified: where could such a wonderful-smelling wind come from to reach the crowded streets of Shinjuku?

"Are you going back to your house in the country?" Tengo asked Fuka-Eri. The trains were jammed; it would take her forever to get home.

Fuka-Eri shook her head. "I have a room in Shinano-machi. Just a few minutes away from here."

"You stay there when it gets too late to go home?"

"Futamatao is too far away."

As before, Fuka-Eri held Tengo's left hand while they were walking to the station. She did it the way a little girl holds a grown-up's hand, but still it made Tengo's heart pound to have his hand held by such a beautiful girl.

When they reached the station, she let go of his hand and bought a ticket to Shinano-machi from the machine.

"Don't worry about the press conference," Fuka-Eri said.

"I'm not worried."

"Even if you don't worry, I can do it okay."

"I know that," Tengo said. "I'm not the least bit worried. I'm sure it will be okay."

Without speaking, Fuka-Eri disappeared through the ticket gate into the crowd.

After leaving Fuka-Eri, Tengo went to a little bar near the Kinokuniya bookstore and ordered a gin and tonic. This was a bar he would go to now and then. He liked the old-fashioned decor and the fact that they had no music playing. He sat alone at the bar and stared at his left hand for a while, thinking nothing in particular. This was the hand that Fuka-Eri had been holding. It still retained her touch. He thought about her chest, its beautiful curves. The shape was so perfect it had almost no sexual meaning.

As he thought about these things, Tengo found himself wanting to talk with his older girlfriend on the telephone – to talk about anything at all: her complaints about child raising, the approval rating of the Nakasone government, it didn't matter. He just wanted to hear her voice. If possible, he wanted to meet her somewhere right away and have sex with her. But calling her at home was out of the question. Her husband might answer. One of her children might answer. He never did the phoning. That was one of the rules they had established.

Tengo ordered another gin and tonic, and while he waited for it he imagined himself in a little boat shooting the rapids. On the phone Komatsu had said, "When we go over the falls, let's do it together in grand style!" But could Tengo take him at his word? Wouldn't Komatsu leap onto a handy boulder just before they reached the falls? "Sorry, Tengo," he would say, "but I just remembered some business I have to take care of. I'll leave the rest of this to you." And the only one to go over the falls in style would be Tengo himself. It was not inconceivable. Indeed, it was all too conceivable.

He went home, went to bed, and dreamed. He hadn't had such a vivid dream in a very long time. He was a tiny piece in a gigantic puzzle. But instead of having one fixed shape, his shape kept changing. And so – of course – he couldn't fit anywhere. As he tried to sort out where he belonged, he was also given a set amount of time to gather the scattered pages of the timpani section of a score. A strong wind swept the pages in all directions. He went around picking up one page at a time. He had to check the page numbers and arrange them in order as his body changed shape like an amoeba. The situation was out of control. Eventually Fuka-Eri came along and grabbed his left hand. Tengo's shape stopped changing. The wind suddenly died and stopped scattering the pages of the score. "What a relief!" Tengo thought, but in that instant his time began to run out. "This is the end," Fuka-Eri informed him in a whisper. One sentence, as always. Time stopped, and the world ended. The earth ground slowly to a halt, and all sound and light vanished.

When he woke up the next day, the world was still there, and things were already moving forward, like the great karmic wheel of Indian mythology that kills every living thing in its path.

CHAPTER 17

Aomame

WHETHER WE ARE HAPPY OR UNHAPPY

Aomame stepped out onto her balcony again the next night to find that there were still two moons in the sky. The big one was the normal moon. It wore a mysterious white coating, as if it had just burrowed its way there through a mountain of ash, but aside from that it was the same old moon she was used to seeing, the moon that Neil Armstrong marked with a first small step but giant leap in that hot summer of 1969. Hanging next to it was a small, green, lopsided moon, nestled shyly by the big moon like an inferior child.

There must be something wrong with my mind, Aomame thought. *There has always been only one moon, and there should only be one now. If the number of moons had suddenly increased to two, it should have caused some actual changes to life on earth. The tides, say, should have been seriously altered, and everyone would be talking about it. I couldn't possibly have failed to notice it until now. This is different from just happening to miss some articles in the paper.*

Or is it really so different? Can I declare that with one hundred percent certainty?

Aomame scowled for a time. *Strange things keep happening around me these days. The world is moving ahead on its own without my being aware of it, as if we're playing a game in which everybody else can move only when I have my eyes closed. Then it might not be so strange for there to be two moons hanging in the sky side by side. Perhaps, at some point when my mind was sleeping, the little one happened along from somewhere in space and decided to settle into the earth's gravitational field, looking like a distant cousin of the moon.*

Police officers were issued new uniforms and new pistols. The police and a radical group staged a wild gun battle in the mountains of Yamanashi. These things occurred without my being aware of them. There was also a news report that the U.S. and the USSR jointly constructed a moon base. Could there be some connection between that and the increase in the number of moons? Aomame probed her memory to see if there had been an article about the new moon in the compact edition of the newspaper she read in the library, but could think of nothing.

She wished that she could ask someone about these things, but she had no idea whom to ask nor how to go about it. Would it be all right for her just to say, "Hey, I think there are two moons in the sky. Do you mind having a look for me?" No, it would be a stupid question under any circumstances. If the number of moons had in fact increased to two, it would be strange for her not to know that. If there was still only the one moon, people would think she had gone crazy.

She lowered herself into the aluminum chair, resting her feet on the balcony railing. She thought of ten different ways of asking the question, and some she even tried out loud, but they all sounded as stupid as the first. *Oh, what the hell. The whole situation defies common sense. There's no way to come up with a sensible question about it, obviously.*

She decided to shelve the question of the second moon for the time being. *I'll just wait and see what happens. It's not*

causing me any practical problems for now. And maybe at some
point I'll notice that it disappeared when I wasn't looking.

She went to the sports club in Hiroo the following afternoon,
taught two martial arts classes, and had one private lesson.
Stopping by the front desk, she was surprised to find a message
for her from the dowager in Azabu, asking her to call when she
was free.

Tamaru answered the phone as always. He explained that
the dowager wondered if Aomame could come to the house
the following day if possible. She wanted the usual program,
to be followed by a light supper.

Aomame said she could come after four and that she would
be delighted to join the dowager for supper. Tamaru confirmed
the appointment, but before he could hang up, Aomame asked
him if he had seen the moon lately.

"The moon?" Tamaru asked. "You mean the moon – up in
the sky?"

"Yes, the moon."

"I can't say I recall consciously looking at it recently. Is
something going on with the moon?"

"Nothing special," Aomame said. "All right, see you after
four tomorrow."

Tamaru hesitated a moment before hanging up.

There were two moons again that night, both two days past
full. Aomame had a glass of brandy in one hand as she stared
at the pair of moons, big and small, as if at an unsolvable puzzle. The more she looked, the more enigmatic the combination
felt to her. If only she could ask the moon directly, "How did
you suddenly come by this little green companion of yours?"!
But the moon would not favor her with a reply.

The moon had been observing the earth close-up longer than
anyone. It must have witnessed all of the phenomena occurring

– and all of the acts carried out – on this earth. But the moon remained silent; it told no stories. All it did was embrace the heavy past with cool, measured detachment. On the moon there was neither air nor wind. Its vacuum was perfect for preserving memories unscathed. No one could unlock the heart of the moon. Aomame raised her glass to the moon and asked, "Have you gone to bed with someone in your arms lately?"

The moon did not answer.

"Do you have any friends?" she asked.

The moon did not answer.

"Don't you get tired of always playing it cool?"

The moon did not answer.

Tamaru met her at the front door as always. "I saw the moon last night!" he said immediately.

"Oh, really?" Aomame said.

"Thanks to you, I started wondering about it. I hadn't stopped and looked at the moon in quite a while. It's nice. Very calming."

"Were you with a lover?"

"Exactly," Tamaru said, tapping the side of his nose. "Is something up with the moon?"

"Not at all," Aomame said, then added cautiously, "It's just that, I don't know, I've been *concerned* about the moon lately."

"For no reason at all?"

"Nothing in particular," Aomame said.

Tamaru nodded in silence. He seemed to be drawing his own conclusions. This man did not trust things that lacked reasons. Instead of pursuing the matter, however, he led Aomame to the sunroom. The dowager was there, dressed in a jersey top and bottom for exercise, seated in her reading chair and listening to John Dowland's instrumental piece "Lachrimae" while reading a book. This was one of her favorite pieces of music. Aomame had heard it many times and knew the melody.

"Sorry for the short notice," the dowager said. "This time slot just happened to open up yesterday."

"You don't have to apologize to me," Aomame said.

Tamaru carried in a tray holding a pot of herbal tea and proceeded to fill two elegant cups. He closed the door on his way out, leaving the two women alone. They drank their tea in silence, listening to Dowland and looking at the blaze of azalea blossoms in the garden. Whenever she came here, Aomame felt she was in another world. The air was heavy, and time had its own special way of flowing.

The dowager said, "Often when I listen to this music, I'm struck by mysterious emotions with regard to time." She seemed almost to have read Aomame's mind. "To think that people four hundred years ago were listening to the same music we're hearing now! Doesn't it make you feel strange?"

"It does," Aomame said, "but come to think of it, those people four hundred years ago were looking at the same moon we see."

The dowager looked at Aomame with a hint of surprise. Then she nodded. "You're quite right about that. Looking at it that way, I guess there's nothing mysterious about people listening to the same music four hundred years apart."

"Perhaps I should have said *almost* the same moon," Aomame said, looking at the dowager. Her remark seemed to have made no impression on the older woman.

"The performance on this CD uses period instruments," the dowager said, "exactly as it was written at the time, so the music sounds pretty much as it did back then. It's like the moon."

Aomame said, "Even if *things* were the same, people's perception of them might have been very different back then. The darkness of night was probably deeper then, so the moon must have been that much bigger and brighter. And of course people didn't have records or tapes or CDs. They couldn't hear proper performances of music anytime they liked: it was always something special."

"I'm sure you're right," the dowager said. "Things are so convenient for us these days, our perceptions are probably that much duller. Even if it's the same moon hanging in the sky, we may be looking at something quite different. Four hundred years ago, we might have had richer spirits that were closer to nature."

"It was a cruel world, though. More than half of all children died before they could reach maturity, thanks to chronic epidemics and malnutrition. People dropped like flies from polio and tuberculosis and smallpox and measles. There probably weren't very many people who lived past forty. Women bore so many children, they became toothless old hags by the time they were in their thirties. People often had to resort to violence to survive. Tiny children were forced to do such heavy labor that their bones became deformed, and little girls were forced to become prostitutes on a daily basis. Little boys, too, I suspect. Most people led minimal lives in worlds that had nothing to do with richness of perception or spirit. City streets were full of cripples and beggars and criminals. Only a small fraction of the population could gaze at the moon with deep feeling or enjoy a Shakespeare play or listen to the beautiful music of Dowland."

The dowager smiled. "What an interesting person you are!"

Aomame said, "I'm a very ordinary human being. I just happen to like reading books. Especially history books."

"I like history books too. They teach us that we're basically the same, whether now or in the old days. There may be a few differences in clothing and lifestyle, but there's not that much difference in what we think and do. Human beings are ultimately nothing but carriers – passageways – for genes. They ride us into the ground like racehorses from generation to generation. Genes don't think about what constitutes good or evil. They don't care whether we are happy or unhappy. We're just a means to an end for them. The only thing they think about is what is most efficient for them."

"In spite of that, we can't help but think about what is good and what is evil. Is that what you're saying?"

The dowager nodded. "Exactly. People *have to* think about those things. But genes are what control the basis for how we live. Naturally, a contradiction arises," she said with a smile.

Their conversation about history ended there. They drank the rest of their herbal tea and proceeded with martial arts training.

That day they shared a simple dinner in the dowager's home.

"A simple meal is all I can offer you, if that's all right," the dowager said.

"That's fine with me," Aomame said.

Tamaru rolled their meal in on a wagon. A professional chef had doubtless prepared the food, but it was Tamaru's job to serve it. He plucked the bottle of white wine from its ice bucket and poured with practiced movements. The dowager and Aomame both tasted the wine. It had a lovely bouquet and was perfectly chilled. The dinner consisted of boiled white asparagus, salade Niçoise, a crabmeat omelet, and rolls and butter, nothing more. All the ingredients were fresh and delicious, and the portions were moderate. The dowager always ate small amounts of food. She used her knife and fork elegantly, bringing one tiny bite after another to her mouth like a small bird. Tamaru stayed in the farthest corner of the room throughout the meal. Aomame was always amazed how such a powerfully built man could obscure his own presence for such a long time.

The two women spoke only in brief snatches during the meal, concentrating instead on what they ate. Music played at low volume – a Haydn cello concerto. This was another of the dowager's favorites.

After the dishes were taken away, a coffeepot arrived. Tamaru poured, and as he backed away, the dowager turned to him with a finger raised.

"Thank you, Tamaru. That will be all."

Tamaru nodded respectfully and left the room, his footsteps silent as always. The door closed quietly behind him. While the two women drank their coffee, the music ended and a new silence came to the room.

"You and I trust each other, wouldn't you say?" the dowager said, looking straight at Aomame.

Aomame agreed – succinctly, but without reservation.

"We share some important secrets," the dowager said. "We have put our fates in each other's hands."

Aomame nodded silently.

This was the room in which Aomame first confessed her secret to the dowager. Aomame remembered the day clearly. She had known that someday she would have to share the burden she carried in her heart with someone. She could keep it locked up inside herself only so long, and already she was reaching her limit. And so, when the dowager said something to draw her out, Aomame had flung open the door.

She told the dowager how her best friend had lost her mental balance after two years of physical violence from her husband and, unable to flee from him, in agony, she had committed suicide. Aomame allowed nearly a year to pass before concocting an excuse to visit the man's house. There, following an elaborate plan of her own devising, she killed him with a single needle thrust to the back of the neck. It caused no bleeding and left no visible wound. His death was treated simply as the result of illness. No one had any suspicions. Aomame felt that she had done nothing wrong, she told the dowager, either then or now. Nor did she feel any pangs of conscience, though this fact did nothing to lessen the burden of having purposely taken the life of a human being.

The dowager had listened attentively to Aomame's long confession, offering no comment even when Aomame occasionally faltered in her detailed account. When Aomame finished her story, the dowager asked for clarification on a few particulars. Then she reached over and firmly grasped Aomame's hand for a very long time.

"What you did was right," she said, speaking slowly and with conviction. "If he had lived, he eventually would have done the same kind of thing to other women. Men like that always find victims. They're made to do it over and over. You severed the evil at the root. Rest assured, it was not mere personal vengeance."

Aomame buried her face in her hands and cried. She was crying for Tamaki. The dowager found a handkerchief and wiped her tears.

"This is a strange coincidence," the dowager said in a low but resolute voice, "but I also once made a man vanish for almost exactly the same reason."

Aomame raised her head and looked at the dowager. She did not know what to say. What could she be talking about?

The dowager continued, "I did not do it directly, myself, of course. I had neither the physical strength nor your special training. But I did make him vanish through the means that I had at my disposal, leaving behind no concrete evidence. Even if I were to turn myself in and confess, it would be impossible to prove, just as it would be for you. I suppose if there is to be some judgment after death, a god will be the one to judge me, but that doesn't frighten me in the least. I did nothing wrong. I reserve the right to declare the justice of my case in anyone's presence."

The dowager sighed with apparent relief before continuing. "So, then, you and I now have our hands on each other's deepest secrets, don't we?"

Aomame still could not fully grasp what the dowager was telling her. She made a man vanish? Caught between deep doubt and intense shock, Aomame's face began to lose its normal shape. To calm her down, the dowager began to explain what had happened, in a tranquil tone of voice.

Circumstances similar to those of Tamaki Otsuka had led her daughter to end her own life, the dowager said. Her daughter had married the wrong man. The dowager had known from the beginning that the marriage would not go well. She could clearly see that the man had a twisted personality. He had already been involved in several bad situations, their cause almost certainly deeply rooted. But no one could stop the daughter from marrying him. As the dowager had expected, there were repeated instances of domestic violence. The daughter gradually lost whatever self-respect and self-confidence she had and sank into a deep depression. Robbed of the strength to stand on her own, she felt increasingly like an ant trapped in a bowl of sand. Finally, she washed down a large number of sleeping pills with whiskey.

The autopsy revealed many signs of violence on her body: bruises from punching and severe battering, broken bones, and numerous burn scars from cigarettes pressed against the flesh. Both wrists showed signs of having been tightly bound. The man apparently enjoyed using a rope. Her nipples were deformed. The husband was called in and questioned by the police. He was willing to admit to some use of violence, but he maintained that it had been part of their sexual practice, under mutual consent, to satisfy his wife's preferences.

As in Tamaki's case, the police were unable to find the husband legally responsible. The wife had never filed a complaint, and now she was dead. The husband was a man of some social standing, and he had hired a capable criminal lawyer. And finally, there was no room for doubt that the death had been a suicide.

"Did you kill the man?" Aomame ventured to ask.

"No, I didn't kill him – not *that* man," the dowager said.

Unclear where this was heading, Aomame simply stared at her in silence.

The dowager said, "My daughter's former husband, that contemptible man, is still alive in this world. He wakes up in bed every morning and walks down the street on his own two feet. Mere killing is not what I had planned for him."

She paused for a moment to allow Aomame to absorb her words fully.

"I have socially destroyed my former son-in-law, leaving nothing behind. It just so happens that I possess that kind of power. The man is a weakling. He has a degree of intelligence, he speaks well, and has gained some social recognition, but he is basically weak and despicable. Men who wield great violence at home against their wives and children are invariably people of weak character. They prey upon those who are weaker than themselves precisely because of their own weakness. Destroying him was easy. Once men like that are destroyed, they can never recover. My daughter died a long time ago, but I have kept watch over him to this day. If he ever shows signs of recovery, I will not allow it to happen. He goes on living, but he might as well be a corpse. He won't kill himself. He doesn't have the courage to do that. And I won't do him the favor of killing him, either. My method is to go on tormenting him mercilessly without letup but without killing him, as though skinning him alive. The man I made vanish was another person. A practical reason made it necessary for me to have him move to another place."

The dowager went on to explain this to Aomame. The year after her daughter killed herself, the dowager set up a private safe house for women who were suffering from the same kind of domestic violence. She owned a small, two-story apartment building on a plot of land adjoining her Willow House property in Azabu and had kept it unoccupied, intending to demolish it before long. Instead, she decided to renovate the building and use it as a safe house for women who had nowhere else to go. She also opened a downtown "consultation office" through which women suffering from domestic violence could seek advice, primarily from lawyers in the metropolitan area. It was staffed by volunteers who took turns doing interviews and giving telephone counseling. The office kept in touch with the dowager at home. Women who needed an emergency shelter would be sent to the safe house, often with children in tow (some of whom were teenage girls who had been sexually abused by their fathers). They would stay there until more permanent arrangements could be made for them. They would be provided with basic necessities – food, clothing – and they would help each other in a kind of communal living arrangement. The dowager personally took care of all their expenses.

The lawyers and counselors made regular visits to the safe house to check on the women's progress and discuss plans for their futures. The dowager would also drop in when she had time, listening to each woman's story and offering her advice. Sometimes she would find them jobs or more permanent places to live. When troubles arose requiring intervention of a physical nature, Tamaru would head over to the safe house and handle them – say, for example, when a husband would learn of his wife's whereabouts and forcibly try to take her back. No one could deal with such problems as quickly and expeditiously as Tamaru.

"There are those cases, however, that neither Tamaru nor I can fully deal with and for which we can find no practical remedy through the law," the dowager said.

Aomame noticed that, as the dowager spoke, her face took on a certain bronze glow and her usual mild-mannered elegance faded until it had disappeared entirely. What took its place was a certain *something* that transcended mere anger or disgust. It was probably that small, hard, nameless core that lies in the deepest part of the mind. In spite of the facial change, however, her voice remained as cool and dispassionate as ever.

"Of course, a person's existence (or nonexistence) cannot be decided on the basis of mere practical considerations – for example, if he is no longer there, it will eliminate the difficulties of divorce, say, or hasten the payment of life insurance. We take such action only as a last resort, after examining all factors closely and fairly, and arriving at the conclusion that the man deserves no mercy. These parasitical men, who can only live by sucking the blood of the weak! These incurable men, with their twisted minds! They have no interest in rehabilitating themselves, and we can find no value in having them continue to live in this world!"

The dowager closed her mouth and momentarily glared at Aomame with eyes that could pierce a rock wall. Then she went on in her usual calm tone, "All we can do with such men is make them vanish one way or another – but always taking care not to attract people's attention."

"Is such a thing possible?"

"There are many ways for people to vanish," the dowager said, pausing to let her words sink in. Then she continued, "I can arrange for people to vanish in certain ways. I have that kind of power at my disposal."

Aomame struggled to understand, but the dowager's words were too obscure.

The dowager said, "You and I have both lost people who were important to us. We lost them in outrageous ways, and we are both deeply scarred from the experience. Such wounds to the heart will probably never heal. But we cannot simply sit and stare at our wounds forever. We must stand up and move on to the next action – not for the sake of our own individual vengeance but for the sake of a more far-reaching form of justice. Will you help me in my work? I need a capable collaborator in whom I can put my trust, someone with whom I can share my secrets and my mission. Will you be that person? Are you willing to join me?"

Aomame took some time to fully comprehend what the dowager had said to her. It was an incredible confession and an equally incredible proposal. Aomame needed even more time to decide how she felt about the proposal. As she sorted this out for herself, the dowager maintained a perfect silence, sitting motionless in her chair, staring hard at Aomame. She was in no hurry. She seemed prepared to wait as long as it took.

Without a doubt, this woman has been enveloped by a form of madness, thought Aomame. *But she herself is not mad or psychologically ill. No, her mind is rock steady, unshakably cool. That fact is backed up by positive proof. Rather than madness, it's something that resembles madness. A correct prejudice, perhaps. What she wants now is for me to share her madness or prejudice or whatever it is. With the same coolheadedness that she has. She believes that I am qualified to do that.*

How long had she been thinking? She seemed to have lost her grasp of time at some point while she was deeply absorbed in her own thoughts. Only her heart continued to tick off the time in its hard, fixed rhythm. Aomame visited several little rooms she possessed inside her, tracing time backward the way a fish swims upstream. She found there familiar sights and long-forgotten smells, gentle nostalgia and severe pain. Suddenly, from some unknown source, a narrow beam of light pierced Aomame's body. She felt as though, mysteriously, she had become transparent. When she held her hand up in the beam, she could see through it. Suddenly there was no longer any weight to her body. At this moment Aomame thought, *Even if I give myself over to the madness – or prejudice – here and now, even if doing so destroys me, even if this world vanishes in its entirety, what do I have to lose?*

"I see," Aomame said to the dowager. She paused, biting her lip. And then she said, "I would like to help in any way I can."

The dowager reached out and grasped Aomame's hands. From that moment onward, Aomame and the dowager shared their secrets, shared their mission, and shared that *something* that resembled madness. It may well have been sheer madness itself, though Aomame was unable to locate the dividing line. The men that she and the dowager together dispatched to a faraway world were ones for whom there were no grounds, from any point of view, for granting them mercy.

"Not much time has gone by since you moved that man in the Shibuya hotel to another world," the dowager said softly. The way she talked about "moving" him to another world, she could as well have been talking about a piece of furniture.

"In another four days, it will be exactly two months."

"Still less than two months, is it?" the dowager went on. "I really shouldn't be asking you to do another job so soon. I would prefer to put at least six months between them. If we space them too closely, it will increase your psychological burden. This is not – how should I put it? – an *ordinary* task. In addition to which, someone might start suspecting that the number of heart attack deaths among men connected with my safe house was a bit too high."

Aomame smiled slightly and said, "Yes, there are so many distrustful people around."

The dowager also smiled. She said, "As you know, I am a very, very careful person. I don't believe in coincidence or forecasts or good luck. I search for the least drastic possibilities in dealing with these men, and only when it becomes clear that no such possibilities exist do I choose the ultimate solution. And when, as a last resort, I take such a step, I eliminate all conceivable risks. I examine all the elements with painstaking attention to detail, make unstinting preparations, and only after I am convinced that it will work do I come to you. Which is why, so far, we have not had a single problem. We haven't, have we?"

"No, you're absolutely right," Aomame said, and she meant it. She would prepare her equipment, make her way to the designated place, and find the situation arranged exactly as planned. She would plunge her needle – once – into the one precise spot on the back of the man's neck. Finally, after making sure that the man had "moved to another place," she would leave. Up to now, everything had worked smoothly and systematically.

"About this next case, though," the dowager continued, "sorry to say, I am probably going to have to ask you to do something far more challenging. Our timetable has not fully matured yet, and there are many uncertainties. I may not be able to give you the kind of well-prepared situation we have provided so far. In other words, things will be somewhat different this time."

"Different how?"

"Well, the man is not someone in an ordinary position," the dowager said. "By which I mean, first of all, that he has extremely tight security."

"Is he a politician or something?"

The dowager shook her head. "No, he is not a politician. I'll tell you more about that later. I've tried to find a solution that would save us from having to send you in, but none of them seems likely to work. No ordinary approach can meet this challenge. I am sorry, but I have not been able to come up with anything other than asking you to do it."

"Is it an urgent matter?" Aomame asked.

"No, it is not especially urgent. Neither is there a fixed deadline by which it must be accomplished. But the longer we put it off, the more people there are who could be hurt. And the opportunity that has been given to us is limited in nature.

There is no way of telling when the next one would come our way."

It was dark out. The sunroom was enveloped in silence. Aomame wondered if the moon was up. But she could not see it from where she was sitting.

"I intend to explain the situation to you in all possible detail. Before I do that, however, I have someone I would like you to meet. Shall we go now to see her?"

"Is she living in your safe house?"

The dowager inhaled slowly and made a small sound in the back of her throat. Her eyes took on a special gleam that Aomame had not seen before.

"She was sent here six weeks ago by our consultation office. For the first four weeks, she didn't say a word. She was in some sort of dazed state and had simply lost the ability to speak. We knew only her name and age. She had been taken into protective custody when she was found sleeping in a train station in terrible condition, and after being passed around from one office to another she ended up with us. I've spent hours talking to her bit by bit. It took a long time for me to convince her that this is a safe place and she doesn't have to be afraid. Now she can talk to some extent. She speaks in a confused, fragmented way, but, putting the pieces together, I've been able to form a general idea of what happened to her. It's almost too terrible to talk about, truly heartbreaking."

"Another case of a violent husband?"

"Not at all," the dowager said drily. "She's only ten years old."

The dowager and Aomame cut through the garden and, unlocking a small gate, entered the adjoining yard. The safe house was a small, wood-frame apartment building. It had been used in the old days as a residence for some of the many servants who had worked for the dowager's family. A two-story structure, the house itself had a certain old-fashioned charm, but it was too age-worn to rent out. As a temporary refuge for women who had nowhere else to go, however, it was perfectly adequate. An old oak tree spread out its branches as if to protect the building, and the front door contained a lovely panel of ornamental glass. There were ten apartments altogether, all full at times but nearly empty at other times. Usually five or six women lived there quietly. Lights shone in the windows of roughly half the rooms now. The place was oddly hushed except for the occasional sounds of small children's voices. The building itself almost appeared to be holding its breath. It lacked the normal range of sounds associated with everyday life. Bun, the female German shepherd, was chained near the front gate. Whenever people approached, she would let out a low growl and then a few barks. The dog had been trained – how or by whom it was not clear – to bark fiercely whenever a man approached, though the person she trusted most was Tamaru.

The dog stopped barking as soon as the dowager drew near. She wagged her tail and snorted happily. The dowager bent down and patted her on the head a few times. Aomame scratched her behind the ears. The dog seemed to remember Aomame. She was a smart dog. For some reason, she liked to eat raw spinach. The dowager opened the front door with a key.

"One of the women here is looking after the girl," the dowager said to Aomame. "I've asked her to live in the same apartment and try not to take her eyes off her. It's still too soon to leave her alone."

The women of the safe house looked after each other on a daily basis and were implicitly encouraged to tell each other stories of what they had been through, to share their pain. Those who had been there for a while would give the newcomers tips on how to live in the house, passing along necessities. The women would generally take turns doing the cooking and cleaning, but there were of course some who wanted only to keep to themselves and not talk about their experiences, and their desire for privacy and silence was respected. The majority of women, however, wanted to talk and interact with other women who had been through similar trials. Aside from prohibitions against drinking, smoking, and the presence of unauthorized individuals, the house had few restrictions.

The building had one phone and one television set, both of which were kept in the common room next to the front door. Here there was also an old living room set and a dining table. Most of the women apparently spent the better part of each day in this room. The television was rarely switched on, and even when it was, the volume was kept at a barely audible level. The women preferred to read books or newspapers, knit, or engage in hushed tête-à-têtes. Some spent the day drawing pictures. It was a strange space, its light dull and stagnant, as if in a transient place somewhere between the real world and the world after death. The light was always the same here, on sunny or cloudy days, in daytime or nighttime. Aomame always felt out of place in this room, like an insensitive intruder. It was like a club that demanded special qualifications for membership. The loneliness of these women was different in origin from the loneliness that Aomame felt.

The three women in the common room stood up when the dowager walked in. Aomame could see at a glance that they had profound respect for the dowager. The dowager urged them to be seated.

"Please don't stop what you're doing. We just wanted to have a little talk with Tsubasa."

"Tsubasa is in her room," said a woman whom Aomame judged to be probably around the same age as herself. She had long, straight hair.

"Saeko is with her. Tsubasa still can't come down, it seems," said a somewhat older woman.

"No, it will probably take a little more time," the dowager said with a smile.

Each of the three women nodded silently. They knew very well what "take more time" meant.

Aomame and the dowager climbed the stairs and entered one of the apartments. The dowager told the small, rather unimposing woman inside that she needed some time with Tsubasa. Saeko, as the woman was called, gave her a wan smile and left them with ten-year-old Tsubasa, closing the door behind her as she headed downstairs. Aomame, the dowager, and Tsubasa took seats around a small table. The window was covered by a thick curtain.

"This lady is named Aomame," the dowager said to the girl. "Don't worry, she works with me."

The girl glanced at Aomame and gave a barely perceptible nod.

"And this is Tsubasa," the dowager said, completing the introductions. Then she asked the girl, "How long has it been, Tsubasa, since you came here?"

The girl shook her head – again almost imperceptibly – as if to say she didn't know.

"Six weeks and three days," the dowager said. "You may not be counting the days, but I am. Do you know why?"

Again the girl gave a slight shake of the head.

"Because time can be very important," the dowager said. "Just counting it can have great significance."

To Aomame, Tsubasa looked like any other ten-year-old girl. She was rather tall for her age, but she was thin and her chest had not begun to swell. She looked chronically malnourished. Her features were not bad, but the face gave only the blandest impression. Her eyes made Aomame think of frosted windows, so little did they reveal of what was inside. Her thin, dry lips gave an occasional nervous twitch as if they might be trying to form words, but no actual sound ever emerged from them.

From a paper bag she had brought with her, the dowager produced a box of chocolates with a Swiss mountain scene on the package. She spread its contents on the table: a dozen pretty pieces of varied shapes. She gave one to Tsubasa, one to Aomame, and put one in her own mouth. Aomame put hers in her mouth. After seeing what they had done, Tsubasa also put a piece of chocolate in her mouth. The three of them ate chocolate for a while, saying nothing.

"Do you remember things from when you were ten years old?" the dowager asked Aomame.

"Very well," Aomame said. She had held the hand of a boy that year and vowed to love him for the rest of her life. A few months later, she had had her first period. A lot of things changed inside Aomame at that time. She left the faith and cut her ties with her parents.

"I do too," the dowager said. "My father took us to Paris when I was ten, and we stayed there for a year. He was a foreign service officer. We lived in an old apartment house near the Luxembourg Gardens. The First World War was in its final months, and the train stations were full of wounded soldiers, some of them almost children, others old men. Paris is breathtakingly beautiful in all seasons of the year, but bloody images are all I have left from that time. There was terrible trench warfare going on at the front, and people who had lost arms and legs and eyes wandered the city streets like abandoned ghosts. All that caught my eye were the white of their bandages and the black of the armbands worn by mourning women. Horse carts hauled one new coffin after another to the cemeteries, and whenever a coffin went by, people would avert their eyes and clamp their mouths shut."

The dowager reached across the table. After a moment of thought, the girl brought her hand out from her lap and laid it in the dowager's hand. The dowager held it tight. Probably, when she was a girl passing horse carts stacked with coffins on the streets of Paris, her father or mother would grasp her hand like this and assure her that she had nothing to worry about, that she would be all right, that she was in a safe place and needn't be afraid.

"Men produce several million sperm a day," the dowager said to Aomame. "Did you know that?"

"Not the exact figure," Aomame said.

"Well, of course, I don't know the exact figure, either. It's more than anyone can count. And they come out all at once. The number of eggs a woman produces, though, is limited. Do you know how many that is?"

"Not exactly, no."

"It's only around four hundred in the course of her lifetime," the dowager said. "And they are not made anew each month: they are all already stored inside the woman's body from the time she is born. After her first period, she produces one ripened egg a month. Little Tsubasa here has all her eggs stored inside her already. They should be pretty much intact – packed away in a drawer somewhere – because her periods haven't started. It goes without saying, of course, that the role of each egg is to be fertilized by a sperm."

Aomame nodded.

"Most of the psychological differences between men and women seem to come from differences in their reproductive systems. From a purely physiological point of view, women live to protect their limited egg supply. That's true of you, of me, and of Tsubasa." Here the dowager gave a wan little smile. "That should be in the past tense in my case, of course."

Aomame did some quick mental calculations. *That means I've already ejected some two hundred eggs. About half my supply is left inside, maybe labeled "reserved."*

"But Tsubasa's eggs will never be fertilized," the dowager

said. "I asked a doctor I know to examine her last week. Her uterus has been destroyed."

Aomame looked at the dowager, her face distorted. Then, tilting her head slightly, she turned toward the girl. She could hardly speak. "Destroyed?"

"Yes, destroyed," the dowager said. "Not even surgery can restore it to its original condition."

"But who would do such a thing?" Aomame asked.

"I'm still not sure," said the dowager.

"The Little People," said the girl.

CHAPTER 18

Tengo

NO LONGER ANY PLACE FOR A BIG BROTHER

Komatsu phoned after the press conference to say that every-thing had gone well.

"A brilliant job," he said with unusual excitement. "I never imagined she'd carry it off so flawlessly. The repartee was downright witty. She made a great impression on everybody."

Tengo was not at all surprised to hear Komatsu's report. Without any strong basis for it, he had not been especially worried about the press conference. He had assumed she would at least handle herself well. But "made a great impres-sion"? Somehow, that didn't fit with the Fuka-Eri he knew.

"So none of our dirty laundry came out, I suppose?" Tengo asked to make sure.

"No, we kept it short and deflected any awkward questions. Though in fact, there weren't any tough questions to speak of. I mean, not even newspaper reporters want to look like bad guys grilling a sweet, lovely, seventeen-year-old girl. Of course, I should add 'for the time being.' No telling how it'll go in the future. In this world, the wind can change direction before you know it."

Tengo pictured Komatsu standing on a high cliff with a grim look on his face, licking his finger to test the wind direction.

"In any case, your practice session did the trick, Tengo. Thanks for doing such a good job. Tomorrow's evening papers will report on the award and the press conference."

"What was Fuka-Eri wearing?"

"What was she wearing? Just ordinary clothes. A tight sweater and jeans."

"A sweater that showed off her boobs?"

"Yes, now that you mention it. Nice shape. They looked brand new, fresh from the oven," Komatsu said. "You know, Tengo, she's going to be a huge hit: girl genius writer. Good looks, maybe talks a little funny, but *smart*. She's got that air about her: you know she's not an ordinary person. I've been present at a lot of writers' debuts, but she's special. And when I say somebody's special, they're really special. The magazine carrying *Air Chrysalis* is going to be in the bookstores in another week, and I'll bet you anything – my left hand and right leg – it'll be sold out in three days."

Tengo thanked Komatsu for the news and ended the call with some sense of relief. They had cleared the first hurdle, at least. How many more hurdles were waiting for them, though, he had no idea.

The next evening's newspapers carried reports of the press conference. Tengo bought four of them at the station after work at the cram school and read them at home. They all said pretty much the same thing. None of the articles was especially long, but compared with the usual perfunctory five-line report, the treatment given to the event was unprecedented. As Komatsu had predicted, the media leapt on the news that a seventeen-year-old girl had won the prize. All reported that the four-person screening committee had chosen the work unanimously after only fifteen minutes of deliberation. That in itself was unusual. For four egotistical writers to gather in a room and be in perfect agreement was simply unheard of. The work was already causing a stir in the industry. A small press conference was held in the same room of the hotel where the award ceremony had taken place, the newspapers reported, and the prizewinner had responded to reporters' questions "clearly and cheerfully."

In answer to the question "Do you plan to keep writing fiction?" she had replied, "Fiction is simply one form for expressing one's thoughts. It just so happens that the form I employed this time was fiction, but I can't say what form I will use next time." Tengo found it impossible to believe that Fuka-Eri had actually spoken in such long continuous sentences. The reporters might have strung her fragments together, filled in the gaps, and made whole sentences out of them. But then again, she might well have spoken in complete sentences like this. He couldn't say anything about Fuka-Eri with absolute certainty.

When asked to name her favorite work of fiction, Fuka-Eri of course mentioned *The Tale of the Heike.* One reporter then asked which part of *The Tale of the Heike* she liked best, in response to which she recited her favorite passage from memory, which took a full five minutes. Everyone was so amazed, the recitation was followed by a stunned silence. Fortunately (in Tengo's opinion), no one asked for her favorite song.

In response to the question "Who was the happiest for you about winning the new writers' prize?" she took a long time to think (a scene that came easily to mind for Tengo), finally answering, "That's a secret."

As far as he could tell from the news reports, Fuka-Eri said nothing in the question-and-answer session that was untrue. Her picture was in all the papers, looking even more beautiful than the Fuka-Eri of Tengo's memory. When he spoke with her in person, his attention was diverted from her face to her physical movements to her changes of expression to the words she formed, but seeing her in a still photograph, he was able to realize anew what a truly beautiful girl she was. A certain glow was perceptible even in the small shots taken at the press conference (in which he was able to confirm that she was wearing the same summer sweater). This glow was probably what Komatsu had called "that air about her: you know she's not an ordinary person."

Tengo folded the evening papers, put them away, and went to the kitchen. There he made himself a simple dinner while drinking a can of beer. The work that he himself had rewritten had won the new writers' prize by unanimous consent, had already attracted much attention, and was on the verge of becoming a bestseller. The thought made him feel very strange. He wanted simply to celebrate the fact, but it also made him feel anxious and unsettled. He had been expecting this to happen, but he wondered if it was really all right for things to move ahead so smoothly.

While fixing dinner, he noticed that his appetite had disappeared. He had been quite hungry, but now he didn't want to eat a thing. He covered the half-made food in plastic wrap and put it away in the refrigerator. Then he sat in a kitchen chair and drank his beer in silence while staring at the calendar on the wall. It was a free calendar from the bank containing photos of Mount Fuji. Tengo had never climbed Mount Fuji. He had never gone to the top of Tokyo Tower, either, or to the roof of a skyscraper. He had never been interested in high places. He wondered why not. Maybe it was because he had lived his whole life looking at the ground.

Komatsu's prediction came true. The magazine containing Fuka-Eri's *Air Chrysalis* nearly sold out the first day and soon disappeared from the bookstores. Literary magazines *never* sold out. Publishers continued to absorb the losses each month, knowing that the real purpose of these magazines was to find and publish fiction that would later be collected and sold in a hardcover edition – and to discover new young writers through the prize competitions. No one expected the magazines themselves to sell or be profitable. Which is why the news that a literary magazine had sold out in a single day drew as much attention as if snow had fallen in Okinawa (though its having sold out made no difference to its running in the red).

Komatsu called to tell him the news.

"This is just great," Komatsu said. "When a magazine sells out, people can't wait to read the piece to find out what it's like. So now the printers are going crazy trying to rush the book version of *Air Chrysalis* out – top priority! At this rate, it doesn't matter whether the piece wins the Akutagawa Prize or not. Gotta sell 'em while they're hot! And make no mistake about it, this is going to be a bestseller, I guarantee you. So, Tengo, you'd better start planning how you're going to spend all your money."

One Saturday-evening newspaper's literary column discussed *Air Chrysalis* under a headline exclaiming that the magazine had sold out in one day. Several literary critics gave their opinions, which were generally favorable. The work, they claimed, displayed such stylistic power, keen sensitivity, and imaginative richness that it was hard to believe a seventeen-year-old girl had written it. It *might* even hint at new possibilities in literary style. One critic said, "The work is not entirely without a regrettable tendency for its more fantastical elements to sometimes lose touch with reality," which was the only negative remark Tengo noticed. But even that critic softened his tone at the end, concluding, "I will be very interested to see what kind of works this young girl goes on to write." No, there was nothing wrong with the wind direction for now.

Fuka-Eri called Tengo four days before the hardcover version of *Air Chrysalis* was due out. It was nine in the morning.

"Are you up," she asked in her usual uninflected way, without a question mark.

"Of course I'm up," Tengo said.

"Are you free this afternoon."

"After four, any time."

"Can you meet me."

"I can," Tengo said.

"Is that last place okay," Fuka-Eri asked.

"Fine," Tengo said. "I'll go to the same café in Shinjuku at four o'clock. Oh, and your photos in the paper looked good. The ones from the press conference."

"I wore the same sweater," she said.

"It looked good on you," Tengo said.

"Because you like my chest shape."

"Maybe so. But more important in this case was making a good impression on people."

Fuka-Eri kept silent at her end, as if she had just set something on a nearby shelf and was looking at it. Maybe she was thinking about the connection between the shape of her chest and making a good impression. The more he thought about it, the less Tengo himself could see the connection.

"Four o'clock," Fuka-Eri said, and hung up.

Fuka-Eri was already waiting for Tengo when he walked into the usual café just before four. Next to her sat Professor Ebisuno. He was dressed in a pale gray long-sleeved shirt and dark gray pants. As before, his back was perfectly straight. He could have been a sculpture. Tengo was somewhat surprised to find the Professor with her. Komatsu had said that the Professor almost never "came down from the mountains."

Tengo took a seat opposite them and ordered a cup of coffee. The rainy season hadn't even started, but the weather felt like midsummer. Even so, Fuka-Eri sat there sipping a hot cup of cocoa. Professor Ebisuno had ordered iced coffee but hadn't touched it yet. The ice had begun to melt, forming a clear layer on top.

"Thanks for coming," the Professor said.

Tengo's coffee arrived. He took a sip.

Professor Ebisuno spoke slowly, as if performing a test of his speaking voice: "Everything seems to be going as planned for now," he said. "You made major contributions to the project. Truly major. The first thing I must do is thank you."

"I'm grateful to hear you say that, but as you know, where this matter is concerned, officially I don't exist," Tengo said. "And officially nonexistent people can't make contributions."

Professor Ebisuno rubbed his hands over the table as if warming them.

"You needn't be so modest," the Professor said. "Whatever the public face of the matter may be, you *do* exist. If it hadn't been for you, things would not have come this far or gone this smoothly. Thanks to you, *Air Chrysalis* became a much better work, deeper and richer than I ever imagined it could be. That Komatsu fellow really *does* have an eye for talent."

Beside him, Fuka-Eri went on drinking her cocoa in silence, like a kitten licking milk. She wore a simple white short-sleeved blouse and a rather short navy-blue skirt. As always, she wore no jewelry. Her long, straight hair hid her face when she leaned forward to drink.

"I wanted to be sure to tell you this in person, which is why I troubled you to come here today," Professor Ebisuno said.

"You really don't have to worry about me, Professor. Rewriting *Air Chrysalis* was a very meaningful project for me."

"I still think I need to thank you for it properly."

"It really isn't necessary," Tengo said. "If you don't mind, though, there's something personal I want to ask you about Eri."

"No, I don't mind, if it's a question I can answer."

"I was just wondering if you are Eri's legal guardian."

The Professor shook his head. "No, I am not. I would like to become her legal guardian if possible, but as I told you before,

I haven't been able to make the slightest contact with her parents. I have no legal rights as far as she is concerned. But I took her in when she came to my house seven years ago, and I have been raising her ever since."

"If that's the case, then, wouldn't the most normal thing be for you to want to keep her existence quiet? If she steps into the spotlight like this, it could stir up trouble. She's a minor, after all . . ."

"Trouble? You mean if her parents sued to regain custody, or if she were forced to return to the commune?"

"Yes, I don't quite get what's involved here."

"Your doubts are entirely justified. But the other side is not in any position to take conspicuous action, either. The more publicity Eri receives, the more attention they are going to attract if they attempt anything involving her. And attention is the one thing they most want to avoid."

"By 'they,' I suppose you mean the Sakigake people?"

"Exactly," the Professor said. "The Religious Juridical Person Sakigake. Don't forget, I've devoted seven years of my life to raising Eri, and she herself clearly wants to go on living with us. Whatever situation her parents are in, the fact is they've ignored her for seven long years. There's no way I can hand her over just like that."

Tengo took a moment to organize his thoughts. Then he said, "So *Air Chrysalis* becomes the bestseller it's supposed to be. And Eri attracts everyone's attention. And that makes it harder for Sakigake to do anything. That much I understand. But how are things supposed to go from there in your view, Professor Ebisuno?"

"I don't know any better than you do," the Professor said matter-of-factly. "What happens from here on out is unknown territory for anybody. There's no map. We don't find out what's waiting for us around the next corner until we turn it. I have no idea."

"You have no idea," Tengo said.

"Yes, it may sound irresponsible of me, but 'I have no idea' is the gist of this story. You throw a stone into a deep pond. Splash. The sound is big, and it reverberates throughout the surrounding area. What comes out of the pond after that? All we can do is stare at the pond, holding our breath."

This brought conversation at the table to a momentary halt. Each of the three pictured ripples spreading on a pond. Tengo waited patiently for his imaginary ripples to settle down before speaking again.

"As I said the first time we met, what we are engaged in is a kind of fraud, possibly an offense to our whole society. A not inconsiderable amount of money may enter the picture as well before long, and the lies are going to snowball until finally the situation is beyond anyone's control. And when the truth comes out, everyone involved – including Eri here – will be hurt in some way, perhaps even ruined, at least socially. Can you go along with that?"

Professor Ebisuno touched the frame of his glasses. "I have no choice but to go along with it."

"But I understand from Mr. Komatsu that you are planning to become a representative of the phony company that he is putting together in connection with *Air Chrysalis,* which means you will be fully participating in Komatsu's plan. In other words, you are taking steps to have yourself smeared in the mud."

"That might well be the end result."

"As far as I understand it, Professor, you are a man of superior intellect, with broad practical wisdom and a unique worldview. In spite of that, you don't know where this plan is headed. You say you can't predict what will come up around the next corner. How a man like you can put himself into such a tenuous, risky position is beyond me."

"Aside from all the embarrassing overestimation of 'a man

like me,' " the Professor said, taking a breath, "I understand what you're trying to say."

A moment of silence followed.

"Nobody knows what is going to happen," Fuka-Eri interjected, without warning. Then she went back into her silence. Her cup of cocoa was empty.

"True," the Professor said. "Nobody knows what is going to happen. Eri is right."

"But you must have some sort of plan in mind, I would think," Tengo said.

"I do have some sort of plan in mind," Professor Ebisuno said.

"May I guess what it is?"

"Of course you may."

"The publication of *Air Chrysalis* might lead to revelations about what happened to Eri's parents. Is that what you mean about throwing a stone in a pond?"

"That's pretty close," Professor Ebisuno said. "If *Air Chrysalis* becomes a bestseller, the media are going to swarm like carp in a pond. In fact, the commotion has already started. After the press conference, requests for interviews started pouring in from magazines and TV. I'm turning them all down, of course, but things are likely to get increasingly overheated as publication of the book draws near. If we don't do interviews, they'll use every tool at their disposal to look into Eri's background. Sooner or later it will come out – who her parents are, where and how she was raised, who's looking after her now. All of that should make for interesting news.

"I'm not doing this for fun or profit. I enjoy my nice, quiet life in the mountains, and I don't want to get mixed up with anything that is going to draw the attention of the public. What I am hoping is that I can spread bait to guide the attention of the media toward Eri's parents. *Where are they now, and what are they doing?* In other words, I want the media to do for me what the police can't or won't do. I'm also thinking that, if it works well, we might even be able to exploit the flow of events to rescue the two of them. In any case, Fukada and his wife are both very important to me – and of course to Eri. I can't just leave them unaccounted for like this."

"Yes, but assuming the Fukadas are in there, what possible reason could there have been for them to have been kept under restraint for seven years? That's a *very long time!*"

"I don't know any better than you do. I can only guess," Professor Ebisuno said. "As I told you last time, the police did a search of Sakigake in connection with the Akebono shootout, but all they found was that Sakigake had absolutely nothing to do with the case. Ever since then, Sakigake has continued steadily to strengthen its position as a religious organization. No, what am I saying? Not steadily: they did it quite rapidly. But even so, people on the outside had almost no idea what they were actually doing in there. I'm sure you don't know anything about them."

"Not a thing," Tengo said. "I don't watch TV, and I hardly read the newspaper. You can't tell by me what people in general know."

"No, it's not just you who don't know anything about them. They purposely keep as low a profile as possible. Other new religions do showy things to get as many converts as they can, but not Sakigake. Their goal is not to increase the number of their believers. They want healthy, young believers who are highly motivated and skilled in a wide variety of professional fields. So they don't go out of their way to attract converts. And they don't admit just anybody. When people show up asking to join, they interview them and admit them selectively. Sometimes they go out of their way to recruit people who have particular skills they are looking for. The end result is a militant, elite religious organization."

"Based on what kind of doctrine?"

"They probably don't have any set scriptures. Or if they do, they're very eclectic. Roughly, the group follows a kind of esoteric Buddhism, but their everyday lives are centered not so much on particular doctrines as on labor and ascetic practice – quite stern austerities. Young people in search of that kind of spiritual life hear about them and come from all over the country. The group is highly cohesive and obsessed with secrecy."

"Do they have a guru?"

"Ostensibly, no. They reject the idea of a personality cult, and they practice collective leadership, but what actually goes on in there is unclear. I'm doing my best to gather what intelligence I can, but very little seeps out. The one thing I can say is that the organization is developing steadily and seems to be very well funded. The land owned by Sakigake keeps expanding, and its facilities are constantly improving. Also, the wall around the property has been greatly reinforced."

"And at some point, the name of Fukada, the original leader of Sakigake, stopped appearing."

"Exactly. It's all very strange. I'm just not convinced by what I hear," Professor Ebisuno said. He glanced at Fuka-Eri and turned back to Tengo. "Some kind of major secret is hidden inside there. I'm sure that, at some point, a kind of realignment occurred in Sakigake's organization. What it consisted of, I don't know. But because of it, Sakigake underwent a major change of direction from agricultural commune to religion. I imagine that something like a coup d'état occurred at that point, and Fukada was swept up in it. As I said before, Fukada was a man without the slightest religious inclinations. He must have poured every ounce of his strength into trying to put a stop to such a development. And probably he lost the battle for supremacy in Sakigake at that time."

Tengo considered this for a moment and said, "I understand what you are saying, but even if you are right, isn't this something that could have been solved just by expelling Fukada from Sakigake, like the peaceful splitting off of Akebono from Sakigake? They wouldn't have had to lock him up, would they?"

"You're quite right about that. Under ordinary circumstances, there would have been no need to take the trouble of locking him up. But Fukada would almost certainly have had his hands on some of Sakigake's secrets by then, things that Sakigake would have found very awkward if they were exposed to the public. So just throwing him out was not the answer.

"As the original founder of the community, Fukada had acted as its virtual leader for years and must have witnessed everything that had been done on the inside. He must have known too much. In addition to which, he himself was quite well known to the public at large. So even if Fukada and his wife wanted to renounce their ties with the group, Sakigake could not simply let them go."

"And so you are trying to shake up the stalemate indirectly? You want to stir up public interest by letting Eri have a sensational debut as a writer, with *Air Chrysalis* a bestseller?"

"Seven years is a very long time, and nothing I have tried over the years has done any good. If I don't take this drastic measure now, the riddle may never be solved."

"So you are using Eri as bait to try to lure a big tiger out of the underbrush."

"No one knows what is going to come out of the underbrush. It won't necessarily be a tiger."

"But you *do* seem to be expecting something violent to happen, I gather."

"True, there is that possibility," the Professor said with a thoughtful air. "You yourself should know that anything can happen inside homogeneous, insular groups."

A heavy silence followed, in the midst of which Fuka-Eri spoke up.

"It's because the Little People came," she said softly.

Tengo looked at her seated beside the Professor. As always, her face lacked anything that might be called an expression.

"Are you saying that something changed in Sakigake because the Little People came?" Tengo asked her.

She said nothing in reply. Her fingers toyed with the top button of her blouse.

Professor Ebisuno then spoke as if taking up where Eri's silence left off. "I don't know what the Little People are supposed to mean, and Eri either can't or won't explain in words what the Little People are. It does seem certain, however, that the Little People played some role in the sudden drastic change of Sakigake from an agricultural commune to a religious organization."

"Or something Little People–ish did," Tengo said.

"That's true," the Professor said. "I don't know, either, whether it was the Little People themselves or something Little People–ish. But it does appear to me, at least, that Eri is trying to say something important by introducing the Little People in her *Air Chrysalis*."

The Professor stared at his hands for a time, then looked up and said, "George Orwell introduced the dictator Big Brother in his novel *1984*, as I'm sure you know. The book was an allegorical treatment of Stalinism, of course. And ever since then, the term 'Big Brother' has functioned as a social icon. That was Orwell's great accomplishment. But now, in the real year 1984, Big Brother is all too famous, and all too obvious. If Big Brother were to appear before us now, we'd point to him and say, 'Watch out! He's Big Brother!' There's no longer any place for a Big Brother in this real world of ours. Instead, these so-called Little People have come on the scene. Interesting verbal contrast, don't you think?"

Looking straight at Tengo, the Professor had something like a smile on his face.

"The Little People are an invisible presence. We can't even tell whether they are good or evil, or whether they have any substance or not. But they seem to be steadily undermining us." The Professor paused, then continued on. "It may be that if we are ever to learn what happened to Fukada and his wife or what happened to Eri, we will first have to find out what the Little People are."

"So, then, is it the Little People that you are trying to lure out into the open?" Tengo asked.

"I wonder, ultimately, whether it is possible for us to lure something out when we can't even tell whether it has substance or not," the Professor said, the smile still playing about his lips. "The 'big tiger' you mentioned could be more realistic, don't you think?"

"Either way, that doesn't change the fact that Eri is being used for bait."

"No, 'bait' is not the right word. She is creating a whirlpool: that is a closer image. Eventually, those at the edge of the whirlpool will start spinning along with it. That is what I am waiting to see."

The Professor slowly twirled his finger in space. Then he continued, "The one in the center of the whirlpool is Eri. There is no need for the one in the center of a whirlpool to move. That is what those around the edge must do."

Tengo listened in silence.

"If I may borrow your unsettling figure of speech, all of us may be functioning as bait, not just Eri." The Professor looked at Tengo with narrowed eyes. "You included."

"All I had to do, supposedly, was rewrite *Air Chrysalis*. I was just going to be a hired hand, a technician. That was how Mr. Komatsu put it to me to begin with."

"I see."

"But things seem to have changed a bit along the way," Tengo said. "Does this mean that you revised his original plan, Professor?"

"No, that is not how I see it. Mr. Komatsu has his intentions and I have my intentions. At the moment, they share the same direction."

"So the plan is proceeding as if the two of you just happened to be riding together."

"I suppose you could say that."

"Two men with different destinations are riding the same horse down the road. Their routes are identical to a certain point, but neither knows what is going to happen after that."

"Well put, like a true writer."

Tengo sighed. "Our prospects are not very bright, I would say. But there's no turning back now, is there?"

"Even if we could turn back, we'd probably never end up where we started," the Professor said.

This brought the conversation to a close. Tengo could think of nothing further to say.

Professor Ebisuno left the café first. He had to see someone in the neighborhood, he said. Fuka-Eri stayed behind. Sitting on opposite sides of the table, Tengo and Fuka-Eri remained silent for a while.

"Are you hungry?" Tengo asked.

"Not really," Fuka-Eri said.

The café was filling up. The two of them left, though neither had been the first to suggest it. For a while they walked the streets of Shinjuku aimlessly. Six o'clock was drawing near, and many people were hurrying toward the station, but the sky was still bright. Early-summer sunlight enveloped the city, its brightness feeling strangely artificial after the underground café.

"Where are you going now?" Tengo asked.

"No place special," Fuka-Eri replied.

"Shall I see you home?" Tengo asked. "To your Shinano-machi condo, I mean. I suppose you'll be staying there today?"

"I'm not going there," Fuka-Eri said.

"Why not?"

She did not reply.

"Are you saying you feel you'd better not go there?"

Fuka-Eri nodded, saying nothing.

Tengo thought about asking her why she felt she had better not go there, but he sensed that it wouldn't get him a straight answer.

"So, will you be going back to the Professor's?"

"Futamatao is too far away."

"Do you have somewhere else in mind?"

"I will stay at your place," Fuka-Eri said.

"That . . . might . . . not . . . be a . . . good idea," Tengo said. "My place is small, I live alone, and I'm sure Professor Ebisuno wouldn't permit it."

"The Professor won't mind," Fuka-Eri said with a kind of shrug of the shoulders. "And I won't mind."

"But I might mind," Tengo said.

"Why."

"Well . . . ," Tengo started to say, but no further words came out. He was not even sure what he had intended to say. This often happened when he was talking with Fuka-Eri. He would momentarily lose track of what he was going to say. It was like sheet music being scattered by a gust of wind.

Fuka-Eri reached out and gently grasped Tengo's left hand in her right hand as if to comfort him.

"You don't get it," she said.

"Don't get what?"

"We are one."

"We are one?" Tengo asked with a shock.

"We wrote the book together."

Tengo felt the pressure of Fuka-Eri's fingers against his palm. It was not strong, but it was even and steady.

"That's true. We wrote *Air Chrysalis* together. And when we are eaten by the tiger, we'll be eaten together."

"No tiger will come out," Fuka-Eri said, her voice unusually grave.

"That's good," Tengo said, though it didn't make him especially happy. A tiger might not come out, but there was no telling what might come out instead.

They stood in front of Shinjuku Station's ticket machines. Fuka-Eri looked up at him, still gripping his hand. People streamed past them on both sides.

"Okay, if you want to stay at my place, you can," Tengo said, resigning himself. "I can sleep on the sofa."

"Thank you," Fuka-Eri said.

Tengo realized this was the first time he had ever heard anything resembling polite language from Fuka-Eri's mouth. No, it might not have been the first time, but he could not recall when he might have heard it before.

WOMEN SHARING A SECRET

"The Little People?" Aomame asked gently, peering at the girl. "Tell us, who are these 'Little People'?"

But having pronounced only those few words, Tsubasa's mouth clamped shut again. As before, her eyes had lost all depth, as though the effort of speaking the words had exhausted most of her energy.

"Somebody you know?" Aomame asked.

Again no answer.

"She has mentioned those words several times before," the dowager said. " 'The Little People.' I don't know what she means."

The words had an ominous ring, a subtle overtone that Aomame sensed like the sound of distant thunder.

She asked the dowager, "Could these 'Little People' have been the ones who injured her?"

The dowager shook her head. "I don't know. But whatever they are, the 'Little People' undoubtedly carry great significance for her."

Hands resting side by side atop the table, the girl sat utterly still, her opaque eyes staring at a fixed point in space.

"What in the world could have happened to her?" Aomame asked.

The dowager replied almost coolly, "There is observable evidence of rape. Repeated rape. Terrible lacerations on the outer lips of her vagina, and injury to the uterus. An engorged adult male sex organ penetrated her small uterus, which is still not fully mature, largely destroying the area where a fertilized egg would become implanted. The doctor thinks she will probably never be able to become pregnant."

The dowager appeared almost intentionally to be discussing these graphic details in the girl's presence. Tsubasa listened without comment and without any perceptible change of expression. Her mouth showed slight movements now and then but emitted no sound. She almost seemed to be listening out of sheer politeness to a conversation about a stranger far away.

"And that is not all," the dowager continued quietly. "Even if some procedure managed to restore the function of her uterus, the girl will probably never want to have sex with anyone. A good deal of pain must have accompanied any penetration that could cause such terrible damage, and it was done to her repeatedly. The memory of that much pain won't simply fade away. Do you see what I mean?"

Aomame nodded. Her fingers were tightly intertwined atop her knees.

"In other words, the eggs prepared inside her have nowhere to go. They – " the dowager glanced at Tsubasa and went on, "have already been rendered infertile."

Aomame could not tell how much of this Tsubasa understood. Whatever her mind was able to grasp, her living emotions appeared to be somewhere else. They were not here, at least. Her heart seemed to have been shut up inside a small, dark room with a locked door, a room located in another place.

The dowager went on, "I am not saying that a woman's only purpose in life is to bear children. Each individual is free to choose the kind of life she wants to lead. It is simply not permissible for someone to rob her by force of her innate right as a woman before she has the opportunity to exercise it."

Aomame nodded in silence.

"Of course it is not permissible," the dowager repeated. Aomame noticed a slight quaver in her voice. She was obviously finding it difficult to keep her emotions in check. "This child ran away, alone, from a certain place. How she was able to manage it, I do not know. But she has nowhere else to go but here. Nowhere else is safe for her."

"Where are her parents?"

The dowager scowled and tapped the tabletop with her fingernails. "We know where her parents are. But they are the ones who allowed this terrible thing to happen. They are the ones she ran away from."

"You're saying that the parents approved of having their own daughter raped?"

"They not only approved of it, they encouraged it."

"But why would anyone . . . ?" Aomame could not find the words to go on.

The dowager shook her head. "I know, it's terrible. Such things should never be allowed to happen. But the situation is a difficult one. This is not a simple case of domestic violence. The doctor said we have to report it to the police, but I asked him not to. He's a good friend, so I managed to convince him to hold off."

"But why didn't you want to report it to the police?" Aomame asked.

"This child was clearly the victim of a savage, inhuman act. Moreover, it was a heinous crime that society should punish with severe criminal penalties," the dowager said. "But even if we were to report it to the police, what could they do? As you see, the child herself can hardly speak. She can't properly explain what happened or what was done to her. And even if she were able to, we have no way to prove it. If we handed her over to the police, she might just be sent back to her parents. There is no place else for her to go, and they *do* have parental rights. Once she was back with them, the same thing would probably be done to her again. We cannot let that happen."

Aomame nodded.

"I am going to raise her myself," the dowager declared. "I will not send her anywhere. I don't care who comes for her – her parents or anyone – I will not give her up. I will hide her somewhere else and take charge of her upbringing."

Aomame sat for a while, looking back and forth between the dowager and the girl.

"So, then, can we identify the man who committed such sexual violence against this child? Was it one man?" Aomame asked.

"We can identify him. He was the only one."

"But there's no way to take him to court?"

"He is a very powerful man," the dowager said. "He can exert his influence on people directly. This girl's parents were under his influence. And they still are. They do whatever he orders them to do. They have no individual character, no powers of judgment of their own. They take his word as the absolute truth. So when he tells them they must give him their daughter, they cannot refuse. Far from it, they do his bidding without question and hand her over gladly, knowing full well what he plans to do to her."

It took Aomame some time to comprehend what the dowager was telling her. She set her mind to work on the problem and put things in order.

"Is this a special group you are talking about?"

"Yes, indeed, a special group that shares a sick and narrow spirit."

"A kind of cult, you mean?" Aomame asked.

The dowager nodded. "Yes, a particularly vicious and dangerous cult."

Of course. It could only be a cult. People who do whatever they are ordered to do. People without individual character or powers of judgment. *The same thing could have happened to me,* Aomame thought, biting her lip.

Of course, people were not embroiled in rape in the Society of Witnesses. In her case at least, it never came to a sexual threat. The "brothers and sisters" around her were all mild-mannered, sincere people. They thought seriously about their faith, and they lived with reverence for their doctrines – to the point of staking their lives on them. But decent motives don't always produce decent results. And the body is not the only target of rape. Violence does not always take visible form, and not all wounds gush blood.

Seeing Tsubasa reminded Aomame of herself at that age. *My own will made it possible for me to escape back then. But when you're as seriously wounded as this girl, it may not be possible to bring yourself back. You might never be able to return your heart to its normal condition again.* The thought sent a stab of pain through Aomame's chest. What she had discovered in Tsubasa was *herself as she might have been.*

"I have to confess something to you," the dowager said softly to Aomame. "I can tell you this now, but the fact is, though I knew it was a disrespectful thing to do, I ran a background check on you."

The remark brought Aomame back to the present. She looked at the dowager.

"It was right after the first time I invited you to the house and we talked. I hope you're not offended."

"No, not at all," Aomame said. "In your situation, it was a natural thing to do. The work we are engaged in is by no means ordinary."

"Exactly. We are walking a very delicate, fine line. We have to be able to trust each other. No matter who the other person is, though, you can't have trust if you don't know what you need to know. So I had them look up everything about you. From the present all the way back into the past. I suppose I should say 'almost everything,' of course. No one can know *everything* about another person. Not even God, probably."

"Or the devil," Aomame said.

"Or the devil," the dowager repeated with a faint smile. "I know that you carry cult-connected psychological scars from when you were a girl. Your parents were – and still are – ardent believers in the Society of Witnesses, and they have never forgiven you for abandoning the faith. That causes you pain even now."

Aomame nodded silently.

"To give you my honest opinion," the dowager went on, "the Society of Witnesses is not a proper religion. If you had been badly injured or come down with an illness that required surgery, you might have lost your life then and there. Any religion that would prohibit life-saving surgery simply because it goes against the literal word of the Bible can be nothing other than a cult. This is an abuse of dogma that crosses the line."

Aomame nodded. The rejection of blood transfusion is the first thing pounded into the heads of Witness children. They are taught that it is far better to die and go to heaven with an immaculate body and soul than to receive a transfusion in violation of God's teaching and go to hell. There is no room for compromise. It's one road or the other: you go either to hell or to heaven. Children have no critical powers. They have no way of knowing whether such a doctrine is correct, either as an idea widely accepted by society or as a scientific concept. All they can do is believe what their parents teach them. *If I had been caught in the position of needing a transfusion when I was little, I'm sure I would have followed my parents' orders and chosen to reject the transfusion and die. Then I supposedly would have been transported to heaven or someplace who-knows-where.*

"Is this cult you're talking about well known?" Aomame asked.

"It's called 'Sakigake.' I'm sure you've heard of it. At one point it was being mentioned in the paper almost every day."

Aomame could not recall having heard the name 'Sakigake,' but rather than say so, she nodded vaguely to the dowager. She felt she had better just leave it at that, aware that she was no longer living in 1984 but in the changed world of 1Q84. That was still just a hypothesis, but one that was steadily increasing in reality with each passing day. There seemed to be a great deal of information in this new world of which she knew nothing. She would have to pay closer attention.

The dowager went on, "Sakigake originally started out as a small agricultural commune run by a core new-left group who had fled from the city, but it suddenly changed direction at one point and turned into a religion. How and why this came about is not well understood."

The dowager paused for breath and then continued speaking.

"Very few people know this, but the group has a guru they call 'Leader.' They view him as having special powers, which he supposedly uses to cure serious illnesses, to predict the future, to bring about paranormal phenomena, and such. They're all elaborate ruses, I'm sure, but they are another reason that many people are drawn to him."

"Paranormal phenomena?"

The dowager's beautifully shaped eyebrows drew together. "I don't have any concrete information on what that is supposed to mean. I've never had the slightest interest in matters of the occult. People have been repeating the same kinds of fraud throughout the world since the beginning of time, using the same old tricks, and still these despicable fakes continue to thrive. That is because most people believe not so much in truth as in things they wish were the truth. Their eyes may be wide open, but they don't see a thing. Tricking them is as easy as twisting a baby's arm."

"Sakigake." Aomame tried out the word. What did it mean, anyway? Forerunner? Precursor? Pioneer? It sounded more like the kind of name that would be attached to a Japanese super-express train than to a religion.

Tsubasa lowered her eyes momentarily when she heard the word "Sakigake," as though reacting to a special sound concealed within it. When she raised her eyes again, her face was as expressionless as before, as if a small eddy had suddenly begun to swirl inside her and had immediately quieted down.

"Sakigake's guru is the one who raped Tsubasa," the dowager said. "He took her by force on the pretext of granting her a spiritual awakening. The parents were informed that the ritual had to be completed before the girl experienced her first period. Only such an undefiled girl could be granted a pure spiritual awakening. The excruciating pain caused by the ritual would be an ordeal she would have to undergo in order to ascend to a higher spiritual level. The parents took him at his word with complete faith. It is truly astounding how stupid people can be. Nor is Tsubasa's the only such case. According to our intelligence, the same thing has been done to other girls in the cult. The guru is a degenerate with perverted sexual tastes. There can be no doubt. The organization and the doctrines are nothing but a convenient guise for masking his individual desires."

"Does this 'guru' have a name?"

"Unfortunately, we haven't learned that yet. He's just called 'Leader.' We don't know what sort of person he is, what he looks like, or anything about his background. No matter how much we dig, the information is not forthcoming. It has been totally blocked. He stays shut up in cult headquarters in the mountains of Yamanashi, and almost never appears in public. Even inside the cult, the number of individuals allowed to see him is highly restricted. He is said to be always in the dark, meditating."

"And we can't allow him to continue unchecked."

The dowager glanced at Tsubasa and nodded slowly. "We can't let there be any more victims, don't you agree?"

"In other words, we have to take steps."

The dowager reached over and laid her hand atop Tsubasa's, steeping herself in a moment of silence. Then she said, "Exactly."

"It is quite certain, then, that he repeatedly engages in these perverted acts?" Aomame asked.

The dowager nodded. "We have proof that he is systematically raping girls."

"If it's true, it's unforgivable," Aomame said softly. "You are right: we can't let there be any more victims."

Several different thoughts seemed to be intertwined and competing for space in the dowager's mind. Then she said, "We must learn a great deal more about this 'Leader' person. We must leave no ambiguities. After all, a human life hangs in the balance."

"This person almost never comes out in public, you say?"

"Correct. And he probably has extremely tight security."

Aomame narrowed her eyes and pictured to herself the specially made ice pick in the back of her dresser drawer, the sharp point of its needle. "This sounds like a very tough job."

"Yes, unusually difficult," the dowager said. She drew her hand back from Tsubasa's and pressed the tip of her middle finger against her eyebrow. This was a sign – not one she displayed very often – that the dowager had run out of ideas.

Aomame said, "Realistically speaking, it would be next to impossible for me to go out to the Yamanashi hills on my own, sneak into this heavily guarded cult, dispatch their Leader, and come out unscathed. It might work in a ninja movie, but . . ."

"I am not expecting you to do any such thing, of course,"

the dowager said earnestly before realizing that Aomame's last remark had been a joke. "It is out of the question," she added with a wan smile.

"One other thing concerns me," Aomame said, looking into the dowager's eyes. "The Little People. Who – or what – are they? What did they do to Tsubasa? We need more information about them."

Finger still pressed against her brow, the dowager said, "Yes, they concern me, too. Tsubasa here hardly speaks at all, but the words 'Little People' have come out of her mouth a number of times, as you heard earlier. They probably mean a lot to her, but she won't tell us a thing about them. She clams up as soon as the topic arises. Give me a little more time. I'll look into this matter, too."

"Do you have some idea how we can learn more about Sakigake?"

The dowager gave her a gentle smile. "There is nothing tangible in this world you can't buy if you pay enough, and I am prepared to pay a lot – especially where this matter is concerned. It may take a little while, but I will obtain the necessary information without fail."

There are some things you can't buy no matter how much you pay, Aomame thought. *For example, the moon.*

Aomame changed the subject. "Are you really planning to raise Tsubasa yourself?"

"Of course, I am quite serious about that. I intend to adopt her legally."

"I'm sure you are aware that the formalities will not be simple, especially given the situation."

"Yes, I am prepared for that," the dowager said. "I will use every means at my disposal, do everything I can. I will not give her up to anyone."

The dowager's voice trembled with emotion. This was the very first time she had displayed such feeling in Aomame's presence. Aomame found this somewhat worrisome, and the dowager seemed to read this in her expression.

"I have never told this to anyone," the dowager said, lowering her voice as if preparing to reveal a long-hidden truth. "I have kept it to myself because it was too painful to speak about. The fact is, when my daughter committed suicide, she was pregnant. Six months pregnant. She probably did not want to give birth to the boy she was carrying. And so she took him with her when she ended her own life. If she had delivered the child, he would have been about the same age as Tsubasa here. I lost two precious lives at the same time."

"I'm sorry to hear that," Aomame said.

"Don't worry, though. I am not allowing such personal matters to cloud my judgment. I will not expose you to needless danger. You, too, are a precious daughter to me. We are already part of the same family."

Aomame nodded silently.

"We have ties more important than blood," the dowager said softly.

Aomame nodded again.

"Whatever it takes, we must liquidate that man," the dowager said, as if trying to convince herself. Then she looked at Aomame. "At the earliest possible opportunity, we must move him to another world – before he injures someone else."

Aomame looked across the table at Tsubasa. The girl's eyes had no focus. She was staring at nothing more than an imaginary point in space. To Aomame, the girl looked like an empty cicada shell.

"But at the same time, we mustn't rush things along," the dowager said. "We have to be careful and patient."

Aomame left the dowager and the girl Tsubasa behind in the apartment when she walked out of the safe house. The dowager had said she would stay with Tsubasa until the girl fell asleep. The four women in the first-floor common room were gathered around a circular table, leaning in closely, engaged in a hushed conversation. To Aomame, the scene did not look real. The women seemed to be part of an imaginary painting, perhaps with the title *Women Sharing a Secret*. The composition exhibited no change when Aomame passed by.

Outside, Aomame knelt down to pet the German shepherd for a while. The dog wagged her tail with happy abandon. Whenever she encountered a dog, Aomame would wonder how dogs could become so unconditionally happy. She had never once in her life had a pet – neither dog nor cat nor bird. She had never even bought herself a potted plant. Aomame suddenly remembered to look up at the sky, which was covered by a featureless gray layer of clouds that hinted at the coming of the rainy season. She could not see the moon. The night was quiet and windless. There was a hint of moonlight filtering through the overcast, but no way to tell how many moons were up there.

Walking to the subway, Aomame kept thinking about the strangeness of the world. If, as the dowager had said, we are nothing but gene carriers, why do so many of us have to lead such strangely shaped lives? Wouldn't our genetic purpose – to transmit DNA – be served just as well if we lived simple lives, not bothering our heads with a lot of extraneous thoughts, devoted entirely to preserving life and procreating? Did it benefit the genes in any way for us to lead such intricately warped, even bizarre, lives?

A man who finds joy in raping prepubescent girls, a powerfully built gay bodyguard, people who choose death over transfusion, a woman who kills herself with sleeping pills while six months pregnant, a woman who kills problematic men with a needle thrust to the back of the neck, men who hate women, women who hate men: how could it possibly profit the genes to have such people existing in this world?

Did the genes merely enjoy such deformed episodes as color-ful entertainment, or were these episodes utilized by them for some greater purpose?

Aomame didn't know the answers to these questions. All she knew was that it was too late to choose any other life for herself. *All I can do is live the life I have. I can't trade it in for a new one. However strange and misshapen it might be, this is it for the gene carrier that is me.*

I hope the dowager and Tsubasa will be happy, Aomame thought as she walked along. *If they can become truly happy, I don't mind sacrificing myself to make it happen. I myself prob-ably have no future to speak of. But I can't honestly believe that the two of them are going to have tranquil, fulfilled lives – or even ordinary lives. The three of us are more or less the same. Each of us has borne too great a burden in the course of our lives. As the dowager said, we are like a single family – but an extended fam-ily engaged in an endless battle, united by deep wounds to the heart, each bearing some undefined absence.*

In the course of pursuing these thoughts, Aomame became aware of her own intense urge for male flesh. *Why, of all things, should I start wanting a man at a time like this?* She shook her head as she walked along, unable to judge whether this increased sexual desire had been brought about by psycholog-ical tension or was the natural cry of the eggs stored inside her or just a product of her own genes' warped machinations. The desire seemed to have very deep roots – or, as Ayumi might say, "I want to fuck like crazy." *What should I do now?* Aomame wondered. *I could go to one of my usual bars and look for the right kind of guy. It's just one subway stop to Roppongi.* But she was too tired for that. Nor was she dressed for seduction: no makeup, only sneakers and a vinyl gym bag. *Why don't I just go home, open a bottle of red wine, masturbate, and go to sleep? That's it. And let me stop thinking about the moon.*

* * *

One glance was all it took for Aomame to realize that the man sitting across from her on the subway home from Hiroo to Jiyugaoka was her type – mid-forties, oval face, hairline beginning to recede. Head shape not bad. Healthy complexion. Slim, stylish black-framed glasses. Smartly dressed: light cotton sport coat, white polo shirt, leather briefcase on lap. Brown loafers. A salaried working man from the look of him, but not at some straitlaced corporation. Maybe an editor at a publishing company, or an architect at a small firm, or something to do with apparel, that was probably it. He was deeply absorbed in a paperback, its title obscured by a bookstore's plain wrapper.

Aomame thought she would like to go somewhere and have hot sex with him. She imagined herself touching his erect penis. She wanted to squeeze it so tightly that the flow of blood nearly stopped. Her other hand would gently massage his testicles. The hands now resting in her lap began to twitch. She opened and closed her fingers unconsciously. Her shoulders rose and fell with each breath. Slowly, she ran the tip of her tongue over her lips.

But her stop was coming up soon. She had to get off at Jiyugaoka. She had no idea how far the man would be going, unaware that he was the object of her sexual fantasies. He just kept sitting there, reading his book, obviously unconcerned about the kind of woman who was sitting across from him. When she left the train, Aomame felt like ripping his damned paperback to shreds, but of course she stopped herself.

Aomame was sound asleep in bed at one o'clock in the morning, having an intensely sexual dream. In the dream, her breasts were large and beautiful, like two grapefruits. Her nipples were hard and big. She was pressing them against the lower half of a man. Her clothes lay at her feet, where she had cast them off. Aomame was sleeping with her legs spread. As she slept, Aomame had no way of knowing that two moons were hanging in the sky side by side. One of them was the big moon that had always hung there, and the other was a new, smallish moon.

Tsubasa and the dowager were also asleep, in Tsubasa's room. Tsubasa wore new checked pajamas and slept curled into a tight little ball in bed. The dowager, still wearing her street clothes, was stretched out in a long chair, a blanket over her knees. She had been planning to leave after Tsubasa fell asleep, but had fallen asleep there. Set back from the street in its hill-top location, the apartment house was hushed, its grounds silent but for the occasional distant scream of an accelerating motorcycle or the siren of an ambulance. The German shepherd also slept, curled up outside the front door. The curtains had been drawn across the window, but they glowed white in the light of a mercury-vapor lamp. The clouds began to part, and from the rift, now and then two moons peeked through. The world's oceans were adjusting their tides.

Tsubasa slept with her cheek pressed against the pillow, her mouth slightly open. Her breathing could not have been any quieter, and aside from the occasional tiny twitch of one shoulder, she barely moved. Her bangs hung over her eyes.

Soon her mouth began to open wider, and from it emerged, one after another, a small troupe of Little People. Each one carefully scanned the room before emerging. Had the dowager awakened at that point, she might have been able to see them, but she remained fast asleep. She would not be waking anytime soon. The Little People knew this. There were five of them altogether. When they first emerged, they were the size of Tsubasa's little finger, but once they were fully on the outside, they would give themselves a twist, as though unfolding a tool, and stretch themselves to their full one-foot height. They all wore the same clothing without distinguishing features, and their facial features were equally undistinguished, making it impossible to tell them apart.

They climbed down from the bed to the floor, and from under the bed they pulled out an object about the size of a Chinese pork bun. Then they sat in a circle around the object and started feverishly working on it. It was white and highly elastic. They would stretch their arms out and, with practiced movements, pluck white, translucent threads out of the air, applying them to the fluffy, white object, making it bigger and bigger. The threads appeared to have a suitably sticky quality. Before long, the Little People themselves had grown to nearly two feet in height. They were able to change their height freely as needed.

Several hours of concentrated work followed, during which time the Little People said nothing at all. Their teamwork was tight and flawless. Tsubasa and the dowager remained sound asleep the whole time, never moving a muscle. All the other women in the safe house enjoyed deeper sleeps than usual. Stretched out on the front lawn, perhaps dreaming, the German shepherd let out a soft moan from the depths of its unconscious.

Overhead, the two moons worked together to bathe the world in a strange light.

CHAPTER 20

Tengo

THE POOR GILYAKS

Tengo couldn't sleep. Fuka-Eri was in his bed, wearing his pajamas, sound asleep. Tengo had made simple preparations for sleeping on the couch (no great imposition, since he often napped there), but he had felt not the slightest bit sleepy when he lay down, so he was writing his long novel at the kitchen table. The word processor was in the bedroom; he was using a ballpoint pen on a writing pad. This, too, was no great imposition. The word processor was undeniably more convenient for writing speed and for saving documents, but he loved the classic act of writing characters by hand on paper.

Writing fiction at night was rather rare for Tengo. He enjoyed working when it was light outside and people were walking around. Sometimes, when he was writing at night while everything was hushed and wrapped in darkness, the style he produced would be a little too heavy, and he would have to rewrite the whole passage in the light of day. Rather than go to that trouble, it was better to write in daylight from the outset.

Writing at night for the first time in ages, though, using a ballpoint pen and paper, Tengo found his mind working smoothly. His imagination stretched its limbs and the story flowed freely. One idea would link naturally with the next almost without interruption, the tip of the pen raising a persistent scrape against the white paper. Whenever his hand tired, he would set the pen down and move the fingers of his right hand in the air, like a pianist doing imaginary scales. The hands of the clock were nearing half past one. He heard strangely few sounds from the outside, as though extraneous noises were being soaked up by the clouds covering the city's sky like a thick cotton layer.

He picked up his pen again and was still arranging words on paper when suddenly he remembered: tomorrow was the day his older girlfriend would be coming. She always showed up around eleven o'clock on Friday mornings. He would have to get rid of Fuka-Eri before then. Thank goodness she wore no perfume or cologne! His girlfriend would be sure to notice right away if the bed had someone else's smell. Tengo knew how observant and jealous she could be. It was fine for her to have sex with her husband now and then, but she became seriously angry if Tengo went out with another woman.

"Married sex is something else," she explained. "It's charged to a separate account."

"A separate account?"

"Under a whole different heading."

"You mean you use a different part of your feelings?"

"That's it. Even if I use the same body parts, I make a distinction in the feelings I use. So it really doesn't matter. I have the ability to do that as a mature woman. But you're not allowed to sleep with other girls and stuff."

"I'm not doing that!" Tengo said.

"Even if you're not having sex with another girl, I would feel slighted just to think such a possibility exists."

"Just to think such a possibility exists?" Tengo asked, amazed.

"You don't understand a woman's feelings, do you? And you call yourself a novelist!"

"This seems awfully unfair to me."

"It may be unfair. But I'll make it up to you," she said. And she did.

Tengo was satisfied with this relationship with his older girl-friend. She was no beauty, at least in the general sense. Her facial features were, if anything, rather unusual. Some might even find her ugly. But Tengo had liked her looks from the start. And as a sexual partner, she was beyond reproach. Her demands on him were few: to meet her once a week for three or four hours, to participate in attentive sex – twice, if possible – and to keep away from other women. Basically, that was all she asked of him. Home and family were very important to her, and she had no intention of destroying them for Tengo. She simply did not have a satisfying sex life with her husband. Her interests and Tengo's were a perfect fit.

Tengo had no particular desire for other women. What he wanted most of all was uninterrupted free time. If he could have sex on a regular basis, he had nothing more to ask of a woman. He did not welcome the unavoidable responsibility that came with dating a woman his own age, falling in love, and having a sexual relationship. The psychological stages through which one had to pass, the hints regarding various possibilities, the unavoidable collisions of expectations: Tengo hoped to get by without taking on such burdens.

The concept of duty always made Tengo cringe. He had lived his life thus far skillfully avoiding any position that entailed responsibility, and to do so, he was prepared to endure most forms of deprivation.

In order to flee from responsibility, Tengo learned early on in life to make himself inconspicuous. He worked hard to negate his presence by publicly displaying very little of his true abilities, by keeping his opinions to himself, and by avoiding situations that put him at the center of attention. He had to survive on his own, without depending on others, from the time he was a child. But children have no real power. And so, whenever a strong wind began to blow, he would have to take shelter and grab onto something to prevent himself from being blown away. It was necessary for him to keep such contrivances in mind at all times, like the orphans in Dickens's novels.

But while it could be said that things had gone well for Tengo so far, several tears had begun to appear in the fabric of his tranquil life since he first laid his hands on the manuscript of Fuka-Eri's *Air Chrysalis*. First of all, he had been dragged almost bodily into Komatsu's dangerous plan. Secondly, the beautiful girl who wrote the book had shaken his heart from a strange angle. And it seemed that the experience of rewriting *Air Chrysalis* had begun to change something inside of him. Now Tengo felt driven by a powerful urge to write *his own* novel. This, of course, was a change for the better. But it was also true that his neat, self-satisfied lifestyle was being tested.

In any case, tomorrow was Friday. His girlfriend would be coming. He had to get rid of Fuka-Eri before then.

Fuka-Eri woke up just after two o'clock in the morning. Dressed in his pajamas, she opened the bedroom door and came out to the kitchen. She drank a big glass of water and, rubbing her eyes, sat down at the kitchen table across from Tengo.

"Am I in your way," Fuka-Eri asked in her usual style free of question marks.

"Not especially," Tengo said. "I don't mind."

"What are you writing."

Tengo closed the pad and set his ballpoint pen down.

"Nothing much," Tengo said. "Anyway, I was just thinking of quitting."

"Mind if I stay up with you a while," she asked.

"Not at all. I'm going to have a little wine. Want some?"

The girl shook her head. "I want to stay out here a while."

"That's fine. I'm not sleepy, either."

Tengo's pajamas were too big on Fuka-Eri. She had the sleeves and cuffs rolled up. Whenever she leaned forward, the collar revealed glimpses of the swell of her breasts. The sight of Fuka-Eri wearing his pajamas made it strangely difficult for Tengo to breathe. He opened the refrigerator and poured the wine left in the bottom of a bottle into a glass.

"Hungry?" Tengo asked. On their way back to his apartment earlier, they had had some spaghetti at a small restaurant near Koenji Station. The portions had not been very big, and several hours had elapsed in the meantime. "I can make you a sandwich or something else simple if you'd like."

"I'm not hungry. I'd rather have you read me what you wrote."

"You mean what I was writing just now?"

"Uh-huh."

Tengo picked up his pen and twirled it between his fingers. It looked ridiculously small in his big hand. "I make it a policy not to show people manuscripts until they're finished and revised. I don't want to jinx my writing."

" 'Jinx.' "

"It's an English word. 'To cause bad luck.' It's a kind of rule of mine."

Fuka-Eri looked at Tengo for several moments. Then she drew the pajama collar closed. "So read me a book."

"You can get to sleep if someone reads you a book?"

"Uh-huh."

"I suppose Professor Ebisuno has read you lots of books."

"Because he stays up all night."

"Did he read you *The Tale of the Heike*?"

Fuka-Eri shook her head. "I listened to a tape."

"So that's how you memorized it! Must have been a very long tape."

Fuka-Eri used two hands to suggest a pile of cassette tapes. "Very long."

"What part did you recite at the press conference?"

" 'General Yoshitsune's Flight from the Capital.' "

"That's the part after the defeat of the Heike where the victorious Genji general Yoshitsune flees from Kyoto, with his brother Yoritomo in pursuit. The Genji have won the war against the Heike, but then the family starts fighting among themselves."

"Right."

"What other sections can you recite from memory?"

"Tell me what you want to hear."

Tengo tried to recall some episodes from *The Tale of the Heike*. It was a long book, with an endless number of stories. Off the top of his head, Tengo named "The Battle of Dan-no-ura."

Fuka-Eri took some twenty seconds to collect her thoughts in silence. Then she began to chant a decisive part of the final sea battle in the original verse:

The Genji warriors had boarded the Heike ships to find
The sailors and helmsmen pierced by arrows or slashed by
    swords,
Their corpses lying in the bilge, leaving no one to steer.
Aboard a small boat, New Middle Counselor Tomomori
Approached the Imperial Ship and said:
"And so it seems to have come to this.
Heave everything unsightly into the ocean."
He ran from stem to stern, sweeping, scrubbing,
Gathering litter, cleaning everything with his own hands.
The ladies-in-waiting asked, "How goes the battle, Counselor?"
"Soon you will behold those marvelous men of the east,"
He replied with caustic laughter.
"How dare you jest at a time like this?" the women cried.

Observing this state of affairs, the Nun of Second
    Rank
Proceeded to carry out the plan
Upon which she had settled long before.
Hooding herself under two dark-gray robes,
She lifted high the hems of her glossy silk split skirt,
Tucked the Imperial Bead Strand under one arm,
Thrust the Imperial Sword under her sash,
And took the Child Emperor himself in her arms.
"Mere woman though I am, I shall never fall into enemy
    hands.
I shall go wherever His Majesty goes.
All you women whose hearts are with him,
Follow us without delay." So saying,
She strode to the gunwale.

His Majesty had turned but eight that year,
Yet he exhibited a maturity far beyond his age.
His handsome countenance radiated an Imperial glow,
And his glossy black hair could cascade down his back past
    the waist.
Confused by all the commotion, he asked,
"Grandmother, where are you taking me?"
She turned to the innocent young Sovereign and,
Fighting back her tears, she said,
"Do you not know yet what is happening?
For having followed the Ten Precepts in your previous life,
You were born to be a Lord commanding
Ten thousand charioteers,
But now, dragged down by an evil karma,
Your good fortune has exhausted itself.
Turn first now to the east,
And say your farewell to the Grand Shrine of Ise.
Then turn toward the west and call upon Amida Buddha

That his heavenly hosts may guide you to the Western Pure
    Land.
This country is no better than a scattering of millet,
A place where hearts know only sadness.
I am taking you, therefore, to a wonderful pure land called
    'Paradise.' "
Her tears escaped as she spoke thus to him.
His Majesty wore a robe of olive-tinged gray,
And his hair was bound on either side in boyish loops.
Tears streaming from his eyes, he joined his darling hands.
First, he bowed toward the east
And spoke his farewell to the Grand Shrine of Ise.
Then he turned to the west and, once he had called upon
    Amida Buddha,
The Nun of Second Rank clasped him to her breast and,
Comforting him with the words,
"There is another capital beneath the waves,"
She plunged ten thousand fathoms beneath the sea.

Listening to her recite the story with his eyes closed, Tengo
felt as though he were hearing it the traditional way, chanted
by a blind priest accompanying himself on the lute, and he was
reminded anew that *The Tale of the Heike* was a narrative poem
handed down through an oral tradition. Fuka-Eri's normal style
of speaking was extremely flat, lacking almost all accent and intonation, but when she launched into the tale, her voice became
startlingly strong, rich, and colorful, as if something had taken
possession of her. The magnificent sea battle fought in 1185 on
the swirling currents between Honshu and Kyushu came vividly
to life. The Heike side was doomed to defeat, and Kiyomori's
wife Tokiko, the "Nun of Second Rank," plunged into the waves
holding her grandson, the child emperor Antoku, in her arms.
Her ladies-in-waiting followed her in death rather than fall into
the hands of the rough eastern warriors. Tomomori, concealing

his grief, jokingly urged the ladies to kill themselves. *You'll have nothing but a living hell if you go on like this,* he had told them. *You had best end your lives here and now.*

"Want me to go on," Fuka-Eri asked.

"No, that's fine. Thank you," Tengo answered, stunned. He understood how those news reporters, at a loss for words, must have felt. "How did you manage to memorize such a long passage?"

"Listening to the tape over and over."

"Listening to the tape over and over, an ordinary person still wouldn't be able to memorize it."

It suddenly dawned on Tengo that precisely to the degree she could not read a book, the girl's ability to memorize what she had heard might be extraordinarily well developed, just as certain children with savant syndrome can absorb and remember huge amounts of visual information in a split second.

"I want you to read me a book," Fuka-Eri said.

"What kind of book would you like?"

"Do you have the book you were talking about with the Professor," Fuka-Eri asked. "The one with Big Brother."

"*1984*? I don't have that one."

"What kind of story is it."

Tengo tried to recall the plot. "I read it once a *long* time ago in the school library, so I don't remember the details too well. It was published in 1949, when 1984 seemed like a time far in the future."

"That's this year."

"Yes, by coincidence. At some point the future becomes reality. And then it quickly becomes the past. In his novel, George Orwell depicted the future as a dark society dominated by totalitarianism. People are rigidly controlled by a dictator named Big Brother. Information is restricted, and history is constantly being rewritten. The protagonist works in a government office, and I'm pretty sure his job is to rewrite words. Whenever a new history is written, the old histories all have to be thrown out. In the process, words are remade, and the meanings of current words are changed. What with history being rewritten so often, nobody knows what is true anymore. They lose track of who is an enemy and who an ally. It's that kind of story."

"They rewrite history."

"Robbing people of their actual history is the same as robbing them of part of themselves. It's a crime."

Fuka-Eri thought about that for a moment.

Tengo went on, "Our memory is made up of our individual memories and our collective memories. The two are intimately linked. And history is our collective memory. If our collective memory is taken from us – is rewritten – we lose the ability to sustain our true selves."

"You rewrite stuff."

Tengo laughed and took a sip of wine. "All I did was touch up your story, for the sake of expedience. That's totally different from rewriting history."

"But that Big Brother book is not here now," she asked.

"Unfortunately, no. So I can't read it to you."

"I don't mind another book."

Tengo went to his bookcase and scanned the spines of his books. He had read many books over the years, but he owned few. He tended to dislike filling his home with a lot of possessions. When he finished a book, unless it was something quite special, he would take it to a used-book store. He bought only books he knew he was going to read right away, and he would read the ones he cared about very closely, until they were ingrained in his mind. When he needed other books he would borrow them from the neighborhood library.

Choosing a book to read to Fuka-Eri took Tengo a long time. He was not used to reading aloud, and had almost no clue which might be best for that. After a good deal of indecision, he pulled out Anton Chekhov's *Sakhalin Island*, which he had just finished reading the week before. He had marked the more interesting spots with paper tags and figured this would make it easy to choose suitable passages to read.

Tengo prefaced his reading with a brief explanation of the book – that Chekhov was only thirty years old when he traveled to Sakhalin Island in 1890; that no one really knew why the urbane Chekhov, who had been praised as one of the most promising young writers of the generation after Tolstoy and Dostoevsky, and who was living a cosmopolitan life in Moscow, would have made up his mind to go off to live on Sakhalin Island, which was like the end of the earth. Sakhalin had been developed primarily as a penal colony, and to most people it symbolized only bad luck and misery. Furthermore, the Trans-Siberian Railway had not yet been built, which meant that Chekhov had to make more than 2,500 miles of his trip in a horse-drawn cart across frozen earth, an act of self-denial that subjected the young man in poor health to merciless suffering. And finally, when he ended his eight-month-long journey to the Far East and published *Sakhalin* as the fruit of his labor, the work did little more than bewilder most readers, who found that it more closely resembled a dry investigative report or gazetteer than a work of literature. People whispered amongst themselves, "Why did Chekhov do such a wasteful, pointless thing at such an important stage in his literary career?" One critic answered scathingly, "It was just a publicity stunt." Another view was that Chekhov had gone there looking for a new subject because he had run out of things to write about. Tengo showed Fuka-Eri the location of Sakhalin on the map included in the book.

"Why did Chekhov go to Sakhalin," Fuka-Eri asked.

"You mean, why do *I* think he went?"

"Uh-huh. Did you read the book."

"I sure did."

"What did you think."

"Chekhov himself might not have understood exactly why he went," Tengo said. "Or maybe he didn't really have a reason. He just suddenly felt like going – say, he was looking at the shape of Sakhalin Island on a map and the desire to go just bubbled up out of nowhere. I've had that kind of experience myself: I'm looking at a map and I see someplace that makes me think, 'I absolutely have to go to this place, no matter what.' And most of the time, for some reason, the place is far away and hard to get to. I feel this overwhelming desire to know what kind of scenery the place has, or what people are doing there. It's like measles – you can't show other people exactly where the passion comes from. It's curiosity in the purest sense. An inexplicable inspiration. Of course, traveling from Moscow to Sakhalin in those days involved almost unimaginable hardships, so I suspect that wasn't Chekhov's only reason for going."

"Name another one."

"Well, Chekhov was both a novelist and a doctor. It could be that, as a scientist, he wanted to examine something like a diseased part of the vast Russian nation with his own eyes. Chekhov felt uncomfortable living as a literary star in the city. He was fed up with the atmosphere of the literary world and was put off by the affectations of other writers, who were mainly interested in tripping each other up. He was disgusted by the malicious critics of the day. His journey to Sakhalin may have been an act of pilgrimage designed to cleanse him of such literary impurities. Sakhalin Island overwhelmed him in many ways. I think it was precisely for this reason that Chekhov never wrote a single literary work based on his trip to Sakhalin. It was not the kind of half-baked experience that could be easily made into material for a novel. The diseased part of the country became, so to speak, a physical part of him, which may have been the very thing he was looking for."

"Is the book interesting," Fuka-Eri asked.

"I found it very interesting. It's full of dry figures and statistics and, as I said earlier, not much in the way of literary color. The scientist side of Chekhov is on full display. But that is the very quality of the book that makes me feel I can sense the purity of the decision reached by Anton Chekhov the individual. Mixed in with the dry records are some very impressive examples of observation of character and scenic description. Which is not to say there is anything wrong with the dry passages that relate only facts. Some of them are quite marvelous. For example, the sections on the Gilyaks."

"The Gilyaks," Fuka-Eri said.

"The Gilyaks were the indigenous people of Sakhalin long before the Russians arrived to colonize it. They originally lived at the southern end of the island, but they moved up to the center when they were displaced by the Ainu, who moved north from Hokkaido. Of course, the Ainu themselves had also been pushed northward – by the Japanese. Chekhov struggled to observe at close hand and to record as accurately as possible the rapidly disappearing Gilyak culture."

Tengo opened to a passage on the Gilyaks. At some points he would introduce suitable omissions and changes to the text in order to make it easily understandable to his listener.

The Gilyak is of strong, thick-set build, and average, even small, in height. Tall stature would hamper him in the taiga. ["That's a Russian forest," Tengo added.] His bones are thick and are distinctive for the powerful development of all the appendages and protuberances to which the muscles are attached, and this leads one to assume firm, powerful muscles and a constant strenuous battle with nature. His body is lean and wiry, without a layer of fat; you do not come across obese, plump Gilyaks. Obviously all the fat is expended in warmth, of which the body of a Sakhalin inhabitant needs to produce such a great deal in order to compensate for the loss engendered by the low temperature and the excessive dampness of the air. It's clear why the Gilyak consumes such a lot of fat in his food. He eats rich seal, salmon, sturgeon and whale fat, meat and blood, all in large quantities, in a raw, dry, often frozen state, and because he eats coarse, unrefined food, the places to which his masticatory muscles are attached are singularly well developed and his teeth are heavily worn. His diet is made up exclusively of animal products, and rarely, only when he happens to have his dinner at home or if he eats out at a celebration, will he add Manchurian garlic or berries. According to Nevelskoy's testimony, the Gilyaks consider working the soil a great sin; anybody who begins to dig the earth or who plants anything will infallibly die. But bread, which they were acquainted with by the Russians, they eat with pleasure, as a delicacy, and it is not a rarity these days in Alexandrovsk or Rykovo to meet a Gilyak carrying a round loaf under his arm.

Tengo stopped reading at that point for a short breather. Fuka-Eri was listening intently, but he could not read any reaction from her expression.

"What do you think? Do you want me to keep reading? Or do you want to switch to another book?" he asked.

"I want to know more about the Gilyaks."

"Okay, I'll keep going."

"Is it okay if I get in bed?" Fuka-Eri asked.

"Sure," Tengo said.

They moved into the bedroom. Fuka-Eri crawled into bed, and Tengo brought a chair next to the bed and sat in it. He continued with his reading.

The Gilyaks never wash, so that even ethnographers find it difficult to put a name to the real colour of their faces; they do not wash their linen, and their fur clothing looks as if it has just been stripped off a dead dog. The Gilyaks themselves give off a heavy, acid smell, and you know you are near their dwellings from the repulsive, sometimes hardly bearable odour of dried fish and rotting fish offal. By each yurt usually lies a drying ground filled to the brim with split fish, which from a distance, especially when the sun is shining on them, look like filaments of coral. Around these drying grounds Kruzenshtern saw a vast number of maggots covering the ground to the depth of an inch.

"Kruzenshtern."

"I think he was an early explorer. Chekhov was a very studious person. He had read every book ever written about Sakhalin."

"Let's keep going."

In winter the yurts are full of acrid smoke which comes from the open fireplace, and on top of all this the Gilyaks, their wives and even the children smoke tobacco. Nothing is known about the morbidity and mortality of the Gilyaks, but one must form the conclusion that these unhealthy hygienic arrangements must inevitably have a bad effect on their health. Possibly it is to this they owe their small stature, the puffiness of their faces, and a certain sluggishness and laziness of movement.

"The poor Gilyaks!" Fuka-Eri said.

Writers give varying accounts of the Gilyaks' character, but all agree on one thing – that they are not a warlike race, they do not like quarrels or fights, and they get along peacefully with their neighbours. They have always treated the arrival of new people with suspicion, with apprehension about their future, but have met them every time amiably, without the slightest protest, and the worst thing they would do would be to tell lies at people's arrival, painting Sakhalin in gloomy colours and thinking by so doing to frighten foreigners away from the island. They embraced Kruzenshtern's travelling companions, and when Shrenk fell ill this news quickly spread among the Gilyaks and aroused genuine sorrow. They tell lies only when trading or talking to a suspicious and, in their opinion, dangerous person, but, before telling a lie, they exchange glances with each other in an utterly childlike manner. Every sort of lie and bragging in the sphere of everyday life and not in the line of business is repugnant to them.

"The wonderful Gilyaks!" Fuka-Eri said.

The Gilyaks conscientiously fulfil commissions they have undertaken, and there has not yet been a single case of a Gilyak abandoning mail halfway or embezzling other people's belongings. They are perky, intelligent, cheerful, and feel no stand-offishness or uneasiness whatever in the company of the rich and powerful. They do not recognize that anybody has power over them, and, it seems, they do not possess even the concept of "senior" and "junior." People say and write that the Gilyaks do not respect family seniority either. A father does not think he is superior to his son, and a son does not look up to his father but lives just as he wishes; an elderly mother has no greater power in a yurt than an adolescent girl. Boshnyak writes that he chanced more than once to see a son striking his own mother and driving her out, and nobody daring to say a word to him. The male members of the family are equal among themselves; if you entertain them with vodka, then you also have to treat the very smallest of them to it as well. But the female members are all equal in their lack of rights; be it grandmother, mother or baby girl still being nursed, they are ill treated in the same way as domestic animals, like an object which can be thrown out, sold or shoved with one's foot like a dog. However, the Gilyaks at least fondle their dogs, but their womenfolk – never. Marriage is considered a mere trifle, of less importance, for instance, than a drinking spree, and it is not surrounded by any kind of religious or superstitious ceremony. A Gilyak exchanges a spear, a boat or a dog for a girl, takes her back to his own yurt and lies with her on a bearskin – and that is all there is to it. Polygamy is allowed, but it has not become widespread, although to all appearances there are more women than men. Contempt toward women, as if for a lower creature or object, reaches such an extreme in the Gilyak that, in the field of the question of women's rights, he does not consider reprehensible even slavery in the literal and crude sense of the word. Evidently with them a woman represents the same sort of trading object as tobacco or nankeen. The Swedish writer Strindberg, a renowned misogynist, who desired that women should be merely slaves and should serve men's whims, is in essence of one and the same mind as the Gilyaks; if he ever chanced to come to northern Sakhalin, they would spend ages embracing each other.

Tengo took a break at that point, but Fuka-Eri remained silent, offering no opinion on the reading. Tengo continued.

They have no courts, and they do not know the meaning of "justice." How hard it is for them to understand us may be seen merely from the fact that up till the present day they still do not fully understand the purpose of roads. Even where a road has already been laid, they will still journey through the taiga. One often sees them, their families and their dogs, picking their way in Indian file across a quagmire right by the roadway.

Fuka-Eri had her eyes closed and was breathing very softly. Tengo studied her face for a while but could not tell whether she was sleeping or not. He decided to turn the page and keep reading. If she was sleeping, he wanted to give her as sound a sleep as possible, and he also felt like reading more Chekhov aloud.

Formerly the Naibuchi Post stood at the river mouth. It was founded in 1866. Mitzul found eighteen buildings here, both dwellings and non-residential premises, plus a chapel and a shop for provisions. One correspondent who visited Naibuchi in 1871 wrote that there were twenty soldiers there under the command of a cadet-officer; in one of the cabins he was entertained with fresh eggs and black bread by a tall and beautiful female soldier, who eulogized her life here and complained only that sugar was very expensive.

Now there are not even traces left of those cabins, and, gazing round at the wilderness, the tall, beautiful female soldier seems like some kind of myth. They are building a new house here, for overseers' offices or possibly a weather center, and that is all. The roaring sea is cold and colourless in appearance, and the tall grey waves pound upon the sand, as if wishing to say in despair: "Oh God, why did you create us?" This is the Great, or, as it is otherwise known, the Pacific, Ocean. On this shore of the Naibuchi river the convicts can be heard rapping away with axes on the building work, while on the other, far distant, imagined shore, lies America . . . to the left the capes of Sakhalin are visible in the mist, and to the right are more capes . . . while all around there is not a single living soul, not a bird, not a fly, and it is beyond comprehension who the waves are roaring for, who listens to them at nights here, what they want, and, finally, who they would roar for when I was gone. There on the shore one is overcome not by connected, logical thoughts, but by reflections and reveries. It is a sinister sensation, and yet at the very same time you feel the desire to stand for ever looking at the monotonous movement of the waves and listening to their threatening roar.

It appeared that Fuka-Eri was now sound asleep. He listened for her quiet breathing. He closed the book and set it on the little table by the bed. Then he stood up and turned the light off, taking one final look at Fuka-Eri. She was sleeping peacefully on her back, her mouth a tight, straight line. Tengo closed the bedroom door and went back to the kitchen.

It was impossible for him to continue with his own writing, though. His mind was now fully occupied by Chekhov's desolate Sakhalin coastal scenes. He could hear the sound of the waves. When he closed his eyes, Tengo was standing alone on the shore of the Sea of Okhotsk, a prisoner of his own meditations, sharing in Chekhov's inconsolable melancholy. What Chekhov must have felt there at the end of the earth was an overwhelming sense of powerlessness. To be a Russian writer at the end of the nineteenth century must have meant bearing an inescapably bitter fate. The more they tried to flee from Russia, the more deeply Russia swallowed them.

After rinsing his wineglass and brushing his teeth, Tengo turned off the kitchen light, stretched out on the sofa, pulled a blanket over himself, and tried to sleep. The roar of the ocean still echoed in his ears, but eventually he began to lose consciousness and was drawn into a deep sleep.

He awoke at eight thirty in the morning. There was no sign of Fuka-Eri in his bed. The pajamas he had lent her were balled up and tossed into the bathroom washing machine, the cuffs and legs still rolled up. He found a note on the kitchen table: "How are the Gilyaks doing now? I'm going home." Written in ballpoint pen on notepaper, the characters were small, square, and indefinably strange, like an aerial view of characters written on a beach in seashells. He folded the paper and put it in his desk drawer. If his girlfriend found something like this when she arrived at eleven, she would make a terrible fuss.

Tengo straightened the bed and returned the fruits of Chekhov's labor to the bookcase. Then he made himself coffee and toast. While eating breakfast, he noticed that some kind of heavy object had settled itself in his chest. Some time had to go by before he figured out what it was. Fuka-Eri's tranquil sleeping face.

Could I be in love with her? No, impossible, Tengo told himself. *It just so happens that something inside her has physically shaken my heart. So, then, why am I so concerned about the pajamas she had on her body? Why did I (almost unconsciously) pick them up and smell them?*

There were too many questions. It was probably Chekhov who said that the novelist is not someone who answers questions but someone who asks them. It was a memorable phrase, but Chekhov applied this attitude not only to his works but to his life as well. His life presented many questions but answered none. Although he knew quite well that he was suffering from an incurable lung disease (as a doctor, he could not help but know), he tried hard to ignore the fact, and refused to believe he was dying until he was actually on his deathbed. He died young, violently coughing up blood.

Tengo left the kitchen table, shaking his head. *My girlfriend is coming today. I have to do laundry and clean the place up now. Thinking is something I can save for later.*

CHAPTER 21

Aomame

NO MATTER HOW FAR AWAY
I TRY TO GO

Aomame went to the ward library and, following the same procedures as before, opened the compact edition of the newspaper on a desk. She was there to read once again about the gun battle between the radical faction and the police that had taken place in Yamanashi Prefecture in the autumn three years earlier. The headquarters of Sakigake, the religious group that the dowager had mentioned, was located in the mountains of Yamanashi, and the gun battle had also occurred in the mountains of Yamanashi. This might have been a mere coincidence, but Aomame was not quite ready to accept that. There might well have been some link between the two. And the expression that the dowager had used – "such a major incident" – also seemed to suggest a connection.

The gunfight had occurred three years earlier, in 1981 (or, according to Aomame's hypothesis, three years prior to 1Q84), on October 19. Having read the news reports during her previous trip to the library, Aomame had fairly detailed knowledge of the facts. This enabled her to skim through that material and concentrate instead on subsequent related articles and analyses that viewed the affair from different angles.

In the first battle, three officers had been killed and two

badly wounded by Chinese-made Kalashnikov automatic rifles. After that, the radical group fled into the mountains with their weapons and the police staged a major manhunt. Fully armed Self-Defense Force paratroopers were also sent in by helicopter. Three radicals who resisted the onslaught were shot to death, two were gravely wounded (one of those died in the hospital three days later, but the fate of the other was not clearly stated in the article), and four others were arrested unharmed or slightly wounded. Wearing high-performance bulletproof vests, the police and Self-Defense troops suffered no further casualties except for one policeman's broken leg when he fell off a cliff in pursuit of the radicals. Only one of the radicals was listed as whereabouts unknown. He had apparently managed to disappear in spite of the extensive search.

Once the initial shock of the gun battle wore off, the newspaper started carrying detailed reports on the origins of the radical group, which was seen as the fallout from the university campus uprisings that occurred around 1970. More than half of the members were veterans of the takeover of Yasuda Hall at the University of Tokyo or the sit-in at Nihon University. After their "fortresses" had fallen to the riot police, these students (and a few faculty members) had been expelled from their universities or become disillusioned with urban political action centered on the university campuses. They overcame their factional differences and started a communal farm in Yamanashi Prefecture. At first they participated in the agricultural commune known as the Takashima Academy, but they were not satisfied with the life there. They reorganized, went independent, bought an abandoned village deep in the mountains at an exceptionally low price, and started farming there. They experienced many hardships at first, but they eventually succeeded in the mail order sale of vegetables when the use of organically grown produce began a quiet boom in the cities. Their farm grew. They were, ultimately, serious, hardworking people whose leader had organized them well. The name of the commune was Sakigake.

Aomame twisted her face into a major grimace and swallowed hard. She let out a deep groan and started tapping the surface of the desk with her ballpoint pen.

She continued reading. She read through the news reports that explained how a deep split grew within the ranks of Sakigake between a moderate group that rejected a violent revolution as acceptable for contemporary Japan, and a radical faction that eventually founded a nearby commune and took the name Akebono. She learned how they were granted religious status by the government in 1979.

After the radical group moved to their own property, they underwent secret military training even as they continued to farm, which gave rise to several clashes with neighboring farmers. One such clash involved water rights over a stream that flowed through Akebono's land. The stream had always been used as a common source of water by farms in the area, but Akebono denied neighboring residents entry. The dispute went on for a number of years, until several Akebono members severely beat a resident who had complained about the barbed wire fence surrounding their land. The Yamanashi Prefectural Police obtained a search warrant and headed for Akebono to question the suspects, only to become involved in a wholly unanticipated shootout.

After Akebono was all but obliterated by the intense gun battle in the mountains, the religious organization Sakigake lost no time in issuing a formal statement. A handsome, young spokesman in a business suit read the document to the media at a press conference. The point of the statement was quite clear. Whatever their relationship might have been in the past, Sakigake and Akebono now had no connection at all. After the two groups parted ways, there had been hardly any contact aside from certain operational matters. They had separated amicably after concluding that, as a community devoted to farming, respect for the law, and longing for a peaceful spiritual world, Sakigake could no longer work with the members of Akebono, who pursued a radical revolutionary ideology. After that, Sakigake had become a religious organization and had been legally certified as a Religious Juridical Person. That such an incident involving bloodshed had occurred was truly unfortunate, and Sakigake wished to express its deep sympathy for the families of the officers who had lost their lives in the course of their duties, but Sakigake was in no way involved. Still, it was an undeniable fact that Sakigake had been the parent organization of Akebono. Consequently, if the authorities deemed it necessary to conduct some sort of investigation in connection with the present incident, Sakigake was fully prepared to comply so as to avoid pointless misunderstanding.

A few days later, as if in response to Sakigake's formal statement, the Yamanashi Prefectural Police entered the organization's precincts with a search warrant. They spent an entire day covering all parts of Sakigake's extensive property and carefully examining their buildings' interiors and their files. They also questioned several members of the group's leadership. The police suspected that the two groups' contacts were as active as ever and that Sakigake was surreptitiously involved in Akebono's activities. But they found no evidence to support this view. Scattered along the trails winding through the beautiful deciduous forest were wood-frame meditation huts where many members dressed in ascetic robes were engaged in religious austerities, nothing more. Nearby, other adherents were engaged in farming. There was an array of well-maintained farming implements and heavy farm machinery. The police found no trace of weapons or anything else suggesting violence. Everything was clean and orderly. There was a nice little dining hall, a lodging house, and a simple (but adequately equipped) medical facility. The two-floored library was well stocked with Buddhist scriptures and books, among which several experts were engaged in studies and translations. Overall, the place seemed less like a religious establishment than the campus of a small private college. The police left deflated, having found almost nothing of value.

Some days later, the group welcomed television and news-paper reporters, who observed much the same scenes the police had found. They were not taken around on carefully controlled tours, as might be expected, but were allowed to wander freely throughout the property unaccompanied, to speak with any-one they wanted to interview, and to write up their discover-ies as they wished. The one restriction agreed upon was that the media would use only television and photographic images approved by the group in order to protect the privacy of indi-vidual members. Several ascetic-robed members of the lead-ership answered reporters' questions in a large assembly hall, explaining the organization's origins, doctrines, and adminis-tration. Their manner of speaking was courteous but direct, eschewing any hint of the kind of propaganda often associated with religious groups. They seemed more like top employees of an advertising agency, skilled presenters, rather than leaders of a religion. The only thing different was the clothes they wore.

We do not have any set, clear-cut doctrine, they explained. We perform theoretical research on early Buddhism and put into actual practice the ascetic disciplines that were engaged in back then, aiming for a more fluid religious awakening. We do not hold that doctrine gives rise to awakening but rather that the individual awakenings come first. This is our fundamental principle. In that sense, our origin differs greatly from those of established religions.

Now, as to our funding: like most other religious organi-zations, we depend in part on the spontaneous contributions of our believers. Our ultimate goal, however, is to establish a frugal, self-sufficient lifestyle through our farming, rather than depending on contributions. For us, "less is more": we aim to achieve spiritual peace through the purification of the body and the discipline of the mind. One after another, people who have sensed the emptiness of competitive society's materialism have entered our gates in search of a different and deeper spiritual axis. Many of them are highly educated professionals with social standing. We are not trying to be one of those "fast food," "new" religions that pretend to take on people's worldly suffering and save anyone and everyone. Salvation of the weak is of course an important task, but it may be best to think of us as a kind of "graduate school," providing a suitable place and appropriate support to people who are strongly motivated to save themselves.

Major differences of opinion arose at one point between us and the people of the Akebono commune concerning matters of administrative policy, and we were at odds with them for a time, but talks between us led to an amicable meeting of the minds. We then separated, each of us following a different path. Akebono pursued its ideals in its own pure-minded and ascetic way, but with those disastrous – and genuinely tragic – results. The single greatest cause was that they had become too doctrinaire and lost touch with actual, living society. For us, too, the event has driven home the message that we must continue to be an organization that keeps a window open to the outside even as we impose ever stricter discipline upon ourselves. We believe that violence solves nothing. We hope you understand that we do not force religion on anyone. We do not proselytize, nor do we attack other religions. All we do is offer an appropriate and effective communal environment to people in search of spiritual awakening.

Most of the journalists present left with a favorable impression of the organization. All of the believers, both men and women, were slim, relatively young (though older people had been spotted on occasion), and beautifully clear-eyed. They were courteous in speech and behavior. None of them evidenced an inclination to speak extensively about their pasts, but most did indeed appear to be highly educated. The lunch served to the journalists had been simple fare (much the same sort of food eaten by believers, supposedly) but delicious in its own way, all ingredients having been freshly harvested on the organization's land.

Subsequently, the media defined Akebono as a mutant offspring that Sakigake had had to shake off. A revolutionary ideology based on Marxism had become outmoded and useless in 1980s Japan. The youth with radical political aspirations in 1970 were now working for corporations, engaged in the forefront of fierce fighting on an economic battlefield. Or else they had put distance between themselves and the battle and clamor of real society, each in search of personal values in a place apart. In any case, the times had changed, and the season for politics was now a thing of the distant past. Sakigake was one hopeful option for a new world; Akebono had no future.

Aomame set down her pen and took a deep breath. She pictured to herself the eyes of Tsubasa, so utterly lacking in expression or depth. Those eyes had been looking at Aomame, but at the same time they had been looking at nothing. Something important was missing.

It's not as simple as all that, Aomame thought. *Sakigake can't be this clean. It has a hidden dark side. The dowager says this "Leader" person is raping preteen girls and calling it a religious act. The media didn't seem to know anything about that. They were only there half a day. They were guided through the orderly facilities for religious practice, they were fed a lunch made with fresh ingredients, they were treated to beautiful explanations of spiritual awakening, and they went home satisfied. They never had a glimpse of what was really going on inside.*

Aomame went straight from the library to a café, where she ordered a cup of coffee and used the phone to call Ayumi at her office, on the number that Ayumi had told her she could call anytime. A colleague picked up the phone. Ayumi was out making rounds but should be back at the station in about two hours, he said. "I'll call again later," Aomame said without giving her name.

She went back to her apartment and dialed the number again two hours later. This time Ayumi answered the phone herself.

"Hi, Aomame, how are you?"

"Fine, how are you?"

"Nothing wrong with me that a good man wouldn't fix. How about you?"

"Same here," Aomame said.

"Too bad," Ayumi said. "There must be something wrong with the world if women like us have to complain to each other about overly healthy sex drives. We'll have to do something about that."

"True, but . . . uh, is it okay for you to be saying stuff like that out loud? You're on duty, right? Isn't anybody else around?"

"Don't worry, you can talk to me about anything."

"Well, I've got a favor to ask if it's something you can do for me. I can't think of anyone else I can go to for this."

"Sure," Ayumi said. "I don't know if I can help or not, but give it a try."

"Do you know of a religious group called Sakigake? It's headquartered in Yamanashi Prefecture, in the hills."

"Sakigake? Hmm." Ayumi took some ten seconds to search her memory. "I think I know it. It's a kind of religious commune, isn't it? The Akebono radicals that started the gun battle in Yamanashi used to belong to it. Three prefectural police-men died in the shootout. It was a real shame. But Sakigake had nothing to do with it. Their compound was searched after the shootout and came up clean. So . . . ?"

"I'd like to know if Sakigake was involved in any kind of incident after the shootout – criminal, civil, anything. But I don't know how to go about looking into such things. I can't read all the compact editions of all the newspapers, but I fig-ured the police probably had some way of finding out."

"It's easy, we just have to do a quick search on our computer – or, at least, I wish I could say that, but I'm afraid computer-ization is not so advanced in Japan's police forces. I suspect it'll take a few more years to get to that stage. So for now, if I wanted to find out about something like that, I'd probably have to ask the Yamanashi Prefectural Police to send copies of the related materials in the mail. And for that I'd first have to fill out a materials request form and get my boss's okay. Of course I'd have to give a good reason for the request. And we're a gov-ernment office, after all, so we're getting paid to make things as complicated as possible."

"I see," Aomame said with a sigh. "So that's out."

"But why do you want to know something like that? Is some friend of yours mixed up in some kind of case connected to Sakigake?"

Aomame hesitated a moment before deciding to tell Ayumi the truth. "Close. It involves rape. I can't go into detail yet, but it's about the rape of young girls. I've been informed that they're systematically raping them in there under cover of religion."

Aomame could sense Ayumi wrinkling her brow at the other end. "The rape of young girls, huh? We can't let that hap-pen," Ayumi said.

"Of course we can't," Aomame said.

"What do you mean by 'young'?"

"Maybe ten, or even younger. Girls who haven't had their first period, at least."

Ayumi went silent for a while. Then, in a flat voice, she said, "I see what you mean. I'll think of something. Can you give me two or three days?"

"Sure. Just let me know."

They spent the next few minutes in unrelated chatter until Ayumi said, "Okay, I've got to get back to work."

After hanging up, Aomame sat in her reading chair by the window and stared at her right hand for a while. Long, slim fingers, closely trimmed nails. Nails well cared for but unpolished. Looking at her nails, Aomame had a strong sense of what a fragile, fleeting thing her own existence was. Something as simple as the shape of her fingernails: it had been decided without her. *Somebody else made the decision, and all I could do was go along with it, like it or not. Who could have decided that this was how my nails would be shaped?*

The dowager had recently said to her, "Your parents were – and still are – ardent believers in the Society of Witnesses." Which meant that they were probably still devoting themselves to missionary work even now. Aomame had a brother four years her senior, a docile young man. At the time Aomame made up her mind to leave home, he was still living according to his parents' instructions, keeping the faith. What could he be doing now? Not that Aomame had an actual desire to know what was happening with her family. To her, they were just a part of her life that had ended. The ties had snapped.

Aomame had struggled for a long time to forget everything that had happened to her before the age of ten. *My life actually started when I was ten. Everything before that was some kind of miserable dream. Let me throw those memories away somewhere.* But try as she might, her heart was constantly being drawn back into that nightmarish world. It seemed to her that almost everything she possessed had its roots sunk in that dark soil and was deriving its nourishment from it. *No matter how far away I try to go, I always have to come back here,* she thought.

I must send that "Leader" into the other world, Aomame told herself, *for my own sake as well.*

A phone call came from Ayumi three nights later.

"I've got some facts for you," she said.

"About Sakigake?"

"Yes. I was mulling it over when all of a sudden I remembered that the uncle of one of my police academy classmates is on the Yamanashi Prefectural Police force – a fairly high-ranking officer. So I tried asking my old classmate. I told him a relative of mine, a young girl, ran into some trouble when she was in the process of converting to that faith, so I was collecting information on Sakigake, and if he wouldn't mind, could he help me? I'm pretty good at making up stuff like that."

"Thanks, Ayumi. I appreciate it," Aomame said.

"So he called his uncle in Yamanashi and explained the situation, and the uncle introduced me to the officer in charge of investigating Sakigake. So I spoke to him directly."

"Oh, wonderful."

"Yup. Well, I had a long talk with him and got all kinds of information about Sakigake, but you probably know everything that was in the papers, so I'll just tell you the stuff that wasn't, the parts that aren't known to the public, okay?"

"That's fine."

"First of all, Sakigake has had a number of legal problems – civil suits, mostly concerning land deals. They seem to have a *lot* of money, and they're buying up all the property around them. Sure, land is cheap in the country, but still. And a lot of times they're pretty much forcing people to sell. They hide their involvement behind fake companies and buy up everything they can get their hands on. That way they start trouble with landowners and local governments. I mean, they operate like any ordinary landshark. Up to now, though, it's all been civil actions, so the police haven't had to get involved. They've come pretty close to crossing the line into criminal territory, but so far things haven't gone public. They *might* be involved with organized crime or politicians. The police back off when politicians are mixed up in it. Of course, it'll be a whole new ball game if something blows up and the prosecutor has to step in."

"So Sakigake is not as clean as it looks where economic activity is concerned."

"I don't know about their ordinary believers, but as far as I can tell from the records of their real estate transactions, the top people in charge of the funds are probably not that clean. Even trying to cast it in the best light, it's almost inconceivable that they would be using their money in search of pure spirituality. And besides, these guys hold land and buildings not just in Yamanashi but in downtown Tokyo and Osaka – first-class properties! Shibuya, Minami-Aoyama, Shoto: the organization seems to be planning to expand its religious activities on a national scale – assuming it's not going to switch from religion to the real estate business."

"I thought they wanted to live in natural surroundings and practice pure, stringent religious austerities. Why in the world would such an organization have to branch out to the middle of Tokyo?"

"And where do they get the kind of cash they're throwing around?" Ayumi added. "There's no way they could have amassed such a fortune selling daikon radishes and carrots."

"Squeezing donations out of their believers."

"That's part of it, I'm sure, but nowhere near enough. They must have some other major source of funds. I also discovered another fact of some concern, something you might be interested in. There are a fair number of believers' children in the compound. They generally attend the local public elementary school, but most of them drop out before long. The school insists that the children follow the standard education program, but the organization won't cooperate. They tell the school that some of their children simply don't want to go there, that they themselves are providing an education for those children, so there is no need to worry about their studies."

Aomame recalled her own experience in elementary school. She could well understand why children from the religion wouldn't want to go to school, where they would be bullied as outsiders or ignored. "The kids probably feel out of place in a public school," she said. "Besides, it's not that unusual for children not to go to school."

"Yes, but according to the teachers who had those kids in their classes, most of them – boys and girls alike – appear to have some kind of emotional problems. They show up normal in first grade, just bright, outgoing children, but year by year they grow less talkative, their faces lose any hint of expression. Eventually they become utterly apathetic and stop coming to school. Almost all of the Sakigake kids seem to go through the same stages and exhibit the same symptoms. The teachers are puzzled and worried about the kids who have stopped coming and stay shut up inside the compound. They want to know if the kids are okay, but they can't get in to see them. Nobody is allowed inside."

These were the same symptoms Tsubasa had, Aomame thought. Extreme apathy, lack of expression, barely talking.

Ayumi said to Aomame, "You imagine the kids in Sakigake are being abused. Systematically. Maybe including rape."

"But the police can't make a move based on unconfirmed accusations by an ordinary citizen."

"Of course not. The police department's just another

bureaucratic government agency, after all. The top brass don't think of anything but their own careers. Some are not like that, but most of them have worked their way up playing it safe, and their goal is to find a cushy job in a related organization or private industry after they retire. So they don't want to touch anything the least bit risky or hot. They probably don't even eat pizza without letting it cool off. It would be an entirely different story if you could bring us a real victim who could prove something in court, but I'm guessing that would be hard for you to do."

"True, it might be hard," Aomame said. "But anyhow, thanks. This is really useful information. I'll have to find a way to thank you."

"Never mind that. Let's just have another night out in Roppongi sometime soon and forget about our problems."

"Sounds good to me," Aomame said.

"Now you're talking!" Ayumi said. "By the way, are you at all interested in playing with handcuffs?"

"Probably not," Aomame said. *Playing with handcuffs?*

"No? Too bad," Ayumi said, sounding genuinely disappointed.

CHAPTER 22

Tengo

THAT TIME COULD TAKE ON DEFORMED SHAPES AS IT MOVED AHEAD

Tengo thought about his brain. Lots of things made him do this.

The size of the human brain had increased four times over the past two and a half million years. In terms of weight, the brain occupied only two percent of the human body, but it consumed some forty percent of the body's total energy (according to a book he had recently read). Owing to the dramatic expansion of the brain, human beings had been able to acquire the concepts of time, space, and possibility.

The concepts of time, space, and possibility.

Tengo knew that time could become deformed as it moved forward. Time itself was uniform in composition, but once consumed, it took on a deformed shape. One period of time might be terribly heavy and long, while another could be light and short. Occasionally the order of things could be reversed, and in the worst cases order itself could vanish entirely. Sometimes things that should not be there at all might be added onto time. By adjusting time this way to suit their own purposes, people probably adjusted the meaning of their existences. In other words, by adding such operations to time, they were able – but just barely – to preserve their own sanity. Surely, if a person had to accept the time through which he had just passed uniformly in the given order, his nerves could not bear the strain. Such a life, Tengo felt, would be sheer torture.

Through the expansion of the brain, people had acquired the concept of temporality, but they simultaneously learned ways in which to change and adjust time. In parallel with their ceaseless consumption of time, people would ceaselessly reproduce time that they had mentally adjusted. This was no ordinary feat. No wonder the brain was said to consume forty percent of the body's total energy!

Tengo often wondered whether he had actually witnessed the memory he retained from the age of one and a half or, at most, two – the scene in which his mother in underclothes let a man who was not his father suck on her breasts. Her arms were wrapped around the man. Could a one- or two-year-old infant distinguish such details and remember them so vividly? Wasn't this a false memory that he had later conveniently fashioned to protect himself?

That was entirely conceivable. At some point Tengo's brain might have subconsciously created the memory of another man (his possibly "real" father) in order to "prove" that he was not the biological child of the man who was supposed to be his father. This was how he tried to eliminate "the man who was supposed to be his father" from the tight circle of blood. By establishing inside himself the hypothetical existence of a mother who must be alive somewhere and a "real" father, he was trying to create a portal leading out of his limited, suffocating life.

The problem with this view was that the memory came with such a vivid sense of reality. It had such an authentic feel, and weight, and smell, and depth. It was stubbornly fastened to the walls of his mind like an oyster clinging to a sunken ship. He could never manage to shake it off, to wash it away. He found it impossible to believe that such a memory was a mere counterfeit that his mind had created in response to some need. It was too real, too solid, to be imaginary.

What if it was real, then? Tengo thought.

His infant self would certainly have been frightened to witness such a scene. Someone else, some other human being, was sucking on breasts that should have been for him – someone bigger and stronger. And it appeared that Tengo's mother had – at least temporarily – forgotten about him, creating a situation that threatened his very survival, small and weak as he was. The primal terror of that moment may have been indelibly imprinted on the photo paper of his mind.

The memory of that terror came rushing back to him when he least expected it, attacking him with all the ferocity of a flash flood, and putting him into a near panic. This terror spoke to him, forcing him to remember: *Wherever you go, whatever you do, you can never escape the pressure of this water. This memory defines who you are, shapes your life, and is trying to send you to a place that has been decided for you. You can writhe all you want, but you will never be able to escape from this power.*

It suddenly occurred to Tengo: *When I lifted the pajamas that Fuka-Eri wore from the washing machine and smelled them, I might have been hoping to find my mother's smell. But why do I have to look for my departed mother's image in, of all things, the smell of a seventeen-year-old girl? There should be a more likely place to look – in the body of my older girlfriend, for one thing.*

Tengo's girlfriend was ten years his senior, but for some reason he never sought his mother's image in her. Neither did he have any particular interest in her smell. She took the lead in most of their sexual activity. Tengo simply did as she directed, hardly thinking, making neither choices nor judgments. She demanded only two things of him: good erections and well-timed ejaculations. "Don't come yet," she would command. "Hold on a little longer." And he would pour all his energy into holding on. "Okay, *now*! Come *now*!" she would whisper by his ear, and he would let go at precisely that point with as intense an ejaculation as he could manage. Then she would praise him, caressing his cheek: "Oh, Tengo! You're wonderful!" Tengo had an innate knack for precision in all realms, including correct punctuation and discovering the simplest possible formula necessary to solve a math problem.

It didn't work this way when he had sex with younger women. He would have to think from beginning to end, making choices and judgments. This made Tengo uncomfortable. All the responsibilities fell on his shoulders. He felt like the captain of a small boat on a stormy sea, having to take the rudder, inspect the setting of the sails, keep in mind the barometric pressure and the wind direction, and modulate his own behavior so as to boost the crew's trust in him. The slightest mistake or accident could lead to tragedy. This felt less like sex than the discharging of a duty. As a result he would tense up and miss the timing of an ejaculation or fail to become erect when necessary. This would only increase his doubts about himself.

Such mistakes never happened with his older girlfriend. She fully appreciated him. She always praised and encouraged him. After the one time he ejaculated prematurely, she was careful never to wear a white slip again. And not just slips: she stopped wearing any white lingerie at all.

That day she was wearing black lingerie – a matching top and bottom – as she performed fellatio on him, fully enjoying the hardness of his penis and the softness of his testicles. Tengo could see her breasts moving up and down, enfolded in the black lace of her bra, as she moved her mouth. To keep himself from coming too soon, he closed his eyes and thought about the Gilyaks.

They have no courts, and they do not know the meaning of "justice." How hard it is for them to understand us may be seen merely from the fact that up till the present day they still do not fully understand the purpose of roads. Even where a road has already been laid, they will still journey through the taiga. One often sees them, their families and their dogs, picking their way in Indian file across a quagmire right by the roadway.

Tengo imagined the scene: the shabbily dressed Gilyaks walking through the thick forest in line beside the road with their dogs and women, hardly speaking. In their concepts of time, space, and possibility, roads did not exist. Rather than walk on a road, they probably gained a clearer grasp of their own raison d'être by making their way quietly through the forest, in spite of the inconvenience.

The poor Gilyaks! Fuka-Eri had said.

Tengo thought of Fuka-Eri's face as she slept. She had fallen asleep wearing Tengo's too-large pajamas, the sleeves and cuffs rolled up. He had lifted them from the washing machine, held them to his nose, and smelled them.

I can't let myself think about that! Tengo told himself, but it was already too late.

The semen surged out of him in multiple violent convulsions and into his girlfriend's mouth. She took it in until he finished, then stepped out of bed and went to the bathroom. He heard her open the spigot, run the water, and rinse her mouth. Then, as if it had been nothing at all, she came back to the bed.

"Sorry," Tengo said.

"I guess you couldn't stop yourself," she said, caressing his nose with her fingertip. "That's okay, it's no big deal. Did it feel *that* good?"

"Fantastic," he said. "I think I can do it again in a few minutes."

"I can hardly wait," she said, pressing her cheek against Tengo's bare chest. She closed her eyes, keeping very still. Tengo could feel the soft breath from her nose against his nipple.

"Can you guess what your chest reminds me of when I see it?" she asked Tengo.

"No idea."

"A castle gate in a Kurosawa samurai movie."

"A castle gate," Tengo said, caressing her back.

"You know, like in *Throne of Blood* or *Hidden Fortress*. There's always a big, sturdy castle gate in those old black-and-white movies of his, all covered with these huge iron rivets. That's what I think of. Thick, solid . . ."

"I don't have any rivets, though."

"I hadn't noticed," she said.

Fuka-Eri's *Air Chrysalis* placed on the bestseller lists the second week after it went on sale, rising to number one on the fiction list in the third week. Tengo traced the process of the book's ascent through the newspapers they kept in the cram school's teachers' lounge. Two ads for the book also appeared in the papers, featuring a photo of the book's cover and a smaller shot of Fuka-Eri wearing the familiar tight-fitting summer sweater that showed off her breasts so beautifully (taken, no doubt, at the time of the press conference). Long, straight hair falling to her shoulders. Dark, enigmatic eyes looking straight at the camera. Those eyes seemed to peer through the lens and focus directly on something the viewer kept hidden deep in his heart, of which he was normally unaware. They did so neutrally but gently. This seventeen-year-old girl's unwavering gaze was disconcerting. It was just a small black-and-white photograph, but the mere sight of it almost certainly prompted many people to buy the book.

Komatsu had sent two copies of the book to Tengo a few days after it went on sale, but Tengo opened only the package, not the vinyl around the books themselves. True, the text inside the book was something he himself had written, and this was the first time his writing had taken the shape of a book, but he had no desire to open it and read it – or even glance at its pages. The sight of it gave him no joy. The sentences and paragraphs may have been his, but the story they comprised belonged entirely to Fuka-Eri. Her mind had given birth to it. His minor role as a secret technician had ended long before, and the work's fate from this point onward had nothing to do with him. Nor should it. He shoved the two volumes into the back of his bookcase, out of sight, still wrapped in vinyl.

For a while after the one night Fuka-Eri slept in his apartment, Tengo's life flowed along uneventfully. It rained a lot, but Tengo paid almost no attention to the weather, which ranked far down on his list of priorities. From Fuka-Eri herself, he heard nothing. The lack of contact probably meant that she had no particular problems for him to solve.

In addition to writing his novel every day, Tengo wrote a number of short pieces for magazines – anonymous jobs that anyone could do. They were a welcome change of pace, though, and the pay was good for the minimal effort involved. Three times a week, as usual, Tengo taught math at the cram school. He burrowed more deeply than ever into the world of mathematics in order to forget his concerns – issues involving *Air Chrysalis* and Fuka-Eri, mainly. Once he entered the mathematical world, his brain switched circuits (with a little click), his mouth emitted different kinds of words, his body began to use different kinds of muscles, and both the tone of his voice and the look on his face changed. Tengo liked the way this change of gears felt. It was like moving from one room into another or changing from one pair of shoes into another.

In contrast to the time he spent performing daily tasks or writing fiction, Tengo was able to attain a new level of relaxation – and even to become more eloquent – when he entered the world of mathematics. At the same time, however, he also felt he had become a somewhat more practical person. He could not decide who might be the real Tengo, but the switch was both natural and almost unconscious. He also knew that it was something he more or less needed.

As a teacher, Tengo pounded into his students' heads how voraciously mathematics demanded logic. Here things that could not be proven had no meaning, but once you had succeeded in proving something, the world's riddles settled into the palm of your hand like a tender oyster. Tengo's lectures took on uncommon warmth, and the students found themselves swept up in his eloquence. He taught them how to practically and effectively solve mathematical problems while simultaneously presenting a spectacular display of the romance concealed in the questions it posed. Tengo saw admiration in the eyes of several of his female students, and he realized that he was seducing these seventeen- or eighteen-year-olds through mathematics. His eloquence was a kind of intellectual foreplay. Mathematical functions stroked their backs; theorems sent warm breath into their ears. Since meeting Fuka-Eri, however, Tengo no longer felt sexual interest in such girls, nor did he have any urge to smell their pajamas.

Fuka-Eri is surely a special being, Tengo realized. *She can't be compared with other girls. She is undoubtedly someone of special significance to me. She is – how should I put it? – an all-encompassing image projected straight at me, but an image I find it impossible to decipher.*

Still, I'd better end any involvement with Fuka-Eri. Tengo's rational mind reached this lucid conclusion. *I should also put as much distance as possible between myself and the piles of* Air Chrysalis *displayed in the front of all the bookstores, and the inscrutable Professor Ebisuno, and that ominously mysterious religious organization. I'd also better keep away from Komatsu, at least for the time being. Otherwise, I'm likely to be carried into even more chaotic territory, pushed into a dangerous corner without a shred of logic, driven into a situation from which I can never extricate myself.*

But Tengo was also well aware that he could not easily withdraw from the twisted conspiracy in which he was now fully involved. He was no Hitchcockian protagonist, embroiled in a conspiracy before he knew what was happening. He had embroiled himself, knowing full well that it contained an element of risk. The machine was already in motion, gaining too much forward momentum for him to stop it. Tengo himself was one of its gears – and an important one at that. He could hear the machine's low groaning, and feel its implacable motion.

Komatsu called Tengo a few days after *Air Chrysalis* topped the bestseller list for the second week in a row. The phone rang after eleven o'clock at night. Tengo was already in bed in his pajamas. He had been reading a book for a while, lying on his stomach, and was just about to turn off the bedside light. Judging from the ring, he knew it was Komatsu. Exactly how, he could not explain, but he could always tell when the call was from Komatsu. The phone rang in a special way. Just as writing had a particular style, Komatsu's calls had a particular ring.

Tengo got out of bed, went to the kitchen, and picked up the receiver. He did not really want to answer the call and would have preferred to go quietly to sleep, to dream of Iriomote cats or the Panama Canal, or the ozone layer, or Basho – anything, as long as it was as far from here as possible. If he didn't answer the phone now, though, it would just ring again in another fifteen minutes or half an hour. Better to take the call now.

"Hey, Tengo, were you sleeping?" Komatsu asked, easygoing as usual.

"I was trying," Tengo said.

"Sorry about that," Komatsu said, sounding not the least bit sorry. "I just wanted to let you know that *Air Chrysalis* is selling well."

"That's great."

"Like hotcakes. They can't keep up. The poor guys at the printer are working through the night. Anyhow, I figured the numbers would be pretty good, of course. The author is a beautiful seventeen-year-old girl. People are talking about it. All the elements are in place for a bestseller."

"Unlike novels written by a thirty-year-old cram school teacher who looks like a bear, you mean."

"Exactly. But still, you couldn't call this a commercial novel. It's got no sex scenes, it's not a tearjerker. Not even I imagined it would sell so spectacularly."

Komatsu paused as if he expected a response from Tengo. When Tengo said nothing, he went on:

"It's not just selling a lot, either. The critical reception is wonderful, too. This is no lightweight drama slapped together on a whim by some youngster. The story itself is outstanding. Of course your superb revision made this possible, Tengo. That was an absolutely perfect piece of work you did."

Made this possible. Ignoring Komatsu's praise, Tengo pressed his fingertips against his temples. Whenever Komatsu openly praised Tengo, it was bound to be followed by something unpleasant.

Tengo asked Komatsu, "So tell me, what's the bad news?"

"How do you know there's bad news?"

"Look what time you're phoning me! There has to be some bad news."

"True," Komatsu said, in apparent admiration. "You've got that special sensitivity, Tengo. I should have known."

Sensitivity's got nothing to do with it, Tengo thought. *It's just plain old experience.* But he said nothing and waited to see what Komatsu was getting at.

"Unfortunately, you're right, I do have a piece of unpleasant news," Komatsu said. He paused meaningfully. Tengo imagined Komatsu at the other end, his eyes gleaming like a mongoose's in the dark.

"It probably has something to do with the author of *Air Chrysalis,* am I right?"

"Exactly. It is about Fuka-Eri. And it's not good. She's been missing for a while."

Tengo's fingers kept pressing against his temples. " 'A while'? Since when?"

"Three days ago, on Wednesday morning, she left her house in Okutama for Tokyo. Professor Ebisuno saw her off. She didn't say where she was going. Later in the day she phoned to say she wouldn't be coming back to the house in the hills, that she was going to spend the night in their Shinano-machi condo. Professor Ebisuno's daughter was also supposed to spend the night there, but Fuka-Eri never showed up. They haven't heard from her since."

Tengo traced his memory back three days, but could think of nothing relevant.

"They have absolutely no idea where she is. I thought she might have contacted you."

"I haven't heard a thing," Tengo said. More than four weeks must have gone by since she spent the night in his apartment.

Tengo momentarily wondered whether he ought to tell Komatsu what she had said back then – that she had better not go back to the Shinano-machi condo. She might have been sensing something ominous about the place. But he decided not to mention it. He didn't want to have to tell Komatsu that Fuka-Eri had stayed at his apartment.

"She's an odd girl," Tengo said. "She might have just gone off somewhere by herself without telling anybody."

"No, I don't think so. She may not look it, but Fuka-Eri is a very conscientious person. She's always very clear about her whereabouts, always phoning to say where she is or where she's going and when. That's what Professor Ebisuno tells me. For her to be out of touch for three full days is not at all usual for her. Something bad might have happened."

"Something bad," Tengo growled.

"The Professor and his daughter are both very worried," Komatsu said.

"In any case, if she stays missing like this, it'll put you in a difficult position, I'm sure," Tengo said to Komatsu.

"True, especially if the police get involved. I mean, think about it: beautiful teenage writer of runaway bestseller disappears! You know the media would go crazy over that one. Then they're going to drag me out for comments as her editor. No good can come of that. I'm strictly a shadow figure, I don't do well in the sunlight. Once something like that gets going the truth could come out at any point."

"What does Professor Ebisuno say?"

"That he's going to file a search request with the police, maybe as soon as tomorrow," Komatsu said. "I got him to hold off for a few days, but it's not something that can be postponed for very long."

"If the media get wind of the search request, they'll be all over this."

"I don't know how the police are going to respond, but Fuka-Eri is the girl of the moment, not just some teenage runaway. Keeping this out of the public eye will likely be impossible."

That might have been exactly what Professor Ebisuno was hoping for, Tengo thought: to cause a sensation using Fuka-Eri as bait, exploit it to clarify the relationship of Sakigake to Fuka-Eri's parents, and learn the couple's whereabouts. If so, then the Professor's plan was working as he had imagined it would. But had the Professor fully grasped how dangerous this might prove to be? He certainly should have: Professor Ebisuno was not a thoughtless person. Indeed, deep thinking was exactly what he did for a living. And besides, there seemed to be a number of important facts surrounding Fuka-Eri's situation of which Tengo was unaware, as though he were trying to assemble a jigsaw puzzle without having been given all the pieces. A wise person would have avoided getting involved from the beginning.

"Do you have any idea where she might be, Tengo?" Komatsu asked.

"Not at the moment."

"No?" Komatsu said with a perceptible note of fatigue in his voice. He was not a man who often let such human failings show. "Sorry I woke you in the middle of the night."

To hear words of apology coming from Komatsu's mouth was also a rare occurrence.

"That's okay," Tengo said. "Given the situation."

"You know, Tengo, if I had my way I would have preferred not to involve you in these real-world complications. Your only job was to do the writing, and you carried that off splendidly. But things never work out as smoothly as we want them to. And, as I said to you once before, we're all shooting the rapids – "

"In the same boat," Tengo mechanically finished the sentence.

"Exactly."

"But come to think of it," Tengo added, "won't *Air Chrysalis* just sell all the more if Fuka-Eri's disappearance becomes news?"

"It's selling enough already," Komatsu said with a note of resignation. "We don't need any more publicity. The only thing a scandal will net us is trouble. What we ought to be thinking about is a nice, quiet spot to land in."

"A spot to land in," Tengo said.

Komatsu made a sound as though he were swallowing some imaginary thing. Then he lightly cleared his throat. "Well, let's have a nice, long talk about that over dinner sometime. After this mess gets cleaned up. Good night, Tengo. You ought to get a good night's rest."

Komatsu hung up. As if he had just had a curse laid on him, Tengo could no longer sleep. He felt tired, but he couldn't get to sleep.

What was this "You ought to get a good night's rest" business? He thought about doing some work at the kitchen table, but he wasn't in the mood. He took a bottle of whiskey from the cabinet, poured some into a glass, and drank it straight in small sips.

Maybe Fuka-Eri had been kidnapped by Sakigake. It seemed entirely plausible to Tengo. A bunch of them had staked out her Shinano-machi condo, forced her into a car, and taken her away. It was by no means impossible, if they had chosen the right moment and acted quickly. Maybe Fuka-Eri had already sensed their presence when she said she had better not go back to the condo.

Both the Little People and air chrysalises actually existed, Fuka-Eri had told Tengo. She had met the Little People in the Sakigake commune when she was being punished for having carelessly let the blind goat die, and she had made an air chrysalis with them for several nights running. As a result, something of great significance had happened to her. She had put the events into a story, and Tengo had refashioned the story into a finished piece of fiction. In other words, he had transformed it into a *commodity,* and that commodity was (to borrow Komatsu's expression) selling like hotcakes. This in turn might be distressing to Sakigake. The stories of the Little People and the air chrysalis might be major secrets that must not be divulged to the outside world. And so, to prevent any further leaks, they had kidnapped Fuka-Eri and shut her up. They had resorted to force, even if it meant risking the possibility that her disappearance might arouse public suspicion.

This was, of course, nothing more than Tengo's hypothesis. He had no evidence he could offer, no way he could prove it. Even if he told people, "The Little People and air chrysalises actually exist," who could possibly take him seriously? First of all, Tengo himself did not know what it meant to say that such things "actually exist."

Another possibility was that Fuka-Eri had become sick of all the hype surrounding her bestseller and had gone into hiding. This was entirely conceivable, of course. It was all but impossible to predict what she would do, but assuming she went into hiding, she would probably have left some kind of message for Professor Ebisuno and his daughter, Azami. There would have been no reason for her to worry them.

It was easy for Tengo to imagine, however, that Fuka-Eri might be in great danger if she had actually been abducted by Sakigake. Just as there had been no word from her parents, all word of Fuka-Eri might be lost. Even if the relationship between Fuka-Eri and Sakigake were revealed (which would not take a very long time), and this gave rise to a media scandal, it would all be for nothing if the police refused to get involved on the grounds that there was "no physical evidence that she was abducted." She might remain locked up somewhere inside the high-walled religious commune. Had Professor Ebisuno concocted a plan that included such a worst-case scenario?

Tengo wanted to call Professor Ebisuno and ask him all these questions, but it was already past midnight, and he could only wait until tomorrow.

The next morning Tengo dialed the number he was given to call Professor Ebisuno's house, but the call did not go through. All he got was the recorded message, "The number you have dialed is not presently in service. Please check the number and dial again." He tried again several times, but always with the same results. He guessed that they had changed phone numbers after Fuka-Eri's debut, due to an onslaught of calls requesting interviews.

Nothing unusual happened during the following week. *Air Chrysalis* went on selling in the same high numbers, coming out again at the top of the national bestseller list. No one contacted Tengo during the week. He tried phoning Komatsu at his office a few times, but he was always out (which was not unusual). Tengo left a message with the editorial office for Komatsu to call, but no call came (which was also not unusual). He read the newspaper every day, but he found no report that a search request had been filed for Fuka-Eri. Could Professor Ebisuno have decided not to file one? Perhaps he had filed a request but the police had not publicized it so as to search for her in secret, or they had not taken it seriously, treating it as just another case of a runaway teenager.

As always, Tengo taught mathematics at the cram school three days a week, continued writing his novel on other days, and spent Friday afternoon having intense sex with his girlfriend when she visited his apartment. But he could not focus. He spent day after day feeling uneasy and muddled, like someone who has mistakenly swallowed a thick swatch of cloud. He began losing his appetite. He would wake up at odd times in the middle of the night, unable to get back to sleep. Then he would think about Fuka-Eri. Where was she now? What was she doing? Whom was she with? What was happening to her? He imagined a variety of situations, all of them, with minor variations, deeply pessimistic. In the scenes he imagined, she was always wearing her thin, tight-fitting sweater that showed off the lovely shape of her breasts. The image made him gasp for breath and only added to his agitation.

It was on the Thursday of the sixth week after *Air Chrysalis* became a permanent fixture on the bestseller list that Fuka-Eri finally got in touch with him.

CHAPTER 23

Aomame

THIS IS JUST THE BEGINNING OF SOMETHING

Aomame and Ayumi were the perfect pair to host intimate but fully erotic all-night sex feasts. Ayumi was petite and cheerful, comfortable with strangers, and talkative. She brought a positive attitude to just about any situation once she had made up her mind to do so. She also had a healthy sense of humor. By contrast, Aomame, slim and muscular, tended to be rather expressionless and reserved, and she found it hard to be witty with a man she was meeting for the first time. In her speech there was a subtle note of cynicism and even hostility, and in her eyes an equally subtle gleam of intolerance. Still, when she felt like it, Aomame gave off a cool aura that naturally attracted men. It was like the sweet, sexually stimulating fragrance that animals or insects give off when necessary. This was not something that could be learned through conscious effort. It was probably inborn. But no – she might well have acquired the fragrance for some reason at a certain stage of life. In any case, this aura subtly aroused not only her sexual partners but also Ayumi, adding color and a positive warmth to their evenings.

Whenever they encountered suitable men, first Ayumi approached them with her natural cheer. Then Aomame would join them at an appropriate moment, creating a unique atmosphere that was part operetta, part film noir. Once things got to that point, the rest was simple. They would move to an appropriate place and (as Ayumi bluntly put it) "fuck like mad." The hardest thing was finding suitable partners. Preferably, they should be two men together – clean, and reasonably good-looking. They had to be at least somewhat intellectual, but too much so could be a problem: boring conversation could turn the evening sterile. They also had to look like men who had money to spend. Obviously, the men paid for the drinks and the hotel rooms.

When they tried to hold a nice little sex feast near the end of June, however (in what would turn out to be their last team activity), they simply could not find suitable men. They put a lot of time into it, changing venues several times, always with the same results. In spite of the fact that it was the last Friday of the month, all the clubs they tried, from Roppongi to Akasaka, were shockingly quiet, almost deserted, giving them no real choice. Maybe it had something to do with the heavy clouds that hung in the sky, as if the whole of Tokyo were in mourning for someone.

"It doesn't look good today," Aomame said. "Maybe we should give up." It was already ten thirty.

Ayumi reluctantly agreed. "I've never seen such a dead Friday night. And here I'm wearing my sexy purple underwear!"

"So go home and get carried away with yourself in the mirror."

"Not even I have the guts to do that in the police dorm bathroom!"

"Anyhow, let's just forget it. We'll have a nice, quiet drink, then head home and go to bed."

"That may be the best thing," Ayumi said. Then, as if she had suddenly recalled something, she added, "Say, let's have a bite to eat before we go home. I've got an extra thirty thousand yen in my purse."

Aomame frowned. "Extra? How come? You're always complaining how little they pay you."

Ayumi scratched the side of her nose. "Actually, the last time, the guy gave me thirty thousand yen. He called it 'taxi fare' and handed it to me when we said good-bye. You know, the time we did it with those real estate guys."

"And you just took it?" Aomame asked, shocked.

"Maybe he thought we were semi-pros," Ayumi said with a chuckle. "I bet it never crossed his mind he was dealing with a cop and a martial arts instructor. Anyhow, what's the difference? I'm sure he makes tons of money in real estate – more than he knows what to do with. I kept it separate, figured I'd spend it with you on a nice meal or something. I mean, money like that you don't want to use on just regular expenses."

Aomame did not tell Ayumi how she felt about this. To have taken money for casual sex with a man she didn't know – she could hardly comprehend the fact that such a thing had occurred. She felt as if she were looking at a twisted image of herself in a warped mirror. Ethically, which was better – taking money for killing men or taking money for having sex with men?

"Tell me," Ayumi asked Aomame uneasily, "does the idea of taking money from a man bother you?"

Aomame shook her head. "It doesn't bother me so much as make me feel a little mystified. But what about you? I would have expected a female cop to feel reluctant to do anything like prostitution."

"Not at all," Ayumi insisted cheerfully. "I have no problem with that. You know, a prostitute is somebody who agrees on a price and gets her money before having sex. The first rule is 'Pay me before you take your pants off.' She couldn't make a living if guys told her, 'Gee, I don't have any money' after it was all over. But when there's no prior negotiation of a price, and afterward the guy gives you a little something for 'taxi fare,' it's just an expression of gratitude. That's different from professional prostitution. There's a clear distinction between the two."

What Ayumi had to say made a certain kind of sense.

The men that Aomame and Ayumi had chosen the last time were in their late thirties or early forties. Both had full heads of hair, but Aomame was willing to compromise on that point. They said they were with a company that dealt in real estate, but judging from their Hugo Boss suits and Missoni Uomo neckties, they were not just ordinary employees of giant conglomerates like Mitsubishi or Mitsui, whose employees were bound by finicky rules, tradition, and endless meetings, but rather they worked for a more aggressive, flexible company with a cool, foreign-sounding name, a place that looked for individual talent and richly rewarded success. One of the men carried keys to a brand-new Alfa Romeo. Tokyo was short on office space, they said. The economy had recovered from the oil shocks and was showing signs of heating up again. Capital was growing ever more fluid, and soon it would be impossible to meet the need for space no matter how many new high-rise buildings they put up.

"Sounds like real estate is where the money is," Aomame said to Ayumi.

"That's true," Ayumi said. "If you have anything extra lying around, you ought to invest it in real estate. Huge amounts of money are just pouring into Tokyo, which is only so big. Land prices are bound to soar. Buy now, and there's no way you can lose. It's like betting on horses when you know you hold the winning ticket. Unfortunately, low-ranking public employees like me don't have anything to spare. But how about you, Aomame? Do you do any investing?"

Aomame shook her head. "I don't trust anything but cash."

Ayumi laughed out loud. "You have the mind of a criminal!"

"The thing to do is keep your cash in your mattress so in a jam, you can grab it and escape out the window."

"That's it!" Ayumi said, snapping her fingers. "Like in *The Getaway*. The Steve McQueen movie. A wad of bills and a shotgun. I love that kind of stuff."

"More than being on the side that enforces the law?"

"Personally, yes," Ayumi said with a smile. "I'm more drawn to outlaws. They're a whole lot more exciting than riding around in a mini patrol car and handing out parking tickets. That's what I like about you."

"Do I look like an outlaw?"

Ayumi nodded. "How should I put it? I don't know, you just have that atmosphere about you, though maybe not like a Faye Dunaway holding a machine gun."

"I don't need a machine gun," Aomame said.

"About that religious commune we were talking about last time, Sakigake . . . ," Ayumi said.

The two were sharing a light meal and a bottle of Chianti at a small, late-night Italian restaurant in Iikura, a quiet neighborhood. Aomame was having a salad with strips of raw tuna, while Ayumi had ordered a plate of gnocchi with basil sauce.

"Uh-huh," Aomame said.

"You got me interested, so I did a little searching on my own. And the more I looked, the fishier it began to smell. Sakigake calls itself a religion, and it even has official certification, but it's totally lacking any religious *substance*. Doctrine-wise, it's kind of deconstructionist or something, just a jumble of *images* of religion thrown together. They've added some new-age spiritualism, fashionable academicism, a return to nature, anticapitalism, occultism, and stuff, but that's all: it has a bunch of flavors, but no substantial core. Or maybe that's what it's all about: this religion's substance is its lack of substance. In

McLuhanesque terms, the medium is the message. Some people might find that cool."

"McLuhanesque?"

"Hey, look, even I read a book now and then," Ayumi protested. "McLuhan was ahead of his time. He was so popular for a while that people tend not to take him seriously, but what he had to say was right."

"In other words, the package itself is the contents. Is that it?"

"Exactly. The characteristics of the package determine the nature of the contents, not the other way around."

Aomame considered this for a moment and said, "The core of Sakigake as a religion is unclear, but that has nothing to do with why people are drawn to it, you mean?"

Ayumi nodded. "I wouldn't say it's amazing how many people join Sakigake, but the numbers are by no means small. And the more people who join, the more money they put together. Obviously. So, then, what is it about this religion that attracts so many people? If you ask me, it's primarily that it doesn't *smell* like a religion. It's very clean and intellectual, and it looks systematic. That's what attracts young professionals. It stimulates their intellectual curiosity. It provides a sense of achievement they can't get in the real world – something tangible and personal. And these intellectual believers, like an elite officers' corps, form the powerful brains of the organization.

"Plus," Ayumi continued, "their 'Leader' seems to have a good deal of charisma. People idolize him. His very presence, you might say, functions like a doctrinal core. It's close in origin to primitive religion. Even early Christianity was more or less like that at first. But *this* guy never comes out in the open. Nobody knows what he looks like, or his name, or how old he is. The religion has a governing council that supposedly runs everything, but another person heads the council and acts as the public face of the religion in official events, though I don't think he's any more than a figurehead. The one who is at the center of the system seems to be this mysterious 'Leader' person."

"Sounds like he wants to keep his identity hidden."

"Well, either he has something to hide or he keeps his existence obscure on purpose to heighten the mysterious atmosphere around him."

"Or else he's tremendously ugly," Aomame said.

"That's possible, I suppose. A grotesque creature from another world," Ayumi said, with a monster's growl. "But anyway, aside from the founder, this religion has too many things that stay hidden. Like the aggressive real estate dealings I mentioned on the phone the other day. Everything on the surface is there for show: the nice buildings, the handsome publicity, the intelligent-sounding theories, the former social elites who have converted, the stoic practices, the yoga and spiritual serenity, the rejection of materialism, the organic farming, the fresh air and lovely vegetarian diet – they're all like calculated photos, like ads for high-class resort condos that come as inserts in the Sunday paper. The packaging is beautiful, but I get the feeling that suspicious plans are hatching behind the scenes. Some of it might even be illegal. Now that I've been through a bunch of materials, that's the impression I get."

"But the police aren't making any moves now."

"Something may be happening undercover, but I wouldn't know about that. The Yamanashi Prefectural Police do seem to be keeping an eye on them to some extent. I kind of sensed that when I spoke to the guy in charge of the investigation. I mean, Sakigake gave birth to Akebono, the group that staged the shootout, and it's just guesswork that Akebono's Chinese-made Kalashnikovs came in through North Korea: nobody's really gotten to the bottom of that. Sakigake is still under some suspicion, but they've got that 'Religious Juridical Person' label, so they have to be handled with kid gloves. The police have already investigated the premises once, and that made it more or less clear that there was no direct connection between Sakigake and the shootout. As for any moves the Public Security Intelligence Agency might be making, we just don't know. Those guys work in absolute secrecy and have never gotten along with us."

"How about the children who stopped coming to public school? Do you know any more about them?"

"No, nothing. Once they stop going to school, I guess, they never come outside the walls of the compound again. We don't have any way of investigating their cases. It would be different if we had concrete evidence of child abuse, but for now we don't have anything."

"Don't you get any information about that from people who have quit Sakigake? There must be a few people at least who become disillusioned with the religion or can't take the harsh discipline and break away."

"There's constant coming and going, of course – people joining, people quitting. Basically, people are free to quit anytime. When they join, they make a huge donation as a 'Permanent Facility Use Fee' and sign a contract stipulating that it is entirely nonrefundable, so as long as they're willing to accept that loss, they can come out with nothing but the clothes on their backs. There's an organization of people who have quit the religion, and they accuse Sakigake of being a dangerous, antisocial cult engaged in fraudulent activity. They've filed a suit and put out a little newsletter, but they're such a small voice they have virtually zero impact on public opinion. The religion has a phalanx of top lawyers, and they've put together a watertight defense. One lawsuit can't budge them."

"Haven't the ex-members made any statements about Leader or the children inside?"

"I don't know," Ayumi said. "I've never read their newsletter. As far as I've been able to check, though, all the dissidents are from the lowest ranks of the group, just small fry.

Sakigake makes a big deal about how they reject all worldly values, but part of the organization is completely hierarchical, sharply divided between the leadership and the rest of them. You can't become a member of the leadership without an advanced degree or specialized professional qualifications. Only elite believers in the leadership group ever get to see or receive direct instruction from Leader or make contact with key figures of the organization. All the others just make their required donations and spend one sterile day after another performing their religious austerities in the fresh air, devoting themselves to farming, or spending hours in the meditation rooms. They're like a flock of sheep, led out to pasture under the watchful eye of the shepherd and his dog, and brought back to their shed at night, one peaceful day after the next. They look forward to the day when their position rises high enough in the organization for them to come into the presence of Big Brother, but that day never comes. That's why ordinary believers know almost nothing about the inner workings of the organization. Even if they quit Sakigake, they don't have any important information they can offer the outside world. They've never even seen Leader's face."

"Aren't there any members of the elite who have quit?"

"Not one, as far as I can tell."

"Does that mean you're not allowed to leave once you've learned the secrets?"

"There might be some pretty dramatic developments if it came to that," Ayumi said with a short sigh. Then she said to Aomame, "So tell me, about that raping of little girls you mentioned: how definite is that?"

"Pretty definite, but there's still no proof."

"It's being done systematically inside the commune?"

"That's not entirely clear, either. We do have one actual victim, though. I've met the girl. They did terrible things to her."

"By 'rape,' do you mean actual penetration?"

"Yes, there's no question about that."

Ayumi twisted her lips at an angle, thinking. "I've got it! Let me dig into this a little more in my own way."

"Don't get in over your head, now."

"Don't worry," Ayumi said. "I may not look it, but I'm very cautious."

They finished their meal, and the waiter cleared the table. They declined to order dessert and, instead, continued drinking wine.

Ayumi said, "Remember how you told me that no men had fooled around with you when you were a little girl?"

Aomame glanced at Ayumi, registering the look on her face, and nodded. "My family was very religious. There was never any talk of sex, and it was the same with all the other families we knew. Sex was a forbidden topic."

"Well, okay, but being religious has nothing to do with the strength or weakness of a person's sex drive. Everybody knows the clergy is full of sex freaks. In fact, we arrest a *lot* of people connected with religion – and with education – for stuff like prostitution and groping women on commuter trains."

"Maybe so, but at least in our circles, there was no hint of that kind of thing, nobody who did anything they shouldn't."

"Well, good for you," Ayumi said. "I'm glad to hear it."

"It was different for you?"

Instead of responding immediately, Ayumi gave a little shrug. Then she said, "To tell you the truth, they messed around with me a lot when I was a girl."

"Who were 'they'?"

"My brother. And my uncle."

Aomame grimaced slightly. "Your brother and uncle?"

"That's right. They're both policemen now. Not too long ago, my uncle even received official commendation as an outstanding officer – thirty years of continuous service, major contributions to public safety in the district and to improvement of the environment. He was featured in the paper once for saving a stupid dog and her pup that wandered into a rail crossing."

"What did they do to you?"

"Touched me down there, made me give them blow jobs."

The wrinkles of Aomame's grimace deepened. "Your brother and uncle?"

"Separately, of course. I think I was ten and my brother maybe fifteen. My uncle did it before that – two or three times, when he stayed over with us."

"Did you tell anybody?"

Ayumi responded with a few slow shakes of the head. "I didn't say a word. They warned me not to, threatened that they'd get me if I said anything. And even if they hadn't, I was afraid if I told, they'd blame *me* for it and punish me. I was too scared to tell anybody."

"Not even your mother?"

"*Especially* my mother," Ayumi said. "My brother had always been her favorite, and she was always telling me how disappointed she was in me – I was sloppy, I was fat, I wasn't pretty enough, my grades in school were nothing special. She wanted a different kind of daughter – a slim, cute little doll to send to ballet lessons. It was like asking for the impossible."

"So you didn't want to disappoint her even more."

"Right. I was sure if I told her what my brother was doing, she'd hate me even more. She'd say it was *my* fault instead of blaming him."

Aomame used her fingers to smooth out the wrinkles in her face. *My mother refused to talk to me after I announced that I was abandoning the faith at the age of ten. She'd hand me notes when it was absolutely necessary to communicate something, but she would never speak. I ceased to be her daughter. I was just "the one who abandoned the faith." I moved out after that.*

"But there was no penetration?" Aomame asked Ayumi.

"No penetration," Ayumi said. "As bad as they were, they

couldn't do anything *that* painful to me. Not even they would demand that much."

"Do you still see this brother and uncle of yours?"

"Hardly ever after I took a job and left the house. But we are relatives, after all, and we're in the same profession. Sometimes I can't avoid seeing them, and when I do I'm all smiles. I don't do anything to rock the boat. I bet they don't even remember that something like that ever happened."

"Don't remember?"

"Sure, *they* can forget about it," Ayumi said. "*I* never can."

"Of course not," Aomame said.

"It's like some historic massacre."

"Massacre?"

"The ones who did it can always rationalize their actions and even forget what they did. They can turn away from things they don't want to see. But the surviving victims can never forget. They can't turn away. Their memories are passed on from parent to child. That's what the world is, after all: an endless battle of contrasting memories."

"True," Aomame said, scowling slightly. *An endless battle of contrasting memories?*

"To tell you the truth," Ayumi said, "I kind of thought that you must have had the same kind of experience as me."

"Why did you think that?"

"I don't know, I can't really explain it, I just sort of figured. Maybe I thought that having wild one-night stands with strange men was a result of something like that. And in your case, I thought I detected some kind of anger, too. Anyhow, you just don't seem like someone who can do the ordinary thing, you know, like everybody else does: find a regular boyfriend, go out on a date, have a meal, and have sex in the usual way with just the one person. It's more or less the same with me."

"You're saying that you couldn't follow the normal pattern

because someone messed around with you when you were little?"

"That's how I felt," Ayumi said. She gave a little shrug. "To tell you the truth, I'm afraid of men. Or, rather, I'm afraid of getting deeply involved with one particular man, of completely taking on another person. The very thought of it makes me cringe. But being alone can be hard sometimes. I want a man to hold me, to put his thing inside me. I want it so bad I can't stand it sometimes. Not knowing the man at all makes it easier. A *lot* easier."

"Because you're afraid of men?"

"I think that's a large part of it."

"I don't think I have any fear of men," Aomame said.

"Is there anything you *are* afraid of?"

"Of course there is," Aomame said. "The thing I'm most afraid of is *me*. Of not knowing what I'm going to do. Of not knowing what I'm doing right now."

"What *are* you doing right now?"

Aomame stared at the wineglass in her hand for a time. "I wish I knew." She looked up. "But I don't. I can't even be sure what world I'm in now, what year I'm in."

"It's 1984. We're in Tokyo, in Japan."

"I wish I could declare that with such certainty."

"You're strange," Ayumi said with a smile. "They're just self-evident truths. 'Declaring' and 'certainty' are beside the point."

"I can't explain it very well, but I can't say they're self-evident truths to me."

"You can't?" Ayumi said as if deeply impressed. "I'm not quite sure what you're talking about, but I will say this: whatever time and place this might be, you do have one person you love deeply, and that's something I can only envy. I don't have anybody like that."

Aomame set her wineglass down on the table and dabbed at her mouth with her napkin. Then she said, "You may be right.

Whatever time and place this might be, totally unrelated to that, I want to see him. I want to see him so badly I could die. That's the only thing that seems certain. It's the only thing I can say with confidence."

"Want me to have a look at the police materials? If you give me the basic information, we might be able to find out where he is and what he's doing."

Aomame shook her head. "Please *don't* look for him. I think I told you before, I'll run into him sometime, somewhere, strictly by chance. I'll just keep patiently waiting for that time to come."

"Like a big, romantic TV series," Ayumi said, impressed. "I love stuff like that. I get chills just thinking about it."

"It's tough on the one who's actually doing it, though."

"I know what you mean," Ayumi said, lightly pressing her fingers against her temples. "But still, even though you're that much in love with him, you feel like sleeping with strange men every once in a while."

Aomame clicked her fingernails against the rim of the thin wineglass. "I *need* to do it. To keep myself in balance as a flesh-and-blood human being."

"And it doesn't destroy the love you have inside you."

Aomame said, "It's like the Tibetan Wheel of the Passions. As the wheel turns, the values and feelings on the outer rim rise and fall, shining or sinking into darkness. But true love stays fastened to the axle and doesn't move."

"Marvelous," Ayumi said. "The Tibetan Wheel of the Passions, huh?"

And she drank down the wine remaining in her glass.

Two days later, a little after eight o'clock at night, a call came from Tamaru. As always, he skipped the preliminary greetings and went straight to business.

"Are you free tomorrow afternoon?"

"I don't have a thing in the afternoon. I can come over whenever you need me."

"How about four thirty?"

Aomame said that would be fine.

"Good," Tamaru said. She could hear his ballpoint pen scratching the time into his calendar. He was pressing down hard.

"How is Tsubasa doing?" Aomame asked.

"She's doing well, I think. Madame is going there every day to look after her. The girl seems to be growing fond of her."

"That's good news."

"Yes, it *is* good news, but something else happened that is not so good."

"Something not so good?" Aomame knew that when Tamaru said something was "not so good," it had to be terrible.

"The dog died," Tamaru said.

"The dog? You mean Bun?"

"Yes, the funny German shepherd that liked spinach. She died last night."

Aomame was shocked to hear this. The dog was maybe five or six years old, not an age for dying. "She was perfectly healthy the last time I saw her."

"She didn't die from illness," Tamaru said, his voice flat. "I found her this morning in pieces."

"In pieces?!"

"As if she had exploded. Her guts were splattered all over the place. It was pretty intense. I had to go around picking up chunks of flesh with paper towels. The force of the blast turned her body inside out. It was as if somebody had set off a small but powerful bomb inside her stomach."

"The poor dog!"

"Oh, well, there's nothing to be done about the dog," Tamaru said. "She's dead and won't be coming back. I can find another guard dog to take her place. What worries me, though, is *what happened*. It wasn't something that any ordinary person could do – setting off a bomb inside a dog like that. For one thing, that dog barked like crazy whenever a stranger approached. This was not an easy thing to carry off."

"That's for sure," Aomame said in a dry tone of voice.

"The women in the safe house are scared to death. The one in charge of feeding the dog found her like that this morning. First she puked her guts out and then she called me. I asked if anything suspicious happened during the night. Not a thing, she said. Nobody heard an explosion. If there had been such a big sound, everybody would have woken up for sure. These women live in fear even in the best of times. It must have been a soundless explosion. And nobody heard the dog bark. It was an especially quiet night, but when morning came, there was the dog, inside out. Fresh organs had been blown all over, and the neighborhood crows were having a great time. For me, though, it was nothing but worries."

"Something weird is happening."

"That's for sure," Tamaru said. "Something weird is happening. And if what I'm feeling is right, this is just the beginning of something."

"Did you call the police?"

"Hell, no," Tamaru said, with a contemptuous little snort. "The police are useless – looking in the wrong place for the wrong thing. They'd just complicate matters."

"What does Madame say?"

"Nothing. She just nodded when I gave her my report," Tamaru said. "All security measures are my responsibility, from beginning to end. It's *my* job."

A short silence followed, a heavy silence having to do with responsibility.

"Tomorrow at four thirty," Aomame said.

"Tomorrow at four thirty," Tamaru repeated, and quietly hung up.

CHAPTER 24

Tengo

WHAT'S THE POINT OF ITS BEING A WORLD THAT ISN'T HERE?

It rained all Thursday morning, not a heavy downpour, but persistent rain. There had been no letup since the previous afternoon. Whenever it seemed about to stop it would start pouring again. June was half gone without a sign the rainy season would ever end. The sky remained dark, as if covered with a lid, and the world wore a heavy dampness.

Just before noon, Tengo put on a raincoat and hat and was headed out to the local market when he noticed a brown padded envelope in his mailbox. It bore no postmark, stamps, or address, and no return address, either. His name had been written with a ballpoint pen in the middle of the front in small, stiff characters that might have been scratched into dry clay with a nail – Fuka-Eri's writing, without question. He tore it open to find a single bare sixty-minute TDK audiotape cassette. No letter or memo accompanied it. It was not in a plastic case, and the cassette bore no label.

After a moment of uncertainty, Tengo decided to forget about shopping and listen to the tape. Back in his apartment, he held the cassette in the air and gave it several shakes. For all the mystery surrounding its arrival, it was obviously just an ordinary mass-produced object. There was nothing suggesting that it would explode after he played it.

Taking off his raincoat, he set a radio cassette player on the kitchen table. He removed the cassette from the padded envelope and inserted it into the player, next to which he placed memo paper and a ballpoint pen in case he wanted to take notes. After looking around to make certain there was no one else present, he pressed the "play" button.

There was no sound at first. This lasted for some time. Just as he was beginning to suspect that it was nothing but a blank tape, there were some sudden bumping sounds like the moving of a chair. Then a light clearing of the throat (it seemed). Then, without warning, Fuka-Eri began to speak.

"Tengo," she said, as if in a sound test. As far as he could recall, this was probably the first time she had actually called him by name.

She cleared her throat again. She seemed tense.

I should write you a letter, but I'm bad at that, so I'll record a tape. It's easier for me to talk this way than on the phone. Somebody might be listening on the phone. Wait, I need water.

Tengo heard what he thought were the sounds of Fuka-Eri picking up a glass, taking a drink, and setting the glass back down on a table. Recorded on tape, her uniquely unaccented manner of speech without question marks or other punctuation sounded even stranger than in conversation. It was almost unreal. On tape, however, as opposed to conversation, she was able to speak several sentences in a row.

I hear you don't know where I am. You might be worried. But you don't have to be. This is not a dangerous place. I wanted to tell you that. I really shouldn't do this, but I felt like I ought to.
[Ten seconds of silence.]

They told me not to tell anyone. That I'm here. The Professor filed a search request with the police to look for me. But they're not doing anything. Kids run away all the time. So I will just stay still here a while.

[Fifteen seconds of silence.]

This place is far away. No one will find me if I don't go out walking. Very far away. Azami will bring this tape to you. Better not send it in the mail. Gotta be careful. Wait, I'll make sure it's recording.

[A click. An empty interval. Another click.]

Good, it's recording.

Children shouting in the distance. Faint sounds of music. These were probably coming through an open window. There might have been a kindergarten nearby.

Thanks for putting me up that time. I needed you to do that. I also needed to get to know you. Thanks for reading the book to me. I felt close to the Gilyaks. Why do the Gilyaks walk through the forest swamps and not on the wide roads.

[Tengo secretly added a question mark at the end.]

Even if the roads are convenient, it's easier for the Gilyaks to keep away from the roads and walk through the forest. To walk on the roads, they would have to completely remake the way they walk. If they remade the way they walk, they would have to remake other things. I couldn't live like the Gilyaks. I would hate for men to hit me all the time. I would hate to live with a lot of maggots around – so dirty! But I don't like to walk on wide roads, either. I need more water.

Fuka-Eri took another drink of water. After a short silence, her glass came back to the table with a clunk. Then there was an interval while she wiped her lips with her fingertips. Didn't this girl realize that tape recorders have pause buttons?

I think it might be trouble for you that I went away. But I don't want to be a novelist, and I don't plan to write anymore. I asked Azami to look up stuff about the Gilyaks for me. She went to the library. The Gilyaks live in Sakhalin and are like the Ainu and American Indians: they don't have writing. They don't leave records. I'm the same. Once it gets written down, the story is not mine anymore. You did a good job of writing my story. I don't think anybody else could do that. But it's not my story anymore. But don't worry. It's not your fault. I'm just walking in a place away from the road.

Here Fuka-Eri inserted another pause. Tengo imagined her trudging along silently, alone, off to the side, away from a road.

The Professor has big power and deep wisdom. But the Little People have just as deep wisdom and big power as he does. Better be careful in the forest. Important things are in the forest, and the Little People are in the forest, too. To make sure the Little People don't harm you, you have to find something the Little People don't have. If you do that, you can get through the forest safely.

Having managed to say all this in one go, Fuka-Eri paused to take a deep breath. She did this without averting her face from the microphone, thereby recording what sounded like a huge gust of wind blowing between buildings. When that quieted down, there came the deep, foghorn-like sound of a large truck honking in the distance. Two short blasts. Apparently Fuka-Eri was in a place not far from a major highway.

[Clearing of throat.] I'm getting hoarse. Thanks for worrying about me. Thanks for liking my chest shape and putting me up in your apartment and lending me your pajamas. We probably can't see each other for a while. The Little People may be mad that they were put into writing. But don't worry. I'm used to the forest. Bye.

There was a click, and the recording ended.

Tengo stopped the tape and rewound to the beginning. Listening to the rain dripping from the eaves, he took several deep breaths and twirled the plastic ballpoint pen in his fingers. Then he set the pen down. He had not taken a single note. He had merely listened in fascination to Fuka-Eri's normally peculiar narrative style. Without resorting to note taking, he had grasped the three main points of her message:

1 She had not been abducted, but was merely in temporary hiding. There was no need to worry about her.

2 She had no intention of publishing any more books. Her story was meant for oral transmission, not print.

3 The Little People possessed no less wisdom and power than Professor Ebisuno. Tengo should be careful.

These were the points she hoped to convey. She also spoke of the Gilyaks, the people who had to stay off broad roads when they walked.

Tengo went to the kitchen and made himself some coffee. While drinking his coffee, he stared aimlessly at the cassette tape. Then he listened to it again from the beginning. This time, just to make sure, he occasionally pushed the pause button and took brief notes. Then he let his eyes make their way through the notes. This led to no new discoveries.

Had Fuka-Eri made her own simple notes at first and followed them as she spoke into the recorder? Tengo could not believe she had done that. She wasn't the type to do such a thing. She had undoubtedly spoken her thoughts into the mike as they came to her in real time (without even pushing the pause button).

What kind of place could she be in? The recorded background noises provided Tengo with few hints. The distant sound of a door slamming. Children's shouts apparently coming in through an open window. A kindergarten? A truck horn. She was obviously not deep in the woods but somewhere in a city. The time of the recording was probably late morning or early afternoon. The sound of the door might suggest that she was not alone.

One thing was clear: Fuka-Eri had gone into hiding on her own initiative. No one had forced her to make the tape: that much was obvious from the sound of her voice and the way she spoke. There was some perceptible nervousness at the beginning, but otherwise it sounded as if she had freely spoken her own thoughts into the microphone.

The Professor has big power and deep wisdom. But the Little People have just as deep wisdom and big power as he does. Better be careful in the forest. Important things are in the forest, and the Little People are in the forest, too. To make sure the Little People don't harm you, you have to find something the Little People don't have. If you do that, you can get through the forest safely.

Tengo played that part back one more time. Fuka-Eri narrated this section somewhat more rapidly than the others. The intervals between sentences were a touch shorter. The Little People were beings who possessed the potential for harming both Tengo and Professor Ebisuno, but he could not discern in Fuka-Eri's tone of voice any suggestion that she had written them off as evil. Judging from the way she spoke of them, they seemed like neutral beings who could go either way. Tengo had misgivings about another passage:

The Little People may be mad that they were put into writing.

If the Little People were, in fact, angry, it stood to reason that Tengo himself would be one of the objects of their anger. He was, after all, one of those most responsible for having publicized their existence in print. Even if he were to beg their forgiveness on the grounds that he had done so without malice, they were not likely to listen to him.

What kind of harm did the Little People inflict on others? Tengo could hardly be expected to know the answer. He rewound the tape again, returned it to the envelope, and stuffed it in a drawer. Putting his raincoat and hat on again, he set out for the market once more in the pouring rain.

Komatsu telephoned after nine o'clock that night. Once again, Tengo knew it was Komatsu before he lifted the receiver. He was in bed, reading. He let the phone ring three times, eased himself out of bed, and sat at the kitchen table to answer the call.

"Hey, Tengo," Komatsu said. "Having a drink?"

"No, I'm sober."

"You may want to take a drink after this call," Komatsu said.

"Must be about something enjoyable."

"I wonder. I don't think it's all that enjoyable. It might have a certain amount of paradoxical humor about it, though."

"Like a Chekhov short story."

"Exactly," Komatsu said. " 'Like a Chekhov short story.' Well said! Your expressions are always concise and to the point, Tengo."

Tengo remained silent. Komatsu went on.

"Things have taken a somewhat problematic turn. The police have responded to Professor Ebisuno's search request by formally initiating a search for Fuka-Eri. I don't think they'll go so far as to actually mount a full-scale search, though, especially since there's been no ransom demand or anything.

They'll probably just go through the motions so it won't be too embarrassing for them if something really does come up. Otherwise, it'll look as if they stood by with their arms folded. The media are not going to let it go so easily, though. I've already gotten several inquiries from the papers. I pretended to know nothing, of course. I mean, there's nothing to say at this point. By now they've probably uncovered the relationship between Fuka-Eri and Professor Ebisuno, as well as her parents' background as revolutionaries. Lots of facts like that are going to start coming out. The problem is with the weekly magazines. Their freelancers or journalists or whatever you call them will start circling like sharks smelling blood. They're all good at what they do, and once they latch on, they don't let go. Their livelihood depends on it, after all. They can't afford to have little things like good taste or people's privacy stand in their way. They may be 'writers' like you, Tengo, but they're a different breed, they don't live in your literary ivory tower."

"So I'd better be careful too, I suppose."

"Absolutely. Get ready to protect yourself. There's no telling what they'll sniff out."

Tengo imagined a small boat surrounded by sharks, but only as a single cartoon frame without a clever twist. "You have to find something the Little People don't have," Fuka-Eri had said. What kind of "something" could that possibly be?

Tengo said to Komatsu, "But isn't this working out the way Professor Ebisuno planned it from the beginning?"

"Well, maybe so," Komatsu said. "Maybe it'll turn out that he was just discreetly using us. But to some extent we knew what he was up to right from the start. He wasn't hiding his plan from us. In that sense, it was a fair transaction. We *could* have said, 'Sorry, Professor, too dangerous, we can't get involved.' That's what any normal editor would have done. But as you know, Tengo, I'm no normal editor. Besides, things were already moving forward by then, and there was a little greed at work on my part, too. Maybe that's why I had let my defenses down somewhat."

There was silence on the telephone – a short but dense silence.

Tengo spoke first. "In other words, *your* plan was more or less hijacked by Professor Ebisuno."

"I suppose you could say that. Ultimately, *his* agenda trumped mine."

Tengo said, "Do you think Professor Ebisuno will be able to make things work his way?"

"Well, *he* certainly thinks he can. He knows how to read a situation, and he has plenty of self-confidence. It just might go his way. But if this new commotion exceeds even Professor Ebisuno's expectations, he might not be able to control the outcome. There's a limit to what one person can do, even the most outstanding individual. So you'd better tighten your seat belt!"

"Not even the tightest seat belt is going to do you any good if your plane crashes."

"No, but at least it makes you feel a little better."

Tengo couldn't help smiling – if somewhat feebly. "Is that the point of this call – the thing that might not be all that enjoyable but might have a certain amount of paradoxical humor about it?"

"To tell you the truth, I am feeling sorry I got you involved in this," Komatsu said in an expressionless voice.

"Don't worry about me. I don't have a thing to lose – no family, no social position, no future to speak of. What I'm worried about is Fuka-Eri. She's just a seventeen-year-old girl."

"That concerns me, too, of course. There's no way it couldn't. But we can rack our brains here and it won't change anything for her. For now, let's just think about how we're going to tie ourselves down somewhere so this storm doesn't blow us away. We'd better keep a close eye on the papers."

"I've been making sure I check the papers every day."

"Good," Komatsu said. "Which reminds me, do you have any idea at all where Fuka-Eri might be? Nothing comes to mind?"

"Not a thing," Tengo said. He was not a good liar. And Komatsu was strangely sensitive about such things. But he did not seem to notice the slight quaver in Tengo's voice. His head was probably too full of himself at that point.

"I'll get in touch with you if anything else comes up," Komatsu said, terminating the call.

The first thing Tengo did after hanging up was pour an inch of bourbon into a glass. Komatsu had been right: he needed a drink.

On Friday Tengo's girlfriend came for her regular visit. The rain had stopped, but every inch of the sky was covered in gray cloud. They had a light meal and got into bed. Even during sex, Tengo went on thinking one fragmentary thought after another, but this did nothing to dull his physical pleasure. As always, she skillfully drew a week's worth of desire out of Tengo and took care of it with great efficiency. She experienced full satisfaction, too, like a talented accountant who finds deep pleasure in the complex manipulation of figures in a ledger. Still, she seemed to notice that something else was on Tengo's mind.

"Hmm, your whiskey level seems to be going down," she said. Her left hand rested on Tengo's thick chest, enjoying the aftertaste of sex. Her third finger bore a smallish but sparkling diamond wedding ring. She was referring to the bottle of Wild Turkey that had been sitting on the shelf for months. Like most older women in sexual relationships with younger men, she was quick to note even tiny changes in his surroundings.

"I've been waking up a lot at night," Tengo said.

"You're not in love, are you?"

Tengo shook his head. "No, I'm not in love."

"Your writing's not going well, then?"

"No, it's moving along – where to, I'm not sure."

"But still, something's bothering you."

"I wonder. I just can't sleep very well. That rarely happens to me. I've always been a sound sleeper."

"Poor Tengo!" she said, caressing his testicles with the palm of the ringless hand. "Are you having nightmares?"

"I almost never dream," Tengo said, which was true.

"I dream a lot. Some dreams I have over and over – so much so that I realize in the dream, 'Hey, I've had this one before.' Strange, huh?"

"What kind of dreams do you have? Tell me one."

"Well, there's my dream of a cottage in a forest."

"A cottage in a forest," Tengo said. He thought about people in forests: the Gilyaks, the Little People, and Fuka-Eri. "What kind of cottage?"

"You really want to know? Don't you find other people's dreams boring?"

"No, not at all. Tell me, if you don't mind," Tengo said honestly.

"I'm walking alone in the forest – not the thick, ominous forest that Hansel and Gretel got lost in, but more of a brightish, lightweight sort of forest. It's a nice, warm afternoon, and I'm walking along without a care in the world. So then, up ahead, I see this little house. It's got a chimney and a little porch, and gingham-check curtains in the windows. It's friendly looking. I knock on the door and say, 'Hello.' There's no answer. I try knocking again a little harder and the door opens by itself. It wasn't completely closed, you see. I walk in yelling, 'Hello! Is anybody home? I'm coming in!' "

She looked at Tengo, gently stroking his testicles. "Do you get the mood so far?"

"Sure, I do."

"It's just a one-room cottage. Very simply built. It has a little kitchen, beds, and a dining area. There's a woodstove in the middle, and dinner for four has been neatly set out on the table. Steam is rising from the dishes. But there's nobody inside. It's as if they were all set to start eating when something strange happened – like, a monster showed up or something, and everybody ran out. But the chairs are not in disarray. Everything is peaceful and almost strangely ordinary. There just aren't any people there."

"What kind of food is on the table?"

She had to think about that for a moment, cocking her head to one side. "I can't remember. Good question: what kind of food is it? I guess the question isn't so much *what* they're eating as that it's freshly cooked and still hot. So anyhow, I sit in one of the chairs and wait for the family that lives there to come back. That's what I'm supposed to do: just wait for them to come home. I don't know why I'm *supposed* to. I mean, it's a dream, so not everything is clearly explained. Maybe I want them to tell me the way home, or maybe I have to *get* something: that kind of thing. So I'm just sitting there, waiting for them to come home, but no matter how long I wait, nobody comes. The meal is still steaming. I look at the hot food and get tremendously hungry. But just because I'm starved, I have no right to touch the food on the table without them there. It would be natural to think that, don't you think?"

"Sure, I'd probably think that," Tengo said. "Of course, it's a dream, so I can't be sure what I would think."

"But soon the sun goes down. The cottage grows dark inside. The surrounding forest gets deeper and deeper. I want to turn the light on, but I don't know how. I start to feel uneasy. Then at some point I realize something strange: the amount of steam rising from the food hasn't decreased at all. Hours have gone by, but it's still nice and hot. Then I start to think that something odd is going on. Something is wrong. That's where the dream ends."

"You don't know what happens after that?"

"I'm sure something must happen after that," she said. "The sun goes down, I don't know how to go home, and I'm all alone in this weird cottage. Something is *about* to happen – and I get the feeling it's not very good. But the dream always ends there, and I keep having the same dream over and over."

She stopped caressing his testicles and pressed her cheek against his chest. "My dream might be suggesting something," she said.

"Like what?"

She did not answer Tengo's question. Instead, she asked her own question. "Would you like to know what the scariest part of the dream is?"

"Yes, tell me."

She let out a long breath that grazed Tengo's nipple like a hot wind blowing across a narrow channel. "It's that *I* might be the monster. The possibility struck me once. Wasn't it because they had seen *me* approaching that the people had abandoned their dinner and run out of the house? And as long as I stayed there, they couldn't come back. In spite of that, I had to keep sitting in the cottage, waiting for them to come home. The thought of that is what scares me so much. It seems so hopeless, don't you think?"

"Or else," Tengo said, "maybe it's your own house, and your self ran away and you're waiting for it to come back."

After the words left his mouth, Tengo realized he should not have spoken them. But it was too late to take them back. She remained silent for a long time, and then she squeezed his testicles hard – so hard he could barely breathe.

"How could you say such a terrible thing?"

"I didn't mean anything by it," Tengo managed to groan. "It just popped into my head."

She softened her grip on his testicles and released a sigh. Then she said, "Now tell me one of your dreams, Tengo."

Breathing normally again, he said, "Like I said before, I almost never dream. Especially these days."

"You must have *some* dreams. Everybody in the world dreams to some extent. Dr. Freud's gonna feel bad if you say you don't dream at all."

"I may be dreaming, but I don't remember my dreams after I wake up. I might have a lingering sensation that I was *having* a dream, but I can never remember what it was about."

She slipped her open palm under Tengo's limp penis, carefully noting its weight, as if the weight had an important story to tell her. "Okay, never mind the dreams. Tell me about the novel you're writing instead."

"I prefer not to talk about a piece of fiction while I'm writing it."

"Hey, I'm not asking you to tell me every last detail from beginning to end. Not even I would ask for that. I know you're a much more sensitive young man than your build would suggest. Just tell me a little something – a part of the setting, or some minor episode, anything at all. I want you to tell me something that nobody else in the world knows – to make up for the terrible thing you said to me. Do you see what I'm saying?"

"I think I might," Tengo said uncertainly.

"Okay, go!"

With his penis still resting on the palm of her hand, Tengo began to speak. "The story is about me – or about somebody modeled on me."

"I'm sure it is," she said. "Am I in it?"

"No, you're not. I'm in a world that isn't here."

"So I'm not in the world that isn't here."

"And not just you. The people who are in this world are not in the world that isn't here."

"How is the world that isn't here different from this world? Can you tell which world you're in now?"

"Of course I can. I'm the one who's writing it."

"What I mean is, for people *other* than you. Say, if I just happened to wander into that world now, could I tell?"

"I think you could," Tengo said. "For example, in the world that isn't here, there are two moons. So you can tell the difference."

The setting of a world with two moons in the sky was something he had taken from *Air Chrysalis*. Tengo was in the process of writing a longer and more complicated story about that same world – and about himself. The fact that the setting was the same might later prove to be a problem, but for now, his overwhelming desire was to write a story about a world with two moons. Any problems that came up later he would deal with then.

"In other words," she said, "if there are two moons up there when night comes and you look at the sky, you can tell, 'Aha! This is the world that isn't here!' "

"Right, that's the sign."

"Do the two moons ever overlap or anything?" she asked.

Tengo shook his head. "I don't know why, but the distance between the two moons always stays the same."

His girlfriend thought about that world for a while. Her finger traced some kind of diagram on Tengo's bare chest.

"Hey, Tengo, do you know the difference between the English words 'lunatic' and 'insane'?" she asked.

"They're both adjectives describing mental abnormality. I'm not quite sure how they differ."

" 'Insane' probably means to have an innate mental problem, something that calls for professional treatment, while 'lunatic' means to have your sanity temporarily seized by the *luna,* which is 'moon' in Latin. In nineteenth-century England, if you were a certified lunatic and you committed a crime, the severity of the crime would be reduced a notch. The idea was that the crime was not so much the responsibility of the person himself as that he was led astray by the moonlight. Believe it or not, laws like that actually existed. In other words, the fact that the moon can drive people crazy was actually recognized in law."

"How do you know stuff like that?" Tengo asked, amazed.

"It shouldn't come as that much of a surprise to you. I've been living ten years longer than you, so I ought to know a lot more than you do."

Tengo had to admit that she was right.

"As a matter of fact, I learned it in an English literature course at Japan Women's University, in a lecture on Dickens. We had an odd professor. He'd never talk about the story itself but go off on all sorts of tangents. But all I wanted to say to you was that one moon is enough to drive people crazy, so if you had two moons hanging in the sky, it would probably just make them that much crazier. The tides would be thrown off, and more women would have irregular periods. I bet all kinds of funny stuff would happen."

"You may be right," Tengo said, after giving it some thought.

"Is that what happens in the world you're writing about? Do people go crazy all the time?"

"No, not really. They do pretty much the same things we do in this world."

She squeezed Tengo's penis softly. "So in the world that isn't here, people do pretty much the same things as those of us who are in this world. If that's the case, then, what's the point of its being a world that isn't here?"

"The point of its being a world that isn't here is in being able to rewrite the past of the world that is here," Tengo said.

"So you can rewrite the past any way you like, as much as you like?"

"That's right."

"Do you want to rewrite the past?"

"Don't *you* want to rewrite the past?"

She shook her head. "No, I don't have the slightest desire to rewrite the past or history or whatever. What I'd like to rewrite is the present, here and now."

"But if you rewrote the past, obviously, the present would change, too. What we call the present is given shape by an accumulation of the past."

She released another deep sigh. Then, as if testing the operation of an elevator, she raised and lowered the hand on which Tengo's penis lay. "I can only say one thing. You used to be a math prodigy and a judo belt holder and you're even writing a long novel. In spite of all that, you don't understand *anything at all* about this world. Not one thing."

Tengo felt no particular shock at this sweeping judgment. These days, not understanding anything had more or less become the normal state of affairs for him. This was not a new discovery.

"It doesn't matter, though, even if you don't understand anything," his older girlfriend said, turning to press her breasts against him. "You're a dreaming math teacher who keeps writing his long novel day after day, and I want you to stay just like that. I love your wonderful penis – the shape, the size, the feel. I love it when it's hard and when it's soft, when you're sick and when you're well. And for the time being, at least, it belongs only to me. It does, doesn't it?"

"That is correct," Tengo assured her.

"I *have* told you that I'm a terribly jealous person, haven't I?"

"You certainly have – jealous beyond reason."

"*All* reason. I've been very consistent that way for many years now." She slowly began moving her fingers in three dimensions. "I'll get you hard again right away. You wouldn't have any objection to that, would you?"

Tengo said that he would have no objection.

"What are you thinking about now?"

"You as a student, listening to a lecture at Japan Women's University."

"The text was *Martin Chuzzlewit*. I was eighteen and wearing a cute pleated dress. My hair was in a ponytail. I was a *very* serious student, and still a virgin. I feel like I'm talking about something from an earlier life. Anyhow, the difference between 'lunatic' and 'insane' was the first bit of knowledge I ever learned at the university. What do you think? Does it get you excited to imagine that?"

"Of course it does," he said, closing his eyes, imagining her pleated dress and her ponytail. A very serious student, a virgin. But jealous beyond all reason. The moon illuminating Dickens's London. The insane people and the lunatics wandering around London. They wore similar hats and similar beards. How was it possible to distinguish one from the other? With his eyes closed, Tengo could not be sure which world he now belonged to.

BOOK 2 JULY–SEPTEMBER

CHAPTER 1

Aomame

IT WAS THE MOST BORING TOWN IN THE WORLD

Although the rainy season had not been declared officially over, the Tokyo sky was intensely blue and the midsummer sun beat down on the earth. With their newly thickened burden of green leaves, the willows once again cast dense, trembling shadows on the street.

Tamaru met Aomame at the front door, wearing a dark summer suit, white shirt, and solid-color tie. There was not a drop of sweat on him. Aomame always found it mysterious that such a big man did not sweat on even the hottest summer days.

He gave her a slight nod, and, after uttering a short greeting that she found barely audible, he said nothing further. Today there was none of their usual banter. He walked ahead of her down a long corridor and did not look back, instead guiding her to where the dowager waited. Aomame guessed that he was in no mood for small talk. Maybe the death of the dog was still bothering him. "We need a new guard dog," he had said on the phone, as if commenting on the weather, though Aomame knew this was no indication of how he actually felt. The female German shepherd had been important to him: they had been close for many years. He had taken her sudden, baffling death as both a personal insult and a challenge. As she looked at silent Tamaru's back, as broad as a classroom blackboard, Aomame could imagine the quiet anger he was feeling.

Tamaru opened the living-room door to let Aomame in, and stood in the doorway awaiting instructions from the dowager.

"We won't be needing anything to drink now," she said.

Tamaru gave her a silent nod and quietly closed the door, leaving the two women alone. A round goldfish bowl, with two goldfish inside, had been placed on the table beside the armchair in which the dowager was sitting – an utterly ordinary goldfish bowl with utterly ordinary goldfish and the requisite green strip of seaweed. Aomame had been in this large, handsome living room any number of times, but had never seen the goldfish before. She felt an occasional puff of cool air against her skin and guessed that the air conditioner must be running on low. On a table behind the dowager stood a vase containing three white lilies. The flowers were large and fleshy white, like little animals from an alien land that were deep in meditation.

The dowager waved Aomame over to the sofa beside her. White lace curtains covered the windows facing the garden, but still the summer afternoon sun was strong. In its light the dowager looked tired, which was unusual for her. Slumped in the big chair, she rested her chin on her hand, eyes sunken, neck more wrinkled than before, lips drained of color. The outer tips of her long eyebrows had dropped a notch, as if they had given up the struggle against gravity. Perhaps the efficiency of her circulatory system had declined: her skin appeared to have white, powdery blotches. She had aged at least five or six years since their last meeting. And today, for a change, it didn't seem to bother her to show such obvious fatigue. This was not normal for her. As far as Aomame had observed, the dowager always tried – with much success – to keep her appearance smart, her inner strength fully mobilized, her posture perfectly erect, her expression focused, and all signs of aging hidden.

Aomame noticed that many things in the house were different today. Even the light had taken on a different color. And the bowl of goldfish, such a common object, did not fit in with the elegant high-ceilinged room full of antique furniture.

The dowager remained silent for a time, chin in hand, staring into the space adjacent to Aomame, where, Aomame knew, there was nothing special to be seen. The dowager simply needed a spot where she could temporarily park her vision.

"Do you need something to drink?" the dowager asked softly.

"No, thanks, I'm not thirsty," Aomame answered.

"There's iced tea over there. Pour yourself a glass if you like."

The dowager pointed toward a side table set next to the door. On it was a pitcher of tea containing ice and lemon slices, and, next to that, three cut-glass tumblers of different colors.

"Thank you," Aomame said, remaining seated and waiting for the dowager's next words.

For a time, however, the dowager maintained her silence. She had something she needed to talk to Aomame about, but if she actually put it into words, the facts contained in the "something" might irretrievably become more definite *as* facts, so she wanted to postpone that moment, if only briefly. Such was the apparent significance of her silence. She glanced at the goldfish bowl next to her chair. Then, as if resigning herself to the inevitable, she finally focused her gaze directly on Aomame. Her lips were clenched in a straight line, the ends of which she had deliberately turned up.

"You heard from Tamaru that the safe house guard dog died, didn't you – in that inexplicable way?"

"Yes, I did."

"After that, Tsubasa disappeared."

Aomame frowned slightly. "Disappeared?"

"She just vanished. Probably during the night. This morning she was gone."

Aomame pursed her lips, searching for something she could say, but the words did not come to her immediately. "But . . . from what you told me last time . . . I thought Tsubasa always had somebody nearby when she slept . . . in the same room . . . as a precaution."

"Yes, that is true, but the woman fell into an unusually deep sleep and was totally unaware that Tsubasa had left. When the sun came up, there was no sign of Tsubasa in the bed."

"So the German shepherd died, and the next day Tsubasa disappeared," Aomame said, as if to verify the accuracy of her understanding.

The dowager nodded. "So far, we don't know for sure if the two events are related, but I think that they are."

Aomame glanced at the goldfish bowl on the table for no particular reason. The dowager followed Aomame's glance. The two goldfish swam coolly back and forth in their glass pond, barely moving their fins. The summer sunlight refracted strangely in the bowl, creating the illusion that one was peering into a mysterious ocean cave.

"I bought these goldfish for Tsubasa," the dowager said by way of explanation, looking at Aomame. "There was a little festival at one of the Azabu shopping streets, so I took her for a walk there. I thought it wasn't healthy for her to be locked up in her room all the time. Tamaru came with us, of course. I bought her the fish at one of the stands. She seemed fascinated by them. She put them in her room and spent the rest of the day staring at them. When we realized she was gone, I brought them here. Now I'm spending a lot of time watching the fish. Just staring at them, doing nothing. Strangely enough, you really don't get tired of watching them. I've never done this before – stared at goldfish so intently."

"Do you have any idea where Tsubasa might have gone?" Aomame asked.

"None whatsoever," the dowager answered. "She doesn't have any relatives. As far as I know, the child has nowhere to go in this world."

"What is the chance that someone took her away by force?"

The dowager gave a nervous little shake of the head, as if she were chasing away an invisible fly. "No, she just left. No one came and forced her to go. If that had happened, it would have awakened someone around her. Those women are all light sleepers. No, I'm sure she made up her mind and left on her own. She tiptoed downstairs, quietly unlocked the front door, and went out. I can see it happening. She didn't make the dog bark – it had died the night before. She didn't even change her clothes. The next day's clothing was all nicely folded nearby, but she went out in her pajamas. I don't think she has any money, either."

Aomame's grimace deepened. "All by herself – in pajamas?"

The dowager nodded. "Yes, where could a ten-year-old girl – all alone, in pajamas, with no money – possibly go in the middle of the night? It's inconceivable, using ordinary common sense. But for some reason, I don't find it all that strange. Far from it. I even get the feeling that it was something that had to happen. We're not even looking for her. I'm not doing anything, just watching the goldfish like this."

She glanced toward the goldfish bowl as she spoke. Then she turned back toward Aomame.

"I know that it would be pointless to search for her. She has gone somewhere out of our reach."

The dowager stopped resting her chin on her hand and, with her hands on her knees, she slowly released a breath that she had held inside for a very long time.

"But why would she have done such a thing?" Aomame asked. "Why would she have left the safe house? She was protected as long as she stayed, and she had nowhere else to go."

"I don't know why. But I feel that the dog's death was the trigger. She loved the dog, and the dog loved her. They were like best friends. The fact that the dog died – and died in such a bloody, incomprehensible way – was a great shock to her. Of course. It was a shock to everyone in the house. Now that I think of it, however, the killing of the dog might have been a kind of message to Tsubasa."

"A message?"

"That she should not stay here. That they knew she was hiding here. That she had to leave. That even worse things might happen to the people around her if she didn't go."

The dowager's fingers ticked off an imaginary interval on her lap. Aomame waited for the rest of what the dowager had to say.

"She probably understood the message and left on her own. I'm sure she didn't leave because she wanted to. She *had* to go, even knowing that she had no place to go. I can hardly stand the thought – that a ten-year-old girl was forced to make such a decision."

Aomame wanted to reach out and hold the dowager's hand, but she stopped herself. There was still more to tell.

The dowager continued, "It was a great shock to me, of course. I feel as if a part of me has been physically torn out. I was planning to formally adopt her, as you know. I knew that things would not work out so easily, but even recognizing all the difficulties involved, it was something I wanted to do. I was in no position to complain to anyone if it did not work out, but, to tell you the truth, at my age, these things take an enormous toll."

Aomame said, "But Tsubasa might suddenly come back one day soon. She has no money, and there's no place she can go . . ."

"I'd like to think you're right, but that is not going to happen," the dowager said, her voice completely flat. "She's only ten years old, but she has ideas of her own. She made up her mind and left. I doubt she would ever decide to come back."

"Excuse me a moment," Aomame said, walking over to the table by the door, where she poured herself some iced tea into a green cut-glass tumbler. She was not particularly thirsty, but she wanted to introduce a pause into the conversation by leaving her seat. She then returned to the sofa, took a sip of tea, and set the tumbler down on the glass tabletop.

The dowager waited for Aomame to settle onto the sofa again and said, "That's enough about Tsubasa for now," stretching her neck and clasping her hands together to give herself an emotional pause. "Let's talk about Sakigake and its Leader. I'll tell you what we have been able to find out. This is the main reason I called you here today. Of course, it also has to do with Tsubasa."

Aomame nodded. She had been expecting this.

"As I told you last time, we absolutely must 'take care of' this Leader. We must transport him into *another world*. You know, of course, that he is in the habit of raping preteen girls, none of whom have had their first period. He makes up 'doctrine' and exploits the religion's system to justify such actions. I have had this researched in as much detail as possible and paid quite a bit of money for the information. It wasn't easy. The cost far exceeded my expectations, but we succeeded in identifying four girls he is likely to have raped. Tsubasa was the fourth."

Aomame lifted her glass and took a sip of iced tea, tasting nothing, as if her mouth were stuffed with cotton that absorbed all flavor.

"We still don't know all the details, but at least two of the girls are still living in the religion's compound," the dowager said. "We're told they serve Leader as his own personal shrine maidens. They never appear before the ordinary believers. We don't know if they stay there of their own free will or are simply unable to run away. We also don't know if there is still a sexual relationship between them and Leader. In any case, they all live in the same place, like a family. The area of Leader's residence is strictly off-limits to ordinary believers. Many things are still shrouded in mystery."

The cut-glass tumbler was beginning to sweat on the tabletop. The dowager paused to catch her breath and then continued.

"We do know one thing for certain. The first of the four victims is Leader's own daughter."

Aomame frowned. Her facial muscles began to move involuntarily, becoming greatly distorted. She wanted to say something, but her voice would not form the words.

"It's true," the dowager said. "They think that the first girl he violated was his own daughter. It happened seven years ago, when she was ten."

The dowager lifted the intercom and told Tamaru to bring them a bottle of sherry and two glasses. They fell silent while they waited for him, each woman putting her thoughts in order. Tamaru came in, carrying a tray with a new bottle of sherry and two slim, elegant crystal glasses. After lining up everything on the table, he twisted open the bottle with a sharp, precise movement, as if wringing a chicken's neck. The sherry gurgled as he poured it. The dowager nodded, and Tamaru bowed and left the room, saying nothing, as usual. Not even his steps made a sound.

The dog is not the only thing that's bothering him, Aomame thought. *The girl's disappearance is another deep wound for him. She was so important to the dowager, and yet she vanished before his very eyes!* Strictly speaking, the girl was not his responsibility. He was not a live-in bodyguard; he slept in his own home at night, a ten-minute walk away, unless some special task kept him at the dowager's. Both the dog's death and the girl's disappearance had happened at night, when he was absent. He could have prevented neither. His job was to protect the dowager and her Willow House. His duties did not extend to security for the safe house, which lay outside the compound. Even so, the events were a personal defeat for Tamaru, an unforgivable slight.

"Are you prepared to take care of that man?" the dowager asked Aomame.

"Fully prepared," Aomame assured her.

"It's not going to be easy," the dowager said. "Of course, none of the work I ask you to do is easy. But this is especially difficult. We'll do everything we can to set it up, but I'm not sure of the extent to which we can guarantee your safety. It will probably involve a greater risk than usual."

"I understand."

"As I have told you before, I would rather not send you into dangerous situations, but to be honest, our choices are limited this time."

"I don't mind," Aomame said. "We can't leave that man alive in this world."

The dowager lifted her glass and let some of her sherry glide over her tongue. Then she watched the goldfish again for a while.

"I've always enjoyed sherry at room temperature on a summer afternoon. I'm not fond of cold drinks on hot days. I'll take a drink of sherry and, a little later, lie down for a nap, and fall asleep before I know it. When I wake up, some of the day's heat is gone. I hope I can die that way – drink a little sherry on a summer afternoon, stretch out on a sofa, drop off to sleep, and never wake up."

Aomame also lifted her sherry glass and took a small sip. She was not fond of sherry, but she definitely needed a drink.

This time the taste got through to her, unlike the iced tea. The alcohol stabbed at her tongue.

"I want you to tell me the truth," the dowager said. "Are you afraid to die?"

Aomame needed no time at all to answer. Shaking her head, she said, "Not particularly – living as myself scares me more."

The dowager gave a fleeting smile that seemed to revive her a little. Her lips now had a touch of color. Maybe speaking with Aomame had helped, or perhaps the sip of sherry was having its effect.

"I believe you said there is a particular man you are in love with."

"Yes, it's true, but the chances of my actually being with him are infinitely close to zero. So even if I were to die, the resulting loss would also be infinitely close to zero."

The dowager narrowed her eyes. "Is there a concrete reason that you think you probably will never be united with him?"

"Not in particular," Aomame said. "Other than the fact that I am me."

"Don't you have any intention of taking the initiative to approach him?"

Aomame shook her head. "The most important thing to me is the fact that I want him with my whole heart."

The dowager kept her eyes fixed on Aomame for a while in apparent admiration. "You are very clear about your own ideas, aren't you?" she said.

"I had to be that way," Aomame said, going through the motions of bringing the sherry glass to her lips. "It was not a matter of choice."

Silence filled the room for a short while. The lilies continued hanging their heads, and the goldfish continued swimming in the refracted summer sunlight.

"We can set things up so that you are alone with Leader," the dowager said. "It won't be easy, and it will take a good deal of time, but I can make it happen. All you have to do is what you always do for us. Except this time, you'll have to disappear afterward. Have plastic surgery. Quit your current job, of course, and go far away. Change your name. Get rid of all your possessions. Become another person. Of course you will be compensated with a suitable payment. I will be responsible for everything else. Is this all right with you?"

Aomame said, "As I said before, I don't have anything to lose. My work, my name, this life of mine in Tokyo: none of them mean anything to me. I have no objections at all."

"And your face? You don't mind if it changes?"

"Would it change for the better?"

"If you wanted, of course we could do that," the dowager replied with a somber expression. "We can make a face according to your wishes – within limits, of course."

"As long as we're at it, I might as well have them do a breast enlargement."

The dowager nodded. "That may be a good idea – for disguise purposes, I mean, of course."

"I'm just kidding," Aomame said, softening her expression. "I'm not exactly proud of them, but I don't mind leaving them just the way they are. They're light and easy to carry. And it would be such a pain to buy all new bras."

"That's nothing. I'd buy you as many as you liked."

"No, I'm kidding about that, too," Aomame said.

The dowager cracked a smile. "Sorry, I'm not used to hearing jokes from you."

"I don't have any objection to plastic surgery," Aomame said. "I've never felt I wanted to have it, but I don't have any reason to refuse it, either. I've never really liked my face, and I don't have anybody who likes it especially, either."

"You'll lose all your friends, too, you know."

"I don't have any 'friends,' " Aomame said, but then Ayumi came to mind. *If I were to just disappear without saying anything to her, she might be sad. She might even feel betrayed.* But there had been a problem with calling her a "friend" right from the start. Aomame was traveling too dangerous a road to make friends with a police officer.

"I had two children," the dowager said. "A boy and a girl. She was three years younger than he. As I told you before, she died – she committed suicide. She had no children. My son and I have had our troubles and have not gotten along well for a very long time. I hardly ever talk to him now. I have three grandchildren, but I haven't seen them for a long time, either. When I die, though, most of my estate will go to my only son and his children, almost automatically. Wills don't carry much force these days, unlike the way it used to be. For now, though, my discretionary funds are quite considerable. I'd like to leave a lot of that money to you, if you succeed in this new task. Please don't misunderstand, though: I'm not trying to buy you off. All I want to say is that I think of you as my own daughter. I wish you *were* my actual daughter."

Aomame gazed quietly at the dowager, who set her sherry glass on the table as if suddenly recalling that she was holding it. She then turned to look at the glossy petals of the lilies behind her. Inhaling their rich fragrance, she looked once again at Aomame.

"As I said before, I was planning to adopt Tsubasa, but now I've lost her, too. I couldn't help her. I did nothing but stand by and watch her disappear alone into the dark of night. And now, I'm getting ready to send you into far greater danger than ever before. I don't really want to do that, but unfortunately, I can't think of any other way to accomplish our goal. All I can do is offer you tangible compensation."

Aomame listened attentively without comment. When the dowager fell silent, the chirping of a bird came clearly through the windowpane. It continued for a while, until the bird flew off somewhere.

"That man must be 'taken care of,' no matter what," Aomame said. "That is the most important thing now. I have nothing but the deepest gratitude for the way you feel about me. I think you know that I rejected my parents and they abandoned me when I was a child; we both had our reasons. I had no choice but to take a path without anything like family affection. In order to survive on my own, I had to adapt myself to such a frame of mind. It wasn't easy. I often felt that I was nothing but scum – some kind of meaningless, filthy residue – which is why I am so grateful to you for what you just said to me. But it's a bit too late for me to change my attitude or lifestyle. This is not true of Tsubasa, however. I'm sure she can still be saved. Please don't resign yourself to losing her so easily. Don't lose hope. Get her back!"

The dowager nodded. "I'm afraid I didn't put it very well. I am of course not resigned to losing her. I will do everything in my power to bring her back. But as you can see, I'm too tired right now. My failure to help her has filled me with a deep sense of powerlessness. I need a little time to get my energy back. On the other hand, I may just be too old. The energy might never come back, no matter how long I wait."

Aomame got up from the sofa and went over to the dowager. Sitting on the arm of her armchair, she grasped the woman's slim, elegant hand.

"You're an incredibly tough woman," Aomame said. "You can go on living with more strength than anybody. You just happen to be exhausted. You ought to lie down and get some rest. When you wake up, you'll be your old self, I'm sure."

"Thank you," the dowager said, squeezing Aomame's hand in return. "You're right: I should probably get some sleep."

"I'll be leaving, then," Aomame said. "I will be waiting to hear from you. I'll put my things in order – not that I own so many 'things' to put in order."

"Prepare yourself to travel light. If there's anything you need, we'll take care of it."

Aomame released the dowager's hand and stood up. "Good night. I'm sure everything is going to go well."

The dowager nodded. Still cradled in her chair, she closed her eyes. Aomame took one last glance at the goldfish bowl and one last whiff of the lilies before she left the high-ceilinged living room.

Tamaru was waiting for her at the front door. Five o'clock had come, but the sun was still high in the sky, its intensity undiminished. The glare of its light reflected off Tamaru's black cordovan shoes, which were perfectly polished as usual. A few white summer clouds appeared in the sky, but they gathered at its corners, where they could not block the sun. The end of the rainy season was not yet near, but there had been several days in a row of midsummer-like weather, complete with the cries of cicadas, which now sounded from the garden's trees. The cries were not very strong. If anything, they seemed somewhat restrained. But they were a positive sign of the season to come. The world was still working as it always did. The cicadas cried, the clouds moved along, Tamaru's shoes were spotless. But all of this seemed fresh and new to Aomame: that the world should continue along as usual.

Aomame asked Tamaru, "Can we talk a little? Do you have time?"

"Fine," Tamaru said. His expression did not change. "I have time. Killing time is part of what I do for a living." He lowered himself into one of the garden chairs by the front door. Aomame sat in the chair next to his. The overhanging eaves blocked the sunlight. The two of them sat in their cool shadow. There was the smell of fresh grass.

"Summer's here already," Tamaru said.

"The cicadas have started crying," Aomame replied.

"They seem a little early this year. This area's going to get very noisy again for a while. That piercing cry hurts your ears.

I heard exactly the same sound when I stayed in the town of Niagara Falls. It just kept going from morning to night without a letup, like a million cicadas."

"So you've been to Niagara Falls."

Tamaru nodded. "It was the most boring town in the world. I stayed there alone for three days and there was nothing to do but listen to the sound of the falls. It was too noisy to read."

"What were you doing alone in Niagara Falls for three days?"

Instead of answering, Tamaru just shook his head.

Tamaru and Aomame went on listening to the faint cries of the cicadas, saying nothing.

"I've got a favor to ask of you," Aomame said.

This seemed to pique Tamaru's interest. Aomame was not in the habit of asking people for favors.

She said, "It's kind of unusual. I hope it doesn't annoy you."

"I don't know if I'll be able to accommodate you, but I'll be glad at least to listen. It's not polite to be annoyed when a lady asks a favor."

"I need a gun," Aomame said flatly. "One that would fit in a handbag. Something with a small recoil but still fairly powerful and dependable. Not a modified fake or one of those Filipino copies. I'll only need to use it once. And one bullet should be enough."

Silence. Tamaru kept his eyes on Aomame the whole time, unwavering.

Then, speaking slowly and carefully, Tamaru said, "You *do* know that it is illegal in this country for an ordinary citizen to own a handgun, don't you?"

"Of course I do."

"And just so you know, let me say this," Tamaru continued. "I have never once been charged with a crime. That is to say, I have no police record. Now, this may be owing to some oversights on the part of the justice system, I don't deny that. But at least as far as the written record is concerned, I'm a good citizen. Honest, upright, pure. I'm gay, but that's not against the law. I pay my taxes as ordered, and I vote in elections – though no candidate I voted for was ever elected. I've even paid all my parking tickets before the due date. I haven't been stopped for speeding in the past ten years. I'm enrolled in the National Health Insurance system. I pay my NHK licensing fee automatically from my bank account, and I carry both an American Express card and a MasterCard. Although I have no intention of doing so now, I could qualify for a thirty-year mortgage if I wanted one, and it always pleases me immensely to think that I am in such a position. In other words, I could be called a pillar of society without the least bit of irony. Do you realize that you are asking such a person to provide you with a gun?"

"Which is why I said I hoped you wouldn't be annoyed."

"Yes, I heard you say that."

"Sorry, but I couldn't think of anyone besides you I could ask."

Tamaru made a small, strangled sound in the back of his throat that could well have been the suppression of a sigh. "Now, just supposing that I were in a position to provide you with what you are asking for, common sense tells me that I would probably want to ask you this: Whom do you intend to shoot?"

Aomame pointed her index finger toward her own temple. "Right here, probably."

Tamaru stared at the finger expressionlessly for a moment. "My next question would probably be, 'Why?' "

"Because I don't want to be captured," Aomame said. "I'm not afraid to die. And although I probably wouldn't like it, I could tolerate going to prison. But I refuse to be held hostage and tortured by some unknown bunch of people. I just don't want to give away anybody's name. Do you see what I am saying?"

"I think I do."

"I don't plan to shoot anybody or to rob a bank. So I don't need some big, twenty-shot semiautomatic. I want something compact without much kick."

"A drug would be another option. It's more practical than trying to get ahold of a gun."

"Taking out a drug and swallowing it would take time. Before I could crush a capsule in my teeth, somebody might stick a hand in my mouth and stop me. With a gun, I could hold the other person off while I took care of things."

Tamaru thought about this for a moment, his right eyebrow slightly raised.

"I'd rather not lose you, if I can help it," he said. "I kind of like you. Personally, that is."

Aomame gave him a little smile. "For a human female, you mean?"

Without changing his expression, Tamaru said, "Male, female, human, dog – I don't have that many individuals I'm fond of."

"No, of course not," Aomame said.

"At the same time, my single most important duty is protecting Madame's health and safety. And I'm – what should I say? – kind of a pro."

"That goes without saying."

"So let me see what I can do. I can't guarantee anything, but I might be able to find somebody I know who can respond to your request. This is a very delicate business, though. It's not like buying an electric blanket by mail order. It might take a week before I can get back to you."

"That would be fine," Aomame said.

Tamaru squinted up at the trees where the cicadas were buzzing. "I hope everything goes well. I'll do whatever I can, within reason."

"Thanks, Tamaru. This next job will probably be my last. I might never see you again."

Tamaru spread his arms, palms up, as if he were standing in a desert, waiting for the rain to fall, but he said nothing. He had big, fleshy palms marked with scars. His hands looked more like parts of a giant machine than of a human body.

"I don't like good-byes," Tamaru said. "I didn't even have a chance to say good-bye to my parents."

"Are they dead?"

"I don't know whether they're alive or dead. I was born on Sakhalin Island the year before the war ended. The south end of Sakhalin was a Japanese territory called Karafuto, but the Soviets occupied it, and my parents were taken prisoner. My father apparently had some kind of job with the harbor facilities. Most of the Japanese civilian prisoners were returned to Japan soon enough, but my parents couldn't go to Japan because they were Koreans who had been sent to Sakhalin as laborers. The Japanese government refused to take them. Once Japan lost the war, Koreans were no longer subjects of the empire of Japan. It was terrible. The government didn't have a shred of sympathy for them. They could have gone to North Korea if they wanted to, but not to the South, because the Soviet Union at the time didn't recognize the existence of South Korea. My parents came from a fishing village near Pusan and had no desire to go to the North. They had no relatives or friends up there. I was still a baby. They put me in the hands of a couple being repatriated to Japan, and those people took me across the straits to Hokkaido. The food situation in Sakhalin at the time was horrendous, and the Soviet army's treatment of their prisoners was terrible. My parents had other small children and must have figured it would be hard to bring me up there. They probably figured they would send me over to Hokkaido first and join me later. Or maybe it was just an excuse to get rid of me. I don't know the details. In any case, we were never reunited. They're probably still in Sakhalin to this day – assuming they haven't died yet."

"You don't remember them?"

"Not a thing. I was just a little over a year old when we separated. The couple kept me for a while and then sent me to a facility for orphans in the mountains near Hakodate, way down near the southern tip of Hokkaido, about as far as you could go from Sakhalin and still be on Hokkaido. They probably couldn't afford to keep me. Some Catholic organization ran the orphanage, which was a *very tough* place. There were tons of orphans after the war, and not enough food or heat for them all. I had to do all kinds of things to survive." Tamaru glanced down at the back of his right hand. "So an adoption was arranged for form's sake, I became a Japanese citizen, and got a Japanese name: Ken'ichi Tamaru. All I know about my original name is the surname: Park – and there are as many Koreans named 'Park' as there are stars in the sky."

Sitting side by side with Tamaru, Aomame listened to the cries of the cicadas.

"You should get another dog," Aomame said.

"Madame says so too. The safe house needs another guard dog, at least. But I just don't feel like it yet."

"I understand. But you should get one. Not that I'm in any position to be advising people."

"I will," Tamaru said. "We do need a trained guard dog, in the end. I'll get in touch with a breeder right away."

Aomame looked at her watch and stood up. There was still some time left until sunset, but already a hint of evening marked the sky – a different blue mixed in with the blue of the afternoon. She could feel some of the lingering effects of the sherry. Could the dowager still be sleeping?

"According to Chekhov," Tamaru said, rising from his chair, "once a gun appears in a story, it has to be fired."

"Meaning what?"

Tamaru stood facing Aomame directly. He was only an inch or two taller than she was. "Meaning, don't bring unnecessary props into a story. If a pistol appears, it has to be fired at some point. Chekhov liked to write stories that did away with all useless ornamentation."

Aomame straightened the sleeves of her dress and slung her bag over her shoulder. "And that worries you – if a pistol comes on the scene, it's sure to be fired at some point."

"In Chekhov's view, yes."

"So you're thinking you'd rather not hand me a pistol."

"They're dangerous. And illegal. And Chekhov is a writer you can trust."

"But this is not a story. We're talking about the real world."

Tamaru narrowed his eyes and looked hard at Aomame. Then, slowly opening his mouth, he said, "Who knows?"

CHAPTER 2

Tengo

I DON'T HAVE A THING
EXCEPT MY SOUL

He set his recording of Janáček's *Sinfonietta* on the turntable and pressed the "auto-play" button. Seiji Ozawa conducting the Chicago Symphony. The turntable started to spin at 33⅓ RPM, the tonearm moved over the edge of the record, and the needle traced the groove. Following the brass introduction, the ornate timpani resounded from the speakers. It was the section that Tengo liked best.

While listening to the music, Tengo faced the screen of his word processor and typed in characters. It was a daily habit of his to listen to Janáček's *Sinfonietta* early in the morning. The piece had retained a special significance for him ever since he performed it as an impromptu high school percussionist. It gave him a sense of personal encouragement and protection – or at least he felt that it did.

He sometimes listened to Janáček's *Sinfonietta* with his older girlfriend. "Not bad," she would say, but she liked old jazz records more than classical – the older the better. It was an odd taste for a woman her age. Her favorite record was a collection of W. C. Handy blues songs, performed by the young Louis Armstrong, with Barney Bigard on clarinet and Trummy Young on trombone. She gave Tengo a copy, though less for him than for herself to listen to.

After sex, they would often lie in bed listening to the record. She never tired of it. "Armstrong's trumpet and singing are absolutely wonderful, of course, but if you ask me, the thing you should concentrate on is Barney Bigard's clarinet," she would say. Yet the actual number of Bigard solos on the record was small, and they tended to be limited to a single chorus. Louis Armstrong was the star of this record. But she obviously loved those few Bigard solos, the way she would quietly hum along with every memorized note.

She said she supposed there might be more talented jazz clarinetists than Barney Bigard, but you couldn't find another one who could play with such warmth and delicacy. His best performances always gave rise to a particular mental image. Tengo could not, off the top of his head, name any other jazz clarinetists, but as he listened to this record over and over, he began to appreciate the sheer, unforced beauty of its clarinet performances – their richly nourishing and imaginative qualities. He had to listen closely and repeatedly for this to happen, and he had to have a capable guide. He would have missed the nuances on his own.

His girlfriend once said, "Barney Bigard plays beautifully, like a gifted second baseman. His solos are marvelous, but where he really shines is in the backup he gives the other musicians. That is *so hard*, but he does it like it's nothing at all. Only an attentive listener can fully appreciate his true worth."

Whenever the sixth tune on the flip side of the LP, "Atlanta Blues," began, she would grab one of Tengo's body parts and praise Bigard's concise, exquisite solo, which was sandwiched between Armstrong's song and his trumpet solo. "Listen to that! Amazing – that first, long wail like a little child's cry! What is it – surprise? Overflowing joy? An appeal for happiness? It turns into a joyful sigh and weaves its way through a beautiful river of sound until it's smoothly absorbed into some perfect, unknowable place. There! Listen! Nobody else can play such thrilling solos. Jimmy Noone, Sidney Bechet, Pee Wee Russell, Benny Goodman: they're all great clarinetists, but none of them can create such perfectly sculptured works of art."

"How come you know so much about old-time jazz?" Tengo once asked.

"I have lots of past lives that you don't know anything about – past lives that no one can change in any way," she said, gently massaging Tengo's scrotum with the palm of her hand.

When he was finished writing for the morning, Tengo walked to the station and bought a paper at the newsstand. This he carried into a nearby café, where he ordered a "morning set" of buttered toast and a hard-boiled egg. He drank coffee and opened the paper while waiting for his food to come. As Komatsu had predicted, there was an article about Fuka-Eri on the human interest page. Not very large, the article appeared above an ad for Mitsubishi automobiles, under the headline "Popular High School Girl Writer Runaway?"

Fuka-Eri (penname of Eriko Fukada, 17), author of the current bestseller *Air Chrysalis,* has been listed as missing, it was revealed yesterday afternoon. According to her guardian, cultural anthropologist Takayuki Ebisuno (63), who filed the search request with the Oume police station, Eriko has failed to return either to her home in Oume City or to her Tokyo apartment since the night of June 27, and there has been no word from her since then. In response to this newspaper's telephone inquiry, Mr. Ebisuno said that Eriko was in her usual good spirits when he last saw her, that he could think of no reason she would want to go into hiding, that she had never once failed to come home without permission, and that he is worried something might have happened to her. The editor in charge of *Air Chrysalis* at the ** publishing company,

Yuji Komatsu, said, "The book has been at the top of the bestseller list for six straight weeks and has garnered a great deal of attention, but Miss Fukada herself has not wanted to make public appearances. We at the company have been unable to determine whether her current disappearance might have something to do with her attitude toward such matters. While young, Miss Fukada is an author with abundant talent from whom much can be expected in the future. We hope that she reappears in good health as soon as possible." The police investigation is proceeding with several possible leads in view.

That was probably about as much as the newspapers could say at this stage, Tengo concluded. If they gave it a more sensational treatment and Fuka-Eri showed up at home two days later as if nothing had happened, the reporter who wrote the article would be embarrassed and the newspaper itself would lose face. The same was true for the police. Both issued brief, neutral statements like weather balloons to see what would happen. The story would turn big once the weekly magazines got ahold of it and the TV news shows turned up the volume. That would not happen for a few more days.

Sooner or later, though, things would heat up, that was for certain. A sensation was inevitable. There were probably only four people in the world who knew that she had not been abducted but was lying low somewhere, alone. Fuka-Eri herself knew it, of course, and Tengo knew it. Professor Ebisuno and his daughter Azami also knew it. No one else knew that the fuss over her disappearance was a hoax meant to attract broad attention.

Tengo could not decide whether his knowledge of the truth was something he should be pleased or upset about. Pleased, probably: at least he didn't have to worry about Fuka-Eri's welfare. She was in a safe place. At the same time it was also clear that Tengo was complicit in this complicated plot. Professor Ebisuno was using it as a lever, in order to pry up an ominous boulder and let the sunlight in. Then he would wait to see what crawled out from under the rock, and Tengo was being forced to stand right next to him. Tengo did not want to know what would crawl out from under the rock. He would prefer not to see it. It was bound to be a huge source of trouble. But he sensed he would have no choice but to look.

After he had drunk his coffee and eaten his toast and eggs, Tengo exited the café, leaving his rumpled newspaper behind. He went back to his apartment, brushed his teeth, showered, and prepared to leave for school.

During the noon break at the cram school, Tengo had a strange visitor. He had just finished his morning class and was reading a few of the day's newspapers in the teachers' lounge when the school director's secretary approached him and said there was someone who wanted to see him. The secretary was a capable woman one year older than Tengo who, in spite of her title, handled virtually all of the school's administrative business. Her facial features were a bit too irregular for her to be considered beautiful, but she had a nice figure and marvelous taste in clothes.

"He says his name is Mr. Ushikawa."

Tengo did not recognize the name.

For some reason, a slight frown crossed her face. "He says he has 'something important' to discuss with you and wants to see you alone if possible."

"Something important?" Tengo asked, taken aback. No one *ever* brought him "something important" to discuss at the cram school.

"The reception room was empty, so I showed him in there. Teachers aren't supposed to use that room without permission, but I figured . . ."

"Thanks very much," Tengo said, and gave her his best smile.

Unimpressed, she hurried off somewhere, the hem of her new agnès b. summer jacket flapping in the breeze.

Ushikawa was a short man, probably in his mid-forties. His trunk had already filled out so that it had lost all sign of a waist, and excess flesh was gathering at his throat. But Tengo could not be sure of his age. Owing to the peculiarity (or the uncommonness) of his appearance, the clues necessary for guessing his age were difficult to find. He could have been older than that, or he could have been younger – anywhere between, say, thirty-two and fifty-six. His teeth were crooked, and his spine was strangely curved. The large crown of his head formed an abnormally flat bald area with lopsided edges. It was reminiscent of a military heliport that had been made by cutting away the peak of a small, strategically important hill. Tengo had seen such a heliport in a Vietnam War documentary. Around the borders of the flat, lopsided area of his head clung thick, black, curly hair that had been allowed to grow too long, hanging down shaggily over the man's ears. Ninety-eight people out of a hundred would probably be reminded by it of pubic hair. Tengo had no idea what the other two would think.

Everything about the man – his face, his body – seemed to have been formed asymmetrically. Tengo noticed this right away. Of course, all people's bodies are asymmetrical to some extent: that in itself was not contrary to the laws of nature. Tengo himself was aware that his own two eyelids had slightly different shapes, and his left testicle hung slightly lower than the right one. Our bodies are not mass-produced in a factory according to fixed standards. But in this man's case, the differences between right and left went far beyond the bounds of common sense. This imbalance, obvious to any observer, could not help but annoy those in his presence and cause them the same kind of discomfort they would feel in front of a funhouse mirror.

The man's gray suit had countless tiny wrinkles, which made

it look like an expanse of earth that had been ground down by a glacier. One flap of his white dress shirt's collar was sticking out, and the knot of his tie was contorted, as if it had twisted itself from the sheer discomfort of having to exist in that place. The suit, the shirt, and the tie were all slightly wrong in size. The pattern on his tie might have been an inept art student's impressionistic rendering of a bowl of tangled, soggy noodles. Each piece of clothing looked like something he had bought at a discount store to fill an immediate need. But the longer Tengo studied them, the sorrier he felt for the clothes themselves, for having to be worn by this man. Tengo paid little attention to his own clothing, but he was strangely concerned about the clothing worn by others. If he had to compile a list of the worst dressers he had met in the past ten years, this man would be somewhere near the top. It was not just that he had terrible style: he also gave the impression that he was deliberately desecrating the very idea of wearing clothes.

When Tengo entered the reception room, the man stood and produced a business card from his card case, handing it to Tengo with a bow. "Toshiharu Ushikawa," it said in both Japanese characters and Roman script. An ordinary enough first name, but "Ushikawa"? "Bull River"? Tengo had never seen that one before. The card further identified the man as "Full-time Director, New Japan Foundation for the Advancement of Scholarship and the Arts," located downtown in Kojimachi, Chiyoda Ward, and gave the foundation's telephone number. Tengo had no idea what kind of organization the New Japan Foundation for the Advancement of Scholarship and the Arts might be, nor what it meant to be a "full-time director" of anything. The business card, though, was a handsome one, with an embossed logo, not a makeshift item. Tengo studied it for several moments before looking at the man again. He felt sure there could not be many people in the world whose appearance was so out of keeping with the grandiose title

"Full-time Director, New Japan Foundation for the Advancement of Scholarship and the Arts."

They sat in easy chairs on opposite sides of a low table and looked at each other. The man gave his sweaty forehead a few vigorous rubs with a handkerchief and returned the pitiful cloth to his jacket pocket. The receptionist brought in two cups of green tea on a tray. Tengo thanked her as she left.

Ushikawa said nothing to her, but to Tengo he said, "Please forgive me for interrupting your break and for arriving without having first made an appointment." The words themselves were polite and formal enough, but his tone was strangely colloquial, and Tengo found it almost offensive. "Have you finished lunch? If you like, we could go out and talk over a meal."

"I don't eat lunch when I'm working," Tengo said. "I'll have something light after my afternoon class, so don't worry."

"I see. Well, then, with your permission, I'll tell you what I have in mind and we can discuss it here. This seems like a nice, quiet place where we can talk without interruption." He surveyed the reception room as though appraising its value. There was nothing special about the room. It had one big oil painting hanging on the wall – a picture of some mountain, more impressive for the weight of its paint than anything else. A vase had an arrangement of flowers resembling dahlias – dull blossoms reminiscent of a slow-witted matron. Tengo wondered why a cram school would keep such a gloomy reception room.

"Let me belatedly introduce myself. As you can see from the card, my name is Ushikawa. My friends all call me 'Ushi,' never 'Ushikawa.' Just plain, old 'Ushi,' as if I were a bull," Ushikawa said, smiling.

Friends? Tengo wondered – out of pure curiosity – what kind of person would ever want to be this man's friend.

On first impression, Ushikawa honestly made Tengo think of some creepy *thing* that had crawled out of a hole in the earth

– a slimy thing of uncertain shape that in fact was not *supposed* to come out into the light. He might conceivably be one of the things that Professor Ebisuno had lured out from under a rock. Tengo unconsciously wrinkled his brow and placed the business card, which was still in his hand, on the table. Toshiharu Ushikawa. That was this man's name.

"I am sure that you are very busy, Mr. Kawana, so with your permission I will abbreviate any preliminary background and proceed directly to the heart of the matter," Ushikawa said.

Tengo answered with a little nod.

Ushikawa took a sip of tea and launched into the business at hand. "You have probably never heard of the New Japan Foundation for the Advancement of Scholarship and the Arts, Mr. Kawana." Tengo nodded. "We are a relatively new foundation that concentrates on selecting and supporting young people – especially those young people who are not yet widely known – who are engaged in original activity in the fields of scholarship and the arts. In other words, our aim is to nourish the budding youth who will carry the next generation on their shoulders in all fields of Japan's contemporary culture. We contract with specialists to propose candidates for us in each category. We choose five artists and scholars each year and provide them with grants. They can do anything they like for one year, no strings attached. All we ask is that they submit a simple report at the end of their year – a mere formality – outlining their activities and results, to be included in the foundation's magazine. Nothing more burdensome than that. We have just begun this activity, so the important thing for us is to produce tangible results. We are, in other words, still in the seed-planting stage. In concrete terms, what this means is that we will provide each recipient with an annual stipend of three million yen."

"Very generous," Tengo said.

"It takes both time and money to build up or discover something important. Of course, time and money are not in themselves a guarantee of great results, but they can't hurt. The total amount of time available is especially limited. The clock is ticking as we speak. Time rushes past. Opportunities are lost right and left. If you have money, you can buy time. You can even buy freedom if you want. Time and freedom: those are the most important things that people can buy with money."

Hearing this, Tengo almost reflexively glanced at his watch. True, time was ticking past without a letup.

"Sorry for taking so much of your time," Ushikawa added, obviously interpreting Tengo's gesture as a demonstration of his own argument. "Let me be quick about this. These days, of course, a mere three million yen is not going to enable a lavish lifestyle, but it ought to help a young person pay the bills very nicely. Which is our basic purpose: to make it possible for recipients to spend a full year concentrating on their research or creative projects without struggling to support themselves. And if the governing board determines at the end-of-year evaluation that the person produced noteworthy results during the period, the possibility remains for the stipend to be extended beyond the single year."

Tengo said nothing but waited for Ushikawa to continue.

"The other day I took the liberty of listening to you lecture for a full hour here at the cram school, Mr. Kawana. Believe me, I found it *very* interesting. I am a total outsider when it comes to mathematics, or should I say I've always been terrible at it and absolutely hated math class in school. I just had to hear the word 'mathematics' to start writhing in agony and to run away as far as I could. But your lecture, Mr. Kawana, was utterly enjoyable. Of course, I didn't understand a thing about the logic of calculus, but just listening to you speak about it, I thought, if it's really so interesting, I ought to start studying math. You can be proud of yourself. You have a special talent – a talent for drawing people in, should I say. I had heard that you were a popular teacher, and I could see why."

Tengo had no idea when or where Ushikawa could have heard him lecture. He always paid close attention to who was in the room when he was teaching, and though he had not memorized every student's face, he could never have missed anyone as strange-looking as Ushikawa, who would have stood out like a centipede in a sugar bowl. He decided not to pursue the matter, however, which would only have prolonged a conversation that was already too long.

"As you must know, Mr. Ushikawa, I'm just an employee here, somebody the cram school hires to teach a few courses," Tengo began, anxious to waste as little time as possible. "I don't do any original research in mathematics. I just take knowledge that is already out there and explain it to students as simply and entertainingly as I can. All I'm doing is teaching them more effective methods for solving problems on college placement tests. I may have a certain talent for that, but I gave up the idea of being a professional researcher in the field a long time ago. For one thing, I couldn't afford to stay in school any longer, and I never thought I had the aptitude or the ability to make a name for myself in the academic world. In that sense, I'm just not the kind of person you're looking for."

Ushikawa hurriedly raised his hand. "No, that's not what I'm getting at at all. I'm sorry, I might have made this more complicated than it has to be. It's true that your math lectures are interesting and unique and original. But I didn't come here today about that. What we have our eye on, Mr. Kawana, is your activity as a novelist."

Tengo was so unprepared for this that he was momentarily at a loss for words.

"My activity as a novelist?"

"Exactly."

"I don't understand. It's true, I've been writing fiction for several years, but nothing of mine has ever been published.

You can't call someone like that a novelist. How could I have possibly attracted your attention?"

At Tengo's reaction, Ushikawa smiled in great delight, revealing a mouthful of horribly crooked teeth. Like seaside pilings that had been hit by huge waves, they pointed off in all directions and were befouled in a great many ways. *They were surely beyond help from orthodontia, but someone should at least teach him how to brush his teeth properly,* Tengo thought.

"That's what makes our foundation unique," Ushikawa said proudly. "The researchers we contract with take note of things that other people have yet to notice. That is one of our goals. As you say, none of your work has been properly published, and we are quite aware of that. But we also know that, under a penname, you have entered various literary magazines' new writers' competitions almost every year. You have not won yet, unfortunately, but a few times your work made it through to the last stage of the screening process, so that, quite naturally, a not inconsiderable number of people got to read them, and several of those people took note of your talent. Our researcher has concluded that you are certain to win a new writers' award in the near future and make your debut as a writer. 'Investing in futures' would be a rather crude way to put it, but as I said before, our aim is to 'nourish the budding youth who will carry the next generation on their shoulders.' "

Tengo picked up his cup and took a drink of his tea, which, by now, was somewhat cool. "So, what you're saying is that I'm a candidate for a grant as a fledgling novelist, is that it?"

"That is it exactly. Except that you're not so much a candidate as a finalist. If you say that you are willing to accept the grant, then I am authorized to finalize the arrangements. If you will be so good as to sign the necessary documents, the three million yen will be transferred electronically into your bank account immediately. You will be able to take six months or a year's leave from this cram school and devote all your energies to writing. We have heard that you are presently writing a long novel. This would be a perfect opportunity, don't you think?"

"How do you know I'm writing a long novel?" Tengo asked with a frown.

Ushikawa gave him another toothy grin, but upon closer inspection, Tengo realized that his eyes were not smiling at all. The glow from them was icy cold.

"Our researchers are eager and capable. They choose a number of candidates and examine them from every angle. Probably a few people around you know that you are writing a novel. Word gets out . . ."

Komatsu knew he was writing a novel, and so did his older girlfriend. Was there anyone else? Probably not.

"I'd like to ask a few things about your foundation," Tengo said.

"Please do. Ask anything at all."

"Where does it get the money it needs to operate?"

"From a certain individual. Or, you might say, from an organization of his. Realistically speaking – just between us – it also serves as one of his many tax write-offs. Of course, quite aside from that, this individual has a deep interest in scholarship and the arts, and he wants to support members of the younger generation. I can't go into any more detail here. The person wishes to remain anonymous – and that includes his organization as well. All day-to-day operations are entrusted to the foundation's committee, of which yours truly is, for now, a member."

Tengo thought about this for a moment, but there really wasn't that much to think about. All he did was put the things that Ushikawa had told him in order.

"Would you mind very much if I smoked?" Ushikawa asked.

"Not at all," Tengo said, pushing a heavy glass ashtray in his direction.

Ushikawa took a box of Seven Stars cigarettes from his

breast pocket, put a cigarette in his mouth, and lit it with a gold lighter. The lighter was slim and expensive-looking.

"So, what do you say, Mr. Kawana?" Ushikawa asked. "Will you do us the honor of accepting our grant? Speaking for myself, quite honestly, after having heard your delightful lecture, I am very much looking forward to seeing what kind of world you go on to create in your literature."

"I am very grateful to you for bringing me this offer," Tengo said. "It's far more than I deserve. But I'm afraid I can't accept it."

Smoke rose from the cigarette between Ushikawa's fingers. He looked at Tengo with his eyes narrowed. "By which you mean . . . ?"

"First of all, I don't like the idea of taking money from people I hardly know. Secondly, as things stand now, I don't really need the money. I have managed well enough so far by teaching three days a week at the cram school and using the other days to concentrate on my writing. I'm not ready to change that lifestyle."

Thirdly, Mr. Ushikawa, I personally don't want to have anything to do with you. Fourthly, no matter how you look at it, there's something fishy about this grant. It just sounds too good to be true. There's something going on behind the scenes. I certainly don't have the best intuition in the world, but I can tell that much from the smell. Tengo, of course, said none of this.

"I see," Ushikawa said, filling his lungs with cigarette smoke and exhaling with a look of deep satisfaction. "I see. I think, in my own way, I understand your view of the matter. What you say is quite logical. But really, Mr. Kawana, there is no need for you to give me your answer right now. Why don't you go home and take a good two or three days to think it over? Take more time to reach your conclusion. We're not in any hurry. It's not a bad offer."

Tengo gave his head a decisive shake. "Thank you, that's

very kind, but it will save us both a lot of time and trouble if we reach a final decision today. I am honored to have been nominated for a grant, and I'm sorry to have put you to the trouble of making a special trip here, but I'm afraid I will have to decline. This is my final conclusion, and there is no possibility that I would reconsider."

Ushikawa nodded a few times and regretfully used the ashtray to crush out the cigarette, from which he had taken only two puffs.

"That's fine, Mr. Kawana. I see where you are coming from, and I want to respect your wishes. I am sorry for having taken up your time. It's unfortunate, but I will have to resign myself to it. I will be going now."

But Ushikawa showed no sign of standing up. He simply treated the back of his head to a thorough scratching and looked at Tengo with narrowed eyes.

"However, Mr. Kawana, you yourself may not be aware of it, but people are expecting great things from you as a writer. You have talent. Mathematics and literature probably have no direct connection, but listening to you lecture on mathematics is like listening to someone tell a story. This is not something that any ordinary person can do. You have something special that needs to be told. That is clear even to the likes of me. So be sure to take care of yourself. Forgive me if I am being oversolicitous, but please try not to become embroiled in extraneous matters, and make up your mind to walk straight down your own path in life."

"Extraneous matters?" Tengo asked.

"For example, you seem to have – how should I put this? – some sort of connection with Miss Eriko Fukada, the author of *Air Chrysalis*. Or at least you have met her a few times, am I correct? By coincidence, I just happened to read in today's paper that she has apparently disappeared. The media will have a field day with this delicious item, I'm sure."

"Assuming I have met Eriko Fukada, is that supposed to mean something?"

Again Ushikawa raised his hand to stop Tengo. It was a small hand, but the fingers were short and stubby. "Now, now, please don't get worked up over this. I don't mean any harm. All I am trying to say is that selling off one's talents and time in dribs and drabs to make ends meet never produces good results. It may sound presumptuous of me to say this, but your talent is a genuine diamond in the rough, and I don't want to see it wasted and ruined on pointless things. If the relationship between you and Miss Fukada becomes public knowledge, Mr. Kawana, someone is bound to seek you out at home. They'll start stalking you, and they'll turn up all kinds of half-truths. They're a persistent bunch."

Tengo stared at Ushikawa, saying nothing. Ushikawa narrowed his eyes and started scratching one of his big earlobes. The ears themselves were small, but Ushikawa's earlobes were strangely big. Ushikawa's physical oddities were an unending source of fascination.

"Now, don't get the wrong idea. My lips are sealed," Ushikawa said, gesturing as if zipping his mouth closed. "I promise you that. I may not look it, but I know how to keep a secret. People say I must have been a clam in a previous life. I'll keep this matter locked up inside as a sign of my personal regard for you. No one else will know."

Finally he stood up and made several attempts to smooth out the tiny wrinkles in his suit but succeeded only in making them more obvious.

"If you should change your mind about the grant, please call the number on my card whenever you feel like it. There is still plenty of time. If this year is no good for you, well, there's always next year." With raised index fingers, Ushikawa mimed the earth revolving around the sun. "We are in no hurry. At least I succeeded in meeting you and having this little talk with you, and I believe that you have gotten our message."

After one more smile, all but flaunting his ruined dentition, Ushikawa turned and left the reception room.

Tengo used the time until his next class to think through Ushikawa's remarks in his head. The man seemed to know that Tengo had participated in the rewrite of *Air Chrysalis*. There were hints of it everywhere in his speech. **All I am trying to say is that selling off one's talents and time in dribs and drabs to make ends meet never produces good results,** Ushikawa had said pointedly.

"We know" – surely, that was the message.

I succeeded in meeting you and having this little talk with you, and I believe that you have gotten *our* message.

Could they have dispatched Ushikawa to see Tengo and offer him the three-million-yen grant for no other purpose than to deliver this message? No, it didn't make sense. There was no need for them to devise such an elaborate plot. They already knew where he was weakest. If they had wanted to threaten Tengo, all they had to do was bring out the facts. Or were they trying to buy him off with the grant? It was all too dramatic. And who were "they," after all? Was the New Japan Foundation for the Advancement of Scholarship and the Arts connected with Sakigake? Did it even exist?

Tengo went to see the secretary, carrying Ushikawa's business card. "I need to ask you to do me another favor," he said.

"What would that be?" she asked, remaining seated at her desk and looking up at Tengo.

"I'd like you to call this number and ask if they're the New Japan Foundation for the Advancement of Scholarship and the Arts. Also, ask whether this director, Mr. Ushikawa, is in. They'll probably say he's not there, so ask when he's due back in the office. If they ask your name, just make something up.

I'd do it myself, except it might be a problem if they recognize my voice."

The secretary dialed the numbers and a standard back-and-forth ensued – a concise exchange between two professionals. When it ended, the secretary reported to Tengo, "The New Japan Foundation for the Advancement of Scholarship and the Arts does exist. A woman answered, probably in her early twenties, a normal receptionist. Mr. Ushikawa actually works there. He's supposed to be back around three thirty. She didn't ask my name – which I certainly would have done."

"Of course," Tengo said. "Anyhow, thanks."

"You're welcome," she said, handing Ushikawa's card back to Tengo. "Is this Mr. Ushikawa the person who came to see you?"

"That's him."

"I barely looked at him, but he seemed kind of creepy."

Tengo put the card into his wallet. "I suspect that impression wouldn't change even if you had more time to look at him," he said.

"I always tell myself not to judge people by their appearance. I've been wrong in the past and had some serious regrets. But the minute I saw this man, I got the feeling he couldn't be trusted. I still feel that way."

"You're not alone," Tengo said.

"I'm not alone," she echoed, as if to confirm the grammatical accuracy of Tengo's sentence.

"That's a beautiful jacket you're wearing," Tengo said, meaning it quite honestly. He wasn't just flattering her. After Ushikawa's crumpled heap of a suit, her stylishly cut linen jacket looked like a lovely piece of fabric that had descended from heaven on a windless afternoon.

"Thank you," she said.

"But just because somebody answered the phone, it doesn't necessarily mean that the New Japan Foundation for the

Advancement of Scholarship and the Arts actually exists."

"That's true. It could be an elaborate ruse. You just have to put in a phone line and hire somebody to answer it. Like in *The Sting*. But why would they go to all that trouble? Forgive me, Tengo, but you don't look like somebody who'd have enough money to squeeze out of you."

"I don't have a thing," Tengo said, "except my soul."

"Sounds like a job for Mephistopheles," she said.

"Maybe I should walk over to this address and see if there's really an office there."

"Tell me what you find out," she said, inspecting her manicure with narrowed eyes.

The New Japan Foundation for the Advancement of Scholarship and the Arts actually existed. After class, Tengo took the subway to Yotsuya and walked to Kojimachi. At the address on Ushikawa's card he found a four-story building with a metal nameplate by the front entrance: "New Japan Foundation for the Advancement of Scholarship and the Arts." The office was on the third floor. Also on that floor were Mikimoto Music Publishers and Koda Accountants. Judging from the scale of the building, none of them could be very big offices. None appeared to be flourishing, either, though their true condition was impossible to judge from outside. Tengo considered taking the elevator to the third floor. He wanted to see what kind of office it was, or at least what its door looked like. But things could prove awkward if he ran into Ushikawa in the hallway.

Tengo took another subway home and called Komatsu's office. For a change, Komatsu was in, and he came to the phone right away.

"I can't talk now," Komatsu said, speaking more quickly than usual, his tone of voice somewhat higher than normal. "Sorry, but I don't think I can talk about anything here right now."

"This is very important," Tengo said. "A very strange guy came to see me at school today. He seemed to know something about my connection with *Air Chrysalis*."

Komatsu went silent for a few seconds at his end. "I think I can call you in twenty minutes. Are you at home?"

Tengo said that he was. Komatsu hung up. While he waited for Komatsu to call, Tengo sharpened two kitchen knives on a whetstone, boiled water, and poured himself some tea. The phone rang exactly twenty minutes later, which was again unusual for Komatsu.

This time Komatsu sounded far calmer than he had before. He seemed to be phoning from a quieter place. Tengo gave him a condensed account of what Ushikawa had said in the reception room.

"The New Japan Foundation for the Advancement of Scholarship and the Arts? Never heard of it. And that three-million-yen grant for you is hard to figure, too. I agree, of course, that you have a great future as a writer, but you still haven't published anything. It's kind of incredible. They've got some ulterior motive."

"That's what I thought."

"Give me a little time. I'll find out what I can about this New Japan Foundation for the Advancement of Scholarship and the Arts. I'll get in touch with you if I learn anything. But this Ushikawa guy knows you're connected with Fuka-Eri, huh?"

"Looks that way."

"That's a bit of a problem."

"Something's starting to happen," Tengo said. "It's fine that Professor Ebisuno managed to pry up his rock, but some kind of monster seems to have crawled out from underneath."

Komatsu sighed into the phone. "It's coming after me, too. The weekly magazines are going crazy. And the TV guys are poking around. This morning the cops came to the office to question me. They've already latched on to the connection between Fuka-Eri and Sakigake. And of course the disappearance of her parents. The media will start blowing up that angle soon."

"What's Professor Ebisuno doing?"

"Nobody's been able to get in touch with him for a while. Phone calls don't go through, and he doesn't get in touch with anybody. He may be having a tough time too. Or he could be working on another secret plan."

"Oh, by the way, to change the subject a bit, have you told anybody that I'm writing a long novel?" Tengo asked Komatsu.

"No, nobody," Komatsu responded immediately. "Why would I tell anyone about that?"

"That's okay, then. Just asking."

Komatsu fell silent for a moment, and then he said, "It's kind of late for me to be saying this, but we might have gotten ourselves into nasty territory."

"Whatever we've gotten ourselves into, there's no backing out now, that's for sure."

"And if we can't back out, all we can do is keep going forward, even if you're right about that monster."

"Better fasten your seat belt," Tengo said.

"You said it," Komatsu said, and hung up.

It had been a long day. Tengo sat at the kitchen table, drinking his cold tea and thinking about Fuka-Eri. What could she be doing all day, locked up alone in her hiding place? Of course, no one ever knew what Fuka-Eri was doing.

In her recorded message, Fuka-Eri had said that the Little People's wisdom and power might cause harm to the Professor and to Tengo. **Better be careful in the forest.** Tengo found himself looking at his surroundings. True, the forest was *their world.*

CHAPTER 3

Aomame

YOU CAN'T CHOOSE HOW YOU'RE BORN, BUT YOU CAN CHOOSE HOW YOU DIE

One night near the end of July, the thick clouds that had long covered the sky finally cleared, revealing two moons. Aomame stood on her apartment's small balcony, looking at the sky. She wanted to call someone right away and say, "Can you do me a favor? Stick your head out the window and look at the sky. Okay, how many moons do you see up there? Where I am, I can see two very clearly. How about where you are?"

But she had no one to whom she could make such a call. Ayumi was one possibility, but Aomame preferred not to further deepen their personal relationship. She was a police-woman, after all. Aomame would more than likely be killing another man before long, after which she would change her face, change her name, move to a different area, and disappear. Obviously, she wouldn't be able to see or contact Ayumi any-more. Once you let yourself grow close to someone, cutting the ties could be painful.

She went back inside, closed the balcony door, and turned on the air conditioner. Then she drew the curtains to place a barrier between herself and the moons. The two moons in the sky were disturbing to her. They subtly disrupted the bal-ance of the earth's gravity, and they seemed to be affecting her physically as well. Her period was not due for a while, but her body felt strangely listless and heavy. Her skin was dry, and her pulse abnormal. She told herself not to think about the moons anymore – even if they were something that she *ought to* think about.

To combat the listlessness, Aomame lay on the carpet to stretch her muscles, systematically engaging one muscle after another that she had little chance to use on a daily basis, and stretching it as far as it would go. Each muscle responded with wordless screams, and her sweat rained down on the floor. She had devised this stretching program herself and modified it each day, making it increasingly radical and effective. It was strictly for her own use. She could not have introduced it into her sports club classes. Ordinary people could never bear that much pain. Most of her fellow instructors screamed for mercy when she tried it on them.

While going through her program, she played a recording of Janáček's *Sinfonietta* conducted by George Szell. The music took twenty-five minutes to play, which was the right amount of time to effectively torture every muscle in her body – neither too short nor too long. By the time the music ended, the turntable stopped, and the automatic tonearm returned to its rest, both her mind and her body felt like rags that had been thoroughly wrung out.

By now, Aomame had memorized every note of *Sinfonietta*. Listening to the music while stretching her body close to its limit, she was able to attain a mysterious calm. She was simultaneously the torturer and the tortured, the forcer and the forced. This sense of inner-directed self-sufficiency was what she wanted most of all. It gave her deep solace. Janáček's *Sinfonietta* was effective background music for that purpose.

Just before ten o'clock that night, the phone rang. Lifting the receiver, she heard Tamaru's voice.

"Any plans for tomorrow?"

"I get out of work at six thirty."

"Think you can stop by after that?"

"I'm sure I can," Aomame said.

"Good," Tamaru said. She could hear his ballpoint pen writing on his calendar.

"Have you found a new dog yet?" Aomame asked.

"Dog? Uh-huh. Another female German shepherd. I still don't know everything about her disposition, but she's been trained in the basics and she seems to obey commands. She arrived about ten days ago and is pretty well settled in. The women are relieved to have a dog again."

"That's good."

"This one's satisfied with ordinary dog food. Less bother."

"Ordinary German shepherds don't eat spinach."

"That was one strange dog. And depending on the season, spinach can be expensive," Tamaru complained nostalgically. After a few seconds' pause, he added, "It's a nice night for moon viewing."

Aomame frowned slightly into the phone. "Where did that come from all of a sudden?"

"Even I am not unaware of natural beauty, I'll have you know."

"No, of course not," Aomame said. *But you're not the type to discuss poetic subjects on the phone without some particular reason, either.*

After another short silence at his end, Tamaru said, "You're the one who brought up moon viewing the last time we talked on the phone, remember? I've been thinking about it ever since, especially when I looked up at the sky a little while ago and it was so clear – not a cloud anywhere."

Aomame was on the verge of asking him how many moons he had seen in that clear sky, but she stopped herself. It was too fraught with danger. Tamaru had told her about his life last time

– about having been raised as an orphan who never knew his parents' faces, about his nationality. He had never spoken at such length before, but he was not a man much given to talking about himself in any case. He had taken a personal liking to Aomame and had more or less opened himself up to her. But ultimately, he was a professional, trained to take the shortest route to see his mission through. There was no point in saying too much to him.

"I think I can get there around seven o'clock tomorrow night after work," she said.

"Fine," Tamaru said. "You'll probably be hungry. The cook is off tomorrow, so we can't serve you anything decent, but if a sandwich or something is all right with you, I can do the preparations."

"Thanks," Aomame said.

"You'll be needing your driver's license, your passport, and your health insurance card. We'd like you to bring those tomorrow. Plus, we'd like a copy of your apartment key. Can you have all those ready for us?"

"Yes, I think so."

"And one more thing. I'd like to see you alone about that business from before. So keep some time open for me after you're through with Madame."

"Business from before?"

Tamaru fell silent for a moment. His silence had all the weight of a sandbag. "I believe there was something you wanted to get ahold of. Have you forgotten?"

"No, of course I remember," Aomame hurried to say. In a corner of her mind, she had still been thinking about the moons.

"Tomorrow at seven, then," Tamaru said and hung up.

The number of moons had not changed the following night. When she took a quick shower after work and left the club, two pale-colored moons had already appeared side by side in the still-bright sky. Aomame stood on the pedestrian footbridge

spanning Gaien-nishi Dori Avenue, leaning against the handrail and gazing at the two moons for a time. No one else made
a point of looking at the moons like this. The people passing by
did no more than cast puzzled glances in Aomame's direction
as she stood there looking up at the sky. They hurried toward
the subway station as if they had absolutely no interest in either
the sky or the moon. As she gazed upward, Aomame began to
feel the same physical lassitude she had experienced the day
before. *I have to stop staring at the moons like this,* she told herself. *It can't have a good effect on me.* But try as she might not to
look at the moons, she could not help feeling their gaze against
her skin. *Even if I don't look at them, they're looking at me. They
know what I'm about to do.*

Using ornate cups from a bygone era, the dowager and
Aomame drank thick hot coffee. The dowager dribbled in a
little milk at the edge of her cup and drank the coffee without
stirring it. She used no sugar. Aomame drank hers black, as
usual. Tamaru served them the sandwiches he had promised.
He had cut them into bite-sized pieces. Aomame ate several.
They were simple cucumber and cheese sandwiches on brown
bread, but were subtly flavored. Tamaru had a fine touch in
making such simple dishes, wielding a kitchen knife with skill,
cutting each of his ingredients to the perfect size and thick-
ness. He knew the proper order with which to undertake each
task. This was all it took to make an amazing difference in how
things tasted.

"Have you finished organizing your things?" the dowager
asked.

"I donated my extra clothing and books to charity. I've
packed a bag with everything I'll need in my new life, ready
to go at any time. The only things left in my apartment are the
basics I'll need for the time being: electrical appliances, cook-
ware, bed and bedding, a few dishes."

"We'll take care of anything that's left. And you don't have to think about your lease or other such details. You can just walk out with the few things you really need in your luggage."

"Should I let them know at work? It could raise suspicions if I suddenly disappeared one day."

The dowager quietly returned her coffee cup to the table. "You don't have to think about that, either."

Aomame responded with a nod. She ate another sandwich and took a sip of coffee.

"By the way, do you have money in the bank?" the dowager asked.

"I have six hundred thousand yen in a regular savings account and two million yen in a CD."

The dowager did some calculations. "There's no problem with your withdrawing up to four hundred thousand yen from the savings account if you do it in stages, but don't touch the CD. It wouldn't be a good idea for you to cancel it all of a sudden. They might be watching your personal affairs. We can't be too careful. I'll cover the difference later. Do you have any other property or assets?"

"There's the money you paid me before. It's just sitting in a safe-deposit box."

"Take the cash out, but don't keep it in your apartment. Think about someplace good to put it."

"All right."

"That's all we need you to do for now. Otherwise, just go about your business as usual, not changing your lifestyle or doing anything that would attract attention. And make sure you don't talk about anything important on the telephone."

Once she had finished saying this much, the dowager settled more deeply into her chair, as if she had used up her entire reserve of energy.

"Has the date been set?" Aomame asked.

"Not yet, unfortunately," the dowager said. "We're still

waiting for them to contact us. The arrangements have been made, but they won't decide their schedule until the last minute. It could be another week, or it could be another month. We don't know the place, either. We just have to ask you to stand by, I'm afraid, on pins and needles."

"I don't mind waiting," Aomame said, "but I wonder if you can give me even a general idea about the 'arrangements.' "

"You'll be giving him a muscle-stretching session," the dowager said. "What you always do. He has some kind of physical problems. They're not life-threatening, but we've heard they give him a lot of trouble. In addition to orthodox medicine, he's tried a number of alternative treatments in an attempt to solve these 'problems' – shiatsu, acupuncture, massage – but none of them seems to help. These physical problems are the only weak spot of this man they call 'Leader.' It's the breach in his defenses that we've been looking for."

The curtains were drawn on the window behind the dowager, concealing the moons, but Aomame could feel their cool gaze against her skin. Their conspiratorial silence seemed to be stealing into the room.

"We have a spy inside the Sakigake organization, and we've used him to pass the word that you are an outstanding expert in muscle stretching. This was not especially difficult, because it happens to be true. Now they are very interested in you. At first, they wanted to bring you into their compound in Yamanashi, but we made it clear that you are far too busy with your work to leave Tokyo. In any case, the man comes to Tokyo at least once a month on business. He stays incognito in a downtown hotel. You will be giving him a stretching session there. All you have to do is take the usual steps with him once you're inside."

Aomame imagined the scene. A hotel room. A man is lying on a yoga mat, and she is stretching his muscles. She can't see his face. On his stomach, he leaves the back of his neck exposed to her, defenseless. She reaches over and takes the ice pick from her bag.

"So he and I can be alone together in his room?" Aomame asked.

The dowager nodded. "Leader keeps his physical problems hidden from others in the organization, so there should be no one else present. You and he will be alone."

"Do they know my name and where I work?"

"They are exceedingly cautious people. They've already done a thorough background check on you and found no problems. We received word yesterday that they will want you to come to where he is staying. They will let us know as soon as the time and place are set."

"I come here so often, don't you think there is some chance they will find our relationship suspicious?"

"I'm just a member of the sports club where you work, and you come to my house as a personal trainer. They have no reason to think that there might be any more to our relationship than that."

Aomame responded with a nod.

The dowager said, "Whenever this Leader person leaves the compound and moves around, he has two bodyguards who accompany him. Both are believers and karate belt holders. We don't know yet if they also carry weapons, but they are apparently good at what they do. They train every day. According to Tamaru, though, they are amateurs."

"Unlike Tamaru."

"Yes, unlike Tamaru. He used to belong to a Self-Defense Force Ranger unit. Those people have it pounded into them to carry out whatever needs to be done to accomplish the mission, and to do it instantly, without the slightest hesitation. The important thing is not to hesitate, no matter who the opponent might be. Amateurs hesitate – especially when the opponent is, say, a young woman."

The dowager sank her head back into the chair and sighed deeply. Then she straightened herself again and looked directly at Aomame.

"The two bodyguards will most likely wait in the next room of the suite while you are administering your treatment to Leader. You'll be alone with him for an hour. That is how we have set things up for now. How it will actually go is anybody's guess. Things can be fluid. Leader never reveals his plan of action until the very last minute."

"How old a man is he?"

"Probably in his mid-fifties. We've heard he's a big man. Unfortunately, we don't know any more than that."

Tamaru was waiting at the front door. She gave him her spare apartment key, driver's license, passport, and health insurance card. He stepped inside and made copies of the documents. After checking to see that he had all the necessary copies, he handed the originals back to Aomame. Then he showed Aomame to his office, which was next to the front door. It was a small, square space lacking any decoration. A tiny window opened to the garden. The wall-mounted air conditioner hummed along. He had Aomame sit in a small wooden chair, while he sat at his desk. On the wall above the desk hung a row of four monitor screens with changeable camera angles. Four video decks constantly recorded their images. The screens showed views outside the walls. The far right one displayed an image of the front door of the safe house where the women were living. The new guard dog was also visible, resting on the ground. It was somewhat smaller than the previous dog.

"The tape didn't show how the dog died," Tamaru said, as if anticipating a question from Aomame. "She wasn't tied up at the time. There's no way she could have untied herself, so possibly someone untied her."

"Someone who could approach without causing her to bark."

"That's what it amounts to."

"Strange."

Tamaru nodded but said nothing. He had thought about the various possibilities so much on his own that he was sick of thinking about them. There was nothing left for him to say to anybody else.

Tamaru reached over and opened a drawer of the cabinet by his desk, taking out a black plastic bag. From the bag he took a faded blue bath towel, and when he spread the towel open, a lustrous black object emerged – a small automatic pistol. Saying nothing, he handed it to Aomame, who also remained silent as she took it. She tested the weight of it in her hand. It was much lighter than it appeared to be. Such a small, light object could deliver death to a human being.

"You just made two major mistakes. Do you know what they were?" Tamaru asked.

Aomame thought over the actions she had just taken but could discover no mistakes. All she had done was take the gun that was handed to her. "I don't know," she said.

"First, when you took the gun, you didn't check to see if it was loaded or not and, if it was loaded, whether the safety was on. The second was that, after you took the gun, you pointed it – even if only for one split second – at me. You broke two absolute rules. Also, you should never put your finger inside the trigger guard if you have no intention of firing the gun."

"I see. I'll be careful from now on."

"Emergency situations aside, you should never handle or hand over or carry a gun that has even one bullet in it. And whenever you see a gun, you should treat it as loaded until you know for sure otherwise. Guns are made to kill people. You can never be too careful with them. Some people might laugh at me for being too cautious, but stupid accidents happen all the time, and the ones who get killed or badly wounded are usually the ones who were laughing."

Tamaru drew a plastic bag from his jacket pocket. Inside were seven new bullets. He set them on his desk. "As you can see, the bullets are not in the gun. The magazine is in place, but it's empty. The chamber is empty, too."

Aomame nodded.

"This is a personal gift from me. Even so, if you don't use it, I'd like to have it back."

"Of course," Aomame said, her voice dry. "But it must have cost you something."

"Don't let that worry you," Tamaru said. "You have other things to worry about. Let's talk about those. Have you ever fired a gun?"

Aomame shook her head. "Never."

"Revolvers tend to be easier to use than automatics, especially for amateurs. Their mechanism is simpler, and it's easier to learn how to operate them, and you're less likely to make mistakes with them. But a good revolver can be bulky and inconvenient to carry around. So I figured an automatic would be better for you. This is a Heckler & Koch HK4. A German make. Weighs 480 grams without bullets. It's small and light, but its 9mm Short cartridges pack a punch, and it has a small recoil. It's not very accurate for long distances, but it's perfect for what you have in mind. Heckler & Koch started up after the war, but this HK4 is based on the Mauser HSc, a well-respected model from before the war. They've been making it since 1968, and it's still widely used. So it's dependable. This is not a new one, but it's been well taken care of by somebody who obviously knew what he was doing. Guns are like cars: you can trust a good used one better than one that's brand-new."

Tamaru took the gun back from Aomame and showed her how to handle it – how to lock and unlock the safety, how to remove and replace the magazine.

"Make sure the safety is on when you take the magazine out.

After you open the catch and pull the magazine out, you pull the slide back and the bullet pops out of the chamber – not now, of course, since the gun isn't loaded. After that, the slide stays open, so then you pull the trigger like this and the slide closes but the hammer stays cocked. You pull the trigger again and the hammer falls. Then you put in a new magazine."

Tamaru went through the sequence of motions with practiced speed. Then he repeated the same sequence slowly, demonstrating each separate operation. Aomame watched intently.

"Now you try it."

Aomame carefully extracted the magazine, pulled the slide back, emptied the chamber, lowered the hammer, and reinserted the magazine.

"That's fine," Tamaru said. Then he took the gun from Aomame, pulled out the magazine, carefully loaded it with seven bullets, and shoved it back into the gun with a loud click. Pulling back the slide, he sent a bullet into the chamber. Then he pushed down a lever on the left side of the gun to set the safety.

"Now do the same thing you did before. Only, this time it's loaded with real bullets. There's one in the chamber, too. The safety is on, but you still shouldn't point the muzzle of the gun toward anyone," Tamaru said.

Taking the loaded gun, Aomame found it noticeably heavier than before. Now it had the unmistakable feel of death. This was a precision tool designed to kill people. She could feel her armpits sweating.

Checking once more to make sure the safety was on, she opened the catch, pulled out the magazine, and set it on the table. Pulling back the slide, she ejected the bullet from the chamber. It fell on the wooden floor with a dry thump. She pulled the trigger to close the slide, and pulled the trigger one more time, lowering the hammer. Then, with a trembling hand, she picked up the bullet from where it lay by her feet.

Her throat was dry, and each breath she took was accompanied by a painful burning sensation.

"Not bad for your first time," Tamaru said, pressing the fallen 9mm bullet back into the magazine. "But you need a lot more practice. Your hands are shaking. You should practice the movements for ejecting and reinserting the magazine several times a day until your hands learn the feel of the gun. You should be able to do it as quickly and automatically as I did. In the dark. In your case, you shouldn't have to change magazines in mid-use, but the movements themselves are the most basic of the basic for people who handle pistols. You have to memorize them."

"Don't I need to practice firing?"

"Well, it's not as if you're going to shoot somebody with this. You're just going to shoot yourself, right?"

Aomame nodded.

"In that case, you don't have to practice firing. You just have to learn to load it, release the safety, and get the feel of the trigger. And anyway, where were you planning to practice firing it?"

Aomame shook her head. She had no idea.

"Also, *how* were you planning to shoot yourself? Here, give it a try."

Tamaru inserted the loaded magazine, checked to make sure the safety was on, and handed the gun to Aomame. "The safety is on," he said.

Aomame pressed the muzzle against her temple. She felt the chill of the steel. Looking at her, Tamaru slowly shook his head several times.

"Trust me, you *don't* want to aim at your temple. It's a lot harder than you think to shoot yourself in the brain that way. People's hands usually shake, and it throws their aim off. You end up grazing your skull, but not killing yourself. You certainly don't want that to happen."

Aomame silently shook her head.

"Look what happened to General Tojo after the war. When the American military came to arrest him, he tried to shoot himself in the heart by pressing the muzzle against his chest and pulling the trigger, but the bullet missed and hit his stomach without killing him. Here you had the top professional soldier in Japan, and to think he didn't know how to kill himself with a gun! They took him straight to the hospital, he got the best care the American medical team could give him, recovered, then was tried and hanged. It's a terrible way to die. A person's last moments are an important thing. You can't choose how you're born, but you can choose how you die."

Aomame bit her lip.

"The surest way is to shove the gun barrel in your mouth and blow your brains out from below. Like this."

Tamaru took the gun from Aomame to demonstrate. She knew that the safety was on, but the sight still made her tense up. She could hardly breathe, as if something were stuck in her throat.

"But even this isn't one hundred percent certain. I actually know a guy who failed to kill himself and ended up in terrible shape. We were together in the Self-Defense Force. He shoved a rifle barrel in his mouth and fired the gun by pressing his big toes against a spoon he had fastened to the trigger. I suppose the barrel must have moved a little. Instead of dying, he became a vegetable. He lived that way for another ten years. It's not so easy for people to end their own lives. It's not like in the movies. There, they do it like nothing, no pain, and it's all over, they're dead. The reality is not like that. You lie in bed for ten years with the piss oozing out of you."

Aomame nodded in silence.

Tamaru took the bullets out of the magazine and gun and put them in a plastic bag. Then he handed Aomame the gun and the bullets separately. "Now it's not loaded."

Aomame took them with a nod.

"Trust me, the smart thing is to think about surviving. It's the most practical thing, too. That's my advice to you."

"I see," Aomame said drily. Then she wrapped a scarf around the Heckler & Koch HK4, which was like a crude machine too, and thrust it to the bottom of her shoulder bag. This made the bag a pound or so heavier, but it didn't change its shape. The HK4 was a small pistol.

"It's not a gun for amateurs," Tamaru said. "Speaking from experience, not much good can come of it. But you should be able to handle it all right. You're like me in some ways. In a pinch, you can put the rules ahead of yourself."

"Probably because the 'self' doesn't really exist."

Tamaru had nothing to say to that.

"You were in the Self-Defense Force?" Aomame asked.

"Yeah, in the toughest unit. They fed us rats and snakes and locusts. They're not inedible, but they sure don't taste good."

"What did you do after that?"

"All kinds of stuff. Security work, mainly as a bodyguard – though maybe that's too fancy a word for what I was doing in some cases. I'm not much of a team player, so I tend to work alone. I was involved in the underworld, too, for a little while, when that was the only thing I could find. I saw a lot of stuff going down – things that most people never have to see in their lifetimes. Still, I never got into the worst of the worst. I was always careful not to cross the line. I'm careful by nature, and I don't think much of the yakuza. So, like I said before, my record is clean. After that, I came here." Tamaru pointed straight down. "My life has been very settled ever since. Not that a stable life is all I'm looking for, but I'd like to try to keep things as they are for now. It isn't easy finding jobs you like."

"No, of course not," Aomame said. "But really, shouldn't I pay you something for this?"

Tamaru shook his head. "No, I don't want your money. The

world moves less by money than by what you owe people and what they owe you. I don't like to owe anybody anything, so I keep myself as much on the lending side as I can."

"Thank you," Aomame said.

"If, by any chance, the cops end up grilling you about where you got the gun, I don't want you giving them my name. And if they do come here, I'll deny everything, of course. They'll never find out anything about my past. If they go after Madame, though, I won't have a leg to stand on."

"I won't give your name, of course."

Tamaru pulled a folded piece of notepaper from his pocket and handed it to Aomame. On it was written a man's name.

Tamaru said, "On July 4, you met this man at the Renoir Café near Sendagaya Station. He gave you the gun and seven bullets, and you paid him five hundred thousand yen in cash. He contacted you after he heard that you were looking for a gun. If he is questioned by police, he is supposed to freely admit to the charges and spend a few years in prison. You don't have to tell them any more than that. As long as they can establish how the gun got into your hands, the police will come off looking good. And you might spend a little while behind bars too, for violating the Firearm and Sword Possession Control Law."

Aomame memorized the name and handed the slip of paper back to Tamaru. He tore it into little pieces and threw it into the wastebasket. Then he said, "Like I said before, I'm very careful by nature. I almost never depend on anybody for anything, and even when I do, I still don't trust them. I never leave things to work themselves out. But what I'm most hoping for in this case is that the gun will come back to me unused. Then no one gets in trouble, no one dies, no one gets hurt, and no one goes to prison."

Aomame nodded. "Meaning, you want me to violate Chekhov's rule."

"Exactly. Chekhov was a great writer, but not all novels have to follow his rules. Not all guns in stories have to be fired," Tamaru said. Then he frowned slightly, as if recalling something. "Oh, yes, I almost forgot something important. I have to give you a pager."

He took a small device from his drawer and set it on the desk. It had a metal clip to attach to clothing or a belt. Tamaru picked up the phone and punched in a three-digit quick-dial code. The phone rang three times, and the pager responded by emitting a series of electronic beeps. After turning up the volume as high as it would go, Tamaru pressed a switch to turn it off. He squinted at the device to make sure it displayed the caller's number, and then handed it to Aomame.

"I'd like you to keep this on you at all times if possible," Tamaru said, "or at least don't get too far away from it. If it rings, that means you have a message from me. An important message. I won't signal you to talk about the weather. Call the number you see in the display. Right away. From a public phone. And one other thing: if you have luggage, put it in a coin locker in Shinjuku Station."

"Shinjuku Station," Aomame repeated.

"It goes without saying that you should be ready to travel light."

"Of course."

Back at her apartment, Aomame closed her curtains and took the Heckler & Koch HK4 and the bullets from her shoulder bag. Sitting at the kitchen table, she practiced ejecting and inserting the empty magazine a few times. Her speed increased with each repetition. Her movements developed a rhythm, and her hands stopped trembling. Then she wrapped the pistol in an old T-shirt and hid it in a shoe box, which she shoved to the back of the closet. The bag of bullets she stored inside the pocket of a raincoat on a hanger. Suddenly very thirsty, she took a pitcher of chilled barley tea from the refrigerator and drank three glassfuls. Her shoulder muscles were tense and stiff, and the sweat of her armpits had an unusual smell. The awareness that she now possessed a pistol was enough to make the world look a little different. Her surroundings had taken on a strange, unfamiliar coloration.

She undressed and took a hot shower to wash off the unpleasant sweat smell. *Not all guns have to be fired,* she told herself in the shower. *A pistol is just a tool, and where I'm living is not a storybook world. It's the real world, full of gaps and inconsistencies and anticlimaxes.*

Two weeks passed uneventfully. Aomame went to work at the sports club as usual, teaching her martial arts and stretching classes. She was not supposed to change her daily pattern. She followed the dowager's instructions as strictly as possible. Coming home, she would eat dinner alone. Afterward, she would close the curtains, sit at the kitchen table, and practice handling the Heckler & Koch HK4 until its weight and hardness, the smell of its machine oil, its brute force and quietness all became a part of her.

Sometimes she practiced blindfolded, using a scarf. Soon she could nimbly load the magazine, release the safety, and pull back the slide without seeing a thing. The terse, rhythmical sound produced by each operation was pleasing to her ears. In the dark, she gradually lost track of the difference between the sounds the implement actually made and her aural perception of the sounds. The boundary between herself and her actions gradually faded until it disappeared entirely.

At least once a day she would stand in front of the bathroom mirror and put the muzzle of the loaded gun in her mouth. Feeling the hardness of the metal against the edges of her teeth, she imagined herself pulling the trigger. That was all it would take to end her life. In the next instant, she would have vanished from this world. To the self she saw standing in the mirror, she said, *A few important points: not to let my hand shake; to brace for the recoil; not to be afraid; and, most important, not to hesitate.*

I could do it now if I wanted to, Aomame thought. *I'd just have to pull my finger inward half an inch. It would be so easy. Why don't I just go ahead and do it?* But she reconsidered and took the pistol from her mouth, returned the hammer to its uncocked position, set the safety, and laid the gun down by the sink between the toothpaste tube and her hairbrush. *No, it's too soon for that. There's something I have to do first.*

As instructed by Tamaru, Aomame kept the pager with her at all times. She set it next to the alarm clock when she slept. She was ready to deal with it whenever it rang, but another week went by in silence.

The pistol in the shoe box, the seven bullets in the raincoat pocket, the silent pager, her handmade ice pick, its deadly point, the suitcase packed with her personal effects; the new face and the new life that must be awaiting her; the bundle of bills in a Shinjuku Station coin locker: Aomame spent the midsummer days in their presence. More and more people went off on full-fledged summer vacations. Shops closed their shutters. The streets had fewer passersby. The number of cars declined, and a hush fell over the city. She sometimes felt she was on the verge of losing track of her location. *Is this actually the real world?* she asked herself. *If it's not, then where should I look for reality?* She had no idea where else to look, and so she had no choice for now but to recognize this as the one and only reality and to use all her strength to ride it out.

I'm not afraid to die, Aomame reassured herself. *What I'm afraid of is having reality get the better of me, of having reality leave me behind.*

She had gotten everything ready. She was emotionally prepared as well. She could leave her apartment at any time, as soon as Tamaru contacted her. But she heard nothing from him. The end of August was approaching. Soon summer would begin to wind down, and the cicadas outside would wring out their final cries. How could a whole month have shot by like this even though each day felt horribly long?

Aomame came home from work at the sports club, threw her sweat-soaked clothes into the hamper, and changed into a tank top and shorts. A violent downpour broke out after noon. The sky turned dark. Pebble-sized raindrops smacked down on the streets, and thunder rumbled. The streets were left soaking wet, but then the sun came out again and used all its energy to evaporate the standing water, shrouding the city in a shimmering curtain of steam. Clouds appeared as the sun was going down, covering the sky in a thick veil and hiding the moons.

She felt the need to relax a bit before preparing her supper. Drinking a cold cup of barley tea and nibbling on some edamame she had steamed earlier, she spread the evening paper on the kitchen table and proceeded to skim it in order, first page to last. Nothing piqued her interest. It was just an ordinary evening paper. When she opened to the human interest pages, however, the first thing to attract her attention was a photo of Ayumi. Aomame caught her breath and frowned.

No, it can't be Ayumi, she thought at first. Aomame assumed she must be mistaken: it was someone who looked a lot like her young policewoman friend. Ayumi would never be so prominently featured in the newspaper, complete with a photo. The more she looked, though, the more certain she became that this was her erstwhile partner in those little sex feasts. In the close-up photo, Ayumi had the hint of a smile on her face – an artificial, uncomfortable smile. The real Ayumi always smiled in a natural, open way with her whole face. This photo looked like one that had been taken for some kind of public album. There was something unnerving in her apparent discomfort.

Aomame did not want to read the article, if possible. If she read the big headline next to the picture, she would be able to guess what had happened. But not reading the article was out of the question. This was reality. Whatever it might be, she could not pass reality by. Aomame took a deep breath and started reading.

Ayumi Nakano (26). Single. Resident of Shinjuku Ward, Tokyo.

The article reported that Ayumi had been found dead in a Shibuya hotel room. She had been strangled with a bathrobe sash. Stark naked, she was handcuffed to the bed, a piece of clothing stuffed in her mouth. A hotel staff person had found the body when inspecting the room before noon. Ayumi and a man had taken the room before eleven o'clock the night before, and the man had left alone at dawn. The charges had been paid in advance. This was not a terribly unusual occurrence in the big city, where the commingling of people gave off heat, often in the form of violence. The newspapers were full of such events. This one, however, had unusual aspects. The victim was a policewoman, and the handcuffs that appeared to have been used as a sex toy were the authentic government-issue type, not the cheap kind sold in porno shops. Quite naturally, this was news that attracted people's attention.

CHAPTER 4

Tengo

IT MIGHT BE BETTER
NOT TO WISH FOR SUCH A THING

*Where is she now, and what could she be doing? Does she still
belong to the Society of Witnesses?*

I sure hope not, Tengo thought. Of course, religious faith was
a matter of individual freedom. He shouldn't be weighing in
on it. But as he recalled, she gave no indication as a young girl
that she enjoyed being a believer in the Society of Witnesses.

In college, Tengo worked part-time in a liquor wholesaler's warehouse. The pay wasn't bad, but moving heavy cases
around was hard work, even for the sturdy Tengo, whose
every joint would ache at the end of the day. By coincidence,
two young fellows who had grown up as "second-generation"
members of the Society of Witnesses worked alongside him.
Both were polite young men, nice guys. They were the same
age as Tengo, and serious workers. They worked without complaint and without cutting corners. Once after work the three
of them went to a bar and had a pint of beer together. The
two of them had been friends since childhood, they said, but a
few years earlier they had abandoned the faith. On separating
from the religion, they had set foot in the real world. As far as
Tengo could see, however, neither of them had fully adapted
to their new world. Because they had been raised in a narrow,
close-knit community, they found it hard to understand and

accept the rules of the broader world. Often they would lose what confidence they had in their own judgments and end up perplexed. They felt liberated by their abandonment of the faith, but they simultaneously retained a nagging suspicion that their decision had been a mistake.

Tengo could not help but sympathize with them. If they had separated from that world while they were still children, before their egos had been firmly established, they would have had a much better chance of adapting to the social mainstream, but once they missed that chance, they had no choice but to live in the Witness community, conforming with its values. Or else, with considerable sacrifice, and depending entirely on their own strength, they had to remake their customs and attitudes from the ground up. When he spoke with them, Tengo would recall the girl and hope that she had not experienced the same pain as these two young men.

After the girl finally let go of his hand and dashed out of the classroom without looking back, Tengo could only stand there, unable to do a thing. She had gripped his left hand with considerable strength, and a vivid sense of her touch remained in that hand for several days. Even after more time went by and the direct sensation began to fade, his heart retained the deep impression she had made there.

Shortly after that, Tengo experienced his first ejaculation. A very small amount of liquid emerged from the tip of his erect penis. It was somewhat thicker than urine and was accompanied by a faintly painful throbbing. Tengo did not realize that this was the precursor of full-fledged semen. He had never seen such a thing before, and it worried him. Something scary might be happening to him. It was not something he could discuss with his father, however, nor could he ask his classmates about it. That night, he woke from a dream (the contents of which he could not remember) to find his underpants slightly damp. It seemed to Tengo as if, by squeezing his hand, the girl had drawn something out of him.

He had no contact with her after that. Aomame maintained the same isolated position in the class, spoke with no one, and recited the usual prayer before lunch in the same clear voice. Even if they happened to pass each other somewhere, her expression exhibited not the slightest change, as if there had been nothing between them – as if she had not even seen Tengo.

Tengo, for his part, took to observing Aomame closely and covertly whenever he had the chance. He realized now, on closer inspection, that she had a nice face – nice enough for him to feel he could like her. She was long and thin, and she always wore faded clothing that was too big for her. When she put on gym clothes, he could tell that her chest had not yet begun to develop. Her face displayed virtually no expression, she hardly ever talked, and her eyes, which always seemed to be focused on something far away, had no sign of life in them. Tengo found this strange, because, on that day when her eyes had looked straight into his, they had been so clear and luminous.

After she squeezed his hand like that, Tengo came to see that this skinny little girl was far tougher inside than the average person. Her grip itself was impressive, but it was more than that. She seemed to possess an even greater strength of mind. Ordinarily she kept this energy hidden where the other students couldn't see it. When the teacher called on her in class, she would say no more than minimally necessary to answer the question (and sometimes not even that much), but her posted test scores were never bad. Tengo guessed that she could earn still better grades if she wanted to, but she might be deliberately holding back on exams so as not to attract attention. Perhaps this was the wisdom with which a child in her position survived: by minimizing her wounds – staying as small as possible, as nearly transparent as possible.

How great it would be, Tengo thought, if only she were a totally ordinary girl with whom he could have a lighthearted conversation! Maybe they could have been good friends. For a ten-year-old boy and girl to become good friends was not easy under any circumstances. Indeed, it might be one of the most difficult accomplishments in the world. But while they ought to have managed the occasional friendly chat, such an opportunity never presented itself to Tengo and Aomame. So rather than make the effort to forge a real relationship with the flesh-and-blood Aomame, Tengo chose to relate to her through the silent realm of imagination and memory.

The ten-year-old Tengo had no concrete image of sex. All he wanted from the girl was for her to hold his hand again if possible. He wanted her to squeeze his hand again someplace where the two of them could be alone. And he wanted her to tell him something – anything – about herself, to whisper some secret about what it meant to be Aomame, what it meant to be a ten-year-old girl. He would try hard to understand it, and that would be the beginning of something, though even now, Tengo still had no idea what that "something" might be.

April came, and the new school year began. Now they were fifth graders, but Tengo and the girl were put into separate classes. Sometimes they would pass each other in the hall or wait at the same bus stop, but the girl continued to act as if she were unaware of Tengo's existence – or at least it appeared that way to Tengo. He could be right next to her and she wouldn't move an eyebrow. She wouldn't even bother to look away from him. As before, all depth and brightness were gone from her eyes. Tengo wondered what that incident in the classroom could have meant. Often it seemed to him like something that had happened in a dream. And yet his hand still retained the vivid feel of Aomame's extraordinary grip. This world was far too full of riddles for Tengo.

Then at some point he realized that the girl named Aomame was no longer in school. She had transferred to another school, but that was all he found out. No one knew where she had moved to. He was probably the only one in the entire elementary school even slightly bothered by the fact that she had ceased to exist among them.

For a very long time after that, Tengo continued to regret his actions – or, more precisely, his *lack* of action. Now, finally, he could think of the words that he should have spoken to her. Inside him at last were the things that he wanted to tell her, the things he should have told her. It would not have been so hard. He should have stopped her on the street and said something. If only he had found a good opportunity and whipped up a tiny bit of courage! But that had been impossible for Tengo. And now the chance was lost forever.

Tengo often thought about Aomame after he graduated from the elementary school and advanced to a public middle school. He started having erections more often and masturbated while thinking of her. He always used his left hand – the hand that retained the touch of her grasp. In his memory, Aomame remained a skinny little girl without breasts, but he was able to bring himself to ejaculation with the thought of her in gym clothes.

In high school, he started dating girls his own age. Their brand-new breasts showed clearly through their clothes, and the sight made it hard for Tengo to breathe. But even so, in bed, before he fell asleep at night, Tengo would move his left hand while thinking of Aomame's flat chest, which lacked even a hint of swelling. There must be something wrong with him, something perverted, Tengo thought.

Once he entered college, though, Tengo no longer thought about Aomame all the time. The main reason for this was that he started dating real women, actually having sex with some of them. Physically, at least, he was a mature man, for whom the image of a skinny little ten-year-old girl in gym clothes had, naturally enough, grown removed from the objects of his desire.

Still, Tengo never again experienced the same intense shuddering of the heart that he had felt when Aomame gripped his hand in the elementary school classroom. None of the women he met in college or after leaving college to the present day made as distinct an impression on his heart as Aomame. He could not find what he was really looking for in any of them. There had been beautiful ones and warmhearted ones and ones who truly cared for him, but they had come and gone, like vividly colored birds perching momentarily on a branch before flying off somewhere. They could not satisfy him, and he could not satisfy them.

Even now, on the verge of turning thirty, Tengo was surprised to find his thoughts drifting back to the ten-year-old Aomame. There she was, in the deserted classroom, staring straight at him with her crystal-clear eyes, her hand tightly gripping his. Sometimes her skinny frame was draped in gym clothes. Or she was walking behind her mother down the Ichikawa shopping mall on a Sunday morning, her lips clamped shut, her eyes staring at a place that was no place.

At such times, Tengo would think, *I guess I'll never be able to detach myself from her.* And he would kick himself again, now that it was too late, for never having spoken to her in the hallway. *If only I had made myself do it! If only I had said something to her, my life might be very different.*

What reminded him of Aomame was buying edamame in the supermarket. He was choosing among the branches of fresh edamame in the refrigerator case when the thought of Aomame came to him quite naturally. Before he knew it, he was standing there, lost in a daydream. How long this went on, he had no idea, but a woman's voice saying, "Excuse me" brought him back. He was blocking access to the edamame section with his large frame.

Tengo stopped daydreaming, apologized to the woman, dropped the edamame branch into his shopping basket, and brought it to the cashier along with his other groceries – shrimp, milk, tofu, lettuce, and crackers. There, he waited in line with the housewives of the neighborhood. It was the crowded evening shopping hour and the cashier was a slow-moving trainee, which made for a long line, but this didn't bother Tengo.

Assuming she was in this line at the cash register, would I know it was Aomame just by looking at her? I wonder. We haven't seen each other in twenty years. The possibility of our recognizing each other must be pretty slim. Or, say we pass on the street and I think, "Could that be Aomame?," would I be able to call out to her on the spot? I can't be sure of that, either. I might just lose heart and let her go without doing a thing. And then I'd be filled with regret again – "Why couldn't I have said something to her – just one word?"

Komatsu often said to Tengo, "What's missing in you is desire and a positive attitude." And maybe he was right. When Tengo had trouble making up his mind, he would think, *Oh well*, and resign himself. That was his nature.

But if, by chance, we were to come face-to-face and were fortunate enough to recognize each other, I would probably open up and tell her everything honestly. We'd go into some nearby café (assuming she had the time and accepted my invitation) and sit across from each other, drinking something, while I told her everything.

There were so many things he wanted to tell her! "I still remember when you squeezed my hand in that classroom. After that, I wanted to be your friend. I wanted to get to know you better. But I just couldn't do it. There were lots of reasons for that, but the main problem was that I was a coward. I regretted it for years. I still regret it. And I think of you all the time." Of course he would not tell her that he had masturbated while picturing her. That would be in a whole different dimension than sheer honesty.

It might be better not to wish for such a thing, though. It might be better never to see her again. *I might be disappointed if I actually met her,* Tengo thought. Maybe she had turned into some boring, tired-looking office worker. Maybe she had become a frustrated mother shrieking at her kids. Maybe the two of them would have nothing in common to talk about. Yes, that was a very real possibility. Then Tengo would lose something precious that he had cherished all these years. It would be gone forever. But no, Tengo felt almost certain it wouldn't be like that. In that ten-year-old girl's resolute eyes and strong-willed profile he had discovered a decisiveness that time could not have worn down.

By comparison, what about Tengo himself?

Such thoughts made him uneasy.

Wasn't Aomame the one who would be disappointed if they met again? In elementary school, Tengo had been recognized by everyone as a math prodigy and received the top grades in almost every subject. He was also an outstanding athlete. Even the teachers treated him with respect and expected great things from him in the future. Aomame might have idolized him. Now, though, he was just a part-time cram school instructor. True, it was an easy job that put no constraints on his solitary lifestyle, but he was far from being a pillar of society. While teaching at the cram school, he wrote fiction on the side, but he was still unpublished. For extra income, he wrote a made-up astrology column for a women's magazine. It was popular, but it was, quite simply, a pack of lies. He had no friends worth mentioning, nor anyone he was in love with. His weekly trysts with a married woman ten years his senior were virtually his sole human contact. So far, the only accomplishment of which he could be proud was his role as the ghostwriter who turned *Air Chrysalis* into a bestseller, but that was something he could never mention to anyone.

Tengo's thoughts had reached this point when the cashier picked up his grocery basket.

He went back to his apartment with a bag of groceries in his arms. Changing into shorts, he took a cold can of beer from the refrigerator and drank it, standing, while he heated a large pot of water. Before the water boiled, he stripped all the leathery edamame pods from the branch, spread them on a cutting board, and rubbed them all over with salt. When the water boiled, he threw them into the pot.

Tengo wondered, *Why has that skinny little ten-year-old girl stayed in my heart all these years? She came over to me after class and squeezed my hand without saying a word. That was all.* But in that time, Aomame seemed to have taken part of him with her – part of his heart or body. And in its place, she had left part of her heart or body inside him. This important exchange had taken place in a matter of seconds.

Tengo chopped a lot of ginger to a fine consistency. Then he sliced some celery and mushrooms into nice-sized pieces. The Chinese parsley, too, he chopped up finely. He peeled the shrimp and washed them at the sink. Spreading a paper towel, he laid the shrimp out in neat rows, like troops in formation. When the edamame were finished boiling, he drained them in a colander and left them to cool. Next he warmed a large frying pan and dribbled in some sesame oil and spread it over the bottom. He slowly fried the chopped ginger over a low flame.

I wish I could meet Aomame right now, Tengo started thinking again. Even if she turned out to be disappointed in him or he was a little disappointed in her, he didn't care. He wanted to see her in any case. All he wanted was to find out what kind of life she had led since then, what kind of place she was in now, what kinds of things gave her joy, and what kinds of things made her sad. No matter how much the two of them had changed, or whether all possibility of their getting together had already been lost, this in no way altered the fact that they had exchanged something important in that empty elementary school classroom so long ago.

He put the sliced celery and mushrooms into the frying pan. Turning the gas flame up to high and lightly jogging the pan, he carefully stirred the contents with a bamboo spatula, adding a sprinkle of salt and pepper. When the vegetables were just beginning to cook, he tossed the drained shrimp into the pan. After adding another dose of salt and pepper to the whole thing, he poured in a small glass of sake. Then a dash of soy sauce and finally a scattering of Chinese parsley. Tengo performed all these operations on automatic pilot. This was not a dish that required complicated procedures: his hands moved on their own with precision, but his mind stayed focused on Aomame the whole time.

When the stir-fried shrimp and vegetables were ready, Tengo transferred the food from the frying pan to a large platter along with the edamame. He took a fresh beer from the refrigerator, sat at the kitchen table, and, still lost in thought, proceeded to eat the steaming food.

I've obviously been changing a lot over the past several months. Maybe you could say I'm growing up mentally and emotionally . . . at last . . . on the verge of turning thirty. Well, isn't that something! With his partially drunk beer in hand, Tengo shook his head in self-derision. *Really, isn't that something! How many years will it take me to reach full maturity at this rate?*

In any case, though, it seemed clear that *Air Chrysalis* had been the catalyst for the changes going on inside him. The act of rewriting Fuka-Eri's story in his own words had produced in Tengo a strong new desire to give literary form to the story inside himself. And part of that strong new desire was a need for Aomame. Something was making him think about Aomame all the time now. At every opportunity, his thoughts would be drawn back to that classroom on an afternoon twenty years earlier the way a strong riptide could sweep the feet out from under a person standing on the shore.

Tengo drank only half his beer and ate only half his shrimp and vegetables. He poured the leftover beer into the sink, and the food he transferred to a small plate, covered it with plastic wrap, and put it in the refrigerator.

After the meal, Tengo sat at his desk, switched on his word processor, and opened his partially written document.

True, rewriting the past probably had almost no meaning, Tengo felt. His older girlfriend had been right about that. No matter how passionately or minutely he might attempt to rewrite the past, the present circumstances in which he found himself would remain generally unchanged. Time had the power to cancel all changes wrought by human artifice, overwriting all new revisions with further revisions, returning the flow to its original course. A few minor facts might be changed, but Tengo would still be Tengo.

What Tengo would have to do, it seemed, was take a hard, honest look at the past while standing at the crossroads of the present. Then he could create a future, as though he were rewriting the past. It was the only way.

> Contrition and repentance
> Tear the sinful heart in two.
> O that my teardrops may be
> A sweet balm unto thee,
> Faithful Jesus.

This was the meaning of the aria from the *St. Matthew Passion* that Fuka-Eri had sung the other day. He had wondered about it and listened again to his recording at home, looking up the words in translation. It was an aria near the beginning of the *Passion* concerned with the so-called Anointing in Bethany. When Jesus visits the home of a leper in the town of Bethany, a woman pours "very costly fragrant oil" on his head. The disciples around him scold her for wasting the precious ointment, saying that she could have sold it and used the money to help the poor. But Jesus quiets the angry disciples and says that the woman has done a good deed. "For in pouring this fragrant oil on my body, she did it for my burial."

The woman knew that Jesus would have to die soon. And so, as though bathing him in her tears, she could do no less than pour the valuable, fragrant oil on his head. Jesus also knew that he would soon have to tread the road to death, and he told his disciples, "Wherever this gospel is preached in the whole world, what this woman has done will also be told as a memorial to her."

None of them, of course, was able to change the future.

Tengo closed his eyes again, took a deep breath, found the words he needed and set them in a row. Then he rearranged them to give the image greater clarity and precision. Finally, he improved the rhythm.

Like Vladimir Horowitz seated before eighty-eight brand-new keys, Tengo curved his ten fingers suspended in space. Then, when he was ready, he began typing characters to fill the word processor's screen.

He depicted a world in which two moons hung side by side in the evening eastern sky, the people living in that world, and the time flowing through it.

"Wherever this gospel is preached in the whole world, what this woman has done will also be told as a memorial to her."

CHAPTER 5

Aomame

THE VEGETARIAN CAT
MEETS UP WITH THE RAT

Once she had managed to comprehend the sheer fact that Ayumi had died, Aomame went through a brief period involving a certain process of mental adjustment. Eventually, when the first phase of the process ended, she began to cry. She cried quietly, even silently, burying her face in her hands, her shoulders quivering, as if she wanted to be sure that no one else in the world could tell that she was crying.

The window curtains were shut tight, but still, someone might be watching. That night Aomame spread the newspaper on the kitchen table, and, in its presence, she cried without interruption. Now and then a sob escaped her, but the rest of the time she cried soundlessly. Her tears ran down her hands and onto the paper.

Aomame did not cry easily in this world. Whenever she felt like crying, she would instead become angry – at someone else or at herself – which meant that it was rare for her to shed tears. Once they started pouring out of her, though, she couldn't stop them. She hadn't had such a long cry since Tamaki Otsuka killed herself. How many years ago had that been? She could not remember. In any case, it had been a *long* time before, and she had cried forever. It went on for days. She ate nothing the whole time, and stayed shut up indoors. Now and then she would replenish the water that she had cried out in tears, and then she would collapse and doze. That was all. The rest of the time she went on weeping. That was the last time she did anything like this.

Ayumi was no longer in this world. She was now a cold corpse that was probably being sent for forensic dissection. When that ended, they would sew her back together, probably give her a simple funeral, send her to the crematorium, and burn her. She would turn into smoke, rise up into the sky, and mix with the clouds. Then she would come down to the earth again as rain, and nurture some nameless patch of grass with no story to tell. But Aomame would never see Ayumi alive again. This seemed warped and misguided, in opposition to the flow of nature, and horribly unfair.

Ayumi was the only person for whom Aomame had been able to feel anything like friendship since Tamaki Otsuka left the world. Unfortunately, however, there had been limits to her friendship. Ayumi was an active-duty police officer, and Aomame a serial murderer. True, she was a murderer motivated by conviction and conscience, but a murderer is, in the end, a murderer, a criminal in the eyes of the law.

For this reason, Aomame had to make an effort to harden her heart and not respond when Ayumi sought to deepen their ties. Ayumi must have realized this to some extent – that Aomame had some kind of personal secret or secrets that caused her deliberately to put a certain distance between them. Ayumi had excellent intuition. At least half of her easy openness was an act, behind which lurked a soft and sensitive vulnerability. Aomame knew this to be true. Her own defensiveness had probably saddened Ayumi, making her feel rejected and distanced. The thought was like a needle stabbing Aomame in the chest.

And so Ayumi had been murdered. She had probably met a man in the city, had drinks with him, and gone to the hotel.

Then, in the dark, sealed room, their elaborate sex game had begun. Handcuffs, a gag, a blindfold. Aomame could picture the scene. The man tightened the sash of his bathrobe around the woman's neck, and as he watched her writhe in agony, his excitement mounted until he ejaculated. But the man tightened the sash with too much force. What was supposed to have ended at the point of crisis did not end.

Ayumi must have feared that such a thing might happen. She needed intense sexual activity at regular intervals. Her flesh needed it – and so, perhaps, did her mind. Like Aomame, she did not want a regular lover. But Ayumi tended to wade in deeper than Aomame. She preferred wilder, riskier sex, and perhaps, unconsciously, she wanted to be hurt. Aomame was different. She was more cautious, and she refused to be hurt by anyone. She would fiercely resist if a man tried such a thing; but Ayumi tended to respond to a man's desire, whatever it might be, and she looked forward to finding out what he would give her in return. It was a dangerous tendency. These sexual partners of hers were, ultimately, passing strangers. It was impossible to find out what desires they possessed, what tendencies they were hiding, until the critical moment. Ayumi herself recognized the danger, of course, which was why she needed a stable partner like Aomame – someone to put on the brakes and watch over her with care.

In her own way, Aomame, too, needed Ayumi, who possessed abilities that she herself happened to lack – an open, cheerful personality that put people at ease, a friendly manner, a natural curiosity, a positive attitude, a talent for interesting conversation, large breasts that attracted attention. All Aomame had to do was stay next to Ayumi with a mysterious smile on her face. The men would want to find out what lay behind that smile. In that sense, Aomame and Ayumi were an ideal team – an invincible sex machine.

I should have been more open and accepting with that girl,

Aomame thought. *I should have reciprocated her feelings and held her tight. That was the one thing she was hoping for – to be accepted and embraced unconditionally, to be comforted by someone, if only for a moment. But I could not respond to her need. My instinct for self-preservation is too strong, and so is my determination to keep Tamaki Otsuka's memory unsullied.*

So Ayumi went out to the city at night alone, without Aomame, to be strangled to death, shackled by the cold steel of genuine handcuffs, blindfolded, her stockings or underwear stuffed in her mouth. The thing that Ayumi had always feared had become a reality. If Aomame had accepted her more willingly, Ayumi would probably not have gone out that night. She would have called and asked Aomame to go with her. They would have gone to a safer place, and checked on each other as they lay in their men's arms. But Ayumi had probably been hesitant to impose on Aomame. And Aomame had never once called Ayumi to suggest an outing.

It was nearly four o'clock in the morning when Aomame found that she could no longer bear to stay alone in her apartment. She stepped into a pair of sandals and went out, walking aimlessly through the predawn streets, wearing only shorts and a tank top. Someone called out to her, but she kept walking straight ahead. She walked until she was thirsty. Then she stopped by an all-night convenience store, bought a large carton of orange juice, and drank it on the spot. Then she went back to her apartment to cry. *I loved Ayumi,* she thought, *even more than I realized. If she wanted to touch me, I should have let her touch me anywhere she liked, as much as she liked.*

The next day's paper carried another report, under the heading "Policewoman Strangled in Shibuya Hotel." The police were doing everything in their power to catch the man, it said, and the woman's fellow officers were utterly perplexed. Ayumi was a cheerful person who was well liked by everyone, a responsible and energetic individual who had always earned high marks for her police work. Several of her relatives, including her father and brother, were also police officers, and their family ties were strong. All were puzzled as to how such a thing could have happened to her.

None of them know, Aomame thought. *But I know. Ayumi had a great emptiness inside her, like a desert at the edge of the earth. You could try watering it all you wanted, but everything would be sucked down to the bottom of the world, leaving no trace of moisture. No life could take root there. Not even birds would fly over it. What had created such a wasteland inside Ayumi, only she herself knew. No, maybe not even Ayumi knew the true cause. But one of the biggest factors had to be the twisted sexual desires that the men around Ayumi had forced upon her. As if to build a fence around the fatal emptiness inside her, she had to create the sunny person that she became. But if you peeled away the ornamental egos that she had built, there was only an abyss of nothingness and the intense thirst that came with it. Though she tried to forget it, the nothingness would visit her periodically – on a lonely rainy afternoon, or at dawn when she woke from a nightmare. What she needed at such times was to be held by someone, anyone.*

Aomame took the Heckler & Koch HK4 from the shoe box, loaded the magazine with practiced movements, released the safety, pulled back the slide, sent a bullet into the chamber, raised the hammer, and aimed the gun at a point on the wall with both hands solidly on the grip. The barrel was rock steady. Her hands no longer trembled. Aomame held her breath, went into a moment of total concentration, and then let out one long breath. Lowering the pistol, she reset the safety and tested the weight of the gun in her hand, staring at its dull gleam. The gun had almost become a part of her body.

I have to keep my emotions in check, Aomame told herself. *Even if I were to punish Ayumi's uncle or brother, they wouldn't know what they were being punished for. And nothing I could do to them now would bring Ayumi back. Poor kid, something like this had to happen sooner or later. Ayumi was on a slow but unavoid-able approach toward the center of a deadly whirlpool. And even if I had been warmer to her, there were probably limits to how much that could have accomplished. It's time for me to stop crying. I'll have to change my attitude again. I'll have to put the rules ahead of my self. That's the important thing, as Tamaru said.*

On the morning of the fifth day after Ayumi died, the pager finally rang. At the time, she was in the kitchen, boiling water to make coffee and listening to the news on the radio. The pager was sitting on the kitchen table. She read the telephone number displayed on the small screen. It was not one she knew. But it had to be a message from Tamaru. She went to a nearby pay phone and dialed the number. Tamaru answered after the third ring.

"All set to go?" Tamaru asked.

"Of course," Aomame answered.

"Here is Madame's message: seven o'clock tonight in the lobby of the Hotel Okura's main building. Dress for work as usual. Sorry for the short notice, but this could only be arranged at the last minute."

"Seven o'clock tonight in the lobby of the Hotel Okura's main building," Aomame repeated mechanically.

"I'd like to wish you luck, but I'm afraid a good luck wish from me won't do any good," Tamaru said.

"Because you don't believe in luck."

"Even if I wanted to, I don't know what it's like," Tamaru said. "I've never seen it."

"That's okay, I don't need good wishes. There's something I'd like you to do for me instead. I have a potted rubber plant in my apartment. I'd like you to take care of it. I couldn't bring myself to throw it out."

"I'll take care of it."

"Thanks."

"A rubber plant's a lot easier to take care of than a cat or a tropical fish. Anything else?"

"Not a thing. Just throw out everything I leave behind."

"When you've finished the job, go to Shinjuku Station and call this number again. I'll give you your next instructions then."

"When I finish the job, I go to Shinjuku Station and call this number again," Aomame repeated.

"I think you know not to write down the telephone number. When you leave home, break the pager and get rid of it somewhere."

"I see. Okay."

"We've lined up everything to the last detail. You don't have to worry about a thing. Just leave the rest to us."

"I won't worry," Aomame said.

Tamaru kept silent for a moment. "Do you want my honest opinion?"

"Sure."

"I don't mean to say that what you two are doing is useless, I really don't. It's your problem, not mine. But I do think that, at the very least, it's reckless. And there's no end to it."

"You may be right," Aomame said. "But it's beyond changing now."

"Like avalanches in the spring."

"Probably."

"But sensible people don't go into avalanche country in avalanche season."

"A sensible person wouldn't be having this conversation with you."

"You may be right," Tamaru had to admit. "Anyhow, are there any relatives we should be contacting in case an avalanche does occur?"

"None at all."

"You mean there aren't any, or they're there but they're not."

"They're there but they're not."

"That's fine," Tamaru said. "It's best to travel light. A rubber plant is just about the ideal family."

"Seeing those goldfish in Madame's house suddenly made me want to have some of my own. They'd be nice to have around. They're little and quiet and probably don't make too many demands. So I went to a shop by my station the next day thinking I was going to buy some, but when I actually saw them in the tank I didn't want them anymore. Instead, I bought this sad little rubber plant, one of the last ones they had."

"I'd say you made the right choice."

"I might never be able to buy goldfish – ever."

"Maybe not," Tamaru said. "You could buy another rubber plant."

A short silence ensued.

"Seven o'clock tonight in the lobby of the Hotel Okura's main building," Aomame said again to reconfirm.

"You just have to sit there. They'll find you."

"They'll find me."

Tamaru cleared his throat. "By the way, do you know the story about the vegetarian cat who met up with the rat?"

"Never heard that one."

"Would you like to?"

"Very much."

"A cat met up with a big male rat in the attic and chased him into a corner. The rat, trembling, said, 'Please don't eat me, Mr. Cat. I have to go back to my family. I have hungry children waiting for me. Please let me go.' The cat said, 'Don't worry, I won't eat you. To tell you the truth, I can't say this too loudly, but I'm a vegetarian. I don't eat any meat. You were lucky to run into me.' The rat said, 'Oh, what a wonderful day! What a lucky rat I am to meet up with a vegetarian cat!' But the very next second, the cat pounced on the rat, held him down with his claws, and sank his sharp teeth into the rat's throat. With his last, painful breath, the rat asked him, 'But Mr. Cat, didn't you say you're a vegetarian and don't eat any meat? Were you lying to me?' The cat licked his chops and said, 'True, I don't eat meat. That was no lie. I'm going to take you home in my mouth and trade you for lettuce.' "

Aomame thought about this for a moment. "What's the point?"

"No point, really. I suddenly remembered the story when we were talking about luck before. That's all. You can take whatever you like from it, of course."

"What a heartwarming story."

"Oh, and another thing. I'm pretty sure they're going to pat you down and search your bag before they let you in. They're a careful bunch. Better keep that in mind."

"I'll keep it in mind."

"All right, then," Tamaru said, "let's meet again somewhere."

"Again somewhere," Aomame repeated by reflex.

Tamaru cut the connection. Aomame looked at the receiver for a moment, grimaced slightly, and put it down. Then, after committing the telephone number displayed on the pager to memory, she deleted it. *Again somewhere,* Aomame repeated to herself. But she knew she would probably never see Tamaru again.

Aomame scoured the morning paper but found nothing on Ayumi's murder. This probably meant that the investigation had turned up nothing new. No doubt all the weekly magazines would be mining the case for every weird angle they could find. A young, active-duty policewoman engages in sex games with handcuffs in a Shibuya love hotel and is strangled, stark naked. Aomame didn't want to read any sensationalistic reports. She had avoided turning on the television ever since it happened, not wanting to hear some female news announcer reporting on Ayumi's death in the usual artificial high-pitched tones.

Of course, she wanted the perpetrator to be caught. He had to be punished, no matter what. But would it make any difference if he were arrested, tried, and all the details of the murder came out? It wouldn't bring Ayumi back, that much was certain. In any case, the sentence would be a light one. It would probably be judged to have been not a homicide but involuntary manslaughter – an accident. Of course, not even a death penalty could make up for what had happened. Aomame closed the paper, rested her elbows on the table, and covered her face with her hands for a while. She thought about Ayumi, but the tears no longer came. Now she was just angry.

She still had a lot of time until seven o'clock in the evening but nothing to do in the meantime, no work at the sports club. Following Tamaru's instructions, she had already deposited her small travel bag and shoulder bag in a coin locker at Shinjuku Station. The travel bag contained a sheaf of bills and enough clothing (including underwear and stockings) for several days. She had been going to Shinjuku once every three days to deposit more coins in the slot and double-check on the contents. She had no need to clean her apartment, and even if she wanted to cook, the refrigerator was nearly empty. Aside from the rubber plant, there was almost nothing left in the room that still had the smell of life. She had gotten rid of everything connected to her personal information. All the drawers were empty. *And as of tomorrow, I won't be here, either. Not a trace of me will be left.*

The clothes she would wear that evening were nicely folded and stacked on the bed. Next to them she had placed a blue gym bag. Inside was a complete set of stretching equipment. She checked the contents of the bag once more for safety's sake:

jersey top and bottom, yoga mat, large and small towels, and small hard case containing the fine-pointed ice pick. Everything was there. She took the ice pick out of the case, pulled off the cork, and touched the point to make sure it was still plenty sharp. To make doubly sure, she gave it a light sharpening with her finest whetstone. She pictured the needle sinking soundlessly into that special point on the back of the man's neck, as if being sucked inside. As usual, everything should end in an instant – no screaming, no bleeding, just a momentary spasm. Aomame thrust the needle back into the cork and carefully returned the ice pick to its case.

Next she pulled the T-shirt-wrapped Heckler & Koch from its shoe box and, with practiced movements, loaded seven 9mm bullets into the magazine. With a dry sound, she sent a cartridge into the chamber. She released the safety catch and set it again. She wrapped the pistol in a white handkerchief and put it in a vinyl pouch. This she hid in a change of underwear.

Now, was there anything else I had to do?

She couldn't think of anything. Standing in the kitchen, Aomame made coffee with the boiled water. Then she sat at the table, drinking it with a croissant.

This may be my last job, Aomame thought. It's also going to be my most important and most difficult job. Once I've finished this assignment, I won't have to kill anyone anymore.

Aomame was not opposed to losing her identity. If anything, she welcomed it. She was not particularly attached to her name or her face and could think of nothing about her past that she would regret losing. *A reset of my life: this may be the one thing I've longed for most.*

Strangely enough, the one thing that Aomame felt she did not want to lose was her rather sad little breasts. From the age of twelve, she had lived with an unwavering dissatisfaction with regard to the shape and size of her breasts. It often occurred to her that she might have been able to live a far more serene life if only her breasts had been a little larger. And yet now, when she was being given a chance to enlarge them (a choice that carried with it a certain necessity), she found that she had absolutely no desire to make the change. They were fine as they were. Indeed, they were just right.

She touched her breasts through her tank top. They were the same breasts as always, shaped like two lumps of dough that had failed to rise – because of a failure to properly combine the ingredients – and subtly different in size. She shook her head. *But never mind. These are me.*

What will be left of me besides these breasts?

Tengo's memory will stay with me, of course. The touch of his hand will stay. My shuddering emotion will stay. The desire to be in his arms will stay. Even if I become a completely different person, my love for Tengo can never be taken from me. That's the biggest difference between Ayumi and me. At my core, there is not nothing. Neither is it a parched wasteland. At my core, there is love. I'll go on loving that ten-year-old boy named Tengo forever – his strength, his intelligence, his kindness. He does not exist here, with me, but flesh that does not exist will never die, and promises unmade are never broken.

The thirty-year-old Tengo inside of Aomame was not the real Tengo. That Tengo was nothing but a hypothesis, as it were, created entirely in Aomame's mind. Tengo still had his strength and intelligence and kindness, and now he was a grown man with thick arms, a broad chest, and big, strong genitals. He could be by her side whenever she wanted him there, holding her tightly, stroking her hair, kissing her. Their room was always dark, and Aomame couldn't see him. All that her eyes could take in was his eyes. Even in the dark, she could see his warm eyes. She could look into them and see the world as he saw it.

Aomame's occasional overwhelming need to sleep with

men came, perhaps, from her wish to keep the Tengo she nur-
tured inside her as unsullied as possible. By engaging in wild
sex with unknown men, what she hoped to accomplish, surely,
was the liberation of her flesh from the desire that bound it.
She wanted to spend time alone with Tengo in the calm, quiet
world that came to her after the liberation, just the two of them
together, undisturbed. Surely that was what Aomame wanted.

Aomame spent several hours that afternoon thinking about
Tengo. She sat on the aluminum chair on her narrow balcony,
looking up at the sky, listening to the roar of the traffic, occasionally holding a leaf of her sad little rubber plant between
her fingers as she thought of him. There was still no moon to
be seen in the afternoon sky. That wouldn't happen for some
hours yet. *Where will I be at this time tomorrow?* Aomame
wondered. *I have no idea. But that's a minor matter compared
with the fact that Tengo exists in this world.*

Aomame gave her rubber plant its last watering, and then
she put Janáček's *Sinfonietta* on the record player. It was the
only record she had kept after getting rid of all the others. She
closed her eyes and listened to the music, imagining the windswept fields of Bohemia. How wonderful it would be to walk
with Tengo in such a place! They would be holding hands, of
course. The breeze would sweep past, soundlessly swaying the
soft green grass. Aomame could feel the warmth of Tengo's
hand in hers. The scene would gradually fade like a movie's
happy ending.

Aomame then lay down on her bed and slept for thirty
minutes, curled up in a ball. She did not dream. It was a sleep
that required no dreaming. When she woke, the hands of the
clock were pointing to four thirty. Using the food still left in
the refrigerator, she made herself some ham and eggs. She
drank orange juice straight from the carton. The silence after
her nap was strangely heavy. She turned on the FM radio to

find Vivaldi's Concerto for Woodwinds playing. The piccolo was trilling away like the chirping of a little bird. To Aomame, this sounded like music intended to emphasize the unreality of her present reality.

After clearing the dishes from the table, Aomame took a shower and changed into the outfit she had prepared weeks ago for this day – simple clothes that made for easy movement: pale blue cotton pants and a white short-sleeved blouse free of ornamentation. She gathered her hair in a bun and put it up, holding it in place with a comb. No accessories. Instead of putting the clothes she had been wearing into the hamper, she stuffed them into a black plastic garbage bag for Tamaru to get rid of. She trimmed her fingernails and took time brushing her teeth. She also cleaned her ears. Then she trimmed her eyebrows, spread a thin layer of cream over her face, and put a tiny dab of cologne on the back of her neck. She inspected the details of her face from every angle in the mirror to be sure there were no problems, and then, picking up a vinyl gym bag with a Nike logo, she left the room.

Standing by the front door, she turned for one last look, aware that she would never be coming back. The thought made the apartment appear unbelievably shabby, like a prison that only locked from the inside, bereft of any picture or vase. The only thing left was the bargain-sale rubber plant on the balcony, which she had bought instead of goldfish. She could hardly believe she had spent years of her life in this place without question or discontent.

"Good-bye," she murmured, bidding farewell not so much to the apartment as to the self that had lived here.

CHAPTER 6

Tengo

WE HAVE VERY LONG ARMS

The situation showed little development for a while. No one contacted Tengo. No messages arrived from Komatsu or Professor Ebisuno or Fuka-Eri. They all might have forgotten him and gone off to the moon. Tengo would have no problem with that if it were true, but things would never work out so conveniently for him. No, they had not gone to the moon. They just had a lot to do that kept them busy day after day, and they had neither the time nor the consideration to let Tengo know what they were up to.

Tengo tried to read the newspaper every day, in keeping with Komatsu's instructions, but – at least in the paper he read – nothing further about Fuka-Eri appeared. The newspaper industry actively sought out events that had already happened, but took a relatively passive attitude toward ongoing events. Thus, it probably carried the tacit message, "Nothing much is happening now." Having no television himself, Tengo did not know how television news shows were handling the case.

As for the weekly magazines, virtually all of them picked up the story. Not that Tengo actually read them. He just saw the magazine ads in the newspaper with their sensational headlines: "Truth about the enigmatic disappearance of the beautiful bestselling teenage author," "*Air Chrysalis* author

Fuka-Eri (17): Where did she disappear to?" " 'Hidden' background of beautiful runaway teenage author." Several of the ads even included Fuka-Eri's photo, the one taken at the press conference. Tengo was, of course, not uninterested in what the articles might say, but he was not about to spend the money it would take to compile a complete set of weeklies. Komatsu would probably let him know if there was anything in them that he should be concerned about. The absence of contact meant that, for the moment, there had been no new developments. In other words, people had still not realized that *Air Chrysalis* had (perhaps) been the product of a ghostwriter.

Judging from the headlines, the media were focused on the identity of Fuka-Eri's father as a once-famous radical activist, the fact that she had spent an isolated childhood in a commune in the hills of Yamanashi, and her present guardian, Professor Ebisuno (a formerly well-known intellectual). And even as the whereabouts of the beautiful, enigmatic teenage author remained a mystery, *Air Chrysalis* continued to occupy the bestseller list. Such questions were enough to arouse people's interest.

If it appeared that Fuka-Eri's disappearance was going to drag on, however, it was probably just a matter of time until investigations would begin to probe into broader areas. Then things might get sticky. If anyone decided to look into Fuka-Eri's schooling, for example, they might discover that she was dyslexic and, possibly for that reason, hardly went to school at all. Her grades in Japanese or her compositions (assuming she wrote any) might come out, and that might naturally lead to the question of how a dyslexic girl had managed to produce such sterling prose. It didn't take a genius to imagine how, at that point, people might start wondering if she had had help.

Such doubts would be brought to Komatsu first. He was the editor in charge of the story and had overseen everything regarding its publication. Komatsu would surely insist that he knew nothing about the matter. With a cool look on his face, he would maintain that his only role had been to pass the author's manuscript on to the selection committee, that he had had nothing to do with the process of its creation. Komatsu was good at keeping a straight face when saying things he didn't believe, though this was a skill mastered by all experienced editors to some degree. No sooner had he denied any knowledge of the deception than he would call Tengo and dramatically say something like, "Hey, Tengo, it's starting: the heat is on," as if he himself were enjoying the mess.

And maybe he was. Tengo sometimes felt that Komatsu had a certain desire for self-destruction. Maybe deep down he was hoping to see the whole plan exposed, a big juicy scandal blow up, and all connected parties blasted into the sky. And yet, at the same time, Komatsu could be a hardheaded realist. He would be more likely to cast his desire aside than to sail over the edge toward destruction.

Komatsu probably had it all figured out so that no matter what happened, he at least would survive. Just how he would manage it in this case, Tengo did not know, but Komatsu probably had his own clever ways of exploiting anything, be it a scandal or even total destruction. He was a shrewd player who was in no position to be criticizing Professor Ebisuno in that regard. But Tengo told himself with some confidence that Komatsu would be sure to contact him if clouds of suspicion began to appear on the horizon concerning the authorship of *Air Chrysalis*. So far, Tengo had merely functioned as a convenient and effective tool for Komatsu, but now he was also Komatsu's Achilles' heel. If Tengo were to disclose all the facts, that would put Komatsu in a terrible position, so Komatsu could not afford to ignore him. All Tengo had to do was wait for Komatsu to call; as long as there was no call, the "heat" was not "on."

Tengo was more interested in what Professor Ebisuno might be doing at the moment. No doubt he was making things happen with the police, hounding them with the possibility that Sakigake was involved in Fuka-Eri's disappearance, exploiting the event to pry open the religious organization's hard shell. But were the police moving in that direction? Yes, they probably were. The media were already foaming at the mouth over the relationship of Fuka-Eri and Sakigake. If the police did nothing and important facts later emerged along that line, they would be attacked for having failed to investigate. In any case, however, their investigation would be carried out behind the scenes, which meant that no substantial new information was to be gleaned from either the weekly magazines or TV news.

Coming home from the cram school one day, Tengo found a thick envelope shoved into his mailbox in the apartment building's front entrance. It bore Komatsu's name as sender, the logo of his publisher, and six special-delivery postmarks. Back in his apartment, Tengo opened it to find copies of all the latest reviews of *Air Chrysalis* and a letter from Komatsu. Deciphering Komatsu's scrawl took a good bit of time.

Tengo–
There have been no major developments so far. They still haven't found Fuka-Eri. The weekly magazines and TV reports are mainly concentrating on the question of her birth and childhood, and fortunately the damage has not spread to us. The book keeps selling more and more, which may or may not be a cause for celebration, it's hard to say. The company's very happy, though, and the boss gave me a certificate of commendation and a cash bonus. I've been working for this publisher for over twenty years, but this is the first time he's ever had anything nice to say about me. It kind of makes me want to see the look on their faces if they found out the truth.

I am enclosing copies of reviews and other articles
regarding *Air Chrysalis*. Have a look at them for your own
enlightenment when you get a chance. I think some of
them will be of special interest to you, and a few will make
you laugh – if you're in the mood for laughing, that is.

I had an acquaintance of mine look into that New Japan
Foundation for the Advancement of Scholarship and the
Arts we talked about. It was set up a few years ago,
received government approval, and is now actively
operating. It has an office and submits its annual financial
reports. It awards grants to a number of scholars and
writers each year – or so they claim. My source can't tell
where they get their money, and he finds the whole thing
just plain fishy. It could be a front established as a tax
write-off. A detailed investigation might turn up some
more information, but we don't have that kind of time and
effort to spare. As I said to you when we last talked, I'm
not quite convinced that a place like that wants to give
three million yen to an unknown writer like you. There's
something going on behind the scenes, and we can't
discount the possibility that Sakigake has something to do
with it. If so, it means they've sniffed out your connection
to *Air Chrysalis*. In any case, it makes sense for you to have
nothing to do with that organization.

Tengo returned Komatsu's letter to the envelope. Why
would Komatsu have bothered to write him a letter? It could
simply be that, as long as he was sending the reviews, he put
a letter in with them, but that was not like Komatsu. If he had
something to tell Tengo, he would have done it on the phone as
usual. A letter like this could remain as evidence in the future.
Cautious Komatsu could not have failed to think about that.
Or possibly Komatsu was less worried about evidence remaining than the possibility of a wiretap.

Tengo looked over at his phone. A wiretap? It had never occurred to him that anyone might be tapping his phone. Though, come to think of it, no one had called him in the past week. Maybe it was common knowledge that this phone was being tapped. He had not even heard from his older girlfriend, who liked talking on the phone. That was very unusual.

Even more unusual was the fact that she had not come to his apartment last Friday. She always called if something came up to prevent her from visiting him – say, her child was home from school with a cold, or her period had started all of a sudden. That Friday, however, she had not contacted him; she simply never showed up. Tengo had prepared a simple lunch for them in anticipation of her arrival, but ended up spending the day alone. Perhaps she was stuck dealing with some emergency, but it was not normal not to have had the slightest word from her. Meanwhile, he was not able to contact her from his end.

Tengo stopped thinking about both his girlfriend and the telephone. He sat at the kitchen table to read the book reviews in order. They had been assembled chronologically, the title of the newspaper or magazine and date of publication written in ballpoint pen in the upper left-hand corner. Komatsu must have had his part-time female assistant do it; he would never have undertaken such drudgery himself. Most of the reviews were positive. Many of the reviewers praised the story's depth and boldness and acknowledged the precision of the style, several of them finding it "incredible" that the work had been written by a seventeen-year-old girl.

Not a bad guess, Tengo thought.

One article called the author "a Françoise Sagan who has absorbed the air of magical realism." This piece, though vague and filled with reservations, generally seemed to be in praise of the work.

More than a few of the reviewers seemed perplexed by – or

simply undecided about – the meaning of the air chrysalis and the Little People. One reviewer concluded his piece, "As a story, the work is put together in an exceptionally interesting way and it carries the reader along to the very end, but when it comes to the question of what *is* an air chrysalis, or who *are* the Little People, we are left in a pool of mysterious question marks. This may well be the author's intention, but many readers are likely to take this lack of clarification as a sign of 'authorial laziness.' While this may be fine for a debut work, if the author intends to have a long career as a writer, in the near future she may well need to explain her deliberately cryptic posture."

Tengo cocked his head in puzzlement. If an author succeeded in writing a story "put together in an exceptionally interesting way" that "carries the reader along to the very end," who could possibly call such a writer "lazy"?

But Tengo, in all honesty, had nothing clear to say to this. Maybe his thoughts on the matter were mistaken and the critic was right. He had immersed himself so deeply in the rewriting of *Air Chrysalis* that he was practically incapable of any kind of objectivity. He now saw the air chrysalis and the Little People as things that existed inside himself. Not even he could honestly say he knew what they meant. Nor was this so very important to him. The most meaningful thing was whether or not one could accept their existence as a fact, and Tengo was able to do this quite readily, which was precisely why he had been able to immerse his heart and soul in rewriting *Air Chrysalis*. Had he not been able to accept the story on its own terms, he would never have participated in the fraud, even if tempted with a fortune or faced with threats.

Still, Tengo's reading of the story was his and his alone. He could not help feeling a certain sympathy for the trusting men and women who were "left in a pool of mysterious question marks" after reading *Air Chrysalis*. He pictured a bunch of dismayed-looking people clutching at colorful flotation rings as they drifted aimlessly in a large pool full of question marks. In the sky above them shone an utterly unrealistic sun. Tengo felt a certain sense of responsibility for having foisted such a state of affairs upon the public.

But who can possibly save all the people of the world? Tengo thought. *You could bring all the gods of the world into one place, and still they couldn't abolish nuclear weapons or eradicate terrorism. They couldn't end the drought in Africa or bring John Lennon back to life. Far from it – the gods would just break into factions and start fighting among themselves, and the world would probably become even more chaotic than it is now. Considering the sense of powerlessness that such a state of affairs would bring about, to have people floating in a pool of mysterious question marks seems like a minor sin.*

Tengo read about half of the *Air Chrysalis* reviews that Komatsu had sent before stuffing them back into the envelope. He could pretty well imagine what the rest were like. As a story, *Air Chrysalis* was fascinating to many people. It had fascinated Tengo and Komatsu and Professor Ebisuno and an amazing number of readers. What more did it have to do?

The phone rang just after nine o'clock Tuesday night. Tengo was listening to music and reading a book. This was his favorite time of day, reading to his heart's content before going to sleep. When he tired of reading, he would fall asleep.

This was the first time he had heard the phone ring in quite a while, and there was something ominous about it. This was not Komatsu calling. The phone had a different ring when it was Komatsu. Tengo hesitated, wondering whether he should pick it up at all. He let it ring five times. Then he lifted the needle from the record groove and picked up the receiver. It might be his girlfriend.

"Mr. Kawana?" a man said. It was the voice of a middle-aged man, soft and deep. Tengo did not recognize it.

"Yes," Tengo said cautiously.

"I'm sorry to call so late at night. My name is Yasuda," the man said in a neutral voice, neither friendly nor hostile, neither impersonal nor intimate.

Yasuda? The name was ordinary enough, but he couldn't think of any Yasudas he knew.

"I'm calling to give you a message," the man said. He then inserted a slight pause, rather like putting a bookmark in between the pages of a book. "My wife will not be able to visit your home anymore, I believe. That is all I wanted to tell you."

Yasuda! That was his girlfriend's name. Kyoko Yasuda. She never had occasion to speak her name in Tengo's presence, which accounted for the lag in recognition. This man on the phone was Kyoko's husband. Tengo felt as if something were stuck in his throat.

"Have I managed to make myself clear?" the man asked, his voice entirely free of emotion – or none that Tengo could hear. He spoke with a slight accent, possibly from Hiroshima or Kyushu. Tengo could not be sure.

"Not be able to visit," Tengo echoed the words.

"Yes, she will no longer be *able* to visit."

Tengo mustered up the courage to ask, "Has something happened to her?"

Silence. Tengo's question hung in space, unanswered. Then the man said, "So what I'm telling you, Mr. Kawana, is that you will probably never see my wife again. I just wanted to let you know that."

The man knew that Tengo had been sleeping with his wife. Once a week. For a year. Tengo could tell that he knew. But the man's voice was strangely lacking in either anger or resentment. It contained something else – not so much a personal emotion as an objective scene: an abandoned, overgrown garden, or a dry riverbed after a major flood – a scene like that.

"I'm not sure what you are trying to – "

"Then let's just leave it at that," the man said, before Tengo could finish. A trace of fatigue was discernible in his voice. "One thing should be perfectly clear. My wife is irretrievably lost. She can no longer visit your home in any form. That is what I am saying."

"Irretrievably lost," Tengo repeated.

"I did not want to make this call, Mr. Kawana. But I couldn't sleep at night if I just let it go and said nothing. Do you think I like having this conversation?"

No sounds of any kind came from the other end when the man stopped talking. He seemed to be phoning from an incredibly quiet place. Either that or the emotion inside him was acting like a vacuum, absorbing all sound waves in the vicinity.

Tengo felt he ought to ask the man a question or two. Otherwise, it seemed, this whole thing would end as a collection of inscrutable hints. He mustn't let the conversation die! But this man had no intention of informing Tengo of any situational details. What kind of question could he ask when the other person had no intention of revealing the actual state of affairs? What kind of words should he give voice to when facing a vacuum? Tengo was still struggling to discover any words that might work when, without warning, the connection was cut. The man had set down the receiver without saying anything and left Tengo's presence. Probably forever.

Tengo kept the dead receiver pressed to his ear for a time. If anyone else was listening in to the call, he might be able to grasp that person's presence. He held his breath and listened, but there were no telltale sounds. All he could hear was the beating of his own heart. The more he listened, the more he felt like a thief who has crept into a stranger's house at night, hidden in the shadows, holding his breath, and waiting for the family to fall asleep.

He boiled some water in a kettle and made green tea to calm

his nerves. Cradling the handleless cup in his hands, he sat at the kitchen table and mentally reviewed the telephone call.

"My wife is irretrievably lost. She can no longer visit your home in any form. That is what I am saying." *In any form:* that phrase disturbed Tengo the most. It suggested something dark, damp, and slimy.

What this man named Yasuda wanted to convey to Tengo, it seemed, was the message that even if his wife *wanted* to visit Tengo's apartment again, it was literally *impossible* for her to carry out that wish. Impossible in what way? In what context? And what did it mean to say that she was "irretrievably lost"? An image formed in his mind of Kyoko Yasuda with serious injuries from an accident or having come down with an incurable disease or her face horribly disfigured by violence. She was confined to a wheelchair or had lost a limb or was wrapped head to toe in bandages, unable to move. Or then again she was being held in an underground room, fastened like a dog on a thick chain. All of these possibilities, however, seemed far-fetched.

Kyoko Yasuda (as Tengo was now calling her in his mind) had hardly ever spoken of her husband. Tengo had learned nothing about him from her – his profession, his age, his looks, his personality, where they had met, when they had married, whether he was skinny or fat, tall or short, or whether or not they got along well. All Tengo knew was that she was not particularly hard-pressed economically (she appeared to be quite comfortable, in fact), and that she seemed dissatisfied with either the frequency or the quality of the sex she had with her husband, though even these were entirely matters of conjecture on his part. She and Tengo spent their afternoons in bed talking of many things, but never once had the subject of her husband come up, nor had Tengo wanted to know about him. He preferred to remain ignorant of the man whose wife he was stealing. It seemed only proper. Now that this new situation had developed, however, he was sorry that he had never asked her about her husband (she would almost certainly have responded frankly if he had asked). Was her husband jealous? Possessive? Did he have violent tendencies?

He tried to put himself in the man's place. How would he feel if the situation were reversed? Say, he has a wife, two small children, and a tranquil home life, but he discovers that his wife is sleeping with another man once a week – a man ten years her junior, and the affair has been going on for over a year. What would he think if he found himself in such a situation? What emotions would rule his heart? Violent anger? Deep disappointment? Vague sadness? Scornful indifference? A sense of having lost touch with reality? Or an indistinguishable blend of several emotions?

No amount of thinking enabled Tengo to hit upon exactly how he would feel. What came to mind through all his hypothesizing was the image of his mother in a white slip giving her breasts to a young man he did not know. *Destiny seems to have come full circle,* Tengo thought. The enigmatic young man was perhaps Tengo himself, the woman in his arms Kyoko Yasuda. The composition was exactly the same; only the individuals had changed. *Does this mean that my life has been nothing but a process through which I am giving concrete form to the dormant image inside me? And how much responsibility do I bear for her having become irretrievably lost?*

Tengo could not get back to sleep again. He kept hearing the voice of the man who called himself Yasuda. The hints that he had left behind weighed heavily on Tengo, and the words he had spoken bore a strange reality. Tengo thought about Kyoko Yasuda. He pictured her face and body in minute detail. He had last seen her on Friday, two weeks prior. As always, they had spent a lot of time having sex. After the phone call from her husband, though, it seemed like something that had happened in the distant past, like an episode out of history.

On his shelf remained several LP records that she had brought from home to listen to in bed with him, all jazz records from long, long ago – Louis Armstrong, Billie Holliday (this one, too, had Barney Bigard as a sideman), some 1940s Duke Ellington. She had listened to them – and handled them – with great care. The jackets had faded somewhat with the years, but the records themselves looked brand-new. Tengo picked up one jacket after another. Gazing at them, he felt with growing certainty that he might never see her again.

Tengo was not, strictly speaking, in love with Kyoko Yasuda. He had never felt that he wanted to spend his life with her or that saying good-bye to her could be painful. She had never made him feel that deep trembling of the heart. But he had grown accustomed to having this older girlfriend as part of his life, and naturally, he had grown fond of her. He looked forward to welcoming her to his apartment once a week and joining his naked flesh with hers. Their relationship was an unusual one for Tengo. He had never been able to feel very close to many women. In fact, most women – whether he was in a sexual relationship with them or not – made Tengo feel uncomfortable. And in order to curb that discomfort, Tengo had to fence off a certain territory inside himself. In other words, he had to keep certain rooms in his heart locked tight. With Kyoko Yasuda, however, such complex operations were unnecessary. First of all, she seemed to grasp exactly what Tengo wanted and what he did not want. And so Tengo counted himself lucky that they had happened to find each other.

Now, however, something had happened, and she was irretrievably lost. For some unknowable reason, she could never visit here *in any form*. And, according to her husband, it was better for Tengo to know nothing about either the reason or its consequence.

*   *   *

Still unable to sleep, Tengo was sitting on the floor, listening to the Duke Ellington record at low volume, when the phone rang again. The hands of the wall clock were pointing to 10:12. Tengo could think of no one other than Komatsu who might call at a time like this, but the ring didn't sound like Komatsu's, which was always more high-strung and impatient. It might be Yasuda again; perhaps he had forgotten to tell Tengo something else. Tengo did not want to answer. Experience had taught him that phone calls at this time of night were never very pleasant. Thinking of his current situation, however, he had no choice but to answer it.

"That is Mr. Kawana, isn't it?" said a man. It was not Komatsu. Nor was it Yasuda. The voice belonged unmistakably to Ushikawa, speaking as if he had a mouthful of water – or some other elusive liquid. His strange face and flat, misshapen head came to Tengo's mind automatically.

"Uh, sorry for calling so late. It's Ushikawa. I know I burst in on you the other day and took much of your valuable time. Today, too, I wish I could have called earlier, but some urgent business came up, and the next thing I knew it was already this late. Believe me, I know you're a real early-to-bed, early-to-rise type, Mr. Kawana, and that's a very admirable thing. Staying up until all hours, frittering away your time, doesn't do anyone any good. The best thing is to go to bed as soon as possible after it gets dark and wake with the sun in the morning. But, I don't know, call it intuition, it just popped into my mind that you might still be up tonight, Mr. Kawana, so even though I knew it was not the most polite thing to do, I decided to give you a call. Have I caught you at a bad time?"

Tengo did not like what Ushikawa was saying, and he did not like it that Ushikawa knew his home phone number. Intuition had nothing to do with it: he had called because he knew perfectly well that Tengo was up, unable to sleep. Maybe he knew that Tengo's lights were on. Could someone be watching this apartment? He could almost picture one of Ushikawa's "eager" and "capable" "researchers" observing Tengo's apartment from somewhere with a pair of high-powered binoculars.

"I am up tonight, in fact," Tengo said. "That 'intuition' of yours is correct. Maybe I drank too much strong green tea."

"That *is* too bad, Mr. Kawana. Wakeful nights often give people useless thoughts. How about it, then, do you mind talking with me a while?"

"As long as it's not about something that makes it harder for me to sleep."

Ushikawa burst out laughing. At his end of the line – someplace in this world – his misshapen head shook in its own misshapen way. "Very funny, Mr. Kawana. Of course, what I have to say may not be as comforting as a lullaby, but the subject itself is not so deadly serious as to keep you awake at night, I assure you. It's a simple question of yes or no. The business about the, uh, grant. It's an attractive proposition, don't you think? Have you thought it over? We have to have your final answer now."

"I believe I declined the grant quite clearly the last time we talked. I appreciate the offer, but I have everything I need at the moment. I'm not hard-pressed financially, and if possible I'd like to keep my life going along at its present pace."

"Meaning, you don't want to be beholden to anyone."

"In a word, yes."

"I suppose that is very admirable of you, Mr. Kawana," Ushikawa said with a sound like a light clearing of the throat. "You want to make it on your own. You want to have as little as possible to do with organizations. I understand how you feel, but I'm concerned about you, Mr. Kawana. Look at the world we live in. Anything could happen at any time. So we all need some kind of insurance, something to lean on, a shelter from the wind. I hate to say this, Mr. Kawana, but at the moment you have, uh, exactly nothing that you can lean on. Not one of the people around you can be counted on, it seems to me: all of them would most likely desert you in a pinch. Am I right? You know what they say – 'Better safe than sorry.' It's important to insure yourself for when the pinch does come, don't you think? And I'm not just talking about money. Money, ultimately, is just a kind of *symbol* of something else."

"I'm not quite sure what you're getting at," Tengo said. That intuitive sense of distaste he experienced when first meeting Ushikawa was creeping up on him again.

"No, of course not. You're still young and healthy. Maybe that's why you don't understand what I am saying. Let me give you an example. Once you pass a certain age, life becomes nothing more than a process of continual loss. Things that are important to your life begin to slip out of your grasp, one after another, like a comb losing teeth. And the only things that come to take their place are worthless imitations. Your physical strength, your hopes, your dreams, your ideals, your convictions, all meaning, or, then again, the people you love: one by one, they fade away. Some announce their departure before they leave, while others just disappear all of a sudden without warning one day. And once you lose them you can never get them back. Your search for replacements never goes well. It's all very painful – as painful as actually being cut with a knife. You will be turning thirty soon, Mr. Kawana, which means that, from now on, you will gradually enter that twilight portion of life – you will be getting older. You are probably beginning to grasp that painful sense that you are *losing something,* are you not?"

Tengo wondered if this man could be dropping hints about Kyoko Yasuda. Perhaps he knew that they had been meeting here once a week, and that recently something had caused her to leave him.

"You seem to know a great deal about my private life," Tengo said.

"No, not at all," Ushikawa insisted. "I'm just talking about life in general. Really. I know very little about your private life."

Tengo remained silent.

"Please, Mr. Kawana," Ushikawa said with a sigh, "be so good as to accept our grant. Frankly speaking, you are in a rather precarious position. We can back you up in a pinch. We can throw you a life preserver. If things go on like this, you might find yourself in an inextricable situation."

"An inextricable situation," Tengo said.

"Exactly."

"Can you tell me specifically what kind of 'situation' you mean?"

Ushikawa paused momentarily. Then he said, "Believe me, Mr. Kawana, there are things it is better not to know. Certain kinds of knowledge rob people of their sleep. Green tea is no match for these things. They might take restful sleep away from you forever. What I, uh, want to say to you is this. Think about it this way: it's as if you opened a special spigot and let a special something out before you knew what was happening, and it's having an effect on the people around you – a rather less-than-desirable effect."

"Do the Little People have anything to do with this?"

It was a shot in the dark, but it shut Ushikawa up for a while. His was a heavy silence, like a black stone sunk to the bottom of a deep body of water.

"I want to know the truth, Mr. Ushikawa. Let's stop throwing riddles at each other and talk more concretely. What has happened to her?"

" 'Her'? I don't know what you mean."

Tengo sighed. This was too delicate a matter to discuss on the phone.

"I'm sorry, Mr. Kawana, but I'm just a messenger sent by my client. For now, my job is to speak of fundamental matters as indirectly as possible," Ushikawa said circumspectly. "I'm sorry if I seem to be deliberately tantalizing you, but I'm only allowed to talk about this in the vaguest terms. And, to tell you the truth, my own knowledge of the matter is quite limited. In any case, though, I really don't know anything about 'her,' whoever she might be. You'll have to be a little more specific."

"All right, then, who are the Little People?"

"Again, Mr. Kawana, I don't know anything at all about these 'Little People' – or at least nothing more than that they appear in the book *Air Chrysalis*. I will tell you this, however: judging from the drift of your remarks, it seems to me that you have let something out of the bag before you yourself knew what it was all about. That can be awfully dangerous under certain circumstances. My client knows very well just how dangerous it is and what kind of danger it poses, and they have a degree of understanding regarding how to deal with the danger, which is precisely why we have tried to extend a helping hand to you. To put it quite bluntly, we have very long arms – long and strong."

"Who is this 'client' you keep mentioning? Someone connected with Sakigake?"

"Unfortunately, I have not been granted the authority to divulge any names," Ushikawa said with what sounded like genuine regret. "I can say, however, without going into detail, that they have their own very special power. Formidable power. We can stand behind you. Please understand – this is our final offer. You are free to take it or leave it. Once you make up your mind, however, there is no going back. So please think about it very carefully. And let me say this: if you are not on their side, regrettably, under certain circumstances, their long arms could, when extended, have certain undesirable – though unintended – effects on you."

"What kind of 'undesirable effects'?"

Ushikawa did not immediately reply to Tengo's question. Instead, Tengo heard what sounded like the faint sucking of saliva at both sides of Ushikawa's mouth.

"I don't know the exact answer to that," Ushikawa said. "They haven't told me anything specific, which is why I am speaking in generalities."

"So, what is it that I supposedly let out of the bag?" Tengo asked.

"I don't know the answer to that, either," Ushikawa said. "At the risk of repeating myself, I am nothing but a hired negotiator. By the time the full reservoir of information reaches me, it's squeezed down to a few droplets. All I'm doing is passing on to you exactly what my client has told me to with the limited authority I have been granted. You may wonder why the client doesn't just contact you directly, which would speed things up, and why they have to use this strange man as an intermediary, but I don't know any better than you do."

Ushikawa cleared his throat and waited for another question, but when there was none, he continued, "Now, Mr. Kawana, you were asking what it is that you let out of the bag, right?"

Tengo said yes, that was right.

"Well, Mr. Kawana, I'm not sure why exactly, but I can't help wondering if it might be something for which a third party couldn't offer a simple solution. I suspect it's something you would need to go out on your own and work up a sweat to find out. And it could very well be that after you've gone through all that and reached a point where you've figured out the answer, it's too late. To me, it seems obvious that you have a, uh, very special talent – a superior and beautiful talent, a talent that ordinary people do not possess. Which is precisely why your recent accomplishment carries an authority that cannot be easily overlooked. And my client appears to value that talent of yours very highly. That is why we are offering you this grant. Unfortunately, however, sheer talent is not enough. And depending upon how you look at it, possessing an outstanding talent that is not sufficient may be more dangerous than possessing nothing at all. That is my impression, however vague, of the recent matter."

"So what you are saying, then, is that your client has sufficient knowledge and ability to tell about such things."

"Hmm, I really can't say about that, don't you think? I mean, nobody can ever declare whether such qualities are 'sufficient.' "

"Why do they need me?"

"If I may use the analogy of epidemic, you people may be playing the role of – pardon me – the main carriers of a disease."

" 'You people?' " Tengo said. "Are you talking about Eriko Fukada and me?"

Ushikawa did not answer the question. "Uh, if I may use a classical analogy here, you people might have opened Pandora's box and let loose all kinds of things in the world. This seems to be what my client thinks you've done, judging from my own impressions. The two of you may have joined forces by accident, but you turned out to be a far more powerful team than you ever imagined. Each of you was able to make up for what the other lacked."

"But that's not a crime in any legal sense."

"That is true. It is not, of course, a, uh, crime in any legal sense, or in any this-worldly sense. If I may be allowed to quote from George Orwell's great classic, however – or, rather, from his novel as a great source of quotations – it is very close to what he called a 'thought crime.' By an odd coincidence, this year just happens to be 1984. Shall we call it a stroke of fate? But I seem to have been talking a bit too much tonight, Mr. Kawana. And most of what I have been saying is nothing but my own clumsy guesswork, pure speculation, without any firm evidence to support it. Because you asked, I have given you my general impressions, that is all."

Ushikawa fell silent, and Tengo started thinking. *His "own clumsy guesswork"? How much of what this man is saying can I believe?*

"Oh, well, I'll have to be calling it a day," Ushikawa said. "It's such an important matter, I'll give you a little more time. Just a little. The clock is counting off the time. Tick-tock, tick-tock, without a break. Please consider our offer carefully once more. I'll probably be getting in touch with you again soon. Good night, then. I'm glad we had a chance to talk. I, uh, hope you will be able to sleep well, Mr. Kawana."

Ushikawa hung up. Tengo stared at the dead receiver in his hand for a while, the way a farmer stares at a withered vegetable he has picked up from his drought-wracked field. These days, a lot of people were hanging up on Tengo.

As he had imagined, restful sleep paid Tengo no visits that night. Until the pale light of dawn began coloring the curtains and the tough city crows woke to begin their day's work, Tengo sat on the floor, leaning against the wall and thinking about his girlfriend and about the long, strong arms reaching toward him from some unknown place. Such thoughts, however, carried him nowhere. They merely circled aimlessly around the same spot.

Tengo looked around and heaved a sigh and realized that he was absolutely alone. Ushikawa had been right. He had nothing and no one to lean on.

CHAPTER 7

Aomame

WHERE YOU ARE ABOUT TO SET FOOT

With its high ceiling and muted lighting, the capacious lobby of the Hotel Okura's main building seemed like a huge, stylish cave. Against the cave walls, like the sighing of a disemboweled animal, bounced the muted conversations of people seated on the lobby's sofas. The floor's thick, soft carpeting could have been primeval moss on a far northern island. It absorbed the sound of footsteps into its endless span of accumulated time. The men and women crossing and recrossing the lobby looked like ghosts tied in place by some ancient curse, doomed to the endless repetition of their assigned roles. Men were armored in tight-fitting business suits. Slim young women were swathed in chic black dresses, here to attend a ceremony in one of the hotel's many reception rooms. They wore small but expensive accessories, like vampire finches in search of blood, longing for a hint of light they could reflect. A large foreign couple loomed like an old king and queen past their prime, resting their tired bodies on thrones in the corner.

In this place so full of legend and suggestion, Aomame was truly out of place, with her pale blue cotton pants, simple white blouse, white sneakers, and blue Nike gym bag. She probably looked like a babysitter sent by her agency to work for a hotel guest, she thought, as she killed time sitting in a big easy chair. *Oh well, I'm not here for socializing.* Sitting there, she sensed that someone was watching her, but, try as she might to scan the area, she could not find anyone who seemed to be focused on her. *Never mind,* she told herself. *Let them look all they want.*

When the hands of her watch hit 6:50, Aomame stood up and went to the ladies' room, carrying her gym bag. She washed her hands with soap and water and checked once more to make sure there were no problems with her appearance. Then, facing the large, clear mirror, she took several deep breaths. This was a spacious restroom, and she was the only one in it. It might be even bigger than her whole apartment. "This is going to be my last job," she said in a low voice to the mirror. *Once I carry this off, I disappear. Poof! Like a ghost. I'm here now, but not tomorrow. In a few days, I'll have a different name and a different face.*

She returned to the lobby and took her seat again, setting the gym bag on the table next to her. In the bag was a small automatic pistol with seven bullets and a sharp needle made for thrusting into the back of a man's neck. *I've got to calm down,* she told herself. *This job is important, and it's my last. I have to be the usual cool, tough Aomame.*

But she could not shake off the awareness that she was not in a normal state. Her breathing was strangely labored, and the heightened speed of her heartbeat concerned her. A film of sweat moistened her armpits. Her skin was tingling. *I'm not just tense, though. I'm having a premonition of something. And the premonition is giving me a warning. It keeps knocking on the door of my mind. It's telling me, "It's still not too late. Get out of here now and forget all this."*

Aomame wanted to heed the warning if she could, abandon everything and turn her back on this hotel lobby. There was something ominous here, the lingering presence of circuitous death – a slow, quiet, but inescapable death. *But I can't just run away with my tail between my legs. That's not the Aomame way to live.*

It was a long ten minutes. Time refused to move ahead. She stayed on the sofa, trying to get her breathing under control. The lobby ghosts kept spouting their hollow reverberations. People drifted silently over the thick carpet like souls groping for their eternal resting places. The only actual noise to reach her ears now and then was the clinking of a coffee set on a tray whenever a waitress passed by. But even that sound contained a dubious secondary sound within it. Things were not heading in a good direction. *If I'm already this tense, I won't be able to do a thing when the time comes.* Aomame closed her eyes and almost by reflex intoned a prayer, the one that she had been taught to recite before every meal from as long ago as she could remember. That had been a long, long time ago, but she remembered every word with perfect clarity –

O Lord in Heaven, may Thy name be praised in utmost purity for ever and ever, and may Thy kingdom come to us. Please forgive our many sins, and bestow Thy blessings upon our humble pathways. Amen.

However grudgingly, Aomame had to admit that this prayer, which had given her nothing but pain in the past, now provided a source of support. The sound of the words calmed her nerves, stopped her fears at the doorway, and helped her breathing to quiet down. She pressed her fingers against her eyelids and repeated the prayer to herself over and over.

"Miss Aomame, I believe," a man said close by. It was the voice of a young man.

Aomame opened her eyes, slowly raised her head, and looked at the owner of the voice. Two young men were standing in front of her. Both wore the same kind of dark suit.

Judging by the fabric and cut, these were not expensive clothes – probably bought right off the rack at a discount store. They didn't quite fit in every detail, but they were admirably free of wrinkles. Perhaps the men pressed them every time they put them on. Neither man wore a tie. One had his white shirt buttoned all the way to the top, while the other wore a kind of gray crew-neck shirt under his suit jacket. They had on the plainest black shoes possible.

The man in the white shirt must have been a good six feet tall, and he wore his hair in a ponytail. He had long eyebrows, the ends of which turned up at a distinct angle like a line graph. His face was serene, with well-balanced features that could have belonged to an actor. The other man must have been five foot five and had a buzz cut and a snub nose. A tiny beard grew at the tip of his chin like a mistakenly applied shadow, and there was a small scar by his right eye. Both men were slim, with sunken cheeks and tanned faces. There was not an ounce of fat to be seen on either of them, and judging from the spread of their suits' shoulders there were some serious muscles underneath. They were probably in their mid- to late twenties. The look in their eyes was deep and sharp, and the eyeballs moved no more than necessary, as with animals on the hunt.

As if by reflex, Aomame stood up from her chair and looked at her watch. The hands pointed to seven o'clock exactly. Right on time.

"Yes, I am Aomame."

Neither man displayed any expression. They did a swift examination of Aomame's attire and looked at the blue gym bag next to her.

"Is this all you brought with you?" Buzzcut asked.

"Yes, this is it," Aomame said.

"That's fine. Let's go, then. Are you ready?" Buzzcut asked. Ponytail said nothing as he kept his eyes on Aomame.

"Yes, of course," Aomame said. She guessed that the shorter man was somewhat older than the other one and the leader of the two.

Buzzcut went ahead with leisurely steps, crossing the lobby toward the elevators. Aomame followed him, gym bag in hand. Ponytail followed about six feet behind her. This meant she was sandwiched between them. *They know what they're doing,* she thought. They walked with erect posture, their gait strong and precise. The dowager had said they both practiced karate. Aomame knew from her martial arts training that in a face-to-face confrontation with these two, there was probably no way she could win. But she did not sense from these men the kind of overpowering menace that Tamaru projected. Defeating them was not entirely out of the question. The first thing she would have to do in hand-to-hand combat would be to render Buzzcut powerless. He called the shots. If Ponytail was her only opponent, she could manage to survive and escape.

The three of them boarded the elevator, and Ponytail pushed the button for the seventh floor. Buzzcut stood next to Aomame, and Ponytail stood in the corner, facing them at an angle. They did all this wordlessly, systematically, like a second baseman and shortstop who live to make double plays.

In the midst of such thoughts, it suddenly dawned on Aomame that her breathing and heartbeat had returned to their normal rhythms. *Nothing to worry about,* she thought. *I'm my usual self – the cool, tough Aomame. Everything will probably go well. No more bad premonitions.*

The elevator door opened soundlessly. Ponytail kept the "Door Open" button depressed while Buzzcut stepped out followed by Aomame, and then he released the button and left the elevator. Buzzcut led the way down the corridor, Aomame followed, and Ponytail continued playing rear guard. The broad corridor was totally deserted: perfectly silent and perfectly clean, well cared for in every detail, befitting a first-class hotel – no trays of used room-service dishes parked in front of doors, no cigarette butts in the ashtray outside the elevator, the fragrance of fresh-cut flowers wafting from well-placed vases. They turned several corners and came to a stop in front of a door. Ponytail knocked twice and then, without waiting for an answer, opened the door with a key card. He stepped inside, looked around to make sure there was nothing wrong, and gave Buzzcut a curt nod.

"Please," Buzzcut said to Aomame drily.

Aomame walked in. Buzzcut came in after her and closed the door, locking it from the inside with a chain. The room was a big one. No ordinary hotel room, it was outfitted with a large set of reception-room furniture and an office desk. The television set and refrigerator were also full-size. This was clearly the living area of a special suite. The window provided a sweeping view of Tokyo at night. It had to be an expensive room. Buzzcut checked his watch and urged Aomame to sit on the sofa. She did as she was told and set her blue gym bag next to her.

"Will you be changing clothes?" Buzzcut asked.

"If possible," Aomame said. "I'd prefer to change into work-out clothes."

Buzzcut nodded. "First we'll have to do a search, if you don't mind. Sorry, but it's part of our job."

"That's fine, search all you want," Aomame said. There was no hint of tension in her voice. If anything, there was a percep-tible touch of amusement at their neurotic attention to detail.

Ponytail came over to Aomame and did a body search to make sure she was not carrying anything suspicious. All she had on was a pair of thin cotton pants and a blouse; it didn't take a search to know there could be nothing hidden under those. He was just going through the motions. His hands seemed tense and stiff. It would have been hard to compliment him on his skill at this. He probably had little experience at doing body searches on women. Buzzcut watched him work, leaning against the desk.

When the body search was over, Aomame opened her gym bag for him. Inside were a thin summer cardigan, a matching jersey top and bottom for work, and two towels, one large and one small. A simple makeup set and a paperback. There was a small beaded purse containing a wallet, a change purse, and a key ring. Aomame handed each item to Ponytail. Finally she took out a black vinyl pouch and unzipped it. Inside was a change of underwear and a few tampons and sanitary napkins.

"I sweat when I work, so I need to have a change of clothes," Aomame said. She took out matching lace-trimmed bra and panties and started to spread them out for Ponytail to see. He blushed slightly and gave several quick nods as if to say, "All right, I've seen enough." Aomame began to suspect that this man could not speak at all.

With unhurried movements, Aomame returned her underthings and sanitary products to the pouch, zipped it closed, and replaced it in the bag. *These guys are amateurs,* she thought. *What kind of bodyguard blushes at the sight of cute lingerie and a few tampons? If Tamaru had been doing this job, he would have searched Snow White down to the hairs of her crotch. He would have examined the bottom of that pouch if it meant digging through a warehouse's worth of bras, camisoles, and panties. Things like that are nothing but rags to him – well, true, he's as gay as they come. At the very least, he would have picked up the pouch to check its weight. And then he would have been sure to find the Heckler & Koch wrapped in a handkerchief (and weighing in at some 500 grams) and the small homemade ice pick in its hard case.*

These guys are amateurs. They may have some skill at karate, and they may have vowed absolute loyalty to their Leader, but they're nothing but a couple of amateurs. Just as the dowager predicted. Aomame had assumed they wouldn't go through a pouch stuffed with women's things, and she had been right. It had been a gamble, of course, but she had not gone so far as to think about what she would do if the gamble hadn't paid off. About all she could have done in that case was pray. But she knew this much: *prayer works.*

Aomame went into the suite's large powder room and changed into her jersey outfit, folding her blouse and cotton pants and placing them in the bag. Next she checked to see that her hair was pinned tightly in place. Then she sprayed her mouth with a breath freshener. She took the Heckler & Koch out of the pouch and, after flushing the toilet to mask the sound, she pulled back the slide to send a bullet into the chamber. Now all she would have to do was release the safety. Finally, she moved the case with the ice pick to the top of the bag where she could have immediate access to it. Once she had finished with these preparations, she faced the mirror and relaxed her tensed expression. *Fine. I've kept my cool so far.*

Coming out of the powder room, Aomame found Buzzcut standing at attention with his back to her, speaking at low volume into a telephone. When he saw her, he cut his call short, quietly hung up the receiver, and gave her a once-over in her jersey outfit.

"All set?" he asked.

"Whenever you are," Aomame said.

"First I have a request to make," Buzzcut said.

Aomame gave him a token smile.

"That you not say a word about tonight to anyone," Buzzcut said. He paused a moment so that his message could sink in. It was as if he had scattered water on dry earth and was waiting for it to be absorbed and disappear. She watched him the whole time without saying anything.

Buzzcut continued, "Pardon me if this sounds crass, but we

are planning to offer you generous remuneration, and we may be requesting your services from time to time in the future. So we would like to ask you to forget anything and everything that happens here tonight. Whatever you see or hear. Everything."

"As you know," Aomame said, adopting a somewhat frosty tone, "my work involves people's bodies, so I believe I am well versed in the ways of professional confidentiality. No information of any kind regarding an individual's body will leave this room. If that is what concerns you, I can assure you there is no need to worry."

"Excellent. That is what we wanted to hear," Buzzcut said. "But let me just add that we would appreciate it if you would view this as a case that goes beyond professional confidentiality in the most general sense. Where you are about to set foot is, so to speak, a sacred space."

"A sacred space?"

"It may sound a bit much, but, believe me, it is no exaggeration. The one you are about to lay eyes on, and to place your hands upon, is a sacred person. There is no other appropriate way to put it."

Aomame nodded, saying nothing. This was no time for remarks from her.

Buzzcut said, "We took the liberty of running a background check on you. I hope you're not offended, but it was something we had to do. We have our reasons for taking every precaution."

Aomame stole a glance at Ponytail as she listened. He was sitting motionless in a chair beside the door, his back perfectly straight, hands on his knees, chin pulled back. He could have been posing for a photo. His eyes were locked on her the whole time.

Buzzcut looked down at his feet as if to check how worn out his black shoes might be, then raised his face and looked at Aomame again. "In short, we found no problems, which is why we have asked you to come today. You have a reputation as a talented instructor, and in fact people think very highly of you."

"Thank you very much," Aomame said.

"I understand you used to be a Society of Witnesses believer. Is that true?"

"Yes, it is. Both of my parents were believers, and they naturally made me one, too, from the time I was born. I didn't choose it for myself, and I left the religion a long time ago."

I wonder if their investigation turned up the fact that Ayumi and I used to go out man hunting in Roppongi? Oh well, it doesn't make any difference. If they did find out, it obviously didn't bother them. Otherwise, I wouldn't be here now.

"We know about that, too," Buzzcut said. "But you did live in faith at one time in your life – that especially impressionable time of early childhood. So I assume you have a good idea what I mean when I speak of something as 'sacred.' In any religion, the sacred lies at the very root of faith. We must never tread upon that world. There is a sacred region into which we dare not stray. The first step of all faith is to recognize its existence, accept it, and revere it absolutely. You do understand what I am trying to say, don't you?"

"I think so," Aomame said, "though whether I accept it or not is another matter."

"Of course," Buzzcut said. "Of course there is no need for you to accept it. It is our faith, not yours. But, transcending the question of belief or nonbelief, you are likely to witness special things – a being who is by no means ordinary."

Aomame kept silent. *A being who is by no means ordinary.*

Buzzcut narrowed his eyes for a time, gauging the meaning of Aomame's silence. Then, speaking unhurriedly, he said, "Whatever you happen to witness today, you must not mention it to anyone on the outside. For that would cause an ineradicable defilement of the holiness, as if a clear, beautiful pond were polluted by a foreign body. Whatever the world at large might think, or the laws of this world might stipulate, that is how we feel about it. If we can count on you, and if you will keep your promise, we can, as I said before, provide you with generous remuneration."

"I see," Aomame said.

"We are a small religious body, but we have strong hearts and long arms," Buzzcut said.

You have long arms, Aomame thought. *I guess I'll be testing to find out just how long they are.*

Leaning against the desk with his arms folded, Buzzcut studied Aomame, as if checking to see whether a picture hanging on the wall was crooked or straight. Ponytail remained motionless, never once taking his eyes off of Aomame.

Buzzcut checked his watch.

"Let's go, then," he said. He cleared his throat once, then moved slowly across the room with the careful steps of a pilgrim crossing the surface of a lake. He gave two soft knocks on the door to the connecting room and, without waiting for a response, pulled the door open, gave a slight bow, and entered. Aomame followed, carrying the gym bag. Sinking step after careful step into the deep carpet, she made sure that her breathing was under control. Her finger was cocked and ready to pull the trigger of the pistol in her imagination. *Nothing to worry about. I'm the same as always.* But still, Aomame was afraid. A chunk of ice was stuck to her spine – ice that showed no sign of melting. *I'm cool, calm, and – deep down – afraid.*

We must never tread upon that world. There is a sacred region into which we dare not stray, Buzzcut had said. Aomame knew what he meant by that. She herself had once lived in a world that placed such a region at its core. *In fact, I might still be living in that world. I just may not be aware of it.*

Aomame soundlessly repeated the words of her prayer with her lips. Then she took one deep breath, made up her mind, and walked into the next room.

CHAPTER 8

Tengo

TIME FOR THE CATS TO COME

Tengo spent the next week or more in a strange silence. One night, the man named Yasuda had called to tell Tengo that his wife had been lost and would never visit Tengo again. An hour later Ushikawa had called to tell him that Tengo and Fuka-Eri were functioning together as a carrier of a "thought crime" epidemic. Each caller had conveyed to Tengo a message containing (he could only believe that it *did* contain) a deep meaning, the way a toga-clad Roman would mount a platform in the middle of the Forum to make a proclamation to concerned citizens. And once each man had spoken his piece, he had hung up on Tengo.

Not one person had contacted Tengo since those two night-time calls. There were no phone calls, no letters, no knocks on the door, no carrier pigeons. Neither Komatsu nor Professor Ebisuno nor Fuka-Eri nor Kyoko Yasuda had anything at all they needed to convey to Tengo.

And Tengo felt as if he had lost all interest in those people. Nor was it just them: he seemed to have lost interest in anything at all. He didn't care about the sales of *Air Chrysalis* or what its author, Fuka-Eri, might be doing now, or what was happening with Komatsu's scheme or whether Professor Ebisuno's coolly conceived plan was progressing well, or how close the media had come to sniffing out the truth, or what kind of moves Sakigake might be making. If the boat they were all riding in was plunging over the falls upside down, there was nothing to do but fall with it. Tengo could struggle all he wanted to at this point, and it would do nothing to change the flow of the river.

He was, of course, worried about Kyoko Yasuda. He had no real idea what was happening to her, but he would spare no effort to help her if he could. Whatever problems she was facing at the moment, however, were out of his reach. There was nothing he could do.

He stopped reading the papers. The world was moving ahead in a direction unconnected with him. Apathy enveloped him as if it were his own personal haze. He was so sick of seeing the piles of *Air Chrysalis* on display that he stopped going to bookstores. He would travel in a straight line from home to the school and back. Most people were enjoying summer vacation, but the cram schools had summer courses, which kept him busier than ever. He welcomed this schedule. At least while he was lecturing, he didn't have to think about anything but mathematics.

He gave up on writing his novel, too. He might sit at his desk, switch on the word processor, and watch the screen light up, but he couldn't find the motivation to write. Whenever he tried to think of anything, snatches of his conversations with Kyoko Yasuda's husband or with Ushikawa would come to mind. He couldn't concentrate on his novel.

My wife is irretrievably lost. She can no longer visit your home in any form.

That was what Kyoko Yasuda's husband had said.

If I may use a classical analogy here, you people might have opened Pandora's box and let loose all kinds of things in the world. The two of you may have joined forces by accident, but you turned out to be a far more powerful team

**than you ever imagined. Each of you was able to make up
for what the other lacked.**

So said Ushikawa.

Both seemed to be trying to say the same thing: Tengo had
unleashed some kind of power before fully comprehending it
himself, and it was having a real impact (probably not a desirable impact) on the world around him. Tengo turned off the
word processor, sat down on the floor, and stared at the telephone. He needed more hints, more pieces of the puzzle. But
no one would give him those. Kindness was one of the things
presently (or permanently) in short supply in the world.

He thought about phoning someone – Komatsu or Professor Ebisuno or Ushikawa. But he couldn't make himself actually do it. He had had enough of their inscrutable, deliberately
cryptic pronouncements. If he sought a hint concerning one
riddle, all they would give him was another riddle. He couldn't
keep up the game forever. Fuka-Eri and Tengo were a powerful
team. That's all they needed to say. Tengo and Fuka-Eri. Like
Sonny and Cher. The Beat Goes On.

Day after day went by. Finally Tengo grew tired of staying
holed up in his apartment, waiting for something to happen. He shoved his wallet and a paperback into his pockets,
put on a baseball cap and sunglasses, and went out, walking with decisive strides as far as Koenji, the nearby station.
There he showed his pass and boarded the Chuo Line inbound
rapid-service train. The car was empty. He had nothing
planned that day. Wherever he went and whatever he did (or
didn't do) was entirely up to him. It was ten o'clock on a windless summer morning, and the sun was beating down.

Wondering if one of Ushikawa's "researchers" might be following him, he paid special attention on the way to the station,
stopping suddenly to glance behind him, but there was no sign
of anyone suspicious. At the station, he purposely went to the

wrong platform and then, pretending to change his mind all
of a sudden, he dashed down the stairs and went to the platform for trains headed in the other direction. But no one else
seemed to take those same maneuvers. He must be having a
typical delusion of being pursued. Of course no one was following him. Not even Tengo knew where he was going or what
he was about to do. He himself was the one who most wanted
to watch his own forthcoming actions from a distance.

The train he had boarded passed Shinjuku, Yotsuya, Ochano-
mizu, and arrived at Tokyo Central Station, the end of the line.
Everyone got off, and he followed suit. Then he sat on a bench
and gave some thought to where he ought to go. *I'm in downtown Tokyo now,* Tengo thought. *I have nothing planned all day.
I can go anywhere I decide to. The day looks as if it's going to be a
hot one. I could go to the seashore.* He raised his head and looked
at the platform guide.

At that point he suddenly realized what he had been doing
all along.

He tried shaking his head a few times, but the idea that
had struck him would not go away. He had probably made
up his mind unconsciously from the moment he boarded the
inbound Chuo Line train at his station in Koenji. He heaved a
sigh, stood up from the bench, went down the platform stairs,
and headed for the Sobu Line platform. On the way, he asked
a station employee for the fastest connection to Chikura,
and the man flipped through the pages of a thick volume of
train schedules. He should take the 11:30 special express train
to Tateyama, transfer there to a local, and he would arrive
at Chikura shortly after two o'clock. He bought a Tokyo–
Chikura round-trip ticket and a reserved seat on the express
train. Then he went to a restaurant in the station and ordered
rice and curry and a salad. He killed time after the meal by
drinking a cup of thin coffee.

Going to see his father was a depressing prospect. He had

never much liked the man, and his father probably had no special love for him, either. Tengo had no idea if his father had any desire to see him. His father had retired from NHK four years earlier and, soon afterward, entered a sanatorium in Chikura that specialized in care for patients with cognitive disorders. Tengo had visited him there no more than twice before – the first time just after the father entered the facility when an administrative procedural problem had required Tengo, as the only relative, to travel out there. The second time had involved a pressing administrative matter as well. Two times: that was it.

The sanatorium stood on a large plot of land across the road from the shoreline. Originally the country villa of a wealthy family connected with one of the prewar zaibatsu – large, influential, family-controlled financial/industrial monopolies – it had been bought as a life insurance company's welfare facility and, more recently, converted into a sanatorium primarily for the treatment of people with cognitive disorders. To an outside observer, it appeared to be an odd combination of elegant old wooden buildings and new three-story reinforced-concrete buildings. The air there was fresh, however, and aside from the roar of the surf, it was always quiet. One could walk along the shore on days when the wind was not too strong. An imposing pine grove lined the garden as a windbreak. And the medical facilities were excellent.

With his health insurance, retirement bonus, savings, and pension, Tengo's father could probably spend the rest of his life there quite comfortably, all because he had been lucky enough to be hired as a full-time employee of NHK. He might not be able to leave behind any sizable inheritance, but at least he could be taken care of, for which Tengo was tremendously grateful. Whether or not the man was his true biological father, Tengo had no intention of taking anything from him or giving him anything. They were two separate human beings who had come from – and were heading toward – entirely different places. By chance, they had spent some years of life together, that was all. It was a shame that things had come to that, Tengo believed, but there was absolutely nothing he could do about it.

Tengo knew that the time had come for him to visit his father again. He didn't much like the idea, and he would have preferred to take a U-turn and go straight back to his apartment. But he already had his round-trip and express-train tickets in his pocket. He was all set to go.

He left the table, paid his bill, and went to the platform to wait for the Tateyama express train to arrive. He scanned his surroundings once more, but saw no likely "researchers" in the area. His only fellow passengers were happy-looking families heading out for a few days at the beach. He took off his sunglasses, shoved them into a pocket, and readjusted his baseball cap. *Who gives a damn?* he thought. *Let them spy on me all they want. I'm going to a seaside town in Chiba to see my father, who is suffering from dementia. He might remember his son, or then again he might not. His memory was already pretty shaky last time. It's probably gotten worse since then. Cognitive disorders move ahead, never back. Or so I've been told. They're like gears that can only move in one direction.*

When the train left Tokyo Station, Tengo took out the paperback he had brought along and started reading it. It was an anthology of short stories on the theme of travel and included one tale about a young man who journeyed to a town ruled by cats. "Town of Cats" was the title. It was a fantastical piece by a German writer with whom he was not familiar. According to the book's editorial note, the story had been written in the period between the two world wars.

Carrying a single bag, the young man is traveling alone at his whim with no particular destination in mind. He goes by train and gets off at any stop that arouses his interest. He takes a room, sees the sights, and stays as long as he likes. When he has had enough, he boards another train. He spends every vacation this way.

One day he sees a lovely river from the train window. Gentle green hills line the meandering stream, and below them lies a quiet-looking, pretty little town with an old stone bridge over the river. The scene attracts him. Tasty river fish should be available in a place like this. The train stops at the station, and the young man steps down with his bag. No one else gets off there. As soon as he alights, the train departs.

No workers man the station, which must see very little activity. The young man crosses the stone bridge and walks into the town. It is utterly still, with no one to be seen. All the shops are shuttered, the town hall deserted. No one occupies the desk at the town's only hotel. He rings the bell, but no one comes out. The place seems totally uninhabited. Perhaps all the people are off napping somewhere. But it is only ten thirty in the morning, way too early for that. Perhaps something caused all the people to abandon the town. In any case, the next train will not come until the following morning, so he has no choice but to spend the night here. He wanders around the town to kill time.

In fact, however, this is a town of cats. When the sun starts to go down, many cats cross the bridge into town – cats of all different kinds and colors. They are much larger than ordinary cats, but they are still cats. The young man is shocked to see this spectacle. He rushes into the bell tower in the center of town and climbs to the top to hide. The cats go about their business raising the shop shutters or seating themselves at their town hall desks to start their day's work. Soon, still more cats come, crossing the bridge into town like the others. They enter the shops to buy things or go to the town hall to handle administrative matters or have a meal at the hotel restaurant or drink beer at the tavern and sing lively cat songs. One plays a concertina and others dance to the music. Because cats can see in the dark, they need almost no lights, but that particular night the glow of the full moon floods the town, enabling the young man to see every detail from his perch in the bell tower. When dawn approaches, the cats close up shop, finish their work or official business, and swarm back across the bridge to where they came from.

By the time the sun comes up, the cats are gone, and the town is deserted again. The young man climbs down, picks one of the hotel beds for himself, and goes to sleep. When he gets hungry, he eats the bread and cooked fish left in the hotel kitchen. When darkness approaches, he hides in the top of the bell tower again and observes the cats' activities until dawn. Trains stop at the station before noon and before evening. If he took the morning train he could continue his journey, and if he took the afternoon train he could go back where he came from. No passengers alight at the station, and no one boards here, either. Still, the trains stop at the station for exactly one minute as scheduled and pull out again. He could take one of the trains and leave the creepy cat town behind. But he doesn't. Being young, he has a lively curiosity and boundless ambition and is ready for adventure. He wants to see more of the strange spectacle of the cat town. If possible, he wants to find out when and how it became a town of cats, how the town is organized, and what the cats are doing there. He is probably the only human being who has ever seen this strange sight.

On the night of the third day, a hubbub breaks out in the square below the bell tower. "Hey, do you smell something human?" one of the cats says. "Now that you mention it, I *thought* there was a funny smell the past few days," another chimes in, twitching his nose. "Me too," says yet another cat. "That's weird. There shouldn't be any humans here," someone adds. "No, of course not. There's no way a human could get into this town of cats." "Still, that smell of theirs is definitely here."

The cats form into groups and search the town from top

to bottom like vigilante bands. Cats have an excellent sense of smell when they want to use it, so it takes them very little time to discover that the bell tower is the source of the smell. The young man hears their soft paws padding their way up the stairs. *That's it, they've got me!* he thinks. His smell seems to have aroused the cats to anger. They have big, sharp claws and white fangs. Humans are not supposed to set foot in this town. He has no idea what terrible fate awaits him if he is discovered, but he is sure they will never let him leave the town alive now that he has learned their secret.

Three cats climb to the top of the bell tower and sniff the air. "Strange," one cat says, twitching his whiskers. "I smell a human, but there's no one here."

"It *is* strange," says a second cat. "But there is definitely no one here. Let's look somewhere else."

"I don't get it, though."

The three cats cock their heads, puzzled, then retreat down the stairs. The young man hears their footsteps going down and fading into the dark of night. He breathes a sigh of relief, but *he* doesn't get it, either. He was literally nose-to-nose with the cats in this small space. There was no way they could have missed him. But for some reason they did not see him. He brings his hand to his eyes and can see it perfectly well. It hasn't turned transparent. Strange. In any case, though, when morning comes, he knows he should go to the station and take the train away from this town. Staying here would be too dangerous. His luck can't last forever.

The next day, however, the morning train does not stop at the station. He watches it pass by without slowing down. The afternoon train does the same. He can even see the engineer seated at the controls. The passengers' faces, too, are visible through the windows. But the train shows no sign of stopping. It is as though people cannot see the young man waiting for a train – or even see the station itself. Once the afternoon train disappears down the track, the place grows quieter than ever. The sun begins to sink. It is time for the cats to come. He knows that he is irretrievably lost. This is no town of cats, he finally realizes. It is the place where he is meant to be lost. It is a place not of this world that has been prepared especially for him. And never again, for all eternity, will the train stop at this station to bring him back to his original world.

Tengo read the story twice. The phrase "the place where he is meant to be lost" attracted his attention. He closed the book and let his eyes wander aimlessly across the drab coastal industrial scene passing by the train window – the flame of an oil refinery, the gigantic gas tanks, the squat but equally gigantic smokestacks shaped like long-range cannons, the line of tractor-trailers and tank trucks moving down the road. It was a scene remote from "Town of Cats," but it had its own sense of fantasy about it, as though it were the netherworld supporting urban life from below.

Soon afterward Tengo closed his eyes and imagined Kyoko Yasuda closed up in her own "lost place," where there were no trains or telephones or mail. During the day there was nothing but absolute loneliness, and with night came the cats' relentless searching, the cycle repeating itself with no apparent end. Apparently, he had drifted off to sleep in his seat – not a long nap, but a deep one. He woke covered in sweat. The train was moving along the southern coastline of the Boso Peninsula in midsummer.

He left the express train in Tateyama, transferred to a local, and went as far as Chikura. Stepping from the train, he caught a whiff of the old familiar smell of the seashore. Everyone on the street was darkly tanned. He took a cab from the station to the sanatorium. At the reception desk, he gave his name and his father's name.

The middle-aged nurse at the desk asked, "Have you by any chance notified us of your intention to visit today?" There was a hard edge to her voice. A small woman, she wore metal-frame glasses, and her short hair had a touch of gray. The ring on her stubby ring finger might have been bought as part of a matching set with the glasses. Her name tag said "Tamura."

"No, it just occurred to me to come this morning and I hopped on a train," Tengo answered honestly.

The nurse gave him a look of mild disgust. Then she said, "Visitors are supposed to notify us before they arrive to see a patient. We have our schedules to keep, and the wishes of the patient must also be taken into account."

"I'm sorry, I didn't know."

"When was your last visit?"

"Two years ago."

"Two years ago," Nurse Tamura said as she checked the list of visitors with a ballpoint pen in hand. "You mean to say that you have not made a single visit in two years?"

"That's right," Tengo said.

"According to our records, you are Mr. Kawana's only relative."

"That is correct."

She set the list on the desk and glanced at Tengo, but she said nothing. Her eyes were not blaming Tengo, just checking the facts. Apparently, Tengo's case was not exceptional.

"At the moment, your father is in group rehabilitation. That will end in half an hour. You can see him then."

"How is he doing?"

"Physically, he's healthy. He has no special problems. It's in the *other* area that he has his ups and downs," she said, touching her temple with an index finger. "I'll leave it to you to see what I mean about ups and downs."

Tengo thanked her and went to pass the time in the lounge by the entrance, sitting on a sofa that smelled like an earlier era and reading more of his book. A breeze passed through now and then, carrying the scent of the sea and the cooling sound of the pine windbreak outside. Cicadas clung to the branches of the trees, screeching their hearts out. Summer was now at its height, but the cicadas seemed to know that it would not last long.

Eventually bespectacled Nurse Tamura came to tell Tengo that he could see his father now that the rehabilitation session was over.

"I'll show you to his room," she said. Tengo got up from the sofa and, passing by a large mirror on the wall, realized for the first time what a sloppy outfit he was wearing – a Jeff Beck Japan Tour T-shirt under a faded dungaree shirt with mismatched buttons, chinos with specks of pizza sauce near one knee, long-unwashed khaki-colored sneakers, a baseball cap: no way for a thirty-year-old son to dress on his first hospital visit to his father in two years. Nor did he have anything with him that might serve as a gift on such an occasion. He had a paperback book shoved into one pocket, nothing more. No wonder the nurse had given him that look of disgust.

As they crossed the sanatorium grounds toward the wing in which his father's room was located, the nurse gave him a general description of the place. There were three wings divided according to the severity of the patient's illness. Tengo's father was now housed in the "moderate" wing. People usually started in the "mild" wing, moved to "moderate," and then to "severe." As with a door that opens in only one direction, backward movement was not an option. There was nowhere to go beyond the "severe" wing – other than the crematorium. The nurse did not add that remark, of course, but her meaning was clear.

His father was in a double room, but his roommate was out attending some kind of class. The sanatorium offered several rehabilitation classes – ceramics, or gardening, or exercise.

Though all were supposedly for "rehabilitation," they did not aim at "recovery." Their purpose, rather, was to slow the advance of the disease as much as possible. Or just to kill time. Tengo's father was seated in a chair by the open window, looking out, hands on his knees. A nearby table held a potted plant. Its flowers had several delicate, yellow petals. The floor was made of some soft material to prevent injury in case of a fall. There were two plain wood-frame beds, two writing desks, and two dressers. Next to each desk was a small bookcase, and the window curtains had yellowed from years of exposure to sunlight.

Tengo did not realize at first that the old man seated by the window was his own father. He had become a size smaller – though "shriveled up" might be more accurate. His hair was shorter and as white as a frost-covered lawn. His cheeks were sunken, which may have been why the hollows of his eyes looked much larger than they had before. Three deep creases marked his forehead. The shape of his head seemed more deformed than it had, probably because his shorter hair made it more obvious. His eyebrows were extremely long and thick, and white hair poked out from both ears. His large, pointed ears were now larger than ever and looked like bat wings. Only the shape of the nose was the same – round and pudgy, in marked contrast to the ears, and it wore a reddish black tinge. His lips drooped at both ends, seemingly ready to drool at any moment. His mouth was slightly open, revealing uneven teeth. Sitting so still at the window, his father reminded Tengo of one of van Gogh's last self-portraits.

Although Tengo entered the room, the man did nothing but glance momentarily in his direction, after which he continued to stare outside. From a distance, he looked less like a human being than some kind of creature resembling a rat or a squirrel – a creature that might not be terribly clean but that possessed all the cunning it needed. It was, however, without a doubt,

Tengo's father – or, rather, the wreckage of Tengo's father. The two intervening years had taken much from him physically, the way a merciless tax collector strips a poor family's house of all its possessions. The father that Tengo remembered was a tough, hardworking man. Introspection and imagination may have been foreign qualities to him, but he had his own moral code and a simple but strong sense of purpose. He was a stoic individual; Tengo never once heard him whine or make excuses for himself. But the man Tengo saw before him now was a mere empty shell, a vacant house deprived of all warmth.

"Mr. Kawana!" the nurse said to Tengo's father in a crisp, clear tone of voice she must have been trained to use when addressing patients. "Mr. Kawana! Look who's here! It's your son!"

His father turned once more in Tengo's direction. His expressionless eyes made Tengo think of two empty swallows' nests hanging from the eaves.

"Hello," Tengo said.

"Mr. Kawana, your son is here from Tokyo!" the nurse said.

His father said nothing. Instead, he looked straight at Tengo as if he were reading a bulletin written in a foreign language.

"Dinner starts at six thirty," the nurse said to Tengo. "Please feel free to stay until then."

Tengo hesitated for a moment after the nurse was gone, and then approached his father, sitting down in the chair that faced his – a faded, cloth-covered chair, its wooden parts scarred from long use. His father's eyes followed his movements.

"How are you?" Tengo asked.

"Fine, thank you," his father said formally.

Tengo did not know what to say after that. Toying with the third button of his dungaree shirt, he turned his gaze toward the pine trees outside and then back again to his father.

"You have come from Tokyo, is it?" his father asked, apparently unable to remember Tengo.

"Yes, from Tokyo."

"You must have come by express train."

"That's right," Tengo said. "As far as Tateyama. There I transferred to a local for the trip here to Chikura."

"You've come to swim?" his father asked.

"I'm Tengo. Tengo Kawana. Your son."

"Where do you live in Tokyo?" his father asked.

"In Koenji. Suginami Ward."

The three wrinkles across his father's forehead deepened. "A lot of people tell lies because they don't want to pay their NHK subscription fee."

"Father!" Tengo called out to him. This was the first time he had spoken the word in a very long time. "I'm Tengo. Your son."

"I don't have a son," his father declared.

"You don't have a son," Tengo repeated mechanically.

His father nodded.

"So, what am I?" Tengo asked.

"You're nothing," his father said with two short shakes of the head.

Tengo caught his breath. He could find no words. Nor did his father have any more to say. Each sat in silence, searching through his tangled thoughts. Only the cicadas sang without confusion, screeching at top volume.

He may be speaking the truth, Tengo felt. *His memory may have been destroyed, and his mind might be sunk in mud, but the words on his lips are probably true.* Tengo understood this intuitively.

"What are you talking about?" Tengo asked.

"You are nothing," his father repeated the words, his voice devoid of emotion. "You were nothing, you are nothing, and you will be nothing."

That's enough, Tengo thought.

He wanted to get up out of his chair, walk to the station, and go back to Tokyo. He had heard what he needed to hear. But he could not stand up. He was like the young man who traveled to the town of cats. He had curiosity. He wanted to know what lay behind those words. He wanted a clearer answer. There was danger lurking there, of course. But if he let this opportunity escape, he would lose any chance to learn the secret about himself forever. It would sink into total chaos.

Tengo arranged and rearranged words in his head until, at last, he was ready to speak them. This was the question he had come close to asking since childhood but could never quite manage to utter.

"What you're saying, then, is that you are not my biological father, correct? You are telling me that there is no blood connection between us, is that it?"

His father looked at him without speaking. It was impossible to tell from his expression whether he had understood the meaning of Tengo's question.

"Stealing radio waves is an unlawful act," his father said, looking into Tengo's eyes. "It is no different from stealing money or valuables, don't you think?"

"You're probably right," Tengo decided to agree for now.

His father nodded several times with apparent satisfaction.

"Radio waves don't come falling out of the sky for free like rain or snow," his father said.

With his lips closed Tengo stared at his father's hands. They were lined up neatly on his knees, right hand on right knee, left hand on left knee, stock still. Small, dark hands, they looked tanned to the core by long years of outdoor work.

"My mother didn't really die of an illness when I was little, did she?" Tengo asked slowly, speaking phrase by phrase.

His father did not answer. His expression did not change, and his hands did not move. His eyes focused on Tengo as if they were observing something unfamiliar.

"My mother left you. She got rid of you and left me behind. She probably went off with another man. Am I wrong?"

His father nodded. "It is not good to steal radio waves. You can't get away with it, doing anything you like."

This man understands my questions perfectly well. He just doesn't want to answer them directly, Tengo felt.

"Father," Tengo addressed him. "You may not actually be my father, but I'll call you that for now because I don't know what else to call you. To tell you the truth, I've never liked you. Maybe I've even hated you most of the time. You know that, don't you? But even supposing you are not my real father and there is no blood connection between us, I no longer have any reason to hate you. I don't know if I can go so far as to be fond of you, but I think that at least I should be able to understand you better than I do now. I have always wanted to know the truth about who I am and where I came from. That's all. But no one ever told me. If you will tell me the truth right now, I won't hate you or dislike you anymore. In fact, I would welcome the opportunity not to have to hate you or dislike you any longer."

His father went on staring at Tengo with expressionless eyes, saying nothing, but Tengo felt he might be seeing the tiniest gleam of light flashing somewhere deep within those empty swallows' nests.

"I am nothing," Tengo said. "You are right. I'm like someone who's been thrown into the ocean at night, floating all alone. I reach out, but no one is there. I call out, but no one answers. I have no connection to anything. The closest thing I have to a family is you, but you hold on to the secret and won't even try to tell me anything. Meanwhile, in this seaside town, your memory goes through repeated ups and downs as it steadily deteriorates day by day. Like your memory, the truth about me is being lost. Without the aid of truth, I am nothing, and I can never be anything. You are right about that, too."

"Knowledge is a precious social asset," his father said in a monotone, though his voice was somewhat quieter than before, as if someone behind him had reached over and turned down the volume. "It is an asset that must be amassed in abundant stockpiles and utilized with the utmost care. It must be handed down to the next generation in fruitful forms. For that reason, too, NHK needs to have all of your subscription fees and – "

This is a kind of mantra for him, thought Tengo. *He has protected himself all these years by reciting such phrases.* Tengo felt he had to smash this obstinate amulet of his, to pull the living human being out from behind the surrounding barrier.

He cut his father short. "What kind of person was my mother? Where did she go? What happened to her?"

His father brought his incantation to a sudden halt.

Tengo went on, "I'm tired of living in hatred and resentment. I'm tired of living unable to love anyone. I don't have a single friend – *not one.* And, worst of all, I can't even love myself. Why is that? Why can't I love myself? It's because I can't love anyone else. A person learns how to love himself through the simple acts of loving and being loved by someone else. Do you understand what I am saying? A person who is incapable of loving another cannot properly love himself. No, I'm not blaming you for this. Come to think of it, you may be such a victim. You probably don't know how to love yourself. Am I wrong about that?"

His father was closed off in silence, lips shut tight. It was impossible to tell from his expression whether he had understood Tengo or not. Tengo also fell silent and settled more deeply into his chair. A breeze blew in through the open window, stirred the sun-bleached curtains and the delicate petals of the potted plant, and slipped through the open door into the corridor. The smell of the sea was stronger than before. The soft sound of pine needles brushing against each other blended with the cries of the cicadas.

His voice softer now, Tengo went on, "A vision often comes to me – the same one, over and over, ever since I can remember.

I suspect it's probably not so much a vision as a memory of something that actually happened. I'm one and a half years old, and my mother is next to me. She and a young man are holding each other. The man is not you. Who he is, I have no idea, but he is definitely not you. I don't know why, but the scene is permanently burned into me."

His father said nothing, but his eyes were clearly seeing something else – something not there. The two maintained their silence. Tengo was listening to the suddenly stronger breeze. He did not know what his father was listening to.

"I wonder if I might ask you to read me something," his father said in formal tones after a long silence. "My sight has deteriorated to the point where I can't read books anymore. I can't follow the words on the page for long. That bookcase has some books. Choose any one you like."

Tengo gave up and left his chair to scan the spines of the volumes in the bookcase. Most of them were historical novels set in ancient times when samurai roamed the land. All the volumes of *Sword of Doom* were there. Tengo couldn't bring himself to read his father some musty old book full of archaic language.

"If you don't mind, I'd rather read a story about a town of cats," Tengo said. "I brought it to read myself."

"A story about a town of cats," his father said, savoring the words. "Please read that to me, if it is not too much trouble."

Tengo looked at his watch. "It's no trouble at all. I have plenty of time before my train leaves. It's an odd story; I don't know if you'll like it or not."

Tengo pulled out his paperback and started reading "Town of Cats." His father listened to him read the entire story, not changing his position in the chair by the window. Tengo read slowly in a clearly audible voice, taking two or three breaks along the way to catch his breath. He glanced at his father whenever he stopped reading but saw no discernible reaction on his face. Was he enjoying the story or not? He could not tell. When he was through reading the story, his father was sitting perfectly still with his eyes closed. He looked as if he could be sound asleep, but he was not. He was simply deep inside the story, and it took him a while to come back out. Tengo waited patiently for that to happen. The afternoon light had begun to weaken and blend with touches of evening. The ocean breeze continued to shake the pines.

"Does that town of cats have television?" his father asked.

"The story was written in Germany in the 1930s. They didn't have television yet back then. They did have radio, though."

"I was in Manchuria, but I didn't even have a radio. There weren't any stations. The newspaper often didn't arrive, and when it did it was two weeks old. There was hardly anything to eat, and we had no women. Sometimes there were wolves roaming around. It was like the edge of the earth out there."

He fell silent for a while, thinking, probably recalling the hard life he led as a young pioneer in distant Manchuria. But those memories soon clouded over, swallowed up into nothingness. Tengo could read these movements of his father's mind from the changing expressions on his face.

"Did the cats build the town? Or did people build it a long time ago and the cats came to live there?" his father asked, speaking toward the windowpane as if to himself, though the question seemed to have been directed to Tengo.

"I don't know," Tengo said. "But it does seem to have been built by human beings long before. Maybe the people left for some reason – say, they all died in an epidemic – and the cats came to live there."

His father nodded. "When a vacuum forms, something has to come along to fill it. Because that's what everybody does."

"That's what everybody does?"

"Exactly."

"What kind of vacuum are *you* filling?"

His father scowled. His long eyebrows came down to hide his eyes. Then he said with a touch of sarcasm in his voice, "Don't you know?"

"I don't know," Tengo said.

His father's nostrils flared. One eyebrow rose slightly. This was the expression he always used when he was dissatisfied with something. "If you can't understand it without an explanation, you can't understand it with an explanation."

Tengo narrowed his eyes, trying to read the man's expression. Never once had his father employed such odd, suggestive language. He always spoke in concrete, practical terms. To say only what was necessary when necessary: that was his unshakable definition of a conversation. But there was no expression on his face to be read.

"I see. So you are filling in some kind of vacuum," Tengo said. "All right, then, who is going to fill the vacuum that you have left behind?"

"You," his father declared, raising an index finger and thrusting it straight at Tengo. "Isn't it obvious? I have been filling in the vacuum that somebody else made, so you will fill in the vacuum that I have made. Like taking turns."

"The way the cats filled in the town after the people were gone."

"Right. Lost like the town," his father said. Then he stared vacantly at his own outstretched index finger as if looking at some mysterious, misplaced object.

"Lost like the town," Tengo repeated his father's words.

"The woman who gave birth to you is not anywhere anymore."

" 'Not anywhere.' 'Lost like the town.' Are you saying she's dead?"

His father made no reply to that.

Tengo sighed. "So, then, who is my father?"

"Just a vacuum. Your mother joined her body with a vacuum and gave birth to you. I filled in that vacuum."

Having said that much, his father closed his eyes and closed his mouth.

"Joined her body with a vacuum?"

"Yes."

"And you raised me. Is that what you're saying?"

After one ceremonious clearing of his throat, his father said, as if trying to explain a simple truth to a slow-witted child, "That is why I said, 'If you can't understand it without an explanation, you can't understand it with an explanation.' "

"So you're telling me that I came out of a vacuum?" Tengo asked.

No answer.

Tengo folded his hands in his lap and looked straight into his father's face once more. *This man is no empty shell, no vacant house. He is a flesh-and-blood human being with a narrow, stubborn soul and shadowed memories, surviving in fits and starts on this patch of land by the sea. He has no choice but to coexist with the vacuum that is slowly spreading inside him. The vacuum and his memories are still at odds, but eventually, regardless of his wishes, the vacuum will completely swallow up whatever memories are left. It is just a matter of time. Could the vacuum that he is confronting now be the same vacuum from which I was born?*

Tengo thought he might be hearing the distant rumble of the sea mixed with the early-evening breeze slipping through the pine branches. Though it could have been an illusion.

CHAPTER 9

Aomame

WHAT COMES AS A PAYMENT
FOR HEAVENLY GRACE

When Aomame walked into the adjoining room, Buzzcut followed and swiftly closed the door. The room was totally dark. Thick curtains covered the window, and all lights had been extinguished. A few rays of light seeped in through a gap between the curtains, serving only to emphasize the darkness of everything else.

It took time for her eyes to adjust to the darkness, as in a movie theater or planetarium. The first thing she saw was the display of an electric clock on a low table. Its green figures read 7:20 P.M. When a few more seconds passed, she could tell that there was a large bed against the back wall. The clock was near the head of the bed. This room was somewhat smaller than the spacious adjoining room, but it was still larger than an ordinary hotel room.

On the bed was a deep black object, like a small mountain. Still more time had to go by before Aomame could tell that its irregular outline indicated the presence of a human body. During this interval, the outline remained perfectly unbroken. She could detect no signs of life. There was no breathing to be heard. The only sound was the soft rush of air from the air conditioner near the ceiling. Still, the body was not dead. Buzzcut's actions were based on the premise that this was a living human being.

This was a very large person, most likely a man. She could not be sure, but the person did not seem to be facing in this direction and did not seem to be under the covers but rather was lying facedown on the made-up bed, like a large animal at the back of a cave, trying not to expend its physical energy while it allows its wounds to heal.

"It is time," Buzzcut announced in the direction of the shadow. There was a new tension in his voice.

Whether or not the man heard Buzzcut's voice was unclear. The dark mound on the bed remained perfectly still. Buzzcut stood stiffly by the door, waiting. The room was enveloped in a silence so deep Aomame could hear someone swallow, and then she realized that the sound of swallowing had come from her. Gripping her gym bag in her right hand, Aomame, like Buzzcut, was waiting for something to happen. The clock display changed to 7:21, then 7:22, then 7:23.

Eventually the outline on the bed began to show a slight degree of motion – a faint shudder that soon became a clear movement. The person must have been in a deep sleep or a state resembling sleep. The muscles awoke, the upper body began to rise, and, in time, the consciousness was regained. The shadow sat straight up on the bed, legs folded. *It's definitely a man*, thought Aomame.

"It is time," Buzzcut said again.

Aomame heard the man release a long breath. It was like a heavy sigh slowly rising from the bottom of a deep well. Next came the sound of a large inhalation. It was as wild and unsettling as a gale tearing through a forest. Then the cycle started again, the two utterly different types of sound repeated, separated by a long silence. This made Aomame feel uneasy. She sensed that she had found her way into a region that was completely foreign to her – a deep ocean trench, say, or the surface of an unknown asteroid: the kind of place it might be possible to reach with great effort, but from which return was impossible.

Her eyes refused to adapt fully to the darkness. She could now see to a certain point but no farther. All that her eyes could reach was the man's dark silhouette. She could not tell which way he was facing or what he was looking at. All she could see was that he was an extremely large man and that his shoulders seemed to rise and fall quietly – but enormously – with each breath. This was not normal breathing. Rather, it was breathing that had a special purpose and function and that was performed with the entire body. She pictured the large movements of his shoulder blades and diaphragm expanding and contracting. No ordinary human being could breathe with such fierce intensity. It was a distinctive method of breathing that could only be mastered through long, intense training.

Buzzcut stood next to her at full attention, back straight, chin in. His breathing was shallow and quick, in contrast to that of the man on the bed. He was trying to minimize his presence as he waited for the intense deep breathing sequence to end: apparently it was an activity the man practiced routinely. Like Buzzcut, Aomame could do nothing but wait for it to end. It was probably a process the man needed to go through to become fully awake.

Finally, the special breathing ended in stages, the way a large machine stops running. The intervals between breaths grew gradually longer, concluding with one long breath that seemed to squeeze everything out. A deep silence fell over the room once again.

"It is time," Buzzcut said a third time.

The man's head moved slowly. He now seemed to be facing Buzzcut.

"You may leave the room," the man said. His voice was a deep, clear baritone – decisive and unambiguous. His body had apparently attained complete wakefulness.

Buzzcut gave one shallow bow in the darkness and left the room the way he had entered it, with no unnecessary movements. The door closed, leaving Aomame alone in the room with the man.

"I'm sorry it's so dark," the man said, most likely to Aomame.

"I don't mind," Aomame said.

"We had to make it dark," the man said softly. "But don't worry. You will not be hurt."

Aomame nodded. Then, recalling that she was in darkness, she said aloud, "I see." Her voice was somewhat harder and higher than normal.

For a time, the man stared at Aomame in the darkness. She felt herself being stared at intensely. His gaze was precise and attentive to detail. He was not so much "looking" at her as "viewing" her. He seemed able to survey every inch of her body. She felt as if he had, in an instant, stripped off every piece of clothing and left her stark naked. But his gaze didn't stop with the skin; it pierced through to her muscles and organs and uterus. *He can see in the dark,* she thought. *He is* viewing *far more than the eyes can see.*

"Things can be seen better in the darkness," he said, as if he had just seen into her mind. "But the longer you spend in the dark, the harder it becomes to return to the world above-ground where the light is. You have to call a stop to it at some point."

Having said this, he spent another interval observing Aomame. There was nothing sexual in his gaze. He was just *viewing* her as an object, the way a boat passenger stares at the shape of a passing island. But this was no ordinary passenger. He was trying to see through to *everything* about the island. With prolonged exposure to such a relentless, piercing gaze, Aomame strongly felt the imperfections of her own fleshly self. This was not how she felt normally. Aside from the size of her breasts, she was, if anything, proud of her body. She trained it daily and kept it beautiful. Her muscles were smooth and taut without the slightest excess flesh. Stared at by this man, however, she could not help but feel that her flesh was a worn-out old bag of meat.

As though he had read her thoughts, the man stopped staring at her. She felt the power suddenly go out of his gaze. It was as if someone had been spraying water with a hose when another person behind the building turned off the spigot.

"Sorry, but could you open the curtains just a bit?" the man asked softly. "I'm sure you could use some light, too, for your work."

Setting the gym bag on the floor, Aomame went over to the window and pulled on the cords at the side to open, first, the thick, heavy curtains and then the inner white lace curtains. Nighttime Tokyo poured its light into the room. Tokyo Tower's floodlights, the lamps lining the elevated expressway, the moving headlights of cars, the lighted windows of high-rise buildings, the colorful rooftop neon signs: they all combined to illuminate the hotel room with that mixed light unique to the big city, but just barely, enough so that Aomame was now able to make out some of the room's furnishings. Aomame saw the light with a pang of familiarity. This was light from the world to which she herself belonged. She suddenly realized how urgently she needed such light. As weak as it was, though, it appeared to be too strong for the man's eyes. Still seated on the bed in the lotus position, he covered his face with his two large hands.

"Are you all right?" Aomame asked.

"Don't worry," he said.

"Shall I close the curtains a bit more?"

"No, that's fine. I have a problem with my retinas. It takes time for them to adjust to light. I'll be all right in a minute. Have a seat over there."

A problem with his retinas? Aomame wondered. People with retinal problems are usually on the verge of going blind. But this was of no concern to Aomame now. She was not here to deal with this man's sight.

While the man was covering his face with his hands and letting his eyes adjust to the light streaming in from the window, Aomame sat on a sofa and watched him. Now it was her turn to study him in detail.

He was a very large man. Not fat, just large. Tall and broad and powerful looking. She had heard about his large size from the dowager, but she had not expected him to be this big. There was, of course, no reason that a religious guru should not be huge. She imagined ten-year-old girls being raped by this big man and found herself scowling. She imagined him naked and mounted on a tiny girl. There was no way for such girls to resist. Even an adult woman would have a difficult time of it.

The man was wearing something like thin sweatpants that narrowed at the ankles with elastic bands, and a solid-color long-sleeved shirt that had a slight, silk-like sheen. The loose-fitting shirt buttoned up the front, but the man had left the top two buttons open. Both the pants and the shirt appeared to be white or a light cream color. These were not pajamas but more like comfortable lounging clothes or an outfit that would look normal under palm trees in southern lands. His bare feet looked big. The broad stone wall of his shoulders brought to mind an experienced martial arts combatant.

After waiting for a pause in Aomame's observation, the man said, "Thanks for coming today."

"It's my job," Aomame said in a voice devoid of emotion. "I go where I'm needed." Even as she spoke, however, she felt like a prostitute who had come when called. Perhaps this was due to the way he had undressed her in the darkness with that penetrating gaze.

"How much do you know about me?" the man asked Aomame, his hands still covering his face.

"How much do I know about you?"

"That's right."

"Almost nothing," Aomame said, choosing her words

carefully. "I have not even been told your name. All I know is that you are the head of a religious organization in Nagano or Yamanashi, that you have some kind of physical problem, and that I may be able to help you with it."

The man gave his head a few quick shakes and took his hands away from his face. Now he and Aomame were looking directly at each other.

His hair was long. His abundant head of hair hung straight down to his shoulders. It had much gray mixed in. The man was probably somewhere in his late forties or early fifties. He had a large nose that occupied a good deal of his face. It was admirably straight and brought to mind a calendar photo of the Alps. The mountain had a broad base and great dignity. It was the first thing one noticed when looking at his face, and it contrasted sharply with his eyes, which were set so deeply into his face that it was hard to tell what they were looking at. Like his body, his face was broad and thick. Clean-shaven, it bore no scars or moles. The features worked well together, producing a look of serenity and intelligence but also something peculiar, out of the ordinary, something that did not inspire easy trust. It was the kind of face that, on first impression, gives people pause. Perhaps it was because the nose was too big. Because of it, the face was missing a certain balance, perhaps the root of what left the observer feeling unsettled. Or perhaps it was the deep-set eyes that did it, the way they gave off the quiet glow of an ancient glacier. Then again, it might have been the cruel impression created by the thin lips, which looked as if they were ready to spit out unpredictable words at any moment.

"And besides that?" he asked.

"Besides that I have heard very little. All I was told was to be prepared to perform stretching exercises. The muscles and joints are my area of expertise. I don't need to know much about my clients' positions or personalities."

Just like a whore, Aomame thought.

"I understand what you are saying," the man said in a deep voice. "But in my case, you might need some explanation."

"I would be glad to listen to anything you might wish to share."

"People call me 'Leader.' But I almost never show my face to anyone. Most of our believers, although they belong to the religion and live in the same compound, have no idea what I look like."

Aomame nodded.

"But here I am, letting you see my face. For one thing, I can hardly ask you to treat me in the dark or blindfolded. And there is also the question of courtesy."

"What I do is not a 'treatment,'" Aomame calmly corrected him. "It is simply the stretching of the muscles. I am not licensed to perform medical procedures. All I do is force people to stretch the muscles they don't normally use or the ones that are difficult to use, and that way we prevent the deterioration of their physical strength."

The man appeared to smile faintly, though it might have been a mere illusion caused by a slight twitching of his facial muscles.

"I am quite aware of that. I simply used the word 'treat' for convenience's sake. Don't worry. All I was trying to say was that you are now seeing something that most people are not able to see, and I wanted you to be aware of that."

"I was warned in there not to say anything about this to anyone," Aomame said, pointing toward the door to the adjoining room. "But none of you need to worry. Nothing that I observe here will find its way outside. I touch many people's bodies in my work. You may be someone in a special position, but to me you are merely one of many people with muscle problems. The only part of you that concerns me is your muscles."

"I hear you were a Society of Witnesses believer as a child."

"It's not as if I chose to become a believer. I was simply raised that way. There is a big difference between the two."

"Indeed, a very big difference," the man said. "But people can never fully divorce themselves from the images implanted during early childhood."

"For better or worse," Aomame said.

"The Witnesses' doctrines are very different from those of the religion that I belong to. If you ask me, any religion that takes the end of the world as one of its central tenets is more or less bogus. In my view, the only thing that ever 'ends' is the individual. That said, the Society of Witnesses is an amazingly tough religion. Its history is not very long, but it has withstood many tests and has steadily continued to increase the number of its believers. There is a lot that can be learned from that."

"It probably just shows how close-minded they've been. The smaller and narrower such a group is, the more firmly they can resist outside pressure."

"You are probably right about that," the man said, pausing for a few moments. "In any case, we're not here to discuss religion."

Aomame said nothing.

"What I want you to understand is the fact that my body has many special things about it."

Aomame, still seated, waited for him to go on.

"As I said before, my eyes can't stand strong light. This symptom appeared some years ago. I had no particular problem until that time, but all at once, at some point, it started. This was the main reason I stopped coming into people's presence. I spend practically all my time in dark rooms."

"I'm afraid I can't do anything for vision problems," Aomame said. "As I said before, the muscles are my area of expertise."

"Yes, I am quite aware of that. And of course I consulted medical specialists. I have been to any number of famous eye doctors and had many tests. But they tell me there is nothing they can do at this point. My retinas have been damaged, but they don't know the cause. The symptoms are slowly progressing. If things go on like this, I will lose my sight before long. As you say, of course, this is a problem that has nothing to do with the muscles. But let me list my physical problems in order, and when I am through, we can think about what you can and cannot do."

Aomame nodded.

"The next problem is that my muscles often go stiff," the man said. "I quite literally 'can't move a muscle.' They become rock hard and stay that way for hours. All I can do at such times is lie down. I don't feel any pain. All the muscles of my body simply become immobile. I can't even move a finger. The only thing I can manage to move, through sheer willpower, is my eyeballs. This happens once or twice a month."

"Do you have any sign beforehand that it is about to happen?"

"First I have spasms. My muscles start twitching all over. That goes on for ten to twenty minutes. After that, my muscles go dead, as if someone has turned off a switch. During those ten or twenty minutes after the warning comes, I go to a place where I can stretch out, and I lie down. Like a boat seeking shelter from a storm in a cove, I wait there in hiding for the paralysis to pass over me. And though the paralysis is complete when it comes, my mind remains fully awake. No, if anything, it is awake with a special clarity."

"You say you have no pain?"

"I lose all sensation. If you jabbed me with a needle, I wouldn't feel it."

"Have you consulted a doctor about that?"

"I have been to all the best hospitals and any number of doctors, but all they can tell me is that this is an unprecedented affliction for which current medical knowledge can do nothing. I have tried traditional Chinese remedies, osteopathic physicians, acupuncture, moxibustion, massage, hot spring cures – everything I could think of – but have had no results worth talking about."

Aomame frowned slightly. "All my approach does is to stimulate the normal bodily functions. I doubt that it will have much effect on such severe problems."

"Yes, I am quite aware of that as well. But I am trying to exhaust every possibility. Even if your method has no effect, that is not your responsibility. Just do to me what you always do. I would like to see how my body responds to it."

Aomame pictured the man's huge body lying motionless in some dark place like a hibernating animal.

"When was the last time you experienced the paralysis?"

"Ten days ago," the man said. "And – this is a bit difficult to bring up, but – there is one more thing I should probably mention."

"Feel free to tell me anything."

"All the time my muscles are in that state of suspended animation, I have an erection."

Aomame's frown deepened. "You mean to say that your sex organ remains hard for hours at a time?"

"That is correct."

"But you have no feeling."

"None at all," he said. "No sexual desire, either. I just harden up. Like a rock, the way my muscles do."

Aomame gave her head a little shake and did her best to resume a normal expression. "I don't believe I can do anything about that, either. It's quite far from my area of expertise."

"This is very difficult for me to talk about, and you probably don't want to hear about it either, but may I tell you a bit more?"

"Please do. Your secrets are safe with me."

"During this interval, it happens that I am physically joined with girls."

"Girls?!"

"I have a number of females around me. Whenever I go into my paralytic state, they take turns mounting me and having sexual relations with me. I have no feeling at all. I feel no sexual pleasure. But I do ejaculate. With each of them."

Aomame kept silent.

He continued, "All together, there are three girls, all in their teens. I am sure you must be wondering why I have such young girls around me and why they must have sex with me."

"Could it be, perhaps, part of a religious practice?"

Still sitting cross-legged on the bed, the man took a deep breath. "It is thought that these paralyses of mine are a form of grace bestowed by heaven, a kind of sacred state. Thus, when I am visited by those states, the girls come to me and join their bodies with mine. They are trying to become impregnated. With my heir."

Aomame looked at him, saying nothing. He also fell silent.

"So, then, what you are telling me is that the girls' purpose is to become pregnant? To carry your child?" Aomame then asked.

"That is correct."

"And during this several-hour period while you lie there paralyzed, you have three ejaculations with these three girls?"

"That is correct."

Aomame could not help but realize that she had gotten herself into a terribly complicated situation. She was about to murder this man, to send him to the other side. Yet here she was, being given the strange secrets of his flesh.

"I don't quite understand the precise nature of your problem. All the muscles of your body become paralyzed once or twice a month. When that happens, your three girlfriends come and have sex with you. True, that is not exactly *normal* in commonsense terms, but – "

"They are not my girlfriends," the man said, cutting her short. "They serve me as shrine maidens. Joining their bodies with mine is one of their duties."

"Duties?"

"It is a role that has been assigned to them – to become pregnant with my heir."

"Assigned by whom?" Aomame asked.

"That would be a long story," the man said. "The problem is that all of this is steadily leading toward the destruction of my flesh."

"So, then, have they gotten pregnant?"

"No, not yet. And there is little possibility that any of them will. They have not started their periods. Still, they are hoping for a miracle through heavenly grace."

"None of them have gotten pregnant. They are not menstruating," Aomame said. "And your flesh is headed for destruction."

"Little by little, the time of each paralytic episode is growing longer. And the episodes are increasing in number. They started seven years ago. Back then, I would have one episode in two or three months. Now it is once or twice a month, and after each paralysis ends, my body is racked by excruciating pain and exhaustion. I have to live this way for a week or more each time. I feel as if my whole body is being stabbed by thick needles. I have intense headaches and an overwhelming fatigue. I find it impossible to sleep, and no medicine has done anything to alleviate the pain."

The man sighed. Then he continued, "The second week after the episode is better than the first, but still the pain never entirely goes away. Intense pain comes over me like a wave several times a day. I can hardly breathe. My organs don't function properly. My joints creak like a machine that needs oiling. My flesh is being devoured and my blood sucked out. I can feel it happening. But what is gnawing away at me is neither cancer nor a parasite. I have had every test they can think of, but they can never find the cause. They tell me I'm the picture of health. Medical science cannot explain my torment. The only conclusion is that this is the price I must pay for the heavenly grace I experience."

This man is surely on the road to destruction, Aomame thought. But she could find no hint of emaciation about him. He seemed sturdily built in every way and appeared to have the discipline to withstand intense pain. And yet she could sense that his flesh was headed for destruction. *This man is diseased. I don't know what his disease might be, but even if I don't take steps to dispatch him right now, he will suffer intense pain as his flesh is slowly destroyed and he encounters inevitable death.*

"I can't stop its progress," the man said, as if he had read Aomame's thoughts. "Every part of me is being eaten away, my body hollowed out, and a horribly painful death awaits me. They'll just throw me away like a useless old car."

" 'They'?" Aomame asked. "Who are 'they'?"

"I am talking about the ones who are eating away at my flesh like this," the man said. "But never mind that. What I am looking for now is some way to have my very real pain eased to some extent. That is what I need more than anything, even if the solution is not complete. This pain is unbearable. At times – at certain times – the pain deepens dramatically, as if it has a direct link to the center of the earth. It is a kind of pain that no one else besides me can grasp. It has robbed me of many things, but in return it has given me much. Deep, special pain bestows deep, special grace – not that the grace alleviates the pain, of course. Nor can it prevent the coming destruction."

A deep silence followed for some moments.

Aomame finally managed to speak. "I know I keep saying the same thing, but I can't help thinking that the techniques at my disposal can do almost nothing for your problem – especially if it is something that has come to you as a payment for heavenly grace."

Leader sat up straight and looked at Aomame with those small, deep-set, glacier-like eyes. Then he opened his long, thin lips.

"No, I think you *can* do something for me – something that *only* you can do."

"I hope you're right."

"I am right, I know it," the man said. "I know a lot of things. If you are willing, I would like to have you start now. Do what you always do."

"I'll try," Aomame said, her voice tense and hollow. *What I always do,* Aomame thought.

CHAPTER 10

Tengo

YOU HAVE DECLINED OUR OFFER

Tengo said good-bye to his father just before six p.m. While he waited for the taxi to come, the two of them sat across from each other by the window, saying nothing. Tengo indulged in his own unhurried thoughts while his father stared hard at the view outside the window, frowning. The sun had dropped down, and the sky's pale blue was slowly deepening.

He had many more questions he wanted to ask, but he knew that there would be no answers coming back. The sight of his father's tightly clenched lips told him that. His father had obviously decided to say nothing more, so Tengo decided not to ask any more. If you couldn't understand something without an explanation, you couldn't understand it with an explanation. As his father had said.

When the time for him to leave drew near, Tengo said, "You told me a lot today. It was indirect and often hard to grasp, but it was probably as honest and open as you could make it."

Tengo looked at his father, but there was no change of expression.

"I still have some things I'd like to ask you, but I know they would only cause you pain. All I can do is guess the rest from what you've told me. You are probably not my father by blood. That is what I assume. I don't know the details, but I have to think that in general. If I'm wrong, please tell me so."

His father made no reply.

Tengo continued, "If my assumption is correct, that makes it easier for me. Not because I hate you, but – as I said before – because I no longer need to hate you. You seem to have raised me as your son even though we had no blood ties. I should be grateful for that. Unfortunately, we were never very good at being father and son, but that's another problem."

Still his father said nothing, his eyes fixed on the outdoor scene like a soldier on guard duty, determined not to miss the next signal flare sent up by the savage tribe on the distant hill. Tengo tried looking out along his father's line of vision, but found nothing resembling a flare. The only things out there were the pine trees tinted with the coming sunset.

"I'm sorry to say it, but there is virtually nothing I can do for you – other than to hope that the process forming a vacuum inside you is a painless one. I'm sure you have suffered a lot. You must have loved my mother as deeply as you knew how. I do get that sense. But she went off somewhere. I don't know whether the man she went with was my biological father or not, and you apparently have no intention of telling me. But in any case she left you. And me, too, an infant. Maybe you decided to raise me because you figured she would come back to you if you had me with you. But she never came back – to you or to me. That must have been hard on you, like living in an empty town. Still, you raised me in that empty town – as if to fill in the vacuum."

His father's expression did not change. Tengo could not tell whether he was understanding – or even hearing – what he was saying.

"My assumption may be wrong, and that might be all for the better. For both of us. But thinking about it that way helps all kinds of things to fit together nicely inside me, and my doubts are more or less resolved."

A pack of crows cut across the sky, cawing. Tengo looked at his watch. It was time for him to leave. He stood up, went over to his father, and put his hand on his shoulder.

"Good-bye, Father. I'll come again soon."

Grasping the doorknob, Tengo turned around one last time and was shocked to see a single tear running down from his father's eye. It shone a dull silver color under the ceiling's fluorescent light. To release that tear, his father must have squeezed every bit of strength from what little emotion he still had left. The tear crept slowly down his father's cheek and fell onto his lap. Tengo opened the door and left the room. He took the cab to the station and boarded the train that had brought him here.

The Tokyo-bound express train from Tateyama was more crowded and noisy than the outbound train had been. Most of the passengers were families returning from a stay at the beach. Looking at them, Tengo thought about being in elementary school. He had never once experienced such a family outing or trip. During the Bon Festival, or New Year's, his father would do nothing but stretch out at home and sleep, looking like some kind of grubby machine with the electricity switched off.

Taking his seat, he thought he might read the rest of his paperback, until he realized he had left it in his father's room. He sighed but then realized on second thought that this was probably just as well. Anything he might read now would probably not register with him. And "Town of Cats" was a story that belonged more in his father's room than in Tengo's possession.

The scenery moved past the window in the opposite order: the dark, deserted strip of coastline pressed in upon by mountains eventually gave way to the more open coastal industrial zone. Most of the factories were still operating even though it was nighttime. A forest of smokestacks towered in the darkness, spitting fire like snakes sticking out their long tongues.

Big trucks' strong headlights flooded the roadway. The ocean beyond looked like thick, black mud.

It was nearly ten o'clock by the time he arrived home. His mailbox was empty. Opening his apartment door, he found the place looking even emptier than usual, the same vacuum he had left behind that morning. The shirt he had thrown on the floor, the switched-off word processor, the swivel chair with the indentation his weight had left in the seat, the eraser crumbs scattered over his desk. He drank two glasses of water, undressed, and crawled straight into bed. Sleep came over him immediately – a deep sleep such as he had not had lately.

When he woke up after eight o'clock the next morning, Tengo realized that he was a brand-new person. Waking up felt good. The muscles of his arms and legs felt free of all stiffness and ready to deal with any wholesome stimulus. His physical weariness was gone. He had that feeling he remembered from childhood when he opened a new textbook at the beginning of the term, ignorant of its contents but sensing the new knowledge to come. He went into the bathroom and shaved. Drying his face and slapping on aftershave lotion, he studied himself in the mirror, confirming that he was, indeed, a new person.

Yesterday's events all seemed as if they had happened in a dream, not in reality. While everything was quite vivid, he noticed touches of unreality around the edges. He had boarded a train, visited the "Town of Cats," and come back. Fortunately, unlike the hero of the story, he had managed to board the train for the return trip. And his experiences in that town had changed Tengo profoundly.

Of course, nothing at all had changed about the actual situation in which he found himself, compelled to walk on dangerous, enigmatic ground. Things had developed in totally unforeseen ways, and he had no idea what was going to happen to him next. Still, Tengo had a strong sense that somehow he would be able to overcome the danger.

I've finally made it to the starting line, Tengo thought. Not that any decisive facts had come to light, but from the things his father had said, and his father's attitude, he had begun to gain some vague understanding of his own origins. That "image" that had long tormented and confused him was no meaningless hallucination. How much it reflected actuality, he could not say with any precision, but it was the single piece of information left him by his mother, and, for better or worse, it comprised the foundation of his life. With that much now clear, Tengo was able to feel that he had lowered a great burden from his back. And, having set it down once and for all, he realized what a heavy load he had been carrying.

A strangely quiet and peaceful two weeks went by, like a calm sea. He taught four days a week at the cram school during summer vacation, and allocated the rest of his time to writing his novel. No one contacted him. Tengo knew nothing about how the Fuka-Eri disappearance case was progressing or whether *Air Chrysalis* was still selling. Nor did he want to know. Let the world move along as it pleased. If it had any business with him, it would be sure to tell him.

August ended, and September came. As he made his morning coffee, Tengo found himself silently wishing that this peaceful time could go on forever. If he said it aloud, some keen-eared demon somewhere might overhear him. And so he kept his wish for continued tranquility to himself. But things never go the way you want them to, and this was no exception. The world seemed to have a better sense of how you wanted things *not* to go.

The phone rang just after ten o'clock that morning. He let it ring seven times, gave up, reached out, and lifted the receiver.

"Can I come over now," a subdued voice asked. As far as Tengo knew, there was only one person in the world who could ask questions without a question mark like that. In the background Tengo could hear some kind of announcement and the sound of car exhausts.

"Where are you now?" Tengo asked.

"At the front door of the Marusho."

His apartment was less than two hundred yards from that supermarket. She was calling from the pay phone out front.

Tengo instinctively glanced around his apartment. "Don't you think it's risky? Somebody might be watching my apartment. And you're supposed to be 'whereabouts unknown.' "

"Somebody might be watching your apartment," she asked, parroting his words.

"Right," Tengo said. "All kinds of weird things have been going on around me, probably having to do with *Air Chrysalis*."

" 'Cause people are mad."

"Probably. They're mad at you, and I think they're a little mad at me, too. Because I rewrote *Air Chrysalis*."

"I don't care," Fuka-Eri said.

"You don't care." Now Tengo was parroting her words. The habit was catching. "About what?"

"Your apartment being watched. If it is."

He was momentarily at a loss for words. "Well, maybe I *do* care," he said at last.

"We should be together," Fuka-Eri said. "Join forces."

"Sonny and Cher," Tengo said. "The strongest male/female duo."

"The strongest what?"

"Never mind. My own little joke."

"I'm coming over."

Tengo was about to say something when he heard the

connection cut. Everybody was hanging up on him. Like chopping down a rope bridge.

Fuka-Eri showed up ten minutes later with a plastic supermarket bag in each arm. She wore a blue-striped long-sleeve shirt and slim jeans. The shirt was a men's shirt, unironed, straight from the clothesline. A canvas bag hung from one shoulder. She wore a pair of oversized sunglasses to hide her face, but it didn't look like an effective disguise. If anything, it would attract attention.

"I thought we should have lots of food," Fuka-Eri said, transferring the contents of the plastic bags to the refrigerator. Most of what she had bought was ready-made food that only needed heating in a microwave oven. There were also crackers and cheese, apples, tomatoes, and some canned goods.

"Where's the microwave?" she asked, looking around the kitchen.

"I don't have one," Tengo said.

Fuka-Eri wrinkled her brow in thought, but had nothing to say. She seemed to have trouble imagining a world without a microwave oven.

"I want you to put me up," she said, as if conveying an objective fact.

"How long?" Tengo asked.

Fuka-Eri shook her head. This meant she didn't know.

"What happened to your hiding place?"

"I don't want to be alone when something happens."

"You think something is going to happen?"

Fuka-Eri did not reply.

"I don't mean to keep repeating myself, but this is not a safe place," Tengo said. "Some kind of people seem to be keeping an eye on me. I don't know who they are yet, but . . ."

"There is no such thing as a safe place," Fuka-Eri said, narrowing her eyes meaningfully and tugging on an earlobe.

Tengo could not tell what this body language was supposed to mean. Probably nothing.

"So it doesn't matter where you are," Tengo said.

"There is no such thing as a safe place," Fuka-Eri repeated.

"You may be right," Tengo said with resignation. "After a certain point, there's no difference in the level of danger. In any case, I have to go to work soon."

"To the cram school."

"Right."

"I'll stay here," Fuka-Eri said.

"You'll stay here," Tengo echoed her. "You should. Just don't go outside, and don't answer if anybody knocks. Don't answer the phone if it rings."

Fuka-Eri nodded silently.

"So, anyhow, what's happening with Professor Ebisuno?"

"They searched Sakigake yesterday."

"You mean, the police searched the Sakigake compound looking for you?" Tengo asked, surprised.

"You aren't reading the papers."

"I'm not reading the papers," Tengo echoed. "I just haven't felt like it lately. So I don't know what's happening. But I would think the Sakigake people would be very upset by that."

Fuka-Eri nodded.

Tengo released a deep sigh. "They must be even angrier than before, like hornets having their nest poked."

Fuka-Eri narrowed her eyes and went into a short silence. She was probably imagining a swarm of furious hornets pouring out of their nest.

"Probably," Fuka-Eri said in a tiny voice.

"So, did they find out anything about your parents?"

Fuka-Eri shook her head. They still knew nothing about them.

"In any case, the organization is angry," Tengo said. "And if the police find out that your disappearance was an act, they'll be mad at you too. And mad at me for covering up for you even though I know the truth."

"Which is precisely why we have to join forces," Fuka-Eri said.

"Did you just say, 'Which is precisely'?"

Fuka-Eri nodded. "Did I say it wrong?" she asked.

Tengo shook his head. "Not at all. The words sounded fresh, that's all."

"If it's a bother for you, I can go somewhere else," Fuka-Eri said.

"I don't mind if you stay here," Tengo said, resigned. "I'm sure you don't have anyplace else in mind, right?"

Fuka-Eri answered with a curt nod.

Tengo took some cold barley tea from the refrigerator and drank it. "Angry hornets would be too much for me, but I'm sure I can manage to look after you."

Fuka-Eri looked hard at Tengo for a few moments. Then she said, "You look different."

"What do you mean?"

Fuka-Eri twisted her lips into a strange angle and then returned them to normal. "Can't explain."

"No need to explain," Tengo said. *If you can't understand it without an explanation, you can't understand it with an explanation.*

As he left the apartment, Tengo said, "When I call, I'll let it ring three times, hang up, and call again. Then you answer. Okay?"

"Okay," Fuka-Eri said. "Ring three times, hang up, call again, answer." She sounded as if she could be translating aloud from an ancient stone monument.

"It's important, so don't forget," Tengo said.

Fuka-Eri nodded twice.

Tengo finished his two classes, went back to the teachers' lounge, and was getting ready to go home. The receptionist came to tell him that the man named Ushikawa was here to see him. She spoke with an apologetic air, like a kind-hearted messenger bearing unwelcome news. Tengo flashed her a bright smile and thanked her. No sense blaming the messenger.

Ushikawa was in the cafeteria by the front lobby, drinking a café au lait as he waited for Tengo. Tengo could not imagine a drink less well suited to Ushikawa, whose strange exterior looked all the stranger amid the energetic, young students. Only the part of the room where he was sitting seemed to have different gravity and air density and light refractivity. Even from a distance, there was no mistaking that he looked like bad news. The cafeteria was crowded between classes, but not one person shared his six-person table. The students' natural instincts led them to avoid Ushikawa, just as antelope keep away from wild dogs.

Tengo bought a coffee at the counter and carried it over to Ushikawa's table, sitting down opposite him. Ushikawa seemed to have just finished eating a cream-filled pastry. The crumpled wrapper lay atop the table, and crumbs stuck to the corner of his mouth. Cream pastries also seemed totally unsuited to Ushikawa.

"It's been quite a while, hasn't it, Mr. Kawana?" Ushikawa said to Tengo, raising himself slightly from his chair. "Sorry to barge in on you again all of a sudden."

Tengo dispensed with the polite chatter and got down to business. "I'm sure you're here for my answer. To the offer you made the other day, that is."

"Well, yes, that is true," Ushikawa said. "In a word."

"I wonder, Mr. Ushikawa, if I can get you to speak a little more concretely and directly today. What is it that you people want from me – in return for this 'grant' thing?"

Ushikawa cast a cautious glance around the room, but there was no one near them, and the cafeteria was so noisy with student voices that there was no danger of their conversation's being overheard.

"All right, then. Let me give you our best deal and lay it all out with total honesty," Ushikawa said, leaning across the table and lowering his voice a notch. "The money is just a pretext. For one thing, the grant is not all that big. The most important thing that my client can offer you is your personal safety. In other words, no harm will come to you. We guarantee it."

"In return for which . . . ?" Tengo said.

"In return for which all they want from you is your silence and forgetting. You participated in this affair, but you didn't know what you were getting yourself into. You were just a foot soldier acting under orders. They won't hold you personally responsible. So all you have to do is forget everything. We can make it as though nothing ever happened. Word will never get out that you ghostwrote *Air Chrysalis*. You are not – and never will be – connected with it in any way. That is what they want from you. And it would be to your advantage as well, I'm sure you see."

"No harm will come to *me*. In other words, harm *will* come to the other participants? Is that what you are saying?"

"That would be handled, uh, '*case by case*,' as they say in English," Ushikawa said with apparent difficulty. "I am not the one who decides, so I can't say specifically, but some steps will have to be taken, I should think."

"And your arms are both long and strong."

"Exactly. *Very* long, and *very* strong, as I mentioned before. So, then, Mr. Kawana, what kind of answer can we hope for from you?"

"Let me first say that for me to accept money from you people is out of the question."

Without speaking, Ushikawa reached for his glasses, took them off, carefully wiped the lenses with a handkerchief he produced from his pocket, and put them back on, as if to say that there might be some sort of connection between his vision and what he had just heard.

"Do I understand this to mean that you have rejected our offer?"

"That is correct."

Ushikawa stared at Tengo through his glasses as if he were looking at an oddly shaped cloud. "And why would that be? In my humble opinion, it is by no means a bad deal for you."

"In the end, all of us connected with the story are in the same boat. It's out of the question for me to be the only one who runs away."

"I'm mystified!" Ushikawa said, as if truly mystified. "I can't understand it. I maybe shouldn't say this, but none of the others are the least bit concerned about you. It's true. They throw a little spare change your way and use you any way they like. And for that you get dragged into the mess. If you ask me, you'd be totally justified to tell them all to go to hell. If it were me, I'd be fuming. But you're ready to protect them. 'It's out of the question for me to be the only one who runs away,' he says! Boat schmoat! I don't get it. Why won't you take it?"

"One reason has to do with a woman named Kyoko Yasuda."

Ushikawa picked up his cold café au lait and winced as he sipped it. "Kyoko Yasuda?"

"You people know something about Kyoko Yasuda," Tengo said.

Ushikawa let his mouth hang open, as if he had no idea what Tengo was talking about. "No, honestly, I don't know a thing about a woman by that name. I swear, really. Who is she?"

Tengo looked at Ushikawa for a while, saying nothing, but he could not read anything on his face. "A woman I know."

"Would she, by any chance, be someone with whom you have a . . . *relationship*?"

Tengo did not reply to that. "What I want to know is whether you people did something to her."

"Did something? No way! We haven't done a thing," Ushikawa said. "I'm not lying. I just told you, I don't know a thing about her. You can't *do* anything to somebody you've never even heard of."

"But you said you hired a capable 'researcher' and investigated every last thing about me. He even hit upon the fact that I had rewritten Eriko Fukada's work. He knows a lot about my private life, too. It only makes sense that he should know about Kyoko Yasuda and me."

"Yes, it's true, we have hired a capable researcher. And he has been finding out about you in great detail. So it could be that he has discovered your relationship with Kyoko Yasuda, as you say. But even assuming he has discovered it, the information has not reached me."

"I was seeing Kyoko Yasuda for quite some time," Tengo said. "I used to see her once a week. In secret. Because she had a family. But suddenly one day, without saying a word to me, she disappeared."

Ushikawa used the handkerchief with which he had wiped his glasses to dab at the sweat on the tip of his nose. "And so, Mr. Kawana, you think that, in one way or another, we have something to do with the fact that this married woman disappeared, is that it?"

"Maybe you informed her husband that she was seeing me."

Ushikawa pursed his lips as if taken aback. "What possible reason could we have for doing such a thing?"

Tengo clenched his fists in his lap. "I keep thinking about something you said on the phone the last time we talked."

"And what could that have been?"

"Once you pass a certain age, life is just a continuous process of losing one thing after another. One after another, things you value slip out of your hands the way a comb loses teeth. People you love fade away one after another. That sort of thing. Surely, you must remember."

"Yes, I remember. I did say something like that the other day. But really, Mr. Kawana, I was just speaking in generalities. I was offering my own humble view of the pain and difficulty of aging. I certainly was not pointing specifically to What's-her-name Yasuda."

"But to my ears it sounded like a warning."

Ushikawa gave his head several vigorous shakes. "Nothing of the sort! It wasn't even remotely meant as a warning. It was simply my personal view. Really, I swear, I don't know anything at all about Mrs. Yasuda. She disappeared?"

Tengo went on, "And you also said this: if I go on refusing to listen to you people, it might have an undesirable effect on everyone around me."

"Yes, I did say something like that."

"Isn't that a warning too?"

Ushikawa stuffed his handkerchief into his jacket pocket and let out a sigh. "True, it might have sounded like a warning, but there, too, I was speaking strictly generally. I'm telling you, Mr. Kawana, I don't know anything about this Mrs. Yasuda. I've never even heard the name. I swear to all the gods and goddesses of heaven and earth."

Tengo studied Ushikawa's face again. This man really might not know anything about Kyoko Yasuda. The expression of bewilderment on his face certainly looked like the real thing. But even if *he* knew nothing, it didn't necessarily mean that *they* hadn't done anything to her. It could just be that they hadn't told him about it.

"It's none of my business, Mr. Kawana, but having an affair with a married woman is a dangerous business. You're a young, healthy single male. You should be able to have any number of single young girls without doing such dangerous things." Having said this, Ushikawa deftly licked the crumbs from the corner of his mouth.

Tengo watched Ushikawa in silence.

Ushikawa said, "Of course, male/female relationships don't work by logic and reason. Even monogamous marriage has its own set of contradictions. I'm telling you for your own good, though, if she has left you, it might be best to let the situation stay as it is. What I'm trying to say is this: there are things in this world that are better left as unknowns. The business about your mother, for example. Learning the truth would just hurt you. And once you do learn the truth, you end up having to take on a certain responsibility for it."

Tengo scowled, holding his breath for a few seconds. "You know something about my mother?"

Ushikawa flicked his tongue over his lips. "Yes, to some extent, I do. Our researcher investigated that area very thoroughly. So if you ever want to learn about that, I can hand you all the materials on your mother as is. As I understand it, you grew up knowing absolutely nothing about her. However, there might be some not-very-pleasant information included in the file."

"Please leave now, Mr. Ushikawa," Tengo said, pushing his chair back and standing up. "I have no desire to talk to you any more. And please don't ever show your face to me again. Whatever 'harm' might be coming to me, it would be better than having to deal with you. I don't want that 'grant' of yours or your guarantees of 'safety.' There's only one thing I want, and that is never to see you again."

Ushikawa showed no discernible reaction to this. Perhaps he had had worse things said to him any number of times. There was even a hint of a smile gleaming deep in his eyes.

"That's fine," Ushikawa said. "I'm glad I got your answer at least. A definite no. You have declined our offer. Clear and easy to understand. I will convey it to my superiors in that form. I am just a lowly errand boy. Now, simply because your answer is no, that doesn't mean that harm will come to you right away. It just *might,* is all I am saying. It might never happen. That's what I am hoping for. No, really, with all my heart. Because I

like you, Mr. Kawana. I'm sure that's the last thing you want –
for me to like you – but that's just the way it is. This nonsensical guy who shows up with nonsensical deals, terrible to look
at. I've never had the problem of being liked too much. But
the simple fact is that I have good feelings toward you, Mr.
Kawana, as unwelcome as you may find them. And I hope that
you go on to achieve great success in life."

Having said this, Ushikawa proceeded to stare at his own
fingers. They were short, stubby fingers. He turned them over
a few times. Then he stood up.

"Well, then, I'll be excusing myself. Now that you mention
it, this will probably be the last time you see me. Yes, I will do
my best to honor your wishes. May things go well for you in
the future. Good-bye."

Ushikawa picked up the worn-out leather case he had set
on the chair and disappeared into the cafeteria's crowd. As he
walked, the mass of young male and female students parted
naturally to make way for him, like medieval village children
trying to avoid a fearsome slave trader.

Tengo dialed his own apartment from the public phone in the
school lobby. He was planning to hang up after three rings, but
Fuka-Eri picked up at the second ring.

"I was going to let it ring three times and then call again. We
had an arrangement," Tengo said wearily.

"I forgot," Fuka-Eri said with apparent unconcern.

"I'm sure I asked you not to forget."

"Want to do it again," Fuka-Eri asked.

"No, never mind, we're talking. Has anything unusual happened since I left?"

"No calls. Nobody came."

"Good. I'm through working. I'll be coming back now."

"A big crow came and cawed outside the window," Fuka-Eri
said.

"He comes every evening. Nothing to worry about. It's like a social call. Anyhow, I should be back by seven."

"Better hurry."

"Why's that?" Tengo asked.

"The Little People are stirring."

"The Little People are stirring," Tengo repeated her words. "In my apartment?"

"No. Somewhere else."

"Somewhere else."

"Way far away."

"But you can hear them."

"I can hear them."

"Does it mean something?" Tengo asked.

"That something extra ordinary is starting."

It took Tengo a moment to realize she meant "extraordinary." "And what kind of extraordinary something would that be?"

"I can't tell that much."

"The Little People are going to make this extraordinary thing happen?"

Fuka-Eri shook her head. He could feel it through the phone. It meant she didn't know.

"Better come back before the thunder starts," she said.

"Thunder?"

"If the train stops running, we'll be apart."

Tengo turned and looked out the window. It was a calm late-summer evening without a cloud in the sky. "It doesn't look like thunder."

"You can't tell from looks."

"I'll hurry," Tengo said.

"Better hurry," Fuka-Eri said, and hung up.

Tengo stepped outside, looked up once again at the clear evening sky, and walked briskly toward Yoyogi Station, Ushikawa's words resounding in his head like a tape on auto-repeat.

What I'm trying to say is this: there are things in this world that are better left as unknowns. The business about your mother, for example. Learning the truth would just hurt you. And once you do learn the truth, you end up having to take on a certain responsibility for it.

And somewhere the Little People are stirring. They apparently have something to do with an extraordinary event that is coming our way. For now, the sky is beautiful and clear, but you can't tell by how things look. Maybe the thunder will roar, the rain will fall, and the trains will stop. Got to hurry back to the apartment. Fuka-Eri's voice was strangely compelling.

"We have to join forces," she had said.

Those long arms were reaching out from somewhere. *We have to join forces. Because we'll be the world's strongest male/female duo.*

The Beat Goes On.

CHAPTER 11

Aomame

BALANCE ITSELF IS THE GOOD

Aomame spread her blue foam yoga mat on the carpeted bedroom floor. Then she told the man to take off his top. He got down from the bed and pulled off his shirt. He looked even bigger without a shirt on. He was deep-chested, with bulging muscles, and had no drooping excess flesh. To all appearances, this was a very healthy body.

Following Aomame's directions, he lay facedown on the mat. Aomame touched his wrist and took his pulse. It was strong and steady.

"Are you doing some kind of regular exercise?" Aomame asked.

"Not really," he said. "Just breathing."

"Just breathing?"

"It's a little different from ordinary breathing," the man said.

"Like you were doing before in the dark, I suppose. Deep, repetitive breathing with all the muscles of your body."

Facedown, he gave a little nod.

Aomame could not quite grasp it. While his intense style of breathing certainly must take a good deal of physical strength, was it possible for mere breathing to maintain such a tight, powerful body?

"What I'm about to do now involves a good deal of pain,"

Aomame said in a voice without inflection. "It has to hurt for it to do any good. On the other hand, I can adjust the amount of pain. So if it hurts, don't just bear it – speak up."

The man paused for a moment before saying, "If there is a pain I've never tasted, I'd like to try it." This sounded mildly sarcastic to her.

"Pain is not fun for anybody."

"But a painful technique is more effective, is that it? I can bear any pain as long as it has meaning."

Aomame allowed herself a momentary facial expression in the pale darkness. Then she said, "I understand. Let's both see how it goes."

As always, Aomame started with the stretching of the shoulder blades. The first thing she noticed when she touched his flesh was its suppleness. This was fine, healthy flesh, fundamentally different in composition from the tired, stiff flesh of the urbanites with whom she dealt at the gym. At the same time, however, she had a strong sense that its natural "flow" was being blocked by something, the way a river's flow can be blocked temporarily by floating timber or other debris.

Leaning her weight into her elbow, Aomame squeezed the man's shoulder upward – slowly at first, but then with a serious application of strength. She knew he was feeling pain – intense pain that would make any ordinary human being cry out. But he bore it in silence. His breathing remained calm, nor was there any hint of a frown on his face. *He tolerates pain well,* she thought. She decided to see how much he could stand. She held nothing back from her next push, until the shoulder blade joint gave out with a dull snap and she could tell that the track had been switched. The man's breathing paused momentarily but immediately resumed its quiet, steady pace.

"Your shoulder blade was tremendously obstructed," Aomame explained, "but that took care of it. Now the flow is back to normal."

She jammed her fingers in under the shoulder blade up to the second joint. The muscles here were meant to be flexible, and once the obstruction was removed they would quickly return to normal.

"That feels much better," the man murmured.

"It must have hurt quite a bit."

"Not more than I could stand."

"I myself have a rather high tolerance for pain, but if someone had done the same thing to me, I'm pretty sure I would have cried out."

"In most cases, one pain is alleviated or canceled out by another pain. The senses are, ultimately, relative."

Aomame placed her hand on his left shoulder blade, felt for the muscles with her fingertips, and determined that they were in about the same condition that the right ones had been. *Let's see just how relative this can be.* "I'll do the left side now. It should hurt about as much as the right side did."

"Do what you need to. Don't worry about me."

"Meaning, I shouldn't hold back at all?"

"No need for that."

Following the same procedure, Aomame corrected the joints and the muscles around the left shoulder blade. As instructed, she did not hold back. Once she had decided she would not hold anything back, Aomame took the shortest possible route without hesitation. The man reacted even more calmly than he had with the right side. He accepted the pain with complete equanimity, making only one brief swallowing sound in his throat. *All right, let's see how much he can stand,* Aomame thought.

She started working on his muscles one after another in order, loosening them up, following her mental checklist. All she had to do was mechanically follow the usual route, like a capable and fearless night watchman making the rounds of his building with a flashlight.

All of his muscles were more or less "blocked," like a region that has suffered a horrible disaster, its waterways obstructed, their embankments collapsed. Any ordinary human being in such a condition would probably not be able to stand up – or even breathe normally. This man was supported by his sturdy flesh and strong will. However despicable his behavior might have been, Aomame could not deny him her professional admiration for his ability to bear such intense pain in silence.

She worked on one muscle after another, forcing it to move, bending and stretching it to the limit, and each time the joint would release a dull pop. She was fully aware that this was something close to torture. She had performed this muscle stretching on many athletes, tough men used to living with physical pain, but even the toughest of them at some point couldn't stop themselves from letting out a cry – or something close to a cry. Some even wet themselves. But this man never even groaned. He was very impressive. Still, it was possible to guess the pain he was feeling from the sweat oozing on the back of his neck. Aomame herself was starting to develop a film of sweat on her body.

It took close to thirty minutes for her to loosen up the muscles on the back of his body. When this was finished, she took a moment's break to wipe the sweat from her forehead.

This is very odd, Aomame thought. *I came here to kill this man. In my bag is the superfine ice pick I made. If I hold its point at the right spot on the back of his neck and punch the handle, it will be all over. He would never know what happened to him as his life came to an instantaneous end and he moved on to another world. That way, in effect, his body would be released from all pain. Instead, I'm spending all my energy to ease the pain that he is feeling in the real world.*

I am probably doing it because this is the work that I have been given to do, Aomame thought. *Whenever I have work*

before me, I have to pour all my strength into getting it done.
That is just the way I am. If I am given the job of curing problem
muscles, then I will pour all my strength into that. If I have to
kill a person and have a proper reason for doing so, I will do that
with all my strength.

Obviously, though, I can't do both at the same time. The two
jobs have conflicting purposes and call for incompatible meth-
ods. I can only do one at a time. At the moment I am trying to
bring this man's muscles back to as normal a state as possible. I
am concentrating my mind on that task and mobilizing all the
strength I can muster up. I can think about the other task after
this one is finished.

At the same time, Aomame was unable to suppress her curiosity. The man's far-from-ordinary illness; the fine, healthy
muscles so terribly obstructed by it; the strong will and powerful flesh that enabled him to bear the intense pain he called his
"payment for heavenly grace": all aroused her curiosity. She
wanted to see what she could do for this man, what kind of
response his flesh would show. It was a matter of both professional curiosity and personal curiosity. *Also, if I killed him now,*
I would have to leave right away. If the job ends too quickly, the
two men in the next room might find it suspicious. I told them
that it would take an hour at the very least.

"I'm halfway done. Now I'll do the second half. Could you
please turn over onto your back?"

The man rolled over slowly like some large aquatic animal
that has been cast up on the shore.

"The pain is definitely lessening," the man said after releasing a long breath. "None of the treatments I have tried thus far
have done as much."

"I am only treating the symptoms, however, not solving the
basic problem. Until you identify the cause, the same thing
will probably keep happening."

"I know that. I considered using morphine, but I would

rather not use drugs if possible. Long-term use of drugs destroys the function of the brain."

"I will go on with the rest of the treatment now," Aomame said. "I gather you are all right with my not holding back."

"It goes without saying."

Aomame emptied her mind and worked on the man's muscles with total concentration. The structure of each muscle in the human body was engraved in her professional memory – its function, the bones to which it was attached, its unique characteristics, its sensitivities. She inspected, shook, and effectively worked on each muscle and joint in order, the way zealous inquisitors used to test every point of pain in their victims' bodies.

Thirty minutes later, they were bathed in sweat, panting like lovers who have just had miraculously deep sex. The man said nothing for a time, and Aomame was at a loss for words.

Finally, the man spoke: "I don't want to exaggerate, but I feel as if every part of my body has been replaced."

Aomame said, "You might experience something of a backlash tonight. During the night your muscles might tighten up tremendously and let out a scream, but don't worry, they will be back to normal tomorrow morning."

If you have a tomorrow morning, Aomame thought.

Sitting cross-legged on the yoga mat, the man took several deep breaths, as though testing the condition of his body. Then he said, "You really do seem to have a special talent."

Aomame toweled the sweat from her face as she said, "What I do is strictly practical. I studied the structure and function of the muscles in college and have expanded my knowledge through actual practice. I've put together my own system by making tiny adjustments to my technique, just doing things that are obvious and reasonable. 'Truth' here is for the most part observable and provable. It also involves a good deal of pain, of course."

The man opened his eyes and looked at Aomame as though intrigued. "So that is what you believe."

"What do you mean?" Aomame asked.

"That truth is strictly something observable and provable."

Aomame pursed her lips slightly. "I'm not saying it is true for all truths, just that it happens to be the case in my professional field. Of course, if it were true in all fields, things in general would be a lot easier to grasp."

"Not at all," the man said.

"Why is that?"

"Most people are not looking for provable truths. As you said, truth is often accompanied by intense pain, and almost no one is looking for painful truths. What people need is beautiful, comforting stories that make them feel as if their lives have some meaning. Which is where religion comes from."

The man turned his neck several times before continuing.

"If a certain belief – call it 'Belief A' – makes the life of that man or this woman appear to be something of deep meaning, then for them Belief A is the truth. If Belief B makes their lives appear to be powerless and puny, then Belief B turns out to be a falsehood. The distinction is quite clear. If someone insists that Belief B is the truth, people will probably hate him, ignore him, or, in some cases, attack him. It means nothing to them that Belief B might be logical or provable. Most people barely manage to preserve their sanity by denying and rejecting images of themselves as powerless and puny."

"But people's flesh – all flesh, with only minor differences – is a powerless and puny thing. This is self-evident, don't you think?"

"I do," the man said. "All flesh, with only minor differences, is a powerless and puny thing doomed soon to disintegrate and disappear. That is an unmistakable truth. But what, then, of a person's spirit?"

"I try my best not to think about the spirit."

"And why is that?"

"Because there is no particular need to think about it."

"Why is there no particular need to think about the spirit? Setting aside the question of whether it has any practical value to do so, thinking about one's own spirit is one of the most indispensable of all human tasks, is it not?"

"I have love," Aomame declared.

Oh, no, what am I doing? she thought. *Talking about love to this man I'm about to kill!*

As a breeze sends ripples over the surface of a quiet pond, a faint smile spread across the man's face, conveying a natural and even friendly emotion.

"Do you think that love is all a person needs?" he asked.

"I do."

"Now, this 'love' of yours – does it have a particular individual as its object?"

"It does," Aomame said. "It is directed toward a specific man."

"Powerless, puny flesh and an absolute love free of shadows . . . ," he murmured. Then, after a brief pause, he added, "You don't seem to have any need for religion."

"Maybe I don't have any need."

"Because your attitude is itself the very essence of religion, as it were."

"You said before that religion offers not so much truth as beautiful hypotheses. Where does that leave the religion that you head?"

"To tell you the truth, I don't consider what I do to be a religious activity," the man said. "What I am doing is listening to the voices and transmitting them to people. I am the only one who can hear the voices. That I can hear them is an unmistakable truth, but I can't prove that their messages *are* the truth. All I can do is to embody their accompanying traces of heavenly grace."

Lightly biting her lip, Aomame set down her towel. She wanted to ask what kinds of grace he was talking about, but she stopped herself. This could go on forever. She still had an important task she had to complete.

"Can you lie facedown again? I'm going to work on loosening up your neck muscles," Aomame said.

The man stretched out his huge frame again on the yoga mat and presented the back of his thick neck to Aomame.

"In any case, you have a *magic touch*," he said, using the English expression.

"Magic touch?"

"Fingers that give off extraordinary power. An acute sense for locating those special points on the body. A special capacity that is granted to very few individuals. This is not something you can learn through study and practice. I have something – a very different kind of something – that came to me in the same way. But as with all forms of heavenly grace, people have to pay a price for the gifts they are given."

"I've never thought of it that way," Aomame said. "I simply developed my techniques through study and a lot of practice. They were not 'granted' to me by anybody."

"I'm not going to get involved in a debate with you. Just remember this: the gods give, and the gods take away. Even if you are not aware of having been granted what you possess, the gods remember what they gave you. They don't forget a thing. You should use the abilities you have been granted with the utmost care."

Aomame looked at her ten fingers. Then she placed them on the back of the man's neck, concentrating all her awareness into her fingertips. The gods give, and the gods take away.

"I'll be through soon. This is the finishing touch," she announced drily to the man's back.

She seemed to hear thunder in the distance. She raised her face and looked out the window. There was nothing to see but the dark sky. Again the sound came, reverberating hollowly in the quiet room.

"It is going to rain any time now," the man declared in a voice without feeling.

Hands on the back of the man's thick neck, Aomame searched for the special spot. This required unusual powers of concentration. She closed her eyes, held her breath, and listened for the flow of his blood there. Her fingertips strained to read detailed information from the elasticity of his skin and the conduction of his body heat. There was only one special spot, and it was exceptionally small. On some people, it was easy to find, but much more difficult on others. This man they called "Leader" was clearly the latter type. This was like trying to find a single coin in a pitch-dark room entirely by feel, while taking care not to make any sound. At last, however, she found it. She placed her fingertip on it and engraved the feel and its precise position into her mind as though marking a map, a special ability that had been imparted to her.

"Please stay in that exact position," Aomame said to the man as he lay there prone. She reached out for the gym bag lying next to them and from it took out the hard case holding the little ice pick.

"One spot is left on the back of your neck where the flow is still blocked," Aomame said calmly, "and I can't seem to resolve it with only the strength of my fingers. If I can remove the blockage in this one place, it should give you great relief from your pain. I want to place one simple acupuncture needle there. Don't worry, I've done this any number of times. Do you mind?"

The man released a deep breath. "I am leaving it entirely up to you. I will accept anything from you that will erase the pain I am feeling."

She took the ice pick from the case and slipped the cork

from its tip. The point had its usual deadly sharpness. She held the ice pick in her left hand and used the index finger of her right hand to locate the point she had found earlier. This was the spot, without the slightest doubt. She placed the point against the spot and took a deep breath. Now all she needed to do was bring her right hand down on the handle like a hammer and drive the needle's exceedingly fine point deep into the spot. Then it would all be over.

But *something* held her back. For some reason, she was unable to bring down the fist she was holding aloft. *With this, it will be all over,* Aomame thought. *With one stroke, I can send this man to the "other side." Then I leave the room looking cool, change my face and name, and take on a new personality. I can do it. Without fear, without pangs of conscience. This man has repeatedly committed loathsome acts that deserve death, there can be no doubt.* But, for some reason, she could not bring herself to do it. What held her right hand back was an incoherent yet persistent doubt. *This is all happening too easily,* her instincts were warning her.

Reason had nothing to do with it. She simply knew: something was wrong. Something was not natural. All her powers and abilities were clashing inside her, their disparate elements engaged in a fierce struggle. Her face performed deep contortions in the darkness.

"What is it?" the man called out. "I'm waiting. I'm waiting for you to finish once and for all."

When she heard this, Aomame finally realized what was holding her back. *This man knows. He knows what I am about to do to him.*

"There is no need for you to hesitate," the man said calmly. "It's all right. What you want is also what I want."

The thunder continued to rumble, but there was no lightning to be seen, just a roar like distant cannons. The battlefield was still far off. The man continued.

"If there were ever a perfect *treatment,* that is it. You did a careful job of stretching out my muscles. I have only the purest respect for your skill. But as you pointed out yourself, it is, ultimately, nothing but a symptomatic treatment. My pain has advanced to the point where it can only be resolved by severing my life at the roots, by going down to the basement and cutting the main switch. You are about to do that for me."

Aomame maintained her pose, the left hand holding the needle against the special spot on the back of his neck, the right hand held aloft. She could move neither forward nor back.

"If you want to put a stop to what you are about to do, there are any number of ways you can do that. It's simple," he said. "Try bringing your right hand down."

As directed, Aomame tried to lower her right hand. But it would not budge. It was frozen in midair, like the hand of a stone statue.

"I have the power to do that – not that it was something I ever hoped to obtain. All right, you can move your right hand now. Now you are in complete control of my life."

Aomame became aware that she could now move her right hand freely. She clenched her fist and opened it. It felt entirely normal. He must have employed something like hypnotism. Whatever it was, it was very powerful.

"They have granted me these special powers, but in return they have impressed certain demands upon me. Their desires have become my desires – implacable desires that I have been unable to defy."

"*They?*" Aomame asked. "Do you mean the Little People?"

"So you know about them. Good. That will save time explaining."

"All I know is that name. I don't know who or what the Little People are."

"Probably no one knows for sure who the Little People are,"

the man said. "All that people are able to learn is that they exist. Have you read Frazer's *The Golden Bough*?"

"No, I haven't."

"It is a very interesting book that has much to teach us. In certain periods of history in several parts of the world – in ancient times, of course – the king was often killed at the end of his reign, usually after a fixed period of ten to twelve years. When the term ended, the people would gather together and slaughter him. This was deemed necessary for the community, and the kings themselves willingly accepted it. The killing had to be cruel and bloody, and it was considered a great honor bestowed upon the one who was king. Now, why did the king have to be killed? It was because in those days the king was the *one who listened to the voices*, as the representative of the people. Such a person would take it upon himself to become the circuit connecting 'us' with 'them.' And slaughtering the *one who listened to the voices* was the indispensable task of the community in order to maintain a balance between the minds of those who lived on the earth and the power manifested by the Little People. In the ancient world, 'to rule' was synonymous with 'listening to the voices of the gods.' Such a system was at some point abandoned, of course. Kings were no longer killed, and kingship became secular and hereditary. In this way, people stopped hearing the voices."

Unconsciously opening and closing her elevated right hand, Aomame listened to what the man was saying.

"*They* have been called by many different names, but in most cases have not been called anything at all. *They were simply there.* The expression 'Little People' is just an expedient. My daughter called them that when she was very young and brought them with her."

"Then you became a king."

The man drew a strong breath in through his nose and held it in his lungs for a time before releasing it slowly. "I am no king. I became *one who listens to the voices.*"

"And now you are seeking to be slaughtered."

"No, it need not be a slaughter. This is 1984, and we are in the middle of the big city. There is no need for a brutal, bloody killing. All you have to do is take my life. It can be neat and simple."

Aomame shook her head and relaxed the muscles of her body. The point of the needle was still pressed against the spot on the back of his neck, but she found it impossible to summon the will to kill this man.

Aomame said, "You have raped many young girls – girls barely ten years old, some perhaps even younger."

"That is true," the man said. "There are aspects to what I did, I must admit, that can be viewed that way in the light of commonly held concepts. In the eyes of earthly law, I am a criminal. I did have physical relations with girls who had still not reached maturity – even if it was something that I myself did not seek."

All that Aomame could do was inhale and exhale deeply. She had no idea how to go about quieting the intense emotional currents streaming through her body. Her face was greatly distorted, and her right and left hands seemed to be longing for entirely different things.

"I would like you to take my life," the man said. "It makes no sense for me to go on living in this world. I should be obliterated in order to maintain the world's balance."

"What would happen after I killed you?"

"The Little People would lose one who listens to their voices. I still have no successor."

"How is it possible to believe this?" Aomame practically spit the words out between her taut lips. "You may just be a sexual pervert trying to justify your despicable actions with convenient rationalizations. There never were any 'Little People,' no voices of the gods, no heavenly grace. You may be just another phony claiming to be a prophet or religious leader."

"See the clock over there?" the man said without lifting his head. "On the right-hand chest of drawers."

Aomame looked to the right. There was a rounded, waist-high chest, on top of which sat a clock embedded in a marble frame – obviously, a heavy object.

"Keep your eyes on it. Don't look away."

As instructed, Aomame kept her neck turned in that direction and fixed her eyes on the clock. Beneath her fingers, she could feel every muscle in the man's body turning to stone and filling with an incredibly intense power. As if in response to that power, the marble clock rose slowly from the surface of the chest. She watched it begin to tremble, as if hesitating, come to rest at a point some three inches in the air, and stay there for a full ten seconds. Then the man's muscles lost their strength, and the clock dropped back to the chest with a dull thud, as if it had just remembered the earth's gravity.

The man took a long time to release a deep, exhausted-sounding breath.

"Even a little thing like that takes a huge amount of energy," he said once he had expelled every last breath in his body. "Enough to shorten my life. But I hope you see it now: at least I am no phony."

Aomame did not answer him. The man took time bringing his strength back with a series of deep breaths. The clock went on silently displaying the time as though nothing had happened. Only its position on top of the chest had shifted slightly on a diagonal. Aomame stared hard at the clock while the second hand made a circuit.

"You do have special powers," Aomame said drily.

"As you have now seen."

"There is an episode involving the devil and Christ in *The Brothers Karamazov,* I recall. The Christ is undergoing harsh austerities in the wilderness when the devil challenges him to perform a miracle – to change a stone into bread. But the Christ ignores him. Miracles are the devil's temptation.'"

"Yes, I know that. I, too, have read *The Brothers Karamazov*. And what you say is true: this kind of showing off doesn't solve a thing. But I had to convince you in the limited amount of time we have, so I went ahead and performed for you."

Aomame remained silent.

"In this world, there is no absolute good, no absolute evil," the man said. "Good and evil are not fixed, stable entities but are continually trading places. A good may be transformed into an evil in the next second. And vice versa. Such was the way of the world that Dostoevsky depicted in *The Brothers Karamazov*. The most important thing is to maintain the balance between the constantly moving good and evil. If you lean too much in either direction, it becomes difficult to maintain actual morals. Indeed, *balance itself is the good.* This is what I mean when I say that I must die in order to keep things in balance."

"I don't feel any need to kill you at this point," Aomame declared. "As you probably know, that is what I came here to do. I can't permit a person like you to exist. I was determined to obliterate you from this world. But I no longer feel that determination. You are suffering terribly, I can tell. You deserve to die slowly, going to pieces bit by bit, in terrible pain. I can't find it in me to grant you an easy death."

Still lying facedown, the man responded with a small nod. "If you were to kill me, my people would be sure to track you down. They are absolute fanatics, and they are powerful and persistent. With me gone, the religion would lose its centripetal force. But once it is formed, a system takes on a life of its own."

Aomame listened to him speak as he lay there facedown.

"What I did to your friend was very bad."

"My friend?"

"Your girlfriend with the handcuffs. Now, what was her name again . . . ?"

A sudden calm filled Aomame. The inner conflict was gone. A heavy silence hung over her now.

"Ayumi Nakano," Aomame said.

"Poor girl."

"Did *you* do that?" Aomame asked coldly. "Are *you* the one who killed Ayumi?"

"No, not at all. I didn't kill her."

"But for some reason you know – that someone killed her."

"Our researcher found out," the man said. "We don't know who killed her. All we know is that your friend, the police-woman, was strangled to death in a hotel."

Aomame's right hand became tightly clenched again. "But you said, 'What I did to your friend was very bad.' "

"That I was unable to prevent it. Whoever may have killed her, the fact is that they always go after your weakest point – the way wolves chase down the weakest sheep in the herd."

"You're saying that Ayumi was a weak point of mine?"

The man did not answer.

Aomame closed her eyes. "But why did they have to kill her? She was such a good person! She would never hurt anyone. Why? Because I am involved in *this*? If so, wouldn't it have been enough just to destroy me?"

The man said, "They can't destroy you."

"Why not?" Aomame asked. "Why can't they destroy me?"

"Because you have long since become a special being."

"Special being?" Aomame asked. "In what way 'special'?"

"You will discover that eventually."

"Eventually?"

"When the time comes."

Aomame screwed up her face again. "I can't understand what you are saying."

"You will at some point."

Aomame shook her head. "In any case, they can't attack me for now. And so they aimed at a weak point near me. In order to give me a warning. To keep me from taking your life."

The man remained silent. It was a silence of affirmation.

"It's too terrible," Aomame said. She shook her head. "What real difference could it possibly have made for them to murder her?"

"No, they are not murderers. They never destroy anyone with their own hands. What killed your friend, surely, was something she had inside of her. The same kind of tragedy would have happened sooner or later. Her life was filled with risk. All *they* did was to provide the stimulus. Like changing the setting on a timer."

Setting on a timer?

"She was no electric oven! She was a living human being! So what if her life was full of risk? She was a dear friend of mine. You people took that from me like nothing at all. Meaninglessly. Callously."

"Your anger is entirely justified," the man said. "You should direct it at me."

Aomame shook her head. "Even if I take your life here, that won't bring Ayumi back."

"No, but it would provide some degree of retaliation against the Little People. You could have your revenge, as it were. They don't want me to die yet. If I die now, it will open up a vacuum – at least a temporary vacuum, until a successor comes into being. It would be a strike against them. At the same time, it would be a benefit to you."

"Someone once said that nothing costs more and yields less benefit than revenge," Aomame said.

"Winston Churchill. As I recall it, though, he was making excuses for the British Empire's budget deficits. It has no moral significance."

"Never mind about morals. You are going to die in agony while some strange *thing* eats you up whether I raise a hand against you or not. I have no reason to sympathize with you for that. Even if the world were to lose all morals and go to pieces, it wouldn't be *my* fault."

The man took another deep breath. "All right, I see what you are saying. How about this, then? Let's make a deal. If you will take my life, I will spare the life of Tengo Kawana. I still have that much power left."

"Tengo," Aomame said. The strength went out of her body. "So you know about that, too."

"I know everything about you. Or perhaps I should say *almost* everything."

"But you can't possibly tell that much. Tengo's name has never taken a step outside my heart."

"Please, Miss Aomame," the man said. Then he released a brief sigh. "There is nothing in this world that never takes a step outside a person's heart. And *it just so happens* – should I say? – that Tengo Kawana has become a figure of no little significance to us at the moment."

Aomame was at a loss for words.

The man said, "But then again, chance has nothing to do with it. Your two fates did not cross through mere happenstance. The two of you set foot in this world because you were meant to enter it. And now that you have entered it, like it or not, each of you will be assigned your proper role here."

"Set foot in this world?"

"Yes, in this year of 1Q84."

"1Q84?" Aomame said, her face greatly distorting. *I made that word up!*

"True, it is a word you made up," the man said, as if reading her mind. "I am just borrowing it from you."

Aomame formed the word 1Q84 in her mouth.

"There is nothing in this world that never takes a step outside a person's heart," Leader repeated softly.

Tengo

MORE THAN I COULD COUNT
ON MY FINGERS

Tengo managed to return to his apartment before the rains came. He hurried on foot from the station to his building. There was not a cloud to be seen in the evening sky, no sign that rain was on its way, no suggestion of coming thunder. None of the people around him was carrying an umbrella. It was the kind of pleasant late-summer evening that called for a draft beer at a baseball game. But he had recently entered a new frame of mind, and that was to assume that anything Fuka-Eri said might be true. *Better to believe than not to believe,* Tengo thought, basing it not so much on logic as experience.

He peeked into his mailbox to find a business envelope with no return address. He tore it open on the spot. Inside was a notice that 1,627,534 yen had been electronically transferred into his bank account. The payer was listed as "Office ERI," which was almost certainly Komatsu's fabricated company. Or possibly Professor Ebisuno had made the transfer. Komatsu had informed Tengo that he would be paid a part of the *Air Chrysalis* royalties as an honorarium, and perhaps this was that "part." No doubt the payment had been listed as an "assistance fee" or "research fee." After checking the figure again, Tengo returned the notice to the envelope and stuffed it into his pocket.

1.6 million yen was a lot of money to Tengo (in fact, he had never received such a lump sum in his life), but he felt neither happy nor surprised. Money was not a major problem for him at this point in time. He had his regular income, which enabled him to get by without undue strain, and for the moment, at least, he had no anxiety about his future. In spite of that, everyone wanted to give him large chunks of money. It was a strange world.

Where the rewriting of *Air Chrysalis* was concerned, however, Tengo had a sneaking suspicion that 1.6 million yen was not sufficient recompense for his having been drawn into *this much* trouble. If, on the other hand, someone were to ask him straight out, "All right, then, how much *would* be a fair amount?," he would have been hard-pressed to come up with a figure. First of all, he did not know if there was such a thing as a fair price for trouble. There must surely be many different kinds of trouble in the world for which there was no way to attach a price or for which there was no one willing to pay. *Air Chrysalis* was still selling well, apparently, which meant that there might be further payments into his account, but the more the deposits increased, the more problems they would give rise to. Each increase in compensation only served to increase the extent of Tengo's involvement with *Air Chrysalis* as an established fact.

He thought about sending the money back to Komatsu first thing tomorrow morning. That would enable him to evade some sort of responsibility. It might also provide some psychological relief. In any case it would establish the fact that he had rejected compensation. Not that it would expunge his moral responsibility or justify the actions he had taken. All it would give him was "possible extenuating circumstances," though it might end up doing just the opposite by making his actions appear all the more suspicious, as though he had returned the money because he felt guilty about it.

As he went on agonizing about the money, his head started to hurt, so he decided to stop. He could think about it again later, when he had time to spare. Money was not a living thing. It wouldn't run off anywhere if he left it alone. Probably.

The problem I have to deal with now is how to give my life a new start, Tengo thought as he climbed the three flights of stairs to his apartment. Having gone to see his father at the southern tip of the Boso Peninsula, he had become generally convinced that the man was not his real father. He felt he had also succeeded in reaching a turning point in his life. It might be the perfect opportunity. Now might be a good time to make a break with all his troubles and start his life over again: a new job, a new place, new relationships. Though not yet entirely confident, he had a kind of presentiment that he might be able to lead a somewhat more coherent life than he had so far.

Before he could do that, however, there were things he had to take care of. He couldn't simply shrug off Fuka-Eri and Komatsu and Professor Ebisuno and disappear somewhere. Of course, he had no obligations toward them, no ethical responsibilities. As Ushikawa had said, where this current matter was concerned, Tengo was the one being put upon by them. Still, though he could claim to have been all but dragged into the situation and to have been ignorant of its underlying plot, the fact was that he had still been involved. He couldn't simply announce that he would have nothing more to do with it and that the others could do as they pleased. Wherever he might go from here on out, he wanted first to bring things to some sort of conclusion and clean up his personal affairs. Otherwise, his fresh new life might be tainted from the outset.

"Tainted" reminded Tengo of Ushikawa. *Ushikawa, huh?* Tengo thought with a sigh. Ushikawa had his hands on some information regarding Tengo's mother, information that he said he could share with Tengo.

If you ever want to learn about that, I can hand you all the materials on your mother as is. However, there might be some not-very-pleasant information included in the file.

Tengo had not even bothered to reply to this. He had no wish to hear news about his mother from Ushikawa's mouth. Any kind of information would be sullied the moment it emerged from that orifice. No, Tengo had no desire to hear such information from *anyone's* mouth. If he was going to be given news about his mother, it had to come not in bits and pieces but as a comprehensive "revelation." It had to be, as it were, a vivid cosmic landscape, the full vast expanse of which could be seen in a split second.

Tengo did not know, of course, if he would be granted such a dramatic revelation sometime in the future. It might never come. But what he needed was something so enormous, on such an overwhelming scale, that it could rival and even surpass the striking images of the "waking dream" that had disoriented and jolted and tormented him over these many years. He needed something that would totally purge him of this image. Fragmentary information would do him no good at all.

These were the thoughts that ran through Tengo's mind as he climbed three flights of stairs.

Tengo stood in front of his apartment door, pulled his key from his pocket, inserted the key in the lock, and turned it. Then, before opening the door, he knocked three times, paused, and knocked twice more. Finally, he eased the door open.

Fuka-Eri was sitting at the table, drinking tomato juice from a tall glass. She was dressed in the same clothes she had been wearing when she arrived – a striped men's shirt and slim blue jeans. But the impression she made on Tengo was very different from the one she had given him that morning. It took

Tengo a while to realize why: she had her hair tied up, revealing her ears and the back of her neck. Those small, pink ears
of hers looked as though they had been daubed with powder
using a soft brush and had just been made a short time ago
for purely aesthetic reasons, not for the practical purpose of
hearing sounds. Or at least they looked that way to Tengo. The
slim, well-shaped neck below the ears had a lustrous glow, like
vegetables raised in abundant sunshine, immaculate and well
suited to morning dew and ladybugs. This was the first time
he had seen her with her hair up, and it was a miraculously
intimate and beautiful sight.

Tengo had closed the door by reaching around behind himself, but he went on standing there in the entrance. Her bared
ears and neck disoriented him as much as another woman's
total nakedness. Like an explorer who has discovered the secret
spring at the source of the Nile, Tengo stared at Fuka-Eri with
narrowed eyes, speechless, hand still clutching the doorknob.

"I took a shower," she said to Tengo as he stood there transfixed. She spoke in grave tones, as though she had just recalled
a major event. "I used your shampoo and rinse."

Tengo nodded. Then, exhaling, he finally wrenched his
hand from the doorknob and locked the door. *Shampoo and
rinse?* He stepped forward, away from the door.

"Did the phone ring after I called?" Tengo asked.

"Not at all," Fuka-Eri said. She gave her head a little shake.

Tengo went to the window, parted the curtains slightly, and
looked outside. The view from the third floor had nothing
unusual about it – no suspicious people lurking there or suspicious cars parked out front, just the usual drab expanse of
this drab residential neighborhood. The misshapen trees lining the street wore a layer of gray dust. The pedestrian guard-
rail was full of dents. Rusty bicycles lay abandoned by the side
of the road. A wall bore the police slogan "Driving Drunk:
A One-Way Street to a Ruined Life." (Did the police have

slogan-writing specialists in their ranks?) A nasty-looking old man was walking a stupid-looking mutt. A stupid-looking woman drove by in an ugly subcompact. Nasty-looking wires stretched from one ugly utility pole to another. The scene outside the window suggested that the world had settled in a place somewhere midway between "being miserable" and "lacking in joy," and consisted of an infinite agglomeration of variously shaped microcosms.

On the other hand, there also existed in the world such unexceptionally beautiful views as Fuka-Eri's ears and neck. In which should he place the greater faith? It was not easy for him to decide. Like a big, confused dog, Tengo made a soft growling noise in his throat, closed the curtains, and returned to his own little world.

"Does Professor Ebisuno know that you're here?" Tengo asked.

Fuka-Eri shook her head. The professor did not know.

"Don't you plan to tell him?"

Fuka-Eri shook her head. "I can't contact him."

"Because it would be dangerous to contact him?"

"The phone may be tapped. Mail might not get through."

"I'm the only one who knows you're here?"

Fuka-Eri nodded.

"Did you bring a change of clothing and stuff?"

"A little," Fuka-Eri said, glancing at her canvas shoulder bag. Certainly "a little" was all it could hold.

"I don't mind," the girl said.

"If you don't mind, of course I don't mind," Tengo said.

Tengo went into the kitchen, put the kettle on to boil, and spooned some tea leaves into the teapot.

"Does your lady friend come here," Fuka-Eri asked.

"Not anymore," Tengo gave her a short answer.

Fuka-Eri stared at Tengo in silence.

"For now," Tengo added.

"Is it my fault," Fuka-Eri asked.

Tengo shook his head. "I don't know whose fault it is. But I don't think it's yours. It's probably my fault. And maybe hers to some extent."

"But anyhow, she won't come here anymore."

"Right, she won't come here anymore. Probably. So it's okay for you to stay."

Fuka-Eri spent a few moments thinking about that. "Was she married," she asked.

"Yes, and she had two kids."

"Not yours."

"No, of course not. She had them before she met me."

"Did you love her."

"Probably," Tengo said. *Under certain limited conditions,* Tengo added to himself.

"Did she love you."

"Probably. To some extent."

"Were you having intercourse."

It took a moment for the word "intercourse" to register with Tengo. It was hard to imagine that word coming from Fuka-Eri's mouth.

"Of course. She wasn't coming here every week to play Monopoly."

"Monopoly," she asked.

"Never mind," Tengo said.

"But she won't come here anymore."

"That's what I was told, at least. That she won't come here anymore."

"She told you that," Fuka-Eri asked.

"No, I didn't hear it directly from her. Her husband told me. That she was *irretrievably lost* and couldn't come here anymore."

"Irretrievably lost."

"I don't know exactly what it means either. I couldn't get

him to explain. There were lots of questions but not many answers. Like a trade imbalance. Want some tea?"

Fuka-Eri nodded.

Tengo poured the boiling water into the teapot, put the lid on, and waited.

"Oh well," Fuka-Eri said.

"What? The few answers? Or that she was lost?"

Fuka-Eri did not reply.

Tengo gave up and poured tea into two cups. "Sugar?"

"A level teaspoonful," Fuka-Eri said.

"Lemon or milk?"

Fuka-Eri shook her head. Tengo put a spoonful of sugar into the cup, stirred it slowly, and set it in front of the girl. He added nothing to his own tea, picked up the cup, and sat at the table across from her.

"Did you like having intercourse," Fuka-Eri asked.

"Did I like having intercourse with my girlfriend?" Tengo rephrased it as an ordinary question.

Fuka-Eri nodded.

"I think I did," Tengo said. "Having intercourse with a member of the opposite sex that you're fond of. Most people enjoy that."

To himself he said, *She was very good at it. Just as every village has at least one farmer who is good at irrigation, she was good at sexual intercourse. She liked to try different methods.*

"Are you sad she stopped coming," Fuka-Eri asked.

"Probably," Tengo said. Then he drank his tea.

"Because you can't do intercourse."

"That's part of it, naturally."

Fuka-Eri stared straight at Tengo again for a time. She seemed to be having some kind of thoughts about intercourse. What she was actually thinking about, no one could say.

"Hungry?" Tengo asked.

Fuka-Eri nodded. "I have hardly eaten anything since this morning."

"I'll make dinner," Tengo said. He himself had hardly eaten anything since the morning, and he was feeling hungry. Also, he could not think of anything to do for the moment aside from making dinner.

Tengo washed the rice, put it in the cooker, and turned on the switch. He used the time until the rice was ready to make miso soup with wakame seaweed and green onions, grill a sun-dried mackerel, take some tofu out of the refrigerator and flavor it with ginger, grate a chunk of daikon radish, and reheat some leftover boiled vegetables. To go with the rice, he set out some pickled turnip slices and a few pickled plums. With Tengo moving his big body around inside it, the little kitchen looked especially small. It did not bother him, though. He was long used to making do with what he had there.

"Sorry, but these simple things are all I can make," Tengo said.

Fuka-Eri studied Tengo's skillful kitchen work in great detail. With apparent fascination, she scrutinized the results of that work neatly arranged on the table and said, "You know how to cook."

"I've been living alone for a long time. I prepare my meals alone as quickly as possible and I eat alone as quickly as possible. It's become a habit."

"Do you always eat alone."

"Pretty much. It's very unusual for me to sit down to a meal like this with somebody. I used to eat lunch here once a week with the woman we were talking about. But, come to think of it, I haven't eaten dinner with anybody for a very long time."

"Are you nervous."

Tengo shook his head. "No, not especially. It's just dinner. It does seem a little strange, though."

"I used to eat with lots of people. We all lived together when I was little. And I ate with lots of different people after I moved to the Professor's. He always had visitors."

He had never heard Fuka-Eri speak so many sentences in a row.

"But you were eating alone all the time you were in hiding?" Tengo asked.

Fuka-Eri nodded.

"Where *were* you in hiding?" Tengo asked.

"Far away. The Professor arranged it for me."

"What were you eating alone?"

"Instant stuff. Packaged food," Fuka-Eri said. "I haven't had a meal like this in a long time."

Fuka-Eri put a lot of time into tearing the flesh of the mackerel from the bones with her chopsticks. She brought the pieces of fish to her mouth and put more time into chewing them, as though she were eating some rare new food. Then she took a sip of miso soup, examined the taste, made some kind of judgment, set her chopsticks on the table, and went on thinking.

Just before nine o'clock, Tengo thought he might have caught the sound of thunder in the distance. He parted the curtains slightly and looked outside. The sky was totally dark now, and across it streamed a number of ominously shaped clouds.

"You were right," Tengo said after closing the curtain. "The weather's looking very ugly out there."

"Because the Little People are stirring," Fuka-Eri said with a somber expression.

"When the Little People begin stirring, it does extraordinary things to the weather?"

"It depends. Weather is a question of how you look at it."

"A question of how you look at it?"

Fuka-Eri shook her head. "I don't really get it."

Tengo didn't get it either. To him, weather seemed to be an independent, objective condition. But he probably couldn't get anywhere pursuing this question further. He decided to ask another question instead.

"Do you think the Little People are angry about something?"

"Something is about to happen," the girl said.

"What kind of something?"

Fuka-Eri shook her head. "We'll see soon."

Together they washed and dried the dishes and put them away, after which they sat facing each other across the table, drinking tea. He would have liked a beer, but decided it might be better to refrain from drinking today. He sensed some kind of danger in the air, and thought he should remain as clear-headed as possible in case something happened.

"It might be better to go to sleep early," Fuka-Eri said, pressing her hands against her cheeks like the screaming man on the bridge in the Munch picture. Not that she was screaming: she was just sleepy.

"Okay, you can use my bed," Tengo said. "I'll sleep on the sofa like before. Don't worry, I can sleep anywhere."

It was true. Tengo could fall asleep anywhere right away. It was almost a talent.

Fuka-Eri only nodded. She looked straight at Tengo for a while, offering no opinions. Then she briefly touched her freshly made ears, as if to check that they were still there. "Can you lend me your pajamas. I didn't bring mine."

Tengo took his extra pajamas from the bedroom dresser drawer and handed them to Fuka-Eri. They were the same pajamas he had lent her the last time she stayed here – plain blue cotton pajamas, washed and folded from that time. Tengo held them to his nose to check for odors, but there were none. Fuka-Eri took them, went to the bathroom to change, and came back to the dining table. Now her hair was down. The pajama legs and arms were rolled up as before.

"It's not even nine o'clock," Tengo said, glancing at the wall clock. "Do you always go to bed so early?"

Fuka-Eri shook her head. "Today is special."

"Because the Little People are stirring outside?"

"I'm not sure. I'm just tired now."

"You *do* look sleepy," Tengo admitted.

"Can you read me a book or tell me a story in bed," Fuka-Eri asked.

"Sure," Tengo said. "I don't have anything else to do."

It was a hot and humid night, but as soon as she got into bed, Fuka-Eri pulled the quilt up to her chin, as if to form a firm barrier between the outside world and her own world. In bed, somehow, she looked like a little girl no more than twelve years old. The thunder rumbling outside the window was much louder than before, as though the lightning were beginning to strike somewhere quite close by. With each thunderclap, the windowpanes would rattle. Strangely, though, there were no lightning flashes to be seen, just thunder rolling across the pitch-dark sky. Nor was there any hint of rain. Something was definitely out of balance.

"They are watching us," Fuka-Eri said.

"You mean the Little People?" Tengo asked.

Fuka-Eri did not answer him.

"They know we're here," Tengo said.

"Of course they know," Fuka-Eri said.

"What are they trying to do to us?"

"They can't do anything to us."

"That's good."

"For now, that is."

"They can't touch us for now," Tengo repeated feebly. "But there's no telling how long that will go on."

"No one knows," Fuka-Eri declared with conviction.

"But even if they can't do anything to us, they *can*, instead, do something to the people around us?" Tengo asked.

"Maybe so."

"Maybe they can make terrible things happen to them?"

Fuka-Eri narrowed her eyes for a time with a deadly serious look, like a sailor trying to catch the song of a ship's ghost. Then she said, "In some cases."

"Maybe the Little People used their powers against my girlfriend. To give me a warning."

Fuka-Eri slipped a hand out from beneath the quilt and gave her freshly made ear a scratching. Then she slipped the hand back inside. "What the Little People can do is limited."

Tengo bit his lip for a moment. Then he said, "Exactly what kinds of things *can* they do, for example?"

Fuka-Eri started to offer an opinion on the matter but then had second thoughts and stopped. Her opinion, unvoiced, sank back into the place it had originated from – a deep, dark, unknown place.

"You said that the Little People have wisdom and power."

Fuka-Eri nodded.

"But they have their limits."

Fuka-Eri nodded.

"And that's because they are people of the forest; when they leave the forest, they can't unleash their powers so easily. And in this world, there exist something like values that make it possible to resist their wisdom and power. Is that it?"

Fuka-Eri did not answer him. Perhaps the question was too long.

"Have you ever met the Little People?" Tengo asked.

Fuka-Eri stared at him vaguely, as though she could not grasp the meaning of his question.

"Have you ever actually seen them?" Tengo rephrased his question.

"Yes," Fuka-Eri said.

"How many of the Little People did you see?"

"I don't know. More than I could count on my fingers."

"But not just one."

"Their numbers can sometimes increase and sometimes decrease, but there is never just one."

"The way you depicted them in *Air Chrysalis*."

Fuka-Eri nodded.

Tengo took this opportunity to ask Fuka-Eri a question he had been wanting to ask her for some time. "Tell me," he said, "how much of *Air Chrysalis* is real? How much of it really happened?"

"What does 'real' mean," Fuka-Eri asked without a question mark.

Tengo had no answer for this, of course.

A great clap of thunder echoed through the sky. The window-panes rattled. But still there was no lightning, no sound of rain. Tengo recalled an old submarine movie. One depth charge after another would explode, jolting the ship, but everyone was locked inside the dark steel box, unable to see outside. For them, there was only the unbroken sound and the shaking of the sub.

"Will you read me a book or tell me a story," Fuka-Eri asked.

"Sure," Tengo said, "but I can't think of a good book for reading out loud. I don't have the book here, but I can tell you a story called 'Town of Cats,' if you like."

" 'Town of Cats.' "

"It's the story of a town ruled by cats."

"I want to hear it."

"It might be a little too scary for a bedtime story, though."

"That's okay. I can sleep, whatever story you tell."

Tengo brought a chair next to the bed, sat down, folded his hands in his lap, and started telling "Town of Cats," with the thunder as background music. He had read the story twice on the express train and once again, aloud, to his father in the sanatorium, so he knew the plot pretty well. It was not such a complex or finely delineated story, nor had it been written in a terribly elegant style, so he felt little hesitation in altering it as he pleased, omitting the more tedious parts or adding episodes that occurred to him as he recited the story for Fuka-Eri.

The original story had not been very long, but telling it took a lot longer than he had imagined because Fuka-Eri would not hesitate to ask any questions that occurred to her. Tengo would interrupt the story each time and give her careful answers, explaining the details of the town or the cats' behavior or the protagonist's character. When they were things not described in the story (which was usually the case), Tengo would make them up, as he had with *Air Chrysalis*. Fuka-Eri seemed to be completely drawn in by "Town of Cats." She no longer looked tired. She would close her eyes sometimes, imagining scenes of the town of cats. Then she would open her eyes and urge Tengo to go on with the story.

When he was through telling her the story, Fuka-Eri opened her eyes wide and stared at Tengo the way a cat widens its pupils to stare at something in the dark.

"Did you go to a town of cats," Fuka-Eri asked Tengo, as if pressing him to reveal a truth.

"*Me?!*"

"You went to *your* town of cats. Then came back on a train."

"Is that what you feel?"

With the summer quilt pulled up to her chin, Fuka-Eri gave him a quick little nod.

"You're quite right," Tengo said. "I went to a town of cats and came back on a train."

"Did you do a purification afterward," she asked.

"Purification? No, I don't think so, not yet."

"You have to do it."

"What kind of purification?"

Instead of answering him, Fuka-Eri said, "If you go to a

town of cats and don't do anything about it afterward, bad stuff can happen."

A great thunderclap seemed to crack the heavens in two. The sound was increasing in ferocity. Fuka-Eri recoiled from it in bed.

"Come here and hold me," Fuka-Eri said. "We have to go to a town of cats together."

"Why?"

"The Little People might find the entrance."

"Because I haven't done a purification?"

"Because the two of us are one," the girl said.

CHAPTER 13

Aomame

WITHOUT YOUR LOVE

"1Q84," Aomame said. "Are you talking about the fact that I am living now in the year called 1Q84, not the *real* 1984?"

"What the real world is: that is a very difficult problem," the man called Leader said as he lay on his stomach. "What it is, is a metaphysical proposition. But *this* is the real world, there is no doubt about that. The pain one feels in this world is real pain. Deaths caused in this world are real deaths. Blood shed in this world is real blood. This is no imitation world, no imaginary world, no metaphysical world. I guarantee you that. But this is not the 1984 you know."

"Like a parallel world?"

The man's shoulders trembled with laughter. "You've been reading too much science fiction. No, this is no parallel world. You don't have 1984 over there and 1Q84 branching off over here and the two worlds running along parallel tracks. The year 1984 no longer exists *anywhere*. For you and for me, the only time that exists anymore is this year of 1Q84."

"We have entered into its time flow once and for all."

"Exactly. We have entered into this place where we are now. Or the time flow has entered us once and for all. And as far as I understand it, the door only opens in one direction. There is no way back."

"I suppose it happened when I climbed down the Metropolitan Expressway's emergency stairway."

"Metropolitan Expressway?"

"Near Sangenjaya," Aomame said.

"The place is irrelevant," the man said. "For you, it was Sangenjaya. But the specific place is not the question. The question here, in the end, is the time. The track, as it were, was switched there, and the world was transformed into 1Q84."

Aomame imagined a number of Little People joining forces to move the device that switches the tracks. In the middle of the night. Under the pale light of the moon.

"And in this year of 1Q84, there are two moons in the sky, aren't there?"

"Correct: two moons. That is the *sign* that the track has been switched. That is how you can tell the two worlds apart. Not that all of the people here can see two moons. In fact, most people are not aware of it. In other words, the number of people who know that this is 1Q84 is quite limited."

"Most people in this world are not aware that the time flow has been switched?"

"Correct. To most people, this is just the plain old everyday world they've always known. This is what I mean when I say, 'This is the real world.'"

"So the track has been switched," Aomame said. "If it had *not* been switched, we would not be meeting here like this. Could that be what you are saying?"

"That is the one thing that no one knows. It's a question of probability. But that is probably the case."

"Is what you are saying an objective fact, or just a hypothesis?"

"Good question. But distinguishing between the two is virtually impossible. Remember how the old song goes, 'Without your love, it's a honky-tonk parade'?" He hummed the melody. "Do you know it?"

" 'It's Only a Paper Moon.' "

"That's it. 1984 and 1Q84 are fundamentally the same in terms of how they work. If you don't believe in the world, and if there is no love in it, then everything is phony. No matter which world we are talking about, no matter what *kind* of world we are talking about, the line separating fact from hypothesis is practically invisible to the eye. It can only be seen with the inner eye, the eye of the mind."

"Who switched the tracks?"

"Who switched the tracks? That is another difficult question. The logic of cause and effect has little power here."

"In any case, *some* kind of will transported me into this world of 1Q84," Aomame said. "A will other than my own."

"That is true. You were carried into this world when the train you were on had its tracks switched."

"Do the Little People have anything to do with that?"

"In this world there are the so-called Little People. Or at least, that is what they are called in this world. But they do not always have a shape or a name."

Aomame bit her lip in thought. Then she said, "What you are saying sounds contradictory to me. Let's assume it was these 'Little People' who switched the track and carried me into this world of 1Q84. Why would they do such a thing if they don't want me to do what I am about to do to you? It would be far more advantageous to get rid of me."

"That is not easy to explain," the man said, his voice lacking all intonation. "But you are a very quick thinker. You might be able to grasp, however vaguely, what I am trying to tell you. As I said before, the most important thing with regard to this world in which we live is for there to be a balance maintained between good and evil. The so-called Little People – or some kind of manifestations of will – certainly do have great power. But the more they use their power, the more another power automatically arises to resist it. In that way, the world maintains a delicate balance. This fundamental principle is the same in any world. Precisely the same thing can be said in this world of 1Q84 that now contains us. When the Little People began to manifest their enormous power, a power opposing the Little People also automatically came into being. And this opposing momentum must have drawn you into the year 1Q84."

Lying like a beached whale on his blue yoga mat, the giant man released a huge breath.

"To continue with the train analogy: it is possible for them to switch tracks, as a result of which the train has entered its current line – the 1Q84 line. One thing they are not able to do, however, is to distinguish one passenger on the train from another – to choose among them. Which means that there may be passengers aboard who, to them, are undesirable."

"Uninvited passengers."

"Exactly."

Again there was a rumble of thunder. This one was much louder than before. But there was no lightning. Just the sound. *Strange,* Aomame thought. *The thunder is so close, but the lightning doesn't flash. And no rain is falling.*

"Have I managed to make myself clear thus far?"

"I'm listening," she said, having already moved the needle away from the spot on his neck. Now she had it pointed cautiously toward empty space. She had to concentrate all her attention on what he was saying.

"Where there is light, there must be shadow, and where there is shadow there must be light. There is no shadow without light and no light without shadow. Karl Jung said this about 'the Shadow' in one of his books: 'It is as evil as we are positive . . . the more desperately we try to be good and wonderful and perfect, the more the Shadow develops a definite will to be black and evil and destructive. . . . The fact is that if one tries beyond one's capacity to be perfect, the Shadow descends to hell and becomes the devil. For it is just as sinful from the standpoint of nature and of truth to be above oneself as to be below oneself."

"We do not know if the so-called Little People are good or evil. This is, in a sense, something that surpasses our understanding and our definitions. We have lived with them since long, long ago – from a time before good and evil even existed, when people's minds were still benighted. But the important thing is that, whether they are good or evil, light or shadow, whenever they begin to exert their power, a compensatory force comes into being. In my case, when I became an 'agent' of the so-called Little People, my daughter became something like an agent for those forces opposed to the Little People. In this way, the balance was maintained."

"Your daughter?"

"Yes, the first one to usher in the so-called Little People was my daughter. She was ten years old at the time. Now she is seventeen. The Little People emerged from the darkness at some point, coming here through her, and they made me their agent. My daughter became a Perceiver and I became a Receiver. Apparently we were suited to such roles by nature. In any case, *they* found *us*. We did not find them."

"And so you raped your own daughter."

"I had congress with her," he said. "That expression is closer to the truth. And the one I had congress with was, strictly speaking, my daughter as a concept. 'To have congress with' is an ambiguous term. The essential point was for us to become one – as Perceiver and Receiver."

Aomame shook her head. "I can't understand what you are saying. Did you have sex with your daughter or didn't you?"

"The answer to that question is, finally, both yes and no."

"Is this true of little Tsubasa as well?"

"Yes, in principle."

"But Tsubasa's uterus was destroyed – not 'in principle' but in reality."

The man shook his head. "What you saw was the outward manifestation of a concept, not an actual substance."

Aomame was unable to follow the swift flow of the conversation. She paused to bring her breathing under control. Then she asked, "Are you saying that a concept took on human shape and ran away on its own two feet?"

"To put it simply."

"The Tsubasa I laid eyes on was not actual substance?"

"Which is why she was retrieved."

"Retrieved," Aomame said.

"She was retrieved and is now being healed. She is receiving the treatment she needs."

"I don't believe you," Aomame declared.

"I can't blame you," the man said without emotion.

Aomame was at a loss to say anything for a time. Then she asked another question. "By violating your daughter, conceptually and ambiguously, you became an agent of the Little People. But simultaneously, your daughter compensated by leaving you and becoming, as it were, an opponent of the Little People. Is this what you are asserting?"

"That is correct. And in order to do so, she had to leave her own *dohta* behind," the man said. "That doesn't mean anything to you, though, does it?"

" '*Dohta*'?" Aomame asked.

"Something like a living shadow. Here another character becomes involved – an old friend of mine. A man I can trust. I put my daughter in his care. Then, not too long ago, yet another character became involved, someone you know very well by the name of Tengo Kawana. Sheer chance brought Tengo and my daughter together as a team."

Time seemed to come to a sudden halt. Aomame could find no words to speak. She went stiff from head to toe, waiting for time to begin to move once again.

The man continued speaking. "Each happened to have

qualities that augmented the other. What Tengo lacked, Eriko possessed, and what Eriko lacked, Tengo possessed. They joined forces to complete a single work. And the fruits of their collaboration turned out to have a great impact. That is to say, in the context of establishing an opposition to the Little People."

"They made a team?"

"Not that the two have a romantic or physical relationship. So there is nothing for you to worry about – if that is what you have in mind. Eriko will never have a romantic relationship with anyone. She has transcended such things."

"What are the fruits of their collaboration, exactly?"

"In order to explain that, I must bring up a second analogy. The two have, so to speak, invented an antibody to a virus. If we take the actions of the Little People to be a virus, Tengo and Eriko have created and spread the antibody to combat it. This is, of course, a one-sided analogy. From the Little People's point of view, Tengo and Eriko are, conversely, the carriers of a virus. All things are arranged as mirrors set face-to-face."

"Is this what you call the compensatory function?"

"Exactly. In joining forces, the man you love and my daughter have succeeded in giving rise to such a function. Which is to say that, in this world, you and Tengo are literally in step with each other."

"But that is not simply a matter of chance, according to you. You say I was led into this world by some form of will. Is that it?"

"That is it exactly. You came with a purpose, led by a form of will, to this world of 1Q84. That you and Tengo have come to have a relationship here – in whatever form it might take – is by no means a product of chance."

"What kind of will, and what kind of purpose?"

"It has not been given to me to explain that, sorry to say," the man said.

"Why are you unable to explain it?"

"It is not that the meaning cannot be explained. But there are certain meanings that are lost forever the moment they are explained in words."

"All right, then, let me try another question," Aomame said. "Why did *I* have to be the one?"

"You still don't understand why, do you?"

Aomame gave her head several strong shakes. "No, I don't understand why. Not at all."

"It is very simple, actually. It is because you and Tengo were so powerfully drawn to each other."

Aomame maintained a long silence. She sensed a hint of perspiration oozing from the pores of her face. It felt as if her whole face were covered by a thin membrane invisible to the naked eye.

"Drawn to each other," she said.

"Yes, to each other. Very powerfully."

An emotion resembling anger welled up inside her as if from nowhere, accompanied by a vague sense of nausea. "I can't believe that. He couldn't possibly remember me."

"No, Tengo knows very well that you exist in this world, and he wants you. To this day, he has never once loved any woman other than you."

Aomame was momentarily at a loss for words, during which time the violent thunder continued at short intervals, and rain seemed to have finally begun to fall. Large raindrops began pelting the hotel room window, but the sound barely reached Aomame.

The man said, "You can believe it or not as you wish. But you would do better to believe it because it is the unmistakable truth."

"You mean to say that he still remembers me even though twenty years have gone by since we last met? Even though we never really spoke to each other?"

"In that empty classroom, you strongly gripped his hand. When you were ten years old. You had to summon up every bit of your courage to do it."

Aomame twisted her face out of shape. "How could *you* possibly know such a thing?"

The man did not answer her. "Tengo never forgot about that. And he has continued to think of you all this time. You would do well to believe it. I know many things. For example, I know that, even now, you think of Tengo when you mastur-bate. You picture him. I am right about that, aren't I?"

Aomame let her mouth fall open slightly, but she was at a total loss for words. All she did was take one shallow breath after another.

The man went on, "It is nothing to be ashamed of. It is a nat-ural human function. Tengo does the same thing. He thinks of you at those times, even now."

"But *how* could you possibly . . . ?"

"How could I possibly know such things? By listening closely. That is my job – to listen to the voices."

She wanted to laugh out loud, and, simultaneously, she wanted to cry. But she could do neither. She could only stay transfixed, somewhere between the two, inclining her center of gravity in neither direction, at a loss for words.

"You need not be afraid," the man said.

"Afraid?"

"You are afraid, just as the people of the Vatican were afraid to accept the Copernican theory. Not even they believed in the infallibility of the Ptolemaic theory. They were afraid of the new situation that would prevail if they accepted the Coperni-can theory. They were afraid of having to reorder their minds to accept it. Strictly speaking, the Catholic Church has still not publicly accepted the Copernican theory. You are like them. You are afraid of having to shed the armor with which you have long defended yourself."

Aomame covered her face with her hands and let out several convulsive sobs. This was not what she wanted to do, but she was unable to stop herself. She would have preferred to appear to be laughing, but that was out of the question.

"You and Tengo were, so to speak, carried into this world on the same train," the man said softly. "By teaming up with my daughter, Tengo took steps against the Little People, and you are trying to obliterate me for other reasons. In other words, each of you, in your own way, is doing something dangerous in a very dangerous place."

"And you are saying that some kind of *will* wanted us to do these things?"

"Perhaps."

"For what conceivable purpose?" No sooner had the question left her mouth than Aomame realized it was pointless. There was no hope she would ever receive a reply.

"The most welcome resolution would be for the two of you to meet somewhere and leave this world hand in hand," the man said, without answering her question. "But that would not be an easy thing to do."

"Not be an easy thing to do," Aomame repeated his words unconsciously.

"Not an easy thing to do, and, sad to say, that is putting it as mildly as possible. In fact, it is just about impossible. The adversary that you two are facing, whatever you care to call it, is a fierce power."

"So then – " Aomame said, her voice dry. She cleared her throat. By now she had overcome her confusion. *This is no time to cry,* she thought. "So then comes your proposition, is that it? I give you a painless death, in return for which you can give me something – a different choice."

"You're very quick on the uptake," the man said, still lying facedown. "That is correct. My proposition is a choice having to do with you and Tengo. It may not be the most pleasant choice. But at least it does give you room to choose."

"The Little People are afraid of losing me," the man said. "They still need me. I am useful to them as their human agent. Finding my replacement will not be easy for them. And at this point in time, they have not prepared my successor. Many difficult conditions have to be met in order to become their agent, and I happen to meet all of them, which makes me a rare find. They are afraid of losing me. If that were to happen, it would give rise to a temporary vacuum. This is why they are trying to prevent you from taking my life. They want to keep me alive a little while longer. The thunder you hear outside is a sign of their anger. But they can't raise a hand against you directly. All they can do is warn you of their anger. For the same reason, they drove your friend to her death using possibly devious methods. And if things go on like this they will almost surely inflict some kind of harm upon Tengo."

"Inflict harm on Tengo?"

"Tengo wrote a story about the Little People and their deeds. Eriko furnished the basic story, and Tengo converted it into an effective piece of writing. It was their collaborative effort, and it acted as an antibody, countering the momentum of the Little People. It was published as a book and became a bestseller, as a result of which, if only temporarily, the Little People found that many potential avenues had been closed for them, and limits were placed on several of their actions. You have probably heard of the book: it is called *Air Chrysalis*."

Aomame nodded. "I've seen articles about the book in the newspaper. And the publisher's advertisements. I haven't read the book, though."

"The one who did the actual writing of *Air Chrysalis* was Tengo. And now he is writing a new story of his own. In *Air Chrysalis* – which is to say, in its world with two moons – he discovered his own story. A superior Perceiver, Eriko inspired the story as an antibody inside him. Tengo seems to have possessed superior ability as a Receiver. That ability may be what brought you here – in other words, what put you onto that train."

Aomame severely distorted her face in the gloom. She had to try her best to follow what this man was saying. "Are you telling me that I was transported into this other world of 1Q84 by Tengo's storytelling ability – or, as you put it, by his power as a Receiver?"

"That is, at least, what I surmise," the man said.

Aomame stared at her hands. Her fingers were wet with tears.

"If things go on as they are now, Tengo will in all likelihood be liquidated. At the moment, he is the number one threat to the so-called Little People. And, after all, this is the real world, where real blood is shed and real deaths occur. Death, of course, lasts forever."

Aomame bit her lip.

"I would like you to think about it this way," the man said. "If you kill me here and eliminate me from this world, the Little People will no longer have any reason to harm Tengo. If I cease to exist as a channel, Tengo and my daughter can obstruct that channel all they want without presenting any threat to them. The Little People will just forget about the two of them and look for a channel somewhere else – a channel with another origin. That will become their first priority. Do you see what I mean?"

"In theory, at least," Aomame said.

"On the other hand, if I am killed, the organization that I have created will never leave you alone. True, it might take them some time to find you because you will surely change your name, change where you live, and maybe even change your face. Still, they will track you down and punish you severely.

That is the kind of *system* that we have created: close-knit, violent, and irreversible. That is one choice you have."

Aomame took time to organize her thoughts about what he had told her. The man waited for his logic to permeate her mind.

Then he went on. "Conversely, if you do not kill me here and now, what will happen? You will simply withdraw from this place and I will go on living. So then the Little People will use all their powers to eliminate Tengo in order to protect me, their agent. The protective cloak he wears is not yet strong enough. They will find his weak point and do everything they can to destroy him because they cannot tolerate any further dissemination of the antibody. Meanwhile, you cease to be a threat, and they no longer have any reason to punish you. That is your other choice."

"In that case," Aomame said, summarizing what the man had told her, "Tengo dies and I go on living – here, in this world of 1Q84."

"Probably," he said.

"But there is no point in my living in a world where Tengo no longer exists. All possibility of our meeting would be lost forever."

"That may be the case from your point of view."

Aomame bit down hard on her lip, imagining such a state of affairs.

"But all I have to go on is what you are saying," she pointed out. "Why do I have to take you at your word? Is there some basis or backing for that?"

The man shook his head. "You are right. There is no basis or backing. It's just what I tell you. But you saw my special powers a little while ago. There are no strings attached to that clock, and it's very heavy. Go look at it yourself. Do you accept what I am saying or don't you? Decide one way or the other. We don't have much time left."

Aomame looked over at the clock on the chest of drawers. Its hands were showing just before nine. The clock was slightly out of place, facing at an odd angle, having been lifted into the air and dropped back again.

The man said, "At this point in this year of 1Q84, there seems to be no way to rescue you both at the same time. You have two possibilities to choose from. In one, you probably die and Tengo lives. In the other, he probably dies and you live. As I said before, it is not a pleasant choice."

"But no other possibilities exist to choose between."

The man shook his head. "At this point in time, you can only choose between those two."

Aomame filled her lungs with air and slowly exhaled.

"It's too bad for you," the man said. "If you had stayed in the year 1984, you would not have been faced with this choice. But at the same time, if you had stayed in 1984, you would almost surely never have learned that Tengo has continued to long for you all this time. It is precisely because you were transported to 1Q84 that you were able to learn this fact – the fact that your hearts are, in a sense, intertwined."

Aomame closed her eyes. *I will not cry,* she thought. *It is not the time to cry yet.*

"Is Tengo really longing for me? Can you swear to that without deception?"

"To this day, Tengo has never loved anyone but you with his whole heart. It is a fact. There is not the slightest room for doubt."

"But still, he never looked for me."

"Well, you never looked for him. Isn't that true?"

Aomame closed her eyes and, in a split second, reviewed the long span of years as if standing on the edge of a sheer cliff, surveying an ocean channel far below. She could smell the sea. She could hear the deep sighing of the wind.

She said, "We should have had the courage to search for each other long ago, I suppose. Then we could have been united in the original world."

"Theoretically, perhaps," the man said. "But you would never have even *thought* such a thing in the world of 1984. Cause and effect are linked that way in a twisted form. You can pile up all the worlds you like and the twisting will never be undone."

Tears poured from Aomame's eyes. She cried for everything she had lost. She cried for everything she was about to lose. And eventually – how long had she been crying? – she arrived at a point where she could cry no longer. Her tears dried up, as if her emotions had run into an invisible wall.

"All right, then," Aomame said. "There is no firm basis. Nothing has been proved. I can't understand all the details. But still, it seems I have to accept your offer. In keeping with your wishes, I will obliterate you from this world. I will give you a painless, instantaneous death so that Tengo can go on living."

"This means that you will agree to my bargain, then?"

"Yes. We have a bargain."

"You will probably die as a result, you know," the man said. "You will be chased down and punished. And the punishment may be terrible. They are fanatics."

"I don't care."

"Because you have love."

Aomame nodded.

The man said, " 'Without your love, it's a honky-tonk parade.' Like in the song."

"You are sure that Tengo will be able to go on living if I kill you?"

The man remained silent for a while. Then he said, "Tengo will go on living. You can take me at my word. I can give you that much without fail in exchange for my life."

"And my life, too," Aomame said.

"Some things can only be done in exchange for life," the man said.

Aomame clenched her fists. "To tell the truth, though, I would have preferred to stay alive and be united with Tengo."

A short silence came over the room. Even the thunder stopped. Everything was hushed.

"I wish I could make that happen," the man said softly. "Unfortunately, however, that is not one of the options. It was not available in 1984 nor is it in 1Q84, in a different sense in each case."

"Our paths would never have crossed – Tengo's and mine – in 1984? Is that what you are saying?"

"Exactly. You would have had no connection whatever, but you likely would have kept on thinking about each other as each of you entered a lonely old age."

"But in 1Q84 I can at least know that I am going to die for him."

The man took a deep breath, saying nothing.

"There is one thing I want you to tell me," Aomame said.

"If I can," the man said, lying on his stomach.

"Will Tengo find out in some form or other that I died for him? Or will he never know anything about it?"

The man thought about the question for a long time. "That is probably up to you."

"Up to me?" Aomame asked with a slight frown. "What do you mean by that?"

The man quietly shook his head. "You are fated to pass through great hardships and trials. Once you have done that, you should be able to see things as they are supposed to be. That is all I can say. No one knows for certain what it means to die until they actually do it."

Aomame picked up a towel and carefully dried the tears still clinging to her face. Then she examined the slender ice pick in her hand again to be certain that its fine point had not been broken off. With her right index finger, she searched again for the fatal point on the back of the man's neck as she had done before. She was able to find it right away, so vividly was it etched into her brain. She pressed the point softly with her fingertip, gauged its resilience, and made sure once again that her intuition was not mistaken. Taking several slow, deep breaths, she calmed the beating of her heart and steadied her heightened nerves. Her head would have to be perfectly clear. She swept away all thoughts of Tengo for the moment. Hatred, anger, confusion, pity: all these she sealed off in a separate space. Error was unacceptable. She had to concentrate her attention on *death itself,* as if focusing a narrow beam of light.

"Let us complete our work," Aomame said calmly. "I must remove you from this world."

"Then I can leave behind all the pain that I have been given."

"Leave behind all the pain, the Little People, a transformed world, those hypotheses . . . and love."

"And love. You are right," the man said as if speaking to himself. "I used to have people I loved. All right, then, let each of us finish our work. You are a terribly capable person, Aomame. I can tell that."

"You, too," Aomame said. Her voice had taken on the strange transparency of one who will deliver death. "You, too, are surely a very capable, superior person. I am sure there must have been a world in which there was no need for me to kill you."

"That world no longer exists," the man said. These were the last words he spoke.

That world no longer exists.

Aomame placed the sharp point against that delicate spot on the back of his neck. Concentrating all her attention, she adjusted the angle of the ice pick. Then she raised her right fist in the air. Holding her breath, she waited for a signal. *No more thinking,* she said to herself. *Let each of us complete our work. That is all. There is no need to think, no need for explanations. Just wait for the signal.* Her fist was as hard as a rock, devoid of feeling.

Outside the window, the thunder-without-lightning rumbled with increased force. Raindrops pelted the glass. The two of them were in an ancient cave – a dark, damp, low-ceilinged cave. Dark beasts and spirits surrounded the entrance. For the briefest instant around her, light and shadow became one. A nameless gust of wind blew through the distant channel. That was the signal. Aomame brought her fist down in one short, precise movement.

Everything ended in silence. The beasts and spirits heaved a deep breath, broke up their encirclement, and returned to the depths of a forest that had lost its heart.

CHAPTER 14

Tengo

A PACKAGE IN HIS HANDS

"Come here and hold me," Fuka-Eri said. "The two of us have to go to the town of cats together one more time."

"Hold you?" Tengo asked.

"You don't want to hold me," Fuka-Eri asked without a question mark.

"No, that's not it. It's just that – I didn't quite get what you were saying."

"This will be a purification," she informed him in uninflected tones. "Come here and hold me. You put on pajamas, too, and turn out the light."

As instructed, Tengo turned out the bedroom ceiling light. He undressed, took out his pajamas, and put them on. *When was the last time I washed these?* he wondered as he slipped into his pajamas. Judging from the fact that he could not remember, it must have been quite some time ago. Fortunately, they did not smell of sweat. Tengo had never sweated very much, and he did not have a strong body odor. *But still,* he reflected, *I ought to wash my pajamas more often. Life is so uncertain: you never know what could happen. One way to deal with that is to keep your pajamas washed.*

He got into bed and gingerly wrapped his arms around Fuka-Eri, who laid her head on Tengo's right arm. She lay very still, like a creature about to enter hibernation. Her body was warm, and so soft as to feel utterly defenseless. But she was not sweating.

The thunder increased in intensity, and now it was beginning to rain. As though crazed with anger, the raindrops slammed sideways against the window glass. The air was damp and sticky, and the world felt as if it might be oozing its way toward its dark finale. The time of Noah's flood might have felt like this. If so, it must have been quite depressing in the violent thunderstorm to have the narrow ark filled with the rhinoceroses, the lions, the pythons, and so forth, all in pairs, all used to different modes of living, with limited communication skills, and the stink something special.

The word "pair" made Tengo think of Sonny and Cher, but Sonny and Cher might not be the most appropriate pair to put aboard Noah's ark to represent humanity. Though they might not be entirely inappropriate, either. *There must be some other couple who would be a more appropriate human sample.*

Embracing Fuka-Eri in bed like this, with her wearing his own pajamas, Tengo had a strange feeling. He even felt as if he might be embracing a part of himself, as if he were holding someone with whom he shared flesh and body odor and whose mind was linked with his.

Tengo imagined the two of them having been chosen as a *pair* to board Noah's ark instead of Sonny and Cher. But even they could hardly be said to be the most appropriate sample of humanity. *The very fact of our embracing each other in bed like this is far from appropriate, no matter how you look at it.* The thought kept Tengo from being able to relax. He decided instead to imagine Sonny and Cher becoming good friends with the python pair on the ark. It was an utterly pointless thing to imagine, but at least it enabled him to relax the tension in his body.

Lying in Tengo's arms, Fuka-Eri said nothing. Nor did she

move or open her mouth. Tengo didn't say anything either. Even embracing Fuka-Eri in bed, he felt almost nothing that could be called sexual desire. To Tengo, sexual desire was fundamentally an extension of a means of communication. And so, to look for sexual desire in a place where there was no possibility of communication seemed inappropriate to him. He realized, too, that what Fuka-Eri was looking for was not his sexual desire. She was looking for *something else* from him, but what that something else was, he could not tell.

The *purpose* of doing so aside, the sheer *act* of holding a beautiful seventeen-year-old girl in his arms was by no means unpleasant. Her ear would touch his cheek now and then. Her warm breath grazed his neck. Her breasts were startlingly large and firm for a girl with such a slim body. He could feel them pressed against him in the area above his stomach. Her skin exuded a marvelous fragrance. It was the special smell of life that could only be exuded by flesh still in the process of formation, like the smell of dew-laden flowers in midsummer. He had often experienced that smell as an elementary school student on his way to early-morning radio exercises.

I hope I don't have an erection, Tengo thought. If he did have an erection, she would know immediately, given their relative positions. If that happened, it would make things somewhat uncomfortable. With what words and in what context could he explain to a seventeen-year-old girl that erections simply happen sometimes, even when not directly driven by sexual desire? Fortunately, however, no erection had happened so far, nor did he have any sign of one. *Let me stop thinking about smells. I have to concentrate my mind on things having as little to do with sex as possible.*

He thought again of the socializing between Sonny and Cher and the two pythons. Would they have anything to talk about? And if so, what could it be? Finally, when his ability to imagine the ark in the storm gave out, he tried multiplying sets of three-digit numbers. He would often do that when he was having sex with his older girlfriend. This would enable him to delay the moment of ejaculation (the moment of ejaculation being something about which she was particularly demanding). Tengo did not know if it would also work to hold off an erection, but it was better than doing nothing. He had to do *something*.

"I don't mind if it gets hard," Fuka-Eri said, as if she had read his mind.

"You don't mind?"

"There is nothing wrong with that."

"There is nothing wrong with that," Tengo said, echoing her words. *Sounds like a grade school kid in sex education.* "*Now, boys, there is nothing shameful or bad about having an erection. But of course you must choose the proper time and occasion.*"

"So, anyhow, has the purification begun?" Tengo asked in order to change the subject.

Fuka-Eri did not reply. Her small, beautiful ear seemed still to be trying to catch something in the rumbling of the thunder. Tengo could tell that much, and so he decided not to say any more. He also gave up trying to multiply three-digit numbers. *If Fuka-Eri doesn't mind, what's the difference if I get hard?* he thought. In any case, his penis showed no signs of movement. For now, it was just peacefully lying in the mud.

"I like your thingy," his older girlfriend had said. "I like its shape and color and size."

"I'm not so crazy about it," Tengo said.

"Why not?" she asked, slipping her palm under Tengo's flaccid penis as if handling a sleeping pet, testing its weight.

"I don't know," Tengo said. "Probably because I didn't choose it for myself."

"You're so weird," she said. "You've got a weird way of thinking."

That had happened once upon a time. Before Noah's flood, probably.

Fuka-Eri's warm, silent breath grazed Tengo's neck in a regular rhythm. Tengo could see her ear in the faint green light from the electric clock or in the occasional flash of lightning, which had finally started. The ear looked like a soft secret cave. *If this girl were my lover, I would probably never tire of kissing her there,* Tengo thought. *While I was inside her, I would kiss that ear, give it little bites, run my tongue over it, blow my breath into it, inhale its fragrance. Not that I want to do that* now. This was just a momentary fantasy based on pure hypothesis concerning what he would do *if* she were his lover. Morally, it was nothing for him to be ashamed of – probably.

But whether this involved a moral question or not, he should not have been thinking about it. Tengo's penis began to wake from its tranquil sleep in the mud, as if it had been poked in its back by a finger. It gave a yawn and slowly raised its head, gradually growing harder until, like a yacht whose sails are filled by a strong northwest tailwind, it achieved a full, unreserved erection. As a result, his hardened penis could not help but press against Fuka-Eri's hip. Tengo released a deep mental sigh. He had not had sex for more than a month following the disappearance of his girlfriend. Probably that was the cause. He should have continued multiplying three-digit figures.

"Don't let it bother you," Fuka-Eri said. "Getting hard is only natural."

"Thank you," Tengo said. "But maybe the Little People are watching from somewhere."

"Just watching. They can't do anything."

"That's good," Tengo said, his voice unsettled. "But it does kind of bother me to think that I'm being watched."

Again a lightning bolt cracked the sky in two, like the

ripping of an old curtain, and the thunder gave the windowpane a violent shake as if *they* were seriously trying to shat-
ter the glass. The glass might actually break before long, it
seemed. The window had a sturdy aluminum frame, but it
might not hold up if such ferocious shaking continued. Big,
hard raindrops went on knocking against the glass like bullets
slamming into a deer.

"The thunderbolts have hardly moved, it seems," Tengo
said. "Lightning storms don't usually go on this long."

Fuka-Eri looked up at the ceiling. "It won't go anywhere for
a while."

"How long a while?"

Fuka-Eri did not answer him. Tengo went on holding
Fuka-Eri apprehensively, his unanswered question and his
useless erection both intact.

"We will go to the cat town again," Fuka-Eri said. "So we
have to sleep."

"Do you think we *can* sleep with all this thunder going?
And it's barely past nine," Tengo said anxiously.

Tengo arranged mathematical formulas in his head. It was
a problem concerning long, complex mathematical formulas,
but he already knew the answer. The assignment was to find
how quickly and by how short a route he could arrive at the
answer. He wasted no time setting his mind in motion, pushing his brain to the point of abuse. But this did nothing to
relieve his erection. Its hardness only seemed to increase.

"We can sleep," Fuka-Eri said.

And she was right. Even in the midst of the violent downpour, surrounded by thunder rattling the building, and beset
by his jangled nerves and his stubborn erection, Tengo drifted
into sleep before he knew it. He couldn't believe such a thing
was possible, and yet . . .

This is total chaos, Tengo thought just before he fell asleep.
I've got to find the shortest route to the solution. Time is running

out, and there's so little space on the examination sheet they distributed. Tick-tock, tick-tock, the clock dutifully counted off time.

He was naked when he awoke, and so was Fuka-Eri. Completely and totally naked. Her breasts were perfect hemispheres. Her nipples were not overly large, and they were soft, still quietly groping for the maturity that was to come. Her breasts themselves were large, however, and fully ripe. They seemed to be virtually uninfluenced by the force of gravity, the nipples turned beautifully upward, like a vine's new tendrils seeking sunlight. The next thing that Tengo became aware of was that Fuka-Eri had no pubic hair. Where there should have been pubic hair there was only smooth, bare white skin, its whiteness giving emphasis to its utter defenselessness. She had her legs spread; he could see her vagina. Like the ear he had been staring at, it looked as if it had just been made only moments before. And perhaps it really had been made only moments before. *A freshly made ear and a freshly made vagina look very much alike,* Tengo thought. Both appeared to be turned outward, trying to listen closely to something – something like a distant bell.

I was sleeping, Tengo realized. He had fallen asleep still erect. And even now he was firmly erect. Had the erection continued the whole time he was sleeping? Or was this a new erection, following the relaxation of the first (like Prime Minister So-and-So's Second Cabinet)? *How long was I sleeping? But what's the difference? I'm still erect now, and it shows no sign of subsiding. Neither Sonny and Cher nor three-digit multiplication nor complex mathematics had managed to bring it down.*

"I don't mind," Fuka-Eri said. She had her legs spread and was pressing her freshly made vagina against his belly. He could detect no hint of embarrassment on her part. "Getting hard is not a bad thing," she said.

"I can't move my body," he said. It was true. He was trying to raise himself, but he couldn't move a finger. He could *feel* his body – feel the weight of Fuka-Eri's body on top of his – feel the hardness of his erection – but his body was as heavy and stiff as if it had been fastened down by something.

"You have no *need* to move it," Fuka-Eri said.

"I *do* have a *need* to move it. It's *my* body," Tengo said.

Fuka-Eri said nothing in response to that.

Tengo could not even be sure whether what he was saying was vibrating in the air as vocal sounds. He had no clear sense that the muscles around his mouth were moving and forming the words he tried to speak. The things he wanted to say were more or less getting through to Fuka-Eri, it seemed, but their communication was as uncertain as a long-distance phone call with a bad connection. She, at least, could get by without hearing what she had no need to hear. But this was not possible for Tengo.

"Don't worry," Fuka-Eri said, moving her body lower down on his. The meaning of her movement was clear. Her eyes had taken on a certain gleam, the hue of which he had never seen before.

It seemed inconceivable that his adult penis could penetrate her small, newly made vagina. It was too big and too hard. The pain should have been enormous. Before he knew it, though, every bit of him was inside her. There had been no resistance whatever. The look on her face remained totally unchanged as she brought him inside. Her breathing became slightly agitated, and the rhythm with which her breasts rose and fell changed subtly for five or six seconds, but that was all. Everything else seemed like a normal, natural part of everyday life.

Having brought Tengo deep inside her, Fuka-Eri remained utterly still, as did Tengo, feeling himself deep inside of her. He remained incapable of moving his body, and she, eyes closed, perched on top of him like a lightning rod, stopped moving. He could see that her mouth was slightly open and her lips were making delicate, rippling movements as if groping in space to form some kind of words. Aside from this, she exhibited no movement at all. She seemed to be holding that posture as she waited for something to happen.

A deep sense of powerlessness came over Tengo. Even though something was about to happen, he had no idea what that something might be, and had no way of controlling it through his own will. His body felt nothing. He could not move. But his penis had feeling – or, rather than feeling, it had what might have been closer to a concept. In any case, *it* was telling him that he was inside Fuka-Eri and that he had the consummate erection. Shouldn't he be wearing a condom? He began to worry. It could be a real problem if she got pregnant. His older girlfriend was extremely strict about birth control, and she had trained Tengo to be just as strict.

He tried as hard as he could to think of other things, but in fact he was unable to think about anything at all. He was in chaos. Inside that chaos, time seemed to have come to a stop. But time never stopped. That was a theoretical impossibility. Perhaps it had simply lost its uniformity. Taking the long view, time moved ahead at a fixed pace. There could be no mistake about that. But if you considered any one particular part of time, it could cease to be uniform. In these momentary periods of slackness, such things as order and probability lost all value.

"Tengo," Fuka-Eri said. She had never called him by his first name before. She said it again: "Tengo," as if practicing the pronunciation of a foreign word. *Why is she calling me by my name all of a sudden?* Tengo wondered. Fuka-Eri then leaned forward slowly, bringing her face close to his. Her partially open lips now opened wide, and her soft, fragrant tongue entered his mouth, where it began a relentless search for unformed words, for a secret code engraved there. Tengo's own tongue responded unconsciously to this movement and soon their tongues were like two young snakes in a spring meadow, newly wakened from their hibernation and hungrily intertwining, each led on by the other's scent.

Fuka-Eri then stretched out her right hand and grasped Tengo's left hand. She took it powerfully, as if to envelope his hand in hers. Her small fingernails dug into his palm. Then, bringing their intense kiss to an end, she righted herself. "Close your eyes."

Tengo did as he was told. Inside his closed eyes he found a deep, gloomy space – so deep that it appeared to extend to the center of the earth. Then a light evocative of dusk broke into this space, the kind of sweet, nostalgic dusk that comes at the end of a long, long day. He could see, suspended in the light, numberless fine-grained cross-section-like particles – dust, perhaps, or pollen, or something else entirely. Eventually the depths began to contract, the light began to grow brighter, and the surrounding objects came into view.

The next thing he knew he was ten years old and in an elementary school classroom. This was real time and a real place. The light was real, and so was his ten-year-old self. He was really breathing the air of the room, smelling its varnished woodwork and the chalk dust permeating its erasers. Only he and the girl were in the room. There was no sign of other children. She was quick to seize the opportunity and she did so boldly. Or perhaps she had been waiting for this to happen. In any case, standing there, she stretched out her right hand and grasped Tengo's left hand, her eyes looking straight into his.

His mouth felt parched. It all happened so suddenly, he had no idea what he should do or say. He simply stood there, letting his hand be squeezed by the girl. Eventually, deep in his loins, he felt a faint but deep throbbing. This was nothing he had ever experienced before, a throbbing like the distant roar of the sea. At the same time actual sounds reached his ears – the shouts of children resounding through the open window, a soccer ball being kicked, a bat connecting with a softball, the high-pitched complaints of a girl in one of the younger classes, the uncertain notes of a recorder ensemble practicing "The Last Rose of Summer." After-school activities.

He wanted to return the girl's grasp with equal force, but the strength would not come into his hand. Part of it was that the girl's grip was too strong. But Tengo realized, too, that he could not make his body move. Why should that be? He couldn't move a finger, as if he were totally paralyzed.

Time seems to have stopped, Tengo thought. He breathed quietly, listening to his own inhalations and exhalations. The sea went on roaring. Suddenly he realized that all actual sounds had ceased. The throbbing in his loins had transformed into something different, something more limited, and soon he felt a particular kind of tingling. The tingling in turn became a fine, dust-like substance that mixed with his hot, red blood, coursing through his veins to all parts of his body, by the power of his hardworking heart. A dense, little, cloud-like thing formed in his chest, changing the rhythm of his breathing and stiffening the beating of his heart.

I'm sure I'll be able to understand the meaning and purpose of this incident sometime in the future, Tengo thought. *What I have to do now, in order to make that happen, is to record this moment in my mind as clearly and accurately as possible.* Now Tengo again was nothing more than a ten-year-old boy who happened to be good at math. A new door stood before him, but he did not know what awaited him on the other side. He felt powerless and ignorant, emotionally confused, and not a little afraid. This much he knew. And the girl, for her part, had no hope of being understood at that moment. All she wanted was to make sure that her feelings were delivered to Tengo, stuffed into a small, sturdy box, wrapped in a spotless sheet of paper, and tied with a narrow cord. She was placing such a package in his hands.

You don't have to open the package right now, the girl was telling him wordlessly. *Open it when the time comes. All you have to do is take it now.*

She already knows all kinds of things, Tengo thought. They were things that he did not know yet. She was the leader in this new arena. There were new rules here, new goals and new dynamics. Tengo knew nothing. *But she knows.*

At length she released the grip of her right hand on Tengo's left hand, and, without saying anything or looking back, she hurried from the big classroom. Tengo stood there all alone. Children's voices resounded through the open window.

In the next second, Tengo realized that he was ejaculating. The violent spasm went on for several seconds, releasing a great deal of semen in a powerful surge. *Where is my semen going?* Tengo's garbled mind wondered. Ejaculating like this after school in a grade school classroom was not an appropriate thing to do. He could be in trouble if someone saw him. But this was not a grade school classroom anymore. Now he realized that he was inside Fuka-Eri, ejaculating toward her uterus. This was not something that he wanted to be doing. But he could not stop himself. Everything was happening beyond his control.

"Don't worry," Fuka-Eri said a short time afterward in her usual flat voice. "*I* will not get pregnant. I haven't started my periods yet."

Tengo opened his eyes and looked at Fuka-Eri. She was still mounted on him, looking down. Her perfect breasts were there in front of him, moving with each calm, regular breath.

Tengo wanted to ask her if this was what "going to the town of cats" meant. What kind of a place *was* the town of cats? He tried to put the question into actual words, but the muscles of his mouth would not budge.

"This was necessary," Fuka-Eri said, as if reading Tengo's mind. It was a concise answer and no answer at all, as usual.

Tengo closed his eyes again. He had gone *there,* ejaculated, and come back *here* again. It had been a real ejaculation discharging real semen. If Fuka-Eri said it was necessary, it had surely been necessary. Tengo's flesh was still paralyzed and had no feeling. And the lassitude that follows ejaculation enveloped his body like a thin membrane.

Fuka-Eri maintained her position for a long time, effectively squeezing out the last drop of semen from Tengo, like an insect sucking nectar from a flower. She literally left not a drop behind. Then, sliding off of Tengo's penis, without a word, she left the bed and went into the bathroom. Tengo realized now that the thunder had stopped. The violent rain had also cleared before he knew it. The thunderclouds, which had stayed so stubbornly fixed above them, had now vanished without a trace. The silence was almost unreal. All he could hear was the faint sound of Fuka-Eri showering in the bathroom. Tengo stared at the ceiling, waiting for the feeling to come back to his flesh. Even after ejaculating, he was still erect, though at least the hardness had abated somewhat.

Part of his mind was still in the grade school classroom. The touch of the girl's fingers remained as a vivid impression in his left hand. He could not lift the hand to look at it, but the palm of that hand probably still had red fingernail marks in it. His heartbeat retained traces of his arousal. The dense cloud had faded from his chest, but its imaginary space near his heart still cried out with its pleasant dull ache.

Aomame, Tengo thought.

I have to see Aomame, Tengo thought. *I have to find her. Why has it taken me so long to realize something so obvious? She handed me that precious package. Why did I toss it aside and leave it unopened all this time?* He thought of shaking his head, but that was something he could not yet do. His body had still not recovered from its paralysis.

Fuka-Eri came back to the bedroom a short time later. Wrapped in a bath towel, she sat on the edge of the bed for a while.

"The Little People are not stirring anymore," she said, like a cool, capable scout reporting on conditions at the front. Then she used her fingertip to draw a little circle in the air – a perfect, beautiful circle such as an Italian Renaissance painter might draw on a church wall: no beginning, no end. The circle hung in the air for a while. "All done."

Having said this, the girl stood and undid her bath towel. Completely naked, she stayed there for a while, as if allowing her damp body to dry naturally in the still air. It was a lovely sight: the smooth breasts, the lower abdomen free of pubic hair.

She bent over and picked up the pajamas where they had fallen on the floor, putting them on directly next to her skin without underwear, buttoning the top and tying the bottom's cord. Tengo watched all this in the darkened room, as if studying an insect undergoing metamorphosis. Tengo's pajamas were too big for her, but she looked comfortable in them. Fuka-Eri slipped into bed, found her narrow space, and rested her head on Tengo's shoulder. He could feel the shape of her little ear against his naked shoulder and her warm breath against the base of his neck. All the while, his paralysis began to fade, just as the tide ebbs when the time comes.

The air was still damp but no longer unpleasantly sticky. Outside, the insects were beginning to chirp. By now Tengo's erection had subsided and his penis was beginning to sink into the peaceful mud again. Things seemed to have run their course, bringing the cycle to an end. A perfect circle had been drawn in the air. The animals had left the ark and scattered across the earth they craved, all the pairs returning to the places where they belonged.

"You'd better sleep," she said. "Very deeply."

Sleep very deeply, Tengo thought. *Sleep, and then wake up. What kind of world will be there tomorrow?*

"No one knows the answer to that," Fuka-Eri said, reading his mind.

CHAPTER 15

Aomame

TIME NOW FOR GHOSTS

Aomame took a spare blanket from the closet and laid it over the man's big body. Then she placed a finger on the back of his neck again and confirmed that his pulse had completely stopped. This man they called "Leader" had already moved on to another world. What kind of world that was, she could not be sure, but it was definitely not 1Q84. In this world, he had now become what would be called "the deceased." The man had crossed the divide that separates life and death, and he had done so without making the slightest sound, with just a momentary shiver, as if he had felt a chill. Nor had he shed a drop of blood. Now he had been released from all suffering, lying silent and dead, facedown on the blue yoga mat. As always, her work had been swift and precise.

She placed the cork on the needle and returned the ice pick to the hard case. This went into the gym bag. She took the Heckler & Koch from the vinyl pouch and slipped it under the waistband of her sweatpants, safety released and bullet in the chamber. The hard metal against her backbone reassured her. Stepping over to the window, she pulled the thick curtain closed and made the room dark again.

She picked up the gym bag and headed for the door. With her hand on the knob, she turned for one last look at the large man lying in the dark room. He appeared only to be sound asleep, as he had when she first saw him. Aomame herself was the only person in the world who knew that he was no longer alive. No, the Little People probably knew, which was why they had stopped the thunder. They knew it would be useless to go on sending such warnings. The life of their chosen agent had come to an end.

Aomame opened the door and stepped into the bright room, averting her eyes from the glare. She closed the door soundlessly. Buzzcut was sitting on the sofa, drinking coffee. On the table was a coffeepot and a large room service tray holding a stack of sandwiches. The sandwiches were half gone. Two unused coffee cups stood nearby. Ponytail was sitting in a rococo chair beside the door, his back straight, as he had been earlier. It seemed as though both men had spent the whole time in the same position, saying nothing. Such was the reserved atmosphere that pervaded the room.

When Aomame came in, Buzzcut set his coffee cup onto its saucer and quietly stood up.

"I'm through," Aomame said. "He's asleep now. It took quite a while. I think it was hard on his muscles. You should let him get some sleep."

"He's sleeping?"

"Very soundly," Aomame said.

Buzzcut looked Aomame straight in the face. He peered deep into her eyes. Then he slowly moved his gaze down to her toes and back again, as if to inspect for possible irregularities.

"Is that normal?"

"Many people react that way, falling into a deep sleep after they have been released from extreme muscular stress. It is not unusual."

Buzzcut walked over to the bedroom door, quietly turned the knob, and opened the door just enough to peer inside. Aomame rested her right hand on the waist of her sweatpants so that she could take the pistol out as soon as anything happened. The man spent some ten seconds observing the situation in the bedroom, then finally drew his face back and closed the door.

"How long do you think he will sleep?" he asked Aomame. "We can't just leave him lying on the floor like that forever."

"He should wake up in two hours or so. It would be best to leave him in that position until then."

Buzzcut checked his watch and gave Aomame a slight nod.

"I see. We'll leave him like that for a while," Buzzcut said. "Would you like to take a shower?"

"I don't need to shower, but let me change my clothes again."

"Of course. Please use the powder room."

Aomame would have preferred not to change her clothes and to get out of there as quickly as possible, but she had to be sure not to arouse their suspicions. She had changed clothes when she arrived, so she must change her clothes on her way out. She went into the bathroom and took off her sweat suit and her sweat-soaked underwear, dried her body with a bath towel, and put on fresh underwear and her original cotton pants and blouse. She shoved the pistol under her belt so that it would not be visible from the outside. She tested various movements of her body to make sure that they would not appear unnatural. She washed her face with soap and water and brushed her hair. Facing the large mirror over the sink, she twisted her face into every scowl she could think of in order to relax any facial muscles that had stiffened from tension. After continuing that for a while, she returned her face to normal. After such prolonged frowning, it took her some moments to recall what her normal face even looked like, but after several attempts she was able to settle on a reasonable facsimile. She glared into the mirror, studying her face in detail. *No problem,* she thought. *This is my normal face. I can even smile if I have to. My hands are not shaking, either. My gaze is steady. I'm the usual cool Aomame.*

Buzzcut, though, had stared hard at her when she first came out of the bedroom. He might have noticed the streaks left by her tears. There must have been something left after all that crying. The thought made Aomame uneasy. He must have found it odd that she would have had to shed tears while stretching a client's muscles. It might have led him to suspect that something strange had occurred. He might have opened the bedroom door, gone in to check on Leader, and discovered that his heart had stopped . . .

Aomame reached around to check the grip of her pistol. *I have to calm down,* she told herself. *I can't be afraid. Fear will show on my face and raise suspicions.*

Resigning herself to the worst, Aomame cautiously stepped out of the bathroom with the gym bag in her left hand, right hand ready to reach for the gun, but there was no sign of anything unusual in the room. Buzzcut stood in the center, his arms folded, eyes narrowed in thought. Ponytail was still in the chair by the door, coolly observing the room. He had the calm eyes of a bomber's tail gunner, accustomed to sitting there all alone, looking at the blue sky, eyes taking on the sky's tint.

"You must be worn out," Buzzcut said. "How about a cup of coffee? We have sandwiches, too."

"Thanks, but I'll have to pass on that. I can't eat right after work. My appetite starts to come back after an hour or so."

Buzzcut nodded. Then he pulled a thick envelope from his inner jacket pocket. After checking its weight, he handed it to Aomame.

The man said, "I believe you will find here something more than the agreed-upon fee. As I said earlier, we strongly urge you to keep this matter a secret."

"Hush money?" Aomame said jokingly.

"For the extra effort we have put you through," the man said, without cracking a smile.

"I have a policy of strict confidentiality, whatever the fee.

That is part of my work. No word of this will leak out under any circumstances," Aomame said. She put the unopened envelope into her gym bag. "Do you need a receipt?"

Buzzcut shook his head. "That will not be necessary. This is just between us. There is no need for you to report this as income."

Aomame nodded silently.

"It must have taken a great deal of strength," Buzzcut said, as if probing for information.

"More than usual," she said.

"Because he is no ordinary person."

"So it would seem."

"He is utterly irreplaceable," he said. "He has suffered terrible physical pain for a very long time. He has taken all of our suffering and pain upon himself, as it were. We can only hope that he can have some small degree of relief."

"I can't say for sure because I don't know the basic cause of his pain," Aomame said, choosing her words carefully, "but I *do* think that his pain may have been reduced somewhat."

Buzzcut nodded. "As far as I can tell, you seem quite drained."

"Perhaps I am," Aomame said.

While Aomame and Buzzcut were speaking, Ponytail remained seated by the door, wordlessly observing the room. His face was immobile; only his eyes moved. His expression never changed. She had no idea whether he was even hearing their conversation. Isolated, taciturn, attentive, he kept watch for any sign of enemy fighter planes among the clouds. At first they would be no bigger than poppy seeds.

After some hesitation, Aomame asked Buzzcut, "This may be none of my business, but drinking coffee, eating ham sandwiches: are these not violations of your religion?"

Buzzcut turned to look at the coffeepot and the tray of sandwiches on the table. Then the faintest possible smile crossed his lips.

"Our religion doesn't have such strict precepts. Alcohol and tobacco are generally forbidden, and there are some prohibitions regarding sexual matters, but we are relatively free where food is concerned. Most of the time we eat only the simplest foods, but coffee and ham sandwiches are not especially forbidden."

Aomame just nodded, offering no opinion on the matter.

"The religion brings many people together, so some degree of discipline is necessary, of course, but if you focus too much on formalities, you can lose sight of your original purpose. Things like precepts and doctrines are, ultimately, just expedients. The important thing is not the frame itself but what is inside the frame."

"And your Leader provides the content to fill the frame."

"Exactly. He can hear the voices that we cannot hear. He is a special person." Buzzcut looked into Aomame's eyes again. Then he said, "Thank you for all your efforts today. And luckily the rain seems to have stopped."

"The thunder was terrible," Aomame said.

"Yes, very," Buzzcut said, though he himself did not seem particularly interested in the thunder and rain.

Aomame gave him a little bow and headed for the door, gym bag in hand.

"Wait a moment," Buzzcut called from behind. His voice had a sharp edge.

Aomame came to a stop in the center of the room and turned around. Her heart made a sharp, dry sound. Her right hand casually moved to her hip.

"The yoga mat," the young man said. "You're forgetting your yoga mat. It's still on the bedroom floor."

Aomame smiled. "He is lying on top of it, sound asleep. We can't just shove him aside and pull it out. I'll give it to you if you like. It's not expensive, and it's had a lot of use. If you don't need it, throw it away."

Buzzcut thought about this for a moment and finally nodded. "Thank you again. I'm sure you're very tired."

As Aomame neared the door, Ponytail stood and opened it for her. Then he bowed slightly. *That one never said a word,* Aomame thought. She returned his bow and started to slip past him.

In that moment, however, a violent urge penetrated Aomame's skin, like an intense electric current. Ponytail's hand shot out as if to grab her right arm. It should have been a swift, precise movement – like grabbing a fly in thin air. Aomame had a vivid sense of its happening *right there.* Every muscle in her body stiffened up. Her skin crawled, and her heart skipped a beat. Her breath caught in her throat, and icy insects crawled up and down her spine. A blazing hot white light poured into her mind: *If this man grabs my right arm, I won't be able to reach for the pistol. And if that happens, I have no hope of winning. He feels it. He feels that I've done something. His intuition recognizes that* something *happened in this hotel room. He doesn't know what, but it is something that should not have happened. His instincts are telling him, "You have to stop this woman," ordering him to wrestle me to the floor, drop his whole weight on me, and dislocate my shoulders. But he has only instinct, no proof. If his feeling turns out to be wrong, he'll be in big trouble. He was intensely conflicted, and now he's given up. Buzzcut is the one who makes the decisions and gives the orders. Ponytail is not qualified. He struggled to suppress the impulse of his right hand and let the tension go out of his shoulder.* Aomame had a vivid sense of the stages through which Ponytail's mind had passed in that second or two.

Aomame stepped out into the carpeted hallway and headed for the elevator without looking back, walking coolly down the perfectly straight corridor. Ponytail, it seemed, had stuck his head out the door and was following her movements with his eyes. She continued to feel his sharp, knifelike gaze piercing her back. Every muscle in her body was tingling, but she refused to look back. She *must not* look back. Only when she turned the corner did she feel the tension go out of her. But still she could not relax. There was no telling what could happen next. She pushed the elevator's "down" button and reached around to hold the pistol grip until the elevator came (which took an eternity), ready to draw the gun if Ponytail changed his mind and came after her. She would have to shoot him without hesitation before he put his powerful hands on her. Or shoot herself without hesitation. She could not decide which. Perhaps she would not be able to decide.

But no one came after her. The hotel corridor was hushed. The elevator door opened with a ring, and Aomame got on. She pressed the button for the lobby and waited for the door to close. Biting her lip, she glared at the floor number display. Then she exited the elevator, walked across the broad lobby, and stepped into a cab waiting for passengers at the front door. The rain had cleared up completely, but the cab had water dripping from its entire chassis, as if it had made its way here underwater. Aomame told the driver to take her to the west exit of Shinjuku Station. As they pulled away from the hotel, she exhaled every bit of air she was holding inside. Then she closed her eyes and emptied her mind. She didn't want to think about anything for a while.

A strong wave of nausea hit her. It felt as if the entire contents of her stomach were surging up toward her throat, but she managed to force them back down. She pressed the button to open her window halfway, sending the damp night air deep into her lungs. Then she leaned back and took several deep breaths. Her mouth produced an ominous smell, as though something inside her were beginning to rot.

It suddenly occurred to her to search in her pants pocket, where she found two sticks of chewing gum. Her hands trembled slightly as she tore off the wrappers. She put the sticks in her mouth and began chewing slowly. Spearmint. The pleasantly familiar aroma helped to quiet her nerves. As she moved her jaw, the bad smell in her mouth began to dissipate. *It's not as if I actually have something rotting inside me. Fear is doing funny things to me, that's all.*

Anyhow, it's all over now, Aomame thought. *I don't have to kill anyone anymore. And what I did was right,* she told herself. *He deserved to be killed for what he did. It was a simple case of just punishment. And as it happened (strictly by chance), the man himself had a strong desire to be killed. I gave him the peaceful death he was hoping for. I did nothing wrong. All I did was break the law.*

Try as she might, however, Aomame was unable to convince herself that this was true. Only moments before, she had killed a far-from-ordinary human being with her own hands. She retained a vivid memory of how it felt when the needle sank soundlessly into the back of the man's neck. That far-from-ordinary feeling was still there, in her hands, upsetting her to no small degree. She opened her palms and stared at them. Something was different, utterly different. But she was unable to discover what had changed, and how.

If she was to believe what he had told her, she had just killed a prophet, one entrusted with the voice of a god. But the master of that voice was no god. It was probably the Little People. A prophet is simultaneously a king, and a king is destined to be killed. She was, in other words, an assassin sent by destiny. By violently exterminating a being who was both prophet and king, she had preserved the balance of good and evil in the world, as a result of which she must die. But when she performed the deed, she struck a bargain. By killing the man and, in effect, throwing her own life away, she would save Tengo's life. That was the content of the bargain. **If she was to believe what he had told her.**

Aomame had no choice but to believe fundamentally in what he had said. He was no fanatic, and dying people do not lie. Most importantly, his words had genuine persuasive power. They carried the weight of a huge anchor. All ships carry anchors that match their size and weight. However despicable his deeds may have been, the man was truly reminiscent of a great ship. Aomame had no choice but to recognize that fact.

Taking care that the driver did not see her, Aomame slipped the Heckler & Koch from her belt, set the safety catch, and put the gun in its pouch, relieving herself of 500 grams of solid, lethal weight.

"Wasn't that thunder something?" the driver said. "And the rain was incredible."

"Thunder?" Aomame said. It seemed to have happened a long time ago, though it had been a mere thirty minutes earlier. Yes, come to think of it, there had been some thunder. "Yes, really, incredible thunder."

"The weather forecast said absolutely nothing about it. It was supposed to be beautiful all day."

She tried to make her mind work. *I have to say something. But I can't think of anything good to say. My brain seems to have fogged over.* "Weather forecasts are never right," she said.

The driver glanced at Aomame in the rearview mirror. Maybe there was something funny about the way she spoke. The driver said, "I hear the water in the streets overflowed and ran down into the Akasaka-Mitsuke subway station onto the tracks. It was because the rain all fell in one small area. They stopped the Ginza Line and the Marunouchi Line. I heard it on the radio news."

The concentrated downpour brought the subway to a stop. Will this have any influence on my actions? I've got to make my brain work faster. I go to Shinjuku Station to get my travel bag and shoulder bag out of a coin locker. Then I call Tamaru for instructions. If I'm going to have to use the Marunouchi Line from Shinjuku, things could get very messy. I only have two hours to make my getaway. Once two hours have gone by, they'll begin to wonder why Leader isn't waking up. They'll probably go into the bedroom and discover that he's drawn his last breath. They'll go into action immediately.

"Do you think the Marunouchi Line is still not running?" Aomame asked the driver.

"I wonder. I really don't know. Want me to turn on the news?"

"Yes, please."

According to Leader, the Little People caused that downpour. They concentrated the intense rain on a small area in the Akasaka District and caused the subway to stop. Aomame shook her head. Maybe they did it on purpose. Things don't always go according to plan.

The driver tuned the radio to NHK. They were broadcasting a music program – folk songs sung by Japanese singers popular in the late sixties. Having listened to such music on the radio as a girl, Aomame remembered it vaguely, but in no way fondly. If anything, the memories it called up for her were unpleasant ones, things she would rather not think about. She put up with it for a while, but there was no sign of news about the subway situation.

"Sorry, that's enough. Could you please turn off the radio?" Aomame said. "I'll just go to Shinjuku Station and see what's happening."

The driver turned off the radio. "That place will be jammed," he said.

As the driver had said, Shinjuku Station was horribly congested. Because the stalled Marunouchi Line connected with the National Railways here, the flow of passengers had been disrupted, and people were wandering in all directions. The evening rush hour had ended, but even so, pushing her way through the crowd was hard work for Aomame.

At last she made her way to the coin locker and took out her shoulder bag and her black imitation-leather travel bag. The travel bag contained the cash she had taken from her safe-deposit box. She took the items out of her gym bag and divided them between the shoulder and travel bags: the envelope of cash she had received from Buzzcut, the vinyl pouch containing the pistol, the hard case with the ice pick. The now useless Nike gym bag she put into a nearby locker, inserted a hundred-yen coin, and turned the key. She had no intention of reclaiming it. It contained nothing that could be traced to her.

Travel bag in hand, Aomame walked around looking for a pay phone in the station. Crowds had formed at every phone. People stood in long lines, waiting their turn to call home and say they would be late because the train had stopped. Aomame put her face into a light frown. *I guess the Little People are not going to let me get away that easily. Leader said they can't touch me directly, but they can interfere with my movements through the back door, using other methods.*

Aomame gave up on waiting her turn for a phone. Leaving the station, she walked a short distance, went into the first café she saw, and ordered an iced coffee. The pink pay phone here was also in use, but at least it had no line. She stood behind a middle-aged woman and waited for her long conversation to end. The woman flashed annoyed glances at Aomame but resigned herself to hanging up after she talked for five more minutes.

Aomame slipped all her coins into the phone and punched in the number she had memorized. After three rings, a mechanical recorded announcement came on: "Sorry, but we can't come to the phone right now. Please leave a message after the beep."

The beep sounded, and Aomame said into the mouthpiece, "Hello, Tamaru, please pick up if you're there."

Someone lifted the receiver, and Tamaru said, "I'm here."

"Good!" Aomame said.

Tamaru seemed to sense an unusual tension in her voice. "Are you all right?" he asked.

"For now."

"How did the job go?"

Aomame said, "He's in a deep sleep. The deepest sleep possible."

"I see," Tamaru said. He sounded truly relieved, and it colored his voice. This was unusual for him. "I'll pass on the news. She'll be glad to hear it."

"It wasn't easy."

"I'm sure it wasn't. But you did it."

"One way or another," Aomame said. "Is this phone safe?"

"I'm using a special circuit. Don't worry."

"I got my bags out of the Shinjuku Station coin locker. Now what?"

"How much time do you have?"

"An hour and a half," Aomame said. She explained briefly. After another hour and a half, the two bodyguards would check the bedroom and find that Leader was not breathing.

"An hour and a half is plenty," Tamaru said.

"Do you think they'll call the police right away?"

"I don't know. Just yesterday, the police went into the group's headquarters to start an investigation. They're still at the questioning stage and haven't launched the investigation itself, but it could be real trouble for them if the head of the religion suddenly turned up dead."

"You think they might just handle it themselves without making anything public?"

"That would be nothing for them. We'll know what happened when we see tomorrow's newspaper – whether they reported the death or not. I'm no gambler, but if I had to make a bet, I'd put my money on their not reporting it."

"They won't just assume it happened naturally?"

"They won't be able to tell by appearances. And they won't know whether it was a natural death or murder without a meticulous autopsy. In any case, the first thing they're going to want to do is talk to you. You were the last one to see him alive, after all. And once they learn that you've cleared out of your apartment and gone into hiding, they'll be pretty sure it was no natural death."

"So then they'll start looking for me – with every resource at their disposal."

"That's for sure," Tamaru said.

"Do you think we can manage to keep me hidden?"

"We've got it all planned out – in great detail. If we follow the plan carefully and persistently, no one's going to find you. The worst thing would be to panic."

"I'm doing my best," Aomame said.

"Keep it up. Act quickly and get time on your side. You're a careful and persistent person. Just keep doing what you're doing."

Aomame said, "There was a huge downpour in the Akasaka area, and the subways have stopped running."

"I know," Tamaru said. "Don't worry, we weren't planning for you to use the subway. You'll be taking a cab and going to a safe house in the city."

"In the city? Wasn't I supposed to be going somewhere far away?"

"Yes, of course you will be going far away," Tamaru said slowly, as if spelling things out for her. "But first we have to get you ready – change your name and your face. And this was a particularly tough job: you must be all keyed up. Nothing good can come of running around crazily at a time like this. Hide out in the safe house for a while. You'll be fine. We'll provide all the support you need."

"Where is this 'safe house'?"

"In the Koenji neighborhood. Maybe twenty minutes from where you are now."

Koenji, Aomame thought, tapping her nails against her teeth. She knew it was somewhere west of the downtown area, but she had never set foot there.

Tamaru told her the address and the name of the condo. As usual, she took no notes but engraved it on her brain.

"On the south side of Koenji Station. Near Ring Road 7. Apartment 303. Press 2831 to unlock the front door."

Tamaru paused while Aomame repeated "303" and "2831" to herself.

"The key is taped to the bottom of the doormat. The apartment has everything you'll need for now, so you shouldn't have to go out for a while. I'll make contact from my end. I'll ring the phone three times, hang up, and call again twenty seconds later. We'd like to avoid having you call."

"I see," Aomame said.

"Were his men tough?" Tamaru asked.

"There were two of them, and both seemed pretty tough. I had some scary moments. But they're no pros. They can't touch you."

"There aren't too many people like me."

"Too many Tamarus could be a problem."

"Could be," Tamaru said.

Carrying her bags, Aomame headed for the station's taxi stand, where she encountered another long line. Subway operations had still not returned to normal, it seemed. She had no choice but to take her place in line.

Joining the many other annoyed-looking commuters and patiently waiting her turn, Aomame mentally repeated the safe house address, the name of the building and apartment number, the code for unlocking the front door, and Tamaru's phone number. She was like an ascetic sitting on a rock on a mountaintop, intoning his precious mantra. Aomame had always had confidence in her powers of memory. She could easily memorize those few bits of information. But these figures were now a lifeline. If she forgot even one of them in this situation, it could put her survival in jeopardy. She had to make sure they were engraved on her brain.

By the time Aomame finally got a taxi, a full hour had passed since she had left Leader's corpse in the hotel room. So far, it was taking her twice as long as she had planned – a delay that the Little People had caused, no doubt. *No, it could be sheer coincidence. Maybe I'm just letting the specter of some nonexistent "Little People" frighten me.*

Aomame gave the driver her destination and then settled back in the seat, closing her eyes. *Right about now, those two guys in their dark suits are probably checking their watches and waiting for their guru to wake up.* Aomame pictured them. Buzzcut was drinking coffee and thinking about all sorts of things. Thinking was his job. Thinking and deciding. Maybe he had grown suspicious: Leader's sleep was all too quiet. But Leader *always* slept soundly, without making noises – no snoring or even heavy breathing. Still, there was always his *presence*. The woman had said that Leader would be sound asleep for at least two hours, that it was important to let him rest quietly so that his muscles could recover. Only an hour had gone by, but something was bothering Buzzcut. Maybe he should check on Leader's condition. What should he do?

Ponytail was the dangerous one, though. Aomame still had a vivid image of that momentary hint of violence he had displayed as she was leaving the hotel room. He was silent, but his instincts were sharp. His fighting skills must also be outstanding – probably much more so than she had imagined until that moment. Her own command of martial arts was surely no match for his. In a fight, he would probably not give her a chance to reach for her gun. Fortunately, though, he was no professional. He had let his rational mind interfere before he put his intuition into action. He was used to taking orders – unlike Tamaru. Tamaru would subdue his opponent and render him powerless before thinking. Action came first – trust the instincts and let rational judgments come later. A split-second's hesitation and it was all over.

Recalling that moment at the door, Aomame felt her underarms growing moist. She shook her head. *I was just lucky. At least I avoided being captured on the spot. I have to be a lot more careful from now on. Tamaru was right: the most important things are to be careful and persistent. Danger comes the moment you relax.*

The driver was a polite-spoken middle-aged man. He pulled out a map, stopped the car, turned off the meter, and kindly found the exact location of the condo building. Aomame thanked him and stepped out of the cab. It was a handsome new six-story building in the middle of a residential area. There was no one at the entrance. Aomame punched in 2831 to unlock the front door, went inside, and rode a clean but narrow elevator up to the third floor. The first thing she did upon exiting the elevator was find the location of the emergency stairway. Then she removed the key taped to the back of the doormat of apartment 303 and used it to go inside. The entryway lights were set to go on automatically when the door opened. The place had that new-apartment smell. All of the furniture and appliances looked brand-new and unused, as if they had just come out of the boxes and plastic wrapping – matching pieces that could have been chosen by a designer to equip a model condo: simple, functional design, free of the smell of daily life.

To the left of the entry was a living/dining room. Off a hallway was a bathroom and beyond that were two rooms. One had a queen-sized bed that was already made. The blinds were closed. Opening the window that faced the street, she heard the traffic on Ring Road 7 like the distant roar of the ocean. Closing it again, she could hear almost nothing. There was a small balcony off the living room. It overlooked a small park across the street. There were swings, a slide, a sandbox, and a public toilet. A tall mercury-vapor lamp made everything unnaturally bright. A large zelkova tree spread its branches over the area. This was a third-floor condo, but there were no other tall buildings nearby from which she might have to worry about being watched.

Aomame thought about the Jiyugaoka apartment she had just vacated. It was in an old building, not terribly clean, with the occasional cockroach, and the walls were thin – not exactly the kind of place to which one became attached. Now, though, she missed it. In this brand-new, spotless condo, she felt like an anonymous person, stripped of memory and individuality.

Aomame opened the refrigerator to find four cans of Heineken chilling in the door. She opened one and took a swallow. Switching on the twenty-one-inch television, she sat down in front of it to watch the news. There was a report on the thunderstorm. The top story concerned the flooding of Akasaka-Mitsuke Station and the stopping of the Marunouchi and Ginza lines. The water overflowing the street had poured down the station steps like a waterfall. Station employees in rain ponchos had piled sandbags at the entrances, but they were obviously too late. The subway lines were still not running, and there was no estimate of when they would return to normal. The reporter thrust a mike at one stranded commuter after another. One man complained, "The morning forecast said it would be clear all day!"

She watched the news program until it ended. Of course, there was no report yet on the death of Sakigake's Leader. Buzzcut and Ponytail were probably still waiting in the next room for the full two hours to pass. Then they would learn the truth. She took the pouch from her travel bag and pulled out the Heckler & Koch, setting it on the dining table. On the new table, the German-made automatic pistol looked terribly crude and taciturn – and black through and through – but at least it gave a focal point to the otherwise impersonal room. *Landscape with Pistol*, Aomame muttered, as if titling a painting. *In any case, I have to keep this within reach at all times – whether I use it to shoot someone else or myself.*

The large refrigerator had been stocked with enough food for her to stay for two weeks or more: fruit, vegetables, and several processed foods ready for eating. The freezer held various meats, fish, and bread. There was even some ice cream. In the cabinets she found a good selection of foods in vacuum pouches and cans, plus spices. Rice and pasta. A generous supply of mineral water. Two bottles of red wine and two white. She had no idea who put these supplies together, but the person had done a very thorough job. For now, she couldn't think of anything that was missing.

Feeling a little hungry, she took out some Camembert, cut a wedge, and ate it with crackers. When the cheese was half gone, she washed a stalk of celery, spread it with mayonnaise, and munched it whole.

Next she examined the contents of the dresser drawers in the bedroom. The top one held pajamas and a thin bathrobe – new ones still in their plastic packs. More well-chosen supplies. The next drawer held three sets of T-shirts, socks, and underwear. All were simple, white things that seemed chosen to match the design of the furniture, and all were still packed in plastic. These were probably the same things they gave to the women staying in the safe house, made of good materials but very much "supplied" by an institution.

The bathroom had shampoo, conditioner, skin cream, and cologne, everything she needed. She rarely put on makeup and so needed few cosmetics. There were a toothbrush, interdental brush, and a tube of toothpaste. They had also thoughtfully supplied her with a hairbrush, cotton swabs, razor, small scissors, and sanitary products. The place was well stocked with toilet paper and tissues. Bath and face towels had been neatly folded and piled in a cabinet. Everything was there.

She looked in the bedroom closet, wondering if, by any chance, she would find dresses and shoes of her size – Armani and Ferragamo, preferably. But no, the closet was empty. There was a limit to how far they could go. They knew the difference between thoroughness and overkill. It was like Jay Gatsby's library: the books were real, but the pages uncut. Besides, she would not need street clothes while she was here. They wouldn't supply things she didn't need. There were plenty of hangers, though.

She used those hangers for the clothes she had brought in her travel bag, taking each piece out, checking it for wrinkles, and hanging it in the closet. She knew that it would be more convenient, as a fugitive, to leave the clothes in her bag rather than hanging them up, but the thing she hated most in the world was wearing creased clothing.

I guess I can never be a coolheaded professional criminal, Aomame thought, *if I'm going to be worried about wrinkled clothes at a time like this!* She suddenly recalled a conversation she had once had with Ayumi.

"The thing to do is keep your cash in your mattress so in a jam you can grab it and escape out the window."

"That's it," Ayumi said, snapping her fingers. **"Like in *The Getaway*. The Steve McQueen movie. A wad of bills and a shotgun. I love that kind of stuff."**

It's not much fun to live like that, Aomame said to the wall.

Aomame went into the bathroom, stripped, and showered. The hot water took off the remaining unpleasant sweat still clinging to her body. Then she went into the kitchen, sat at the counter, and took another swallow from her beer can while toweling her hair.

In the course of this one day, several things have taken a decisive step forward, Aomame thought. *The gears have turned forward with a click. And gears that have turned forward never turn back. That is one of the world's rules.*

Aomame picked up the gun, turned it upside down, and put the muzzle into her mouth. The steel felt horrendously cold and hard against her teeth. She caught the faint scent of grease. *This is the best way to blow the brains out. Pull the hammer, squeeze the trigger. Everything ends – just like that. No need to think. No need to run around.*

Aomame was not particularly afraid of dying. *I die, Tengo lives. He goes on living in this 1Q84, this world with two moons. But I'm not in it. I don't get to meet him in this world. Or any world. At least, that's what Leader says.*

Aomame took another slow scan of the room. *It's like a model apartment,* she thought. *Clean and uniform, with every need supplied. But distant and devoid of individuality. Papier-mâché. It wouldn't be very pleasant to die in a place like this. But even if you changed the backdrop to something more desirable, is there really a pleasant way to die in this world? And come to think of it, isn't this world we live in itself like a gigantic model room? We come in, sit down, have a cup of tea, gaze out the window at the scenery, and when the time comes we say thank you and leave. All the furniture is fake. Even the moon hanging in the window may be made of paper.*

But I love Tengo. Aomame murmured the words aloud. "I love Tengo." *This is no honky-tonk parade. 1Q84 is the real world, where a cut draws real blood, where pain is real pain, and fear is real fear. The moon in the sky is no paper moon. It – or they – are real moons. And in this world, I have willingly accepted death for Tengo's sake. I won't let anyone call this fake.*

Aomame looked at the round clock on the wall. A simple design, by Braun. Well matched to the Heckler & Koch. The clock was the only thing hanging on the walls of this apartment. The clock hands had passed ten. Just about time for the two men to find Leader's corpse.

In the bedroom of an elegant suite at the Hotel Okura, a man had breathed his last. A big man. A man who was far from ordinary. He had moved on to another world. No one could do anything to bring him back.

Time now for ghosts.

CHAPTER 16

Tengo

LIKE A GHOST SHIP

What kind of world will be there tomorrow?

"No one knows the answer to that," Fuka-Eri said.

But the world to which Tengo awoke did not appear especially changed from the world he had seen as he fell asleep the night before. The bedside clock said it was just after six. Outside, it was fully light, the air perfectly clear. A wedge of light came in through the curtains. Summer was winding down, it seemed. The cries of the birds were sharp and clear. Yesterday's violent thunderstorm felt like an apparition – or else something that had happened in an unknown place in the distant past.

The first thing that came to Tengo's mind upon waking was that Fuka-Eri might have disappeared during the night. But no, there she was, next to him, sound asleep, like a little animal in hibernation. Her face was beautiful in sleep, a few narrow strands of black hair against her white cheek forming a complex pattern, her ears hidden. Her breathing was soft. Tengo stared at the ceiling for a while, listening. Her breathing sounded like a tiny bellows.

He retained a vivid tactile memory of last night's ejaculation. He had actually released semen – a lot of semen – inside this young girl. The thought made his head swim. But now that morning was here, it seemed as unreal as that violent storm, like something that happened in a dream. He had experienced wet dreams several times in his teens. He would have a realistic sexual dream, ejaculate, and then wake up. The events had all happened in the dream, but the release of semen was real. What he felt now was a lot like that.

It had not been a wet dream, though. He had unquestionably come inside Fuka-Eri. She had deliberately penetrated herself with his penis and squeezed every drop of semen out of him. He had simply followed her lead. He had been totally paralyzed at the time, unable to move a finger. And as far as he was concerned, he was coming while in the elementary school classroom, not in Fuka-Eri, who later told him there was no chance she'd become pregnant because she had no periods. He couldn't fully grasp that such a thing had actually happened. But it *had* actually happened. As a real event in the real world. Probably.

He got out of bed, got dressed, went to the kitchen, boiled water, and made coffee. While making the coffee, he tried to put his head in order, like arranging the contents of a desk drawer. He couldn't get things straight, though. All he succeeded in doing was rearranging the items in the drawer, putting the paper clips where the eraser had been, the pencil sharpener where the paper clips had been, and the eraser where the pencil sharpener had been, exchanging one form of confusion for another.

After drinking a fresh cup of coffee, he went to the bathroom and shaved while listening to a baroque music program on the FM radio: Telemann's partitas for various solo instruments. This was his normal routine: make coffee in the kitchen, drink it, and shave while listening to *Baroque Music for You* on the radio. Only the musical selections changed each day. Yesterday it had almost certainly been Rameau's keyboard music.

The commentator was speaking.

Telemann won high praise throughout Europe in the early eighteenth century, but came to be disdained as too prolific by people in the nineteenth century. This was no fault of Telemann's, however. The purposes for which music is composed underwent great changes as the structure of European society changed, leading to this reversal in his reputation.

Is this the new world? he wondered.

He took another look at his surroundings. Still there was no sign of change. For now, there was no sign of disdainful people. In any case, what he had to do was shave. Whether the world had changed or not, no one was going to shave for him. He would have to do it himself.

When he was through shaving, he made some toast, buttered and ate it, and drank another cup of coffee. He went into the bedroom to check on Fuka-Eri, but she was still in a very deep sleep, it seemed: she hadn't moved at all. Her hair still formed the same pattern on her cheek. Her breathing was as soft as before.

For the moment, he had nothing planned. He would not be teaching at the cram school. No one would be coming to visit, nor did he have any intention of visiting anyone. He could spend the day any way he liked. Tengo sat at the kitchen table and continued writing his novel, filling in the little squares on the manuscript paper with a fountain pen. As always, his attention became focused on his work. Switching channels in his mind made everything else disappear from his field of vision.

It was just before nine when Fuka-Eri woke. She had taken off his pajamas and was wearing one of Tengo's T-shirts – the Jeff Beck Japan Tour T-shirt he was wearing when he visited his father in Chikura. Her nipples showed clearly through the shirt, which could not help but revive in Tengo the feeling of last night's ejaculation, the way a certain date brings to mind related historical facts.

The FM radio was playing a Marcel Dupré organ piece. Tengo stopped writing and fixed her breakfast. Fuka-Eri drank Earl Grey tea and ate strawberry jam on toast. She devoted as much time and care to spreading the jam on the toast as Rembrandt had when he painted the folds in a piece of clothing.

"I wonder how many copies your book has sold," Tengo said.

"You mean *Air Chrysalis*?" Fuka-Eri asked.

"Uh-huh."

"I don't know," Fuka-Eri said, lightly creasing her brow. "A *lot*."

Numbers were not important to her, Tengo thought. Her "a *lot*" brought to mind clover growing on a broad plane as far as the eye could see. The clover suggested only the idea of "a lot," but no one could count them all.

"A lot of people are reading *Air Chrysalis*," Tengo said.

Saying nothing, Fuka-Eri inspected how well she had spread the jam on her toast.

"I'll have to see Mr. Komatsu. As soon as possible," Tengo said, looking at Fuka-Eri across the table. As always, her face showed no expression. "You *have* met Mr. Komatsu, haven't you?"

"At the press conference."

"Did you talk?"

Fuka-Eri gave her head a slight shake, meaning they had hardly talked at all.

Tengo could imagine the scene vividly. Komatsu was talking his head off at top speed, saying everything he was thinking – or *not* thinking – while she hardly opened her mouth or listened to what he had to say. Komatsu was not concerned about that. If anyone ever asked Tengo for a concrete example of two perfectly incompatible personalities, he would name Fuka-Eri and Komatsu.

Tengo said, "I haven't seen Mr. Komatsu for a *very* long time. And I haven't heard from him, either. He must be very busy these days. Ever since *Air Chrysalis* became a bestseller, he's been swept up in the circus. It's about time, though, for us to get together and have a serious talk. We've got all kinds of problems to discuss. *Now* would be a good chance to do that, since you're here. How about it? Want to see him together?"

"The three of us?"

"Uh-huh. That'd be the quickest way to settle things."

Fuka-Eri thought about this for a moment. Or else she was imagining something. Then she said, "I don't mind. If we can."

If we can, Tengo repeated mentally. It had a prophetic sound.

"Are you thinking we might not be able to?" Tengo asked with some hesitation.

Fuka-Eri did not reply.

"Assuming we can, we'll meet him. Are you okay with that?"

"Meet him and do what?"

" 'Meet him and do what'? Well, first I'd return some money to him. A fairly good-sized payment was transferred into my bank account the other day for my rewriting of *Air Chrysalis,* but I'd rather not take it. Not that I have any regrets about having done the work. It was a great inspiration for my own writing and guided me in a good direction. And it turned out pretty well, if I do say so myself. It's been well received critically and the book is selling. I don't believe it was a mistake for me to take it on. I just never expected it to blow up like this. Of course, I am the one who agreed to do it, and I certainly have to take responsibility for that. But I just don't want to be paid for it."

Fuka-Eri gave her shoulders a little shrug.

Tengo said, "You're right. It might not change a thing. But I'd like to make it clear where I stand."

"Who for?"

"Well, mainly for myself," Tengo said, lowering his voice somewhat.

Fuka-Eri picked up the lid of the jam jar and stared at it as if she found it fascinating.

"But it may already be too late," Tengo said.

Fuka-Eri had nothing to say to that.

When Tengo tried phoning Komatsu's office after one o'clock (Komatsu never came to work in the morning), the woman who answered said that Komatsu had not been in for the past several days. That was all she knew. Or, if she knew more, she obviously had no intention of sharing it with Tengo. He asked her to connect him with another editor he knew. Tengo had written short columns under a pseudonym for the monthly magazine edited by this man, who was two or three years older than Tengo and generally well disposed toward him, in part because they had graduated from the same university.

"Komatsu has been out for over a week now," the editor said. "He called in on the third day to say he wouldn't be coming to work for a while because he wasn't feeling well, and we haven't seen him since. The guys in the book division are going crazy. He's in charge of *Air Chrysalis* and so far he's handled everything himself. He's *supposed* to restrict himself to the magazine side of things, but he ignored that fact and hasn't let anybody else lay a finger on this project, even when it went into book production. So if he takes off now, nobody knows what to do. If he's really sick, I suppose there's nothing we can say, but still . . ."

"What's wrong with him?"

"I don't know. All he said was he's not feeling well. And then he hung up. Haven't heard a word from him since. We wanted to ask him a few things and tried calling him, but all we got was the answering machine. Nobody knows what to do."

"Doesn't he have a family?"

"No, he lives alone. He used to have a wife and a kid, but I'm pretty sure he's been divorced for a long time. He doesn't tell anybody anything, so I don't really know, but that's what I've heard."

"Anyhow, it's strange that he's been out a week and you've only heard from him once."

"Well, you know Komatsu. Common sense isn't really his thing."

Receiver in hand, Tengo thought about this remark. "It's true, you never know what he'll do next. He's socially awkward and he can be self-centered, but as far as I know he's not irresponsible about his work. I don't care how sick he is, he wouldn't just let everything go and not contact the office when *Air Chrysalis* is selling like this. He's not that bad."

"You're absolutely right," the editor said. "Maybe somebody should go to his place and see what's up. There was all that trouble with Sakigake over Fuka-Eri's disappearance, and we still don't know where she is. Something might have happened. I can't believe he'd fake being sick so he could take off from work and hide out with Fuka-Eri, right?"

Tengo said nothing. He could hardly tell the man that Fuka-Eri was right there in front of him, cleaning her ears with a cotton swab.

"And not just this case. Everything involving this book. I don't know, there's something wrong with it. We're glad it's selling so well, but there's something about it that's not quite right. And I'm not the only one: a lot of people at the company feel that way about it. Oh, by the way, Tengo, did you have something you wanted to talk to Komatsu about?"

"No, nothing special. I haven't talked to him for a while, so I was just wondering what he's up to."

"Maybe the stress of it all finally got to him. Anyhow, *Air Chrysalis* is the first bestseller this company has ever had. I'm looking forward to this year's bonus. Have you read the book?"

"Of course, I read the manuscript when it was submitted for the competition."

"Oh, that's right. You were a screener."

"I thought it was well written and pretty interesting, too."

"Oh, it's interesting all right, and well worth a read."

Tengo detected an ominous ring to his remark. "But something about it bothers you?"

"Well, this is just an editor's intuition. You're right: it *is* well written. A little *too* well written for a debut by a seventeen-year-old girl. And now she's disappeared. And we can't get in touch with her editor. The book is like one of those old ghost ships with nobody aboard: it just keeps sailing along, all sails set, straight down the bestseller seaway."

Tengo managed a vague grunt.

"It's creepy. Mysterious. Too good to be true. This is just between you and me, but people around here are whispering that Komatsu himself might have fixed up the manuscript – more than common sense would allow. I can't believe it, but if it's true, we could be holding a time bomb."

"Maybe it was just a series of lucky coincidences."

"Even so, good luck can only last so long," the editor said.

Tengo thanked him and ended the call.

After hanging up, Tengo said to Fuka-Eri, "Mr. Komatsu hasn't been to work for the past week. They can't get in touch with him."

Fuka-Eri said nothing.

"The people around me seem to be disappearing one after another," Tengo said.

Still Fuka-Eri said nothing.

Tengo suddenly recalled the fact that people lose fifty million skin cells every day. The cells get scraped off, turn into invisible dust, and disappear into the air. *Maybe we are nothing but skin cells as far as the world is concerned. If so, there's nothing mysterious about somebody suddenly disappearing one day.*

"I may be next," Tengo said.

Fuka-Eri gave her head a tight, little shake. "Not you," she said.

"Why not me?"

"Because I did a purification."

Tengo contemplated this for several seconds without reaching a conclusion. He knew from the start that no amount of thinking could do any good. Still, he could not entirely forgo the effort to think.

"In any case, we can't see Mr. Komatsu right now," Tengo said. "And I can't give the money back to him."

"The money is no problem," Fuka-Eri said.

"Then what is a problem?" Tengo asked.

Of course, he did not receive an answer.

Tengo decided to follow through on last night's resolution to search for Aomame. If he spent the whole day in a concentrated effort, he should at least be able to come up with some kind of clue. But in fact, it turned out not to be that easy. He left Fuka-Eri in his apartment (after warning her repeatedly not to open the door for anyone) and went to the telephone company's main office, which had a complete set of telephone books for every part of the country, available for public use. He went through all the phone books for Tokyo's twenty-three central wards, looking for the name "Aomame." Even if he didn't find Aomame herself, a relative might be living there, and he could ask that person for news of Aomame.

But he found no one with the name Aomame. He broadened his search to include the entire Tokyo metropolis and still found no one. He further broadened his search to include the entire Kanto region – the prefectures of Chiba, Kanagawa, and Saitama. At that point, his time and energy ran out. After glaring at the phone books' tiny type all day, his eyeballs were aching.

Several possibilities came to mind.

1 She was living in a suburb of the city of Utashinai on Hokkaido.

2 She had married and changed her name to "Ito."

3 She kept her number unlisted to protect her privacy.

4 She had died in the spring two years earlier from a virulent influenza.

There must have been any number of possibilities besides these. It didn't make sense to rely strictly on the phone books. Nor could he read every one in the country. It could be next month before he finally reached Hokkaido. He had to find another way.

Tengo bought a telephone card and entered a booth at the telephone company. From there he called their old elementary school in Ichikawa and asked the female office worker who answered the phone to look up the address they had on file for Aomame, saying he wanted to reach her on alumni association business. The woman seemed kind and unhurried as she went through the roster of graduates. Aomame had transferred to another school in the fifth grade and was not a graduate. Her name therefore did not appear in the roster, and they did not know her current address. It would be possible, however, to find the address to which she moved at the time. Did he want to know that?

Tengo said that he did want to know that.

He took down the address and telephone number, "c/o Koji Tasaki" in Tokyo's Adachi Ward. Aomame had apparently left her parents' home at the time. Something must have happened. Figuring it was probably hopeless, Tengo tried dialing the phone number. As he had expected, the number was no longer in use. It had been twenty years, after all. He called Information and gave them the address and the name Koji Tasaki, but learned only that no telephone was listed under that name.

Next Tengo tried finding the phone number for the head-quarters of the Society of Witnesses, but no contacts were listed for them in any of the phone books he perused – nothing under "Before the Flood," nothing under "Society of Witnesses" or anything else of that ilk. He tried the classified directory under "Religious Organizations" but found nothing. At the end of this struggle, Tengo concluded that they probably didn't want anyone contacting them.

This was, upon reflection, rather odd. They showed up all the time. They'd ring the bell or knock on the door, uncon-cerned that you might be otherwise occupied – be it baking a soufflé, soldering a connection, washing your hair, training a mouse to do tricks, or thinking about quadratic functions – and, with a big smile, invite you to study the Bible with them. They had no problem coming to see you, but you were not free to go to see them (unless you were a believer, probably). You couldn't ask them one simple question. This was rather inconvenient.

But even if he did manage to find the Society's phone num-ber and get in touch with them, it was hard to imagine that such a wary organization would freely disclose information on an individual believer. No doubt they had their reasons for being so guarded. Many people hated them for their extreme, eccentric doctrines and for the close-minded nature of their faith. They had caused several social problems, as a result of which their treatment often bordered on persecution. It had probably become second nature for them to protect their com-munity from a less-than-welcoming outside world.

In any case, Tengo's search for Aomame had been shut down, at least for now. He could not immediately think of what additional search methods might remain. Aomame was such an unusual name, you could never forget it once you'd heard it. But in trying to trace the footsteps of one single human being who bore that name, he quickly collided with a hard wall. It might be quicker to go around asking Society of Witnesses members directly. Headquarters would probably doubt his motives and refuse to tell him anything, but if he were to ask some individual member, he felt, they would probably be kind enough to tell him. But Tengo did not know even one member of the Society of Witnesses. Come to think of it, no one from the Society had knocked on his door for a good ten years now. Why did they not come when you wanted them and come only when you didn't want them?

One possibility was to put a classified ad in the paper. "Aomame, please contact me immediately. Kawana." Stupid sounding. Tengo couldn't believe that Aomame would bother to contact him even if she saw such an ad. It would probably just end up scaring her away. "Kawana" was not such a common name, either, but Tengo couldn't believe that Aomame would still remember it. Kawana – who's that? She simply wouldn't contact him. And besides, who read classified ads, anyway?

Another approach might be to hire a private detective. They should know how to look for people. They have their methods and connections. The clues Tengo already had might be enough for them to find her right away. And it probably wouldn't be too expensive. But that might be something to set aside as a last resort, Tengo thought. He would try a little harder to see what he could come up with himself.

When the daylight began to fade, he went home to find Fuka-Eri sitting on the floor, listening to records – old jazz records left by his girlfriend. Record jackets were spread on the floor – Duke Ellington, Benny Goodman, Billie Holliday. Spinning on the turntable just then was Louis Armstrong singing "Chantez les Bas," a memorable song. It reminded him of his girlfriend. They had often listened to this one between bouts of lovemaking. Near the end, the trombonist, Trummy Young, gets carried away, forgets to end his solo at the agreed-upon point, and plays an extra eight bars. "Here, this is the part," his girlfriend had explained to him. When it ended, it was Tengo's job to get out of bed naked, go to the next room, and turn the LP over to play the second side. He felt a twinge of nostalgia recalling those days. Though he never thought the relationship would last forever, he had not expected it to end so abruptly.

Tengo felt odd seeing Fuka-Eri listening intently to the records that Kyoko Yasuda had left behind. Wrinkling her brow in complete concentration, she seemed to be trying to hear something beyond the old music, straining to see the shadow of something in its tones.

"You like this record?"

"I listened to it a lot," Fuka-Eri said. "Is that okay."

"Sure, it's okay. But aren't you bored here all by yourself?"

Fuka-Eri gave her head a little shake. "I have stuff to think about."

Tengo wanted to ask Fuka-Eri about what had happened between them during the thunderstorm. *Why did you do that?* He couldn't believe that Fuka-Eri had any sexual desire for him. It must have been an act that somehow took shape unconnected with sex. If so, what possible meaning could it have had?

Even if he asked her about it outright, though, he doubted he would receive a straight answer. And Tengo couldn't quite bring himself to broach a subject like that directly on such a peaceful, quiet September evening. It was an act that had been performed in hiding at a dark hour in a dark place in the midst of a raging thunderstorm. Brought out into everyday circumstances, the nature of its meaning might change.

So Tengo approached the question from a different angle, one that admitted a simple yes-or-no answer. "You don't have periods?"

"No" was Fuka-Eri's curt reply.

"You've never had even one?"

"No, not even one."

"This may be none of my business, but you're seventeen years old. It's probably not normal that you've never had a period."

Fuka-Eri gave a little shrug.

"Have you seen a doctor about it?"

Fuka-Eri shook her head. "It wouldn't do any good."

"Why wouldn't it do any good?"

Fuka-Eri did not answer. She gave no sign that she had even heard the question. Maybe her ears had a special valve that sensed a question's appropriateness or inappropriateness, opening and closing as needed, like a mermaid's gills.

"Are the Little People involved in this, too?" Tengo asked.

Again no answer.

Tengo sighed. He couldn't think of anything else to ask that would enable him to approach a clarification of last night's events. The narrow, uncertain path gave out at that point, and only a deep forest lay ahead. He checked his footing, scanned his surroundings, and looked up to the heavens. This was always the problem with talking to Fuka-Eri. All roads inevitably gave out. A Gilyak might be able to continue on even after the road ended, but for Tengo it was impossible.

Instead he brought up a new subject. "I'm looking for a certain person," he said. "A woman."

There was no point in talking about this to Fuka-Eri. Tengo was fully aware of that. But he wanted to talk about it to someone. He wanted to hear himself telling someone – anyone – what he was thinking about Aomame. Unless he did so, he felt Aomame would grow even more distant from him.

"I haven't seen her for twenty years. I was ten when I last saw her. She and I are the same age. We were in the same class in elementary school. I've tried different ways of finding her without any luck."

The record ended. Fuka-Eri lifted it from the turntable, narrowed her eyes, and sniffed the vinyl a few times. Then, handling it carefully by the edges so as not to leave fingerprints on it, she slipped it into its paper envelope and slid the envelope into the record jacket – gently, lovingly, like transferring a sleeping kitten to its bed.

"You want to see this person," Fuka-Eri asked without a question mark.

"Yes, she is very important to me."

"Have you been looking for her for twenty years," Fuka-Eri asked.

"No, I haven't," Tengo said. While searching for the proper words to continue, Tengo folded his hands on the table. "To tell you the truth, I just started looking for her today."

"Today," she said.

"If she's so important to you, why have you never looked for her until today?" Tengo asked for Fuka-Eri. "Good question."

Fuka-Eri looked at him in silence.

Tengo put his thoughts into some kind of order. Then he said, "I've probably been taking a long detour. This girl named Aomame has been – how should I put this? – at the center of my consciousness all this time without a break. She has functioned as an important anchor to my very existence. In spite of that fact – is it? – I guess I haven't been able to fully grasp her significance to me *precisely* because she has been all too close to the center."

Fuka-Eri stared at Tengo. It was impossible to tell from her expression whether this young girl had the slightest comprehension of what he was saying. But that hardly mattered. Tengo was half talking to himself.

"But it has finally hit me: she is neither a concept nor a symbol nor a metaphor. She actually exists: she has warm flesh and a spirit that moves. I never should have lost sight of that warmth and that movement. It took me twenty years to understand something so obvious. It always takes me a while to think of things, but this is a little too much. It may already be too late. But one way or another, I want to find her."

With her knees on the floor, Fuka-Eri straightened up, the shape of her nipples showing through the Jeff Beck T-shirt.

"Ah-oh-mah-meh," Fuka-Eri said slowly, as if pondering each syllable.

"Yes. Green Peas. It's an unusual name."

"You want to meet her," Fuka-Eri asked without a question mark.

"Yes, of course I want to meet her," Tengo said.

Fuka-Eri chewed her lower lip as she took a moment to think about something. Then she looked up as if she had hit upon a new idea and said, "She might be very close by."

CHAPTER 17

Aomame

PULL THE RAT OUT

The seven a.m. television news carried a big report on the Akasaka-Mitsuke subway station's flooding, but there was no mention of the death of Sakigake's Leader in a suite at the Hotel Okura. When NHK's news ended, Aomame switched channels and watched the news on a few other channels, but none of them announced that large man's painless death.

They hid his body, Aomame thought, scowling. Tamaru had predicted such a possibility, but she had found it hard to believe that they would actually do it. Somehow they had managed to carry Leader's corpse from the Hotel Okura suite, load it into a car, and take it away. He was a big man, and the corpse must have been tremendously heavy. The hotel was full of guests and employees. Security cameras were everywhere. How had they succeeded in carrying the corpse to the hotel's underground parking lot without having anyone notice?

They must have transported the body at night to the head-quarters in Yamanashi and then held a discussion of what to do with it. At least they were not going to formally report his death to the police. Once you've hidden something, you have to keep it hidden.

Aomame, of course, had no idea how they intended to fill the vacuum created by Leader's death. But they would exhaust every means available to them to maintain the organization. As the man himself had said, the system would endure with or without a leader. Who could inherit Leader's mantle? That problem had nothing to do with Aomame. Her assignment had been to liquidate Leader, not to crush a religion.

She thought about the two bodyguards in their dark suits. Buzzcut and Ponytail. When they got back to headquarters, would they be held responsible for having allowed Leader to be wiped out before their very eyes? Aomame imagined their next assignment: "Find that woman, no matter what. Don't come back here until you do." It was possible.

She ate an apple for breakfast, but she had almost no appetite. Her hands still retained the sensation of driving the needle into the back of the man's neck. While peeling the apple with a small knife in her right hand, she felt a slight trembling in her body – a trembling she had never experienced before. When she had killed someone in the past, the memory of it had nearly faded after a night's sleep. Though it never felt good to take a person's life, those were all men who didn't deserve to go on living. They inspired more disgust than human pity. But this time was different. Objectively, what this man had been doing was perhaps an affront to humanity. But he himself was, in many senses, an extraordinary human being, and his extraordinariness, at least in part, appeared to transcend standards of good and evil. Ending his life had also been something extraordinary. It had left a strange kind of resonance in her hands – an extraordinary resonance.

What he had left behind was a "promise." This was the conclusion to which Aomame's thoughts led her. The weight of that promise was left in her hands as a *sign*. She understood this. The sign might not fade from her hands – ever.

The phone rang shortly after nine a.m. It was Tamaru. It rang three times, stopped, and started again twenty seconds later.

"They didn't call the police after all," Tamaru said. "It's not on the TV news or in the paper."

"He *did* die, though. I'm sure of that."

"Yes, of course, I know. No question he died. There were a few movements around there. They've already cleared out of the hotel. They called in several people from their city branch office in the middle of the night, probably to help deal with the body. They're good at things like that. Around one a.m., an S-Class Mercedes and a Toyota Hiace van left the hotel parking lot. Both had dark glass and Yamanashi plates. They were probably back in Sakigake headquarters by sunrise. The police investigated the compound the day before yesterday, but it wasn't a full-scale operation, and all the officers were long gone by then. Sakigake has a big incinerator. If you threw a body in there, it wouldn't leave a bone, just clean smoke."

"Creepy."

"They're a creepy bunch, all right. Even if their Leader is dead, the organization will keep moving for a while, like a snake that keeps going even after its head is cut off. Head on or off, it knows exactly where it's headed. Nobody can say what will happen in the future. It might die. Or grow a new head."

"He was no ordinary man."

Tamaru offered no opinion on that matter.

"Completely different from the others," Aomame said.

Tamaru took a moment to gauge the resonance of her words. Then he said, "Yes, I can imagine this was different from the others. But we'd better start thinking about what happens *from now on,* and be a little more practical. Otherwise you won't be able to survive."

Aomame thought she should say something, but the words would not come. The trembling was still there in her body.

"Madame tells me she wants to talk to you," Tamaru said. "Can you talk?"

"Of course," Aomame said.

The dowager took the phone. Aomame could sense relief in her voice.

"I am so grateful to you, more than I can ever say. You handled this one perfectly."

"Thank you very much. But I don't think I'll be able to do it again," Aomame said.

"No, I realize that. We asked too much of you. I'm so happy you're all right. We won't be asking you to do this anymore. This was the last time. We have prepared a place for you to settle into. You won't have to worry about a thing. Just lie low for a while in the safe house. In the meantime, we'll make arrangements for you to move into your new life."

Aomame thanked her.

"Do you have everything you need there? If not, let us know. I'll have Tamaru take care of it right away."

"No, thank you. As far as I can tell, everything I need is here."

The dowager lightly cleared her throat. "Now, this is something I want you to keep in mind. What we did was absolutely right. We punished the man for his crimes and prevented him from committing any more. There will be no more victims. We put a stop to that. You must not let this bother you."

"He said the same thing."

" 'He'?"

"Sakigake's Leader. The man I took care of last night."

The dowager remained silent for a full five seconds. Then she said, "He knew?"

"Yes, he knew I was there to take care of him, and still he let me in. He was, if anything, hoping for death. His body had already suffered serious injury and was heading toward a slow but inevitable end. All I did was speed up the process somewhat and provide relief to a body tortured by intense pain."

The dowager seemed seriously shocked to hear this. Again she was at a loss for words, something most unusual for her.

"You mean to say – " the dowager said, looking for the right words, "that he himself was hoping for punishment for his deeds?"

"What he wanted was to end his painful life as soon as possible."

"And he made up his mind to let you kill him."

"Exactly."

Aomame said nothing about the bargain she had struck with Leader. In exchange for letting Tengo go on living in this world, she herself would have to die: this was an agreement known only to Aomame and the man. No one else was to be told.

Aomame said, "The things he did were deviant and deserving of death, but he was no ordinary human being. Or at least he possessed something special."

"Something special?" the dowager said.

"It's hard to explain," Aomame said. "It was at the same time both a special power or gift and a cruel burden. It was, I think, eating him alive from the inside."

"Could it be that this special *something* urged him on toward his deviant behavior?"

"Probably."

"In any case, you put a stop to it."

"That is true," Aomame said, her voice dry.

Holding the receiver in her left hand, Aomame spread out her right hand, with its lingering sensation of death, and stared at the palm. What did it mean to "have ambiguous congress" with those girls? Aomame could neither understand it nor explain it to the dowager.

"As always, I made the death appear to have been a natural one, but they will probably not do us the favor of seeing it that way. Given the circumstances, I'm sure they will conclude that I had something to do with it. And as you know, his death has not been reported to the police yet."

"Whatever steps they choose to take, we will do everything

in our power to protect you," the dowager said. "They have their organization, but we have strong connections and ample funds. Also, you are a careful, intelligent person. We won't let them have their way."

"Have you not yet found Tsubasa?" Aomame asked.

"We still don't know where she went. My thought is that she is in the Sakigake compound. She has nowhere else to go. We haven't found a way to bring her back yet, but I suspect that Leader's death has put the group into a state of confusion. We may be able to do something to exploit that confusion in order to save her. That child must be protected."

That child in the safe house was not actual substance, according to Leader. She was merely one form of a concept and had since been "retrieved." But Aomame could hardly say this to the dowager now. Aomame herself did not know what it meant. She did, however, remember the levitation of the marble clock. She had seen it happen with her own eyes.

Aomame asked, "How many days will I be hiding out in this safe house?"

"You should assume it will be from four days to a week. After that you will be given a new name and situation and moved to a faraway place. Once you have settled down there, we will have to cut off all contact with you for your own safety. I won't be able to see you for a while. Considering my age, I might never be able to see you again. It might have been better if I had never lured you into this troublesome business. I have thought about that many times. Then I would not have had to lose you this way. But – "

The dowager's voice caught in her throat. Aomame waited quietly for her to continue speaking.

"But I have no regrets. Everything was more or less destined to happen. I had to involve you. I had no choice. A very strong force was at work, and that is what has moved me. Still, I feel bad for you that it has come to this."

"On the other hand, we have shared something, something important, something we could not have shared with anyone else, something we could not have had any other way."

"Yes, you are right," the dowager said.

"Sharing it was something that I needed, too."

"Thank you for saying that. It gives me a measure of salvation."

Aomame was also pained to think that she could no longer see the dowager, who was one of the few ties she possessed with the outside world.

"Be well," Aomame said.

"You, too," the dowager said. "And be happy."

"If possible," Aomame said. Happiness was one of the farthest things away from her.

Tamaru came on the phone.

"You haven't used *it* so far, have you?" he asked.

"No, not yet."

"Try your best not to use it."

"I'll keep that in mind."

After a momentary pause, Tamaru said, "I think I told you the other day that I grew up in an orphanage in the mountains of Hokkaido."

"You were put in there after you were evacuated from Sakhalin when you were separated from your parents."

"There was a boy in that orphanage two years younger than I was. He was mixed: half Japanese, half black. I think his father was a soldier from the American base in Misawa. I don't know about his mother, but she was probably a prostitute or a bar hostess. She abandoned him soon after he was born, and he was put in the orphanage. He was a lot bigger than me, but not very smart. The other kids teased him, of course, mainly because his color was different. You know how that goes."

"I guess."

"I wasn't Japanese, either, so it fell to me one way or another to be his protector. Our situations were similar – a Korean evacuee and the illegitimate mixed-race kid of a black guy and a whore. You can't get much lower than that. But it did me good: it toughened me up. Not him, though. He could never be tough. Left on his own, he would have died for sure. In that place, you had to have a quick wit or be a tough fighter if you wanted to survive."

Aomame waited quietly for him to go on.

"He was bad at everything. He couldn't do anything right. He couldn't button his own shirt or wipe his ass. Carving, though, was something else. He was great at that. Give him a few carving tools and a block of wood and before you knew it he had made a really fine carving. No sketches or anything: the image would pop into his head and he would produce an accurate three-dimensional figure, tremendously detailed and realistic. He was a kind of genius. It was amazing."

"A savant," Aomame said.

"Yes, sure. I learned about that stuff later, the so-called savant syndrome. People with extraordinary powers. But nobody knew about that back then. People assumed he was mentally retarded or something – a kid with a slow brain but gifted hands that made him good at carving. For some reason, though, the only thing he would ever carve was rats. He could do those beautifully. They looked alive from any angle. But he never, ever carved anything but rats. Everybody would urge him to carve some other animal – a horse or a bear – and they even took him to the zoo for that purpose, but he never showed the slightest interest in other creatures. So then they just gave up and let him have his way, making nothing but rats. He made rats of every shape and size and pose. It was strange, I guess. By which I mean that there *weren't* any rats in the orphanage. It was too cold there, and there was nothing for them to eat. The place was too poor even for rats. Nobody could figure out why he was so fixated on rats. . . . Well, anyway, word got out about the rats he was making. The local paper carried a story, and people started asking to buy them. The head of the orphanage, a Catholic priest, got a craft shop to carry the carved rats and sell them to tourists. They must have brought in some decent money, but of course none of it ever came back to the boy. I don't know what they did with it, but I suspect the top people in the orphanage used it for themselves. All the boy ever got was more carving tools and wood to keep making rats in the workshop. True, he was spared the hard fieldwork; all he had to do was carve rats by himself while the rest of us were out. He was lucky to that extent."

"What finally happened to him?"

"I really don't know. I ran away from the orphanage when I was fourteen and lived on my own after that. I headed straight for the ferry, crossed over to the main island, and I haven't set foot in Hokkaido since then. The last I saw him, he was bent over a workbench, concentrating on his carving. You couldn't get through to him at those times, so we never even said good-bye. If he's still alive, I imagine he's still carving rats somewhere. It was all he could do."

Aomame kept silent and waited for the rest of the story.

"I often think of him even now. Life in the orphanage was terrible. They fed us next to nothing, and we were always hungry. The winters were *cold*. The work was harsh, and the older kids bullied us something awful. But he never seemed to find the life there all that painful. He appeared to be happy as long as he could carve. Sometimes he would go half mad when he picked up his carving tools, but otherwise he was a truly docile little fellow. He didn't make trouble for anyone but just kept quietly carving his rats. He'd pick up a block of wood and stare at it for a long time until he could see what kind of rat in what kind of pose was lurking inside. It took a long while before he could see the figure, but once that happened, all he had to do was pull the rat out of the block with his knives. He often used to say that: 'I'm going to pull the rat out.' And the rats he *pulled out* looked as if they might start moving at any moment. He kept on freeing these imaginary rats that were locked up in their blocks of wood."

"And you were the boy's protector."

"Yes, but not because I wanted to be. I just ended up in that position. And once you were given a position, you had to live up to it, no matter what. That was the rule. Say, if one of the other boys took away his carving tools just to be nasty, I would go and beat him up. Even if the other kid was older or bigger or there was more than one of them, I had to beat him up. Of course, there were times when *they* beat *me* up. Lots of times. But it didn't matter whether I won or lost those fights: I always got the tools back for him. That was the main thing. See what I mean?"

"I think so," Aomame said. "But finally you had to abandon him."

"Well, I had to go on living. I couldn't stay with him forever, taking care of him. I didn't have that luxury, obviously."

Aomame opened her right hand again and stared at it.

"I've seen you holding a little carved rat now and then. Did he make that?"

"Yes, he gave me a little one. I took it when I ran away. I keep it with me."

"You know, Tamaru, you're not the kind of guy who usually talks about himself. Why now?"

"One thing I wanted to tell you is that I often think of him," Tamaru said. "Not that I want to see him again or anything. I really don't. We wouldn't have anything to talk about, for one thing. It's just that I still have this vivid image of him 'pulling rats out' of blocks of wood with total concentration, and that has remained an important mental landscape for me, a reference point. It teaches me something – or tries to. People need things like that to go on living – mental landscapes that have meaning for them, even if they can't explain them in words. Part of why we live is to come up with explanations for these things. That's what I think."

"Are you saying that they're like a basis for us to live?"

"Maybe so."

"I have such mental landscapes, too."

"You'd better handle them with care."

"I will."

"I have one more thing to say, and that is that I will do everything I can to protect you. If there's somebody I have to beat up, I'll go out and beat them up. Win or lose, I won't abandon you."

"Thank you."

A few tranquil seconds of silence followed.

"Don't leave that apartment for a while. Just think of it as a jungle one step outside your door. Okay?"

"Got it," Aomame said.

The connection was cut. Hanging up, Aomame realized how tightly she had been gripping the receiver.

What Tamaru wanted to convey to me was that I'm now an indispensable part of their family, that ties once formed will never be cut, Aomame thought. *We are bound by artificial blood, so to speak.* Aomame was grateful to Tamaru for having delivered that message. He must have realized what a painful time this was for Aomame. It was precisely because he thought of her as a member of the family that he had begun to share some of his secrets.

To think that such a close connection could only be formed through violence was almost too much for Aomame to bear. *We can only share these deep feelings because of my unique circumstances: I've broken the law, killed several people, and now someone is after me and may even kill me. Would it have been possible to form such a relationship if murder had not been involved? Could we have formed such bonds of trust if I were not an outlaw? I doubt it.*

She watched the TV news, drinking tea. There were no more reports on the flooding of the Akasaka-Mitsuke subway station. Once the water receded the next day and the trains were running normally again, it had become old news. The death of Sakigake's Leader was still not public knowledge. Only a handful of people knew about that. Aomame imagined the large man's corpse being consumed by the high-temperature incinerator. Tamaru had said that not a single bone would be left. Unrelated to either grace or pain, everything would become smoke and blend into the early-autumn sky. Aomame could picture the smoke and the sky.

There was a report on the disappearance of the seventeen-year-old girl who wrote the bestselling book *Air Chrysalis*. Eriko Fukada, or "Fuka-Eri," as she was known, had been missing for over two months. The police had received a search request from her guardian and were carrying on a thorough investigation, but nothing had come to light as yet, the announcer said. The screen showed a stack of copies of *Air Chrysalis* in a bookstore, and a poster with the photo of the beautiful author hung on the store wall. A young female bookstore clerk was interviewed: "The book is still selling like crazy. I bought a copy myself and read it. It's really good – very imaginative! I hope they find out where Fuka-Eri is soon."

The report said nothing about a relationship between Eriko Fukada and Sakigake. The media were very cautious when religious organizations were involved.

In any case, Eriko Fukada was missing. She had been violated by her father when she was ten years old. They had had "ambiguous congress," if Aomame was to accept his terminology. Through that act, they had led the Little People into him. *How did he put it, again? That's it – they were Perceiver and Receiver. Eriko Fukada was the one who perceived, and her father was the one who received. Then the man started to hear special voices. He became the agent of the Little People and the founder of the religion called Sakigake. She left the religion after that. Then, as a force against the Little People, she teamed up with Tengo and wrote the novella* Air Chrysalis, *which became a bestseller. Now, for some reason or other, she has disappeared, and the police are looking for her.*

Meanwhile, last night, using a specially made ice pick, I killed Eriko Fukada's father, leader of the religion called Sakigake. People from the religion transported his corpse from the hotel and secretly "disposed" of it. Aomame could not imagine how Eriko Fukada would deal with the news of her father's death. *It was a death that he himself asked for, a painless "mercy killing," but the fact is that I used these hands of mine to end the life of a human being. A person's life may be a lonely thing by nature, but it is not isolated. To that life other lives are linked, and I surely have to bear some responsibility for those as well.*

Tengo is also deeply involved in these events. The Fukadas – father and daughter – are what bind us together: Perceiver and Receiver. Where could Tengo be now, and what is he doing? Could he have something to do with the disappearance of Eriko Fukada? Are the two of them still working together? The television news, of course, tells me nothing about Tengo's fate. So far, no one seems to know that he was the actual writer of Air Chrysalis. *But I know.*

It appears that he and I are narrowing the distance between us bit by bit. Circumstances carried us into this world and are bringing us closer together as though we are being drawn into a great whirlpool. It may be a lethal whirlpool. But Leader suggested that we would never find each other outside such a lethal place, just as violence creates certain kinds of pure relationships.

She took a deep breath. Then she reached out toward the Heckler & Koch on the table and assured herself of its hardness.

She imagined its muzzle being shoved into her mouth and her finger tightening on the trigger.

A large crow suddenly appeared on her balcony, perched on the railing, and let out a number of piercing cries. Aomame and the crow observed each other through the glass. The crow moved the big, bright eye on the side of his head, watching Aomame's movements in the room. He seemed to understand the significance of the pistol in her hand. Crows were intelligent animals. They knew that this block of steel had great importance. Somehow or other, they knew.

The crow spread its wings and flew off as suddenly as it had arrived, apparently having seen what it was supposed to see. Once it was gone, Aomame stood up, turned off the television, and sighed, hoping that the crow was not a spy for the Little People.

Aomame practiced her usual stretching on the living-room carpet. She worked her muscles to the limit for an hour, passing the time with the appropriate pain. One by one, she summoned up each muscle of her body and subjected it to an intense, detailed interrogation. She had the name, function, and quality of each muscle minutely engraved in her mind, missing none. She sweated profusely, working her lungs and heart to the fullest, and switching the channels of her consciousness. She listened to the flow of the blood in her veins, and received the wordless messages that her heart was issuing. The muscles of her face contorted every which way as she sank her teeth into the messages.

Next she washed the sweat off in the shower. She stepped on the scale to make sure there had been no major change in her weight. Confirming in the mirror that the size of her breasts and the shape of her pubic hair had not changed, she scowled immensely. This was her morning ritual.

When she was finished in the bathroom, she changed into a

jersey sportswear top and bottom for easy movement. Then, to kill time, she decided to examine the contents of the apartment again, beginning with the kitchen: the foods and the eating and cooking utensils. She memorized each item and devised a plan for which foods she would prepare and eat in what order. She estimated that, even if she never set foot outside the apartment, she could live here for at least ten days without going hungry, and she could make it last two weeks if she was careful in parceling out the supplies. They had stocked the place with that much food.

Then she went through the non-food items: toilet paper, tissues, laundry detergent, rubber gloves. Nothing was missing. The shopping had been done with great care. A woman must have participated in the preparations – probably an experienced housewife, judging from the obvious care that had been lavished on the task. Someone had meticulously calculated what and how much would be needed for a healthy thirty-year-old single woman to live here alone for a short time. This was not something a man could have done – though perhaps it would be possible for a highly observant gay man.

The bedroom linen closet was well stocked with sheets, blankets, and spare pillows, all with the smell of new linen, and all plain white. Ornamentation had been carefully avoided, there being no need for taste or individuality.

The living room had a television, a VCR, and a small stereo with a record player and a cassette deck. On the wall opposite the window, there was a waist-high wooden sideboard. She bent over and opened it to find some twenty books lined up inside. Someone had done their best to assure that Aomame would not be bored while hiding out here. The books were all new hardcover volumes that showed no evidence of having been opened. Most of them were recent, probably chosen from displays of current bestsellers at a large bookstore. The person had exercised some standards of selection – if not exactly taste – in choosing about half fiction and half non-fiction. *Air Chrysalis* was among them.

With a little nod, Aomame picked it up and sat on the living-room sofa in the warm sunshine. It was not a thick book. It was light, and the type was large. She looked at the dust jacket and at the name of the author, "Fuka-Eri," printed there, balanced the book on her palm to gauge its weight, and read the publisher's copy on the colorful band around the jacket. Then she sniffed the book for that special smell that new books have. Though his name was nowhere printed on it, Tengo's presence was here. The text printed inside it had passed through Tengo's body. She calmed herself and opened to the first page.

Her teacup and the Heckler & Koch were both where she could reach them.

CHAPTER 18

Tengo

THAT LONELY, TACITURN SATELLITE

"She might be very close by," Fuka-Eri said after some moments of biting her lip in serious thought.

Tengo unfolded and refolded his hands on the table, looking into Fuka-Eri's eyes. "Very close by? You mean here, in Koenji?"

"Within walking distance."

How do you know that? Tengo wanted to ask her, but he was at least prescient enough to know that he would not get an answer to such a question. She needed practical questions that could be answered with a simple yes or no.

"Are you saying that I can meet Aomame if I look for her in this neighborhood?" Tengo asked.

Fuka-Eri shook her head. "You can't meet her just by walking around."

"She's within walking distance, but I can't find her just by walking around. Is that what you are saying?"

"Because she's hiding."

"Hiding?"

"Like a wounded cat."

Tengo got an image of Aomame curled up under a moldy-smelling porch somewhere. "Why? Is she hiding from someone?" he asked.

This, of course, she did not answer.

"But the fact that she is *hiding* must mean that she is in some kind of critical situation, doesn't it?"

"Crit-i-cal sit-choo-ay-shun," Fuka-Eri said, echoing Tengo, with a look on her face like that of a child being shown a bitter medicine. She probably didn't like the sound of the words.

"Like, someone is chasing after her," Tengo said.

Fuka-Eri cocked her head slightly, meaning she didn't understand. "But she is not going to stay here forever."

"Our time is limited."

"Yes, limited."

"But now she is sitting somewhere like a wounded cat, so she won't be out taking walks."

"No, she won't do that," the beautiful young girl said with conviction.

"In other words, I'd have to look for her someplace special."

Fuka-Eri nodded.

"What kind of special place would that be?" Tengo asked.

Needless to say, he received no answer.

"You remember some things about her," Fuka-Eri said after a short pause. "One of them might help."

"Might help," Tengo said. "Are you saying that if I remember something about her, I might get a hint about where she is hiding?"

Without answering, she gave a little shrug. The gesture might have contained an affirmative nuance.

"Thank you," Tengo said.

Fuka-Eri gave him a tiny nod, like a contented cat.

Tengo prepared lunch in the kitchen. Fuka-Eri was intently choosing records from the record shelf. Not that he had a lot of records there, but it took her time to choose. At the end of her deliberations, she took out an old Rolling Stones album, put it on the turntable, and lowered the tonearm. It was a record that he had borrowed from somebody in high school and, for some reason, never given back. He hadn't heard it in years.

Listening to tracks like "Mother's Little Helper" and "Lady Jane," he made rice pilaf using ham and mushrooms and brown rice, and miso soup with tofu and wakame. He boiled cauliflower and flavored it with curry sauce he had prepared. He made a green bean and onion salad. Cooking was not a chore for Tengo. He always used it as a time to think – about everyday problems, about math problems, about his writing, or about metaphysical propositions. He could think in a more orderly fashion while standing in the kitchen and moving his hands than while doing nothing. Today, however, no amount of thinking would tell him what kind of "special place" Fuka-Eri had been talking about. Trying to impose order on something where there had never been any was a waste of effort. The number of places he could arrive at was limited.

The two of them sat across from each other eating dinner. Their conversation was virtually nonexistent. Like a bored married couple, they transported the food to their mouths in silence, each thinking – or not thinking – separate thoughts. It was especially difficult to distinguish between the two in Fuka-Eri's case. When the meal ended, Tengo drank coffee and Fuka-Eri ate a pudding she found in the refrigerator. Whatever she ate, her expression never changed. Chewing seemed to be the only thing she was thinking about.

Tengo sat at his desk, and, following Fuka-Eri's suggestion, he tried hard to recall something about Aomame.

You remember some things about her. One of them might help.

But Tengo could not concentrate. Another Rolling Stones record was playing. "Little Red Rooster" – a performance from the time Mick Jagger was crazy about Chicago blues. Not bad, but not a song written for people engaged in deep thinking or in the midst of seriously digging through old memories. The

Rolling Stones were not a band much given to such kindness. He needed someplace quiet where he could be alone.

"I'm going out for a while," Tengo said.

Studying the Rolling Stones album jacket in her hand, Fuka-Eri nodded, as if to say, "Fine."

"If anyone comes here, don't open the door for them," Tengo said.

Tengo walked toward the station wearing a navy-blue long-sleeved T-shirt, chinos from which the crease had long since faded, and sneakers. Just before reaching the station, he turned into a bar called Barleyhead and ordered a draft beer. The place served drinks and snacks. It was small enough so that twenty customers filled it up. He had come here any number of times before. Young people made it quite noisy late at night, but there were relatively few customers in the hour between seven and eight, when the mood was nice and hushed. It was perfect for sitting alone in a corner and reading a book while drinking a beer. The chairs were comfortable, too. He had no idea where the bar's name came from or what it meant. He could have asked one of the employees, but he was not good at small talk with strangers, and not knowing the source of the name didn't really matter. It was just a pleasant bar that happened to be named Barleyhead.

Fortunately, no music was playing. Tengo sat at a table by a window, drinking Carlsberg draft and munching on mixed nuts from a small bowl, thinking about Aomame. Picturing Aomame meant that Tengo himself became a ten-year-old boy again. It also meant that he experienced a major turning point in his life once again. After Aomame grasped his hand when they were ten, he refused to make any more rounds with his father doing NHK subscription collections. Shortly after that he experienced a definite erection and his first ejaculation. That was a watershed in his life. Of course, the transformation would have come – sooner or later – whether or not Aomame grasped his hand, but Aomame urged him on and promoted the change as if she had given his back a gentle shove.

He stared at the open palm of his left hand for a long time. *That ten-year-old girl grasped this hand and hugely changed something inside me, but I can't give a reasonable explanation of how such a thing could have happened. Still, the two of us understood each other and accepted each other in a very natural way in every last particular – almost miraculously so. Such things don't happen all that often in this life. For some people, they might never happen.* At the time, however, Tengo had not been able to fully comprehend the event's decisive meaning. And not just back then. He had not *truly* been able to understand its meaning until almost the present moment. He had only vaguely embraced the girl's image in his heart over the years.

She was thirty now, and her outward appearance might be very different from what he remembered from when they were ten. She must have grown taller, her chest developed, and her hairstyle must have changed. If she left the Society of Witnesses, she was probably wearing makeup. She might be sporting expensive, stylish clothing. Tengo found it hard to imagine Aomame striding down the street wearing a Calvin Klein suit and high heels. But such a thing was, of course, conceivable. People grow up, and when they grow up they change. *She could be in this bar right this moment without my realizing it.*

Tipping back his beer glass, Tengo took another look at his surroundings. She was somewhere close by. Within walking distance. Fuka-Eri said so. And Tengo accepted Fuka-Eri at her word. If she said it, it must be true.

The only other customers in the room were a young couple, probably students, sitting at the bar, engaged in an intense and intimate conversation, their foreheads practically touching. Seeing them, Tengo felt a profound loneliness, the sort he had not experienced for a very long time. *I'm alone in this world,* he thought. *I have no ties with anyone.*

Tengo closed his eyes and concentrated on the elementary school classroom once again. He had closed his eyes and visited that place last night, too – with a tremendously concrete sense of reality – when he and Fuka-Eri joined bodies during the violent thunderstorm. Because of that, the picture he conjured now came back with special vividness, as if it had been cleansed of all dust by last night's rain.

Unease and expectation and fear scattered to the farthest corners of the spacious classroom, and hid themselves in the room's many objects like cowardly little animals. Tengo was able to re-create the scene in meticulous detail – the blackboard with its partially erased mathematical formulas, the broken pieces of chalk, the cheap, sun-damaged curtains, the flowers in the vase on the teacher's podium (though he couldn't tell what type), the children's paintings pinned to the wall, the world map behind the podium, the smell of the floor wax, the waving of the curtains, the children's shouts coming through the window. His eyes could trace each omen or plan or riddle they contained.

During those several seconds when Aomame was holding his hand, Tengo had seen many things and accurately seared each image on his retinas, like a camera taking a photograph. These images comprised one of the basic landscapes that helped him survive his pain-filled teens. The scene always included the strong sensation of the girl's fingers. Her right hand never failed to encourage Tengo during the agonizing process of becoming an adult. *Don't worry, I'm with you,* the hand declared.

You are not alone.

She is in hiding, Fuka-Eri had said. Like a wounded cat.

Come to think of it, this was a strange coincidence. Fuka-Eri herself was in hiding here. She wouldn't set foot outside of

Tengo's apartment. In this same section of Tokyo, two women were lying low, running away from something. Both women had deep connections with Tengo. Could that be significant? Or was it a mere coincidence?

No answers were forthcoming, of course, just an aimless bunch of questions. Too many questions, too few answers. It was always like this.

When he finished his beer, a young waiter came over and asked him if he would like something else. Tengo hesitated a moment and then requested a bourbon on the rocks and another bowl of mixed nuts. "The only bourbon we have is Four Roses, if that's okay." Tengo said it would be okay. Anything at all. Then he went back to thinking about Aomame. The fragrance of a baking pizza wafted toward him from the kitchen.

From whom could Aomame possibly be hiding? The police? But Tengo could not believe that she had become a criminal. What kind of crime could she have committed? No, it could not be the police who were chasing her. Whoever or whatever it might be, the law surely had nothing to do with it.

Maybe they're the same ones who are after Fuka-Eri, it suddenly occurred to Tengo. *The Little People? Why would the Little People have to pursue Aomame?*

But if they *are really the ones pursuing Aomame, am I at the center of this?* Tengo of course had no idea why *he* had to be the pivotal figure in such a chain of events, but if there was a connection between the two women, Fuka-Eri and Aomame, it could not be anyone other than Tengo himself. *Without even being aware of it, I may have been using some kind of power to draw Aomame closer to me.*

Some kind of power?

He stared at his hands. *I don't get it. Where could I have that kind of power?*

His Four Roses on the rocks arrived along with a new bowl

of nuts. He took a swallow of Four Roses, and, taking several nuts in the palm of his hand, he shook them like dice.

Anyhow, Aomame is in this neighborhood. Within walking distance. That's what Fuka-Eri says. And I believe it. I'd be hard-pressed to explain why, but I do believe it. Still, how can I go about finding Aomame in her hiding place? It's hard enough finding someone living a normal life, but the task obviously becomes more challenging when someone is deliberately hiding. Should I go through the streets calling her name on a loudspeaker? Sure, like that's going to get her to step right up. It would just alert others to her presence and expose her to added danger.

There must be something else I should recall about her, Tengo thought.

"You remember some things about her. One of them might help," Fuka-Eri had said. But even before she said that to him, Tengo had long suspected that he might have failed to recall an important fact or two regarding Aomame. It had begun to make him feel uneasy now and then, like a pebble in his shoe. The feeling was vague but persistent.

Tengo swept his mind clean, as if erasing a blackboard, and started unearthing memories again – memories of Aomame, memories of himself, memories of the things around them, dredging the soft, muddy bottom like a fisherman dragging his net, putting the items in order and mulling them over with great care. Ultimately, though, these were things that had happened twenty years earlier. As vividly as he might recall them, there was a limit to how much he could bring back.

It occurred to him to try thinking about lines of vision. What had Aomame been looking at? And what had Tengo himself been looking at? *Let me think back along our moving lines of vision and the flow of time.*

The girl was holding his hand and looking straight into his eyes. Her line of vision never wavered. Tengo, initially at a loss to understand her actions, sought an explanation in her eyes. *This must be some kind of misunderstanding or mistake,* Tengo had thought. But there was no misunderstanding or mistake here. What he realized was that the girl's eyes were almost shockingly deep and clear. He had never seen eyes of such absolute clarity. They were like two springs, utterly transparent, but too deep to see the bottoms. He felt he might be sucked inside if he went on looking into them. And so he had no choice but to turn away from them.

He looked first at the floorboards beneath his feet, then at the entrance to the empty classroom, and finally he bent his neck slightly to look outside through the window. All this time, Aomame's gaze never wavered. She kept staring at Tengo's eyes even as he looked outside the window. He could feel her line of vision stinging his skin and her fingers gripping his left hand with unwavering strength and with complete conviction. She was not afraid. There was nothing she had to fear. And she was trying to convey that feeling to Tengo through her fingertips.

Because their encounter followed the cleaning of the classroom, the window had been left wide open for fresh air, and the white curtains were softly waving in the breeze. Beyond them stretched the sky. December had come, but it was still not that cold. High up in the sky floated a cloud – a straight, white cloud that retained a vestige of autumn, like a brand-new brushstroke across the sky. And there was something else there, hanging beneath the cloud. The sun? No, it was not the sun.

Tengo held his breath, pressed his fingers to his temple and tried to peer into a still-deeper place in his memory, tracing a frail thread of consciousness that was ready to snap at any moment.

That's it. The moon was up there.

Sunset was still some time away, but there it was – the moon – standing out against the sky, about three-quarters full. Tengo was impressed that he could see such a large, bright moon while it was still so light out. He remembered that. The unfeeling chunk of rock hung low in the sky as if, having nothing better to do, it was suspended on an invisible thread. It had a certain artificial air about it. At first glance, it looked like a fake moon used as a stage prop. But it was the actual moon, of course. Nobody would take the time and effort to hang a fake moon in a real sky.

Suddenly Tengo realized that Aomame was no longer looking at him. Her line of vision was turned in the same direction as his. Like him, Aomame was staring at the moon in broad daylight, still gripping his hand, her face deadly serious. He looked at her eyes again. They were not as clear as before. That had been a special, momentary clarity, and in its place he now could see something hard and crystalline. It was at once beguiling and severe, with a quality reminiscent of frost. Tengo could not grasp its meaning.

Eventually the girl seemed to have made up her mind. She suddenly released her grip on his hand, turned her back on him, and rushed out of the room without a word or a backward glance, leaving Tengo in a deep vacuum.

Tengo opened his eyes, relaxed his mental concentration, released a deep breath, and took a swallow of his bourbon. He felt the whiskey pass through his throat and down his gullet. He took another breath and exhaled. He could no longer see Aomame. She had turned her back on him and left the classroom, erasing herself from his life.

Twenty years went by.

It was the moon, Tengo thought.

I was looking at the moon, and so was Aomame. That gray chunk of rock hanging in the still-bright sky at three thirty in the afternoon. That lonely, taciturn satellite. We stood side by side, looking at that moon. But what does it mean? That the moon will guide me to her?

It suddenly crossed Tengo's mind that back then, Aomame might have entrusted the moon with her feelings. She and the moon might have reached a kind of secret agreement. Her gaze at the moon contained something frighteningly serious that could stir the imagination this way.

Tengo had no idea, of course, what Aomame had offered to the moon that time, but he could well imagine what the moon had given her: pure solitude and tranquillity. That was the best thing the moon could give a person.

Tengo paid his bill and walked out of the Barleyhead. Then he looked up at the sky but could not find the moon. The sky was clear, and the moon should be up, but it could not be seen from street level with buildings all around. Hands thrust in his pockets, Tengo walked from one street to the next, looking for the moon. He wanted to go someplace with an open field of vision, but finding such a place in a neighborhood like Koenji was no easy matter. The area was so flat that finding even a slight incline involved a major effort, and there were no hills at all. The best place might be the roof of a tall building with a view in all directions, but he couldn't see the kind of building in the area that let people up to the roof.

As he went on walking around aimlessly, Tengo recalled that there was a playground nearby, one that he often passed on walks. It was not a large playground, but it probably had a slide. If he climbed that, he should be able to have a better view of the sky. It wasn't a tall slide, but the view should be better than from street level. He headed for the playground. His watch hands were pointing to nearly eight o'clock.

There was no one in the playground. A tall mercury-vapor lamp stood in the middle, illuminating every corner of the place. There was a large zelkova tree, its leaves still thick and luxuriant. There were several low shrubs, a water fountain, a bench, swings, and a slide. There was also a public toilet, but it had been locked by a worker at sunset, perhaps to keep vagrants out. During the daytime, young mothers brought their children who were not yet old enough for kindergarten, and kept up their lively chattering while the children played. Tengo had observed such scenes any number of times. Once the sun went down, however, almost no one visited this place.

Tengo climbed the slide and, still standing, looked up at the night sky. A new six-story condo stood on the north side of the park. He had never noticed it before. It must have been built quite recently. It blocked the northern sky like a wall. Only low buildings stood on the other three sides of the playground. Tengo turned to scan the area and found the moon in the southwest, hanging over an old two-story house. It was about three-quarters full. *Just like the moon of twenty years ago,* Tengo thought. *Exactly the same size and shape. A complete coincidence. Probably.*

But this bright moon, hanging in the early-autumn night sky, had sharp, clear outlines and the introspective warmth characteristic of this season. The impression it gave was very different from that of the moon at three thirty in the December afternoon sky. Its calm, natural glow had the power to soothe and heal the heart like the flow of clear water or the gentle stirring of tree leaves.

Standing on the very top of the slide, Tengo looked up at that moon for a very long time. From the direction of Ring Road 7 came the blended sound of different-sized tires, like the roar of the sea. All at once the sound reminded Tengo of the sanatorium where his father was staying on the Chiba shore.

The city's earthly lights blotted out the stars as always. The sky was nice and clear, but only a few stars were visible, the very bright ones that twinkled as pale points here and there. Still, the moon stood out clearly against the sky. It hung up there faithfully, without a word of complaint concerning the city lights or the noise or the air pollution. If he focused hard on the moon, he could make out the strange shadows formed by its gigantic craters and valleys. Tengo's mind emptied as he stared at the light of the moon. Inside him, memories that had been handed down from antiquity began to stir. Before human beings possessed fire or tools or language, the moon had been their ally. It would calm people's fears now and then by illuminating the dark world like a heavenly lantern. Its waxing and waning gave people an understanding of the concept of time. Even now, when darkness had been banished from most parts of the world, there remained a sense of human gratitude toward the moon and its unconditional compassion. It was imprinted upon human genes like a warm collective memory.

Come to think of it, I haven't looked hard at the moon like this for a very long while, Tengo thought. *When could the last time have been? Living one hectic day after another in the city, you tend to look down at the ground. You forget to even look at the night sky.*

It was then that Tengo realized there was another moon hanging in the sky. At first, he thought it might be an optical illusion, a mere trick of light rays, but the more he looked at it, the surer he became that there was a second moon with solid outlines up there. His mind went blank as he stared in its direction, open-mouthed. *What am I seeing?* He could not make up his mind. The outline and the substance refused to overlap, as when word and concept fail to cohere.

Another moon?

He closed his eyes, opened his palms, and rubbed his cheeks. *What's wrong with me? I didn't drink that much.* He drew in a long, quiet breath and then quietly expelled it. He checked to be sure his mind was clear. *Who am I? Where am I now? What am I doing?* he asked himself in the darkness behind his closed eyelids. *It's September 1984, I'm Tengo Kawana, I'm in a playground in Koenji in Suginami Ward, and I'm looking up at the moon in the night sky. No doubt about it.*

Then he slowly opened his eyes and looked at the sky again, carefully, his mind calm, but still there were two moons.

This is no illusion. There are two moons. Tengo balled his hand into a fist and kept it that way for a long time.

The moon was as taciturn as ever. But it was no longer alone.

CHAPTER 19

Aomame

WHEN THE *DOHTA* WAKES UP

Air Chrysalis was a fantastical story, but it took the form of a very readable novella narrated from beginning to end in a simple, colloquial style, by a ten-year-old girl. It was not overly complex in terms of its vocabulary or logic, and it did not contain long-winded explanations or wordy expressions. The words and style of the young narrator were universally appealing – concise and, in most cases, pleasant – but they explained almost nothing about the events that unfolded. Rather, the girl simply let the narrative flow as she recounted what she had seen with her own eyes, never stopping to consider "What is going on here?" or "What could this mean?" The book moved forward at an easy pace appropriate to the story she was telling. Her readers followed along, very naturally adopting her point of view, and before they knew it, they were in another world – a world that was *not this world,* a world in which the Little People made air chrysalises.

Reading the first ten pages, Aomame felt herself responding strongly to the novel's style. If indeed this was Tengo's creation, he was certainly a talented writer. The Tengo that Aomame knew was primarily a mathematical genius. He was said to be a prodigy, easily able to solve mathematical problems that were too difficult for most adults. His grades had been outstanding in other subjects, too, if not quite up to his work in mathematics. He was also physically big and an all-around athlete, but Aomame did not recall anything about his being an especially good writer. Probably that talent was obscured at the time in the shadow of his mathematics.

On the other hand, Tengo might have done nothing more than transfer the author's narrative voice to the page just as he had initially read it. His own originality might not have contributed much of anything to the style. She felt, though, that this was not the case. While the writing was deceptively simple, a closer read revealed that it was in fact calculated and arranged with great care. No part of it was overwritten, but at the same time it had everything it needed. Figurative expressions were kept to a minimum, but the descriptions were still vivid and richly colored. Above all, the style had a wonderfully musical quality. Even without reading it aloud, the reader could recognize its deep sonority. This was not writing that flowed naturally from the pen of a seventeen-year-old girl.

Having ascertained all this, Aomame proceeded to read the rest with great care.

The heroine is a young girl. She belongs to a small mountain community known as the "Gathering." Her mother and father live a communal life in the Gathering. She has no brothers or sisters. Because she was brought here shortly after her birth, the girl has virtually no knowledge of the outside world. All three members of the family have busy schedules that give them little opportunity to spend time together in relaxed conversation, but still they are close. The girl spends her days in the local elementary school while her parents are primarily engaged in farm work. The children also help with the farming when they have free time.

The adults of the Gathering all hate the outside world. At every opportunity, they like to say that the world in which they live is a beautiful, solitary island floating in a sea of "cap-i-tal-izum," a "for-tress." The girl does not know what they mean by "cap-i-tal-izum" (or the other word they sometimes use, "ma-teer-ee-al-izum"), but, judging from the scornful tone they use whenever they speak the words, cap-i-tal-izum and ma-teer-ee-al-izum must be very twisted things that are opposed to nature and *rightness*. The girl has been taught that, in order to keep her body and her thoughts clean, she must limit her contact with the outside world. Otherwise, her mind will become "po-loo-ted."

The Gathering is composed of some fifty relatively young men and women, divided into two groups. One group aims at "rev-a-loo-shun," while the other group aims at "peese." The girl's parents tend to belong to the "peese" group. Her father is the oldest member of that group, and he has played a central role since the founding of the Gathering.

The ten-year-old girl cannot, of course, give a logical explanation of the opposition of the two groups, nor does she understand the difference between "rev-a-loo-shun" and "peese." She has only the vague impression that "rev-a-loo-shun" is a kind of pointed way of thinking, while "peese" has a rather more rounded shape. Each "way of thinking" has its own shape and color, which wax and wane like the moon. That is about all she understands.

The girl does not know much about how the Gathering came into being, either. She has been told that, almost ten years earlier, just after she was born, there was a big movement in society, and people stopped living in the city and came out to an isolated village in the mountains. She does not know much about the city. She has never ridden on a subway or taken an elevator. She has never seen a building with more than three stories. There is just too much she doesn't know about. All she can understand are the things around her that she can see and touch.

Still, the girl's low-angled line of vision and unadorned

narrative voice vividly and naturally depict the small community called the Gathering, its makeup and scenery, and the customs and ways of thinking of the people who live there.

Despite the split in the residents' ways of thinking, their sense of solidarity is strong. They share the conviction that it is good to live separately from "cap-i-tal-izum," and they are well aware that even though the shape and color of their ways of thinking may differ, they have to stand together if they hope to survive. They are barely able to make ends meet. People work hard every day without a break. They grow vegetables, barter with the neighboring villages, sell their surplus products, avoid the use of mass-produced items as much as possible, and generally spend their lives in nature. When they must use an electrical appliance, they find one in a pile of discards somewhere and repair it. Almost all the clothes they wear are used items sent to them from somewhere else.

Some members of the community, unable to adapt to this pure but difficult life, eventually leave the Gathering, but others come to join it. New members outnumber those who leave, and so the Gathering's population gradually increases. This is a welcome trend. The abandoned village in which they make their life has many homes that can be lived in with a few repairs, and many fields remaining that can be farmed. The community is delighted to have new workers.

The number of children in the community varies between eight and ten. Most of the children were born in the Gathering. The eldest child is the heroine of the story, the girl. The children attend a local elementary school, walking together to and from the school each day. They are required by law to attend a school in the district, and the Gathering's founders believe that preserving good relations with the people of the district is indispensable to the survival of the community. The local children, however, are unnerved by the children of the Gathering, and they either avoid them or bully them, as a result of which the Gathering children move as one. They stay together to protect themselves, both from physical harm and from "po-loo-shun" of the mind.

Quite separate from the district public school, the Gathering has its own school, and members take turns teaching the children. This is not a great burden, since most of the members are highly educated, and several of them hold teaching certificates. They make their own textbooks and teach the children basic reading, writing, and arithmetic. They also teach the basics of chemistry, physics, physiology, biology, and the workings of the outside world. The world has two systems, "cap-i-tal-izum" and "com-yoon-izum," that hate each other. Both systems, though, have big problems, so the world is generally moving in a direction that is not good. "Com-yoon-izum" was originally an outstanding ideology with high ideals, but it was twisted out of shape by "self-serving politicians." The girl was shown a photograph of one of the "self-serving politicians." With his big nose and big, black beard, the man made her think of the king of the devils.

There is no television in the Gathering, and listening to the radio is not allowed except on special occasions. Newspapers and magazines are also limited. News that is considered necessary is reported orally during dinner at the Assembly Hall. The people respond to each item of news with cheers or groans – far more often with groans. This is the girl's only experience of media. She has never seen a movie. She has never read a cartoon. She is only allowed to listen to classical music. There is a stereo set in the Assembly Hall and lots of records that someone probably brought in as a single collection. During free moments, it is possible to listen to a Brahms symphony or a Schumann piano piece or Bach keyboard music or religious music. These are precious times for the girl and virtually her only entertainment.

* * *

Then one day something happens that makes it necessary for the girl to be punished. She has been ordered that week to take care of the Gathering's small herd of goats each morning and night, but, overwhelmed with her homework and other daily chores, one night it slips her mind. The next morning, the oldest animal, a blind goat, is found cold and dead. As her punishment, the girl is to be isolated from the rest of the Gathering for ten days.

That particular goat was thought by the community to have a special significance, but it was quite old, and some kind of illness had sunk its talons into the goat's wasted body, so whether anyone took care of it or not, there was no hope it would recover. Still, that does not lessen the severity of the girl's crime in any way. She is blamed not only for the death of the goat itself but for the dereliction of her duties. Isolation is one of the most serious punishments that the Gathering can impose.

The girl is locked in a small, old earthen storehouse with the dead blind goat. The storehouse is called the Room for Reflection. Anyone who has broken the Gathering's rules goes there in order to reflect upon his or her offense. No one speaks to the girl while she is in isolation. She must endure ten full days of total silence. A minimal amount of water and food is brought to her, but the storehouse is dark, cold, and damp, and it smells of the dead goat. The door is locked from the outside. In one corner of the room is a bucket where she can relieve herself. High on one wall is a small window that admits the light of the sun and the moon. A few stars can also be seen through it when the sky is not clouded over. There is no other light. She stretches out on the hard mattress on top of the board floor, wraps herself in two old blankets, and spends the night shivering. It is April, but the nights are cold in the mountains. When darkness falls, the dead goat's eye sparkles in the starlight. Afraid, the girl can hardly sleep.

On the third night, the goat's mouth opens wide. It has been pushed open from the inside, and out of the mouth comes a number of tiny people, six in all. They are only four inches high when they first emerge, but as soon as they set foot on the ground, they begin to grow like mushrooms sprouting after the rain. Even so, they are no more than two feet tall. They tell the girl that they are called the Little People.

This is like "Snow White and the Seven Dwarfs," the girl thinks, recalling a story her father read to her when she was little. *But there's one missing.*

"If you'd rather have seven, we can be seven," one of the Little People says to her in a soft voice. Apparently, they can read her mind. She counts them again, and now there are seven. The girl does not find this especially strange, however. The rules of the world had already changed when the Little People came out of the goat's mouth. Anything could happen after that.

"Why did you come out of the dead goat's mouth?" she asks, noticing that her voice sounds odd. Her manner of speaking is also different from usual, probably because she has not spoken with anyone for three days.

"Because the goat's mouth turned into a passageway," one of the Little People with a hoarse voice says. "We didn't know it was a dead goat until we actually came out."

A screechy-voiced one adds, "We don't mind at all, though. A goat, a whale, a peapod: as long as it's a passageway."

"You made the passageway, so we thought we'd give it a try and see where it came out," the soft-voiced one says.

"*I* made the passageway?" the girl says. No, it does not sound like her own voice.

"You did us a favor," says one of the Little People with a small voice.

Some of the others voice their agreement.

"Let's play," says one with a tenor voice. "Let's make an air chrysalis."

"Yes," replies a baritone. "Since we went to all the trouble of coming here."

"An air chrysalis?" the girl asks.

"We pluck threads out of the air and make a home. We make it bigger and bigger!" the bass says.

"A home? Who is it for?" the girl asks.

"You'll see," the baritone says.

"You'll see when it comes out," the bass says.

"Ho ho," another one takes up the beat.

"Can I help?" the girl asks.

"Of course," the hoarse one says.

"You did us a favor," the tenor says. "Let's work together."

Once the girl begins to get the hang of it, plucking threads out of the air is not too difficult. She has always been good with her hands, so she is able to master this operation right away. If you look closely, there are lots of threads hanging in the air. You can see them if you try.

"Yes, that's it, you're doing it right," the small-voiced one says.

"You're a very clever girl. You learn quickly," says the screechy-voiced one.

All the Little People wear the same clothing and their faces look alike, but each one has a distinctly different voice.

The clothing they wear is utterly ordinary, the kind that can be seen anywhere. This is an odd way to put it, but there is no other way to describe their clothing. Once you take your eyes off their clothes, you can't possibly remember what they looked like. The same can be said of their faces, the features of which are neither good nor bad. They are just ordinary features, the kind that can be seen anywhere. Once you take your eyes off their faces, you can't possibly remember what they looked like. It is the same with their hair, which is neither long nor short, just ordinary hair. One thing they do not have is any smell.

When the dawn comes and the cock crows and the eastern sky lightens, the seven Little People stop working and begin stretching. Then they hide the partially finished air chrysalis – which is only about the size of a baby rabbit – in the corner of the room, probably so that the person who brings the meals will not see it.

"It's morning," says the one with the small voice.

"The night has ended," says the bass.

Since they have all these different voices, they ought to form a chorus, the girl thinks.

"We have no songs," says the tenor.

"Ho ho," says the keeper of the beat.

The Little People all shrink down to their original four-inch size, form a line, and enter the dead goat's mouth.

"We'll be back tonight," the small-voiced one says before closing the goat's mouth from the inside. "You must not tell anyone about us."

"If you do tell someone about us, something very bad will happen," the hoarse one adds for good measure.

"Ho ho," says the keeper of the beat.

"I won't tell anyone," the girl says.

And even if I did, they wouldn't believe me. The girl has often been scolded by the grown-ups around her for saying what is in her mind. People have said that she does not distinguish between reality and her imagination. The shape and color of her thoughts seem to be very different from those of other people. She can't understand what they consider so wrong about her. In any case, she had better not tell anyone about the Little People.

After the Little People have disappeared and the goat's mouth has closed, the girl does a thorough search of the area where they hid the air chrysalis, but she is unable to find it. They did such a good job of hiding it! The space is confined, but still she can't discover where it might be. Where could they have hidden it?

After that, she wraps herself in the blankets and goes to sleep – her first truly restful sleep in a long time: no dreams, no interruptions. She enjoys the unusually deep sleep.

The dead goat stays dead all day, its body stiff, its eyes clouded like marbles. When the sun goes down, though, and darkness comes to the storehouse, the eye sparkles in the starlight, the mouth snaps open, and the Little People emerge, as if guided by the light. This time there are seven from the beginning.

"Let's pick up where we left off last night," the hoarse-voiced one says.

Each of the other six voices his approval in his own way.

The seven Little People and the girl sit in a circle around the chrysalis and continue to work on it, plucking white threads from the air and adding them to the chrysalis. They hardly speak, concentrating their energies on the job. Engrossed in moving her hands, the girl is not bothered by the night's coldness. She is hardly aware of the passing of time, and she feels neither bored nor sleepy. The chrysalis grows in size, slowly but visibly.

"How big are we going to make it?" the girl asks when dawn is nearing. She wants to know if the job will be done within the ten days she is locked in the storehouse.

"As big as we can," the screechy-voiced one replies.

"When it gets to a certain size, it will break open all by itself," the tenor says gleefully.

"And something will come out," the baritone says in vibrant tones.

"What kind of thing?" the girl asks.

"What will come out?" the small-voiced one says.

"Just you wait!" the bass says.

"Ho ho," says the keeper of the beat.

"Ho ho," the other six join in.

*   *   *

A peculiar darkness pervaded the novella's style. As she became aware of it, Aomame frowned slightly. This was like a fabulous children's story, but hidden down deep somewhere it had a strong, dark undercurrent. Aomame could hear its ominous rumble beneath the story's simple phrases, a gloomy suggestion of illness to come – a deadly illness that quietly gnaws away a person's spirit from the core. What brought the illness with them was the chorus-like group of seven Little People. *There is something unhealthy here, without question,* Aomame thought. And yet she could hear in their voices something that she recognized in herself – something almost fatally familiar.

Aomame looked up from the book and recalled what Leader had said about the Little People before he died.

"We have lived with them since long, long ago – from a time before good and evil even existed, when people's minds were still benighted."

Aomame went on reading the story.

The Little People and the girl continue working, and after several days the air chrysalis has grown to something like the size of a large dog.

"My punishment ends tomorrow. After that I'll get out of here," the girl says to the Little People as dawn is beginning to break.

The seven Little People listen quietly to what the girl is telling them.

"So I won't be able to make the air chrysalis with you anymore."

"We are very sorry to hear that," the tenor says, sounding genuinely sorry.

"You helped us very much," the baritone says.

The one with the screechy voice says, "But the chrysalis is almost finished. It will be ready once we add just a little bit more."

The Little People stand in a row, staring at the air chrysalis as if to measure the size of what they have made so far.

"Just a tiny bit more!" the hoarse-voiced one says as if leading the chorus in a monotonous boatman's song.

"Ho ho," intones the keeper of the beat.

"Ho ho," the other six join in.

The girl's ten days of isolation end and she returns to the Gathering. Her communal life starts again, and she is so busy following all the rules that she has no more time to be alone. She can, of course, no longer work on the air chrysalis with the Little People. Every night before she goes to bed, she imagines to herself the seven Little People continuing to sit around the air chrysalis and make it bigger. It is all she can think about. It even feels as if the whole air chrysalis has actually slipped inside her head.

The girl is dying to know what could possibly be inside the air chrysalis. What will appear when the chrysalis ripens and pops open? She is filled with regret to think that she cannot witness the scene with her own eyes. *I worked so hard helping them to make it, I should be allowed to be there when it opens.* She even thinks seriously of committing another offense so that she can be punished with another period of isolation in the storehouse. But even if she were to go to all that trouble, the Little People might not appear. The dead goat has been carried away and buried somewhere. Its eye will not sparkle in the starlight again.

The story goes on to describe the girl's daily life in the community – the disciplined schedule, the fixed tasks, the guidance and care she provides the other children as the oldest child in the community, her simple meals, the stories her parents read her before bedtime, the classical music she listens to whenever she can find a spare moment. A life without "po-loo-shun."

The Little People visit her in dreams. They can enter people's dreams whenever they like. They tell her that the air chrysalis is about to break open, and they urge her to come and see it. "Come to the storehouse with a candle after sunset. Don't let anyone see you."

The girl cannot suppress her curiosity. She slips out of bed and pads her way to the storehouse carrying the candle she has prepared. No one is there. All she finds is the air chrysalis sitting quietly where it has been left on the storehouse floor. It is twice as big as it was when she last saw it, well over four feet long. Its entire surface radiates a soft glow, and its beautifully curved shape has a waist-like narrowed area in the middle that was not there before, when it was smaller. The Little People have obviously been working hard. The chrysalis is already breaking open. A vertical crack has formed in its side. The girl bends over and peers in through the opening.

She discovers that she herself is inside the chrysalis. She stares at this other self of hers lying naked on her back, eyes closed, apparently unconscious, not breathing, like a doll.

One of the Little People speaks to her – the one with the hoarse voice: "That is your *dohta*," he says, and then clears his throat.

The girl turns to find the seven Little People fanned out behind her in a row.

"*Dohta*," she says, mechanically repeating the word.

"And what you are called is '*maza*,' " the bass says.

"*Maza* and *dohta*," the girl says.

"The *dohta* serves as a stand-in for the *maza*," the screechy-voiced one says.

"Do I get split in two?" the girl asks.

"Not at all," the tenor says. "This does not mean that you are split in two. You are the same you in every way. Don't worry. A *dohta* is just the shadow of the *maza*'s heart and mind in the shape of the *maza*."

"When will *she* wake up?"

"Very soon. When the time comes," the baritone says.

"What will this *dohta* do as the shadow of my heart and mind?" the girl asks.

"She will act as a Perceiver," the small-voiced one says furtively.

"Perceiver," the girl says.

"Yes," says the hoarse one. "She who perceives."

"She conveys what she perceives to the Receiver," the screechy one says.

"In other words, the *dohta* becomes our passageway," the tenor says.

"Instead of the goat?" the girl asks.

"The dead goat was only a temporary passageway," the bass says. "We must have a living *dohta* as a Perceiver to link the place we live with this place."

"What does the *maza* do?" the girl asks.

"The *maza* stays close to the *dohta*," the screechy one says.

"When will the *dohta* wake up?" the girl asks.

"Two days from now, or maybe three," the tenor says.

"One or the other," says the one with the small voice.

"Make sure you take good care of this *dohta*," the baritone says. "She is *your dohta*."

"Without the *maza*'s care, the *dohta* cannot be complete. She cannot live long without it," the screechy one says.

"If she loses her *dohta*, the *maza* will lose the shadow of her heart and mind," the tenor says.

"What happens to a *maza* when she loses the shadow of her heart and mind?" the girl asks.

The Little People look at each other. None of them will answer the question.

"When the *dohta* wakes up, there will be two moons in the sky," the hoarse one says.

"The two moons cast the shadow of her heart and mind," the baritone says.

"There will be two moons," the girl repeats mechanically.

"That will be a sign. Watch the sky with great care," the small-voiced one says furtively. "Watch the sky with great care," he says again. "Count the moons."

"Ho ho," says the keeper of the beat.

"Ho ho," the other six join in.

The girl runs away.

There was something mistaken there. Something wrong. Something greatly misshapen. Something opposed to nature. The girl knows this. She does not know what the Little People want, but the image of herself inside the air chrysalis sends shivers through her. She cannot possibly live with her living, moving other self. She has to run away from here. As soon as she possibly can. Before her *dohta* wakes up. Before that second moon appears in the sky.

In the Gathering it is forbidden for individuals to own money. But the girl's father once secretly gave her a ten-thousand-yen bill and some coins. "Hide this so that no one can find it," he told her. He also gave her a piece of paper with someone's name, address, and telephone number written on it. "If you ever have to run away from this place, use the money to buy a train ticket and go there."

Her father must have known back then that something bad might happen in the Gathering. The girl does not hesitate. Her actions are swift. She has no time to say good-bye to her parents.

From a jar she buried in the earth, she takes out the ten-thousand-yen bill and the coins and the paper. During class, she tells the teacher she is not feeling well and gets permission to go to the nurse's office. Instead she leaves the school and takes a bus to the station. She presents her ten-thousand-yen bill at the window and buys a ticket to Takao, west of Tokyo.

The man at the window gives her change. This is the first time in her life she has ever bought a ticket or received change or gotten on a train, but her father gave her detailed instructions, and she has memorized what she must do.

As indicated on the paper, the girl gets off the train at Takao Station on the Chuo Line, and she uses a public telephone to call the number her father gave her. The man who answers is an old friend of her father's, an artist who paints in the traditional Japanese style. He is ten years older than her father and he lives in the hills with his daughter near Mount Takao. His wife died a short time before. The daughter is named Kurumi and she is one year younger than the girl. As soon as he hears from the girl, the man comes to get her at the station, and he warmly welcomes this young escapee into his home.

The day after she is taken into the painter's home, the girl looks at the sky from her room and discovers that the number of moons up there has increased to two. Near the usual moon a smaller second moon hangs like a slightly shriveled green pea. *My* dohta *must have awakened,* the girl thinks. The two moons cast the shadow of her heart and mind. Her heart gives a shudder. *The world has changed. And something is beginning to happen.*

The girl hears nothing from her parents. Perhaps no one in the Gathering has noticed her disappearance. That is because her other self, her *dohta,* has remained behind. The two of them look exactly alike, so most people can't tell the difference. Her parents, of course, should be able to tell that the *dohta* is not the actual girl, that she is nothing but the girl's other self, that their actual daughter has run away from the Gathering, leaving the *dohta* behind in her place. There is only one place where the girl might have gone, but still her parents never try to contact her. This in itself might be a wordless message to the girl to stay away.

The girl goes to school irregularly. The new outside world is simply too different from the world of the Gathering where she grew up. The rules are different, the aims are different, the words they use are different. For this reason, she has trouble making friends in this new world. She can't get used to life in the school.

In middle school, however, she befriends a boy. His name is Toru. He is small and skinny, and his face has several deep wrinkles like that of a monkey. He seems to have suffered from a serious illness when little and can't participate in strenuous activities. His backbone is somewhat curved. At recess time, he always stays by himself, reading a book. Like the girl, he has no friends. He is too small and too ugly. During one lunch break, the girl sits next to him and starts to talk to him. She asks about the book he is reading. He reads it aloud to her. She likes his voice, which is small and hoarse but very clear to her. The stories he tells with that voice all but carry her away. He reads prose so beautifully that it sounds as if he is reciting poetry. Soon she is spending every lunchtime with him, sitting very still and listening with deep attention to the stories he reads her.

Before long, however, Toru is lost to the girl. The Little People snatch him away from her.

One night an air chrysalis appears in Toru's room. The Little People make it bigger and bigger each night while he sleeps, and they show the scene to the girl through her dreams. The girl can do nothing to stop them. Eventually the chrysalis reaches full size and a vertical split appears in its side, just as it happened with the girl. But inside this chrysalis are three big, black snakes. The three snakes are tightly intertwined, so tightly that no one – including themselves – can pull them apart. They look like a shiny perpetual *tangle* with three heads. The snakes are terribly angry that they cannot pull free. They writhe in a frantic effort to separate themselves from each other, but the more they writhe, the more entangled they become. The Little People show these creatures to the girl. The boy called Toru sleeps on beside them, unaware. Only the girl can see all this.

The boy suddenly falls ill a few days later and is sent to a distant sanatorium. The nature of his illness is not disclosed. In any case, Toru will surely never return to the school. He has been irretrievably lost.

The girl realizes that this is a message from the Little People. Apparently they cannot do anything to the girl, a *maza*, directly. What they can do instead is harm and even destroy the people around her. But they cannot do this to just anyone – they cannot touch her guardian, the painter, or his daughter, Kurumi. Instead they choose the weakest ones for their prey. They dragged the three black snakes from the depths of the boy's mind and woke them from their slumber. By destroying the boy, they have sent a warning to the girl and are trying their best to bring her back to her *dohta*. "*You*, finally, are the one who caused this to happen," they are telling her.

The girl returns to her loneliness. She stops going to school. Making friends with someone can only expose that person to danger. That is what it means to live beneath two moons. That is what she has learned.

The girl eventually makes up her mind and begins fashioning her own air chrysalis. She is able to do this. The Little People said that they had come to her world down a passageway from the place they belong. If that is the case, she herself should be able to go to that place down a passageway in the opposite direction. If she goes there, she can learn the secrets regarding why she is here and what the meaning of "*maza*" and "*dohta*" could be. She might also succeed in saving the lost Toru. The girl begins making a passageway. All she has to do is pluck threads from the air and weave a chrysalis. This will take time, but if she does take the time, she can do it.

Sometimes, however, she becomes unsure and confusion overtakes her. *Am I really a* maza? *Couldn't I have switched places somewhere with my* dohta? The more she thinks about it, the less certain she becomes. *How can I prove that I am the real me?*

The story ends symbolically when the girl is opening the door of her passageway. It says nothing about what will happen beyond the door – probably because it has not happened yet.

Dohta, Aomame thought. *Leader used that word before he died. He said that his own daughter had run away, leaving her* dohta *behind, in order to establish a force opposed to the Little People. It might have actually happened. And I am not the only one to see two moons.*

Still, Aomame felt she could understand why this novella had gained such a wide readership. Although it was a story about the fantastical experiences of a girl placed in unusual circumstances, it also had something that called forth people's natural sympathies. It probably aroused some subconscious something, which was why readers were pulled in and kept turning pages.

Tengo undoubtedly had contributed much to the book's literary qualities, its vivid, precise descriptions, but she could not confine her admiration to that fact alone. She had to focus on the parts of the story where the Little People enter the action. For Aomame, this was a highly *practical* story – a virtual instruction manual – upon which hinged the life and death of actual people. She needed to gain concrete knowledge from it, to add whatever solidity and detail she could to her understanding of the world into which she had strayed.

Air Chrysalis was not just a wild fantasy dreamed up by a seventeen-year-old girl. The names may have been changed, but Aomame firmly believed that the majority of things depicted in it were unmistakable reality as experienced firsthand by the girl herself. Fuka-Eri had recorded those events from her own life as accurately as possible in order to reveal those hidden secrets to the world at large, to inform large numbers of people of the existence and the deeds of the Little People.

The *dohta* that the girl had left behind must have become a passageway for the Little People and guided them to Leader, the girl's father, who was then transformed by them into a Receiver. They then drove the Akebono members, who were of no use to them, into a suicidal bloodbath, and transformed the remaining Sakigake group into a smart, militant, and xeno-phobic religious organization, which was probably the most comfortable and convenient environment for the Little People.

Aomame wondered if Fuka-Eri's *dohta* had been able to survive for long without her *maza*. The Little People had said that it was virtually impossible for a *dohta* to go on living with-out her *maza*. And what about a *maza*? What was it like for her to live after having lost the shadow of her heart and mind?

After the girl escaped from Sakigake, the Little People had probably used the same process to make more new *doh-tas*, their purpose being to widen and stabilize the passage-way by which they came and went, like adding new lanes to a highway. This was how the *dohtas* became Perceivers for the Little People and played the role of shrine maidens. Tsubasa had been one of them. If Leader had sexual relations not with the girls' actual *mazas* but with their other selves, their *doh-tas*, then Leader's expression – "ambiguous congress" – made sense. It also explained Tsubasa's flat, depthless eyes and her near inability to speak. Aomame had no idea how or why the *dohta*, Tsubasa, had escaped from the religious organization, but she had almost certainly been put into an air chrysalis and "retrieved" to be taken back to her *maza*. The bloody killing of the dog had been a warning from the Little People, like what was done to Toru in the story.

The *dohtas* wanted to become pregnant with Leader's child,

but, lacking substance themselves, they were not menstruating. Still, according to Leader, their desire to become pregnant was intense. Why should that have been?

Aomame shook her head. There was still much that she did not understand.

Aomame wished that she could tell this to the dowager as soon as possible – that the man might actually have raped nothing more than the girls' shadows; that they might not have had to kill him after all.

But even if she explained these things, it would not be easy for her to get the dowager to believe her. Aomame knew how the dowager would feel. The dowager – or any sane person – would have trouble accepting as fact this stuff about the Little People, *mazas, dohtas,* or air chrysalises. To sane people, these things would seem like nothing more than the kinds of fabrications that appear in fiction, no more real than the Queen of Hearts or the white rabbit with the watch in *Alice in Wonderland.*

But Aomame herself had *actually* seen two moons – the old one and the new one – hanging in the sky. She had actually been living under their light. She had felt their lopsided gravity in her skin. And with her own hands she had killed the man called Leader in a dark hotel room.

Aomame did not know what the Little People were hoping to accomplish by taking control of Sakigake. Perhaps they wanted things that transcended good and evil, but the young protagonist of *Air Chrysalis* intuitively recognized those things as *not right,* and she tried to strike back in her own way. Her vehicle was her story. Tengo became her partner to help get the story going. Tengo himself probably did not understand the meaning of what he was doing at that point, and he might not understand it even now.

In any case, the story called *Air Chrysalis* was the important key.

Everything started from this story.
But where do I fit into it?
From the moment I heard Janáček's Sinfonietta *and climbed down the escape stairs from the traffic jam on the Metropolitan Expressway, I was drawn into this world with two moons in the sky, into this enigma-filled world of 1Q84. What could it mean?*

She closed her eyes and continued to think.

I have probably been drawn into the passageway of the "force opposed to the Little People" created by Fuka-Eri and Tengo. That force carried me into this side. What other explanation could there be? And the role I am playing in this story is by no means small. I may even be one of the central characters.

Aomame looked at her surroundings. *In other words, I am in the story that Tengo set in motion. In a sense, I am inside him – inside his body,* she realized. *I am inside that shrine, so to speak.*

I saw an old science fiction movie on television long ago. It was the story of a small group of scientists who shrank their bodies down to microscopic size, boarded a submarine-like vehicle (which had also been shrunk down), and entered their patient's blood vessels, through which they gained entry to his brain in order to perform a complex operation that would have been impossible under ordinary circumstances. Maybe my situation is like that. I'm in Tengo's blood and circulating through his body. I battled the white blood cells that attacked the invading foreign body (me) as I headed for the root cause of the disease, and I must have succeeded in "deleting" that cause when I killed Leader at the Hotel Okura.

Aomame was able to warm herself somewhat with such thoughts. *I carried out my assigned mission. It was a difficult mission, that is for sure, and I was afraid, but I carried it off coolly and flawlessly in the midst of all that thunder – and perhaps with Tengo looking on.* She felt proud of what she had accomplished.

To continue with the blood analogy, I should soon be drawn into a vein, spent, having served my purpose. Before long, I will be expelled from the body. That is the rule by which the body's system works – an inescapable destiny. But so what? I am inside Tengo now, enveloped by his warmth, guided by his heartbeat, guided by his logic and his rules, and perhaps by the very language he is writing. How marvelous to be inside him like this!

Still sitting on the floor, Aomame closed her eyes. She pressed her nose against the pages of the book, inhaling its smells – the smell of the paper, the smell of the ink. She quietly gave herself up to its flow, listening hard for the sound of Tengo's heart.

This is the kingdom, she thought.

I am ready to die, anytime at all.

CHAPTER 20

Tengo

THE WALRUS AND THE MAD HATTER

No doubt about it: there were two moons.

One was the moon that had always been there, and the other was a far smaller, greenish moon, somewhat lopsided in shape, and much less bright. It looked like a poor, ugly, distantly related child that had been foisted on the family by unfortunate events and was welcomed by no one. But it was undeniably there, neither a phantom nor an optical illusion, hanging in space like other heavenly bodies, a solid mass with a clear-cut outline. Not a plane, not a blimp, not an artificial satellite, not a papier-mâché moon that someone made for fun. It was without a doubt a chunk of rock, having quietly, stubbornly settled on a position in the night sky, like a punctuation mark placed only after long deliberation or a mole bestowed by destiny.

Tengo stared at the new moon for a long time as if to challenge it, never averting his gaze, hardly even blinking. But no matter how long he kept his eyes locked on it, it refused to budge. It stayed hunkered down in its spot in the sky with silent, stonehearted tenacity.

Tengo unclenched his right fist and, almost unconsciously, gave his head a slight shake. *Damn, it's the same as in* Air

Chrysalis*! A world with two moons hanging in the sky side by side. When a* dohta *is born, a second moon appears.*

"That will be a sign. Watch the sky with great care," one of the Little People said to the girl.

Tengo was the one who wrote those words. Following Komatsu's advice, he had made his description of the new moon as concrete and detailed as possible. It was the part on which he had worked the hardest. The look of the new moon was almost entirely Tengo's creation.

Komatsu had said, "Think of it this way, Tengo. Your readers have seen the sky with one moon in it any number of times, right? But I doubt they've seen a sky with two moons in it side by side. When you introduce things that most readers have *never* seen before into a piece of fiction, you have to describe them with as much precise detail as possible."

It made a lot of sense.

Still looking up at the sky, Tengo shook his head again. The newly added moon was absolutely the same size and shape as the one for which he had invented a description. Even the figurative language that he had used fit this one almost perfectly.

This can't be, Tengo thought. *What kind of reality mimics fictional creations?* "No, this can't be," he actually said aloud. Or tried to. His voice barely worked. His throat was parched, as if he had just run a very long distance. *There's no way this can be. That's a fictional world, a world that does not exist in reality.* It was a world in a fantastic story that Fuka-Eri had told Azami night after night and that Tengo himself had fleshed out.

Could this mean, then – Tengo asked himself – *that this is the world of the novel? Could I have somehow left the real world and entered the world of* Air Chrysalis *like Alice falling down the rabbit hole? Or could the real world have been made over so as to match exactly the story of* Air Chrysalis*? Does this mean that the world that used to be – the familiar world with only one moon – no longer exists anywhere? And could the power of* *the Little People have something to do with this in one way or another?*

He looked around, hoping for answers, but all that appeared before his eyes was the perfectly ordinary urban residential neighborhood. He could find nothing about it that seemed odd or unusual – no Queen of Hearts, no walrus, no Mad Hatter. There was nothing in his surroundings but an empty sandbox and swings, a mercury-vapor lamp emitting its sterile light, the spreading branches of a zelkova tree, a locked public toilet, a new six-story condo (only four units of which had lighted windows), a ward notice board, a red vending machine with a Coca-Cola logo, an illegally parked old-model green Volkswagen Golf, telephone poles and electric lines, and primary-color neon signs in the distance. The usual city noise, the usual lights. Tengo had been living here in Koenji for seven years. Not because he particularly liked it, but because he had just happened to find a cheap apartment that was not too far from the station. It was convenient for commuting, and moving somewhere else would have been too much trouble, so he had stayed on. But he at least knew the neighborhood inside and out and would have noticed any change immediately.

How long had there been more than one moon? Tengo could not be sure. Perhaps there had been two moons for years now and he simply hadn't noticed. He had missed lots of things that way. He wasn't much of a newspaper reader, and he never watched television. There were countless things that everybody knew but him. Perhaps something had occurred just recently to increase the number of moons to two. He wanted to ask someone, "Excuse me, this is a strange question, but how long have there been two moons? I just thought you might know." But there was nobody there to ask – literally, not even a cat.

No, there *was* someone there. Nearby, someone was using a hammer to pound a nail into a wall. *Bang bang bang.* The sound kept up without a break, a very hard nail going into a very hard wall. Who could be pounding nails at a time like this? Puzzled, Tengo looked around, but he could see no wall, nor was there anyone pounding nails.

A moment later, Tengo realized that he was hearing the sound of his own heart. Spurred on by adrenaline, his heart was pumping surges of blood through his body. It pounded in his ears.

The sight of the two moons gave Tengo a slight dizzy feeling, as if it had put his nervous system out of balance. He sat down on top of the slide, leaning against the handrail, and closed his eyes, fighting the dizziness. He felt as if the force of gravity around him had subtly changed. Somewhere the tide was rising, and somewhere else the tide was receding. Their faces devoid of expression, people were moving back and forth between "insane" and "lunatic."

In his dizziness, it suddenly occurred to Tengo that the image of his mother wearing a white slip had not attacked him for a very long time. He had almost forgotten that he had been tormented by that illusion for years. When could he have last seen it? He could not recall exactly, but it was probably around the time he started writing his new novel. For some unfathomable reason, his mother's ghost had stopped haunting him from that point onward.

Instead, Tengo now sat on top of a slide in a playground in Koenji, looking at a pair of moons in the sky. An inscrutable new world silently surrounded him like lapping dark water. Perhaps a new trouble had chased out the old one. Perhaps the old, familiar riddle had been replaced by a fresh, new one. The thought came to Tengo without irony. Nor did he feel any need to complain about it. *Whatever the composition of this new world might be, I surely have no choice but to accept it in silence. There's no way to pick and choose. Even in the world that existed until now, there was no choice. It's the same thing. And besides,* he asked himself, *even if I wanted to lodge a complaint, who is there for me to complain to?*

The hard, dry sound of his heart continued, but the dizzy sensation was gradually subsiding. With his heart pounding in his ears, Tengo leaned his head against the handrail of the slide and looked at the two moons hanging in the Koenji sky. What a strange sight it was – a new world with a new moon. Everything was uncertain, and ultimately ambiguous. *But there is one thing I can declare with certainty,* Tengo thought: *No matter what happens to me in the future, this view with two moons hanging up there side by side will never – ever – seem ordinary and obvious to me.*

What kind of secret pact had Aomame concluded with the moon that time, Tengo wondered. And he recalled the deadly serious look in her eye as she stared at the moon in broad daylight. What could she have offered the moon?

And what is going to happen to me from now on?

At ten years old, as a frightened boy standing before the room's big door, Tengo had wondered this again and again while Aomame continued to grip his hand in the empty classroom. Even now Tengo continued to wonder that same thing. He felt the same anxiety, the same fear, the same trembling. The door now was new and bigger. The moon was hanging there again, but this time there were two moons, not one.

Where could Aomame be?

Tengo scanned the area again from his perch on the slide, but nowhere could he find what he was hoping to discover. He spread out his left hand and struggled to find some clue, but there was nothing in his palm besides its natural deeply carved lines. In the flat light of the mercury-vapor lamp they looked like the canals on the surface of Mars, but they told him absolutely nothing. The most he could glean from this big hand was the fact that he had come a very long way since the age of ten – all the way to the top of this slide in a little Koenji playground where two moons were hanging in the sky.

Where could Aomame be? Tengo asked himself again. *Where is she hiding?*

"She might be very close by," Fuka-Eri had said. "Within walking distance."

Supposedly somewhere close by, could Aomame also see the two moons?

Yes, I'm sure she can, Tengo thought. He had no proof, of course, but he had a mysterious conviction that it must be true. She could see what he could see, without a doubt. He balled his left hand into a tight fist and pounded on the surface of the slide hard enough to hurt.

That is why it has to happen: we have to run into each other somewhere within walking distance of this place. Someone is after Aomame, and she's hiding like a wounded cat. I don't have much time to find her. But where could she be? Tengo had no idea.

"Ho ho," called the keeper of the beat.

"Ho ho," the other six joined in.

CHAPTER 21

Aomame

WHAT SHOULD I DO?

That night, Aomame stepped out onto the balcony in her slippers and gray jersey workout clothes to look at the moons. She was holding a cup of cocoa. It was the first time in a very long time that she felt like drinking cocoa, but the sight of a can of Van Houten cocoa in a kitchen cabinet had suddenly inspired her. Two moons – a big one and a little one – hung in the perfectly clear southwestern sky. Instead of sighing, she produced a tiny moan. A *dohta* had been born from an air chrysalis, and now there were two moons. 1984 had changed to 1Q84. The old world had vanished, and she could never get back to it.

Sitting on the balcony's garden chair, taking little sips of the hot cocoa and looking at the two moons through narrowed eyes, Aomame tried to recall things from the old world. All she could bring back at the moment, however, was the potted rubber plant she had left in her apartment. Where could it be now? Was Tamaru looking after it as he had promised? *Of course. There's nothing to worry about,* Aomame told herself: *Tamaru is a man who keeps his word. He might kill you without hesitation if necessary, but even so, he would care for your rubber plant to the end.*

But why am I so concerned about that rubber plant?

Aomame had barely thought about the thing until the

day she left it behind in her apartment. It was nothing but a sad-looking rubber plant, its color pale and dull, its poor health obvious at a glance. It had carried an 1,800-yen price tag in a special sale, but the cashier had further dropped the price to 1,500 yen without being asked, and if Aomame had bargained it might have gotten cheaper still. It had obviously remained unsold for a long time, and all the way home she had regretted having bought it on impulse, not only because it was sad-looking, bulky, and hard to carry, but because it was a living thing.

That was the first time in her life that she had owned something alive. Whether a pet or a potted plant, she had never bought one or received one or found one. The rubber plant was her very first experience of living with a thing that had a life of its own. The moment she had seen the two little red goldfish in the living room and heard from the dowager that she had bought them for Tsubasa at a night stall in a street fair, Aomame had wanted to have her own fish – badly. She could hardly keep her eyes off them. Where had this desire come from all of a sudden? Perhaps she felt envious of Tsubasa. No one had ever bought Aomame anything at a street fair – or even taken her to one. Ardent members of the Society of Witnesses, faithful in every way to the teachings of the Bible, her parents had disdained and avoided all the secular world's festivals.

And so Aomame had made up her mind to go to a discount store near the station in her Jiyugaoka neighborhood and buy a goldfish. If no one was going to buy her a goldfish and bowl, then she would do it herself. *What's wrong with that?* she had thought. *I'm a grown-up, I'm thirty years old, and I live in my own apartment. I've got bricks of money piled up in my safe-deposit box. I don't have to ask anyone's permission to buy myself a damned goldfish.*

But when she went to the pet department and saw actual goldfish swimming in the tank, their lacy fins waving,

Aomame felt incapable of buying one. She could not help but feel that paying money to take ownership of a living organism was inappropriate. It made her think, too, of her own young self. The goldfish was powerless, trapped in a small glass bowl, unable to go anywhere. This fact did not appear to bother the goldfish itself. It probably had nowhere it wanted to go. But to Aomame this was a matter of genuine concern.

She had felt none of this when she saw the two goldfish in the dowager's living room. They had appeared to be enjoying themselves swimming in their glass bowl so elegantly, the summer light rippling through the water. Living with goldfish seemed like a wonderful thought. It should add a certain richness to her own life. But the sight of the goldfish in the pet department of the discount store by the station only made Aomame feel short of breath. *No, it's out of the question. I can't possibly keep a goldfish.*

What caught her eye at that point was the rubber plant, over in a corner of the store. It seemed to have been shoved into the least noticeable spot in the place, hiding like an abandoned orphan. Or at least it appeared so to Aomame. It was lacking in color and sheen, and its shape was out of kilter, but with hardly a thought in her head, she bought it – not because she liked it but because she *had to* buy it. And in fact, even after she brought it home and set it down, she hardly looked at it except on those rare occasions when she watered it.

Once she had left it behind, however, and realized that she would never see it again, Aomame couldn't stop herself from worrying about the plant. She frowned hugely, the way she often did when she wanted to scream out loud in confusion, stretching every muscle in her face until she looked like a completely different person. When she had finished distorting her face into every possible angle, Aomame finally returned it to normal.

Why am I so concerned about that rubber plant?

* * *

In any case, I know for sure that Tamaru will treat the plant well. He is used to loving and caring for living things. Unlike me. He treats his dogs like second selves. He even uses his spare time to go through the dowager's garden, inspecting her plants in great detail. When he was in the orphanage, he risked his own life to protect a younger boy with impaired abilities. I could never do anything like that, Aomame thought. *I can't afford to take responsibilities for others' lives. It's all I can do to bear the weight of my own life and my own loneliness.*

"Loneliness" reminded Aomame of Ayumi.

Some man had handcuffed her to a bed in a love hotel, violently raped her, and strangled her to death with a bathrobe sash. As far as Aomame knew, the perpetrator had not been taken into custody. *Ayumi had a family and colleagues, but she was lonely – so lonely that she had to experience such a horrible death. Still, I wasn't there for her. She wanted something from me, that was certain. But I had my own secrets – and my own loneliness – that had to be protected. I could never share them with Ayumi. Why did she choose me, of all people, when there are so many others in this world?*

Aomame closed her eyes and pictured the potted rubber plant that she had left in her empty apartment.

Why am I so concerned about that rubber plant?

Aomame spent the next several minutes crying. *What's wrong with me?* she wondered, shaking her head. *I'm crying too much these days.* Crying was the last thing she wanted to do. But she couldn't stop the tears. Her shoulders trembled. *I've got nothing left. Anything of value I ever possessed has disappeared, one thing after another. Everything is gone – except for the warmth of my memory of Tengo.*

I've got to stop this crying, Aomame told herself. *Here I am, inside of Tengo, like the scientists in* Fantastic Voyage. *Yes, that's it! The movie's title was* Fantastic Voyage. Satisfied that she had recalled the title, Aomame calmed down and stopped crying. *No matter how many tears I shed, it's not going to solve anything. I've got to go back to being the cool, tough Aomame.*

Who wants that to happen?

I want that to happen.

She looked at her surroundings. There were still two moons in the sky.

"That will be a sign. Watch the sky with great care," one of the Little People, the small-voiced one, had said.

"Ho ho," said the keeper of the beat.

Just then Aomame noticed something: she was not the only person looking up at the moons. She could see a young man in the playground across the street. He was sitting on top of the slide and looking in the same direction that she was. *He is seeing two moons, just like me,* she knew intuitively. *No mistake, he is looking at what I am looking at. He can tell: there are two moons in this world. But Leader had said that not everyone living in this world could see both moons.*

There was no room for doubt: this large young man was looking at a pair of moons in the sky. *I'd bet anything on that. I can tell. He's sitting there, looking at the big, yellow moon and the small, lopsided, greenish mossy-colored moon. He appears to be thinking hard about their meaning. Could he too have drifted into 1Q84? Maybe he is confused, unable to grasp the meaning of this new world. Yes, that must be it. That must be why he had to climb to the top of the slide in this playground at night, staring at the moons all alone, mentally listing all the possibilities, all the hypotheses he could think of, and examining them in detail.*

But no, that might not be it at all. He could be working for Sakigake. He could be here looking for me.

The thought set Aomame's heart racing. Her right hand unconsciously reached for the automatic pistol in her waistband, tightening on its hard grip.

It was impossible, though, to find any sense of tension or urgency in the man on the slide, and there was nothing about him that suggested violence. He was just sitting up there alone, his head against the handrail, looking straight up at the moons in the sky, absorbed in his own thoughts. Aomame was on her third-story balcony, and he was down below. She sat in the garden chair, looking down at the man through the gap between the balcony's opaque plastic screen and the metal railing. Even if he were to look up toward Aomame, he would probably not be able to see her, but in any case the man appeared to be completely engrossed, staring at the sky without the slightest sense that someone might be staring at him.

Aomame calmed herself down and quietly released the breath that she was holding in. She relaxed the tension in her fingers and took her hand from the pistol. Maintaining her position, she continued to observe the man. From her vantage point, she could only see his profile. The playground's mercury-vapor lamp cast its bright light on him from above. He was a tall man with broad shoulders. He had a stiff-looking head of hair, cut short, and he wore a long-sleeved T-shirt, its sleeves rolled up to his elbows. Not exactly handsome, but he had good, solid features, and the shape of his head was not bad. If he were a little older and his hair thinning, he would be quite nice-looking.

Then Aomame suddenly knew:

It was Tengo.

No, she thought, *that couldn't possibly be.* She gave her head several short, sharp shakes. *No way. I must be wrong. Things don't work out like that.* She found it impossible to breathe normally. Her body wasn't working right. Thought and action refused to sync. *I've got to take another good look at him,* she thought, but for some reason she couldn't get her eyes to focus. Something seemed to be causing the vision of her right and left eyes to become hugely different, all of a sudden. She unconsciously twisted her features out of shape.

What should I do?

She got out of her garden chair and looked around help-lessly. Then she recalled that there had been a small pair of Nikon binoculars in the sideboard, and she went in to get them. She hurried back to the balcony holding the binoculars and looked at the slide. The young man was still there. In the same position, in profile, looking at the sky. With trembling fingers, she focused the binoculars and looked at his profile close-up, holding her breath, concentrating. No doubt about it: it was Tengo. Twenty years might have gone by, but she knew for sure: it could not be anyone but Tengo.

What most surprised Aomame was that Tengo's appearance had hardly changed from the time he was ten, as if the ten-year-old boy had aged directly into a thirty-year-old man. This was not to say that he looked childish. His body and his head were, of course, far bigger than they used to be, and his features were now those of an adult. His facial expression had a new depth to it. The hands resting on his knees were big and strong, very different from the hand she had grasped in that elementary school classroom twenty years earlier. Even so, the aura projected by his physical presence was the same. His solid, massive body gave her a deep, natural sense of warmth and security. She felt a strong desire to press her cheek against his chest, and that filled her with joy. He was sitting on a play-ground slide, looking at the sky, staring hard at exactly the same things that she was looking at – the two moons. *Yes, it is possible for us to see the same things.*

What should I do?

Aomame had no idea what to do next. She set the binoculars in her lap and clenched her fists – tightly enough for her nails to leave marks in her skin. Her clenched fists were trembling slightly.

What should I do?

She listened to her labored breathing. Before she knew it, her body seemed to have split down the middle. One half was willing to accept the fact that Tengo was right there in front of her. The other half refused to accept it, trying to convince itself that this was not happening. Inside her, these two forces clashed, each trying to drag her in its own direction. It was as if every bit of her flesh was being shredded, her joints torn apart, her bones smashed.

Aomame wanted to run straight to the playground, climb the slide, and speak to Tengo there. But what should she say? She didn't know how to move the muscles of her mouth. Could she manage to squeeze out a few words? "My name is Aomame. I held your hand in an elementary school classroom in Ichikawa twenty years ago. Do you remember me?"

Is that what she should say?

There should be something a little better.

The other Aomame gave her an order: "Stay hidden on this balcony. There's nothing more you can do. You know that. You struck a bargain with Leader last night: you would save Tengo and help him to go on living in this world by throwing away your own life. That was the gist of your bargain. The contract has been concluded. You have sent Leader to the other world and agreed to offer your own life. What good would it do you now to see Tengo and talk about the past? And what would you do if he didn't remember you or if he knew you only as 'that strange girl who used to say the creepy prayers'? Then how would you feel as you went to your death?"

The thought made her go stiff all over. She began to shiver uncontrollably, as if she had caught a bad cold and might freeze to the core. She hugged herself for a time, shivering, but never once did she take her eyes off Tengo sitting on top of the slide and looking at the sky. He might disappear somewhere the moment she looked away from him.

She wanted Tengo to hold her in his arms, to caress her with his big hands. She wanted her whole body to feel his warmth, to have him stroke her from head to toe and warm her up. *I want him to take away this chill I feel in my body's core. Then I want him to come inside me and stir me with all his might, like a spoon in a cup of cocoa, slowly, to the very bottom. If he would do that for me, I wouldn't mind dying right then and there. Really.*

No, can that really be true? Aomame thought. *If that really happened, I might not want to die anymore. I might want to stay with him forever and ever. My resolve to die might simply evaporate, like a drop of dew in the morning sun. Or then again, I might feel like killing him, shooting him first with the Heckler & Koch, and then blowing my own brains out. I can't begin to predict what would happen or what I would be capable of.*

What should I do?

Aomame could not decide. Her breathing became harsh. A jumble of thoughts came to her, one after another, tangled thoughts defying all her attempts to impose order upon them. What was right? What was wrong? She knew only one thing for sure: she wanted those thick arms of his to be holding her right now. What happened after that would happen: let God or the devil decide.

Aomame made up her mind. She went to the bathroom and wiped away the traces of her tears. She looked in the mirror and swiftly straightened her hair. Her face was an absolute mess. Her eyes were bloodshot. Her outfit was terrible – faded jersey workout clothes with a weird bulge in back where she had a 9mm automatic pistol shoved into her waistband. This was no way to present herself to the man for whom she'd been burning with desire for twenty years. Why wasn't she wearing something a little more decent? But it was too late. She had no time to be changing clothes. She slipped on a pair of sneakers and ran down three floors on the condo building's emergency stairway, crossed the street, entered the empty playground, and walked to the slide, where there was no sign of Tengo. Bathed in the artificial light of the mercury-vapor lamp, the top of the slide was deserted – darker, colder, and emptier than the far side of the moon.

Could it have been a hallucination?

No, it was no hallucination, Aomame told herself, out of breath. *Tengo was there until a moment ago, without a doubt.* She climbed to the top of the slide and stood there, looking all around. *No sign of anybody. But he could not have gone very far. He was here until a very few minutes ago – four or five minutes at the most. If I run, I should be able to catch up with him.*

But Aomame changed her mind. She stopped herself almost by force. *No, I can't do that. I don't even know which way he walked from here. I don't want to be running aimlessly around the streets of Koenji at night. That is not something I should be doing.* While Aomame had hesitated on the balcony, wondering what she should do, Tengo had climbed down from the slide and left. *Come to think of it, this is the fate I have been handed. I hesitated and hesitated and momentarily lost my powers of judgment, and in that time Tengo went away. That is what happened to me.*

It's just as well this way, Aomame told herself. *It's probably the best thing that could have happened. At least I succeeded in finding Tengo. I saw him just across the street. I trembled with the possibility of having his arms around me. If only for a few moments, I was able to taste that intense joy and anticipation.* She closed her eyes and grasped the slide handrail, biting her lip.

Aomame sat down on top of the slide in the same posture that Tengo had adopted. She looked up at the southwestern sky, where the two moons, large and small, hung side by side. Until only moments ago, she had been watching Tengo from the balcony of her apartment, where her deep hesitation seemed to be lingering still.

1Q84: that is the name given to this world. I entered it six months ago without meaning to, and now I am about to leave it quite deliberately. Tengo will stay here after I am gone. I have no idea, of course, what kind of world it will be for Tengo. There is no way I can see it through to the end. But so what? I am going to die for him. I was unable to live for myself: that possibility had already been stripped from me. Instead, I will be able to die for him. That is enough. I can die smiling.

This is no lie.

Aomame struggled to feel whatever hint of Tengo's presence might be left at the top of the slide, but no warmth of any kind remained there. The night wind, with its presentiment of autumn, cut through the leaves of the zelkova tree, removing all traces of Tengo. Even so, Aomame went on sitting there, looking up at the moons, bathed in their odd, emotionless light. The city sounds blended together into one urban noise surrounding her with its basso continuo. She thought of the little spiders that had spun their webs on the emergency stairway of the Metropolitan Expressway. Were those spiders still alive and maintaining their webs?

She smiled.

I'm ready, she thought. *I've made my preparations.*

But there was one place she would have to visit first.

CHAPTER 22

Tengo

AS LONG AS THERE ARE
TWO MOONS IN THE SKY

After climbing down from the slide and leaving the playground, Tengo wandered aimlessly through the streets of
Koenji, from one block to the next, hardly conscious of where
his feet were taking him. He tried to organize the jumble of
ideas in his head, but unified thinking was beyond him now,
probably because he had thought about too many different
things at once while sitting on the slide: about the increase in
the number of moons, about blood ties, about a new chapter in his life, about his dizzyingly realistic daydream, about
Fuka-Eri and *Air Chrysalis,* and about Aomame, who was
probably in hiding somewhere nearby. With his head a confused tangle of thoughts, Tengo felt his powers of concentration being tested to the limit. He wished he could just go to
bed and be fast asleep. He could continue this process in the
morning. No amount of additional thinking would bring him
any clarity now.

Back at his apartment, he found Fuka-Eri sitting at his desk,
intently sharpening pencils with a small pocketknife. Tengo
always kept ten pencils in his pencil holder, but now there
were at least twenty. She had done a beautiful job of sharpening them. Tengo had never seen such beautifully sharpened
pencils. Their points were like needles.

"You had a phone call," she said, checking the sharpness of the current pencil with her finger. "From Chikura."

"You weren't supposed to be answering the phone."

"It was an important call."

She had probably been able to tell it was important from the ring.

"What was it about?" Tengo asked.

"They didn't say."

"But it was from the sanatorium in Chikura, right?"

"They want a call."

"They want me to call them?"

"Today. Even if it's late."

Tengo sighed. "You don't know the number, I suppose."

"I do."

She had memorized the number. Tengo wrote it down. Then he looked at the clock. Eight thirty.

"What time did they call?" he asked.

"A little while ago."

Tengo went to the kitchen and drank a glass of water. Resting his hands on the edge of the sink, he closed his eyes and confirmed that his brain was functioning normally. Then he went to the phone and dialed the number. Perhaps his father had died. Or at least it was a life-and-death issue of some sort. They would not have called this late if it were not about something important.

A woman answered the phone. Tengo gave his name and said he was calling in response to an earlier message.

"Mr. Kawana's son?" the woman asked.

"Yes," Tengo said.

"We met here the other day," she said.

Tengo pictured the middle-aged nurse with metal-framed glasses. He could not recall her name.

He uttered a few polite words, adding, "I gather you called earlier?"

"Yes, I did. I'll connect you with the doctor in charge so you can talk to him directly."

With the receiver pressed against his ear, Tengo waited – and waited – for the doctor to pick up. "Home on the Range" seemed as if it would go on playing forever. Tengo closed his eyes and pictured the sanatorium on the Boso Peninsula shore. The thickly overlapping pine trees, the sea breeze blowing through them, the Pacific Ocean waves breaking endlessly on the beach. The hushed entryway lobby without visitors. The sound of movable beds being wheeled down the corridors. The sun-damaged curtains. The well-pressed white uniforms of the nurses. The thin, flat coffee in the lunchroom.

Finally, the doctor picked up the phone.

"Sorry to keep you waiting. I got an emergency call from one of the other sickrooms a few minutes ago."

"That's fine," Tengo said. He tried to recall what his father's doctor looked like, until it occurred to him that he had never met the man. His brain was still not functioning properly. "So, is something wrong with my father?"

The doctor paused a moment and then said, "Well, it's not that something in particular happened today, just that his condition has not been good lately. I hate to tell you this, but he is in a coma."

"You mean, he's completely unconscious?"

"Exactly."

Tengo struggled to make his brain work. "Did he come down with something that made him go into a coma?"

"Properly speaking, no," the doctor said with apparent difficulty.

Tengo waited.

"It's difficult to explain on the phone, but there is not one particular thing wrong with him. He does not have cancer or pneumonia or any other illness that we can name. Medically speaking, we can't see any distinguishing symptoms. We don't know what the cause might be, but in your father's case, it appears that his natural life-sustaining force is visibly weakening. And since we don't know the cause, we don't know what treatment to apply. We are continuing to feed him intravenously, but this is strictly treating the symptoms."

"Is it all right for me to ask you a very direct question?" Tengo asked.

"Yes, of course," the doctor said.

"Are you saying that my father is not going to last much longer?"

"That might be a strong possibility if he stays in his current condition."

"So he's more or less wasting away of old age?"

The doctor made a vague sound into the phone. Then he said, "Your father is still in his sixties, not yet ready to 'waste away of old age.' He is basically healthy. We haven't found anything wrong with him other than his impaired cognitive abilities. He gets rather good scores on the periodic strength tests we perform. We are not aware of a single problem he might have."

The doctor stopped talking at that point. Then he went on:

"But . . . come to think of it . . . observing him these past few days, there may be some degree of what you call 'wasting away of old age.' His physical functions overall have declined, and he seems to be losing the will to live. Normally, these symptoms don't emerge until the patient passes his mid-eighties. When a person gets that old, we often see him grow tired of living and abandon the effort to maintain life. But I have no idea why that should be happening to a man in his sixties like Mr. Kawana."

Tengo bit his lip and gave this some thought.

"When did the coma start?" Tengo asked.

"Three days ago," the doctor said.

"You mean he hasn't awakened for three days?"

"Not once."

"And his vital signs are gradually weakening?"

The doctor said, "Not drastically, but as I just said, the level of his life-sustaining force is gradually – but visibly – going down, like a train dropping its speed little by little as it begins to stop."

"How much time do you think he has left?"

"I can't say for sure. If his present condition continues as is, he might have another week in the worst case," the doctor said.

Tengo changed his grip on the receiver and bit his lip again.

"I'll be there tomorrow," Tengo said. "Even if you hadn't called, I was thinking of going there soon. But I'm glad you called. I'm very grateful to you."

The doctor seemed relieved to hear this. "Please do come. The sooner you see him the better, I think. He may not be able to talk to you, but I'm sure your father will be glad you're here."

"He is completely unconscious, though, isn't he?"

"Yes. He is not conscious."

"Do you think he is in pain?"

"For now, no, probably not. That is the one silver lining in all this. He is sound asleep."

"Thank you very much," Tengo said.

"You know, Mr. Kawana," the doctor said, "your father was a very easy patient to take care of. He never gave anyone any trouble."

"He's always been like that," Tengo said. Then, thanking the doctor once again, he ended the call.

Tengo warmed his coffee and drank it at the kitchen table, sitting across from Fuka-Eri.

"You'll be leaving tomorrow," Fuka-Eri asked.

Tengo nodded. "Tomorrow morning I have to take the train and go to the cat town again."

"You're going to the cat town," Fuka-Eri asked without expression.

"You will be waiting here," Tengo asked. Living with Fuka-Eri, he had become used to asking questions without question marks.

"I will be waiting here."

"I'll go to the cat town alone," Tengo said. He took a sip of coffee. Then it suddenly occurred to him to ask her, "Do you want something to drink?"

"White wine if you have some."

Tengo opened the refrigerator to see if he had any chilled white wine. In back he found a bottle of Chardonnay he had recently bought on sale. The label had a picture of a wild boar. He pulled the cork, poured some into a wineglass, and placed it before Fuka-Eri. After some hesitation, he poured himself a glass as well. He was definitely more in the mood for wine than coffee. It was a bit too chilled, and a bit too sweet, but the alcohol calmed Tengo's nerves somewhat.

"You'll be going to the cat town tomorrow," Fuka-Eri asked again.

"I'll take a train first thing in the morning," Tengo said.

Tipping back his glass of white wine, Tengo recalled that he had ejaculated into the body of the beautiful seventeen-year-old girl now sitting across the table from him. It had happened only the night before, but it seemed like something that had occurred in the distant past – almost a historical event. Still, the sensation of it remained as vivid as ever inside him.

"The number of moons increased," Tengo said, as if sharing a secret, slowly turning the wineglass in his hand. "When I looked at the sky a little while ago, there were two moons – a big, yellow one and a small, green one. They might have been there from before, but I never noticed them. I finally realized it just a little while ago."

Fuka-Eri had nothing to say regarding the fact that the number of moons had increased, nor could Tengo discern any sense of surprise at the news. Her expression had not changed at all. She did not even give her usual little shrug. It did not appear to *be* news to her.

"I don't have to tell you that having two moons in the sky is the same as the world of *Air Chrysalis*," Tengo said. "And the new moon looks exactly as I described it – the same size and color."

Fuka-Eri had nothing to say. She never answered questions that needed no answers.

"Why do you think such a thing has happened? How *could* such a thing have happened?"

Still no answer.

Tengo decided to ask her directly, "Could this mean that we have entered into the world depicted in *Air Chrysalis*?"

Fuka-Eri spent several moments carefully examining the shapes of her fingernails. Then she said, "Because we wrote the book together."

Tengo set his wineglass on the table. Then he asked Fuka-Eri, "We wrote *Air Chrysalis* and published it. It was a joint effort. Then the book became a bestseller, and information regarding the Little People and *mazas* and *dohtas* was revealed to the world. As a result of that, you and I together entered into this newly altered world. Is that what it means?"

"You are acting as a Receiver."

"I'm acting as a Receiver," Tengo said, echoing her words. "True, I wrote about Receivers in *Air Chrysalis,* but I didn't understand any of that. What does a Receiver do, specifically?"

Fuka-Eri gave her head a little shake, meaning she could not explain it.

"If you can't understand it without an explanation, you can't understand it with an explanation," Tengo's father had said.

"We had better stay together," Fuka-Eri said, "until you find her."

Tengo looked at Fuka-Eri for a time, trying to read her expression, but as always, there was no expression on her face to read. Unconsciously, he turned aside to look out the window, but there were no moons to be seen, only an ugly, twisted mass of electric lines.

"Does it take some special talent to act as a Receiver?"

Fuka-Eri moved her chin slightly up and down, meaning that some talent was required.

"But *Air Chrysalis* was originally *your* story, a story *you* wrote from scratch. It came from inside of *you*. All I did was take on the job of fixing the style. I was just a technician."

"Because we wrote the book together," Fuka-Eri said as before.

Tengo unconsciously brought his fingertips to his temple. "Are you saying I was acting as a Receiver from then on without even knowing it?"

"From before that," Fuka-Eri said. She pointed her right index finger at herself and then at Tengo. "I'm a Perceiver, and you're a Receiver."

"In other words, you 'perceive' things and I 'receive' them?"

Fuka-Eri gave a short nod.

Tengo frowned slightly. "So you knew that I was a Receiver or had a Receiver's special talent, and that's why you let me rewrite *Air Chrysalis*. Through me, you turned what you had perceived into a book. Is that it?"

No answer.

Tengo undid his frown. Then, looking into Fuka-Eri's eyes, he said, "I still can't pinpoint the exact moment, but I'm guessing that around that time, I had already entered this world with two moons. I've just overlooked that fact until now. I never had occasion to look up at the night sky, so I never noticed that the number of moons had increased. That's it, isn't it?"

Fuka-Eri kept silent. Her silence floated up and hung in the air like fine dust. This was dust that had been scattered there only moments before by a swarm of moths from a special space. For a while, Tengo looked at the shapes the dust had made in the air. He felt he had become a two-day-old evening paper. New information was coming out day after day, but he was the only one who knew none of it.

"Cause and effect seem to be all mixed up," Tengo said, recovering his presence of mind. "I don't know which came before and which came after. In any case, though, we are now inside this new world."

Fuka-Eri raised her face and peered into Tengo's eyes. He might have been imagining it, but he thought he caught a hint of an affectionate gleam in her eyes.

"In any case, the original world no longer exists," Tengo said.

Fuka-Eri gave a little shrug. "We will go on living here."

"In the world with two moons?"

Fuka-Eri did not reply to this. The beautiful seventeen-year-old girl tensed her lips into a perfectly straight line and looked directly into Tengo's eyes – exactly the way Aomame had looked into the ten-year-old Tengo's eyes in the empty classroom, with strong, deep mental concentration. Under Fuka-Eri's intense gaze, Tengo felt he might turn into stone, transforming into the new moon – the lopsided little moon. A moment later, Fuka-Eri finally relaxed her gaze. She raised her right hand and pressed her fingertips to her temple as if she were trying to read her own secret thoughts.

"You were looking for someone," the girl asked.

"Yes."

"But you didn't find her."

"No, I didn't find her," Tengo said.

He had not found Aomame, but instead he had discovered the two moons. This was because he had followed Fuka-Eri's suggestion to dig deep into his memory, as a result of which he had thought to look at the moon.

The girl softened her gaze somewhat and picked up her wineglass. She held a mouthful of wine for a while and then swallowed it carefully, like an insect sipping dew.

Tengo said, "You say she's hiding somewhere. If that's the case, it won't be easy to find her."

"You don't have to worry," the girl said.

"I don't have to worry," Tengo echoed her words.

Fuka-Eri nodded deeply.

"You mean, I'm going to find her?"

"She is going to find you," Fuka-Eri said in a voice like a breeze passing over a field of soft grass.

"Here, in Koenji?"

Fuka-Eri inclined her head to one side, meaning she did not know. "Somewhere," she said.

"Somewhere *in this world*," Tengo said.

Fuka-Eri gave him a little nod. "As long as there are two moons in the sky."

Tengo thought about this for a moment and said with some resignation, "I guess I have no choice but to believe you."

"I perceive and you receive," Fuka-Eri said thoughtfully.

"You perceive and I receive," Tengo said.

Fuka-Eri nodded.

And is that why we joined our bodies? Tengo wanted to ask Fuka-Eri. *In that wild storm last night. What did that mean?* But he did not ask those questions, which might have been inappropriate, and which he knew she never would have answered.

If you can't understand it without an explanation, you can't understand it with an explanation, Tengo's father said somewhere.

"You perceive and I receive," Tengo repeated once again. "The same as when I rewrote *Air Chrysalis*."

Fuka-Eri shook her head. Then she pushed her hair back, revealing one beautiful, little ear as though raising a transmitter's antenna.

"It is not the same," Fuka-Eri said. "You changed."

"I changed," Tengo repeated.

Fuka-Eri nodded.

"How have I changed?"

Fuka-Eri stared for a long time into the wineglass she was holding, as if she could see something important inside.

"You will find out when you go to the cat town," the beautiful girl said. Then, with her ear still showing, she took a sip of white wine.

CHAPTER 23

Aomame

PUT A TIGER IN YOUR TANK

Aomame woke at just after six o'clock in the morning. It was a clear, beautiful day. She made herself a pot of coffee, toasted some bread, and boiled an egg. While eating breakfast, she checked the television news to confirm that there was still no report of the Sakigake Leader's death. They had obviously disposed of the body in secret without filing a report with the police or letting anyone else know. No problem with that. A dead person was still a dead person no matter how you got rid of him.

At eight o'clock she showered, gave her hair a thorough brushing at the mirror, and applied a barely perceptible touch of lipstick. She put on stockings. Then she put on the white silk blouse she had hanging in the closet and completed her outfit with her stylish Junko Shimada suit. While shaking and twisting her body a few times to help her padded underwire bra conform more comfortably to her shape, she found herself again wishing that her breasts could have been somewhat bigger. She must have had that same thought at least 72,000 times while looking in the mirror. *But so what? I can think what I want as many times as I want. This could be the 72,001st time, but what's wrong with that? As long as I'm alive, I can think what I want, when I want, any way I want, as much as I want, and nobody can tell me any different.* She put on her Charles Jourdan high heels.

She stood at the full-length mirror by the front door and checked to see that her outfit was flawless. She raised one shoulder slightly and considered the possibility that she might look something like Faye Dunaway in *The Thomas Crown Affair.* Faye Dunaway played a coolheaded insurance investigator in that movie – a woman like a cold knife: sexy, great-looking in a business suit. Of course Aomame didn't look like Faye Dunaway, but the atmosphere she projected was somewhat close – or at least not entirely different. It was that special atmosphere that only a first-class professional could exude. In addition, her shoulder bag contained a cold, hard automatic pistol.

Putting on her slim Ray-Ban sunglasses, she left the apartment. She crossed the street to the playground, walked up to the slide where Tengo had been sitting, and replayed last night's scene in her head. It had happened twelve hours earlier. The actual Tengo had been right there – *just across the street from me. He sat there for a long time, alone, looking up at the moons* – the same two moons that she had been looking at.

It felt almost like a miracle to Aomame – a kind of revelation – that she had come so close to Tengo. *Something* had brought her into his presence. And the event, it seemed, had largely restructured her physical being. From the moment she woke up in the morning, she had continued to feel a sort of friction throughout her entire body. *He appeared before me and departed. We were not able to speak to or touch each other. But in that short interval, he transformed many things inside me. He literally stirred my mind and body the way a spoon stirs a cup of cocoa, down to the depths of my internal organs and my womb.*

She stood there for a full five minutes, one hand on a step of the slide, frowning slightly, jabbing at the ground with the sharp heel of her shoe. She was checking the degree to which she had been stirred both physically and mentally, and savoring the sensation. Finally, she made up her mind, walked out of the playground to the nearest big street, and caught a cab.

"I want you to go out to Yohga first, then take the Metropolitan Expressway Number 3 inbound until just before the Ikejiri exit," she announced to the driver, who was understandably confused by these instructions.

"So, miss, can you tell me exactly what your final destination is?" he asked, his tone rather on the easygoing side.

"The Ikejiri exit. For now."

"Well, then, it would be *much* closer to go straight to Ikejiri from here. Going all the way out to Yohga would be a huge detour. And at this time of the morning, the inbound lanes of Number 3 are going to be completely jammed. They'll hardly be moving. I'm as sure of that as I am that today is Wednesday."

"I don't care if the expressway is jammed. I don't care if today is Thursday or Friday or the Emperor's Birthday. I want you to get on the Metropolitan Expressway from Yohga. I've got all the time in the world."

The driver was a man in his early thirties. He was slim, with a long, pale face, and looked like a timid grazing animal. His chin stuck out like those of the stone faces on Easter Island. He was looking at Aomame in his rearview mirror, trying to decide from her expression whether his current passenger was totally bonkers or just an ordinary human being in a complicated situation. It was not easy for him to tell, though, especially from the image in the small mirror.

Aomame took her wallet out of her shoulder bag and thrust a brand-new ten-thousand-yen bill toward his face. The money looked as if it had just been printed.

"No change needed, and no receipt," Aomame said curtly.

"So keep your opinions to yourself and do what you're told. Go first to Yohga, get on the expressway, and go to Ikejiri. This should cover the fare even if we get caught in traffic."

"It's more than enough, of course," the driver said, though he still seemed dubious. "Do you have some special business on the expressway?"

Aomame shook the bill at him like a pennant in the wind. "If you don't want to take me, I'll get out and find another cab. So make up your mind, please. *Now.*"

The driver stared at the ten-thousand-yen bill for a good ten seconds with his brows knit. Then he made up his mind and took the money. After holding the bill up to the light to check its authenticity, he shoved it into his business bag.

"All right, then, let's go, Metropolitan Expressway Number 3. It's going to be badly backed up, though, I'm telling you, miss. And there's no exit between Yohga and Ikejiri. No toilet, either. So if there's any chance you might need to go, better take care of it now."

"Don't worry, just take me straight there."

The driver made his way out of the network of residential streets to Ring Road Number 8 and joined the thick traffic heading for Yohga. Neither he nor Aomame said a word. He listened to the news, and she was lost in thought. As they neared the entrance to the Metropolitan Expressway, the driver lowered the radio's volume and asked Aomame a question.

"This may be none of my business, miss, but are you in some special line of work?"

"I'm an insurance investigator," Aomame said without hesitation.

"An insurance investigator," the driver repeated her words carefully, as if tasting a new food.

"I find evidence in cases of insurance fraud," Aomame said.

"Wow," the driver said, obviously impressed. "Does

Metropolitan Expressway Number 3 have something to do with this insurance fraud stuff?"

"It does indeed."

"Just like that movie, isn't it?"

"What movie?"

"It's a really old one, with Steve McQueen. I don't remember what it's called."

"*The Thomas Crown Affair*," Aomame said.

"Yeah, that's it. Faye Dunaway plays an insurance investigator. She's a specialist in theft insurance. McQueen is this rich guy who commits crimes for fun. That was a great movie. I saw it when I was in high school. I really liked the music. It was very cool."

"Michel Legrand."

The driver hummed the first few bars of the theme song. Then he looked in the mirror for another close look at Aomame.

"Come to think of it, miss, something about you reminds me of Faye Dunaway."

"Thank you," Aomame said, struggling somewhat to hide the smile that formed around her lips.

The inbound side of Metropolitan Expressway Number 3 was, as the driver had predicted, beautifully backed up. The slowdown started less than a hundred yards from the entrance, an almost perfect specimen of chaos, which was exactly what Aomame wanted. The same outfit, the same road, the same traffic jam. Unfortunately, Janáček's *Sinfonietta* was not playing on the car radio, and the sound quality didn't measure up to that of the stereo in the Toyota Crown Royal Saloon, but that would have been asking for too much.

The cab inched ahead, hemmed in by trucks. It would stay in one place for a long time and then unpredictably creep ahead. The young driver of the refrigerated truck in the next lane was absorbed in his *manga* magazine during the long stops. The middle-aged couple in a cream Toyota Corona Mark II sat looking straight ahead, frowning, but never saying a word to each other. They probably had nothing to talk about, or maybe they *had* talked and now they were silent as a result. Aomame settled deeply into her seat. The taxi driver listened to the broadcast on his radio.

The cab finally passed a sign for Komazawa as it continued to crawl along toward Sangenjaya at a snail's pace. Aomame looked up now and then to stare out the window. *I won't be seeing this neighborhood anymore. I'm going somewhere far away.* But she was not about to start feeling nostalgic for the streets of Tokyo. All the buildings along the expressway were ugly, stained with the soot of automobile exhaust, and they carried garish billboards. The sight weighed on her heart. *Why do people have to build such depressing places? I'm not saying that every nook and cranny of the world has to be beautiful, but does it have to be this ugly?*

Finally, after some time, a familiar area entered Aomame's field of vision – the place where she had stepped out of the cab. The middle-aged driver had told her, as if hinting at some deeper significance, that there was an emergency stairway at the side of the roadway. Just ahead was the large billboard advertising Esso gasoline. A smiling tiger held up a gas hose. It was the same billboard as before.

"Put a tiger in your tank."

Aomame suddenly noticed that her throat was dry. She coughed once, thrust her hand into her shoulder bag, and took out a box of lemon-flavored cough drops. After putting a drop in her mouth, she returned the box to the bag. While her hand was in there, she gave the handle of the Heckler & Koch a strong squeeze, reassured by its weight and hardness. *Good,* she thought. The cab moved ahead somewhat.

"Get into the left lane, will you?" Aomame said to the driver.

"The right lane is moving better," he objected softly. "And the Ikejiri exit is on the right. If I get into the left lane here, I'll just have to move over again."

Aomame was not ready to accept his objections. "Never mind, just get into the left lane."

"If you say so, miss," the driver said with resignation.

Leaning over and sticking his hand out the front passenger window, he signaled to the refrigerated truck behind him in the left lane. After making sure the driver had seen him, he raised the window again and squeezed the cab into the left lane. They moved ahead another fifty yards until the traffic came to a full stop again.

"Now open the door for me. I'm getting out here," Aomame said.

"Getting out?" the driver asked, astonished. He made no move to pull the lever that opened the passenger door. "Here?!"

"Yes, this is where I'm getting out. I have something to do here."

"But we're right in the middle of the Metropolitan Expressway. It would be too dangerous to get out here, and even if you did, there's no place you could go."

"Don't worry, there's an emergency stairway right there."

"Emergency stairway." He shook his head. "I don't know if there's an emergency stairway or not, but if anyone found out I let a passenger out in a place like this, I'd be in big trouble with the cab company *and* the expressway management company. So please, miss, give me a break . . ."

"Sorry, I *have to* get out here," Aomame said. She took another ten-thousand-yen bill from her wallet, gave it a snap, and shoved it at the driver. "I know I'm asking you to do something you shouldn't do. This will pay for your trouble. So please stop arguing and let me out."

The driver did not take the money, but he gave up and pulled the lever. The left-side passenger door opened.

814 | BOOK 2 JULY–SEPTEMBER

"No, thanks, you've already paid me more than enough. But please be careful. The expressway doesn't have shoulders, and no matter how backed up the traffic might be, it's very dangerous for anybody to walk up here."

"Thank you," Aomame said. After stepping out, she knocked on the passenger-side front window and had him lower the glass. Leaning inside, she thrust the ten-thousand-yen bill into the driver's hand.

"Never mind, just take it. Don't worry, I have more money than I know what to do with."

The driver looked back and forth between the bill and Aomame's face.

Aomame said, "If this gets you into trouble with the police or the company, just tell them I threatened you with a pistol. You had no choice but to let me out. That'll shut them up."

The driver seemed unable to grasp what she was saying. More money than she knew what to do with? Threatened him with a pistol? Still, he took the money, probably fearing that she might do something even more unreasonable if he refused.

Just as she had done before, Aomame made her way between the expressway's sidewall and the cars in the left lane, heading toward Shibuya. She had some fifty yards to pass. People in the cars looked at her, incredulous, but Aomame did not let them bother her. She walked ahead with long, confident strides, her back straight, like a fashion model on the Paris runway. The wind stirred her hair. Trucks speeding along the wide-open lanes heading in the other direction shook the roadway. The Esso billboard grew larger as she approached, until finally she reached the familiar emergency turnout.

Everything looked as it had before – the metal barrier, the yellow box next to it containing an emergency telephone.

This is where the year 1Q84 started, Aomame thought.

One world took the place of another from the time I climbed down this emergency stairway to Route 246 below. So I'm going to try climbing down again. The first time I did it, it was April, and I was wearing my beige coat. Now it's early September, and the weather is too hot for a coat. Aside from the coat, though, I'm wearing exactly the same outfit I had on that day, when I killed that awful man who worked in oil – my Junko Shimada suit and Charles Jourdan high heels. White blouse. Stockings and white underwire bra. I pulled my miniskirt up to step over the barrier and climbed down the emergency stairway from here.

I'll try doing the same thing again – purely out of curiosity. I just want to know what will happen if I do the same thing in the same place wearing the same outfit. I'm not hoping this will save me. I'm not especially afraid to die. If it comes to that, I'll do it without hesitation. I can die smiling. But Aomame did not want to die ignorant, failing to grasp how things worked. *I want to push myself to my limits, and if things don't work out, then I can give up. But I will do everything I can until the bitter end. That is how I live.*

Aomame leaned over the metal barrier and looked for the emergency stairway. It was not there.

She looked again and again, with the same result. The emergency stairway had vanished.

Aomame bit her lip and twisted her face out of shape.

This is not the wrong place. It was definitely this turnout. Everything around here looks the same. The Esso billboard is right there. The emergency stairway existed in that place in the world of 1984. Aomame had found it easily, exactly where the strange taxi driver had said it would be. She had been able to step over the barrier and climb down. But in the world of 1Q84, the emergency stairway no longer existed.

Her exit was blocked.

Aomame untwisted her face and carefully observed her surroundings. She looked up at the Esso billboard again. Gas hose in hand, curly tail held high, the tiger looked out from the frame with a sly, knowing glance and a happy smile – a smile so utterly joyful it seemed to say that any greater satisfaction was an impossibility.

Yes, of course, Aomame thought.

She had known it from the start. Leader had said so before she killed him in the Hotel Okura suite: there was no way to return from 1Q84 to 1984. The door to this world only opened in one direction.

Even so, Aomame needed to confirm this fact with her own two eyes. It was her nature. And now she had confirmed it. It was all over. The proof was finished. QED.

Aomame leaned against the metal barrier and looked up at the sky. The weather was perfect. Several long, narrow clouds traced straight lines across a deep blue background. She could view the sky far into the distance. It didn't seem like a city's sky. But there were no moons to be seen. Where could the moons have gone? *Oh well, a moon is a moon, and I am me. Each of us has a different way to live. We each have our own plans.*

If she had been Faye Dunaway, at this point Aomame would have taken out a slim cigarette and coolly lit it with a cigarette lighter, elegantly narrowing her eyes. But Aomame did not smoke, and she had neither cigarettes nor a lighter with her. About all she had in her bag was a box of lemon cough drops. That plus a steel 9mm automatic pistol and a specially made ice pick she had used to stab a number of men in the back of the neck. Both might be somewhat more lethal than cigarettes.

She looked at the backed-up line of cars. Inside their vehicles, people were staring intently at her. Of course. Not often did people have the chance to see an ordinary citizen walking along the Metropolitan Expressway, and especially not a young woman, wearing a miniskirt and spike heels, with green sunglasses and a smile on her lips. Anyone who did *not* look must have something wrong with them.

The majority of vehicles stuck on the roadway were large trucks. They were bringing all sorts of goods from all sorts of places to Tokyo. The drivers had probably been at the wheel all night. And now they were stuck in this fated morning traffic jam. They were bored, fed up, and tired. All they wanted was to take a bath, shave, lie down, and go to sleep. They stared blankly at Aomame, as if they were looking at some unfamiliar animal. They were too tired to engage with her positively.

Wedged between these many trucks, like a graceful antelope caught in a herd of clumsy rhinoceros, was a silver Mercedes-Benz coupe. Its beautiful body, looking fresh from the factory, reflected the newly risen morning sun. Its hubcaps had been color coordinated with the body. The car was an import, with its steering wheel on the left side. The driver's window was down, and a well-dressed middle-aged woman was looking straight at Aomame. Givenchy sunglasses. Hands visible on the steering wheel. Rings glittering.

The woman had a kind face, and she seemed to be worried about Aomame. She was obviously wondering what a well-dressed young woman was doing out on the roadway of the Metropolitan Expressway and what could have caused her to be there. She looked ready to call out to Aomame. If asked, she might drive her anywhere she wanted to go.

Aomame took off her Ray-Bans and put them in the pocket of her suit top. Squinting in the bright morning light, she spent some time rubbing the dents left on either side of her nose by the glasses. She ran her tongue across her dry lips and caught the faint taste of lipstick. She looked up at the clear sky and checked the ground under her feet once.

She opened her shoulder bag and slowly drew out the Heckler & Koch, dropping the bag at her feet to free up her hands. With her left hand, she released the safety catch and pulled back the slide, sending a round into the chamber. She performed the sequence of movements rapidly and precisely with a few satisfying clicks. She lightly shook the gun in her hand, testing its weight. The gun itself weighed 480 grams, to which the weight of seven bullets was added. *No question, it's loaded.* She could tell by the difference in weight.

A smile still played around Aomame's straight lips. People were focused on her actions. No one was surprised to see her pull a gun out of her bag – or at least they did not show surprise on their faces. Maybe they didn't believe it was a real gun. *It is, though,* Aomame told them mentally.

Next she turned the gun upward and thrust the muzzle into her mouth. Now it was aimed directly at her cerebrum – the gray labyrinth where consciousness resided.

The words of a prayer came to her automatically, with no need to think. She intoned them quickly with the muzzle of the gun still in her mouth. *Nobody can hear what I am saying, I'm sure. But so what? As long as God can hear me.* When a little girl, Aomame could hardly understand the phrases she was reciting, but the words had permeated her to the core. She had to be sure to recite them before her school lunches, all by herself, but in a loud voice, unconcerned about the curious stares and scornful laughter of the other children. *The important thing is that God is watching you. No one can avoid his gaze.*

Big Brother is watching you.

O Lord in Heaven, may Thy name be praised in utmost purity for ever and ever, and may Thy kingdom come to us. Please forgive our many sins, and bestow Thy blessings upon our humble pathways. Amen.

The nice-looking middle-aged lady at the wheel of the brand-new Mercedes-Benz was still looking straight at Aomame. Like the other people watching, she seemed unable to grasp the meaning of the gun that Aomame was holding. *If she understood, she would have to look away from me,* Aomame thought. *If she sees my brain splatter in all directions, she probably won't be able to eat her lunch today – or her dinner. I won't blame you if you look the other way,* Aomame said to her wordlessly. *I'm not over here brushing my teeth. I've got this German-made automatic pistol, a Heckler & Koch, shoved in my mouth. I've said my prayers. You should know what that means.*

Here is my advice to you – important advice. Don't look at anything. Just drive your brand-new Mercedes-Benz straight home – your beautiful home, where your precious husband and children are waiting – and go on living your peaceful life. This is not something that someone like you should see. This is an ugly pistol, a real gun, loaded with seven ugly 9mm bullets. And, as Anton Chekhov said, once a gun appears in a story, it has to be fired at some point. That is what we mean by "a story."

But the middle-aged lady would not look away from Aomame. Resigned, Aomame gave her head a little shake. *Sorry, but I can't wait any longer. My time is up. Let's get the show on the road.*

Put a tiger in your tank.

"Ho ho," said the keeper of the beat.

"Ho ho," the six other Little People joined in.

"Tengo!" said Aomame, and started to squeeze the trigger.

CHAPTER 24

Tengo

AS LONG AS THIS WARMTH REMAINS

Tengo took a morning special express train from Tokyo Station to Tateyama, changed there to a local, and rode it as far as Chikura. The morning was clear and beautiful. There was no wind, and there was hardly a wave to be seen on the ocean. Summer was long gone. He wore a thin cotton jacket over a short-sleeved shirt, which turned out to be exactly right for the weather. Without bathers, the seaside town was surprisingly deserted and quiet. *Like a real town of cats,* Tengo thought.

He had a simple lunch by the station and took a taxi to the sanatorium, arriving just after one o'clock. The same middle-aged nurse greeted him at the reception desk – the woman who had taken his phone call the night before. Nurse Tamura. She remembered Tengo and was somewhat friendlier than she had been the first time, even managing a little smile, perhaps influenced by Tengo's nicer outfit.

She guided Tengo first to the lunchroom and poured him a cup of coffee. "Please wait here. The doctor will come to see you," she said. Ten minutes later, his father's doctor appeared, drying his hands with a towel. Flecks of white were beginning to appear among the stiff hairs of his head. He was probably around fifty. He was not wearing a white jacket, as if he had just completed some task. Instead he wore a gray sweatshirt, matching gray sweatpants, and an old pair of jogging shoes. He was well built and looked less like a doctor than a college sports coach who had never been able to rise past Division II.

The doctor told Tengo pretty much the same thing he had said on the phone the night before. Judging from his expression and his words, he seemed genuinely saddened when he said, "I'm sorry to say there is almost nothing we can do for him medically at this point. The only thing left to do is let him hear his son's voice. It might enhance his will to live."

"Do you think he can hear what people say?" Tengo asked.

The doctor frowned thoughtfully as he sipped his luke-warm green tea. "To tell you the truth, not even I know the answer to that. Your father is in a coma. He shows absolutely no physical response when we speak to him. There have been cases, though, where someone in a deep coma has been able to hear people talking and sometimes even understand what was being said."

"But you can't tell by looking at them."

"No, we can't."

"I can stay here until six thirty tonight," Tengo said. "I'll sit with him all day and talk to him as much as possible. Let's see if it does any good."

"Please let me know if he shows any kind of reaction," the doctor said. "I'll be around here somewhere."

A young nurse showed Tengo to his father's room. She wore a name badge that read "Adachi." His father had been moved to a private room in the new wing, the wing for more serious patients. In other words, the gears had advanced one more notch. There was nowhere else to move after this. It was a drab little room, long and narrow, and more than half filled by the bed. Beyond the window stretched the pine woods that acted as a windbreak. The dense grove looked like a wall, separating the sanatorium from the vitality of the real world. The nurse went out, leaving Tengo alone with his father, who lay on his back, sound asleep. Tengo sat on a small wooden stool by the bed and looked at his father.

Near the head of the bed stood an intravenous feeding device, the liquid in its plastic bag being sent into a vein in his father's arm through a tube. A catheter had been inserted to catch urine, surprisingly little of which had been collected. His father seemed to have shrunk another size or two since the month before. His emaciated cheeks and chin wore perhaps two days' growth of white beard. His father had always had sunken eyes, but now they were more deeply set than ever. Tengo couldn't help wondering if it might be necessary to pull the eyeballs up from their holes with some kind of medical device. His eyelids were tightly shut at the bottoms of those caverns like lowered shutters, and his mouth was slightly open. Tengo couldn't hear his father's breathing, but, bringing his ear close, he could feel the slight movement of air. Life was being quietly maintained there at a minimal level.

The doctor's words on the phone last night – "like a train, dropping its speed little by little as it begins to stop" – began to feel terribly real to Tengo. This "father" train was gradually lowering its speed, waiting for its momentum to run down, and preparing to come to a quiet stop in the middle of an empty prairie. At least there was no longer a single passenger aboard, no one to raise a complaint even if the train came to a halt. That was the only salvation.

Tengo felt he ought to start talking to his father, but he did not know what he should say, how he should say it, or what tone of voice to use. *All right, say something,* he told himself, but no meaningful words came to mind.

"Father," he ventured in a whisper, but no other words followed.

He got up from the stool, approached the window, and looked at the well-tended lawn and garden and the sky stretching high above the pine woods. A solitary crow sat perched on

a large antenna, glaring at the area with disdain as it caught
the sunlight. A combination transistor radio/alarm clock had
been placed near the head of the bed, but his father required
neither of its functions.

"It's me – Tengo. I just came from Tokyo. Can you hear
me?" he said, standing at the window, looking down at his
father, who did not respond at all. After vibrating in the air for
a moment, the sound of his voice was absorbed without a trace
by the void that had come to occupy the room.

This man is trying to die, Tengo thought. He could tell by
looking at the deeply sunken eyes. *He made up his mind to end
his life, and then he closed his eyes and went into a deep sleep. No
matter what I say to him, no matter how much I try to rouse him,
it will be impossible to overturn his resolution.* Medically speaking, he was still alive, but life had already ended for this man.
He no longer had the reason or the will to continue to struggle.
All that Tengo could do was respect his father's wishes and let
him die in peace. The look on his face was utterly tranquil. He
did not seem to be suffering at all. As the doctor had said on
the phone, that was the one salvation.

Still, Tengo had to speak to his father, if only because he had
promised the doctor that he would do so. The doctor seemed to
be caring for his father with genuine warmth. Secondly, there
was the question of what he thought of as "courtesy." Tengo
had not had a full-fledged conversation with his father for a
very long time, not even small talk. The truth was that Tengo
had probably been in middle school the last time they had had
a real conversation. Tengo hardly ever went near their home
after that, and even when he had some business that required
him to go to the house, he did his best to avoid seeing his father.

Now, having made a de facto confession to Tengo that he
was not his real father, the man could lay down his burden at
last. He looked in some way relieved. *That means that each of
us was able to lay down his burden – at the last possible moment.*

Here was the man who had raised Tengo as his own son, listing him as such in the family register despite the absence of blood ties, and raising him until he was old enough to fend for himself. *I owe him that much. I have some obligation to tell him how I have lived my life thus far, as well as some of the thoughts I have had in the course of living that life,* Tengo thought. *No, it's not so much an obligation as a courtesy. It doesn't matter if the things I am saying reach his ears or whether telling him serves any purpose.*

Tengo sat on the stool by the bed once again and began to narrate a summary of his life to date, beginning from the time he left the house and started living in the judo dorm when he entered high school. From that time onward, he and his father had lost nearly all points of contact, creating a situation in which neither had the least concern for what the other was doing. Tengo felt he should probably fill in such a large vacuum as best he could.

Ultimately, however, there was almost nothing for Tengo to tell about his life in high school. He had entered a private high school in Chiba Prefecture that had a strong reputation for its judo program. He could easily have gotten into a better school, but the conditions offered him by that school were the best. They waived his tuition and allowed him to live in the dormitory, providing him with three meals a day. Tengo became a star member of the judo team, studied between practice sessions (he could maintain some of the highest grades in his class without having to study too hard), and he earned extra money during vacations by doing assorted manual labor with his teammates. With so much to do, he found himself pressed for time day after day. There was little to say about his three years of high school other than that it was a busy time for him. It had not been especially enjoyable, nor had he made any close friends. He never liked the school, which had a lot of rules. He did what he had to do in order to get along with his teammates, but they weren't really on the same wavelength. In all honesty, Tengo never once felt totally committed to judo as a sport. He needed to win in order to support himself, so he devoted a lot of energy to practice in order not to betray others' expectations. It was less a sport to him than a practical means of survival – a job. He spent the three years of high school wanting to graduate so that he could begin living a more serious life as soon as possible.

Even after entering college, however, he continued with judo, living basically the same life as before. Keeping up his judo meant he could live in the dormitory and thus be spared any difficulty in finding a place to sleep or food to eat (minimal though it was). He also received a scholarship, though it was nowhere nearly enough to get by on. His major was mathematics, of course. He studied fairly hard and earned good grades in college, too. His adviser even urged him to continue into graduate school. As he advanced into the third year and then the fourth year of college, however, his passion for mathematics as an academic discipline rapidly cooled. He still liked mathematics as much as ever, but he had no desire to make a profession of research in the field. It was the same as it had been with judo. It was fine as an amateur endeavor, but he had neither the personality nor the drive to stake his whole life on it, which he well knew.

As his interest in mathematics waned and his college graduation drew near, his reasons for continuing judo evaporated and he had no idea what path he should next pursue. His life seemed to lose its center of gravity – not that he had ever really had one, but up to that point, other people had placed certain demands and expectations upon him, and responding to them had kept him busy. Once those demands and expectations disappeared, however, there was nothing left worth talking about. His life had no purpose. He had no close friends. He was drifting and unable to concentrate his energies on anything.

He had a number of girlfriends during his college years, and a lot of sexual experience. He was not handsome in the usual sense. He was not a particularly sociable person, nor was he especially amusing or witty. He was always hard up for money and wasn't at all stylish. But just as the smell of certain kinds of plants attracts moths, Tengo was able to attract certain kinds of women – and very strongly, at that.

He discovered this fact around the time he turned twenty (which was just about the time he began losing his enthusiasm for mathematics as an academic discipline). Without doing anything about it himself, he always had women who were interested enough to take the initiative in approaching him. They wanted him to hold them in his big arms – or at least they never resisted him when he did so. He couldn't understand how this worked at first and reacted with a good deal of confusion, but eventually he got the hang of it and learned how to exploit this ability, after which Tengo was rarely without a woman. He never had a positive feeling of love toward any of them, however. He just went with them and had sex with them. They filled each other's emptiness. Strange as it may seem, he never once felt a strong emotional attraction to any of the women who had a strong emotional attraction to him.

Tengo recounted these developments to his unconscious father, choosing his words slowly and carefully at first, more smoothly as time went by, and finally with some passion. He even spoke as honestly as he could about sexual matters. *There's no point getting embarrassed about such things now,* he told himself. His father lay faceup, unmoving, his deep sleep unbroken, his breathing unchanged.

A nurse came before three o'clock, changed the plastic bag of intravenous fluid, replaced the bag of collected urine with an empty one, and took his father's temperature. She was a strongly built, full-bosomed woman in her late thirties. The name on her tag read "Omura." Her hair was pulled into a tight bun on the back of her head, with a ballpoint pen thrust into it.

"Has there been any change in his condition?" she asked Tengo while recording numbers on a clipboard with the ballpoint pen.

"None at all. He's been fast asleep the whole time," Tengo said.

"Please push that button if anything happens," she said, pointing toward the call switch hanging over the head of the bed. Then she shoved the ballpoint pen back into her hair.

"I see."

Shortly after the nurse went out, there was a quick knock on the door and bespectacled Nurse Tamura poked her head in.

"Would you like to have a bite to eat? You could go to the lunchroom."

"Thanks, but I'm not hungry yet," Tengo said.

"How is your father doing?"

Tengo nodded. "I've been talking to him the whole time. I can't tell whether he can hear me or not."

"It's good to keep talking to them," she said. She smiled encouragingly. "Don't worry, I'm sure he can hear you."

She closed the door softly. Now it was just Tengo and his father in the little room again.

Tengo went on talking.

He graduated from college and started teaching mathematics at a cram school in the city. No longer was he a math prodigy from whom people expected great things, nor was he a promising member of a judo team. He was a mere cram school instructor. But that very fact made Tengo happy. He could catch his breath at last. For the first time in his life, he was free: he could live his own life as he wanted to without having to worry about anyone else.

Eventually, he started writing fiction. He entered a few of

his finished stories in competitions, which led him to become acquainted with a quirky editor named Komatsu. This editor gave him the job of rewriting *Air Chrysalis,* a story by a seventeen-year-old girl named Fuka-Eri (whose real name was Eriko Fukada). Fuka-Eri had created the story, but she had no talent for writing, so Tengo took on that task. He did such a good job that the piece won a debut writer's prize from a magazine and then was subsequently published as a book that became a huge bestseller. Because the book was so widely discussed, the selection committee for the Akutagawa Prize, the most prestigious literary award, kept their distance from it. So while it did not win that particular prize, the book sold so many copies that Komatsu, in his typically brusque way, said, "Who the hell needs *that*?"

Tengo had no confidence that his story was reaching his father's ears, and even if it was, he had no way of telling whether or not his father was understanding it. He felt his words had no impact and he could see no response. Even if his words were getting through, Tengo had no way of knowing if his father was even interested. Maybe the old man just found them annoying. Maybe he was thinking, "Who gives a damn about other people's life stories? Just let me sleep!" All Tengo could do, though, was continue to say whatever came to his mind. He couldn't think of anything better to do while crammed into this little room with his father.

His father never made the slightest movement. His eyes were closed tightly at the bottom of those two deep, dark hollows. He might as well have been waiting for winter to come and the hollows to fill up with snow.

"I can't say that things are going all that well for the moment, but if possible I'd like to make my living by writing – not just rewriting somebody else's work but writing what I want to write, the way I want to write it. Writing – and especially fiction writing – is well suited to my personality, I think. It's good to have something you want to do, and now I finally have it. Nothing of mine has ever been published with my name on it, but that ought to happen soon enough. I'm really not a bad writer, if I do say so myself. At least one editor gives me some credit for my talent. I'm not worried on that front."

And I seem to have the qualities needed to be a Receiver, Tengo thought of adding. *So much so that I have been drawn into the fictional world that I myself have written.* But this was no place to start talking about such complicated matters. That was a whole different story. He decided to change the subject.

"A more pressing problem for me is that I have never been able to love anyone seriously. I have never felt unconditional love for anyone since the day I was born, never felt that I could give myself completely to that one person. Never once."

Even as he said this, Tengo found himself wondering if this miserable-looking old man before him had ever experienced loving someone with his whole heart. Perhaps he had seriously loved Tengo's mother, which may have been why he was willing to raise Tengo as his own child, even though he knew they had no blood tie. If so, that meant he had lived a far more spiritually fulfilling life than Tengo.

"The one possible exception is a girl I remember very well. We were in the same class in the third and fourth grades in Ichikawa. Yes, I'm talking about something that happened a good twenty years ago. I was very strongly drawn to her. I've thought about her all this time, and even now I still think about her a lot. But I never really talked to her. She changed schools, and I never saw her again. But something happened recently that made me want to find her. I finally realized that I need her, that I want to see her and talk to her about all kinds of things. But I haven't been able to track her down. I suppose I should have started looking for her a lot sooner. It might have been much easier then."

Tengo fell silent, waiting for the things he had talked about so far to sink into his father's mind – or, rather, to sink into his own mind. Then he started speaking again.

"Yes, I was too much of a coward where these things were concerned. The same reason kept me from investigating my own family register. If I wanted to find out whether my mother really died or not, I could have looked it up easily. All I had to do was go to the city hall and look up the record. In fact, I thought about doing it any number of times. I even walked as far as the city hall. But I couldn't make myself request the documents. I was afraid to see the truth before my eyes. I was afraid to expose it with my own hands. And so I waited for it to happen by itself, naturally."

Tengo released a sigh.

"Oh well, all that aside, I should have started looking for the girl a lot sooner. I took a huge detour. I couldn't get myself going. I just – how should I put this? – I'm a coward when it comes to matters of the heart. That is my fatal flaw."

Tengo got up from the stool, went to the window, and looked out at the pine woods. The wind had died. He couldn't hear the roar of the ocean. A large cat was crossing the garden. Judging from its sagging middle, it was probably pregnant. It lay down at the base of a tree, spread its legs, and started licking its belly.

Leaning against the windowsill, Tengo continued to speak to his father.

"But anyhow, lately it has begun to seem as if my life has finally started to change. I feel that way. To tell you the truth, I hated you for a long time. From the time I was little, I used to think that I didn't belong in such a miserable little place, that I was someone who deserved to be in more comfortable circumstances. I felt it was unfair for you to treat me as you did. My classmates all seemed to be living happy, satisfying lives. Kids whose gifts and talents were far inferior to mine were having much more fun than I was every day. I used to seriously wish that you were not my father. I imagined that this had to be some mistake; you couldn't possibly be my real father; there couldn't possibly be any blood relationship."

Tengo looked out of the window again at the cat. It was still absorbed in licking its swollen belly, unaware that it was being watched. Tengo kept his gaze on the cat as he continued talking.

"I don't feel that way anymore. Now I think that I was in the right circumstances for me and had the right father. I really mean it. To tell you the truth, I was a useless human being, a person of no value. In a sense, I'm the one who ruined me: I did it myself. I can see that now. I was a math prodigy when I was little, that's for sure. Even I know I had a real talent. Everybody kept their eye on me and made a big deal over me. But ultimately, it was a talent that had no hope of developing into anything meaningful. It was *just there.* I was always a big boy and good at judo, and I always did well in the prefectural tournaments. But when I went out into the wider world, there were lots of guys who were stronger than I was. I was never chosen to represent my university in the national tournaments. This was a great shock to me, and for a while I no longer knew who I was. But that was only natural, because in fact I was nobody."

Tengo opened the bottle of mineral water he had brought with him and took a drink. Then he sat down on the stool again.

"I told you this before, but I'm grateful to you. I believe I'm not your real son. I'm almost sure of it. I'm grateful to you for having raised me even though we had no blood tie. I'm sure it wasn't easy for a man to raise a small child alone. Now, though, when I recall how you took me around on your NHK collections, I feel sick at heart. I have only terrible memories of that. But I'm sure that you could think of no other way to communicate with me. How should I put it? It was probably the best you could do. That was your only point of contact with society, and you wanted to show me what it was like out there. I can see that now. Of course, you also calculated that having a child with you would make it easier for you to collect the money. But that wasn't all you had in mind, I suspect."

Tengo paused briefly to let his words sink in and to organize his own thoughts.

"Of course, as a child, I couldn't see it that way. It was just embarrassing and painful to me – that I had to go around with you making collections while my classmates spent their Sundays having fun. I can't tell you how much I hated it when Sundays came around. But now, at least to some extent, I can understand what you did. I'm not saying that it was right. It left me with scars. It was hard for a child. But what's done is done. Don't let it bother you. One good thing it did was to make me tougher. I learned firsthand that it's not easy making your way through this world."

Tengo opened his hands and looked at his palms for a while.

"I'm going to go on living one way or another. I think I can do a better job of it from now on, without such pointless detours. I don't know what you want to do. Maybe you just want to go on sleeping quietly, without ever waking up again. That's what you should do if you want to. I can't stand in your way if that's what you are hoping for. All I can do is let you go on sleeping. In any case, I wanted to say all this to you – to tell you what I have done so far in life and what I am thinking. Maybe you would have preferred not to hear any of this, and if that's the case, I'm sorry to have inflicted it on you. Anyhow, I have nothing more to tell you. I've pretty much said everything I thought I ought to say. I won't bother you anymore. Now you can sleep as much as you like."

After five o'clock, Nurse Omura, the one with the ballpoint pen in her hair, came to the room and checked the amount of intravenous fluid in the bag. This time she did not check his father's temperature.

"Anything to report?" she asked.

"Not really. He's just been sleeping the whole time," Tengo answered.

The nurse nodded. "The doctor will be here soon. How late can you stay here today, Mr. Kawana?"

Tengo glanced at his watch. "I'll be catching the train just before seven, so I can stay as late as six thirty."

The nurse wrote something on his father's chart and put the pen back into her hair.

"I've been talking to him all afternoon, but he doesn't seem to hear me," Tengo said.

The nurse said, "If I learned anything in nursing school, it's that bright words make the eardrums vibrate brightly. They have their own bright sound. So even if the patient doesn't understand what you're saying, his eardrums will physically vibrate on that bright wavelength. We're taught to always talk to the patient in a big, bright voice whether he can hear you or not. It definitely helps, whatever the logic involved. I can say that from experience."

Tengo thought about this remark. "Thank you," he said. Nurse Omura nodded lightly and, with a few quick steps, left the room.

After that, Tengo and his father maintained a long silence. Tengo had nothing more to say, but the silence was not an uncomfortable one for him. The afternoon light was gradually fading, and hints of evening hung in the air. The sun's last rays moved silently and stealthily through the room.

Tengo suddenly wondered if he had said anything to his father about the two moons. He had the feeling that he had probably not done so. Tengo was now living in a world with two moons. "It's a very strange sight, no matter how many times I see it," he wanted to say, but he also felt that there wouldn't be much point to mentioning it. The number of moons in the sky was of no concern to his father. This was a problem that Tengo would have to handle on his own.

Ultimately, though, whether this world (or *that* world) had only one moon or two moons or three moons, there was only one Tengo. What difference did it make? Whatever world he was in, Tengo was just Tengo, the same person with his own unique problems and his own unique characteristics. The real question was not in the moons but in Tengo himself.

Half an hour later, Nurse Omura came into the room again. For some reason, she no longer had a pen in her hair. Where could it have gone? Tengo found himself strangely concerned about the pen. Two male staff members came with her, wheeling a movable bed. Both men were stockily built and dark-complexioned, and neither of them said a word. They might have been foreigners.

"We have to take your father for some tests, Mr. Kawana," the nurse said. "Would you like to wait here?"

Tengo looked at the clock. "Is something wrong with him?"

The nurse shook her head. "No, not at all. We just don't have the testing equipment in this room, so we're taking him to where it is. It's nothing special. The doctor will probably talk to you afterward."

"I see. I'll wait here."

"You could go to the lunchroom for some hot tea. You should get some rest."

"Thank you," Tengo said.

The two men gently lifted his father's thin body, with the intravenous tubes still attached, and transferred him to the wheeled bed, moving the bed and intravenous stand into the corridor with quick, practiced movements. Still they did not say a word.

"This won't take too long," the nurse said.

But his father did not return to the room for a long time. The light coming in the window grew slowly weaker, but Tengo did not turn on the lamp. If he did so, he felt, something important here would be lost.

An indentation remained in the bed where his father had been lying. His father now probably weighed next to nothing, but still he had left a clear impression of his shape. Looking at the indentation, Tengo had a strong feeling that he had been left behind in this world all alone. He even felt that the dawn might never come again, once the sun had set tonight.

Sitting on the stool by the bed, steeped in the colors of the approaching evening, Tengo stayed in the same position, lost in thought. Then suddenly it occurred to him that he had not actually been thinking at all but had been aimlessly submerging himself in a vacuum. He stood up slowly, went to the toilet, and relieved himself. After washing his face with cold water, he dried his face with his handkerchief and looked at himself in the mirror. Then, recalling what the nurse had said, he went downstairs to the lunchroom and drank some hot green tea.

His father had still not been brought back to the room when Tengo returned there after twenty minutes downstairs. Instead, what he found, in the hollow that his father had left in the bed, was a white object that he had never seen before.

Nearly five feet in length, it had smooth, beautiful curves. At first sight, it seemed to be shaped like a peanut shell, its entire surface covered with something like short, soft down that emitted a faint but even glow. In the rapidly darkening room, the pale bluish light enveloped the object softly. The thing lay still in the bed, as if to fill the individual space that his father had temporarily left behind. Tengo halted in the doorway, hand on the knob, staring at the mysterious object. His lips seemed to move somewhat, but no words emerged from them.

What is *this thing?* Tengo asked himself as he stood there, frozen to the spot, eyes narrowed. How had this come to be here in his father's place? No doctor or nurse had brought it in, that much was obvious. Around it hovered some special kind of air that was out of sync with reality.

Then it suddenly hit him: *This is an air chrysalis!*

This was the first time that Tengo had ever seen an air chrysalis. He had described some in great detail in the novella, but of course he had never seen a real one with his own eyes, and he had never thought of them as things that actually existed. But what he saw before him now was the very object his mind had imagined and his words had described: an air chrysalis. He experienced such a violent sense of déjà vu that it felt as if a metal band had been tightened around his stomach. Nevertheless, he stepped inside the room and closed the door. Better not let anyone see him. He swallowed the saliva that had been collecting in his mouth, making a strange sound in his throat.

Tengo crept toward the bed, stopping when there was no more than a yard between him and it, examining the air chrysalis in greater detail. Now he could be sure that it looked exactly like the picture he had drawn of an air chrysalis at the time he wrote the story. He had done a simple pencil sketch before attempting to create a description of an air chrysalis, first putting the image in his mind into visual form and then transferring it into words. He had left the picture pinned to the wall over his desk while he rewrote *Air Chrysalis*. It was shaped more like a cocoon than a chrysalis, but "air chrysalis" was the only name by which Fuka-Eri (and Tengo himself) could possibly call the thing.

During his revision, Tengo had created most of the external features of an air chrysalis and added them to his descriptions, including the gracefully narrowed waist in the middle and the swelling, round, decorative protuberance at either end. These came entirely from Tengo's mind. There had been no mention of them in Fuka-Eri's original narrative. To Fuka-Eri, an air chrysalis was simply that – an air chrysalis, something midway between an object and a concept – and she seemed to feel little need to describe its appearance in words. Tengo had to invent all the details himself, and the air chrysalis that he was now seeing had these same details exactly: the waist in the middle and the lovely protuberances at either end.

This is the very air chrysalis I sketched and described, Tengo thought. *The same thing happened with the two moons.* For some reason, every detail he had put into writing had now become a reality. Cause and effect were jumbled together.

All four of Tengo's limbs felt a strange, nervous, twisting sensation, and his flesh began to crawl. He could no longer distinguish how much of this present world was reality and how much of it fiction. How much of it belonged to Fuka-Eri, how much was Tengo's, and how much was "ours"?

A small tear had opened at the very top of the air chrysalis: the chrysalis was about to break in two. The gap that had formed was perhaps an inch long. If he bent over and brought his eye to the opening, he could probably see what was inside. But Tengo could not find the courage to do so. He sat down on the stool by the bed, staring at the air chrysalis while his shoulders rose and fell imperceptibly as he struggled to bring his breathing under control. The white chrysalis lay there still, emitting its faint glow, quietly waiting, like a mathematical proposition, for Tengo to approach it.

What could possibly be inside the chrysalis?

What was it trying to show him?

In the novella *Air Chrysalis,* the young girl protagonist discovers her own other self inside. Her *dohta.* She leaves her *dohta* behind and runs away from the community alone. But what could possibly be inside of Tengo's air chrysalis? (Tengo felt intuitively that this air chrysalis must be *his own.*) Was it something good or something evil? Was it something that would guide him somewhere or something that would stand in his way? And who could possibly have sent this air chrysalis to him here?

Tengo knew quite well that he was being asked to act. But he could not find the courage that would enable him to stand and look inside the chrysalis. He was afraid. The thing inside the chrysalis might wound him or greatly change his life. The thought caused Tengo to grow stiff, sitting on the little stool like someone who has lost a place of refuge. He was feeling the same kind of fear that had kept him from looking up his parents' family register or searching for Aomame. He *did not want to know* what was inside the air chrysalis that had been prepared for him. If he could get by without knowing what was in there, that was how he wanted to walk out of this room. If possible, he wanted to leave this room *now*, get on the train, and go back to Tokyo. He wanted to close his eyes, block his ears, and burrow himself in his own little world.

But Tengo also knew that this was impossible. *If I leave here without seeing what is inside, I'll regret it for the rest of my life. I'll probably never be able to forgive myself for having averted my eyes from that* something, *whatever it might be.*

Tengo remained seated on the stool for a long time, unsure of what he should do, unable to go either forward or back. Folding his hands on his knees, he stared at the air chrysalis on the bed, glancing occasionally out the window, as if hoping to escape. The sun had set, and a pale afterglow was slowly enveloping the pine woods. Still there was no wind, nor could he hear the sound of the waves. It was almost mysteriously quiet. And as the room's darkness increased, the light emitted by the white object became deeper and more vivid. The chrysalis itself seemed like a living thing to Tengo, with its soft glow of life, its unique warmth, its nearly imperceptible vibration.

Finally Tengo made up his mind, stood up from the stool,

and leaned over the bed. Running away now was out of the question. He couldn't live forever like a frightened child, averting his eyes from the things before him. Only by learning the truth – whatever that truth might be – could people be given the right kind of power.

The tear in the air chrysalis was unchanged, neither bigger nor smaller than before. Squinting, he looked in through the opening, but he could not see very far inside. It was dark in there, and a thin membrane seemed to be stretched across the space inside. Tengo steadied his breathing and made sure his hands were not shaking. Then he put his fingers into the inch-long opening and slowly spread it apart, as if opening the two leaves of a double sliding door. It opened easily with little resistance and no sound, as if it had been waiting for his hands.

Now the light of the air chrysalis itself was softly illuminating its interior, like light reflected from snow. He was able to see inside, however dimly.

What Tengo found in there was a beautiful ten-year-old girl.

She was sound asleep. She wore a simple white dress or nightgown free of decoration, her small hands folded on top of her flat chest. Tengo knew instantly who this was. She had a slender face, and her lips formed a straight line, as if drawn with a ruler. Perfectly straight bangs lay over a smooth, well-shaped forehead. Her little nose seemed to be searching for something, aimed tentatively upward into space. Her cheekbones stretched slightly to either side. Her eyes were closed, but Tengo knew what they would look like when they opened. How could he not know? He had lived for twenty years holding the image of this girl in his heart.

"Aomame," Tengo said aloud.

The girl was sound asleep – a deep and utterly natural sleep, with the faintest possible breathing. The beating of her heart was too ephemeral to be heard. She did not have enough strength to raise her eyelids. The *time for that* had not come yet.

Her conscious mind was not here but rather somewhere far away. Still, the word that Tengo had spoken was able to impart the slightest vibration to her eardrums. It was her name.

Aomame heard the call from far away. *Tengo,* she thought. She formed the word clearly with her mouth, though it didn't move the lips of the girl in the air chrysalis or reach Tengo's ears.

As if his soul had been snatched, Tengo stared insatiably at the girl, taking one shallow breath after another. Her face looked totally peaceful, without the slightest shadow of sadness or pain or anxiety. Her thin, little lips seemed ready to begin moving at any moment to form meaningful words. Her eyelids appeared ready to open. Tengo prayed from the heart for this to happen. His prayer took no precise words, but his heart spun this formless prayer and sent it out into space. The girl, however, showed no sign of waking.

"Aomame," Tengo called again.

There were things he had to say to Aomame, feelings he had to convey to her. He had been living with them, keeping them inside, for years. But all that Tengo could do now was speak her name.

"Aomame," he called.

He dared then to reach out and touch the hand of the girl who lay in the air chrysalis, placing his big grown-up hand on hers. This was the little hand that had so tightly grasped the hand of his ten-year-old self. This hand had come straight for him, wanting him, giving him encouragement. The unmistakable warmth of life was there in the hand of the girl asleep inside the pale glow. *Aomame came here to convey her warmth to me,* Tengo thought. *That was the meaning of the package she handed to me in that classroom twenty years ago.* Now at last he was able to open the package and view its contents.

"Aomame," Tengo said. "I will find you, no matter what."

* * *

After the air chrysalis had gradually lost its glow and disappeared, as if sucked into the darkness, and the young Aomame had disappeared as well, Tengo found himself unable to judge whether all of this had really happened. But his fingers retained the touch and the intimate warmth of her little hand.

This warmth will almost surely never fade, Tengo thought, sitting aboard the special express train heading for Tokyo. Tengo had lived for the past twenty years with the memory of her touch. He should be able to go on living with this new warmth.

The express train traced a huge arc along the ocean shore beneath the towering mountains, until it reached a point along the coast where the two moons were visible, hanging side by side in the sky above the quiet sea. They stood out sharply – the big, yellow moon and the small, green one – vivid in outline but their distance impossible to grasp. In their light, the ocean's tiny ripples shone mysteriously like scattered shards of glass. As the train continued around the curve, the two moons moved slowly across the window, leaving those delicate shards behind, like wordless hints, until they disappeared from view.

Once the moons were gone, the warmth returned to Tengo's chest. Faint as it was, the warmth was surely there, conveying a promise like a lamp a traveler sees in the far distance.

I will go on living in this world, Tengo thought, closing his eyes. He did not know yet how this world was put together or under what principles it moved, and he had no way of predicting what would happen there. But that was all right. He didn't have to be afraid. Whatever might be waiting for him, he would survive in this world with two moons, and he would find the path he needed to take – as long as he did not forget this warmth, as long as he did not lose this feeling in his heart.

He kept his eyes closed like this for a long time. Eventually, he opened his eyes to stare into the darkness of the early-autumn night beyond the window. The ocean had long since disappeared.

I will find Aomame, Tengo swore to himself again, *no matter what happens, no matter what kind of world it may be, no matter who she may be.*

BOOK 3 OCTOBER–DECEMBER

CHAPTER 1

Ushikawa

SOMETHING KICKING AT THE FAR EDGES OF CONSCIOUSNESS

"I wonder if you would mind not smoking, Mr. Ushikawa," the shorter man said.

Ushikawa gazed steadily at the man seated across the desk from him, then down at the Seven Stars cigarette between his fingers. He hadn't lit it yet.

"I'd really appreciate it," the man added politely.

Ushikawa looked puzzled, as if he were wondering how such an object possibly found its way into his hand.

"Sorry about that," he said. "I won't light up. I just took it out without thinking."

The man's chin moved up and down, perhaps a half inch, but his gaze didn't waver. His eyes remained fixed on Ushikawa's. Ushikawa stuck the cigarette back in its box, the box in a drawer.

The taller of the two men, the one with a ponytail, stood in the doorway, leaning so lightly against the door frame that it was hard to tell if he was actually touching it. He stared at Ushikawa as if he were a stain on the wall. *What a creepy pair,* Ushikawa thought. This was the third time he had met with these men, and they made him uneasy every time.

Ushikawa's cramped office had a single desk, and the shorter of the two men, the one with a buzz cut, sat across from him. He was the one who did the talking. Ponytail didn't say a word. Like one of those stone guardian dogs at the entrance to a Shinto shrine, he stood stock-still, not moving an inch, watching Ushikawa.

"It has been three weeks," Buzzcut noted.

Ushikawa picked up his desk calendar, checked what was written on it, and nodded. "Correct. It has been exactly three weeks since we last met."

"And in the meantime you haven't reported to us even once. As I've mentioned before, Mr. Ushikawa, every moment is precious. We have no time to waste."

"I completely understand," Ushikawa replied, fiddling with his gold lighter in place of the cigarette. "There's no time to waste. I am well aware of this."

Buzzcut waited for Ushikawa to go on.

"The thing is," Ushikawa said, "I don't like to talk in fits and starts. A little of this, a little of that. I would like to wait until I start to see the big picture and things begin to fall into place and I can see what's behind all this. Half-baked ideas can only lead to trouble. I know this sounds selfish, but that's the way I do things."

Buzzcut gazed coolly at Ushikawa. Ushikawa knew the man didn't think much of him, not that this really worried him much. As far as he could recall, no one had ever had a good impression of him. He was used to it. His parents and siblings had never liked him, and neither had his teachers or classmates. It was the same with his wife and children. If someone *did* like him, now *then* he would be concerned. But the other way around didn't faze him.

"Mr. Ushikawa, we would like to respect your way of doing things. And I believe we have done that. So far. But things are different this time. I'm sorry to say we don't have the luxury of waiting until we know all the facts."

"I understand," Ushikawa said, "but I doubt you've just been sitting back all this time waiting for me to get in touch. I suspect you've been running your own investigations?"

Buzzcut didn't respond. His lips remained pressed in a tight horizontal line, and his expression didn't give anything away. But Ushikawa could tell that he wasn't far from the truth. Over the past three weeks, their organization had geared up, and, although they had probably used different tactics from Ushikawa, they had been searching for the woman. But they must not have found anything, which is why they had turned up again in Ushikawa's office.

"It takes a thief to catch a thief," Ushikawa said, spreading his hands wide, as if disclosing some fascinating secret. "Try to hide something, and this thief can sniff it out. I know I'm not the most pleasant-looking person, but I do have a nose for things. I can follow the faintest scent to the very end. Because I'm a thief myself. I have to do things my way, at my own pace. I completely understand that time is pressing, but I would like you to wait a little longer. You have to be patient, otherwise the whole thing may collapse."

Ushikawa toyed with his lighter. Buzzcut's eyes patiently followed Ushikawa's movements, and then he looked up.

"I would appreciate it if you would tell me what you've found, even if it's incomplete. Granted, you have your own way of doing things, but if I don't take something concrete back to my superiors, we'll be in a tough spot. I think you're in a bit of a precarious situation yourself, Mr. Ushikawa."

These guys really are *up a creek,* Ushikawa realized. The two of them were martial arts experts, which is why they were selected to be Leader's bodyguards. Despite that, Leader had been murdered right under their noses. Not that there was actually any evidence that he had been murdered – several doctors in the religion had examined the body and found no external injuries. But medical equipment within the religion was rudimentary at best. And time was of the essence. If a thorough, legal autopsy had been performed by a trained pathologist, they might very well have discovered evidence of foul play, but it was too late now. The body had been secretly disposed of within the Sakigake compound.

At any rate, these two bodyguards had failed in their assignment to protect Leader, and their position in the religion was shaky. Their role now was to locate this woman, after she had seemingly vanished into thin air. The order was out: leave no stone unturned until they found her. But so far they had come up empty-handed. They were trained bodyguards, but when it came to finding missing persons, they lacked the right skills.

"I understand where you're coming from," Ushikawa replied. "And I will tell you some things I've discovered. Not the whole story, but I can reveal parts of it."

Buzzcut sat there for a while, his eyes narrowed. And then he nodded. "That would be fine. We have uncovered a few details ourselves, things you may already be aware of, or perhaps not. We should share whatever information we have."

Ushikawa put the lighter down and tented his fingers on top of the desk.

"The young woman, Aomame," he began, "was asked to come to a suite at the Hotel Okura, and helped Leader to relax his muscles by working his body through a series of stretching exercises. This was at the beginning of September, on the evening of that tremendous thunderstorm. Aomame treated him for around an hour in a separate room, then left Leader while he slept. She told you to let him sleep undisturbed for two hours, and you followed her instructions. But Leader wasn't asleep. He was already dead. There were no external injuries, and it appeared to be a heart attack. Right after this, the woman vanished. She had cleared out of her apartment beforehand. The place was empty. And the next day her resignation letter arrived at the sports club. Everything seemed to follow a preset plan. The inevitable conclusion is that this Miss Aomame was the one who murdered Leader."

Buzzcut nodded. It all sounded correct to him.

"Your goal is to get to the bottom of what actually occurred," Ushikawa added. "Whatever it takes, you need to catch this woman."

"If this Aomame really is the one who killed Leader, we need to know why, and who's behind it."

Ushikawa looked down at his ten fingers resting on the desk, as if they were some curious object he had never set eyes on before. He raised his head and looked at the man across from him.

"You've already run a background check on Aomame's family, correct? All of her family members are devout members of the Witnesses. Her parents are still quite active and they have continued to proselytize door to door. Her older brother, who is thirty-four, works at the religion headquarters in Odawara. He is married and has two children. His wife is also a devout Witness. Aomame is the only one in the family who left the religion – an apostate, they called her – and she was essentially disowned. I have found no evidence that the family has had any contact with her for nearly the last twenty years. I think it's impossible her family would hide her. At the age of eleven, she cut all ties with her family, and has been on her own pretty much ever since. She lived with her uncle for a while, but since she entered high school she has effectively been independent. Quite an impressive feat. And quite a strong-willed woman."

Buzzcut didn't say a word. He might have already had all this information.

"There is no way that the Witnesses are involved," Ushikawa went on. "They are well known to be pacifists, following the principle of nonresistance. It's not possible that their organization itself was aiming to take Leader's life. On that we can be agreed, I think."

Buzzcut nodded. "The Witnesses aren't involved in this. That much I know. Just to be sure, though, we had a talk with her brother. We took *every possible precaution*. But he didn't know anything."

"By *every possible precaution* you don't mean ripping off his fingernails, do you?"

Buzzcut ignored the question.

"Don't look so upset," Ushikawa said. "I'm joking. I'm sure her brother knew nothing about her actions or her where-abouts. I'm a born pacifist myself and would never do something so harsh, but that much I can figure out. Aomame has nothing to do with either her family or the Witnesses. Still, she couldn't have pulled off something this complicated on her own. Things were carefully arranged, and she just followed the plan. And that was also a pretty nimble vanishing act she pulled. She had to have a lot of help and a generous amount of funding. There's got to be someone – or some organization – who is backing her, someone who wanted Leader dead. They're the ones that plotted all this. Agreed?"

Buzzcut nodded. "Generally speaking, yes."

"But there's no clue what sort of organization we're talking about," Ushikawa said. "I assume you checked out her friends and acquaintances?"

Buzzcut silently nodded.

"And – let me guess – you found no friends to speak of," Ushikawa said. "No friends, no boyfriend. She has a few acquaintances at work, but outside of work she doesn't hang out with anybody. At least I wasn't able to find any evidence of her having any close relationship with anyone. Why would that be? She is a young, healthy, decent-looking woman."

Ushikawa glanced at Ponytail, standing by the door, seemingly frozen in time. He was devoid of all expression to begin with, so what was there to change? Does this guy even have a name? Ushikawa wondered. He wouldn't be surprised if he didn't.

"You two are the only ones who have actually seen Miss Aomame," Ushikawa said. "How about it? Did you notice anything unusual about her?"

Buzzcut shook his head slightly. "As you said, she is a fairly attractive young woman. Not beautiful enough to turn heads, though. A very quiet, calm person. She seemed quite confident in her abilities as a physical therapist. But nothing else really leapt out at us. It's strange, in fact, how little of an impression her outward appearance made. I can't even remember much about her face."

Ushikawa again glanced over at Ponytail by the door. Perhaps he had something to add? But he didn't look like he was about to open his mouth.

Ushikawa looked back at Buzzcut. "I'm sure you checked out Miss Aomame's phone record for the past few months?"

Buzzcut shook his head. "We haven't done that yet."

"You should," Ushikawa smiled. "It's definitely worth checking out. People call all sorts of places and get all sorts of calls. Investigate a person's phone records and you get a good idea of the kind of life they lead. Miss Aomame is no exception. It's no easy thing to get ahold of private phone records, but it can be done. It takes a thief to catch one, right?"

Buzzcut was silent, waiting for him to continue.

"In looking over Miss Aomame's phone records, several facts came to light. Quite unusually for a woman, she doesn't like talking on the phone. There weren't so many calls, and those that she made didn't last long. Occasionally there were some long calls, but these are the exception. Most of the calls were to her workplace, but since she works freelance half the time, she also made calls related to private business – in other words, appointments she made directly with clients rather than going through the sports club desk. There were quite a few calls like that. But as far as I could tell, none of them were suspicious."

Ushikawa paused, and as he examined the nicotine stains on his fingers from a number of angles, he thought about cigarettes. He lit an imaginary cigarette, inhaled the imaginary smoke, and exhaled.

"There were two exceptions, however. Two calls were to the police. Not 911 calls, but to the Traffic Bureau in the Shinjuku police station. And there were several calls from the station to her. She doesn't drive, and policemen can't afford private lessons at an expensive gym. So it must mean she has a friend working in that division. Who it is, though, I have no idea. One other thing that bothered me is that she had several long conversations with an unknown number. The other party always called her. She never once called them. I tried everything but couldn't trace the number. Obviously there are numbers that can be manipulated so that the party's name remains undisclosed. But even these, with some effort, should be traceable. I tried my best, but I couldn't find out anything. It's locked up tight. Quite extraordinary, really."

"This other person, then, can do things that aren't ordinary."

"Exactly. Professionals are definitely involved."

"Another thief," Buzzcut said.

Ushikawa rubbed his bald, misshapen head with his palm, and grinned. "That's right. Another thief – and a pretty formidable one at that."

"So at least we understand that professionals are backing her," Buzzcut commented.

"Correct. Miss Aomame is connected to some sort of organization. And this isn't some organization run by amateurs in their spare time."

Buzzcut lowered his eyelids halfway and studied Ushikawa. Then he turned around, toward the door. His eyes met Ponytail's, and Ponytail gave a slight single nod to indicate he understood their conversation. Buzzcut turned his gaze back to Ushikawa.

"So?" Buzzcut asked.

"So – " Ushikawa said, "it's my turn to ask you the questions. Do you have any idea which group or organization might want to rub out Leader?"

Buzzcut's long eyebrows became one as he frowned. Three wrinkles appeared above his nose.

"Listen, Mr. Ushikawa. Think about it. We are a religious organization. We seek a peaceful heart and a spiritual life. We live in harmony with nature, spending our days farming and in religious training. Who could possibly view us as an enemy? What is there to gain?"

A vague smile played around the corners of Ushikawa's mouth. "There are fanatics in every area of life. Who knows what kind of ideas fanatics will come up with?"

"We have no idea who could be behind this," Buzzcut replied, his face blank, ignoring Ushikawa's sarcasm.

"What about Akebono? There are still members of that group at large, aren't there?"

Buzzcut shook his head once more, this time decisively, meaning this was impossible. Anyone connected with Akebono must have been so thoroughly crushed that there were no fears about them. So there was no trace of Akebono left.

"Fine. So you have no idea who it could be either. The reality is, though, that some organization somewhere targeted your Leader and took his life. Very cleverly, very efficiently. And then they vanished, leaving nothing behind. Like smoke."

"And we have to find out who is behind this."

"Without getting the police involved."

Buzzcut nodded. "This is our problem, not a legal problem."

"Fine," Ushikawa said. "Understood. You've made that clear. But there's one more thing I would like to ask you."

"Go ahead," Buzzcut said.

"How many people within your religion know that Leader has died?"

"There would be the two of us," Buzzcut said. "And the two other people who helped transport the body. Subordinates of mine. Only five of the council know about this. That would make nine people. We haven't told his three shrine maidens yet, but they will find out soon enough. They serve him personally, so we can't hide it from them for very long. And then there's you, Mr. Ushikawa. Of course you know about it too."

"So all together, thirteen people."

Buzzcut didn't reply.

Ushikawa sighed deeply. "May I speak frankly?"

"Please do," Buzzcut said.

"I know it doesn't do much good to say this now," Ushikawa said, "but when you found out Leader was dead you should have contacted the police immediately. You should have made his death public. This kind of major event can't be hidden forever. Any secret known by more than ten people isn't a secret anymore. You could soon find yourself in a lot of trouble."

Buzzcut's expression didn't change. "It is not my job to decide. I just follow orders."

"So who makes the decisions?"

No reply.

"The person who has taken over for Leader?"

Buzzcut maintained his silence.

"Fine," Ushikawa said. "Someone above you instructed you to take care of Leader's corpse behind closed doors. In your organization, orders from above can't be questioned. But from a legal standpoint this clearly involves willful destruction and disposal of a dead body, which is quite a serious crime. You're aware of this, I'm sure."

Buzzcut nodded.

Ushikawa sighed deeply again. "I mentioned this before, but if by some chance the police get involved, please make it clear that I was never informed of Leader's death. Criminal charges are the last thing I need."

"You were never told about Leader's death," Buzzcut said. "We hired you as an outside investigator to locate a woman named Aomame, that's all. You have done nothing illegal."

"That works," Ushikawa said.

"You know, we had no desire to have an outsider like yourself find out about Leader's death. But you're the one who conducted the initial background check on Aomame, the one who cleared her. So you're already involved. We need your help to locate her. And we need you to keep the whole thing confidential."

"Keeping secrets is what my profession is all about. There is nothing to worry about. I assure you that no one else will ever hear about this from me."

"If it does get out, and we find out that you were the source, this could lead to something unpleasant."

Ushikawa looked down at his desk again, at the ten plump fingers resting on it. He looked surprised to discover that these fingers were his.

"Something unpleasant," he repeated, and looked up.

Buzzcut's eyes narrowed slightly. "Above all we have to keep Leader's death a secret. And we're not concerned about the means we use to accomplish this."

"I will keep your secret. Rest assured," Ushikawa said. "So far, we've worked together perfectly well. I've done a number of things behind the scenes that would have been hard for you to do openly. The work hasn't always been easy, but the compensation is more than adequate. So okay – double zippers on my mouth. I have no religious beliefs, but Leader helped me personally, so I am doing all I possibly can to locate Miss Aomame. I will do my utmost to uncover what is behind this. And I'm starting to see some progress. So please, be patient for just a while longer. Before too long, I should have some good news."

Buzzcut shifted ever so slightly in his chair. Standing by

the door, Ponytail shifted in tandem, moving his weight to his other leg.

"Is this all the information you're able to share?" Buzzcut asked.

Ushikawa mulled this over. "As I said, Miss Aomame called the Traffic Bureau of the Shinjuku Metropolitan Police Precinct twice, and the other party called her a number of times. I don't know the other party's name yet. It's the police. I can't just ask them. But an idea did flash through this inept brain of mine. There was something I remembered about the Traffic Bureau in the Shinjuku Precinct. I thought about it a lot, wondering what it was that was clinging to the edges of my pathetic memory. It took quite some time before it came to me. It's no fun growing old, no fun at all. The drawers where you store memories get harder to open. I used to be able to just yank them open with no problem, but this time it took me a good week before it finally dawned on me."

Ushikawa stopped talking, and a theatrical smile rose to his lips. He gazed at Buzzcut, who waited patiently for him to go on.

"In August of this year, a young female police officer with the Traffic Bureau in the Shinjuku Precinct was found strangled to death in a love hotel in Maruyama Ward, in Shibuya. Stark naked, handcuffed with her own police-issue handcuffs. Naturally this caused a scandal. The phone conversations between Miss Aomame and the Shinjuku Precinct were in the several months before this incident. There were no calls at all after the murder. What do you think? Too much to see this as mere coincidence?"

Buzzcut was silent for a while, then finally spoke. "So you're saying that the person Aomame contacted was this female police officer who was murdered?"

"The officer's name was Ayumi Nakano. Age twenty-six. A very charming-looking young woman. She came from a police family. Her father and older brother were both in the force. She was a fairly top-ranked officer. Needless to say, the police have tried very hard to locate the murderer, but with no luck so far. I apologize for being so forward with this question, but is there any chance that you might know something about this incident?"

Buzzcut's eyes, staring at Ushikawa, were cold, as if only minutes ago he had been extracted from a glacier. "I'm not sure what you mean," he said. "Are you thinking that we may in some way be involved in this incident? That one of us took this female police officer to a disreputable hotel, handcuffed her, and strangled her to death?"

Ushikawa pursed his lips and shook his head. "Don't be absurd! The thought never crossed my mind. All I'm asking is whether you have any ideas about this case. Anything at all. I would welcome even the smallest clue. No matter how hard I try to squeeze out whatever I can from this brain of mine, I can't find a connection between these two murders."

Buzzcut gazed at Ushikawa for a time, as if measuring something. Then he slowly let out his breath. "I understand. I will let my superiors know," he said. He took out a pocket notebook and made some notes. "Ayumi Nakano. Twenty-six. Traffic Bureau, Shinjuku Precinct. Possibly connected with Aomame."

"Exactly."

"Anything else?"

"There's one more thing. Someone within your religion must have brought up Miss Aomame's name. Someone who knew of a fitness trainer in Tokyo who was very good at stretching exercises. As you pointed out, I was hired to investigate the woman's background. I'm not trying to excuse myself, but I did my absolute best. Yet I didn't find anything out of the ordinary, nothing at all suspicious. She's as clean as they come. And you all asked her to come to the suite at the Hotel Okura. So who was it who recommended her in the first place?"

"I don't know."

"You don't know?" Ushikawa exclaimed. He looked like a child who has just heard a word he doesn't understand. "You mean that while someone within your religion must have first raised Miss Aomame's name, no one can recall who it was? Is that what you're saying?"

"Correct," Buzzcut replied, his expression unchanged.

"That's pretty weird," Ushikawa said, in a tone that reflected just how odd he found it.

Buzzcut didn't say a word.

"So we don't know when her name came up, or from whom, and things went forward seemingly on their own. Is that what you're saying?"

"To tell you the truth, the one who most enthusiastically supported the idea was Leader himself," Buzzcut said, choosing his words carefully. "Within the leadership, some thought it might be dangerous to allow a complete stranger to take care of Leader like that. As bodyguards we felt the same way. But Leader wasn't worried. In fact, he is the one who insisted that we go forward with it."

Ushikawa picked up his lighter again, flipped open the top, and flicked it on, as if testing it. Then he quickly snapped the top shut.

"I always heard Leader was a very cautious person," he said.

"He was. Very careful, very cautious," Buzzcut said. Silence continued for a time.

"There is one more thing I would like to ask," Ushikawa said. "About Tengo Kawana. He was seeing an older, married woman named Kyoko Yasuda. She came to his apartment once a week, and they would spend some intimate time together. He's young, so that's only to be expected. But suddenly one day her husband calls him, telling him she won't be paying him any more visits. And he hasn't heard a peep from her since."

Buzzcut frowned. "I don't understand why you're telling me

this. Are you saying that Tengo Kawana was involved in all this?"

"I wouldn't go that far. It's just that something has been bothering me. Whatever the circumstances might be, you would expect the woman to at least give him a call. But she hasn't gotten in touch. She just vanished, without a trace. Loose ends bother me, so that's why I posed the question, to be on the safe side. Do you know anything about this?"

"Personally, I have no knowledge about this woman," Buzzcut said in a flat tone. "Kyoko Yasuda. She had a relationship with Tengo Kawana."

"She was married, and ten years older than him."

Buzzcut noted down the name in his notebook. "I will let my superiors know."

"That's fine," Ushikawa said. "By the way, have you located the whereabouts of Eriko Fukada?"

Buzzcut raised his head and stared at Ushikawa as if he were examining a crooked picture frame. "And why should we know where Eriko Fukada is?"

"You're not interested in locating her?"

Buzzcut shook his head. "It is not our concern. She is free to go wherever she wants."

"And you're not interested in Tengo Kawana either?"

"He has nothing to do with us."

"At one time it seemed like you were quite interested in both of them," Ushikawa said.

Buzzcut narrowed his eyes for a moment, then opened his mouth. "At this point we are focused solely on Aomame."

"Your focus shifts from day to day?"

Buzzcut's lips parted a fraction, but he didn't reply.

"Mr. Buzzcut, have you read the novel Eriko Fukada wrote, *Air Chrysalis*?"

"No, I have not. In the religion we are strictly forbidden to read anything other than books on Sakigake doctrine. We can't even touch them."

"Have you ever heard the term *Little People*?"

"No," Buzzcut said, without missing a beat.

"That's fine," Ushikawa replied.

Their conversation came to an end. Buzzcut slowly rose from his chair and straightened the collar of his jacket. Ponytail took one step forward from the wall.

"Mr. Ushikawa, as I mentioned before, time is of the essence." Buzzcut stood and looked down at Ushikawa, who had remained seated. "We have to locate Aomame as soon as possible. We are doing our very best, and we need you to do the same, from a different angle. If Aomame isn't found, it could be bad for both of us. You are, after all, one of the few who know an important secret."

"With great knowledge comes great responsibility."

"Exactly," Buzzcut replied without a trace of emotion. He turned and swiftly exited the room. Ponytail followed Buzzcut out, noiselessly shutting the door.

After they had left, Ushikawa pulled open a desk drawer and switched off the tape recorder inside. He opened the lid of the recorder, extracted the cassette tape, and wrote the date and time on it with a ballpoint pen. For a man with his sort of odd looks, his handwriting was neat and graceful. He grabbed the pack of Seven Stars cigarettes beside him, extracted one, and lit it with his lighter. He took a long puff, exhaled deeply toward the ceiling, then closed his eyes for a moment. He opened his eyes and looked over at the wall clock. The clock showed 2:30. *What a creepy pair indeed,* Ushikawa told himself once more.

If Aomame isn't found, it could be bad for both of us, Buzzcut had said.

Ushikawa had twice visited the headquarters of Sakigake, deep in the mountains of Yamanashi Prefecture, and had seen the huge incinerator in the woods behind the compound. It was built to burn garbage and waste, but since it operated at an extremely high temperature, if you threw a human corpse inside there wouldn't be a single bone left. He knew that in fact several people's bodies had been disposed of in this way. Leader's body was probably one of them. Naturally enough, Ushikawa didn't want to suffer the same fate. Someday he would die, but if possible he would prefer something a bit more peaceful.

But there were some facts that Ushikawa hadn't revealed. Ushikawa preferred not to show all his cards at once. It was okay to show them a few of the lower-value cards, but the face cards he kept hidden. One needed some insurance – like the secret conversation he had recorded. When it came to this kind of game, Ushikawa was an expert. These young body-guards had nowhere near the experience he had.

Ushikawa had gotten ahold of Aomame's private client list. As long as you don't mind the time and effort, and you know what you're doing, you can get ahold of almost any kind of information. Ushikawa had made a decent enough investiga-tion of the backgrounds of the twelve private clients. Eight women and four men, all of them of high social standing and fairly well off. Not a single one the type who would lend a hand to an assassin. But one of them, a wealthy woman in her sev-enties, provided a safe house for women escaping domestic violence. She allowed battered women to live in a two-story apartment building on the extensive grounds of her estate, next door to her house.

This was, in itself, a wonderful thing to do. There was noth-ing suspicious about it. Yet something bothered Ushikawa, kicking around the edges of his consciousness. And as this vague notion rattled around in his mind, Ushikawa tried to pinpoint what it was. He was equipped with an almost animal-like sense of smell, and he trusted his intuition more than anything. His sense of smell had saved him a few times. *Violence* was perhaps the keyword here. This elderly woman had a special awareness of the violent, and thus went out of her way to protect those who were its victims.

Ushikawa had actually gone over to see this safe house. The wooden apartment building was on a rise in Azabu, prime real estate. It was a fairly old building, but had character. Through the grille of the front gate, he saw a beautiful flower bed in front of the entrance, and an extensive garden. A large oak cast a shadow onto the ground. A small die-cut plate glass was set into the front door. It was the kind of building that was fast disappearing from Tokyo.

For all its tranquillity, the building was heavily secured. The walls around it were high, and topped with barbed wire. The solid metal gate was securely locked, and a German shepherd patrolled the grounds and barked loudly if anyone approached. There were several cameras set up to scan the vicinity. Hardly any pedestrians walked on the road in front of the apartment building, so one couldn't loiter there long. It was a quiet residential area, with several embassies nearby. If a strange-looking man like Ushikawa were seen loitering, someone would be sure to question his presence.

The security was a little too tight. For a place meant to shelter battered women, they went a bit overboard. Ushikawa felt he would have to find out all there was to know about this safe house. No matter how tightly it was guarded, he would somehow have to pry it open. No – the more tightly it was guarded, the more he had to pry it open. And to do so, he would have to wrack his brain to come up with a plan.

Ushikawa recalled the part of his conversation with Buzzcut concerning the Little People.

"*Have you ever heard the term* Little People?"

"*No.*"

The reply had come a little too fast. If you had never heard that name before, you would normally pause a beat before answering. Little People? You would let the sound roll around in your mind for a second to see if anything clicked. And then you would reply. That's what most people would do.

Buzzcut had heard the term *Little People* before. Ushikawa didn't know if he knew what it meant or what it was, but it was definitely not the first time he'd heard it.

Ushikawa extinguished his now stubby cigarette. He was lost in thought for a while, and then he pulled out a new cigarette and lit it. He had decided years ago not to worry about getting lung cancer. If he wanted to concentrate, he had to get some nicotine into his system. Who knew what his fate was, even two or three days down the road? So what was the point in worrying about how his health would be fifteen years from now?

As he smoked his third Seven Stars, an idea came to him. *Ah!* he thought. *This might actually work.*

CHAPTER 2

Aomame

ALONE, BUT NOT LONELY

When it got dark she sat on a chair on the balcony and gazed out at the playground across the street. This was the most important part of her daily schedule, the focal point of her life. On sunny days, cloudy days, even when it rained, she kept a close watch, without missing a day. As October came around, the air grew cooler. On cold nights she wore many layers, kept a blanket for her legs, and sipped hot cocoa. She watched the slide until ten thirty, then took a leisurely bath to warm herself up, and went to bed.

Of course, there was a possibility that Tengo might appear even in the daytime. But most likely he wouldn't. If he was going to show up at the park, it would be after the mercury-vapor lamp went on and the moon was in the sky. Aomame had a quick supper, dressed so she could run outside, straightened her hair, then sat down on a garden chair and fixed her gaze on the slide. She always had an automatic pistol and a pair of small Nikon binoculars with her. Fearing that Tengo might appear if she went inside to the bathroom, she restricted her drinks to the hot cocoa.

Aomame kept up her watch without missing a day. She didn't read, didn't listen to music, just stared at the park, her ears poised to catch any sound outside. She rarely even changed her position in the chair. She would raise her head from time to time and – if it was a cloudless night – look at the sky to make sure there were still two moons. And then she would quickly shift her gaze back to the park. As Aomame kept a close watch on the park, the moons kept a close watch over her.

But Tengo didn't come.

Not many people visited the playground at night. Occasionally young lovers would appear. They would sit on a bench, hold hands, and, like a pair of tiny birds, exchange a few short, nervous kisses. But the park was too small, and too well lit. Soon they would grow restless and move on. Someone might show up to use the public toilet, find the door locked, and go away disappointed (or perhaps angry). The occasional office worker on his way home from work would sometimes sit alone on the bench, head bowed, undoubtedly hoping to sober up. Or maybe he just didn't want to go straight home. And there was an old man who took his dog for a walk late at night. Both the dog and the man were taciturn, and looked like they had given up all hope.

Most of the time, though, the playground was empty at night. Not even a cat ran across it. Just the mercury-vapor lamp's anonymous light illuminating the swings, the slide, the sandbox, the locked public toilet. When Aomame looked at this scene for a long time, she began to feel as if she had been abandoned on a deserted planet. Like that movie that showed the world after a nuclear war. What was the title?

On the Beach.

Still, Aomame sat there, her mind focused as she kept watch over the playground. As if she were a sailor who had climbed a tall mast and was scanning the vast ocean in search of schools of fish, or the ominous shadow of a periscope. Her watchful pair of eyes were on the lookout for one thing only – Tengo Kawana.

Perhaps Tengo lived in some other town, and had just happened to be passing by that night. In that case, the chances of his revisiting this park were close to zero. But Aomame didn't think so. When he sat on the slide that night, something about his manner, and his clothes, made her feel that he was taking a late-night stroll in the neighborhood, that he had stopped by the park and climbed up the slide. Probably to get a better look at the moons. Which meant he must live within walking distance.

In the Koenji District it wasn't easy to find a place to see the moon. The area was mostly flat, with hardly any tall buildings from which you could look at the sky. This made the slide in the playground a decent place to do so. It was quiet, and no one would bother you. If he decided he wanted to look at the moon again, he would show up – Aomame was certain of it. But then the next moment a thought struck her: *Things might not work out that easily. Maybe he's already found a better place to view the moon.*

Aomame gave a short, decisive shake of her head. She shouldn't overthink things. *The only choice I have is to believe that Tengo will return to this playground, and to wait here patiently until he does. I can't leave – this is the only point of contact between him and me.*

Aomame hadn't pulled the trigger.

It was the beginning of September. She was standing in a turnout on the Metropolitan Expressway No. 3, in the midst of a traffic jam, bathed in bright morning sunlight as she stuck the black muzzle of a Heckler & Koch in her mouth. Dressed in a Junko Shimada suit and Charles Jourdan high heels.

People were watching her from their cars, as if something was about to occur but they had no idea what. There was a middle-aged woman in a silver Mercedes coupe. There were suntanned men looking down at her from the high cab of a freight truck. Aomame planned to blow her brains out right before their very eyes with a 9mm bullet. Taking her life was the only way she could vanish from this 1Q84 world. That way she would be able to save Tengo's life. At least Leader had promised that. He had promised that much, and sought his own death.

Aomame didn't find it particularly disappointing that she had to die. Everything, she felt, had already been decided, ever since she was first pulled into this 1Q84 world. *I'm just following the plan that has already been laid out. Continuing to live, alone, in this unreasonable world – where there are two moons in the sky, one large, one small, where something called Little People control the destiny of others – what meaning could it have anyway?*

In the end, though, she didn't pull the trigger. At the last moment she relaxed her right index finger and removed the muzzle from her mouth. Like a person surfacing from deep under water she took a long breath, and exhaled, as if replacing every molecule of air within her.

She stopped moving toward death because she had heard a distant voice. At that point, she was in a soundless space. From the moment she put pressure on the trigger, all noise around her vanished. She was wrapped in silence, as if at the bottom of a pool. Down there, death was neither dark nor fearful. Like amniotic fluid to a fetus, it was natural, self-evident. *This isn't so bad,* Aomame thought, and almost smiled. That was when she heard a voice.

The voice sounded far away, as if coming from a distant time. She didn't recognize it. It reached her only after many twists and turns, and in the process it lost its original tone and timbre. What was left was a hollow echo, stripped of meaning. Still, within that sound, Aomame could detect a warmth she hadn't felt for years. The voice seemed to be calling her name.

She relaxed her finger on the trigger, narrowed her eyes,

and listened carefully, trying to hear the words the voice was saying. But all she could make out, or thought that she made out, was her name. The rest was wind whistling through a hollow space. In the end the voice grew distant, lost any meaning at all, and was absorbed into the silence. The void enveloping her disappeared, and, as if a cork had been pulled, the noise and clamor around her rushed in. And she no longer wanted to die.

Maybe I can see Tengo one more time at that little playground, she thought. *I can die after that. I'll take a chance on that happening. Living – not dying – means the possibility of seeing Tengo again. I want to live,* she decided. It was a strange feeling. *Had she ever experienced that feeling before in her life?*

She released the hammer of the automatic pistol, set the safety, and put it inside her shoulder bag. She straightened up, put on her sunglasses, and walked in the opposite direction of traffic back to her taxi. People silently watched her, in her high heels, striding down the expressway. She didn't have to walk for long. Even in the traffic jam, her taxi had managed to inch forward and had come up to where she was now standing.

Aomame knocked on the window and the driver lowered it.

"Can I get in again?"

The driver hesitated. "That thing you put in your mouth over there looked like a pistol."

"It was."

"A real one?"

"No way," Aomame replied, curling her lips.

The driver opened the door, and she climbed in. She took the bag off her shoulder and laid it on the seat and wiped her mouth with her handkerchief. She could still taste the metal and the residue of gun oil.

"So, did you find an emergency stairway?" the driver asked.

Aomame shook her head.

"I'm not surprised. I never heard of an emergency stairway

anywhere around here," the driver said. "Would you still like to get off at the Ikejiri exit?"

"Yes, that would be fine," Aomame replied.

The driver rolled down his window, stuck his hand out, and pulled over into the right lane in front of a large bus. The meter in the cab was unchanged from when she had gotten out.

Aomame leaned back against the seat, and, breathing slowly, she gazed at the familiar Esso billboard. The huge tiger was looking in her direction, smiling, with a gas hose in his paw. *Put a Tiger in Your Tank,* the ad read.

"Put a tiger in your tank," she whispered.

"Excuse me?" the driver said, glancing at her in the rear-view mirror.

"Nothing. Just talking to myself."

I think I'll stay alive here a bit longer, and see with my own eyes what's going to happen. I can still die after that – it won't be too late. Probably.

The day after she gave up on killing herself, Tamaru called her. So Aomame told him that the plan had changed – that she was going to stay put, and not change her name or get plastic surgery.

On the other end of the line Tamaru was silent. Several theories noiselessly aligned themselves in his mind.

"In other words, you're saying you don't want to move to another location?"

"Correct," Aomame replied. "I would like to stay here for the time being."

"That place is not set up to hide someone for an extended period."

"If I stay inside and don't go out, they shouldn't find me."

"Don't underestimate them," Tamaru said. "They will do everything they can to pinpoint who you are and hunt you down. And you won't be the only one in danger. It could involve those around you. If that happens, I could be put in a difficult position."

"I'm very sorry about that. But I need a bit more time."

"*A bit more time?* That's a little vague," Tamaru said.

"That's the only way I can put it."

Tamaru was silent, in thought. He seemed to have sensed how firm her decision was.

"I have to keep my priorities straight," he said. "Do you understand that?"

"I think so."

Tamaru was silent again, and then continued.

"All right. I just wanted to make sure I wasn't misunderstanding. Since you insist on staying, you must have your reasons."

"I do," Aomame said.

Tamaru briefly cleared his throat. "As I have told you before, we have committed to take you someplace safe, and far away – to erase any trail, change your face and name. Maybe it won't be a total transformation, but as close to total as we can manage. I thought we were agreed on this."

"Of course I understand. I'm not saying I don't like the plan itself. It's just that something unexpected occurred, and I need to stay put for a while longer."

"I am not authorized to say yes or no to this," Tamaru said, making a faint sound in the back of his throat. "It might take a while to get an answer."

"I'll be here," Aomame said.

"Glad to hear it," Tamaru said, and hung up.

The phone rang the next morning, just before nine. Three rings, then it stopped, and rang again. It had to be Tamaru.

Tamaru launched right in without saying hello. "Madame also is concerned about you staying there for very long. It is just a safe house, and it is not totally secure. Both of us agree that it's best to move you somewhere far away, somewhere more secure. Do you follow me?"

"I do."

"But you are a calm, cautious person. You don't make stupid mistakes, and I know you are committed. We trust you implicitly."

"I appreciate that."

"If you insist that you want to stay in that place for a *bit* longer then you must have your reasons. We don't know what your rationale is, but I'm sure it's not just a whim. So she is thinking that she would like to follow your wishes as much as she can."

Aomame said nothing.

Tamaru continued. "You can stay there until the end of the year. But that's the limit."

"After the first of the year, then, I need to move to another place."

"Please understand we are doing our very best to respect your wishes."

"I understand," Aomame said. "I'll be here until the end of the year, then I will move."

But this wasn't her real intention. She didn't plan to take one step out of this apartment until she saw Tengo again. If she mentioned this now, though, complications would set in. She could delay things for over three months, until the end of the year. After that she would consider what to do next.

"Fine," Tamaru said. "We'll deliver food and other necessities once a week. At one p.m. each Tuesday the supply masters will stop by. They have a key, so they can get in on their own. They will only go to the kitchen, nowhere else. While they are at the apartment, I want you to go into the back bedroom and lock the door. Don't show your face, or speak. When they're leaving, they will ring the doorbell once. Then you can come out of the bedroom. If there's anything special you need, let me know right now and I'll have it included in the next delivery."

"It would be nice to have equipment so I could do some strength training," Aomame said. "There's only so much you can do exercising and stretching without equipment."

"Full-scale gym equipment is out of the question, but we could supply some home equipment, the kind that doesn't take up much space."

"Something very basic would be fine," Aomame said.

"A stationary bike and some auxiliary equipment for strength training. Would that do it?"

"That would be great. If possible, I'd also like to get a metal softball bat."

Tamaru was silent for a few seconds.

"A bat has many uses," Aomame explained. "Just having it next to me makes me calm. It's like I grew up with a bat in my hand."

"Okay. I'll get one for you," Tamaru said. "If you think of anything else you need, write it on a piece of paper and leave it on the kitchen counter. I'll make sure you get it the next time we bring supplies."

"Thank you. But I think I have everything I need."

"How about books and videos and the like?"

"I can't think of anything I particularly want."

"How about Proust's *In Search of Lost Time*?" Tamaru asked. "If you've never read it this would be a good opportunity to read the whole thing."

"Have you read it?"

"No, I've never been in jail, or had to hide out for a long time. Someone once said unless you have those kinds of opportunities, you can't read the whole of Proust."

"Do you know anybody who has read the whole thing?"

"I've known some people who have spent a long period in jail, but none were the type to be interested in Proust."

"I'd like to give it a try," Aomame said. "If you can get ahold of those books, bring them the next time you bring supplies."

"Actually, I already got them for you," Tamaru said.

The so-called supply masters came on Tuesday afternoon at one p.m. on the dot. As instructed, Aomame went into the back bedroom, locked it from the inside, and tried not to make a sound. She heard the front door being unlocked and people opening the door and coming in. Aomame had no idea what kind of people these "supply masters" were. From the sounds they made she got the feeling there were two of them, but she didn't hear any voices. They carried in several boxes and silently went about putting things away. She heard them at the sink, rinsing off the food they had bought and then stacking it in the fridge. They must have decided beforehand who would be in charge of what. They unwrapped some boxes, and she could hear them folding up the wrapping paper and containers. It sounded like they were wrapping up the kitchen garbage as well. Aomame couldn't take the bag of garbage downstairs to the collection spot, so she had to have somebody take it for her.

The people seemed to do their work efficiently, with no wasted effort. They tried not to make any unnecessary noise, and their footsteps, too, were quiet. They were finished in about twenty minutes. Then they opened the front door and left. She heard them lock the front door from the outside, and then the doorbell rang once as a signal. To be on the safe side, Aomame waited fifteen minutes. Then she exited the bedroom, made sure no one else was there, and locked the dead bolt on the front door.

The large fridge was crammed full of a week's worth of food. This time it wasn't the kind of food you popped in the microwave, but mostly fresh groceries: a variety of fruits and vegetables; fish and meat; tofu, wakame, and natto. Milk, cheese, and orange juice. A dozen eggs. So there wouldn't be any extra garbage, they had taken everything out of their original containers and then neatly rewrapped them in plastic wrap. They had done a good job understanding the type of food she normally ate. *How would they know this?* she wondered. A stationary bicycle was set down next to the window, a small but high-end model. The digital display on it showed speed, distance, and calories burned. You could also monitor rpms and heart rate. There was a bench press to work on abs, deltoids, and triceps, the kind of equipment that was easy to assemble and disassemble. Aomame was quite familiar with it. It was the newest type, a very simple design yet very effective. With these two pieces of equipment she would have no trouble keeping in shape.

A metal bat in a soft case was there as well. Aomame took it out of the case and took a few swings. The shiny, new silver bat swished sharply through the air. The old familiar heft of it calmed her. The feel of the bat in her hands brought back memories of her teenage years, and the time she had spent with Tamaki Otsuka.

All seven volumes of *In Search of Lost Time* were piled up on the dining table. They were not new copies, but they appeared to be unread. Aomame flipped through one. There were several magazines, too – weekly and monthly magazines – and five brand-new videos, still in their plastic wrap. She had no idea who had chosen them, but they were all new movies she had never seen. She was not in the habit of going to movie theaters, so there were always a lot of new films that she missed.

There were three brand-new sweaters in a large department-store shopping bag, in different thicknesses. There were two thick flannel shirts, and four long-sleeved T-shirts. All of them were in plain fabric and simple designs. They were all the perfect size. There were also some thick socks and tights. If she was going to be here until December, she would need them. Her handlers knew what they were doing.

She took the clothes into the bedroom and folded them to store in drawers or hung them on hangers in the closet. She had gone back to the kitchen and was drinking coffee when the phone rang. It rang three times, stopped, then rang again.

"Did you get everything?" Tamaru asked.

"Yes, thank you. I think I have everything I need now. The exercise equipment is more than enough. Now I just have to crack open Proust."

"If there is anything that we've overlooked, don't hesitate to tell me."

"I won't," Aomame said. "Though I don't think it would be easy to find anything you have overlooked."

Tamaru cleared his throat. "This might not be my business, but do you mind if I give you a warning?"

"Go right ahead."

"Unless you have experienced it, being shut up in a small place by yourself, unable to see or talk to anyone else, is not the easiest thing in the world. No matter how tough a person might be, eventually he is going to make a sound. Especially when someone is after you."

"I haven't been living in very spacious places up till now."

"That could be an advantage," Tamaru said. "Still, I want you to be very careful. If a person remains tense for a long time he might not notice it himself, but it's like his nerves are a piece of rubber that has been stretched out. It's hard to go back to the original shape."

"I'll be careful," Aomame said.

"As I said before, you are a very cautious person. You're practical and patient, not overconfident. But no matter how careful a person might be, once your concentration slips, you will definitely make one or two mistakes. Loneliness becomes an acid that eats away at you."

"I don't think I'm lonely," Aomame declared. She said this half to Tamaru, and half to herself. "I'm all alone, but I'm not lonely."

There was silence on the other end of the phone, as if Tamaru were giving serious thought to the difference between being alone and being lonely.

"At any rate I'll be more cautious than I have been," Aomame said. "Thank you for the advice."

"There is one thing I'd like you to understand," Tamaru said. "We will do whatever we can to protect you. But if some emergency situation arises – what that might be, I don't know – you may have to deal with it yourself. I can run over there as fast as possible and still might not make it in time. Depending on the situation, I may not be able to get there at all. For instance, if it is no longer desirable for us to have a connection with you."

"I understand completely. I plan to protect myself. With the bat, and with the *thing you gave me.*"

"It's a tough world."

"Wherever there's hope there's a trial," Aomame said.

Tamaru was silent again for a moment, and then spoke. "Have you heard about the final tests given to candidates to become interrogators for Stalin's secret police?"

"No, I haven't."

"A candidate would be put in a square room. The only thing in the room is an ordinary small wooden chair. And the interrogator's boss gives him an order. He says, 'Get this chair to confess and write up a report on it. Until you do this, you can't leave this room.' "

"Sounds pretty surreal."

"No, it isn't. It's not surreal at all. It's a real story. Stalin actually did create that kind of paranoia, and some ten million people died on his watch – most of them his fellow countrymen. And we *actually* live in that kind of world. Don't ever forget that."

"You're full of heartwarming stories, aren't you."

"Not really. I just have a few set aside, just in case. I never received a formal education. I just learned whatever looked useful, as I experienced it. *Wherever there's hope there's a trial.* You're exactly right. Absolutely. Hope, however, is limited, and generally abstract, while there are countless trials, and they tend to be concrete. That is also something I had to learn on my own."

"So what kind of confession did the interrogator candidates extract from the chairs?"

"That is a question definitely worth considering," Tamaru said. "Sort of like a Zen koan."

"Stalinist Zen," Aomame said.

After a short pause, Tamaru hung up.

That afternoon she worked out on the stationary bike and the bench press. Aomame enjoyed the moderate workout, her first in a while. Afterward she showered, then made dinner while listening to an FM station. In the evening she checked the TV news (though not a single item caught her interest). After the sun had set she went out to the balcony to watch the playground, with her usual blanket, binoculars, and pistol. And her shiny brand-new bat.

If Tengo doesn't show up by then, she thought, *I guess I will see out this enigmatic year of 1Q84 in this corner of Koenji, one monotonous day after another. I'll cook, exercise, check the news, and work my way through Proust – and wait for Tengo to show up at the playground. Waiting for him is the central task of my life. Right now that slender thread is what is barely keeping me alive. It's like that spider I saw when I was climbing down the emergency stairway on the Metropolitan Expressway No. 3. A tiny black spider that had spun a pathetic little web in a corner of the grimy steel frame and was silently lying in wait. The wind from under the bridge had blown the spider web, which hung there precariously, tattered and full of dust. When I first saw it, I thought it was pitiful. But right now I'm in the same situation.*

I have to get ahold of a recording of Janáček's Sinfonietta. *I need it when I'm working out. It makes me feel connected. It's as if that music is leading me to something. To what, though, I can't say.* She made a mental note to add that to the next list of supplies.

It was October now. There were less than three months left of her reprieve. The clock kept ticking away, ceaselessly. Aomame sank down into her garden chair and continued to watch the slide in the playground through the plastic blinds. The little children's playground looked pale under the mercury-vapor lamp. The scene made Aomame think of deserted hallways in an aquarium at night. Invisible, imaginary fish were swimming noiselessly through the trees, never halting their silent movements. And two moons hung in the sky, waiting for Aomame's acknowledgment.

"Tengo," she whispered. "Where are you?"

CHAPTER 3

Tengo

THE ANIMALS ALL WORE CLOTHES

In the afternoons Tengo would visit his father in the hospital, sit next to his bed, open the book he brought, and read aloud. After reading five pages he would take a short break, then read five more pages. He read whatever book he happened to be reading on his own at the time. Sometimes it was a novel, or a biography, or a book on the natural sciences. What was most important was the act of reading the sentences aloud, not the contents.

Tengo didn't know if his father actually heard his voice. His face never showed any reaction. This thin, shabby-looking old man had his eyes closed, and he was asleep. He didn't move at all, and his breathing wasn't audible. He was breathing, but unless you brought your ear very close, or held a mirror up to his nose to see if it clouded, you couldn't really tell. The liquid in the IV drip went into his body, and a tiny amount of urine oozed out the catheter. The only thing that revealed that he was alive was this silent, slow movement in and out. Occasionally a nurse would shave his beard with an electric razor and use a tiny pair of scissors with rounded-off tips to clip the white hairs growing out of his ears and nose. She would trim his eyebrows as well. Even though he was unconscious, these continued to grow. As he watched his father, Tengo started to have doubts about the difference between a person being alive and being dead. *Maybe there really wasn't much of a difference to begin with,* he thought. *Maybe we just decided, for convenience's sake, to insist on a difference.*

At three the doctor came and gave Tengo an update on his father's condition. The explanation was always concise, and it was nearly the same from one day to the next. There was no change. The old man was simply asleep, his life gradually fading away. In other words, death was approaching, slowly but certainly, and there was nothing medically speaking that could be done. Just let him lie here, quietly sleeping. That's about all the doctor could say.

In the evenings two male nurses would come and take his father to an examination room. The male nurses differed depending on the day, but both of them were taciturn. Perhaps the masks they wore had something to do with it, but they never said a word. One of them looked foreign. He was short and dark skinned, and was always smiling at Tengo through his mask. Tengo could tell he was smiling by his eyes. Tengo smiled back and nodded.

Anywhere from a half hour to an hour later, his father would be brought back to his room. Tengo had no idea what kind of examinations they were conducting. While his father was gone he would go to the cafeteria, have some hot green tea, and stay about fifteen minutes before going back to the hospital room. All the while he held on to the hope that when he returned an air chrysalis would once again materialize, with Aomame as a young girl lying inside. But all that greeted him in the gloomy hospital room was the smell of a sick person and the depressions left behind in the empty bed.

Tengo stood by the window and looked at the scene outside. Beyond the garden and lawn was the dark line of the pine windbreak, through which came the sound of waves. The rough waves of the Pacific. It was a thick, darkish sound, as if many souls were gathered, each whispering his story. They seemed to be seeking more souls to join them, seeking even more stories to be told.

Before this, in October, Tengo had twice taken day trips, on his days off, to the sanatorium in Chikura. He would take the early-morning express train. Once there, he would sit beside his father's bed, and talk to him sometimes. There was nothing even close to a response. His father just lay there, faceup, sound asleep. Tengo spent most of his time gazing out the window. As evening approached he waited for something to happen, but nothing ever did. The sun would silently sink, and the room would be wrapped in the gathering gloom. He would ultimately give up, leave, and take the last express train back to Tokyo.

Maybe I should be more patient, stay with him longer, Tengo thought once. *Maybe visiting him for the day and then leaving isn't enough. What's needed, perhaps, is a deeper commitment.* He had no concrete evidence that this was true. He just felt that way.

After the middle of November he took the vacation leave he had accumulated, telling the cram school that his father was in critical condition and he needed to look after him. This in itself wasn't a lie. He asked a classmate from college to take over his classes. He was one of the relatively few people with whom Tengo had kept in touch, albeit just once or twice a year. Even in the math department, which had more than its share of oddballs, this guy was particularly odd, as well as smart beyond compare. After graduating, though, he didn't get a job or go on to grad school. Instead, when he felt like it, he taught math at a private cram school for junior high students. Other than that, he read, went fly fishing, and did whatever he wanted. Tengo happened to know, however, that he was a very capable teacher. The thing was, he was tired of being so capable. Plus, he was from a wealthy family and there was no need for him to force himself to work. He had substituted for Tengo once before and the students had liked him. Tengo called him and explained the situation, and he immediately agreed to step in.

There was also the question of what to do about Fuka-Eri. Tengo couldn't decide if leaving this naive girl behind in his apartment for a long time was the right thing to do. And besides, she was trying to hide out, to stay out of sight. So he asked her directly. "Are you okay on your own here for a while? Or would you like to go someplace else, temporarily?"

"Where are you going," Fuka-Eri asked, a serious look in her eyes.

"To the cat town," Tengo explained. "My father won't regain consciousness. He's been in a deep sleep for a while. They say he might not last long."

He didn't say a word about the air chrysalis appearing in the hospital room bed one evening. Or how Aomame appeared inside as a young girl, asleep. Or how the air chrysalis was exactly as Fuka-Eri had described it in her novel, down to the last detail. Or how he was secretly hoping that it would again appear before him.

Fuka-Eri narrowed her eyes, pursed her lips, and stared straight at Tengo, as if trying to make out a message written in tiny letters. Almost unconsciously he touched his face, but it didn't feel as though something was written on it.

"That's fine," Fuka-Eri said after a while, and she nodded several times. "Do not worry about me. I will stay at home." After thinking for a moment she added, "Right now there is no danger."

"Right now there is no danger," Tengo repeated.

"Do not worry about me," she said again.

"I'll call you every day."

"Do not get abandoned in the cat town."

"I'll be careful," Tengo said.

Tengo went to the supermarket and bought enough food so Fuka-Eri wouldn't have to go shopping, all things that would be simple to prepare. Tengo was well aware that she had neither the ability nor the desire to do much cooking. He wanted to avoid coming back in two weeks to a fridge full of mushy, spoiled food.

He stuffed a vinyl bag full of clothes and toiletries, a few books, pens, and paper. As usual he took the express train from Tokyo Station, changed to a local train at Tateyama, and got off at Chikura. He went to the tourist information booth in front of the station to look for a fairly inexpensive hotel. It was the off-season, so he had no trouble finding a room in a simple Japanese-style inn that catered mainly to people coming to fish. The cramped but clean room smelled of fresh tatami. The fishing harbor was visible from the second-floor window. The charge for the room, which included breakfast, was cheaper than he had expected.

"I don't know yet how long I'll be staying," Tengo said, "but I'll go ahead and pay for three days." The proprietress of the inn had no objection. The doors shut at eleven, and bringing a woman to his room would be problematic, she explained in a roundabout way. All this sounded fine to him. Once he settled into his room, he phoned the sanatorium. He told the nurse (the same middle-aged nurse he had met before) that he would like to visit his father at three p.m. and asked if that would be convenient. That would be fine, she replied. "Mr. Kawana just sleeps all the time," she said.

Thus began Tengo's days at the cat town beside the sea. He would get up early, take a walk along the shore, watch the fishing boats go in and out of the harbor, then return to the inn for breakfast. Breakfast was exactly the same every day – dried horse mackerel and fried eggs, a quartered tomato, seasoned dried seaweed, miso soup with shijimi clams, and rice – but for some reason it tasted wonderful every morning. After breakfast he would sit at a small desk and write. He hadn't written in some time and found the act of writing with his fountain pen enjoyable. Working in an unfamiliar place, away from your daily routine, was invigorating. The engines of the fishing boats chugged monotonously as they pulled into the harbor. Tengo liked the sound.

The story he was writing began with a world where there were two moons in the sky. A world of Little People and air chrysalises. He had borrowed this world from Fuka-Eri's *Air Chrysalis,* but by now it was entirely his own. As he wrote, his mind was living in that world. Even when he lay down his pen and stood up from the desk, his mind remained there. There was a special sensation of his body and his mind beginning to separate, and he could no longer distinguish the real world from the fictional. The protagonist of the story who entered the cat town probably experienced the same sensation. Before he knew it, the world's center of gravity had shifted. And the protagonist would (most likely) be unable to ever board the train to get out of town.

At eleven Tengo had to leave his room so they could clean it. When the time came he stopped writing, went out, walked to the front of the station, and drank coffee in a nearby coffee shop. Occasionally he would have a light sandwich, but usually he ate nothing. He would then pick up the morning paper and check it closely to see if there was any article that might have something to do with him. He found no such article. *Air Chrysalis* had long since disappeared from the bestseller lists. Number one on the list now was a diet book entitled *Eat as Much as You Want of the Food You Love and Still Lose Weight.* What a great title. The whole book could be blank inside and it would still sell.

After he finished his coffee and was done with the paper,

Tengo took the bus to the sanatorium. He usually arrived between one thirty and two. He chatted a bit with the nurse who was always at the front desk. When Tengo began staying in the town and visiting his father every day, the nurses grew kinder to him, and treated him in a friendly way – as warmly as the prodigal son's family must have welcomed him back home.

One of the younger nurses always gave an embarrassed smile whenever she saw Tengo. She seemed to have a crush on him. She was petite, wore her hair in a ponytail, and had big eyes and red cheeks. She was probably in her early twenties. But ever since the air chrysalis had appeared with the sleeping girl inside, all Tengo could think about was Aomame. All other women were faint shadows in comparison. An image of Aomame was constantly playing at the edges of his mind. Aomame was alive somewhere in this world – he could *feel* it. He knew she must be searching for him, which is why on that evening she chose to find him. She had not forgotten him either.

If what I saw wasn't an illusion.

Sometimes he remembered his older girlfriend, and wondered how she was. *She's irretrievably lost now,* her husband had said on the phone. She can no longer visit your home. *Irretrievably lost.* Even now those words gave Tengo an uncomfortable, uneasy feeling. They had an undeniably ominous ring.

Still, she became less and less of a presence in his mind as time went on. He could recall the afternoons they had spent together only as events in the past, undertaken to fulfill certain goals. Tengo felt guilty about this. But before he had known it, gravity had changed. It had shifted, and it wouldn't be going back to its original location.

When he arrived at his father's room, Tengo would sit in the chair next to his bed and briefly greet him. Then he would explain, in chronological order, what he had done since the previous night. He hadn't done much. He had gone back to town on the bus, had a simple dinner at a restaurant, drunk a beer, returned to the inn, and read. He'd gone to bed at ten. In the morning he would take a walk, eat breakfast, and work on his novel for about two hours. He repeated the same things every day, but even so, Tengo gave the unconscious man a detailed report on all his activities. There was no response from his listener. It was like talking to a wall. A formality he had to go through. Still, sometimes simple repetition has meaning.

Then Tengo would read from the book he had brought along. He didn't stick to just one book. He would read aloud the book that he himself was reading at the time. If a manual for an electric lawn mower had been his current reading material, that's what he would have read. Tengo read in a deliberately clear voice, slowly, so that it was easy to understand. That was the one thing he made sure to do.

The lightning outside grew steadily stronger and for a while the greenish light illuminated the road, but there was no rumble of thunder. Maybe there was thunder, but he felt unfocused. It was as if he couldn't hear it. Rainwater flowed in small rivers along the road. After wading through the water, customers came into the shop, one after another.

His friend turned and stared. He went strangely quiet. There was a sudden commotion as customers pushed toward them, making it hard to breathe.

Someone cleared his throat, perhaps because a piece of food had gotten stuck; it was a strange voice, more of a snuffling cough, as if it were a dog.

Suddenly there was a huge flash of lightning that shone all the way inside the place, illuminating the people on the dirt floor. And just then a clap of thunder sounded, ready to crack the roof. Surprised, he stood up, and the crowd of people at the entrance turned as one to face him. Then he saw that theirs were the faces of animals – dogs or foxes, he wasn't sure – and the animals all wore clothes, and some of them had long tongues hanging out, licking around the corners of their mouths.

Tengo read to there and looked at his father's face. "The end," he said. The story stopped there.

No reaction.

"What do you think?"

As expected, there was no response from his father.

Sometimes he would read what he himself had written that morning. After he had read it, he would rewrite in ballpoint pen the parts he wasn't satisfied with, and reread the parts he had edited. If he still wasn't satisfied at the way it sounded, he would rewrite it again, and then read the new version.

"The rewritten version is better," he said to his father, as if hoping he would agree. His father, predictably, didn't express an opinion. He didn't say that it was better, or that the earlier version was better, or that there really wasn't much of a difference between the two. The lids on his sunken eyes were shut tight, like a sad house with its heavy shutters lowered.

Sometimes Tengo would stand up from his chair and stretch and go to the window and look at the scenery outside. After several overcast days, it was raining. The continual afternoon rain made the pine windbreak dark and heavy. He couldn't hear the waves at all. There was no wind, just the rain falling straight down from the sky. A flock of black birds flew by in the rain. The hearts of those birds were dark, and wet, too. The inside of the room was also wet. Everything there, pillows, books, desk, was damp. But oblivious to it all – to the weather, the damp, the wind, the sound of the waves – his father continued in an uninterrupted coma. Like a merciful cloak, paralysis enveloped his body. After a short break Tengo went back to reading aloud. In the damp, narrow room, that was all he was able to do.

When he tired of reading aloud, Tengo sat there, gazing at the form of his sleeping father and trying to surmise what kinds of things were going through his brain. Inside – in the inner parts of that stubborn skull, like an old anvil – what sort of consciousness lay hidden there? Or was there nothing left at all? Was it like an abandoned house from which all the possessions and appliances had been moved, leaving no trace of those who had once dwelled there? Even if it was, there should be the occasional memory or scenery etched into the walls and ceilings. Things cultivated over such a long time don't just vanish into nothingness. As his father lay on this plain bed in the sanatorium by the shore, at the same time he might very well be surrounded by scenes and memories invisible to others, in the still darkness of a back room in his own vacant house.

The young nurse with the red cheeks would come in, smile at Tengo, then take his father's temperature, check how much remained in the IV drip, and measure the amount of urine he had produced. She would note all the numbers down on a clipboard. Her actions were automatic and brisk, as if prescribed in a training manual. Tengo watched this series of movements and wondered how she must feel to live her life in this sanatorium by the sea, taking care of senile old people whose prognosis was grim. She looked young and healthy. Beneath her starched uniform, her waist and her breasts were compact but ample. Golden down glistened on her smooth neck. The plastic name tag on her chest read *Adachi*.

What could possibly have brought her to this remote place, where oblivion and listless death lay hovering over everything? Tengo could tell she was a skilled and hardworking nurse. She was still young and worked quite efficiently. She could have easily worked in some other field of health care, something more lively and engaging, so why did she choose this sad sort of place to work? Tengo wondered. He wanted to find out the reason and the background. If he did ask her, he knew she would be honest. He could sense that about her. But it would be better not to get involved, Tengo decided – this was, after all, the cat town. Some day he would have to get on the train and go back to the world from which he came.

The nurse finished her tasks, put the clipboard back, and gave Tengo an awkward smile.

"His condition is unchanged. The same as always."

"So he's stable," Tengo said in as cheerful a voice as he could manage. "To put a positive spin on it."

A half-apologetic smile rose to her lips and she inclined her head just a touch. She glanced at the book on his lap. "Are you reading that to him?"

Tengo nodded. "I doubt he can hear it, though."

"Still, it's a good thing to do," the nurse said.

"Maybe it is, or maybe it isn't, but I can't think of anything else I can do."

"But not everybody else would do that."

"Most people have busier lives than I do," Tengo said.

The nurse looked like she was about to say something, but she hesitated. In the end she didn't say a thing. She looked at his sleeping father, and then at Tengo.

"Take care," she said.

"Thanks," Tengo answered.

After Nurse Adachi left, Tengo waited a while, then began reading aloud once more.

In the evening, when his father was wheeled on a gurney to the examination room, Tengo went to the cafeteria, drank some tea, then phoned Fuka-Eri from a pay phone.

"Is everything okay?" Tengo asked her.

"Yes, everything is okay," she said. "Just like always."

"Everything's fine with me, too. Doing the same thing every day."

"But time is moving forward."

"That's right," Tengo said. "Every day time moves forward one day's worth."

And what has gone forward can't go back to where it came from.

"The crow came back again just a little while ago," Fuka-Eri said. "A big crow."

"In the evening that crow always comes up to the window."

"Doing the same thing every day."

"That's right," Tengo said. "Just like us."

"But it doesn't think about time."

"Crows can't think about time. Probably only humans have the concept of time."

"Why," she asked.

"Humans see time as a straight line. It's like putting notches on a long straight stick. The notch here is the future, the one on this side is the past, and the present is this point right here. Do you understand?"

"I think so."

"But actually time isn't a straight line. It doesn't have a shape. In all senses of the term, it doesn't have any form. But since we can't picture something without form in our minds, for the sake of convenience we understand it as a straight line. At this point, humans are the only ones who can make that sort of conceptual substitution."

"But maybe we are the ones who are wrong."

Tengo mulled this over. "You mean we may be wrong to see time as a straight line?"

No response.

"That's a possibility. Maybe we're wrong and the crow is

right. Maybe time is nothing at all like a straight line. Perhaps it's shaped like a twisted doughnut. But for tens of thousands of years, people have probably been seeing time as a straight line that continues on forever. And that's the concept they based their actions on. And until now they haven't found anything inconvenient or contradictory about it. So as an experiential model, it's probably correct."

"Experiential model," Fuka-Eri repeated.

"After taking a lot of samples, you come to view one conjecture as actually correct."

Fuka-Eri was silent for a time. Tengo had no idea if she had understood him or not.

"Hello?" Tengo said, checking if she was still there.

"How long will you be there," Fuka-Eri asked, omitting the question mark.

"You mean how long will I be in Chikura?"

"Yes."

"I don't know," Tengo answered honestly. "All I can say right now is that I'll stay here until certain things make sense. There are some things I don't understand. I want to stay for a while and see how they develop."

Fuka-Eri was silent on the other end again. When she was silent it was like she wasn't there at all.

"Hello?" Tengo said again.

"Don't miss the train," Fuka-Eri said.

"I'll be careful," Tengo replied, "not to be late for the train. Is everything okay with you?"

"One person came here a while ago."

"What kind of person?"

"An N – H – K person."

"A fee collector from NHK?"

"Fee collector," she asked, again without the question mark.

"Did you talk to him?" Tengo asked.

"I did not understand what he was saying."

She apparently had no idea what NHK was. The girl lacked some essential cultural knowledge.

"It will take too long to explain over the phone," Tengo said, "but basically it's a large organization. A lot of people work there. They go around to all the houses in Japan and collect money every month. You and I don't need to pay, because we don't receive anything from them. I hope you didn't unlock the door."

"No, I did not unlock it. Like you told me."

"I'm glad."

"But he said, 'You are a thief.' "

"You don't need to worry about that," Tengo said.

"We have not stolen anything."

"Of course we haven't. You and I haven't done anything wrong."

Fuka-Eri was again silent on the other end of the line.

"Hello?" Tengo said.

Fuka-Eri didn't reply. She might have already hung up. Though he didn't hear any sound that indicated this.

"Hello?" Tengo repeated, this time more loudly.

Fuka-Eri coughed lightly. "That person knew a lot about you."

"The fee collector?"

"Yes. The N – H – K person."

"And he called you a thief."

"No. He didn't mean me."

"He meant me?"

Fuka-Eri didn't reply.

"Anyway," Tengo said, "I don't have a TV. So I'm not stealing anything from NHK."

"But that person was very angry that I didn't unlock the door."

"It doesn't matter. Let him be angry. But no matter what happens, no matter what anyone tells you, never, ever unlock the door."

"I won't unlock it."

After saying this, Fuka-Eri suddenly hung up. Or perhaps it wasn't so sudden. Perhaps for her, hanging up the phone at that point was an entirely natural, even logical act. To Tengo's ear, though, it sounded abrupt. But Tengo knew that even if he were to try his hardest to guess what Fuka-Eri was thinking and feeling, it wouldn't do any good. As an experiential model.

Tengo hung up the phone and went back to his father's room.

His father had not been brought back to his room yet. The bed still had a depression in it from his body. No air chrysalis was there. In the room, darkened by the dim, chill dusk, the only thing present was the slight trace of the person who had occupied it until moments ago.

Tengo sighed and sat down on the chair. He rested his hands on his lap and gazed for a long while at the depression in the sheets. Then he stood, went to the window, and looked outside. The rain had stopped, and the autumn clouds lingered over the pine windbreak. It would be a beautiful sunset, the first in some time.

Tengo had no idea why the fee collector *knew a lot* about him. The last time an NHK fee collector had come around had been about a year ago. At that time he had stood at the door and politely explained to the man that there was no TV in his apartment. He never watched TV, he continued. The fee collector hadn't been convinced, but he had left without saying any more, muttering some snide remark under his breath.

Was it the same fee collector who had come today? He had the impression that that man had also said something about his being a *thief.* It was a bit odd that the same collector would show up a year later and say he *knew a lot* about Tengo. They had only stood at the door and chatted for five minutes or so, that's all.

Whatever. What was important was that Fuka-Eri had kept the door locked. The fee collector wouldn't be paying another visit anytime soon. He had a quota to meet and had to be tired of standing around quarreling with people who refused to pay their subscription fees. In order not to waste time, he would skip the troublesome customers' places and collect the fees from people who didn't have a problem paying.

Tengo looked again at the hollow his father had left in the bed, and he remembered all the pairs of shoes his father had worn out. As his father had pounded the Tokyo pavement collecting fees, he had consigned countless pairs of shoes to oblivion. All of the shoes looked the same – cheap, no-nonsense leather shoes, black, with thick soles. He had worn them hard, until they were worn out and falling apart, the heels warped out of shape. As a boy, every time Tengo saw these terribly misshapen shoes it pained him. He didn't feel sorry for his father, but for the shoes. They reminded him of a pitiful work animal, driven as hard as possible and hovering on the verge of death.

But come to think of it, wasn't his father now like a work animal about to die? No different from a worn-out pair of leather shoes?

Tengo gazed out the window again as the colors of the sunset deepened in the western sky. He remembered the air chrysalis emitting a faint, pale light, and Aomame, as a young girl, sleeping inside.

Would that air chrysalis ever appear here again?

Was time really a straight line?

"It seems I've reached a deadlock," Tengo mumbled to the wall. "There are too many variables. Even for a former child prodigy, it's impossible to find an answer."

The walls didn't have a response. Nor did they express an opinion. They simply, and silently, reflected the color of the setting sun.

CHAPTER 4

Ushikawa

OCCAM'S RAZOR

Ushikawa found it hard to get his head around the idea that the elderly dowager who lived in a mansion in Azabu could somehow be involved with the assassination of Sakigake's Leader. He had dug up background information on her. She was a well-known figure in society, so the investigation had not taken much effort. Her husband had been a prominent businessman in the postwar era, influential in the political sphere. His business focused mainly on investments and real estate, though he had also branched out into large-scale retail stores and transport-related businesses. After her husband's death in the mid-1950s, the woman had taken over his company. She had a talent for managing business, as well as an ability to sense impending danger. In the late 1960s she felt that the company had overextended itself, so she deliberately sold – at a high price – its stock in various fields, and systematically downsized the business. She put all her physical and mental strength into the remaining areas. Thanks to this, she was able to weather the era of the oil shock that occurred soon after with minimal damage and set aside a healthy amount of liquid assets. She knew how to turn other people's crises into golden opportunities for herself.

She was retired now and in her mid-seventies. She had an

abundance of money, which allowed her to live in comfort in her spacious mansion, indebted to no one. But why would a woman like that deliberately plot to murder someone?

Even so, Ushikawa decided to dig a little deeper. One reason was that he couldn't find anything else that even resembled a clue. The second reason was that there was something about this safe house that bothered him. There was nothing especially unnatural about providing a free shelter for battered women. It was a sound and useful service to society. The dowager had the financial resources, and the women must be very grateful to her for her kindness. The problem was that the security at that apartment building – the heavy locked gate, the German shepherd, the surveillance cameras – was too tight for a facility of its type. There was something excessive about it.

The first thing Ushikawa did was check the deed for the land and the house that the dowager lived in. This was public information, easily ascertained by a trip to city hall. The deed to both the land and the house were in her name alone. There was no mortgage. Everything was quite clear-cut. As private assets, the property tax would come to quite a sum, but she probably didn't mind paying such an amount. The future inheritance tax would also be huge, but this didn't seem to bother her, which was unusual for such a wealthy person. In Ushikawa's experience, nobody hated paying taxes more than the rich.

After her husband's death, she continued to live alone in that enormous mansion. No doubt she had a few servants, so she wasn't totally alone. She had two children, and her son had taken over the company. The son had three children. Her daughter had married and died fifteen years ago of an illness. She left no children behind.

This much was easy to find out. But once he tried to dig deeper into the woman's background, a solid wall loomed up out of nowhere, blocking his way. Beyond this, all paths were closed. The wall was high, and the door had multiple locks. What Ushikawa did know was that this woman wanted to keep anything private about her completely out of public view. And she had poured considerable effort and money into carrying out that policy. She never responded to any sort of inquiry, never made any public statements. And no matter how many materials he raked through, not once did he come up with a photograph of her.

The woman's number was listed in the Minato Ward phone book. Ushikawa's style was to tackle things head on, so he went ahead and dialed it. Before the phone had rung twice, a man picked up.

Ushikawa gave a phony name and the name of some investment firm and said, "There's something I would like to ask the lady of the house about, regarding her investment funds."

The man replied, "She isn't able to come to the phone. But you can tell me whatever she needs to know." His businesslike tone sounded mechanical, manufactured.

"It's company policy not to reveal these things to anyone other than the client," Ushikawa explained, "so if I can't speak with her directly now, I can mail the documents to her. She will have them in a few days."

"That would be fine," the man said, and hung up.

Ushikawa wasn't particularly disappointed that he couldn't speak to the dowager. He wasn't expecting to. What he really wanted to find out was how concerned she was about protecting her privacy. Extremely so, it would appear. She seemed to have several people with her in the mansion who kept a close guard over her. The tone of this man who answered the phone – her secretary, most likely – made this clear. Her name was printed in the telephone directory, but only a select group could actually speak to her. All others were flicked away, like ants who had crawled into the sugar bowl.

*　*　*

Pretending to be looking for a place to rent, he made the rounds of local real estate agencies, indirectly asking about the apartment building used as the safe house. Most of the agents had no idea there was an apartment building at that address. This neighborhood was one of the more upscale residential areas in Tokyo. These agents only dealt with high-end properties and couldn't be bothered with a two-story, wooden apartment building. One look at Ushikawa's face and clothes, too, and they essentially gave him the cold shoulder. If a three-legged, waterlogged dog with a torn-off tail and mange had limped in the door, they would have treated it more kindly than they treated him.

Just when he was about to give up, a small local agency that seemed to have been there for years caught his eye. The yellowed old man at the front desk said, "Ah, that place," and volunteered information. The man's face was shriveled up, like a second-rate mummy, but he knew every nook and cranny of the neighborhood and always jumped at the chance to bend someone's ear.

"That building is owned by Mr. Ogata's wife, and yes, in the past it was rented out as apartments. Why she happened to have that building, I don't really know. Her circumstances did not exactly demand that she manage an apartment building. I imagine she mostly used it to house their employees. I don't know much about it now, but it seems to be used for battered women, kind of like those *kakekomidera*, temples in the old days that sheltered wives running away from abusive husbands. Anyway, it isn't going to fatten a real estate agent's wallet."

The old man laughed, with his mouth shut. He sounded like a woodpecker.

"A *kakekomidera*, eh?" Ushikawa said. He offered him a Seven Stars cigarette. The old man took it, let Ushikawa light it for him with his lighter, and took a deep, appreciative drag on it. This is exactly what the Seven Stars must long for, Ushikawa mused – to be enjoyed so thoroughly.

"Women whose husbands smack them around and run away, their faces all puffed up, they – they take shelter there. They don't have to pay rent."

"Like a kind of public service," Ushikawa said.

"Yes, that sort of thing. They had this extra apartment building so they used it to help people in trouble. She's tremendously wealthy, so she could do whatever she wanted, without worrying about making money. Not like the rest of us."

"But why did Mrs. Ogata start doing that? Was there something that led up to it?"

"I don't know. She's so rich that maybe it's like a hobby?"

"Well, even if it is a hobby," Ushikawa said, beaming, "that's a wonderful thing, to help people in trouble like that. Not everyone with money to burn takes the initiative to help others."

"Of course it's a nice thing to do," the old man agreed. "Years ago I used to hit my old lady all the time, so I'm not one to talk." He opened his mouth, showing off his missing teeth, and guffawed, as if hitting your wife every once in a while were one of life's notable pleasures.

"So I take it that several people live there now?" Ushikawa asked.

"I go past there when I take a walk every morning, but you can't see anything from outside. But it does seem like a few people are living there. I guess there will always be men in the world who beat their wives."

"There are always far more people in the world who make things worse, rather than help out."

The old man guffawed again loudly, his mouth wide open. "You got that right. There are a lot more people who do bad things than do good."

The old man seemed to have taken a liking to Ushikawa. This made Ushikawa uncomfortable.

"By the way, what sort of person is Mrs. Ogata?" Ushikawa asked, trying to sound casual.

"I really don't know that much about her," the old man replied, knitting his brow like the spirit of an old, withered tree. "She lives a very quiet, reserved life. I've done business here for many years, but at most I've just caught glimpses of her from afar. When she goes out she always has a chauffeur, and her maids do all the shopping. She has a man who is like her personal secretary and he takes care of most everything. I mean, she's a well-bred, wealthy woman, and you can't expect her to talk with the hoi polloi." The old man frowned, and from the midst of those wrinkles came a wink, directed at Ushikawa.

By hoi polloi, the old man with the yellowed face seemed to be talking about a group composed primarily of two people: himself and Ushikawa.

Ushikawa asked another question. "How long has Mrs. Ogata been active in providing a safe house for victims of domestic violence?"

"I'm not really sure. I've only heard from others that the place is a kind of *kakekomidera*. But about four years ago, people started to go in and out of that apartment building. Four or five years, something like that." The old man lifted the teacup to his lips and drank his cold tea. "It was about then that they built a new gate and the security got tighter. It's a safe house, after all, and if anyone can just wander in, the folks who live there won't be able to relax."

The old man seemed to come back to the present. He looked at Ushikawa a bit suspiciously. "So – you said you're looking for a reasonably priced place to rent?"

"That's correct."

"Then you better try somewhere else. This neighborhood is full of expensive mansions and even if there are places for rent that come on the market, they're all high-end rentals aimed at foreigners who work in the embassies. A long time ago there were a lot of regular people who lived around here, ones who weren't so wealthy. As a matter of fact, finding places for them is how our business got started. But there aren't any afford-able houses left, so I'm thinking of closing the business. Land prices in Tokyo have skyrocketed and small fry like me can't handle it anymore. Unless you have bags of cash to spare, I suggest you try elsewhere."

"I'll do that," Ushikawa said. "The truth is, I am a bit strapped. I'll try some other location."

The old man breathed out cigarette smoke and a sigh. "But once Mrs. Ogata passes, you can bet that mansion will disap-pear. That son of hers is a real go-getter, and there's no way he's going to let a prime piece of real estate like that in a premium area just sit around. He'll knock it down in a flash and put up an ultra-high-end condo. He may very well be drawing up the blueprints as we speak."

"If that happens this whole neighborhood won't be quite as serene as it is now."

"Yup, you won't recognize it."

"You mentioned her son. What business is he in?"

"Basically he's in real estate. The same as me. But the differ-ence between us is like chalk and cheese. Like a Rolls-Royce and an old bicycle. He takes a huge amount of capital and then makes investments on his own, one after another. He licks up all the honey himself, without leaving a drop behind. Nothing spills over in my direction, I can tell you that. The world sucks, that's for sure."

"I was just walking around a while ago and wandered all around the outskirts of that mansion. I was impressed. It's quite a place."

"Well, it's definitely the best residence in this neighbor-hood. When I picture those beautiful willow trees being chopped down, it hurts." The old man shook his head as if he really were in pain. "I can only hope that Mrs. Ogata lives a little longer."

"I hear you," Ushikawa agreed.

Ushikawa found a listing for the Center for Victims of Domestic Violence in the phone book and decided to contact them. It was a nonprofit organization, run by volunteers and headed by several lawyers. Ushikawa made an appointment in the name of his phony office, the New Japan Foundation for the Advancement of Scholarship and the Arts. He led them to believe he might be a potential donor, and they set the time for the appointment.

Ushikawa proffered his business card (which was the same as the one he had given to Tengo) and explained how one of the purposes of his foundation was to pinpoint an outstanding nonprofit organization that was making a real contribution to society, and provide them with a grant. Though he couldn't reveal who the sponsor was, the grant could be used in any way the recipient wished. The only requirement was to submit a simple report by the end of the year.

Ushikawa's appearance didn't inspire any goodwill or trust, and the young lawyer he spoke with eyed him warily at first. However, they were chronically short on funds, and had to accept any support, no matter the source.

"I'll need to know more about your activities," Ushikawa said. The lawyer explained how they had started the organization. Ushikawa found this history boring, but he listened carefully, his expression one of devoted interest. He made all the appropriate noises, nodded in all the right places, and kept his expression docile and open. As he did, the lawyer warmed up to him. Ushikawa was a highly trained listener, adopting such a sincere and receptive manner that he almost always succeeded in putting the other person at ease.

He found the opportunity to casually nudge the conversation

in the direction of the safe house. For the unfortunate women who are running away from domestic violence, he asked, if they can't find an appropriate place to go, where do they end up living? He put on an expression that showed his deep sympathy for these women whose fate was like that of leaves tossed about in some outrageously strong wind.

"In instances like that we have several safe houses where they can go," the young lawyer replied.

"Safe houses?"

"Temporary refuges. There aren't many, but there are places that charitable people have offered us. One person has even provided an entire apartment building for us to use."

"An entire apartment building," Ushikawa said, sounding impressed. "I guess some people can be quite generous."

"That's right. Whenever our activities are covered in newspapers or magazines, inevitably we'll get a call from people wanting to help out. Without offers from people like that, we would never be able to keep this organization going, since we depend almost entirely on contributions."

"What you're doing is very meaningful," Ushikawa said.

The lawyer flashed him a vulnerable smile. *Nobody's easier to fool,* Ushikawa thought, *than the person who is convinced that he is right.*

"How many women would you say are living in that apartment building now?"

"It depends, but – let's see – I would say usually four or five," the lawyer said.

"About that charitable person who provided that apartment building," Ushikawa said, "how did this person get involved? I'm thinking there must have been some event that led up to this interest."

The lawyer tilted his head. "I really don't know. Though in the past this person was, it seems, involved in similar activities, on an individual level. As far as we're concerned, we're just grateful for this individual's kindness. We don't ask the reasons behind it."

"Of course," Ushikawa nodded. "I assume you keep the locations of your safe houses secret?"

"Correct. We have to make sure that the women are protected, plus many of our donors prefer to remain anonymous. I mean, we're dealing with acts of violence, after all."

They talked for a while longer, but Ushikawa was unable to extract any more useful information. What Ushikawa knew were the following facts: the Center for Victims of Domestic Violence had begun operations in earnest four years ago. Not long afterward, a certain "donor" had contacted them and offered them use of a vacant apartment building as a safe house. The donor had read about their activities in the newspaper. The donor had set one condition, namely, that the donor's name never be revealed. Still, from what was said, Ushikawa could deduce that, beyond any doubt, the "donor" was the elderly dowager living in Azabu, the one who owned the old apartment building.

"Thank you so much for taking the time to speak with me," Ushikawa said warmly to the idealistic young lawyer. "Your organization is certainly making a valuable contribution. I'll present what I have learned here to our board of directors. We should be getting in touch with you fairly soon. In the meantime, my very best wishes for your continued success."

Next, Ushikawa began to investigate the death of the dowager's daughter. The daughter had married an elite bureaucrat in the Ministry of Transport and was only thirty-six when she died. He didn't know the cause yet. Not long after she died, her husband left the Ministry of Transport. These were the only facts Ushikawa had unearthed so far. He didn't know why the husband had left the ministry, or what sort of life he had led afterward. The Ministry of Transport was not the sort of government office that willingly revealed information regarding its inner workings to ordinary citizens. But Ushikawa had a sharp sense of smell, and something smelled fishy. He couldn't believe that losing his wife would have made the man so overcome with grief that he would quit his job and go into hiding.

Ushikawa knew there weren't many thirty-six-year-old women who died of illness. Not that there weren't some. No matter how old you are, or how blessed your circumstances, you can suddenly fall ill and die – from cancer, a brain tumor, peritonitis, acute pneumonia. The human body is a fragile thing. But for an affluent woman of thirty-six to join the ranks of the dead – in all likelihood it was not a natural death, but either an accident or suicide.

Let me speculate here, Ushikawa said to himself. *Following the famous rule of Occam's razor, I'll try to find the simplest possible explanation. Eliminate all unnecessary factors, boil it all down to one logical line, and then look at the situation.*

Let's say the dowager's daughter didn't die of illness but by suicide. Ushikawa rubbed his hands together as he pondered this. *It wouldn't be too hard to pretend that a suicide was actually death by illness, especially for someone with money and influence. Take this a step further and say that this daughter was the victim of domestic violence, grew despondent, and took her own life. Certainly not an impossibility. It was a well-known fact that certain members of the so-called elite had disgusting personalities and dark, twisted tendencies, as if they had taken more than the share of darkness allotted to them.*

If that were the case, what would the rich old dowager do? Would she call it fate, say that nothing else could be done, and give up? Not very likely. She would take suitable revenge against whatever force had driven her daughter to her untimely end. Ushikawa felt he had a better understanding of the dowager. She was a daring, bright woman, with a clear vision and a strong will. And she would spare neither fortune nor influence to avenge the death of the one she loved.

Ushikawa had no way of knowing what kind of retaliation she had actually taken toward her daughter's husband, since all trace of him had vanished into thin air. He didn't think that the dowager had gone so far as to take the man's life. But he had no doubt that she had taken some sort of decisive action. And it was hard to believe that she had left any trail behind.

Ushikawa's conjectures thus far seemed to make sense, though he had no proof. His theory, however, did clear up a lot of questions. Licking his lips, Ushikawa vigorously rubbed his hands together. Beyond this point, though, things started to get a little hazy.

The dowager had set up the safe house to sublimate her desire for revenge, turning it into something more useful and positive. Then, at the sports club she frequented, she got to know the young instructor Aomame, and somehow – he had no idea how – they came to a secret understanding. After meticulous preparation, Aomame got access to the suite at the Hotel Okura and murdered Leader. The method she used was unclear. Aomame might be quite proficient in murdering people using a special technique. As a result, despite being closely guarded by two very dedicated and able bodyguards, Leader wound up dead.

Up to this point, the threads tying his conjectures held together – barely – but when it came to linking Sakigake's Leader to the center for battered women, Ushikawa was at a total loss. At this point his thought process hit a roadblock and a very sharp razor neatly severed all the threads.

What Sakigake wanted from Ushikawa at this point were answers to two questions: Who planned the murder of Leader? and Where was Aomame?

Ushikawa was the one who had run the original background

check on Aomame, and he had found nothing suspicious about her at all. But after she had left, Leader expired. And right after that, Aomame disappeared. *Poof* – like a gust of smoke in the wind. Sakigake had to have been very upset with Ushikawa, convinced that his investigation hadn't been thorough enough.

But in fact, as always, his investigation left nothing to be desired. As he had told Buzzcut, Ushikawa was a stickler for making sure all the bases were covered. He could be faulted for not having checked her phone records beforehand, but unless there was something extraordinarily suspicious about a situation, that wasn't something he normally did. And as far as he could tell from his investigations, there wasn't a single suspect thing about Aomame.

Ushikawa didn't want them to be upset with him forever. They paid him well, but they were a dangerous bunch. Ushikawa was one of the few who knew how they had secretly disposed of Leader's body, which made him a potential liability. He knew he had to come up with something concrete to show them so they would know he was a valuable resource, someone worth keeping alive.

He had no proof that the old dowager from Azabu was mixed up in Leader's murder. At this point it was pure speculation. He did know that some deep secret lay hidden inside that mansion with its magnificent willows. Ushikawa's sense of smell told him this, and his job was to bring that truth to light. It wouldn't be easy. The place was under heavy guard, with professionals involved.

Yakuza?

Perhaps. Businessmen, those involved in real estate in particular, are often involved in secret negotiations with yakuza. When the going gets rough, the yakuza get called in. It was possible the old dowager might be making use of their influence. But Ushikawa wasn't very certain of this – the old dowager was too well bred to deal with people like them. Also, it was hard to imagine that she would use yakuza to protect women who were victims of domestic violence. Probably she had her own security apparatus in place, one that she paid for herself. Her own personal system she had refined. It would cost her, but then, she wasn't hurting for funds. And this system of hers might employ violence when there was a perceived need.

If Ushikawa's hypothesis was correct, then Aomame must have gone into hiding somewhere far away, with the aid of the old dowager. They would have carefully erased any trail, given her a new identity and a new name, possibly even a new face. If that was the case, then it would be impossible for Ushikawa's painstaking little private investigation to track her down.

At this point the only thing to do was to try to learn more about the dowager. His hope was that he would run across a seam that would lead him to discover something about Aomame's whereabouts. Things might work out, and then again they might not. But Ushikawa had some strong points: his sharp sense of smell and his tenaciousness. He would never let go of something once he latched onto it. *Besides these,* he asked himself, *what other talents do I have worth mentioning? Do I have other abilities I can be proud of?*

Not one, Ushikawa answered himself, convinced he was right.

CHAPTER 5

Aomame

NO MATTER HOW LONG YOU
KEEP QUIET

Aomame didn't find it painful to be shut away, living a monotonous, solitary existence. She got up every day at six thirty
and had a simple breakfast. Then she would spend an hour or
so doing laundry, ironing, or mopping the floor. For an hour
and a half in the morning she used the equipment Tamaru
had obtained for her to do a strenuous workout. As a fitness
instructor she was well versed in how much stimulation all the
various muscles needed every day – how much exercise was
just right, and how much was excessive.

Lunch was usually a green salad and fruit. The afternoon
was spent sitting on the sofa and reading, or taking a short
nap. In the evening she would spend an hour preparing dinner, which she would finish before six. Once the sun set, she
would be out on the balcony, seated on her garden chair, keeping watch over the playground. Then to bed at ten thirty. One
day was the same as the next, but she never felt bored.

She was not very social to begin with, and never had a problem going long stretches without seeing or talking with other
people. Even when she was in elementary school, she seldom
talked with her classmates. More accurately, unless it was
absolutely necessary, no one else ever spoke to her.

Compared with the harsh days of her childhood, being holed up in a neat little apartment, not talking to anybody, was nothing. Compared with staying silent while those around her chatted away, it was much easier – and more natural – to be silent in a place where she was all alone. And besides, she had a book she should read. She had started reading the Proust volumes that Tamaru had left for her. She read no more than twenty pages a day. She read each and every word carefully, working her way through each day's reading. Once she finished that section, she read something else. And just before bed she made sure to read a few pages of *Air Chrysalis*. This was Tengo's writing, and it had become a sort of manual she followed to live in 1Q84.

She also listened to music. The elderly dowager had sent over a box of classical music cassettes: Mahler symphonies, Haydn chamber music, Bach keyboard pieces – all varieties and types of classical music. There was a tape of Janáček's *Sinfonietta* as well, which she had specifically requested. She would listen to the *Sinfonietta* once a day as she noiselessly went through her exercise routine.

Autumn quietly deepened. She had the feeling that her body was slowly becoming transparent. Aomame tried her best to keep her mind clear of any thoughts, but it was impossible not to think of anything. Nature abhors a vacuum. At the very least, though, she felt that now there was nothing for her to hate. There was no need to hate her classmates and teacher anymore. Aomame was no longer a helpless child, and no one was forcing her to practice a religion now. There was no need to hate the men who beat up women. The anger she had felt before, like a high tide rising up within her – the overwrought emotions that sometimes made her want to smack her fists against the closest wall – had vanished before she'd realized it. She wasn't sure why, but those feelings were entirely gone. She was grateful for this. As much as possible, she wanted never to hurt anyone, ever again. Just as she didn't want to hurt herself.

On nights when she found it hard to sleep, she thought of Tamaki Otsuka and Ayumi Nakano. When she closed her eyes, the memory of holding their bodies close came rushing back to her. Both of them had had soft, lustrous skin and warm bodies. Gentle, profound bodies, with fresh blood coursing through them, hearts beating regular, blessed beats. She could hear them sigh softly and giggle. Slender fingers, hardened nipples, smooth thighs. . . . But these two women were no longer in the world.

Like dark, soft water, sadness took over Aomame's heart, soundlessly, and with no warning. The best antidote at a time like this was to just shut off that stream of memories and think only of Tengo. Focus, and recall the touch of the ten-year-old boy's hand as she had held it for a fleeting moment. And then she called forth from memory the thirty-year-old Tengo sitting on top of the slide, she imagined what it would feel like to be held in those large, strong arms.

He was almost within reach.

Maybe if I hold out my hand the next time, I really will be able to reach him. In the darkness she closed her eyes and immersed herself in that possibility. She gave herself up to her longing.

But if I never do see him again, she thought, her heart trembling, *then what?* Things had been a whole lot simpler when there was no actual point of contact between them. Meeting the adult Tengo had been a mere dream, an abstract hypothesis. But now that she had seen the *real* him before her very eyes, his presence was more concrete, more powerful, than it had ever been before. She *had* to see him, to have him hold her, caress every part of her. Just the very thought that this might not come to pass made her feel as if her heart and body were being ripped in two.

Maybe back there in front of the Esso tiger on the billboard, I should have shot that 9mm bullet into my skull. Then I wouldn't have to live like this, feeling such sadness and pain. But she just couldn't pull the trigger. She had heard a voice. From far off, someone calling her name. *I might be able to see Tengo again,* she had thought – and once this thought had struck her, she had to go on living. Even if what Leader had said was true, that doing so would make things dangerous for Tengo, she had no other choice. She had felt an unbearably strong surge of the life force, beyond the bounds of logic. The upshot was that she was burning with a fierce desire for him. It was a thirst that wouldn't quit, and a premonition of despair.

A realization struck her. *This is what it means to live on. When granted hope, a person uses it as fuel, as a guidepost to life. It is impossible to live without hope.* Aomame's heart clenched at the thought, as if every bone in her body were suddenly creaking and screaming out.

She sat at the dining table and picked up the automatic pistol. She pulled back the slide, sending a bullet into the chamber, thumbed back the hammer, and stuck the muzzle in her mouth. Just a touch more pressure with her trigger finger and all this sadness would disappear. *Just a touch more. One more centimeter. No, if I pull my finger just five millimeters toward me, I will shift over to a silent world where there are no more worries. The pain will only last an instant. And then there will be a merciful nothingness.* She closed her eyes. The Esso tiger from the billboard, gas hose in hand, grinned at her. *Put a Tiger in Your Tank.*

She pulled the hard muzzle out of her mouth and slowly shook her head.

I can't die. In front of the balcony is the playground. The slide is there, and as long as I have the hope that Tengo will show up again, I won't be able to pull this trigger. This possibility drew her back from the brink. One door closed inside her heart and another door opened, quietly, without a sound. Aomame pulled the slide again, ejecting the bullet, set the safety, and placed the pistol back on the table. When she closed her eyes she sensed something in the darkness, a faint light, fading away by the moment. What it could be, she had no idea.

She sat down on the sofa and focused on the pages of *Swann's Way*. She imagined the scenes depicted in the story, trying hard not to let other thoughts intrude. Outside a cold rain had started to fall. The weather report on the radio said a gentle rain would continue until the next morning. A weather front was stalled out in the Pacific – like a lonely person, lost in thought, oblivious of time.

Tengo won't be coming, she thought. The sky was covered from one end to the other with thick clouds, blocking out the moon. Still she would probably go out onto the balcony, a hot cup of cocoa in hand, and watch the playground. She would keep binoculars and the pistol nearby, wear something decent enough so that she could quickly run outside, and gaze at the slide in the rain. This was the only meaningful act she could undertake.

At three p.m., someone at the entrance of the building rang her bell. Aomame ignored it. It wasn't possible that anyone would be visiting her. She had the kettle on for tea, but to be on the safe side she switched off the gas and listened. The bell rang three or four times and then was silent.

About five minutes later a bell rang again. This time it was the doorbell to her apartment. Now someone was inside the building, right outside her door. The person may have followed a resident inside, or else had rung somebody else's bell and talked their way in. Aomame kept perfectly still. *If somebody comes, don't answer,* Tamaru had instructed her. *Set the dead bolt and don't make a sound.*

The doorbell must have rung ten times. A little too

persistent for a salesman – they usually give up at three rings. As she held her breath, the person began to knock on the door with his fist. It wasn't that loud a sound, but she could sense the irritation behind it. "Miss Takai," a low, middle-aged man's voice said. A slightly hoarse voice. "Miss Takai. Can you please answer the door?"

Takai was the fake name on the mailbox.

"Miss Takai, I know this isn't a good time, but I would like to see you. Please."

The man paused for a moment, waiting for a response. When there was none, he knocked on the door again, this time a little louder.

"I know you're inside, Miss Takai, so let's cut to the chase and open the door. I know you're in there and can hear me."

Aomame picked up the automatic pistol from the table and clicked off the safety. She wrapped the pistol in a towel and held it by the grip.

She had no idea who this could be, nor what he could possibly want. His anger seemed directed at her – why, she had no clue – and he was determined to get her to open the door. Needless to say, in her present position this was the last thing she wanted.

The knocking finally stopped and the man's voice echoed again in the hallway.

"Miss Takai, I am here to collect your NHK fee. That's right, good old NHK. I know you're at home. No matter how much you try to stay quiet, I can tell. Working this job for so many years, I know when someone is really out, and when they're just pretending. Even when a person tries to stay very quiet, there are still signs he's there. People breathe, their hearts beat, their stomachs continue to digest food. Miss Takai, I know you're in there, and that you're waiting for me to give up and leave. You're not planning to open the door or answer me. Because you don't want to pay the subscription fee."

The man's voice was louder than it needed to be, and it reverberated down the hallway of the building. That was his intention – calling out the person's name so loudly that it would make them feel ridiculed and embarrassed. And so it would be a warning to all the neighbors. Aomame kept perfectly silent. She wasn't about to respond. She put the pistol back on the table. Just to be sure, though, she kept the safety off. The man could just be pretending to be an NHK fee collector. Seated at the dining table, she stared at the front door.

She wanted to stealthily pad over to the door, look through the peephole, and check out what kind of person he was. But she was glued to the chair. Better not do anything unnecessary – after a while he would give up and leave.

The man, however, seemed ready to deliver an entire lecture.

"Miss Takai, let's not play hide and seek anymore, okay? I'm not doing this because I like to. Even I have a busy schedule. Miss Takai, I know you watch TV. And everyone who watches TV, without exception, has to pay the NHK subscription fee. You may not like it, but that's the law. Not paying the fee is the same as stealing, Miss Takai, you don't want to be treated as a thief because of something as petty as this, do you? This is a fancy building you live in, and I don't think you will have any trouble paying the fee. Right? Hearing me proclaim this to the world can't be much fun for you."

Normally Aomame wouldn't care if an NHK fee collector was making a racket like this. But right now she was in hiding, trying to keep out of sight. She didn't want anything to attract the attention of other residents. But there was nothing she could do about it. She had to keep still and wait until he went away.

"I know I'm repeating myself, Miss Takai, but I am sure you're in there, listening to me. And you're thinking this: Why, of all places, did you have to choose *my* apartment to stand outside of? I wonder, too, Miss Takai. It's probably because I don't like people pretending not to be at home. Pretending not to be at home is just a temporary solution, isn't it? I want you to open the door and tell me to my face that you don't have any intention of paying the NHK fee. You would feel much better, and so would I. That would leave some room for discussion. Pretending to be out is not the way to go. It's like a pitiful little rat hiding in the dark. It only sneaks out when people aren't around. What a miserable way to live your life."

This man's lying, Aomame thought. *That's just ridiculous, that he can sense when somebody is at home. I haven't made a sound. His real goal is to just stand in front of a random apartment, make a racket, and intimidate all the other residents, to make people decide they would prefer to pay the fee than to have him plant himself outside their door like that. This man must have tried the same tactics elsewhere and had good results.*

"Miss Takai, I know you find me unpleasant. I can understand perfectly what you're thinking. And you're right – I *am* an unpleasant person. I'm aware of that. But you have to understand, Miss Takai, that pleasant people don't make good fee collectors. There are tons of people in the world who have decided they aren't going to pay the NHK subscription fee, and if you're going to collect from people like that you can't always act so nice. I would rather leave with no problem, just say, *Is that right? You don't want to pay the fee? I understand. Sorry to bother you.* But I can't. Collecting the fee is my job, and besides, personally I don't like it when people pretend not to be at home."

The man stopped and paused. And then he knocked on the door ten times in a row.

"Miss Takai, you must be finding this annoying. Aren't you starting to feel like a real thief by now? Think about it. We're not talking about a lot of money here. Enough to buy a modest dinner at your neighborhood chain restaurant. Just pay it, and you won't be treated like a thief. You won't have anyone yelling at you outside or banging on your door anymore. Miss Takai, I know you're hiding in there. You think you can hide and get away from me forever. Well – go ahead and try. You can keep as quiet as you like, but one of these days somebody is going to find you. You can't act so sneaky forever. Consider this: there are people a whole lot poorer than you all over Japan who faithfully pay their fee every month. Is that fair?"

Fifteen knocks on the door followed. Aomame counted them.

"I get it, Miss Takai. You're pretty stubborn too. Fine. I'll be going now. I can't stand outside here forever. But rest assured, I'll be back. Once I decide on something, I don't give up easily. And I don't like people pretending to be out. I'll be back, and I'll knock on your door. I'll keep banging on your door until the whole world has heard it. I promise you this, a promise just between you and me. All right? Well, I'll be seeing you soon."

She didn't hear any footsteps. Perhaps he had on rubber soles. Aomame stayed still there for five minutes, staring at the door. The hallway outside was quiet again, and she couldn't hear a thing. She crept to the front door, summoned her courage, and peered out the peephole. No one was there.

She reset the safety on the pistol and took some deep breaths to get her heart rate back down. She switched on the gas, heated up water, made green tea, and drank it. *It was only an NHK collector,* she told herself. But there was something malicious, sick even, about his voice. Whether this was directed at her personally or at the fictitious Miss Takai, she couldn't tell. Still, that husky voice and persistent knock disturbed her, like something clammy sticking to your bare skin.

Aomame undressed and took a shower. She carefully scrubbed herself in the hot water. After she finished and had put on clean clothes, she felt a bit better. The clammy sensation was gone. She sat down on the sofa and drank the rest of the tea. She tried to read her book but couldn't concentrate on the words. Fragments of the man's voice came back to her.

"You think you can hide and get away from me forever. Well – go ahead and try. You can keep as quiet as you like, but one of these days somebody is going to find you."

She shook her head. The man just said whatever nonsense popped into his head, yelling things just to make people feel bad. *He doesn't know a thing about me – what I've done, why I'm here.* Still, her heart wouldn't stop pounding.

You can keep as quiet as you like, but one of these days somebody is going to find you.

The fee collector's words sounded like they had deeper implications. *Maybe it was just a coincidence,* she thought, *but that man knew exactly what to say to upset me.* Aomame gave up reading and closed her eyes as she lay on the sofa.

Tengo, where are you? she wondered. She said it out loud. "Tengo, where are you?" *Find me now. Before someone else does.*

CHAPTER 6

Tengo

BY THE PRICKING OF MY THUMBS

Tengo led a very orderly life in the small town by the sea. Once his days fell into a pattern, he tried his best to keep them that way. He wasn't sure why he did so, but it seemed important. In the morning he would take a walk, work on his novel, then go to see his father in the sanatorium and read whatever he had at hand. Then he would go back to his room and sleep. One day followed the next like the monotonous rhythm of the work songs farmers sing as they plant their rice paddies.

There were several warm nights, followed by surprisingly cold ones. Autumn advanced a step, then retreated, but was steadily deepening. The change in seasons didn't bring any change to Tengo's life, however – he simply modeled each day on the one preceding it. He tried his best to become an invisible observer, staying quiet, keeping the effect of his presence to a minimum, silently waiting for *that time* to come. As the days passed, the difference between one day and the next grew fainter. A week passed, then ten days. But the air chrysalis never materialized. In the afternoon when his father was at the examination room, the only thing on his bed was the small, pitiful, person-shaped depression.

Was that just a one-time event? Tengo thought, biting his lip as he sat in the small room in the gathering twilight. *A special revelation never to appear again? Or did I just see an illusion?* No one answered him. The only sound that reached him was the roar of the far-off sea, and the wind blowing through the pine windbreak.

Tengo wasn't certain that he was doing the right thing. Maybe the time he was spending here, in this room in a sanatorium in a town far from Tokyo, was meaningless. Even if it was, though, he didn't think he could leave. Here in this room, he had seen the air chrysalis, and inside, in a faint light, the small sleeping figure of Aomame. He had *touched* it. Even if this was a one-time event, even if it was nothing more than a fleeting illusion, he wanted to stay as long as he possibly could, tracing with his mind's eye the scene as he had witnessed it.

Once they discovered that he was not going back to Tokyo, the nurses began to act more friendly. They would take a short break between tasks and stop to chat. If they had a free moment they came to his father's room to talk with him. They brought him tea and cakes. Two nurses alternated in caring for Tengo's father – Nurse Omura, who was in her mid-thirties (she was the one who wore her hair up with a ballpoint pen stuck through her bun), and Nurse Adachi, who had rosy cheeks and wore her hair in a ponytail. Nurse Tamura, a middle-aged nurse with metal-framed glasses, usually staffed the reception desk, but if they happened to be shorthanded she would pitch in and care for his father too. All three of them seemed to take a personal interest in Tengo.

Except for his special hour at twilight, Tengo had plenty of time on his hands and talked with them about all kinds of things. It was more like a question-and-answer session, though, with the nurses asking questions about his life and Tengo responding as honestly as he could.

The nurses talked about their own lives as well. All three had been born in this area, had entered nursing school after high

school, and had become nurses. They all found work at the sanatorium monotonous and boring, the working hours long and
irregular, but they were happy to be able to work in their home-
town. The work was much less stressful than being at a general
hospital, where they would face life-and-death situations on
a daily basis. The old people in the sanatorium gradually lost
their memory and died, not really understanding their situation. There was little blood, and the staff minimized any pain.
No one was brought there by ambulance in the middle of the
night, and there were no distraught, sobbing families to deal
with. The cost of living was low in the area, so even with a salary
that wasn't the most generous they were able to comfortably get
by. Nurse Tamura, the one with glasses, had lost her husband
five years earlier in an accident, and lived in a nearby town with
her mother. Nurse Omura, who wore the ballpoint pen in her
hair, had two little boys and a husband who drove a cab. Young
Miss Adachi lived in an apartment on the outskirts of town with
her sister, who was three years older and worked as a hair stylist.

"You are such a kind person, Tengo," Nurse Omura said as
she changed an IV bag. "There's no one else I know who comes
here to read aloud to an unconscious patient."

The praise made Tengo uncomfortable. "I just happen to
have some vacation days," he said. "But I won't be here all that
long."

"No matter how much free time someone might have, they
don't come to a place like this because they want to," she said.
"Maybe I shouldn't say this, but these are patients who will
never recover. As time passes it makes people get more and
more depressed."

"My father asked me to read to him. He said he didn't mind
what I read. This was a long time ago, when he was still conscious. Besides, I don't have anything else to do, so I might as
well come here."

"What do you read to him?"

"All kinds of things. I just pick whatever book I'm in the midst of reading, and read aloud from wherever I've left off."

"What are you reading right now?"

"Isak Dinesen's *Out of Africa*."

The nurse shook her head. "Never heard of it."

"It was written in 1937. Dinesen was from Denmark. She married a Swedish nobleman, moved to Africa just before the First World War, and they ran a plantation there. After she divorced him, she continued to run the plantation on her own. The book is about her experiences at the time."

The nurse took his father's temperature, noted it on his chart, then returned the ballpoint pen to her hair and brushed back her bangs. "I wonder if I could hear you read for a bit," she said.

"I don't know if you'll like it," Tengo said.

She sat down on a stool and crossed her legs. They were sturdy looking, fleshy, but nicely shaped. "Just go ahead and read, if you would."

Tengo slowly began to read from where he had left off. It was the kind of passage that was best read slowly, like time flowing over the African landscape.

When in Africa in March the long rains begin after four months of hot, dry weather, the richness of growth and the freshness and fragrance everywhere are overwhelming.

But the farmer holds back his heart and dares not trust to the generosity of nature, he listens, dreading to hear a decrease in the roar of the falling rain. The water that the earth is now drinking in must bring the farm, with all the vegetable, animal and human life on it, through four rainless months to come.

It is a lovely sight when the roads of the farm have all been turned into streams of running water, and the farmer wades through the mud with a singing heart, out to the flowering and dripping coffee-fields. But it happens in the middle of the rainy season that in the evening the stars show themselves through the thinning clouds; then he stands outside his house and stares up, as if hanging himself on to the sky to milk down more rain. He cries to the sky: "Give me enough and more than enough. My heart is bared to thee now, and I will not let thee go except thou bless me. Drown me if you like, but kill me not with caprices. No *coitus interruptus,* heaven, heaven!"

"*Coitus interruptus?*" the nurse asked, frowning.
"She's the kind of person who doesn't mince words."
"Still, it seems awfully graphic to use when you're addressing God."
"I'm with you on that," Tengo said.

Sometimes a cool, colourless day in the months after the rainy season calls back the time of the *marka mbaya,* the bad year, the time of the drought. In those days the Kikuyu used to graze their cows round my house, and a boy amongst them who had a flute, from time to time played a short tune on it. When I have heard this tune again, it has recalled in one single moment all our anguish and despair of the past. It has got the salt taste of tears in it. But at the same time I found in the tune, unexpectedly surprisingly, a vigour, a curious sweetness, a song. Had those hard times really had all these in them? There was youth in us then, a wild hope. It was during those long days that we were all of us merged into a unity, so that on another planet we shall recognize one another, and the things cry to each other, the cuckoo clock and my books to the lean-fleshed cows on the lawn and the sorrowful old Kikuyus: "You also were there. You also were part of the Ngong farm." That bad time blessed us and went away.

"That's a wonderful passage," the nurse said. "I can really picture the scene. Isak Dinesen's *Out of Africa,* you said?"

"That's right."

"You have a nice voice, too. It's deep, and full of emotion. Very nice for reading aloud."

"Thanks."

The nurse sat on the stool, closed her eyes for a while, and breathed quietly, as if she were still experiencing the afterglow of the passage. Tengo could see the swell of her chest under her uniform rise and fall as she breathed. As he watched this, Tengo remembered his older girlfriend. Friday afternoons, undressing her, touching her hard nipples. Her deep sighs, her wet vagina. Outside, beyond the closed curtains, a tranquil rain was falling. She was feeling the heft of his balls in her hand. But these memories didn't arouse him. The scenery and emotions were distant and vague, as though seen through a thin film.

Some time later the nurse opened her eyes and looked at Tengo. Her eyes seemed to read his thoughts. But she was not accusing him. A faint smile rose to her lips as she stood up and looked down at him.

"I have to be going." She patted her hair to check that the ballpoint pen was there, spun around, and left the room.

Every evening he called Fuka-Eri. Nothing really happened today, she would tell him. The phone had rung a few times, but she followed instructions and didn't answer. "I'm glad," Tengo told her. "Just let it ring."

When Tengo called her he would let it ring three times, hang up, then immediately dial again, but she didn't always follow this arrangement. Most of the time she picked up on the first set of rings.

"We have to follow our plan," Tengo cautioned her each time this happened.

"I know who it is. There is no need to worry," Fuka-Eri said.

"You know it's me calling?"

"I don't answer the other phone calls."

I guess that's possible, Tengo thought. He himself could sense when a call was coming in from Komatsu. The way it rang was sort of nervous and fidgety, like someone tapping their fingers persistently on a desktop. But this was, after all, just a feeling. It wasn't as if he knew who was on the phone.

Fuka-Eri's days were just as monotonous as Tengo's. She never set foot outside the apartment. There was no TV, and she didn't read any books. She hardly ate anything, so at this point there was no need to go out shopping.

"Since I'm not moving much there's not much need to eat," Fuka-Eri said.

"What are you doing by yourself every day?"

"Thinking."

"About what?"

She didn't answer the question. "There's a crow that comes, too."

"The crow comes once every day."

"It comes many times, not just once," she said.

"Is it the same crow?"

"Yes."

"Nobody else comes?"

"The N-H-K person came again."

"Is it the same NHK person as before?"

"He says, *Mr. Kawana, you're a thief,* in a loud voice."

"You mean he yells that right outside my door?"

"So everyone else can hear him."

Tengo pondered this for a moment. "Don't worry about that. It has nothing to do with you, and it's not going to cause any harm."

"He said he knows you are hiding in here."

"Don't let it bother you," Tengo said. "He can't tell that. He's just saying it to intimidate me. NHK people do that sometimes."

Tengo had witnessed his father do exactly the same thing

any number of times. A Sunday afternoon, his father's voice, filled with malice, ringing out down the hallway of a public housing project. Threatening and ridiculing the resident. Tengo lightly pressed the tips of his fingers against his temple. The memory brought with it a heavy load of other baggage.

As if sensing something from his silence, Fuka-Eri asked, "Are you okay."

"I'm fine. Just ignore the NHK person, okay?"

"The crow said the same thing."

"Glad to hear it," Tengo said.

Ever since he saw two moons in the sky, and an air chrysalis materializing on his father's bed in the sanatorium, nothing surprised Tengo very much. Fuka-Eri and the crow exchanging opinions by the windowsill wasn't hurting anybody.

"I think I'll be here a little longer. I can't go back to Tokyo yet. Is that all right?"

"You should be there as long as you want to be."

And then she hung up. Their conversation vanished in an instant, as if someone had taken a nicely sharpened hatchet to the phone line and chopped it in two.

Afterward Tengo called the publishing company where Komatsu worked. He wasn't in. He had put in a brief appearance around one p.m. but then had left, and the person on the phone had no idea where he was or if he was coming back. This wasn't that unusual for Komatsu. Tengo left the number for the sanatorium, saying that was where he could be found during the day, and asked that Komatsu call back. If he had left the inn's number and Komatsu ended up calling in the middle of the night, that would be a problem.

The last time he had heard from Komatsu had been near the end of September, just a short talk on the phone. Since then Komatsu hadn't been in touch, and neither had Tengo. For a three-week period starting at the end of August, Komatsu had disappeared. He had called the publisher with some vague excuse, claiming he was ill and needed time off to rest, but hadn't called afterward, as if he were a missing person. Tengo was concerned, but not overly worried. Komatsu had always done his own thing. Tengo was sure that he would show up before long and saunter back into the office.

Such self-centered behavior was usually forbidden in a corporate environment. But in Komatsu's case, one of his colleagues always smoothed things over so he didn't get in trouble. Komatsu wasn't the most popular man, but somehow there always seemed to be a willing person on hand, ready to clean up whatever mess he left behind. The publishing house, for its part, was willing, to a certain extent, to look the other way. Komatsu was self-centered, uncooperative, and insolent, but when it came to his job, he was capable. He had handled, on his own, the bestseller *Air Chrysalis*. So they weren't about to fire him.

As Tengo had predicted, one day Komatsu simply returned, without explaining why he was away or apologizing for his absence, and came back to work. Tengo heard the news from another editor he worked with who happened to mention it.

"So how is Mr. Komatsu feeling?" Tengo asked the editor.

"He seems fine," the man replied. "Though he seems less talkative than before."

"Less talkative?" Tengo asked, a bit surprised.

"How should I put it – he's *less sociable* than before."

"Was he really quite sick?"

"How should I know?" the editor said, apathetically. "He says he's fine, so I have to go with that. Now that he's back we've been able to take care of the work that has been piling up. While he was away there were all sorts of things to do with *Air Chrysalis* that were a real pain, things I had to take care of in his absence."

"Speaking of *Air Chrysalis,* are there any developments in the case of the missing author, Fuka-Eri?"

"No, no updates. No progress at all, and not any idea where the author is. Everybody is at their wits' end."

"I've been reading the newspapers but haven't seen a single mention of it recently."

"The media has mostly backed off the story, or maybe they're deliberately distancing themselves from it. And the police don't appear to be actively pursuing the case. Mr. Komatsu will know the details, so he would be the one to ask. But as I said, he has gotten a bit less talkative. Actually he's not himself at all. He used to be brimming with confidence, but he has toned that down, and has gotten more introspective, I guess you would say, just sitting there half the time. He's more difficult to get along with, too. Sometimes it seems like he has totally forgotten that there are other people around, like he is all by himself inside a hole."

"Introspective," Tengo said.

"You'll know what I mean when you talk with him."

Tengo had thanked him and hung up.

A few days later, in the evening, Tengo called Komatsu. He was in the office. Just like the editor had told him, the way Komatsu spoke had changed. Usually the words slipped out smoothly without a pause, but now there was awkwardness about him, as if he were preoccupied. *Something must be bothering him,* Tengo thought. At any rate, this was no longer the cool Komatsu he knew.

"Are you completely well now?" Tengo asked.

"What do you mean?"

"Well, you took a long break from work because you weren't feeling well, right?"

"That's right," Komatsu said, as if he had just recalled the fact. A short silence followed. "I'm fine now. I'll tell you all about it sometime, before long. I can't really explain it at this point."

Sometime, before long. Tengo mulled over the words. There was something odd about the sound of Komatsu's voice. The sense of distance that you would normally expect was missing, and his words were flat, without any depth.

Tengo found an appropriate point in the conversation to say good-bye, and hung up. He decided not to bring up *Air Chrysalis* or Fuka-Eri. Something in Komatsu's tone indicated he was trying to avoid these topics. Had Komatsu ever had trouble discussing anything before?

This phone call, at the end of September, was the last time he had spoken to Komatsu. More than two months had passed since then. Komatsu usually loved to have long talks on the phone. Tengo was, as it were, the wall against which Komatsu hit a tennis ball. Maybe he was going through a period when he just didn't want to talk to anyone, Tengo surmised. Everybody has times like that, even somebody like Komatsu. And Tengo, for his part, didn't have anything pressing he had to discuss with him. *Air Chrysalis* had stopped selling and had practically vanished from the public eye, and Tengo knew exactly where the missing Fuka-Eri happened to be. If Komatsu had something he needed to discuss, then he would surely call. No calls simply meant he didn't have anything to talk about.

But Tengo was thinking that it was getting about time to call him. *I'll tell you all about it sometime, before long.* Komatsu's words had stuck with him, oddly enough, and he couldn't shake them.

Tengo called his friend who was subbing for him at the cram school, to see how things were going.

"Everything's fine," his friend replied. "How is your father doing?"

"He has been in a coma the whole time," Tengo explained. "He's breathing, and his temperature and blood pressure are low but stable. But he's unconscious. I don't think he's in any pain. It's like he has gone over completely to the dream world."

"Not such a bad way to go," his friend said, without much emotion. What he was trying to say was *This might sound a little insensitive, but depending on how you look at it, that's not such a bad way to die.* But he had left out such prefatory remarks. If you study for a few years in a mathematics department, you get used to that kind of abbreviated conversation.

"Have you looked at the moon recently?" Tengo suddenly asked. This friend was probably the only person he knew who wouldn't find it suspicious to be asked, out of the blue, about the moon.

His friend gave it some thought. "Now that you mention it, I don't recall looking at the moon recently. What's going on with the moon?"

"When you have a chance, would you look at it for me? And tell me what you think."

"What I think? From what standpoint?"

"Any standpoint at all. I would just like to hear what you think when you see the moon."

A short pause. "It might be hard to find the right way to express what I think about it."

"No, don't worry about expression. What's important are the most obvious characteristics."

"You want me to look at the moon and tell you what I think are the most obvious characteristics?"

"That's right," Tengo replied. "If nothing strikes you, then that's fine."

"It's overcast today, so I don't think you can see the moon, but when it clears up I'll take a look. If I remember."

Tengo thanked him and hung up. *If he remembers.* This was one of the problems with math department graduates. When it came to areas they weren't interested in, their memory was surprisingly short-lived.

When visiting hours were over and Tengo was leaving the sanatorium he said good-bye to Nurse Tamura, the nurse at the reception desk. "Thank you. Good night," he said.

"How many more days will you be here?" she asked, pressing the bridge of her glasses on her nose. She seemed to have finished her shift, because she had changed from her uniform into a pleated dark purple skirt, a white blouse, and a gray cardigan.

Tengo came to a halt and thought for a minute. "I'm not sure. It depends on how things go."

"Can you still take time off from your job?"

"I asked somebody to teach my classes for me, so I should be okay for a while."

"Where do you usually eat?" the nurse asked.

"At a restaurant in town," he replied. "They only provide breakfast at the inn so I go someplace nearby and eat their set meal, or a rice bowl, that sort of thing."

"Is it good?"

"I wouldn't say that. Though I don't really notice what it tastes like."

"That won't do," the nurse said, looking displeased. "You have to eat more nutritious food. I mean, look – these days your face reminds me of a horse sleeping standing up."

"A horse sleeping standing up?" Tengo asked, surprised.

"Horses sleep standing up. You've never seen that?"

Tengo shook his head. "No, I never have."

"Their faces look like yours," the middle-aged nurse said. "Go check out your face in the mirror. At first glance you can't tell they're asleep, but if you look closely you will see that their eyes are open, but they aren't seeing anything."

"Horses sleep with their eyes open?"

The nurse nodded deeply. "Just like you."

For a moment Tengo did think about going to the bathroom and looking at himself in the mirror, but he decided against it. "I understand. I'll try to eat better from now on."

"Would you care to go out to get some *yakiniku*?"

"*Yakiniku*?" Tengo didn't eat much meat. He didn't usually crave it. But now that she had brought it up, he thought it might be good to have some meat for a change. His body might indeed be crying out for more nourishment.

"All of us were talking about going out now to eat some *yakiniku*. You should join us."

"All of us?"

"The others finish work at six thirty and we'll meet afterward. There will be three of us. Interested?"

The other two were Nurse Omura and Nurse Adachi. The three of them seemed to enjoy spending time together, even after work. Tengo considered the idea of going out to eat *yakiniku* with them. He didn't want to disrupt his simple lifestyle, but he couldn't think of a plausible excuse in order to refuse. It was obvious to them that in a town like this Tengo would have plenty of free time on his hands.

"If you don't think I'll be a bother."

"Of course you won't," the nurse said. "I don't invite people out if I think they'll be a bother. So don't hesitate to come with us. It will be nice to have a healthy young man along for a change."

"Well, healthy I definitely am," Tengo said in an uncertain voice.

"That is the most important thing," the nurse declared, giving it her professional opinion.

It wasn't easy for all three nurses to be off duty at the same time, but once a month they managed it. The three of them would go into town, eat something nutritious, have a few drinks, sing karaoke, let loose, and blow off some steam. They definitely needed a change of scenery. Life in this rural town was monotonous, and with the exception of the doctors and other nurses at work, the only people they saw were the elderly, those devoid of memory and signs of life.

The three nurses ate and drank a lot, and Tengo couldn't keep up. As they got livelier, he sat beside them, quietly eating a moderate amount of grilled meat and sipping his draft beer so he didn't get drunk. After they left the *yakiniku* place, they went to a bar, bought a bottle of whiskey, and belted out karaoke. The three nurses took turns singing their favorite songs, then teamed up to do a Candies number, complete with choreographed steps. Tengo was sure they had practiced, they were that good. Tengo wasn't into karaoke, but he did manage one Yosui Inoue song he vaguely remembered.

Nurse Adachi was normally reserved, but after a few drinks, she turned animated and bold. Once she got a bit tipsy, her red cheeks turned a healthy tanned color. She giggled at silly jokes and leaned back, in an entirely natural way, on Tengo's shoulder. Nurse Omura had changed into a light blue dress and had let down her hair. She looked three or four years younger and her voice dropped an octave. Her usually brisk, businesslike manner was subdued, and she moved languidly, as if she had taken on a different personality. Only Nurse Tamura, with her metal-framed glasses, looked and acted the same as always.

"My kids are staying with a neighbor tonight," Nurse Omura explained. "And my husband has to work the night shift. You have to take advantage of times like this to just go out and have fun. It's important to get away from it all sometimes. Don't you agree, Tengo?"

The three nurses had started calling him by his first name. Most people around him seemed to do that naturally. Even his students called him "Tengo" behind his back.

"Yes, that's for sure," Tengo agreed.

"We just have to get out sometimes," Nurse Tamura said,

sipping a glass of Suntory Old whiskey and water. "We're just flesh and blood, after all."

"Take off our uniforms, and we're just ordinary women," Miss Adachi said, and giggled at her comment.

"Tell me, Tengo," Nurse Omura said. "Is it okay to ask this?"

"Ask what?"

"Are you seeing anybody?"

"Yes, tell us," Nurse Adachi said, crunching down on some corn nuts with her large, white teeth.

"It's not an easy thing to talk about," Tengo said.

"We don't mind if it's not easy to talk about," the experienced Nurse Tamura said. "We have lots of time, and we would love to hear about it. I'm dying to hear this hard-to-talk-about story."

"Tell us, tell us!" Nurse Adachi said, clapping her hands lightly and giggling.

"It's not all that interesting," Tengo said. "It's kind of trite and pointless."

"Well, then just cut to the chase," Nurse Omura said. "Do you have a girlfriend, or not?"

Tengo gave in. "At this point, I'm not seeing anyone."

"Hmm," Nurse Tamura said. She stirred the ice in her glass with a finger and licked it. "That won't do. That won't do at all. A young, vigorous man like yourself without a girlfriend, it's such a waste."

"It's not good for your body, either," the large Nurse Omura said. "If you keep it stored inside you for a long time, you'll go soft in the head."

Young Nurse Adachi was still giggling. "You'll go soft in the head," she said, and poked her forehead.

"I did have someone until recently," Tengo said, somewhat apologetically.

"But she left?" Nurse Tamura said, pushing up the bridge of her glasses.

Tengo nodded.

"You mean she dumped you?"

"I don't know," Tengo said, inclining his head. "Maybe she did. I think I probably was dumped."

"By any chance is that person – a lot older than you?" Nurse Tamura asked, her eyes narrowed.

"Yes, she is," Tengo said. How did she know that?

"Didn't I tell you?" Nurse Tamura said, looking proudly at the other two nurses. They nodded.

"I told the others that," Nurse Tamura said, "that you were going out with an older woman. Women can sniff out these things."

"Sniff, sniff," went Nurse Adachi.

"On top of that, maybe she was already married," Nurse Omura said in a lazy tone. "Am I right?"

Tengo hesitated for a moment and then nodded. Lying was pointless.

"You bad boy," Nurse Adachi said, and poked him in the thigh.

"Ten years older," Tengo said.

"Goodness!" Nurse Omura exclaimed.

"Ah, so you had an experienced, older married woman loving you," Nurse Tamura, herself a mother, said. "I'm envious. Maybe I should do that myself. And comfort lonely, gentle young Tengo here. I might not look it, but I still have a pretty decent body."

She grabbed Tengo's hand and was about to press it against her breasts. The other two women managed to stop her. Even if you were letting your hair down, there was a line that shouldn't be crossed between nurses and a patient's relative. That's what they seemed to think – or else they were afraid that someone might spot them. It was a small town, and rumors spread quickly. Maybe Nurse Tamura's husband was the jealous type. Tengo had enough problems and didn't want to get caught up in any more.

"You're really something," Nurse Tamura said, wanting to change the subject. "You come all this way here, sit by your father's bedside for hours a day reading aloud to him . . . Not many people would do that."

Young Nurse Adachi tilted her head a bit. "I agree, he really is something. I really respect you for that."

"You know, we're always praising you," Nurse Tamura said.

Tengo's face reddened. He wasn't in this town to nurse his father. He was staying here hoping to again see the air chrysalis, and the faint light it gave off, and inside it, the sleeping figure of Aomame. That was the only reason he remained here. Taking care of his unconscious father was only a pretext. But he couldn't reveal the truth. If he did, he would have to start by explaining an air chrysalis.

"It's because I never did anything for him up till now." Awkwardly, he scrunched up his large frame in the narrow wooden chair, sounding uncomfortable. But the nurses found his attitude appealingly humble.

Tengo wanted to tell them he was sleepy so he could get up and go back to his inn, but he couldn't find the right opportunity. He wasn't the type, after all, to assert himself.

"Yes, but – " Nurse Omura said, and cleared her throat. "To get back to what we were talking about, I wonder why you and that married woman ten years older than you broke up. I imagine you were getting along all right? Did her husband find out or something?"

"I don't know the reason," Tengo said. "At one point she just stopped calling, and I haven't heard from her since."

"Hmm," Nurse Adachi said. "I wonder if she was tired of you."

Nurse Omura shook her head. She held one index finger pointing straight up and turned to her younger colleague. "You still don't know anything about the world. You don't get it at all. A forty-year-old married woman who snags a young, vigorous, delicious young man like this one and enjoys him to the fullest doesn't then just up and say *Thanks. It was fun. Bye!* It's impossible. Of course, the other way around happens sometimes."

"Is that right?" Nurse Adachi said, inclining her head just a fraction. "I guess I'm a bit naive."

"Yes, that's the way it is," Nurse Omura declared. She looked at Tengo for a while, as if stepping back from a stone monument to examine the words chiseled into it. Then she nodded. "When you get a little older you'll understand."

"Oh, my – it's been simply ages," Nurse Tamura said, sinking deeper into her chair.

For a time the three nurses were lost in a conversation about the sexual escapades of someone he didn't know (another nurse, he surmised). With his glass of whiskey and water in hand, Tengo surveyed these three nurses, picturing the three witches in *Macbeth*. The ones who chant "Fair is foul, and foul is fair," as they fill Macbeth's head with evil ambitions. But Tengo wasn't seeing the three nurses as evil beings. They were kind and straightforward women. They worked hard and took good care of his father. Overworked, living in this small, less-than-stimulating fishing town, they were just letting off steam, as they did once every month. But when he witnessed how the energy in these three women, all of different generations, was converging, he couldn't help but envision the moors of Scotland – a gloomy, overcast sky, a cold wind and rain howling through the heath.

In college he had read *Macbeth* in English class, and somehow a few lines remained with him.

> *By the pricking of my thumbs,*
> *Something wicked this way comes,*
> *Open, locks,*
> *Whoever knocks!*

Why should he remember only these lines? He couldn't even recall who spoke them in the play. But they made Tengo think of that persistent NHK collector, knocking at the door of his apartment in Koenji. Tengo looked at his own thumbs. They didn't feel pricked. Still, Shakespeare's skillful rhyme had an ominous ring to it.

Something wicked this way comes . . .

Tengo prayed that Fuka-Eri wouldn't unlock the door.

CHAPTER 7

Ushikawa

I'M HEADING YOUR WAY

For a while Ushikawa had to give up collecting more information on the elderly dowager in Azabu. The security around her was just too tight, and he knew he would come smack up against a high wall whatever direction he went in. He wanted to find out more about the safe house, but it was too risky hanging out in the neighborhood any longer. There were security cameras, and given his looks, Ushikawa was too conspicuous. Once the other party was on its guard, things could get a bit sticky, so he decided to stay away from the Willow House and try a different approach.

The only different approach he could come up with, though, was to reinvestigate Aomame. He had already asked a PI firm he had worked with to collect more information on her, and he did some of the legwork himself, questioning people involved with her. Nothing suspicious or opaque surfaced. Ushikawa frowned, sighing deeply. *I must have overlooked something,* he thought. *Something critical.*

Ushikawa took out an address book from a drawer of his desk and dialed a number. Whenever he needed information that could only be obtained illegally, this was the number he called. The man on the other end lived in a much darker world than

Ushikawa. As long as you paid, he could dig up almost any information you needed. The more tightly guarded the information, the higher the fee.

Ushikawa was after two pieces of information. One was personal background on Aomame's parents, who were still devout members of the Witnesses. Ushikawa was positive that the Witnesses had a central database with information on all their members. They had numerous followers throughout Japan, with much coming and going between the headquarters and the regional branches. Without a centralized database, the system wouldn't run smoothly. Their headquarters was located in the suburbs of Odawara. They owned a magnificent building on a generous plot of land, and had their own factory to print pamphlets, and an auditorium and guest facilities for followers from all over the country. All their information was sourced from this location, and you could be sure it was under strict control.

The second piece of information was Aomame's employment record at the sports club. Ushikawa wanted to know the details of her job there, and the names of her personal clients. This kind of information wouldn't be as closely guarded. Not that you could waltz in, say, "I wonder if you would mind showing me Miss Aomame's file, please?," and have them gladly hand it over.

Ushikawa left his name and phone number on the machine. Thirty minutes later he got a call back.

"Mr. Ushikawa," a hoarse voice said.

Ushikawa related the particulars of what he was looking for. He had never actually met the man. They always did business by phone, with materials sent over by special delivery. The man's voice was a bit husky, and he occasionally cleared his throat. He might have had something wrong with it. There was always a perfect silence on the other end of the line, as if he were phoning from a soundproof room. All Ushikawa could hear was the man's voice, and the grating sound of his breathing. Beyond that, nothing. The sounds he heard were all a bit exaggerated. *What a creepy guy,* Ushikawa thought each time. *The world is sure full of creepy guys,* he mused, knowing full well that, objectively speaking, this category would include himself. He had secretly nicknamed the man Bat.

"In both cases, then, you're after information concerning the name Aomame, right?" Bat said huskily, and cleared his throat.

"Correct. It's an unusual name."

"You want every bit of information I can get?"

"As long as it involves the name Aomame, I want it all. If possible, I would also like a photo of her, with a clear shot of her face."

"The gym should be easy. They aren't expecting anyone to steal their information. The Witnesses, though, are a different story. They're a huge organization, with a lot of money, and tight security. Religious organizations are some of the hardest groups to crack. They keep things tight to protect their members' personal security, and there are always tax issues involved."

"Do you think you can do it?"

"There are ways to pry open the door. What is more difficult is making sure you close it afterward. If you don't do that, you'll have a homing missile chasing you."

"You make it sound like a war."

"That's exactly what it is. Some pretty scary things might pop out," the man rasped. Ushikawa could tell from his tone of voice that this battle was something he enjoyed.

"So, you'll take it on for me?"

The man lightly cleared his throat. "All right. But it'll cost you."

"How much are we talking about, roughly?"

The man gave him an estimate. Ushikawa had to swallow

before he accepted. He had put aside enough of his own funds to cover it, and if the man came through, he could get reimbursed later on.

"How long will it take?"

"I assume this is a rush job?"

"Correct."

"It's hard to give an exact estimate, but I'm thinking a week to ten days."

"Fine," Ushikawa said. He would have to let Bat determine the pace.

"When I've gathered the material, I'll call you. I'll definitely get in touch before ten days are up."

"Unless a missile catches up with you," Ushikawa said.

"Exactly," Bat said, totally blasé.

After he hung up, Ushikawa hunched over his desk, turning things over in his mind. He had no idea how Bat would gather the information via some *back door*. Even if he asked, he knew he wouldn't get an answer. The only thing for sure was that his methods weren't legal. He would start by trying to bribe somebody inside. If necessary he might try trespassing. If computers were involved, things could get complicated.

There were only a few government offices and companies that managed information by computer. It cost too much and took too much effort. But a religious organization of national scale would have the resources to computerize. Ushikawa himself knew next to nothing about computers. He did understand, however, that computers were becoming an indispensable tool for gathering information. Earlier ways of finding information – going to the National Diet Library, sitting at a desk with piles of bound, small-sized editions of old newspapers, or almanacs – might soon become a thing of the past. The world might be reduced to a battlefield, the smell of blood everywhere, where computer managers and hackers fought it out. No, "the smell of blood" isn't accurate, Ushikawa decided. It was a war, so there was bound to be some bloodshed. But there wouldn't be any smell. What a weird world. Ushikawa preferred a world where smells and pain still existed, even if the smells and pain were unendurable. Still, people like Ushikawa might become out-of-date relics.

But Ushikawa wasn't pessimistic. He had an innate sense of intuition, and his unique olfactory organ let him sniff out and distinguish all sorts of odors. He could physically feel, in his skin, how things were trending. Computers couldn't do this. This was the kind of ability that couldn't be quantified or systematized. Skillfully accessing a heavily guarded computer and extracting information was the job of a hacker. But deciding which information to extract, and sifting through massive amounts of information to find what is useful, was something only a flesh-and-blood person could do.

Maybe I am just an ugly, middle-aged, outdated man, Ushikawa thought. *Nope, no maybes about it. I am, without a doubt, one ugly, middle-aged, outdated man. But I do have a couple of talents nobody else has. And as long as I have these talents, no matter what sort of weird world I find myself in, I'll survive.*

I'm going to get you, Miss Aomame. You are quite clever, to be sure. Skilled, and cautious. But I'm going to chase after you until I catch you. So wait for me. I'm heading your way. Can you hear my footsteps? I don't believe you can. I'm like a tortoise, hardly making a sound. But step by step, I am getting closer.

But Ushikawa felt something else pressing on him from behind. Time. Pursuing Aomame meant simultaneously shaking off time, which was in pursuit of him. He had to track her down quickly, clarify who was backing her, and present it all, nice and neat, on a plate to the people from Sakigake. He had been given a limited amount of time. It would be too late to find out everything, say, three months from now. Up until recently he had been a very valuable person to them. Capable and accommodating, well versed in legal matters, a man they could count on to keep his mouth shut. Someone who could work off the grid. But in the end, he was simply a hired jack-of-all-trades. He wasn't one of them, a member of their family. He was a man without a speck of religious devotion. If he became a danger to the religion, they might eliminate him with no qualms whatever.

While he waited for Bat to return his call, Ushikawa went to the library to look into the history and activities of the Witnesses. He took notes and made copies of relevant documents. He liked doing research at a library. He liked the feeling of accumulating knowledge in his brain. It was something he had enjoyed ever since he was a child.

Once he had finished at the library, he went to Aomame's apartment in Jiyugaoka, to make sure once more that it was unoccupied. The mailbox still had her name on it, but no one seemed to be living there. He stopped by the office of the real estate agent who handled the rental.

"I heard that there was a vacant apartment in the building," Ushikawa said, "and I was wondering if I could rent it."

"It is vacant, yes," the agent told him, "but no one can move in until the beginning of February. The rental contract with the present occupant doesn't expire until the end of next January. They are going to be paying the monthly rent the same as always until then. They have moved everything out and the electricity and water have been shut off. But the lease remains intact."

"So until the end of January, they're paying rent for an empty apartment?"

"Correct," the real estate agent said. "They said they will pay the entire amount owed on the lease so they would like us to keep the apartment as it is. As long as they pay the rent, we can't object."

"It's a strange thing – wasting money to pay for an empty apartment."

"Well, I was concerned myself, so I had the owner accompany me and let me in to take a look at the place. I wouldn't want there to be a mummified body in the closet or anything. But nothing was there. The place had been nicely cleaned. It was simply empty. I have no idea, though, what the circumstances are."

Aomame was obviously no longer living there. But for some reason they still wanted her listed as nominally renting the place, which is why they were paying four months' rent for an empty apartment. Whoever *they* were, they were cautious, and not hurting for money.

Precisely ten days later, in the early afternoon, Bat called Ushikawa's office in Kojimachi.

"Mr. Ushikawa," the hoarse voice said. In the background, there was the usual emptiness – a complete lack of any sound.

"Speaking."

"Do you mind if we talk now?"

"That would be fine," Ushikawa said.

"The Witnesses had very tight security. But I was expecting that. I was able to get the information related to Aomame okay."

"No homing missile?"

"Nothing so far."

"Glad to hear it."

"Mr. Ushikawa," the man said, and he cleared his throat a few times. "I'm really sorry, but could you put out the cigarette?"

"Cigarette?" he asked, glancing at the Seven Stars between his fingers. Smoke silently swirled up toward the ceiling. "You're right, I am smoking, but how can you tell?"

"Obviously I can't smell it. Just hearing your breathing makes it hard for me to breathe. I have terrible allergies, you see."

"I see. I hadn't noticed. My apologies."

The man cleared his throat a few times. "I'm not blaming you, Mr. Ushikawa. I wouldn't expect you to notice."

Ushikawa crushed the cigarette out in the ashtray and poured some tea he had been drinking over it. He stood up and opened the window wide.

"I put out the cigarette, opened the window, and let in some fresh air. Not that the air outside is all that clean."

"Sorry for the trouble."

Silence continued for about ten seconds. A total, absolute quiet.

"So, you were able to get the information from the Witnesses?" Ushikawa asked.

"Yes. Quite a lot, actually. The Aomame family are devout, long-time members, so there was plenty of material related to them. It is probably easiest if I give you the whole file, and then at your end you decide what is important material and what isn't."

Ushikawa agreed. That was what he had been hoping for.

"The sports club wasn't much of a problem – just open the door, go in, do your job, shut the door, that's it. Time was kind of limited, so I grabbed everything I could. There's a lot of material here too. I'll send over a folder with both sets of material. As usual, in exchange for the fee."

Ushikawa wrote down the fee that Bat gave him. It was about twenty percent higher than the estimate. Not that he had a choice.

"I don't want to use the mail this time, so a messenger will bring it over to your place tomorrow. Please have the fee ready. And as usual, don't expect a receipt."

"All right," Ushikawa replied.

"I mentioned this before, but I will repeat it just to make sure. I was able to get all the available information on the topic you asked me to look into. So even if you aren't satisfied with it, I take no responsibility. I did everything that was technically possible. Compensation was for the time and effort involved, not the results. So please don't ask me to give your money back if you don't find the information you're looking for. I would like you to acknowledge this point."

"I do," Ushikawa replied.

"Another thing is that I wasn't able to obtain a photograph of Miss Aomame, no matter how much I tried," Bat said. "All photos of her have been carefully removed."

"Understood. That's okay," Ushikawa said.

"Her face may be different by now," Bat commented.

"Maybe so," Ushikawa said.

Bat cleared his throat several times. "Well, that's it," he said, and hung up.

Ushikawa put the phone back in its cradle, sighed, and placed a new cigarette between his lips. He lit it with his lighter, and slowly exhaled smoke in the direction of the phone.

The next afternoon, a young woman visited his office. She was probably not yet twenty. She had on a short white dress that revealed the curves of her body, matching white high heels, and pearl earrings. Her earlobes were large for her small face. She was barely five feet tall. She wore her hair long and straight, and her eyes were big and bright. She looked like a fairy in training. The woman looked straight at Ushikawa and smiled a cheerful, intimate smile, as if she were viewing something precious she would never forget. Neatly aligned white teeth peeked out happily from between her tiny lips. Perhaps it was just her business smile. Very few people did not flinch when they came face-to-face with Ushikawa for the first time.

"I have brought the materials that you requested," the woman said, and extracted two large, thick manila envelopes from the cloth bag hanging from her shoulders. As if she were a shamaness transporting an ancient stone lithograph, she held up the envelopes in front of her, then carefully placed them on Ushikawa's desk.

From a drawer Ushikawa took out the envelope he had ready and passed it over to her. She opened the envelope, extracted the sheaf of ten-thousand-yen bills, and counted them as she stood there. She was very adept at counting, her beautiful, slim fingers moving swiftly. She finished counting, returned the bills to the envelope, and put the envelope in her cloth bag. She showed Ushikawa an even bigger, warmer smile than before, as if nothing could have made her happier than to meet him.

Ushikawa tried to imagine what connection this woman could have with Bat. Passing along the material, receiving payment. That was perhaps the only role she played.

After the small woman had left, Ushikawa stared at the door for the longest time. She had shut the door behind her, but there was still a strong sense of her in the room. Maybe in exchange for leaving a trace of herself behind, she had taken away a part of Ushikawa's soul. He could feel that new void within his chest. *Why did this happen?* he wondered, finding it odd. *And what could it possibly mean?*

After about ten minutes, he finally took the materials out of the envelopes, which had been sealed with several layers of adhesive tape. The inside was stuffed with a jumble of print-outs, photocopies, and original documents. Ushikawa didn't know how Bat had accomplished it, but he had certainly come up with a lot of material in such a short time. As always, the man did an impressive job. Still, faced with that bundle of documents, Ushikawa was hit by a deep sense of impotence. No matter how much he might rustle around in it, would he ever arrive anywhere? Or would he spend a small fortune just to wind up with a stack of wastepaper? The sense of powerlessness he experienced was so deep that he could stare as much as he wanted into the well and never get a glimpse of its bottom.

Everything Ushikawa could see was covered in a gloomy twilight, like an intimation of death. *Perhaps this was due to something that woman left behind,* he thought. *Or perhaps due to something she took away with her.*

Somehow, though, Ushikawa recovered his strength. He patiently went through the stack of materials until evening, copying the information he felt was important into a notebook, organizing it under different categories. By concentrating on this, he was able to dispel the mysterious listlessness that had grabbed hold of him. And by the time it grew dark and he switched on his desk lamp, Ushikawa was thinking that the information had been worth every yen he had paid for it.

He began by reading through the material from the sports club. Aomame was a highly skilled trainer, popular with the members. Along with teaching general classes, she was also a personal trainer. Looking through the copies of the daily schedule he could figure out when, where, and how she trained these private clients. Sometimes she trained them individually at the club, sometimes she went to their homes. Among the names of her clients was a well-known entertainer, and a politician. The dowager of the Willow House, Shizue Ogata, was her oldest client.

Her connection with Shizue Ogata began not long after Aomame started working at the club four years earlier, and continued until just before she disappeared. This was exactly the same period during which the two-story apartment building at the Willow House became a safe house for victims of domestic violence. Maybe it was a coincidence, but maybe not. At any rate, according to the records, their relationship appeared to have deepened over time.

Perhaps a personal bond had grown between Aomame and the old dowager. Ushikawa's intuition sensed this. At first it started out as the relationship between a sports club instructor and a client, but at a certain point, the nature of this relationship changed. As Ushikawa went through the businesslike descriptions in chronological order, he tried to pinpoint that moment. Something happened that transformed their relationship beyond that of mere instructor and client. They formed a close personal relationship that transcended the difference in age and status. This may even have led to some secret emotional understanding between the two, a secret understanding that eventually led Aomame down the path to murder Leader at the Hotel Okura. Ushikawa's sense of smell told him so.

But what *was* that path? And what secret understanding did they have?

That was as far as Ushikawa's conjectures could take him.

Most likely, domestic violence was one factor in it. At first glance this seemed to be a critical theme for the older woman. According to the records, the first time Shizue Ogata came in contact with Aomame was at a self-defense class. It wasn't very common for a woman in her seventies to take a self-defense class. Something connected with violence must have brought the old lady and Aomame together.

Or maybe Aomame herself had been the victim of domestic violence. And Leader had committed domestic violence. Perhaps they found out about this and decided to punish him. But these were all simply hypotheses, and these hypotheses didn't square with the image Ushikawa had of Leader. Certainly people, no matter who they are, have something hidden deep down inside, and Leader was a deeper person than most. He was, after all, the driving force behind a major religious organization. Wise and intelligent, he also had depths no one else could access. But say he really had committed domestic violence? Would these acts have been so significant to these women that, when they learned of them, they planned out a meticulous assassination – one of them giving up her identity, the other risking her social standing?

One thing was for sure: the murder of Leader was not carried out on a whim. Behind it stood an unwavering will, a clear-cut, unclouded motivation, and an elaborate system – a system that had been meticulously crafted using a great deal of time and money.

The problem was that there was no concrete proof to back up his conjectures. What Ushikawa had before him was nothing more than circumstantial evidence based on theories. Something that Occam's razor could easily prune away. At this stage he couldn't report anything to Sakigake. Still, he knew he was on to something. There was a certain smell to it, a distinctive texture. All the elements pointed in a single direction. Something to do with domestic violence made the dowager direct Aomame to kill Leader and then hide her away. Indirectly, all the information Bat had provided him supported this conclusion.

Plowing through the materials dealing with the Witnesses took a long time. There were an enormous number of documents, most of them useless to Ushikawa. The majority of the materials were reports on what Aomame's family had contributed to the activities of the Witnesses. As far as these documents were concerned, Aomame's family were earnest, devout followers. They had spent the better part of their lives propagating the religion's message. Her parents presently resided in Ichikawa, in Chiba Prefecture. In thirty-five years they had moved twice, both times within Ichikawa. Her father, Takayuki Aomame (58), worked in an engineering firm, while her mother, Yasuko (56), wasn't employed. The couple's eldest son, Keiichi Aomame (34), had worked in a small printing company in Tokyo after graduating from a prefectural high school in Ichikawa, but after three years he quit the company and began working at the Witnesses' headquarters in Odawara. There he also worked in printing, making pamphlets for the religion, and was now a supervisor. Five years earlier he had married a woman who was also a member of the Witnesses. They had two children and rented an apartment in Odawara.

The record for the eldest daughter, Masami Aomame, ended when she was eleven. That was when she abandoned the faith. And the Witnesses seemed to have no interest at all in anyone who had left the faith. To the Witnesses, it was the same as if Masami Aomame had died at age eleven. After this, there wasn't a single detail about what sort of life she led – not even whether or not she was alive.

In this case, Ushikawa thought, *the only thing to do is visit the parents or the brother and ask them. Maybe they will provide me with some hint.* From what he gathered from the documentary evidence, he didn't imagine they would be too pleased to answer his questions. Aomame's family – as far as Ushikawa could see it, that is – were narrow-minded in their thinking, narrow-minded in the way they lived. They were people who had no doubt whatsoever that the more narrow-minded they became, the closer they got to heaven. To them, anyone who abandoned the faith, even a relative, was traveling down a wicked, defiled path. Who knows, maybe they didn't even think of them as relatives anymore.

Had Aomame been the victim of domestic violence as a girl?

Maybe she had, maybe she hadn't. Even if she had, her parents most likely would not have seen this as abuse. Ushikawa knew very well how strict members of the Witnesses were with their children. In many cases this included corporal punishment.

But would a childhood experience like that form such a deep wound that it would lead a person, after she grew up, to commit murder? This wasn't out of the realm of possibility, but Ushikawa thought it was pushing the limits of conjecture to an extreme. Carrying out a premeditated murder on one's own wasn't easy. It was dangerous, to begin with, and the emotional toll was enormous. If you got caught, the punishment was stiff. There had to be a stronger motivation behind it.

Ushikawa picked up the sheaf of documents and carefully reread the details about Masami Aomame's background, up to age eleven. Almost as soon as she could walk, she began accompanying her mother to proselytize. They went from door to door handing out pamphlets, telling people about the judgment to come at the end of the world and urging them to join the faith. Joining meant you could survive the end of the world. After that, the heavenly kingdom would appear. A church member had knocked on Ushikawa's door any number of times. Usually it was a middle-aged woman, wearing a hat or holding a parasol. Most wore glasses and stared fixedly at him with eyes like those of a clever fish. Often she had a child along. Ushikawa pictured little Aomame trundling around from door to door with her mother.

Aomame didn't attend kindergarten, but went into the local neighborhood municipal public elementary school in Ichikawa. And when she was in fifth grade she withdrew from the Witnesses. It was unclear why she left. The Witnesses didn't record each and every reason a member renounced the faith. Whoever fell into the clutches of the devil could very well stay there. Talking about paradise and the path to get there kept members busy enough. The righteous had their own work to do, and the devil, his – a spiritual division of labor.

In Ushikawa's brain someone was knocking on a cheaply made, plywood partition. "Mr. Ushikawa! Mr. Ushikawa!" the voice was yelling. Ushikawa closed his eyes and listened carefully. The voice was faint, but persistent. *I must have overlooked something,* he thought. *A critical fact must be written here, somewhere, in these very documents. But I can't see it. The knock must be telling me this.*

Ushikawa turned again to the thick stack of documents, not just following what was written, but trying to imagine actual scenes in his mind. Three-year-old Aomame going with her mother as she spread the gospel door to door. Most of the time people slammed the door in their faces. Next she's in elementary school. She continues proselytizing. Her weekends are taken up entirely with propagating their faith. She doesn't have any time to play with friends. She might not even have had any friends. Most children in the Witnesses were bullied and shunned at school. Ushikawa had read a book on the Witnesses and was well aware of this. And at age eleven she left the religion. That must have taken a great deal of determination. Aomame had been raised in the faith, had had it drummed into her since she was born. The faith had seeped into every fiber of her being, so she couldn't easily slough it off, like changing clothes. That would mean she was isolated within the home. They wouldn't easily accept a daughter who had renounced the faith. For Aomame, abandoning the faith was the same as abandoning her family.

When Aomame was eleven, what in the world had happened to her? What could have made her come to that decision?

The Ichikawa Municipal ** Elementary School. Ushikawa tried saying the name aloud. *Something had happened there. Something had most definitely happened . . .* He inhaled sharply. *I've heard the name of that school before,* he realized.

But where? Ushikawa had no ties to Chiba Prefecture. He had been born in Urawa, a city in Saitama, and ever since he came to Tokyo to go to college – except for the time he lived in Chuorinkan, in Kanagawa Prefecture – he had lived entirely within the twenty-three wards of Tokyo. He had barely set foot in Chiba Prefecture. Only once, as he recalled, when he went to the beach at Futtsu. So why did the name of an elementary school in Ichikawa ring a bell?

It took him a while to remember. He rubbed his misshapen head as he concentrated. He fumbled through the dark recesses of memory, as if sticking his hand deep down into mud. It wasn't so long ago that he first heard that name. Very recently, in fact. Chiba Prefecture . . . Ichikawa Municipal ** Elementary School. Finally he grabbed onto one end of a thin rope.

Tengo Kawana. That's it – Tengo Kawana was from Ichikawa! And I think he attended a municipal public elementary school in town, too.

Ushikawa pulled down from his document shelf the file on Tengo. This was material he had compiled a few months back, at the request of Sakigake. He flipped through the pages to confirm Tengo's school record. His plump finger came to rest on Tengo's name. It was just as he had thought: Masami Aomame had attended the same elementary school as Tengo Kawana. Based on their birthdates, they were probably in the same year in school. Whether they were in the same class or not would require further investigation. But there was a high probability they knew each other.

Ushikawa put a Seven Stars cigarette in his mouth and lit up with his lighter. He had the distinct feeling that things were starting to fall into place. He was connecting the dots, and though he was unsure of what sort of picture would emerge, before long he should be able to see the outlines.

Miss Aomame, can you hear my footsteps? Probably not, since I'm walking as quietly as I can. But step by step I'm getting closer. I'm a dull, silly tortoise, but I'm definitely making progress. Pretty soon I'll catch sight of the rabbit's back. You can count on it.

Ushikawa leaned back from his desk, looked up at the ceiling, and slowly let the smoke rise up from his mouth.

CHAPTER 8

Aomame

NOT SUCH A BAD DOOR

Except for the silent men who brought supplies every Tuesday afternoon, for the next two weeks no one else visited Aomame's apartment. The man who claimed to be an NHK fee collector had insisted that he would be back. He had been determined, or at least that was the way it sounded to Aomame. But there hadn't been a knock on the door since. Maybe he was busy with another route.

On the surface, these were quiet, peaceful days. Nothing happened, nobody came by, the phone didn't ring. To be on the safe side, Tamaru called as little as possible. Aomame always kept the curtains closed, living as quietly as she could so as not to attract attention. After dark, she turned on the bare minimum number of lights.

Trying to stay as quiet as possible, she did strenuous workouts, mopped the floor every day, and spent a lot of time preparing meals. She asked for some Spanish-language tapes and went over the lessons aloud. Not speaking for a long time makes the muscles around the mouth grow slack. She had to focus on moving her mouth as much as she could, and foreign language drills were good for that. Plus Aomame had long fantasized about South America. If she could go anywhere, she would like to live in a small, peaceful country in South

America, like Costa Rica. She would rent a small villa on the coast and spend the days swimming and reading. With the money she had stuffed in her bag she should be able to live for ten years there, if she watched her expenses. She couldn't see them chasing her all the way to Costa Rica.

As she practiced Spanish conversation Aomame imagined a quiet, peaceful life on the Costa Rican beach. Could Tengo be a part of her life there? She closed her eyes and pictured the two of them sunbathing on a Caribbean beach. She wore a small, black bikini and sunglasses and was holding Tengo's hand. But a sense of reality, the kind that would move her, was missing from the picture. It was nothing more than an ordinary tourist brochure photo.

When she ran out of things to do, she cleaned the pistol. She followed the manual and disassembled the Heckler & Koch, cleaned each part with a cloth and brush, oiled them, and then reassembled it. She made sure the action was smooth. By now she had mastered the operation and the pistol felt like a part of her body.

She would go to bed at ten, read a few pages in her book, and fall asleep. Aomame had never had trouble falling asleep. As she read, she would get sleepy. She would switch off the bedside lamp, rest her head on the pillow, and shut her eyes. With few exceptions, when she opened her eyes again it was morning.

Ordinarily she didn't tend to dream much. Even if she did, she usually had forgotten most of the dream by the time she woke up. Sometimes faint scraps of her dream would get caught on the wall of her consciousness, but she couldn't retrace these fragments back to any coherent narrative. All that remained were small, random images. She slept deeply, and the dreams she did have came from a very deep place. Like fish that live at the bottom of the ocean, most of her dreams weren't able to float to the surface. Even if they did, the difference in water pressure would force a change in their appearance.

But after coming to live in this hiding place, she dreamed every night. And these were clear, realistic dreams. She would be dreaming and wake up in the middle of a dream, unable to distinguish whether she was in the real world or the dream world. Aomame couldn't remember ever having had this experience before. She would look over at the digital clock beside her bed. The numbers would say 1:15, 2:37, or 4:07. She would close her eyes and try to fall asleep again, but it wasn't easy. The two different worlds were silently at odds within her, fighting over her consciousness, like the mouth of a river where the seawater and the fresh water flow in.

Not much I can do about it, she told herself. *I'm not even sure if this world with two moons in the sky is the* real *reality or not. So it shouldn't be so strange, should it? That in a world like this, if I fall asleep and dream, I find it hard to distinguish dream from reality? And let's not forget that I've killed a few men with my own hands. I'm being chased by fanatics who aren't about to give up, and I'm hiding out. How could I* not *be tense, and afraid? I can still feel the sensation, in my hands, of having murdered somebody. Maybe I'll never be able to sleep soundly the rest of my life. Maybe that's the responsibility I have to bear, the price I have to pay.*

The dreams she had – at least the ones she could recall – fell into three set categories.

The first was a dream about thunder. She is in a dark room, with thunder roaring continuously. But there is no lightning, just like the night she murdered Leader. There is something in the room. Aomame is lying in bed, naked, and something is wandering about around her, slowly, deliberately. The carpet is thick, and the air lies heavy and still. The windowpane rattles slightly in the thunder. She is afraid. She doesn't know what is there in the room. It might be a person. Maybe it's an animal. Maybe it's neither one. Finally, though, whatever it is leaves the room. Not through the door, nor by the window. But still its presence fades away until it has completely disappeared. She is alone now in the room.

She fumbles for the light near her bed. She gets out of bed, still naked, and looks around the room. There is a hole in the wall opposite her bed, a hole big enough for one person to barely make it through. The hole isn't in a set spot. It changes shape and moves around. It shakes, it moves, it grows bigger, it shrinks – as if it's alive. *Something* left through that hole. She stares into the hole. It seems to be connected to something else, but it's too dark inside to see, a darkness so thick that it's as if you could cut it out and hold it in your hand. She is curious, but at the same time afraid. Her heart pounds, a cold, distant beat. The dream ends there.

The second dream took place on the shoulder of the Metropolitan Expressway. And here, too, she is totally nude. Caught in the traffic jam, people leer at her from their cars, shamelessly ogling her naked body. Most are men, but there are a few women, too. The people are staring at her less-than-ample breasts and her pubic hair and the strange way it grows, all of them evaluating her body. Some are frowning, some smiling wryly, others yawning. Others are staring intently at her, their faces blank. She wants to cover herself up – at least her breasts and groin, if she can. A scrap of cloth would do the trick, or a sheet of newspaper. But there is nothing around her she can pick up. And for some reason (she has no idea why) she can't move her arms. From time to time the wind blows, stimulating her nipples, rustling her pubic hair.

On top of this – as if things couldn't get any worse – it feels like she is about to get her period. Her back feels dull and heavy, her abdomen hot. What should she do if, in front of all these people, she starts bleeding?

Just then the driver's-side door of a silver Mercedes coupe

opens and a very refined middle-aged woman steps out. She's wearing bright-colored high heels, sunglasses, and silver earrings. She's slim, about the same height as Aomame. She wends her way through the backed-up cars, and when she comes over she takes off her coat and puts it on Aomame. It's an eggshell-colored spring coat that comes down to her knees. It's light as a feather. It's simple, but obviously expensive. The coat fits her perfectly, like it was made for her. The woman buttons it up for her, all the way to the top.

"I don't know when I can return it to you. I'm afraid I might bleed on it," Aomame says.

Without a word, the woman shakes her head, then weaves her way back through the cars to the Mercedes coupe. From the driver's side it looks like she lifts her hand in a small wave to Aomame, but it may be an illusion. Wrapped in the light, soft spring coat, Aomame knows she is protected. Her body is no longer exposed to anyone's view. And right then, as if it could barely wait, a line of blood drips down her thigh. Hot, thick, heavy blood. But as she looks at it she realizes it isn't blood. It's colorless.

The third dream was hard to put into words. It was a rambling, incoherent dream without any setting. All that was there was a feeling of being in motion. Aomame was ceaselessly moving through time and space. It didn't matter when or where this was. All that mattered was this movement. Everything was fluid, and a specific meaning was born of that fluidity. But as she gave herself up to it, she found her body growing transparent. She could see through her hands to the other side. Her bones, organs, and womb became visible. At this rate she might very well no longer exist. After she could no longer see herself, Aomame wondered what could possibly come then. She had no answer.

* * *

At two p.m. the phone rang and Aomame, dozing on the sofa, leapt to her feet.

"Is everything going okay?" Tamaru asked.

"Yes, fine," Aomame replied.

"How about the NHK fee collector?"

"I haven't seen him at all. Maybe he was just threatening me, saying he would be back."

"Could be," Tamaru said. "We set it up so the NHK subscription fee is automatically paid from a bank account, and an up-to-date sticker is on the door. Any fee collector would be bound to see it. We called NHK and they said the same thing. It must be some kind of clerical error."

"I just hope I don't have to deal with him."

"Yes, we need to avoid any kind of attention. And I don't like it when there are mistakes."

"But the world is full of mistakes."

"The world can be that way, but I have my own way of doing things," Tamaru said. "If there is anything that bothers you – anything at all – make sure you get in touch."

"Is there anything new with Sakigake?"

"Everything has been quiet. I imagine something is going on below the surface, but we can't tell from the outside."

"I heard you had an informant within the organization."

"We've gotten some reports, but they're focused on details, not the big picture. It does seem as if they are tightening up control of the faith. The faucet has been shut."

"But they are definitely still after me."

"Since Leader's death, there has clearly been a large gap left in the organization. They haven't decided yet who is going to succeed him, or what sort of policies Sakigake should take. But when it comes to pursuing you, opinion is unwavering and unanimous. Those are the facts we have been able to find out."

"Not very heartwarming facts, are they."

"Well, with facts what's important is their weight and accuracy. Warmth is secondary."

"Anyway," Aomame said, "if they capture me and the truth comes to light, that will be a problem for you as well."

"That is why we want to get you to a place they can't reach, as soon as we can."

"I know. But I need you to wait a little longer."

"*She* said that we would wait until the end of the year. So of course that's what I'll do."

"I appreciate it."

"I'm not the one you should be thanking."

"Be that as it may," Aomame said. "There is one item I'd like to add to the list the next time you bring over supplies. It's hard to say this to a man, though."

"I'm like a rock wall," Tamaru said. "Plus, when it comes to being gay, I'm in the big leagues."

"I would like a home pregnancy test."

There was silence. Finally Tamaru spoke. "You believe there's a need for that kind of test."

It wasn't a question, so Aomame didn't reply.

"Do you think you might be pregnant?" Tamaru asked.

"No, that isn't the reason."

Tamaru quickly turned this over in his mind. If you were quiet, you could actually hear the wheels turning.

"You don't think you're pregnant. Yet you need a pregnancy test."

"That's right."

"Sounds like a riddle to me."

"All I can tell you is that I would like to have the test. The kind of simple home test you can pick up in a drugstore is fine. I'd also appreciate a handbook on the female body and menstruation."

Tamaru was silent once more – a hard, concentrated silence.

"I think it would be better if I called you back," he said. "Is that okay?"

"Of course."

He made a small sound in the back of his throat, and hung up the phone.

The phone rang again fifteen minutes later. It had been a long while since Aomame had heard the dowager's voice. She felt like she was back in the greenhouse. That humid, warm space where rare butterflies flutter about, and time passes slowly.

"Are you doing all right there?"

"I'm trying to keep to a daily routine," Aomame replied. Since the dowager wanted to know, Aomame gave her a summary of her daily schedule, her exercising and meals.

"It must be hard for you," the dowager said, "not being able to go outside. But you have a strong will, so I'm not worried about you. I know you will be able to get through it. I would like to have you leave there as soon as possible and get you to a safer place, but if you want to stay there longer, I will do what I can to honor your wishes."

"I am grateful for that."

"No, I'm the one who should be grateful to you. You have done a wonderful thing for us." A short silence followed, and then the dowager continued. "Now, I understand you have requested a pregnancy test."

"My period is nearly three weeks late."

"Are your periods usually regular?"

"Since they began when I was ten, I have had a period every twenty-nine days, almost without fail. Like the waxing and waning of the moon. I've never skipped one."

"You are in an unusual situation right now. Your emotional balance and physical rhythm will be thrown off. It's possible your period might stop, or the timing may be off."

"It has never happened before, but I understand how it could."

"According to Tamaru you don't see how you could be pregnant."

"The last time I had sexual relations with a man was the middle of June. After that, nothing at all."

"Still, you suspect you might be pregnant. Is there any evidence for that? Other than your period being late?"

"I just have a feeling about it."

"A feeling?"

"A feeling inside me."

"A feeling that you have conceived?"

"Once we talked about eggs, remember? The evening we went to see Tsubasa. About how women have a set number of them?"

"I remember. The average woman has about four hundred eggs. Each month, she releases one of them."

"Well, I have the distinct sensation that one of those eggs has been fertilized. I don't know if *sensation* is the right word, though."

The dowager pondered this. "I have had two children, so I think I have a very good idea of what you mean by *sensation*. But you're saying you've been impregnated without having had sex with a man. That is a little difficult to accept."

"I know. I feel the same way."

"I'm sorry to have to ask this, but is it possible you've had sexual relations with someone while you weren't conscious?"

"That is not possible. My mind is always clear."

The dowager chose her words carefully. "I have always thought of you as a very calm, logical person."

"I've always tried to be," Aomame said.

"In spite of that, you think you are pregnant without having had sex."

"I think that *possibility exists*. To put it more accurately,"

Aomame replied. "Of course, it might not make any sense even to consider it."

"I understand," the dowager said. "Let's wait and see what happens. The pregnancy kit will be there tomorrow. It will come at the same time and in the same way as the rest of the supplies. We will include several types of tests, just to be sure."

"I really appreciate it," Aomame said.

"If it does turn out that you are pregnant, when do you think it happened?"

"I think it was that night when I went to the Hotel Okura. The night there was a storm."

The dowager gave a short sigh. "You can pinpoint it that clearly?"

"I calculated it, and that night just happened to be the day when I was most fertile."

"Which would mean that you are two months along."

"That's right," Aomame said.

"Do you have any morning sickness? This would normally be when you would have the worst time of it."

"No, I don't feel nauseous at all. I don't know why, though."

The dowager took her time, and carefully chose her next words. "If you do the test and it does turn out you're pregnant, how do you think you'll react?"

"I suppose I'll try to figure out who the child's biological father could be. This would be very important to me."

"But you have no idea."

"Not at the moment, no."

"I understand," the dowager said, calmly. "At any rate, whatever does happen, I will always be with you. I'll do everything in my power to protect you. I want you to remember that."

"I'm sorry to cause so much trouble at a time like this," Aomame said.

"It's no trouble at all," the dowager said. "This is the most important thing for a woman. Let's wait for the test results, and then decide what we'll do. Just relax."

And she quietly hung up.

Someone knocked at the door. Aomame was in the bedroom doing yoga, and she stopped and listened carefully. The knock was hard and insistent. She remembered that sound.

She took the automatic pistol from the drawer and switched off the safety. She pulled back the slide to send a round into the chamber. She stuck the pistol in the back of her sweatpants and softly padded out to the dining room. She gripped the softball bat in both hands and stared at the door.

"Miss Takai," a thick, hoarse voice called out. "Are you there, Miss Takai? NHK here, come to collect the subscription fee."

Plastic tape was wrapped around the handle of the bat so it wouldn't slip.

"Miss Takai, to repeat myself, I know you're in there. So please stop playing this silly game of hide-and-seek. You're inside, and you're listening to my voice."

The man was saying almost exactly the same things he had said the previous time, like a tape being replayed.

"I told you I would be back, but you probably thought that was just an empty threat. You should know that I always keep my promises. And if there are fees to collect, I most definitely will collect them. You're in there, Miss Takai, and you're listening. And you're thinking this: If I just stay patient, the collector will give up and go away."

He knocked on the door again for some time. Twenty, maybe twenty-five times. *What sort of hands does this man have?* Aomame wondered. *And why doesn't he use the doorbell?*

"And I know you're thinking this, too," the fee collector said, as if reading her mind. "You are thinking that this man must have pretty tough hands. And that his hands must hurt, pounding on the door like this so many times. And there is another thing you are thinking: Why in the world is he knocking, anyway? There's a doorbell, so why not ring that?"

Aomame grimaced.

The fee collector continued. "No, I don't want to ring the bell. If I do, all you hear is the bell ringing, that's all. No matter who pushes the bell, it makes the same harmless little sound. Now, a knock – *that* has personality. You use your physical body to knock on something and there's a flesh-and-blood emotion behind it. Of course my hand does hurt. I'm not Superman, after all. But it can't be helped. This is my profession. And every profession, no matter high or low, deserves respect. Don't you agree, Miss Takai?"

Knocks pounded on the door again. Twenty-seven in all, powerful knocks with a fixed pause between each one. Aomame's hands grew sweaty as they gripped the bat.

"Miss Takai, people who receive the NHK TV signal have to pay the fee – it's the law. There are no two ways about it. It is a rule we have to follow. So why don't you just cheerfully pay the fee? I'm not pounding on your door because I want to, and I know you don't want this unpleasantness to go on forever. You must be thinking, Why do I have to go through this? So just cheerfully pay up. Then you can go back to your quiet life again."

The man's voice echoed loudly down the hallway. *This man is enjoying the sound of his own voice,* Aomame thought. *He's getting a kick out of insulting people, making fun of them and abusing them.* She could sense the perverse pleasure he was getting from this.

"You're quite the stubborn lady, aren't you, Miss Takai. I'm impressed. You're like a shellfish at the bottom of a deep ocean, maintaining a strict silence. But I know you're in there. You're there, glaring at me through the door. The tension is making your underarms sweat. Do I have that right?"

Thirteen more knocks. Then he stopped. Aomame realized she was, indeed, sweating under her arms.

"All right. That's enough for today. But I'll be back soon. I'm starting to grow fond of this door. There are lots of doors in the world, and this one is not bad at all. It is definitely a door worth knocking on. At this rate I won't be able to relax unless I drop by here regularly to give it a few good knocks. Good-bye, Miss Takai. I'll be back."

Silence reigned. The fee collector had apparently left for good, but she hadn't heard any footsteps. Maybe he was pretending to have left and was waiting outside the door. Aomame gripped the bat even tighter and waited a couple of minutes.

"I'm still here," the fee collector suddenly announced. "Ha! You thought I left, didn't you? But I'm still here. I lied. Sorry about that, Miss Takai. That's the sort of person I am."

She heard him cough. An intentionally grating cough.

"I've been at this job for a long time. And over the years I've become able to picture the people on the other side of the door. This is the truth. Quite a few people hide behind their door and try to get away with not paying the NHK fee. I've been dealing with them for decades. Listen, Miss Takai."

He knocked three times, louder than he ever had.

"Listen, Miss Takai. You're very clever at hiding, like a flounder on the sea floor covered in sand. *Mimicry*, they call it. But in the end you won't be able to escape. Someone will come and open this door. You can count on it. As a veteran NHK fee collector, I guarantee it. You can hide as cleverly as you like, but in the final analysis mimicry is deception, pure and simple. It doesn't solve a thing. It's true, Miss Takai. I'll be on my way soon. Don't worry, this time for real. But I'll be back soon. When you hear a knock, you'll know it's me. Well, see you, Miss Takai. Take care!"

She couldn't hear any footsteps this time, either. She waited five minutes, then went up to the door and listened carefully. She squinted through the peephole. No one was outside. This time the fee collector really had left, it seemed.

Aomame leaned the metal bat up against the kitchen counter. She slid the round out of the pistol's chamber, set the safety, wrapped it back up in a pair of thick tights, and returned it to the drawer. She lay down on the sofa and closed her eyes. The man's voice still rang in her ears.

But in the end you won't be able to escape. Someone will come and open this door.

At least this man wasn't from Sakigake. They would take a quieter, more indirect approach. They would never yell in an apartment hallway, insinuate things like that, putting their target on guard. That was not their MO. Aomame pictured Buzzcut and Ponytail. They would sneak up on you without making a sound. And before you knew it, they would be standing right behind you.

Aomame shook her head, and breathed quietly.

Maybe he really was an NHK fee collector. If so, it was strange that he didn't notice the sticker that said they paid the subscription fee automatically. Aomame had checked that the sticker was pasted to the side of the door. Maybe the man was a mental patient. But the things he said had a bit too much reality to them for that. *The man certainly did seem to sense my presence on the other side of the door. As if he had sniffed out my secret, or a part of it.* But he did not have the power to open the door and come in. The door had to be opened from inside. *And I'm not planning on opening it.*

No, she thought, *it's hard to say that for sure. Someday I might open the door. If Tengo were to show up at the playground, I wouldn't hesitate to open the door and rush outside. It doesn't matter what might be waiting for me.*

Aomame sank down into the garden chair on the balcony and gazed as usual through the cracks in the screen at the playground. A high school couple were sitting on the bench underneath the zelkova tree, discussing something, serious expressions on their faces. Two young mothers were watching their children, not yet old enough for kindergarten, playing in the sandbox. They were deep in conversation yet kept their eyes glued to their children. A typical afternoon scene in a park. Aomame stared at the top of the slide for a long time.

She brought her hand down to her abdomen, shut her eyes, and listened carefully, trying to pick up the voice. Something was definitely alive inside her. A small, living something. She knew it.

Dohta, she whispered.

Maza, something replied.

CHAPTER 9

Tengo

BEFORE THE EXIT IS BLOCKED

The four of them had *yakiniku,* then went to another place where they sang karaoke and polished off a bottle of whiskey. It was nearly ten p.m. when their cozy but boisterous little party broke up. After they left the bar, Tengo took Nurse Adachi back to her apartment. The other two women could catch a bus near the station, and they casually let things work out that way. Tengo and the young nurse walked down the deserted streets, side by side, for a quarter of an hour.

"Tengo, Tengo, Tengo," she sang out. "Such a nice name. *Tengo.* It's so easy to say."

Nurse Adachi had drunk a lot, but her cheeks were normally rosy so it was hard to tell, just by looking at her face, how drunk she really was. Her words weren't slurred and her footsteps were solid. She didn't seem drunk. Though people had their own ways of being drunk.

"I always thought it was a weird name," Tengo said.

"It isn't at all. *Tengo.* It has a nice ring to it and it's easy to remember. It's a wonderful name."

"Speaking of which, I don't know your first name. Everybody calls you Ku."

"That's my nickname. My real name is Kumi. Kind of a nothing name."

"*Kumi Adachi,*" Tengo said aloud. "Not bad. Compact and simple."

"Thank you," Kumi Adachi said. "But putting it like that makes me feel like a Honda Civic or something."

"I meant it as a compliment."

"I know. I get good mileage, too," she said, and took Tengo's hand. "Do you mind if I hold your hand? It makes it more fun to walk together, and more relaxed."

"I don't mind," Tengo replied. Holding hands like this with Kumi Adachi, he remembered Aomame and the classroom in elementary school. It felt different now, but there was something in common.

"I must be a little drunk," Kumi said.

"You think so?"

"Yup."

Tengo looked at the young nurse's face again. "You don't look drunk."

"I don't show it on the outside. That's just the way I am. But I'm wasted."

"Well, you were knocking them back pretty steadily."

"I know. I haven't drunk this much in a long time."

"You just have to get out like this sometimes," Tengo said, quoting Mrs. Tamura.

"Of course," Kumi said, nodding vigorously. "People have to get out sometimes – have something good to eat, have some drinks, belt out some songs, talk about nothing in particular. But I wonder if you ever have times like that. Where you just get it out of your system, to clear your head? You always seem so cool and composed, Tengo."

Tengo thought about it. Had he done anything lately to unwind? He couldn't recall. If he couldn't recall, that probably meant he hadn't. The whole concept of *getting something out of his system* was something he might be lacking.

"Not so much, I guess," Tengo admitted.

"Everybody's different."

"There are all sorts of ways of thinking and feeling."

"Just like there are lots of ways of being drunk," the nurse said, and giggled. "But it's important, Tengo."

"You may be right," he said.

They walked on in silence for a while, hand in hand. Tengo felt uneasy about the change in the way she spoke. When she had on her nurse's uniform, Kumi was invariably polite. But now in civilian clothes, she was more outspoken, probably partly due to the alcohol. That informal way of talking reminded him of someone. Somebody had spoken the same way. Someone he had met fairly recently.

"Tengo, have you ever tried hashish?"

"Hashish?"

"Cannabis resin."

Tengo breathed in the night air and exhaled. "No, I never have."

"How about trying some?" Kumi Adachi asked. "Let's try it together. I have some at home."

"You have hashish?"

"Looks can be deceiving."

"They certainly can," Tengo said vaguely. So a healthy young nurse living in a seaside little town on the Boso Peninsula had hashish in her apartment. And she was inviting him to smoke some.

"How did you get ahold of it?" Tengo asked.

"A girlfriend from high school gave it to me for a birthday present last month. She had gone to India and brought it back." Kumi began swinging Tengo's hand with her own in a wide arc.

"But there's a stiff penalty if you're caught smuggling pot into the country. The Japanese police are really strict about it. They have pot-sniffing dogs at the airports."

"She's not the type to worry about little details," Kumi said.

"Anyhow, she got through customs okay. Would you like to try it? It's high-quality stuff, very potent. I checked into it, and medically speaking there's nothing dangerous about it. I'm not saying it isn't habit forming, but it's much milder than tobacco, alcohol, or cocaine. Law enforcement says it's addictive, but that's ridiculous. If you believe that, then pachinko is far more dangerous. You don't get a hangover, so I think it would be good for you to try it to blow off some steam."

"Have you tried it yourself?"

"Of course. It was fun."

"Fun," Tengo repeated.

"You'll understand if you try it," Kumi said, and giggled. "Say, did you know? When Queen Victoria had menstrual cramps she used to smoke marijuana to lessen the pain. Her court doctor actually prescribed it to her."

"You're kidding."

"It's true. I read it in a book."

Which book? Tengo was about to ask, but decided it was too much trouble. That was as far as he wanted to go picturing Queen Victoria having menstrual cramps.

"So how old were you on your birthday last month?" Tengo asked, changing subjects.

"Twenty-three. A full-fledged adult."

"Of course," Tengo said. He was already thirty, but yet to have a sense of himself as an adult. It just felt to him like he had spent thirty years in the world.

"My older sister is staying over tonight at her boyfriend's, so I'm by myself. So come on over. Don't be shy. I'm off duty tomorrow so I can take it easy."

Tengo searched for a reply. He liked this young nurse. And she seemed to like him, too. But she was inviting him to her place. He looked up at the sky, but it was covered with thick gray clouds and he couldn't see the moons.

"The other day when my girlfriend and I smoked hashish,"

Kumi began, "that was my first time, but it felt like my body was floating in the air. Not very high, just a couple of inches. You know, floating at that height felt really good. Like it was just right."

"Plus you won't hurt yourself if you fall."

"Yeah, it's just the right height, so you can feel safe. Like you're being protected. Like you're wrapped in an air chrysalis. I'm the *dohta,* completely enveloped in the air chrysalis, and outside I can just make out *maza.*"

"*Dohta?*" Tengo asked. His voice was surprisingly hard. "*Maza?*"

The young nurse was humming a tune, swinging their clasped hands as they walked down the deserted streets. She was much shorter than Tengo, but it didn't seem to bother her at all. An occasional car passed by.

"*Maza* and *dohta.* It's from the book *Air Chrysalis.* Do you know it?" she asked.

"I do."

"Have you read it?"

Tengo silently nodded.

"Great. That makes things easier. I *love* that book. I bought it in the summer and read it three times. I hardly ever read a book three times. And as I was smoking hashish for the first time in my life I thought it felt like I was inside an air chrysalis myself. Like I was enveloped in something and waiting to be born. With my *maza* watching over me."

"You saw your *maza*?" Tengo asked.

"Yes, I did. From inside the air chrysalis you can see outside, to a certain extent. Though you can't see in from outside. That's how it's structured. But I couldn't make out her expression. She was a vague outline. But I knew it was my *maza.* I could feel it very clearly. That this person was my *maza.*"

"So an air chrysalis is actually a kind of womb."

"I guess you could say that. I don't remember anything from

when I was in the womb, so I can't make an exact comparison," Kumi Adachi said, and giggled again.

It was the kind of cheaply made two-story apartment building you often find in the suburbs of provincial cities. It looked fairly new, yet it was already starting to fall apart. The outside stairway creaked, and the doors didn't quite hang right. Whenever a large truck rolled by outside, the windows rattled. The walls were thin, and if anyone were to practice a bass guitar in one of the apartments, the whole building would end up being one large sound box.

Tengo wasn't all that drawn to the idea of smoking hashish. He had a sane mind, yet he lived in a world with two moons. There was no need to distort the world any more than that. He also didn't have any sexual desire for Kumi Adachi. Certainly he did feel friendly toward this young twenty-three-year-old nurse. But friendliness and sexual desire were two different things, at least for Tengo. So if she hadn't mentioned *maza* and *dohta,* most likely he would have made up an excuse and not gone inside. He would have taken a bus back, or, if there weren't any buses, he would have had her call a cab, and then returned to the inn. This was, after all, the cat town. It was best to avoid any dangerous spots. But once Kumi mentioned the words *maza* and *dohta,* Tengo couldn't turn down her invitation. Maybe she could give him a hint as to why the young Aomame had appeared in the air chrysalis in the hospital room.

The apartment was a typical place for two sisters in their twenties living together. There were two small bedrooms, plus a combined kitchen and dining room that connected to a tiny living room. The furniture looked thrown together from all over, with no unifying style. Above the laminated dining table there hung a tacky imitation Tiffany lamp, quite out of place. If you were to open the curtain, with its tiny floral pattern, outside there was a cultivated field, and beyond that, a thick, dark grove of various trees. The view was nice, with nothing to obstruct it, but far from heartwarming.

Kumi sat Tengo down on the love seat in the living room – a gaudy, red love seat – facing the TV. She took out a can of Sapporo beer from the fridge and set it down, with a glass, in front of him.

"I'm going to change into something more comfortable, so wait here. I'll be right back."

But she didn't come back for a long time. He could hear the occasional sound from behind the door across the narrow corridor – the sound of drawers that didn't slide well, opening and closing, the thud of things clunking to the ground. With each thud, Tengo couldn't help but look in that direction. Maybe she really was drunker than she looked. He could hear a TV through the thin walls of the apartment. He couldn't make out what the people were saying, but it appeared to be a comedy show, and every ten or fifteen seconds there was a burst of laughter from the audience. Tengo regretted not having turned down her invitation. At the same time, though, in a corner of his mind he felt it was inevitable that he had come here.

The love seat was cheap, and the fabric itched whenever his skin touched it. Something bothered him, too, about the shape of it, and he couldn't get comfortable no matter how he shifted around. This only amplified his sense of unease. Tengo took a sip of beer and picked up the TV remote from the table. He stared at it for a time, as if it were some odd object, and then hit the on button. He surfed through a few channels, finally settling on an NHK documentary about railroads in Australia. He chose this program simply because it was quieter than the others. While an oboe piece played in the background, a woman announcer was calmly introducing the elegant sleeper cars in the line that ran across the whole of Australia.

Tengo sat there in the uncomfortable love seat, unenthusiastically following the images on the screen, but his mind was on *Air Chrysalis*. Kumi Adachi had no idea that he was the one who had really written the book. Not that it mattered – what did matter was that while he had written such a detailed description of the air chrysalis, Tengo knew next to nothing about it. What *was* an air chrysalis? And what did *maza* and *dohta* signify? He had no idea what they meant when he wrote *Air Chrysalis,* and he still didn't. Still, Kumi liked the book and had read it three times. How could such a thing be possible?

Kumi came back out as the show was discussing the dining-car menu. She plunked down on the love seat next to Tengo. It was so narrow their shoulders touched. She had changed into an oversized long-sleeved shirt and faded cotton pants. The shirt had a large smiley face on it. The last time Tengo had seen a smiley face was the beginning of the 1970s, back when Grand Funk Railroad rattled the jukeboxes with their crazy loud songs. But the shirt didn't look that old. Somewhere, were people still manufacturing smiley-face shirts?

Kumi took a fresh beer from the fridge, loudly popped it open, poured it in her glass, and chugged down a third of it. She narrowed her eyes like a satisfied cat and pointed at the TV screen. In between red cliffs the train was traveling down an endlessly straight line.

"Where is this?"

"Australia," Tengo said.

"Australia," Kumi Adachi said, as if searching the recesses of memory. "The Australia in the Southern Hemisphere?"

"Right. The Australia with the kangaroos."

"I have a friend who went to Australia," Kumi said, scratching next to her eye. "It was right during the kangaroo mating season. He went to one town and the kangaroos were doing it all over the place. In the parks, in the streets. Everywhere."

Tengo thought he should make a comment, but he couldn't

think of anything. Instead he took the remote and turned off the TV. With the TV off, the room suddenly grew still. The sound of the TV next door, too, was gone. The occasional car would pass by on the road outside, but other than that it was a quiet night. If you listened carefully, though, there was a muffled, far-off sound. It was steady and rhythmic, but Tengo had no idea what it was. It would stop for a time, then start up again.

"It's an owl," the nurse explained. "He lives in the woods nearby. He hoots at night."

"An owl," Tengo repeated vaguely.

Kumi rested her head on his shoulder and held his hand. Her hair tickled his neck. The love seat was still uncomfortable. The owl continued hooting knowingly off in the woods. That voice sounded encouraging to Tengo, but at the same time like a warning. Or maybe a warning that contained a note of encouragement. It was a very ambiguous sound.

"Tell me, do you think I'm too forward?" Kumi Adachi asked.

Tengo didn't reply. "Don't you have a boyfriend?"

"That's a perplexing question," she said, indeed looking a bit perplexed. "Most of the smart young men head off to Tokyo as soon as they graduate from high school. There are no good colleges here, and not enough decent jobs, either. They have no other choice."

"But you're here."

"Yes. Considering the lousy pay they give us, the work is pretty hard. But I kind of like living here. The problem is finding a boyfriend. I'm open to it if I find someone, but there aren't so many chances."

The hands of the clock on the wall pointed to just before eleven. If he didn't go back to the inn by the eleven o'clock curfew, he wouldn't be able to get in. But Tengo couldn't rouse himself from the cramped love seat. His body just wouldn't listen. Maybe it was the shape of the chair, or maybe he was drunker than he thought. He listened vaguely to the owl's hooting, felt Kumi's hair tickle his neck, and gazed at the faux Tiffany lamp.

Kumi Adachi whistled cheerfully as she prepared the hashish. She used a safety razor to slice thin slices off a black ball of hash, stuffed the shavings into a small, flat pipe, and then, with a serious look on her face, lit a match. A unique, sweetly smoky smell soon filled the room. Kumi took the first hit. She inhaled deeply, held it in her lungs for a long time, then slowly exhaled. She motioned to Tengo to do the same. Tengo took the pipe and followed her example. He tried to hold the smoke in his lungs as long as possible, and then let it out ever so slowly.

They leisurely passed the pipe back and forth, never exchanging a word. The neighbor next door switched on his TV and they could hear the comedy show again. The volume was a bit louder than before. The happy laughter of the studio audience swelled up, the laughter only stopping during the commercials.

They took turns smoking for about five minutes, but nothing happened. The world around Tengo was unchanged – colors, shapes, and smells were the same as before. The owl kept on hooting in the woods, Kumi Adachi's hair on his neck still itched. The two-person love seat remained uncomfortable. The second hand on the clock ticked away at the same speed and the people on TV kept on laughing out loud when someone said something funny, the kind of laugh that you could laugh forever but never end up happy.

"Nothing's happening," Tengo said. "Maybe it doesn't work on me."

Kumi lightly tapped his knee twice. "Don't worry. It takes time."

And she was right. Finally it hit him. He heard a click, like a secret switch being turned on, and then something inside his head sloshed thickly. It felt like tipping a bowl of rice porridge sideways. *My brain is vibrating,* Tengo thought. This was a new experience for him – considering his brain as an object apart from the rest of him, physically experiencing the viscosity of it. The deep hoot of the owl came in through his ears, mixed with the porridge inside, and melted into it.

"The owl is inside me," Tengo commented. The owl had become a part of his consciousness, a vital part that couldn't be separated out.

"The owl is the guardian deity of the woods. He knows all and gives us the wisdom of the night," Kumi said.

But where and how should he seek this wisdom? The owl was everywhere, and nowhere. "I can't think of a question to ask him," Tengo said.

Kumi Adachi held his hand. "There's no need for questions. All you need to do is go into the woods yourself. That way is much simpler."

He could hear laughter again from the comedy next door. Applause as well. The show's assistant, off camera, was probably holding up cue cards to the audience that said *Laugh* and *Applaud.* Tengo closed his eyes and thought of the woods, of himself going into the woods. Deep in the dark forest was the realm of the Little People. But the owl was still there too. The owl knows all and gives us the wisdom of the night.

Suddenly all sound vanished, as if someone had come up behind him stealthily and stuck corks in his ears. Someone had closed one lid, while someone else, somewhere, had opened another lid. Entrance and exit had switched.

Tengo found himself in an elementary school classroom.

The window was wide open and children's voices filtered in from the schoolyard. The wind blew, almost as an afterthought, and the white curtains waved in the breeze. Aomame was beside him, holding his hand tightly. It was the same scene as always – but something was different. Everything he could see was crystal clear, almost painfully clear, fresh and focused down to the texture. He could make out each and every detail of the forms and shapes of things around him. If he reached out his hand, he could actually touch them. The smell of the early-winter afternoon hit him strongly, as if what had been covering up those smells until then had been yanked away. Real smells. The set smells of the season: of the blackboard erasers, the floor cleaner, the fallen leaves burning in the incinerator in a corner of the schoolyard – all these were mixed inseparably together. When he breathed in these scents, he felt them spread out deep and wide within his mind. The structure of his body was being reassembled. His heartbeat was no longer just a heartbeat.

For an instant, he could push the door of time inward. Old light mixed with the new light, the two becoming one. The old air mixed in with the new to become one. *It is this light, and this air*, Tengo thought. He understood everything now. Almost everything. *Why couldn't I remember this smell until now? It's so simple. It's such a straightforward world, yet I didn't get it.*

"I wanted to see you," Tengo said to Aomame. His voice was far away and faltering, but it was definitely his voice.

"I wanted to see you, too," the girl said. The voice sounded like Kumi Adachi's. He couldn't make out the boundary between reality and imagination. If he tried to pin it down, the bowl slipped sideways and his brains sloshed around.

Tengo spoke. "I should have started searching for you long ago. But I couldn't."

"It's not too late. You can still find me," the girl said.

"But how can I find you?"

No response. The answer was not put into words.

"But I know I can find you," Tengo said.

The girl spoke. "Because I could find *you*."

"You found me?"

"Find me," the girl said. "While there's still time."

Like a departed soul that had failed to leave in time, the white curtain soundlessly and gently wavered. That was the last thing Tengo saw.

When he came to, he was lying in a narrow bed. The lights were out, the room faintly lit by the streetlights filtering in through a gap in the curtains. He was wearing a T-shirt and boxers. Kumi wore only her smiley-face shirt. Underneath the long shirt, she was nude. Her soft breasts lay against his arm. The owl was still hooting in Tengo's head. The woods lingered inside him – he was still clinging to the nighttime woods.

Even in bed like this with the young nurse, he felt no desire. Kumi seemed to feel the same way. She wrapped her arms around his body and giggled. What was so funny? Tengo had no idea. Maybe somebody, somewhere, was holding out a sign that said *Laugh*.

What time could it be? He lifted his head to look for a clock but couldn't see any. Kumi suddenly stopped laughing and wrapped her arms around his neck.

"I was reborn," she said, her hot breath brushing his ear.

"You were reborn," Tengo said.

"Because I died once."

"You died once," Tengo repeated.

"On a night when there was a cold rain falling," she said.

"Why did you die?"

"So I would be reborn like this."

"You would be reborn," Tengo said.

"More or less," she whispered very quietly. "In all sorts of forms."

Tengo pondered this statement. What did it mean to *be reborn more or less, in all sorts of forms*? His brain was heavy, and was brimming with the germs of life, like some primeval sea. Not that these led him anywhere.

"Where do air chrysalises come from, anyway?"

"That's the wrong question," Kumi said, and chuckled.

She twisted her body on top of his and Tengo could feel her pubic hair against his thighs. Thick, rich hair. It was like her pubic hair was a part of her thinking process.

"What is necessary in order to be reborn?" Tengo asked.

"The biggest problem when it comes to being reborn," the small nurse said, as if revealing a secret, "is that people aren't reborn for their own sakes. They can only do it for someone else."

"Which is what you mean by *more or less, in all sorts of forms.*"

"When morning comes you will be leaving here, Tengo. Before the exit is blocked."

"When morning comes I'll be leaving here," Tengo repeated the nurse's words.

Once more she rubbed her rich pubic hair against his thigh, as if to leave behind some sort of *sign.* "Air chrysalises don't come from somewhere. They won't come no matter how long you wait."

"You know that."

"Because I died once," she said. "It's painful to die. Much more painful than you imagine, Tengo. You are utterly lonely. It's amazing how completely lonely a person can be. You had better remember that. But you know, unless you die once, you won't be reborn."

"Unless you die once, you won't be reborn," Tengo confirmed.

"But people face death while they're still alive."

"People face death while they're still alive," Tengo repeated, unsure of what it meant.

The white curtain continued to flutter in the breeze. The air in the classroom smelled of a mixture of blackboard erasers and cleaner. There was the scent of burning leaves. Someone was practicing the recorder. The girl was squeezing his hand tightly. In his lower half he felt a sweet ache, but he didn't have an erection. That would come later on. The words *later on* promised him eternity. Eternity was a single long pole that stretched out without end. The bowl tipped a bit again, and again his brains sloshed to one side.

When he woke up, it took Tengo a while to figure out where he was, and to piece together the events of the previous night. Bright sunlight shone in through the gap between the flowery curtains, while birds whistled away noisily outside. He had been sleeping in an uncomfortable, cramped position in the narrow bed. He found it hard to believe he could have slept the whole night in such a position. Kumi was lying beside him, her face pressed into the pillow, sound asleep. Her hair was plastered against her cheeks, like lush summer grass wet with dew. *Kumi Adachi,* Tengo thought. A young nurse who just turned twenty-three. His wristwatch had fallen to the floor. The hands showed 7:20 – 7:20 in the morning.

Tengo slipped quietly out of bed, careful not to wake Kumi, and looked out the window through a crack in the curtains. There was a cabbage field. Rows of cabbages crouched stolidly on the dark soil. Beyond the field was the woods. Tengo remembered the hoot of the owl. Last night it had definitely been hooting. The wisdom of the night. Tengo and the nurse had listened to it as they smoked hashish. He could still feel her stiff pubic hair on his thigh.

Tengo went to the kitchen, scooped up water from the faucet with his hands, and drank. He was so thirsty he drank and drank, and still wanted more. Other than that, nothing else had changed. His head didn't hurt, and his body wasn't listless. His mind was clear. But somehow, inside him, things seemed to flow a bit too well – as if pipes had been carefully, and professionally, cleaned. In his T-shirt and boxers he padded over to the toilet and took a good long pee. In the unfamiliar mirror, his face didn't look like his own. Tufts of hair stood up here and there on his head, and he needed a shave.

He went back to the bedroom and gathered up his clothes. His discarded clothes lay mixed in with Kumi's, scattered on the floor. He had no memory of when, or how, he had undressed. He located both socks, tugged on his jeans, buttoned up his shirt. As he did, he stepped on a large, cheap ring. He picked it up and put it on the nightstand next to the bed. He tugged on his crew-neck sweater and picked up his windbreaker. He checked that his wallet and keys were in his pocket. The young nurse was sleeping soundly, the blanket pulled up to just below her ears. Her breathing was quiet. Should he wake her up? Even though they hadn't – he was pretty sure – *done* anything, they had spent the night in bed together. It seemed rude to leave without saying good-bye. But she was sleeping so soundly, and she had said this was her day off. Even if he did wake her, what were they supposed to do then?

He found a memo pad and ballpoint pen next to the telephone. *Thanks for last night,* he wrote. *I had a good time. I'm going back to my inn. Tengo.* He wrote down the time. He placed the memo on the nightstand, and put the ring he had picked up on top, as a paperweight. He then slipped on his worn-out sneakers and left.

He walked down the road for a while, until he came across a bus stop. He waited there for five minutes and soon a bus heading for the station arrived. The bus was full of noisy high school boys and girls, and he rode with them to the end of the line. The people at the inn took his unshaven eight a.m. arrival in stride. It didn't seem to be that out of the ordinary for them. Without a word, they briskly prepared his breakfast.

As he ate his hot breakfast and drank tea, Tengo went over the events of the previous night. The three nurses had invited him out and they went to have *yakiniku*. Then on to

a bar, where they sang karaoke. Then he went to Kumi Adachi's apartment, where they smoked Indian hashish, while an
owl hooted outside. Then his brain felt like it had changed into
hot, thick porridge. And suddenly he was in his elementary
school classroom in winter, he could smell the air, and he was
talking with Aomame. Then Kumi, in bed, was talking about
death and resurrection. There were wrong questions, ambiguous answers. The owl in the woods went on hooting, people on
a TV show went on laughing.

His memory was patchy and there were definitely several
gaps. But the parts he did recall were amazingly vivid and
clear. He could retrace each and every word they spoke. Tengo
recalled the last thing Kumi said. It was both advice and a
warning.

*When morning comes you will be leaving here, Tengo. Before
the exit is blocked.*

Maybe this was the right time to leave. He had taken off
from his job and come to this town hoping to see ten-year-old
Aomame inside the air chrysalis once more. And he had spent
nearly two weeks going every day to the sanatorium, reading
aloud to his father. But the air chrysalis had never appeared.
Instead, when he was about to give up, Kumi Adachi had prepared a different kind of vision just for him. And in it he was
able once more to see Aomame as a girl, and speak with her.
Find me, Aomame had said. *While there's still time.* Actually, it
may have been Kumi who said that. Tengo couldn't tell. Not
that it mattered. Kumi had died once, and been reborn. Not
for herself, but for someone else. For the time being, Tengo
decided to believe what he had heard from her. It was important to do so. At least, he was pretty sure it was.

This was the cat town. There was something specific that
could only be found here. That's why he had taken the train
all the way to this far-off place. But everything he found here
held an inherent risk. If he believed Kumi's hints, these risks

could be fatal. *By the pricking of my thumbs, something wicked this way comes.*

It was time to go back to Tokyo – before the exit was blocked, while the train still stopped at this station. But before that he needed to go to the sanatorium again, and say good-bye to his father. There were things he still needed to clarify.

CHAPTER 10

Ushikawa

GATHERING SOLID LEADS

Ushikawa traveled to Ichikawa. It felt like quite a long excursion, but actually Ichikawa was just over the river in Chiba Prefecture, not far from downtown Tokyo. At the station he boarded a cab and gave the driver the name of the elementary school. It was after one p.m. when he arrived at the school. Lunch break was over and classes had just begun for the afternoon. He heard a chorus singing in the music room and a gym class was playing soccer outside. Children were yelling as they chased after the ball.

Ushikawa didn't have good memories of his own days in elementary school. He wasn't good at sports, particularly any kind that involved a ball. He was short, a slow runner, had astigmatism, and was uncoordinated. Gym class was a nightmare. His grades in other classes were excellent, though. He was pretty bright and applied himself to his schoolwork (which led to passing the difficult bar exam when he was only twenty-five). But nobody liked him, or respected him. Not being good at sports may have been one reason. And then there was his face. Since he was a child, he had had this big, ugly face, with a misshapen head. His thick lips sagged at the corners and looked as if they were about to drool at any moment, though they never actually did. His hair was frizzy and unruly. These were not the sort of looks to attract others.

In elementary school he hardly ever spoke. He knew he could be eloquent if necessary, but he didn't have any close friends and never had the opportunity to show others how well spoken he could be. So he always kept his mouth shut. He kept his ears open and listened closely to whatever anyone else had to say, aiming to learn something from everything he heard. This habit eventually became a useful tool. Through this, he discovered a number of important realities, including this one: most people in the world don't really use their brains to think. And people who don't think are the ones who don't listen to others.

At any rate, his elementary school days were not a page of his life that Ushikawa enjoyed reminiscing over. Just thinking that he was about to visit an elementary school depressed him. Despite any differences between Saitama and Chiba prefectures, elementary schools were pretty much alike anywhere you went in Japan. They looked the same and operated on the same principles. Still, Ushikawa insisted on going all the way to visit this school in Ichikawa himself. This was important, something he couldn't leave up to anyone else. He had called the school's front office and already had an appointment for one thirty.

The vice principal was a petite woman in her mid-forties, slim, attractive, and nicely dressed. *Vice principal?* Ushikawa was puzzled. He had never heard that term before. But it was ages ago when he graduated from elementary school. Lots of things must have changed since then. The woman must have dealt with many people over the years, for she didn't blink an eye when faced with Ushikawa's extraordinary features. Or perhaps she was just a very well-mannered person. She showed Ushikawa to a tidy reception room and invited him to take a seat. She sat down in the chair across from him and smiled broadly, as if wondering what sort of enjoyable conversation they were about to have.

She reminded Ushikawa of a girl who had been in his class in school. The girl had been pretty, got good grades, was kind and responsible. She was well brought up and good at piano. She was one of the teacher's favorites. During class Ushikawa spent a lot of time gazing at her, mainly at her back. But he never once talked with her.

"I understand that you're looking into one of the graduates of our school?" the vice principal asked.

"I'm sorry, I should have given you this before," Ushikawa said, and passed her his business card. It was the same card he had given Tengo, the one with his title on it: Full-time Director, New Japan Foundation for the Advancement of Scholarship and the Arts. What he told the woman was the same fabricated story he had told Tengo. Tengo Kawana, who had graduated from this school, had become a writer and was on a short list to receive a grant from the foundation. Ushikawa was just running an ordinary background check on him.

"That's wonderful news," the vice principal said, beaming. "It's a great honor for our school, and we will do everything we can to help you."

"I was hoping to meet and speak directly with the teacher who taught Mr. Kawana," Ushikawa said.

"I'll check into that. It's more than twenty years ago, so she may be retired already."

"I appreciate that," Ushikawa said. "If it's all right, there's one other thing I would like you to look into, if you would."

"And what would that be?"

"There was a girl in the same year, I believe, as Mr. Kawana, a Miss Masami Aomame. Would you be able to check into whether she was in the same class as Mr. Kawana?"

The vice principal looked a bit dubious. "Is this Miss Aomame in some way connected with the question of funding for Mr. Kawana?"

"No, it's not that. In one of the works by Mr. Kawana, there is a character who seems to be modeled on someone like Miss Aomame, and I have a few questions of my own on this topic that I need to clear up. It's nothing very involved. Basically a formality."

"I see," the vice principal said, the corners of her lips rising ever so slightly. "I am sure you understand, however, that in some cases we may not be able to give you information that might touch on a person's privacy. Grades, for instance, or reports on a pupil's home environment."

"Of course, I'm fully aware of that. All we are after is information on whether or not she was actually in the same class as Mr. Kawana. And if she was, I would appreciate it very much if you could give me the name and contact information for the teacher in charge of their class at the time."

"I understand. That shouldn't be a problem. Miss Aomame, was it?"

"Correct. It's written with the characters for green and peas. An uncommon name."

Ushikawa wrote the name "Masami Aomame" in pen on a page on his pocket notebook and passed the page to the vice principal. She looked at it for a few seconds, then placed it in the pocket of a folder on her desk.

"Could you please wait here for a few minutes? I'll go check our staff records. I'll have the person in charge photocopy whatever can be made public."

"I'm sorry to bother you with this when you are obviously so busy," Ushikawa said.

The vice principal's flared skirt swished prettily as she exited the room. She had beautiful posture, and she moved elegantly. Her hairstyle was attractive too. She was clearly aging gracefully. Ushikawa shifted in his seat and killed time by reading a paperback book he had brought along.

*   *   *

The vice principal came back fifteen minutes later, a brown business envelope clutched to her breast.

"It turns out that Mr. Kawana was quite the student. He was always at the top of his class as well as a very successful athlete. He was especially good at arithmetic and mathematics, and even in elementary school he was able to solve high-school-level problems. He won a math contest and was written up in the newspaper as a child prodigy."

"That's amazing," Ushikawa said.

"It's odd that while he was touted as a math prodigy, today he has distinguished himself in literature."

"Abundant talent is like a rich vein of water underground that finds all sorts of places to gush forth. Presently he is teaching math while writing novels."

"I see," the vice principal said, raising her eyebrows at a lovely angle. "Unlike Tengo, there wasn't much on Masami Aomame. She transferred to another school in fifth grade. She was taken in by relatives in Adachi Ward in Tokyo and transferred to a school there. She and Tengo Kawana were classmates in third and fourth grades."

Just as I suspected, Ushikawa thought. *There was some connection between the two of them.*

"A Miss Ota was in charge of their class then. Toshie Ota. Now she's teaching at a municipal elementary school in Narashino."

"If I contact that school, perhaps I will be able to get in touch with her?"

"We have already made the call," the vice principal said, smiling faintly. "When we explained the situation, she said she would be very pleased to meet with you."

"I really appreciate that," Ushikawa said. *She wasn't just a pretty face,* he thought, *but an efficient administrator, too.*

On the back of her business card, the vice principal wrote down the teacher's name and the phone number of the school, the Tsudanuma elementary school, and handed it to Ushikawa. Ushikawa carefully stashed the card in his billfold.

"I heard that Miss Aomame was raised with some sort of religious background," Ushikawa said. "We are a bit concerned about this."

The vice principal frowned, tiny lines forming at the corners of her eyes. The kind of subtle, charming, intelligent lines acquired only by middle-aged women who have taken great care to train themselves.

"I'm sorry, but that is not a subject we can discuss here," she said.

"It touches on areas of personal privacy, doesn't it," Ushikawa asked.

"That's correct. Especially issues dealing with religion."

"But if I meet with this Miss Ota, I might be able to ask her about this."

The vice principal inclined her slender jaw slightly to the left and smiled meaningfully. "If Miss Ota wishes to speak as a private individual, that is no concern of ours."

Ushikawa stood up and politely thanked her. She handed him the brown business envelope. "The materials we could copy are inside. Documents pertaining to Mr. Kawana. There's a little bit, too, concerning Miss Aomame. I hope it's helpful to you."

"I'm sure it will be. Thank you very much for all you have done. You've been very kind."

"When the results of that grant are decided, you'll be sure to let us know, won't you? This will be a great honor for our school."

"I'm positive there will be a good outcome," Ushikawa said. "I have met him a number of times and he is a talented young man with a promising future."

Ushikawa stopped at a diner in front of Ichikawa Station, ate a simple lunch, and looked through the material in the envelope. There was a basic record of attendance at the school for both Tengo and Aomame, as well as records of awards given to Tengo for his achievements in academics and sports. He did indeed seem to be an extraordinary student. He probably never once thought of school as a nightmare. There was also a copy of a newspaper article about the math contest he had won. It was an old article and the photo wasn't very clear, but it was obviously Tengo as a boy.

After lunch Ushikawa phoned the Tsudanuma elementary school. He spoke with Miss Ota, the teacher, and made an appointment to meet her at four at her school. After four I'm free to talk, she had said.

I know it's my job, Ushikawa sighed, *but two elementary schools in one day is a bit much.* Just thinking about it made him depressed. But so far it had been worth the effort. He now had proof that Tengo and Aomame were classmates for two years – a huge step forward.

Tengo had helped Eriko Fukada to revise *Air Chrysalis* into a decent novel, and make it a bestseller. Aomame had secretly murdered Eriko's father, Tamotsu Fukada, in a suite at the Hotel Okura. It would appear that they shared the goal of attacking, in their own ways, the religious organization Sakigake. Perhaps they were working together. That's what most people would conclude.

But it wouldn't do to tell that duo from Sakigake about this – not yet. Ushikawa didn't like to reveal information in fits and starts. He much preferred gathering as much information as he could, making absolutely sure of all the facts, and then, when he had solid proof, revealing the results with a flourish. It was a theatrical gesture he still retained from his days as a lawyer. He would act self-deprecating so that other people would let down their guard. Then, just when things were drawing to a conclusion, he would bring forth his irrefutable evidence and turn the tables.

As he rode the train to Tsudanuma, Ushikawa mentally assembled a number of hypotheses.

Tengo and Aomame might be lovers. They wouldn't have been lovers when they were ten, of course, but it was possible to see them, after they graduated from elementary school, running into each other and growing intimate. And for some reason – the reason was still unclear – they decided to work together to destroy Sakigake. This was one hypothesis.

As far as Ushikawa could tell, however, there was no evidence of Tengo and Aomame having a relationship. Tengo had maintained an ongoing affair with a married woman ten years older than himself. If Tengo had been deeply involved with Aomame, he would not then regularly cheat on her with another woman – he wasn't adroit enough to pull that off. Ushikawa had previously investigated Tengo's habits over a two-week period. He taught math at a cram school three days a week, and on the other days he was mostly alone in his apartment. Writing novels, most likely. Other than occasionally shopping or going for a walk, he seldom left his place. It was a very monotonous, simple lifestyle, easy to fathom. There was nothing mysterious about it. Somehow Ushikawa just couldn't picture him involved in a plot that involved murdering someone.

Personally, Ushikawa liked Tengo. Tengo was an unaffected, straightforward young man, independent and self-reliant. As is often the case with physically large people, he tended to be a bit slow on the uptake at times, but he wasn't sly or cunning in the least. He was the kind of guy who, once he decided on a course of action, never deviated from it. The kind who would never make it as a lawyer or a stockbroker. Rather, he was more likely to get tripped up and stumble at the most critical juncture. He would make a good math teacher and novelist, though. He wasn't particularly sociable or eloquent, but he did appeal to a certain type of woman. In a nutshell, he was the polar opposite of Ushikawa.

In contrast to what he knew about Tengo, Ushikawa knew next to nothing about Aomame – other than her background with the Witnesses and that she had later been a star softball player. When it came to her personality – her way of thinking, her strong points and weaknesses, what sort of private life she led – he was clueless. The facts that he had assembled were nothing more than what you would find on a résumé.

But while comparing the backgrounds of Tengo and Aomame, some similarities came to light. First of all, both of them must have had unhappy childhoods. Aomame was dragged all over town by her mother to proselytize, slogging from house to house, ringing doorbells. All the Witness children were made to do that. In Tengo's case, his father was an NHK fee collector. This was another job that involved making the rounds from one house to the next. Had Tengo been dragged along with him? Maybe he had. If Ushikawa had been Tengo's father, he probably would have taken Tengo with him on his rounds. Having a child with you helped you collect more fees, and you saved on babysitting money – two birds with one stone. For Tengo this couldn't have been much fun. Perhaps these two children even passed each other on the streets of Ichikawa.

Second, as they grew older, Tengo and Aomame worked hard to win athletic scholarships so they could get far away from home as quickly as possible. And both of them turned out to be superb athletes. They both must have been pretty talented to begin with. But there was also a reason they *had to be superb*. Being an athlete was a way to be recognized by others, and having outstanding records in sports was just about the only way they could win their independence. This was the valuable ticket they needed to survive. They thought differently from average teenagers. They confronted the world differently.

When he thought about it, Ushikawa realized his own situation somewhat resembled theirs.

I'm from an affluent family and had no need to get a scholarship. I always had plenty of spending money. But in order to get into a top university, and pass the bar exam, I had to study like mad, just like Tengo and Aomame. I had no time to have fun like my classmates. I had to abstain from all worldly pleasures – not that I had much chance of obtaining them to begin with – and focus solely on my studies. I was always stuck between feelings of inferiority and superiority. I often used to think I was like Raskolnikov, except I never met Sonia.

Enough about me. Thinking about that won't change anything. I have to get back to Tengo and Aomame.

Say Tengo and Aomame did happen to run across each other sometime in their twenties and started talking. They would have been so amazed at all the things they had in common. And there would be so many things they had to talk about. Maybe they found themselves attracted to each other, as a man and a woman. Ushikawa had a vivid mental image of this scene – a fateful meeting, the ultimate romantic moment.

But had such a meeting actually taken place? Had a romance blossomed? Ushikawa didn't know. But it would make sense if they had actually met. That would explain how they joined forces to attack Sakigake, each of them from a different angle – Tengo with his pen, Aomame no doubt with some special skill she had. Somehow, though, Ushikawa couldn't warm to this hypothesis. On one level it all made sense, but he wasn't convinced.

If indeed Tengo and Aomame did have such a deep relationship, there would be evidence. This fateful meeting would have had fateful results, and this would not have passed unnoticed by Ushikawa's observant eyes. Aomame might have been able to hide it, but not Tengo.

In general, Ushikawa saw things logically. Without proof, he couldn't go forward. However, he also trusted his natural intuition. When it came to a scenario where Tengo and

Aomame had conspired together, his intuition shook its head no. It was just a little shake, but insistent nonetheless. Maybe the two of them weren't even aware of each other's existence. Maybe it *just turned out* that they were both simultaneously involved with Sakigake.

Even if it was hard to picture such a coincidence, Ushikawa's intuition told him that this hypothesis felt more likely than the conspiracy theory. The two of them, driven by different motives, and approaching things from different angles, just happened to simultaneously shake Sakigake to the core. Two story lines at work, with different starting points but running parallel to each other.

The question was, would the Sakigake twosome accept such a convenient hypothesis? *No way,* Ushikawa concluded. Instead, they would jump at the conspiracy theory, for they loved anything that hinted of sinister plots. Before he handed over any raw information, he needed solid proof. Otherwise they would be misled and it might wind up hurting him.

As Ushikawa rode the train from Ichikawa to Tsudanuma, he pondered all this. Without realizing it, he must have been frowning, sighing, and glaring into space, because an elementary-school girl in the seat across from him was looking at him oddly. To cover his embarrassment, he relaxed his expression and rubbed his balding head. But this gesture only ended up making the little girl frightened, and just before Nishi-Funabashi Station, she leapt to her feet and rushed away.

He spoke with Toshie Ota in her classroom after school. She looked to be in her mid-fifties. Her appearance was the polar opposite of the refined vice principal back at the Ichikawa elementary school. Miss Ota was short and stocky and, from behind, had a weird sort of gait, like a crustacean. She wore tiny metal-framed glasses, but the space between her eyebrows was flat and broad and you could clearly see the downy hair growing there. She had on a wool suit of indeterminate age, though no doubt it was already out of fashion by the time it was manufactured, and it carried with it a faint odor of moth-balls. The suit was pink, but an odd sort of pink, like some other color had been accidentally mixed in. They had probably been aiming for a classy, subdued sort of hue, but because they didn't get it right, the pink of her suit sank deeply back into diffidence, concealment, and resignation. Thanks to this, the brand-new white blouse peeking out of the collar looked like some indiscreet person who had wandered into a wake. Her dry hair, with some white strands mixed in, was pinned back with a plastic clip, probably the nearest thing she had had on hand. Her limbs were on the beefy side, and she wore no rings on her stubby fingers. There were three thin wrinkles at her neckline, sharply etched, like notches on the road of life. Or maybe they were marks to commemorate when three wishes had come true – though Ushikawa had serious doubts that this had ever happened.

The woman had been Tengo Kawana's homeroom teacher from third grade until he graduated from elementary school. Teachers changed classes every two years, but in this case she had happened to be in charge of his class for all four. Aomame was in her class in only third and fourth grades.

"I remember Mr. Kawana very well," she said.

In contrast to her gentle-looking exterior, her voice was strikingly clear and youthful. It was the kind of voice that would pierce the farthest reaches of a noisy classroom. *Your profession really molds you,* Ushikawa thought, impressed, sure that she must be a most capable teacher.

"Mr. Kawana was an outstanding pupil in every area of school. I have taught countless students in a number of schools, for over twenty-five years, yet I have never run across a student as brilliant as he was. He outdid everyone in anything he tried. He was quite personable and had strong leadership qualities. I knew he could make it in any field he chose. In elementary school he particularly stood out in arithmetic and math, but I wasn't so surprised to hear that he has been a success in literature."

"I understand that his father was an NHK fee collector."

"Yes, that's right," the teacher said.

"Mr. Kawana told me that his father was quite strict," Ushikawa said. This was just a shot in the dark.

"Exactly so," she said, without hesitating. "His father did have a strict way about him. He was proud of his work – a wonderful thing – but this seemed to be a burden at times for Tengo."

Ushikawa had skillfully tied topics together and teased out the details from her. This was his forte – to let the other person do the talking, as much as possible. Tengo hated having to tag along with his father on his rounds on the weekend, she told him, and in fifth grade he ran away from home. "It was more like he was kicked out rather than ran away," she explained. So Tengo *had* been forced to go with his father to collect the fees, Ushikawa mused. And – just as he thought – this must have taken an emotional toll on the boy.

Miss Ota had taken the temporarily homeless Tengo into her home for the night. She prepared a bed for him, and made sure he ate breakfast the next morning. That evening she went to Tengo's house and convinced his father to take him back. From the way she talked about this event, you would have thought it was the highlight of her entire life. She told him too about how they happened to run into each other again at a concert when Tengo was in high school. Tengo had played the timpani, wonderfully, she added.

"It was Janáček's *Sinfonietta*. Not an easy piece, by any means. Tengo had first taken up the timpani only a few weeks before. But even with such little preparation he played his part beautifully. It was miraculous."

This lady has deep feelings for Tengo, Ushikawa thought admiringly. *Almost a kind of unconditional love. What would it feel like to be loved that deeply by someone else?*

"Do you remember Masami Aomame?" Ushikawa asked.

"I remember her very well," the teacher replied. But her voice wasn't as happy as when she had talked about Tengo. The tone of her voice had dropped two notches on the scale.

"Quite an unusual name, isn't it?" Ushikawa said.

"Yes, very unusual. But I don't remember her just because of her name."

A short silence followed.

"I heard her family were devout members of the Witnesses," Ushikawa said, sounding her out.

"Could you keep this between just the two of us?" the teacher asked.

"Of course. I won't repeat it to anyone."

The woman nodded. "There is a large branch office of the religion in Ichikawa, so I have had several children from the Witnesses in my class over the years. As a teacher this led to some delicate problems I had to address. But no one was as devout as Miss Aomame's parents."

"In other words, they were uncompromising."

As if recalling the time, the teacher bit her lip. "Exactly. When it came to their principles they were extremely firm, and I think they sought the same strict obedience from their children. This made Miss Aomame quite isolated in the class."

"So in a sense she was someone rather special."

"She was," the teacher admitted. "But you can't blame the child for this. Responsibility for it lies in the intolerance that can take over a person's mind."

The teacher explained more about Aomame. Generally the other children just ignored her. They tried to treat her as if she *wasn't there*. She was a foreign element, brandishing strange principles that bothered others. The class was all in agreement on this. Aomame reacted by keeping a low profile.

"I tried to do my best, but children's unity is stronger than you might think, and the way Miss Aomame reacted to this was to transform herself into something close to a ghost. Nowadays we would have referred her to counseling, but such a system wasn't in place back then. I was still young, and it took all I had to get everybody in the class on the same page. Though I'm sure that sounds like I'm trying to excuse myself."

Ushikawa could understand what she was getting at. Being an elementary school teacher was hard work. To a certain extent, you had to let the children figure out things on their own.

"There is always just a thin line separating deep faith from intolerance," Ushikawa said. "And it's very hard for people to do anything about it."

"Absolutely," the woman said. "But still, at a different level there should have been something I could do. I tried talking with Miss Aomame any number of times, but she would barely respond. She had a very strong will, and once she was set on something she wouldn't change her mind. She was quite bright, very quick-witted, with a strong desire to learn. But she tried hard to suppress any of that, to keep it from showing. Probably *not standing out* was her only way of protecting herself. I'm sure if she had been living in a normal environment she would have been an outstanding pupil. I feel really bad looking back on it now."

"Did you ever speak with her parents?"

The teacher nodded. "Many times. Her parents came to school to complain about religious persecution. When they did, I asked them to try to make more of an effort to help their daughter fit in to the class. I asked if they could bend their principles just a little. They refused point-blank. Their top priority was keeping true to the rules of their faith. To them the highest happiness lay in going to heaven, and life in this profane world was merely transient. But this was the logic of an adult worldview. Unfortunately, I could never get them to see how much pain it was causing their young daughter to be ignored in class, shunned by the other children – how this would lead to an emotional wound that might never heal."

Ushikawa told her how Aomame was a leading softball player on teams in college and in a company, and how she was working as a very capable fitness instructor in a high-class sports club. Or rather, *had been working* until recently, he should have said, but he didn't insist on making the distinction.

"I'm very glad to hear that," the woman said. She blushed slightly. "I'm so relieved to hear that she grew up all right, and is healthy and independent now."

"There was one thing, though, that I wasn't able to find out," Ushikawa said, a seemingly innocent smile rising to his lips. "Do you think it was possible that Tengo Kawana and Miss Aomame had a close personal relationship?"

The woman teacher linked her fingers together and thought about this. "That may have been possible. But I never saw it myself, or heard about it. I find it hard to picture any child in that class ever being really friendly with Miss Aomame. Perhaps Tengo did reach out to her. He was a very kind, responsible sort of boy. But even supposing it did happen, Miss Aomame wouldn't have opened up that easily. She was like an oyster stuck on a rock. It can't easily be pried open."

The teacher stopped for a moment, and then added, "It pains me to have to put it this way, but there was nothing I could do at the time. As I said before, I was inexperienced and not very effective."

"If Mr. Kawana and Miss Aomame did have a close relationship, that would have caused quite a sensation in class, and you would have heard of it. Am I right?"

The teacher nodded. "There was intolerance on both sides."

"It has been very helpful to be able to talk with you," Ushikawa said, thanking her.

"I hope what I've said about Miss Aomame won't become an obstacle in awarding the grant," the teacher said worriedly. "As the teacher in charge of the class I had ultimate responsibility for problems like that arising in the classroom. It wasn't the fault of either Tengo or Miss Aomame."

Ushikawa shook his head. "Please don't worry about that. I'm merely checking the background behind a work of fiction. Religious issues, as I'm sure you know, can be very complicated. Mr. Kawana is a major talent, and I know he will soon make a name for himself."

Hearing this, the teacher gave a satisfied smile. Something in her small eyes caught the sunlight and glistened, like a glacier on the faraway face of a mountain. She is remembering Tengo when he was a boy, Ushikawa surmised. It was twenty-some years ago, but for her it was like yesterday.

As he waited near the main gate of the school for the bus back to Tsudanuma Station, Ushikawa thought about his own teachers in elementary school. Did they still remember him? Even if they did, it wouldn't make their eyes sparkle with a friendly glimmer.

What he had verified was very close to his hypothesis. Tengo was the top student in his class, and he was popular. Aomame had no friends and was ignored by everyone. There was little possibility that the two of them would have gotten close. They were simply too unalike. Plus, when she was in fifth grade Aomame moved out of Ichikawa and went to another school. Any connection was severed then.

If he had to list one thing they had in common in elementary school, it would be this: they had both unwillingly had to obey their parents. Their parents' goals might have been different – proselytizing and fee collection – but both Tengo and Aomame were required to traipse all over town with their parents. In class they were in totally different positions, yet both of them must have been equally lonely, searching desperately for *something*. Something that would accept them unconditionally and hold them close. Ushikawa could imagine their feelings. In a sense, these were feelings that he shared.

Okay, Ushikawa said to himself. He was seated in an express train from Tsudanuma back to Tokyo, arms folded. *Okay, now what? I was able to find some connections between Tengo and Aomame. Very interesting connections. Unfortunately, however, this doesn't prove anything.*

There's a tall stone wall towering in front of me. It has three doors, and I have to choose one. Each door is labeled. One says Tengo, *one says* Aomame, *and the third says* the Dowager from Azabu. *Aomame vanished, as they say, like smoke. Without a trace. And the Azabu Willow House is locked up tight as a bank vault. Nothing I can do to get in. Which leaves only one door.*

It looks like I'll be sticking with Tengo for the time being, Ushikawa decided. *There's no other choice – a perfect example of the process of elimination. So perfect an example, it makes me want to print it up in a pamphlet and hand it out to people on the street. Hi, how are you? Check out the process of elimination.*

Tengo, always the nice young man. Mathematician and novelist. Judo champion and teacher's pet. Right now he's the only way to unravel this knotty tangle. The more I think about it, the less I seem to understand, like my brain is a tub of tofu past its expiration date.

So what about Tengo? Did he see the whole picture here? Probably not. As far as Ushikawa could make out, Tengo was doing things through trial and error, taking detours where he found the need. *He must be confused himself, trying out various hypotheses. Still, he was a born mathematician. A master at fitting together the pieces of a puzzle. And he probably has a lot more pieces of the puzzle than I do.*

For the time being I'll keep watch over Tengo Kawana. I'm sure he'll lead me somewhere – *if I get lucky, right to Aomame's hideout.* Ushikawa was a master at sticking to somebody, like a remora to a shark. Once he made up his mind to latch onto someone, there was no way they could shake free of him.

Once he had decided, Ushikawa closed his eyes and switched off his thinking process. *Time to get a little shut-eye,* he thought. It had been a rough day, given that he had had to visit two elementary schools out in crummy old Chiba Prefecture and listen to two female schoolteachers, a beautiful vice principal and a teacher who walked like a crab. After that you need to relax. Soon his huge misshapen head began to bob up and down in time to the movement of the train, like a life-sized sideshow doll that spat out unlucky fortunes.

The train was crowded, but no one dared sit down beside him.

CHAPTER 11

Aomame

A SERIOUS SHORTAGE OF BOTH LOGIC AND KINDNESS

On Tuesday morning Aomame wrote a memo to Tamaru explaining how the man calling himself an NHK fee collector had come again – how he had banged on the door and yelled, insulting Aomame (or a person named Takai who lived there), berating her. The whole thing was too much, too bizarre. She needed to remain vigilant.

Aomame placed the memo in an envelope, sealed it, and put it on the kitchen table. She wrote the initial *T* on the envelope. The men who delivered supplies would make sure it got to Tamaru.

Just before one p.m. she went into her bedroom, locked the door, lay down in bed, and continued where she had left off with Proust. At one o'clock on the dot the doorbell rang once. After a pause the door was unlocked and the supply team came inside. As always, they briskly resupplied the fridge, got the garbage together, and checked the supplies on the shelves. In fifteen minutes they had finished their appointed tasks, left the apartment, shut the door, and locked it from the outside. Then the doorbell rang once again as a signal – the same procedure as usual.

Just to be on the safe side, Aomame waited until the clock

showed 1:30 before she came out of her bedroom and went to the kitchen. The memo to Tamaru was gone, replaced by a paper bag on the table with the name of a pharmacy printed on it. There was also a thick book Tamaru had gotten for her, *The Women's Anatomical Encyclopedia.* Inside the paper bag there were three different home pregnancy tests. She opened the boxes one by one and read over the instructions, comparing them. They were all the same. You could use the tests if your period was a week or more late. The tests were 95 percent accurate, but if they were positive, the instructions said – in other words, if they did show you were pregnant – then you should be examined by a medical specialist as soon as possible. You should not jump to conclusions. The tests indicated merely the *possibility* that one was pregnant.

The test itself was simple. Just urinate into a clean container and then dip the indicator stick into it. Or, alternately, urinate directly onto the stick. Then wait a few minutes. If the color changes to blue you're pregnant, if it doesn't change color, you're not. In one version, if two vertical lines appear in the little window, you're pregnant. One line, and you're not. The details might vary but the principle was the same. The presence or absence of human chorionic gonadotropin in urine indicated whether or not you were pregnant.

Human chorionic gonadotropin? Aomame frowned. She had been a female for thirty years and had never once heard that term. *All this time, some crazy substance was stimulating her sex glands?*

Aomame opened up *The Women's Anatomical Encyclopedia. Human chorionic gonadotropin is secreted during the early stages of pregnancy,* the book said, *and helps maintain the corpus luteum. The corpus luteum secretes progestogens and estrogen to preserve the inner lining of the womb and prevent menstruation. In this way the placenta gradually takes form. In seven to nine weeks, once the placenta is complete, there is no more need for the corpus luteum and the role of the human chorionic gonado-tropin is over.*

In other words, this hormone was secreted from the time of implantation for seven to nine weeks. The timing was a little tricky in her case. One thing she could say was that if the test came back positive, she was without a doubt pregnant. If it was negative, then the conclusion wouldn't be so clear-cut. It was possible that she had passed the time when she was secreting the hormone.

She didn't feel the need to urinate. She went to the fridge, took out a bottle of mineral water, and had two glasses. But she still didn't feel the need to go. *Well, no need to rush it,* she thought. She forgot about the pregnancy kits for a while and sat down on the sofa and concentrated on Proust.

It was after three when she felt the need to urinate. She peed into a container she found and stuck the test strip in it. As she watched, the strip changed color, until it was a vivid blue. A lovely shade of blue that would work well as the color of a car. A small blue convertible with a tan top. How great it would feel to drive along the coast in a car like that, racing through the summer breeze. But in the bathroom of an apartment in the middle of the city, in the deepening autumn, what this blue told her was the fact that she was pregnant – or, at least, that there was a 95 percent chance of it. Aomame stood in front of the mirror and gazed at the thin strip of paper, now blue. No matter how long she stared, the color wasn't about to change.

Just to be sure, she tried another test. This one instructed you to "urinate directly onto the tip of the stick." But since she wouldn't feel the need to pee for a while she dipped the stick into the container of urine. Freshly collected urine. Pee directly on it or dip it in pee – what is the difference? You would get the same result. Two vertical lines clearly appeared in the little plastic window. This, too, told Aomame she *might be pregnant.*

Aomame poured the urine into the toilet and flushed it down. She wrapped the test strip in a wad of tissue and threw it in the trash, and rinsed the container in the bath. She went to the kitchen and drank two more glasses of water. *Tomorrow I will try again and do the third test,* she thought. *Three is a good number to stop at. Strike one, strike two.* Waiting, with bated breath, for the final pitch.

Aomame boiled some water and made hot tea, sat down on the sofa, and continued reading Proust. She laid out some cheese biscuits on one of a set of matching plates and munched on them as she sipped her tea. A quiet afternoon, perfect for reading. Her eyes followed the printed words, but nothing stayed with her. She had to reread the same spot several times. She gave up, shut her eyes, and she was driving a blue convertible, the top down, speeding along the shore. The light breeze, fragrant with the smell of the sea, rustled her hair. A sign along the road had two vertical lines. These meant *Warning: You May Be Pregnant.*

Aomame sighed and tossed her book aside.

She knew very well there was no need to try the third test. She could do it a hundred times and the result would be the same. It would be a waste of time. *My human chorionic gonadotropin would still maintain the same attitude toward my womb – keeping the corpus luteum intact, obstructing my period from coming, helping form the placenta. Face it: I'm pregnant. The human chorionic gonadotropin knows that. And so do I. I can feel it as a pinpoint in my lower abdomen. It's still tiny – nothing more than* a hint of something. *But eventually it will have a placenta, and grow bigger. It will take nutrition from me and, in the dark, heavy liquid, grow – steadily, unceasingly.*

This was the first time she had been pregnant. She was always a very careful person, and only trusted what she could see with her own eyes. When she had sex she made absolutely sure her partner used a condom. Even when she was drunk, she never failed to check. As she had told the dowager, ever since her first menstruation at age ten, she had never missed a period. Her periods were regular, never more than a day late. Her cramps were light. She merely bled for a few days, that was all. It never got in the way of her exercising or playing sports.

She got her first period a few months after holding Tengo's hand in the elementary school classroom. Somehow, she felt that the two events were connected. The feel of Tengo's hand may have stirred something inside her. When she told her mother she got her period, her mother made a face, like it was one more burden to add to all the others she carried. It's a little early, her mother commented. But that didn't bother Aomame. It was her problem, not her mother's or anybody else's. She had stepped into a brand-new world.

And now she was pregnant.

She thought about her eggs. *Of my allotted four hundred or so, one of them (near the middle of the bunch, she imagined) went and got herself fertilized. Most likely on that September night, during the terrible storm. In a dark room when I murdered a man. When I stuck a sharp needle from the base of his neck into the lower part of his brain. But that man was completely different from the men I had killed before. He knew he was about to be murdered, and he wanted it to happen. I actually gave him what he* wanted. *Not as punishment, but more as an act of mercy. In exchange for which, he gave me what I was seeking. An act of negotiation carried out in a deep, dark place. Very quietly, fertilization took place that night. I know it,* she thought.

With these hands I took a man's life, and almost simultaneously, a new life began inside me. Was this part of the transaction?

Aomame shut her eyes and stopped thinking. Her head empty, something silently flowed inside. And before she knew it, she was praying.

O Lord in Heaven, may Thy name be praised in utmost purity for ever and ever, and may Thy kingdom come to us. Please forgive our many sins, and bestow Thy blessings upon our humble pathways. Amen.

Why would a prayer come to my lips at a time like this? I don't believe in things like heaven or paradise or the Lord, yet the words are chiseled into my brain. Ever since I was three or four and didn't even know what they meant, I could recite this prayer from memory. If I made the slightest mistake, I got the back of my hands smacked with a ruler. Though you couldn't normally see it, when something happened it would rise to the surface, like a secret tattoo.

What would my mother say if I told her I got pregnant without having had sex? She might see it as a terrible sacrilege against her faith. In any case, it was a kind of immaculate conception – though Aomame was certainly not a virgin. But still. Or maybe her mother wouldn't be bothered to even deal with it, not even listen to her. *Because she sees me as a failure, someone who long ago had fallen from her world.*

Let me think about it in a different way, Aomame thought. *I won't try to force an explanation on the inexplicable, but instead I'll examine the phenomenon from a different angle, as the riddle that it is.*

Am I seeing this pregnancy as something good, something to be welcomed? Or as something unwelcome, something inappropriate?

I can't reach a conclusion no matter how hard I think about it. I'm still in a state of shock. I'm mixed up, confused. In certain ways I feel split in two. And understandably I'm having trouble swallowing this new reality.

Yet Aomame also had to recognize that she was watching this little heat source with a positive sense of anticipation. She simply had to see what happened to this thing growing inside her. Obviously she was anxious and scared. *It* might be more than she could imagine. It might be a hostile foreign entity that greedily devoured her from the inside. She could imagine all sorts of negative possibilities. But she was in thrall to a healthy curiosity. Like a sudden flash of light in the dark, a thought abruptly sprang to her mind.

Maybe this is Tengo's child inside my womb.

Aomame frowned a bit and considered this. *Why do I have to be pregnant with Tengo's child?*

How about looking at it like this? she thought. *On that chaotic night, when so much took place, some process was at work in this world and Tengo sent his semen into my womb. Somehow, through a gap in the thunder and rain, the darkness and the murder, a special kind of passageway opened, through some logic I can't understand. Just for an instant. And in that instant we took advantage of the passageway. I took that opportunity to greedily accept Tengo into me. I became pregnant. Egg 201 – or was it 202? – grabbed onto one of his millions of spermatozoa, a single sperm cell that was as healthy and clever and straightforward as the one who produced it.*

That's a pretty wild idea. It doesn't make any sense. I could try to explain it until I went hoarse and nobody would ever believe me. But the whole notion of me being pregnant itself doesn't make any sense. But remember – this is the year 1Q84. A strange world where anything can happen.

What if this really is Tengo's child? she wondered.

That morning at the turnout on Metropolitan Expressway No. 3 through Tokyo, I didn't pull the trigger. I really went there, and stuck the muzzle in my mouth, planning to die. I wasn't afraid of death, because I was dying to save Tengo. But some higher power acted on me and snatched me away from death. From far away I heard a voice calling my name. Maybe it called me because I was pregnant? Was something trying to tell me of this new life inside me?

Aomame recalled the dream, and the refined older woman

who put her coat on her to cover her nakedness. *She got out of her silver Mercedes and gave me her light, soft eggshell-colored coat. She knew then that I was pregnant, and she gently protected me from people's stares, the cold wind, and other vicious things.*

This was a good sign.

Aomame's tight face relaxed, her expression returned to normal. *Someone is watching over me, protecting me,* she believed. *Even in this 1Q84 world, I'm not alone. Probably.*

Aomame took her now cold tea over to the window. She went out to the balcony and sank into the garden chair so no one could spot her, and gazed out through the gaps in the screen at the playground. She tried to think of Tengo. For some reason, though, today her thoughts just wouldn't go to him. What she saw instead was the face of Ayumi Nakano. Ayumi was smiling cheerfully, a totally natural, unreserved smile. The two of them were at a restaurant seated across from each other, drinking wine. They were both pretty drunk. The excellent Burgundy in their blood gently coursed through their bodies, giving the world around them a faint purplish tinge.

"But still," Ayumi said, "it seems to me that this world has a serious shortage of both logic and kindness."

"Oh well, no problem," Aomame said. "The world's going to end before we know it."

"Sounds like fun."

"And the kingdom is going to come."

"I can hardly wait," Ayumi said.

Why did I talk about the kingdom then, I wonder? Aomame found it odd. *Why would I suddenly bring up a kingdom that I don't even believe in? And not long after that Ayumi died.*

I think when I mentioned the kingdom, the mental image I had was different from the kingdom the Witnesses believe in. Probably it was a more personal kind of kingdom, which is why the term could slip out so naturally. But what sort of kingdom do I believe in? What sort of kingdom do I think will appear after the world has been destroyed?

She gently laid her hands on her stomach and listened carefully. No matter how hard she listened, she didn't hear a thing.

Ayumi Nakano was cast off by this world. Her hands were tightly bound with cold handcuffs, and she was choked to death with a rope (and, as far as Aomame knew, the murderer had yet to be caught). An official autopsy was conducted, then she was sewn back up, taken to a crematorium, and burned. The person known as Ayumi Nakano no longer existed in this world. Her flesh and her blood were lost forever. She only remained in the realm of documents and memory.

No, maybe that's not entirely true. Maybe she was still alive and well in 1984. Still grumbling that she wasn't allowed to carry a pistol, still sticking parking tickets under the wipers of illegally parked cars. Still going around to high schools to teach girls about contraception. "If he doesn't have on a condom, girls, then there shouldn't be any penetration."

Aomame desperately wanted to see Ayumi. If she could climb back up that emergency stairway on the Metropolitan Expressway No. 3 and return to the world of 1984, then maybe she would see her again. *Maybe there Ayumi is still alive, and I'm not being chased by these Sakigake freaks. Maybe we could stop by that restaurant on Nogizaka again and enjoy another glass of Burgundy. Or perhaps –*

Climb back up that emergency stairway?

Like rewinding a cassette tape, Aomame retraced her thoughts. *Why haven't I thought of that before? I tried to go down that emergency stairway again but couldn't find the entrance. The stairway, which should have been across from the Esso billboard, had vanished. But maybe if I took it from the opposite direction it would work out – not climb* down *the stairway but go* up. *Slip into that storage area under the expressway and go*

*the opposite direction, back up to the Metropolitan Expressway
No. 3. Go back up the passage. Maybe that's the answer.*

Aomame wanted to race out that very minute to Sangenjaya and see if it was possible. *It might actually work out. Or
maybe it wouldn't. But it was worth trying. Wear the same suit,
the same high heels, and climb back up that spiderweb-infested
stairway.*

But she suppressed the impulse.

*No, it won't work. I can't do that. It was because I came to the
1Q84 world that I was able to see Tengo again, and to be pregnant with what is most likely his child. I have to see him one more
time in this new world. I have to meet him again. Face-to-face. I
can't leave this world until that happens.*

Tamaru called her the following afternoon.

"First, about the NHK fee collector," Tamaru began. "I called
the NHK business office and checked into it. The fee collector who covers the Koenji District said he had no memory of
knocking on the door of apartment 303. He said he checked
beforehand that there was a sticker on the door indicating that
the fee was paid automatically from the account. Plus he said
there was a doorbell, so he wouldn't have knocked. He said
that would only make his hand hurt. And on the day the fee
collector was at your place, this man was making the rounds
in another district. I don't think he's lying. He's a fifteen-year
veteran, and he has a reputation as a very patient, courteous
person."

"Which means – " Aomame said.

"Which means that there's a strong possibility that the
fee collector who came to your place was a fake – someone
pretending to be from NHK. The person I talked to on the
phone was concerned about this too. The last thing they want
are phony NHK collectors popping up. The person in charge
asked to see me and get more details. As you can imagine, I

turned him down. There was no actual harm done, and I don't want it to get all blown out of proportion."

"Maybe he was a mental patient? Or someone who's after me?"

"I don't think anyone pursuing you would act like that. It wouldn't do any good, and would actually put you on your guard."

"If the man was crazy, I wonder why he would choose this particular door. There are lots of other doors around. I'm always careful to make sure no light leaks out, and I'm very quiet. I always keep the curtains closed and never hang laundry outside to dry. But still that guy picked this door to bang on. He knows I'm hiding inside here – or at least he insists he knows that – and he tries whatever he can to get me to open up."

"Do you think he's going to come back?"

"I don't know. But if he's really serious about getting me to open up, I'm betting he'll keep coming back until I do."

"And that unsettles you."

"I wouldn't say it unsettles me, exactly," Aomame replied. "I just don't like it."

"I don't like it either, not one little bit. But even if that phony collector comes back again, we can't call NHK or the police. And if you call me and I race over, he will probably have vanished by the time I get there."

"I think I can handle it myself," Aomame said. "He can be as intimidating as he wants, but all I have to do is keep the door shut."

"I'm sure he will use whatever means he can to intimidate you."

"No doubt," Aomame said.

Tamaru cleared his throat for a moment and changed the subject.

"Did you get the test kits all right?"

"It was positive," Aomame said straight out.

"A hit, in other words."

"Exactly. I tried two tests and the results were identical."

There was silence. Like a lithograph with no words carved on it yet.

"No room for doubt?" Tamaru asked.

"I knew it from the start. The tests merely confirmed it."

Tamaru silently rubbed the lithograph for a time with the pads of his fingers.

"I have to ask a pretty forward question," he said. "Do you plan to have the baby? Or are you going to deal with it?"

"I'm not going to *deal with* it."

"Which means you will give birth."

"If things go smoothly, the due date will be between June and July of next year."

Tamaru did the math in his head. "Which means we will have to make some changes in our plans."

"I'm sorry about that."

"No need to apologize," Tamaru said. "All women have the right to give birth. We have to protect that right as much as we can."

"Sounds like a Declaration of Human Rights," Aomame said.

"I'm asking this again just to make sure, but you have no idea who the father is?"

"Since June I haven't had a sexual relationship with anyone."

"So this is a kind of immaculate conception?"

"I imagine religious people would get upset if you put it that way."

"If you do anything out of the ordinary, you can be sure someone, somewhere, will get upset," Tamaru said. "But when you're dealing with a pregnancy, it's important to get a specialist to check you over. You can't just stay shut up in that room waiting it out."

Aomame sighed. "Let me stay here until the end of the year. I promise I won't be any trouble."

Tamaru was silent for a while. Then he spoke. "You can stay there until the end of the year, like we promised. But once the new year comes, we have to move you to a less dangerous place, where you can easily get medical attention. You understand this, right?"

"I do," Aomame said. She wasn't fully convinced, though. *If I don't see Tengo,* she thought, *will I really be able to leave here?*

"I got a woman pregnant once," Tamaru said.

Aomame didn't say anything for a time. "You? But I thought you were – "

"Gay? I am. A card-carrying homosexual. I have always been that way, and I imagine I always will be."

"But still you got a woman pregnant."

"Everybody makes mistakes," Tamaru said, with no hint of humor. "I don't want to go into the details, but it was when I was young. I did it once, but *bang*! A bull's-eye."

"What happened to the woman?"

"I don't know," Tamaru said.

"You don't know?"

"I know how she was up to her sixth month. But after that I have no idea."

"If you get to the sixth month, abortion is not an option."

"That's my understanding."

"So there's a high possibility she had the baby," Aomame said.

"Most likely."

"If she really did have the baby, don't you want to see it?"

"I'm not that interested," Tamaru said without missing a beat. "That's not the kind of life I lead. What about you? Would you want to see your child?"

Aomame gave it some thought. "I am someone whose parents threw her away when she was small, so it's hard for me to imagine what it would be like to have my own child. I have no good model to follow."

"Still, you're going to be bringing that child into the world – into this violent, mixed-up world."

"It's because I'm looking for love," Aomame said. "Not love between me and the child, though. I haven't reached that stage yet."

"But the child is part of that love."

"I think so, in one way or another."

"But if things don't turn out like you expect, and that child isn't part of the love you're looking for, then he'll end up hurt. Just like the two of us."

"It's possible. But I don't sense that will happen. Call it intuition."

"I respect intuition," Tamaru said. "But once the ego is born into this world, it has to shoulder morality. You would do well to remember that."

"Who said that?"

"Wittgenstein."

"I'll keep it in mind," Aomame said. "If your child was born, how old would it be?"

Tamaru did the math in his head. "Seventeen."

"Seventeen." Aomame imagined a seventeen-year-old boy, or girl, shouldering morality.

"I'll let Madame know about this," Tamaru said. "She has been wanting to talk with you directly. As I have said a number of times, however, from a security standpoint I am none too happy about the idea. On a technical level I'm taking all necessary precautions, but the telephone is still a risky means of communication."

"Understood."

"But she is very concerned about what has happened, and is worried about you."

"I understand that, too. And I'm grateful for her concern."

"It would be the smart thing to trust her, and follow her advice. She is a very wise person."

"Of course," Aomame said.

But apart from that, Aomame told herself, *I need to hone my own mind and protect myself. The dowager is certainly a very wise person. And she wields a considerable amount of power. But there are some things she has no way of knowing. I doubt she knows what principles the year 1Q84 is operating on. I mean – has she even noticed that there are two moons in the sky?*

After she hung up, Aomame lay on the sofa and dozed for a half hour. It was a short, deep sleep. She dreamed, but her dream was like a big, blank space. Inside that space she was thinking about things. And she was writing, with invisible ink, in that pure white notebook. When she woke up, she had an indistinct yet strangely clear image in her mind. *I will give birth to this child. This little life will be safely born into the world.* Like Tamaru had put it, as an unavoidable bearer of morality.

She laid her palm on her abdomen and listened. She couldn't hear a thing. For now.

CHAPTER 12

Tengo

THE RULES OF THE WORLD
ARE LOOSENING UP

After he finished breakfast, Tengo took a shower. He washed his hair and shaved at the sink, then changed into the clothes he had washed and dried. He left the inn, bought the morning edition of the paper at a kiosk at the station, and went to a coffee shop nearby and had a cup of hot black coffee.

There wasn't much of interest in the newspaper. At least as far as this particular morning's paper was concerned, the world was a dull, boring place. It felt like he was rereading a paper from a week ago, not today. Tengo folded up the paper and glanced at his watch. It was nine thirty. Visiting hours at the sanatorium began at ten.

It didn't take long to pack for the trip back home. He didn't have much luggage, just a few changes of clothes, toiletries, a few books, and a sheaf of manuscript paper. He stuffed it all inside his canvas shoulder bag. He slung the bag over his shoulder, paid his bill for the inn, and took a bus from the station to the sanatorium. It was the beginning of winter, and there were few people this morning heading to the beach. Tengo was the only one getting out at the stop in front of the sanatorium.

At the reception desk he wrote his name and the time in

the visitors' log. A young nurse he had never seen before was stationed at the reception desk. Her arms and legs were terribly long and thin, and a smile played around the corners of her lips. She made him think of a kindly spider guiding people along the path through a forest. Usually it was Nurse Tamura, the middle-aged woman with glasses, who sat at the reception desk, but today she wasn't there. Tengo felt a bit relieved. He had been dreading any suggestive comments she might make because he had accompanied Kumi Adachi back to her apartment the night before. Nurse Omura, too, was nowhere to be seen. They might have been sucked into the earth without a trace. Like the three witches in *Macbeth*.

But that was impossible. Kumi Adachi was off duty today, but the other two nurses said they were working as usual. They must just be working somewhere else in the facility right now.

Tengo went upstairs to his father's room, knocked lightly, twice, and opened the door. His father was lying on the bed, sleeping as always. An IV tube came out of his arm, a catheter snaked out of his groin. There was no change from the day before. The window was closed, as were the curtains. The air in the room was heavy and stagnant. All sorts of smells were mixed together – a medicinal smell, the smell of the flowers in the vase, the breath of a sick person, the smell of excreta – all the smells that life brings with it. Even if the life force here was weak, and his father was unconscious, metabolism went on unchanged. His father was still on this side of the great divide. Being alive, if you had to define it, meant emitting a variety of smells.

The first thing Tengo did when he entered the sickroom was go straight to the far wall, where he drew the curtains and flung open the window. It was a refreshing morning, and the room was in desperate need of fresh air. It was chilly outside, but not what you would call cold. Sunlight streamed in and the curtain rustled in the sea breeze. A single seagull, legs tucked neatly underneath, caught a draft of wind and glided over the pine trees. A ragged line of sparrows sat on an electrical line, constantly switching positions like musical notes being rewritten. A crow with a large beak came to rest on top of a mercury-vapor lamp, cautiously surveying his surroundings as he mulled over his next move. A few streaks of clouds floated off high in the sky, so high and far away that they were like abstract concepts unrelated to the affairs of man.

With his back to the patient, Tengo gazed for a while at this scene outside. Things that are living and things that are not. Things that move and things that don't. What he saw out the window was the usual scenery. There was nothing new about it. The world has to move forward. Like a cheap alarm clock, it does a halfway decent job of fulfilling its assigned role. Tengo gazed blankly at the scenery, trying to postpone facing his father even by a moment, but he couldn't keep delaying forever.

Finally Tengo made up his mind, turned, and sat down on the stool next to the bed. His father was lying on his back, facing the ceiling, his eyes shut. The quilt that was tucked up to his neck was neat and undisturbed. His eyes were deeply sunken. It was like some piece was missing, and his eye sockets couldn't support his eyeballs, which had quietly caved in. Even if he were to open his eyes, what he would see would be like the world viewed from the bottom of a hole.

"Father," Tengo began.

His father didn't answer. The breeze blowing in the room suddenly stopped and the curtains hung limply, like a worker in the midst of a task suddenly remembering something else he had to do. And then, after a while, as if gathering itself together, the wind began to blow again.

"I'm going back to Tokyo today," Tengo said. "I can't stay here forever. I can't take any more time off from work. It's not much of a life, but I do have a life to get back to."

There was a two- to three-day growth of whiskers on his

father's cheeks. A nurse shaved him with an electric razor, but not every day. His whiskers were salt-and-pepper. He was only sixty-four, but he looked much older, like someone had mistakenly fast-forwarded the film of his life.

"You didn't wake up the whole time I was here. The doctor says your physical condition is still not so bad. The strange thing is, you're almost as healthy as you used to be."

Tengo paused, letting the words sink in.

"I don't know if you can hear what I'm saying or not. Even if the words are vibrating your eardrums, the circuit beyond that might be shot. Or maybe the words I speak are actually reaching you but you're unable to respond. I don't really know. But I have been talking to you, and reading to you, on the assumption that you can hear me. Unless I assume that, there's no point in me speaking to you, and if I can't speak to you, then there's no point in me being here. I can't explain it well, but I'm sensing something tangible, as if the main points of what I'm saying are, at least, getting across."

No response.

"What I'm about to say may sound pretty stupid. But I'm going back to Tokyo today and I don't know when I might be back here. So I'm just going to say what's in my mind. If you find it dumb, then just go ahead and laugh. If you *can* laugh, I mean."

Tengo paused and observed his father's face. Again, there was no response.

"Your body is in a coma. You have lost consciousness and feeling, and you are being kept alive by life-support machines. The doctor said you're like a living corpse – though he put it a bit more euphemistically. Medically speaking, that's what it probably is. But isn't that just a sham? I have the feeling your consciousness isn't lost at all. You have put your body in a coma, but your consciousness is off somewhere else, alive. I've felt that for a long time. It's just a feeling, though."

Silence.

"I can understand if you think this is a crazy idea. If I told anybody else, they would say I was hallucinating. But I have to believe it's true. I think you lost all interest in this world. You were disappointed and discouraged, and lost interest in everything. So you abandoned your physical body. You went to a world apart and you're living a different kind of life there. In a world that's inside you."

Again more silence.

"I took time off from my job, came to this town, rented a room at an inn, and have been coming here every day and talking to you – for almost two weeks now. But I wasn't just doing it to see how you were doing or to take care of you. I wanted to see where I came from, what sort of bloodline I have. None of that matters anymore. I am who I am, no matter who or what I'm connected with – or not connected with. Though I do know that you are the one who is my father. And that's fine. Is this what you call a reconciliation? I don't know. Maybe I just reconciled with myself."

Tengo took a deep breath. He spoke in a softer tone.

"During the summer, you were still conscious. Your mind was muddled, but your consciousness was still functioning. At that time I met a girl here, in this room, again. After they took you to the examination room she *appeared*. I think it must have been something like her alter ego. I came to this town again and have stayed here this long because I have been hoping I could see her one more time. Honestly, that's why I came."

Tengo sighed and brought his hands together on his lap.

"But she didn't come. What brought her here last time was a thing called an air chrysalis, a capsule she was encased in. It would take too long to explain the whole thing, but an air chrysalis is a product of the imagination, a fictitious object. But it's not fictitious anymore. The boundary between the real world and the imaginary one has grown obscure. There are two moons in the sky now. These, too, were brought over from the world of fiction."

Tengo looked at his father's face. Could he follow what Tengo was saying?

"In that context, saying your consciousness has broken away from your body and is freely moving about some other world doesn't sound so farfetched. It's like the rules that govern the world have begun to loosen up around us. As I said before, I have this strange sense that you are *actually doing that*. Like you have gone to my apartment in Koenji and are knocking on the door. You know what I mean? You announce you're an NHK fee collector, bang hard on the door, and yell out a threat in a loud voice. Just like you used to do all the time when we made the rounds in Ichikawa."

He felt a change in the air pressure in the room. The window was open, but there was barely any sound coming in. There was just the occasional burst of chirping sparrows.

"There is a girl staying in my apartment in Tokyo. Not a girlfriend or anything – something happened and she's taking shelter there temporarily. A few days ago she told me on the phone about an NHK collector who came by, how he knocked on the door, and what he did and said out in the corridor. It was strange how closely it resembled the methods you used to use. The words she heard were exactly the same lines I remember, the expressions I was hoping I could totally erase from my memory. And I'm thinking now that that fee collector might actually have been you. Am I wrong?"

Tengo waited thirty seconds. His father didn't twitch a single eyelash.

"There's just one thing I want: for you to never knock on my door again. I don't have a TV. And those days when we went around together collecting fees are long gone. I think we already agreed on that, that time in front of my teacher – I don't remember her name, the one who was in charge of my class. A short lady, with glasses. You remember that, right? So don't knock on my door ever again, okay? And not just my place. Don't knock on any more doors anywhere. You're not an NHK fee collector anymore, and you don't have the right to scare people like that."

Tengo stood up, went to the window, and looked outside. An old man in a bulky sweater, clutching a cane, was walking in front of the woods. He was probably just taking a stroll. He was tall, with white hair, and excellent posture. But his steps were awkward, as if he had forgotten how to walk, as if with each step forward he was remembering how to do it. Tengo watched him for a while. The old man slowly made his way across the garden, then turned the corner of the building and disappeared. It didn't look like he had recalled the art of walking. Tengo turned to face his father.

"I'm not blaming you. You have the right to send your consciousness wherever you want. It's your life, and your consciousness. You have your own idea of what is right, and you're putting it into practice. Maybe I don't have the right to say these things. But you need to understand: *you are not an NHK fee collector anymore.* So you shouldn't pretend to be one. It's pointless."

Tengo sat down on the windowsill and searched for his next words in the air of the cramped hospital room.

"I don't know what kind of life you had, what sorts of joys and sorrows you experienced. But even if there was something that left you unfulfilled, you can't go around seeking it at other people's doors. Even if it is at the place you're most familiar with, and the sort of act that is your forte."

Tengo gazed silently at his father's face.

"I don't want you to knock on anybody's door anymore. That's all I ask of you, Father. I have to be going. I came here every day talking to you in your coma, reading to you. And I think at least a part of us has reconciled, and I think that reconciliation has actually taken place in the real world. Maybe you won't like it, but you need to come back here again, to *this* side. This is where you belong."

Tengo lifted his shoulder bag and slung it across his shoulder. "Well, I'll be off, then."

His father said nothing. He didn't stir and his eyes remained shut – the same as always. But somehow it seemed like he was thinking about something. Tengo was quiet and paid careful attention. It felt to him like his father might pop open his eyes at any moment and abruptly sit up in bed. But none of that happened.

The nurse with the spidery limbs was still at the reception desk as he left. A plastic name tag on her chest said *Tamaki*.

"I'm going back to Tokyo now," Tengo told her.

"It's too bad your father didn't regain consciousness while you were here," she said, consolingly. "But I'm sure he was happy you could stay so long."

Tengo couldn't think of a decent response. "Please tell the other nurses good-bye for me. You have all been so helpful."

He never did see bespectacled Nurse Tamura or busty Nurse Omura and her ever-present ballpoint pen. It made him a little sad. They were outstanding nurses, and had always been kind to him. But perhaps it was for the best that he didn't see them. After all, he was slipping out of the cat town alone.

As the train pulled out of Chikura Station, he recalled spending the night at Kumi Adachi's apartment. It had only just happened yesterday. The gaudy Tiffany lamp, the uncomfortable love seat, the TV comedy show he could hear from next door. The hooting of the owl in the woods. The hashish smoke, the smiley-face shirt, the thick pubic hair pressed against his leg. It had been less than a day, but it felt like long ago. His mind felt unstable. Like an unbalanced set of scales, the core of his memories wouldn't settle down in one spot.

Suddenly anxious, Tengo looked around him. Was this reality

actually real? Or had he once again boarded the wrong reality? He asked a passenger nearby and made sure this train was indeed headed to Tateyama. *It's okay, don't worry,* he told himself. *At Tateyama I can change to the express train to Tokyo.* He was drawing farther and farther away from the cat town by the sea.

As soon as he changed trains and took his seat, as if it could barely wait, sleep claimed him. A deep sleep, like he had lost his footing and fallen into a bottomless hole. His eyelids closed, and in the next instant his consciousness had vanished. When he opened his eyes again, the train had passed Makuhari. The train wasn't particularly hot inside, yet he was sweating under his arms and down his back. His mouth had an awful smell, like the stagnant air he had breathed in his father's sick room. He took a stick of gum out of his pocket and popped it in his mouth.

Tengo was sure he would never visit that town again – at least not while his father was alive. While there was nothing in this world that he could state with one hundred percent certainty, he knew there was probably nothing more he could do in that seaside town.

When he got back to the apartment, Fuka-Eri wasn't there. He knocked on the door three times, paused, then knocked two more times. Then he unlocked the door. Inside, the apartment was dead silent. He was immediately struck by how neat and clean everything was. The dishes were neatly stacked away in the cupboard, everything on the table and desk was neatly arranged, and the trash can had been emptied. There were signs that the place had been vacuumed as well. The bed was made, and no books or records lay scattered about. Dried laundry lay neatly folded on top of the bed.

The oversized shoulder bag that Fuka-Eri used was also gone. It didn't appear, however, that she had remembered something she had to do or that something had suddenly come up and she had hurriedly left. Nor did it look like she had just gone out for a short time. Instead, all indications were that she had decided to leave for good, that she had taken her time cleaning the apartment and then left. Tengo tried picturing her pushing around the vacuum cleaner and wiping here and there with a wet cloth. It just didn't fit her image at all.

He opened the mail slot inside the front door and found the spare key. From the amount of mail, she must have left yesterday or the day before. The last time he had called her had been in the morning two days earlier, and she had still been in the apartment. Last night he had had dinner with the three nurses and had gone back to Kumi's place. What with one thing and another, he had forgotten to call her.

Normally she would have left a note behind in her unique cuneiform-like script, but there was no sign of one. She had left without a word. Tengo wasn't particularly surprised or disappointed. No one could predict what the girl was thinking or what she would do. She just showed up when she wanted to, and left when she felt like it – like a capricious, independent-minded cat. In fact, it was unusual for her to have stayed put this long in one place.

The refrigerator was more full of food than he had expected. He guessed that a few days earlier, Fuka-Eri must have gone out and done some shopping on her own. There was a pile of steamed cauliflower as well, which seemed to have been cooked recently. Had she known that Tengo would be back in Tokyo in a day or two? Tengo was hungry, so he fried some eggs and ate them with the cauliflower. He made some toast and drank two mugs of coffee.

Next he phoned his friend who had covered for him at school and told him he expected to be back at work at the beginning of the week. His friend updated him on how much they had covered in the textbook.

"You really helped me out. I owe you one."

"I don't mind teaching," the friend said. "I even enjoy it at times. But I found that the longer you teach, the more you feel like a total stranger to yourself."

Tengo had often had an inkling of the same thing.

"Anything out of the ordinary happen while I was gone?"

"Not really. Oh, you did get a letter. I put it in a drawer in your desk."

"A letter?" Tengo asked. "From whom?"

"A thin young girl brought it by. She had straight hair down to her shoulders. She came up to me and said she had a letter to give to you. She spoke sort of strangely. I think she might be a foreigner."

"Did she have a large shoulder bag?"

"She did. A green shoulder bag. Stuffed full of things."

Fuka-Eri may have been afraid to leave the letter behind in his apartment, scared that someone else might read it, or take it away. So she went directly to the cram school and gave it to his friend.

Tengo thanked his friend again and hung up. It was already evening, and he didn't feel like taking the train all the way to Yoyogi to pick up the letter. He would leave it for tomorrow.

Right afterward he realized he had forgotten to ask his friend about the moon. He started to dial again but decided against it. Most likely his friend had forgotten all about it. This was something he would have to resolve on his own.

Tengo went out and aimlessly sauntered down the twilight streets. With Fuka-Eri gone, his apartment was too quiet and he couldn't settle down. When they had been living together he didn't really sense her presence all that much. He followed his daily routine, and she followed hers. But without her there, Tengo noticed a human-shaped void she had left behind.

It wasn't because he was attracted to her. She was a beautiful, attractive young girl, for sure, but since Tengo first met her he had never felt anything like desire for her. Even after sharing the same apartment for so long, he never felt anything stirring within his heart. *How come? Is there some reason I shouldn't feel sexual desire for her?* he wondered. It was true that on that stormy night they had had intercourse. But it wasn't what he had wanted. It had all been *her* doing.

Intercourse was exactly the right word to describe the act. She had climbed on top of Tengo, who had been numb and unable to move, and inserted his penis inside her. Fuka-Eri had seemed to be in some transcendent state then, like a fairy in the throes of a lewd dream.

Afterward they lived together in the tiny apartment as if nothing had happened. The storm had stopped, morning came, and Fuka-Eri acted like she had completely forgotten the incident. And Tengo didn't bring it up. He felt that if she really had forgotten, it was better to let her stay that way. It might be best if he himself forgot it too. Still, the question remained – why had she suddenly done such a thing? Was there some objective behind it all? Or had she been temporarily possessed?

There was only one thing Tengo knew for sure: *it wasn't an act of love.* Fuka-Eri had a natural affinity for Tengo – that seemed certain. But it was farfetched to believe that she loved him, or desired him, or felt anything even close to these emotions. *She felt no sexual desire for anyone.* Tengo wasn't confident in his powers of observation when it came to people, but still he couldn't quite imagine Fuka-Eri passionately making love with a man, her breath hot and heavy. Or even engaged in not-so-passionate sex. That just wasn't her.

These thoughts ran through his head as he walked the streets of Koenji. The sun had set and a cold wind had picked up, but he didn't mind. He liked to think while he walked, then sit down at his desk and give form to his thoughts. That was his way of doing things. That was why he walked a lot. It might rain, it might be windy, he didn't care. As he walked he found

himself in front of a bar called Mugiatama – "Ears of Wheat."
Tengo couldn't think of anything better to do, so he popped
inside and ordered a Carlsberg draft beer. The bar had just
opened and he was the only customer. He stopped thinking
for a while, kept his mind a blank, and slowly sipped his beer.

But just like nature abhors a vacuum, Tengo wasn't afforded
the leisure of keeping his mind blank for long. He couldn't
help thinking of Fuka-Eri. Like a scrap of a dream, she wended
her way into his mind.

**That person may be very close. Somewhere you can walk
to from here.**

*Fuka-Eri had said this. Which is why I went out to look for
her. And came inside this bar. What other things did she say?*

**Do not worry. Even if you cannot find that person, that
person will find you.**

Just as Tengo was searching for Aomame, Aomame was
searching for him. Tengo hadn't really grasped that. He had
been caught up in *himself* searching for her. It had never
occurred to him that Aomame might be looking for *him* too.

I perceive and you receive.

This was also something Fuka-Eri had said. She perceives
it, and Tengo receives it. But Fuka-Eri only made clear what
she perceived when she felt like it. Whether she was operating
on some principle or theory, or merely acting on a whim,
Tengo couldn't tell.

Again Tengo remembered the time they had intercourse. The
beautiful seventeen-year-old climbed on top of him and put

his penis inside her. Her ample breasts moved lithely in the air, like ripe fruit. She closed her eyes in rapture, her nostrils flaring with desire. Her lips formed something that didn't come together as actual words. He could see her white teeth, her pink tongue darting out from between them every now and then. Tengo had a vivid memory of that scene. His body may have been numb, but his mind was clear. And he had a rock-hard erection.

But no matter how clearly he relived the scene in his head, Tengo didn't feel any stir of sexual excitement. And it didn't cross his mind to want to have sex with her again. He hadn't had sex for the nearly three months since that encounter. More than that, he hadn't even come once. For him this was quite unusual. He was a healthy, thirty-year-old single guy, with a normal sex drive, the sort of desire that had to be taken care of one way or another.

Still, when he was in Kumi Adachi's apartment, in bed with her, her pubic hair pressing against his leg, he had felt no desire at all. His penis had remained flaccid the whole time. Maybe it was the hashish. But that wasn't the reason, he decided. On that stormy night when he had had sex with Fuka-Eri, she had taken *something* important away, from his heart. Like moving furniture out of a room. He was convinced of it.

Like what, for instance?

Tengo shook his head.

When he had polished off the beer, he ordered a Four Roses on the rocks and some mixed nuts. Just like the last time.

Most likely his erection on that stormy night was *too* perfect. It was far harder, and bigger, than he had ever experienced. It didn't look like his own penis. Smooth and shiny, it seemed less an actual penis than some conceptual symbol, and when he ejaculated it was powerful, heroic even, the semen copious and thick. This must have reached her womb, or even beyond. It was the perfect orgasm.

But when something is so complete, there has to be a reaction. That's the way things go. *What kind of erections have I had since?* Tengo wondered. He couldn't recall. Maybe he hadn't even had one. Or if he had, it was obviously not very memorable, a subpar hard-on. If his erection had been a movie, it would have been low budget, straight to video. Not an erection even worth discussing. Most likely.

Maybe I'm fated to drift through life with nothing but second-rate erections, he asked himself, *or not even second-rate ones? That would be a sad sort of life, like a prolonged twilight. But depending on how you look at it, it might be unavoidable.* At least once in his life he had had the perfect erection, and the perfect orgasm. It was like the author of *Gone With the Wind*. Once you have achieved something so magnificent, you have to be content with it.

He finished his whiskey, paid the bill, and continued wandering the streets. The wind had picked up and the air was chillier than before. *Before the world's rules loosen up too much,* he thought, *and all logic is lost, I have to find Aomame.* Nearly the only hope he could cling to now was the thought that he might run across her. *If I don't find her, then what value is there to my life?* he wondered. She had been here, in Koenji, in September. If he were lucky, she was still in the same place. Not that he could prove it – but all he could do right now was pursue that possibility. *Aomame is somewhere around here. And she is searching for me, too. Like two halves of a coin, each seeking the other.*

He looked up at the sky, but he couldn't see the moons. *I have to go someplace where I can see the moon,* Tengo decided.

CHAPTER 13

Ushikawa

IS THIS WHAT THEY MEAN BY BACK TO SQUARE ONE?

Ushikawa's appearance made him stand out. He did not have the sort of looks suited for stakeouts or tailing people. As much as he might try to lose himself in a crowd, he was as inconspicuous as a centipede in a cup of yogurt.

His family wasn't like that at all. Ushikawa's family consisted of his parents, an older and younger brother, and a younger sister. His father ran a health clinic, where his mother was the bookkeeper. Both brothers were outstanding students, attended medical school, and became doctors. His older brother worked in a hospital in Tokyo, while his younger brother was a research doctor at a university. When his father retired, his older brother was due to take over the family clinic in Urawa, a suburb of Tokyo. Both brothers were married and had one child. Ushikawa's sister had studied at a college in the United States and was now back in Japan, working as an interpreter. She was in her mid-thirties but still single. All his siblings were slim and tall, with pleasantly oval features.

In almost every respect, particularly in looks, Ushikawa was the exception in his family. He was short, with a large, misshapen head and unkempt, frizzy hair. His legs were stumpy and bent like cucumbers. His popping eyes always looked startled, and he had a thick layer of flesh around his neck. His eyebrows were bushy and large and nearly came together in the middle. They looked like two hairy caterpillars reaching out to each other. In school he had generally gotten excellent grades, but his performance in some subjects was erratic and he was particularly hopeless at sports.

In this affluent, self-satisfied, elite family, he was the foreign element, the sour, dissonant note that ruined the familial harmony. In family photos he looked like the odd man out, the insensitive outsider who had pushed his way into the group and had his picture taken with them.

The other members of his family couldn't understand how someone who didn't resemble them in the least could be one of them. But there was no mistaking the fact that his mother had given birth to him, with all the attendant labor pains (her recollection was how particularly painful that birth had been). No one had laid him at their doorstep in a basket. Eventually, someone recalled that there was a relative who also had an oversized, misshapen head – Ushikawa's grandfather's cousin. During the war he had worked in a metal shop in Koto Ward in Tokyo, but he died in the massive air raid in the spring of 1945. His father had never met the man, though he had a photo of him in an old album. When the family saw the photo, they exclaimed, "It all makes sense now!" Ushikawa and his uncle were such peas in a pod that you would think that Ushikawa was the man reincarnated. The genetic traits of this uncle had, for whatever reason, surfaced once more.

The Ushikawa family of Urawa, Saitama Prefecture, would have been the perfect family – in both looks and academic and career achievements – if only Ushikawa hadn't existed. They would have been the kind of memorable, photogenic family that anyone would envy. But with Ushikawa in the mix, people tended to frown and shake their heads. People might begin to think that somewhere along the line a joker or two had tripped up the goddess of beauty. No, they *definitely* must think this, his parents decided, which is why they tried their hardest to keep him out of the public eye or at least make sure he didn't stand out (though the attempt was always pointless).

Being put in this situation, however, never made Ushikawa feel dissatisfied, sad, or lonely. He wasn't sociable to begin with and usually preferred to stay in the shadows. He wasn't particularly fond of his brothers and sister. From Ushikawa's perspective, they were irretrievably shallow. To him, their minds were dull, their vision narrow and devoid of imagination, and all they cared about was what other people thought. More than anything, they were completely lacking in the sort of healthy skepticism needed to attain any degree of wisdom.

Ushikawa's father was a moderately successful doctor of internal medicine in the countryside, but he was so utterly boring that talking with him gave you chest pains. Like the king whose touch turned everything to gold, every single word he uttered turned into insipid grains of sand. But as a man of few words he was able – probably unintentionally – to conceal how boring and ignorant he really was. In contrast, his mother was a real talker, a hopeless snob. Money was everything to her, and she was self-centered and proud, loved anything gaudy and showy, and could always be counted on to bad-mouth other people in a shrill voice. Ushikawa's older brother had inherited his father's disposition; his younger brother had his mother's. His sister was very independent. She was irresponsible and had no consideration for others. As the baby of the family, she had been totally pampered and spoiled by her parents.

All of which explained why, since he was a boy, Ushikawa had kept to himself. When he came home from school, he had shut himself in his room and gotten lost in books. He had no friends other than his dog, so he never had the chance to talk with someone about what he had learned, or debate anyone.

Still, he was convinced that he was a clear, eloquent, logical thinker, and he patiently honed these abilities all by himself. For instance, he would propose an idea for discussion and debate it, taking both sides. He would passionately argue in support of the proposition, then argue – just as vigorously – against it. He could identify equally with either of the two positions and was completely and sincerely absorbed by whatever position he happened to be supporting at the moment. Before he had realized it, these exercises had given him the talent to be skeptical about his own self, and he had come to the recognition that most of what is generally considered the truth is entirely relative. Subject and object are not as distinct as most people think. If the boundary separating the two isn't clear-cut to begin with, it is not such a difficult task to intentionally shift back and forth from one to the other.

In order to use logic and rhetoric more clearly and effectively, he filled his mind with whatever knowledge he could find – both what he thought would be useful and what he was pretty sure was the opposite. He chose things he agreed with, and things that, initially, he opposed. It wasn't cultivation and learning in the usual sense that he was after, but more tangible information – something you could actually handle, something with a real shape and heft.

That huge, misshapen head of his turned out to be the perfect container for these quantities of accumulated information. Thanks to all this, he was far more erudite than any of his contemporaries. If he felt like it, he knew he could shoot down anybody in an argument – not just his siblings or classmates, but his teachers and parents as well. But he didn't want to attract any kind of attention if he could avoid it, so he kept this ability hidden. Knowledge and ability were tools, not things to show off.

Ushikawa began to think of himself as a nocturnal creature, concealed in a dark forest, waiting for prey to wander by. He waited patiently for an opportunity, and when it came he would leap out and grab it. But until that point, he couldn't let his opponent know he was there. It was critical to keep a low profile and catch the other person off guard. Even as an elementary school pupil, he had thought this way. He never depended on others or readily revealed his emotions.

Sometimes he imagined how his life would be if he had been born a little better-looking. He didn't need to be handsome. There was no need to look that impressive. He just needed to be normal-looking, or enough so that people wouldn't turn and stare. *If only I had been born like that,* he wondered, *what sort of life would I have led?* But this was a supposition that exceeded his powers of imagination. Ushikawa was too Ushikawa-like, and there was no room in his brain for such hypotheses. It was precisely because of his large, misshapen head, his bulging eyes, and his short, bandy legs that he was who he was, a skeptical young boy, full of intellectual curiosity, quiet but eloquent.

As the years passed the ugly boy grew up into an ugly youth, and before he knew it, into an ugly middle-aged man. At every stage of his life, people continued to turn and stare. Children would stare unabashedly at him. *When I become an ugly old man,* Ushikawa sometimes thought, *then maybe I won't attract so much attention.* But he wouldn't know for sure. Maybe he would end up the ugliest old man the world had ever seen.

At any rate, he was not equipped with the skills needed to blend into the background. And to make matters worse, Tengo knew what he looked like. If he was discovered hanging around outside Tengo's building, the whole operation would come crashing down.

In situations like this, Ushikawa normally hired someone from a PI agency. Ever since he was a lawyer, he had made use of these sorts of organizations, which mostly employed former policemen who were adept at digging up information, shadowing people, and conducting surveillance. But in this case, he didn't want to involve any outsiders. Things were too touchy, and a serious crime – murder – was involved. Besides, Ushikawa wasn't even sure what he might gain by putting Tengo under surveillance.

What Ushikawa wanted was to make clear the *connection* between Tengo and Aomame, but he wasn't even sure what Aomame looked like. He had tried all sorts of methods but had yet to come up with a decent photo. Even Bat hadn't been able to obtain one. Ushikawa had looked at her high school graduation album, but in the class photo her face was tiny and somehow unnatural-looking, like a mask. In the photo of her company softball team she had on a wide-brimmed cap and her face was in shadow. So even if Aomame were to pass him on the street, he would have no way of knowing if it was really her. He knew she was nearly five feet six inches tall and had a trim body and good posture. Her eyes and cheekbones were distinctive, and she wore her hair down to her shoulders. But there were plenty of women in the world who fit that description.

So it looked like Ushikawa would have to undertake the surveillance by himself. He would have to keep his eyes open, patiently waiting for something to happen, and, when it did, instantly react. He couldn't ask someone else to handle such a delicate undertaking.

Tengo was living on the third floor of an old, three-story concrete apartment building. At the entrance was a row of mailboxes for all the residents, one of them with a name tag on it that said *Kawana*. Some of the mailboxes were rusty, the paint peeling off. They all had locks, but most of the residents left them unlatched. The front door of the building was unlocked, and anyone could go inside.

The dark corridor inside had that special odor you find in older apartment buildings. It is a peculiar mix of smells – of unrepaired leaks, old sheets washed in cheap detergent, stale tempura oil, a dried-up poinsettia, cat urine from the weed-filled front yard. Live there long enough and you would probably get used to the smell. But no matter how used to it you got, the fact remained that this was not a heartwarming odor.

Tengo's apartment faced the main road. It wasn't all that noisy, but there was a fair amount of foot traffic. An elementary school was nearby and at certain times of day there were large groups of children outside. Across from the building was a clump of small single-family homes, two-story houses with no garden. Just down the road were a liquor store and a stationery store catering to elementary school children. And two blocks farther down was a small police substation. There was nowhere to hide, and if he were to stand by the road and look up at Tengo's apartment – even if Tengo didn't discover him – the neighbors would be sure to cast a suspicious eye his way. And since he was such an *unusual*-looking character, the locals' alert level would be ratcheted up a couple of levels. He might be mistaken for a pervert waiting for the kids to get out of school, and neighbors might call the police.

In surveillance the first requirement is finding a suitable place from which to watch, a place to track your target's movements and maintain a steady supply of water and food. The ideal situation would be to have a room from which Ushikawa could see Tengo's apartment. He could set up a camera with a telephoto lens on a tripod and keep watch over movement in the apartment and who came in and out. Since he was alone on the assignment, twenty-four-hour coverage was impossible, but Ushikawa figured he could cover it for ten hours a day. Needless to say, however, finding a suitable place was going to be tricky.

Even so, Ushikawa walked the neighborhood, searching. He wasn't the type to give up easily. Tenaciousness was, after all, his forte. But after pounding the pavement of every nook and cranny of the neighborhood, Ushikawa called it quits. Koenji was a densely populated residential area, flat with no tall buildings. The number of places from which Tengo's apartment was visible was very limited, and there was not a single one he thought he could use.

Whenever Ushikawa had trouble coming up with a good idea, he liked to take a long, lukewarm soak in the tub, so he went back home and drew a bath. As he lay in the acrylic bathtub, he listened to Sibelius's violin concerto on the radio. He didn't particularly want to listen to Sibelius – and Sibelius's concerto wasn't exactly the right music to listen to at the end of a long day as you soaked in the tub. Perhaps, he mused, Finnish people liked to listen to Sibelius while in a sauna during their long nights. But in a tiny, one-unit bathroom of a two-bedroom condo in Kohinata, Bunkyo Ward, Sibelius's music was too emotional, too tense. Not that this bothered him – as long as there was some background music, he was fine. A concerto by Rameau would do just as well, nor would he have complained if it had been Schumann's *Carnaval*. The radio station just happened to be broadcasting Sibelius's violin concerto. That was all there was to it.

As usual, Ushikawa let half his mind go blank and thought with the other half. David Oistrakh's performance of Sibelius went through the blank half of his mind, like a gentle breeze wafting in through a wide-open entrance and out through a wide-open exit. Maybe it was not the most laudable way of appreciating music. If Sibelius knew his music was being treated this way, it was easy to imagine how those large eyebrows would frown, the folds of his thick neck coming together. But Sibelius had died long ago, and even Oistrakh had long since gone to his grave. So Ushikawa could do as he pleased and let the music filter from right to left, as the unblank half of his brain toyed with random thoughts.

In times like these, Ushikawa didn't like to have a set objective. He let his thoughts run free, as if he were releasing dogs on a broad plain. He would tell them to go wherever they wanted and do whatever they liked, and then he would just let them go. He sank down in the bathwater up to his neck, closed his eyes, and, half listening to the music, let his mind wander. The dogs frolicked around, rolled down slopes, gamboled after each other tirelessly, chased pointlessly after squirrels, then came back, covered in mud and grass, and Ushikawa patted their heads and fastened their collars back on. The music came to an end. Sibelius's violin concerto was a roughly thirty-minute piece – just the right length. The next piece, the announcer intoned, is Janáček's *Sinfonietta*. Ushikawa had a vague memory of hearing the name of the piece before, but he couldn't remember exactly. When he tried to recall, his vision turned strangely cloudy and indistinct, as if a cream-colored mist had settled over his eyeballs. He must have stayed too long in the bath, he decided. He gave up, switched off the radio, got out of the bathtub, wrapped a towel around his waist, and got a beer from the fridge.

Ushikawa lived by himself. He used to have a wife and two small daughters. They had bought a house in the Chuorinkan District in Yamato, in Kanagawa Prefecture. It was a small house, but they had a garden and a dog. His wife was good-looking enough, and his daughters were even pretty. Neither daughter had inherited anything of Ushikawa's looks, which was a great relief.

Then, like a sudden blackout on the stage between acts, he was alone. He found it hard to believe that there had ever been a time when he had a family and lived with them in a house in the suburbs. Sometimes he was even sure the whole thing must be a misunderstanding, that he had unconsciously fabricated this past for himself. But it had actually happened. He had actually had a wife he shared a bed with and two children who shared his bloodline. In his desk drawer, he had a family photo of the four of them. They were all smiling happily. Even the dog seemed to be grinning.

There was no likelihood that they would ever be a family again. His wife and daughters lived in Nagoya now. The girls had a new father, the kind of father with normal looks who wouldn't embarrass them when he showed up at parent-teacher conference day. The girls hadn't seen Ushikawa for nearly four years, but they didn't seem to regret this. They never even wrote to him. It didn't bother Ushikawa much either that he couldn't see his daughters. This didn't mean that his daughters weren't important to him. It was just that now his top priority was simply keeping himself secure, so for the time being he had to switch off any unnecessary emotional circuits and focus on the tasks at hand.

Plus, he knew this: that no matter how far away his daughters went from him, his blood still flowed inside them. His daughters might forget all about him, but that blood would not lose its way. Blood had a frighteningly long memory. And the sign of that large head would, sometime, somewhere in the future, reappear, in an unexpected time and unexpected place. When it did, people would sigh and remember that Ushikawa had once existed.

Ushikawa might be alive to witness this eruption, or perhaps not. It didn't really matter. He was satisfied just to know that it was *possible*. It wasn't like he was hoping for revenge. Rather, he felt content to know that he was, unavoidably, an inherent part of the world's structure.

He sat down on his sofa, plopped his stubby legs up on the table, and, as he sipped his beer, a thought suddenly came to him. *It might not work out,* he thought, *but it was worth trying. It's so simple – why hadn't it occurred to me?* he wondered, finding it odd. *Maybe the easiest things are the hardest to come up with. Like they say, people miss what's going on right under their noses.*

The next morning Ushikawa went to Koenji again. He saw a real estate agency, went inside, and asked if there were any apartments available for rent in Tengo's building. But this agency didn't handle that building. All rentals in that apartment building were handled by an agency in front of the station.

"I sort of doubt there are any units available," the agent said. "The rent is reasonable, and it's a convenient location, so few people move out."

"Well, I'll ask anyway, just to make sure," Ushikawa said.

He stopped by the agency in front of the station. A young man in his early twenties was the one who dealt with him. The man had jet-black hair, hardened with gel to the consistency of a bird's nest. He wore a bright white shirt and a brand-new tie. He probably hadn't been working there long. He still had marks from pimples on his cheeks. The man flinched a bit when he looked at Ushikawa, but soon recovered and gave him a pleasant, professional smile.

"You're in luck, sir," the young man said. "The couple on the first floor had some family issues that arose and they had to move out quickly, so one of the units has been vacant for a week. We finished cleaning it yesterday but haven't advertised it yet. It's on the first floor so it might be a bit noisy, and it doesn't get a lot of sun, but it's a wonderful location. There is one condition of the contract, however: in five or six years the owner plans to completely rebuild the place, so when you receive notice of that renovation six months ahead of time, you'll need to move out, with no complaints. Plus, there's no parking lot there."

"Not a problem," Ushikawa replied. He didn't plan to stay there that long, and he didn't have a car.

"Excellent. If you agree to those conditions, then you can

move in at once. I imagine you would like to see the apartment first?"

"Yes, of course," Ushikawa replied. The young man took a key out of a desk drawer and passed it to him.

"I'm very sorry, but I have an errand to run, so if you don't mind, could you check out the place by yourself? The apartment is empty, and all you need to do is drop off the key on your way back."

"That sounds fine," Ushikawa said, "but what if I'm some evil man who never gives the key back, or makes a copy and sneaks in later to ransack the place? What would you do then?"

The young man stared in surprise at Ushikawa for a time. "Yes, good point. I see. Just to be on the safe side, could you give me a card?"

Ushikawa took out one of his New Japan Foundation for the Advancement of Scholarship and the Arts business cards and handed it to him.

"Mr. Ushikawa," the young man frowned as he read the name. But then he looked relieved. "You don't look to me like someone who would do something bad."

"Much appreciated," Ushikawa replied. And he smiled, a smile as meaningless as the title listed on his card.

No one had ever told him this before. Maybe it meant his looks were too unusual for him to ever do anything bad. It would be too easy for anyone to describe him, and a simple matter to draw a police sketch. If a warrant were issued for his arrest, he wouldn't last three days.

The apartment was nicer than he had imagined. Tengo's third-floor apartment was two stories directly above, so it was impossible to observe his place. But the front entrance was visible from his window so he could see when Tengo entered and exited the building, and spot anyone visiting him. He could just camouflage a telephoto lens and take pictures of each person's face.

In order to rent this apartment he had to pay two months' security deposit: one month's rent up front, plus a fee equivalent to the second month's rent. The rent itself wasn't that high, and the security deposit would be returned when the lease was up, but still, this all came to a hefty sum. Having just paid Bat, his resources were severely depleted, but he knew he had to rent that apartment. There was no other choice. Ushikawa went back to the real estate agency, took out the cash he had already prepared in an envelope, and signed the lease. The lease was with the New Japan Foundation for the Advancement of Scholarship and the Arts. He told them he would mail them a certified copy of the foundation's registry later. This didn't seem to faze the young real estate agent. Once the lease was signed, the agent again handed him the keys.

"Mr. Ushikawa, the apartment is ready for you to move in today. The electricity and water are on, but you will have to be present when they turn on the gas, so please contact Tokyo Gas yourself. What will you do about a phone?"

"I'll handle that myself," Ushikawa said. It took a lot of time and effort to get a contract with the phone company, and a workman would have to come to the apartment to install it. It was easier to use a nearby pay phone.

Ushikawa went back to the apartment and drew up a list of items he would be needing. Thankfully the previous resident had left the curtains up. They were old, flowery curtains, but as long as they were curtains, he felt lucky to have them. Curtains of some kind were indispensable to a stakeout.

The list of necessary items wasn't all that long. The main things he would need were food and drinking water, a camera with a telephoto lens, and a tripod. The rest of his list included toilet paper, a heavy-duty sleeping bag, portable kerosene containers, a camping stove, a sharp knife, a can opener, garbage bags, basic toiletries, and an electric razor, several towels, a flashlight, and a transistor radio. The minimal amount of clothes and a carton of cigarettes. That was about it. No need for a fridge, a table, or bedding. As long as he had a place to keep out of the weather, he considered himself lucky. Ushikawa returned to his own house and put a single reflex and a tele-photo lens in a camera bag, as well as an ample amount of film. He then stuffed all the items on his list into a travel bag. He bought the additional things he still needed in the shopping district in front of Koenji Station.

He set up his tripod next to the window, attached the lat-est Minolta automatic camera to it, screwed on the telephoto lens, aimed it at the level of the faces of anyone who came in or exited the building, and set the camera to manual. He made it so he could use a remote control to work the shutter and set the motor drive. He fashioned a cardboard cone to go around the lens so that light wouldn't reflect off the lens. From the out-side, part of a paper tube was visible at one end of the slightly raised curtain, but no one would ever notice it. No one would ever imagine that someone was secretly photographing the entrance of such a nondescript apartment building.

Ushikawa took a few test shots of people coming in and out of the building. Because of the motor drive he was able to get three quick shots of each person. As a precaution he wrapped a towel around the body of the camera to muffle any noise. As soon as he finished the first roll, he took it to the photo store next to the station. The clerk placed it in a machine that would automatically develop and print the photos. It handled great numbers of photos at high speed, so no one ever noticed or cared about the images printed on them.

The photos came out fine – not very artistic, to be sure, but serviceable. The faces of the people entering and exiting the building were clear enough to distinguish one from another. On the way back from the photo shop, Ushikawa bought some mineral water and several cans of food. And he bought a carton of Seven Stars at a smoke shop. Holding his bags of purchases in front of him to hide his face, he returned to the apartment and sat down again in front of the camera. As he kept watch over the entrance he drank some water, ate canned peaches, and smoked a couple of cigarettes. The electricity was on, but for some reason not the water. When he turned on the tap there was a rumbling sound in the wall, but nothing came out. Something had to be holding them up from turning on the water. He thought of contacting the real estate agent, but, wanting to limit his trips in and out of the building, he decided to wait and see. No running water meant he couldn't use the toilet, so instead he peed into an old bucket the cleaning company had conveniently forgotten to take away.

The impatient early-winter twilight came quickly and the room grew totally dark, but still he didn't turn on the lights. Ushikawa rather welcomed the darkness. The light came on at the entrance and he continued to survey the faces that passed by under the yellowish light.

As evening came, the foot traffic into and out of the building increased a bit, though the number of people was still not that great. It was, after all, a small apartment building. Tengo was not among them, and neither was anyone who could possibly be Aomame. Tengo was scheduled to teach at the cram school today. He would be coming back in the evening. He didn't usually stop off anywhere on the way home after work. He preferred to make his own dinner rather than eat out, and he liked to eat alone while reading. Ushikawa knew all this. But Tengo didn't come home. Perhaps he was meeting someone after work.

A variety of people lived in the building, everyone from young, single working people, to college students, to couples with small children, to elderly people living alone – people from all walks of life. But all of them entered the frame of the lens, unaware they were under surveillance. Despite some differences in age and circumstances, every one of them looked worn out, tired of life. They appeared hopeless, abandoned by ambition, their emotions worn away, with only resignation and numbness filling the void left behind. As if they had just had a tooth pulled, their faces were dark, their steps heavy.

But he may have been mistaken. Some of them may have actually been enjoying life to the fullest. Once they opened their doors, there was some breathtaking little paradise waiting just for them. Perhaps some of them were pretending to live a Spartan life to avoid getting audited by the Tax Bureau. This was possible. But through the telephoto lens, they all looked like dead-end city dwellers not going anywhere in life, clinging to a cheap apartment scheduled to be torn down.

That night Tengo didn't make an appearance and Ushikawa saw no one who could be connected to him. When ten thirty rolled around, he decided to call it a day. He hadn't quite settled into a routine and didn't want to push it. *There will be many days to come,* he decided, *so this is enough for now.* He did a variety of stretches to loosen his stiff muscles, then ate a sweet *anpan* bun, poured coffee from his thermos into the cap, and drank it. He tried the faucet in the sink, and now the water was running. He washed his face with soap, brushed his teeth, and took a good, long pee. He leaned back against the wall and smoked a cigarette. He longed for a sip of whiskey, but he had decided that as long as he was here, he wouldn't touch a drop of alcohol.

He stripped to his underwear and snuggled into the sleeping bag. The cold made him tremble slightly. At night the empty apartment was unexpectedly chilly. He thought he might need a small electric space heater.

As he lay shivering, alone in the sleeping bag, he recalled the days when he had been surrounded by his family. He didn't particularly miss those days. His life now was so completely different that these memories merely popped up to illustrate that fact. Even when he was living with his family, Ushikawa had felt lonely. He never opened up to anyone and thought that his ordinary life would never last. Deep down he was convinced that one day it would all too easily fall apart – his busy days as a lawyer, his generous income, his nice house in Chuorinkan, his not-bad-looking wife, his cute daughters, both attending private elementary school, his pedigreed dog. So when his life steadily fell apart bit by bit and he was left all alone, he was actually relieved. *Thank God,* he thought. *Nothing to worry about now. I'm back right where I started.*

Is this what it means to go back to square one?

He curled up like a maggot in the sleeping bag and stared at the dark ceiling. He had sat in the same position for too long and his joints ached. Shivering in the cold, making do with a cold bun for dinner, standing watch over the entrance of a cheap apartment that was ready to be torn down, watching the unattractive people coming in and out, peeing into a wash bucket. *Is this what it means to go back to square one?* he asked again. He remembered something he had forgotten to do. He crawled out of the sleeping bag, poured the urine in the bucket into the toilet, pushed the wobbly handle, and flushed it down. The sleeping bag had just started to warm up, and he had hesitated to get out. *Just leave it,* he had thought – but if he happened to slip in the dark he would regret it. Afterward he crawled back into the sleeping bag and shivered in the cold again.

Is this what it means to go back to square one?

Most likely. He had nothing left to lose, other than his life. It was all very clear-cut. In the darkness, a razor-thin smile came to Ushikawa's lips.

CHAPTER 14

Aomame

THIS LITTLE ONE OF MINE

For the most part, Aomame's life had become filled with confusion. She felt as though she were blindly groping around in the dark. Ordinary logic and reason didn't function in this 1Q84 world, and she couldn't predict what was going to happen to her next. She felt sure, though, that she would survive the next few months and give birth to the baby. This was nothing more than a hunch, though a strong one. Everything was proceeding on the premise that she would give birth to this child. She could just sense it.

She remembered the last words that Leader had spoken. "You are fated to pass through great hardships and trials," he had said. "Once you have done that, you should be able to see things as they are supposed to be."

He *knew* something. Something vital. *And he had tried – in vague and ambiguous terms – to give me this message,* Aomame thought. *The hardship he spoke of may have been when I took myself to the brink of death, when I took the pistol to that spot in front of the Esso sign, meaning to kill myself. But I came back, without dying, and discovered I was pregnant. This, too, might have been preordained.*

As they entered December, the winds grew fierce for a few days. The fallen zelkova leaves whipped against the plastic screen on the balcony with a dry, biting sound. The cold wind let out a warning as it whistled between the bare branches of the trees. The caws of the crows grew sharper, keener. Winter had arrived.

Every day, she became even more convinced that the baby growing in her womb was Tengo's child, until this theory became an established fact. It wasn't logical enough to convince a third party, but it made sense to her. It was obvious.

If I'm pregnant without having had sex, who could the man possibly be other than Tengo?

In November she had begun putting on weight. She couldn't go outside, but she more than made up for it by continuing to work out and strictly watching her diet. After age twenty she never weighed more than 115 pounds. But one day the scale showed she weighed 119, and after that her weight never dropped below it. She felt like her face, too, had rounded out. No doubt this *little one* wanted its mother to plump up.

Together with this *little one* she continued to keep watch over the playground at night, hoping to spot the silhouette of a large young man sitting alone on the slide. As she gazed at the two moons, lined up side by side in the early-winter sky, Aomame rubbed her belly through the blanket. Occasionally tears would well up for no reason. She would find a tear rolling down her cheek and falling to the blanket on her lap. Maybe it was because she was lonely, or because she was anxious. Or maybe pregnancy had made her more sensitive. Or maybe it was merely the cold wind stimulating the tear ducts to produce tears. Whatever the reason, Aomame let the tears flow without wiping them away.

Once she had cried for a while, at a certain point the tears would stop, and she would continue her lonely vigil. *No*, she thought, *I'm not that lonely. I have this* little one *with me. There are two of us – two of us looking up at the two moons, waiting for Tengo to appear.* From time to time she would pick up her binoculars and focus on the deserted slide. Then she would pick up the automatic pistol to check its heft and what it felt like. *Protecting myself, searching for Tengo, and providing this* little one *with nourishment. Those are my duties now.*

One time, as the cold wind blew and she kept watch over the playground, Aomame realized she believed in God. It was a sudden discovery, like finding, with the soles of your feet, solid ground beneath the mud. It was a mysterious sensation, an unexpected awareness. Ever since she could remember, she had always hated this thing called God. More precisely, she rejected the people and the system that intervened between her and God. For years she had equated those people and that system with God. Hating them meant hating God.

Since the moment she was born *they* had been near her, controlling her, ordering her around, all in the name of God, driving her into a corner. In the name of God, they stole her time and her freedom, putting shackles on her heart. They preached about God's kindness, but preached twice as much about his wrath and intolerance. At age eleven, Aomame made up her mind and was ultimately able to break free from that world. In doing so, though, much had been sacrificed.

If God didn't exist, then how much brighter my life would be, how much richer. Aomame often thought this. Then she should be able to share all the beautiful memories that normal children had, without the constant anger and fear that tormented her. And then how much more positive, peaceful, and fulfilling her life might be.

Despite all this, as she sat there, her palm resting on her belly, peeking through the slats of the plastic boards at the deserted playground, she couldn't help but come to the realization that she believed in God. When she had mechanically repeated the words of the prayer, when she brought her hands together, she had believed in a God outside the conscious realm. It was a feeling that had seeped into her marrow, something that could not be driven away by logic or emotion. Even hatred and anger couldn't erase it.

But this isn't their God, she decided. *It's my God. This is a God I have found through sacrificing my own life, through my flesh being cut, my skin ripped off, my blood sucked away, my nails torn, all my time and hopes and memories being stolen from me. This is not a God with a form. No white clothes, no long beard. This God has no doctrine, no scripture, no precepts. No reward, no punishment. This God doesn't give, and doesn't take away. There is no heaven up in the sky, no hell down below. When it's hot, and when it's cold, God is simply* there.

From time to time, she would recall Leader's final words before he died. She could never forget his rich baritone. Just like she could never forget the feeling of stabbing a needle into the back of his neck.

Where there is light, there must be shadow, where there is shadow, there must be light. There is no shadow without light and no light without shadow. . . . We do not know if the so-called Little People are good or evil. This is, in a sense, something that surpasses our understanding and our definitions. We have lived with them since long, long ago – from a time before good and evil even existed, when people's minds were still benighted.

Are God and the Little People opposites? Or two sides of the same thing?

Aomame had no idea. What she did know was that she had to protect this *little one* inside her. And to do so it became necessary to somehow believe in God. Or to recognize the fact that she believed in God.

Aomame pondered the idea of God. God has no form, yet is

able to take on any form. The image she had was of a stream-lined Mercedes coupe, a brand-new car just delivered from the dealer. An elegant, middle-aged woman coming out of that car, in the middle of an expressway running through the city, offering her beautiful spring coat to the naked Aomame. To protect her from the chilly wind, and people's rude stares. And then, without a word, getting back in her silver coupe. The woman knew – that Aomame had a baby within her. That Aomame had to be protected.

She began to have a new dream. In the dream she is imprisoned in a white room. A small, cube-shaped room, no windows, a single door. A plain bed, no frills, on which she lies sleeping, faceup. A light hanging over the bed illuminates her hugely swollen belly. It doesn't look like her own body, but it is definitely a part of Aomame's flesh. It is getting close to the time for the baby's delivery.

The room is guarded by Buzzcut and Ponytail. The duo is dead set against making any more errors. They made a mistake once and they need to recover their reputation. Their assignment is to make sure that Aomame does not leave this room, and that no one enters. They wait for the birth of the *little one*. It seems they plan to snatch it away from Aomame the moment it is born.

Aomame calls out, desperately seeking help. But this room is built of special material. The walls, floor, and ceiling immediately absorb any sound. She can't even hear her own scream. Aomame prays that the woman in the Mercedes coupe will come and rescue her – her and the *little one*. But her voice is sucked, in vain, into the walls of that white room.

The *little one* absorbs nourishment through its umbilical cord, and is growing larger by the minute. Hoping to break out of that lukewarm darkness, it kicks against the walls of her womb. Hoping for light, and freedom.

Tall Ponytail sits in a chair beside the door, hands in his lap, staring at a point in space. Perhaps a small, dense cloud is floating there. Buzzcut stands next to the bed. They wear the same dark suits as before. Buzzcut raises his arm from time to time to glance at his watch, like somebody waiting for an important train to pull into the station.

Aomame can't move her arms and legs. It doesn't feel like she is tied down, but still she can't move. There is no feeling in her fingers. She has a premonition that her labor pains are about to begin. Like that fateful train drawing nearer to the station, exactly on schedule. She can hear the slight vibration of the rails as it gets closer.

And then she wakes up.

She took a shower to wash off the sweat and changed clothes. She tossed her sweaty clothes into the washer. There was no way she wanted to have this dream, but it came upon her anyway. The details sometimes changed, but the place and outcome were always the same: the cube-shaped white room, the approaching labor pains, the duo in their bland, dark suits.

The two men knew she was pregnant with the *little one* – or they were going to find out. Aomame was prepared. If need be, she would have no problem pumping all the 9mm bullets she had into Ponytail and Buzzcut. The God that protected her was also, at times, a bloody God.

A knock came at the door. Aomame sat down on a stool in the kitchen and gripped the automatic pistol tight, the safety off. Outside a cold rain had been falling since morning. The world was enveloped in the smell of winter rain.

The knocks stopped. "Hello, Miss Takai," a man's voice said on the other side of the door. "It's me, your friendly NHK collector. Sorry to bother you again, but I'm back to collect the subscription fee. I know you're there, Miss Takai."

Aomame faced the door and silently spoke. We called NHK

and asked about this. You're nothing but someone posing as an NHK man. Who *are* you? And what do you want here?

"When people receive things, they have to pay for them. That's the way the world works. You receive a TV signal, so you have to pay the fee. Receiving without paying isn't fair. It's the same as stealing."

His voice echoed loudly in the hallway. A hoarse, but piercing voice.

"My personal feelings are not involved in this at all. I don't hate you, and I'm not trying to punish you whatsoever. It's just that I can't stand when things are unfair. People have to pay for what they receive. Miss Takai, as long as you don't open up, I'll be back again and again to bang on your door. And I don't think that's what you want. I'm not some unreasonable old coot. If we talk, I'm sure we can come to an understanding. So would you be kind enough to open the door?"

The knocking continued.

Aomame gripped the pistol tighter. *This man must know I'm having a baby.* A thin sheen of sweat formed under her arms and on the tip of her nose. *I am never going to open this door. He can try to use a duplicate key, or try to force it open, but if he does I'm going to empty this entire clip into his belly – NHK collector or not.*

No, that probably wouldn't happen. And she knew it. He couldn't open the door. As long as she didn't open it from the inside, the door was set up so it couldn't be opened. Which is why the man got so irritated and voluble, using every verbal trick in the book trying to make her tense and on edge.

Ten minutes later, the man left. But only after he had, in a thunderous voice, threatened and ridiculed her, slyly tried to win her over to his side, denounced her in no uncertain terms, and finally announced he would be back to pay her another visit.

"You can't escape, Miss Takai. As long as you get the TV signal I will be back. I'm not the kind of man who gives up so easily. That's just my personality. Well, we will be seeing each other again very soon."

She didn't hear his footsteps, but he was no longer standing outside the door. Aomame peeked through the peephole to make sure. She set the safety on the pistol and washed her face in the sink. Her armpits were soaked. As she changed to a fresh shirt she stood, naked, in front of the mirror. Her stomach still wasn't showing enough to notice, but she knew an important secret lay hidden within.

She spoke to the dowager on the phone. After Tamaru had gone over a few points with her, he handed the phone to the dowager without a word. They used a roundabout way of speaking, avoiding any clear-cut terms. At least at first.

"We have already secured a new place for you," the dowager said. "There you can perform the *task you've been planning on*. It's a safe place and you can get checked out regularly by a specialist. If you're willing, you can move there as soon as you would like."

Should she tell the dowager about the people who were after her little one? *How in her dreams the guys from Sakigake were trying to get hold of her child? How the phony NHK collector using all his wiles to get her to open the door was probably after the same thing?* But Aomame gave up the idea. She trusted the dowager, and respected her deeply. But that wasn't the issue. *Which world was she living in?* For the time being, that was the point.

"How have you been feeling?" the dowager asked.

"Everything seems to be going well so far," Aomame replied.

"I'm very glad to hear it," the dowager said. "But your voice seems different somehow. Maybe I'm just imagining things, but you sound a little tense and guarded. If there's anything that's bothering you, anything at all, please don't hesitate to tell us. We might be able to help you."

"I think being in one place for so long has made me anxious, maybe, without my even realizing it. But I'm taking good care of myself. That's my field, after all," Aomame replied, careful with her tone of voice.

"Of course," the dowager responded. She paused again. "A little while ago a suspicious man was hanging around our place for a couple of days. He seemed mainly interested in checking out the safe house. I asked the three women staying there to look at the pictures on our security cameras, but none of them recognized him. It might be somebody who's after you."

Aomame frowned slightly. "You mean they've figured out our connection?"

"I'm not sure about that. We're at the point where we *need to consider* that possibility, though. This man looks quite unusual. He has a big, misshapen head. The top is flat, and he's balding. He's short, with stubby arms and legs, and stocky. Does that sound at all familiar?"

A misshapen head? "From the balcony I keep a close eye on the people walking down the street, but I've never seen anyone that fits that description. He sounds like the kind of person you couldn't miss."

"Exactly. He sounds like a colorful circus clown. If he's the one *they* selected and sent to check us out, I would say it's an odd choice."

Aomame agreed. Sakigake wouldn't deliberately send a person who stood out like that to reconnoiter. They couldn't be that desperate for help. Which meant that the man probably had nothing to do with the religion, and that Sakigake still didn't know about her relationship with the dowager. But then who was this man, and what was he doing checking out the safe house? Maybe he was the same man who pretended to be an NHK fee collector and kept on bothering her? She had no proof. She had just mentally linked the fee collector's eccentric manner and the description of this other weird man.

"If you see him, please get in touch. We may have to take steps."

"Of course I will get in touch right away," Aomame replied.

The dowager was silent again. This was rather unusual, for usually when they talked on the phone she was quite no-nonsense, and hated to waste any time.

"Are you well?" Aomame asked casually.

"The same as always. I have no complaints," the dowager said. But Aomame could hear a faint hesitation in her voice – something else that was unusual.

Aomame waited for her to continue.

Finally, as if resigned to it, the dowager spoke. "It's just that recently I feel old more often than I used to. Especially after you left."

"I never left," Aomame said brightly. "I'm still here."

"I know. You're there and we can still speak on the phone. It's just that when we were able to meet regularly and exercise together, some of your vitality rubbed off on me."

"You have a lot of your own vitality to begin with. All I did was help bring it out. Even if I'm not there, you should be able to make it on your own."

"To tell you the truth, I thought the same thing until a while ago," the dowager said, giving a laugh that was best characterized as dry. "I was confident that I was a special person. But time slowly chips away at life. People don't just die when their time comes. They gradually die away, from the inside. And finally the day comes when you have to settle accounts. Nobody can escape it. People have to pay the price for what they've received. I have only just learned that truth."

You have to pay the price for what you've received. Aomame frowned. It was the same line that the NHK collector had spoken.

"On that night in September, when there was the huge thunderstorm, this thought suddenly came to me," the dowager said. "I was in my house, alone in the living room, anxious about you, watching the flashes of lightning. And a flash of lightning lit up this truth for me, right in front of my eyes. That night I lost you, I also lost something inside me. Or perhaps several things. Something central to my existence, the very support for who I am as a person."

"Was anger a part of this?" Aomame ventured.

There was a silence, like after the tide had gone out. Finally the dowager spoke. "You mean was my anger among the things I lost then? Is that what you're asking?"

"Yes."

The dowager slowly breathed in. "The answer to your question is – yes. That's what happened. In the midst of that tremendous lightning, the seething anger I had had was suddenly gone – at least, it had retreated far away. It was no longer the blazing anger I used to have. It had transformed into something more like a faintly colored sorrow. I thought such an intense anger would last forever. . . . But how do you know this?"

"Because the same thing happened to me," Aomame said, "that night when there was all that thunder."

"You're talking about your own anger?"

"That's right. I can't feel the pure, intense anger I used to have anymore. It hasn't completely disappeared, but like you said, it has withdrawn to someplace far away. For years this anger has occupied a large part of me. It's been what has driven me."

"Like a merciless coachman who never rests," the dowager said. "But it has lost power, and now you are pregnant. Instead of being angry."

Aomame calmed her breathing. "Exactly. Instead of anger, there's a *little one* inside me. Something that has nothing to do with anger. And day by day it is growing inside me."

"I know I don't need to say this," the dowager said, "but you need to take every precaution with it. That is another reason you need to move as soon as possible to a more secure location."

"I agree, but before that happens, there's something I need to take care of."

After she hung up, Aomame went out to the balcony, looked down through the plastic slats at the afternoon road below, and gazed at the playground. Twilight was fast approaching. *Before 1Q84 is over,* she thought, *before they find me, I have to find Tengo.*

No matter what it takes.

CHAPTER 15

Tengo

NOT SOMETHING
HE'S ALLOWED TO TALK ABOUT

Tengo left the bar, Mugiatama, and wandered the streets, lost in thought. Eventually, he made up his mind and headed toward the small children's playground – the place where he had first discovered two moons in the sky. *I will climb the slide like last time,* he thought, *and look up at the sky once more.* He might be able to see the moons from there again. And they might tell him something.

As he walked, he wondered when exactly he had last visited the playground. He couldn't recall. The flow of time wasn't uniform anymore, the sense of distance uncertain. But it probably had been in the early autumn. He remembered wearing a long-sleeved T-shirt. And now it was December.

A cold wind was blowing the mass of clouds off toward Tokyo Bay. The free-form clouds looked stiff and hard, as if made of putty. The two moons were visible, occasionally hiding behind the clouds. The familiar yellow moon, and the new, smaller green moon, both of them past full, about two-thirds size. The smaller moon was like a child hiding in its mother's skirts. The moons were in almost the same location as the time he saw them before, as if they had been patiently waiting for Tengo's return.

There was no one else in the playground. The mercury-vapor lamp shone brighter than before, a cold, harsh light. The bare branches of the zelkova tree reminded him of ancient white bones. It was the sort of night when you would expect to hear an owl. But there were no owls to be found in the city's parks. Tengo tugged the hood of his yacht parka over his head and stuck his hands in the pockets of his leather jacket. He climbed up the slide, leaned against the handrail, and gazed up at the two moons as they appeared, then disappeared, among the clouds. Beyond that, the stars twinkled silently. The amorphous filth that hangs over the city was blown away in the wind, leaving the air pure and clear.

Right now, how many people besides me have noticed these two moons? Tengo considered this. Fuka-Eri knew about it, because this was something that she initiated. Most likely. Other than her, though, nobody he knew had mentioned that the number of moons had increased. Have people not noticed? Or they don't dare to bring it up in conversation? Is it just common knowledge? Either way, other than the friend who filled in for him at the cram school, Tengo hadn't asked anybody about the moons. Actually, he had been careful not to bring it up in conversation, like it was some morally inappropriate subject.

Why?

Perhaps the moons wanted it that way, Tengo thought. *Maybe these two moons are a special message meant just for me, and I am not permitted to share this information with anyone else.*

But this was a strange way to see it. Why would the number of moons be a personal message? And what could they be trying to tell him? To Tengo it seemed less a message than a kind of complicated riddle. And if it's a riddle, then who made it? Who's *not permitting* things?

The wind rushed between the branches of the zelkova tree, making a piercing howl, like the coldhearted breath leaking out between the teeth of a person who has lost all hope. Tengo gazed at the moons, not paying much attention to the sound of the wind, sitting there until his whole body was chilled to the bone. It must have been around fifteen minutes. No, maybe more. His sense of time had left him. His body, initially warmed by the whiskey, now felt hard and cold, like a lonely boulder at the bottom of the sea.

The clouds continued to scud off toward the south. No matter how many were blown away, others appeared to take their place. There was an inexhaustible source of clouds in some land far to the north. Decisive people, minds fixed on the task, clothed in thick, gray uniforms, working silently from morning to night to make clouds, like bees make honey, spiders make webs, and war makes widows.

Tengo looked at his watch. It was almost eight. The playground was still deserted. Occasionally people would walk by quickly on the street in front. People who have finished work and are on the way home all walk the same way. In the new six-story apartment building on the other side of the street the lights were on in half the units. On windy winter nights, a window with a light shining in it acquires a gentle warmth. Tengo looked from one lit window to the next, in order, like looking up at a huge luxury cruise liner from a tiny fishing boat bobbing in the night sea. As if by prearrangement, all the curtains at the windows were closed. Seen from a freezing-cold slide in a park at night, they looked like a totally different world – a world founded on different principles, a world that ran by different rules. Beyond those curtains there must be people living their quite ordinary lives, peaceful and content.

Quite ordinary lives?

The only image that Tengo had of *quite ordinary lives* was stereotypical, lacking depth and color. A married couple, probably with two kids. The mother has on an apron. Steam rising from a bubbling pot, voices around the dining table – that's as far as his imagination took him before plowing into a solid wall. What would a *quite ordinary* family talk about around the dinner table? He had no memory himself of ever talking with his father at the dinner table. They each just stuffed food into their mouths, silently, whenever they felt like it. And what they ate was hard to call a real meal.

After checking out all the illuminated windows in the building, Tengo again looked up at the pair of moons. But no matter how long he waited, neither moon said anything to him. Their faces were expressionless as they floated in the sky beside each other, like a precarious couplet in need of reworking. Today there was no message. That was the only thing they conveyed to Tengo.

The clouds swept tirelessly toward the south. All sizes and shapes of clouds appeared, then disappeared. Some of them had very unusual shapes, as if they had their own unique thoughts – small, hard, clearly etched thoughts. But Tengo wanted to know what the moons were thinking, not the clouds.

He finally gave up and stood, stretching his arms and legs, then climbed down from the slide. *That's all I can do. I was able to see that the number of moons hasn't changed, and I will leave it at that for now.* He stuck his hands in the pockets of his leather jacket, left the playground, and strode back to his apartment. As he walked he suddenly thought of Komatsu. It was about time for them to talk. He had to sort out, even if just barely, what had transpired between them. And Komatsu, too, had some things he must need to talk to Tengo about. Tengo had left the number of the sanatorium in Chikura with Komatsu's office, but he had never heard from him. He would give Komatsu a call tomorrow. Before that, though, he needed to go to the cram school and read the letter that Fuka-Eri had left for him.

Fuka-Eri's letter was in his desk drawer, unopened. For such a tightly sealed envelope, it was a short letter. On a page and a half of notebook paper, in blue ink, was her writing, that distinctive cuneiform-like script, the kind of writing that would be more appropriate on a clay tablet than notebook paper. Tengo knew it must have taken her a long time to write like that.

Tengo read the letter over and over. She *had to get out of* his place. *Right this minute,* she had written, because they were being *watched.* She had underlined these three places with a soft, thick pencil. Terribly eloquent underlining.

Who was watching us, and *how* she knew this – about this she said nothing. In the world that Fuka-Eri lived in, it seemed that facts were not conveyed directly. Like a map showing buried pirate treasure, things had to be connected through hints and riddles, ellipses and variations. He had grown used to it and, for the time being, provisionally, accepted whatever Fuka-Eri announced. When she said that they were being *watched,* no doubt they actually were being watched. When she felt that she *had to get out,* that meant the time had come for her to leave. The first thing to do was to accept all those statements as one comprehensive fact. Later on he could discover, or surmise, the background, the details, the basis for these hypotheses – or else just give up on it from the very beginning.

We're being watched.

Did this mean people from Sakigake had found Fuka-Eri? They knew about his relationship with her. They had uncovered the fact that he was the one, at Komatsu's request, who rewrote *Air Chrysalis,* which would explain why Ushikawa tried to get closer to Tengo. And if that was true, then there was a distinct possibility his apartment was under surveillance.

If this was true, though, they were really taking their time. Fuka-Eri had settled down in his apartment for nearly three months. These were organized people, people with real power and influence. If they had wanted to, they could have grabbed her anytime. There was no need to go to all the trouble of putting his apartment under surveillance. And if they really were watching her, they wouldn't let her just leave.

The more Tengo tried to follow the logic of it, the more confused he got. All he concluded was that *they weren't trying to grab Fuka-Eri.* Maybe at a certain point they had changed objectives. They weren't after Fuka-Eri, but someone connected to her. For some reason they no longer viewed Fuka-Eri as a threat to Sakigake. If you accept that, though, then why go to the trouble of putting Tengo's apartment under surveillance?

Tengo used the pay phone at the cram school to call Komatsu's office. It was Sunday, but Tengo knew that he liked to come in and work on the weekend. The office could be a nice place, he liked to say, if there was nobody else there. But no one answered. Tengo glanced at his watch. It was eleven a.m., too early for Komatsu to show up at work. He started his day, and it didn't matter what day of the week it was, after the sun had reached its zenith. Tengo, on a chair in the cafeteria, sipped the weak coffee and reread the letter from Fuka-Eri. As always she used hardly any kanji at all, and no paragraphs or punctuation.

Tengo you are back from the cat town and are reading this letter   that's good but we're being *watched* so I *have to get out* of this place *right this minute* do not worry about me but I can't stay here any longer as I said before the person you are looking for is within walking distance of here   but be careful not to let somebody see you

Tengo read this telegram-like letter again three times, then folded it and put it in his pocket. As before, the more he read it, the more believable her words became. He was being watched by someone. Now he accepted this as a certainty. He looked up and scanned the cram school cafeteria. Class was in session so the cafeteria was nearly deserted. A handful of students were there, studying textbooks or writing in their notebooks. But he didn't spot anyone in the shadows stealthily spying on him.

A basic question remained: If they weren't watching Fuka-Eri, then why would there be surveillance here? Were they interested in Tengo himself, or was it his apartment? Tengo considered this. This was all at the level of conjecture. Somehow, he didn't feel he was the object of their interest. His role in *Air Chrysalis* was long past.

Fuka-Eri had barely taken a step out of his apartment, so her sense that she was being *watched* meant that his apartment was under surveillance. But where could somebody keep his place under watch? The area where he lived was a crowded urban neighborhood, but Tengo's third-floor apartment was, oddly enough, situated so that it was almost out of anyone's line of sight. That was one of the reasons he liked the place and had lived there so long. His older girlfriend had liked the apartment for the same reason. "Putting aside how the place looks," she often said, "it's amazingly tranquil. Much like the person who lives here."

Just before the sun set each day, a large crow would fly over to his window. This was the crow Fuka-Eri had talked about on the phone. It settled in the window box and rubbed its large, jet-black wings against the glass. This was part of the crow's daily routine, to rest for a spell outside his apartment before homing back to its nest. This crow seemed to be curious about the interior of Tengo's apartment. The large, inky eyes on either side of its head shifted swiftly, gathering information through a gap in the curtain. Crows are highly intelligent animals, and extremely curious. Fuka-Eri claimed to be able to talk with this crow. Still, it was ridiculous to think that a crow could be somebody's tool to reconnoiter Tengo's apartment.

So how were they watching him?

* * *

On the way home from the station Tengo stopped by a super-market and bought some vegetables, eggs, milk, and fish. Standing at the entrance to his building, paper bag in hand, he glanced all around just to make sure. Nothing looked suspicious, the same scene as always – the electric lines hanging in the air like dark entrails; the small front yard, its lawn withered in the winter cold; the rusty mailboxes. He listened carefully, but all he could hear was the distinctive, incessant background noise of the city, like the faint hum of wings.

He went into his apartment, put away the food, then went over to the window, drew back the curtains, and inspected the scene outside. Across the road were three old houses, two-story homes built on minuscule lots. The owners were all long-term, elderly residents, people with crabby expressions who loathed any kind of change, so they weren't about to welcome a newcomer to their second floor. Plus, even if someone was on the second floor and leaned way out the window, all they would be able to see was a glimpse of his ceiling.

Tengo closed the window, boiled water, and made coffee. As he sat at the dining table and drank it, he considered every scenario he could think of. Someone nearby was keeping him under watch. And Aomame was (or *had been*) within walking distance. Was there some connection between the two? Or was it all mere coincidence? He thought long and hard, but he couldn't reach a conclusion. His thoughts went around and around, like a poor mouse stuck in an exitless maze allowed only to smell the cheese.

He gave up thinking about it and glanced through the newspaper he had bought at the station kiosk. Ronald Reagan, just reelected president that fall, had taken to calling Prime Minister Yasuhiro Nakasone *Yasu*, and Nakasone was calling him *Ron*. It might have been the way the photo was taken, but the two of them looked like a couple of men in the construction industry discussing how they were going to switch to cheap, shoddy building material. Riots in India following the assassination of Indira Gandhi were still ongoing, with Sikhs being butchered throughout the country. In Japan there was an unprecedented bumper crop of apples. But nothing in the paper aroused Tengo's interest.

He waited until the clock showed two and then called Komatsu's office once more.

As always, it took twelve rings before Komatsu picked up. Tengo wasn't sure why, but it always seemed hard for him to get to the phone.

"Tengo, it's been a while," Komatsu said. His voice sounded like the old Komatsu. Smooth, a bit forced, difficult to pin down.

"I took two weeks off from work and was in Chiba. I just got back last night."

"You said your father wasn't doing so well. It must have been hard on you."

"Not really. He's in a deep coma, so I just spent time with him, gazing at his sleeping face. The rest of the time I was at the inn, writing."

"Still, you're talking about a life-or-death situation, so it couldn't have been easy for you."

Tengo changed the subject. "When we talked last, quite a while ago, you mentioned having to talk with me about something."

"I remember," Komatsu said. "I would like to have a nice long talk with you, if you're free?"

"If it's something important, maybe the sooner the better?"

"Yes, sooner is better."

"Tonight could work for me."

"That would be fine. I'm free tonight, too. Say, seven?"

"Seven it is," Tengo said.

Komatsu told him to meet him in a small bar near his office, a place Tengo had been to a number of times. "It's open on Sundays," Komatsu added, "but there are hardly any people there then. So we can have a nice, quiet talk."

"Is this going to be a long story?"

Komatsu thought about this. "I'm not sure. Until I actually tell it to you, I have no idea how long it will be."

"That's all right. I'll be happy to listen. Because we're in the same boat together, right? Or have you changed to another?"

"No, not at all," Komatsu said, his tone more serious. "We're still in the same boat. Anyway, I'll see you at seven. I'll tell you everything then."

After he hung up, Tengo sat down at his desk, switched on his word processor, and typed up the story he had written out in fountain pen at the inn in Chikura. As he reread the story, he pictured the town in his mind: the sanatorium, the faces of the three nurses; the wind from the sea rustling through the pine trees, the pure white seagulls floating up above. Tengo stood up, pulled back the curtains, opened the sliding glass door, and deeply inhaled the cold air.

Tengo you are back from the cat town and are reading this letter   that's good

So wrote Fuka-Eri in her letter. But this apartment he had returned to was under surveillance. There could even be a hidden camera right here in the room. Anxious now that he had thought of this, Tengo scoured every corner of the apartment. But he found no hidden camera, no electronic bugs. This was, after all, an old, tiny, one-room unit, and anything like that would be next to impossible to keep hidden.

Tengo kept typing his manuscript until it grew dark. It took him much longer than he expected because he rewrote parts as he typed. He stopped for a moment to turn on the desk lamp and realized that the crow hadn't come by today. He could tell when it came by from the sound, the large wings rubbing against the window. It left behind faint smudge marks on the glass, like a code waiting to be deciphered.

At five thirty he made a simple dinner. He wasn't that hungry, but he had barely eaten anything for lunch. *Best to get something in my stomach,* he figured. He made a tomato and wakame salad and ate a slice of toast. At six fifteen he pulled on a black, high-neck sweater and an olive-green corduroy blazer and left the apartment. As he exited the front door he stopped and looked around again, but nothing caught his eye – no man hiding in the shadows of a telephone pole, no suspicious-looking car parked nearby. Even the crow wasn't there. But this made Tengo all the more uneasy. All the seemingly benign things around him seemed to be watching him. Who knew if the people around – the housewife with her shopping basket; the silent old man taking his dog for a walk; the high school students, tennis rackets slung over their shoulders, pedaling by, ignoring him – might be part of a cleverly disguised Sakigake surveillance team.

I'm being paranoid, Tengo told himself. *I need to be careful, but it's no good to get overly jumpy.* He hurried on toward the station, shooting an occasional glance behind him to make sure he wasn't being followed. If he was being shadowed, Tengo was sure he would know it. His peripheral vision was better than most people's, and he had excellent eyesight. After glancing back three times, he was certain that there was no one tailing him.

He arrived at the bar at five minutes before seven. Komatsu was not there yet, and Tengo was the first customer of the evening. A lush arrangement of bright flowers was in a large vase on the counter and the smell of freshly cut greenery wafted toward him. Tengo sat in a booth in the back and ordered a draft beer. He took a paperback out of the pocket of his jacket and began reading.

Komatsu came at seven fifteen. He had on a tweed jacket, a

light cashmere sweater, a cashmere muffler, wool trousers, and suede shoes. His *usual outfit*. High-quality, tasteful clothes, nicely worn out. When he wore these, the clothes looked like he had been born in them. Maybe any new clothes he bought he then slept in and rolled around in. Maybe he washed them over and over and laid them out to dry in the shade. Only once they were broken in and faded would he wear them in front of others. At any rate, the clothes did make him look like a veteran editor. From the way he was dressed, that was the only possible thing he *could* be. Komatsu sat down across from Tengo and also ordered a draft beer.

"You seem the same as ever," Komatsu commented. "How is the new novel coming?"

"I'm getting there, slowly but surely."

"I'm glad to hear it. Writers have to keep on writing if they want to mature, like caterpillars endlessly chewing on leaves. It's like I told you – taking on the rewrite of *Air Chrysalis* would have a good influence on your own writing. Was I right?"

Tengo nodded. "You were. Doing that rewrite helped me learn a lot about fiction writing. I started noticing things I had never noticed before."

"Not to brag or anything, but I know exactly what you mean. You just needed the right *opportunity*."

"But I also had a lot of hard experiences because of it. As you are aware."

Komatsu's mouth curled up neatly in a smile, like a crescent moon in winter. It was the kind of smile that was hard to read.

"To get something important, people have to pay a price. That's the rule the world operates by."

"You may be right. But I can't tell the difference between what's important and the price you have to pay. It has all gotten too complicated."

"Complicated it definitely is. It's like trying to carry on a phone conversation when the wires are crossed. Absolutely," Komatsu said, frowning. "By the way, do you know where Fuka-Eri is now?"

"I don't know where she is at present, no," Tengo said, choosing his words carefully.

"*At present*," Komatsu repeated meaningfully.

Tengo said nothing.

"But until a short while ago she was living in your apartment," Komatsu said. "At least, that's what I hear."

Tengo nodded. "That's right. She was at my place for about three months."

"Three months is a long time," said Komatsu. "And you never told anybody."

"She told me not to tell anyone, so I didn't. Including you."

"But now she isn't there anymore."

"Right. She took off when I was in Chikura, and left behind a letter. I don't know where she is now."

Komatsu took out a cigarette, stuck it in his mouth, and lit a match. He narrowed his eyes and looked at Tengo.

"After she left your place Fuka-Eri went back to Professor Ebisuno's house, on top of the mountain in Futamatao," he said. "Professor Ebisuno contacted the police and withdrew the missing person's report, since she had just gone off on her own and hadn't been kidnapped. The police must have interviewed her about what happened. She is a minor, after all. I wouldn't be surprised if there's an article in the paper about it before long, though I doubt it will say much. Since nothing criminal was involved, apparently."

"Will it come out that she stayed with me?"

Komatsu shook his head. "I don't think Fuka-Eri will mention your name. You know how she is. It can be the cops she's talking to, the military police, a revolutionary council, or Mother Teresa – once she has decided not to say something, then mum's the word. So I wouldn't let that worry you."

"I'm not worried. I would just like to know how things are going to work out."

"Whatever happens, your name won't be made public. Rest assured," Komatsu said. His expression turned serious. "But there is something I need to ask you. I hesitate to bring it up."

"How come?"

"Well, it's very – personal."

Tengo took a sip of beer and put the glass back on the table. "No problem. If it's something I can answer, I will."

"Did you and Fuka-Eri have a sexual relationship? While she was staying at your place, I mean. Just a simple yes or no is fine."

Tengo paused for a moment and slowly shook his head. "The answer is no. I didn't have that kind of relationship with her."

Tengo made an instinctive decision that he shouldn't reveal what had taken place between them on that stormy night. Besides, it wasn't really what you would call a sex act. There was no sexual desire involved, not in the normal sense. On either side.

"So you didn't have a sexual relationship."

"We didn't," Tengo said, his voice dry.

Komatsu scrunched up his nose. "Tengo, I'm not doubting you. But you did hesitate before you replied. Maybe something close to sex happened? I'm not blaming you. I'm just trying to ascertain certain facts."

Tengo looked straight into Komatsu's eyes. "I wasn't hesitating. I just felt weird, wondering why in the world you were so concerned about whether Fuka-Eri and I had a sexual relationship. You're usually not the type to stick your head into other people's private lives. You avoid that."

"I suppose," Komatsu said.

"Then why are you bringing something like that up now?"

"Who you sleep with or what Fuka-Eri does is basically

none of my business." Komatsu scratched the side of his nose. "As you have pointed out. But as you are well aware, Fuka-Eri isn't just some ordinary girl. How should I put it? Every action she takes is significant."

"Significant," Tengo repeated.

"Logically speaking, all the actions that everybody takes have a certain significance," Komatsu said. "But in Fuka-Eri's case they have a *deeper meaning*. Something about her is different that way. So we need to be certain of whatever facts we can."

"By *we*, who do you mean, exactly?" Tengo asked.

Komatsu looked uncharacteristically nonplussed. "Truth be told, it's not me who wants to know whether the two of you had a sexual relationship, but Professor Ebisuno."

"So Professor Ebisuno knows that Fuka-Eri stayed at my apartment?"

"Of course. He knew that the first day she showed up at your place. Fuka-Eri told him where she was."

"I had no idea," Tengo said, surprised. She had told him she hadn't revealed to anyone where she was. Not that it mattered much now. "There's one thing I just don't get. Professor Ebisuno is her legal guardian and protector, so you would expect him to pay attention to things like that. But in the crazy situation we're in now you would think his top priority would be to make sure she's safe – not whether she's staying chaste or not."

Komatsu raised one corner of his lips. "I don't really know the background. He just asked me to find out – to see you and ask whether the two of you had a physical relationship. That is why I asked you this, and the answer was no."

"That's correct. Fuka-Eri and I did not have a physical relationship," Tengo said firmly, gazing steadily into Komatsu's eyes. Tengo didn't feel like he was lying.

"Good, then," Komatsu said. He put another Marlboro between his lips, and lit a match. "That's all I need to know."

"Fuka-Eri is an attractive girl, no question about it," Tengo said. "But as you are well aware, I have gotten mixed up in something quite serious, unwillingly. I don't want things to get any more complicated than they are. Besides, I was seeing somebody."

"I understand perfectly," Komatsu said. "I know you're a very clever person when it comes to things like that, with a very mature way of thinking. I will tell Professor Ebisuno what you said. I'm sorry I had to ask you. Don't let it bother you."

"It doesn't especially bother me. I just thought it was strange, why such a thing like that would come up at this point." Tengo paused for a moment. "What was it you wanted to tell me?"

Komatsu had finished his beer and ordered a Scotch highball from the bartender.

"What's your pleasure?" he asked Tengo.

"I'll have the same," Tengo said.

Two highballs in tall glasses were brought over to their table.

"Well, first of all," Komatsu began after a long silence, "I think that as much as possible we need to unravel some things about the situation that we've gotten entangled in. After all, we're all in the same boat. By *we* I mean the four of us – you, me, Fuka-Eri, and Professor Ebisuno."

"A very interesting group," Tengo said, but his sarcasm didn't seem to register with Komatsu.

Komatsu went on. "I think each of the four of us had his own expectation regarding this plan, and we're not all on the same level, or moving in the same direction. To put it another way, we weren't all rowing our oars at the same rhythm and at the same angle."

"This isn't the sort of group you would expect to be able to work well together."

"That might be true."

"And our boat was headed down the rapids toward a waterfall."

"Our boat was indeed headed down the rapids toward a waterfall," Komatsu admitted. "I'm not trying to make excuses, but from the start this was an extremely simple plan. We fool everybody, we make a bit of money. Half for laughs, half for profit. That was our goal. But ever since Professor Ebisuno got involved, the plot has thickened. A number of complicated subplots lie just below the surface of the water, and the water is picking up speed. Your reworking of the novel far exceeded my expectations, thanks to which the book got great reviews and had amazing sales. And then this took our boat off to an unexpected place – a somewhat perilous place."

Tengo shook his head slightly. "It's not a somewhat perilous place. It's an *extremely dangerous place.*"

"You could be right."

"Don't act like this doesn't concern you. You're the one who came up with this idea in the first place."

"Granted. I'm the one who had the idea and pushed the start button. Things went well at first, but unfortunately as it progressed I lost control. I do feel responsible for it, believe me. Especially about getting you involved, since I basically forced you into it. But it's time for us to stop, take stock of where we are, and come up with a plan of action."

After getting all this out, Komatsu took a breath and drank his highball. He picked up the glass ashtray and, like a blind man feeling an object all over to understand what it is, carefully ran his long fingers over the surface.

"To tell you the truth," he finally said, "I was imprisoned for seventeen or eighteen days somewhere. From the end of August to the middle of September. The day it happened I was in my neighborhood, in the early afternoon, on my way to work. I was on the road to the Gotokuji Station. This large black car stopped beside me and the window slid down and someone called my name. I went over, wondering who it could be, when two men leapt out of the car and dragged me inside.

Both of them were extremely powerful. One pinned my arms back, and the other put chloroform or something up to my nose. Just like in a movie, huh? But that stuff really does the trick, believe me. When I came to, I was being held in a tiny, windowless room. The walls were white, and it was like a cube. There was a small bed and a small wooden desk, but no chair. I was lying on the bed."

"You were kidnapped?" Tengo asked.

Komatsu finished his inspection of the ashtray, returned it to the table, and looked up at Tengo. "That's right. A real kidnapping. Like in that old movie, *The Collector*. I don't imagine most people in the world ever think they will end up kidnapped. The idea never occurs to them. Right? But when they kidnap you, believe me, you're kidnapped. It's kind of – how shall I put it? – surreal. You can't believe you are *actually* being kidnapped by someone. Could you believe it?"

Komatsu stared at Tengo, as if looking for a reply. But it was a rhetorical question. Tengo was silent, waiting for him to continue. He hadn't touched his highball. Beads of moisture had formed on the outside, wetting the coaster.

CHAPTER 16

Ushikawa

A CAPABLE, PATIENT, UNFEELING MACHINE

The next morning Ushikawa again took a seat by the window and continued his surveillance through a gap in the curtain. Nearly the same lineup of people who had come back to the apartment building the night before, or at least people who looked the same, were now exiting. Their faces were still grim, their shoulders hunched over. A new day had barely begun and yet they already looked fed up and exhausted. Tengo wasn't among them, but Ushikawa went ahead and snapped photos of each and every face that passed by. He had plenty of film and it was good practice so he could be more efficient at stealthily taking photos.

When the morning rush had passed and he saw that everyone who was going out had done so, he left the apartment and slipped into a nearby phone booth. He dialed the Yoyogi cram school and asked to speak with Tengo.

"Mr. Kawana has been on leave for the last ten days," said the woman who answered the phone.

"I hope he's not ill?"

"No, someone in his family is, so he went to Chiba."

"Do you know when he will be back?"

"I'm afraid I haven't asked him that," the woman said.

Ushikawa thanked her and hung up.

Tengo's family, as far as Ushikawa knew, meant just his father – the father who used to be an NHK fee collector. Tengo still didn't know anything about his mother. And as far as Ushikawa was aware, Tengo and his father had always had a bad relationship. Yet Tengo had taken more than ten days off from work in order to take care of his sick father. Ushikawa found this hard to swallow. How could Tengo's antagonism for his father soften so quickly? What sort of illness did his father have, and where in Chiba was he in the hospital? There should be ways of finding out, though it would take at least a half a day to do so. And he would have to put his surveillance on hold while he did.

Ushikawa wasn't sure what to do. If Tengo was away from Tokyo, then it was pointless to stake out this building. It might be smarter to take a break from surveillance and search in another direction. He should find out where Tengo's father was a patient, or investigate Aomame's background. He could meet her classmates and colleagues from her college days and from the company she used to work for, and gather more personal information. Who knows but this might provide some new clues.

But after mulling it over, he decided to stay put and continue watching the apartment building. First, if he suspended his surveillance at this point, it would put a crimp in the daily rhythm he had established, and he would have to start again from scratch. Second, even if he located Tengo's father, and learned more about Aomame's friendships, the payoff might not be worth the trouble. Pounding the pavement on an investigation can be productive up to a point, but oddly, once you pass that point, nothing much comes of it. He knew this through experience. Third, his intuition told him, in no uncertain terms, to *stay put* – to stay right where he was, watch all the faces that passed by, and let nothing get by him.

So he decided that, with or without Tengo, he would continue to stake out the building. If he stayed put, by the time Tengo came back Ushikawa would know each and every face. Once he

knew all the residents, then he would know in a glance if someone was new to the building. *I'm a carnivore,* Ushikawa thought.
*And carnivores have to be forever patient. They have to blend in
with their surroundings and know everything about their prey.*

Just before noon, when the foot traffic in and out of the
building was at its most sparse, Ushikawa left the apartment.
He tried to disguise himself a bit, wearing a knit cap and a
muffler pulled up to his nose, but still he couldn't help but
draw attention to himself. The beige knit cap perched on top of
his huge head like a mushroom cap. The green muffler looked
like a big snake coiled around him. Trying a disguise didn't
work. Besides, the cap and muffler clashed horribly.

Ushikawa stopped by the film lab near the station and
dropped off two rolls of film to be developed. Then he went to
a soba noodle shop and ordered a bowl of soba noodles with
tempura. It had been a while since he had had a hot meal. He
savored the tempura noodles and drank down the last drop of
broth. By the time he finished he was so hot he had started to
perspire. He put on his knit cap, wrapped the muffler around
his neck again, and walked back to the apartment. As he
smoked a cigarette, he lined up all the photos that he had had
printed on the floor. He collated the photos of people going
out in the morning and the ones of people coming back, and
if any matched he put them together. In order to easily distinguish them, he made up names for each person, and wrote the
names on the photos with a felt-tip pen.

Once the morning rush hour was over, hardly any residents
left the building. One young man – a college student, by the
looks of him – hurried out around ten a.m., a bag slung over
his shoulder. An old woman around seventy and a woman in
her mid-thirties also went out but then returned lugging bags
of groceries from a supermarket. Ushikawa took their photos
as well. During the morning the mailman came and sorted the
mail into the various mailboxes at the entrance. A deliveryman

with a cardboard box came in and left, empty-handed, five minutes later.

Once an hour Ushikawa left his camera and did some stretching for five minutes. During that interval his surveillance was put on hold, but he knew from the start that total coverage by one person was impossible. It was more important to make sure his body didn't get numb. His muscles would start to atrophy and then he wouldn't be able to react quickly if need be. Like Gregor Samsa when he turned into a beetle, he deftly stretched his rotund, misshapen body on the floor, working the kinks out of his tight muscles.

He listened to AM radio with an earphone to keep from getting bored. Most of the daytime programs appealed to housewives and elderly listeners. The people who appeared on the programs told jokes that fell flat, pointlessly burst out laughing, gave their moronic, hackneyed opinions, and played music so awful you felt like covering your ears. Periodically they gave blaring sales pitches for products no one could possibly want. At least this is how it all sounded to Ushikawa. But he wanted to hear people's voices, so he endured listening to the inane programs, wondering all the while why people would produce such idiotic shows and go to the trouble of using the airwaves to disseminate them.

Not that Ushikawa himself was involved in an operation that was so lofty and productive – hiding behind the curtains in a cheap one-room apartment, secretly snapping photos of people. He couldn't very well criticize the actions of others.

It was not just now, either. Back when he was a lawyer it was the same. He couldn't remember having done anything that helped society. His biggest clients ran small and medium-sized financial firms and had ties to organized crime. Ushikawa created the most efficient ways to disperse their profits and made all the arrangements. Basically, it was money laundering. He was also involved in land sharking: when investors had their eyes on an area, he helped drive out longtime residents so they could knock down their houses and sell the remaining large lot to condo builders. Huge amounts of money rolled in. The same type of people were involved in this as well. He also specialized in defending people brought up on tax-evasion charges. Most of the clients were suspicious characters that an ordinary lawyer would hesitate to have anything to do with. But as long as a client wanted him to represent him – and as long as a certain amount of money changed hands – Ushikawa never hesitated. He was a skilled lawyer, with a decent track record, so he never hurt for business. His relationship with Sakigake began in the same way. For whatever reason, Leader took a personal liking to him.

If he had followed the path that ordinary lawyers take, Ushikawa would probably have found it hard to earn a living. He had passed the bar exam not long after he left college, and he had become a lawyer, but he had no connections or influential backers. With his looks, no prestigious law firm would ever hire him, so if he had stayed on a straight and narrow path he would have had very few clients. There can't be many people in the world who would go out of their way to hire a lawyer who looked as unappealing as Ushikawa, plus pay the high fees involved. The blame might lie with TV law dramas, which have conditioned people to expect lawyers to be both bright and attractive.

So as time went on, Ushikawa became linked with the underworld. People in the underworld didn't care about his looks. In fact, his peculiar appearance was one element that helped them trust and accept him, since neither of them were accepted by the ordinary world. They recognized his quick mind, his practical abilities, his eloquence. They put him in charge of moving vast sums of money (a task they couldn't openly undertake), and compensated him generously. Ushikawa quickly learned the ropes – how to evade the authorities while still doing what was barely legal. His intuitiveness and strong will were a big help. Unfortunately, though, he got too greedy, made some assumptions he shouldn't have, and went over the line. He avoided criminal punishment – barely – but was expelled from the Tokyo Bar Association.

Ushikawa switched off the radio and smoked a Seven Stars. He breathed the smoke deep into his lungs, then leisurely exhaled. He used an empty can of peaches as an ashtray. If he went on like this, he would probably die a miserable death. Before long he would make a false step and fall alone in some dark place. *Even if I left this world, I doubt anyone would notice. I would shout out from the dark, but no one would hear me. Still, I have to keep soldiering on until I die, the only way I know how. Not a laudable sort of life, but the only life I know how to live.* And when it came to *not very laudable things*, Ushikawa was more capable than almost anyone.

At two thirty a young woman wearing a baseball cap exited the building. She had no bags with her and quickly strode across Ushikawa's line of sight. He hurriedly pushed the motor drive switch in his hand and got off three quick shots. It was the first time he had seen her. She was a beautiful young girl, thin and long limbed with wonderful posture, like a ballerina. She looked about sixteen or seventeen and had on faded jeans, white sneakers, and a man's leather jacket. Her hair was tucked into the collar of the jacket. After leaving the building the girl took a couple of steps, then stopped, frowned, and looked intently up above the electric pole in front. She then lowered her gaze to the ground and started off again. She turned left and disappeared from Ushikawa's sight.

That girl looks like somebody, he thought. Somebody he knew, that he had seen recently. With her looks she might be a TV personality. Ushikawa never watched anything on TV but news, and had never been interested in cute girl TV stars.

Ushikawa pushed his memory accelerator to the floor and

shifted his brain into high gear. He narrowed his eyes and squeezed his brain cells hard, like wringing out a dishrag. His nerves ached painfully with the effort. And suddenly it came to him: that *somebody* was none other than Eriko Fukada. He had never seen her in person, only a photo of her in the literary column of the papers. But the sense of aloof transparency that hung over her was exactly the same impression he had gotten from the tiny black-and-white photo of her in the paper. She and Tengo must have met each other during the rewriting of *Air Chrysalis*. It was entirely possible that she had grown fond of Tengo and was lying low in his apartment.

Almost without thinking, Ushikawa grabbed his knit cap, yanked on his navy-blue pea coat, and wrapped his muffler around his neck. He left the building and trotted off in the direction he had last seen her.

She was a very fast walker. *It might be impossible to catch up with her,* he thought. But she was carrying nothing, which meant she wasn't going far. Instead of shadowing her and risking drawing her attention, wouldn't it make more sense to wait patiently for her to return? Ushikawa pondered this, but couldn't stop following her. The girl had a certain illogical something that shook him. The same feeling as the moment at twilight when a mysteriously colored beam of light conjures up a special memory.

After a while he spotted her. Fuka-Eri had stopped in front of a tiny stationery store and was peering intently inside, where something had undoubtedly caught her interest. Ushikawa casually turned his back on her and stood in front of a vending machine. He took some coins out and bought a can of hot coffee.

Finally the girl took off again. Ushikawa laid the half-finished can of coffee at his feet and followed her at a safe distance. The girl seemed to be concentrating very hard on the act of walking, as if she were gliding across the surface of a placid lake. Walk in this special way, and you won't sink or get your shoes wet. It was as if she had grasped the key to doing this.

There was something different about this girl. She had a special something most people didn't. Ushikawa didn't know a lot about Eriko Fukada. From what he had gathered, she was Leader's only daughter, had run away from Sakigake at age ten, had grown up in the household of a well-known scholar named Professor Ebisuno, and had written a novel entitled *Air Chrysalis,* which was reworked by Tengo Kawana and became a bestseller. But she was supposedly missing now – a missing person's report had been filed with the police, and the police had searched Sakigake headquarters not long ago.

The contents of *Air Chrysalis* were problematic for Sakigake, it appeared. Ushikawa had bought the novel and read through it carefully, though which parts were troublesome, and for what reason, he had no idea. He found the novel fascinating and well written. But to him, it seemed a harmless work of fantasy and he was sure the rest of the world must agree. Little People emerge from a goat's mouth, create an air chrysalis, the main character splits into *maza* and *dohta,* and there are two moons. So where in the midst of this fantastical story are there elements that would damage Sakigake if they came out?

But when Eriko Fukada was in the public eye, it would have been too risky to take any action against her. Which is why, Ushikawa surmised, they wanted him to approach Tengo. In Ushikawa's view Tengo was a mere bit player in the bigger scheme of things. Ushikawa still couldn't grasp why they were so fixated on Tengo. But as Ushikawa was just a foot soldier in these operations, he had to unquestioningly follow orders. The problem was, Tengo had quickly rejected the generous proposal that Ushikawa had worked hard to create, and the plan he had made to forge a connection with Tengo had come to a screeching halt. Right when he had been trying to think of another approach, Eriko Fukada's father, Leader, had died, and things were left as they were.

So Ushikawa was in the dark regarding Sakigake's focus. He didn't even know who was in charge now that they had lost Leader. In any case, they were trying to locate Aomame, find out why Leader had been murdered, and who was behind it. No doubt they would mete out some pretty harsh punishment on whoever had done it. And they were determined not to get the law involved.

So what about Eriko Fukada? What was Sakigake's take now on *Air Chrysalis*? Did they still view the book as a threat?

Eriko Fukada didn't slow down or turn around, like a homing pigeon heading straight to her goal. He soon determined that that *goal* was a midsized supermarket, the Marusho. Shopping basket in hand, Fuka-Eri went from one aisle to another, selecting various canned and fresh foods. Just selecting a single head of lettuce took time, as she examined it from every possible angle. *This is going to take a while,* Ushikawa thought. He left the supermarket, went across the street to a bus stop, and pretended to be waiting for a bus while he kept an eye on the store's entrance.

But no matter how long he waited, the girl didn't emerge. Ushikawa started to get worried. Maybe she had left by another exit? As far as he could tell, though, the market had only the one door, facing the main street. Probably shopping was just taking time for her. Ushikawa recalled the serious, strangely depthless eyes of the girl as she contemplated heads of lettuce and decided to sit tight. Three buses came and went. Each time Ushikawa was the only one left behind. He regretted not having brought a newspaper. He could have hidden behind it. When you are shadowing someone a newspaper or magazine is an absolute must. But there was nothing he could do – he had dropped everything and rushed out of the apartment empty-handed.

When Fuka-Eri finally emerged, his watch showed 3:35.

The girl didn't glance his way but marched off in the direction from which she had come. Ushikawa let some time pass and then set off in pursuit. The two shopping bags she carried looked heavy, but she carried them lightly, tripping down the street like a water skipper skimming across a puddle.

What an odd young woman, Ushikawa thought again as he kept her in sight. *It's like watching some rare exotic butterfly. Pleasant to watch, but you can't touch it, for as soon as you do, it dies, its brilliance gone.* That would put an end to his exotic dream.

Ushikawa quickly calculated whether it made sense to let the Sakigake duo know he had discovered Fuka-Eri's whereabouts. It was a tough decision. If he did tell them he had located her, he would definitely score some points. At the very least, it wouldn't hurt his standing with them – he could show them he was making decent progress. But if he got too involved with Fuka-Eri, he might very well miss the chance to find the real object of his search, Aomame. That would be a disaster. So what should he do? He stuffed his hands deep into the pockets of his pea coat, pulled the muffler up to his nose, and continued following her, keeping a longer distance between them than before.

Maybe I'm only following her because I wanted to see her. The thought suddenly occurred to him. Just watching her stride along the road, bags of groceries clutched to her, made his chest grow tight. Like a person hemmed in between two walls, he could go neither forward nor back. His breathing turned ragged and forced, and he found it almost impossible to breathe, like he was caught up in a tepid blast of wind. A thoroughly strange feeling he had never experienced.

At any rate, I'll let her go for a while. I'll stick to the original plan and focus on Aomame. Aomame is a murderer. It doesn't matter what reason she may have had for doing it – she deserves to be punished. Turning her over to Sakigake didn't bother him. But this young girl was different. She was a quiet little creature living deep in the woods, with pale wings like the shadow of a spirit. *Just observe her from a distance,* he decided.

Ushikawa waited a while after Fuka-Eri had disappeared into the entrance of the apartment, grocery bags in hand, before he went in. He went to his room, took off his muffler and cap, and plopped back down in front of the camera. His cheeks were cold from the wind. He smoked a cigarette and drank some mineral water. His throat felt parched, as if he had eaten something very spicy.

Twilight fell, streetlights snapped on, and it was getting near the time people would be coming home. Still wearing his pea coat, Ushikawa held the remote control for the shutter and intently watched the entrance to the building. As the memory of the afternoon sunlight faded, his empty room rapidly grew chilly. It looked like tonight would be much colder than last night. Ushikawa considered going to the discount electrical goods store in front of the station and buying an electric space heater or electric blanket.

Eriko Fukada came out of the entrance again at four forty-five. She had on the same black turtleneck sweater and jeans, but no leather jacket. The tight sweater revealed the swell of her breasts. She had generous breasts for such a slim girl. Ushikawa watched this lovely swelling through his view-finder, and as he did again he felt the same tightness and difficulty breathing.

Since she wasn't wearing a jacket, she couldn't be going far. As before, she stopped at the entrance, narrowed her eyes, and looked up above the electric pole in front. It was getting dark, but if you squinted you could make out the outlines of things. She stood there for a while as if searching for something. But she apparently didn't find what she was looking for. She gave up looking above the pole and, like a bird, twisted her head and gazed at her surroundings. Ushikawa pushed the remote button and snapped photos of her.

As if she had heard the sound of the shutter, Fuka-Eri turned to look right in the direction of the camera. Through the viewfinder Ushikawa and Fuka-Eri were face-to-face. Ushikawa could see her face quite clearly. He was looking through a telephoto lens, after all. On the other end of the lens, though, Fuka-Eri was staring steadily right at him. Deep within the lens, she could see him. Ushikawa's face was clearly reflected within those soft, jet-black eyes. He found it strange that they were directly in touch like this. He swallowed. *This can't be real. From where she is, she can't see anything. The telephoto lens is camouflaged, the sound of the shutter dampened by the towel wrapped around it, so there's no way she could hear it from where she is.* Still, there she stood at the entrance, staring right at where he was hiding. That emotionless gaze of hers was unwavering as it stared straight at Ushikawa, like starlight shining on a nameless, massive rock.

For a long time – Ushikawa had no idea just how long – the two of them stared at each other. Suddenly Fuka-Eri twisted around and strode through the entrance, as if she had seen all that she needed to see. After she disappeared, Ushikawa let all the air out of his lungs, waited a moment, then breathed fresh air in deeply. The chilled air became countless thorns, stinging his lungs.

People were coming back, just like last night, passing under the light at the entrance, one after another. Ushikawa, though, was no longer gazing through his viewfinder. His hand was no longer holding the shutter remote. The girl's open, unreserved gaze had plucked the strength right out of him – as if a long steel needle had been stabbed right into his chest, so deep it felt like it was coming out the other side.

The girl *knew* that he was secretly watching her, that she was being photographed by a hidden camera. He couldn't say how, but Fuka-Eri knew this. Maybe she understood it through some special tactile sense she possessed.

He really needed a drink, to fill a glass of whiskey to the brim and drink it down in one gulp. He considered going out to buy a bottle. There was a liquor store right nearby. But he gave it up – drinking wouldn't change anything. On the other side of the viewfinder, she had seen him. *That beautiful girl saw me, my misshapen head and dirty spirit, hiding here, secretly snapping photos.* Nothing could change that fact.

Ushikawa left his camera, leaned back against the wall, and looked up at the stained ceiling. Soon everything struck him as empty. He had never felt so utterly alone, never felt the dark to be this intense. He remembered his house back in Chuorinkan, his lawn and his dog, his wife and two daughters, the sunlight shining there. And he thought of the DNA he had given to his daughters, the DNA for a misshapen head and a twisted soul.

Everything he had done seemed pointless. He had used up all the cards he'd been dealt – not that great a hand to begin with. He had taken that lousy hand and used it as best he could to make some clever bets. For a time things looked like they were going to work out, but now he had run out of cards. The light at the table was switched off, and all the players had filed out of the room.

That evening he didn't take a single photo. Leaning against the wall, he smoked Seven Stars, and opened another can of peaches and ate it. At nine he went to the bathroom, brushed his teeth, tugged off his clothes, slipped into the sleeping bag, and, shivering, tried to sleep. The night was cold, but his shivering wasn't just brought on by the cold alone. The chill seemed to be arising from inside his body. *Where in the world did I come from?* he asked himself in the dark. *And where the hell am I going?*

The pain of her gaze still stabbed at him. Maybe it would never go away. *Or was it always there,* he wondered, *and I just didn't notice it?*

*　　*　　*

The next morning, after a breakfast of cheese and crackers washed down by instant coffee, he pulled himself together and sat back down in front of the camera. As he did the day before, he observed the people coming and going and took a few photos. Tengo and Fuka-Eri, though, were not among them. Instead it was more hunched-over people, carried by force of habit into the new day. The weather was fine, the wind strong. People's white breath swirled away in the air.

I'm not going to think of anything superfluous, Ushikawa decided. *Be thick-skinned, have a hard shell around my heart, take one day at a time, go by the book. I'm just a machine. A capable, patient, unfeeling machine. A machine that draws in new time through one end, then spits out old time from the other end. It exists in order to exist.* He needed to revert back again to that pure, unsullied cycle – that perpetual motion that would one day come to an end. He pumped up his willpower and put a cap on his emotions, trying to rid his mind of the image of Fuka-Eri. The pain in his chest from her sharp gaze felt better now, little more than an occasional dull ache. *Good. Can't ask for more. I'm a simple system again,* he told himself, *a simple system with complex details.*

Before noon he went to the discount store near the station and bought a small electric space heater. He then went to the same noodle place he had been to before, opened his newspaper, and ate an order of hot tempura soba. Before going back to his apartment he stood at the entrance and gazed above the electric pole at the spot Fuka-Eri had been so focused on yesterday, but he found nothing to draw his attention. All that was there were a transformer and thick black electric lines entwined like snakes. What could she have been looking at? Or was she looking *for* something?

Back in his room, he switched on the space heater. An orange light flickered into life and he felt an intimate warmth on his skin. It was not enough to fully heat the place, but it was much better than nothing. Ushikawa leaned against the wall, folded his arms, and took a short nap in a tiny spot of sunlight. A dreamless sleep, a pure blank in time.

He was pulled out of this happy, deep sleep by the sound of a knock. Someone was knocking on his door. He bolted awake and gazed around him, unsure for a moment of his surroundings. He spotted the Minolta single-lens reflex camera on a tripod and remembered he was in a room in an apartment in Koenji. Someone was pounding with his fist on the door. As he hurriedly scraped together his consciousness, Ushikawa thought it was odd that someone would knock on the door. There was a doorbell – all you had to do was push the button. It was simple enough. Still this person insisted on knocking – pounding it for all he was worth, actually. Ushikawa frowned and checked his watch. One forty-five. One forty-five p.m., obviously. It was still light outside.

He didn't answer the door. Nobody knew he was here, and he wasn't expecting any visitors. It must be a salesman, or someone selling newspaper subscriptions. Whoever it was might need him, but he certainly didn't need them. Leaning against the wall, he glared at the door and maintained his silence. The person would surely give up after a time and go away.

But he didn't. He would pause, then start knocking once more. A barrage of knocks, nothing for ten or fifteen seconds, then a new round. These were firm knocks, nothing hesitant about them, each knock almost unnaturally the same as the next. From start to finish they were demanding a response from Ushikawa. He grew uneasy. Was the person on the other side of the door maybe – Eriko Fukada? Coming to complain to him about his despicable behavior, secretly photographing people? His heart started to pound. He licked his lips with his thick tongue. But the banging against this steel door could only be that of a grown man's fist, not that of a girl's.

Or had she informed somebody else of what Ushikawa was up to, and that person was outside the door? Somebody from the rental agency, or maybe the police? That couldn't be good. But the rental agent would have a master key and could let himself in, and the police would announce themselves. And neither one would bang on the door like this. They would simply ring the bell.

"Mr. Kozu," a man called out. "Mr. Kozu!"

Ushikawa remembered that Kozu was the name of the previous resident of the apartment. His name remained on the mailbox. Ushikawa preferred it that way. The man outside must think Mr. Kozu still lived here.

"Mr. Kozu," the man intoned. "I know you're in there. I can sense you're holed up inside, trying to stay perfectly quiet."

A middle-aged man's voice, not all that loud, but slightly hoarse. At the core his voice had a hardness to it, the hardness of a brick fired in a kiln and carefully allowed to dry. Perhaps because of this, his voice echoed throughout the building.

"Mr. Kozu, I'm from NHK. I've come to collect your monthly subscription fee. So I would appreciate it if you'd open the door."

Ushikawa wasn't planning to pay any NHK subscription fee. *It might be faster,* he thought, *to just let the man in and show him the place. Tell him, look, no TV, right?* But if he saw Ushikawa, with his odd features, shut up alone in an apartment in the middle of the day without a stick of furniture, he couldn't help but be suspicious.

"Mr. Kozu, people who have TVs have to pay the subscription fee. That's the law. Some people say they never watch NHK, so they're not going to pay. But that argument doesn't hold water. Whether you watch NHK or not, if you have a TV you have to pay."

So it's just a fee collector. Let him get it out of his system. Don't respond, and he'll go away. But how could he be so sure there's someone in this apartment? After he came back an hour or so ago, Ushikawa hadn't been out again. He hardly made a sound, and he always kept the curtains closed.

"Mr. Kozu, I know very well that you are in there," the man said, as if reading Ushikawa's thoughts. "You must think it strange that I know that. But I do know it – that you're in there. You don't want to pay the NHK fee, so you're trying to not make a sound. I'm perfectly aware of this."

The homogeneous knocks started up again. There would be a slight pause, like a wind instrument player pausing to take a breath, then once more the pounding would start, the rhythm unchanged.

"I get it, Mr. Kozu. You have decided to ignore me. Fine. I'll leave today. I have other things to do. But I'll be back. Mark my words. If I say I'll be back, you can count on it. I'm not your average fee collector. I never give up until I get what is coming to me. I never waver from that. It's like the phases of the moon, or life and death. There is no escape."

A long silence followed. Just when Ushikawa thought he might be gone, the collector spoke up again.

"I'll be back soon, Mr. Kozu. Look forward to it. When you're least expecting it, there will be a knock on the door. *Bang bang!* And that will be me."

No more knocks now. Ushikawa listened intently. He thought he heard footsteps fading down the corridor. He quickly went over to his camera and fixed his gaze on the entrance to the apartment. The fee collector should finish his business in the building soon and be leaving. He had to check and see what sort of man he was. NHK collectors wear uniforms, so he should be able to spot him right away. But maybe he wasn't really from NHK. Maybe he was pretending to be one to try to get Ushikawa to open the door. Either way, he had to be someone Ushikawa had never seen before. The remote for the shutter in his right hand, he waited expectantly for a likely-looking person to appear.

For the next thirty minutes, though, no one came into or out of the building. Eventually a middle-aged woman he had seen a number of times emerged and pedaled off on her bike. Ushikawa had dubbed her "Chin Lady" because of the ample flesh dangling below her chin. A half an hour later Chin Lady returned, a shopping bag in the basket of her bike. She parked her bike in the bike parking area and went into the building, bag in hand. After this, a boy in elementary school came home. Ushikawa's name for him was "Fox," since his eyes slanted upward. But no one who could have been the fee collector appeared. Ushikawa was puzzled. The building had only one way in and out, and he had kept his eyes glued to the entrance every second. If the collector hadn't come out, that could only mean he was *still inside.*

He continued to watch the entrance without a break. He didn't go to the bathroom. The sun set, it grew dark, and the light at the entrance came on. But still no fee collector. After six, Ushikawa gave up. He went to the bathroom and let out all the pee he had been holding in. The man was definitely still in the building. Why, he didn't know. It didn't make any sense. But that weird fee collector had decided to stay put.

The wind, colder now, whined through the frozen electric lines. Ushikawa turned on the space heater, and as he smoked a cigarette he tried to make sense of it all. *Why did the man have to speak in such an aggressive, challenging tone? Why was he so positive that someone was inside the apartment? And why hadn't he left the building? If he hasn't left here, then where is he?*

Ushikawa left the camera, leaned against the wall, and stared for the longest time at the orange filament of the space heater.

CHAPTER 17

Aomame

I ONLY HAVE ONE PAIR OF EYES

It was a windy Saturday, nearly eight p.m., when the phone rang. Aomame was wearing a down jacket, a blanket on her lap, sitting on the balcony. Through a gap in the screen, she kept an eye on the slide in the playground, which was illuminated by the mercury-vapor lamp. Her hands were under the blanket so they wouldn't get numb. The deserted slide looked like the skeleton of some huge animal that had died in the Ice Age.

Sitting outside on a cold night might not be good for the baby, but Aomame decided it wasn't cold enough to present a problem. No matter how cold you may be on the outside, amniotic fluid maintained nearly the same temperature as blood. There are plenty of places in the world way colder and harsher, she concluded. And women keep on having babies, even there. But above all, this cold was something she felt she had to endure if she wanted to see Tengo again.

As always, the large yellow moon and its smaller green companion floated in the winter sky. Clouds of assorted sizes and shapes scudded swiftly across the sky. The clouds were white and dense, their outlines sharply etched, and they looked to her like hard blocks of ice floating down a snowmelt river to the sea. As she watched the clouds, appearing from somewhere only to disappear again, Aomame felt she had been transported to a spot near the edge of the world. This was the northern frontier of reason. There was nothing north of here – only the chaos of nothingness.

The sliding glass door was open just a crack, so the ringing phone sounded faint, and Aomame was lost in thought, but she didn't miss the sound. The phone rang three times, stopped, then twenty seconds later rang one more time. It had to be Tamaru. She threw aside the blanket, slid open the cloudy glass door, and went inside. It was dark inside and the heat was at a comfortable level. Her fingers still cold, she lifted the receiver.

"Still reading Proust?"

"But not making much progress," Aomame replied. It was like an exchange of passwords.

"You don't like it?"

"It's not that. How should I put it – it's a story about a different place, somewhere totally unlike here."

Tamaru was silent, waiting for her to go on. He was in no hurry.

"By different place, I mean it's like reading a detailed report from a small planet light-years away from *this world* I'm living in. I can picture all the scenes described and understand them. It's described very vividly, minutely, even. But I can't connect the scenes in that book with where I am now. We are physically too far apart. I'll be reading it, and I find myself having to go back and reread the same passage over again."

Aomame searched for the next words. Tamaru waited as she did.

"It's not boring, though," she said. "It's so detailed and beautifully written, and I feel like I can grasp the structure of that lonely little planet. But I can't seem to go forward. It's like I'm in a boat, paddling upstream. I row for a while, but then when I take a rest and am thinking about something, I find myself back where I started. Maybe that way of reading suits me now, rather than the kind of reading where you forge ahead to find out what happens. I don't know how to put it exactly, but there is a sense of time wavering irregularly when you try to forge ahead. If what is in front is behind, and what is behind is in front, it doesn't really matter, does it. Either way is fine."

Aomame searched for a more precise way of expressing herself.

"It feels like I'm experiencing someone else's dream. Like we're simultaneously sharing feelings. But I can't really grasp what it means to be simultaneous. Our feelings seem extremely close, but in reality there's a considerable gap between us."

"I wonder if Proust was aiming for that sort of sensation."

Aomame had no idea.

"Still, on the other hand," Tamaru said, "time in this real world goes ever onward. It never stands still, and never reverses course."

"Of course. In the real world time goes forward."

As she said this Aomame glanced at the glass door. But was it really true? That time was always flowing forward?

"The seasons have changed, and we are getting close to the end of 1984," Tamaru said.

"I doubt I'll finish *In Search of Lost Time* by the end of the year."

"It doesn't matter," Tamaru said. "Take your time. It was written over fifty years ago. It's not like it's crammed with hot-off-the-press information or anything."

You might be right, Aomame thought. *But maybe not.* She no longer had much trust in time.

"Is that *thing inside you* doing all right?" Tamaru asked.

"So far, so good."

"I'm glad to hear it," Tamaru said. "By the way, you heard about the short balding guy who has been loitering outside the Willow House, right?"

"I did. Is he still hanging around?"

"No. Not recently. He did for a couple of days and then he

disappeared. But he went to the rental agencies in the area, pretending to be looking for an apartment, gathering information about the safe house. This guy really stands out. As if that weren't bad enough, his clothes are awful. So everyone who talked with him remembers him. It was easy to track his movements."

"He doesn't sound like the right type to be doing investigations or reconnaissance."

"Exactly. With looks like those, he's definitely not cut out for that kind of work. He has a huge head, too, like one of those Fukusuke good-luck dolls. But he does seem to be good at what he does. He knows how to pound the pavement and dig up information. And he seems quite sharp. He doesn't skip what is important, and he ignores what isn't."

"And he was able to gather a certain amount of information on the safe house."

"He knows it's a refuge for women fleeing domestic violence, and that the dowager has provided it free of charge. I think he must also have discovered that the dowager is a member of the sports club where you worked, and that you often visited her mansion to do private training sessions with her. If I were him, I would have been able to find out that much."

"You're saying he's as good as you are?"

"As long as you don't mind the effort involved, you can learn how to best gather information and train yourself to think logically. Anyone can do that much."

"I can't believe there would be that many people like that in the world."

"Well, there are a few. Professionals."

Aomame sat down and touched the tip of her nose. It was still cold from being outside.

"And that man isn't hanging around outside the mansion anymore?" Aomame asked.

"I think he recognizes that he stands out too much. And

he knows about the security cameras. So he gathered as much information as he could in a short time and then moved on."

"So he knows about the connection between me and the dowager, that this is more than just a relationship between a sports club trainer and a wealthy client, and that the safe house is connected, too. And that we were involved in some sort of project together."

"Most likely," Tamaru said. "As far as I can tell, the guy is getting close to the heart of things. Step by step."

"From what you're saying, though, it sounds like he's working on his own, not as part of some larger organization."

"I had the same impression. Unless they had some special ulterior motive, a large organization would never hire a conspicuous man like that to undertake a secret investigation."

"So why is he doing this investigation – and for whom?"

"You got me," Tamaru said. "All I know is he's good at what he does and he's dangerous. Anything beyond that is just speculation. Though my own modest speculation leads me to believe that, in some form or another, Sakigake is involved."

Aomame considered this prospect. "And the man has moved on."

"Right. I don't know where he has gone, though. But if I had to make a logical guess I would say that he is trying to track you down."

"But you told me it was next to impossible to find this place."

"Correct. A person could investigate all he wanted and never discover anything that linked the dowager to the apartment. Any possible connection has been erased. But I'm talking about the short term. If it's long term, chinks in the armor will appear, just where you least expect them. You might wander outside, for instance, and be spotted. That's just one possibility."

"I don't go outside," Aomame insisted. But this wasn't entirely true. She had left the apartment twice: once when she ran over to the playground in search of Tengo, the other time when she took the taxi to the turnout on the Metropolitan Expressway No. 3, near Sangenjaya, in search of an exit. But she couldn't reveal this to Tamaru.

"Then how is he going to locate this place?"

"If I were him, I would take another look at your personal information. Consider what kind of person you are, where you came from, what kind of life you have led up till now, what you're thinking, what you're hoping for in life, what you're not hoping for. I would take all the information I could get my hands on, lay it all out on a table, verify it, and dissect it from top to bottom."

"Expose me, in other words."

"That's right. Expose you under a cold, harsh light. Use tweezers and a magnifying glass to check out every nook and cranny, to discover patterns in the way you act."

"I don't get it. Would an analysis like that really turn up where I am now?"

"I don't know," Tamaru said. "It might, and it might not. It depends. I'm just saying *that's what I would do*. Because I can't think of anything else. Every person has his set routines when it comes to thinking and acting, and where there's a routine, there's a weak point."

"It sounds like a scientific investigation."

"People need routines. It's like a theme in music. But it also restricts your thoughts and actions and limits your freedom. It structures your priorities and in some cases distorts your logic. In the present situation, you don't want to move from where you are now. At least until the end of the year you have refused to move to a safer location – because you're searching for *something* there. And until you find that something you can't leave. Or you don't want to leave."

Aomame was silent.

"What that might be, or how much you really want it, I have

no idea. And I don't plan to ask. But from my perspective that *something* constitutes your personal weak point."

"You may be right," Aomame admitted.

"And Bobblehead's going to follow that. He will mercilessly trace that personal element that's restraining you. He thinks it will lead to a breakthrough – provided he is as skilled as I imagine and is able to trace fragmentary clues to arrive at that point."

"I don't think he will be able to," Aomame said. "He won't be able to find a path. Because it's something that is found only in my heart."

"You're a hundred percent sure of that?"

Aomame thought about it. "Not a hundred percent. Call it ninety-eight."

"Well, then you had better be very concerned about that two percent. As I said, this guy is a professional. He is very smart, and very persistent."

Aomame didn't reply.

"A professional is like a hunting dog," Tamaru said. "He can sniff out what normal people can't smell, hear what they can't pick up. If you do the same things everyone else does, in the same way, then you're no professional. Even if you are, you're not going to survive for long. So you need to be vigilant. I know you are a very cautious person, but you have to be much more careful than you have been up till now. The most important things aren't decided by percentages."

"There's something I would like to ask you," Aomame said.

"What would that be?"

"What do you plan to do if Bobblehead shows up there again?"

Tamaru was silent for a moment. The question seemed to have caught him by surprise. "I probably won't do anything. I'll just leave him be. There's nothing he can do around here."

"But what if he starts to do something that bothers you?"

"Like what, for instance?"

"I don't know. Something that's a nuisance."

Tamaru made a small sound in the back of his throat. "I think I would send him a message."

"As a fellow professional?"

"I suppose. But before I actually did anything, I would need to find out who he's working with. If he has backup, I could be the one in danger instead of him. I would want to make sure of that before I did anything."

"Like checking the depth of the water before jumping in a pool."

"That is one way of putting it."

"But you believe he is acting on his own. You said he probably doesn't have any backup."

"I did, but sometimes my intuition is off," Tamaru said. "And unfortunately, I don't have eyes in the back of my head. At any rate, I would like you to keep an eye out, all right? See if there's anyone suspicious around, any change in the scenery outside, anything out of the ordinary. If you notice anything unusual, no matter how small, make sure you let me know."

"I understand. I will be careful," Aomame said. She didn't need to be told. *I'm looking for Tengo, so I won't miss the most trivial detail. Still, like Tamaru said, I only have one pair of eyes.*

"That's about it from me," he said.

"How is the dowager?" Aomame asked.

"She is well," Tamaru replied. Then he added, "Though she seems kind of quiet these days."

"She never was one to talk much."

Tamaru gave a low growl in the back of his throat, as if his throat were equipped with an organ to express special emotions. "She is even quieter than usual."

Aomame pictured the dowager, alone on her chair, a large watering can at her feet, endlessly watching butterflies. Aomame knew very well how quietly the old lady breathed.

"I will include a box of madeleines with the next supplies," Tamaru said as he wound up the conversation. "That might have a positive effect on the flow of time."

"Thank you," Aomame said.

Aomame stood in the kitchen and made cocoa. Before going back outside to resume her watch, she needed to warm up. She boiled milk in a pan and dissolved cocoa powder in it. She poured this into an oversized cup and added a cap of whipped cream she had made ahead of time. She sat down at the dining table and slowly sipped her cocoa as she reviewed her conversation with Tamaru. *The man with the large, misshapen head is laying me out bare under a cold, harsh light. He's a skilled professional, and dangerous.*

She put on the down jacket, wrapped the muffler around her, and, the cup of half-drunk cocoa in hand, went out again to the balcony. She sat down on the garden chair and spread the blanket on her lap. The slide was deserted, as usual. But just then she spotted a child leaving the playground. It was strange for a child to be visiting the playground alone at this hour. A stocky child wearing a knit cap. She was looking at him from well above, through a gap in the screen on the balcony, and the child quickly cut across her field of vision and disappeared into the shadows of the building. His head seemed too big for a child, but it might just have been her imagination.

It certainly wasn't Tengo, so Aomame gave it no more thought and turned back to the slide. She sipped her cocoa, warming her hands with the cup, and watched one bank of clouds after another scud across the sky.

Of course, it wasn't a child that Aomame saw for a moment, but Ushikawa. If the light had been better, or if she had seen him a little longer, she would have noticed that his large head wasn't that of a child. It would have dawned on her that that dwarfish, huge-headed person was none other than the man Tamaru had described. But Aomame had only glimpsed him for a few seconds, and at less than the ideal angle. Luckily, for the same reasons, Ushikawa hadn't spotted Aomame out on the balcony.

At this point, a number of "if"s came to mind. *If* Tamaru had hung up a little earlier, *if* Aomame hadn't made cocoa while mulling over things, she would have seen Tengo, on top of the slide, gazing up at the sky. She would have raced out of the room, and they would have been reunited after twenty years.

If that had happened, however, Ushikawa, who had been tailing Tengo, would have noticed that this was Aomame, would have figured out where she lived, and would have immediately informed the duo from Sakigake.

So it's hard to say if Aomame's not seeing Tengo at this point was an unfortunate or fortunate occurrence. Either way, as he had done before, Tengo climbed up to the top of the slide and gazed steadily at the two moons floating in the sky and the clouds crossing in front. Ushikawa watched Tengo from the shadows. In the interim Aomame left the balcony, talked with Tamaru on the phone, and made her cocoa. In this way, twenty-five minutes elapsed. A fateful twenty-five minutes. By the time Aomame had put on her down jacket and returned to the balcony, Tengo had left the playground. Ushikawa didn't immediately follow after him. Instead, he stayed at the playground, checking on something he needed to make sure of. When he had finished, he quickly left the playground. It was during those few seconds that Aomame spotted him from the balcony.

The clouds were still racing across the sky, moving south, over Tokyo Bay and then out to the broad Pacific. After that, who knows what fate awaited them, just as no one knows what happens to the soul after death.

At any rate, the circle was drawing in tighter. But Tengo and Aomame weren't aware that the circle around them was closing in. Ushikawa sensed what was happening, since he was actively taking steps to tighten it, but even he couldn't see the big picture. He didn't know the most important point: that the distance between him and Aomame was now no more than a couple dozen meters. And unusually for Ushikawa, when he left the playground his mind was incomprehensibly confused.

By ten it was too cold to stay outside, so Aomame reluctantly got up and went back into the warm apartment. She undressed and climbed into a hot bath. As she soaked in the water, letting the heat take away the lingering cold, she rested a hand on her belly. She could feel the slight swelling there. She closed her eyes and tried to feel the *little one* that was inside. There wasn't much time left. Somehow she had to let Tengo know: that she was carrying his child. And that she would fight desperately to protect it.

She dressed, got into bed, lay on her side in the dark, and fell asleep. Before she fell into a deep sleep she had a short dream about the dowager.

Aomame is in the greenhouse at the Willow House as they watch butterflies together. The greenhouse is like a womb, dim and warm. The rubber tree she left behind in her old apartment is there. It has been well taken care of and is so green that she hardly recognizes it. A butterfly from a southern land that she has never seen before is resting on one of its thick leaves. The butterfly has folded its brightly colored wings and seems to be sleeping peacefully. Aomame is happy about this.

In the dream her belly is hugely swollen. It seems near her due date. She can make out the heartbeat of the *little one*. Her heartbeat and that of the *little one* blend together into a pleasant, joint rhythm.

The dowager is seated beside her, her back ramrod straight as always, her lips a straight line, quietly breathing. The two of them don't talk, in order not to wake the sleeping butterfly. The dowager is detached, as if she doesn't notice that Aomame is next to her. Aomame of course knows how closely the dowager protects her, but even so, she can't shake a sense of unease. The dowager's hands in her lap are too thin and fragile. Aomame's hands unconsciously feel for the pistol, but can't find it.

She is swallowed up by the dream, yet at the same time aware it is a dream. Sometimes Aomame has those kinds of dreams, where she is in a distinct, vivid reality but knows it isn't real. It is a detailed scene from a small planet somewhere else.

In the dream, someone opens the door to the greenhouse. An ominous cold wind blows in. The large butterfly opens its eyes, spreads its wings, and flutters off, away from the rubber tree. Who is it? She twists her head to look in that direction. But before she can see who it is, the dream is over.

She was sweating when she woke up, an unpleasant, clammy sweat. She stripped off her damp pajamas, dried herself with a towel, and put on a new T-shirt. She sat up in bed for a time. *Something bad might be about to happen. Somebody might be trying to get the* little one. *And whoever that is might be very close by.* She had to find Tengo – there was not a moment to lose. But other than watching the playground every night, there wasn't a thing she could do. Nothing other than what she was already doing – carefully, patiently, dutifully, keeping her eyes open, trained on this one tiny section of the world, that single point at the top of the slide. Even with such focus, though, a person can overlook things. Because she only has one pair of eyes.

Aomame wanted to cry, but the tears wouldn't come. She lay down again in bed, rested her palms on her stomach, and quietly waited for sleep to overtake her.

CHAPTER 18

Tengo

WHEN YOU PRICK A PERSON WITH A NEEDLE, RED BLOOD COMES OUT

"Nothing happened for three days after that," Komatsu said. "I ate the food they gave me, slept at night in the narrow little bed, woke up when morning came, and used the small toilet in one corner of the room. The toilet had a partition for privacy, but no lock on it. There was still a lot of residual summer heat at the time, but the ventilator shaft seemed to be connected to an AC, so it didn't feel hot."

Tengo listened to Komatsu's story without comment.

"They brought food three times a day. At what time, I don't know. They took my watch away, and the room didn't have a window, so I didn't even know if it was day or night. I listened carefully but couldn't hear a sound. I doubt anyone could hear any sound from me. I had no idea where they had taken me, though I did have a vague sense that we were somewhere off the beaten track. Anyhow, I was there for three days, and nothing happened. I'm not actually certain it was three days. They brought me nine meals altogether, and I ate them when they brought them. The lights in the room were turned out three times, and I slept three times. Usually I'm a light, irregular sleeper, but for some reason I slept like a log. It's kind of strange, if you think about it. Do you follow me so far?"

Tengo silently nodded.

"I didn't say a word for the entire three days. A young man brought my meals. He was thin and had on a baseball cap and a white medical face mask. He wore a kind of sweatshirt and sweatpants, and dirty sneakers. He brought my meals on a tray and then took them away when I was finished. They used paper plates and flimsy plastic knives, forks, and spoons. The food they brought was ordinary prepared food in silver foil packages – not very good, but not so bad you wouldn't eat it. They didn't bring much each meal, and I was hungry, so I ate every bite. This was kind of weird, too. Usually I don't have much of an appetite, and if I'm not careful, sometimes I even forget to eat. They gave me milk and mineral water to drink. They didn't provide coffee or tea. No single-malt whiskey or draft beer. No smokes, either. But what're you going to do? It wasn't like I was lounging around some nice hotel."

As if he had just remembered that now he could smoke at his leisure, Komatsu pulled out a red Marlboro pack, stuck a cigarette between his lips, and lit it with a paper match. He sucked the smoke deep into his lungs, exhaled, and then frowned.

"The man who brought the meals never said a word. He must have been ordered by his superiors not to say anything. I'm sure he was at the bottom of the totem pole, a kind of all-purpose gofer. I think he must have been trained in one of the martial arts, though. He had a sort of focus to the way he carried himself."

"You didn't ask him anything?"

"I knew that if I spoke to him, he wouldn't respond, so I just kept quiet and let things be. I ate the food they brought me, drank my milk, went to bed when they turned out the lights, woke up when they turned them back on. In the morning the young guy would come and bring me an electric razor and toothbrush, and I would shave and brush my teeth. When I was done he would take them back. Other than toilet paper, there was nothing else to speak of in the room. They didn't let me take a shower or change my clothes, but I never felt like taking a shower or changing. There was no mirror in the room, but that didn't bother me. The worst thing was definitely the boredom. I mean, from the time I woke up till the time I went to sleep, I had to sit there alone, not speaking to anyone, in this white, completely square, dice-like room. I was bored to tears. I'm kind of a print junkie, I always need to have something to read with me – a room-service menu, you name it. But I didn't have any books, newspapers, or magazines. No TV or radio, no games. No one to talk to. Nothing to do but sit in the chair and stare at the floor, the walls, the ceiling. It was a totally absurd feeling. I mean, you're walking down the road when some people jump out of nowhere, grab you, put chloroform or something over your nose, drag you off somewhere, and hold you in a strange, windowless little room. A weird situation no matter how you cut it. And you get so bored you think you're going to lose your mind."

Komatsu stared with deep feeling at the cigarette between his fingers, the smoke curling up, then flicked the ash into the ashtray.

"I think they must have thrown me into that tiny room for three days, with nothing to do, trying to get me to break down. They seemed to know what they were doing when it came to breaking a person's spirit, pushing someone to the edge. On the fourth day – after I had my fourth breakfast, in other words – two other men came in. I figured this was the pair that had kidnapped me. I was attacked so suddenly that I didn't get a good look at their faces. But when I saw them on the fourth day, it started to come back to me – how they had pulled me into the car so roughly that I thought they were going to twist my arm off, how they had stuffed a cloth soaked with some kind of drug on my nose and mouth. The two of them didn't say a word the whole time, and it was over in an instant."

Remembering the events, Komatsu frowned.

"One of them wasn't very tall, but he was solidly built, with a buzz cut. He had a deep tan and prominent cheekbones. The other one was tall, with long limbs, sunken cheeks, his hair tied up behind him in a ponytail. Put them side by side and they looked like a comedy team. You've got your tall, thin one, and your short, stocky one with a goatee. But I could tell at a glance these were no comedians. They were a dangerous pair. They would never hesitate to do whatever had to be done, without making a big scene. They acted very relaxed, which made them all the more scary, and their eyes were frighteningly cold. They both wore black cotton trousers and white short-sleeved shirts. They were probably in their mid- to late twenties, the one with the buzz cut maybe a little older than the other one. Neither one wore a watch."

Tengo was silent, waiting for him to go on.

"Buzzcut did all the talking. Ponytail just stood there in front of the door, ramrod straight, without moving a muscle. It seemed like he was listening to our conversation, but then again, maybe not. Buzzcut sat down right across from me in a folding metal chair he had brought, and talked. There were no other chairs, so I sat on the bed. The guy had no facial expression at all. His mouth moved when he spoke, but other than that, his face was frozen, like a ventriloquist's dummy."

The first thing Buzzcut said when he sat down across from Komatsu was this: "Are you able to guess who we are, and why we brought you here?"

"No, I can't," Komatsu replied.

Buzzcut stared at Komatsu for a while with his depthless eyes. "But say you had to make a guess," he went on, "what would you say?" His words were polite enough, but his tone was forceful, his voice as hard and cold as a metal ruler left for a long time in a fridge.

Komatsu hesitated, but then said, honestly, that if he were forced to make a guess, he would say it had something to do with the *Air Chrysalis* affair. Nothing else came to mind. "That would mean you two are probably from Sakigake," he continued, "and we are in your compound."

Buzzcut neither confirmed nor denied what Komatsu had said. He just stared at him. Komatsu kept silent as well.

"Let's talk, then, based on that hypothesis," Buzzcut quietly began. "What we're going to say from now on is an extension of that hypothesis of yours, all based on the assumption that this is indeed the case. Is that acceptable?"

"That would be fine," Komatsu replied. They were going to talk about this as indirectly as they could. This was not a bad sign. If they were planning not to let him out of here alive, they wouldn't go to the trouble.

"As an editor at a publishing house, you were in charge of publishing Eriko Fukada's *Air Chrysalis*. Am I correct?"

"You are," Komatsu admitted. This was common knowledge.

"Based on our understanding, there was some fraud involved in the publication. *Air Chrysalis* received a literary prize for debut novelists from a literary journal. But before the selection committee received the manuscript, a third party rewrote it considerably at your direction. After the work was secretly revised, it won the prize, was published as a book, and became a bestseller. Do I have my facts correct?"

"It depends on how you look at it," Komatsu said. "There are times when a submitted manuscript is rewritten, on advice of the editor – "

Buzzcut put his hand up to cut him off. "There's nothing dishonest about the author revising parts of the novel based on the editor's advice. You're right. But having a third party rewrite the work is unscrupulous. Not only that, but forming a phony company to distribute royalties – I don't know how this would be interpreted from a legal standpoint, but morally speaking these actions would be roundly condemned. It's inexcusable. Newspapers and magazines would have a field day over it, and your company's reputation would suffer. I'm sure you understand this very well, Mr. Komatsu. We know all the facts, and have incontrovertible proof we can reveal to the world. So it's best not to try to talk your way out of it. It's a waste of time, for both of us."

Komatsu nodded.

"If it did come to that, obviously you would have to resign from the company. Plus, you know that you would be black-balled from the field. There would be no place left for you in publishing. For legitimate work, at least."

"I imagine not," Komatsu said.

"But at this point only a limited number of people know the truth," Buzzcut said. "You, Eriko Fukada, Professor Ebisuno, and Tengo Kawana, who rewrote the book. And just a handful of others."

Komatsu chose his words carefully. "According to our working hypothesis, this *handful of others* would be members of Sakigake."

Buzzcut nodded, barely. "Yes. According to our hypothesis, that would be the case."

Buzzcut paused, allowing the hypothesis to sink in. And then he went on.

"And if that hypothesis is indeed true, then *they* can do whatever they want to you. They can keep you here as their guest of honor for as long as they like. No problem at all. Or, if they wanted to shorten the length of your stay, there are any number of other choices they can make – including ones that would be unpleasant for both sides. Either way, they have the power and the means. I believe you already have a pretty good grasp of that."

"I think I do," Komatsu replied.

"Good," Buzzcut said.

Buzzcut raised a finger, and Ponytail left the room. He soon returned with a phone. He plugged it into a jack on the wall and handed the phone to Komatsu. Buzzcut directed him to call his company.

"You have had a terrible cold and a fever and have been in bed for a few days. It doesn't look like you'll be able to come in to work for a while. Tell them that and then hang up."

Komatsu asked for one of his colleagues, briefly explained what he had to say, and hung up without responding to his questions. Buzzcut nodded and Ponytail unplugged the phone from the jack and took the phone and left the room. Buzzcut intently studied the back of his hands, then turned to Komatsu. There was a faint tinge of kindness in his voice.

"That's it for today," he said. "We'll talk again another day. Until then, please consider carefully what we have discussed."

The two of them left, and Komatsu spent the next ten days in silence, in that room. Three times a day the masked young man would bring in the mediocre meals. After the fourth day, Komatsu was given a change of clothes – a cotton pajama-like top and bottom – but until the very end, they didn't let him take a shower. The most he could do was wash his face in the tiny sink attached to the toilet. His sense of time's passage grew more uncertain.

Komatsu thought that he had been taken to the cult's headquarters in Yamanashi. He had seen it on TV. It was deep in the mountains, surrounded by a tall fence, like some independent realm. Escape, or finding help, was out of the question. If they did end up killing him (which must be what they had meant by an *unpleasant choice*), his body would never be found. He had never felt death so real, or so close.

Ten days after he had made that forced call to his company (most likely ten days, though he wouldn't bet on it), the same duo made another appearance. Buzzcut seemed thinner than before, which made his cheekbones all the more prominent.

His cold eyes were now bloodshot. As before, he sat down on the folding chair he had brought, across the table from Komatsu. He didn't say a word for a long time. He simply stared at Komatsu with his red eyes.

Ponytail looked the same. Again he stood, ramrod straight, in front of the door, his emotionless eyes fixed on an imaginary point in space. They were again dressed in black trousers and white shirts, most likely a sort of uniform.

"Let's pick up where we left off last time," Buzzcut finally said. "We were saying that we can do whatever we like with you."

Komatsu nodded. "Including choices that wouldn't be pleasant for either side."

"You really do have a great memory," Buzzcut said. "You are correct. An unpleasant outcome is looming."

Komatsu was silent. Buzzcut went on.

"*In theory*, that is. Practically speaking, *they* would much prefer not to make an extreme choice. If you were suddenly to disappear now, Mr. Komatsu, that would lead to unwanted complications. Just like it did when Eriko Fukada disappeared. There aren't many people who would be sad if you were gone, but you're a respected editor, prominent in your field. And I'm sure that if you fall behind in your alimony payments, your wife will have something to say about it. For *them*, this would not be a very favorable development."

Komatsu gave a dry cough and swallowed.

"They're not criticizing you personally, or trying to punish you. They understand that in publishing *Air Chrysalis* you weren't intending to attack a specific religious organization. At first you didn't even know the connection between the novel and that organization. You perpetrated this fraud for fun and out of ambition. And money became a factor, too, as things developed. It's very hard for a mere company employee to pay alimony and child support, isn't it? And you brought Tengo Kawana – an aspiring novelist and cram school instructor who didn't know anything about the circumstances – into the mix. The plan itself was smart, but your choice of the novel and the writer? Not so much. And things got more complicated than you imagined. You were like ordinary citizens who had wandered across the front lines and stepped into a minefield. You can't go forward, and can't go back. Am I correct in this, Mr. Komatsu?"

"That might sum it up, I suppose," Komatsu replied.

"There still seem to be some things you don't entirely understand," Buzzcut said, his eyes narrowing a fraction. "If you did, you wouldn't pretend that this has nothing to do with you. Let's make things crystal clear. You are, frankly, in the middle of a minefield."

Komatsu silently nodded.

Buzzcut closed his eyes, and ten seconds later opened them. "This situation has put you in a bind, but understand that it has created some real problems for *them* as well."

Komatsu took the plunge and spoke. "Do you mind if I ask you a question?"

"If it's something I can answer."

"By publishing *Air Chrysalis* we created a little trouble for the religious organization. Is that what you're saying?"

"More than a *little* trouble," Buzzcut said. He grimaced slightly. "The voice no longer speaks to them. Do you have any idea what that means?"

"No," Komatsu croaked, his voice dry.

"Fine. I can't explain any more to you than that. And it's better for you not to know. *The voice no longer speaks to them.* That's all I can tell you now." Buzzcut paused. "And this unhappy turn of events was brought about by the publication of *Air Chrysalis.*"

Komatsu posed a question. "And did Eriko Fukada and

Professor Ebisuno expect that by making *Air Chrysalis* public, they would bring about this *unhappy turn of events*?"

Buzzcut shook his head. "No, I don't think Professor Ebisuno knew things would turn out this way. It's unclear what Eriko Fukada's intentions were. Saying it was unintentional is just conjecture. But even if you assume it was intentional, I don't believe it was her intention."

"People read *Air Chrysalis* as a fantasy novel," Komatsu said. "A harmless, dreamy little tale written by a high school girl. Actually the novel was criticized quite a lot for being a bit too surreal. No one ever suspected that some great secret, or concrete information, was exposed in the pages of the book."

"I imagine you're right," Buzzcut said. "The vast majority of people would never notice. But that's not the issue. Those secrets should never have been made public. *In any form whatsoever.*"

Ponytail stood rooted to a spot in front of the door, staring at the wall, at some prospect that no one else could see.

"What *they* want is to get the voice back," Buzzcut said, choosing his words. "The well hasn't run dry. It has just sunk down deeper, where it can't be seen. It will be quite difficult to restore, but it can be done."

Buzzcut looked deep into Komatsu's eyes. He looked like he was measuring the depths of something inside, like eyeballing a room to see if a piece of furniture would fit.

"As I said earlier, all of you have wandered into a minefield. You can't go forward, and you can't go back. What *they* can do is show you the path, so you can get out safely. If they do, you'll have a narrow escape, and they'll peacefully manage to get rid of some bothersome intruders."

Buzzcut folded his arms.

"We would like you to quietly withdraw from all this. They aren't really concerned if you leave here in one piece. But it will present problems if we make a lot of noise here right now. So,

Mr. Komatsu, I will show you the way to retreat. I will guide you back to a safe place. What I ask for in return is the following: You must stop publishing *Air Chrysalis*. You won't print any more copies, or reprint it in paperback. And all advertising for the book will cease. And you will sever all connections with Eriko Fukada. What do you say? You have enough influence to handle that."

"It won't be easy, but maybe I can manage it," Komatsu said.

"Mr. Komatsu, we didn't bring you all the way here to talk about *maybes*." Buzzcut's eyes grew even redder and sharper. "We're not asking you to collect all the copies of the book that are out there. Do that, and the media would jump on the story. And we know your influence doesn't extend that far. We would just like you to quietly take care of things. We can't undo what has already happened. Once something's ruined, it can't go back to the way it was. What *they* would like is to remove this from the spotlight. Do you follow me?"

Komatsu nodded.

"Mr. Komatsu, as I have explained, there are several facts here that must not come to light. If they did, all those involved would suffer repercussions. So for the sake of both parties, we would like to conclude a truce. They will not hold you responsible beyond this point. Peace will be guaranteed. You will have nothing further to do with *Air Chrysalis*. This isn't such a bad deal, you know."

Komatsu thought it over. "All right. I will begin by making sure *Air Chrysalis* is no longer published. It may take some time, but I'll find a way. And speaking personally, I can put this entire matter out of my mind. I think Tengo Kawana can do the same. He wasn't enthusiastic about it from the very beginning. I got him involved against his will. His role in this is long past. And I don't think Eriko Fukada will be a problem. She said that she doesn't plan to write any more novels. Professor Ebisuno is the only one whose reaction I can't gauge.

Ultimately he wanted to determine if his friend, Tamotsu Fukada, was all right. He wants to know where he is now and what he's doing. Whatever I might tell him, he may continue to pursue information on Mr. Fukada."

"Tamotsu Fukada is dead," Buzzcut said. His voice was quiet, uninflected, but there was something terribly heavy within.

"*Dead?*" Komatsu asked.

"It happened recently," Buzzcut said. He took a deep breath and slowly exhaled. "He died of a heart attack. It was over in a moment, and he didn't suffer. Due to the circumstances, we didn't submit a notification of death, and we held the funeral secretly at our compound. For religious reasons the body was incinerated, the bones crushed and sprinkled in the nearby mountains. Legally, this constitutes desecration of a body, but it would be difficult to make a formal case against us. But this is the truth. We never lie when it comes to matters of life and death. I would like you to let Professor Ebisuno know about this."

"A natural death."

Buzzcut nodded deeply. "Mr. Fukada was a very important person for us. No – important is too trite a term to express what he was. He was a giant. His death has only been reported to a limited number of people. They grieved deeply for the loss. His wife – Eriko Fukada's mother – died several years ago of stomach cancer. She refused chemotherapy, and passed away within our treatment facility. Her husband, Tamotsu, cared for her to the end."

"Even so, you didn't file a notification of her death," Komatsu asked.

No words of denial came.

"And Tamotsu Fukada passed away recently."

"Correct," Buzzcut said.

"Was this after *Air Chrysalis* was published?"

Buzzcut's gaze went down to the table for a moment, then he raised his head and looked at Komatsu.

"That's right. Mr. Fukada passed away after *Air Chrysalis* was published."

"Are the two events related?" Komatsu dared to ask.

Buzzcut didn't say anything for a while, pondering how he should respond. Finally, as if he had made up his mind, he spoke. "Fine. I think it might be best to let Professor Ebisuno know all the facts, so he will understand. Mr. Tamotsu Fukada was the real Leader, the *one who hears the voice.* When his daughter, Eriko Fukada, published *Air Chrysalis,* the voice stopped speaking to him, and at that point Mr. Fukada himself put an end to his existence. It was a natural death. More precisely, he put an end to his own existence naturally."

"Eriko Fukada was the daughter of Leader," Komatsu murmured.

Buzzcut gave a concise, abbreviated nod.

"And Eriko Fukada ended up driving her father to his death," Komatsu continued.

Buzzcut nodded once more. "That is correct."

"But the religion still continues to exist."

"The religion does still exist," Buzzcut replied, and he stared at Komatsu with eyes like ancient pebbles frozen deep within a glacier. "Mr. Komatsu, the publication of *Air Chrysalis* has done more than a little damage to Sakigake. However, *they* are not thinking to punish you for this. There is nothing to be gained from punishing you at this point. They have a mission they must accomplish, and in order to do so, quiet isolation is required."

"So you want everyone to take a step back and forget it all happened."

"In a word, yes."

"Was it absolutely necessary to kidnap me in order to get this message across?"

Something akin to an expression crossed Buzzcut's face for the first time, a superficial emotion, located somewhere in the interstice between humor and sympathy. "They went to the trouble of bringing you here because *they* wanted you to understand the seriousness of the situation. They didn't want to do anything drastic, but if something is necessary, they don't hesitate. They wanted you to really feel this, viscerally. If all of you do not keep your promise, then something quite unpleasant will occur. Do you follow me?"

"I do," Komatsu replied.

"To tell you the truth, Mr. Komatsu, you were very fortunate. Because of all the heavy fog you may not have noticed this, but you were just a few inches from the edge of a cliff. It would be best if you remember this. At the moment *they* do not have the freedom to deal with you. There are many more pressing matters at hand. And in that sense, too, you are quite fortunate. So while this good fortune still continues . . ."

As he said this he turned his palms faceup, like someone checking to see if it was raining. Komatsu waited for his next words, but there weren't any. Now that he had finished speaking, Buzzcut looked exhausted. He slowly rose from his chair, folded it, and exited the cube-shaped room without so much as a glance back. The heavy door closed, the lock clicking shut. Komatsu was left all alone.

"They kept me locked away in that square little room for four more days. We had already discussed what was important. They had told me what they wanted to say and we had come to an agreement. So I couldn't see the point of keeping me there any longer. That duo never appeared again, and the young man in charge of me never uttered a word. I ate the same monotonous food, shaved with the electric razor, and spent my time staring at the ceiling and the walls. I slept when they turned off the lights, woke up when they switched them on.

And I pondered what Buzzcut had told me. What really struck me most was the fact that he said *we were fortunate*. Buzzcut was right. If these guys wanted to, they could do anything they wanted. They could be as cold-blooded as they liked. While I was locked up in there, I really came to believe this. I think they must have kept me locked up for four more days knowing that would be the result. They don't miss a beat – they're very meticulous."

Komatsu picked up his glass and took a sip of the highball.

"They drugged me again with chloroform or whatever, and when I woke up it was daybreak and I was lying on a bench in Jingu Gaien. It was the end of September, and the mornings were cold. Thanks to this I actually did wind up with a cold and a fever and I really was in bed for the next three days. But I guess I should consider myself fortunate if that's the worst that happened to me."

Komatsu seemed to be finished with his story. "Did you tell this to Professor Ebisuno?" Tengo asked.

"Yes, after I was released, and a few days after my fever broke, I went to his house on the mountain. I told him pretty much what I told you."

"What was his reaction?"

Komatsu drained the last drop of his highball and ordered a refill. He urged Tengo to do the same, but Tengo shook his head.

"Professor Ebisuno had me repeat the story over and over and asked a lot of detailed questions. I answered whatever I could. I could repeat the same story as many times as he wished. I mean, after I last spoke with Buzzcut, I was locked up alone for four days in that room. I had nobody to talk to, and plenty of time on my hands. So I went over what he had told me and was able to accurately remember all the details. Like I was a human tape recorder."

"But the part about Fuka-Eri's parents dying was just

something they claimed happened. Right?" Tengo asked.

"That's right. They insisted it happened, but there's no way to verify it. They didn't file a death notice. Still, considering the way Buzzcut sounded, it didn't seem like he was making it up. As he said, Sakigake considers people's lives and deaths a sacred thing. After I finished my story, Professor Ebisuno was silent for a time, thinking it over. He really thinks about things deeply, for a long time. Without a word, he stood up, left the room, and didn't come back for quite a while. I think he was trying to accept his friends' deaths, trying to understand them as inevitable. He may have already half expected that they were no longer of the world and had resigned himself to that fact. Still, actually being told that two close friends have died has got to hurt."

Tengo remembered the bare, spartan living room, the chilly, deep silence, the occasional sharp call of a bird outside the window. "So," he asked, "have we actually backed our way out of the minefield?"

A fresh highball was brought over. Komatsu took a sip.

"No conclusion was reached right then. Professor Ebisuno said he needed time to think. But what other choice do we have than to do what they told us? I got things rolling right away. At work I did everything I could and stopped them from printing additional copies of *Air Chrysalis*, so in effect it's out of print. There will be no paperback edition, either. The book already sold a lot of copies and made the company plenty of money, so they won't suffer a loss. In a large company like this you have to have meetings about it, the president has to sign off on it – but when I dangled before them the prospect of a scandal connected with a ghostwriter, the higher-ups were terrified and in the end did what I wanted. It looks like I'll be given the silent treatment from now on, but it's okay. I'm used to it."

"Did Professor Ebisuno accept what they said about Fuka-Eri's parents being dead?"

"I think so," Komatsu said. "But I imagine it will take some time for it to really sink in, for him to fully accept it. As far as I could tell, those guys were serious. They would make a few concessions, but I think they're hoping to avoid any more trouble. Which is why they resorted to kidnapping – they wanted to make absolutely sure we got the message. And they didn't need to tell me about how they secretly incinerated the bodies of Mr. and Mrs. Fukada. Even though it would be hard to prove, desecration of bodies is a major crime. But still they brought it up. They laid their cards on the table. That's why I think most of what Buzzcut told me was the truth. Maybe not every detail, but the overall picture, at least."

Tengo went over what Komatsu had told him. "Fuka-Eri's father was *the one who heard the voice*. A prophet, in other words. But when his daughter published *Air Chrysalis* and it became a bestseller, the voice stopped speaking to him, and as a result the father died a natural death."

"Or rather he put an end to his own existence *naturally*," Komatsu said.

"And so it's critical for Sakigake to gain a new prophet. If the voice stops speaking, then the religion's whole reason for existence is lost. So they don't have the time to worry about the likes of us. In a nutshell, that's the story, right?"

"I think so."

"*Air Chrysalis* contains information of critical importance to them. When it was published and became widely read, the voice went silent. But what critical information could the book be pointing toward?"

"During those last four days of my confinement I thought a lot about that," Komatsu said. "*Air Chrysalis* is a pretty short novel. In the story the world is filled with Little People. The ten-year-old girl who is the protagonist lives in an isolated community. The Little People secretly come out at night and create an air chrysalis. The girl's alter ego is inside the chrysalis and a mother-daughter relationship is formed – the *maza* and the *dohta*. There are two moons in that world, a large one and a small one, probably symbolizing the *maza* and the *dohta*. In the novel the protagonist – based on Fuka-Eri herself, I think – rejects being a *maza* and runs away from the community. The *dohta* is left behind. The novel doesn't tell us what happened to the *dohta* after that."

Tengo stared for a time at the ice melting in his glass.

"I wonder if the *one who hears the voice* needs the *dohta* as an intermediary," Tengo said. "It's through her that he can hear the voice for the first time, or perhaps through her that the voice is translated into comprehensible language. Both of them have to be there for the message of the voice to take its proper form. To borrow Fuka-Eri's terms, there's a Receiver and a Perceiver. But first of all the air chrysalis has to be created, because the *dohta* can only be born through it. And to create a *dohta*, the *proper maza* must be there."

"That's your opinion, Tengo."

Tengo shook his head. "I wouldn't call it an opinion. As I listened to you summarize the plot, I just thought that must be the way it is."

As he rewrote the novel, and afterward, Tengo had pondered the meaning of the *maza* and the *dohta*, but he was never quite able to grasp the overall picture. But now, as he talked with Komatsu, the pieces gradually fell into place. Though he still had questions: Why did an air chrysalis materialize above his father's bed in the hospital? And why was Aomame, as a young girl, inside?

"It's a fascinating system," Komatsu said. "But isn't it a problem for the *maza* to be separated from the *dohta*?"

"Without the *dohta*, it's hard to see the *maza* as a complete entity. As we saw with Fuka-Eri, it's difficult to pinpoint exactly what that means, but there is something missing – like a person who has lost his shadow. What the *dohta* is like without the *maza,* I have no idea. Probably they're both incomplete, because, ultimately, the *dohta* is nothing more than an alter ego. But in Fuka-Eri's case, even without the *maza* by her side, the *dohta* may have been able to fulfill her role as a kind of medium."

Komatsu's lips were stretched in a tight line for a while, then turned up slightly. "Are you thinking that everything in *Air Chrysalis* really took place?"

"I'm not saying that. I'm just making an assumption – hypothesizing that it's all real, and going from there."

"All right," Komatsu said. "So even if Fuka-Eri's alter ego goes far away from her body, she can still function as a medium."

"Which explains why Sakigake isn't forcing her to return, even if they know her whereabouts. Because in her case, even if the *maza* isn't nearby, the *dohta* can still fulfill her duties. Maybe their connection is that strong, even if they're far apart."

"Okay . . ."

Tengo continued, "I imagine that they have multiple *dohta*s. The Little People must use the chance to create many air chrysalises. They would be anxious if all they had was one Perceiver. Or the number of *dohta*s who can function correctly might be limited. Maybe there is one powerful, main *dohta,* and several weaker auxiliary *dohta*s, and they function collectively."

"So the *dohta* that Fuka-Eri left behind was the main *dohta,* the one who functions properly?"

"That seems possible. Throughout everything that has happened, Fuka-Eri has always been at the center, like the eye of a hurricane."

Komatsu narrowed his eyes and folded his hands together on the table. When he wanted to, he could really focus on an issue.

"You know, Tengo, I was thinking about this. Couldn't you hypothesize that the Fuka-Eri we met is actually the *dohta* and what was left behind at Sakigake was the *maza*?"

This came as a bit of a shock. The idea had never occurred to Tengo. For him, Fuka-Eri was an actual person. But put it that way, and it started to sound possible. I have no *periods*. So there's no chance I'll get *pregnant*. Fuka-Eri had announced this, after they had had intercourse that night. If she was nothing more than an alter ego, her inability to get pregnant would make sense. An alter ego can't reproduce itself – only the *maza* can do it. Still, Tengo couldn't accept that hypothesis – that it was possible he had had intercourse with her alter ego, not the real Fuka-Eri.

"Fuka-Eri has a distinct personality. And her own code of conduct. I sort of doubt an alter ego could have those."

"Exactly," Komatsu agreed. "If she has nothing else, Fuka-Eri does have her own distinct personality and code of conduct. I would have to agree with you on that one."

Still, Fuka-Eri was hiding a secret, a critical code hidden away inside this lovely girl, a code he had to crack. Tengo sensed this. Which one was the real person and which one the alter ego? Or was the whole notion of classifying into "real" and "alter ego" a mistake? Maybe Fuka-Eri was able, depending on the situation, to manipulate both her real self and her alter ego?

"There are several things I still don't understand," Komatsu said, resting his hands on the table and staring at them. For a middle-aged man, his fingers were long and slender.

"The voice has stopped speaking, the water in the well has dried up, the prophet has died. What will happen to the *dohta* after that? She won't follow him in death like widows do in India."

"When there's no more Receiver, there's no need for a Perceiver."

"If we take your hypothesis a step further, that is," Komatsu said. "Did Fuka-Eri know that would be the result when she wrote *Air Chrysalis*? That Sakigake man told me it wasn't intentional. At least it wasn't *her* intention. But how could he know this?"

"I don't know," Tengo said. "But I just can't see Fuka-Eri intentionally driving her father to his death. I think her father was facing death for some other reason. Maybe that's why she left in the first place. Or maybe she was hoping that her father would be freed from the voice. I'm just speculating, though, and I have nothing to back it up."

Komatsu considered this for a long time, wrinkles forming on either side of his nose. Finally he sighed and glanced around. "What a strange world. With each passing day, it's getting harder to know how much is just hypothetical and how much is real. Tell me, Tengo, as a novelist, what is your definition of reality?"

"When you prick a person with a needle, red blood comes out – that's the real world," Tengo replied.

"Then this is most definitely the real world," Komatsu said, and he rubbed his inner forearm. Pale veins rose to the surface. They were not very healthy-looking blood vessels – blood vessels damaged by years of drinking, smoking, an unhealthy lifestyle, and various literary intrigues. Komatsu drained the last of his highball and clinked the ice around in the empty glass.

"Could you go on with your hypothesis? It's getting more interesting."

"They are looking for a successor to the *one who hears the voice*," Tengo said. "But they also have to find a new, *properly functional dohta*. A new Receiver will need a new Perceiver."

"In other words, they need to find a new *maza* as well. And in order to do so, they have to make a new air chrysalis. That sounds like a pretty large-scale operation."

"Which is why they're so deadly serious."

"Exactly."

"But they can't be going about this blind," Tengo said. "They've got to have somebody in mind."

Komatsu nodded. "I got that impression, too. That's why they wanted to get rid of us as fast as they could – so we don't bother them anymore. I think we were quite a blot on their personal landscape."

"How so?"

Komatsu shook his head. He didn't know either.

"I wonder what message the voice told them until now. And what connection there is between the voice and the Little People."

Komatsu shook his head listlessly again. This, too, went beyond anything the two of them could imagine.

"Did you see the movie *2001: A Space Odyssey*?"

"I did," Tengo said.

"We're like the apes in the movie," Komatsu said. "The ones with shaggy black fur, screeching out some nonsense as they dance around the monolith."

A new pair of customers came into the bar, sat down at the counter like they were regulars, and ordered cocktails.

"There's one thing we can say for sure," Komatsu said, sounding like he wanted to wind things down. "Your hypothesis is convincing. It makes sense. I always really enjoy having these talks with you. But we're going to back out of this scary minefield, and probably never see Fuka-Eri or Professor Ebisuno again. *Air Chrysalis* is nothing more than a harmless fantasy novel, with not a single piece of concrete information in it. And what that voice is, and what message it's transmitting, have nothing to do with us. We need to leave it that way."

"Get off the boat and get back to life onshore."

Komatsu nodded. "You got it. I'll go to work every day, gathering manuscripts that don't make a difference one way or another in order to publish them in a literary journal. You will go to cram school and teach math to promising young people, and in between teaching, you'll write novels. We'll each go back to our own peaceful, mundane lives. No rapids, no waterfalls. We'll quietly grow old. Any objection?"

"We don't have any other choice, do we?"

Komatsu stretched out the wrinkles next to his nose with his finger. "That's right. We have no other choice. I can tell you this – I don't want to ever be kidnapped again. Being locked up in that room once is more than enough. If there were a next time, I might not see the light of day. Just the thought of meeting that duo again makes my heart quake. They only need to glare at you and you would keel over."

Komatsu turned to face the bar and signaled with his glass for a third highball. He stuck a fresh cigarette in his mouth.

"But why haven't you told me this until now? It has been quite some time since the kidnapping, over two months. You should have told me earlier."

"I don't know," Komatsu said, slightly inclining his head. "You're right. I was thinking I should tell you, but I kept putting it off. I'm not sure why. Maybe I had a guilty conscience."

"Guilty conscience?" Tengo said, surprised. He had never expected to hear Komatsu say that.

"Even I can have a guilty conscience," Komatsu said.

"About what?"

Komatsu didn't reply. He narrowed his eyes and rolled the unlit cigarette around between his lips.

"Does Fuka-Eri know her parents have died?" Tengo asked.

"I think she probably does. I imagine at some point Professor Ebisuno told her about it."

Tengo nodded. Fuka-Eri must have known about it a long time ago. He had a distinct feeling she did. He was the only one who hadn't been told.

"So we get out of the boat and return to our lives onshore," Tengo repeated.

"That's right. We edge away from the minefield."

"But even if we want to do that, do you think we can go back to our old lives that easily?"

"All we can do is try," Komatsu said. He struck a match and lit the cigarette. "What specifically bothers you?"

"Lots of things around us are already starting to fall into strange patterns. Some things have already been transformed, and it may not be easy for them to go back the way they were."

"Even if our lives are on the line?"

Tengo gave an ambiguous shake of his head. He had been feeling for some time that he was caught up in a strong current, one that never wavered. And that current was dragging him off to some unknown place. But he couldn't really explain it to Komatsu.

Tengo didn't reveal to Komatsu that the novel he was writing now carried on the world in *Air Chrysalis*. Komatsu probably wouldn't welcome the news. And Sakigake would certainly be less than pleased. If he wasn't careful, he might step into a different minefield, or get the people around him mixed up in it. But a narrative takes its own direction, and continues on, almost automatically. And whether he liked it or not, Tengo was a part of that world. To him, this was no longer a fictional world. This was the real world, where red blood spurts out when you slice open your skin with a knife. And in the sky in this world, there were two moons, side by side.

CHAPTER 19

Ushikawa

WHAT HE CAN DO
THAT MOST PEOPLE CAN'T

It was a quiet, windless Thursday morning. Ushikawa woke as usual before six and washed his face with cold water. He brushed his teeth as he listened to the NHK news on the radio, and he shaved with the electric razor. He boiled water in a pot, made instant ramen, and, after he finished eating, drank a cup of instant coffee. He rolled up his sleeping bag, stowed it in the closet, and sat down at the window in front of his camera. The eastern sky was beginning to grow light. It looked like it was going to be a warm day.

The faces of all the people who left for work in the morning were etched in his mind. There was no need to take any more photos. From seven to eight thirty they hurried out of the apartment building to the station – the usual suspects. Ushikawa heard the lively voices of a group of elementary school pupils heading off for school. The children's voices reminded him of when his daughters were little. His daughters had thoroughly enjoyed elementary school. They took piano and ballet lessons, and had lots of friends. To the very end, Ushikawa had found it hard to accept that he had these ordinary, happy kids. How could someone like him possibly be the father of children like these?

After the morning rush, almost no one came in or out of the

building. The children's lively voices had disappeared. Ushikawa laid aside the remote control for the shutter, leaned against the wall, smoked a cigarette, and kept an eye on the entrance through a gap in the curtain. As always, just after ten a.m., the mailman came on his small red motorcycle and adeptly sorted the mail into all the boxes. From what Ushikawa could make out, half of it was junk mail, stuff that would be tossed away, unopened. As the sun rose higher, the temperature went up, and most of the people along the street took off their coats.

It was after eleven when Fuka-Eri appeared at the entrance to the building. She wore the same black turtleneck as before, a gray short coat, jeans, sneakers, and dark sunglasses. And an oversized green shoulder bag slung diagonally across her shoulder. The bag was bulging with, no doubt, all sorts of things. Ushikawa left the wall he was leaning against, went over to the camera on the tripod, and squinted through the viewfinder.

The girl was leaving there, that much he understood. She had stuffed all her belongings in that bag and was setting off for somewhere else. She would never be back there again. He could sense it. *Maybe she decided to leave here,* he thought, *because she noticed I was staking out the place.* The thought made his heart race.

As she stepped out of the entrance, she came to a halt and stared up at the sky like she had done before, searching for something among the tangle of electric lines and the transformers. Her sunglasses caught the light and glittered. Had she found what she was looking for? Or maybe not? He couldn't read her expression through the sunglasses. She must have stood there, frozen, for a good thirty seconds, gazing up at the sky. Then, almost as an afterthought, she turned her head and looked straight at the window behind which Ushikawa was hiding. She took off her sunglasses and stuck them in a coat pocket. She frowned and focused her gaze right on the camouflaged telephoto lens. *She knows,* Ushikawa thought once again. *The girl knows I'm hiding in here, that she's being secretly watched.* And she was looking at him in the opposite direction, watching Ushikawa through the lens and back through the viewfinder. Like water flowing backward though a curved pipe. Ushikawa felt the flesh crawl on both his arms.

Fuka-Eri blinked every few moments. Like independent, silent living creatures, her eyelids slowly went up and down in a studied way. Nothing else moved. She stood there like some lofty bird with neck twisted, staring straight at Ushikawa. He couldn't pull his eyes away from her. It felt as if the entire world had come to a momentary halt. There was no wind, and sounds no longer made the air vibrate.

Finally Fuka-Eri stopped looking at him. She raised her head again and gazed up at the sky, as she had done a moment before. This time, though, she stopped after a couple of seconds. Her expression was unchanged. She took the dark sunglasses out of her pocket, put them on again, and headed toward the street. She walked with a smooth, unhesitant stride.

I should go out and follow her. Tengo isn't back yet, and I have the time to find out where she's going. It couldn't hurt to find out where she's moving to. But somehow Ushikawa couldn't stand up from the floor. His body was numb. That sharp gaze she had sent through the viewfinder had robbed him of the strength he needed to take action.

It's okay, Ushikawa told himself as he sat there on the floor. *Aomame is the one I have to locate. Eriko Fukada is a fascinating girl, but she's not my main priority here. She's just a supporting actress. If she's leaving, why not just let her go?*

Once on the main street, Fuka-Eri hurried off toward the station. She didn't look back. Through the gap in the sun-bleached curtains, Ushikawa watched as she went. Once the green shoulder bag, swinging back and forth, disappeared from view, he practically crawled away from the camera and leaned against the wall again, waiting for his strength to return.

He took out a Seven Stars, lit it, and inhaled the smoke deeply. But the cigarette was tasteless.

His strength didn't return. His arms and legs still felt numb. He suddenly realized a strange space had formed inside him, a kind of pure hollow. This space signified a simple lack, a nothingness. Ushikawa sat there in the midst of this unknown void, unable to rise. He felt a dull pain in his chest – not exactly pain, but more like the difference in air pressure at the point where the material and the immaterial meet.

He sat for a long time at the bottom of that void, leaning against the wall, smoking tasteless cigarettes. *When that girl left, she left behind this void. No, maybe not. Maybe she just showed me something that was already there, inside me.*

Ushikawa knew that Eriko Fukada had literally shaken him to his core. Her unwavering, pointed gaze shook him not only physically, but to the center of his being, like someone who had fallen passionately in love. He had never felt this way before in his life.

No, that can't be right, he thought. *Why should I be in love with that girl? We have to be the most ill-matched pair one could possibly imagine.* He didn't need to check himself out in the mirror to confirm this. But it wasn't just about looks. *In every possible aspect,* he decided, *no one is further removed from her than me.* Sexually, he wasn't attracted to her. As far as sexual desire was concerned, a couple of times a month Ushikawa called a prostitute he knew, and that was enough. Call her up, have her over to a hotel room, and have sex – like going to the barber.

It had to be something on a more spiritual level, Ushikawa concluded. It was hard to accept, but Ushikawa and that lovely girl had – while staring at each other through opposite ends of the camouflaged telephoto lens – reached a kind of understanding that emanated from the deepest, darkest recesses of their beings. It had happened in an instant, yet they had laid bare their very souls. And then she had gone off, leaving Ushikawa behind, alone in this void.

The girl knew I was secretly observing her through this tele-photo lens, and she must have known, too, that I followed her to the supermarket near the station. She never looked back even once then, but she definitely knew I was there. But he hadn't seen any criticism in her eyes. Ushikawa felt that somehow, in some far-off, deep place, she had understood him.

The girl had shown up, then left. *We came from different directions, our paths happened to cross, our eyes met for an instant, then we moved off in different directions once more. I probably won't ever run across Eriko Fukada again.*

Leaning against the wall, Ushikawa looked through the gap in the curtain and watched people coming and going. Maybe Fuka-Eri would come back. Maybe she would remember something important she had left back in the apartment. But she didn't. She had made up her mind to move on to some-where else, and she would never return.

Ushikawa spent the afternoon feeling deeply powerless. This sense of impotence was formless, weightless. His blood moved slowly, sluggishly, through his veins. It was as if his vision were covered by a fine mist, while the joints in his arms and legs felt creaky and dull. When he shut his eyes, the ache of her gaze stabbed at his ribs, the ache rolling in and out like gentle waves at the shore, rolling in again, then receding. Sometimes the pain was so great it made him wince. At the same time, though, Ushikawa realized it gave him a warm feeling, like nothing he had ever experienced.

His wife and two daughters, his snug little house with a lawn in Chuorinkan – they had never made him feel this warm. He had always had something like a clod of frozen dirt stuck in his heart – a hard, cold core he had always lived with. He had never even felt it as cold. For him this was the *normal tempera-ture*. Even so, Fuka-Eri's gaze had, if even for a moment, melted that icy core. And it brought on the dull ache. The warmth and the pain came as a pair, and unless he accepted the pain, he wouldn't feel the warmth. It was a kind of trade-off.

In a little sunny spot, Ushikawa experienced the pain and the warmth simultaneously. Quietly, without moving a muscle. It was a calm, peaceful winter's day. People on the street passed through the delicate sunshine as they strolled by, but the sun was steadily moving west, hidden in the shadow of the building, and the little pool of sunlight he was in soon disappeared. The warmth of the afternoon was gone, and the cold of the night was gathering around him.

Ushikawa sighed deeply and reluctantly peeled himself away from the wall. His body still had a lingering numbness, but not enough to stop him from moving about the room. He finally rose to his feet, stretched his limbs, and moved his short, thick neck around to work out the kinks. He balled his fists, then stretched out his fingers, again and again. Then he got down on the tatami and did his usual stretching exercises. All his joints crackled dully, and his muscles slowly regained their normal suppleness.

It was now the time of day when people came back from work and school. *I need to continue to keep a watch over them,* he told himself. *This isn't a question of whether I want to or not, or whether it's the right thing to do. Once I start something, I have to see it through.*

Ushikawa sat down again behind the camera. It was completely dark outside now, and the light at the entrance had come on. *It must be on a timer,* he thought. Like nameless birds returning to their shabby nests, people stepped into the entrance. Tengo Kawana wasn't among them, but Ushikawa figured he would be back before long. He couldn't take care of his sick father forever. Most likely he would be back in Tokyo before the new week started, so he could return to work. Within a few days – or maybe even today or tomorrow.

I may well be just a cheerless, grubby little creature, a bug on the damp underside of a rock. So be it – I'll be the first to admit it. But I'm a relentlessly capable, patient, tenacious bug. I don't give up easily. Once I get ahold of a clue, I pursue it to the bitter end. I'll climb up the highest wall you've got. I have to get back that cold core inside me. Right now, that's exactly what I need.

Ushikawa rubbed his hands together in front of the camera, and checked to make sure all ten fingers were working properly.

There are lots of things ordinary people can do that I can't. That's for sure. Playing tennis, skiing, for instance. Working in a company, having a happy family. On the other hand, there are a few things I can do that most other people can't. And I do these few things very, very well. I'm not expecting applause or for people to shower me with coins. But I do need to show the world what I'm capable of.

At nine thirty Ushikawa ended his surveillance for the day. He heated a can of chicken soup over the portable stove and carefully sipped it with a spoon. He ate two cold rolls, then polished off an apple, peel and all. He peed, brushed his teeth, spread out his sleeping bag, stripped down to his underwear, and snuggled inside. He zipped the bag up to his neck and curled up like a bug.

And thus Ushikawa's day was over. It hadn't been a very productive day. All he had been able to do was watch Fuka-Eri exit the building with all her belongings. He didn't know where she had gone. *Somewhere,* but *where*? Inside the sleeping bag he shook his head. Wherever she went, it didn't concern him. After a time his frozen body warmed up, his mind faded, and he fell into a deep sleep. Once more, the tiny frozen core occupied a solid place in his soul.

Nothing much happened the next day. Two days later was Saturday, another warm, peaceful day. Most people slept in during the morning. Ushikawa, though, sat by the window, listening to a tiny radio – the news, traffic updates, the weather report.

Just before ten a large crow flew up and stood at the empty front steps of the building. The crow looked around meticulously, moving its head a few times like it was nodding. It bobbed its thick large beak up and down, its brilliant black feathers glistening in the sunlight. The mailman pulled up on his small red motorcycle and the crow reluctantly spread its wings wide and flew off. As it flew away it squawked once. After the mailman had sorted all the mail into the mailboxes and left, a flock of sparrows twittered over. They bustled around the entrance but found nothing worthwhile and flew away. Next it was a striped cat's turn. He had on a flea collar and probably belonged to a neighbor. Ushikawa had never seen the cat before. The cat peed in the dried-up flower bed, sniffed the result, and – apparently displeased with what it found – twitched its whiskers, as if it were bored. Tail up, it disappeared behind the building.

In the morning several residents exited the building. From the way they were dressed, it looked like they were going out for a relaxed day, or going shopping in the neighborhood – one or the other. Ushikawa knew almost all their faces by now, but he had not a speck of interest in their personalities or private lives. He never even tried to imagine them.

Your own lives are surely very important to each one of you. Very precious to you. I get it. But to me they don't matter one way or the other. To me, you're just flimsy paper dolls walking across a stage. There's only one thing I'm asking of all of you – remain paper dolls and don't interfere with my job here.

"Isn't that right, Mrs. Pear?" He had given the woman currently passing this nickname, because she was pear shaped with a huge rear end. "You're just a cutout paper doll. You're not real. Do you realize that? Though you are a bit on the chunky side for a paper doll."

As he thought this, though, everything in the scene before him began to seem meaningless, to *not matter one way or the other*. Maybe the scene in front of him didn't exist in the first place. Maybe *he* was the one being deceived, by cutout people who didn't really exist. Ushikawa grew uneasy. Being locked up in this empty apartment, day after day, spying on people, must be getting to him – something that would definitely get on a person's nerves. He decided to verbalize his thoughts, to pull himself out of this funk.

"G'morning, there, Long Ears," he said, looking through the viewfinder and addressing a tall, thin old man. The tips of the old man's ears stuck out like horns from beneath his white hair. "Out for a walk? Walking's good for you. It's nice out today, so have a good time. I would love to take a walk and stretch my limbs a bit, but I'm stuck here keeping watch over this crummy entrance day after day."

The old man had on a cardigan and wool trousers, and had excellent posture. He would look perfect taking a faithful white dog out for a walk, but pets weren't allowed in the building. Once the old man was gone, Ushikawa was suddenly struck by a sense of impotence. *This surveillance is going to end up being a waste of time*, he decided. *My intuition is worthless, and all the hours I've spent in this vacant room are leading me exactly nowhere. All I have to show for it is a set of frayed nerves, worn away like the bald head of a Jizo statue that passing children rub for good luck.*

After twelve Ushikawa ate an apple and some cheese and crackers, and a rice ball with pickled plum inside. He then leaned back against the wall and fell asleep. It was a short, dreamless sleep, yet when he awoke he couldn't remember where he was. His memory was a perfectly square, perfectly empty box. The only thing in the box was empty space. Ushikawa gazed around the space. He found it wasn't just a void, but a dim room – empty, cold, without a stick of furniture.

He didn't recognize the place. There was an apple core on an unfolded newspaper next to him. Ushikawa felt confused. *Why am I in such a weird place?*

Finally it came to him, and he remembered what he had been doing: staking out the entrance to Tengo's apartment. *That's right. That's why I have this single-lens reflex Minolta with a telephoto lens.* He remembered the old man with white hair and long ears out for a walk alone. Like birds flying home to their nests at twilight, memories gradually returned to the empty box. And two solid facts emerged:

1 Eriko Fukada has left.

2 Tengo Kawana hasn't come back yet.

No one was in Tengo Kawana's third-floor apartment. The curtains were drawn, and silence enveloped the deserted space. Other than the compressor of the fridge switching on from time to time, nothing disturbed the silence. Ushikawa let his imagination wander over the scene. Imagining a deserted room was a lot like imagining the world after death. Suddenly he remembered the NHK fee collector and his obsessive knocking. He had kept constant watch but never saw any trace that this mysterious man had left the building. *Could he be a resident here? Or was it someone who lived here who liked to pretend to be a fee collector to harass the other residents? If the latter, what would possibly be the point?* This was a very morbid theory, but what else could explain such a strange situation? Ushikawa had no idea.

Tengo Kawana showed up at the entrance to the apartment building just before four that afternoon. He wore an old windbreaker with the collar turned up, a navy-blue baseball cap, and a travel bag slung over his shoulder. He didn't pause at the entrance, didn't glance around, and went straight inside. Ushikawa's mind was still a bit foggy, but he couldn't miss that large figure.

"Welcome back, Mr. Kawana," Ushikawa muttered aloud, and snapped three photos with the motor-drive camera. "How's your father doing? You must be exhausted. Please rest up. Nice to come home, isn't it, even to a miserable place like this. By the way, Eriko Fukada moved out, with all her belongings, while you were gone."

But his voice didn't reach Tengo. He was just muttering to himself. Ushikawa glanced at his watch and wrote a memo in his notebook. *3:56 p.m., Tengo Kawana back home from trip.*

At the same moment that Tengo appeared at the entrance, a door somewhere opened wide and Ushikawa felt reality returning. Like air rushing into a vacuum, his nerves were instantly sharp, his body filled with a fresh vitality. He was again a useful part of the outside world. There was a satisfying click as things fell into place. His circulation sped up, and just the right amount of adrenaline surged through his body. *Good, this is how it should be. This is the way I'm supposed to be, the way the world is supposed to be.*

It was after seven p.m. when Tengo appeared at the entrance again. The wind had picked up after sunset, and the temperature had dropped. Tengo wore a sweater under a windbreaker with faded jeans. He stepped outside and stood there, looking around, but he didn't see anything. He glanced at where Ushikawa was hiding, but didn't pick out the observer. *He's different from Eriko Fukada,* Ushikawa thought. *She's special. She can see what others can't. But you, Tengo – for better or worse you're an ordinary person. You can't see me sitting here.*

Seeing that nothing had changed outside, Tengo zipped his jacket up to his neck, stuck his hands in his pockets, and walked out onto the main road. Ushikawa hurriedly put on his knit cap, wrapped the muffler around his neck, slipped on his shoes, and went out to follow Tengo.

Tengo strolled slowly down the street and turned around to look behind him a few times, but Ushikawa was careful and Tengo didn't see him. Tengo seemed to have something on his mind. Perhaps he was thinking about Fuka-Eri being gone. He was apparently heading toward the station. Maybe he was going to take a train somewhere? That would make tailing him difficult. The station was well lit, and on a Saturday night there wouldn't be many passengers. Ushikawa would be extremely conspicuous. In that case, it would be smarter to give up.

But Tengo wasn't heading toward the station. He walked for a while and then turned down a nearly deserted street and came to a halt in front of a bar named Mugiatama. It was a bar for young people, by the look of it. Tengo glanced at his watch to check the time, stood there pondering for a few seconds, then went inside. *Mugiatama,* Ushikawa thought. He shook his head. *What a stupid name for a bar.*

Ushikawa hid in the shadow of a telephone pole and checked out his surroundings. Tengo was probably going to have a couple of drinks there and a bite to eat, so it would take at least a half hour. Worst-case scenario, Ushikawa would have to stay put for an hour. He looked around for a good place nearby to kill time while he watched the people going in and out of the bar. Unfortunately, though, there was just a milk distributor, a small Tenrikyo meeting hall, and a rice wholesaler, and all of them were closed. *Man, I never get a break,* he thought. The strong northwest wind blew the clouds swiftly by. The warmth of the daytime seemed like a dream now. Ushikawa wasn't relishing the idea of standing in the freezing cold for thirty minutes to an hour, doing nothing.

Maybe I should give it up. Tengo's just having a meal here. There is no need to go to all the trouble of shadowing him. Ushikawa considered popping in to some place himself, having a hot meal, then going home. Tengo would come back home before long. That was a very attractive choice. Ushikawa pictured himself in a cozy little restaurant, enjoying a piping hot bowl of *oyakodon* – rice topped with chicken and eggs. These last few days he hadn't eaten anything worth mentioning. Some hot sake would hit the spot too. In this cold, one step outside and you'll sober up quick.

But another scenario came to him. Tengo might be meeting somebody at Mugiatama. When Tengo left his apartment, he went straight there, and he checked his watch just before he went in. Someone might be waiting for him inside, or might be on his way. If that was the case, Ushikawa had to know who this person was. His ears might freeze off, but he had to stand watch and see who went into the bar. He resigned himself to this, wiping the picture of *oyakodon* and hot sake from his mind.

The person he's meeting might be Fuka-Eri. Or Aomame. Ushikawa pulled himself together. *After all, perseverance is my strong point.* If there was a glimmer of hope, he clung to it desperately. The rain could pelt him, the wind could blow, he could be burned by the sun and beaten with a stick, but he would never let go. Once you let go, you never know when you will get ahold of it again. He knew full well there were more painful things than this in the world – a thought that helped him endure his own suffering.

He leaned against the wall, in the shadows of the telephone pole and a sign advertising the Japanese Communist Party, and kept a sharp watch over the front door of Mugiatama. He wrapped the green muffler up to his nose and stuck his hands inside the pockets of his pea coat. Other than occasionally extracting a tissue from his pocket to blow his nose, he didn't move an inch. Announcements over the PA system at Koenji Station would filter over, on the wind, from time to time. Some pedestrians looked nervous when they saw Ushikawa huddled in the shadows, and hurried past. Since it was dark, though, they couldn't make out his features. His stocky frame loomed in the shadows like some ominous ornament and sent people scurrying away in fright.

What could Tengo be drinking and eating in there? The more he thought about it, the hungrier, and colder, he got. But he couldn't help imagining it. *Anything's fine – doesn't have to be hot sake or* oyakodon. *I just want to go someplace warm and have a regular meal. But if I can stand being out here in the cold, I can take anything.*

Ushikawa had no choice. There was no other path for him to take than this one, freezing in the cold wind until Tengo finished his meal. Ushikawa thought about his home in Chuo-rinkan, and the dining table there. There must have been hot meals on that table every day, but he couldn't recall them. *What in the world did I eat back then?* It was like something out of antiquity. Long, long ago, a fifteen-minute walk from Chuo-rinkan Station on the Odakyu Line, there had been a newly built house and a warm, inviting dinner table. Two little girls played piano, and a small pedigreed puppy scampered about the tiny garden and lawn.

Tengo came out of the bar thirty-five minutes later. Not bad. It could have been a lot worse, Ushikawa reassured himself. The thirty-five minutes had been terrible, but it was certainly better than an awful hour and a half. His body was chilled, but at least his ears hadn't frozen. While Tengo was in the bar, there was no one going in or out of Mugiatama who caught Ushikawa's attention. Just one couple went inside, and no one came out. Tengo must have just had a few drinks and a light meal. Keeping the same distance as before, Ushikawa followed behind him. Tengo walked down the same street, most likely headed back to his apartment.

But Tengo turned off this street and headed down a road

that Ushikawa had never been on before. It looked like Tengo was not on his way home after all. Ushikawa was convinced that he was still lost in thought, maybe even more so than before. He didn't glance back this time. Ushikawa kept track of the scenery passing by, checked the street signs, trying to memorize the route so he could retrace it later on. Ushikawa wasn't familiar with this area, but from the increasing buzz of traffic, like the rushing of a river, he surmised they must be getting closer to the Ring Road. Before long Tengo picked up the pace. Getting closer to his destination, perhaps.

Not bad. So this guy is heading somewhere. It was worth tailing him after all.

Tengo quickly cut through a residential street. It was a Saturday night, with a cold wind blowing, so everyone else was inside, in front of the TV, enjoying a hot drink. The street was practically deserted. Ushikawa followed behind Tengo, making sure to keep enough distance between them. Tengo was an easy type of person to shadow. He was tall and big-boned, and wouldn't get lost in a crowd. He just forged on ahead and didn't get sidetracked. He was always looking slightly down, thinking. He was essentially a straightforward, honest man, not the type to hide anything. *Totally different from me,* Ushikawa thought.

Ushikawa's wife had also liked to hide things. No – it wasn't that she liked to hide things, she couldn't help it. Ask her what time it was, and she probably wouldn't tell you the correct time. Ushikawa wasn't like this. He only hid things when it was necessary, only when it pertained to work. If someone asked him the time and there was no reason for him to be dishonest, he would tell them, and be nice about it. Not like his wife. She even lied about her age, shaving four years off. When they submitted the documents for their marriage license he found out how old she really was, but pretended not to notice. Ushikawa couldn't fathom why she had to lie about something that was going to come out anyway. Who cared if his wife happened to be seven years older?

As they got even farther from the station, there were fewer people on the street. Eventually Tengo turned into a little park, a nothing little playground in one corner of a residential district. The park was deserted. *Of course it is,* Ushikawa thought. *Who feels like spending time in a playground on a cold, windy December night?* Tengo passed under the cold light of a mercury-vapor lamp and headed straight toward the slide. He stepped onto it and climbed to the top.

Ushikawa hid behind a phone booth and kept an eye on Tengo. A *slide*? Ushikawa frowned. Why does a grown man have to climb to the top of a slide on a freezing cold night like this? This wasn't near Tengo's apartment. There must be some reason he would go out of his way to come here. It wasn't exactly the most appealing playground. It was cramped and shabby. In addition to the slide there were two swings, a small jungle gym, and a sandbox. A single mercury-vapor lamp that looked like it had illuminated the end of the world more than a few times, a single crude, leafless zelkova tree. A locked-up public toilet was the perfect canvas for graffiti. There was not a thing in this park to warm people's hearts, or to stimulate the imagination. Perhaps on a bracing May afternoon there might be something. But on a windy December night? Forget it.

Was Tengo meeting up with somebody here? Waiting for somebody to show? Ushikawa didn't think so. Tengo didn't give any signs to indicate that he was looking for someone. When he entered the park, he ignored all the other equipment. The only thing on his mind seemed to be the slide. *Tengo came here to climb up that slide.*

Maybe he had always liked to sit on top of slides when he needed to think. Maybe the top of a slide in a park at night was the perfect place to think about the plot of the novel he was writing, or mathematical formulas. Maybe the darker it was, the colder the wind blew, the shabbier the park, the better he could think. What or how novelists (or mathematicians) thought was way beyond anything Ushikawa could imagine. His practical mind told him that he had to stay put, patiently keeping an eye on Tengo. His watch showed exactly eight p.m.

Tengo sat down on top of the slide, as if folding his large frame. He looked up at the sky. He moved his head back and forth, then settled on a single spot, and gazed upward, his head still.

Ushikawa recalled a sentimental old pop song by Kyu Saka-moto. It began: *Look up at the night sky / see the little stars.* He didn't know how the rest of it went and he really didn't care to know. Sentiment and a sense of justice were Ushikawa's two weakest areas. Up on top of the slide, was Tengo feeling senti-mental as he gazed at the stars?

Ushikawa tried looking up at the sky himself, but he couldn't see any stars. Koenji, Suginami Ward, Tokyo, was not the best place to observe the night sky. Neon signs and lights along the street dyed the whole sky a weird color. Some people, if they squinted hard, might be able to make out a few stars, but that would require extraordinary vision and concentration. On top of that, the clouds tonight were blowing hard across the sky. Still, Tengo sat motionless on top of the slide, his eyes on a fixed point in the sky.

What a pain in the butt this guy is, Ushikawa decided. What possible reason could there be to sit on a slide, gaze up at the sky, and ponder things on a windy winter night like this? Not that he had any right to criticize Tengo. Ushikawa had taken it upon himself, after all, to secretly observe Tengo, and shadow him. Tengo was a free citizen and had every right to look at what he wanted, where he wanted, the whole year round.

Still, it's damn cold. He had needed to pee for some time, but had held it in. The public toilet was locked, though, and even in a deserted place like this he couldn't very well just pee next to a phone booth. *Come on,* he thought, stamping his feet, *can't you just get up and leave already? You might be lost in thought, overtaken by sentiment, deep into your astronomical observations, but Tengo – you gotta be freezing too. Time to go back to your place and warm up, don't you think? Neither of us has anyone waiting for us, but it's still a hell of a lot better than hanging out here and freezing our rear ends off.*

Tengo didn't seem about to get up, though. He finally stopped gazing at the sky, and he turned his attention to the apartment building across the way. It was a new condo, six stories tall, with lights on in about half the windows. Tengo stared at the building. Ushikawa did the same but found nothing that caught his attention. It was just an ordinary condo. It was not an exclusive building, but fairly high-class nonetheless. High-quality design, expensive tile exterior. The entrance was beautiful and well lit. It was a different animal entirely from the cheap, slated-to-be-torn-down place that Tengo called home.

As he gazed up at the condo, was Tengo wishing he could live in a place like that? Ushikawa didn't think so. As far as Ushikawa knew, Tengo wasn't the type to care about where he lived. Just like he didn't care much about clothes. Most likely he was happy with his shabby apartment. A roof over your head and a place to keep out of the cold – that was enough for him. Whatever was running through his head up there on the slide must be something else.

After Tengo had looked at all the windows in the condo, he turned his gaze once more to the sky. Ushikawa followed suit. From where he was hidden, the branches of the zelkova tree, the electric lines, and the other buildings got in the way. He could only see half the sky. What particular point in the sky Tengo was looking at wasn't at all clear. Countless clouds ceaselessly scudded across the sky like some overwhelming army bearing down on them.

Eventually, Tengo stood up and silently climbed down from the slide, like a pilot having just landed after a rough solo flight at night. He cut across the playground and left. Ushikawa hesitated, then decided not to follow him. Most likely Tengo was on his way back to his place. Plus Ushikawa had to pee like crazy. After he saw Tengo disappear, he went into the playground, hustled behind the public toilet, and in the darkness where no one could see him, he peed into a bush. His bladder was ready to burst.

He finally finished peeing – the operation taking as long as it would take a long freight train to cross a bridge – zipped up his pants, shut his eyes, and gave a deep sigh of relief. His watch showed 8:17. Tengo had been on top of the slide for about fifteen minutes. Ushikawa checked again that Tengo wasn't around and headed toward the slide. He clambered up the ladder with his short, bandy legs, sat down on the very top of the freezing slide, and looked up. What could he have been staring at so intently?

Ushikawa had pretty good eyesight. Astigmatism made his eyes a bit out of balance, but generally he could get by every day without glasses. Still, no matter how hard he looked, he couldn't make out a single star. What caught his attention instead was the large moon in the sky, about two-thirds full. Its dark, bruised exterior was clearly exposed between the clouds. Your typical winter moon. Cold, pale, full of ancient mysteries and inklings. Unblinking like the eyes of the dead, it hung there, silent, in the sky.

Ushikawa gulped. For a while, he forgot to breathe. Through a break in the clouds, there was another moon, a little way apart from the first one. This was much smaller than the original moon, slightly warped in shape, and green, like it had moss growing on it. But it was undoubtedly a moon. No star was that big. And it couldn't be a satellite. Yet there it was, pasted onto the night sky.

Ushikawa shut his eyes, then a few seconds later opened them again. This must be an illusion. *That kind of thing can't be there.* But no matter how many times he opened and closed his eyes, the little moon was still in the sky. Passing clouds hid it occasionally, but once they passed by, there it was, in the same exact spot.

This is what Tengo was looking at. Tengo Kawana had come to this playground to see this scene, or perhaps to check that it still existed. He has known for some time that there are two moons. No doubt about it. He didn't look at all surprised to see it. On top of the slide, Ushikawa sighed deeply. *What kind of crazy world is this?* he asked himself. *What sort of world have I gotten myself into?* But no answer came. Swept by countless clouds racing by, the two moons – one big, one small – hung in the sky like a riddle.

There's one thing I can say for sure, he decided. *This isn't the world I came from. The earth I know has only one moon. That is an undeniable fact. And now it has increased to two.*

Ushikawa began to have a sense of déjà vu. *I've seen the same thing before somewhere,* he thought. He focused, desperately searching his memory. He frowned, grit his teeth, dredging the dark sea bottom of his mind. And it finally hit him. *Air Chrysalis.*

He looked around, but all he saw was the same world as always. White lace curtains were drawn in windows in the condo across the street, peaceful lights on behind them. Nothing out of the ordinary. *Only the number of moons was different.*

He carefully climbed down from the slide, and hurriedly left the playground as if running from the eyes of the moons. *Am I going nuts?* he wondered. *No, that can't be it. I'm not going crazy. My mind is like a brand-new steel nail – hard, sober, straight. Hammered at just the right angle, into the core of reality. There's nothing wrong with me. I'm completely sane.*

It's the world around me that's gone crazy.

And I have to find out why.

CHAPTER 20

Aomame

ONE ASPECT OF MY TRANSFORMATION

On Sunday the wind had died down. It was a warm, calm day, totally different from the night before. People took off their heavy coats and enjoyed the sunshine. Aomame, however, did not enjoy the nice weather – she spent the day as always, shut away in her room, the curtains closed.

As she listened to Janáček's *Sinfonietta*, the sound down low, she stretched and then turned to her exercise machine to do some resistance training. She was gradually adding routines to her training workout and it now took nearly two hours to complete. Afterward she cooked, cleaned the apartment, and lay on the sofa to read *In Search of Lost Time*. She had finally begun volume three, *The Guermantes Way*. She tried her best to keep busy. She only watched TV twice a day – the NHK news broadcasts at noon and seven p.m. As always, nothing big was going on – no, actually, lots of big events were happening in the world. People all around the world had lost their lives, many of them in tragic ways – train wrecks, ferry boats sinking, plane crashes. A civil war went on with no end in sight, an assassination, a terrible ethnic massacre. Weather shifts had brought on drought, floods, famine. Aomame deeply sympathized with the people caught up in these tragedies and disasters, but even so, not a single thing had occurred that had a direct bearing on her.

Neighborhood children were playing in the playground across the street, shouting something. She could hear the crows gathered on the roof, cawing out the latest gossip. The air had that early-winter city smell.

It suddenly hit her that ever since she had been living in this condo she had never once felt any sexual desire. Not once had she felt like having sex. She hadn't even masturbated. Maybe it was due to her pregnancy and her body's hormonal changes. Still, Aomame was relieved. This wasn't exactly the place to find a sexual outlet, should she decide she had to sleep with someone. She was happy, too, to not have any more periods. Her periods had never been heavy, but still she felt as if she had set down a load she had been carrying forever. It was one less thing to have to think about.

In the three months that she had been here, her hair had grown long. In September it had barely touched her shoulders, but now it was down to her shoulder blades. When she was a child her mother had always trimmed it short, and from junior high onward, because sports had been her life, she had never let it grow out. It felt a bit too long now, but she couldn't very well cut it herself. She trimmed her bangs, but that was all. She kept her hair up during the day and let it down at night. And then, while listening to music, she brushed it a hundred strokes, something you can only do if you have plenty of time on your hands.

Normally she wore almost no makeup, and now especially there was no need for it. But she wanted to keep a set daily routine as much as she could, so she made sure to take good care of her skin. She massaged her skin with creams and lotions, put on a face mask before bedtime. She was basically a very healthy person, and just a little extra care was all it took for her skin to be beautiful and lustrous. Or maybe this, too, was a by-product of being pregnant? She had heard that pregnant women had beautiful skin. Either way, when she sat at her mirror, let down her hair, and examined her face, she did feel she looked prettier than ever before. Or at least she was taking on the composure of a mature woman. Probably.

Aomame had never once felt beautiful. No one had ever told her that she was. Her mother treated her like she was an ugly child. "If only you were prettier," her mother always said – meaning if she were prettier, a cuter child, they could recruit more converts. So Aomame had always avoided looking at herself in mirrors. When she absolutely had to, she quickly, efficiently, checked out her reflection.

Tamaki Otsuka had told her she liked her features. *Not bad at all*, she had said. *They are actually very nice. You should have more confidence.* That had made Aomame happy. She was just entering puberty, and her friend's warm words calmed her. *Maybe I'm not as ugly as my mother said I was,* she began to think. But even Tamaki had never called her *beautiful.*

Now, however, for the first time in her life, Aomame saw something beautiful in her face. She was able to sit in front of the mirror longer than ever before and examine her face more thoroughly. She wasn't being narcissistic. She inspected her face from a number of angles, as if it were somebody else's. Had she really become beautiful? Or was it her way of appreciating everything that had changed, not her face itself? Aomame couldn't decide.

Occasionally she would put on a big frown in the mirror. Her frowning face looked the same as it always had. The muscles in her face stretched in all directions, her features unraveled, each distinct from the other. All possible emotions in the world gushed out from her face. It was neither beautiful nor ugly. From one angle she looked demonic, from a different angle comic. And from yet another angle her face was a chaotic jumble. When she stopped frowning her facial muscles gradually relaxed, like ripples vanishing on the surface of water, and her usual features returned. And then Aomame discovered a new, slightly different version of herself.

"You should smile more naturally," Tamaki had often told her. "Your features are gentle when you smile, so it's a shame that you don't do so more often." But Aomame could never smile easily, or casually, in front of people. When she forced it, she ended up with a tight sneer, which made others even more tense and uncomfortable. Tamaki was different: she had a natural, cheerful smile. People meeting her for the first time immediately felt friendly toward her. In the end, though, disappointment and despair drove Tamaki to take her own life, leaving Aomame – who couldn't manage a decent smile – behind.

It was a quiet Sunday. The warm sunshine had led many people to the playground across the road. Parents stood around, their children playing in the sandbox or on the swings. Some kids were playing on the slide. Elderly people sat on the benches, intently watching the children at play. Aomame went out on her balcony, sat on her garden chair, and half-heartedly watched through a gap in the screen. It was a peaceful scene. Time was marching on in the world. Nobody there was under threat of death, nobody there was on the trail of a killer. Nobody there had a fully loaded 9mm automatic pistol wrapped in tights in her dresser drawer.

Will I ever be able to participate in that quiet, normal world again? Aomame asked herself. *Will there ever come a day when I can lead this* little one *by the hand, go to the park, and let it play on the swings, on the slides? Lead my daily life without thinking about who I will kill next, or who will kill me? Is that possible in this 1Q84 world? Or is it only possible in some other world? And most important of all – will Tengo be beside me?*

Aomame stopped looking at the park and went back inside. She closed the sliding glass door and shut the curtains. She couldn't hear the children's voices now and a sadness tugged at her. She was cut off from everything, stuck in a place that was locked from the inside. *I'll stop watching the playground during the day. Tengo won't come in the daytime.* What he was looking for was a clear view of the two moons.

After she had a simple dinner and washed the dishes, Aomame dressed warmly and went out on the balcony once more. She lay the blanket on her lap and sank back in the chair. It was a windless night. The kind of clouds that watercolor artists like lingered faintly in the sky, a test of the artist's delicate brushstrokes. The larger moon, which was not blocked by the clouds, was two-thirds full and shone bright, distinct light down on the earth below. At this time of evening, from where she sat Aomame couldn't see the second, smaller moon. It was just behind a building, but Aomame knew *it was there*. She could feel its presence. No doubt it would soon appear before her.

Ever since she had gone into hiding, she had been able to intentionally shut thoughts out of her mind. Especially when she was on the balcony like this, gazing at the playground, she could make her mind a complete blank. She kept her eyes focused on the playground, especially on the slide, but she wasn't thinking of anything – no, her mind might have been thinking of something, but this was mostly below the surface. What her mind was doing below the surface, she had no idea. At regular intervals something would float up, like sea turtles and porpoises poking their faces through the surface of the water to breathe. When that happened, she knew that indeed she *had been thinking of something* up till then. Then her consciousness, lungs full of fresh oxygen, sank back below the surface. It was gone again, and Aomame no longer thought of anything. She was a surveillance device, wrapped in a soft cocoon, her gaze absorbed in the slide.

She was seeing the park, but at the same time she was seeing nothing. If anything new came across her line of vision, her mind would react immediately. But right now nothing new was happening. There was no wind. The dark branches of the zelkova tree stuck out, unmoving, like sharp probes pointed toward the sky. The whole world was still. She looked at her watch. It was after eight. Today might end as always, with nothing out of the ordinary. A Sunday night, as quiet as could be.

The world stopped being still at exactly 8:23.

She suddenly noticed a man on top of the slide. He sat down and looked up at one part of the sky. Aomame's heart shrunk to the size of a child's fist, and stayed that size so long she was afraid it would never start pumping again. But it just as quickly swelled up to normal size and started beating again. With a dull sound it began furiously pumping fresh blood throughout her body. Aomame's mind quickly broke through to the surface of the water, shook itself, and stood by, ready to take action.

It's Tengo, she thought instinctively.

But once her vision cleared, she knew it wasn't him. The man sitting there was short, like a child, with a large square head, wearing a knit hat. The knit hat was stretched out oddly because of the shape of his head. He had a green muffler wrapped around his neck and wore a navy-blue coat. The muffler was too long, and the buttons on his coat were straining around his stomach, ready to pop. Aomame knew this was the *child* she had seen last night coming out of the park. But this was no child. He was more near middle age. He was short and stocky, with short limbs. And his head was abnormally large, and misshapen.

Aomame remembered what Tamaru had said about the man with a head as large as a Fukusuke good-luck doll, the one they had nicknamed Bobblehead. The person who had been loitering around outside the Azabu Willow House, checking out the safe house. This man on top of the slide perfectly fit the description Tamaru had given her last night. That weird man hadn't given up on his investigation, and now he had crept up on her. *I have to get the pistol. Why of all nights did I leave it back in the bedroom?* Aomame took a deep breath, let the chaos of her heart settle and her nerves calm down. *I mustn't panic. There's no need for the pistol at this point.*

The man wasn't, after all, watching her building. Seated at the top of the slide, he was staring at the sky like Tengo had done, at the very same spot. And he seemed lost in thought. He didn't move a muscle for the longest time, like he had forgotten how to move. He didn't pay any attention to the direction of her room. This confused Aomame. *What's going on? This man came here searching for me. He's probably a member of Sakigake. No doubt at all he's a skilled pursuer. I mean, he was able to follow the trail all the way from the Azabu mansion to here. For all that, there he is now, defenseless, exposed, staring vacantly at the night sky.*

Aomame stealthily rose to her feet, slid open the glass door a crack, slipped inside, and sat down in front of the phone. With trembling hands she began dialing Tamaru's number. She had to report this to him – that she could see Bobblehead from where she was, on top of a slide in a playground across the street. Tamaru would decide what to do, and would no doubt deftly handle the situation. But after punching in the first four numbers she stopped, the receiver clutched in her hand, and bit her lip.

It's too soon, Aomame thought. *There are still too many things we don't know about this man. If Tamaru simply sees him as a risk factor and* takes care of him, *all those* things we don't know about him *will remain unknown. Come to think of it, the man is doing exactly what Tengo did the other day. The same slide, the same pose, the same part of the sky, as if he's retracing Tengo's movements. He must be seeing the two moons as well.* Aomame understood this. *Maybe this man and Tengo are linked in some way. And maybe this man hasn't noticed yet that I'm hiding out in an apartment in this building, which is why he's sitting there, defenseless, his back to me.* The more she thought about it, the more persuasive she found this theory. *If that's true, then following the man might lead me right to Tengo. Instead of searching me out, this guy can serve as my guide.* The thought made her heart contract even more, and then start to pound. She laid down the phone.

I'll tell Tamaru about it later, she decided. *There's something I have to do first. Something risky, because it involves the pursued following the pursuer. And this man is no doubt a pro. But even so I can't let this golden opportunity slip by. This may be my last chance. And from the way he looks, he seems to be in a bit of a daze, at least for the moment.*

She hurried into the bedroom, opened the dresser drawer, and took out the Heckler & Koch semiautomatic. She flicked off the safety, racked a round into the chamber, and reset it. She stuffed the pistol into the back of her jeans and went out to the balcony again. Bobblehead was still there, staring at the sky. His misshapen head was perfectly still. He seemed totally captivated by what he was seeing in the sky. Aomame knew how he felt. *That was most definitely a captivating sight.*

Aomame went back inside and put on a down jacket and a baseball cap. And a pair of nonprescription glasses with a simple black frame, enough to give her face a different appearance. She wound a gray muffler around her neck and put her wallet and apartment key in her pocket. She ran down the stairs and went out of the building. The soles of her sneakers were silent as she stepped out on the asphalt. It had been so long since she had felt hard, steady ground beneath her feet, and the feeling encouraged her.

As she walked down the road she checked that Bobblehead was still in the same place. The temperature had dropped significantly after the sun had set, but there was still no wind. She actually found the cold pleasant. Her breath white, Aomame walked as silently as she could past the entrance to the park. Bobblehead showed no sign that he had noticed her. His gaze was fixed straight up from the slide, on the sky. From where she was, Aomame couldn't see them, but she knew that at the end of his gaze there were two moons – one large, one small. No doubt they were snuggled up close to each other in the freezing, cloudless sky.

She passed by the park, and when she got to the next corner, she turned and retraced her steps. She hid in the shadows and watched the man on the slide. The pistol against her back was as hard and cold as death, and the feeling soothed her.

She waited five minutes. Bobblehead slowly got to his feet, brushed off his coat, and gazed up one more time at the sky. Then, as if he had made up his mind, he clambered down the steps of the slide. He left the park and walked off in the direction of the station. Shadowing him wasn't particularly hard. There were few people on a residential street on a Sunday night, and even keeping her distance, she wouldn't lose him. He also had not the slightest suspicion that someone was observing him. He never looked back, kept walking at a set pace, the pace people keep when they're preoccupied. *How ironic*, Aomame thought. *The pursuer's blind spot is that he never thinks* he's *being pursued.*

After a while it dawned on her that Bobblehead wasn't heading toward Koenji Station. Back in the apartment, using a Tokyo map of all twenty-three wards, she had gone over the district again and again until she had memorized the local geography so she would know what direction to take in an emergency. So though he was initially headed toward the station, she knew that when he turned at one corner he was going in a different direction. Bobblehead didn't know the neighborhood, she noticed. Twice he stopped at a corner, looked around as if unsure where to go, and checked the address plaques on telephone poles. He was definitely not from around here.

Finally Bobblehead picked up the pace. Aomame surmised that he was back on familiar territory. He walked past a municipal elementary school, down a narrow street, and went inside an old three-story apartment building.

Aomame waited for five minutes after the man had disappeared inside. Bumping into him at the entrance was the last thing she wanted. There were concrete eaves at the entrance, a round light bathing the front door in a yellowish glow. She looked everywhere but couldn't find a sign for the name of the building. Maybe the apartment building didn't have a name. Either way, it had been built quite a few years ago. She memorized the address indicated on the nearby telephone pole.

After five minutes she headed toward the entrance. She passed quickly under the yellowish light and hurriedly opened the door. There was no one in the tiny entrance hall. It was an empty space, devoid of warmth. A fluorescent light on its last legs buzzed above her. The sound of a TV filtered in from somewhere, as did the shrill voice of a child pestering his mother.

Aomame took her apartment key out of the pocket of her down jacket and lightly jiggled it in her hands so if anyone saw her it would look like she lived in the building. She scanned the names on the mailboxes. One of them might be Bobblehead's. She wasn't hopeful but thought it worth trying. It was a small building, with not that many residents. When she ran across the name *Kawana* on one of the boxes, all sound faded away.

She stood frozen in front of that mailbox. The air felt terribly thin, and she found it hard to breathe. Her lips, slightly parted, were trembling. Time passed. She knew how stupid and dangerous this was. Bobblehead could show up any minute. Still, she couldn't tear herself away from the mailbox. One little card with the name *Kawana* had paralyzed her brain, frozen her body in place.

She had no positive proof that this resident named Kawana was Tengo Kawana. Kawana wasn't that common a name, but certainly not as unusual as Aomame. But if, as she surmised, Bobblehead had some connection with Tengo, then there was a strong possibility that this *Kawana* was none other than Tengo Kawana. The room number was 303, coincidentally the same number as the apartment where she was currently staying.

What should I do? Aomame bit down hard on her lip. Her mind kept going in circles and couldn't find an exit. *What should I do?* Well, she couldn't stay planted in front of the mailbox forever. She made up her mind and walked up the uninviting concrete stairs to the third floor. Here and there on the gloomy floor were thin cracks from years of wear and tear. Her sneakers made a grating noise as she walked.

Aomame now stood outside apartment 303. An ordinary steel door with a printed card saying *Kawana* in the name slot. Just the last name. Those two characters looked brusque, inorganic. At the same time, a deep riddle lay within them. Aomame stood there, listening carefully, her senses razor sharp. But she couldn't hear any sound at all from behind the door, or even tell if there was a light on inside. There was a doorbell next to the door.

Aomame was confused. She bit her lip and contemplated her next step. *Am I supposed to ring the bell?* she asked herself.

Or was this some clever trap? Maybe Bobblehead was hiding behind the door, like an evil dwarf in a dark forest, an ominous smile on his face as he waited. *He deliberately revealed himself on top of that slide to lure me over here and take me captive. Fully aware that I'm searching for Tengo, he's using that as bait. A low-down, cunning man who knows exactly what my weak point is. That's the only way he could ever get me to open my door from the inside.*

She checked that no one else was around and pulled the pistol out of her jeans. She flicked off the safety and stuffed the pistol into the pocket of her down jacket so she could get to it easily. She gripped the pistol in her right hand, finger on the trigger, and with her left hand pressed the doorbell.

The doorbell rang inside the apartment. A leisurely chime, out of step with her racing heart. She gripped the pistol tight, waiting for the door to open. But it didn't. And there didn't seem to be anyone peering out at her through the peephole. She waited a moment, then rang the bell again. The bell was loud enough to get all the people in Suginami Ward to raise their heads and prick up their ears. Aomame's right hand on the pistol grip started to sweat a little. But there was no response.

Better leave, she decided. *The Kawana who lives in 303, whoever he is, isn't at home. And that ominous Bobblehead is still lurking somewhere in this building. Too dangerous to stay any longer.* She rushed down the stairs, shooting a glance at the mailbox as she passed, and left the building. Head down, she hurried under the yellow light and headed toward the street. She glanced back to make sure no one was following her.

There were lots of things she needed to think about, and an equal number of decisions she had to make. She felt in her pocket and reset the safety on the pistol. Then, away from any possible prying eyes, she shoved the pistol in the back of her jeans. *I can't get my expectations or hopes up too high,* she told herself. *The Kawana who lived there might be Tengo. And then again he might not. Once you get your hopes up, your mind starts acting on its own. And when your hopes are dashed you get disappointed, and disappointment leads to a feeling of helplessness. You get careless and let your guard down. And right now,* she thought, *that's the last thing I can afford.*

I have no idea how much Bobblehead knows. But the reality is that he's getting close to me. Almost close enough to reach out and touch. I need to pull myself together and stay alert. I'm dealing with someone who is totally dangerous. The tiniest mistake could be fatal. First of all, I have to stay away from that old apartment building. He's hiding in there, scheming how to capture me – like a poisonous, blood-sucking spider who has spun a web in the darkness.

By the time she got back to her apartment Aomame's mind was made up. There was but one path she could follow.

This time she dialed Tamaru's entire number. She let it ring twelve times, then hung up. She took off her cap and coat, returned the pistol to the drawer, then gulped down two glasses of water. She filled the kettle and boiled water for tea. She peeked through a gap in the curtain at the park across the street, to make sure no one was there. She stood in front of the bathroom mirror and brushed her hair. Even after that her fingers didn't work right. The tension remained. She was pouring hot water in the teapot when the phone rang. It was Tamaru, of course.

"I just saw Bobblehead," she told him.

Silence. "By *just saw him* you mean he's not there anymore?"

"That's right," Aomame said. "A little while ago he was in the park across from my building. But he's not there anymore."

"How long ago do you mean by *a little while ago*?"

"About forty minutes ago."

"Why didn't you call me forty minutes ago?"

"I had to follow him right away and didn't have the time."

Tamaru exhaled ever so slowly, as if squeezing out the breath. "Follow him?"

"I didn't want to lose him."

"I thought I told you never to go outside."

Aomame chose her words carefully. "But I can't just sit by when danger's approaching me. Even if I had called you, you wouldn't have been able to get here right away. Right?"

Tamaru made a small sound in the back of his throat. "So you followed Bobblehead."

"It looks like he had no idea at all he was being followed."

"A pro can act like that," Tamaru cautioned.

Tamaru was right. It all might have been an elaborate ruse. Not that she would admit that. "I'm sure you would be able to do that, but as far as I could tell, Bobblehead isn't on the same level. He may be skilled, but he's different from you."

"He might have had backup."

"No. He was definitely on his own."

Tamaru paused for a moment. "All right. So did you find out where he was heading?"

Aomame told him the address of the building and described its exterior. She didn't know which apartment he was in. Tamaru took notes. He asked a few questions, and Aomame answered as accurately as she could.

"You said that when you first saw him he was in the park across the street from you," Tamaru said.

"Correct."

"What was he doing there?"

Aomame told him – how the man was sitting on top of the slide and staring at the night sky. She didn't mention the two moons. That was only to be expected.

"Looking at the sky?" Tamaru asked. Aomame could hear the gears shift in his mind.

"The sky, or the moon, or the stars. One of those."

"And he let himself be exposed like that, defenseless, on the slide."

"That's right."

"Don't you find that odd?" Tamaru asked. His voice was hard and dry, reminding her of a desert plant that could survive a whole year on one day's worth of rain. "That man had run you down. He was one step away from you. Pretty impressive. Yet there he was, on top of a slide, leisurely gazing up at the night sky, not paying any attention to the apartment where you live. It doesn't add up."

"I agree – it doesn't make much sense. Be that as it may, I couldn't very well let him go."

Tamaru sighed. "But I still think it was dangerous."

Aomame didn't say anything.

"Did following him help you get any closer to solving the riddle?" Tamaru asked.

"No," Aomame said. "But there was one thing that caught my attention."

"Which was?"

"When I looked at the mailboxes I saw that a person named Kawana lives on the third floor."

"So?"

"Have you heard of *Air Chrysalis*? The bestselling novel this past summer?"

"Even I read newspapers, you know. The author, Eriko Fukada, was the daughter of a follower of Sakigake. She disappeared and they suspected she was abducted by the cult. The police investigated it. I haven't read the novel yet."

"Eriko Fukada isn't just the daughter of a follower. Her father was Leader, the head of Sakigake. She's the daughter of the man I sent on to the *other side*. Tengo Kawana was hired by the editor as a ghostwriter, and rewrote *Air Chrysalis*. In reality the novel is a joint work between the two of them."

A long silence descended. Long enough to walk to the end of a long, narrow room, look up something in a dictionary, and walk back. Finally Tamaru broke the silence.

"You have no proof that the Kawana who lives in that building is Tengo Kawana."

"Not yet, no," Aomame admitted. "But if he is the same person, then this all makes sense."

"Certain parts do mesh together," Tamaru said. "But how do you know that this Tengo Kawana ghostwrote *Air Chrysalis*?

That can't have been made public. It would have caused a major scandal."

"I heard it from Leader himself. Right before he died, he told me."

Tamaru's voice turned a little cold. "Don't you think you should have told me this before?"

"At the time I didn't think it was so important."

There was silence again for a time. Aomame couldn't tell what Tamaru was thinking, but she knew he didn't like excuses.

"Okay," he finally said. "We'll put that on hold. Let's cut to the chase. What you're trying to say is that Bobblehead marked this Tengo Kawana. And using that as a lead, he was tracking down your whereabouts."

"That's what I think."

"I don't get it," Tamaru said. "Why would Tengo Kawana be a lead to find you? There isn't any connection between you and Kawana, is there? Other than that you dealt with Eriko Fukada's father, and Tengo was the ghostwriter for her novel."

"There *is* a connection," Aomame said, her voice flat.

"There's a direct relationship between you and Tengo Kawana. Is that what you're saying?"

"He and I were in the same class in elementary school. And I believe he's the father of my baby. But I can't explain any more beyond that. It's very – how should I put it? – personal."

On the other end of the phone she heard a ballpoint pen tapping on a desk. That was the only sound she could hear.

"Personal," Tamaru repeated, in a voice that sounded like he had spied some weird creature on top of a rock in a garden.

"I'm sorry," Aomame said.

"I understand. It's a very personal thing. I won't ask anymore," Tamaru said. "So, specifically, what do you want from me?"

"Well, the first thing I would like to know is if the Kawana who lives in that building is actually Tengo Kawana. If it were possible, I would like to make sure of that myself, but it's too risky to go there again."

"Agreed."

"And Bobblehead is probably holed up somewhere in that building, planning something. If he's getting close to locating me, we have to do something about it."

"He already knows a certain amount about the connection between you and the dowager. He has painstakingly hauled in these various leads and is trying to tie them all together. We can't ignore him."

"I have one other request of you," Aomame said.

"Go ahead."

"If it is really Tengo Kawana living there, I don't want any harm to come to him. If it's unavoidable that he is going to get hurt, then I want to take his place."

Tamaru was silent again for a time. No more ballpoint pen tapping this time. There were no sounds at all, in fact. He was considering things in a world devoid of sound.

"I think I can take care of the first two requests," Tamaru said. "That's part of my job. But I can't say anything about the third. It involves very personal things, and there's too much about it I don't understand. Speaking from experience, taking care of three items at once isn't easy. Like it or not, you end up prioritizing."

"I don't mind. You can prioritize them however you like. I just want you to keep this in mind: while I'm still alive, I have to meet Tengo. There's something I have to tell him."

"I'll keep it in mind," Tamaru said. "While there's still spare room in my mind, that is."

"Thank you."

"I have to report what you have told me to the dowager. This is a rather delicate issue, and I can't decide things on my own. So I'll hang up for now. Listen – do not go outside anymore. Lock the door and stay put. If you go outside, it could cause problems. Maybe it already has."

"But it helped me find out a few things about him."

"All right," Tamaru said, sounding resigned. "From what you have told me, it sounds like you did an excellent job. I'll admit that. But don't let your guard down. We don't know yet what he's got up his sleeve. And considering the situation, most likely he has an organization behind him. Do you still have the thing I gave you?"

"Of course."

"Best to keep it nearby."

"Will do."

A short pause, then the phone connection went dead.

Aomame sank back into the bathtub, which she had filled to the brim, and while she warmed up, she thought about Tengo – the Tengo who might or might not be living in an apartment in that old building. She pictured the uninviting steel door, the slot for the name card, the name *Kawana* printed on the card. *What kind of place was beyond that door? And what kind of life was he living?*

In the hot water she touched her breasts, rubbing them. Her nipples had grown larger and harder than before, and more sensitive. *I wish these were Tengo's hands instead of mine,* she thought. She imagined his hands, large and warm. Strong, but surely gentle. If her breasts were enveloped in his hands – how much joy, and peace, she would feel. Aomame also noticed that her breasts were now slightly larger. It was no illusion. They definitely were swollen, the curves softer. *It's probably due to my pregnancy. Or maybe they just got bigger, unrelated to being pregnant. One aspect of my transformation.*

She put her hands on her abdomen. It was still barely swollen, and she didn't have any morning sickness, for some reason. But there was a *little one* hidden within. She knew it. *Wait a moment,* she thought. *Maybe they're not after my life, but after this little one? As revenge for me killing Leader, are they trying to get to it, along with me?* The thought made her shudder. Aomame was doubly determined now to see Tengo. Together, the two of them had to protect the *little one. I have had so many precious things stolen from me in my life. But this is one I am going to hold on to.*

She went to bed and read for a while, but sleep didn't come. She shut her book, and gently rolled into a ball to protect her abdomen. With her cheek against the pillow, she thought of the winter moon in the sky above the park, and the little green moon beside it. *Maza* and *dohta.* The mixed light of the two moons bathing the bare branches of the zelkova tree. At this very moment Tamaru must be figuring out a plan, his mind racing at top speed. She could see him, brows knit, tip of his ballpoint pen tapping furiously on the desktop. Eventually, as if led by that monotonous, ceaseless rhythm, the soft blanket of sleep wrapped itself around her.

CHAPTER 21

Tengo

SOMEWHERE INSIDE HIS HEAD

The phone was ringing. The hands on his alarm clock showed 2:04. Monday, 2:04 a.m. It was still dark out and Tengo had been sound asleep. A peaceful, dreamless sleep.

First he thought it was Fuka-Eri. She would be the only person who would possibly call at this ungodly hour. Or it could be Komatsu. Komatsu didn't have much common sense when it came to time. But somehow the ring didn't sound like Komatsu. It was more insistent, and business-like. And besides, he had just seen Komatsu a few hours earlier.

One option was to ignore the call and go back to sleep – Tengo's first choice. But the phone kept on ringing. It might go on ringing all night, for that matter. He got out of bed, bumping his shin as he did, and picked up the receiver.

"Hello," Tengo said, his voice still slurry from sleep. It was like his head was filled with frozen lettuce. There must be some people who don't know you're not supposed to freeze lettuce. Once lettuce has been frozen, it loses all its crispness – which for lettuce is surely its best characteristic.

When he held the receiver to his ear, he heard the sound of wind blowing. A capricious wind rushing through a narrow valley, ruffling the fur of beautiful deer bent over to drink from a clear stream. But it wasn't the sound of wind. It was someone's breathing, amplified by the phone.

"Hello," Tengo repeated. Was it a prank call? Or perhaps the connection was bad.

"Hello," the person on the other end said. A woman's voice he had heard before. It wasn't Fuka-Eri. Nor was it his older girlfriend.

"Hello," Tengo said. "Kawana here."

"Tengo," the person said. They were finally on the same page, though he still didn't know who it was.

"Who's calling?"

"Kumi Adachi," the woman said.

"Oh, hi," Tengo said. Kumi Adachi, the young nurse who lived in the apartment with the hooting owl. "What's going on?"

"Were you asleep?"

"Yes," Tengo said. "How about you?"

This was a pointless question. People who are sleeping can't make phone calls. *Why did I say such a stupid thing?* he wondered. *It must be the frozen lettuce in my head.*

"I'm on duty now," she said. She cleared her throat. "Mr. Kawana just passed away."

"Mr. Kawana just passed away," Tengo repeated, not comprehending. Was someone telling him he himself had just died?

"Your father just breathed his last breath," Kumi said, rephrasing.

Tengo pointlessly switched the receiver from his right hand to his left. "Breathed his last breath," he repeated.

"I was dozing in the nurses' lounge when the bell rang, just after one. It was the bell for your father's room. He has been in a coma for so long, and he couldn't ring the bell by himself, so I thought it was odd, and went to check it out. When I got there his breathing had stopped, as had his heart.

I woke up the on-call doctor and we tried to revive him, but couldn't."

"Are you saying my father pressed the call button?"

"Probably. There was no one else who could have."

"What was the cause of death?" Tengo asked.

"I really can't say, though he didn't seem to have suffered. His face looked very peaceful. It was like – a windless day at the end of autumn, when a single leaf falls from a tree. But maybe that's not a good way to put it."

"No, that's okay," Tengo said. "That's a good way of putting it."

"Tengo, can you get here today?"

"I think so." His classes at the cram school began again today, Monday, but for something like this, he would be able to get out of them.

"I'll take the first express train. I should be there before ten."

"I would appreciate it if you would. There are all sorts of *formalities* that have to be taken care of."

"Formalities," Tengo said. "Is there anything in particular I should bring with me?"

"Are you Mr. Kawana's only relative?"

"I'm pretty sure I am."

"Then bring your registered seal. You might need it. And do you have a certificate of registration for the seal?"

"I think I have a spare copy."

"Bring that, too, just in case. I don't think there's anything else you especially need. Your father arranged everything beforehand."

"Arranged everything?"

"Um, while he was still conscious, he gave detailed instructions for everything – the money for his funeral, the clothes he would wear in the coffin, where his ashes would be interred. He was very thorough when it came to preparations. Very practical, I guess you could say."

"That's the kind of person he was," Tengo said, rubbing his temple.

"I finish my rotation at seven a.m. and then am going home to sleep. But Nurse Tamura and Nurse Omura will be on duty in the morning and they can explain the details to you."

"Thank you for all you've done," Tengo said.

"You're quite welcome," Kumi Adachi replied. And then, as if suddenly remembering, her tone turned formal. "My deepest sympathy for your loss."

"Thank you," Tengo said.

He knew he couldn't go back to sleep, so he boiled water and made coffee. That woke him up a bit. Feeling hungry, he threw together a sandwich of tomatoes and cheese that were in the fridge. Like eating in the dark, he could feel the texture but very little of the flavor. He then took out the train schedule and checked the time for the next express to Tateyama. He had only returned two days earlier from the cat town, on Saturday afternoon, and now here he was, setting off again. This time, though, he would probably only stay a night or two.

At four a.m. he washed his face in the bathroom and shaved. He used a brush to tame his cowlicks but, as always, was only partly successful. *Let it be,* he thought, *it will fall into place before long.*

His father's passing didn't particularly shock Tengo. He had spent two solid weeks beside his unconscious father. He already felt that his father had accepted his impending death. The doctors weren't able to determine what had put him into a coma, but Tengo knew. His father had simply decided to die, or else had abandoned the will to live any longer. To borrow Kumi's phrase, as a "single leaf on a tree," he turned off the light of consciousness, closed the door on any senses, and waited for the change of seasons.

*   *   *

From Chikura Station he took a taxi and arrived at the seaside sanatorium at ten thirty. Like the previous day, Sunday, it was a calm early-winter day. Warm sunlight streamed down on the withered lawn, as if rewarding it, and a calico cat that Tengo had never seen before was sunning itself, leisurely grooming its tail. Nurse Tamura and Nurse Omura came to the entrance to greet him. Quietly, they each expressed their condolences, and Tengo thanked them.

His father's body was being kept in an inconspicuous little room in an inconspicuous corner of the sanatorium. Nurse Tamura led Tengo there. His father was lying faceup on a gurney, covered in a white cloth. In the square, windowless room, the white fluorescent light overhead made the white walls even brighter. On top of a waist-high cabinet was a glass vase with three white chrysanthemums, probably placed there that very morning. On the wall was a round clock. It was an old, dusty clock, but it told the time correctly. Its role, perhaps, was to be a witness of some kind. Besides this, there were no furniture or decorations. Countless bodies of elderly people must have passed through here – entering without a word, exiting without a word. A straightforward but solemn atmosphere lay over the room like an unspoken fact.

His father's face didn't look much different from when he was alive. Even up close, it didn't seem like he was dead. His color wasn't bad, and perhaps because someone had been kind enough to shave him, his chin and upper lip were strangely smooth. There didn't seem to be all that much difference from when he was alive, deeply asleep, except that now the feeding tubes and catheters were unnecessary. Leave the body like this, though, and in a few days decay would set in, and then there would be a big difference between life and death. But the body would be cremated before that happened.

The doctor with whom Tengo had spoken many times before came in, expressed his sympathy, then explained what had led up to his father's passing. He was very kind, very thorough in his explanation, but it really all came down to one conclusion: *the cause of death was unknown.* None of their tests had ever determined what was wrong with him. The closest the doctor could say was that Tengo's father died of old age – but he was still only in his mid-sixties, too young for such a diagnosis.

"As the attending physician I'm the one who fills out the death certificate," the doctor said hesitantly. "I'm thinking of writing that the cause of death was 'heart failure brought on by an extended coma,' if that is all right with you?"

"But actually the cause of death was not 'heart failure brought on by an extended coma.' Is that what you're saying?"

The doctor looked a bit embarrassed. "True, until the very end we found nothing wrong with his heart."

"But you couldn't find anything wrong with any of his other organs."

"That's right," the doctor said reluctantly.

"But the form requires a clear cause of death?"

"Correct."

"This isn't my field, but right now his heart is stopped, right?"

"Of course. His heart has stopped."

"Which is a kind of organ failure, isn't it?"

The doctor considered this. "If the heart beating is considered normal, then yes, it is a sort of organ failure, as you say."

"So please write it that way. 'Heart failure brought on by an extended coma,' was it? I have no objection."

The doctor seemed relieved. "I can have the death certificate ready in thirty minutes," he said. Tengo thanked him. The doctor left, leaving only bespectacled Nurse Tamura behind.

"Shall I leave you alone with your father?" Nurse Tamura asked Tengo. Since she had to ask – it was standard procedure – the question sounded a bit matter-of-fact.

"No, there's no need. Thanks," Tengo said. Even if he were

left alone with his father, there was nothing in particular he wanted to say to him. It was the same as when he was alive. Now that he was dead, there weren't suddenly all sorts of topics Tengo wanted to discuss.

"Would you like to go somewhere else, then, to discuss the arrangements? You don't mind?" Nurse Tamura asked.

"I don't mind," Tengo replied.

Before Nurse Tamura left, she faced the corpse and brought her hands together in prayer. Tengo did the same. People naturally pay their respects to the dead. The person had, after all, just accomplished the personal, profound feat of dying. Then the two of them left the windowless little room and went to the cafeteria. There was no one else there. Bright sunlight shone in through the large window facing the garden. Tengo stepped into that light and breathed a sigh of relief. There was no sign of the dead there. This was the world of the living – no matter how uncertain and imperfect a world it might be.

Nurse Tamura poured hot roasted *hojicha* tea into a teacup and passed it to him. They sat down across from each other and drank their tea in silence for a while.

"Are you staying over somewhere tonight?" Nurse Tamura asked.

"I'm planning to stay over, but I haven't made a reservation yet."

"If you don't mind, why don't you stay in your father's room? Nobody's using it, and you can save on hotel costs. If it doesn't bother you."

"It doesn't bother me," Tengo said, a little surprised. "But is it all right to do that?"

"We don't mind. If you're okay with it, it's okay with us. I'll get the bed ready later."

"So," Tengo said, broaching the topic, "what am I supposed to do now?"

"Once you get the death certificate from the attending

physician, go to the town office and get a permit for cremation, and then take care of the procedures to remove his name
from the family record. Those are the main things you need to
do now. There should be other things you'll need to take care
of – his pension, changing names on his savings account – but
talk to the lawyer about those."

"Lawyer?" This took Tengo by surprise.

"Mr. Kawana – your father, that is – spoke with a lawyer
about the procedures for after his death. Don't let the word
lawyer scare you. Our facility has a lot of elderly patients, and
since many are not legally competent, we have paired up with
a local law office to provide consultations, so people can avoid
legal problems related to division of estates. They also make up
wills and provide witnesses. They don't charge a lot."

"Did my father have a will?"

"I can't really say anything about it. You'll need to talk to
the lawyer."

"I see. Can I see him soon?"

"We got in touch with him, and he'll be coming here at
three. Is that all right? It seems like we're rushing things, but
I know you're busy, so I hope you don't mind that we went
ahead."

"I appreciate it." Tengo was thankful for her efficiency. For
some reason all the middle-aged women he knew were very
efficient.

"Before that, though, make sure you go to the town office,"
Nurse Tamura said, "get his name removed from your family
record, and get a permit for cremation. Nothing can happen
until you've done that."

"Well, then I have to go to Ichikawa. My father's permanent
legal residence should be Ichikawa. If I do that, though, I won't
be able to make it back by three."

The nurse shook her head. "No, soon after he came here
your father changed his official residence from Ichikawa to

Chikura. He said it should make things easier if and when the time came."

"He was well prepared," Tengo said, impressed. It was as if he knew from the beginning that this was where he would die.

"He was," the nurse agreed. "No one else has ever done that. Everyone thinks they will just be here for a short time. Still, though . . . ," she began to say, and stopped, quietly bringing her hands together in front of her to suggest the rest of what she was going to say. "At any rate, you don't need to go to Ichikawa."

Tengo was taken to his father's room, the room where he spent his final months. The sheets and covers had been stripped off, leaving only a striped mattress. There was a simple lamp on the nightstand, and five empty hangers in the narrow closet. There wasn't a single book in the bookshelf, and all his personal effects had been taken away. But Tengo couldn't recall what personal effects had been there in the first place. He put his bag on the floor and looked around.

The room still had a medicinal smell, and you could still detect the breath of a sick person hanging in the air. Tengo opened the window to let in fresh air. The sun-bleached curtain fluttered in the breeze like the skirt of a girl at play. *How wonderful it would be if Aomame were here,* he thought, *just holding my hand tight, not saying a word.*

He took a bus to the Chikura town hall, showed them the death certificate, and received a permit for cremation. Once twenty-four hours had passed since the time of death, the body could be cremated. He also applied to have his father's name removed from the family record, and received a certificate to that effect. The procedures took a while, but were almost disappointingly simple – nothing that would cause any soul searching. It was no different from reporting a stolen car.

Nurse Tamura used their office copier to make three copies of the documents he received.

"At two thirty, before the lawyer comes, someone will be here from Zenkosha, a funeral parlor," Mrs. Tamura said. "Please give him one copy of the cremation permit. The person from the funeral parlor will take care of the rest. While he was still alive, your father talked to the funeral director and decided on all the arrangements. He also put enough money aside to cover it, so you don't need to do anything. Unless you have an objection."

"No, no objection," Tengo said.

His father had left hardly any belongings behind. Old clothes, a few books – that was all.

"Would you like something as a keepsake? All there is, though, is an alarm clock radio, an old self-winding watch, and reading glasses," Nurse Tamura said.

"I don't want anything," Tengo told her. "Just dispose of it any way you like."

At precisely two thirty the funeral director arrived, dressed in a black suit. He moved silently. A thin man, in his early fifties, he had long fingers, large eyes, and a single dry, black wart next to his nose. He seemed to have spent a great deal of time outdoors, because his face was suntanned all over, down to the tips of his ears. Tengo wasn't sure why, but he had never seen a fat funeral director. The man explained the main procedures for the funeral. He was very polite and spoke slowly, deliberately, as if indicating that they could take all the time they needed.

"While your father was alive, he said he wanted as simple a funeral as possible. He wanted a simple, functional casket, and he wanted to be cremated as is. He did not want any ceremony, no scriptures read, no posthumous Buddhist name, or flowers, or a eulogy. And he didn't want a grave. He instructed me to have his ashes simply put in a suitable communal facility. That is, if there are no objections . . ."

He paused and looked entreatingly at Tengo with his large eyes.

"If that is what my father wanted, then I have no objection," Tengo said, looking straight back at those eyes.

The funeral director nodded, and cast his eyes down. "Today would be the wake, and for one night we will have the body lie in state in our funeral home. So we will need to transport the body to our place. The cremation will take place tomorrow at one thirty in the afternoon in a crematorium nearby. I hope this is satisfactory?"

"I have no objection."

"Will you be attending the cremation?"

"I will," Tengo said.

"There are some who do not like to attend, and it is entirely up to you."

"I will be there," Tengo said.

"Very good," the man said, sounding a little relieved. "I'm sorry to bother you with this now, but this is the same amount I showed your father while he was still alive. I would appreciate it if you would approve it."

The funeral director, his long fingers like insect legs, extracted a statement from a folder and passed it to Tengo. Tengo knew almost nothing about funerals, but he could see this was quite inexpensive. He had no objection. He borrowed a ballpoint pen and signed the agreement.

The lawyer came just before three and he and the funeral director stood there chatting for a moment – a clipped conversation, one specialist to another. Tengo couldn't really follow their conversation. The two of them seemed to know each other. This was a small town. Probably everybody knew everybody else.

Near the morgue was an inconspicuous back door, and the

funeral parlor's small van was parked just outside. Except for the driver's window, all the windows were tinted black, and the jet-black van was devoid of any sign or markings. The thin funeral director and his white-haired assistant moved Tengo's father onto a rolling gurney and pushed it toward the van. The van had been refitted to have an especially high ceiling and rails onto which they slid the body. They shut the back doors of the van with an earnest thud, the funeral director turned to Tengo and bowed, and the van pulled away. Tengo, the lawyer, Nurse Tamura, and Nurse Omura all faced the rear door of the black Toyota van and brought their hands together in prayer.

Tengo and the lawyer talked in a corner of the cafeteria. The lawyer looked to be in his mid-forties, and was quite obese, the exact opposite of the funeral director. His chin had nearly disappeared, and despite the chill of winter his forehead was covered with a light sheen of sweat. *He must sweat something awful in the summer,* Tengo thought. His gray wool suit smelled of mothballs. He had a narrow forehead, and above it an overabundance of thick, luxurious black hair. The combination of the obese body and the thick hair didn't work. His eyelids were heavy and swollen, his eyes narrow, but behind them was a friendly glint.

"Your father entrusted me with his will. The word *will* implies something significant, but this isn't like one of those wills from a detective novel," the lawyer said, and cleared his throat. "It's actually closer to a simple memo. Let me start by briefly summarizing its contents. The will begins by outlining arrangements for his funeral. I believe the gentleman from Zenkosha has explained this to you?"

"Yes, he did. It's to be a simple funeral."

"Very good," the lawyer said. "That was your father's wish, that everything be done as plainly as possible. The funeral expenses will be paid out of a reserve fund he set aside, and medical and other expenses will come out of the security deposit your father paid when he checked into this facility. There will be nothing you will have to pay for out of your own pocket."

"He didn't want to owe anybody, did he?"

"Exactly. Everything has been prepaid. Also, your father has money in an account at the Chikura post office, which you, as his son, will inherit. You will need to take care of changing it over to your name. To do that, you'll need the proof that your father has been removed from the family register, and a copy of your family register and seal certificate. You should go directly to the Chikura post office and sign the necessary documents yourself. The procedures take some time. As you know, Japanese banks and the post office are quite particular about filling in all the proper forms."

The lawyer took a large white handkerchief out of his coat pocket and wiped the sweat from his forehead.

"That's all I need to tell you about the inheritance. He had no assets other than the post office account – no insurance policies, stocks, real estate, jewelry, art objects – nothing of this sort. Very straightforward, you could say, and fuss free."

Tengo nodded silently. It sounded like his father. But taking over his postal account made Tengo feel a little depressed. It felt like being handed a pile of damp, heavy blankets. If possible, he would rather not have it. But he couldn't say this.

"Your father also entrusted an envelope to my care. I have brought it with me and would like to give it to you now."

The thick brown envelope was sealed tight with packing tape. The obese lawyer took it from his black briefcase and laid it on the table.

"I met Mr. Kawana soon after he came here, and he gave this to me then. He was still – conscious then. He would get confused occasionally, but he was generally able to function fine. He told me that when he died, he would like me to give this envelope to his legal heir."

"*Legal heir*," Tengo repeated, a bit surprised.

"Yes. That was the term he used. Your father didn't specify anyone in particular, but in practical terms you would be the only legal heir."

"As far as I know."

"Then, as instructed, here you go," the lawyer said, pointing to the envelope on the table. "Could you sign a receipt for it, please?"

Tengo signed the receipt. The brown office envelope on the table looked anonymous and bland. Nothing was written on it, neither on the front nor on the back.

"There's one thing I would like to ask you," Tengo said to the lawyer. "Did my father ever mention my name? Or use the word *son*?"

As he mulled this over, the lawyer pulled out his handkerchief again and mopped his brow. He shook his head slightly. "No, Mr. Kawana always used the term *legal heir*. He didn't use any other terms. I remember this because I found it odd."

Tengo was silent. The lawyer collected himself and spoke up.

"But you have to understand that Mr. Kawana knew you were the only legal heir. It's just that when we spoke he didn't use your name. Does that bother you?"

"Not really," Tengo said. "My father was always a bit odd."

The lawyer smiled, as if relieved, and gave a slight nod. He handed Tengo a new copy of their family register. "If you don't mind, since it was this sort of illness, I would like you to check the family register so we can make sure there are no legal problems with the procedure. According to the record, you are Mr. Kawana's sole child. Your mother passed away a year and a half after giving birth to you. Your father didn't remarry, and raised you by himself. Your father's parents and siblings are already deceased. So you are clearly Mr. Kawana's sole legal heir."

After the lawyer stood up, expressed his condolences, and

left, Tengo remained seated, gazing at the envelope on the table. His father was his real blood father, and his mother was *really* dead. The lawyer had said so. So it must be true – or, at least, a fact, in a legal sense. But it felt like the more facts that were revealed, the more the truth receded. Why would that be?

Tengo returned to his father's room, sat down at the desk, and struggled to open the sealed envelope. The envelope might contain the key to unlocking some mystery. Opening it was difficult. There were no scissors or box cutters in the room, so he had to peel off the packing tape with his fingernails. When he finally managed to get the envelope open, the contents were in several other envelopes, all of them in turn tightly sealed. Just the sort of thing he expected from his father.

One envelope contained 500,000 yen in cash – exactly fifty crisp new ten-thousand-yen bills, wrapped in layers of thin paper. A piece of paper included with it said *Emergency cash.* Definitely his father's writing, small letters, nothing abbreviated. This money must be in case there were unanticipated expenses. His father had anticipated that his *legal heir* wouldn't have sufficient funds on hand.

The thickest of the envelopes was stuffed full of newspaper clippings and various award certificates, all of them about Tengo. His certificate from when he won the math contest in elementary school, and the article about it in the local paper. A photo of Tengo next to his trophy. The artistic-looking award Tengo received for having the best grades in his class. He had the best grades in every subject. There were various other articles that showed what a child prodigy Tengo had been. A photo of Tengo in a judo gi in junior high, grinning, holding the second-place banner. Tengo was really surprised to see these. After his father had retired from NHK, he left the company housing he had been in, moved to another apartment in Ichikawa, and finally went to the sanatorium in Chikura.

Probably because he had moved by himself so often, he had hardly any possessions. And father and son had basically been strangers to each other for years. Despite this, his father had lovingly carried around all these mementos of Tengo's child-prodigy days.

The next envelope contained various records from his father's days as an NHK fee collector. A record of the times when he was the top producer of the year. Several simple certificates. A photo apparently taken with a colleague on a company trip. An old ID card. Records of payment to his retirement plan and health insurance. . . . Though his father worked like a dog for NHK for over thirty years, the amount of material left was surprisingly little – next to nothing when compared with Tengo's achievements in elementary school. Society might see his father's entire life as amounting to almost zero, but to Tengo, it wasn't *next to nothing*. Along with a postal savings book, his father had left behind a deep, dark shadow.

There was nothing in the envelope to indicate anything about his father's life before he joined NHK. It was as if his father's life began the moment he became an NHK fee collector.

He opened the final envelope, a thin one, and found a single black-and-white photograph. That was all. It was an old photo, and though the contrast hadn't faded, there was a thin membrane over the whole picture, as if water had seeped into it. It was a photo of a family – a father, a mother, and a tiny baby. The baby looked less than a year old. The mother, dressed in a kimono, was lovingly cradling the baby. Behind them was a torii gate at a shrine. From the clothes they had on, it looked like winter. Since they were visiting a shrine, it was most likely New Year's. The mother was squinting, as if the light were too bright, and smiling. The father, dressed in a dark coat, slightly too big for him, had frown lines between his eyes, as if to say he didn't take anything at face value. The baby looked confused by how big and cold the world could be.

The young father in the photo had to be Tengo's father. He looked much younger, though he already had a sort of surprising maturity about him, and he was thin, his eyes sunken. It was the face of a poor farmer from some out-of-the-way hamlet, stubborn, skeptical. His hair was cut short, his shoulders a bit stooped. That could only be his father. This meant that the baby must be Tengo, and the mother holding the baby must be Tengo's mother. His mother was slightly taller than his father, and had good posture. His father was in his late thirties, while his mother looked to be in her mid-twenties.

Tengo had never seen the photograph before. He had never seen anything that could be called a family photo. And he had never seen a picture of himself when he was little. They couldn't afford a camera, his father had once explained, and never had the opportunity to take any family photos. And Tengo had accepted this. But now he knew it was a lie. They *had* taken a photo together. And though their clothes weren't exactly luxurious, they were at least presentable. They didn't look as if they were so poor they couldn't afford a camera. The photo was taken not long after Tengo was born, sometime between 1954 and 1955. He turned the photo over, but there was no date or indication of where it had been taken.

Tengo studied the woman. In the photo her face was small, and slightly out of focus. If only he had a magnifying glass! Then he could have made out more details. Still, he could see most of her features. She had an oval-shaped face, a small nose, and plump lips. By no means a beauty, though sort of cute – the type of face that left a good impression. At least compared with his father's rustic face she looked far more refined and intelligent. Tengo was happy about this. Her hair was nicely styled, but since she had on a kimono, he couldn't tell much about her figure.

At least as far as they looked in this photo, no one could call them a well-matched couple. There was a great age difference between them. Tengo tried to imagine his parents meeting each other, falling in love, having him – but he just couldn't see it. You didn't get that sense at all from the photo. So if there wasn't an emotional attachment that brought them together, there must have been some other circumstances that did. No, maybe it wasn't as dramatic as the term *circumstances* made it sound. Life might just be an absurd, even crude, chain of events and nothing more.

Tengo tried to figure out if the mother in this photo was the mysterious woman who appeared in his daydreams, or in his fog of childhood memories. But he realized he didn't have any memories of the woman's face whatsoever. The woman in his memory took off her blouse, let down the straps of her slip, and let some unknown man suck her breasts. And her breathing became deeper, like she was moaning. That's all he remembered – some man sucking his mother's breasts. The breasts that should have been his alone were stolen away by somebody else. A baby would no doubt see this as a grave threat. His eyes never went to the man's face.

Tengo returned the photo to the envelope, and thought about what it meant. His father had cherished this one photograph until he died, which might mean he still cherished Tengo's mother. Tengo couldn't remember his mother, for she had died from illness when he was too young to have any memories of her. According to the lawyer's investigation, Tengo was the only child of his mother and his father, the NHK fee collector, a fact recorded in his family register. But official documents didn't guarantee that that man was Tengo's biological father.

"I don't have a son," his father had declared to Tengo before he fell into a coma.

"So, what am I?" Tengo had asked.

"You're nothing," was his father's concise and peremptory reply.

His father's tone of voice had convinced Tengo that there

was no blood connection between him and this man. And he had felt freed from heavy shackles. As time went on, however, he wasn't completely convinced that what his father had said was true.

I'm nothing, Tengo repeated.

Suddenly he realized that his young mother in the photo from long ago reminded him of his older girlfriend. Kyoko Yasuda was her name. In order to calm his mind, he pressed his fingers hard against the middle of his forehead. He took the photo out again and stared at it. A small nose, plump lips, a somewhat pointed chin. Her hairstyle was so different he hadn't noticed at first, but her features did somewhat resemble Kyoko's. But what could that possibly mean?

And why did his father think to give this photo to Tengo after his death? While he was alive he had never provided Tengo with a single piece of information about his mother. He had even hidden the existence of this family photo. One thing Tengo did know was that his father never intended to explain the situation to him. Not while he was alive, and not even now after his death. *Look, here's a photo,* his father must be saying. *I'll just hand it to you. It's up to you to* figure it out.

Tengo lay faceup on the bare mattress and stared at the ceiling. It was a painted white plywood ceiling, flat with no wood grain or knots, just several straight joints where the boards came together – the same scene his father's sunken eyes must have viewed during the last few months of life. Or maybe those eyes didn't see anything. At any rate his gaze had been directed there, at the ceiling, whether he had been seeing it or not.

Tengo closed his eyes and tried to imagine himself slowly moving toward death. But for a thirty-year-old in good health, death was something far off, beyond the imagination. Instead, breathing softly, he watched the twilight shadows as they moved across the wall. He tried to not think about anything. Not thinking about anything was not too hard for Tengo. He was too tired to keep any one particular thought in his head. He wanted to catch some sleep if he could, but he was over-tired, and sleep wouldn't come.

Just before six p.m. Nurse Omura came and told him dinner was ready in the cafeteria. Tengo had no appetite, but the tall, busty nurse wouldn't leave him alone. You need to get some-thing, even a little bit, into your stomach, she told him. This was close to a direct order. When it came to telling people how to maintain their health, she was a pro. And Tengo wasn't the type – especially when the other person was an older woman – who could resist.

They took the stairs down to the cafeteria and found Kumi Adachi waiting for them. Nurse Tamura was nowhere to be seen. Tengo ate dinner at the same table as Kumi and Nurse Omura. Tengo had a salad, cooked vegetables, and miso soup with asari clams and scallions, washed down with hot *hojicha* tea.

"When is the cremation?" Kumi asked him.

"Tomorrow afternoon at one," Tengo said. "When that's done, I'll probably go straight back to Tokyo. I have to go back to work."

"Will anyone else be at the cremation besides you, Tengo?"

"No, no one else. Just me."

"Do you mind if I join you?" Kumi asked.

"At my father's cremation?" Tengo asked, surprised.

"Yes. Actually I was pretty fond of him."

Tengo involuntarily put his chopsticks down and looked at her. Was she really talking about his father? "What did you like about him?" he asked her.

"He was very conscientious, never said more than he needed to," she said. "In that sense he was like my father, who passed away."

"Huh," Tengo said.

"My father was a fisherman. He died before he reached fifty."

"Did he die at sea?"

"No, he died of lung cancer. He smoked too much. I don't know why, but fishermen are all heavy smokers. It's like smoke is rising out of their whole body."

Tengo thought about this. "It might have been better if my father had been a fisherman too."

"Why do you think that?"

"I'm not really sure," Tengo replied. "The thought just occurred to me – that it would have been better for him than being an NHK fee collector."

"If your father had been a fisherman, would it have been easier for you to accept him?"

"It would have made many things simpler, I suppose."

Tengo pictured himself as a child, early in the morning on a day when he didn't have school, heading off on a fishing boat with his father. The stiff Pacific wind, the salt spray hitting his face. The monotonous drone of the diesel engine. The stuffy smell of the fishing nets. Hard, dangerous work. One mistake and you could lose your life. But compared with being dragged all over Ichikawa to collect subscription fees, it would have to be a more natural, fulfilling life.

"But collecting NHK fees couldn't have been easy work, could it?" Nurse Omura said as she ate her soy-flavored fish.

"Probably not," Tengo said. At least he knew it wasn't the kind of job he could handle.

"Your father was really good at his job, wasn't he?" Kumi asked.

"I think he was, yes," Tengo said.

"He showed me his award certificates," Kumi said.

"Ah! Darn," Nurse Omura said, suddenly putting down her chopsticks. "I totally forgot. Darn it! How could I forget something so important? Could you wait here for a minute? I have something I have to give you, and it has to be today."

Nurse Omura wiped her mouth with a napkin, stood up, and hurried out of the cafeteria, her meal half eaten.

"I wonder what's so important?" Kumi said, tilting her head.

Tengo had no idea.

As he waited for Nurse Omura's return, he dutifully worked his way through his salad. There weren't many others eating dinner in the cafeteria. At one table there were three old men, none of them speaking. At another table a man in a white coat, with a sprinkling of gray hair, sat alone, reading the evening paper as he ate, a solemn look on his face.

Nurse Omura finally trotted back. She was holding a department-store shopping bag. She took out some neatly folded clothes.

"I got this from Mr. Kawana about a year or so ago, while he was still conscious," the large nurse said. "He said when he was put in the casket he would like to be dressed in this. So I sent it to the cleaners and had them store it in mothballs."

There was no mistaking the NHK fee collector's uniform. The matching trousers had been nicely ironed. The smell of mothballs hit Tengo. For a while he was speechless.

"Mr. Kawana told me he would like to be cremated wearing this uniform," Nurse Omura said. She refolded the uniform neatly and put it back in the shopping bag. "So I'm giving it to you now. Tomorrow, give this to the funeral home people and make sure they dress him in it."

"Isn't it a problem to have him wear this? The uniform was just on loan to him, and when he retired it should have been returned to NHK," Tengo said, weakly.

"I wouldn't worry about it," Kumi said. "If we don't say anything, who's going to know? NHK isn't going to be in a tight spot over a set of old clothes."

Nurse Omura agreed. "Mr. Kawana walked all over the place, from morning to night, for over thirty years for NHK. I'm sure it wasn't always pleasant. Who cares about one uniform? It's not like you're using it to do something bad or anything."

"You're right. I still have my school uniform from high school," Kumi said.

"An NHK collector's uniform and a high school uniform aren't exactly the same thing," Tengo interjected, but no one took up the point.

"Come to think of it, I have my old school uniform in the closet somewhere too," Nurse Omura said.

"Are you telling me you put it on sometimes for your husband? Along with white bobby socks?" Kumi said teasingly.

"Hmm – now that's a thought," Nurse Omura said, her chin in her hands on the table, her expression serious. "Probably get him all hot and bothered."

"Anyway . . . ," Kumi said. She turned to Tengo. "Mr. Kawana definitely wanted to be cremated in his NHK uniform. I think we should help him make his wish come true. Don't you think so?"

Tengo took the bag containing the uniform and went back to the room. Kumi Adachi came with him and made up the bed. There were fresh sheets, with a still-starchy fragrance, a new blanket, a new bed cover, and a new pillow. Once all this was arranged, the bed his father had slept in looked totally transformed. Tengo randomly thought of Kumi's thick, luxuriant pubic hair.

"Your father was in a coma for so long," Kumi said as she smoothed out the wrinkles in the sheets, "but I don't think he was completely unconscious."

"Why do you say that?" Tengo asked.

"Well, he would sometimes send messages to somebody."

Tengo was standing at the window gazing outside, but he spun around and looked at Kumi. "Messages?"

"He would tap on the bed frame. His hand would hang down from the bed and he would knock on the frame, like he was sending Morse code. Like this."

Kumi lightly tapped the wooden bed frame with her fist.

"Don't you think it sounds like a signal?"

"That's not a signal."

"Then what is it?"

"He's knocking on a door," Tengo said, his voice dry. "The front door of a house."

"I guess that makes sense. It does sound like someone knocking on a door." She narrowed her eyes to slits. "So are you saying that even after he lost consciousness he was still making his rounds to collect fees?"

"Probably," Tengo said. "Somewhere inside his head."

"It's like that story of the dead soldier still clutching his trumpet," Kumi said, impressed.

There was nothing to say to this, so Tengo stayed silent.

"Your father must have really liked his job. Going around collecting NHK subscription fees."

"I don't think it's a question of liking or disliking it," Tengo said.

"Then what?"

"It was the one thing he was best at."

"Hmm. I see," Kumi said. She pondered this. "But that might very well be the best way to live your life."

"Maybe so," Tengo said as he looked out at the pine windbreak. It might really be so.

"What's the one thing you can do best?"

"I don't know," Tengo said, looking straight at her. "I honestly have no idea."

CHAPTER 22

Ushikawa

THOSE EYES LOOKED RATHER FULL OF PITY

Tengo showed up at the entrance to the apartment building on Sunday evening, at six fifteen. As soon as he stepped outside he halted and gazed around, as if looking for something. First to the right, then the left. Then from left to right. He looked up at the sky, then down at his feet. But nothing seemed to be out of the ordinary, as far as he was concerned.

Ushikawa didn't follow him then. Tengo was carrying nothing with him. His hands were stuffed in the pockets of his unpleated chinos. He had on a high-neck sweater and a well-worn olive-green corduroy jacket, and his hair was unruly. A thick paperback book peeped out of a jacket pocket. Ushikawa figured he must be going out to eat dinner in a nearby restaurant. *Fine,* he decided, *just let him go where he wants.*

Tengo had several classes he had to teach on Monday. Ushikawa had found this out by phoning the cram school. Yes, a female office worker had told him, Mr. Kawana will be teaching his regular classes from the beginning of the week. Good. From tomorrow, then, Tengo was finally going back to his normal schedule. Knowing him, he probably wouldn't be going far this evening. (If Ushikawa had followed him that night, he would have found out that Tengo was on his way to meet with Komatsu at the bar in Yotsuya.)

Just before eight, Ushikawa threw on his pea coat, muffler, and knit hat and, looking around him as he did, hurried out of the building. Tengo had not yet returned at this point. If he was really eating somewhere in the neighborhood, it was taking longer than it should. If Ushikawa was unlucky, he might actually bump into him on his way back. But he was willing to run the risk, since there was something he absolutely had to do, and it had to be done now, at this time of night.

He relied on his memory of the route as he turned several corners, passed a few semi-familiar landmarks, and though he hesitated a few times, unsure of the direction, he eventually arrived at the playground. The strong north wind of the previous day had died down, and it was warm for a December evening, but as expected, the park was deserted. Ushikawa double-checked that there was no one else around, then climbed up the slide. He sat down on top of the slide, leaned back against the railing, and looked up at the sky. The moons were there, almost in the same location as the night before. A bright moon, two-thirds full. Not a single cloud nearby. And beside it, a small green, misshapen moon snuggled close.

So it's no mistake, then, Ushikawa thought. He exhaled and shook his head. He wasn't dreaming or hallucinating. Two moons, one big, one small, were definitely visible there, above the leafless zelkova tree. The two moons looked like they had stayed put since last night, waiting for him to return to the top of the slide. They knew that he would be back. As if prearranged, the silence around them was suggestive. And the moons wanted Ushikawa to share that silence with them. *You can't tell anybody else about this,* they warned. They held an index finger, covered with a light dusting of ash, to their mouths to make sure he didn't say a thing.

As he sat there, Ushikawa moved his facial muscles this way

and that, to make sure there wasn't something unnatural or unusual about this feeling he was having. He found nothing unnatural about it. For better or for worse, this was his normal face.

Ushikawa always saw himself as a realist, and he actually was. Metaphysical speculation wasn't his thing. If something really existed, you had to accept it as a reality, whether or not it made sense or was logical. That was his basic way of thinking. Principles and logic didn't give birth to reality. Reality came first, and the principles and logic followed. So, he decided, he would have to begin by accepting this reality: that there were two moons in the sky.

The rest of it he would think about later. He sat there, trying not to think, completely absorbed in observing the two moons. He tried to get used to the scene. *I have to accept these guys* as they are, he said to himself. He couldn't explain why something like this could be possible, but it wasn't a question he needed to delve into deeply at this point. The question was *how to deal with it.* That was the real issue. To do so he needed to start by accepting what he was seeing, without questioning the logic of it.

Ushikawa was there for some fifteen minutes. He sat, leaning against the railing of the slide, hardly moving a muscle. Like a diver slowly acclimatizing his body to a change in water pressure, he let himself be bathed in the light from these moons, let it seep into his skin. Ushikawa's instinct told him this was important.

Finally this small man with a misshapen head stood up, climbed down from the slide, and, completely caught up in indescribable musings, walked back to the apartment building. Things looked a little different from when he came. *Maybe it's the moonlight,* he told himself. *That moonlight is gradually displacing how things appear.* Thanks to this, he took the wrong turn a number of times. Before he walked inside the building he looked up at the third floor to check that Tengo's lights were still off. Tengo was still out. It didn't seem likely that he had just gone out to eat someplace nearby. Maybe he was meeting somebody? And maybe that somebody was Aomame. Or Fuka-Eri. *Have I let a golden opportunity slip through my fingers?* he wondered. But it was too late to worry about it now. It was too risky to tail Tengo every time he went out. Tengo only had to spot him once to bring the whole operation crashing down.

Ushikawa went back to his apartment and removed his coat, muffler, and hat. He opened a tin of corned beef, spread some on a roll, and ate it, standing up in the kitchen. He drank a container of lukewarm canned coffee. Nothing had any taste. He could feel the texture of the food, but he couldn't taste anything. Whether this was the fault of the food and drink or his own sense of taste, he couldn't say. Maybe it could be blamed on those two moons. He heard a faint doorbell ring somewhere. A pause, then it rang again. He didn't care. It wasn't his chime ringing, but somebody else's, far away, on a different floor.

He finished his sandwich, drained the coffee, then leisurely smoked a cigarette to bring his mind back to reality. He reconfirmed what it was he had to do here, and sat down behind the camera at the window. He switched on the electric space heater and warmed his hands in front of the orange light. It was Sunday evening, not yet nine. Traffic into and out of the building was sparse, but Ushikawa was determined to see what time Tengo returned.

A moment later a woman in a black down jacket came out of the entrance, a woman he had never seen before. She had on a gray muffler up to her mouth, dark-framed glasses, and a baseball cap – the perfect getup to hide yourself from prying eyes. She was empty-handed and was walking briskly, taking long strides. Instinctively Ushikawa switched on the camera's motor drive and snapped three quick shots. He had to find out where she was going, but by the time he had gotten to his feet, the woman had reached the road and vanished into the night. Ushikawa frowned and gave up. At the pace she was walking, by the time he got his shoes on and chased after her, it would be too late to catch up.

He did an instant replay in his mind of what he had just seen. The woman was about five feet six inches tall, and wore narrow blue jeans and white sneakers. All her clothes looked strangely brand-new. He would put her at mid-twenties to about thirty. Her hair was stuffed in her collar, so he couldn't tell how long it was. The puffy down jacket made it hard to tell what sort of figure she had, but judging from her legs, she must be fairly slim. Her good posture and quick pace indicated she was young and healthy. She must be into sports. All these characteristics fit the Aomame that Ushikawa knew about, though he couldn't make too many assumptions. Still, she seemed to be very cautious. You could tell how tense her whole body was, like an actress being stalked by paparazzi.

Let's suppose for the moment, he thought, *that this was Aomame.*

She came here to see Tengo, but Tengo was out somewhere. The lights in his place were off. She came to see him, but there was no answer when she knocked, so she gave up and left. Maybe she was the one who had been ringing the doorbell. But something about this didn't make sense. Aomame was being pursued, and should be trying to stay out of sight. Why wouldn't she have called Tengo ahead of time to make sure he would be at home? That way she wouldn't unnecessarily expose herself to danger.

Ushikawa mulled this over as he sat in front of the camera, but he couldn't come up with a working hypothesis that made any sense. The woman's actions – disguising herself in this non-disguise, leaving the place where she was hiding – didn't fit what Ushikawa knew about her. She was more cautious and careful than that. The whole thing left him befuddled.

Anyhow, he decided he would go to the photo shop near the station tomorrow and develop the film he had taken. This mystery woman should be in the photos.

He kept watch with his camera until past ten, but after the woman left no one else came in or out of the building. The entrance was silent and deserted, like a stage abandoned after a poorly attended performance. Ushikawa was puzzled about Tengo. As far as he knew, he rarely stayed out this late, and he had classes to teach tomorrow. Maybe he had already come home while Ushikawa was out, and had long since gone to bed?

After ten Ushikawa realized how exhausted he was. He could barely keep his eyes open. This was unusual, since he normally kept late hours. Usually he could stay up as late as he needed. But tonight, sleep was bearing down on him from above, like the stone lid of an ancient coffin.

Maybe I looked at those two moons for too long, he thought, *absorbed too much of their light.* Their vague afterimage remained in his eyes. Their dark silhouettes numbed the soft part of his brain, like a bee stinging and numbing a caterpillar, then laying eggs on the surface of its body. The bee larvae use the paralyzed caterpillar as a convenient source of food and devour it as soon as they're born. Ushikawa frowned and shook this ominous image from his mind.

Fine, he decided. *I can't wait here forever for Tengo to get back. When he gets back is entirely up to him, and he'll just go to sleep as soon as he does. He doesn't have anywhere else to come back to besides this apartment. Most likely.*

Ushikawa listlessly tugged off his trousers and sweater and, stripped to his long-sleeved shirt and long johns, slipped into his sleeping bag. He curled up and soon fell asleep. It was a deep sleep, almost coma-like. As he was falling asleep he

1208 | BOOK 3 OCTOBER–DECEMBER

thought he heard a knock at the door. But by then his consciousness had shifted over to another world and he couldn't distinguish one thing from another. When he tried, his body creaked. So he kept his eyes shut, didn't try to figure out what the sound could mean, and once more sank down into the soft muddy oblivion of sleep.

It was about thirty minutes after Ushikawa fell into this deep sleep that Tengo came back home after meeting Komatsu. He brushed his teeth, hung up his jacket – which reeked of cigarette smoke – changed into pajamas, and went to sleep. Until a phone call came at two a.m. telling him that his father was dead.

When Ushikawa awoke, it was past eight a.m., Monday morning, and Tengo was already on the express train to Tateyama, fast asleep to make up for the hours he had missed. Ushikawa sat behind his camera, waiting to catch Tengo on his way to the cram school, but of course he never made an appearance. At one p.m. Ushikawa gave up. He went to a nearby public phone and called the cram school to see if Tengo was teaching his regular classes today.

"Mr. Kawana had a family emergency, so his classes are canceled for today," the woman on the phone said. Ushikawa thanked her and hung up.

Family emergency? The only family Tengo had was his father. His father must have died. If that was the case, then Tengo would be leaving Tokyo again. *Maybe he had already left while I was sleeping. What was wrong with me? I slept so long I missed him.*

At any rate, Tengo is now all alone in the world, thought Ushikawa. A lonely man to begin with, he was now even lonelier. Utterly alone. Before he was even two, his mother had been strangled to death at a hot springs resort in Nagano Prefecture. The man who murdered her was never caught. She had left her husband and, with Tengo in tow, had absconded with a young man. *Absconded* – a quite old-fashioned term. Nobody uses it anymore, but for a certain kind of action it's the perfect term. Why the man killed her wasn't clear. It wasn't even clear if that man had been the one who murdered her. She had been strangled at night with the belt from her robe, in a room at an inn. The man she had been with was gone. It was hard not to suspect him. When Tengo's father got the news, he came from Ichikawa and took back his infant son.

Maybe I should have told Tengo about this, Ushikawa thought. *He has a right to know. But he told me he didn't want to hear anything about his mother from the likes of me, so I didn't say anything. Well, what are you going to do? That's not my problem, it's his.*

At any rate, whether Tengo is here or not, I have to keep up my surveillance of this place, Ushikawa told himself. *Last night was that mysterious woman who looked a lot like Aomame. I have no proof it's her, but there's a strong possibility it is. That's what my misshapen head is telling me. And if that woman is Aomame, she'll be back to visit Tengo before long. She doesn't know yet that his father has died.* These were Ushikawa's deductions as he mulled over the situation. Tengo must have gotten the news about his father during the night and set off early this morning. And there must be some reason why the two of them couldn't get in touch by phone. Which means she would definitely be coming back here. Something was so important to her that she would come here, despite the danger. This time he was going to find out where she was going.

Doing so might also begin to explain why there were two moons. This was a fascinating question that Ushikawa was dying to solve. But really it was of secondary importance. His job was to find out where Aomame was hiding, and hand her over, nice and neat, to the creepy Sakigake duo. *Until I do so, whether there are two moons or only one,* he decided, *I have*

*to be realistic. That has always been my strong point. It's what
defines me.*

Ushikawa went to the photo store near the station and handed
over five thirty-six-exposure rolls of film. Once the film had
been processed and printed, he went to a nearby chain restaurant and looked through them in chronological order while
eating a meal of chicken curry. Most were photos of people he
was now familiar with. There were three people he was most
interested in: Fuka-Eri and Tengo, and last night's mystery
woman.

Fuka-Eri's eyes made him nervous. Even in the photo she
was staring straight into his face. *No doubt about it,* Ushikawa
thought. She *knew* she was being observed. She probably knew
about the hidden camera, too, and that he was taking photos.
Her clear eyes saw through everything, and they didn't like
what Ushikawa was up to. That unwavering gaze stabbed mercilessly to the depths of his heart. There was no excuse whatsoever for the activities he was engaged in. At the same time,
though, she wasn't condemning him, or despising him. In a
sense, those gorgeous eyes forgave him. *No, not forgiveness,*
Ushikawa decided, rethinking it. Those eyes *pitied* him. She
knew how ugly Ushikawa's actions were, and she felt compassion for him.

Looking at her eyes, he had felt a sharp stab of pain between
his ribs, as if a thick knitting needle had been thrust in. He felt
like a twisted, ugly person. *So what?* he thought. *I really am
twisted and ugly.* The natural, transparent pity that colored her
eyes sank deep into his heart. He would have much preferred
to be openly accused, reviled, denounced, and convicted.
Much better even to be beaten senseless with a baseball bat.
That he could stand. But not *this.*

Compared with her, Tengo was much easier to deal with. In
the photo he was standing at the entrance, also looking in his

direction. Like Fuka-Eri, he carefully examined his surroundings. But there was nothing in his eyes. Pure, ignorant eyes like those couldn't locate the camera hidden behind the curtains, or Ushikawa.

Ushikawa turned to the photos of the *mystery woman*. There were three photos. Baseball cap, dark-framed glasses, gray muffler up to her nose. It was impossible to make out her features. The lighting was poor in all the photos, and the baseball cap cast a shadow over her face. Still, this woman perfectly fit his mental image of Aomame. He picked up the photos and, like checking out a poker hand, went through them in order, over and over. The more he looked at them, the more convinced he was that this had to be Aomame.

He called the waitress over and asked her about the day's dessert. Peach pie, she replied. Ushikawa ordered a piece and a refill of coffee.

If this isn't Aomame, he thought as he waited for the pie, *then I might never see her as long as I live.*

The peach pie was much tastier than expected. Juicy peaches inside a crisp, flaky crust. Canned peaches, no doubt, but not too bad for a dessert at a chain restaurant. Ushikawa ate every last bite, drained the coffee, and left the restaurant feeling content. He picked up three days' worth of food at a supermarket, then went back to the apartment and his stakeout in front of the camera.

As he continued his surveillance of the entrance, he leaned back against the wall, in a sunny spot, and dozed off a few times. This didn't bother him. He felt sure he hadn't missed anything important while he slept. Tengo was away from Tokyo at his father's funeral, and Fuka-Eri wasn't coming back. She knew he was continuing his surveillance. The chances were slim that the *mystery woman* would visit while it was light out. She would be cautious, and wait until dark to make a move.

* * *

But even after sunset the *mystery woman* didn't appear. The same old lineup came and went – shopping bags in hand, out for an evening stroll, those coming back from work looking more beaten and worn out than when they had set off in the morning. Ushikawa watched them come and go but didn't snap any photos. There wasn't any need. Ushikawa was focused on only three people. Everyone else was just a nameless pedestrian. But to pass time Ushikawa called out to them, using the nicknames he had come up with.

"Hey, Chairman Mao." (The man's hair looked like Mao Tse-tung's.) "You must have worked hard today."

"Warm today, isn't it, Long Ears – perfect for a walk."

"Evening, Chinless. Shopping again? What's for dinner?"

Ushikawa kept up his surveillance until eleven. He gave a big yawn and called it a day. After he brushed his teeth, he stuck out his tongue and looked at it in the mirror. It had been a while since he had examined his tongue. Something like moss was growing on it, a light green, like real moss. He examined this moss carefully under the light. It was disturbing. The moss adhered to his entire tongue and didn't look like it would come off easily. *If I keep up like this,* he thought, *I'm going to turn into a Moss Monster. Starting with my tongue, green moss will spread here and there on my skin, like the shell of a turtle that lives in a swamp.* The very thought was disheartening.

He sighed, and in a voiceless voice decided to stop worrying about his tongue. He turned off the light, slowly undressed in the dark, and snuggled into his sleeping bag. He zipped the bag and curled up like a bug.

It was dark when he woke up. He turned to check the time, but his clock wasn't where it should be. This confused him. His long-standing habit was to always check for the clock before he went to sleep. So why wasn't it there? A faint light came in through a gap in the curtain, but it only illuminated a corner of the room. Everywhere else was wrapped in middle-of-the-night darkness.

Ushikawa felt his heart racing, working hard to pump adrenaline through his system. His nostrils flared, his breathing was ragged, like he had woken in the middle of a vivid, exciting dream.

But he wasn't dreaming. Something really *was* happening. Somebody was standing right next to him. Ushikawa could sense it. A shadow, darker than the darkness, was looming over him, staring down at his face. His back stiffened. In a fraction of a second, his mind regrouped and he instinctively tried to unzip the sleeping bag.

In the blink of an eye, the person wrapped his arm around Ushikawa's throat. He didn't even have time to get out a sound. Ushikawa felt a man's strong, trained muscles around his neck. This arm constricted his throat, squeezing him mercilessly in a viselike grip. The man never said a word. Ushikawa couldn't even hear him breathing. He twisted and writhed in his sleeping bag, tearing at the inner nylon lining, kicking with both feet. He tried to scream, but even if he could, it wouldn't help. Once the man had settled down on the tatami he didn't budge an inch, except for his arm, which gradually increased the amount of force he applied. A very effective, economical movement. As he did, pressure grew on Ushikawa's windpipe, and his breathing grew weaker.

In the midst of this desperate situation, what flashed through Ushikawa's mind was this: *How had the man gotten in here?* The door was locked, the chain inside set, the windows bolted shut. *So how did he get in? If he picked the lock, it would have made a sound.*

This guy is a real pro. If the situation called for it, he wouldn't hesitate to take a person's life. He is trained precisely for this. Was he sent by Sakigake? Have they finally decided to get rid of me? Did they conclude that I was useless to them, a hindrance they had to get rid of? If so, they're flat-out wrong. I'm one step away from locating Aomame. Ushikawa tried to speak, to tell the man this. *Listen to me first,* he wanted to plead. But no voice would come. There wasn't enough air to vibrate his vocal cords, and his tongue in the back of his mouth was a solid rock.

Now his windpipe was completely blocked. His lungs desperately struggled for oxygen, but none was to be found, and he felt his body and mind split apart. His body continued to writhe inside the sleeping bag, but his mind was dragged off into the heavy, gooey air. He suddenly had no feeling in his arms and legs. *Why?* his fading mind asked. *Why do I have to die in such an ugly place, in such an ugly way?* There was no answer. An undefined darkness descended from the ceiling and enveloped everything.

When he regained consciousness, Ushikawa was no longer inside the sleeping bag. He couldn't feel his arms or legs. All he knew was that he had on a blindfold and his cheek felt pressed up against the tatami. He wasn't being strangled anymore. His lungs audibly heaved like bellows breathing in new air. Cold, winter air. The oxygen made new blood, and his heart pumped this hot red liquid to all his nerve endings at top speed. He coughed wretchedly and focused on breathing. Gradually, feeling was returning to his extremities. His heart pounded hard in his ears. *I'm still alive,* Ushikawa told himself in the darkness.

Ushikawa was lying facedown on the tatami. His hands were bound behind him, tied up in something that felt like a soft cloth. His ankles were tied up as well – not tied so tightly, but in an accomplished, effective way. He could roll from side to side, but that was all. Ushikawa found it astounding that he was alive, still breathing. *So that wasn't death,* he thought. It had come awfully close to death, but it wasn't death itself. A sharp pain remained, like a lump, on either side of his throat.

He had urinated in his pants and his underwear was wet and starting to get clammy. But it wasn't such a bad sensation. In fact he rather welcomed it. The pain and cold were signs that he was still alive.

"You won't die that easily," the man's voice said. Like he had been reading Ushikawa's mind.

CHAPTER 23

Aomame

THE LIGHT WAS DEFINITELY THERE

It was past midnight, the day had shifted from Sunday to Monday, but still sleep wouldn't come.

Aomame finished her bath, put on pajamas, slipped into bed, and turned out the light. Staying up late wouldn't accomplish a thing. For the time being she had left it all up to Tamaru. Much better to get some sleep and think again in the morning when her mind was fresh. But she was wide awake, and her body wanted to be up and moving. It didn't look like she would be getting to sleep anytime soon.

She gave up, got out of bed, and threw a robe over her pajamas. She boiled water, made herbal tea, and sat at the dining table, slowly sipping it. A thought came to her, but what it was exactly, she couldn't say. It had a thick, furtive form, like far-off rain clouds. She could make out its shape but not its outline. There was a disconnect of some kind between shape and outline. Mug in hand, she went over to the window, and looked out at the playground through a gap in the curtains.

There was no one there, of course. Past one a.m. now, the sandbox, swings, and slide were deserted. It was a particularly silent night. The wind had died down, and there wasn't a single cloud in the sky, just the two moons floating above the frozen branches of the trees. The position of the moons had shifted with the earth's rotation, but they were still visible.

Aomame stood there, thinking about Bobblehead's run-down apartment building, and the name card in the slot on the door of apartment 303. A white card with the typed name *Kawana*. The card wasn't new, by any means. The edges were curled up, and there were faint moisture stains on it. The card had been in the slot for some time.

Tamaru would find out for her if it was really Tengo Kawana who lived there, or someone else with the same last name. At the latest, he would probably report back by tomorrow. He wasn't the kind of person who wasted time. Then she would know for sure. *Depending on the outcome,* she thought, *I might actually see Tengo before much longer.* The possibility made it hard to breathe, like the air around her had suddenly gotten thin.

But things might not work out that easily. Even if the person living in 303 was Tengo Kawana, Bobblehead was hidden away somewhere in the same building. And he was planning something – what, she didn't know, but it couldn't be good. He was undoubtedly hatching a clever plan, breathing down their necks, doing what he could to prevent them from seeing each other.

No, there's nothing to worry about, Aomame told herself. *Tamaru can be trusted. He's more meticulous, capable, and experienced than anyone I know. If I leave it up to him, he will fend off Bobblehead for me. Bobblehead is a danger not just to me, but to Tamaru as well, a risk factor that has to be eliminated.*

But what if Tamaru decides that it isn't advisable for Tengo and me to meet, then what will I do? If that happens, then Tamaru will surely cut off any possibility of Tengo and me ever seeing each other. Tamaru and I are pretty friendly, but his top priority is what will benefit the dowager and keep her out of harm's way. That's his real job – he isn't doing all this for my sake.

This made her uneasy. Getting Tengo and her together, letting them see each other again – where did this fall on Tamaru's list of priorities? She had no way of knowing. Maybe telling Tamaru about Tengo had been a fatal mistake. *Shouldn't I have taken care of everything myself?*

But what's done is done. I've told Tamaru everything. I had no choice. Bobblehead must be lying in wait for me, and it would be suicide to waltz right in all alone. Time is ticking away and I don't have the leisure to put things on hold and see how they might develop. Opening up to Tamaru about everything, and putting it all in his hands, was the best choice at the time.

Aomame decided to stop thinking about Tengo – and stop looking at the moons. The moonlight wreaked havoc on her mind. It changed the tides in inlets, stirred up life in the woods. She drank the last of her herbal tea, left the window, went to the kitchen, and rinsed out the mug. She longed for a sip of brandy, but she knew she shouldn't have any alcohol while pregnant.

She sat on the sofa, switched on the small reading lamp beside it, and began rereading *Air Chrysalis*. She had read the novel at least ten times. It wasn't a long book, and by now she had nearly memorized it. But she wanted to read it again, slowly, attentively. She figured she might as well, since she wasn't about to get to sleep. There might be something in it she had overlooked.

Air Chrysalis was like a book with a secret code, and Eriko Fukada must have told the story in order to get a message across. Tengo rewrote it, creating something more polished, more effective. They had formed a team to create a novel with a wider appeal. As Leader had said, it was a collaborative effort. If Leader was to be believed, when *Air Chrysalis* became a bestseller and certain secrets were revealed within, the Little People lost their power, and the *voice* no longer spoke. Because of this, the well dried up, the flow was cut off. This is how much influence the novel had exerted.

She focused on each line as she read.

By the time the clock showed 2:30, she was already two-thirds of the way through the novel. She closed the book and tried to put into words the strong emotions she was feeling. Though she wouldn't go so far as to call it a revelation, she had a strong, specific image in her mind.

I wasn't brought here by chance.

This is what the image told her.

I'm here because I'm supposed to be.

Up until now, she thought, *I believed I was dragged into this 1Q84 world not by my own will. Something had intentionally engaged the switch so the train I was on was diverted from the main line and entered this strange new world. Suddenly I realized I was here – a world of two moons, haunted by Little People. Where there is an entrance, but no exit.*

Leader *had explained it this way just before he died. The train is the story that Tengo wrote, and I was trapped inside that tale. Which explains exactly why I am here now – entirely passive, a confused, clueless bit player wandering in a thick fog.*

But that's not the whole picture, Aomame told herself. **That's not the whole picture at all.**

I am not just some passive being mixed up in this because someone else willed it. That might be partly true. But at the same time I chose to be here.

I chose to be here of my own free will.

She was sure of this.

And there's a clear reason I'm here. One reason alone: so I can meet Tengo again. If you look at it the other way around, that's the only reason why this world is inside of me. Maybe it's a paradox, like an image reflected to infinity in a pair of facing mirrors. I am a part of this world, and this world is a part of me.

There was no way for Aomame to know what sort of plot Tengo's new story contained. Most likely there were two moons in that world, and it was frequented by Little People. That was about as far as she could speculate. *This might be Tengo's story,* she thought, *but* it's my story, too. This much she understood.

She realized this when she got to the scene where the young girl, the protagonist, was working to create an air chrysalis every night in the shed with the Little People. As she read through this detailed, clear description, she felt something warm and oozy in her abdomen, a sort of melting warmth with a strange depth. Though tiny, there was an intense heat source there. What that heat source was, and what it meant, was obvious to her – she didn't need to think about it. The *little one.* It was emitting heat in response to the scene in which the protagonist and the Little People together weaved the air chrysalis.

Aomame put the book on the table next to her, unbuttoned her pajama top, and rested a hand on her belly. She could feel the heat being given off, almost like a dim orange light was there inside her. She switched off the reading lamp, and in the darkened bedroom stared hard at that spot, a luminescence almost too faint to see. But the light was definitely there – no mistake about it. *I am not alone. We are connected through this, by experiencing the same story simultaneously.*

And if that story is mine as well as Tengo's, then I *should be able to write the story line too. I should be able to comment on what's there, maybe even rewrite part of it. I have to be able to. Most of all, I should be able to decide how it's going to turn out. Right?*

She considered the possibility.

Okay, but how do I do it?

Aomame didn't know, though she knew it had to be possible. At this point it was a mere theory. In the silent darkness she pursed her lips and contemplated. This was critical, and she had to put her mind to it.

The two of us are a team. Like Tengo and Eriko Fukada made up a brilliant team when they created Air Chrysalis, *Tengo and I are a team for this new story. Our wills – or maybe some undercurrent of our wills – are becoming one, creating this complex story and propelling it forward. This process probably takes place on some deep, invisible level. Even if we aren't physically together, we are connected, as one. We create the story, and at the same time the story is what sets us in motion. Right?*

But I have a question. A very important question.

In this story that the two of us are writing, what could be the significance of this little one? *What sort of role will it play?*

Inside my womb is a subtle yet tangible heat that is emitting a faint orange light, exactly like an air chrysalis. Is my womb playing the role of an air chrysalis? Am I the maza, *and the* little one *my* dohta? *Is the Little People's will involved in all this – in my being pregnant with Tengo's child, although we didn't have sex? Have they cleverly usurped my womb to use as an air chrysalis? Using me as a device to extract another new* dohta?

No. That's not what's going on. She was positive about it. *That's not possible.*

The Little People have lost their power. Leader said so. *The popularity of the novel* Air Chrysalis *essentially blocked what they normally do. So they must not know about this pregnancy. But who – or what power – made this pregnancy possible? And why?*

Aomame had no idea.

What she did know was that this *little one* was something she and Tengo had formed. That it was a precious, priceless life. She placed her hand on her abdomen again, pressing gently against the outline of that faint orange glow. She let the warmth she felt there slowly permeate her whole body. *I've got to protect this* little one, *at all costs,* she told herself. *Nobody is ever going to take it away from me, or harm it. The two of us have to keep it safe.* In the darkness, she made up her mind.

She went into the bedroom, took off her robe, and got into bed. She lay faceup, and once more touched her abdomen and felt the warmth there. Her feeling of unease was gone. She knew what had to be done. *I have to be stronger,* she told herself. *My mind and body have to be one.* Finally sleep came, silently, like smoke, and wrapped her in its embrace. Two moons were still floating in the sky, side by side.

CHAPTER 24

Tengo

LEAVING THE CAT TOWN

Tengo's father's corpse was dressed in his neatly ironed NHK fee collector's uniform and placed inside the simple coffin. Probably the cheapest coffin available, it was a sullen little casket that looked only slightly more sturdy than the boxes for castella cakes. The deceased was a small person, yet there was barely any room to spare. The casket was made of plywood, and had minimal ornamentation. "Is this casket all right?" the funeral director had asked, making sure. "It's fine," Tengo replied. This was the casket his father had chosen from the catalog, for which he had prepaid. If the deceased had no problem with it, then neither did Tengo.

Dressed in his NHK uniform, lying in the crude coffin, his father didn't look dead. He looked like he was taking a nap on a work break and would soon get up, put on his cap, and go out to collect the rest of the fees. The uniform, with the NHK logo sewed into it, looked like a second skin. He was born in this uniform and would leave this world in the same way as he went up in flames. When Tengo actually saw him in it, he couldn't imagine his father wearing anything else. Just like Wagner's warriors on their funeral pyre could only be dressed in armor.

Tuesday morning, in front of Tengo and Kumi Adachi, the

lid of the coffin was closed, nailed shut, then placed inside the hearse. It wasn't much of a hearse, just the same businesslike Toyota van they had used to transport his body to the funeral home. This hearse, too, must have been the cheapest available. *Stately* was the last word you would use to describe it. And there was certainly no *Götterdämmerung* music as a send-off. But Tengo couldn't find anything to complain about, and Kumi didn't seem to have any problems with it either. What was more important was that a person had vanished from the face of the earth, and those left behind had to grasp what that entailed. The two of them got into a taxi and followed the black van.

They left the seaside road, drove a short way into the hills, and arrived at the crematorium. It was a relatively new building but utterly devoid of individuality. It seemed less a crematorium than some sort of factory or government office building. The garden was lovely and well tended, though the tall chimney rising majestically into the sky hinted that this was a facility with a special mission. The crematorium must not have been very busy that day, since the casket was taken right away. The casket was gently laid inside the incinerator, then the heavy lid was shut, like a submarine hatch. The old man in charge, wearing gloves, turned and bowed to Tengo, then hit the ignition switch. Kumi turned to the closed lid and put her hands together in prayer, and Tengo followed suit.

During the hourlong cremation, Tengo and Kumi waited in the building's lounge. Kumi bought two cans of hot coffee from the vending machine and they silently drank them as they sat side by side on a bench, facing a large picture window. Outside was a spacious lawn, dried up now in the winter, and leafless trees. Two black birds were on one of the branches. Tengo didn't know what kind of bird they were. They had long tails, and though small, they gave loud, sharp squawks. When they called out, their tails stood on end. Above the trees was the broad, cloudless, blue winter sky. Beneath her cream-colored duffle coat, Kumi wore a short black dress. Tengo wore a black crew-neck sweater under a dark gray herringbone jacket. His shoes were dark brown loafers. It was the most formal outfit he owned.

"My father was cremated here too," Kumi said. "All the people who attended were smoking like crazy. There was a cloud of smoke hanging up near the ceiling. Maybe to be expected, since they were all fishermen."

Tengo pictured it. A gaggle of sunburned men, uncomfortable in their dark suits, puffing away, mourning a man who had died of lung cancer. Now, though, Tengo and Kumi were the only ones in the lounge. It was quiet all around. Other than an occasional chirp from the birds in the trees, nothing else broke the silence – no music, no voices. Peaceful sunlight poured in through the picture window and formed a taciturn puddle at their feet. Time was flowing leisurely, like a river approaching an estuary.

"Thank you for coming with me," Tengo said after the long silence.

Kumi reached out and put her hand on top of his. "It's hard doing it alone. Better to have somebody with you."

"You may be right," Tengo admitted.

"It's a terrible thing when a person dies, whatever the circumstances. A hole opens up in the world, and we need to pay the proper respects. If we don't, the hole will never be filled in again."

Tengo nodded.

"The hole can't be left open," Kumi went on, "or somebody might fall in."

"But in some cases the dead person has secrets," Tengo said. "And when the hole's filled in, those secrets are never known."

"I think that's necessary too."

"How come?"

"Certain secrets can't be left behind."

"Why not?"

Kumi let go of his hand and looked at him right in the face. "There's something about those secrets that only the deceased person can rightly understand. Something that can't be explained, no matter how hard you try. They're what the dead person has to take with him to his grave. Like a valuable piece of luggage."

Tengo silently looked down at the puddle of light at his feet. The linoleum floor shone dully. In front of him were his worn loafers and Kumi's simple black pumps. They were right in front of him but looked miles away.

"There must be things about you, too, Tengo, that you can't explain to others?"

"Could be," Tengo replied.

Kumi didn't say anything, and crossed her slim black-stockinged legs.

"You told me you died once before, didn't you?" Tengo asked.

"Um. I did die once. On a lonely night when a cold rain was falling."

"Do you remember it?"

"I think so. I've dreamt about it for a long time. A very realistic dream, always exactly the same. So I have to believe that it happened."

"Was it like reincarnation?"

"Reincarnation?"

"Where you're reborn. Transmigration."

Kumi gave it some thought. "I wonder. Maybe it was. Or maybe it wasn't."

"After you died, were you cremated like this?"

Kumi shook her head. "I don't remember that far, since that would be after I died. What I remember is the *moment I died*. Someone was strangling me. A man I had never seen before."

"Do you recall his face?"

"Of course. I saw him many times in my dreams. If I ran across him on the street, I would recognize him right away."

"What would you do if you saw him in real life?"

Kumi rubbed her nose, as if checking to see if it was still there. "I've thought about that too – what I would do if I ran across him on the street. Maybe I would run away. Or maybe I would follow him so he wouldn't notice me. Unless I was actually put in that situation, I don't know what I would do."

"If you followed him, what would you do then?"

"I don't know. But maybe that man holds some vital secret about me. And if I play my cards right, he might reveal it to me."

"What kind of secret?"

"For instance, the reason why *I'm here.*"

"But that guy might kill you again."

"Maybe," Kumi said, lips slightly pursed. "I know it's dangerous. It might be better to just run away. But still the secret draws me in. Like when there's a dark entrance and cats can't help but peep in."

The cremation was over, and Tengo and Kumi, following tradition, picked up select bones from his father's remains and placed them in a small urn. The urn was handed to Tengo. He had no idea what he should do with it, though he knew he couldn't just abandon it. So he clutched the vase in his hands as he and Kumi took a taxi to the station.

"I will take care of any remaining details," Kumi told him in the cab. After a moment she added, "If you would like, I could see about interring the bones, too."

Tengo was startled. "You can do that?"

"I don't see why not," Kumi said. "There are some funerals where not a single person from the family attends."

"That would be a big help," Tengo said. And he handed her the urn, feeling a little guilty, but honestly relieved. *I will probably never see these bones again*, he thought. *All that is left will be memories, and eventually they, too, will vanish like dust.*

"I'm from here, so I think I can take care of it. It's better if you go back to Tokyo right away. We all like you a lot here, but this isn't a place you should stay for long."

I'm leaving the cat town, Tengo mused.

"Thank you for everything you've done," Tengo said.

"Tengo, do you mind if I give you some advice? I know I have no right to do so."

"Of course."

"Your father may have had a secret that he took with him to the other side. And that seems to be causing you confusion. I think I can understand how you feel. But you shouldn't peep anymore into that dark entrance. Leave that up to cats. If you keep doing so, you will never go anywhere. Better to think about the future."

"The hole has to be closed up," Tengo said.

"Exactly," Kumi said. "The owl says the same thing. Do you remember the owl?"

"Of course."

The owl is the guardian deity of the woods, knows all, and gives us the wisdom of the night.

"Is that owl still hooting in the woods?"

"The owl's not going anywhere," Kumi replied. "He'll be there for a long time."

Kumi saw him off on the train to Tateyama – as though she needed to make sure, with her own eyes, that he had boarded the train and left town. She stood on the platform and kept waving to him, until he couldn't see her anymore.

It was seven p.m. on Tuesday when he got back to his apartment in Koenji. Tengo turned on the lights, sat down at his dining table, and looked around the room. The place looked the same as when he had left early the previous morning. The curtains were closed tight, and there was a printout of the story he was writing on top of his desk. Six neatly sharpened pencils in a pencil holder, clean dishes still in the rack in the sink. Time was silently ticking by, the calendar on the wall indicating that this was the final month of the year. The room seemed even more *silent* than ever. A little *too* silent. Something excessive seemed included in that silence. Though maybe he was imagining it. Maybe it was because he had just witnessed a person vanishing right before his eyes. The hole in the world might not yet be fully closed up.

He drank a glass of water and took a hot shower. He shampooed his hair thoroughly, cleaned his ears, clipped his nails. He took a new pair of underwear and a shirt from his drawer and put them on. He had to get rid of all the smells that clung to him, the smells of the cat town. *We all like you a lot here, but this isn't a place you should stay for long,* Kumi Adachi had told him.

He had no appetite. He didn't feel like working or opening a book. Listening to music held no appeal. His body was exhausted, but his nerves were on edge, so he knew that even if he lay down he wouldn't get any sleep. Something about the silence seemed contrived.

It would be nice if Fuka-Eri were here, Tengo thought. *I don't care what silly, meaningless things she might talk about. Her fateful lack of intonation, the way her voice rose at the end of questions – it's all fine by me. I haven't heard her voice in a while and I miss it.* But Tengo knew that she wouldn't be coming back to his apartment again. Why he knew this, he couldn't say exactly. But he knew she would never be there again. Probably.

He wanted to talk with someone. *Anyone.* His older girlfriend would be nice, but he couldn't reach her. She was *irretrievably lost.*

He dialed Komatsu's office number, his direct extension, but nobody answered. After fifteen rings he gave up.

He tried to think of other people he could call, but there wasn't anyone. He thought of calling Kumi, but realized he didn't have her number.

His mind turned to a dark hole somewhere in the world, not yet filled in. Not such a big hole, but very deep. *If I look in that hole and speak loudly enough, would I be able to talk with my father? Will the dead tell me what the truth is?*

"If you do that, you'll never go anywhere," Kumi Adachi had told him. "Better to think about the future."

I don't agree. That's not all there is to it. Knowing the secret may not take me anywhere, but still, I have to know the reason why it won't. If I truly understand the reason, maybe I will be able to go somewhere.

Whether you are my real father or not doesn't matter anymore, Tengo said to the dark hole. *Either one is fine with me. Either way, you took a part of me with you to the grave, and I remain here with a part of you. That fact won't change, whether we are related by blood or not. Enough time has passed for that to be the case, and the world has moved on.*

He thought he heard an owl hooting outside, but it was only his ears playing tricks on him.

CHAPTER 25

Ushikawa

COLD OR NOT, GOD IS PRESENT

"You won't die that easily," the man's voice said from behind him. Like he had been reading Ushikawa's mind. "You just lost consciousness for a moment. Though you were right on the edge of it."

It was a voice he had never heard before. Neutral, utterly devoid of expression. Not too high or low, neither too hard nor too soft. The kind of voice that announces airplane departures or stock market reports.

What day of the week is it? Ushikawa thought randomly. *Must be Monday night. No, technically it might already be Tuesday.*

"Ushikawa," the man said. "You don't mind if I call you Ushikawa, do you?"

Ushikawa didn't reply. There was silence for a good twenty seconds. Then, without warning, the man gave him a short, clipped punch to his left kidney. Silent, but a punch with force behind it. Excruciating pain shot through his whole body. All his internal organs clenched, and until the pain had subsided a little he couldn't breathe. Finally he was able to get out a dry wheeze.

"I asked you politely, and I expect a reply. If you still can't talk, then just nod or shake your head. That's enough. That's what it means to be polite," the man said. "It's okay to call you Ushikawa?"

Ushikawa nodded several times.

"Ushikawa. An easy name to remember. I went through the wallet in your trousers. Your driver's license and business cards were in there. Full-time Director, New Japan Foundation for the Advancement of Scholarship and the Arts. A pretty fancy title, wouldn't you say? What would a Full-time Director of the New Japan Foundation for the Advancement of Scholarship and the Arts be doing shooting photos with a hidden camera in a place like this?"

Ushikawa was silent. He still couldn't get the words out easily.

"You had best reply," the man said. "Consider this a warning. If your kidney bursts, it'll hurt like hell the rest of your life."

"I'm doing surveillance on the residents," Ushikawa finally managed to say. His voice was unsteady, cracking in spots. To him, blindfolded, it didn't sound like his own.

"You mean Tengo Kawana."

Ushikawa nodded.

"The Tengo Kawana who ghostwrote *Air Chrysalis*."

Ushikawa nodded again and then had a fit of coughing. The man knew all this already.

"Who hired you to do this?" the man asked.

"Sakigake."

"That much I could figure out, Ushikawa," the man said. "The question is why, at this late date, Sakigake would want to keep watch over Tengo Kawana's movements. Tengo Kawana can't be that important to them."

Ushikawa's mind raced, trying to figure out who this man was and how much he knew. He didn't know who the man was, but it was clear Sakigake hadn't sent him. Whether that was good news or bad, Ushikawa didn't know.

"There is a question pending," the man said. He pressed a finger against Ushikawa's left kidney. Very hard.

"There's a woman he's connected with," Ushikawa groaned.

"Does this woman have a name?"

"Aomame."

"Why are they pursuing Aomame?" the man asked.

"She brought harm to Leader, the head of Sakigake."

"Brought harm," the man said, as if verifying the phrase. "You mean she killed him, right? To put it more simply."

"That's right," Ushikawa said. He knew he couldn't hide anything from this man. Sooner or later he would have to talk.

"It's a secret within the religion."

"How many people in Sakigake know this secret?"

"A handful."

"Including you."

Ushikawa nodded.

"So you must occupy a very high position."

"No," Ushikawa said, and shook his head, his bruised kidney aching. "I'm simply a messenger. I just happened to find out about it."

"In the wrong place at the wrong time. Is that what you're saying?"

"I think so."

"By the way, Ushikawa, are you working alone?"

Ushikawa nodded.

"I find that strange. Normally a team would conduct surveillance. To do a decent job of it, you would also need someone to run supplies, so three people at the minimum. And you're already deeply connected with an organization. Doing it all alone strikes me as unnatural. In other words, I'm not exactly pleased with your reply."

"I am not a follower of the religion," Ushikawa said. His breathing had calmed down and he was finally able to speak close to normally. "I was hired by them. They call on me when they think it's more convenient to hire an outsider."

"As a Full-time Director of the New Japan Foundation for the Advancement of Scholarship and the Arts?"

"That's just a front. There's no such organization. It was mainly set up by Sakigake for tax purposes. I'm an individual contractor, with no ties to the religion. I just work for them."

"A mercenary of sorts."

"No, not a mercenary. I'm collecting information at their request. If anything rough needs to get done, it's handled by other people."

"So, Ushikawa, you were instructed by Sakigake to do surveillance here on Tengo, and probe into his connection with Aomame."

"Correct."

"No," the man said. "That's the wrong answer. If Sakigake knew for a fact that there's a connection between Aomame and Tengo Kawana, they wouldn't have sent you by yourself on the stakeout. They would have put together a team of their own people. That would reduce the chance for mistakes, and they could resort to force if need be."

"I'm telling you the truth. I'm just doing what the people above me told me to do. Why they're having me do it alone, I have no idea." The pitch of Ushikawa's voice was still unsteady, and it cracked in places.

If he finds out that Sakigake doesn't yet know the connection between Aomame and Tengo, Ushikawa thought, *I might be whacked right here and now. If I'm no longer in the picture, then nobody will be any the wiser about their connection.*

"I'm not very fond of incorrect answers," the man said in a chilly tone. "I think you of all people are well aware of that. I wouldn't mind giving your kidney another punch, but if I hit you hard my hand will hurt, and permanently damaging your kidney isn't what I came here to do. I have no personal animosity toward you. I have just one goal, to get the right answer. So I'm going to try a different approach. I'm sending you to the bottom of the sea."

The bottom of the sea? Ushikawa thought. *What is this guy talking about?*

The man pulled something out of his pocket. There was a rustling sound like plastic rubbing together, and then something covered Ushikawa's head. A plastic bag, the thick freezer bag kind. Then a thick, large rubber band was wrapped around his neck. *This guy is trying to suffocate me,* Ushikawa realized. He tried breathing in but got a mouthful of plastic instead. His nostrils were blocked as well. His lungs were screaming for air, but there wasn't any. The plastic molded tight to his whole face like a death mask. Soon all his muscles started to convulse violently. He tried to reach out to rip away the bag, but his hands wouldn't move. They were tied tight behind his back. His brain blew up like a balloon and felt ready to explode. He tried to scream. He *had* to get air. But no sound came out. His tongue filled his mouth as his consciousness drained away.

Finally the rubber band was taken from his neck, the plastic bag peeled away from his head. Ushikawa desperately gulped down the air in front of him. For a few minutes he bent forward, breathing mightily, like an animal lunging at something just out of reach.

"How was the bottom of the sea?" the man asked after Ushikawa's breathing had settled down. His voice was, as before, expressionless. "You went quite deep down. I imagine you saw all sorts of things you've never seen before. A valuable experience."

Ushikawa couldn't respond. His voice wouldn't come.

"Ushikawa, as I have said a number of times, I am looking for the correct answer. So I'll ask you once again: Were you instructed by Sakigake to track Tengo Kawana's movements and search for his connection with Aomame? This is a critical point. A person's life is on the line. Think carefully before you answer. I'll know if you're lying."

"Sakigake doesn't know about this," Ushikawa managed to stammer.

"Good, that's the correct answer. Sakigake doesn't know yet about the connection between Aomame and Tengo Kawana. You haven't told them yet. Is that correct?"

Ushikawa nodded.

"If you had answered correctly from the start, you wouldn't have had to visit the bottom of the sea. Pretty awful, wasn't it?"

Ushikawa nodded.

"I know. I went through the same thing once," the man said, as easily as if he were chatting about some trivial gossip. "Only people who have experienced it know how horrible it really is. You can't easily generalize about pain. Each kind of pain has its own characteristics. To rephrase Tolstoy's famous line, all happiness is alike, but each pain is painful in its own way. I wouldn't go so far, though, as to say you *savor* it. Don't you agree?"

Ushikawa nodded. He was still panting a little.

The man went on. "So let's be frank with each other, and totally honest. Does that sound like a good idea, Ushikawa?"

Ushikawa nodded.

"Any more incorrect answers and I'll have you take another walk on the bottom of the sea. A longer, more leisurely stroll this time. We'll push the envelope a bit more. If we botch it, you might not come back. I don't think you want to go there. What do you say, Ushikawa?"

Ushikawa shook his head.

"It seems like we have one thing in common," the man said. "We're both lone wolves. Or maybe dogs who got separated from the pack? Rogue operators who don't fit in with society. People who have an instinctive dislike of organizations, or aren't accepted by any organization. We take care of business alone – decide things on our own, take action on our own, take responsibility on our own. We take orders from above, but have no colleagues or subordinates. All we depend on is our brain and our abilities. Do I have it right?"

Ushikawa nodded.

The man continued. "That's our strength, but also at times our weak point. For example, in this case I think you were a little too eager to be successful. You wanted to sort it out by yourself, without informing Sakigake. You wanted to wrap things up neatly and take all the credit. That's why you let your guard down, isn't it?"

Ushikawa nodded once more.

"Why did you have to take things that far?"

"Because it was my fault Leader died."

"How so?"

"I'm the one who ran the background check on Aomame. I did a thorough check on her before letting her see Leader. And I couldn't find anything suspicious at all."

"But she got close to Leader hoping to kill him, and actually did deliver a fatal blow. You messed up your assignment, and you knew that someday you would have to answer for it. You're just a disposable outsider, after all. And you know too much for your own good. To survive this, you knew you had to deliver Aomame's head to them. Am I correct?"

Ushikawa nodded.

"Sorry about that," the man said.

Sorry about that? Ushikawa's misshapen head pondered this. Then it came to him.

"Are you the one who planned Leader's murder?" he asked.

The man didn't respond. But Ushikawa took his silence as not necessarily a denial.

"What are you going to do with me?" Ushikawa asked.

"What indeed. Truth be told, I haven't decided yet. I'm going to take my time and think about it. It all depends on how you play this," Tamaru said. "I still have a few questions I want to ask you."

Ushikawa nodded.

"I would like you to tell me the phone number of your contact at Sakigake. You must report to someone there."

Ushikawa hesitated a moment, but then told him the number. With his life hanging in the balance, he wasn't about to hide it. Tamaru wrote it down.

"His name?"

"I don't know his name," Ushikawa lied. Tamaru didn't seem to mind.

"Pretty tough characters?"

"I'd say so."

"But not real pros."

"They're skilled, and they follow orders from the top, no questions asked. But they're not pros."

"How much do they know about Aomame?" Tamaru asked. "Do they know where she's hiding?"

Ushikawa shook his head. "They don't know yet, which is why I stayed here doing surveillance on Tengo Kawana. If I knew where Aomame is, I would have moved operations over there a long time ago."

"Makes sense," Tamaru said. "Speaking of which, how did you figure out the connection between Aomame and Tengo Kawana?"

"Legwork."

"How so?"

"I reviewed her background, from A to Z. I went back to her childhood, when she was attending the public elementary school in Ichikawa. Tengo Kawana is also from Ichikawa, so I wondered if there could have been a connection. I went to the elementary school to look into it, and sure enough, they were in the same class for two years."

Tamaru made a low, catlike growl deep in his throat. "I see.

A very tenacious investigation, Ushikawa, I must say. It must have taken a lot of time and energy. Impressive."

Ushikawa said nothing. There wasn't a question pending.

"To repeat my question," Tamaru said, "at the present time you are the only one who knows about the connection between Aomame and Tengo Kawana?"

"*You* know about it."

"Not counting me. Those you associate with."

Ushikawa nodded. "I am the only one involved who knows, yes."

"You're telling the truth?"

"I am."

"By the way, did you know that Aomame is pregnant?"

"Pregnant?" Ushikawa said. His voice revealed his surprise. "Whose child is it?"

Tamaru didn't answer his question. "You really didn't know?"

"No, I didn't. Believe me."

Tamaru silently considered his response for a moment, and then spoke.

"All right. It does appear that you didn't know this. I'll believe you. On another topic: you were sniffing around the Willow House in Azabu for a while. Correct?"

Ushikawa nodded.

"Why?"

"The lady who owns it went to a local sports club and Aomame was her personal trainer. It seems they had a close personal relationship. That lady also set up a safe house for battered women on the grounds of her estate. The security there was extremely tight. In my opinion, a little too tight. So I assumed Aomame might be hiding in that safe house."

"And then what happened?"

"I decided that wasn't the case. The lady has plenty of money and power. If she wanted to hide Aomame, she wouldn't do it so close at hand. She would put her somewhere far away. So I gave up checking out the Azabu mansion and turned my attention to Tengo Kawana."

Tamaru gave a low growl again. "You have excellent intuition. You're very logical, not to mention patient. Kind of a waste to have you be an errand boy. Have you always been in this line of work?"

"I used to be a lawyer," Ushikawa said.

"I see. You must have been very good. But I imagine you got carried away, botched up things, and took a fall. These are hard times now, and you're working for next to nothing as an errand boy for this new religious group. Do I have this right?"

Ushikawa nodded. "Yes, that about sums it up."

"Nothing you can do about it," Tamaru said. "For mavericks like us it's not easy to live a normal, everyday life. It might look like we're doing okay for a while, but then we definitely trip up. That's the way the world operates." Tamaru cracked his knuckles, a sharp, ominous sound. "So does Sakigake know about the Willow House?"

"I haven't told anyone," Ushikawa replied truthfully. "When I said that something about the mansion smells fishy, that was my own conjecture, nothing more. The security was too tight for me to confirm anything."

"Good," Tamaru said.

"You were the one who made sure of that, weren't you?"

Tamaru didn't answer.

"Up till now you've answered truthfully," Tamaru said. "In general, at least. Once you sink to the bottom of the sea, you lose the power to lie. If you tried to lie now, it would show in your voice. That's what fear will do to you."

"I'm not lying," Ushikawa said.

"Glad to hear it," Tamaru said. "No one wants to feel any more pain than they have to. By the way, have you heard of Carl Jung?"

Under the blindfold Ushikawa instinctively frowned. *Carl Jung? What was this guy getting at?*

"Carl Jung the psychologist?"

"Exactly."

"I know a little about him," Ushikawa said carefully. "He was born at the end of the nineteenth century in Switzerland. He was a disciple of Freud's, but broke with him. He coined the term 'collective unconscious.' That's about all I know."

"That's plenty," Tamaru said.

Ushikawa waited for him to continue.

"Carl Jung," Tamaru said, "had an elegant house in a quiet lakeside residential area of Zurich, and lived an affluent life with his family. But he needed a place where he could be alone in order to meditate on weighty issues. He found a small parcel of land on one corner of the lake in an area called Bollingen and built a small house there. Not exactly a villa or anything that grand. He piled the stones one by one himself and constructed a round house with high ceilings. The stones had been taken from a nearby quarry. In those days in Switzerland you had to have a stonemason's license in order to build anything out of stone, so Jung went to the trouble of obtaining a license. He even joined the stonemasons' guild. Building this house, and doing it with his own hands, was very important to him. His mother's death also seemed to be one of the major factors that led to him constructing this home."

Tamaru paused for a moment.

"This house was dubbed the 'Tower.' He designed it so it resembled the village huts he had seen on a trip to Africa. The inside was one big open space where everything went on. A very simple residence. He felt this was all one needed to live. The house had no electricity, gas, or running water. He got water from the nearby mountains. What he found out later, though, was that this was just an archetype and nothing else. As time went on, he found it necessary to build partitions and divisions in the house, and a second floor, and later he added on several wings. He created paintings himself on the wall. These were suggestive of the development and split in individual consciousness. The whole house functioned as a sort of three-dimensional mandala. It took him twelve years to complete the entire house. For Jungian researchers, it's an extremely intriguing building. Have you heard of this before?"

Ushikawa shook his head.

"The house is still standing on the banks of the lake in Zurich. Jung's descendants manage it, but unfortunately it's not open to the public, so people can't view the interior. Rumor has it, though, that at the entrance to the original tower there is a stone into which Jung carved some words with his own hand. 'Cold or Not, God Is Present.' That's what he carved into the stone himself."

Tamaru paused again.

" 'Cold or Not, God Is Present,' " he intoned, quietly, once more.

"Do you know what this means?"

Ushikawa shook his head. "No, I don't."

"I can imagine. I'm not sure myself what it means. There's some kind of deep allusion there, something difficult to interpret. But consider this: in this house that Carl Jung built, piling up the stones with his own hands, at the very entrance, he found the need to chisel out, again with his own hands, these words. I don't know why, but I've been drawn to these words for a long time. I find them hard to understand, but the difficulty in understanding makes it all the more profound. I don't know much about God. I was raised in a Catholic orphanage and had some awful experiences there so I don't have a good impression of God. And it was always cold there, even in the summer. It was either really cold or outrageously cold. One or the other. If there is a God, I can't say he treated me very well. Despite all this, those words of Jung's quietly sank deep into the folds of my soul. Sometimes I close my eyes and repeat them over and over, and they make me strangely calm. 'Cold or Not, God Is Present.' Sorry, but could you say that out loud?"

" 'Cold or Not, God Is Present,' " Ushikawa repeated in a weak voice, not really sure what he was saying.

"I can't hear you very well."

" 'Cold or Not, God Is Present.' " This time Ushikawa said it as distinctly as he could.

Tamaru shut his eyes, enjoying the overtones of the words. Eventually, as if he had made up his mind about something, he took a deep breath and let it out. He opened his eyes and looked at his hands. He had on disposable latex gloves so he wouldn't leave behind any fingerprints.

"I'm sorry about this," Tamaru said in a low voice. His tone was solemn. He took out the plastic bag again, put it over Ushikawa's head, and wrapped the thick rubber band around his neck. His movements were swift and decisive. Ushikawa was about to protest, but the words didn't form, and they never reached anyone's ears. *Why is he doing this?* Ushikawa thought from inside the plastic bag. *I told him everything I know. So why does he have to kill me?*

In his head, about to burst, he thought of his little house in Chuorinkan, and about his two young daughters. And the dog they owned. The dog was small and low to the ground and Ushikawa never could bring himself to like it. The dog never liked him, either. The dog wasn't very bright, and barked incessantly. It chewed the rugs and peed on the new flooring in the hallway. It was a totally different creature from the clever mutt he had had as a child. Still, Ushikawa's final conscious thoughts in this life were of the silly little dog scampering around the lawn in their backyard.

Tamaru watched as Ushikawa, his body tightly bound into a ball, writhed on the tatami like some huge fish out of water. Ushikawa's arms and legs were tied behind him, so no matter how much he struggled, the neighbors next door wouldn't hear a thing. Tamaru knew very well what a hideous way to die this was. But it was the most efficient, cleanest way to kill someone. No screams, no blood. Tamaru followed the second hand on his Tag Heuer diver's watch. After three minutes Ushikawa stopped thrashing around. His body trembled slightly, as if resonating to something, and then the trembling stopped. Tamaru looked at his wristwatch for another three minutes. He felt Ushikawa's wrist for a pulse and confirmed that all signs of life had vanished. There was a faint whiff of urine. Ushikawa had lost control of his bladder again, this time emptying it completely. Understandable, considering how much he had suffered.

Tamaru removed the rubber band and peeled away the plastic bag. The bag had been partly sucked into his mouth. Ushikawa's eyes were wide, his mouth open and twisted to one side in death. His dirty, irregular teeth were bared, his tongue with its greenish moss visible. It was the kind of expression Munch might have painted. Ushikawa's normally misshapen head looked even more lopsided. He must have suffered terribly.

"I'm sorry about this," Tamaru said. "I didn't do it because I wanted to."

Tamaru used his fingers to relax the muscles of Ushikawa's face, straighten out the jaw, and make his face more presentable. He used a kitchen towel to wipe away the drool from Ushikawa's mouth. It took a while, but his face began to look a bit better. At least a person looking at it wouldn't avert their eyes. But no matter how hard he tried, he couldn't get Ushikawa's eyes to shut.

"Shakespeare said it best," Tamaru said quietly as he gazed at that lumpish, misshapen head. "Something along these lines: if we die today, we do not have to die tomorrow, so let us look to the best in each other."

Was this from *Henry IV*, or maybe *Richard III*? Tamaru couldn't recall. To him, though, that wasn't important, and he doubted Ushikawa wanted to know the precise reference. Tamaru untied his arms and legs. He had used a soft, towel-like rope, and he had a special way of tying it so as to not leave marks. He took the rope, the plastic bag, and the heavy-duty rubber band and stowed them in a plastic bag he had brought with him for that purpose. He rummaged through Ushikawa's belongings and collected every photo he had taken. He put the camera and tripod in the bag as well. It would only lead to trouble if it got out that Ushikawa had been conducting surveillance. People would ask who he was watching, and the chances were pretty good that Tengo Kawana's name would surface. He took Ushikawa's notebook, too, crammed full of detailed notes. He made sure to collect anything of importance. All that was left behind were the sleeping bag, eating utensils, extra clothes, and Ushikawa's pitiful corpse. Finally, Tamaru took out one of Ushikawa's business cards, the ones that said he was Full-time Director, New Japan Foundation for the Advancement of Scholarship and the Arts, and pocketed it.

"I'm really sorry," Tamaru said again as he was leaving.

Tamaru went into a phone booth near the station, inserted a telephone card into the slot, and dialed the number Ushikawa had given him. It was a local Tokyo number, Shibuya Ward by the look of it. The phone rang six times before someone answered.

Tamaru skipped the preliminaries and told him the address and room number of the apartment in Koenji.

"Did you write it down?"

"Could you repeat it?"

Tamaru did so. The man wrote it down and read it back.

"Ushikawa is there," Tamaru said. "You are familiar with Ushikawa?"

"Ushikawa?"

Tamaru ignored what he said and continued. "Ushikawa is there, and unfortunately he isn't breathing anymore. It doesn't look like a natural death. There are several business cards with Full-time Director, New Japan Foundation for the Advancement of Scholarship and the Arts on them in his business card holder. If the police find these, eventually they will figure out the connection with you. That wouldn't be to your advantage, I imagine. Best to dispose of everything as soon as you can. That's what you're good at."

"Who are you?" the man asked.

"Let's just say I'm a kind informant," Tamaru said. "I'm not so fond of the police myself. Same as you."

"Not a natural death?"

"Well, he didn't die of old age, or very peacefully."

The man was quiet for a moment. "What was this Ushikawa doing there?"

"I don't know. You would have to ask him the details, and as I explained, he's not in a position to respond."

The man on the other end of the line paused. "You must be connected with the young woman who came to the Hotel Okura?"

"That's not the sort of question to which you can expect an answer."

"I'm one of the people who met her. Tell her that and she'll understand. I have a message for her."

"I'm listening."

"We're not planning to harm her," the man said.

"My understanding is that you are trying your best to track her down."

"That's right. We've been trying to locate her for some time."

"Yet you're telling me you don't plan to harm her," Tamaru said. "Why is that?"

There was a short silence before the response came.

"At a certain point the situation changed. Leader's death was deeply mourned by everyone. But that's over, finished. Leader was ill, and, in a sense, he was hoping to put an end to his suffering. So we don't plan to pursue Aomame any further regarding this matter. Instead, we would simply like to talk with her."

"About what?"

"Areas of common interest."

"That's just what *your people* want. You may feel the need to speak with her, but maybe that isn't what she wants."

"There should be room for discussion. There are things that we can provide you. Freedom, for instance, and safety. Knowledge and information. Can't we find a neutral place to discuss this? Name the location. We will go wherever you say. I guarantee her safety, one hundred percent – and not just hers, but the safety of everyone involved. There's no need to run away anymore. I think this is a reasonable request, for both sides."

"That's what you say," Tamaru said. "But there is no reason I should trust you."

"At any rate, I would appreciate it if you would let Aomame know," the man said patiently. "Time is of the essence, and we're still willing to meet you halfway. If you need more proof of our reliability, we'll provide it. You can call here anytime and get in touch with us."

"I wonder if you could give me a few more details. Why is she so important to you? What happened to bring about this transformation?"

The man took a short breath before he replied. "We have to keep hearing the voice. For us it's like a never-ending well. And we can't ever lose it. That's all I can tell you at this time."

"And you need Aomame in order to keep that well."

"It's hard to explain. It's connected, but that's all I can say."

"What about Eriko Fukada? You don't need her anymore?"

"No, not anymore. We don't care where she is, or what she's doing. Her mission is finished."

"What mission?"

"That's sensitive information," the man said after a pause. "I'm sorry, but I can't reveal anything more at this time."

"I suggest you consider your position very carefully," Tamaru said. "In this game we're playing, it's my serve. We can get in touch with you anytime we want, but you can't get in touch with us. You don't even know who we are. Correct?"

"You're right. You do have the advantage. We don't know who you are. But this isn't something we should speak about on the phone. I've already said too much, more than I'm authorized to."

Tamaru was silent for some time. "All right. We'll consider your proposal. We need to talk it over on our end. I will probably be getting in touch with you later."

"I will be waiting to hear from you," the man said. "As I said before, this could be to the advantage of both sides."

"What if we ignore your proposal, or reject it?"

"Then we would have to do things our way. We have a certain amount of power, and unfortunately, things might get a little rough. This could cause problems for everyone involved. No matter who you are, you won't come through this unscathed. I don't see how that could be the ideal outcome for either of us."

"You may be right. But it will take a while before we get to that point. And as you said, time is of the essence."

The man gave a small cough. "It might take time. Or maybe not so much."

"You won't know unless you try."

"Exactly," the man said. "There's one more important thing I need to point out. To borrow your metaphor, in this game it's your serve. But it doesn't seem to me like you're familiar with the basic rules of the game."

"That's another thing you can't know unless you actually try it."

"If you do try it and it doesn't work, that would be a shame."

"For both of us," Tamaru said.

A short, suggestive silence followed.

"What do you plan to do about Ushikawa?" Tamaru asked.

"We'll take charge of him at the earliest opportunity. As early as tonight."

"The apartment is unlocked."

"Much appreciated," the man said.

"By the way, will you all deeply mourn Ushikawa's death?"

"We deeply mourn any person's death."

"You should mourn over him. He was, in his own way, a capable man."

"But not capable *enough*. Is that what you're saying?"

"No man is capable enough to live forever."

"So you say," the man said.

"Yes, I do think that. Don't you?"

"I'll wait for your call," the man said, without answering, his voice cold.

Tamaru silently hung up the phone. There was no need for any more talk. If he wanted to talk further, he would call them. He left the phone booth and walked to where he had parked his car – an old, drab, dark blue Toyota Corolla van, totally inconspicuous. He drove for fifteen minutes, pulled up next to an empty park, checked that there was no one watching, and tossed the plastic bag with the rope and the rubber band into a trash can. Plus the surgical gloves.

"They deeply mourn any person's death," Tamaru said in a low voice as he started the engine and snapped on his seatbelt. *Good – that's what's most important*, he thought. *Everyone's death should be mourned. Even if just for a short time.*

CHAPTER 26

Aomame

VERY ROMANTIC

The phone rang at just past noon on Tuesday. Aomame was seated on her yoga mat, legs wide apart, stretching her iliopsoas muscles. It was a much more strenuous exercise than it looked. A light sheen of perspiration was starting to seep through her shirt. She stopped, wiped her face with a towel, and answered the phone.

"Bobblehead is no longer in that apartment," Tamaru said, as always omitting any sort of greeting. No *hello*s for him.

"He's not there anymore?"

"No, he's not. He was persuaded."

"Persuaded," Aomame repeated. She imagined this meant that Tamaru had, through some means, forcibly removed Bobblehead.

"Also, the person named Kawana who lives in that building is the Tengo Kawana you have been looking for."

The world around Aomame expanded, then contracted, as if it were her own heart.

"Are you listening?" Tamaru asked.

"I am."

"But Tengo Kawana isn't in his apartment right now. He has been gone for a couple of days."

"Is he all right?"

"He's not in Tokyo now, but he's definitely all right. Bobble-head rented an apartment in Tengo's building, and was waiting there for you to come see Tengo. He had set up a hidden camera and was keeping watch over the entrance."

"Did he take my picture?"

"He took three photos of you. It was nighttime, and you had on a hat, glasses, and a muffler, so you can't see any facial details in the photos. But it's you. If you had gone there one more time, things could have gotten sticky."

"So I made the right choice leaving things up to you?"

"If there is such a thing as a right choice here."

"Anyway," Aomame said, "I don't have to worry about him."

"That man won't be trying to do you any harm anymore."

"Because you *persuaded* him."

"I had to adjust some things as we went, but in the end, yes," Tamaru said. "I got all the photos. Bobblehead's aim was to wait until you showed up, and Tengo Kawana was merely the bait he was using to reel you in. So I can't see that they would have any reason now to harm Tengo. He should be fine."

"That's a relief," Aomame said.

"Tengo teaches math at a cram school in Yoyogi. He is apparently an excellent teacher, but he only works a few days a week, so he doesn't make much money. He's still single, and he lives modestly in that simple apartment."

When Aomame closed her eyes she could hear her heartbeat inside her ears. The boundary between herself and the world seemed blurred.

"Besides teaching math at the cram school, he is writing a novel. A long one. Ghostwriting *Air Chrysalis* was just a side job. He has his own literary ambitions, which is a good thing. A certain amount of ambition helps a person grow."

"How did you find all this out?"

"He's gone now, so I let myself into his apartment. It was locked, not that I would count that as a lock. I feel bad about invading his privacy, but I needed to do a basic check. For a man living alone, he keeps his place clean. He had even scrubbed the gas stove. The inside of his fridge was very neat, no rotten cabbage or anything tucked away in the back. I could see he had done some ironing as well. Not a bad partner for you to have. As long as he isn't gay, I mean."

"What else did you find out?"

"I called the cram school and asked about his teaching schedule. The girl who answered the phone said that Tengo's father passed away late Sunday night in a hospital somewhere in Chiba Prefecture. He had to leave Tokyo for the funeral, and his Monday classes were canceled. She didn't know when or where the funeral would take place. His next class is on Thursday, so it seems he will be back by then."

Aomame remembered that Tengo's father was an NHK fee collector. On Sundays Tengo had made the rounds of his father's collection route with him. She and Tengo had run across each other a number of times on the streets of Ichikawa. She couldn't remember his father's face very well. He was a small, thin man who wore a fee collector's uniform. He didn't look at all like Tengo.

"Since there's no more Bobblehead, is it all right if I go see Tengo?"

"That's not a good idea," Tamaru shot back. "Bobblehead was *persuaded,* but I had to get in touch with Sakigake to get them to take care of one last piece of business. There was one particular article I didn't want to fall into the hands of the authorities. If that had been discovered, the residents of the apartment would have been gone over with a fine-tooth comb, and your friend might have gotten mixed up in it too. It would have been difficult for me to wrap up everything by myself. If the authorities spotted me lugging that article out in the middle of the night and questioned me, I don't know how I would talk my way out of it. Sakigake has the manpower and the resources, and that's the sort of thing they're used to. Like the time they transported another article out of the Hotel Okura. Do you follow what I'm saying?"

In her mind Aomame translated Tamaru's terminology into more straightforward vocabulary. "So this *persuasion* got rather rough, I take it."

Tamaru gave a low groan. "I feel bad about it, but that man knew too much."

"Was Sakigake aware of what Bobblehead was doing in that apartment?"

"He was working for them, but on that front he was acting on his own. He hadn't yet reported to his superiors on what he was doing. Fortunately for us."

"But by now they must know that he was *up to something*."

"Correct. So you had best not go near there for a while. Tengo Kawana's name and address have to be on their checklist. I doubt they know yet about the personal connection between you and Tengo. But when they search for the reason Bobblehead was in that apartment, Tengo's name will surface. It's only a matter of time."

"If we're lucky, it might be some time before they discover it. They might not make the connection between Bobblehead's death and Tengo right away."

"If we're lucky," Tamaru said. "If they're not as meticulous as I think they are. But I never count on luck. That's how I've survived all these years."

"So I shouldn't go near that apartment building."

"Correct," Tamaru said. "We made a narrow escape, and we can't be too careful."

"I wonder if Bobblehead figured out that I'm hiding in this apartment."

"If he had, right now you would be somewhere I couldn't get to."

"But he came so close."

"He did. But that was just coincidence, nothing more."

"That's why he could sit there on the slide, totally exposed."

"Right," Tamaru said. "He had no idea that you were watching him. He never expected it. And that was his fatal mistake. I said that, didn't I? That there is a very fine line between life and death?"

A few seconds of silence descended on them. A heavy silence that a person's – any person's – death brings on.

"Bobblehead might be gone, but the cult is still after me."

"I'm not so sure about that," Tamaru said. "At first they wanted to grab you and find out what organization planned Leader's murder. They know you couldn't have done it on your own. It was obvious that you must have had backup. If they had caught you, you would have been in for some tough questioning."

"Which is why I needed a pistol," Aomame said.

"Bobblehead was well aware of all this," Tamaru went on. "He knew the cult was after you to grill you and punish you. But somehow the situation has drastically shifted. After Bobblehead left the stage, I spoke with one of the cult members. He said they have no plans to do you any harm. He asked me to give you this message. It could be a trap, but it sounded genuine to me. The guy explained that Leader was actually hoping to die, that it was a kind of self-destruction. So there's no need anymore to punish you."

"He's right," Aomame said in a dry tone. "Leader knew from the outset that I had gone there to kill him. And he wanted me to kill him."

"His security detail hadn't seen through you, but Leader had."

"That's right. I don't know why, but he knew everything beforehand," Aomame said. "He was *waiting for me* there."

Tamaru paused briefly, and then said, "What happened?"

"We made a deal."

"This is the first I've heard of it," Tamaru said, his voice stiff.

"I never had the opportunity to tell you."

"Tell me what sort of deal you made."

"I massaged his muscles for a good hour, and all the while he talked. He knew about Tengo. And somehow he knew about the connection between Tengo and me. He told me he wanted me to kill him. He wanted to escape the terrible physical pain he was in as soon as possible. If I would give him death, he said, he would spare Tengo's life for me. So I made up my mind and took his life. Even if I hadn't carried it out, he already had one foot in the grave, and when I considered the kinds of things he had done, I almost felt like letting him stay as he was, in such agony."

"You never reported to Madame about this deal you made."

"I went there to kill Leader, and I carried out my assignment," Aomame said. "The issue with Tengo was private."

"All right," Tamaru said, sounding half resigned. "You most definitely did carry out your assignment, I'll give you that. And the issue of Tengo Kawana is indeed a private matter. But somewhere either before or after this, you became pregnant. That's not something that can be easily overlooked."

"Not *before or after*. I got pregnant on that very night, the night of the huge rainstorm and terrible lightning that hit the city. On the same exact night when I *dealt with* Leader. As I said before, without any sex involved."

Tamaru sighed. "Considering what we're talking about, I either have to believe you or not believe you, one or the other. I have always found you to be a trustworthy person and I want to believe you, but I can't fathom the logic. Understand, I am a person who can only follow deductive reasoning."

Aomame was silent.

Tamaru went on. "Is there a cause-and-effect relationship between Leader's murder and this mysterious pregnancy?"

"I really can't say."

"Is it possible that the fetus inside you is Leader's child? That he used some method – what that would be I have no idea – and impregnated you? If that's true, then I understand why they're trying to get ahold of you. They need a successor to Leader."

Aomame clutched the phone tight and shook her head. "That's impossible. This is Tengo's child. I know it for a fact."

"That's another thing I have to either trust you on or not."

"Beyond that, I can't explain anything."

Tamaru sighed again. "All right. For the time being I'll accept what you're saying – that this baby is yours and Tengo's, and that you know this for a fact. Still, I don't see how it makes sense. At first they wanted to capture you and punish you severely, but at a certain point something happened – or they found out something. Now they *need you.* They said they guarantee your safety, and that they have something to offer you, and they want to meet directly to discuss this. What could have happened to account for this sudden turnaround?"

"They don't need me," Aomame said. "They need what's inside my belly. Somewhere along the line they realized this."

"Ho, ho," one of the Little People intoned from somewhere.

"Things are moving a bit too fast for me," Tamaru said. He gave a little groan again in the back of his throat. "I still don't see the logical connection here."

Well, nothing's been logical since the two moons appeared, Aomame thought. *That's what stole the logic from everything.* Not that she said this aloud.

"Ho, ho," six other Little People joined in.

"They need someone to *hear the voice,*" Tamaru said. "The man I talked with on the phone was insistent about that. If they lose the voice, it could be the end of the religion. What hearing the voice actually means, I have no idea. But that's what the man said. Does this mean that the child inside you is the *one who hears the voice*?"

Aomame laid a gentle hand on her abdomen. *Maza and dohta*, she thought to herself. *The moons can't hear about this.*

"I'm not – really sure," Aomame said, carefully choosing her words. "But I can't think of any other reason they would need me."

"But why would this child have that kind of special power?"

"I don't know." *In exchange for his life, maybe Leader entrusted his successor to me*, she thought. *In order to accomplish that, on that stormy night he might have temporarily opened the circuits where worlds intersect, and joined Tengo and me as one.*

Tamaru went on. "No matter who the father of that child is, or whatever abilities that child may or may not have when it's born, you have no intention of negotiating with the cult, correct? You don't care what they give you in exchange. Even if they solve all the riddles you've been wondering about."

"I'll never do it," Aomame said.

"Despite your intentions, they may take *what they want* by force. By any means necessary," Tamaru said. "Plus, you have a weak spot: Tengo Kawana. Perhaps the only weak spot you have, but it's a big one. When they discover that, that's where they'll focus their attack."

Tamaru was right. Tengo was both her reason for living and her Achilles' heel.

Tamaru went on. "It's too dangerous for you to stay there any longer. You need to move to a more secure location before they figure out the connection between you and Tengo."

"There are no more secure places in *this world*," Aomame said.

Tamaru mulled over her opinion. "Tell me what you're thinking," he said quietly.

"First, I have to see Tengo. Until that happens, I can't leave here. No matter how dangerous it might be."

"What are you going to do when you see him?"

"I know what I need to do."

Tamaru was silent for a moment. "You're crystal clear on that?"

"I don't know if it will work out, but I know what I have to do. I'm crystal clear on that, yes."

"But you're not planning on telling me what it involves."

"I'm sorry, but I can't. Not just you, but anybody. If I told anyone about it, at that instant it would be disclosed to the whole world."

The moons were listening carefully. So were the Little People. And this very room she was in. She couldn't let it out of her heart, not one centimeter. She had to surround her heart with a thick wall so nothing could escape.

On the other end of the line Tamaru was tapping the tip of a ballpoint pen on a desk. Aomame could hear the dry, rhythmic noise. It was a lonely sound, lacking any resonance.

"Okay, then let's get in touch with Tengo Kawana. Before that, though, Madame must agree to it. The task I've been given is to move you, as soon as possible, to another location. But you said you can't leave there until you see Tengo. It doesn't look like it will be easy to explain the reason to her. You understand that, right?"

"It's very difficult to logically explain the illogical."

"Exactly. As difficult as finding a real pearl in a Roppongi oyster bar. But I'll do my best."

"Thank you," Aomame said.

"What you're insisting on doesn't make sense to me, no matter how I look at it. Still, the more I talk with you, the more I feel that maybe I can accept it. I wonder why."

Aomame kept silent.

"Madame trusts you and believes in you," Tamaru said, "so if you insist on it that much, I can't see her finding a reason not to let you see Tengo. You and Tengo seem to have an unwavering connection to each other."

"More than anything in the world," Aomame said.

More than anything in any *world,* she repeated to herself.

"Even if I say it's too dangerous, and refuse to contact Tengo, you'll still go to that apartment to see him."

"I'm sure I will."

"And no one can stop you."

"It's pointless to try."

Tamaru paused for a moment. "What message would you like me to give Tengo?"

"Come to the slide after dark. After it gets dark, anytime is fine. I will be waiting. If you tell him Aomame said this, he'll understand."

"Okay. I'll let him know. *Come to the slide after dark.*"

"If he has something important he doesn't want to leave behind, tell him to bring it with him. But tell him he has to be able to keep both hands free."

"Where are you going to take that luggage?"

"Far away," Aomame said.

"How far away?"

"I don't know," Aomame said.

"All right. As long as Madame gives her permission, I'll let Tengo know. And I will do my best to keep you safe. But there's still danger here. We're dealing with desperate men. You need to protect yourself."

"I understand," Aomame said quietly. Her palm still lay softly on her abdomen. *Not just myself,* she thought.

After she hung up, she collapsed onto the sofa. She closed her eyes and thought about Tengo. She couldn't think of anything else. Her chest felt tight, and it hurt, but it was a good sort of pain. It was the kind of pain she could put up with. Tengo was so close, almost within reach. Less than a ten-minute walk away. The very thought warmed her to her core. *Tengo is a bachelor, and teaches math at a cram school. He lives in a neat, humble little apartment. He cooks, irons, and is writing a long novel.* Aomame envied Tamaru. If it were possible, she would like to get into Tengo's apartment like that, when he was out. Tengo's Tengo-less apartment. In the deserted silence she wanted to touch each and every object there – check out how sharp his pencils were, hold his coffee cup, inhale the odor of his clothes. She wanted to take that step first, before actually coming face-to-face with him.

Without that prefatory knowledge, if they were suddenly together, just the two of them, she couldn't imagine what she should say. The thought made it hard to breathe, and her mind went blank. There were too many things. Still, when it came down to it, perhaps nothing needed to be said. The things she most wanted to tell him would lose their meaning the moment she put them into words.

All she could do now was simply wait – calmly, with eyes wide open. She prepared a bag so she could run outside as soon as she spotted Tengo. She stuffed an oversized black leather shoulder bag with everything she would need so she wouldn't have to come back here. There weren't all that many things. Some cash, a few changes of clothes, and the Heckler & Koch, fully loaded. That was about it. She put the bag where she could get to it at a moment's notice. She took her Junko Shimada suit from the hanger in the closet and, after checking that it wasn't wrinkled, hung it on the wall in the living room. She also took out the white blouse that went with the suit, stockings, and her Charles Jourdan high heels. And the beige spring coat. The same outfit she was wearing when she climbed down the emergency stairway on Metropolitan Expressway No. 3. The coat was a bit thin for a December evening, but she had no other choice.

After getting all this ready, she sat in the garden chair on the balcony and looked out through the slit in the screen at the slide in the park. Tengo's father died late Sunday night. A minimum of twenty-four hours had to elapse between the time a person died and the time they could be cremated. She was sure there was a law that said that. Tuesday would be the earliest they could do the cremation. Today was Tuesday. The earliest Tengo would be back in Tokyo from *wherever* after the funeral would be this evening. And then Tamaru could give him the message. So Tengo wouldn't be coming to the park anytime before that. Plus, it was still light out.

On his death, Leader set this little one *inside my womb,* she thought. *That's my working supposition. Or maybe I should say intuition. Does this mean I'm being manipulated by the will he left behind, being led to a destination that he established?*

Aomame grimaced. *I can't decide anything. Tamaru surmised that I got pregnant with the* one who hears the voice *as a result of Leader's plan. Probably as an air chrysalis. But why does it have to be* me? *And why does my partner have to be Tengo?* This was another thing she couldn't explain.

Be that as it may, things are moving forward around me, even though I can't figure out the connections, or sort out the principles at work behind them, or see where things are headed. I've just wound up entangled in it all. Until now, that is, she told herself.

Her lips twisted and she grimaced even more.

From now on, things will be different. Nobody else's will is going to control me anymore. From now on, I'm going to do things based on one principle alone: my own will. I'm going to protect this little one, *whatever it takes. This is my life, and my child. Somebody else may have programmed it for their own purposes, but there's no doubt in my mind that this is Tengo's and my child. I'll never hand it over to anyone else. Never. From here on out, I'm the one in charge. I'm the one who decides what's good and what's bad – and which way we're headed. And people had better remember that.*

The phone rang the next day, Wednesday, at two in the afternoon.

"I gave him the message," Tamaru said, as usual omitting any greeting. "He's in his apartment now. I talked to him this morning on the phone. He will be at the slide tonight at precisely seven."

"Did he remember me?"

"He remembered you well. He seems to have been searching all over for you."

It was just as Leader said. Tengo is looking for me. That's all I need to know. Aomame's heart was filled with an indescribable joy. No other words in this world had any meaning for her.

"He will be bringing something important with him then, as you asked. I'm guessing that this will include the novel he's writing."

"I'm sure of it," Aomame said.

"I checked around that humble building he lives in. All looks clear to me. No suspicious characters hanging around. Bobblehead's apartment is deserted. Everything's quiet, but not too quiet. Those guys took care of the article during the night and left. They probably thought it wouldn't be good to stay too long. I made sure of this, so I don't think I overlooked anything."

"Good."

"*Probably,* though, is the operative word here, *at least for now.* The situation is changing by the moment. And obviously I'm not perfect. I might be overlooking something important. It is possible that those guys might turn out to be one notch ahead of me."

"Which is why it all comes down to me needing to protect myself."

"As I said."

"Thank you for everything. I'm very grateful to you."

"I don't know what you plan to do from now on," Tamaru said, "but if you do go somewhere far away, and I never see you again, I know I'll feel a little sad. You're a rare sort of character, a type I've seldom come across before."

Aomame smiled into the phone. "That's pretty much the impression I wanted to leave you with."

"Madame needs you. Not for the work you do, but on a personal level, as a companion. So I know she feels quite sad that she has to say good-bye like this. She can't come to the phone now. I hope you'll understand."

"I do," Aomame said. "I might have trouble, too, if I had to talk with her."

"You said you're going far away," Tamaru said. "How far away are we talking about?"

"It's a distance that can't be measured."

"Like the distance that separates one person's heart from another's."

Aomame closed her eyes and took a deep breath. She was on the verge of tears, but was able to hold it together.

"I'm praying that everything will go well," Tamaru said quietly.

"I'm sorry, but I may have to hold on to the Heckler & Koch," Aomame said.

"That's fine. It's my gift to you. If it gets troublesome to have, just toss it into Tokyo Bay. The world will take one small step closer to disarmament."

"I might end up never firing the pistol. Contrary to Chekhov's principle."

"That's fine, too," Tamaru said. "Nothing could be better than not firing it. We're drawing close to the end of the twentieth century. Things are different from back in Chekhov's time. No more horse-drawn carriages, no more women in corsets. Somehow the world survived the Nazis, the atomic bomb, and modern music. Even the way novels are composed has changed drastically. So it's nothing to worry about. But I do have a question. You and Tengo are going to meet on the slide tonight at seven."

"If things work out," Aomame said.

"If you do see him, what are you going to do there?"

"We're going to look at the moon."

"Very romantic," Tamaru said, gently.

CHAPTER 27

Tengo

THE WHOLE WORLD
MAY NOT BE ENOUGH

On Wednesday morning when the phone rang, Tengo was still asleep. He hadn't been able to fall asleep until nearly dawn, and the whiskey he had drunk still remained in him. He got out of bed, and was surprised to see how light it was outside.

"Tengo Kawana?" a man said. It was a voice he had never heard before.

"Yes," Tengo replied. The man's voice was quiet and businesslike, and he was sure it must be more paperwork regarding his father's death. But his alarm clock showed it was just before eight a.m. Not the time that a city office or funeral home would be calling.

"I am sorry to be calling so early, but I was rather in a hurry." Something urgent. "What is it?" Tengo's brain was still fuzzy.

"Do you recall the name Aomame?" the man asked.

Aomame? His hangover and sleepiness vanished. His mind reset quickly, like after a short blackout in a stage play. Tengo regripped the receiver.

"Yes, I do," he replied.

"It's quite an unusual name."

"We were in the same class in elementary school," Tengo said, somehow able to get his voice back to normal.

The man paused. "Mr. Kawana, do you have interest at this moment in talking about Aomame?"

Tengo found the man's way of speaking odd. His diction was unique, like listening to lines from an avant-garde translated play.

"If you do not have any interest, then it will be a waste of time for both of us. I'll end this conversation right away."

"I am interested," Tengo said hurriedly. "Sorry, but what is your connection here?"

"I have a message from her," the man said, ignoring his question. "Aomame is hoping to see you. What about you, Mr. Kawana? Would you care to see her as well?"

"I would," Tengo said. He coughed and cleared his throat. "I have been wanting to see her for a long time."

"Fine. She wants to see you. And you are hoping to see her."

Tengo suddenly realized how cold the room was. He grabbed a nearby cardigan and threw it over his pajamas.

"So what should I do?" Tengo asked.

"Can you come to the slide after dark?" the man said.

"The slide?" Tengo asked. What was this guy talking about?

"She said if I told you that, you would understand. She would like you to come to the top of the slide. I'm merely telling you what Aomame said."

Tengo's hand went to his hair, which was a mass of cowlicks and knots after sleeping. *The slide. Where I saw the two moons. It's got to be* that *slide.*

"I think I understand," he replied, his voice dry.

"Fine. Also, if there is something valuable you would like to take with you, make sure you have it on you. So you're all set to move on, far away."

"*Something valuable I would like to take with me?*" Tengo repeated in surprise.

"Something you don't want to leave behind."

Tengo pondered this. "I'm not sure I totally understand,

but by moving on far away, do you mean never coming back here?"

"I wouldn't know," the man said. "As I said previously, I am merely transmitting her message."

Tengo ran his fingers through his tangled hair and considered this. *Move on?* "I might have a fair amount of papers I would want to bring."

"That shouldn't be a problem," the man said. "You are free to choose whatever you like. However, when it comes to luggage, I have been asked to tell you that you should be able to keep both hands free."

"Keep both hands free," Tengo repeated. "So, a suitcase wouldn't work, would it?"

"I wouldn't think so."

From the man's voice it was hard to guess his age, looks, or build. It was the sort of voice that provided no tangible clues. Tengo felt he wouldn't remember the voice at all, as soon as the man hung up. Individuality or emotions – assuming there were any to begin with – were hidden deep down, out of sight.

"That's all that I need to relay," the man said.

"Is Aomame well?" Tengo asked.

"Physically, she's fine," the man said, choosing his words carefully. "Though right now she's caught in a somewhat tense situation. She has to watch her every move. One false step and it might all be over."

"*All be over,*" Tengo repeated mechanically.

"It would be best not to be too late," the man said. "Time has become an important factor."

Time has become an important factor, Tengo repeated to himself. *Was there an issue with this man's choice of words? Or am I too much on edge?*

"I think I can be at the slide at seven tonight," Tengo said. "If for some reason I'm not able to come tonight, I'll be there tomorrow at the same time."

"Understood. And you know which slide we're talking about."

"I think so."

Tengo glanced at the clock. He had eleven hours to go.

"By the way, I heard that your father passed away on Sunday. My deepest condolences."

Tengo instinctively thanked him, but then wondered how this man could possibly know about his father.

"Could you tell me a little more about Aomame?" Tengo said. "For instance, where she is, and what she does?"

"She's single. She works as a fitness instructor at a sports club in Hiroo. She's a first-rate instructor, but circumstances have changed and she has taken leave from her job. And, by sheer coincidence, she has been living not far from you. For anything beyond that, I think it best you hear directly from her."

"Even what sort of *tense situation* she's in right now?"

The man didn't respond. Either he didn't want to answer or he felt there was no need. For whatever reason, people like this seemed to flock to Tengo.

"Today at seven p.m., then, on top of the slide," the man said.

"Just a second," Tengo said quickly. "I have a question. I was warned by someone that I was being watched, and that I should be careful. Excuse me for asking, but did they mean you?"

"No, they didn't mean me," the man said immediately. "It was probably someone else who was watching you. But it is a good idea to be cautious, as that person pointed out."

"Does my being under surveillance have something to do with Aomame's unusual situation?"

"*Somewhat tense* situation," the man said, correcting him. "Yes, most likely there is some sort of connection."

"Is this dangerous?"

The man paused, and chose his words carefully, as if separating out varieties of beans from a pile. "If you call not being able to see Aomame anymore something dangerous, then yes, there is definitely danger involved."

Tengo mentally rearranged this man's roundabout phrasing into something he could understand. He didn't have a clue about the background or the circumstances, but it was obvious that things were indeed fraught.

"If things don't go well, we might not be able to see each other ever again."

"Exactly."

"I understand. I'll be careful," Tengo said.

"I'm sorry to have called so early. It would appear that I woke you up."

Without pausing, the man hung up. Tengo gazed at the black receiver in his hand. As he had predicted, as soon as they hung up, the man's voice had vanished from his memory. Tengo looked at the clock again. Eight ten. *How should I kill all this time between now and seven p.m.?* he wondered.

He started by taking a shower, washing his hair, and untangling it as best he could. Then he stood in front of the mirror and shaved, brushed his teeth, and flossed. He drank some tomato juice from the fridge, boiled water, ground coffee beans and made coffee, toasted a slice of bread. He set the timer and cooked a soft-boiled egg. He concentrated on each action, taking more time than usual. But still it was only nine thirty.

Tonight I will see Aomame on top of the slide.

The thought sent his senses spinning. His hands and legs and face all wanted to go in different directions, and he couldn't gather his emotions in one place. Whatever he tried to do, his concentration was shot. He couldn't read, couldn't write. He couldn't sit still in one place. The only thing he seemed capable of was washing the dishes, doing the laundry, straightening up his drawers, making his bed. Every five minutes he would stop whatever he was doing and glance at the clock. Thinking about time only seemed to slow it down.

Aomame knows.

He was standing at the sink, sharpening a cleaver that really didn't need to be sharpened. *She knows I've been to the slide in that playground a number of times. She must have seen me, sitting there, staring up at the sky. Otherwise it makes no sense.* He pictured what he looked like on top of the slide, lit up by the mercury-vapor lamp. He had had no sense of being observed. Where had she been watching him from?

It doesn't matter, Tengo thought. *No big deal. No matter where she saw me from, she recognized me.* The thought filled him with joy. *Just as I've been thinking of her, she's been thinking of me.* Tengo could hardly believe it – that in this frantic, labyrinth-like world, two people's hearts – a boy's and a girl's – could be connected, unchanged, even though they hadn't seen each other for twenty years.

But why didn't Aomame call out to me then, when she saw me? Things would be so much simpler if she had. And how did she know where I live? How did she – or that man – find out my phone number? He didn't like to get calls, and had an unlisted number. You couldn't get it even if you called the operator.

There was a lot that remained unknown and mysterious, and the lines that constructed this story were complicated. Which lines connected to which others, and what sort of cause-and-effect relationship existed, was beyond him. Still, ever since Fuka-Eri showed up in his life, he felt he had been living in a place where questions outnumbered answers. But he had a faint sense that this chaos was, ever so slowly, heading toward a denouement.

At seven this evening, though, at least some questions will be cleared up, Tengo thought. *We'll meet on top of the slide. Not as a helpless ten-year-old boy and girl, but as an independent, grown-up man and woman. As a math teacher in a cram school and a sports club instructor. What will we talk about then? I have no idea. But we will talk – we need to fill in the blanks between us, exchange information about each other. And – to borrow the phrasing of the man who called – we might then* move on *some-*where. *So I need to make sure to bring what's important to me, what I don't want to leave behind – and pack it away so that I can have both hands free.*

I have no regrets about leaving here. I lived here for seven years, taught three days a week at the cram school, but never once felt it was home. Like a floating island bobbing along in the flow, it was just a temporary place to rest, and nothing more. My girlfriend is no longer here. Fuka-Eri, too, who shared the place briefly – gone. Tengo had no idea where these two women were now, or what they were doing. They had simply, and quietly, vanished from his life. If he left the cram school, someone else would surely take over. The world would keep on turning, even without him. If Aomame wanted to *move on somewhere* with him, there was nothing to keep him from going.

What could be the important thing he should take with him? Fifty thousand yen in cash and a plastic debit card – that was the extent of the assets he had at hand. There was also one million yen in a savings account. No – there was more. His share of the royalties from *Air Chrysalis* was in the account as well. He had been meaning to return it to Komatsu but hadn't gotten around to it. Then there was the printout of the novel he had begun. He couldn't leave that behind. It had no real value to anyone else, but to Tengo it was precious. He put the manuscript in a paper bag, then stuffed it into the hard, russet nylon shoulder bag he used when he went to the cram school. The bag was really heavy now. He crammed floppy disks into the pocket of his leather jacket. He couldn't very well take his word processor along with him, but he did add his notebooks and fountain pen to his luggage. *What else?* he wondered.

He remembered the envelope the lawyer had given him in Chikura. Inside were his father's savings book and seal, a copy of their family record, and the mysterious family photo (if indeed that was what it was). It was probably best to take that with him. His elementary school report cards and the NHK commendations he would leave behind. He decided against taking a change of clothes or toiletries. They wouldn't fit in the now-bulging bag, and besides, he could buy them as needed.

Once he had packed everything in the bag, he had nothing left to do. There were no dishes to wash, no shirts left to iron. He looked at the wall clock again. Ten thirty. He thought he should call his friend to take over his classes at the cram school, but then remembered that his friend was always in a terrible mood if you phoned before noon.

Tengo lay down on his bed, fully clothed, and let his mind wander through various possibilities. The last time he saw Aomame was when he was ten. Now they were both thirty. They had both gone through a lot of experiences in the interim. Good things, things that weren't so good (probably slightly more of the latter). *Our looks, our personalities, the environment where we live have all gone through changes,* he thought. *We're no longer a young boy and a young girl.* Is the Aomame over there really the Aomame he had been searching for? And was he the Tengo Kawana she had been looking for? Tengo pictured them on the slide tonight looking at each other, disappointed at what they saw. Maybe they wouldn't find anything to talk about. That was a real possibility. Actually, it would be kind of strange if it didn't turn out that way.

Maybe we shouldn't meet again. Tengo stared up at the ceiling. *Wasn't it better if they kept this desire to see each other hidden within them, and never actually got together? That way, there would always be hope in their hearts. That hope would be a small, yet vital flame that warmed them to their core – a tiny flame to cup one's hands around and protect from the wind, a flame that the violent winds of reality might easily extinguish.*

Tengo stared at the ceiling for a good hour, two conflicting emotions surging through him. More than anything, he wanted to meet Aomame. At the same time, he was afraid to see her. The cold disappointment and uncomfortable silence that might ensue made him shudder. His body felt like it was going to be torn in half. But he *had* to see her. This is what he had been wanting, what he had been hoping for with all his might, for the last twenty years. No matter what disappointment might come of it, he knew he couldn't just turn his back on it and run away.

Tired of staring at the ceiling, he fell asleep on the bed, still lying faceup. A quiet, dreamless sleep of some forty or forty-five minutes – the deep, satisfying sleep you get after concentrating hard, after mental exhaustion. He realized that for the last few days he had only slept in fits and starts and hadn't gotten a good night's sleep. Before it got dark, he needed to rid himself of the fatigue that had built up. He had to be rested and relaxed when he left here and headed for the playground. He knew this instinctively.

As he was falling asleep, he heard Kumi Adachi's voice – or he felt like he heard it. *When morning comes you'll be leaving here, Tengo. Before the exit is blocked.*

This was Kumi's voice, and at the same time it was the voice of the owl at night. In his memory the voices were mixed, and hard to distinguish from each other. What Tengo needed then more than anything was wisdom – the wisdom of the night that had put down roots into the soil. A wisdom that might only be found in the depths of sleep.

At six thirty Tengo slung his bag diagonally across his shoulders and left his apartment. He had on the same clothes as the last time he went to the slide: gray windbreaker and old leather jacket, jeans, and brown work boots. All of them were worn but they fit well, like an extension of his body. *I probably won't ever be back here again,* he thought. As a precaution he took the typed cards with his name on them out of the door slot and the mailbox. *What would happen to everything else?* He decided not to worry about it for now.

As he stood at the entrance to the apartment building, he peered around cautiously. If he believed Fuka-Eri, he was being watched. But just as before, there was no sign of surveillance. Everything was the same as always. Now that the sun had set, the road in front of him was deserted. He set off for the station, at a slow pace. He glanced back from time to time to make sure he wasn't being followed. He turned down several narrow streets he didn't need to take, then came to a stop and checked again to see if anyone was tailing him. *You have to be careful,* the man on the phone had cautioned. *For yourself, and for Aomame, who's in a* tense situation.

But does the man on the phone really know Aomame? Tengo suddenly wondered. *Couldn't this be some kind of clever trap?* Once this thought took hold, he couldn't shake off a sense of unease. If this really was a trap, then Sakigake had to be behind it. As the ghostwriter of *Air Chrysalis* he was probably – no, make that *definitely* – on their blacklist. Which is why that weird guy, Ushikawa, came to him with that suspicious story about a grant. On top of that, Tengo had let Fuka-Eri hide out in his apartment for three months. There were more than enough reasons for the cult to be upset with him.

Be that as it may, Tengo thought, inclining his head, *why would they go to the trouble of using Aomame as bait to lure me into a trap? They already know where I am. It's not like I'm running away and hiding. If they have some business with me, they should approach me directly. There's no need to lure me out to that slide in the playground. Things would be different if the opposite were true – if they were using me as bait to get Aomame.*

But why lure her out?

He couldn't understand it. Was there, by chance, some connection between Aomame and Sakigake? Tengo's deductive reasoning hit a dead end. The only thing he could do was to ask Aomame herself – assuming he could meet her.

At any rate, as the man on the phone said, he would have to be cautious. Tengo scrupulously took a roundabout route and made sure no one was following him. Once certain of that, he hurried off in the direction of the playground.

He arrived at the playground at seven minutes to seven. It was dark out already, and the mercury-vapor lamp shone its even, artificial illumination into every nook and cranny of the tiny park. The afternoon had been lovely and warm, but now that the sun had set the temperature had dropped sharply, and a cold wind was blowing. The pleasant Indian summer weather they had had for a few days had vanished, and real winter, cold and severe, had settled in for the duration. The tips of the zelkova tree's branches trembled, like the fingers of some ancient person shaking out a warning, with a desiccated, raspy sound.

Lights were on in several of the windows in the buildings nearby, but the playground was deserted. Tengo's heart under the leather jacket beat out a slow but heavy rhythm. He rubbed his hands together repeatedly, to see if they had normal sensation. *Everything's fine,* he told himself. *I'm all set. Nothing to be afraid of.* He made up his mind and started climbing up the ladder of the slide.

Once on top, he sat down as he had before. The bottom of the slide was cold and slightly damp. With his hands in his pockets, he leaned against the railing and looked up at the sky. There were clouds of all sizes – several large ones, several small ones. Tengo squinted and looked for the moons, but at the moment they weren't visible, hidden behind the clouds. These weren't dense, heavy clouds, but rather smooth white ones. Still, they were thick and substantial enough to hide the moons from his gaze. The clouds were gliding slowly from north to south. The wind didn't seem too strong. Or maybe the clouds were actually higher up than they looked? At any rate, they weren't in much of a hurry.

Tengo glanced at his watch. The hands showed three past seven, ticking away the time ever more accurately. Still no Aomame. Tengo spent several minutes gazing at the hands of his watch as if they were something extraordinary. Then he shut his eyes. Like the clouds on the wind, he was in no hurry. If things took time, he didn't mind. He stopped thinking and gave himself over to the flow of time. At this moment, time's natural, even flow was the most important thing.

With his eyes closed, he carefully listened to the sounds around him, as if searching for stations on a radio. He could hear the ceaseless hum of traffic on the expressway. It reminded him of the Pacific surf at the sanatorium in Chikura. A few seagull calls must have been mixed in as well. He could hear the intermittent beep as a large truck backed up, and a huge dog barking a short, sharp warning. Far away someone was shouting out a person's name. He couldn't tell where all these sounds were coming from. With his eyes closed for this long, each and every sound lost its sense of direction and distance. The freezing wind swirled up from time to time, but he didn't feel the cold. Tengo had temporarily forgotten how to feel or react to all stimulations and sensations.

He was suddenly aware of someone sitting beside him, holding his right hand. Like a small creature seeking warmth, a hand slipped inside the pocket of his leather jacket and clasped his large hand. By the time he became fully aware, it had already happened. Without any preface, the situation had jumped to the next stage. *How strange,* Tengo thought, his eyes still closed. *How did this happen?* At one point time was flowing along so slowly that he could barely stand it. Then suddenly it had leapt ahead, skipping whatever lay between.

This person held his big hand even tighter, as if to make sure he was *really there*. Long smooth fingers, with an underlying strength.

Aomame. But he didn't say it aloud. He didn't open his eyes. He just squeezed her hand in return. He remembered this hand. Never once in twenty years had he forgotten the feeling. Of course, it was no longer the tiny hand of a ten-year-old girl. Over the past twenty years her hand had touched many things. It had clasped untold numbers of objects in every possible shape. And the strength within it had grown. Yet Tengo knew right away: this was the very same hand. The way it squeezed his own hand and the feeling it was trying to convey were exactly the same.

Inside him, twenty years dissolved and mixed into one complex, swirling whole. Everything that had accumulated over the years – all he had seen, all the words he had spoken, all the values he had held – all of it coalesced into one solid, thick pillar in his heart, the core of which was spinning like a potter's wheel. Wordlessly, Tengo observed the scene, as if watching the destruction and rebirth of a planet.

Aomame kept silent as well. The two of them on top of the freezing slide, wordlessly holding hands. Once again they were a ten-year-old boy and girl. A lonely boy, and a lonely girl. A classroom, just after school let out, at the beginning of winter. They had neither the power nor the knowledge to know what they should offer to each other, what they should be seeking. They had never, ever, been truly loved, or truly loved someone else. They had never held anyone, never been held. They had no idea, either, where this action would take them. What they entered then was a doorless room. They couldn't get out, nor could anyone else come in. The two of them didn't know it at the time, but this was the only truly complete place in the entire world. Totally isolated, yet the one place not tainted with loneliness.

How much time had passed? Five minutes, perhaps, or was it an hour? Or a whole day? Or maybe time had stood still. What did Tengo understand about time? He knew he could stay like this forever, the two of them silent on top of the slide, holding hands. He had felt that way at age ten, and now, twenty years on, he felt the same.

He knew, too, that it would take time for him to acclimate himself to this new world that had come upon him. His entire way of thinking, his way of seeing things, the way he breathed, the way he moved his body – he would need to adjust and rethink every single element of life. And to do that, he needed to gather together all the time that existed in this world. No – maybe the whole world wouldn't be enough.

"Tengo," Aomame whispered, a voice neither low or high – a voice holding out a promise. "Open your eyes."

Tengo opened his eyes. Time began to flow again in the world.

"There's the moon," Aomame said.

CHAPTER 28

Ushikawa

AND A PART OF HIS SOUL

The fluorescent light on the ceiling shone down on Ushikawa's body. The heat was turned off, and a window was open, so the room was as freezing as an icehouse. Several conference tables had been shoved together in the center of the room, and on top of them, Ushikawa lay faceup. He had on winter long johns, and an old blanket was thrown on top of him. Under the blanket, his stomach was swollen, like an anthill in a field. A small piece of cloth covered his questioning, opened eyes – eyes that no one had been able to close. His lips were slightly parted, lips from which no breath or words would ever slip out again. The crown of his head was flatter, and more enigmatic-looking, than it had been while he was alive. Thick, black, frizzy hair – reminiscent of pubic hair – shabbily surrounded that crown.

Buzzcut had on a navy-blue down jacket, while Ponytail was wearing a brown suede rancher's coat with a fur-trimmed collar. Both were slightly ill-fitting, as if they had hurriedly grabbed them from a limited supply of clothing that happened to be on hand. They were indoors, but their breath was white in the cold. The three of them were the sole occupants of the room. Buzzcut, Ponytail, and Ushikawa. There were three aluminum-sash windows on one wall, near the ceiling, and one of them was wide open to help keep the temperature down. Other than the tables with the body, there was no other furniture. It was an entirely bland, no-nonsense room. Placed there, even a corpse – even Ushikawa's – looked like a colorless, utilitarian object.

No one was talking. The room was utterly devoid of sound. Buzzcut had a lot to ponder, and Ponytail never spoke anyway. Buzzcut was lost in thought, pacing back and forth in front of the table that held Ushikawa's body. Except for the moment when he reached the wall and had to turn around, his pace never slackened. His leather shoes were totally silent as they trod upon the cheap, light yellow-green carpeting. As usual, Ponytail staked out a spot near the door and stood there, motionless, legs slightly apart, back straight, staring off at an invisible point in space. He didn't seem tired or cold, not at all. The only evidence that he was still among the living was an occasional rapid burst of blinks, and the measured white breath that left his mouth.

Earlier that day, a number of people had gathered in that freezing room to discuss the situation. One of Sakigake's high-ranking members had been on a trip and it had taken a day to get everyone together. The meeting was secret, and they spoke in hushed tones so no one outside could hear. All this time, Ushikawa's corpse had lain there on the table, like a sample at an industrial machinery convention. Rigor mortis had set in on the corpse, and it would be another three days before that broke and the body was pliable again. Everyone shot the occasional quick glance at the body as they discussed several practical matters.

While they were discussing things there was no sense – even when the talk turned to the deceased – that they were paying respects to him or feeling regret for his passing. The stiff, stocky corpse simply reminded them of certain lessons, and reconfirmed a few reflections on life. Nothing more. Once time has passed, it can't be taken back. If death brings about any resolution, it's one that only applies to the deceased. Those sorts of lessons, those sorts of reflections.

What should they do with Ushikawa's body? They knew the answer before they began. Ushikawa had died of unnatural causes, and if he were discovered, the police would launch an all-out investigation that would inevitably uncover his connection with Sakigake. They couldn't risk that. As soon as the rigor mortis was gone, they would secretly transport the corpse to the industrial-sized incinerator on the grounds of their compound and dispose of it. Soon it would become nothing but black smoke and white ash. The smoke would be absorbed into the sky, the ash would be spread on the fields as fertilizer for the vegetables. They had performed the same operation a number of times, under Buzzcut's supervision. Leader's body had been too big, so they had "handled" it by using a chain saw to cut it into pieces. There was no need to do so this time, for Ushikawa was nowhere near as big. Buzzcut was grateful for that. He didn't like any operations that got too gory. Whether it was dealing with the living or the dead, he preferred not to see any blood.

His superior asked Buzzcut some questions. Who could have killed Ushikawa? And what was Ushikawa doing in that rented apartment in Koenji, anyway? As head of security, Buzzcut had to respond, though he really didn't know the answers.

Before dawn on Tuesday he had gotten the call from that mysterious man (who was, of course, Tamaru) and learned that Ushikawa's body was in the apartment. Their conversation was at once practical and indirect. As soon as he hung up, Buzzcut immediately put out a call to a couple of followers in Tokyo. They changed into work uniforms, pretending to be movers, and headed out to the apartment in a Toyota HiAce van. Before they went inside, they made sure it wasn't a trap. They parked the van and one of them scouted out the surroundings for anything suspicious. They needed to be very cautious. The police might be lying in wait, ready to arrest them as soon as they set foot in the place, something they had to avoid at all costs.

They had brought along a container, the kind used in moving, and somehow were able to stuff the already-stiff body inside. Then they shouldered it out of the building and into the bed of the van. It was late at night, and cold, so fortunately there was no one else around. It took some time to comb through the apartment to make sure no telling evidence was left behind. Using flashlights, they searched every square inch, but they found nothing incriminating, just food, a small electric space heater, a sleeping bag, and a few other basic necessities. The garbage can was mainly full of empty cans and plastic bottles. It appeared that Ushikawa had been holed up there doing surveillance. Buzzcut's sharp eye noted the indentations in the tatami near the window that indicated the presence of a camera tripod, though there was no camera and there were no photographs. The person who had taken Ushikawa's life must have also taken the camera away, along with the film. Since Ushikawa was dressed only in his underwear, he must have been attacked while asleep. The attacker must have silently slipped inside the apartment. It looked like Ushikawa had suffered horribly, for his underwear was completely saturated with urine.

Buzzcut and Ponytail were the only ones in the van when they transported the body to Yamanashi. The other two stayed behind in Tokyo to handle anything that might come up. Ponytail drove the entire way. The HiAce left the Metropolitan Expressway, got onto the Chuo Highway, and headed west. It was still dark out and the expressway was nearly deserted, but they kept their speed under the limit. If the police stopped them now it would be all over. Their license plates – both front and rear – were stolen, and the container in back contained a dead body. There would be no way to talk their way out of that situation. The two of them were silent for the entire trip.

When they arrived at the compound at dawn, a Sakigake doctor examined Ushikawa's body and confirmed that he had died of suffocation. There were no signs of strangulation around the neck, however. The doctor guessed that a bag or something that didn't leave any evidence must have been placed over the victim's head. There were no marks, either, to indicate that the victim's hands and feet had been tied. He didn't appear to have been beaten or tortured. His expression didn't show any signs of agony. If you had to describe his expression, you would say it was one of pure confusion, as if he had been asking a question he knew wouldn't be answered. It was obvious that he had been murdered, but the corpse was remarkably untouched, which the doctor found odd. Whoever had killed him may have massaged his features after his death, to give him a calmer, more natural expression.

"Whoever did this was a real professional," Buzzcut explained to his superior. "There are no marks on him at all. He probably never had a chance to even scream. It happened in the middle of the night, and if he had yelled out in pain, everyone in the building would have heard him. This is the work of a professional hit man."

But why had Ushikawa ended up murdered by a professional killer?

Buzzcut chose his words carefully. "I think Mr. Ushikawa must have stepped on somebody's tail, someone he never should have crossed. Before he even realized what he had done."

Was this the same person who had disposed of Leader?

"I don't have any proof, but the chances are pretty good," Buzzcut said. "And I think Mr. Ushikawa must have undergone something close to torture. I don't know what exactly was done to him, but he definitely was interrogated ruthlessly."

How much did he say?

"I'm sure he told everything he knew," Buzzcut said. "I have no doubt about it. But Ushikawa only had limited knowledge of what was going on. So I don't think that anything he told them will come back to hurt us."

Buzzcut didn't have access to everything that was going on within Sakigake, though he knew a lot more than an outsider.

By professional, do you mean this person is connected to organized crime? the superior asked.

"This isn't the work of the yakuza or organized criminals," Buzzcut said, shaking his head. "They're less subtle and more gory. They wouldn't do something this intricate. Whoever killed Ushikawa was sending us a message. He's telling us he has a sophisticated system backing him up, and if anybody tries anything, there will be consequences. And that we should keep our noses out of it."

It?

Buzzcut shook his head. "What exactly he means by that, I don't know. Ushikawa was working on his own. I asked him any number of times to give me a progress report, but he insisted that he still didn't have enough material. I think he wanted to gather all the facts together by himself first. Which is why he was the only one who knew what was going on when he was murdered. It was Leader himself who had originally singled out Ushikawa. He worked as a kind of independent agent. He didn't like organizations. Considering the chain of command, I wasn't in a position to give him orders."

Buzzcut wanted to make it absolutely clear how far his responsibility extended. Sakigake was itself an established organization. All organizations have rules, and breaking these rules could lead to punishment. He did not want to be blamed for mishandling this affair.

Who was Ushikawa watching in that apartment building?

"We don't know yet. Normally you would expect it to be someone who lives in the building, or in the vicinity. The men I left back in Tokyo are investigating as we speak, but they haven't reported in yet. It will take some time. It might be best if I go back to Tokyo and look into it myself."

Buzzcut wasn't all that confident in the abilities of the men he had left behind. They were devoted, but not the sharpest pencils in the box. And he hadn't explained the situation in much detail to them. It would be much more efficient for him to take charge directly. They should go through Ushikawa's office as well, though the man on the phone might have already beaten them to it. His superior, however, didn't permit him to return to Tokyo. Until things got a bit clearer, he and Ponytail were to stay put. That was an order.

Was Aomame the person Ushikawa had been watching?

"No, it couldn't have been Aomame," Buzzcut said. "If Aomame had been there, he would have immediately reported it. That would have completed his assignment. I think the person he had under watch was connected to – or *might* have been connected to – Aomame's whereabouts. Otherwise it doesn't add up."

And while he had that person under surveillance, someone found out about him, and took steps to stop him?

"That would be my guess," Buzzcut said. "He was getting too close to something dangerous. He may have found some vital clue. If there had been several people on the surveillance work, they could have watched each other's backs and things might have ended up differently."

You spoke directly to that man on the phone. Does it look as though we'll be able to meet Aomame and talk with her?

"I really can't predict. I would imagine, though, that if Aomame isn't willing to negotiate with us, the chances are slim that there will be any meeting. That would be my guess. Everything depends on how she wants to play it."

They should be pleased that we're willing to overlook what happened to Leader and guarantee her safety.

"They want more information. Such as, why do we want to meet with Aomame? Why are we seeking a truce? What exactly are we hoping to negotiate?"

The fact that they want to learn more means they don't have any solid information.

"Exactly. But we don't have any solid information about them, either. We still don't even know the reason they went to all the time and trouble to concoct a plan to murder Leader."

Either way, while we wait for their reply, we have to keep on searching for Aomame. Even if it means stepping on somebody's tail.

Buzzcut paused a moment, and then spoke. "We have a close-knit organization here. We can put a team together and get them out in the field in no time at all. We have a sense of purpose and high morale. People are literally willing to sacrifice themselves, if need be. But from a purely technical perspective, we're nothing more than a band of amateurs. We haven't had any specialized training. Compared with us, the other side are consummate professionals. They know what they're doing, they take action calmly, and they never hesitate. They seem like real veterans. As you're aware, Mr. Ushikawa was no slouch himself."

How exactly do you propose to continue the search?

"At present I think it's best to pursue the *valuable lead* that Mr. Ushikawa himself unearthed. Whatever it may be."

Meaning we don't have any valuable leads of our own?

"Correct," Buzzcut admitted.

No matter how dangerous it might become, and what sacrifices have to be made, we have to find and secure this woman Aomame. As quickly as possible.

"Is this what the voice has directed us to do?" Buzzcut asked. "That we should secure Aomame as quickly as possible? By whatever means necessary?"

His superior didn't reply. Information beyond this was above Buzzcut's pay grade. He was not one of the top brass, merely the head foot soldier. But Buzzcut knew that this was the final message given by *them,* most likely the final "voice" that the shrine maidens had heard.

As Buzzcut paced in front of Ushikawa's corpse in the freezing-cold room, a thought suddenly flashed through his head. He came to an abrupt halt, frowning, his brow knit, as he tried to grab hold of it. The moment he stopped pacing, Pony-tail moved. A fraction. He let out a deep breath, and shifted his weight from one foot to the other.

Koenji, Buzzcut thought. He frowned slightly, searching the dark depths of memory. Ever so cautiously, he pulled at a thin thread, tugging it toward him. *Somebody else involved in this affair lives in Koenji. But who?*

He took a thick, crumpled memo pad out of his pocket and flipped through it. Tengo Kawana. His address was in Koenji, Suginami Ward. The same exact address, in fact, as the building in which Ushikawa died. Only the apartment numbers were different – the third floor and the first floor. Had Ushikawa been secretly watching Tengo's movements? There was no doubt about it. The two of them living in the same building was too big a coincidence.

But why, in this situation, did Ushikawa have to trace Tengo's movements? Buzzcut hadn't recalled Tengo's address up till now because he was no longer concerned about him. Tengo was nothing more than a ghostwriter. There had been nothing else about him that they needed to know. Sakigake's interest was now entirely focused on locating Aomame. Despite this, Ushikawa had focused all his attention on the cram school instructor, setting up an elaborate stakeout. And losing his own life in the bargain. *Why?*

Buzzcut couldn't figure it out. Ushikawa clearly had some sort of lead. He must have thought that sticking close to Tengo would lead him to Aomame – which is why he went to the trouble of securing that apartment, setting up a camera on a tripod, and observing Tengo, probably for some time. But what connection could there be between Tengo and Aomame?

Without a word, Buzzcut left the room, went into the room next door – which was heated – and made a phone call to Tokyo, to a unit in a condo in Sakuragaoka in Shibuya. He ordered one of his subordinates to immediately go back to Ushikawa's apartment in Koenji and keep watch over Tengo's movements. Tengo is a large man, with short hair, so you can't miss him, he instructed him. If he leaves the building, the two of you are to tail him, but make sure he doesn't spot you. Don't let him out of your sight. Find out where he's going. At all costs, you've got to keep him under surveillance. We'll join you as soon as we can.

Buzzcut went back to the room that held Ushikawa's body and told Ponytail they would be leaving right away for Tokyo. Ponytail gave a slight nod. He didn't ask for an explanation. He grasped what was asked of him and leapt into action. After they left the room, Buzzcut locked it so that no outsiders would have access. They went out of the building and chose, from a line of ten cars, a black Nissan Gloria. They got in, and Ponytail turned the key, already in the ignition, and started the engine. As per their rules, the car's gas tank was full. Ponytail would drive, as usual. The license plates for the Gloria sedan were legal, the registration clean, so even if they exceeded the speed limit a bit, it wouldn't be a problem.

They had been on the highway for a while by the time it occurred to Buzzcut that he hadn't gotten permission from his superiors to go back to Tokyo. This could come back to haunt him, but it was too late now. There wasn't a moment to lose.

He would have to explain the situation to them after he got to Tokyo. He frowned a bit. Sometimes the restrictions disgusted him. The number of rules increased, but never decreased. Still, he knew he couldn't survive outside the system. He was no lone wolf. He was one cog among many, following orders from above.

He switched on the radio and listened to the regular eight o'clock news. When the broadcast was done, Buzzcut turned off the radio, adjusted his seat, and took a short nap. When he woke up he felt hungry – *How long has it been since I've had a decent meal?* he wondered – but there was no time to stop at a rest area for a bite to eat. They were in too much of a hurry.

By this time, however, Tengo had been reunited with Aomame on top of the slide in the park. Buzzcut and Ponytail had no idea where Tengo was headed. Above Tengo and Aomame, the two moons hung in the sky.

Ushikawa's body lay there in the frozen darkness. No one else was in the room. The lights were off, the door locked from the outside. Through the windows near the ceiling, pale moonlight shone in. But the angle made it impossible for Ushikawa to see the moon. So he couldn't know if there was one moon, or two.

There was no clock in the room, so it was unclear what time it was. Probably an hour or so had passed since Buzzcut and Ponytail had left. If someone else had been there, he would have seen Ushikawa's mouth suddenly begin to move. He would have been frightened out of his wits. This was a terrifying, wholly unexpected event. Ushikawa had long since expired and his body was stiff as a board. Despite this, his mouth continued to tremble slightly. Then, with a dry sound, it opened wide.

If someone had been there, he would no doubt have expected Ushikawa to say something. Some pearls of wisdom that only the dead could impart. Terrified, the person would have waited with bated breath. What secret could he be about to reveal?

But no voice came out. What came out were not words, not a drawn-out breath, but six tiny people, each about two inches tall. Their little bodies were dressed in tiny clothes, and they trod over the greenish mossy tongue, clambering over the dirty, irregular teeth. One by one they emerged, like miners returning to the surface after a hard day's labor. But unlike miners their clothes and faces were sparkling clean, not soiled at all. They were free of all dirt and wear.

Six Little People came out of Ushikawa's mouth and climbed down to the conference table, where each one shook himself and gradually grew bigger. When needed, they could adjust their size, but they never grew taller than a yard or shorter than an inch. When they grew to between twenty-four and twenty-eight inches tall, they stopped shaking and then, in order, descended from the table to the floor. The Little People's faces had no expression. But they weren't like masks. They had quite ordinary faces – smaller, but no different from yours or mine. It's just that, at that moment, they felt no need for any expression.

They seemed neither in a hurry nor too relaxed. They had exactly the right amount of time for the work that they needed to do. That time was neither too long nor too short. Without any obvious signal, the six of them quietly sat down on the floor in a circle. It was a perfect little circle, precisely two yards in diameter.

Wordlessly, one of them reached out and grabbed a single thin thread from the air. The thread was about six inches long, nearly a transparent white, almost creamy color. He placed the thread on the floor. The next person did exactly the same, the same color and thread length. The next three followed suit. Only the last one did something different. He stood up, left the circle, clambered back up on the conference table, reached out, and plucked one frizzy hair from Ushikawa's misshapen head. The hair came out with a tiny *snap*. This was his substitute thread. With practiced hands the first of the Little People wove together those five air threads and the single hair from Ushikawa's head.

And thus the Little People made a new air chrysalis. No one talked now, or chanted out a rhythm. They silently pulled threads from the air, plucked hairs from Ushikawa's head, and – in a set, smooth rhythm – briskly wove together an air chrysalis. Even in the freezing room their breath wasn't white. If anyone else had been there to see it, he might have found this odd too. Or perhaps he wouldn't have even noticed, given all the other surprising things going on.

No matter how intently the Little People worked (and they never stopped), completing an air chrysalis in one night was out of the question. It would take at least three days. But they didn't appear to be rushing. It would be another two days before Ushikawa's rigor mortis had passed and his body could be taken to the incinerator. They were well aware of this. If they got most of it done in two nights, that would be fine. They had enough time for what they needed to do. And they never got tired.

Ushikawa lay on the table, bathed in pale moonlight. His mouth was wide open, as were his unclosable eyes, which were covered by thick cloth. In their final moment, those eyes had seen a house, and a tiny dog scampering about a small patch of lawn.

And a part of his soul was about to change into an air chrysalis.

CHAPTER 29

Aomame

I'LL NEVER LET GO OF
YOUR HAND AGAIN

"Tengo, open your eyes," Aomame whispered. Tengo opened his eyes. Time began to flow again in the world.

"There's the moon," Aomame said.

Tengo raised his face and looked up at the sky. The clouds had parted and above the bare branches of the zelkova tree he could make out the moons. A large yellow moon and a smaller, misshapen green one. *Maza* and *dohta*. The glow colored the edges of the passing clouds, like a long skirt whose hem had been accidentally dipped in dye.

Tengo turned now to look over at Aomame sitting beside him. She was no longer a skinny, undernourished ten-year-old girl, dressed in ill-fitting hand-me-downs, her hair crudely trimmed by her mother. There was little left of the girl she had been, yet Tengo knew her at a glance. This was clearly Aomame and no other. Her eyes, brimming with expression, were the same, even after twenty years. Strong, unclouded, clear eyes. Eyes that knew exactly what they longed for. Eyes that knew full well what they should see, and weren't going to let any-one get in her way. And those eyes were looking right at him. Straight into his heart.

Aomame had spent the last twenty years somewhere

unknown to him. During that time, she had grown into a beautiful woman. Instantly and without reservation, Tengo absorbed all those places, and all that time, and they became a part of his own flesh and blood. They were his places now. His time.

I should say something, Tengo thought, but no words would come. He moved his lips, just barely, searching for proper words in the air, but they were nowhere to be found. All that came out from between his lips were swirls of white breath, like a wandering solitary island. As she gazed into his eyes, Aomame gave a slight shake of her head, just once. Tengo understood what that meant. *You don't have to say a thing.* She continued to hold his hand inside his pocket. She didn't let go, not even for a moment.

"We're seeing the same thing," Aomame said quietly as she gazed deep into his eyes. This was, at once, a question and a confirmation.

"There are two moons," Aomame said.

Tengo nodded. *There are two moons.* He didn't say this aloud. For some reason his voice wouldn't come. He just thought it.

Aomame closed her eyes. She curled up and pressed her cheek against his chest. Her ear was right above his heart. She was listening to his thoughts. "I needed to know this," Aomame said. "That we're in the same world, seeing the same things."

Tengo suddenly noticed that the whirling pillar rising up inside him had vanished. All that surrounded him now was a quiet winter night. There were lights on in a few of the windows in the apartment building across the way, hinting at people other than themselves alive in this world. This struck the two of them as exceedingly strange, even as somehow illogical – that other people could also exist, and be living their lives, in the same world.

Tengo leaned over slightly and breathed in the fragrance of Aomame's hair. Beautiful, straight hair. Her small, pink ears peeped out like shy little creatures.

It was such a long time, Aomame thought.

It was such a long time, Tengo thought too. At the same time, though, he noticed how the twenty years that had passed now held no substance. It had all passed by in an instant, and took but an instant to be filled in.

Tengo took his hand out of his pocket and put it around her shoulder. Through his palm he could feel the wholeness of her body. He raised his face and looked up at the moons again. Through breaks in the clouds, the odd pair of moons was still bathing the earth in a strange mix of color. The clouds made their way leisurely across the sky. Under that light, Tengo once again keenly felt the mind's ability to relativize time. Twenty years was a long time. But Tengo knew that if he were to meet Aomame in another twenty years, he would feel the same way he did now. Even if they were both over fifty, he would still feel the same mix of excitement and confusion in her presence. His heart would be filled with the same joy and certainty.

Tengo kept these thoughts to himself, but he knew that Aomame was listening carefully to these unspoken words. Her little pink ear pressed against his chest. She was hearing everything that went on in his heart, like a person who can trace a map with his fingertip and conjure up vivid, living scenery.

"I want to stay here forever and forget all about time," Aomame said in a small voice. "But there's something the two of us have to do."

We have to move on, Tengo thought.

"That's right, we have to move on," Aomame said. "The sooner the better. We don't have much time left. Though I can't yet put into words where we're going."

There's no need for words, Tengo thought.

"Don't you want to know where we're going?" Aomame asked.

Tengo shook his head. The winds of reality had not

extinguished the flame in his heart. There was nothing more significant.

"We will never be apart," Aomame said. "That's more clear than anything. We will never let go of each other's hand again."

A new cloud appeared and gradually swallowed up the moons. The shadow enveloping the world grew one shade deeper.

"We have to hurry," Aomame whispered. The two of them stood up on the slide. Once again their shadows became one. Like little children groping their way through a dark forest, they held on tightly to each other's hand.

"We're going to leave the cat town," Tengo said, speaking aloud for the first time. Aomame treasured this fresh, new-born voice.

"The cat town?"

"The town at the mercy of a deep loneliness during the day and, come night, of large cats. There's a beautiful river running through it, and an old stone bridge spanning the river. But it's not where we should stay."

We call this world *by different names,* Aomame thought. *I call it* the year 1Q84, *while he calls it the* cat town. *But it all means the same thing.* Aomame squeezed his hand even tighter.

"You're right, we're going to leave the cat town now. The two of us, together," Aomame said. "Once we leave this town, day or night, we will never be apart."

As the two of them hurried out of the park, the pair of moons remained hidden behind the slowly moving clouds. The eyes of the moons were covered. And the boy and the girl, hand in hand, made their way out of the forest.

CHAPTER 30

Tengo

IF I'M NOT MISTAKEN

After they left the park, they walked out onto the main street and hailed a cab. Aomame told the driver to take them to San-genjaya, via Route 246.

For the first time, Tengo noticed what Aomame was wearing. She had on a light-colored spring coat, too thin for this cold time of year. The coat was belted in front. Underneath was a nicely tailored green suit. The skirt was short and tight. She had on stockings and lustrous high heels, and carried a black leather shoulder bag. The bag was bulging and looked heavy. She wasn't wearing any gloves or a muffler, no rings or necklace or earrings, no hint of perfume. To Tengo, what she had on, and what she had omitted, looked entirely natural. He could think of nothing that needed to be added or removed.

The taxi sped down Ring Road 7 toward Route 246. Traffic was flowing along unusually smoothly. For a long time after they got in the taxi, the two of them didn't speak. The radio in the taxi was off, and the young driver was very quiet. All the two of them heard was the ceaseless, monotonous hum of tires. Aomame leaned against Tengo, still clutching his large hand. If she let go she might never find him again. Around them the night city flowed by like a phosphorescent tide.

*   *   *

"There are several things I need to say to you," Aomame said, after a while. "I don't think I can explain everything before we arrive *there*. We don't have that much time. But maybe if we had all the time in the world I still couldn't explain it."

Tengo shook his head slightly. There was no need to explain everything now. They could fill in all the gaps later, as they went – if there were indeed gaps that needed to be filled. Tengo felt that as long as it was something the two of them could share – even a gap they had to abandon or a riddle they never could solve – he could discover a joy there, something akin to love.

"What do I need to know about you at this point?" Tengo asked.

"What do you know about me?" Aomame asked in return.

"Almost nothing," Tengo said. "You're an instructor at a sports club. You're single. You've been living in Koenji."

"I know almost nothing about you, too," Aomame said, "though I do know a few small things. You teach math at a cram school in Yoyogi. You live alone. And you're the one who really wrote *Air Chrysalis*."

Tengo looked at her face, his lips parted in surprise. There were very few people who knew this about him. Did she have some connection with the cult?

"Don't worry. We're on the same side," she said. "If I told you how I came to know this, it would take too long. But I do know that you wrote *Air Chrysalis* together with Eriko Fukada. And that you and I both entered a world where there are two moons in the sky. And there's one more thing. I'm carrying a child. I believe it's yours. For now, these are the important things you ought to know."

"You're *carrying my child*?" The driver might be listening, but Tengo wasn't worrying about it at this point.

"We haven't seen each other in twenty years," Aomame said, "but yes, I'm carrying your child. I'm going to give birth to your child. I know it sounds totally crazy."

Tengo was silent, waiting for her to continue.

"Do you remember that terrible thunderstorm in the beginning of September?"

"I remember it well," Tengo said. "The weather was nice all day, then after sunset it turned stormy, with wild lightning. Water flowed down into the Akasaka-Mitsuke Station and they had to shut down the subway for a while." *The Little People are stirring,* Fuka-Eri had said.

"I got pregnant the night of that storm," Aomame said. "But I didn't have *those sorts of* relations with anyone on that day, or for several months before and after."

She paused and waited until this reality had sunk in, then continued.

"But *it* definitely happened that night. And I'm certain that the child I'm carrying is yours. I can't explain it, but I know it's *true.*"

The memory of the strange sexual encounter he had with Fuka-Eri that night came back to him. Lightning was crashing outside, huge drops of rain lashing the window. The Little People were indeed stirring. He was lying there, faceup in bed, his whole body numb, and Fuka-Eri straddled him, inserted his penis inside her, and squeezed out his semen. She looked like she was in a complete trance. Her eyes were closed from start to finish, as if she were lost in meditation. Her breasts were ample and round, and she had no pubic hair. The whole scene was unreal, but he knew it had really happened.

The next morning, Fuka-Eri had acted as if she had no memory of the events of the previous night, or else tried to give the impression that she didn't remember. To Tengo it had felt more like a business transaction than sex. On that stormy night, Fuka-Eri used his body to collect his semen, down to the very last drop. Even now, Tengo could recall that strange sensation. Fuka-Eri had seemed to become a totally different person.

"There is something I recall," Tengo said dryly. "Something that happened to me that night that logic can't explain."

Aomame looked deep into his eyes.

"At the time," he went on, "I didn't know what it meant. Even now, I'm not sure. But if you did get pregnant that night, and there's no other possible explanation for it, then the child inside you has to be mine."

Fuka-Eri must have been the conduit. That was the role she had been assigned, to act as the passage linking Tengo and Aomame, physically connecting the two of them over a limited period of time. Tengo knew this must be true.

"Someday I'll tell you exactly what happened then," Tengo said, "but right now I don't think I have the words to explain it."

"But you really believe it, right? That the *little one* inside me is your child?"

"From the bottom of my heart," Tengo said.

"Good," Aomame said. "That's all I wanted to know. As long as you believe that, then I don't care about the rest. I don't need any explanations."

"So you're pregnant," Tengo asked again.

"Four months along," Aomame said, guiding his hand to rest on her belly.

Tengo was quiet, seeking signs of life there. It was still very tiny, but his hand could feel the warmth.

"Where are we moving on to? You, me, and the *little one.*"

"Somewhere that's not here," Aomame replied. "A world with only one moon. The place where we belong. Where the Little People have no power."

"Little People?" Tengo frowned slightly.

"You described the Little People in detail in *Air Chrysalis.* What they look like, what they do."

Tengo nodded.

"They really exist in this world," Aomame said. "Just like you described them."

When he had rewritten the novel, he had thought the Little People were merely the figment of the active imagination of a seventeen-year-old girl. Or that they were at most a kind of metaphor or symbol. But Tengo could now believe that the Little People really existed, that they had real powers.

"Not just the Little People," Aomame said, "but all of it really exists in this world – air chrysalises, *maza* and *dohta*, two moons."

"And you know the pathway out of *this world*?"

"We'll take the pathway I took to get into this world so that we can get out of it. That's the only exit I can think of." She added, "Do you have the manuscript of the novel you're writing?"

"Right here," Tengo said, lightly tapping the russet-colored bag slung over his shoulder. It struck him as strange. How did she know about this?

Aomame gave a hesitant smile. "I just know."

"It looks like you know a lot of things," Tengo said. It was the first time he had seen her smile. It was the faintest of smiles, yet he felt the tides start to shift all over the world. He knew it was happening.

"Don't let go of it," Aomame said. "It's very important for us."

"Don't worry. I won't."

"We came into *this world* so that we could meet. We didn't realize it ourselves, but that was the purpose of us coming here. We faced all kinds of complications – things that didn't make sense, things that defied explanation. Weird things, gory things, sad things. And sometimes, even beautiful things. We were asked to make a vow, and we did. We were forced to go through hard times, and we made it. We were able to accomplish the goal that we came here to accomplish. But danger is closing in fast. They want the *dohta* inside of me. You know what the *dohta* signifies, I imagine."

Tengo took a deep breath. "You're having our *dohta* – yours and mine."

"I don't know all the details of whatever principle's behind it, but I'm giving birth to a *dohta*. Either through an air chrysalis, or else I'm the air chrysalis. And they're trying to get ahold of all three of us. To make a new system so they can *hear the voice*."

"But what's my role in this? Assuming I have a role beyond being the father of the *dohta*."

"You are – " Aomame began, and stopped. The next words wouldn't come. There were several gaps that remained, gaps they would have to work together, over time, to fill in.

"I decided to find you," Tengo said, "but I couldn't. *You* found *me*. I actually didn't do anything. It seems – how should I put it? – unfair."

"Unfair?"

"I owe you a lot. But in the end, I wasn't much help."

"You don't owe me anything," Aomame said firmly. "You're the one who guided me this far. In an invisible way. The two of us are one."

"I think I saw that *dohta*," Tengo said. "Or at least what the *dohta signifies*. It was you as a ten-year-old, asleep inside the faint light of an air chrysalis. I could touch her fingers. It only happened once."

Aomame leaned her head on Tengo's shoulder. "We don't owe each other anything. Not a thing. But what we do need to worry about is protecting this *little one*. They're closing in. Almost on top of us. I can hear their footsteps."

"I won't ever let anyone else get the two of you – you or the *little one*. Now that we've met each other, we've found what we were looking for when we came to this world. This is a dangerous place. But you said you know where there's an exit."

"I think so," Aomame said. "If I'm not mistaken."

CHAPTER 31

Tengo and Aomame

LIKE A PEA IN A POD

Aomame recognized the spot as they got out of the taxi. She stood at the intersection looking around and found the gloomy storage area, surrounded by a metal panel fence, down below the expressway. Leading Tengo by the hand, she crossed at the crosswalk and headed toward it.

She couldn't remember which of the metal panels had the loose bolts, but after patiently testing each one, she found a space that a person could manage to slip through. Aomame bent down and, careful to keep her clothes from getting snagged, slipped inside. Tengo hunched down as much as his large body would allow, and followed behind her. Inside the storage area, everything was exactly as it had been in April, when Aomame had last seen it. Discarded, faded bags of cement, rusty metal pipes, weary weeds, scattered old waste-paper, splotches of hardened white pigeon excrement here and there. In eight months, nothing had changed. During that time, perhaps no one had ever set foot in here. It was like a sandbar on a main highway in the middle of the city – a completely abandoned, forgotten little spot.

"Is this the place?" Tengo asked, looking around.

Aomame nodded. "If there's no exit here, then we're not going anywhere."

In the darkness Aomame searched for the emergency stairway she had climbed down, the narrow stairs linking the expressway and the ground below. *The stairway* has to be here, she told herself. *I have to believe it.*

And she found it. It was actually closer to a ladder than a stairway. It was shabbier and more rickety than she remembered. She was amazed that she had managed to clamber down it before. At any rate, though, here it was. All they needed to do now was climb up, step by step, instead of down. She took off her Charles Jourdan high heels, stuffed them into her bag, and slung the bag across her shoulders. She stepped onto the first rung of the ladder in her stocking feet.

"Follow me," Aomame said, turning around to Tengo.

"Maybe I should go first?" Tengo asked worriedly.

"No, I'll go first." This was the path she had come down, and she would have to be the first to climb back up.

The stairway was colder than when she had come down it. Her hands got so numb that she thought she would lose all feeling. The wind whipped between the support columns under the expressway. It was much more sharp and piercing than it had been before. The stairway was aloof and uninviting. It promised her nothing.

At the beginning of September when she had searched for the stairway on the expressway, it had vanished. The route had been blocked. Yet now the route from the storage area, going up, was still here, just as she had predicted. She had had a feeling that if she started from this direction, she would find it. *If this* little one *inside me,* she thought, *has any special powers, then it will surely protect me and show me the right way to go.*

The stairway existed, but whether it *really* connected up to the expressway, she didn't know. It might be blocked halfway, a dead end. In this world, anything could happen. The only thing to do was to climb up with her own hands and feet and find out what was there – and what was not.

She cautiously climbed up one step after another. She looked down and saw Tengo right behind her. A fierce wind howled, making her spring coat flutter. It was a cutting wind. The hem of her short skirt had crept up to her thighs. The wind had made a mess of her hair, plastering it against her face and blocking her vision, so much so that she found it hard to breathe. Aomame regretted not having tied her hair back. *And I should have worn gloves, too,* she thought. *Why didn't I think of that?* But regretting it wasn't going to be any help. She had only thought to wear exactly the same thing as before. She had to cling to the rungs and keep on climbing.

As she shivered in the cold, patiently climbing upward, she looked over at the balcony of the apartment building across the road. A five-story building made of brown brick tiles, the same building she had seen when she had climbed down. Lights were on in half the rooms. It was so close by she could almost reach out and touch it. It might lead to trouble if one of the residents happened to spot them climbing up the emergency stairway like this in the middle of the night. The two of them were lit up well under the lights from Route 246.

Fortunately, no one appeared at any of the windows. All the curtains were drawn tight. This was only to be expected, really. Who was going to come out on their balcony in the middle of a freezing night to watch an emergency stairway on an expressway?

There was a potted rubber plant on one of the balconies, crouching down next to a grubby lawn chair. In April when she had climbed down she had seen the same rubber plant – a much more pathetic little plant than the one she had left behind at her apartment in Jiyugaoka. This little rubber plant must have been there the whole eight months, huddled in the same exact spot. It was faded and bedraggled, shoved away into the most inconspicuous spot in the world, completely forgotten, probably hardly ever watered. Still, that little plant gave

Aomame courage and certainty as she struggled up the rickety stairway, her hands and legs freezing, her mind anxious and confused. *It's okay,* she told herself, *I'm on the right track. At least I'm following the same path I took when I came here, from the opposite direction. This little rubber plant has been a landmark for me. A sober, solitary landmark.*

When I climbed down the stairs back then, I came across a few spiderwebs. And I thought of Tamaki Otsuka, how during summer break in high school we took a trip together, and at night, in bed, we stripped naked and explored each other's bodies. Why had that memory suddenly come to her then, of all times, while climbing down an emergency stairway on the expressway? As she now climbed in the opposite direction, Aomame thought again of Tamaki. She remembered her smooth, beautifully shaped breasts. *So different from my own underdeveloped chest,* she thought. *But those beautiful breasts are now gone forever.*

She thought of Ayumi Nakano, the lonely policewoman who, one August night, wound up in a hotel room in Shibuya, handcuffed, strangled with a bathrobe belt. A troubled young woman walking toward the abyss of destruction. She had had beautiful breasts as well.

Aomame mourned the deaths of these two friends deeply. It saddened her to think that these women were forever gone from the world. And she mourned their lovely breasts – breasts that had vanished without a trace.

Please, she pleaded. *Protect me. I beg you – I need your help.* She believed that her voiceless words had reached the ears of her unfortunate friends. *They'll protect me. I know it.*

When she finally came to the top of the ladder, she was faced with a catwalk that connected up to the side of the road. The catwalk had a low railing, and she would have to crouch low to pass through. Beyond the catwalk was a zigzagging stairway. Not a proper stairway, really, but certainly a far cry better than the ladder. As Aomame recalled, once she ascended the stairs she would come out onto the turnout along the expressway. Trucks barreling down the road sent shocks that rocked the catwalk, as if it were a small boat hit from the side by a wave. The roar of the traffic had increased.

She checked that Tengo, who had come to the top of the ladder, was right behind her, and she reached out and took his hand. His hand was warm. She found it odd that his hand could be so warm on such a cold night, after holding on to a freezing ladder.

"We're almost there," Aomame said in his ear. With the traffic noise and the wind she had to raise her voice. "Once we get up those stairs we'll be on the expressway."

That is, if the stairs aren't blocked, she thought, but she kept this thought to herself.

"You were planning to climb these stairs from the beginning?" Tengo asked.

"Right. If I could locate them."

"And you went to the trouble of dressing like that. Tight skirt, high heels. Not exactly the right outfit to wear to climb steep stairs."

Aomame smiled again. "I had to wear these clothes. Someday I'll explain it to you."

"You have beautiful legs," Tengo said.

"You like them?"

"You bet."

"Thanks," Aomame said. On the narrow catwalk she reached up and gently kissed his ear. A crumpled, cauliflower-like ear. His ear was freezing cold.

She turned back, proceeded along the catwalk, and began climbing up the narrow, steep stairs. Her feet were freezing, her fingertips numb. She was careful not to slip. She continued up the stairs, brushing away her hair as the wind whipped by. The freezing wind brought tears to her eyes. She held on tightly to the handrail so she could keep her balance in the swirling wind, and as she took one cautious step after another, she thought of Tengo right behind her. Of his large hand, and his freezing-cold cauliflower ear. Of the *little one* sleeping inside her. Of the black automatic pistol inside her shoulder bag. And the seven 9mm cartridges in the clip.

We have to get out of this world. To do that I have to believe, from the bottom of my heart, that these stairs will lead to the expressway. I believe, she told herself. She suddenly remembered something Leader had said on the stormy night, before he died. Lyrics to a song. She could recall them all, even now.

It's a Barnum and Bailey world,
    Just as phony as it can be,
But it wouldn't be make-believe
    If you believed in me.

No matter what happens, no matter what I have to do, I have to make it real, not make-believe. No – the two of us, Tengo and I, have to do that. We have to make it real. We have to put our strength together, every last ounce of strength we possess. For our sake, and for the sake of this little one.

Aomame stopped on a landing halfway up and turned around. Tengo was still there. She reached out her hand, and Tengo took it. She felt the same warmth as before, and it gave her a certain strength. She reached up again and brought her mouth close to his ear.

"You know, once I almost gave up my life for you," she said. "Just a little more and I would have died. A couple of millimeters more. Do you believe me?"

"I do," Tengo said.

"Will you tell me you believe it from the bottom of your heart?"

"I believe it from the bottom of my heart," Tengo replied.

Aomame nodded, and let go of his hand. She faced forward and began climbing the stairs again.

A few minutes later, she reached the top and came out onto Metropolitan Expressway No. 3. The stairway hadn't been blocked. Before she scrambled over the metal fence, she reached up with the back of her hand and wiped away the cold tears in her eyes.

Tengo looked around without saying a word. Finally, he said, as if impressed, "It's Metropolitan Expressway No. 3. This is the exit out of this world, isn't it."

"That's right," Aomame replied. "It's the entrance and the exit."

Tengo helped her from behind as she clambered over the fence, her tight skirt riding up to her hips. Beyond the fence was a turnout just big enough for two cars. This was the third time she had been here. The large Esso billboard was right in front of her. *Put a Tiger in Your Tank.* The same slogan. The same tiger. She stood there in her stocking feet without a word. She inhaled the car exhaust deep into her lungs. This was the most refreshing air she could possibly imagine. *I'm back,* Aomame thought. *We're back.*

The traffic on the expressway was bumper to bumper, just as she had left it. The Shibuya-bound traffic was barely inching along. This surprised her, and she wondered why. *Whenever I come here, the traffic's always backed up. But at this time of day it's pretty rare for the lanes heading into the city on Expressway No. 3 to be like this. There must be an accident somewhere up ahead.* The lanes going the other direction were flowing along nicely but the ones heading into the city were crushingly crowded.

Tengo climbed over the metal fence, lifting one foot up high to nimbly leap over, then came to stand beside her. They stood there together, wordlessly watching the throng of traffic, like people standing beside the Pacific Ocean for the first time in their lives, awestruck at the waves crashing on the shore.

The people in the barely moving cars stared back at them. They seemed confused, uncertain how to react. Their eyes were filled less with curiosity than suspicion. What could this young couple possibly be up to? They had suddenly popped up out of the dark and were standing in a turnout on the expressway. The woman had on a fashionable suit, but her coat was a thin spring one, and she was standing there in stocking feet, with no shoes. The man was stocky, and was wearing a well-worn leather jacket. Both of them had bags slung diagonally across their shoulders. Had their car broken down? Had they been in an accident? There was no sign of any car nearby. And they didn't look like they were asking for help.

Aomame finally pulled herself together and took her high heels out of her bag. She tugged the hem of her skirt down, put the strap of her bag over one shoulder, and tied the belt on her coat. She licked her dry lips, straightened her hair with her fingers, took out a handkerchief, and wiped away her tears. And she once more nestled close to Tengo.

Just as they had done on that December day twenty years earlier, in a classroom after hours, they stood silently side by side, holding hands. They were the only two people in the world. They watched the leisurely flow of cars before them. But they saw nothing. What they were seeing, what they were hearing – none of it mattered. The sights around them – the sounds, the smells – had all been drained of meaning.

"So, we're in a different world now?" Tengo managed to say.

"Most likely," Aomame said.

"Maybe we should make sure."

There was only one way to make sure, and they didn't need to put it into words. Silently, Aomame raised her face and looked up at the sky. At nearly the same instant, Tengo did so too. They were searching for the moon. Considering the angle, the moon should be somewhere above the Esso billboard. But they couldn't find it. It seemed to be hidden behind the clouds. The clouds were flowing toward the south, sedately moving along in the wind. The two of them waited – no need to rush. They had plenty of time. Enough time to recover the time they had lost. The time they shared. No need to panic. A pump in one hand, a knowing smile on his face, the Esso tiger, in profile, watched over the two of them holding hands.

Aomame was struck by a sudden thought. Something was different, but she couldn't put her finger on it. She narrowed her eyes and focused. And then it hit her. The left side of the Esso tiger's face was toward them. But in her memory it was his *right* side that had faced the world. *The tiger had been reversed.* Her face instinctively grimaced, her heart skipped a beat or two. It felt like something inside her had changed course. But could she really say for sure? *Is my memory really that accurate?* Aomame wasn't certain. She just *had a feeling* about it. Sometimes our memory betrays us.

Aomame kept her doubts to herself. She shut her eyes for a moment to let her breathing and heart rate get back to normal, and waited for the clouds to pass.

People continued to stare at the two of them through the car windows. What are these two looking at? And why are they clutching each other's hand so tightly? A number of them craned their heads, trying to see what the couple was staring at, but all that was visible were white clouds and an Esso billboard. *Put a Tiger in Your Tank,* the billboard tiger's profile said, facing to the left, urging those driving by to consume even more gasoline, his orange-striped tail jauntily raised to the sky.

The clouds finally broke and the moon came into view.

There was just one moon. That familiar, yellow, solitary moon. The same moon that silently floated over fields of pampas grass, the moon that rose – a gleaming, round saucer – over the calm surface of lakes, that tranquilly beamed down on the rooftops of fast-asleep houses. The same moon that brought the high tide to shore, that softly shone on the fur of animals and enveloped and protected travelers at night. The moon that, as a crescent, shaved slivers from the soul – or, as a new moon, silently bathed the earth in its own loneliness. *That* moon. The moon was fixed in the sky right above the Esso billboard, and there was no smaller, misshapen greenish moon beside it. It was hanging there, taciturn, beholden to no one. Simultaneously, the two of them looked at the same scene. Wordlessly Aomame clutched Tengo's hand. The feeling of an internal backflow had vanished.

We're back in 1984, Aomame told herself. *This isn't 1Q84 anymore. This is the world of 1984, the world I came from.*

But is it? Could the world really go back so easily to what it was? Hadn't Leader, just before he died, asserted that there was no pathway back to the old world?

Could this be another, altogether different place? Did we move from one world to yet another, third world? Where the Esso tiger shows us the left side of his face, not his right? Where new riddles and new rules await us?

It might well be, Aomame thought. *At least at this point I can't swear that it isn't. But there is one thing I can say for sure. No matter how you look at it, this isn't that world, with its two moons in the sky. And I am holding Tengo's hand. The two of us entered a dangerous place, where logic had no purpose, and we managed to survive some terrible ordeals, found each other, and slipped away. Whether this place we've arrived in is the world we started out from or a whole new world, what do I have to be afraid of? If there are new trials ahead for us, we just have to overcome them, like we've done before. That's all. But at least we're no longer alone.*

Believing in what she needed to believe, she relaxed, leaning back against Tengo's large body. She pressed her ear against his chest and listened to his heartbeat, and gave herself up to his arms. Just like a pea in a pod.

"Where should we go now?" Tengo asked Aomame after some time had passed. They couldn't stay here forever. That much was clear. But there was no shoulder on the Metropolitan Expressway. The Ikejiri exit was relatively close, but even in a traffic jam like this it was too dangerous for a pedestrian to walk through the backup of cars. They were certain, too, that holding out their thumbs to hitchhike wasn't likely to get them any rides. They could use the emergency phone to call for help from the Japan Highway Public Corporation, but then they would have to come up with a reasonable explanation for why they were stranded. Even if they were able to make it on foot to the Ikejiri exit, the toll collector would be sure to question them. Going back down the same stairs they had climbed up was out of the question.

"I don't know," Aomame said.

She really had no idea what they should do, or where they should go. Once they had climbed the emergency stairway, her role was over. She was too drained to think, or make a judgment call. There wasn't a drop left in her tank. She could only let some other power take over.

O Lord in Heaven, may Thy name be praised in utmost purity for ever and ever, and may Thy kingdom come to us. Please forgive our many sins, and bestow Thy blessings upon our humble pathways. Amen.

The prayer flowed out from her like a conditioned reflex. She didn't have to think about it. Each individual word had no meaning. The phrases were nothing more than sounds to her now, a list of signs and nothing more. Still, as she mechanically recited the prayer, a strange feeling came over her, something you might even call reverence. Something deep inside her struck a chord in her heart. *Despite all that happened, I never lost myself,* she thought. *Thank goodness I can be here, as me. Wherever* here *is.*

May Thy kingdom come, Aomame intoned once more, like she had done in elementary school before lunch, so many years ago. Whatever that might mean, she wished it. *May Thy kingdom come.*

Tengo stroked her hair, as if combing it.

Ten minutes later Tengo was able to flag down a passing taxi. At first they couldn't believe their eyes. A single taxi, absent of any passengers, was slowly making its way along the traffic jam on the expressway. Tengo raised a skeptical hand, the back door swung open right away, and they climbed aboard, quickly, hurriedly, afraid that this phantom would vanish. The young driver, wearing glasses, turned to face them.

"Because of the traffic jam I would like to get off at the Ikejiri exit coming up, if that's all right with you?" the driver asked. He had a rather high-pitched voice for a man, but it wasn't irritating.

"That would be fine," Aomame replied.

"It's actually against the law to pick up passengers on the expressway."

"Which law would that be?" Aomame asked. Her face, reflected in the rearview mirror, wore a slight frown.

The driver couldn't come up with the name of the law that prohibits picking up passengers on highways. Plus, Aomame's face in the rearview mirror was starting to frighten him a little.

"Well, whatever," the driver said, abandoning the topic. "Anyway, where would you like to go?"

"You can let us off near Shibuya Station," Aomame said.

"I haven't set the meter," the driver said. "I'll just charge you for the distance after we get off the expressway."

"Why were you on the expressway with no passenger?" Tengo asked him.

"It's sort of a long story," the driver said, his voice etched with fatigue. "Would you like to hear it?"

"I would," Aomame said. Long and boring was fine by her. She wanted to hear people's stories in this new world. There might be new secrets there, new hints.

"I picked up a fare, a middle-aged man, near Kinuta Park, and he asked me to take him near Aoyama Gakuin University. He wanted me to take the expressway since there would be too much traffic around Shibuya. At this point, there wasn't any bulletin about a traffic jam on the expressway. Traffic was supposed to be moving along just fine. So I did what he asked and got on the expressway at Yoga. But then there was an accident around Tani, apparently, and you can see the result. Once we were stuck, we couldn't even get to the Ikejiri exit to get off. Meanwhile, the passenger spied a friend of his. Around Komazawa, when we weren't moving an inch, there was a silver Mercedes coupe next to us that just happened to be driven by a woman who was a friend of his. They rolled down the windows and chatted and she wound up inviting him to ride with her. The man apologized and asked if he could pay up and go over to her car. Letting a passenger out in the middle of a highway is unheard of, but since we actually weren't moving, I couldn't say no. So the man got into the Mercedes. He felt bad about it, so he added a little extra to what he paid to sweeten the deal. But still it was annoying. I mean, I couldn't move at all. Anyway, bit by bit I made my way here, nearly to the Ikejiri exit. And then I saw you raising your hand. Pretty hard to believe, don't you think?"

"I can believe it," Aomame said concisely.

That night the two of them stayed in a high-rise hotel in Akasaka. They turned the lights out, undressed, got into bed, and held each other. There was a lot they needed to talk about, but that could wait till morning. They had other priorities. Without a word passing between them, they leisurely explored each other's bodies in the dark. With their fingers and palms, one by one, they checked where everything was, what they were shaped like. They felt excited, like little children on a treasure hunt in a secret room. Once they found each part, they kissed it with a seal of approval.

After they had leisurely finished this process, Aomame held Tengo's hard penis in her hand – just like years before, when she had held his hand in the classroom after school. It felt harder than anything she had ever known, miraculously hard. Aomame spread her legs, moved close, and slowly inserted him inside of her. Straight in, deep inside. She closed her eyes in the darkness and gulped a deep and dark intake of breath. Then, ever so slowly, she exhaled. Tengo felt her hot breath on his chest.

"I've always imagined being held by you like this," Aomame said, whispering in his ear as she stopped moving.

"Having sex with me?"

"Yes."

"Since you were ten you've been imagining *this*?" Tengo asked.

Aomame laughed. "No, that came when I was a little older."

"I've been imagining the same thing."

"Being inside me?"

"That's right," Tengo said.

"Is it like you imagined?"

"I still can't believe it's real," Tengo admitted. "I feel like I'm imagining things."

"But this is real."

"It feels too good to be real."

In the darkness Aomame smiled. And she kissed him. They explored each other's tongues.

"My breasts are kind of small, don't you think?" Aomame said.

"They're just right," Tengo said, cupping them.

"You really think so?"

"Of course," he said. "If they were any bigger then it wouldn't be you."

"Thank you," Aomame said. "They're not just small," she added, "but the right and left are also different sizes."

"They're fine the way they are," Tengo said. "The right one's the right one, the left one's the left. No need to change a thing."

Aomame pressed an ear against his chest. "I've been lonely for so long. And I've been hurt so deeply. If only I could have met you again a long time ago, then I wouldn't have had to take all these detours to get here."

Tengo shook his head. "I don't think so. This way is just fine. This is exactly the right time. For both of us."

Aomame started to cry. The tears she had been holding back spilled down her cheeks and there was nothing she could do to stop them. Large teardrops fell audibly onto the sheets like rain. With Tengo buried deep inside her, she trembled slightly as she went on crying. Tengo put his arms around her and held her. He would be holding her close from now on, a thought that made him happier than he could imagine.

"We needed that much time," Tengo said, "to understand how lonely we really were."

"Start moving," Aomame breathed in his ear. "Take your time, and do it slowly."

Tengo did as he was told. He began pumping slowly. Breathing quietly, listening to his heartbeat. Aomame clung to him like she was drowning. She gave up crying, gave up thinking, distanced herself from the past, from the future, and became one with his movements.

Near dawn they slipped on hotel bathrobes, stood next to the large window, and sipped the red wine they had ordered from room service. Aomame took just a token sip. They didn't need to sleep yet. From their room on the seventeenth floor they could enjoy watching the moon to their hearts' content. The clouds had drifted away, and nothing impeded their view. The dawn moon had moved quite a distance, though it still hovered just above the city skyline. The moon was an ashy white, and looked about ready to fall to earth, its job complete.

At the front desk Aomame had asked for a room high up with a view of the moon, even if it cost more. "That's the most important thing – having a nice view of the moon," she said.

The clerk was kind to this young couple who had shown up without a reservation. It also helped that the hotel wasn't busy. She felt kindly toward the couple from the moment she set eyes on them. She had the bellboy go up to look at the room to make sure it had the view they wanted, and only then handed Aomame the key to the junior suite. She gave them a special discount, too.

"Is it a full moon or something tonight?" the woman clerk asked Aomame, her interest aroused. Over the years she had heard every kind of demand, hope, and desire from guests you could imagine. But this was a first, having guests who were looking for a room with a good view of the moon.

"No," Aomame replied. "The moon's past full. It's about two-thirds full. But that doesn't matter. As long as we can see it."

"You enjoy watching the moon, then?"

"It's important to us," Aomame smiled. "More important than you can know."

Even as dawn approached, the number of moons didn't increase. It was just the same old familiar moon. The one and only satellite that has faithfully circled the earth, at the same speed, from before human memory. As she stared at the moon, Aomame softly touched her abdomen, checking one more time that the *little one* was there, inside her. She could swear her belly had grown from the night before.

I still don't know what sort of world this is, she thought. *But whatever world we're in now, I'm sure this is where I will stay. Where we will stay. This world must have its own threats, its own dangers, must be filled with its own type of riddles and contradictions. We may have to travel down many dark paths, leading who knows where. But that's okay. It's not a problem. I'll just have to accept it. I'm not going anywhere. Come what may, this is where we'll remain, in this world with one moon. The three of us – Tengo and me, and the* little one.

Put a tiger in your tank, the Esso tiger said, his left profile toward them. But either side was fine. That big grin of his facing Aomame was natural and warm. *I'm going to believe in that smile,* she told herself. *That's what's important here.* She did her own version of the tiger's smile. Very naturally, very gently.

She quietly stretched out a hand, and Tengo took it. The two of them stood there, side by side, as one, wordlessly watching the moon over the buildings. Until the newly risen sun shone upon it, robbing it of its nighttime brilliance. Until it was nothing more than a gray paper moon, hanging in the sky.

Grateful acknowledgment is made to the following for permission to reprint previously published material:

Oneworld Classics Ltd.: Excerpts from *Sakhalin Island* by Anton Chekhov, translated by Brian Reeve, copyright © 2007 by Brian Reeve. Reprinted by permission of Oneworld Classics Ltd.

The Estate of Isak Dinesen and Rungstedlundfonden: Excerpts from *Out of Africa* by Isak Dinesen, copyright © 1937 by Karen Blixen and copyright renewed 1965 by Rungstedlundfonden. First published by Penguin Books 1954. Reprinted by permission of The Estate of Isak Dinesen and Rungstedlundfonden.

Chappell Music Ltd. and Carlin Music Corporation: Excerpt from "It's Only a Paper Moon," music by Harold Arlen, lyrics by Billy Rose and E. Y. "Yip" Harburg, copyright © 1933 (renewed) by WB Music Corp. (ASCAP) and Glocca Morra Music Corp. (ASCAP). All rights reserved.